EVERYMAN'S LIBRARY

EVERYMAN,
I WILL GO WITH THEE,
AND BE THY GUIDE,
IN THY MOST NEED
TO GO BY THY SIDE

THE RAJ QUARTET

PAUL SCOTT

THE RAJ QUARTET

VOLUME ONE

THE JEWEL IN THE CROWN
THE DAY OF THE SCORPION

WITH AN INTRODUCTION BY
HILARY SPURLING

EVERYMAN'S LIBRARY
Alfred A. Knopf   New York   London   Toronto

297

THIS IS A BORZOI BOOK
PUBLISHED BY ALFRED A. KNOPF

First included in Everyman's Library, 2007

US website: www.randomhouse.com/everymans

ISBN: 978-0-307-26396-4 (US)
1-85715-297-2 & 978-1-85715-297-5 (UK)

A CIP catalogue reference for this book is available from the
British Library

Book design by Barbara de Wilde and Carol Devine Carson

Typeset in the UK by AccComputing, North Barrow, Somerset

Printed and bound in Germany by GGP Media GmbH, Pössneck

CONTENTS

INTRODUCTION

In 1964 Paul Scott set out across India on a journey that he knew would make or break him as a novelist. He was forty-three years old with eight published novels behind him, none of which had done more than scratch the surface of the kind of book he had been struggling for twenty years to write about India. This journey was a last desperate gamble that brought him to the verge of mental and physical collapse. At the same time it strengthened and expanded his creative grasp, enabling him to break through as a writer to levels of emotional and intuitive understanding inaccessible to the conscious mind. It led directly to the *Raj Quartet*, the four linked novels he produced as soon as he got back from what became a voyage of self-discovery, a way of confronting his own inner demons and, through them, the dark hidden underside of British imperial India.

Scott put himself into the first of his four books as its narrator, the nameless stranger who turns up near the beginning without introduction or explanation in the luxuriant garden of the MacGregor house in Mayapore. The writer at that stage was still groping his way forward, absorbing impressions, probing and piecing his narrative together, like the observant stranger in his fictional garden with its cascades of bougainvillaea, its jasmine and canna lilies, its patches of brilliant sunlight heightened by the dense blue-black shadows of neem, pipul, tamarind and banyan trees:

The range of green is extraordinary, palest lime, bitter emerald, mid-tones, neutral tints. The textures of the leaves are many and varied, they communicate themselves through sight to imaginary touch, exciting the finger-tips: leaves coming into the tenderest flesh, superbly in their prime, crisping to old age ... In the shadows there are ... odours of sweet and necessary decay, numerous places layered with the cast-off fruit of other years softened into compost, feeding the living roots that lie under the garden massively, in hungry immobility.

On one level this passage grew from memories of a real garden belonging to the Indian couple who were Scott's hosts

in Calcutta in 1964. On another it explores the garden of the
mind where the novelist broods and ponders, ranging back
and forth over the present and the past, sensing underlying
shapes and patterns, watching new life stir in the tangled
undergrowth of the subject beginning at last to come within
his imaginative reach. It is a potent and accurate image of the
writer at work.

On his return from India in 1964, Scott sat down at once to
write *The Jewel in the Crown*, the opening movement of the *Raj
Quartet*. The whole sequence covers a period of five years, the
final inglorious phase of Britain's imperial dominion during
World War II, leading up to the handover of power in 1947,
the speedy retreat of the British, and the massacres precipitated
by the division of India from Pakistan as both countries became
independent. The *Quartet* starts with the rape of a white woman
during the Quit India riots that mobilized resentment against
the British in 1942. It ends five years later with the murder of
a Muslim – a body falling from a railway carriage, butchered
by Hindu terrorists on an ambushed train that moves off again,
after a brief bloody interval, to complete its interrupted journey
across the subcontinent: 'It was the smooth gliding motion
away from a violent situation which one witness never forgot.
"Suddenly you had the feeling that the train, the wheels, the
lines weren't made of metal but of something greasy and
evasive."'

Railway journeys play a vital part in the *Raj Quartet*. Trains
make connections, they move through time and space, they
may be used to ferry themes as well as people. This particular
train with its cargo of dead or dying Muslims also carries, in
separate carriages, a party of British imperialists heading for
home in August 1947: departing civil servants, police and army
personnel, sahibs and memsahibs moving towards Indian Independence, the splendid ceremonial dissolution of the Raj, the
breakdown of civil authority, and its terrible consequences for
countless unofficial victims. The observer in the passage quoted
above – the witness uneasily aware of the greasiness and
evasion inherent in this process – is a young British conscript
posted to India in wartime, Sergeant Guy Perron, who provides
a linking commentary, or consciousness, in the last of the four

novels, *A Division of the Spoils*. Perron is a professional historian who becomes, like the anonymous stranger in the first novel, a spokesman or stand-in for the author himself. He represents, so to speak, the historian in Scott.

Scott's own first contact with India had come when he was drafted into the Indian army as an officer cadet in 1943. He knew nothing about the country, didn't particularly want to go there and responded, as soon as he landed, with shock and revulsion. He felt lonely, homesick and ill. He loathed the heat, the dirt and the poverty, disliked the army, and was so baffled and appalled by the arrogant complacency of the British in India that he would in the end spend the greater part of his adult life unravelling its implications (his imaginative engagement in the *Raj Quartet* was with the British, not the Indians, who – apart from the wonderfully perceptive and detailed character of Hari Kumar – remain more or less on the sidelines). Scott in those days knew exactly where he stood, politically speaking. Young, liberal-minded, highly critical, he never doubted the wisdom of handing India straight back to its inhabitants, a conviction that deepened over the next three years as he became steadily more fascinated by the place and its people. He sailed home to England in May, 1946, and, by August, he was getting worrying letters from friends left behind, both Indian and English, containing news of riots in Calcutta, looting, rape, murder, and even more alarming premonitions of worse to come in case of partition.

It would be nearly another twenty years before he returned to try to make sense of a process he had seen, or glimpsed, coming to an end as a young man. By this time he had come to recognize the end of empire as unfinished business. His wholesale contempt for the Raj had grown less confident, and so had his initial conviction that the behaviour and attitudes of British India had nothing whatsoever to do with him. On the face of it Scott had little or no connection with the imperial ruling elite. He was born in London into a family of shabby gentility on his father's side and, on his mother's, the same working-class background as the sleeping soldiers contemplated by Perron in a Bombay guardroom in the last volume of the *Quartet*:

The faces were those of urban Londoners and belonged to streets of terraced houses that ended in one-man shops: newsagent-tobacconist, fish and chip shop, family grocer, and a pub at the corner where the high road was. What could such a face know of India? And yet India was there, in the skull, and the bones of the body. Its possession had helped nourish the flesh, warm the blood of every man in the room, sleeping and waking.

Scott himself quoted this passage to show that his link with India ran through his mother's people as well as his father's, and that the British withdrawal was part of what he called his personal luggage. He was thinking of a character named Barbie Batchelor, a retired elderly missionary in *The Towers of Silence*, the *Quartet*'s third volume, who turns up at the hill station of Pankot with a large tin trunk from which she cannot be parted. As Barbie herself is shunted round Pankot, moving from house to house and from one family to the next, the trunk becomes a fearful nuisance, constantly having to be sent for, stowed away, brought out again and sorted through, ending up capsized in transit with its contents spilt all over the road. 'I see now,' Scott wrote afterwards, 'that her trunk of missionary relics, which gives her so much trouble throughout the book . . . is really a symbol for the luggage I am conscious of carrying with me every day of my life – the luggage of my past, of my personal history and of the world's history.' This was what made him a writer. It is why he always insisted he was not a historical novelist, and why his books still reverberate so insistently for readers today. 'One is not ruled by the past, one does not rule or re-order it, one simply *is* it, in the same way that one is as well the present and part of the future.'

At the end of his life, Scott attempted to define his achievement for a class of postgraduate students at an American midwest university. He drew up a chart on the blackboard, beginning before World War I with Britain at the height of her power, wealth and influence in possession of an empire that covered a quarter of the globe, and ending after World War II with the election of a British Labour government, the creation of a welfare state at home and the abandonment of empire abroad. He saw the changes signalled by these two events – each promoted in its day as a glorious liberation, each producing with time increasingly sour and disruptive consequences – reflected consciously or unconsciously in the contemporary novel. He defined postwar British fiction as 'the end of the party and the beginning of the washing up'. For a hard-drinking, heavy-smoking host like Scott, the end of a party meant stacking the dirty dishes, rounding up the empties, finishing off the whisky bottle, holding some sort of inquest over broken glasses and cigarette burns on the carpet, going over any rows that had blown up, working out who had come (and who left) with whom, who was on speaking terms and who wasn't. It is a characteristically unromantic image of what Scott himself was doing in the *Raj Quartet*. 'You write for an age,' he told his students, indicating his chart on the blackboard, 'and this is my age.'

He came in the end to see the precipitate unprepared handover of power by the British as a disaster, the final tragic failure of a long relationship between the two countries. Its root causes run underground through the *Raj Quartet*. Scott's persistence was unwelcome, indeed virtually unheard-of at the time in Britain where, for many years after Independence, people refused to think about India. His novels were attacked or dismissed almost unanimously from opposite directions. On the one hand his younger, more fashion-conscious contemporaries complained that he glamorized the past, apparently by the very act of recognizing its existence and writing about it. On the other hand, an older generation of readers saw him as a troublemaker hellbent on raking over dead embers of rancour, bitterness and betrayal much better left undisturbed. By the time Scott completed the last of his four novels, the Raj and its repercussions seemed to most people to have been safely consigned to ancient history.

A quarter of a century after Scott's return journey to India when, as his biographer, I crossed the subcontinent in his footsteps, I often felt like ancient history myself. At one point I stayed alone in a small town high in the Western Ghats at the hotel immortalized by Scott in his last novel, *Staying On*, a kind of afterthought or pendant to the *Quartet*. He had first gone there as a young conscript in 1943 when it was a smart little outfit beside the parade ground, full of British army officers, the centre of social life in a bustling garrison town. Long before I got there it had become a ghost hotel. My high bare dusty room contained nothing but a chest and a bed shrouded in an elephant-grey mosquito net the size of a small marquee. As the only woman on the premises, probably the only English visitor anyone there could remember, I seemed to have stepped into another world peopled by ghosts – the ghosts of the British and their former glory in their obsolete hotel. In fact the place turned out not to be dead at all. Its life had simply shifted to the bar in the compound outside with piped music, lights strung in the trees, and a crowd of young Indians coming and going, drinking and talking, paying no attention to the phantoms forgotten in their silent unvisited rooms.

Subsequent events have proved Scott right when he said that the ghosts of the past can neither be ignored nor forgotten. His driving principle as a novelist was what he called a vigorous sense of history, 'vigorous because it pruned ruthlessly that other weakening sense so often found with the first, the sense of nostalgia, the desire to *live* in the past'. Scott feared and mistrusted nostalgia. He said the denial of memory was a terrible thing but its opposite – the tendency to romanticize the past – could be just as destructive. The *Quartet* took him a decade to write, and twenty years' preparation before that. 'Imagination is not enough,' he said: 'You have to have knowledge too.' But knowledge was not easily available at that stage. Official records were blocked, documentary evidence largely inaccessible, and people in both countries proved reluctant to talk.

Scott operated for years in a kind of limbo alongside men like Sir Conrad Corfield, a former head of the Political Department in India who had been strongly critical of government policy, and General Mohan Singh, founder of the Indian National Army, a patriotic resistance force proscribed and suppressed by the British. Both had written memoirs (both gave copies to Scott) that were repeatedly rejected by publishers on the grounds that the subject was of no public interest. A whole generation of British colonial adminstrators found themselves treated as figures of fun in retirement, while their views were for all practical purposes suppressed. In India Scott's attempts to find out more about the activities of the INA met with closed doors. 'My not very thrusting attempts in Delhi to be shown pertinent archives were not successful,' he explained, adding unexpectedly: 'I didn't persist because as a novelist ... the reluctance interested me almost as much, if not more than the archives would have done.'

The novelist in Scott was transfixed by the widespread and deep-rooted amnesia that confronted him on all sides. The end of the Raj had been an abrupt and humilating defeat for the British, who reacted by turning away from what was generally agreed to be a closed chapter, and vehemently resisting any attempt to reopen it. Scott was accused at the time and afterwards of a sneaking desire to return to the bad old days of colonial supremacy. 'To forget strikes me as the quickest way of making the same mistakes again ...' was his austere response. 'I'm not sure that there is any such thing as forgetting, but there are tender conspiracies of silence – and these may engender ignorance, always a dangerous thing.'

Scott did not condone the Raj. He looked long and hard at its many failures, its inhumanity, smugness, self-righteousness and rigidity. His treatment of individual characters in the *Quartet* may be sympathetic, but his collective portrayal of the British is far from flattering. When an Indian friend asked him what he meant by the title of the second of the four novels, *The Day of the Scorpion,* he explained that scorpions live under stones because they are sensitive to heat: 'There was an old belief that, if you surrounded them with a ring of fire, they committed suicide. But actually they are shrivelled by the heat, and when they dart their tails, they're not committing suicide but trying to attack. Well, that's what so much of the British in India was all about. They were driven out of their places in the end by a number of pressures – and were scorched by fires they had really set fire to themselves.'

The fires the British lit themselves have been smouldering ever since. Already in the 1960s Scott traced the growing racial tensions of contemporary Britain back to much earlier failures of foresight and strategic planning. 'History seems to have overtaken me,' he wrote to an Indian friend in Bombay when war broke out between India and Pakistan, adding sadly as the fighting dragged on: 'All this is in my book, you know.' He struggled long and hard against the collective inertia cloaking British determination to disclaim responsibility for the consequences of imperial collapse: the greasy and evasive, perennial human instinct to glide smoothly away from violent disturbance. He confronted unpopular issues in the *Raj Quartet*, and reached unpalatable conclusions. He said it was part of the novelist's job to confront what he saw as a pervasive, obstinate and pusillanimous spirit of withdrawal from the problems of the modern world.

Scott got small thanks for his pains, relatively grudging critical esteem and little public recognition until he won the Booker Prize for *Staying On* in 1976, a few months before he died. He would surely have raised a sardonic eyebrow to see the *Quartet*, so widely underrated in his lifetime, turned after his death into one of the most successful television adaptations ever made under the overall title, *The Jewel in the Crown*. The series precipitated a wave of overwhelming nostalgia for the Raj in the early 1980s, which saw trendy Raj restaurants and pubs springing up all over Britain, serving Raj drinks in Raj interiors – potted palms, brass fittings, rattan furniture – to customers wearing Raj clothes in white or biscuit-coloured linen. Scott himself would have been the first to recognize this wave of fakery, fancy-dress and make-believe, however absurd in rational terms, as a perfectly natural human instinct to sidestep the implications of too much clearsightedness.

Granada TV's *Jewel in the Crown*, sensitive and scrupulously faithful though it was, remained at bottom a superbly directed and acted family saga. What it lacked was the majestic breadth and sweep of the novelist's imagination, the shifting temporal and spatial perspectives that give such richness of tone and colour to Scott's panorama of unheroic characters pursuing prosaic occupations in mundane settings. The domestic concerns of the human figures occupying the foreground of the *Raj Quartet* – the wrecked lives of Hari Kumar and his lover in the first of the four novels, the rifts and tensions threatening the shaky equilibrium of the Layton family in the last – acquire depth and gravity from the sense of historical and political tides turning in the background.

Professional historians recognized from the start the intellectual force and originality of the *Raj Quartet*. Scott's portrait of modern British India penetrated deeper and further than anyone else had gone (or indeed could go) at the time. In the early years of the civil rights movement in the United States, he was the first to confront directly the nature and extent of British colonial racism, the unacknowledged colour bar that was as much a reality in imperial India as segregation in the American South. His exposure of routine secret brutality and coercion within the British police and security forces was generally dismissed in Scott's day, by even his greatest admirers, as more or less preposterous fictional licence. Documentary backing, forthcoming only long after his death, led to the kind of widespread historical reappraisal already forestalled in essence by the *Raj Quartet*.

If Scott saw history as an active force for the promotion of understanding, tolerance and freedom, his strength as a novelist was imaginative rather than analytical. The emotional heart of the *Raj Quartet* lies not with the lucid and logical objectivity of observers like Guy Perron but with their opposite number, the least theoretical and most practical of men, a character whom Perron initially distrusts, subsequently despises, and eventually detests with unqualified venom. This is the formidable Major Merrick whose career progresses steadily throughout the four volumes, shifting him from one rung to the next up the official ladder of command and trust, until he reaches his high point (and his dreadful end) in *A Division of the Spoils*. In so far as the *Quartet* may be said to have a villain, it is Ronald Merrick, who believes implicitly in the Raj and its panoply of racial privilege and power. 'He believes we've abandoned the principles we used to live by,' Perron explains,

what he would call the English upper- and ruling-class principle of knowing oneself superior to all other races especially black and having a duty to guide and correct them. He's been sucked in by all that Kiplingesque double-talk that transformed India from a place where plain ordinary greedy Englishmen carved something out for themselves ... into one where they appeared to go voluntarily into exile for the good of their souls and the uplift of the native.

Merrick is a man of the past as well as a man of action. His insistence on the virtues of a world that no longer exists, perhaps never existed, makes him dangerously attractive in time of trouble, when 'his absolutely inflexible and unshakable sense of his own authority' comes as a relief even to people who mistrust his methods. The kind of man always welcome in a tight spot, Merrick slowly comes to seem (as someone said of a similar character in one of Scott's earlier novels) more like *the man who brings the tight spot with him*. For all his impressive public reputation, he is in private a sadistic bully and blackmailer. He wins the confidence of his victims before driving them to despair and, in at least one case, to suicide. He lacks entirely what Perron calls 'that liberal instinct which is so dear to historians that they lay it out like a guideline through the unmapped forests of prejudice and self-interest as though this line, and not the forest, is our history'.

Scott explores that dark, unvisited forest principally through Merrick: through glimpses of his background and upbringing, his social and emotional deprivation, his private obsessions, the sources of his indomitable will, and his undoubted power to charm. This is by no means an unsympathetic portrait. On the contrary, Scott somehow manages to make the reader look through Merrick's eyes and, seeing the world in the same light as Merrick sees it, understand how his conduct might have appeared to him a series of sound, bold, eminently justifiable moves in pursuit of honourable ends. Merrick's baleful influence is chiefly apparent through the ruined lives of his prisoners – Hari Kumar, Corporal Pinker, Havildar Khan (the 'poor weary shagged-out shamed and insulted havildar' who hangs himself in *A Division of the Spoils* in the course of interrogation at Merrick's hands). Each represents a landmark in Scott's attempt to map the irrational impulses that operate in regions far from the historian's searchlight of conscious understanding.

He said that the original seeds of *The Jewel in the Crown* were planted in his mind by the affair of the Jallianwallah Bagh, when British troops fired on a trapped and helpless Indian crowd in 1919. The two related fictional incidents that set the *Quartet* in motion – the attacks on Edwina Crane and Daphne Manners, each of whom eventually dies in consequence – had a historical precedent from the same period. The roots of vengeance, repression and inhumanity, running invisibly underground through time and space, are massively present even in the quietest, least eventful and most elegiac of the four novels, the third in the sequence, *The Towers of Silence*. It takes place largely in 1943–4 among the isolated Anglo-Indian community of Pankot, mostly spinsters, widows, wives with sons or husbands away at the front. It is set against the background of distant European war, Japanese invasion of the subcontinent, defeat and dispersal on all sides; and it charts the gradual reluctant acceptance by one small section of the British civilian population in India that their time is up. 'This sense of danger, of the sea-level rising, swamping the plains, threatening the hills, this sense of imminent inundation, was one to which people were now not unaccustomed....'

It was the historian, Professor Sir Max Beloff, who pointed out that Scott spoke for the other half, the wives and daughters of British India, passive watchers in places like Pankot who play no part in the decision-making process, who remain often barely conscious of its existence, let alone its ramifications behind the scenes, and who yet must gather their energies to receive and absorb its impact. The whole novel is focussed through the eyes of the missionary Barbie Batchelor, the obscure elderly owner of the battered tin trunk, who finds herself professionally redundant at the beginning of the book, and who spirals slowly downwards in the course of it through successive circles of loneliness, rejection, homelessness and humiliation to madness and death. Barbie ends up a speechless outcast with no recollection of the past, forcibly restrained by cold water and winding sheets behind bars in the Samaritan Hospital at Ranpur. It is a grim and graphic image of the denial or suppression of memory. Barbie's fate is parallelled by the experience of Susan Layton, the younger and prettier of the two Layton sisters, who starts the book as a radiant bride, and who also finishes by succumbing, if only temporarily, to insanity and incarceration. Susan's dog, which has pined in its mistress's absence, causes perturbation when glimpsed by a guest at a garden party given to mark the first of many enforced departures from Pankot:

xix

She ... was staring, horrified, at a patch of petal-strewn grass, a corridor between long rectangular beds of rose-trees, bush and standard, vagrant-looking with green reversionary shoots pale and erectile, already sucking the life out of the roots. Along this path the creature crawled, slunk, towards them; a black spectre of famine worn to its hooped rib cage and the arched column of its backbone. A thin dribble of saliva hung from its open mouth ... The others stayed where they were, watching the apparition approach the verandah steps slowly, dragging one leg, pausing every few paces to rest, droop-headed, before struggling on, its eyes upturned ... showing blood-shot whites.

Images like this horrifying hound help bear the weight of a novel that comes down in the end with an almost Shakespearian sense of ordinary people: people who have no individual existence for the historian: shallow, cowardly, small-minded people activated by prejudice and self-interest: the sort of people who provide the casualties and mop up the damage when greater men, like Caesar, cry havoc and let slip the dogs of war.

Scott's first stop, on reaching India in 1964 in search of what eventually became the *Raj Quartet*, was a flat with a balcony overlooking the nineteenth-century law courts on the Oval *maidan* in Bombay. If there is one particular passage where Perron may be said to stand for his creator, it is near the beginning of *A Division of the Spoils* when he, too, looks across from a Bombay balcony to the dark bulk of the Law Courts:

For a moment – perhaps under the influence of that symbol of the one thing the British could point to if asked in what way and by what means they had unified the country, the single rule of law – he felt a pressure, as soft and close to his cheek as a sigh: the combined sigh of countless unknown Indians and of past and present members of the glittering insufferable *raj* ...

This was what Scott tried to do: to speak for (or catch the sigh of) countless unknown, unrepresented, insignificant members of the Raj: to preserve them from the dangers of misrepresentation, the denial of memory, the distortions of nostalgia: to insist that their history is neither disposable nor detachable from the present and the future. He was, as he once said himself of E. M. Forster in *Passage to India*, a prophetic writer. He foresaw what others preferred not to see, and often he did not like what he saw. Sometimes he found it unbearable. It was this stern, insistent, prophetic vision that dismayed his contemporaries, and made him in the end one of the most powerful and perceptive novelists of the twentieth century.

Hilary Spurling

HILARY SPURLING is the author of *Paul Scott: A Life* and biographies of Henri Matisse, Ivy Compton-Burnett and Sonia Orwell.

SELECT BIBLIOGRAPHY

PAUL SCOTT, *Staying On*, Heinemann, London, 1977.

PAUL SCOTT, *My Appointment with the Muse. Essays, 1961–75*, ed. Shelley C. Reece, Heinemann, London, 1986.

HILARY SPURLING, *Paul Scott. A Life*, Hutchinson, London, and Norton, New York, 1990.

ROBIN MOORE, *Paul Scott's Raj*, Heinemann, London, 1990.

JUDITH M. BROWN and WILLIAM ROGER LOUIS, *The Oxford History of the British Empire, vol. 4, The Twentieth Century*, Oxford University Press, 1998.

CHRONOLOGY

DATE	AUTHOR'S LIFE	LITERARY CONTEXT
1916	Tom Scott, a commercial artist from Leeds, marries Frances Mark, a shop clerk from south London.	Tagore: *Fruit Gathering*. Joyce: *A Portrait of the Artist as a Young Man*.
1917		Kipling: *A Diversity of Creatures*. Eliot: *Prufrock and Other Observations*.
1919		Maugham: *The Moon and the Sixpence*. Woolf: *Night and Day*.
1920	Paul Scott born 25 March in Southgate, north London, the second son of Tom and Frances Scott.	Fitzgerald: *This Side of Paradise*. Wharton: *The Age of Innocence*. Lawrence: *Women in Love*.
1924		Forster: *A Passage to India*. Ford: *Parade's End* (to 1928).
1926		Maugham: *The Casuarina Tree*. Kipling: *Debits and Credits*.
1929	Paul and elder brother Peter enter Winchmore Hill Collegiate School.	Tagore: *Farewell, My Friend*. Faulkner: *The Sound and the Fury*. Hemingway: *A Farewell to Arms*. Graves: *Goodbye to All That*.
1930		Sassoon: *Memoirs of an Infantry Officer*. Pritchett: *The Spanish Virgin and Other Stories*.
1931		Premchand: 'Deliverance'. Woolf: *The Waves*. Waugh: *Remote People*.
1932		Tagore: *Sheaves, Poems and Songs*. Premchand: *Arena of Action*. Huxley: *Brave New World*. Waugh: *Black Mischief*.
1933	Financial concerns force Tom Scott to move family in with his sisters at their fashion studio, Wyphurst.	Werfel: *The Forty Days of Musa Dagh*. Maugham: *Ah King*. Hemingway: *Winner Take Nothing*.

Easter Rising in Dublin. Offensive on the Somme. Lloyd George becomes prime minister and forms war cabinet. Lucknow Pact: Muslim League and Indian National Congress agree to work together to campaign for self-government.
Bolshevik Revolution in Russia. US joins war. Balfour Declaration supports a Jewish national home in Palestine.

Versailles peace conference. Montague-Chelmsford reforms reorganize central legislature but fall short of Indian expectations. Demonstrations against British rule become widespread; massacre of peaceful protesters by British troops at Amritsar (Jallianwallah Bagh).
League of Nations formed. Beginning of Gandhi's programme of non-cooperation with British in India. Government of Ireland Act provides for separate parliaments for North and South.

Ramsay Macdonald forms first Labour government in Britain (January–November). Death of Lenin.
General Strike in Britain. Germany admitted to League of Nations.

Gandhi nominates Jawaharlal Nehru to succeed him as leader of Congress movement. Wall Street crash. Beginning of worldwide economic depression. Second Labour government under MacDonald. First non-stop flight from England to India.

Gandhi begins civil disobedience campaign in India. First in series of Round Table Conferences on India in London (to 1933). Nazis win seats from the moderates in German election.

Delhi Pact: Gandhi suspends campaign of disobedience. Labour government resigns; replaced by a National Coalition under MacDonald. Statute of Westminster establishes legal status of dominions of British Commonwealth. Clampdown on demonstrators in India; 60,000 Congress activists are imprisoned. Gandhi's hunger strike against the treatment of untouchables. Unemployed marchers clash with police in London. Landslide victory for Democrat F. D. Roosevelt in US presidential election.

Hitler becomes chancellor of Germany; National Socialist party declared only legal party. Roosevelt's 'New Deal' strategies revealed. Japan withdraws from League of Nations. Gandhi's hunger strike against British oppression in India.

DATE	AUTHOR'S LIFE	LITERARY CONTEXT
1934	Peter leaves the Collegiate School and finds work as a car salesman. Family finances deteriorate. Paul withdraws from school and seeks employment; joins accountant's office in Piccadilly run by C. T. Payne.	Fitzgerald: *Tender is the Night*. Waugh: *A Handful of Dust*; *Ninety-two Days*. Orwell: *Burmese Days*.
1935		Compton-Burnett: *A House and its Head*. Anand: *Untouchable*. Narayan: *Swami and Friends*. Isherwood: *Mr Norris Changes Trains*. Day-Lewis: *A Time to Dance*.
1936	Scotts move to Cannon Road, near Southgate High Street.	Anand: *Coolie*. Premchand: *The Gift of a Cow*. Faulkner: *Absalom, Absalom!*
1937		Anand: *Two Leaves and a Bud*. Orwell: *The Road to Wigan Pier*. Kumar: *Tyagapatra*. Hemingway: *To Have and Have Not*. Narayan: *The Bachelor of Arts*.
1938		Rao: *Kanthapura*. Greene: *Brighton Rock*. Narayan: *The Dark Room*. Spring: *O Absalom!* Day-Lewis: *Overtures to Death*.
1939	Tom Scott installs family in new home in Bourne Hill, Palmers Green. Peter and Paul have separate bedrooms for first time.	Anand: *The Village*. Isherwood: *Goodbye to Berlin*. Joyce Cary: *Mister Johnson*.
1940	Drafted to serve in British Army.	Greene: *The Power and the Glory*. Anand: *Across the Black Waters*. Spring: *Fame is the Spur*. Thomas: *Portrait of the Artist as a Young Dog*. Hemingway: *For Whom the Bell Tolls*.
1941	Bomb destroys Wyphurst; aunts Laura and Florrie both killed. Poetic trilogy *I, Gerontius* published in the Resurgam young poets series. Meets nurse	Fitzgerald: *The Last Tycoon*. Mackenzie: *Monarch of the Glen*. Joyce Cary: *Herself Surprised*.

HISTORICAL EVENTS

Night of the Long Knives in Germany. Unrest in Spain. Gandhi resigns from Congress Party.

Second Government of India Act creates a central legislature; provincial government handed over to elected Indian representatives. Burma separated from India. German government announces Nuremberg Laws, legitimizing persecution of Jews. Italy invades Abyssinia; League of Nations applies economic sanctions. Baldwin succeeds MacDonald as prime minister.

German troops enter Rhineland. Spanish Civil War (to 1939). Rome-Berlin Axis allies Hitler with Mussolini. Anti-Comintern Pact agreed by Germany and Japan. Abdication of Edward VIII.
Basque village of Guernica destroyed by German bomber planes. Chamberlain becomes prime minister. Japan invades China.

Germany annexes Austria. Munich crisis.

Nazi-Soviet Pact. Hitler invades Poland; World War II begins. Gandhi calls on world to disarm. The Indian subcontinent contributes largest volunteer army in history (some 2.5 million service men and women) to the Allied cause.
Muslim League adopts Pakistan Resolution, which demands an independent state for Muslims. Churchill becomes prime minister. British Expeditionary Force evacuated from Dunkirk. Battle of Britain. New Intelligence Corps created by Army Order 112. The Blitz. Italy joins the war as ally to Germany.

Germans invade USSR. Japanese attack Pearl Harbor; US enters war. Japanese invasion of Burma.

DATE	AUTHOR'S LIFE	LITERARY CONTEXT
1941 *cont.*	Nancy Edith (Penny) Avery while stationed in Torquay; they marry on 23 October.	
1942	'Mylor Creek' printed in Wrey Gardiner's *Poetry Quarterly*.	Anand: *The Sword and the Sickle*. Camus: *The Stranger*.
1943	Sails for India from Liverpool on board RMS *Britannic* in draft RZGXG. Attends Royal Indian Army Service Corps training school at Kakul in Kashmir (to 1944).	Eliot: *Four Quartets*.
1944	Further training at Motor Transport School in Lahore and at Air Supply depot in Chaklala near Rawalpindi. Joins No 1 Indian Air Supply Company; becomes second in command of one of three sections, operating behind lines at Comilla. Company relocated to Imphal, where Paul is promoted to captain in command. Accompanies flights supplying army in Burma.	Hartley: *The Shrimp and Anemone*, first novel in *The Eustace and Hilda Trilogy* (to 1947). Compton-Burnett: *Elders and Betters*. Joyce Cary: *The Horse's Mouth*.
1945	Departs for Malaya under Operation Zipper. Japanese have announced unconditional surrender by arrival on Penang Island; Paul and his section enlisted for mopping-up operations.	Orwell: *Animal Farm*. Waugh: *Brideshead Revisited*. Narayan: *The English Teacher*. Waltari: *The Egyptian*.
1946	Returns to India and locates members of No 1 Company at Chas Transit Camp near Bihar. Repatriation orders arrive end of April. Reunited in England with Penny who is now living on Hampden Way, Southgate; returns to work as an audit clerk. Introduced to Joyce Weiner, who is establishing herself as a literary and theatrical agent. Offered job as bookkeeper for new publishing venture Falcon and Grey Walls Press.	Thomas: *Deaths and Entrances*. Peake: *Titus Groan*.

CHRONOLOGY

Japanese capture Rangoon and consolidate position in Burma. Fall of Singapore. Formation of INA (Indian National Army). Indian Congress rejects British proposal for postwar self-government; Quit India campaign is launched. German troops reach Stalingrad. North Africa campaign; battle of El-Alamein.

Subhas Chandra Bose assumes leadership of INA. Famine in Bengal leaves 3 million people dead. Germans retreat in Russia, Africa and Italy.

Normandy landings. Japanese troops driven out of Burma. Liberation of Paris. Red Army reaches Belgrade and Budapest.

Unconditional surrender of Germany; Hitler commits suicide. US drops atomic bombs on Hiroshima and Nagasaki. End of World War II. United Nations founded. Death of Roosevelt; Truman becomes US president. Britain establishes military administration in Malaya.

Royal Indian Navy mutiny starts in Bombay, spreading throughout India. Congress Party rejects Britain's plan for Indian Independence. All-India Muslim League demands creation of separate sovereign Islamic state of Pakistan; violent clashes between Hindus and Muslims ensue, claiming lives of 5,000 people in Calcutta alone. Nuremberg trials. 'Iron Curtain' speech by Churchill.

DATE	AUTHOR'S LIFE	LITERARY CONTEXT
1947	Promoted to company secretary of Falcon and Grey Walls Press. Daughter Carol Vivien born 7 March.	Camus: *The Plague*. Rao: *The Cow of the Barricades*. Snow: *The Light and the Dark*. Mackenzie: *Whisky Galore*.
1948	*Pillars of Salt* wins award in Jewish playwriting competition; published by Gollancz with three other winners as *Four Jewish Plays*. Second daughter Sally Elizabeth born 30 May. Paul moves new family nearer Hampstead, to Brooklands Rise.	Desani: *All About H. Hatterr*. Greene: *The Heart of the Matter*.
1949		Bowen: *The Heat of the Day*. Orwell: *Nineteen Eighty-four*. Narayan: *Mr Sampath*. Peake: *Gormenghast*.
1950	Paul resigns from Falcon and Grey Walls Press. BBC buys radio play *Lines of Communication* for 90 guineas (broadcast early 1951). Following rejections from 17 publishers Scott decides not to pursue first novel *Dazzling Crystal*. Begins working as a literary agent with Pearn, Pollinger and Higham in Covent Garden.	
1951		Snow: *The Masters*. Hanley: *The Consul at Sunset*. Chaudhuri: *Autobiography of an Unknown Indian*. Powell: *A Question of Upbringing*, first novel in sequence *A Dance to the Music of Time* (to 1975). Salinger: *The Catcher in the Rye*. Masters: *Nightrunners of Bengal*.
1952	Novel *Johnny Sahib* published by Eyre & Spottiswoode in UK; earns Eyre & Spottiswoode Literary Fellowship Prize.	Beckett: *Waiting for Godot*. Prescott: *The Man on a Donkey*. Waugh: *Men at Arms*, first novel in *The Sword of Honour Trilogy* (to 1961).
1953	Falcon and Grey Walls Press goes into liquidation; publisher Peter Baker is sentenced to prison for fraud and forgery. *The Alien Sky*.	Hanley: *The Year of the Lion*. Anand: *Private Life of an Indian Prince*. Peake: *Mr Pye*. Eliot: *The Confidential Clerk*. Hartley: *The Go-Between*.

CHRONOLOGY

Indian Independence Act: India partitioned into two dominions, India (Hindu) and Pakistan (Muslim). Burmese independence hero General Aung Sang assassinated. Britain announces that Burma will become independent by 1948.

Burma celebrates independence. Assassination of Mahatma Gandhi. Sri Lanka gains independence from UK with dominion status. Communist coup in Czechoslovakia. Jewish state of Israel established. State of Emergency declared in Malaya following murder of British planters; Malayan Communist Party, Malayan People's Army and Old Comrades' Association banned. Soviet blockade of West Berlin. Apartheid introduced in South Africa.

Chinese Revolution. North Atlantic Treaty signed. Eire leaves Commonwealth, becoming Republic of Ireland. Indian Police Services succeeds Imperial Police, under auspices of first Union Home Minister Sardar Patel.

Royal Indian Army Service Corps becomes Army Service Corps. Korean War (to 1953). Mother Teresa founds the Missionaries of Charity in Calcutta.

India becomes a Republic within the British Commonwealth; first national general election confirms Congress Party dominance. First Indian Five-Year Plan.

Eisenhower elected US president. Accession of Elizabeth II in UK.

Death of Stalin. European Court of Human Rights set up in Strasbourg.

DATE	AUTHOR'S LIFE	LITERARY CONTEXT
1954	Promoted to junior director of Pearn, Pollinger and Higham. Scotts move to a larger home in Hampstead Garden Suburb, on Addison Way. *The Alien Sky* (radio play).	Thomas: *Under Milk Wood*. K. Amis: *Lucky Jim*. Masters: *Bhowani Junction*. Snow: *The New Men*. Markandaya: *Nectar in the Sieve*. Murdoch: *Under the Net*.
1955		White: *The Tree of Man*. Narayan: *Waiting for the Mahatma*. Nabokov: *Lolita*. Greene: *The Quiet American*. Murdoch: *The Flight from the Enchanter*.
1956	*A Male Child*. BBC broadcasts TV adaptation of *The Alien Sky*.	Singh: *Train to Pakistan*. Burgess: *Time for a Tiger*, first novel in *The Malayan Trilogy* (to 1959). Wilson: *Anglo-Saxon Attitudes*. Mahfouz: *The Cairo Trilogy* (to 1957). Pillai: *Chemmeen*.
1957	Gives old typewriter to Penny, who uses it to begin writing her own novels.	Moraes: *A Beginning*. Day-Lewis: *Pegasus*. Braine: *Room at the Top*. Nabokov: *Pnin*. White: *Voss*. Murdoch: *The Sandcastle*.
1958	Tom Scott dies at home aged 88. Frances Scott moves into Addison Way; following family disagreements she goes to stay with Arthur Pridmore, father of her daughter-in-law by Peter. Frances and Arthur are married 6 December. Arranges a new assistant for David Higham in order to be able to take two days a week for writing. *The Mark of the Warrior. Sahibs & Memsahibs* (radio play).	Jhabvala: *Esmond in India*. Achebe: *Things Fall Apart*. Lamapedusa: *The Leopard*.
1959	Scotts celebrate delivery of *The Chinese Love Pavilion* manuscript with a holiday at Tamariu in Spain but Paul's heavy drinking becomes a cause for concern. Announces resignation to David Higham.	Chaudhuri: *A Passage to England*. Avery: *The Margaret Days*. Waterhouse: *Billy Liar*. Peake: *Titus Alone*. Spark: *Memento Mori*.

CHRONOLOGY

Indo-Chinese Treaty. Vietnam War begins.

Warsaw Pact formed. Eden becomes prime minister. West Germany joins NATO. Final territorial acquisition of British Empire: Royal Navy lands on uninhabited islet 'Rockall' in North Atlantic.

Second Five-Year Plan aims to increase Indian national income by 25 percent. Islam made state religion in Egypt. Pakistan becomes first Islamic republic but remains in the Commonwealth. Soviets invade Hungary. Suez crisis.

Ghana becomes independent under Dr Kwame Nkrumah. European Economic Community founded. Malaya achieves independence and membership of the Commonwealth under Tengku Abdul Rahman.

Fifth Republic in France.

Communism installed in Cuba under new premier Fidel Castro.

DATE	AUTHOR'S LIFE	LITERARY CONTEXT
1960	Begins life as a full-time writer. First TV appearance: interviewed by Peter Green for ABC's *Book Man*. Takes on a fiction column in The *New Statesman*. *The Chinese Love Pavilion*.	Avery: *The Marigold Summer*. Malgonkar: *Distant Drum*. Moraes: *Poems*. Rao: *The Serpent and the Rope*. Spark: *The Ballad of Peckham Rye*. Manning: *The Great Fortune*, first novel in *The Balkan Trilogy* (to 1965).
1961		Avery: *Nurse Has Four Cases*. Markandaya: *A Silence of Desire*. Naipaul: *A House for Mr Biswas*. White: *Riders in the Chariot*. Wilson: *The Old Men at the Zoo*. Spark: *The Prime of Miss Jean Brodie*.
1962	Stands in for Howard Spring on *Country Life* magazine. *Birds of Paradise*.	Malgonkar: *Combat of Shadows*. Nabokov: *Pale Fire*. Braine: *Life at the Top*. Burgess: *A Clockwork Orange*.
1963	Elected fellow of the Royal Society of Literature. *The Bender*.	Avery: *Sister Bollard*. Fowles: *The Collector*. West: *The Shoes of the Fisherman*. Malgonkar: *The Princes*. Markandaya: *Possession*. Spark: *The Girls of Slender Means*.
1964	Makes return visit to India; spends time in Bombay, Madras, Timmapuram in Andhra Pradesh and Calcutta. Diagnosed with amoebiasis, accounting for illness and depression of 20 years since army days; receives treatment in Paris. *The Corrida at San Feliu*.	Malgonkar: *A Bend in the Ganges*. Naipaul: *An Area of Darkness*. Snow: *The Corridors of Power*. Isherwood: *A Single Man*.
1965		Das: *Summer in Calcutta*. Rao: *Cat and Shakespeare*. Fowles: *The Magus*. Tagore: *The Housewarming*. Moraes: *John Nobody*.
1966	Penny suffers a series of debilitating accidents. *The Jewel in the Crown* (*The Raj Quartet*).	Markandaya: *A Handful of Rice*. Bulgakov: *The Master and Margarita*.

CHRONOLOGY

Macmillan makes 'wind of change' speech in Cape Town. State of
Maharashtra established, incorporating city of Bombay. Republic of Somalia
declared. Independence of Cyprus; UK retains 2 military bases on the
island. Nigeria gains independence within the Commonwealth. John F.
Kennedy wins US presidency.

Third Five-Year Plan propels India into ranks of ten most industrialized
countries; population rises to 434 million. Yuri Gagarin becomes first man in
space. Sierra Leone becomes independent. Union of South Africa withdraws
from Commonwealth. Erection of Berlin Wall. Taganyika gains
independence under prime minister Julius Nyerere.

Ne Win stages successful coup; Burma becomes a socialist one-party state.
Jamaica, Trinidad and Tobego gain independence within the
Commonwealth. Uganda becomes independent under Milton Obote.
Sino-Indian border clashes. Cuban missile crisis.
Nigeria becomes an independent republic. Profumo affair; prime minister
Macmillan resigns. Assassination of Kennedy; Johnson becomes US
president. Zanzibar and Kenya achieve independence within the
Commonwealth.

Death of Indian prime minister Nehru; succeeded by Shastri. In USSR
Khrushchev deposed and replaced by Brezhnev.

Death of Winston Churchill. Gambia becomes an independent state within
the Commonwealth. Civil war breaks out in Dominican Republic; Johnson
orders US intervention. Sustained bombing of targets in North Vietnam by
US aircraft. Indo-Pakistan War. Tamil riots against Hindi language; English
confirmed as official language of India.
Mrs Indira Gandhi, daughter of Nehru, becomes prime minister of India.
Republic of Botswana established with Seretse Khama as president. British
colony of Basutoland becomes independent state of Lesotho. Barbados gains
independence within the Commonwealth.

DATE	AUTHOR'S LIFE	LITERARY CONTEXT
1967	Penny, still unwell, undergoes a series of tests and treatments.	Das: *The Descendants.* Márquez: *One Hundred Years of Solitude.*
1968	*The Day of the Scorpion* (*The Raj Quartet*).	Clarke: *2001: A Space Odyssey.* Braine: *The Crying Game.*
1969	Departs for India, visiting on his trip Bombay, Agra, Jaipur in Rajasthan, and Belgaum. Mother Frances dies.	Markandaya: *The Coffer Dams.* Fowles: *The French Lieutenant's Woman.* Roth: *Portnoy's Complaint.* First Booker Prize awarded.
1970	Penny takes 3-month nursing refresher course and proceeds to nurse at Middlesex Hospital three days a week.	Updike: *Bech: A Book.* Spark: *The Driver's Seat.*
1971	Carol marries musician Larry McLaughlin. *The Towers of Silence* (*The Raj Quartet*); wins *Yorkshire Post* book of the year award for finest fiction.	Updike: *Rabbit Redux.* Tagore: *The Broken Nest.*
1972	Paul flies to Bombay for a lecture tour organized by the British Council. Takes on a fortnightly column in *Country Life.*	Farrell: *The Siege of Krishnapur.* Malgonkar: *The Devil's Wind.*
1973		Das: *The Old Playhouse and Other Poems.* Markandaya: *Two Virgins.* Jhabvala: *A New Dominion.* Pynchon: *Gravity's Rainbow.* M. Amis: *The Rachel Papers.*
1974		
1975	Flies to US to give series of lectures at universities in Texas, Maryland and Illinois. *A Division of Spoils* (*The Raj Quartet*).	Rushdie: *Grimus.* Das: *Manas.* McEwan: *First Loves, Last Rites.* Jhabvala: *Heat and Dust.* Levi: *The Periodic Table.*

CHRONOLOGY

HISTORICAL EVENTS

Six-Day War between Israel and Arab states. Argentinian-born guerrilla hero Che Guevara shot dead in Bolivia.

Student unrest in US and throughout Europe. Martin Luther King assassinated; violent reaction throughout US. Enoch Powell makes inflammatory speech in Birmingham regarding continued immigration from Commonwealth to Britain. Czechoslovakia invaded by Soviet troops. Richard Nixon elected US president. Swaziland becomes independent within the Commonwealth, marking end of UK's colonial ties with Africa. US troops begin to withdraw from Vietnam. Astronaut Neil Armstrong becomes first man on the moon. British army deployed to support Royal Ulster Constabulary for counter-terrorism and public order operations.

Black September conflict in Jordan (to 1971). Chilean Salvador Allende becomes world's first democratically elected Marxist head of state.

Northern Ireland activates internment law. India recognizes independence of East Pakistan as Bangladesh. Indira Gandhi strips Indian princes of their titles and abolishes privy purses.

'Bloody Sunday' in Londonderry, Northern Ireland; direct rule imposed by British government. Pakistan leaves the Commonwealth. President Amin expels Ugandan Asians. Israeli building at Olympic Village near Munich attacked by Arab guerrillas. Strategic Arms Limitation Treaty (SALT I) signed by US and USSR.
Chilean president Allende and at least 2,700 others killed in coup led by General Pinochet. Arab–Israeli War.

Conference of Islamic heads of state in Lahore recognizes Palestine Liberation Organization and pursuit of Jerusalem's return to Arab control. Coalminers hold full-scale strike in UK. People's Front formed in India. Resignation of Nixon following Watergate scandal.
State of emergency declared in India due to growing strikes and unrest (to 1977). End of Vietnam War. Civil war between Christians and Muslims in Lebanon (to 1990).

DATE	AUTHOR'S LIFE	LITERARY CONTEXT
1976	Penny leaves Paul and takes refuge at Chiswick Women's Aid. Paul assumes a visiting professorship, teaching writing and modern literature at University of Tulsa in Oklahoma. *Staying On*. Professor Max Beloff, an historian, writes first academic study of *The Raj Quartet*.	Das: *Alphabet of Lust*. Rao: *Comrade Kirillov*.
1977	Departs for US for fall semester at Tulsa. Falls seriously ill; examinations reveal severe cirrhosis of the liver and advanced colon cancer. Stops drinking and cuts down on cigarettes, but refuses to leave teaching post. Carol receives Booker Prize in London on his behalf for *Staying On*. Penny moves back to Addison Way for Paul's return in December.	Desai: *Fire on the Mountain*. Manning: *The Danger Tree*, first novel in *The Levant Trilogy* (to 1980). Fowles: *Daniel Martin*.
1978	Dies 1 March in Middlesex Hospital, London.	Greene: *The Human Factor*. Kaye: *The Far Pavilions*. Murdoch: *The Sea, The Sea*.

HISTORICAL EVENTS

Soweto massacre in South Africa. Saddam Hussein becomes president of Iraq. Death of Chairman Mao in China. Jimmy Carter elected US president.

First defeat of Congress Party in India since Independence; Desai becomes prime minister. Prime Minister Bhutto of Pakistan overthrown by military and later hanged (1979).

P. W. Botha comes to power in South Africa.

THE JEWEL IN THE CROWN

To Dorothy Ganapathy
with love

CONTENTS

PART ONE

MISS CRANE

IMAGINE, THEN, a flat landscape, dark for the moment, but even so conveying to a girl running in the still deeper shadow cast by the wall of the Bibighar Gardens an idea of immensity, of distance, such as years before Miss Crane had been conscious of standing where a lane ended and cultivation began: a different landscape but also in the alluvial plain between the mountains of the north and the plateau of the south.

It is a landscape which a few hours ago, between the rainfall and the short twilight, extracted colour from the spectrum of the setting sun and dyed every one of its own surfaces that could absorb light: the ochre walls of the houses in the old town (which are stained too with their bloody past and uneasy present); the moving water of the river and the still water of the tanks, the shiny stubble, the ploughed earth, of distant fields; the metal of the grand trunk road. In this landscape trees are sparse, except among the white bungalows of the civil lines. On the horizon there is a violet smudge of hill country.

This is the story of a rape, of the events that led up to it and followed it and of the place in which it happened. There are the action, the people, and the place; all of which are interrelated but in their totality incommunicable in isolation from the moral continuum of human affairs.

In the Bibighar Gardens case there were several arrests and an investigation. There was no trial in the judicial sense. Since then people have said there was a trial of sorts going on. In fact, such people say, the affair that began on the evening of August 9th, 1942, in Mayapore, ended with the spectacle of two nations in violent opposition, not for the first time nor as yet for the last because they were then still locked in an imperial embrace of such long standing and subtlety it was no longer possible for them to know whether they hated or loved one another, or what it was that held them together and seemed to have confused the image of their separate destinies.

*

In 1942, which was the year the Japanese defeated the British
army in Burma and Mr Gandhi began preaching sedition in India,
the English then living in the civil and military cantonment of
Mayapore had to admit that the future did not look propitious.
They had faced bad times before, though, and felt that they could
face them again, that now they knew where they stood and
there could be no more heart-searching for quite a while yet
about the rights and wrongs of their colonial-imperialist policy
and administration.

As they were fond of putting it at the club, it was a question
of first things first, and when they heard that Miss Crane, the
supervisor of the district's Protestant mission schools, had taken
Mr Gandhi's picture down from the walls of her study and no
longer entertained Indian ladies to tea but young English soldiers
instead, they were grateful to her as well as amused. In peace
time opinions could be as diverse and cranky as you wished. In
war you had to close the ranks; and if it was to be a question of
sides Miss Crane seemed to have shown at last which she was
really on.

What few people knew was that the Indian ladies themselves
had taken the initiative over the question of tea on Tuesdays at
Edwina Crane's bungalow. Miss Crane suspected that it was the
ladies' husbands who had dissuaded them from making the
weekly appearance, not only because Mr Gandhi's picture had
gone but in case such visits could have been thought of, in this
explosive year, as a buttering-up of the *raj*. What hurt her most
was that none of the ladies had bothered to discuss their reasons
with her. They had one by one or two by two just stopped coming and made feeble excuses when she met any of them in the
bazaar or on her way to the mission schoolrooms.

She was sorry about the ladies whom she had always encouraged to be frank with her, but not at all sorry about Mr Gandhi's
portrait. The ladies had an excuse. Mr Gandhi did not. She
believed he was behaving abominably. She felt, in fact, let down.
For years she had laughed at Europeans who said that he was not
to be trusted, but now Mr Gandhi had extended what looked
like an open invitation to the Japanese to come and help him rid
India of the British – and if he thought that they would be the
better masters then she could only assume he was out of his

senses or, which was worse, revealing that his philosophy of non-violence had a dark side that added up to total invalidation of its every aspect. The Japanese, apparently, were to do his violence for him.

Reacting from her newly found distrust of the Mahatma and her disappointment in the behaviour of the ladies (the kind of disappointment she had actually become no stranger to) she wondered whether her life might not have been spent better among her own people, persuading them to appreciate the qualities of Indians, instead of among Indians, attempting to prove that at least one Englishwoman admired and respected them. She had to admit that a searching analysis of her work would show that in the main the people she had got on with best of all were those of mixed blood; which seemed, perhaps, to emphasize the fact that she was neither one thing nor the other herself – a teacher without real qualifications, a missionary worker who did not believe in God. She had never been wholly accepted by Indians and had tended to reject the generality of the English. In this there was a certain irony. The Indians, she thought, might have taken her more seriously if she had not been a representative of the kind of organization they were glad enough to make use of but of which old suspicions died hard. By the same token, if she had not worked for the mission she would, she believed, never have acquired an admiration for the Indians through love and respect for their children, nor been led to such sharp criticism of her own race, in whose apparently neglectful and indifferent care the future of those children and the present well-being of their parents were held. She had never been slow to voice her criticism. And this, possibly, had been a mistake. The English always took such criticism so personally.

However, Miss Crane was of a generation that abided by (even if it did not wholly believe in) certain simple rules for positive action. It was, she told herself, never too late to mend, or try to mend. Thinking of the young British soldiers who were in Mayapore in ever-increasing numbers, and remembering that most of them looked fresh out from home, she wrote to the Station Staff Officer, had an interview with him, and arranged to entertain a party of up to a dozen at a time at tea every Wednesday afternoon from five o'clock until six-thirty. The SSO thanked her for her generosity and said he wished more people realized what it meant to an English lad to be in a home again, if only for an hour or two. For all their flag-wagging the ladies of the cantonment tended to have a prejudice against the British Other Rank. The SSO did not say this but the implication was there. Miss Crane guessed from his speech and manner that he had risen from the ranks himself. He said he hoped she would not have cause to regret her invitation. Young soldiers, although mostly maligned, were indeed apt to be clumsy and noisy. She had only to ring him up if things proved too much for her or if she had anything to complain about. She smiled and reminded him that the life she led had never been sheltered and she had often heard herself referred to in Mayapore as a tough old bird.

The soldiers who came to Miss Crane's bungalow for tea spoke with cockney accents but they were not clumsy. With one exception, a boy called Barrett, they handled the bone china with big-fisted dexterity. They were not too shy and not over noisy. The parties always ended on a gratifyingly free and easy note. Afterwards, she stood on the front verandah and waved them down the path that led through her pretty, well-kept garden. Outside the gate they lit cigarettes and went back to barracks in a comradely bunch making some clatter with their boots on the hard surface of the road. Having helped her old Indian servant Joseph to clear away, Miss Crane then retired to her room to read reports and deal with letters from the head-quarters of the mission, and – since the soldiers' tea was on a Wednesday and Thursday was her day to visit and stay overnight at the school in Dibrapur, seventy-five miles away – prepare her Gladstone bag for the journey and look out a tin of boiled sweets as a gift for the Dibrapur children. While she did these things she also found time to think about the soldiers.

There was one particular boy who came regularly of whom she was very fond. His name was Clancy. He was what middle-class people of her own generation would have called one of nature's gentlemen. It was Clancy who sat down last and stood up first, Clancy who saw to it that she had a piece of her own fruit cake and that she did not go sugarless for want of the passing back up the table of the bowl. He always asked how she was, and gave the most lucid answers to her inquiries about their training and sports and communal life in the barracks. And whereas the others called her Mum, or Ma'am, Clancy called her Miss Crane. She was herself meticulous in the business of getting to know their names and dignifying them with the prefix Mister. She knew that private soldiers hated to be called by their surnames alone if the person talking to them was a woman. But although she never omitted to say Mister Clancy when addressing him, it was as Clancy that she thought of him. It was a nice name, and his friends called him that, or Clance.

Clancy, she was glad to notice, was liked by his comrades. His attentiveness to her wasn't resented, or laughed at. He seemed to be a natural leader. He commanded respect. He was good-looking and fitted his uniform of khaki shirt and shorts better than the other boys. Only his accent, and his hands – with torn finger-nails, never quite clean of vestiges of oil and grease from handling rifles and guns – marked him as an ordinary member of the herd.

Sometimes, when they had gone and she worked on her files and thought about them, she was sad. Some of those boys, Clancy more easily than the others because he was bound to get a position of responsibility, might be killed. She was also sad, but in a different way, when the thought passed through her head, as it couldn't help doing, that probably they all laughed at her on the quiet and talked about her when she wasn't there to hear as the old maid who served up char and wads.

She was, as mission headquarters knew, an intelligent and perceptive woman whose understanding, common sense and organizing ability, more than made up for what in a woman connected with a Christian mission were of doubtful value: her agnosticism, for instance, and her fundamentally anti-British, because pro-Indian, sympathies.

Edwina Crane had lived in India for thirty-five of her fifty-seven years. She was born in London in 1885 of moderately well-to-do middle-class parents; her mother died early and she spent her youth and young womanhood looking after her lost lonely father, a schoolmaster who became fond of the bottle and his own company so that gradually the few friends they had drifted away along with the pupils who attended his private school. He died in an Edwardian summer when she was twenty-one, leaving her penniless and fit for nothing, she felt, except the job of paid companion or housekeeper. The scent of lime trees in fading flower stayed with her afterwards as the smell of death. She thought she was lucky when the first job she got was as governess to a spoiled little boy who called her Storky and tried to shock her once with a precocious show of sexuality in the night-nursery.

She was not shocked. In the later stages of her father's illness she had had to deal with his incontinence, and before that with his drunken outbursts in which he had not been above telling her those facts of life she had not already learned or ridiculing her for her long nose and plain looks and slender hopes of marriage. Sober, he was always ashamed, but too uncourageous to tell her so. She understood this, and because of it learned to value courage in others and try hard, not always successfully, to show it herself. In some ways her father was like a child to her. When he was dead she wept, then dried her eyes and sold most of the few remaining possessions to pay for a decent funeral, having refused financial help from the rich uncle who had kept away during her father's lifetime and moral support from the poor cousins who reappeared at his death.

So the little boy did not shock her. Neither did he enchant her. Living alone with her father she had tended to believe that he and she were of a kind apart, singled out to support a special cross compounded of genteel poverty and drunkenness, but the wealthy and temperate household in which she had now come to live seemed unhappy too, and this had the effect of making the world she knew look tragically small just at the moment when it might have been opening up. It was the desire she had to find a place in an unknown world that would come at her as new and fresh and, if not joyful, then at least adventurous and worthwhile, that made her apply for a post as travelling nurse-companion to a lady making the passage back to India with two young children. The lady, who had a pale face and looked deli-cate, but turned out resilient, explained that if proved satisfac-tory, the person who obtained the post could stay on in India after they arrived, with a view to acting as governess. If unsatisfactory, such a person would easily find a similar job with a family taking the passage home, failing which her passage home would be paid. The lady seemed to take a fancy to her and so Miss Crane was employed.

The voyage was pleasant because Mrs Nesbitt-Smith treated her like a member of the family, and the children, a blue-eyed girl and a blue-eyed boy, both said they loved her and wanted her to live with them for ever. When they reached Bombay, Major Nesbitt-Smith met them and treated her like one of the family too; but Miss Crane could not help noticing from then on that the major's wife gradually withdrew, and by the time they reached the husband's station in the Punjab was treating her not exactly like a servant but like a poor relation with whom the family had somehow got saddled and so for the present made use of. It was Miss Crane's first experience of social snobbery abroad, which was never the same as snobbery at home because it was complicated by the demands, sometimes conflicting, of white solidarity and white supremacy. Her employers felt a duty to accord her a recognition they would have withheld from the highest-born Indian, at the same time a compulsion to place her on one of the lowest rungs of the ladder of their own self-contained society – lower outside the household than in, where, of course, she stood in a position far superior to that of any native servant. Miss Crane disapproved of this preoccupation with the question of who was who and why. It went against the increasingly liberal grain of her strengthening conscience. It also seemed to make life very difficult. She thought that Mrs Nesbitt-Smith was sometimes hard put to it to know what expression to wear when talking to her and decided that the confusion she must often have been in accounted for the frequent look of concern, almost of pain, at having to speak at all.

She was with the Nesbitt-Smiths for three years. She had a strong constitution which meant she was seldom ill even in that difficult climate. She was fond of the children and reacted to the politeness of the servants by overcoming the shyness she had been used to feel at home. There was, as well, India, which at first had seemed strange, even frightening, but presently full of compensations that she found difficult to name but felt in her heart. She had few friends and still felt isolated from people as individuals, but she was aware now of a sense of community. That sense sprang, she knew, from the seldom-voiced but always insistent, even when mute, clan-gathering call to solidarity that was part of the social pattern she had noted early on and disapproved of. She still disapproved of it but was honest enough to recognize it as having always been a bleak but real enough source of comfort and protection. There was a lot to fear in India, and it was good to feel safe, to know that indifferently as Mrs Nesbitt-Smith might sometimes treat her, Mrs Nesbitt-Smith and her like would always rally round if she found herself in any kind of danger from outside the charmed circle of privilege on whose periphery she spent her days. She knew that the India she found full of compensations was only the white man's India. But it was an India of a kind, and that at least was a beginning.

At this stage she fell in love, not with the young assistant chaplain to the station who sometimes conducted the services at the local Protestant church (which would have been a possible match, indeed was one that in her good moods Mrs Nesbitt-Smith chaffed her about and smilingly pushed her towards) but hopelessly and secretly with a Lieutenant Orme who was as handsome as Apollo, as kind, gentle and gay with her as any hero in a romantic novel, as ignorant or unheeding of her regard as his good looks so well enabled him to be in a station remarkable that year for the number of pretty well-placed girls of whom he could have his pick: hopelessly in love, because she had no chance; secretly, because she found she did not blush or act awkwardly in his presence, and Mrs Nesbitt-Smith, even had she bothered to observe the reactions of her children's governess to a man so splendidly equipped, in every sense, as Lieutenant Orme, would not have been able to tell that Miss Crane had longings in directions which were, by tradition, totally closed to her. That she neither blushed nor acted awkwardly puzzled Miss Crane. Her heart beat when he stood close by and perhaps there came a slight dryness into her mouth, but her feelings, she decided, must have been too intense, too adult, for her to act like the fluttering stupid girls who knew nothing of the world's reality.

When Lieutenant Orme was posted away, still uncommitted and with his usual glittering luck, as ADC to a general, to the frenzied disappointment of up to twenty pretty girls, as many plain ones and all their mothers, no one, Miss Crane believed, could have suspected the extent to which his departure darkened her own life. Only the children, her two most intimate human contacts, noticed that her manner changed. They gazed at her through those still remarkably blue but now older and calculating upper-middle-class eyes and said, 'What's wrong, Miss

Crane? Have you got a pain, Miss Crane?' and danced round her singing, 'Old Crane's got a pain,' so that she lost her temper, slapped them and sent them away screaming through shadow and sunlight to be comforted by the old ayah of whom, she knew, they had become fonder.

Before the next hot weather began Major Nesbitt-Smith's regiment was ordered home. 'I and the children will be going on ahead,' she overheard Mrs Nesbitt-Smith say to a friend, 'and of course Crane will be coming with us.' Speaking of her to others Mrs Nesbitt-Smith usually referred to her as Crane, but as Miss Crane to her face and the children, and, in rare moments of warmth and gratitude, as Edwina, as when for instance she lay in her darkened punkah-cooled room with Miss Crane kneeling by her bedside soothing with cologne one of her raging headaches.

For many days after the news of the regiment's impending return to England, Miss Crane went about her duties with no particular thoughts in her head because she had firmly put Lieutenant Orme out of them some time ago and nothing had come to take his place. 'And he,' she said to herself presently, 'was a fancy, a mere illusion that never stood a chance of becoming real for me. Now that I've banished the illusion from my thoughts I can see them for what they are, what they have always been, empty, starved, waiting to be filled. How will they be filled at home, in England? By care of the children as they grow, and become old, beyond me? By substituting different children for these and a different Mrs Nesbitt-Smith for this one? Households that are not the same household and yet the same? And so on, year after year, as Crane, Miss Crane, and sometimes, increasingly rarely, until no more, Edwina?'

In the evenings between five o'clock – when the children had had their tea and became the temporary sole charge of the ayah for play and bath – and seven o'clock when she supervised their supper before going in to dine alone or, if circumstances permitted, with the family, Miss Crane was free. Mostly she spent those two short hours in her room, having her own bath, resting, reading, writing an occasional letter to another of her kind who had exchanged this station for another or gone back to England. But now she began to feel restless and took to putting on her boots and – parasol opened and protectively raised – walking

down the lane of the civil lines in which the Nesbitt-Smiths'
bungalow stood. The lane was shaded by trees that thinned out
gradually as the bungalows gave way to open cultivated fields.
Sometimes she walked in the opposite direction, towards the
cantonment bazaar beyond which lay the railway station and the
native town which she had entered only on one occasion – with
a group of laughing ladies and timid companions in carriages,
stoutly accompanied by gentlemen – to inspect a Hindu temple
which had frightened her, as the native town had frightened her
with its narrow dirty streets, its disgusting poverty, its raucous
dissonant music, its verminous dogs, its starving, mutilated
beggars, its fat white sacred Brahmini bulls and its ragged population of men and women who looked so resentful in comparison with the servants and other officiating natives of the
cantonment.

On the day that she found herself questioning the prospect of
a future that was, as it were, an image seen in a series of mirrors
that reflected it until it became too small for the eye to see –
a diminishing row of children and Nesbitt-Smiths and Edwina
Cranes – the walk she went on at five was the one that brought
her out to the open spaces where the road led on into the far
distance. Reaching this point, she stopped, afraid to go farther.
The sun was still hot, still high enough to make her narrow her
eyes as she gazed from under the brim of her hat and the cotton
canopy of the parasol, towards the horizon of the flat, wide,
immense Punjabi plain. It seemed impossible, she thought, that
the world continued beyond that faraway boundary, that somewhere it changed its nature, erupted into hills and forests and
ranges of mountains whose crests were white with eternal snows
where rivers had their source. It seemed impossible too that
beyond the plains there could be an ocean where those rivers
had their end. She felt dwarfed, famished in the spirit, pressed
down by a tremendous weight of land, and of air and incompre-
hensible space that even the flapping, wheeling crows had
difficulty keeping up in. And she thought for a moment that she
was being touched by the heavy finger of a god; not the familiar
uplifting all-forgiving God she went through the motions of
praying to, but one neither benign nor malign, neither creating
nor destroying, sleeping nor waking, but existing, and leaning
his weight upon the world.

Acknowledging that women such as herself tended to turn to if not actually to seek sanctuary in religion, she walked on the following evening in the other direction and when she came to the Protestant church she turned into the compound and went up the broad gravel path, past the hummocky graves marked by the headstones of those who had died far from home, but who in their resting place, had they woken, might have been comforted by the English look of the church and its yard and the green trees planted there. The side door of the church was on the latch. She went in and sat in a pew at the back, stared at the altar and gazed at the darkening east window of stained glass which she saw every Sunday in the company of the Nesbitt-Smiths.

The god of this church was a kind, familiar, comfortable god. She had him in her heart but not in her soul. She believed in him as a comforter but not as a redeemer. He was very much the god of a community, not of the dark-skinned community that struggled for life under the weight of the Punjabi sky but of the privileged pale-faced community of which she was a marginal member. She wondered whether she would be Crane to Him, or Miss Crane, or Edwina. If she thought of Him as the Son she would, she presumed, be Edwina, but to God in His wrath, undoubtedly Crane.

'Miss Crane?'

Startled by the voice she looked over her shoulder. It was the senior chaplain, an elderly man with a sharp pink nose and a fringe of distinguishing white hair surrounding his gnomic head. His name was Grant, which caused restrained smiles during services when he intoned prayers that began Grant, O Lord, we beseech Thee. She smiled now, although she was embarrassed being found by him there, betraying herself as a woman in need almost certainly not of rest but of reassurance. A plain somewhat horse-faced woman in her middle twenties, alone in an empty Protestant church, on a day when no service was due, was somehow already labelled. In later years, Miss Crane came to look upon that moment as the one that produced in her the certainty of her own spinsterhood.

'You are resting from your labours,' Mr Grant said in his melodious congregational voice, and added, more directly, when she had nodded and looked down at her lap, 'Can I be of any help, child?' so that without warning she wanted to weep because child was what her father had often called her in his sober, loving moments. However, she did not weep. She had not wept since her father's death and although there would come a time when she did once more it had not arrived yet. Speaking in a voice whose steadiness encouraged her, she said, 'I'm thinking of staying on,' and, seeing the chaplain's perplexity, the way he glanced round the church as if something had begun to go on there which nobody had bothered to forewarn him of but which Miss Crane knew about and thought worth staying for, she explained, 'I mean in India, when the Nesbitt-Smiths go home.'

The chaplain said, 'I see,' and frowned, perhaps because she had called them the Nesbitt-Smiths. 'It should not be difficult, Miss Crane. Colonel and Mrs Ingleby, for instance, strike me as worth approaching. I know you are well thought of. Major and Mrs Nesbitt-Smith have always spoken highly.'

The future looked dark, a blank featureless territory with, in its centre, a pinprick of light that seemed to be all that was left of Edwina Crane.

'I think I should like,' she said, giving expression to a thought that had never properly been a thought until now, 'to train for the Mission.'

He sat down next to her and together they watched the east window.

'Not,' she went on, 'no, not to carry the Word. I am not a truly religious woman.' She glanced at him. He was still watching the window. He did not seem to be particularly upset by her confession. 'But there are schools, aren't there?' she said. 'I meant train to teach at the mission schools.'

'Ah yes, I see, to teach not our own children but those of our dark brethren in Christ?'

She nodded. She found herself short of breath. He turned to look at her fully, and asked her, 'Have you seen the school here?'

Yes, she had seen the school, close to the railway station, but – 'Only from the outside,' she told him.

'Have you ever talked to Miss Williams?'

'Who is Miss Williams?'

'The teacher. But then you would be unlikely to know her. She is a lady of mixed blood. Would you like to visit the school?'

'Very much.'

The chaplain nodded and presently, after the appearance of having thought more deeply, said, 'Then I will arrange it, and if you are of the same mind I will write to the superintendent in Lahore, not that there is anything much for you to judge by in Miss Williams's little school.' He shook his head. 'No, Miss Crane. This isn't an area where we've had much success, although more than the Catholics and the Baptists. There are of course a great number of schools throughout the country, of various denominations, all committed to educating what I suppose we must call the heathen. In this matter the Church and the missions have always led the way. The government has been, shall we say, slow to see the advantages. So, perhaps, have the Indians. The school here, for instance. A handful of children at the best of times. At the times of the festivals none. I mean, of course, the Hindu and Muslim festivals. The children come, you see, mainly for the chappattis, and in the last riots the school was set fire to, but that was before your time.'

The mission school was not the one she had had in mind which was close to the railway, the Joseph Wainwright Christian School, a substantial building, a privately endowed school for Eurasian children, the sons and daughters of soldiers, railway officials and junior civil servants whose blood had been mixed with that of the native population. The mission school was on the outskirts of the native town itself, a poor, small, rectangular building with a roof of corrugated iron in a walled compound bare of grass, with nothing to identify it apart from the cross roughly painted on the yellow stucco above the door. She was too ashamed to admit her mistake to Mr Grant, who had brought her in a tonga, and now handed her down and led her through the opening in the wall where once, before the last riots, there might have been a gate.

To come with him at midday she had had to obtain permission from Mrs Nesbitt-Smith and explain her reason for wanting leave of absence from the task of teaching the young Nesbitt-Smiths. Mrs Nesbitt-Smith had stared at her as if she were mad and exclaimed, 'Good heavens, Crane! What on earth has possessed you?' And then added, with what looked like genuine concern, which was touching and therefore far more upsetting than the outburst, 'You'd be with blacks and half-castes, cut off from your own kind. And besides, Edwina, we're all very fond of you.'

She was undoubtedly acting like a fool, far from sure even that she was acting on an impulse she had interpreted correctly. To begin with, to have confused the Eurasian school with the mission school proved how ignorant she was of what was there under her own nose, proved how little was really known by people such as herself about the life of the town they were supposed to have a duty to, a duty whose proper execution earned them the privileges they enjoyed. If she had not even known where this particular mission school was, what, she wondered, could she hope to contribute to other mission schools or deserve to gain from them?

The door of the school was open. There was a sound of children singing. When they reached the door the singing stopped. Mr Grant said that Miss Williams was expecting them and then stood aside. She crossed the threshold directly into the schoolroom. The woman on the dais said, 'Stand up, children,' and motioned with her arms at the pupils who were seated on several rows of benches, facing her. They stood up. A phrase written in block capitals on the blackboard drew Miss Crane's attention. Welcome Miss Crane Mem. At another sign from the teacher the children chanted it slowly. 'Welcome, Miss Crane Mem.' Trying to say, 'Thank you', she found her tongue and the roof of her mouth dry. The visit on which she had set out in the role of a suppliant for employment was looked upon here as the visit of an inquisitive memsahib. She was terrified of the obligation this put her under and of the stuffy white-washed room, the rows of children and the smell of burning cowpats that was coming through the open door and windows from the back of the compound where no doubt the God-sent chappattis were being cooked. And she was afraid of Miss Williams, who wore a grey cotton blouse, long brown skirt and black button boots, and was younger than she and sallow-complexioned in the way that some of the most insufferable of the European women were who had spent a lifetime in the country; only in Miss Williams's case the sallowness denoted a half-Indian origin, the kind of origin for which Miss Crane had been taught to feel a certain horror.

Miss Williams left the dais on which there were the teacher's desk and only one chair. Invited, Miss Crane sat, and the chaplain stood next to her. He had said, 'Miss Crane, this is Miss Williams,' but had not said, 'Miss Williams, this is Miss Crane,' and as Miss Crane sat down she attempted to smile at the girl to apologize for an omission not her own, but her lips were as parched as her mouth, and she was conscious, then, of an expression growing on her face similar to that which she had seen so often on Mrs Nesbitt-Smith's. It became etched more deeply when at last she submitted to the duty to look at the children, found herself the lone, inarticulate object of their curiosity and awe, perhaps their fear. The simple dress she had put on, her best in order to look her best – white muslin with a frilled hem but no other decoration beyond the mother-of-pearl buttons down the pleated choker; and the hat, a straw boater perched squarely upon her piled-up hair; the folded parasol of white cotton with a pink lining, a gift from Mrs Nesbitt-Smith last Christmas – now seemed to envelop her, to encumber her with all the pompous frippery of a class to which she did not belong.

At Miss Williams's command a little girl, barefoot and dressed in a shapeless covering that looked like sacking, but whose pigtail was decked with flowers for the occasion, came forward with a nosegay, curtsied and held the nosegay up. Miss Crane took it. Again she tried to say 'Thank you', but her words must have been unintelligible because the little girl had to look at Miss Williams for confirmation that the ritual of presentation was over. Neither seeing nor smelling the flowers, Miss Crane held them to her nose, and when she looked up again the little girl was back in her place, standing with the other little girls in the front row.

'I think,' Mr Grant said, 'that the children may sit down again, don't you, Miss Crane? Then presently they can either sing the song or say the poem I'm sure Miss Williams here has been rehearsing hard all morning.'

For a moment Miss Crane stared helplessly at the flowers in her lap, aware that Miss Williams and Mr Grant were both watching her, both waiting for her. She nodded her head, ashamed because in the first public duty of her life she was failing.

Sitting down when Miss Williams told them to, the children

were silent. Miss Crane thought that they had sensed her discomfort and had interpreted it as displeasure or boredom. She forced herself to look at Miss Williams and say, 'I should love to hear the song,' then remembered Mr Grant had said poem or song, and added, 'or the poem. Or both. Please let them do what they have rehearsed.'

Miss Williams turned to the class and said in her slow, curiously accented English, 'Now children, what shall we sing? Shall we sing the song about There is a Friend?' and then, 'Achchha,' a word Miss Crane knew well enough, but which was followed by rapid words in Hindustani she could not catch because they sped by too quickly. I can't, she thought, even speak the language properly, so how can I hope to teach?

Once more the children got to their feet. Miss Williams beat time in the air, slowly, and sang the first line of the hymn which otherwise Miss Crane might not easily have recognized; and then paused, beat again and set them all singing, unevenly, shyly, and in voices still unused to the odd, flat, foreign scale.

> 'There's a Friend for little children
>   Above the bright blue sky,
> A Friend Who never changes,
>   Whose love will never die;
> Our earthly friends may fail us,
>   And change with changing years,
> This Friend is always worthy,
>   Of that dear Name He bears.
>
> There's a rest for little children,
>   Above the bright blue sky,
> Who love the Blessed Saviour
>   And to the Father cry;
> A rest from every turmoil,
>   From sin and sorrow free,
> Where every little pilgrim
>   Shall rest eternally.'

As they sang Miss Crane looked at them. They were a ragged little band. As a child the hymn had been one of her favourites and if it had been sung as English children sang it, with a piano or organ accompaniment, as it used to be sung in her father's shabby school, she might have been borne down by an intensity of feeling, or regret and sadness for a lost world, a lost comfort, a lost magic. But she was not borne down, nor uplifted. She felt an incongruity, a curious resistance to the idea of subverting these children from worship of their own gods to worship of one she herself had sung to when young but now had no strong faith in. But she had, too, a sudden passionate regard for them. Hungry, poor, deprived, hopelessly at a disadvantage, they yet conveyed to her an overwhelming impression of somewhere – and it could only be there, in the Black Town – being loved. But love, as their parents knew, was not enough. Hunger and poverty could never be reduced by love alone. There were, to begin with, free chappattis.

And it came to Miss Crane then that the only excuse she or anyone of her kind had to be there, alone, sitting on a chair, holding a nosegay, being sung to, the object of the awe of un-instructed children, was if they sat there conscious of a duty to promote the cause of human dignity and happiness. And then she was no longer really ashamed of her dress, or deeply afraid of the schoolhouse or of the smell of burning cowpats. The cow-pats were all that there was for fuel, the schoolhouse was small and stuffy because there was not enough money spent, not enough available, to make it large and airy, and her dress was only a symbol of the status she enjoyed and the obligations she had not to look afraid, not to be afraid, to acquire a personal grace, a personal dignity, as much as she could of either, as much as was in her power, so that she could be a living proof of there being, somewhere in the world, hope of betterment.

When the singing was sung and she had said, in halting Hindustani, 'Thank you. It was very good,' she asked Miss Williams whether she could stay while they had their chappattis and perhaps watch some of their games, and then, if Miss Williams had time to answer, ask one or two questions about the kind of work a teacher was required to do.

And so Miss Crane set out on the long and lonely, difficult and sometimes dangerous road that led her, many years later, to Mayapore, where she was superintendent of the district's Protes-tant mission schools.

*

Although she had taken Mr Gandhi's portrait down, there was one picture, much longer in her possession, which she kept hanging on the wall above the desk in her combined bedroom and study. She had had it since 1914, the fifth year of her service in the mission, the year in which she left the school in Muzzafirabad, where she had assisted a Mr Cleghorn, to take over on her own account the school in Ranpur.

The picture had been a gift, a parting token of esteem. The head of the mission himself had presided over the gathering at which the presentation was made, although it was Mr Cleghorn who handed the gift over while the children clapped and cheered. In the drawer of her desk she still had the inscribed plate that had been fixed to the frame. The plate was of gilt, now discoloured, and the lettering of the inscription was black, faded, but still legible. It said: 'Presented to Edwina Lavinia Crane, in recognition of her courage, by the staff and pupils of the School of the Church of England Mission, Muzzafirabad, NWFP.'

Before she reached Ranpur she removed the plate because she was embarrassed by the word courage. All she had done was to stand on the threshold of the schoolhouse, into which she had already herded the children, and deny entry – in fluent Urdu, using expressions she could hardly have repeated to her superiors – to a detachment of half-hearted rioters. At least, she had assumed they were half-hearted, although later, only an hour later, they or more determined colleagues sacked and burned the Catholic mission house down the road, attacked the police station and set off for the civil lines where the military dispersed them by shooting one of the ringleaders and firing the rest of their volleys into the air. For four days the town lived under martial law and when peace was restored Miss Crane found herself disagreeably in the public eye. The District Magistrate called on her, accompanied by the District Superintendent of Police, and thanked her. She felt it imperative to say that she was by no means certain she had done the right thing, that she wondered, in fact, whether it wouldn't have been better to have let the rioters in to burn whatever it was they wanted to get rid of, the prayer books or the crucifix. She had refused to let them and so they had gone away angrier than ever, and burned the Catholics to the ground and caused a great deal of trouble.

When Mr Cleghorn returned from leave, anxious for news of what he had only heard as rumour, she decided to apply for a transfer so that she could get on with her job without constant reminders of what she thought of as her false position. She told Mr Cleghorn that it was quite impossible to teach children who, facing her, saw her as a cardboard heroine and no doubt had, each of them, only one eye on the blackboard because the other was fixed on the doorway, expectant of some further disturbance they wanted her to quell. Mr Cleghorn said that he would be sorry to see her go, but that he quite understood and that if she really meant what she said he would write personally to mission headquarters to explain matters.

When the instructions for her transfer came she discovered that she had been promoted by being put in sole charge of the school at Ranpur. Before she left there was a tea, and then the presentation of the picture – a larger, more handsomely framed copy of the picture on the wall behind her desk in the Muzzafirabad schoolroom, a semi-historical, semi-allegorical picture entitled *The Jewel in Her Crown*, which showed the old Queen (whose image the children now no doubt confused with the person of Miss Crane) surrounded by representative figures of her Indian Empire: princes, landowners, merchants, money-lenders, sepoys, farmers, servants, children, mothers, and remarkably clean and tidy beggars. The Queen was sitting on a golden throne, under a crimson canopy, attended by her temporal and spiritual aides: soldiers, statesmen and clergy. The canopied throne was apparently in the open air because there were palm trees and a sky showing a radiant sun bursting out of bulgy clouds such as, in India, heralded the wet monsoon. Above the clouds flew the prayerful figures of the angels who were the benevolent spectators of the scene below. Among the statesmen who stood behind the throne one was painted in the likeness of Mr Disraeli holding up a parchment map of India to which he pointed with obvious pride but tactful humility. An Indian prince, attended by native servants, was approaching the throne bearing a velvet cushion on which he offered a large and sparkling gem. The children in the school thought that this gem was the jewel referred to in the title. Miss Crane had been bound to explain that the gem was simply representative of tribute, and that the jewel of the title was India herself, which had been transferred from the rule of the British East India Company to the rule of the British crown in 1858, the year after the Mutiny when the sepoys in the service of the Company (that first set foot in India in the seventeenth century) had risen in rebellion, and attempts had been made to declare an old moghul prince king in Delhi, and that the picture had been painted after 1877, the year in which Victoria was persuaded by Mr Disraeli to adopt the title Empress of India.

The Jewel in Her Crown was a picture about which Miss Crane had very mixed feelings. The copy that already hung on the classroom wall in Muzzafirabad when she first went there as assistant to Mr Cleghorn she found useful when teaching the English language to a class of Muslim and Hindu children. This is the Queen. That is her crown. The sky there is blue. Here there are clouds in the sky. The uniform of the sahib is scarlet. Mr Cleghorn, an ordained member of the Church and an enthusiastic amateur scholar of archaeology and anthropology, and much concerned with the impending, never-got-down-to composition of a monograph on local topography and social customs, had devoted most of his time to work for the Church and for the older boys in the middle school. He did this at the expense of the junior school, as he was aware. When Miss Crane was sent to him from Lahore in response to his requests for more permanent help in that field of his responsibility he had been fascinated to notice the practical use she made of a picture which, to him, had never been more than something hanging on the wall to brighten things up.

He was fond of remarking on it, whenever he found her in class with half a dozen wide-eyed children gathered round her, looking from her to the picture as she took them through its various aspects, step by step. 'Ah, the picture again, Miss Crane,' he would say, 'admirable, admirable. I should never have thought of it. To teach English and at the same time love of the English.'

She knew what he meant by love of the English. He meant love of their justice, love of their benevolence, love – anyway – of their good intentions. As often as she was irritated by his simplicity, she was touched by it. He was a good man: tireless, inquisitive, charitable. Mohammedanism and Hinduism, which still frightened her in their outward manifestations, merely amused him: as a grown man might be amused by the grim, colourful but harmless games of children. If there were times when she thought him heedless of the misery of men, she could not help knowing that in his own way he never forgot the glory of God. Mr Cleghorn's view was that God was best served, best glorified, by the training and exercise of the intellect. Physically timid – as she knew him to be from his fear of dogs, his mortal terror, once, of a snake which the watchman had to be sent for to despatch, his twitching cheeks and trembling hands when they were met on one or two occasions on the outskirts of villages by delegations of men who looked fierce but were actually friendly – he was morally courageous, and for this she admired him.

He fought long and hard for any money he thought the mission could afford and he could spend well. He had an ear and an eye for injustice and had been known to plead successfully with the District Magistrate for suspension of sentences or quashing of convictions in cases he believed deserved it. Mr Cleghorn – the District Magistrate used to say – was wasted in the Church and should have gone into the Civil.

He showed most determination, however, in promoting the education of boys of the middle-class – Anglo-Indians, Hindus, Muslims, Sikhs. If they had above average intelligence they were all one to him, all 'children whom the Lord has blessed with brains and sensibilities'. His work here was chiefly that of detecting just where a youth's talents lay and in persuading him and his parents to set a course in that direction. 'Look at young Shankar Ram,' he might say to Miss Crane, who had but the vaguest notion which Shankar Ram he referred to, 'he says he wants to be a civil servant. They all want to be civil servants. What chance has he got, though, beyond the post office and telegraphs? He should be an engineer. It may not be in his blood, but it is in his heart and mind.' And so he would set about depressingly often without success looking for ways, for means, for opportunities to send young Shankar Ram out into the great world beyond Muzzafirabad to build bridges. In this, Miss Crane used to think, Mr Cleghorn looked remarkably unlike any ordinary man of God, for the Shankar Ram in question, ninety-nine times out of a hundred, turned out to be as far away from conversion to Christianity as the women of India were from social emancipation. And over the question of women, British or Indian, Mr

Cleghorn was infuriatingly conservative. Women's interests were his blind spot. 'Your sex is made, alas,' he said once, 'and yet not alas, no, Heaven be praised, your sex is made, Miss Crane, for marriage or for God,' and in the one intimate moment there ever was between them, took her hand and patted it, as if to comfort her for the fact that the first, the temporal of these blessings, was certainly denied her.

Sometimes Miss Crane wanted to point to the picture on the wall which showed the old Queen resplendent on her throne and say to him, 'Well there, anyway, was a woman of affairs,' but never did, and was touched when she unwrapped the presentation parcel and saw an even gaudier copy of the enigmatic picture; touched because she knew that Mr Cleghorn, deeply considering the parting gift she might most value, had characteristically hit upon the one she could have done without.

But a couple of days later, as he saw her into the Ladies' First-Class compartment of a train, while young Joseph, a poor boy who had worked in the mission kitchens but had asked to serve and was coming with her, was seeing to the luggage, Mr Cleghorn handed her his own personal gift which, unwrapped as the train moved out into the bleak frontier landscape, turned out to be a copy of a book called *Fabian Essays in Socialism*, edited by Mr George Bernard Shaw. It was inscribed to 'My friend and colleague, Edwina Crane', signed, 'Arthur St John Cleghorn', and dated July 12th, 1914.

This book she still had, in the bookcase in her room in Mayapore.

When she paused in the work she was doing at her desk, as she felt entitled to do at her age, which was one for contemplation as well as action, she would sometimes glance at the picture and find her attention fixed on it. After all these years it had acquired a faint power to move her with the sense of time past, of glory departed, even although she knew there had never been glory there to begin with. The India of the picture had never existed outside its gilt frame, and the emotions the picture was meant to conjure up were not much more than smugly pious. And yet now, as always, there was a feeling somewhere in it of shadowy dignity.

It still stirred thoughts in her that she found difficult to analyse.

She had devoted her life, in a practical and unimportant way, to trying to prove that fear was evil because it promoted prejudice, that courage was good because it was a sign of selflessness, that ignorance was bad because fear sprang from it, that knowledge was good because the more you knew of the world's complexity the more clearly you saw the insignificance of the part you played. It was, possibly, Miss Crane felt, this concept of personal insignificance which, lying like the dark shadows of the rain clouds behind the gaudy colours of the picture of the Queen and her subjects, informed them with a graver splendour. There was, for Miss Crane, in the attitude of the old Queen on her throne, something ironically reminiscent of the way she herself had sat years ago on a dais, dressed in white muslin; and the message that she was always trying to read into this stylized representation of tribute and matriarchal care was one that conveyed the spirit of dignity without pomp, such as a mother, her own mother, had conveyed to her as a child, and the importance of courageously accepting duties and obligations, not for self-aggrandizement, but in self-denial, in order to promote a wider happiness and well-being, in order to rid the world of the very evils the picture took no account of: poverty, disease, misery, ignorance and injustice.

And it was because (turning late, but perhaps not too late, to her own countrymen) she saw in a young man called Private Clancy, beneath the youthful brash male urge to thrust himself into prominence (and she was not blind to that aspect of his behaviour) a spark of tenderness, an instinct for self-denial that made him see to it that she had a slice of cake and sweetened tea, and, perhaps (she admitted it) because he reminded her physically in his plebeian way of the privileged and handsome Lieutenant Orme (who was killed in the First World War and won a posthumous VC) that she thought of Clancy more often than she thought of his more plodding comrades. The tenderness, she guessed, was wafer-thin, but it was there, she believed; there, for instance, in his cheery attitude to Joseph with whom he cracked good-natured jokes in soldier's Urdu that set the old servant grinning and looking forward to the soldiers' visits; there in his friendship with the boy called Barrett who was clumsy, dull, ugly and unintelligent. In fact it was his friendship with Barrett, as much as his special politeness to her and attitude

to Joseph, and the way he and Barrett never missed coming
to tea, that caused her to consider what she really meant, in
Clancy's case, by tenderness; caused her, indeed, consciously to
use that word in her thoughts about him. She knew that boys
like Clancy often made friends of those whose physical and
mental attributes would show their own superior ones to the
best advantage. She knew that in choosing Barrett as what she
understood was called a mucker, Clancy was simply conforming
to an elementary rule of psychological behaviour. But whereas
in the normal way Barrett would have been used by a boy like
Clancy as a butt, frequently mocked, defended only if others
tried to mock him, she felt that Clancy never used Barrett to
such a purpose. While Clancy was present the others never
mocked him. Poor Barrett was a primitive. In that spry company
he could have stood out like a scarecrow in a field of cocky
young green wheat. For Miss Crane, for a while, he did, but
then she noticed that for the others he did not, or no longer
did, and she thought that this was because over a period,
through Clancy's influence, Barrett had been accepted as one
of them, that with Clancy's help Barrett had developed facets
of his personality that they recognized as those of the norm,
and, through Clancy's insistence, no longer noticed facets they
must at first have thought foreign.

It was Barrett who – when the rains came and tea had to be
indoors, and she gave the soldiers the run of the bungalow and
even remembered to provide ashtrays and cigarettes and invite
them to smoke rather than spend an hour and a half in an agony
of deprivation whose relief she had originally noticed but not
easily understood in the way they all lighted up directly they
got to the gate on the first leg of the journey home – Barrett
who first commented on the picture of the old Queen on her
canopied throne; commented on in his dull-ox way, simply by
going up to and staring at it, Clancy who spoke for both of
them by joining Barrett and then saying, 'It's what they call an
allegorical picture, isn't it, Miss Crane?' using the word with a
kind of pride in his hard-won education that she found
endearing and a bit shattering, because, watching Barrett looking at the picture, she had been on the point of saying, 'It's
really an allegory, Mr Barrett,' but had not, remembering that
Barrett would not begin to know what an allegory was.

'Yes, it is an allegory,' she said.

'It's a nice old picture,' Clancy said. 'A very nice old picture. Things were different those days, weren't they, Miss Crane?'

She asked him what he meant. He said, 'Well, I mean, sort of simpler, sort of cut and dried.'

For a while Miss Crane considered this, then said, 'More people thought they were. But they weren't really. You could almost say things are simpler now. After all these years there can't be any doubt. India *must* be independent. When the war's over, we've *got* to give her up.'

'Oh,' Clancy said, looking at the picture still, and not at her. 'I really meant about God and that, and people believing. I don't know much about the other thing, except a bit what Congress is and old Gandhi says, and if you ask me, Miss Crane, he's barmy.'

'Barmy's right,' Barrett said dutifully.

Miss Crane smiled.

'I used to have his picture up too. Over there. You can see where it was.'

They turned to look where she pointed: the upright oblong patch of paler distemper, all that was left to Miss Crane of the Mahatma's spectacled, smiling image, the image of a man she had put her faith in which she had now transferred to Mr Nehru and Mr Rajagopalachari who obviously understood the different degrees of tyranny men could exercise and, if there had to be a preference, probably preferred to live a while longer with the imperial degree in order not only to avoid submitting to but to resist the totalitarian. Looking at Clancy and Barrett and imagining in their place a couple of indoctrinated storm-troopers or ancestor-worshippers whose hope of heaven lay in death in battle, she knew which she herself preferred. There was in this choice, she realized, a residual grain of that old instinct to stay within the harbour of the charmed circle, an understanding of the magic of kind safeguarding kind and of the reliance she could place in a boy, for instance, such as Clancy, should poor old Joseph suddenly go berserk and come into the room armed and mad and dangerous to pay her back for imaginary wrongs, or real wrongs she had not personally done him but had done representatively because she was of her race and of her colour, and he could not in his simple rage any longer distinguish between individual and crowd.

But there was as well in her choice, she believed, an intellectual as well as emotional weight tipping the scales in favour of
lads like Clancy who, ignorant as they might be of the source
and direction of its flow, were borne nevertheless on the surface
of waters native to them, waters she had come to think of as
constituting the moral drift of history; waters of a river that had
to toss aside logs thrown into it by prejudice or carry them with
it towards the still invisible because still far-distant sea of perfect
harmony where the debris would become water-logged and rotten, finally disintegrate, or be lost, like a matchstick in a majestic
ocean. Clancy, after all, was not simply Clancy or Clance, but
the son of his father and of his father's fathers, and so long as
they stayed at home the English – for all their hypocrisy, or even
because of it – had always done as much as any other European
race to undam the flow; as much, perhaps a fraction more,
because of their isolation, their unique position in the European
landmass, a position that hampered their physical invasion but
not the subtler invasion of their minds by the humane concepts
of classical and Renaissance Europe that rose into the air and
flew like migratory birds to wherever they were perennially
welcome.

It was, Miss Crane believed, this ability of Clancy's to hear
the faint rumble, which was all that was audible to him of the
combined thunder of centuries of flight, that enabled him to say,
partly in sorrow, partly in pride – life patently being better for
his own kind now than then – 'Things were different those days,
sort of simpler, sort of cut and dried.' He felt, however unconsciously, the burden of the freedom to think, to act, worship or
not worship, according to his beliefs; the *weight* left on the world
by each act of liberation; and if in his relative innocence he read
a religious instead of a social message into the picture that provoked his comment, well, Miss Crane told herself, it came to
the same thing in the end. God, after all, was no more than a
symbol, the supreme symbol of authority here on earth; and
Clancy was beginning to understand that the exercise of authority was not an easy business, especially if those who exercised it
no longer felt they had heaven on their side.

That year the rains were late. They reached Mayapore towards
the end of June. The young soldiers suffered from the extreme

heat that preceded them, welcomed the first downpours, but by the end of the second week of July were complaining about the damp and the humidity.

Miss Crane had become used to ignoring the weather. In the dry she wore wide-brimmed hats, cotton or woollen dresses and sensible shoes; in the wet, blouses and gaberdine skirts, gumboots when necessary, with a lightweight burberry cape and an oilskin-covered sola topee. For transport in and around Mayapore she rode a ramshackle-looking but sturdy Raleigh bicycle; the car – a ten-year-old Ford – was kept for longer runs. In the past the Ford had taken her as far as Calcutta, but she no longer trusted it for that. On the few occasions – once or twice a year – that she needed to go to Calcutta she now went by train, and she went alone because Joseph, aged fifty in a land whose native expectation of life was still less than forty years, felt too old to accompany her. He fretted if away from Mayapore, and pretended that he did not trust the chaukidar to guard the bungalow from thieves. Joseph shopped, did the cooking, looked after the stores and supervised the sweeper, a twelve-year-old girl from the bazaar. In the hot weather he slept on the verandah; in the cold and in the wet, on a camp-bed in the storeroom. He still went regularly to church, on Sunday evenings, and borrowed her bicycle for that purpose. The church – that of the mission, not the church of St Mary in the civil lines – was situated not far from Miss Crane's bungalow, close to the Mandir Gate bridge, one of the two bridges that spanned the river-bed that divided the civil lines from the native town.

On the native town side of the Mandir Gate bridge was to be found the Tirupati temple within whose precincts was a shrine that sheltered the recumbent figure of the sleeping Vishnu. Between the Mandir Gate bridge, on the civil lines side, and the second bridge, the Bibighar bridge, lived the Eurasian community, close at hand to the depots, godowns and offices of the railway station. The railway followed the course of the riverbed. The tracks crossed the roads that led to the bridges. At the bridgeheads on the civil lines side, consequently, there were level-crossings whose gates, when closed to let railway traffic through, sealed both bridges off, making a barrier between the European and the native populations. When the gates of the level-crossings were shut, road traffic coming from the town to the civil lines became congested on the bridges. Miss Crane, returning on her bicycle from the native town, was sometimes held up in such congestions, hemmed in by other cyclists and by pedestrians, clerks going back to work at District Head-quarters after lunch in their homes, servants returning to the civil bungalows after shopping in the bazaar for vegetables; tailors on their way to measure a sahib or a sahib's lady who preferred the work and the prices of the bazaar tailors to those of the cantonment tailor, Darwaza Chand; pedlars with boxes on their heads, farmers driving their buffalo carts back to villages in the plains north of the cantonment, women and children going begging or scavenging; and, occasionally, car-borne Euro-peans, a bank official or businessman, the District Superinten-dent of Police, the Station Commander, English and Indian Army officers in yellow-painted fifteen-hundredweight trucks. Sometimes on these journeys she would see and nod to, but never speak to, the white woman – said to be mad – who dressed like a nun, kept a refuge for the sick and the dying and was called Sister Ludmila by the Indians.

Miss Crane used the Mandir Gate bridge into the native town in order to go from her bungalow to the Chillianwallah Bazaar school, a journey that took her past the church of the mission and the principal mission school, over the bridge, past the Tiru-pati temple, through narrow dirty streets of open shop fronts, past the gateway of the Chillianwallah bazaar itself where fish, meat and vegetables were sold, and into an even narrower street, a dark alleyway between old, crumbling houses, down whose centre ran an open water-duct. The alley was a cul-de-sac. At its closed-in head were the high wall and arched gateway of the bazaar school. The gateway opened into a narrow mud com-pound where the children played. Stunted banana trees gave a little shade in the early mornings and late afternoons. The mud was reddish brown, baked hard by the sun and pressed flat by the pupils' bare feet. Even in the wet monsoon an afternoon's sunshine would dry and harden it to its old concrete consistency.

The Chillianwallah Bazaar schoolhouse was a two-storey building with steps up to a verandah with shuttered balconied windows above the verandah roof. At least seventy years old, the house had been the property of Mr Chillianwallah, a Parsee who left Bombay and made a fortune in Mayapore out of government building contracts in the 1890s. Mr Chillianwallah had built the barracks in the civil lines, the church of St Mary, the bungalow presently lived in by the Deputy Commissioner, and – in a phil-anthropic fit – the bazaar in the native town. Still in the throes of that fit he presented the house in the alley to the church of St Mary, and until the mission built a more substantial school-house in the civil lines, opposite the mission church, the house in the alley had been its only foothold on the shaky ladder of conversion. For several years after the building of the larger mission school in the civil lines in 1906, the Chillianwallah house and compound had been used by the mission as a place of refuge for the old and sick and dying but as the civil lines school became filled to overflowing with the children of Eurasians, and the numbers of Indian children attending fell away, the mission reopened the house in the alley for lessons in the hope of regaining the foothold they had virtually lost, and the old and sick and dying had some thirty years to wait for the coming of Sister Ludmila.

The Chillianwallah Bazaar school was now the second of Miss Crane's responsibilities in Mayapore District. Her third was in Dibrapur, near the coalmines; her first the larger school in the civil lines, opposite the mission church, where in co-operation with a succession of English teachers whose qualifications to teach were more apparent than her own and whose religious convictions put hers to shame, she supervised the work of the Anglo-Indian class mistresses and taught mathematics and English to the older Eurasian and Indian Christian girls. From this school most of the pupils passed into the Government Higher School whose foundation in 1920 had done much to undermine the mission's influence.

The teacher at the Chillianwallah Bazaar school, whose pupils were all Indian, was a middle-aged, tall, thin, dark-skinned Madrassi Christian, Mr F. Narayan: the F for Francis, after St Francis of Assisi. In his spare time, of which he had a great deal, and to augment his income, of which he had little, Mr Narayan wrote what he called Topics for the local English-language weekly newspaper, *The Mayapore Gazette*. In addition, his ser-vices were available as a letter-writer, and these were services used by both his Hindu and Muslim neighbours. He could con-verse fluently in Urdu and Hindi and the local vernacular, and wrote an excellent Urdu and Hindi script, as well as his native Tamil and acquired Roman-English. In Europe, Miss Crane thought, a man of his accomplishments might have gone a long way – in the commercial rather than the pedagogic field. She suspected him, because Joseph had hinted at it, of selling contraceptives to Christian and progressive Hindu families. She did not disapprove, but was amused because Mr Narayan himself had an ever-pregnant wife, and a large, noisy, undisciplined family of boys and girls.

His wife Mary Narayan, as dark-skinned as himself, was a girl he brought back one year from leave in Madras. He said she was a Christian too, but Miss Crane doubted it, never having seen her go to church but instead, on more than one occasion, entering and leaving the Tirupati temple. He said she was now twenty-five, which Miss Crane doubted as well. She wouldn't have been surprised if Mrs Narayan had only been thirteen or fourteen at the time Francis Narayan married her.

Mr and Mrs Narayan lived in the upstairs rooms of the Chillianwallah Bazaar school. Their children, three girls and two boys to date (apart from the one still suckling whose sex she had somehow never made a note of) sat on the front benches in the schoolroom and were, Miss Crane had begun to notice, virtually the only regular attendants. On Sunday mornings, Mr Narayan and his two eldest children – one boy, John Krishna, and a girl, Kamala Magdalene – left the house in the Chillianwallah Bazaar in a cycle-tonga driven by a convert called Peter Paul Akbar Hossain, precariously negotiated the water-duct down the cul-de-sac, crossed the Mandir Gate bridge, and attended the service at the mission church where Mr Narayan also assisted with the collection. His wife, he said, had to stay at home to look after the younger children. Miss Crane took this information, too, with a pinch of salt. She wondered whether it might be interesting to stand outside the Tirupati temple on a Sunday morning to see whether Mrs Narayan's absence from the mission church was due to the stronger call of Lord Venkataswara, the god of the temple whose image was taken from the sanctuary once a year and carried down to the banks of the river to bless all those from whom he received the prescribed sacrifice.

But on Sunday mornings Miss Crane was otherwise engaged. She went to the service at St Mary's, cycling there rain or shine

along the tidy, tree-lined, geometrically laid out roads of the
cantonment, holding an umbrella up if the weather was inclement. Miss Crane's umbrella was a cantonment joke. In the rains,
reaching the side door, parking the Raleigh, she worked the
canopy vigorously up and down to shake the drops from it. This
flapping bat-wing noise was audible to those in the pews closest
to the door, the pews on the lectern side of the church, whose
English occupants smiled at the unmistakable sounds of Miss
Crane's arrival, much as years before other people in another
church had smiled when Mr Grant offered up his prayers.

The other congregational joke about Miss Crane was over her
tendency to fall asleep during the sermon, which she did with
great discretion, maintaining a ramrod back and squared shoulders, so that only her closed eyes gave the game away, and even
her closed eyes seemed, initially, no more than a likely sign of
her preoccupation with images conjured by the chaplain's words
which, for a moment, she thought of having a closer personal
look at. Her eyes closed, then opened; presently closed again,
only to open again. The third time that the lids snapped shut –
abruptly, never slowly or heavily – they usually stayed shut; and
Miss Crane was then away; and only a slight backward jerk of
her head when the chaplain said Now God the Father God the
Son and the congregation exhaled a corporate sigh of relief,
proved that she hadn't heard a word and that the eyes she now
just as abruptly opened had been closed in sleep.

Her violent shaking of the umbrella – not unlike the sound
of alighting angry angels – and her firm fast sleep during the
service, her reputation for outspokenness, her seeming imper-
viousness to the little drops of condescension falling from those
who, in the way these things were reckoned, were above her
in social station – all these had contributed to the idea the
Mayapore English had of her as a woman whose work for
the missionaries had broadened rather than narrowed her. There
was certainly nothing sanctimonious about Edwina Crane. The
somewhat grudging personal regard she was held in was
increased by her refusal to be browbeaten on the women's
committees she sat on. Since the war began the English ladies
of Mayapore had not been slow to recognize the need and
answer the call for committees: knitting-bee committees, troops
entertainment committees, social welfare committees, Guides

recruitment committees, War Week committees, committees
to direct the voluntary work done in the hospital and the Greenlawns nursing home and by the ladies who had in mind the
welfare of the children of Indian mothers working on the road
extension and proposed airstrip out at Banyaganj and in the
British–Indian Electrical factory. Called in originally to help
with the Guides recruitment by Mrs White, the wife of the
Deputy Commissioner, she was now a member of the social
welfare, the voluntary hospital workers and the Indian mothers
committees and if among themselves the ladies spoke of her in
tones that would have suggested to a stranger that Miss Crane
was only a mission school teacher and as many rungs below
them as it was socially possible to be and still be recognized,
they themselves collectively understood that actual denigration
was not intended, and individually respected her even if they
thought her 'cranky about the natives'.

It was the wife of the Deputy Commissioner who was responsible for creating an image of Miss Crane which the ladies of
Mayapore had now come to regard as definitive of her. 'Edwina
Crane,' Mrs White said, 'has obviously missed her vocation.
Instead of wasting her time in the missions and thumping the
old tub about the iniquities of the British Raj and the intolerable
burdens borne by what her church calls our dark brethren, she
should have been headmistress of a good school for girls, back
in the old home counties.'

Until the war Miss Crane had not gone out much in European
society. Occasional dinners with the chaplain and his wife (it was
the chaplain who was responsible for calling the station's attention to Miss Crane's tendency to sleep during his sermons), an
annual invitation to the Deputy Commissioner's garden party
and once a year to his bungalow during the cold months when
his wife 'dined the station' – these had been the main events on
her white social calendar, indeed still were, but her work on the
committees had widened the circle of English women who were
ready to stop and talk to her in the cantonment bazaar or invite
her to coffee or tea, and the particular dinner at the Deputy
Commissioner's to which Miss Crane now went was the one to
which higher-ranking English were invited, and eminent Indians such as Lady Chatterjee, widow of Sir Nello Chatterjee who
had founded the Mayapore Technical College.

For these full-dress occasions, Miss Crane wore her brown silk: a dinner gown that revealed the sallow-skinned cushion of flesh below her now prominent collar-bones. She decorated the dress with a posy of artificial flowers, cut and shaped out of purple and crimson velvet. The dress had half sleeves. She wore elbow-length gloves of brown lisle silk so cut at the wrists that the hands of the gloves could be removed to reveal her own bony brown hands. Her greying hair, for these occasions, would be combed more loosely above her forehead and gathered into a coil that hung a fraction lower than usual at the back of her neck. Her fingers, unadorned, were short-nailed, thin but supple. From her, as her table-companions knew, came a scent of geranium and mothballs, the former of which grew fainter as the evening progressed, and the latter stronger, until both were lost for them in the euphoria of wine and brandy.

On her wrist before and after dinner, and on her lap during it, she carried a home-made sachet handbag of brown satin lined with crimson silk. The brown satin did not quite match, nor did it complement, the brown of her dress. In the bag which could be drawn open and shut on brown silk cords was a silver powder compact – which was the source of the geranium smell – a plain lawn handkerchief, the ignition key of the Ford, a few soiled rupee notes, her diary of engagements, a silver pencil with a red silk tassel, and a green bottle of smelling salts. At the DC's dinners Miss Crane drank everything she was offered: sherry, white burgundy, claret and brandy, and always smelled the salts before setting off home in the car, to clear her head, which Mrs White had been relieved to find was a strong enough one for her not to fear the possibility of Miss Crane being overcome and letting the side down.

Reaching home, driving the Ford into the corrugated-iron garage beside the bungalow, she would be met by old Joseph and scolded for being late. In the house she drank the milk that he had warmed and re-warmed, ate the biscuits he had put out on a doily-covered plate, took the aspirin he said she needed, and retired, answering his 'God bless you, madam' with her own 'Goodnight', entered her room and slowly, tiredly, got rid of the long skirted encumbrance which in the morning Joseph would air and put back in the chest where she kept her few bits of finery and spare linen; put it there proudly because his mistress was a

Mem in spite of the bicycle, the topee and the gumboots and her work which took her into the stinking alleys of the heathen, native town.

By this summer of 1942 Miss Crane had been in Mayapore for seven years, and during them she had seen many Europeans come and go. The Deputy Commissioner and his wife, Mr and Mrs White, had been there only four years, since 1938, the year that the previous DC, an irritable widower called Stead, had retired, nursing a grievance that he had never been promoted Divisional Commissioner or sent to the Secretariat. The Assistant Commissioner and his wife, Mr and Mrs Poulson, had come to Mayapore shortly afterwards. The Poulsons were friends of the Whites; in fact White had especially asked for Poulson to be sent to Mayapore. Ronald Merrick, the District Superintendent of Police, was a bachelor, a young man sometimes over-anxious, it was said, to excel in his duties, quarrelsome at the club, but sought after by the unmarried girls. He had been in the town only two years. Only the District and Sessions Judge, who together with the DC and the Superintendent of Police formed the triumvirate of civil authority in the District, had been in Mayapore as long as Miss Crane, but he was an Indian. His name was Menen and Miss Crane had never met him to talk to. Menen was a friend of Lady Chatterjee who lived on the Bibighar bridge side of the civil lines in the old MacGregor House, so called because rebuilt by a Scotsman of that name on the foundations of the house built by a prince in the days when Mayapore was a Native State. The raja had been deposed in 1814 and the state annexed by the East India Company, absorbed into the province of whose score of districts it now ranked as second in size and importance.

Although Lady Chatterjee was the leader of Indian society in Mayapore, Miss Crane scarcely knew her. She met her at the Deputy Commissioner's but had never been to the MacGregor House which, it was said, was the one place where English and Indians came together as equals, or at least without too much caution on the part of the Indians or too much embarrassment on the part of the English. Miss Crane did not actually regret never going to the MacGregor House. She thought Lady Chatterjee overwesternized, a bit of a snob, socially and intellectually;

amusing enough to listen to at the DC's dinner-table but not in
the drawing-room afterwards, when the women were alone for
a while and Lady Chatterjee asked questions of them which Miss
Crane thought were calculated to expose them as lacking in
social background at home or cosmopolitan experience abroad,
finally lapsing into dignified silence and letting the English
small-talk get under way without attempting to contribute to it,
content to wait for the men to rejoin them when she would
again have the opportunity of sparkling and making everybody
laugh. The English women found Lady Chatterjee easier-going
if they had the men with them. They were all, Miss Crane con-
cluded, rather afraid of her. And Lady Chatterjee, Miss Crane
thought, was – although not afraid of them – certainly on her
guard, as stuffy in her own way as the English women. For Miss
Crane she seemed to have no feelings whatsoever; a disinterest
that might have been due to her discovery by direct questioning
at the first dinner they attended together that Miss Crane had
no degree, in fact no qualifications to teach other than the rough
and ready training she had received years ago in Lahore after
leaving the service of the Nesbitt-Smiths. On the other hand,
Lady Chatterjee's indifference was equally probably due to a disapproval of missions and missionaries and of anyone connected
with them. Westernized though she was, Lady Chatterjee was
of Rajput stock, a Hindu of the old ruling-warrior caste. Short,
thin, with greying hair cut in European style, seated upright on
the edge of a sofa, with the free end of her saree tight-wound
round her shoulders, and her remarkably dark eyes glittering at
you, her beaky Rajput nose and pale skin proclaiming both
authority and breeding, she looked every inch a woman whom
only the course of history had denied the opportunity of fully
exercising the power she was born to.

Widowed some years earlier by the death of a husband who
had been older than she and by whom she had had no children,
an Indian who was knighted for his services to the Crown and
his philanthropy to his own countrymen, Lady Chatterjee, so
far as Miss Crane was concerned, now seemed to be continuing
what must have been Sir Nello's policy of getting the best out
of both worlds. She thought this in rather bad taste. Friends in
the old days of Sir Henry Manners and his wife who, for a time,
had been Governor and Governor's lady of the province, Lady

Chatterjee still went annually to Rawalpindi or Kashmir to stay with Lady Manners, now a widow like herself; and a Manners girl, Daphne, a niece of Sir Henry, rather plain, big-boned and as yet unmarried, was working in the hospital at Mayapore for the war effort and living in the MacGregor House as Lady Chatterjee's guest. It was, no doubt, Lady Chatterjee's standing with distinguished English people like old Lady Manners as much as the position she enjoyed in Mayapore as Sir Nello's widow and as member of the board of Governors of the Technical College, member of the committee of the purdah hospital in the native town, that caused her to be treated with such outward consideration by the leaders of the English colony. With the DC and his wife she was on Christian name terms. (She had not been with Stead, their predecessor in office.) She was always welcome at the DC's bungalow. She played bridge there and Mrs White played bridge at the MacGregor House. But whatever from the Whites' point of view in this cordiality ranked as part of their duty to be seen as well as felt to be the representatives of a government that had at heart the well-being of all the people living in the district, Indian or British, there certainly seemed to be from all accounts a genuine sympathy and understanding between them and Sir Nello's widow.

But − and this was what interested Miss Crane − at the MacGregor House, said to be equally welcome were Indians: barristers, teachers, doctors, lawyers, municipal officers, higher civil servants, among whom were men of the local Congress Party sub-committee, and men not of that committee but known for the possibly even greater vehemence of their anti-British views.

How often such men found themselves at the MacGregor House face to face with the liberal English, Miss Crane did not know; neither did she know whether Lady Chatterjee would hope by such confrontations to dampen their anti-British ardour or inspire even more radical feelings in the hearts of the liberal English. All she knew was that from her own point of view Lady Chatterjee appeared to lack the true liberal instinct herself. She admitted, though, that behind her lack of empathy for Lady Chatterjee there were probably the particular kinds of blindness and deafness that followed social rebuff. Admitting this, she also admitted a more fundamental truth.

And that truth was that after virtually a lifetime of service in the mission schools she was lonely. Since the death of old Miss de Silva who had been the teacher in Dibrapur, there was not a man or a woman in Mayapore, in India, anywhere, British or Indian, she could point to as a friend of the sort to whom she could have talked long and intimately. When, in the May of 1942, Mr Gandhi demanded that the British should leave India – leave her, he said, 'to God, or to anarchy', which meant leaving her to the Japanese – and she took down his portrait and her Indian ladies stopped coming to tea, she saw that the bungalow would not be particularly empty without them because they had not looked on her as a person, but only as a woman who represented something they felt ought to be represented. She also saw that she herself had looked on the teas not as friendly but as meaningful gatherings. There was no one else in Mayapore to drop by, nowhere in Mayapore she could casually drop by at herself. Such acts of dropping by as were undertaken by herself or others were for reasons other than human intimacy. Now the soldiers came in place of the ladies, on a different day, Wednesday and not Tuesday (as though to keep Tuesdays free in case the ladies underwent a change of heart). And in the case of the soldiers there had probably been a notice put up in the Regimental Institute: 'Personnel wishing to avail themselves of an invitation to tea on Wednesday afternoons at the home of Miss E. Crane, superintendent of the Church of England Mission Schools (Mayapore District) should give their names to their Unit Welfare Officer.'

Sometimes she wondered to what extent her decision to entertain the soldiers had been due to an instinct finally to find refuge in that old privileged circle that surrounded and protected the white community. Her social and political beliefs were, she could not help realizing, by the standards of the present day, somehow old-fashioned, over-simplified. Lacking a real education she had matured slowly and had, she supposed, grasped hold of the ideas of a generation previous to her own as if they were mint-new. Events had gone ahead of her, taking with them younger people who were, in their opinions, in advance of her. She understood, it seemed, little of practical present-day politics. This comparative ignorance defined the gulf that separated her not only from the younger liberal English people such as she met

at the Deputy Commissioner's and whom she found it difficult
to talk to, but from Lady Chatterjee who, lending half an ear to
what she might have to say about Indian independence and the
sacred duty of the British to grant it, conveyed at once an
impression of having heard it all too long ago for it to be worth
hearing again.

'I am,' Miss Crane told herself, 'a relic of the past,' mentally
crossed out 'of the past' as a redundant clause, and looked up at
the picture of the old Queen, stared at it waiting for it to reveal
something simple but irrefutable that perhaps the MacGregor
House set had lost sight of. What seemed to her so extraordinary
was that although her own ladies had stopped coming to tea the
parties at the MacGregor House continued. The English community apparently saw nothing wrong in this even though they
knew they now had their backs to a wall that the Indians seemed
set on removing, brick by brick. It was, they said, the duty of
people like the DC and his wife to keep their ears to the ground,
and where better to do that than at the MacGregor House? It
was rumoured, for instance, that on instructions from Government the DC had already prepared a list of Congress party members in the Mayapore district who would have to be arrested
under the Defence of India Rules if Congress voted in favour
of Mr Gandhi's civil disobedience resolution, a resolution under
which the British would be called upon to leave India on pain
of finding the realm impossible to defend, their armies on the
Assam–Burma frontier impossible to feed, clothe, arm or support; impossible, for the simple reason that there would be no
one who was willing to operate the railways, the posts and telegraphs, the docks, the depots, the factories, the mines, the banks,
the offices, or any of the administrative and productive services
of a nation they had exploited for over two hundred years and,
by failing to defend Burma, brought to the point of having to
succumb to yet another set of imperialistic warmongers.

Miss Crane feared such an uprising. For her the only hope for
the country she loved lay in the coming together at last of its
population and its rulers as equal partners in a war to the death
against totalitarianism. If Congress had not resigned from the
provincial ministries in 1939 in a fit of pique because the Viceroy
without going through the motions of consulting them had
declared war in the name of the King-Emperor on India's behalf,

and if Mr Gandhi had not had a brainstorm and seized the moment of Britain's greatest misfortune to press home his demands for political freedom, if things had been left to Mr Nehru who obviously found Gandhi an embarrassment and to Mr Rajagopalachari (who had headed the provincial ministry in Madras and had wanted to arm and train the entire nation to fight the Japanese) then at this moment, Miss Crane believed, an Indian cabinet would have been in control in Delhi, Lord Linlithgow would have been Governor-General of a virtually independent dominion and all the things that she had hoped and prayed for to happen in India would have happened, and the war would be under process of firm and thoughtful prosecution.

Sometimes Miss Crane woke up in the night and lay sleepless, listening to the rain, and was alarmed, conscious of dangers that were growing and which people were preparing to face but not to understand, so that virtually they were not facing them at all. We only understand, she said, the way to meet them, or, sometimes, the way to avert them.

But on this occasion they were not averted.

In the first week of August Miss Crane caught one of her rare colds. She had never believed in running risks with her health. She telephoned to the school in Dibrapur to say that she would not be coming on the Thursday but would come on the following Saturday. Then she went home and put herself to bed and sweated the chill out. By the weekend she felt perfectly fit again. And so on the morning of the 8th of August – on the day on which Congress were to vote on Mr Gandhi's resolution – Miss Crane set off in her Ford the seventy-odd miles to Dibrapur.

The school in Dibrapur, the third of Miss Crane's responsibilities in Mayapore District, was situated in comparative isolation, on the road midway between the village of Kotali and the town of Dibrapur itself. Dibrapur lay on the southern border of the Mayapore District. There was no church, no European population. The Dibrapur mines, so-called, were now administered from Aligarh in the adjoining district of the province.

Most of the children who attended the school came from Kotali. They had only three miles to walk. If they went to the school run by the District Board in a neighbouring village the distance was four miles. The mission schoolhouse had been built in its isolated position years ago so that it could serve the surrounding villages as well as Dibrapur. Since the expansion of the Government's own educational programme and the setting up of primary schools by District Boards the mission school had not lost many pupils for the simple reason that it had never attracted many. The Kotali children came because it was nearer and a few children still came from Dibrapur because at the mission school the English language was taught. The Dibrapur children were usually the sons – very occasionally the daughters – of shopkeepers, men who fancied their male offspring's chances as government contractors or petty civil servants and who knew that the gift of conversing fluently in English was therefore invaluable. And so, from Dibrapur, up to half a dozen boys and two or three girls would tramp the three miles every day to the school of the mission, carrying with them, like the children from Kotali, their food-tins and their canvas bags. In the school of the mission there were no chappattis; only instruction, good intentions and medicine for upset stomachs.

Having stood now for nearly thirty years the Dibrapur schoolhouse was in constant need of some kind of repair, and, in the summer of 1942, certainly a coat of whitewash that it would have to wait for until the end of the rains. What it most urgently needed was attention to the roof and during this summer Miss Crane's thoughts in connexion with the school had been almost exclusively concerned with the estimates periodically obtained by Mr Chaudhuri, the teacher, and the Allocation, which in crude terms meant the money available. So far Mr Chaudhuri had failed to obtain an estimate from any local builder that came within sight of balancing what had to be spent with what there was to spend. He did not seem to have much of a head for business or talent for bargaining. 'We need,' Miss Crane had been thinking, 'another five hundred rupees. We need, in fact, more; not only a repair to the roof, but a new roof, in fact practically a new school.' Sometimes she could not help wondering whether they also needed a new teacher-in-charge, but always put the thought out of her head as uncharitable, as one sparked off by personal prejudice. The fact that for one reason or another she and Mr Chaudhuri had never hit it off should not, she realized, blind her to his remarkable qualities as a teacher.

Mr Chaudhuri had held the Dibrapur appointment for not

quite a year. His predecessor, old Miss de Silva, a Eurasian
woman from Goa, had been dead for just a bit longer. With
Mary de Silva's death Miss Crane had lost the last person in the
world who called her Edwina. On her first visit to Dibrapur as
superintendent, seven years ago, the older woman – fat, white-
haired, ponderous, and with a voice as dark and forthcoming as
her extraordinary popping black eyes – had said, 'You got the
job *I* wanted. My name's Mary de Silva. My mother was as black
as your hat.'

'Mine's Edwina Crane,' Miss Crane said, shaking the pudgy,
man-strong hand, 'I didn't *know* you wanted the job, and my
mother's been dead for longer than I care to remember.'

'Well in that case I'll call you Edwina, if you don't mind. I'm
too old to bow and scrape to a *new* superintendent. And also if
you don't mind we'll start by talking about the bloody roof.'

So they had talked about the roof, and the walls, and the tube-
well that wanted resinking in another place, and then about the
children, and Mary de Silva's intention to send, by hook or
crook, a boy called Balarachama Rao to the Government Higher
School in Mayapore. 'His parents won't hear of it. But *I'll* hear
of it. Where do *you* stand, Edwina Crane?'

'In matters of this sort, Mary de Silva,' she replied, 'I stand to
do what the teachers on the spot advise me should be done.'

'Then find a decent lodging in Mayapore for Master Balarachama. That's the snag. He's got no place to live if he's admitted.
The parents say they've no relatives there. Which is nonsense.
Indians have relatives *every*where. I ought to know.' Her skin
was no sallower than little Miss Williams's had been.

Miss Crane found lodgings in Mayapore for Balarachama and
spent a month, which is to say most of her time in four weekly
visits to Dibrapur, persuading his parents to let him go. When
she had at last succeeded Mary de Silva said, 'I'm not going to
thank you. It was your duty. And it was mine. But come back
now and help me break into the bottle of rum I've been saving
since Christmas.' So she went back with Mary de Silva to the
bungalow the Chaudhuris now lived in, half a mile down
the road from the school, and drank rum, heard the story of
Mary de Silva's life and told her own. There had been many
other occasions of drinking rum and lime in Mary de Silva's
living-room, discreetly, but in enough quantity for tongues to

be loosened and for Miss Crane to feel that here, in Dibrapur, with Mary de Silva, she had come home again after a lifetime travelling. For six years she went weekly to Dibrapur, and stayed the night with Mary de Silva. 'It's not necessary you know,' Miss de Silva said, 'but it's nice. The last superintendent only came once a month and never stayed the night. That was nice too.'

At the end of the six years, when the roof of the school had been repaired once and needed repairing again, and the new tube-well had been sunk, the walls patched and painted twice, there came the day she reached the schoolhouse and found it closed, and, driving on to Mary de Silva's bungalow, found the old teacher in bed, lying quietly, temporarily deserted by the servant who had gone down to Dibrapur to fetch the doctor. Miss de Silva was mumbling to herself. When she had finished what she had to say, and nodded, her eyes focused on Miss Crane. She smiled and said, 'Well, Edwina. I'm for it. You might see to the roof again,' then closed her eyes and died as if someone had simply disconnected a battery.

After seeing Mary de Silva's body safely and quickly transported to Mayapore and buried in the churchyard of St Mary, Miss Crane put the task of finding a temporary teacher into the hands of Mr Narayan to give him something to do, and went back to Dibrapur to reopen the school and keep it going until the temporary arrived. She also wrote to the headquarters of the mission to report Miss de Silva's death and the steps she had taken to keep the school going until a permanent appointment was made. She recommended a Miss Smithers, with whom she had worked in Bihar. She did not get Miss Smithers. She got first of all a cousin of Mr Narayan who drank, and then, from Calcutta, Mr D. R. Chaudhuri, BA, BSc – qualifications which not only astonished her but made her suspicious. Mission headquarters had been rather astounded too, so she gathered from their letter, but not suspicious. Mr Chaudhuri did not profess to be a Christian, they told her, on the other hand he did not profess any other religion. He had resigned from an appointment in a Government training college and had asked the mission to employ him in the humblest teaching capacity. They had offered him several posts, all of which he declined until, suddenly, the post in Dibrapur fell vacant, and this, from their description, had appealed to him as 'the right kind of beginning'. 'He will be wasted in Dibrapur, of course, and is unlikely to be with you for long,' they wrote, in confidence. 'He will be accompanied by his wife, so perhaps you would arrange to see that the late Miss de Silva's bungalow is made ready for them. We understand he has private but limited means. You will find Mr Chaudhuri a reserved young man and, by and large, unwilling to discuss the reasons for his decision to abandon a more distinguished academic career. We have, however, satisfied ourselves from interviews with Mr Chaudhuri and inquiries outside, that his wish to teach young children in the villages arises from a genuine sympathy for the depressed classes of his own race and a genuine belief that educated men like himself should more often be prepared to sacrifice their private interests in the interest of the country as a whole. It appears, too, that he feels his work in this direction should be with schools such as our own, not because of the religious basis of our teaching but because he has a low opinion of the local government primary schools and thinks of them as staffed by teachers to whom politics are more important than any educational consideration.'

In spite of this promising situation there had been between herself and Mr Chaudhuri right from the beginning what Miss Crane thought of as an almost classical reserve – classical in the sense that she felt they each suspected the other of hypocrisy, of unrevealed motives, of hiding under the thinnest of liberal skins deeply conservative natures, so that all conversations they had that were not strictly to do with the affairs of the school seemed to be either double-edged or meaningless.

For weeks Miss Crane fought against her own reserve. She did not minimize her grief for and memories of Miss de Silva when it came to analysing the possible causes of it. Knowing that Mr Chaudhuri had been told she visited Miss de Silva once a week, she visited him once a week too and stayed overnight in old Miss de Silva's bungalow, now unrecognizable as the same place, furnished as it was by Mr and Mrs Chaudhuri in the westernized-Indian style. She did this in case he should misunderstand her not doing it; at the same time she was aware that he might have taken her visits as a sign of her not trusting in his competence. She continued the visits in the hope that eventually she would feel at home there once more.

Tall, wiry, and square-shouldered, Mr Chaudhuri had the

fine-boned face of a Bengali, was handsome in a way Miss Crane recognized but did not personally consider handsome. With every feature and plane of his face sharp and prominent and in itself indicative of strength, the whole face, for her, still suggested weakness – and yet not weakness, because even weakness required to be conveyed as a special expression, and Mr Chaudhuri's face was capable of conveying only two: blank indifference or petulant annoyance. His smile, she saw, would have been pleasant if it had ever got up into his eyes as well.

His English was excellent, typically Indian in its inflexions and rhythms, but fluent as spoken and crisply correct when written. He also taught it very well. He made Mr Narayan, by comparison, look and sound like a bazaar comedian. And yet, with Mr Narayan, Miss Crane found conversation easy and direct. Not so with Mr Chaudhuri. There had been a period in her career when, highly sensitive herself to the sensitivity of Indians who knew the English language, even some of its subtlest nuances, but seldom if ever the rough and tumble of its everyday idiom, she had inured herself to the temptation to say things like, Don't be silly; or, Nonsense. For some years now, though, she had not bothered to put a curb on her tongue, and wished she never had. When you chose your words the spontaneity went out of the things you wanted to say. She had learned to hate the feeling it gave her of unnaturalness. If she had always been as outspoken as she was now, she thought, then even if she had made enemies she might also have made friends. By developing self-confidence in the manner of her speech earlier in her career she believed she might have developed an inner confidence as well, the kind that communicated itself to people of another race as evidence of sincerity, trustworthiness. Too late for that, the outspokenness, she knew, often looked to Indians like the workaday thoughtless rudeness of any Englishwoman. Only Englishwomen themselves admired it, although with men like Mr Narayan she could conduct a slanging match and feel no bones were broken. With Mr Chaudhuri she found herself reverting to the soft phrase, the cautious sentiment, and then spoiling whatever effect this had had by letting slip words that came more easily to her. She had said Nonsense! to him early on in their association and had seen at once that her tenuous hold on his willingness to co-operate was temporarily lost. From this unfortunate set-back they had never made much advance. If Mrs Chaudhuri had been a more sophisticated woman Miss Crane felt she might have made progress with Mr Chaudhuri through intimate contact with his wife, but apart from a High School education and her years spent at the feet of a music teacher, Mrs Chaudhuri was uninstructed in the ways of the sophisticated world and had a remarkably old-fashioned notion of the role of a wife.

Before Miss Crane set out in the Ford for Dibrapur on the morning of the 8th of August Joseph tried to dissuade her from going. He said there would be trouble. He had heard rumours.

She said, 'We are always hearing rumours. Does that stop you from doing your work? Of course not. I have work in Dibrapur. So to Dibrapur I must go.'

He offered to come with her.

'And who will look after the house, then?' she asked. 'No, Joseph, for both of us it is business as usual.'

It was business as usual all the way to Dibrapur, which she reached at four o'clock in the afternoon, having stopped on the way to eat her sandwiches and drink coffee from the flask. In the villages there were people who shouted Quit India! and others who asked for baksheesh. Driving slowly to avoid hitting cows and buffalo, dogs, hens and children, she smiled and waved at the people whatever they shouted.

In Kotali, the last village before the schoolhouse, she stopped the car and spoke to some of the mothers whose children went to Mr Chaudhuri for lessons. The mothers said nothing about trouble. She did not mention it herself. They would know better than she what was to be expected. Kotali looked very peaceful. Leaving the village behind she met the children making their way home, carrying their food-tins and canvas bags. Their average age was eight. She stopped the car again and distributed some of the boiled sweets.

Reaching the schoolhouse she drove into the compound. Here there were trees and shade. She found Mr Chaudhuri tidying up the schoolroom: 'Is there any news?' she asked, rather hoping that if trouble were coming and this were to be an eleventh hour it would be made productive of something more than politeness.

'News?' he replied. 'What sort of news, Miss Crane?'

'Of the Congress vote.'

'Oh, that,' he said. 'No, I have not listened.'

In the room of the schoolhouse that served as an office there was a radio. Sometimes Mr Chaudhuri used the radio as a medium of instruction. She turned it on now. There was music. She switched off. It was European music. The only music she ever listened to when with the Chaudhuris was Indian classical music.

'Perhaps, however,' he said, 'there is news of the roof?'

'No, there isn't. I've checked through all the estimates again and there's not one that's low enough. Can't you find someone to do it cheaper?'

'I have tried all who are willing to do it at all. If we wait much longer even the low estimates will go up. And these people cannot work for nothing.'

She was about to say, Well, that's not what I'm asking, I'm not asking them to do it for nothing. She would have said that to Mr Narayan. She held back from saying it to Mr Chaudhuri. Instead she said, 'No. Well, come on. I'd like a cup of tea.' And even that sounded brusque.

Mr Chaudhuri closed the school, padlocked the door, and joined her in the Ford. At his bungalow tea was not ready. He did not apologize; but while she was resting on her bed, waiting to be called, she heard him taking his wife to task for not ordering things better. When tea was ready it was served on the verandah. Mrs Chaudhuri did not join them. She moved between kitchen and verandah, carrying things with her own hands, smiling but saying little, and when there seemed to be nothing more that they wanted stood in the shadow of the doorway, pretending not to be there, but watching her husband for the slightest indication from him that something had been forgotten, or was wrong, or needed to be replenished.

'It is *this*,' Miss Crane often told herself, 'this awful feudal attitude to his wife that makes it difficult for me to like him.'

But it was not that. In the evenings Mrs Chaudhuri sometimes sang to them. Directly she was seated cross-legged on the rush mat, gently supporting the onion-shaped tamboura, she became a different woman; self-assured, holding her bony body gracefully erect, not unlike the way Lady Chatterjee held hers when sitting on a sofa at the DC's. After Mrs Chaudhuri had sung a couple of songs Mr Chaudhuri would say, almost under his breath, 'It is enough,' and then Mrs Chaudhuri would rise, take up the tamboura and disappear into an inner room. And Miss Crane knew that Mr and Mrs Chaudhuri loved one another, that Mr Chaudhuri was not a tyrant, that the woman herself preferred the old ways to the new because for her the old ways were a discipline and a tradition, a means of acquiring and maintaining peace of mind and inner stillness.

On this night, the night of August the 8th, which Miss Crane felt in her bones was a special night, one of crisis, she longed to make Mr Chaudhuri talk, to find the key to his reticence, a way of breaking down his reserve. It would have been easier for her if he had been as old-fashioned in his manners as his wife, because then their association would have been of an altogether different kind. But he was not. He was westernized. He wore European clothes at the school and, at least when she was staying with them, at home. They ate at a table, seated on hardwood chairs and talked about art and music and the affairs of the school, but never politics. There was a cloth on the table, there were knives and forks to eat with, and ordinary china plates. At dinner Mrs Chaudhuri sat with them, although she took almost no part in the conversation and ate practically nothing. A woman servant waited on them, the same woman who did the cooking. Miss Crane would have felt more comfortable if the woman had been an untouchable because that would have proved, in the Chaudhuris, emancipation from the rigidity of caste. But the woman was a Brahmin.

They had coffee in the room that overlooked the verandah, in which she and Miss de Silva had sat on old cane chairs, but where they now sat on low divans with their feet on Kashmiri rugs. Miss de Silva had been content with an oil lamp; Mr Chaudhuri had rigged up an electric light that ran from a generator in the compound. They sat in the unflattering light of one naked electric bulb around which moths and insects danced their nightly ritual of primitive desire for what might burn their wings. At this point, between the eating and the singing, Mrs Chaudhuri always left them, presumably to help or supervise the woman in the kitchen. Tonight Miss Crane drank the bitter coffee, more conscious than ever of the unsympathetic silence

that always fell directly she and Mr Chaudhuri were alone. She
longed to know the news but accepted in its place as proof that
in one respect at least the night was normal: the croaking –
beyond the verandah – of the frogs who had come out in their
invisible battalions after the evening rains.

She wanted to say: Mr Chaudhuri, what honestly is the school
to you? but did not. To say that to a man was to question a course
which, to judge by his actions, he had set his mind, even his
heart on.

'You are a fool, Edwina Crane,' she told herself later as she
undressed, preparing for bed. 'You have lost another opportunity, because hearts are no longer set on anything and minds
function as the bowels decide, and Mr Chaudhuri would talk if
you knew the questions to ask and the way to ask them. But he
is of that younger generation of men and women who have seen
what I have seen, understood what I understand, but see and
understand other things as well.'

And so she slept, and woke at four, as if aware that at such an
hour people of her colour might have cause to be wakeful, on
their guard. For at this hour the old man in spectacles was also
woken and taken, and the Deputy Commissioner in Mayapore
was woken, and warned, and told to set in motion those plans
whose object was to prevent, to deter. And in the morning,
having slept again only fitfully, Miss Crane was also woken and
told by Mr Chaudhuri that on the day before in Bombay the
Congress had voted in favour of the working committee's resolution, that the Mahatma was arrested, that the entire working
committee were arrested, that this no doubt was the signal for
arrests all over the country. At nine she walked to the school
with Chaudhuri to take the Sunday-morning Bible class and
found that only the children from Kotali had arrived. So she sent
him on his bicycle into Dibrapur. He returned shortly before
eleven and told her that the shops were closing in the town, that
the police were out in force, that the rumour was that three of
the municipal officers had been arrested by order of the District
Superintendent of Police in Mayapore and taken to Aligarh, that
crowds were collecting and threatening to attack the post office
and the police station.

*

'Then I'll ring Mayapore and find out what is happening there,' Miss Crane said.

She put down the reports she had been co-ordinating. There was a telephone in Mr Chaudhuri's bungalow.

'You can't,' he told her. 'I have already tried. The lines have probably been cut.'

'I see. Well then. One of us must take the children back to Kotali, rather than risk anything happening to them here. So I'd better do that and be getting on my way. You had better go back to look after Mrs Chaudhuri, and perhaps keep an eye on the school if you can manage it.'

Mr Chaudhuri looked round the shabby little room and then at Miss Crane.

'There is nothing to safeguard here,' he said, 'except the children. Take them in the car and I will come with you on my bicycle. If there are bad people on the road you will be safer if I am also seen.'

'Oh, I shall be safe enough. What about your wife?'

'You are the only English person here,' he said. 'My wife will be all right. They may well come here after they have finished with the post office and the police station, or whatever it is they have in mind. They may come from either direction. So we will both go with the children to Kotali.'

Miss Crane looked round the room too. The schoolhouse had always reminded her of the one she visited years ago with Mr Grant. Mr Chaudhuri was right. There wasn't much in the building worth saving, except the building itself, and even the worth of that was doubtful. She doubted, too, that either of them, in present circumstances, could stand in the doorway and successfully deny entry to an angry crowd. She glanced at Chaudhuri, remembering Muzzafirabad where she had been alone.

'You seem pessimistic,' she said.

'I have seen the people and heard the talk.'

'You're sure about the telephone?'

'Yes, I am sure.'

For a moment they looked at each other straight, and Miss Crane thought: This is the way it happens when there is real trouble — the little seed of doubt, of faint distrust, of suspicion that the truth is not actually being told. If the phone is cut, then it is cut. If it is not cut perhaps Mr Chaudhuri has picked it up, got no immediate answer and jumped to conclusions. Or it may not be cut and Mr Chaudhuri may know that it is not but tells me it is because he wants me to set off on the road to Kotali.

'Very well, Mr Chaudhuri,' she said. 'I think you are right. We'll cram the kids into the Ford somehow and you can come along on your bike.'

He said, 'One thing I hope you understand. I am not afraid to stay here. If you wish the building to be protected I will stay and chance my arm.'

'If they find it empty they may leave it alone,' she said.

'It is as I was thinking.'

She nodded, and stood up, collecting the reports, putting them tidily together, edge to edge. Chaudhuri waited. She said, 'Tell me your honest opinion. Is it serious this time?'

'It is serious.'

They always know, she thought, and then: This is how it happens too, to call them 'they' as though they are different.

'All right then, Mr Chaudhuri. Perhaps you'd collect the children together.'

He nodded, went to the door and out to the courtyard at the back where the children were playing.

She put the reports into her brief-case and then remembered that her gladstone bag, although already packed for the journey home, was still at Mr Chaudhuri's bungalow. She went out, called to him above the yelling of the children to whom he had just broken the news that school was over.

'My bag,' she shouted. 'It's at the bungalow. I'll pop down and get it and say goodbye to your wife.'

'I have sent my wife to the house of a friend,' Mr Chaudhuri shouted back. 'And your bag is in the car. I brought it with me.'

'Thanks,' she said, and went back into the office for the brief-case. She switched on the radio. Again there was only music, from All-India Radio, English music for the forces. She left the radio on while she closed the straps of the briefcase. The radio was a life-line of sorts. I am calm, she thought, automatically calm, as in 1914, and 1919, and 1930, other times. Over thirty-five years I have become used to sudden alarms. But I am also afraid. In such circumstances I am always a bit afraid. And I am ashamed, and am always ashamed, because of my suspicions – this time first over the telephone, and now over the gladstone bag.

'Mr Chaudhuri,' she called, going to the doorway. 'When they're ready bring them round to the front and I'll get the car started.'

And in my voice, she said to herself, there – always there – the note of authority, the special note of *us* talking to *them*, which perhaps passes unnoticed when what we talk about is the small change of everyday routine but at times of stress always sounds like taking charge. But then, she thought, we are, we are in charge. Because we have an obligation and a responsibility. In this present instance her main responsibility lay seventy miles away in Mayapore. Things were always worse in the towns.

When she brought the car from its shelter at the side of the schoolhouse, Mr D. R. Chaudhuri, BA, BSc, was standing waiting, with the children of the poor and the sometimes hungry gathered round him, playing their games.

In times of civil disturbance news or rumours of riots in the towns attracted from the villages men whose main preoccupation was the prospect of loot. This is what Mr Chaudhuri had in mind when he spoke of bad people on the road between Dibrapur and Kotali, and Miss Crane knew that in leaving Dibrapur behind they were probably running into trouble as well as away from it.

There was also the question, for her, of continuing on from Kotali the seventy-odd miles through village after village to Mayapore. In this southern part of the district the land was slightly undulating, but still open, with cultivation on both sides of a good metalled road, and few trees. At least on most parts of the road you would be able to see trouble coming from a distance. From experience Miss Crane knew what to look out for: in the dry weather, when the dirt strips on either side of the metal were powdered to the consistency of ground chalk, the cloud of dust which as it got nearer revealed men strung out across the road; in the wet, the same men, but more suddenly, without the earlier warning of the dust they raised, so that at first glimpse you could already make out that some were carrying staves. Starting from one village, three or four men in the course of several miles could become a score. A car, coming at speed, showing no signs of stopping, could scatter them at the last moment, but still be vulnerable to the stones they might pick up at the car's approach. Miss Crane had, once in her life, in the troubles of 1919, run such a gauntlet, but the car she was in that time was driven by a determined young European policeman who had come to rescue her from an outlying schoolhouse where, as her superintendent back at headquarters had suspected, she was virtually a prisoner.

'Whether I could do the same as the young policeman,' she thought, 'blowing the horn and driving like mad, will depend on the size of the crowd.' Mr Chaudhuri could not drive. She did not know whether to be glad or sorry.

The size of the crowd depended on three things: the nature of the disturbance in the town which dictated the likely quantity of loot to be expected; the general temper of the surrounding villages and the number of men in each of them who had time and inclination to take the opportunity of filling their pockets; and finally the degree of control that the village headmen and rural police were able to exercise.

Each village had its watchman or chaukidar, a paid servant of the Government, and the villages were organized in groups under police detachments. A gang reaching a village where the police post was effectively manned, might then be dispersed. At a post where the police decided to look the other way or judged from the temper of the crowd that it was wiser to lock themselves in, the crowd passed by; and grew.

Reaching the village of Kotali with the cargo of laughing children, Mr Chaudhuri still pedalling some distance behind, Miss Crane was met by the chaukidar and the headman and several men and women who had been on the point of setting out to bring the children back from school. The chief constable in charge of the police post in Garhwar, the next village along the road, had sent a message to say that he could no longer get through on the telephone to sub-divisional police headquarters in Dibrapur, that he assumed trouble had broken out following the news of Mr Gandhi's arrest, and that the people of Kotali should therefore be on their guard to protect their property and their lives from dacoits and rioters.

The people of Kotali were, the headman said, very angry with the chief constable in Garhwar. They said he must have been warned at least the day before to expect trouble, and had not bothered to tell them. If they had been told they would not have let the children go to school that morning. The mothers thanked Miss Crane for returning them safely and offered her some tea, which she drank by the roadside, sitting on the chair they brought out and put under a tree. They gave Mr Chaudhuri tea as well.

'I shall pray for rain,' she told him, smiling. 'There's nothing like a good downpour to cool people off. If it's wet they'll stay at home.'

Mr Chaudhuri said nothing. He finished his tea and walked away and spoke for some time to the chaukidar and the headman. When he came back Miss Crane was finishing her second cup. She was hungry but had refused the offer of food.

'You must stay here, Miss Crane,' Mr Chaudhuri told her. 'In this village everyone is your friend because of the children. It is dangerous to drive to Mayapore.'

She shook her head, put the cup down on the tray a young girl stood holding in readiness. 'No,' she said, 'I have to be getting on.'

'They will look after you. The headman invites you to stay in his home.'

'It's very kind of him and I truly appreciate it, but I must try to get back.'

'Then stay for just an hour or two only. I will go back to Dibrapur. Who knows but that it is all a storm in a teapot? If it is then you can stay one more night in the bungalow and go to Mayapore tomorrow. The telephone will probably be working again by then.'

'And if it isn't all a storm in a teapot?'

'Then you shouldn't go to Mayapore at all. You should stay here where everyone is your friend.'

'I've got friends in Mayapore too. And Mr Chaudhuri, I also have responsibilities. I know you mean it kindly but I do really have to be getting on.'

'You have had nothing to eat.'

'I'm not hungry.'

'I will get you something to eat.'

'I don't think I *could* eat. You see this sort of thing always makes me feel a bit sick.' It wasn't true. This sort of thing always made her ravenously hungry. But if she stayed for the food, she thought, her determination to be on her way might weaken.

Mr Chaudhuri raised his arms slightly, a gesture of surrender. 'Then I am coming with you,' he said, 'we had better go now,' and turned away, ignoring her reply of, 'Don't be silly, it's quite unnecessary,' went to speak again to the chaukidar and the headman. Two or three of the children gathered round her. To please her they recited 'One, Two, Buckle my Shoe'. She laughed and said that it was well done. Mr Chaudhuri was walking up the road to the headman's house. He glanced back and indicated he would not be very long. A mother came with a plate covered by a napkin. Beneath it there were piping hot chappattis. More tea was offered. Another woman brought a bowl of dal, and a spoon. She waved the spoon aside and began to eat, breaking off bits of chappatti and scooping the dal up with them. The sweat was forming on her forehead. It was so hot and humid. While she ate the people stood watching. I hate it, she thought, I have always hated it, this being watched, like something in a zoo, seated on a chair, under a tree, by the roadside.

'You see,' she said to Mr Chaudhuri when he came back, 'they've forced it on me.'

'It is for kindness,' he said, as if giving her a lesson she had never learned properly, 'and for hospitality.'

'Well, I know that,' she couldn't help replying. 'But help me out with the chappattis. There are far more here than I can cope with.'

'No,' he said, 'they are for you. Try to finish them. Do not give offence. I also will eat. They are preparing. Then we will go to Mayapore.'

'What about Mrs Chaudhuri?' she asked.

'She is safe with her friend. They will send someone from here to tell her where I have gone.'

After a moment, looking up, catching his watchful eye, she said, 'Thank you, Mr Chaudhuri,' and then, after a bit of difficulty, 'I should have been afraid alone.'

In the next village, Garhwar, the police were waiting, squatting by the roadside in the shade of a banyan tree. Near the tree there was a whitewashed Hindu shrine. The priest in charge of the shrine sat half-naked on the hard-mud verandah of his hut, watching them. The police were armed with sticks. Seeing the car approach, the head constable got up from his haunches and flagged them to a stop. It was his duty to warn her, he told Miss Crane in Urdu, having saluted her and glanced at Mr Chaudhuri, that it was dangerous to proceed. He had been instructed to stand by and to expect trouble.

'When were you so instructed?' Miss Crane asked, also in Urdu.

He had been instructed early that morning to stand by, and yesterday to be prepared for trouble.

'You should have sent a message at once to Kotali,' she said.

He had sent a message to Kotali. He had done so on his own initiative. He had not been instructed to send any message but only to stand by and be prepared for trouble.

'You should have sent a message yesterday, but it's no matter,' Miss Crane said. Perhaps he would be good enough to tell her if he had any information about what was happening in Mayapore and between Garhwar and Mayapore.

'I have no information,' he said. 'The telephone line to Dibrapur is now out of order.'

'You mean cut?'

It was possible that it was cut. Also possible that it was just out of order. It was because he had been warned to stand by and to expect trouble and because immediately afterwards he found the telephone out of order that he had sent messages to Kotali and to the other villages in his jurisdiction. He had sent the messages by ordinary men and women from Garhwar as he could not afford to send any of his men in case trouble came suddenly. He had done everything possible. There was not much he could do with a handful of men if real trouble came. There were many bad people in the villages. His life and the lives of his men were in danger. Perhaps the memsahib would tell the sub-inspector sahib in Tanpur that Head Constable Akbar Ali in Garhwar was standing by as instructed but was without means of communication.

'Shall we reach Tanpur safely then, do you think?' Miss Crane asked.

He did not know, but the police in the Tanpur division of the district, under whose jurisdiction the Dibrapur sub-division came, were all men of character and determination. He thought it possible that she would reach Tanpur, but it was his duty to warn her that it was dangerous to proceed, and of course he could not answer for the division beyond Tanpur, where there were many villages full of bad people who might be converging on Tanpur, and perhaps on Mayapore, if Mayapore was in a state of civil disturbance. But Sub-Inspector Govindas Lal Sahib in Tanpur would no doubt be in a better position to advise her about that.

They reached Tanpur at two o'clock. Tanpur was a small town, dirty, poor, and smelling of ordure. The police who were out in force, patrolling the main street, consisted of six men and the assistant sub-inspector. But there was no sign of Sub-Inspector Govindas Lal who, his assistant said, had been trying to make contact with the District Superintendent Sahib's head-quarters in Mayapore and had gone out an hour ago in a truck with one constable and three linesmen from the posts and tele-graphs to find out where the wires were cut between Tanpur and Mayapore. The lines were also cut between Tanpur and Dibrapur, but the line to Mayapore was the most vital. Mr Chaudhuri told the assistant sub-inspector that the police post in Garhwar was also cut off, but that they had seen no lines down between there and Tanpur itself, or indeed any lines down all the way from the schoolhouse in Dibrapur. The assistant sub-inspector explained that to telephone from Garhwar to Tanpur or from Tanpur to Garhwar the call had to go through the Dibrapur exchange, and that it looked as though the lines must have been cut close to the Dibrapur exchange or even that the Dibrapur posts and telegraphs had been destroyed.

'Is it safe to proceed?' Mr Chaudhuri asked.

'Who can say?' the man replied. 'If no harm has come to the sub-inspector sahib, then you will find him on the road ahead.' In Tanpur itself there had been crowds collecting in the morning but the sub-inspector sahib had persuaded them to disperse. He had put it about that the military were on their way from Maya-pore to maintain order. The shops were still closed, which was contrary to regulations, but the people were staying in their homes and the last instructions from Mayapore, early that morn-ing, were to the effect that crowds should be persuaded to dis-perse if possible, but not provoked. The shopkeepers could have been forced to open their shops, but if people were not to be provoked it was better to let them stay shut. So far, then, all was quiet, but if the sub-inspector sahib did not return soon he did not know how long this state of affairs would continue. 'But we are pulling on all right,' he said to Miss Crane, suddenly, in English.

'We'll see the sub-inspector and tell him.'

But they did not see the sub-inspector. Five miles beyond Tanpur they found what looked like his truck, upside down on the roadside where it had been overturned in the place where it must have been parked, next to a telegraph pole. If the truck belonged to the sub-inspector then he had found where the wires were cut, but not been given time to repair them. They lay tangled and coiled in the ditch at the side of the road.

'We must go back,' Mr Chaudhuri said. 'They have abducted Sub-Inspector Govindas Lal.'

'And the linesmen,' Miss Crane pointed out.

'Perhaps it was the linesmen who abducted him. The posts and telegraphs people are sometimes very bolshie.'

'But there were only three linesmen. And the sub-inspector had a man with him and was probably armed. There must have been other men.'

'Which is why we should turn back, Miss Crane.'

The sky was clouded over, but there was still no rain. 'It's ridiculous,' she said. 'Yesterday I drove along this road and every-thing was as quiet as the grave and safe as houses. Now suddenly there are cut telegraph wires, upturned trucks and vanished sub-inspectors of police. It is really very *silly*.' She laughed. 'No, Mr Chaudhuri, if you like I'll take you back to Tanpur, but I shall press on afterwards to Mayapore because I've just seen the *funny* side. But if I take you back to Tanpur the people will know we've gone back for a good reason, and then it will come out about the sub-inspector. And the assistant sub-inspector will probably panic and the funny side might stop being funny.'

Mr Chaudhuri was silent for a while. Presently he sighed and said, 'I don't follow your reasoning, Miss Crane. It is an example no doubt of British phlegm. You are mad. And I am mad to let you go, let alone go with you. All I ask is that if we see a crowd of people on the road, you put your foot hard on the accelerator.'

She turned her head and again they looked at each other straight. She had stopped smiling, not because she was annoyed with him for calling her mad or had already stopped seeing the funny side, but because she felt there was between them an unexpected mutual confidence, confidence of the kind that could spring up between two strangers who found themselves thrown together quite fortuitously in difficult circumstances that might turn out to be either frightening or amusing.

And for Miss Crane there was something else besides, a feeling she had often had before, a feeling in the bones of her shoulders and in the base of her skull that she was about to go over the hump thirty-five years of effort and willingness had never really got her over; the hump, however high or low it was, which, however hard you tried, still lay in the path of thoughts you sent flowing out to a man or woman whose skin was a different colour from your own. Were it only the size of a pebble, the hump was always there, disrupting the purity of that flow, the purity of the thoughts.

'Yes, I will try,' she said, 'try to put my foot down and keep it there,' and then wished that there were words she could use that would convey to him the regard she held him in at that moment, a regard deeper, harder than that she had felt for the ragged singing children years ago; deeper, harder, because her regard for the children had sprung partly from her pity for them – and for Mr Chaudhuri she had no pity; only respect and the kind of affection that came from the confidence one human being could feel in another, however little had been felt before.

'Then,' Mr Chaudhuri said, 'let us proceed.' His lips looked very dry. He was afraid, and so was she, but now perhaps they both saw the comic side, and she did not have to say anything special to him just because his skin was brown or because she had never understood him. After all, he had never fully understood her either. She set the car in motion again and after a while she began to sing. Presently to her surprise and pleasure he joined in. It was the song she always liked the children to learn. All over India, she thought, there were brown and off-white children and adults who could sing the song or, at least, remember it if they ever heard it again and, perhaps, remember it in connexion with Miss Crane Mem. She sang it now, not sentimentally, but with joy, not piously, but boldly, almost as though it were a jolly march. When they had sung it right through once, they began again.

'There's a *Friend* for little *chil*dren
  Ab*ove* the bright blue *sky,*
A *Friend* Who never *changes,*
  Whose *love* will never *die;*
De *da,* de da, de *da, dum*
  And *change* with changing *years,*
This *Friend* is always *worthy* −'

Ahead of them the rioters were spread out across the road.

'I can't,' she said, as the car got nearer.

'You must,' he said. 'Blow the horn, keep blowing it and press the accelerator, *press.*'

He leaned out of the window to show his dark Bengali face, and waved his arm in a motion demanding right of way. 'Faster,' he shouted at her. 'Faster, you're slowing down, keep pressing and blowing.'

'I shall kill someone,' she shouted back. 'I can't. I can't. Why don't they move away?'

'Let them be killed. Faster. And blow!'

For a moment, closing on the crowd, she thought she and Mr Chaudhuri had won, that the men were moving to give way, but then they cohered again into a solid mass. They must have seen her white face. A man in front began to wave his arms, commanding them to stop.

'Keep going!' Mr Chaudhuri shouted. 'Close your eyes if you must but keep going!'

She tightened her mouth preparing to obey, but failed. She couldn't drive into a mass of living creatures. 'I'm sorry,' she cried, and began to press on the brake pedal. She stopped the car some twenty yards from the man who was waving his arms, but kept the engine running. 'They weren't going to move, they'd have died. I'm sorry.'

'Don't speak,' Mr Chaudhuri said. 'Now leave it to me. Don't speak.' He put a hand on her wrist. 'Trust me,' he said. 'I know you never have, but trust me now. Do whatever I say. *Whatever* I say.'

She nodded. 'I trust you. I'll do what you say.' In her physical panic there was a kind of exhilaration as though she were drunk on the Deputy Commissioner's brandy. 'But don't run risks. I'm not worth risks. I'm old and it's all gone and I've failed.' She laughed. The men were approaching, swaggering. 'After all, it's me they want,' she said. 'Not you. So that's it. If this is where it ends for me, let it end.'

'Please, Miss Crane,' he said, 'don't be ridiculous.'

The car was surrounded now. She found it difficult to distinguish face from face. They all looked the same, they all smelt the same: of liquor and garlic and sweat-soaked cotton cloth. Most were dressed in white homespun shirts and dhotis. Some wore the white Congress cap. They were chanting the words that the whole of India, it seemed to her, had been chanting since early in the spring. *Quit India! Quit India!* Mr Chaudhuri was talking to the leader. The leader was asking what he was doing riding in a car with an Englishwoman. Mr Chaudhuri was not answering his questions but trying to shout him down, trying to tell him that Miss Crane was an old friend of India, that only that morning she had saved the lives of many Indian children from drunken power-mad policemen and was on her way to a secret meeting of the Congress Committee in Mayapore whose confidence she enjoyed and whose efforts to overthrow the English she wholeheartedly endorsed.

The leader said he did not believe Mr Chaudhuri. Mr Chaudhuri was a traitor. No self-respecting Indian male would ride with a dried-up virgin memsahib who needed to feel the strength of a man inside her before she could even look like a woman, and what would Mr Chaudhuri do if they decided to take the memsahib out of the car and show her what women were for and what men could do? Not, the leader said, spitting on to the bonnet of the Ford, that he would waste his strength and manhood on such a dried-up old bag of bones. 'She speaks Hindi,' Mr Chaudhuri said, 'and hears these insults. Are you not ashamed to speak so of a *guru*, a teacher, as great a *guru* as Mrs Annie Besant, and a follower of the Mahatma? Great evil will come to you and your seed if you so much as lay a finger on her.'

'Then we will lay one on you, brother,' the leader said, and dragged open the door, whose lock Miss Crane had failed, month after month, to have repaired. 'Go,' Mr Chaudhuri said, as he was taken out. 'Go now. It's all right. No harm will come to me.'

'Pigs!' she cried in Urdu, trying to hold on to Mr Chaudhuri's arm, using the words she had used years ago, in Muzzafirabad.

'Sons of pigs, cow-eaters, impotent idolaters, fornicators, abhorred of the Lord Shiva . . .'

'Go!' shrieked Mr Chaudhuri, from outside the car, kicking the door shut, his arms held by four men, 'or do you only take orders from white men? Do you only keep promises you make to your own kind?'

'No!' she shouted back. 'No, no! I don't!' and, pressing the accelerator, released the brake, nearly stalling the engine so that the car jerked, paused, and jerked again, throwing the laughing men away from the bonnet, and then it leapt away so that they had to jump out of its path. A couple of hundred yards further on she stopped and looked back. Three of the men were chasing after the car. Behind them Mr Chaudhuri was being pushed from one man to the other. A stick was brought down heavily on his shoulders. She shouted, 'No! No! Mr Chaudhuri!' and opened the door, climbed out. The three men held their arms out, laughing, and called, 'Ah, memsahib, memsahib,' and came towards her. Remembering, she reached into the car and found the starting handle, stood in the road, threatening them with it. They laughed louder and struck postures of mock defence and defiance, jumped about grinning, like performing monkeys. Mr Chaudhuri had his head covered by his hands. The sticks were coming down, thwack, thwack. Then he was on his knees, and then out of sight, surrounded by the men who were beating him. Miss Crane cried out, 'Devils! Devils!' and began to move towards the three men, still waving the starting handle. They moved back, pretending to be alarmed. The youngest of them reached into his dhoti as if about to expose himself, shouted something at her. Suddenly they turned and ran back to their leader who had called out to them. The other rioters were standing over Mr Chaudhuri who lay unmoving in the middle of the road. A couple of them were going through his pockets. The leader was now pointing at the car. Five or six men left the group surrounding Mr Chaudhuri and came towards Miss Crane. Instinctively she backed, but held her ground next to the car. Reaching her they pushed her aside, roughly, angrily, as if ashamed they had not yet summoned up the courage to disobey their leader and attack her. Bending to the task they got their weight under the running-board and the mudguards and began to heave rhythmically, until of a sudden the car turned over.

From this display of strength one of them, anyway, got courage. Turning from the car he came at Miss Crane, raised his hand and hit her across the face, once, twice, then pushed her back towards the ditch and, using both arms, tumbled her down the three-foot embankment. Falling, she lost consciousness. When she came to and had collected her senses and strength she scrambled up the bank on her hands and knees and found the Ford burning and the rioters in the distance.

Limping, she walked to where Mr Chaudhuri still lay. Reaching him she knelt and said, 'Mr Chaudhuri,' but could not touch him because of his bloody face and open eyes and the awful thing that had happened to the side of his head. 'No,' she said, 'no, it isn't true. Oh God. Oh God, forgive me. Oh God, forgive us all,' and then covered her face and wept, which she had not done for years, and continued weeping for some time.

She dried her eyes by wiping them on the sleeve of her blouse, once, twice, three times. She felt the first heavy drops of rain. Her raincape had been in the back of the car. She said, in anguish, 'But there's nothing to cover him with, nothing, nothing,' and stood up, crouched, got hold of his feet and dragged him to the side of the road.

'I can't help it,' she said, as if to him, when he lay bloody and limp and inhuman in the place she had dragged him to. 'There's nothing I can do, nothing, nothing,' and turned away and began to walk with long unsteady strides through the rain, past the blazing car, towards Mayapore. As she walked she kept saying, 'Nothing I can do. Nothing. Nothing.'

A hundred yards past the car she stopped. 'But there is,' she said, and turned and walked back until she reached Mr Chaudhuri's body. She sat down in the mud at the side of the road, close to him, reached out and took his hand.

'It's taken me a long time,' she said, meaning not only Mr Chaudhuri, 'I'm sorry it was too late.'

As Mr Poulson said afterwards, the troubles in Mayapore began for him with the sight of old Miss Crane sitting in the pouring rain by the roadside holding the hand of a dead Indian. On that day, the day of the arrests of members of the Congress sub-committees in the district, Mayapore itself had been quiet. The uprising got off to a slow start. Only Dibrapur and the outlying

districts appeared to have jumped the gun. Mr Poulson set off
from Mayapore in the afternoon, in a car, accompanied by one
of Mr Merrick's inspectors of police, and a truck-load of constables, to investigate rumours of trouble in the sub-divisions
that couldn't be contacted by telephone, and although when he
reached the village of Candgarh he found the sub-inspector of
police from Tanpur, one constable and three linesmen from posts
and telegraphs, locked in the police post, it was not until he
proceeded along the road to Tanpur and found first of all Miss
Crane's burnt-out car and then Miss Crane herself that he really
began to take the troubles seriously.

The troubles which Mr Poulson and several others began by
not taking seriously took until the end of August to put down.
Everyone in Mayapore at that time would have a different story
to tell, although there were stories of which each individual had
common knowledge. There was, to begin with, the story of
Miss Crane, although that was almost immediately lost sight
of following the rape of the English girl in the Bibighar Gardens
on the night of August the 9th, at an hour when Miss Crane was
lying in the first delirium of pneumonia in a bed in the Mayapore
General Hospital. Later, when Miss Crane found it impossible
to identify any of the men arrested that day in Tanpur, for a
short while she came again into prominence. People wondered
whether she was genuinely at a loss to recognize her own
attackers and Mr Chaudhuri's murderers, or whether she was
being obstinate, over-zealous in the business of being fair at all
costs to the bloody blacks.

But the Bibighar Gardens affair was not lost sight of. It seemed
to the European population to be the key to the whole situation
they presently found themselves in, the sharpest warning of the
most obvious danger to all of them, but most especially to the
women. Afterwards it was never clear whether the steps taken
by the authorities following the rape of the English girl in the
Bibighar Gardens sparked off worse riots than had been planned
or whether the riots would have taken place in any case. There
were some who said one thing and some the other. Those who
held that there would have been little or no rioting if it hadn't
been for the rape and the steps taken to avenge it believed that
the men the Deputy Commissioner had ordered to be arrested
on the morning of the 9th August were the right ones to have

arrested, and that the action taken in regard to the Bibighar
Gardens affair had caused worse disorders than the civil disobedience that was stopped by the arrests. Those who held that
there would have been disorders in any event and that the Bibighar Gardens affair was purely symptomatic of general treachery
said that the members of the local Congress committees whom
Mr White had no alternative but to arrest were simply figure-
heads, and that the real ringleaders of the intended rebellion had
been under cover in places like Tanpur and Dibrapur. But at the
time, there was no distinguishing cause from effect and the
events of the following three weeks were of the kind that could
only be dealt with as and when they arose.

It was not until the first week of September, the first week of
quiet, that Miss Crane returned from hospital to her bungalow,
and another fortnight was to pass before she felt strong enough
to attempt to take up the reins again. It was therefore some six
or seven weeks after the beginning of the uprisings in Mayapore
district and some three or four weeks after their end, that on a
Tuesday afternoon Miss Crane once more opened her home to
soldiers from the barracks.

They would be, she knew, changed in some respects from
the boys they were before the riots began. In hospital, and since,
she had closed her mind to stories of the troubles, but she knew
that the military had been called out in aid of the civil power, that
for three or four days Mr White was said to have lost his head
and handed Mayapore over to the control of the local Brigade
Commander. She had heard Indians say, although she had tried
not to listen, that in those few days of Brigadier Reid, things
had been almost as bad as in the days of General Dyer in Amritsar
in 1919. There had not been any indiscriminate shooting of
unarmed civilians, but there had been, apart from controlled
shootings and consequent deaths, the forcible feeding with beef
– if the story were to be believed – of six Hindu youths who
were suspected or guilty of the rape in the Bibighar Gardens.
There had been no public whippings, as in General Dyer's day,
when youths were clapped to a triangle in the open street and
flogged simply as suspects in an attack on an Englishwoman, but
there were rumours that the youths who had been forcibly fed
with beef had also been whipped and had now disappeared into
the anonymous mass of those imprisoned with or without trial.

In the native town itself, as Mr Francis Narayan repeatedly

told her, there had been many charges by mounted police, and firing by the military to disperse crowds and punish looters and fire-raisers. In the district as a whole, as in many other provinces of India, there had been widespread disruption of railways, posts, telegraphs, looting of warehouses, shops, houses and Government grain and seed stores (which the people would be sorry for next year, Mr Narayan pointed out, if the crops failed). Police posts had been attacked, policemen murdered. In one subdivision of the district, so it was rumoured, the Indian magistrate had run the Congress flag up over his courthouse, released prisoners from custody, fined liberals and moderates, illicitly collected revenues and hidden away money that should have been paid into the treasury. Miss Crane suspected that the story was apocryphal, but there did seem to be evidence that one of Mr White's Indian subordinates was in disgrace and, since order was restored, had spent an hour weeping at the Deputy Commissioner's bungalow.

She was, in fact, too old a hand to believe everything told her as incontrovertible truth, and too old a hand not to know that her simple soldiers who had found themselves fresh out from England, suddenly acting in aid of the civil power to reduce rebellion in a colonial empire they knew little about but must now think badly of (remembering home and the blitz and their comrades dead on the plains around Mandalay), would find it difficult to make sense of what had happened, and why it had happened, and why, now that it was over, the English and the Indians had apparently patched their quarrel and come together once more in a compulsive harmony.

There was in that word compulsive, she knew, the idea of a key to the situation, the idea of there being somewhere in this curious centuries-long association a kind of love with hate on the obverse side, as on a coin. But Miss Crane found herself now too tired, too easily weighed down by the sheer pressure of the climate and the land and the hordes of brown faces and the sprinkling of stiff-lipped white ones, to channel any of her remaining pneumonia-sapped energy into solving moral and dialectical problems. But she wished that in the days when she had had the energy, days which had ended abruptly on the road from Tanpur, she had taken one of the soldiers aside – and she was thinking of Clancy – and said:

'For years, since the eighteenth century, and in each century since, we have said at home, in England, in Whitehall, that the day would come when our rule in India will end, not bloodily, but in peace, in — so we made it seem — a perfect gesture of equality and friendship and love. For years, for nearly a century, the books that Indians have read have been the books of our English radicals, our English liberals. There has been, you see, a seed. A seed planted in the Indian imagination and in the English imagination. Out of it was to come something sane and grave, full of dignity, full of thoughtfulness and kindness and peace and wisdom. For all these qualities are in us, in you, and in me, in old Joseph and Mr Narayan and Mr White and I suppose in Brigadier Reid. And they were there, too, in Mr Chaudhuri. For years we have been promising and for years finding means of putting the fulfilment of the promise off until the promise stopped looking like a promise and started looking only like a sinister prevarication, even to me, let alone to Indians who think and feel and know the same as me. And the tragedy is that between us there is this little matter of the colour of the skin, which gets in the way of our seeing through each other's failings and seeing into each other's hearts. Because if we saw through *them*, into *them*, then we should know. And what we should know is that the promise is a promise and will be fulfilled.'

But she had never said this to anyone, even to Clancy. And the day came when Clancy reappeared, coming in force with his mates who had heard that the old maid had had a bad time and been brave and nearly died, and they were anxious to make her laugh and feel happy, so that she would forget her troubles and know that she was among friends, stout lads who had been through it a bit themselves, and who were grateful to her for the small thing she did for them that reminded them of home and safety.

But throughout that tea-time, not one of them, not even Clancy, so much as looked at old Joseph, so when they had gone and she had helped Joseph clear away but found no words to heal the wound to the old man's pride and self-respect, she left him to finish and, going into her room, took down the picture of the old Queen and locked it away, in the chest, against the time when there might, remotely, be an occasion to put it back up again.

PART TWO

THE MACGREGOR HOUSE

Dooliya le aō
re morē babul ke kaharwa.
Chali hoon sajan ba ke des.

(O my father's servants, bring my palanquin.
I am going to the land of my husband)

(A morning raga.)
Translation by Dipali Nag

Next, there is the image of a garden: not the Bibighar garden but the garden of the MacGregor House: intense sunlight, deep and complex shadows. The range of green is extraordinary, palest lime, bitter emerald, mid-tones, neutral tints. The textures of the leaves are many and varied, they communicate themselves through sight to imaginary touch, exciting the finger-tips: leaves coming into the tenderest flesh, superbly in their prime, crisping to old age; all this at the same season because here there is no autumn. In the shadows there are dark blue veils, the indigo dreams of plants fallen asleep, and odours of sweet and necessary decay, numerous places layered with the cast-off fruit of other years softened into compost, feeding the living roots that lie under the garden massively, in hungry immobility.

From the house there is the sound of a young girl singing. She sings a raga, the song of the young bride saying goodbye to her parents, before setting out on the journey to her new home far away. There are ragas for morning and evening. This one is for morning. The dew is not yet off the ground. The garden is still cool. A blue-black crow with a red-yellow beak swoops from the roof of the house looking for its breakfast. Where the sunlight strikes the lawn the dew is a scattering of crystals.

Surrounding the lawn there are bushes of bougainvillaea, white and red. Some of the bushes are hybrids and have branches that bear sprays of both colours. Elsewhere there are jasmine and beds of dark-red canna lilies. The house stands in the middle of the garden, protected from the outside world by close-formed battalions of trees: neem, pipul, gol mohur, tamarind, casuarina and banyan; it goes back to the late eighteenth century and was built by a prince who conceived a passion for a singer of classical music. To build a house and install a woman in it is an expensive way to beg her favours. It was said that he came to visit her morning and evening, and that she sang to him, the same songs perhaps that the girl is singing now, and that he became enamoured finally only of her voice and was content to listen while she instructed the pupils he permitted her to receive. Scheherazade told stories to postpone the hour of her execution. The singer sang to guard her honour. When the singer died the prince grieved. People said he died of a broken heart. The house was deserted, closed. Like the state it decayed, fell into ruin. The prince's son succeeded to the *gaddi*. He despised his father for his futile attachment to the singer. He would let no one live there. He built another house nearby, the Bibighar, where he kept his courtesans. He was a voluptuary. He emptied the treasury. His people starved. An Englishman at his court was poisoned and so the new prince was deposed, imprisoned, his state annexed, and his people were glad of it until time lay over the memory of the old bad but not the badness of the present. The decayed house of the singer was rebuilt by a red-faced Scottish nabob called MacGregor who feared God and favoured Muslims, and was afraid of temples. The story goes that he burnt the Bibighar to the ground because he said it had been an abomination. He died at the hands of mutinous sepoys.

His young wife is the first ghost. She comes dressed in the fashion of the times and stands on the verandah, swaying to and fro, as if nursing her dead baby, but her arms are empty. There is blood on her torn bodice. Her name is Janet MacGregor. A Muslim servant called Akbar Hossain died defending her.

MacGregor rebuilt the singer's house more than a hundred years ago on the decayed princely foundations, with money got, it was rumoured, from bribes. Foursquare, there is a flagged, inner courtyard; on the outer aspect, verandahs with rounded arches shading the upper as well as the ground-floor rooms. The brickwork is stuccoed and painted cream that always dries yellow. Stone steps lead from the gravel driveway to the front entrance. In the arches of the verandahs green chicks can be lowered or rolled up according to the season and the time of day. On the upper verandah there is a balustrade, but not on the lower whose level is three feet from the ground. Ranged along the ground, in front of it, there are clay pots filled with shrubs and flowers, and climbing plants that have embraced the pillars of the arches. An old man with a grizzled head, dressed in a white vest and khaki shorts that expose the knobs and sinews of his rheumatic legs, tends the plants and the flowers. This is Bhalu. His black skin is burnt purple. His bare toes cling to the gravel and are as horny as the shell of a tortoise.

It was on the stone steps leading to the verandah that the girl stumbled at the end of her headlong flight in the dark from the Bibighar Gardens; stumbled, fell, and crawled on her hands and knees the rest of the way to safety and into the history of a troubled period.

Yes, I remember Miss Crane, old Lady Chatterjee says. Long ago as it is, I still regret having thought of her at the time as a mediocre person but I only ever met her at Connie and Robin White's, and only at those awful dull dinners poor Connie had to give as Mrs Deputy C when she needed Miss Crane as an extra woman to make up her table and balance the bachelors. Miss Crane wasn't my cup of tea. With one or two exceptions such as Connie White and Ethel Manners the European women never were and those who come out to India now don't seem to be anybody's except their husbands' and not always then. They're mostly lumps. In those days they were nearly all harpies. I used to think Miss Crane would have been a harpy if she'd got married and had a position to keep up. As it was, she was a lump with a harpy exterior, the kind of person who had nothing much to say but gave the impression of thinking a lot, which is all right in a man but distasteful in a woman. There aren't many women in positions of real authority and so it seems to me the rest of us have a duty to speak our minds. It's the only way the world can judge us unless we are among the fortunate few who are allowed to express themselves through action. Otherwise we have to rely on our tongues. I'm thinking of talk in mixed company. Woman-chatter has never greatly appealed to me because the minds that are spoken between the withdrawal from the dining-room and the return of the gents usually prove to be empty and you might as well give yourself a rest and think of something bleak and cool like snow.

I wrote Miss Crane off as mediocre because although she chatted quite pleasantly and intelligently over coffee she was mostly mumchance at the dinner table. Oh, not mumchance *tout court*. No. She never struck me as shy, although she was probably afraid of me. Her silence was of the ominous kind, which is where the idea of harpy came in because nothing was more ominous than the silence of a European harpy. But true harpy silence is always accompanied by a sly look or a vulgar little grimace from one harpy to another. There was nothing of that kind of harpy about Miss Crane. And then, over coffee, which is the time real harpies bare their talons, she showed herself, as I have said, surprisingly capable of *chat*, chat of an ingenuous nature, and this suggested lumpishness and made me think of her as another woolly liberal, a poor woman who had struggled hard against odds, even injustice, or plain bad luck, and had had to latch on to something both soothing to the mind and enlivening to the physique, like struggling through the monsoon on that dotty bicycle of hers to check that all the children were learning to be unselfish and public-spirited and keeping clean and reasonably well-fed in the process.

There was that typical silliness of a picture of Mr Gandhi that she took down or was said to have taken down because she decided the old boy was being naughty whereas of course he was simply being astute. The English have always revered saints but hated them to be shrewd. English people who thought Gandhi a saint were identifying themselves with the thousands or millions of Indians who said he *was*, but saintliness to an Indian means quite a different thing than it means to an Englishman. An English person automatically thinks of a saint as someone who is going to be martyred, a man whose logic isn't going to work in a final show-down with the severely practical world, a man in fact who is a saint *per se*. Apart from occasional temptations (for which they prescribe hair-shirts) they expect these saints of theirs to be so *un*earthbound that they have one foot in heaven already. And of course by heaven they mean the opposite of earth. They divide the material from the spiritual with their usual passion for tidiness and for people being orderly and knowing their place. On the other hand, to the Hindu there can't be this distinction. For him the material world is illusory and Heaven a name for personal oblivion. Personally I have always found the material world far from illusory and have never welcomed as pleasurable the idea of mindless embodiment in a dull corporate state of total peace, which is how you could describe the Hindu concept of God. The point is, though, that on this difficult journey from illusion to oblivion *anything* counts as practical, because everything is speculative. Well, but to come back to Mr Gandhi, the Hindus called him a saint because for thirty years he was the most *active* Hindu on the scene, which may sound like a paradox to European ears but after all, given our bodies, to travel from illusion to oblivion requires tremendous mental and physical stamina – and, if you are anxious to shorten the journey for others, a notable degree of leadership and a high content of hypnotic persuasion in oratory. But as for Western religious *mores*, well, to get from the practical world of affairs to an impractical heaven requires nothing but an act we're all capable of, dying I mean, although disappointment in the event undoubtedly follows. Irreligious as I am I can't help being contemptuous of the laziness of western religions, and I can't help criticizing myself for not being even a bad Hindu. But at least I don't make the kind of mistake Miss Crane made. If Mr Gandhi thought of his material acts as largely illusory, as private steps taken in public towards his own desirable personal merging with the absolute, I really do as a practical woman have to admire his shrewdness, his perfect timing in putting the cat among the pigeons.

But for Miss Crane, poor woman, pigeons were vulnerable creatures and cats soft little beasts, and both had lessons to learn. I found out a lot about her when all that awful business was over, in fact I tried to make up for my previous bad judgment, but by then she was difficult to get to know, and in the event there wasn't much time. Rather late in the day I invited her here, but she never came. So I called on her once or twice. Her virtues were still less obvious to me than her failings. She still gave me the impression she thought pigeons were to be taught the benefits of giving themselves up and cats the advantages of restraint. Both benefits and advantages were spiritual and therefore for her divisible from the material kind – which to me, passionately committed to what goes on around me, is a nullification of nature. I am not a Hindu but I *am* an Indian. I don't *like* violence but I believe in its inevitability. It is so *positive*. I hate negation. I sit here in the MacGregor House in a positive state of old age, bashing off here and there and everywhere whenever the mingy old government gives me a P form, and it doesn't worry me in the least that in the new India I seem already to be an anachronism, a woman who remembers everything too well quite to make her mark as a person worth listening to today. You could say that the same thing has happened to Mr Nehru for whom I have always had a fondness because he has omitted to be a saint. I still have a fondness for him because the only thing about him currently discussed with any sort of lively passion is the question of who is to succeed him. I suppose we are still waiting for the Mahatma because the previous one disappointed and surprised us by becoming a saint and martyr in the western sense when that silly boy shot him. I'm sure there's a lesson in that for us. If the old man were alive today I believe he'd dot us all one on the head with his spinning-wheel and point out that if we go on as we are we shall end up believing in saints the way you English do and so lose the chance of ever having one again in our public life. I have a feeling that when it was written into our constitution that we should be a secular state we finally put the lid on our Indian-ness, and admitted the *legality* of our long years of living in sin with the English. Our so-called independence *was* rather like a shot-gun wedding. The only Indians who don't realize that we are now really westerners are our peasants. I suppose they'll cotton on to it one day, and then they'll want to be westerners too, like practically everyone else in the East and Far East.

She sits, then, an old Rajput lady, wound in a dark silk saree whose glittering threads catch the light, with her white hair cut short, waved, tinted with the blue of dust from an enamelled Rajputana sky, much as years before she sat erect on the edge of a sofa and frightened Edwina Crane into the realization that to work to, and put her trust in, the formula of a few simple charitable ideas was not enough.

*

But Miss Crane (the old lady goes on), if you are really interested in her, well let me explain why in the end I changed my opinion of her. She was not mediocre. She showed courage and that's the most difficult thing in the world for any human being to show and the one I respect most, especially physical courage. I usually suspect cant in all the chat that goes on about moral courage. Moral courage smells of refusal. The physical sort is like an invitation, and I find that open. I find it appealing. And in any case, you know, physical courage is not without morality. We speak of moral courage as if it's on a higher human plane, but physical courage is usually informed by moral courage too, and often couldn't be expressed without it. Perhaps you could say the same the other way round. Perhaps these notions of courage are western notions, divisible in the usual western way that says black is black, and white is white, and right is the opposite of wrong.

What an old mess I'm in with my Rajput blood, my off-white skin, my oriental curiosity, my liking for the ways of your occidental civilization, and my funny old tongue that is only properly at home in English. At my age I smoke too many cigarettes and drink too much black-market whisky. I adore the Gothic monstrosities of the old public buildings of Bombay and the temple by the sea at Mahabalipuram. I think Corbusier did an interesting job at Chandigarh and the Taj Mahal brings a stupid lump into my throat. Did you ever see what they call the floating palace at Udaipur? Or the long vista from the Arc du Carrousel through the Place de la Concorde the whole length of the Champs Elysées at night with the traffic clustered at the Etoile? Or the city of London deserted on a Sunday morning when the sun is shining in October? The Malayan archipelago from the air? The toe of Italy from 40,000 feet up in a Comet? New York by night from the Beekman Tower, the first sight of Manhattan from the deck of a liner coming up the Hudson late in the afternoon? An old woman drawing water from a well in a village in Andhra Pradesh, or my great-niece Parvati playing the tamboura and singing a morning or evening raga? Well, of course you've seen *her*. But have you understood yet who she is?

These are not divisible, are they, these sights and people I've listed except, I suppose, in the minds of the people who encounter them and decide their meaning. Oh dear, I'm as bad as you, as any of us. Even when I'm not looking for a meaning one springs naturally to my mind. Do you think it is a disease?

Have the other half and then we'll bash off in and have dinner.

In the MacGregor House there is a room where the late Sir Nello Chatterjee deposited souvenirs of a life-time's magpie habit of picking up whatever caught his eye that might be reckoned a curiosity. He obviously engaged in a love affair with cuckoo clocks and cheap brightly coloured leatherwork, mostly orange, of the kind bought from bumboats at the Red Sea side of the Suez Canal. Perhaps the leatherwork celebrated a boyish delight not so much in the pouffes, purses and handbags, as in the lucky dip of baskets and ropes by which they were raised for inspection from the bobbing coracle-bazaars to the austere rock-firm height of the deck of an ironclad ocean-going steamer. He can seldom have resisted the temptation to possess the risen prize, or the obverse temptation to feel the feathery weight of the basket going down empty, weighted only by the coins or notes which were his response to and interpretation of the bargaining gestures of the fezzed nightgowned figure precariously astride below.

The pouffes and purses are scattered round this room in the MacGregor House, curiously dry and lifeless, like seaweed taken from its element, but also capable of bringing to the nose of a knowledgeable traveller the recollected smell of oil and water, of the faint stagnation that seems to surround a big ship directly it stops moving. India also seems to be at anchor. The cuckoo clocks are silent, ornate artificial bowers gathering dust, harbouring behind their shutters a score or more of startled birds who are probably hysterical from long incarceration and imminent expectation of winding and release. In Sir Nello's day the visitor to the room was entertained by the simultaneous cacophonous display of each bird's jack-in-a-box emergence, a sight Lady Chatterjee says she remembers as putting her in mind of a fantasy she suffered after visiting the morgue in Paris with an amorous medical student. Normally kept embalmed in their own disuse by her orders even when Sir Nello was alive, they have remained so, permanently, since his death. The visitor is discouraged from asking for a command performance; instead, invited to admire the stuffed tiger prowling in a nightmare of immobility on a wooden plinth, the glassed ivory replica of the Albert Memorial that plays 'Home Sweet Home' on a mechanical dulcimer, shells and stones from the Connecticut shore, a bronze miniature of the Eiffel Tower, little medallions from the kiosks in the Notre Dame Cathedral that are cold with the blessing of the commercial piety they evoke. There are paper lanterns that were carried away from a restaurant in Singapore in exchange for the payment of Sir Nello's grasping admiration and substantial appetite, the mangy boots of some Mongolian merchant encountered in Darjeeling after a journey over the Himalaya and engaged in Sir Nello's brand of thrusting acquisitive conversation. There are no weapons, no illuminated Moghul manuscripts or ancient jewellery, no Brobdingnagian trappings purloined from a flattered and impecunious prince's elephant stables: nothing of value except in the terms one eccentric might use of another eccentric's relics. There is, for instance, under glass, the old briar pipe that long ago was filled and tamped by the broad but increasingly shaky finger of Sir Henry Manners, one-time Governor of the province in which the town of Mayapore played, in 1942, its peculiar historic role, but Manners was gone ten years before that, carried temporarily away by retirement to Kashmir and then off permanently by the claret and the sunshine which he loved, and a disease which even now is curable only in Paris, Athens and Mexico and of which he knew nothing until it ate through the walls of his intestines and attacked his liver, which the doctors described as a cancerous invasion. And Sir Nello has been dead almost as many years, of a simple heart failure. They had been friends and their wives had been friends and, as widows, remained so right up until Lady Manners's death in 1948.

Of an admirable quartet – admirable because they overcame that little obstacle of the colour of the skin – only Lili Chatterjee survives to recall directly the placid as well as the desperate occasions. Of the other actors Reid has gone, and the girl, and young Kumar into oblivion, probably changing his name once more. The Whites and the Poulsons and young Ronald Merrick seem to be lost, temporarily at least, in the anonymity of time or other occupations. Miss Crane set fire to herself. They are the chance victims of the hazards of a colonial ambition. Museums, though, arrest history in its turbulent progress. So – the MacGregor House.

*

'When I first saw Daphne,' Lady Chatterjee said, referring to the girl, old Lady Manners's niece, 'she struck me as, well, good-natured but inept. She was big and rather clumsy. She was always dropping things.'

The MacGregor House still echoes faintly to the tinkling of shattered glass that can't be traced to present accident or blamed on any servant. Both Lili Chatterjee and her great-niece Parvati tread lightly and the servants go barefoot: so how account for the occasional sound of stoutly shod feet mounting the stairs or crossing the tiled floor of the main hall except by admitting Miss Manners's continuing presence? Through the insistent weeping of the summer rains there would be, one imagines, a singing of songs other than the ragas, in a voice not Parvati's, and the songs would be too recent to be attributable to Janet MacGregor. In any case Janet was a girl who can be imagined as given more to silence than sound, even at the end with the blood on her bodice and death approaching. Was the blood that of her baby or her husband? Perhaps it was her own. History doesn't record the answer or even pose the question. Janet MacGregor is a private ghost, an invisible marginal note on the title deeds of the Mac-Gregor House that passed from European to Indian ownership when Sir Nello bought it in the early nineteen-thirties to mark the occasion of his return to the province and district of his birth. Lili Chatterjee was his second wife, fifteen years his junior. He had no children from either, which accounted possibly for the cuckoo clocks. And Nello was Lili's second husband. Her first was a Rajput prince who broke his neck at polo. She had no children by this athletic heir to a sedentary throne. And this, perhaps, followed by her similarly unproductive life with Nello accounts for her air of unencumbered wisdom, her capacity for free comment and advice. Widow first of a prince she was also the daughter of one. Her education began in Geneva and ended in Paris. For her second husband, reduced as she had been by academic training and worldly experience from a state of privilege to one of common-sense, she chose a man who had a talent for making money as well as for spending it. There were – perhaps still are although she does not mention them – blood relations who never spoke to her again for marrying out of the Rajput into the Vaisya caste. Sir Nello's father had only been a pleader in the courts of law.

And Nello's grandfather (she says) and his grandfather's fathers were only prosperous merchants and small landowners. Nello used to have some old family property still, out near Tanpur, but it all went a long time ago. I think Nello gave some away to the peasants. He told me he had, but it may just have been a yarn, he may have got the idea from Tolstoy. He adored *Resurrection*. And he was very impressionable and eager to act out what he was impressed by. We Indians often are. Nello was a terrific mimic. He did Henry Manners at a party once and the Governor heard about it. So next time they met – Nello used to be called in quite often in an advisory capacity over questions of industrialization in the province – next time they met Henry said, Well come on, Chatterjee, let's see it. And the point about Nello is that he couldn't resist doing the man right in front of him. He liked an audience that could judge him by the highest standards. That's how they became friends and why Henry gave him that old briar pipe you've seen in the glass case. Henry said he thought Nello's imitation would be even better if he had a real pipe in his mouth and not just an imaginary one. Of course, it wasn't better, but Nello pretended it was, and that's very Indian too, to pretend rather than give offence. Nello didn't even like the feel of the pipe in his mouth. He never smoked. Or drank. In fact on the quiet he was a bit of a glutton for self-denial, which is probably why he made a lot of money. And he was half-serious about religion. He said to me once, 'Lili, what would you say if I became *sannyasi*?' You know what that means? It means when a man chucks everything up, leaves his home and family and bashes off with a staff and a begging-bowl. So I said, 'Well, Nello, I'd bash off with you.' So that put paid to that.

It's the fourth stage, you know, *sannyasa*, the fourth and last, on earth anyway. I mean in the Hindu code of how you should live your life. The first stage is training and discipline and celibacy, the next is raising a family and establishing a household. In the third stage – I suppose you'd call it middle-age, what you English call a man's prime, but really a time when your children are beginning to find you a bit of a bore and think their ideas best – in the third stage you prepare to loosen the bonds. You make sure your children are married off and provided for, and you bless your grandchildren and try not to stand in anybody's way. Then you reach the fourth. You bash off into the forest

before you become a doddering old burden, and try to make up
for lost time in the business of earning religious merit, which of
course you can earn all your life but earn best near the end when
you give up your worldly possessions, reject the world's claims
and try to forget Self. Of course, the English are always aghast
at the idea of *sannyasa*. They think it's awful, opting out of your
responsibilities like that and then expecting to live off the charity
of strangers. I always point out to them that they have their
sannyasis too: all those poor old people nobody wants who get
sent to Twilight Homes. You must admit the Hindus are practical. You needn't bother your head about the religious side. It's
like the cow in that respect. The cow became holy and beef
unclean to stop the peasants eating it when they were hungry.
If they ate their cows there'd be no milk, no bullocks to pull the
carts to take stuff to the market or to help plough the fields or
draw the water or turn the grindstone. Well, everybody knows
that. But it's the same with *sannyasa*. We persuade old people to
bash off and make one less mouth to feed by making them think
it's a way of acquiring merit. And we make sure they're fed and
not left to starve by persuading people who can afford it to
believe they acquire merit too every time they give a wandering
sannyasi a copper or a few grains of rice. We do have our own
special brand of social security, you see. And we've had it far
longer than anyone else. And nobody pays taxes for it.

Women can also become *sannyasi*. Shall *I*, do you think? Is
the MacGregor House becoming my ashram? These days I'm
much alone as you can guess from my talking your head off like
this. But I was really thinking of Miss Crane. You say her name
was Edwina. That's something I didn't know. I find it rather
difficult to get used to. I should have thought of her more as
Mildred. Anyway, to me she has always been Crane, Miss Crane.
A bird with long legs and elongated neck trying to flap its way
out of danger, too slowly, you know, like in slow motion at the
movies. On one of those three or four occasions I went to see
her after the trouble, when people were saying she was already
round the bend, I tried to get her to tell me why she'd resigned
from the mission. There weren't any pictures on the walls. But
there were these two blank spaces where you could see pictures
had been. Well, I knew about one blank space, but not the other.
I said, 'I see you're beginning to pack.' Mr Gandhi had gone, as

I knew, but I was curious to know what the other picture had been. A picture of Mr Nehru? The founder of the mission? The Light of the World?

But all she said was, 'No, I shan't need to pack,' so I guessed the mission johnnies had given her permission to stay on in the bungalow. You must visit it. It's still there. I went past it the other day on my way to the Purdah Hospital. I'm still on the committee, still making a nuisance of myself. Look out they say, here comes old Chatters. I bash off there the second Tuesday of every month and usually go the Bibighar bridge way but they're resurfacing the road and you get stuck for ages in the traffic, so this time we went by the Mandir Gate bridge, and Shafi took the wrong turning, stupid fellow. So there we were, not going past the old mission church but Miss Crane's bungalow. I haven't been down that road for years. It seems to be full of banias who've moved in from the bazaar. There was this big gross fellow on Miss Crane's little verandah picking his toes and listening to his transistor, and I think there were a couple of goats eating what there was of the grass and half a dozen children playing tag. She had such a pretty garden, too. Horticulture was the only subject we seemed to have in common. I told her she must come and see the garden here when she felt up to it, but she never did. The garden here at the MacGregor House is the same as it was then, so you can imagine it in those days. Bhalu grows the same flowers in the same beds year after year. He's always been an orderly type of man. Daphne used to pick the marigolds for the table, but she did tend to trample the edges of the beds and she'd only been with me a few days before Bhalu came and begged me to stop young memsahib trying to help him. Because he *grew* the flowers he thought he should be allowed to cut them. I told him the young memsahib liked flowers and wanted to help and although she was always smiling had had a lot of unhappiness and had lost all her family except her Auntie Ethel, so we had to be patient, but perhaps try to get her interested in ferns and evergreens which always grow wild in the shrubbery and made much *chic*-er decorations than marigolds. Now it's Parvati who picks the marigolds. But she's as light as a feather and old Bhalu's only too glad to have extra time to snooze and dream he's back in the army, looking after Colonel James Sahib's garden. I haven't the faintest idea who Colonel James was, but as Bhalu

gets older the colonel gets more and more VIP in his imagination, and now it seems the colonel can't have been anything less
than personal aide to the Viceroy. It used to be a status symbol
for an Indian family to hire a servant who'd worked for the old-
style British. It still is, but that kind of servant is getting so old
now, and useless, that it's better to get someone from the bazaar
and train them up. Bhalu used to refer to Nello as the Chota
Sahib. Indians were always called that by servants who'd worked
for *your* people, to distinguish them from British burra Sahibs.
Burra means big, and chota means small. But you must know
that too. Nello always laughed, but I think it hurt him a bit,
knowing his head gardener called him a chota sahib.

I wish Daphne had known Nello, but of course he died several
years before she came to stay with me. They had the same sense
of fun. In a big girl that kind of thing is more noticeable, isn't
it? Or do I mean that big girls are jollier than ordinary size ones?
But tiny girls are often jolly too, aren't they? I mean tiny English
girls. Indian girls are mostly tiny. Look at Parvati now. If they're
big they're awfully earnest and sometimes violent. They seem
to act as if they have a special position to keep up. If they're
taller than their husbands the situation becomes fraught. I was
an inch shorter than Nello and five inches shorter than my first
husband Ranji.

I'm trying to remember how tall Miss Crane was. Taller than
I of course, but medium English height probably. The neck and
the legs and the nose are all I vividly remember. I mostly saw
her sitting down or sitting up. Dinner at Connie White's, and
then when I visited her at the British General Hospital and at
her bungalow after she'd been discharged but still wasn't well
enough to get up. She received me the first time I went to her
bungalow lying on a charpoy on the verandah. It was difficult
seeing her in the British hospital. The English friends I had who
were ill usually went to the Greenlawns nursing home and had
private rooms they couldn't afford. If I wanted to visit there
I could always fix it with Doctor Mayhew. And if anyone was
in the general hospital they always seemed to have a room in the
private wing and all I had to do then was ring Ian Macintosh
who was the Civil Surgeon and ask him to tell someone to warn
the sister-in-charge. But Miss Crane was in the public wing in
a ward with three or four other beds and Ian was out of station

the day I decided to go. I'd never been in at the main reception before. The girl there – she was Anglo-Indian, but as white as a European – said I couldn't see Miss Crane, and when I insisted she kept me waiting in the hall and only pretended to have sent a message to the ward sister. What she had done was send a warning up to her. It was rather silly because Daphne had been doing voluntary work at the hospital and she *lived* with me, but because I was an Indian I wasn't really allowed in, anyway, not welcome. There wasn't actually a rule about it, just an unwritten one. I could have gone to the military wing because there were Indian King's commissioned officers on the station. That meant I could have visited say Lieutenant Shashardri or his wife, but the civil wing was sacrosanct. When Mrs Menen who was the wife of the District and Sessions Judge was ill she had a room in the nursing home, which Ian Macintosh always insisted should be multi-racial, provided people could pay for a room there. Although even then there was an unwritten rule that an Indian patient had to be of a certain type to get a bed. It didn't matter much and never caused any trouble because if an Indian was rich enough to afford it but not the right type his wife anyway was almost bound to be the kind of woman who wouldn't dream of going anywhere but the Purdah Hospital.

Anyway, there I was, the day I went to visit Miss Crane, sat down in the hall, hoping I looked as if I hadn't the slightest idea that anything was wrong, and after a bit all these lumpy QAs and harpy VADs started popping into reception on some excuse or other but actually to see if the rumour were true, that an Indian woman had had the brass to present herself at the desk and expect to be allowed up into the wards. I felt like something in a zoo, but then we often did in those days. I would probably have been sitting there still if Bruce Mayhew who had a consultant appointment there hadn't come whirling in and stopped dead and said, 'Hello, Lili, what on earth are you doing sitting *there*?' I told him I'd come to visit Miss Crane and that the girl at reception was trying to get hold of the ward-sister for me. I didn't want to get the receptionist into trouble, but of course Bruce knew what was happening. He said there was no need to bother the ward-sister and that he was going up there himself and would take me. When we got into the room where Miss Crane was he stayed with us long enough to make it clear to the

other English women in the ward that I was *somebody*. Not that
it made any difference. When Bruce went out one of them rang
the bell. Ordinarily a nurse would have answered it, but the
ward-sister came in herself. I know Bruce spoke to her on his
way out because he told me so afterwards. He went specially to
her cubby-hole and apologized for taking a visitor in to see Miss
Crane without her permission. He didn't say who I was because
he knew it wasn't necessary. I mean he knew she had been told
an Indian woman had been trying to get in, and that she had
intentionally locked herself in her cubby-hole so that she
couldn't be 'found'. Anyway, in she stalked a few minutes after
Bruce had gone and only a few seconds after this woman had
rung the bell. She stopped in her tracks as if amazed to see
anyone there. She said, 'What are you doing here, don't you
know visitors aren't allowed at this time of day?' I told her
Doctor Mayhew had given me permission because no one had
been able to find her. Oh, *I* am in charge of this ward, not
Doctor Mayhew, she said, please leave at once. Was it you who
rang the bell, Miss Crane? As if Miss Crane had rung to get me
thrown out. And before Miss Crane could say anything, this
woman who'd actually rung piped up, No, it was me who rang,
my rest is being disturbed. She sounded like the wife of a foreman from the British–Indian Electrical. Cockney, overlaid with
a year or two of listening to how the wives of the directors
spoke. I'm sorry. That's awfully snob of me, isn't it, but I was
upset and angry not only because of what was happening, but
also because I saw I'd probably put myself in the wrong over the
question of official visiting hours. But Daphne had always said
nobody took any notice of them and just wandered about at
almost any old time. And there *were* other people going in to
visit patients. It was my bad luck that there was nobody visiting
any of these other women in Miss Crane's ward just then. And
what was so awfully unfair was the fact that poor old Miss Crane
had only had two visitors the whole time she'd been there – the
chaplain and Mr Poulson who really only saw her officially. The
poor man didn't have time for more than that. It was he who
rescued her, you remember. After she'd come through the pneumonia he had to ask her a lot of questions about the men who
had killed Mr Chaudhuri. He didn't *have* to do that, it was really
Ronald Merrick's job, but Mr Poulson and Mr White knew

Miss Crane had to be treated gently and they knew Merrick wasn't a gentle sort of man. And Miss Crane hadn't been helpful with her answers. She wasn't popular any longer in the hospital. People thought she was holding something back so that an Indian killer would go free. When I visited her she'd been in the hospital three weeks and had only just been taken out of a side ward into this room with the lumps and harpies. Bruce Mayhew had told me on the way up that he appreciated my coming to see her. She had almost no white friends. For a day or two at the beginning she'd been thought a lot of in the hospital because she'd come through a bad time in the first riots. They would have liked her to be a heroine of the kind that breathed fire and got a few rioters swinging on the end of a rope. But she didn't breathe fire, and although in the end they got some of the men who'd led the mob and killed Mr Chaudhuri, that was due to the tenacity of the sub-inspector in Tanpur, and people thought justice would have been done quicker if Miss Crane had helped with proper descriptions. I suppose it didn't help her, my going to see her, and certainly didn't help me, my going to see *her*, although there was nothing much that would have helped *me* in the circumstances. The few white friends she had were the kind who hadn't the time to go and see her, and her Indian friends weren't the kind who'd have dared even to try. Some of the soldiers from the barracks clubbed together and sent her flowers and there were a few gifts from poor Indians like Mr Narayan who taught at the Chillianwallah school. Probably more gifts of that kind than ever reached her. The hospital staff wouldn't even have to look at the card to tell whether flowers came from an Indian or a European. I expect a lot were thrown away, so that she never had the chance of knowing how much the Indians liked her, not just for not giving evidence that wasn't absolutely in line with what she remembered, but for herself. I know Connie White and Mavis Poulson always *meant* to go and see her in hospital, but things were in such a frightful state, almost a state of siege, they never had the proper opportunity. It must have made her feel loved by no one. And about my own visit, you must bear in mind that Indians were hardly popular among the whites just then, and then of course, there was the other business, too. They all knew I was the woman in whose house Daphne was staying. It's what I told

myself when I'd got over the anger and annoyance of being
thrown out by that harpy sister.

What made being thrown out more or less bearable was the
fact that Miss Crane didn't seem to care whether I stayed or
went, so the situation resolved itself. The sister stood over the
bed and I got up and Miss Crane said, 'Thank you for visiting
me, Lady Chatterjee.' But the way she said it made it sound as
if I were too late, or she were too late, or as if nothing that
happened now could alter the way she saw things. A couple of
days later Bruce rang me and said any time I wanted to visit Miss
Crane I only had to appear at the reception desk. He'd kicked up
an awful fuss apparently. He said the hospital staff simply hadn't
realized who I was. I said, Oh Bruce, of course they realized. If
I'd been just Mrs Chatterjee the whole thing would have been
a joke to them, something they could score over and then forget.
But being Lady Chatterjee, the widow of a man knighted by
their own King, that made it awfully serious, something they
really had to take a stand over, quite apart from the personal
jealousy they might feel not being Knights' ladies themselves.
After all, practically every Indian who had them gave up his title
and honours about this time and returned his decorations to the
Viceroy for forwarding to King George or whatever, and that
was thought frightful. If it wasn't thought frightful it was
thought only right, because the Europeans always looked on
Indian titles as a bit of a joke. If Nello had been alive I expect
he'd have reverted to plain Mister along with the rest of them.
These days a lot of people still use their titles even though they're
not recognized by Government but in *those* days people used to
say to me, Why don't you drop the Lady? Nello would have
dropped the Sir. So I said I can't choose a course of action for a
husband who's dead. If I drop the Lady I'm really dishonouring
him, just for my own peace of mind. Anyway, he *deserved* his title.

There were people in Mayapore who said I only kept up with
Lady Manners for snob reasons, *Indian* snob reasons, like calling
an English person by his Christian name. They said the same
when I had Daphne come to live here at the MacGregor House.
She was Henry Manners's brother's daughter. Connie White
told me people tried to snub Daphne in places like the Gymkhana, snub her by pretending not to know where Daphne was
staying so that they could smirk or look shocked when she said

the MacGregor House. She didn't go to the club much – at least not at first – because I wasn't allowed in there, even as a guest. The Deputy Commissioner himself couldn't have got me past the door. Even the Viceroy couldn't. She only went to show friendly to the girls she worked with at the hospital, but then Ronald Merrick tried to set his cap at her and began to take her out and around and she was at the club with him several times. That was another bad mark against her. Mr Merrick was just about the most eligible bachelor on the station. He was quite good-looking, if a man with a permanent sneer in his eyes can ever be called that, but the main thing about him was his position as District Superintendent of Police. All the unmarried girls who didn't mind too much that he had no 'family' to speak of had hopes of hooking him. He'd never taken much notice of them so they didn't take very kindly to Daphne for apparently getting hold of him without so much as a finger raised. Neither Robin White nor Jack Poulson liked him much, but they said he was good at his job. Judge Menen couldn't stand him, but never said so in so many words. I had him round at the MacGregor House because I'd been on good terms with his predecessor, a rather older man called Angus MacGilvray. I thought Mr Merrick would be annoyed if he didn't even get an invitation, but I was surprised when he accepted it. He only came, though, because it was here he had the opportunity to meet Indians socially. You could see his mind working away, storing up little things that were said, so that he could go home and make a note on the confidential files that were kept so that whenever there was any civil trouble the most influential congress wallahs and anyone who ranked as dangerous could be locked up right away. I guessed he cottoned on to Daphne because he saw it as a duty to be on terms with someone who might let slip things that were going on here that were kept from him when he visited. He saw the MacGregor House as a sort of Cliveden, a hot-bed of Indian intrigue, a forcing-house for English reds – which of course would be the opposite of Cliveden-ish, but you know what I mean. But I was wrong, I think. His reasons for cottoning on to Daphne were much more complicated than that. By the time I realized how complicated, it was too late.

I often wish I could have that time all over again, but knowing what I know now. Not just for Daphne's sake, but for Miss

Crane's sake. I think I could have stopped Miss Crane from becoming *sannyasi* in that especially horrible way. It's all right to give everything up as long as you realize just what it is you've *had*. Poor Miss Crane didn't. That last time I saw her at the bungalow, when she was sitting in her room and I noticed the two blank spaces on the walls, she said, 'Lady Chatterjee, why do you come to see me?' And all I could think of to say was, 'To see if you want anything.' Well, I ask you, what was the good of that? Can you imagine a woman of Miss Crane's temperament admitting that she needed help? What should I have said, do you think? Said instead of what I did say? Well, if she were there now, and not that fat fellow picking his toes and listening to film music on his little radio, I think I'd say, 'Because neither of us must give up, and I can see you're about to.'

I must get my times sorted out. I work it out that I paid her *three* visits, not four. The first time in the hospital, and then on the occasion when she was still laid up but at home and I found her resting on the verandah with that old servant of hers hovering about, watching from the doorway to make sure she wasn't upset, and then a few weeks later when I'd heard about her resignation which came as a surprise to everybody. After my first visit to the bungalow I thought I should keep away for a while, but then people told me she'd had her soldiers to tea again. So I thought, Now's the time. Now we can get to know each other. But I didn't go right then. I had so much to do. I didn't go until I heard about her resignation and that people were saying she must have gone a bit bats. I called one afternoon. The servant was on the verandah, which of course was perfectly normal, but I realized he was on guard. He said Miss Crane was very busy and couldn't see anyone and I was about to go when she called out, Who is it? and he went inside, then came out again and said I could go in. She was in her bedroom, sitting in an armchair. She didn't get up and didn't ask me to sit down, but I sat all the same and it was then she said, Lady Chatterjee, why do you come to see me? I thought for a moment, and then came out with this silly remark, To see if you want anything. It's kind of you, she said, but there's nothing I want. I said, I hear you've resigned from the mission. She simply nodded her head. I looked round the room, as you do, don't you, when you're with someone in a room you've just heard they're going away from. And I saw those two blank spaces on the walls, one of which must have been made by Gandhi and the other by some-one else. So I made this remark about packing already. Oh, I shan't need to pack, she said, and then after a bit, while I was trying to work out why, she *smiled*, but to herself, not to me, so I thought, Well, it's true. She's nuts. It was because I thought, Oh, she's nuts, that I didn't ask what she meant, didn't say, The mission johnnies are going to *give* you the bungalow then? I didn't ask because it seemed so unlikely and I thought her answer would only add to the feeling I had that she was off her head, and I didn't feel up to coping with the embarrassment of having it proved. So I left it at that, she wouldn't need to pack. Poor Miss Crane. I ought to have followed up, I ought to have said, Why? Not that she'd have come right out with the real answer. The awful thing is it was in my mind afterwards that it may have been only then, when we were sitting there talking about not needing to pack, that she really understood why she wasn't going to pack, saw why there wouldn't be any need. That smile, you see, coming some while after she'd said, Oh I shan't pack, I shan't be packing, I shan't need to. Then she changed the subject. She asked how Daphne was. How is Miss Manners? Like that, in that tone of voice, of someone asking about a *colleague*, as if between them they represented something, which I suppose they did. She didn't know young Kumar. If she'd known about Hari Kumar I expect she'd have said, How is Miss Manners? in the same tone as before but added, Is it true what I hear, what I hear about what they've done to young Mr Kumar?

Dinner is the only meal Parvati has with the family, such as the family is: that is to say, Lili Chatterjee and young Parvati, the two of them. When there are no guests there is this picture to be had of them sharing one end of the long polished dining-room table, with two places laid close together, the old woman and the young girl, talking in English because even now that is the language of Indian society, in the way that half a century ago French was the language of polite Russians.

The man who serves them is quite young, too young to have been more than a small lad about the house at the time Miss Manners lived there, and actually he was not even that. He is a

recent acquisition. He is from the south, a cousin of some kind
of Bhalu, the old gardener. It amuses Lady Chatterjee that
although it was on Bhalu's recommendation that Ram Dass,
whom she calls Ramu, got the job of houseboy he has since
had little to do with the gardener because Bhalu's position is so
inferior to his own. He will not even admit a family connection.
Sometimes from the servants' quarters behind the house you can
hear them quarrelling. The cook despises them both. He has
cooked for a maharanee in his time. There is a girl sweeper called
Sushila. Lady Chatterjee turns a blind eye to evidence that the
Muslim driver, the handsome grinning Shafi, sleeps with
Sushila. It is difficult to get enough servants and their wage
demands get higher every year. Some of the rooms in the Mac-
Gregor House are shut up.

With all the chicks lowered the house is dark and cool even
at midday. The ceilings are very high. In such rooms human
thought is in the same danger as an escaped canary would be,
wheeling up and up, round and round, fluttering in areas of
shadow and in crevices you can imagine untouched by any
human hand since the house was rebuilt by MacGregor. In these
rooms, at night, even the artificial illumination of lamps and
brackets fails to reach the remoter angles and areas that would
lie far beyond the reach of a man standing on the shoulders of
another. It is best to depend upon a humdrum eye-level for
impressions; the strain on the neck otherwise is no less acute
than the strain on the senses then of other years impinging on
the present. There is in any case always a lulling feeling of imme-
diacy in these ground-floor rooms, the present lying as it does
in the lower levels, like the mist of a young day in ancient hollows. It is in going upstairs that the feeling of mounting into the
past first comes and ever afterwards persists, no matter how many
times the routine journey is undertaken. Bedrooms, after all, are
more specifically the repositories of their old occupants' intimate
sensations than the public rooms below.

Collecting a key from some arcane source or other – a guest
never penetrates the barrier from behind which the control and
ordering of the household is directed – Lady Chatterjee goes up
the broad uncarpeted polished wood staircase that curves from
the black and white tiled hall to the complex of landings and
corridors and opens the mahogany, brass-knobbed door of the

room where Miss Manners slept and which she still calls Daphne's room. It smells musty, as unused as the late Sir Nello's museum of schoolboy curios which suitably enough lies directly below it, with a view to the garden when the chicks are raised and a continuing view through the gaps between the bushiness of the shorter trees to the plains that surround Mayapore and the smudge of hills on the horizon. There is the spire of St Mary's church, a mile or two distant, still standing, still as irrelevant to its background as any architecture, Anglo or Indian, seems to be in this strangely unfinished landscape that makes the mono-tonous chanting of the crows which are never at rest sound like the cries of creatures only partially evolved, not yet born, but sharpened already by desires the world will eventually recognize as hunger.

In the desk there are two of the letters Miss Manners wrote to her aunt which Lady Manners afterwards gave to Lili Chatterjee, perhaps not wanting them herself, or the recollections they stirred; and these, possibly, reveal similar hungers and contrast-ing desires: unco-ordinated, irrelevant. She must have written them – unless she wrote them at night when the crows fitfully slept, impatient of morning – to the same accompaniment they are read to all this time after. The letters, read to the accom-paniment of this continuing unchanging sound, are curiously dead, strangely inarticulate. Why pretend otherwise? They do not resurrect the writer. They are merely themselves; like the photograph of Miss Manners which is signed with a calligraphic flourish by one Subhas Chand who used to take portraits of those people on the station who wanted a record for friends and relatives of what Mayapore had done to them. Subhas Chand, Lady Chatterjee says, had a booth in the shop of the chemist, Dr Gulab Singh Sahib. And Clancy was pictured there, in full-face, as his handsome pushing self in spotless khaki drill, and in matey combination with the rustic Barrett, staring out at the world from a background (again irrelevant) of draped velvet and gothic fern (maidenhair in a brass bowl on a romantic revival monumental column around which graveyard ivy is invisible but naggingly present to the impressionable eye).

The pictures of Clancy lie irrelevant too, like gifts kept from a Christmas cracker, among the rest of Miss Crane's unclaimed personal effects which have somehow been preserved at Mission

Headquarters in Calcutta; mouldering relics not of Miss Crane alone but also of sustained Christian honesty, and of the disinterested shrugs of distant Crane cousins, offspring of those poor ones who on her father's death turned up for the funeral in the mild hope of benefit and then departed, putting her out of mind and of temptation's reach of their own slender pockets in case the brave funeral face and declarations of self-sufficiency turned out to be untrustworthy. Having already seen in Calcutta pictures of Clancy, the Subhas Chand technique and signature, the quality of the matt-surfaced sepia paper he used for his prints (small cabinet size), all strike harmonious echoes of recognition when the picture of Miss Manners, memorially enclosed in a silver-plated frame, is first lifted from its place on the dressing-table which she sat at combing her apparently curly short-cut sepia hair.

You can't from this (Lady Chatterjee says, rubbing at a speck of tarnish on the frame) get a real idea of her personality. I think looking at pictures of people you don't or didn't know but only know about is intensely unsatisfactory. Of course, it's fascinating to see for the first time a portrait of someone like that, someone whose name was at one time on a lot of people's lips, as they say. You're probably feeling that now, but once the initial curiosity has been satisfied there's a sense of anti-climax, isn't there? Or perhaps even of no climax at all because you can't be absolutely sure the picture is anything like a good likeness or even that it's a picture of the right person? Do you know, I sometimes take a second look at pictures of myself and Nello – that one downstairs taken at the garden party in Simla for instance, where we're sandwiched between Lord Willingdon and the Aga Khan, and I think: Is that really Nello? Did I really look like that? Did I ever smile in quite such a smug way? Almost coy-smug, glancing at something that has caught my eye but isn't in the picture. Since I can't even guess what it could have been that caught my eye, let alone remember what it was, I begin to wonder whether the woman in the picture (who anyway doesn't *feel* like me) isn't an impersonator, and the plump chap with her a man who isn't Nello but is taking Nello off almost as success-fully as Nello used to take off Henry Manners. Willingdon and the Aga Khan look all right, but then when you meet and chat to blokes as high up as that you tend to look at them in only two dimensions, which is the way the camera looks at them too, so the photographic result is bound to seem authentic.

Daphne had this picture taken by Subhas Chand two or three months after she came to stay here. It wasn't her idea. Lady Manners wrote me and said: Tell Daphne I'd like a picture of her for my birthday but not to bother to frame it because I've got trunks full of frames from Henry's old Rogues' Gallery. It's what she and Henry called their collection of photographs. The Rogues' Gallery. Everything from old daguerreotypes of Henry's pa with his foot on a dead buffalo to groups taken at some beano with all the princes except one scowling at the camera because Henry's handsome aide had got the protocol wrong and stood a chap with a nine-gun salute closer to the Governor than a chap with eleven guns. And then there were all the snaps given to Henry and Henry's pa by servants – timid old boys pretending to look like tribesmen, all white whiskers and lopsided turbans. Henry never threw a single snap away. They all got framed and went with him wherever they were posted. When he died, Ethel had them packed up and put into trunks. I often wonder who this old silver frame originally had in it. I inherited it complete with Daphne's picture along with the two letters. I think if Daphne had given me a copy too, at the time she bashed off to Subhas Chand to have her picture taken for her Aunt Ethel's birthday, I think if I'd always had it, I'd see it as far more like Daphne than I do. But it came afterwards. It came here into this house, into this bedroom, when Daphne wasn't alive to come back in herself. I expect I resented it. It's always struck me as not quite belonging. It's Daphne all right – she had that kind of hopeful smile – perhaps she'd nearly knocked over one of old Subhas Chand's spotlights just before she sat down, and was still thinking: There I go again, just like me, catch me in a china shop, Auntie. It's a sweet smile though, isn't it? And that's come through. But photographers like Subhas Chand always make people's skin look like wax. There's not the tiniest crack in it anywhere, and around the eyes where there ought to be cracks, lines anyway, it's all been smoothed out by touching up and the real Daphne simply isn't looking out of them.

She had a habit of blinking whenever she began to speak, as if she couldn't get out the first word or two with her eyes open. And often she shut her eyes at the end of what she was saying.

When she shut her eyes this little smile you see in the photograph used to come on automatically, as if her eyelids and lips
were working off the same set of nerves. And it *was* nervousness
that made her do it. I used to think of it as affectation. I met her
for the first time when I went up to Pindi to spend Christmas
with Ethel Manners. It was Daphne's first Christmas in India
and Ethel wanted to cheer her up. I'd expected to find someone
mopey, instead there she was, blinking at me and chatting at
me. I sensed the affectation before I pinpointed the mannerism,
before I *noticed* the blinking, but once I'd separated the cause
from the effect I realized that what I called affectation was nothing more complicated than straightforward shyness. The eye-
shutting and the smiling were to give herself confidence in
company. Once she got used to you the mannerism disappeared.
But it came back at once if a stranger came into the room. People
instinctively liked her, though, and she never gave in to her shyness, she never seemed at a loss for a word.

What old Subhas Chand hasn't been able to disguise, at least
from me, is that this is the portrait of a girl who was more comfortable in specs. She had to wear them to read or to write letters.
According to the oculists, she really needed them all the time but
her aunt discouraged her and said specs were a lot of nonsense
for young people. What she meant was that specs just weren't
attractive, especially on a girl. I discouraged her too, not because
I thought specs could be unattractive, but because I knew you
could cure bad sight by exercises, splashing the eyes with cold
water, looking alternately from short to long distances, looking
up from concentrated work like writing a letter or reading a
book and focusing on some fixed object in the room several feet
away. But Auntie, she used to say, she got into the habit of calling
me Auntie, I can't see into long distances, I can't even see short
distances properly. She used to stand at the window there, putting her specs on and taking them off. Eventually she made out
where the hills are. She wanted so much to see everything there
was to see. India was what we used to call a thing with her. She'd
always wanted to come out. She was born in the Punjab but
didn't remember any of it because her mother couldn't stand the
climate and her father resigned from his service and went home
into private practice when Daphne was still almost a baby. He
was IMS. Years younger than his brother Henry. I don't think

he minded leaving India at the time. He obviously chose to be
a doctor instead of an administrator so that he wouldn't have to
compete with clever brother Henry all his life. By all accounts
his wife, Daphne's mother, was a tartar. She had to have everything her own way and she was a frightful snob. India obviously
didn't suit her as the wife of a junior man in the IMS. Law and
medicine are the two things we Indians have always shone at so
I expect George – Daphne's dad – had too many Indian colleagues for Mrs George's liking. She wanted him to be what
today you people call a Top Person, with rooms in Harley Street
and masses of top hospital appointments. But when he was in a
fair way to getting what she wanted she changed her tack and
saw herself as a leader of county society, so then there was the
flat in town and the house in Wiltshire and poor George
working himself to death bashing off from one place to the
other. You can tell the effect it had on him from something
Daphne said to me. She said, 'Poor daddy always regretted
leaving India, didn't he? I wish he were here with me now to
see it all again.' There were times when I thought she worked
doubly hard at knowing India simply to make up to her father
for what he had missed and probably admitted regretting having
given up just to please her mother. And like all those apparently
frail women who can't stand the Indian climate Daphne's
ma turned out as strong as an ox. At least until she got cancer.
And in my opinion that is a disease of the strong rather than of
the weak.

Picture her then: Daphne Manners, a big girl (to borrow a none
too definite image from Lady Chatterjee) leaning on the balcony
outside her bedroom window, gazing with concentration (as one
might gaze for two people, one being absent, once deprived,
since dead, and now regretted) at a landscape calculated to
inspire in the most sympathetic western heart a degree of
cultural shock. There is (even from this vantage point above a
garden whose blooms will pleasurably convey scent if you bend
close enough to them) a pervading redolence, wafting in from
the silent, heat-stricken trembling plains; from the vast panorama of fields, from the river, from the complex of human dwellings (with here and there, spiky or bulbous, a church, a mosque,
a temple), from the streets and lanes and the sequestered white

bungalows, the private houses, the public buildings, the station, from the rear quarters of the MacGregor House. A smell. Could it be of ordure?

After a few months the newcomer will cease to notice it. Ubiquitous, it translates itself from repellent through almost attractive because familiar stages into an essence distilled by an empirically committed mind, so that an old hand, temporarily bereft of it, nostalgically remembering it in some less malodorous place, will describe it to himself as the sub-continental equivalent of acrid wood-smoke at the end of a burnished copper autumn. But let the old hand's bereavement be of comparatively short duration: European leave, a rarefied, muscular effort above the Himalayan snow lines. Let it not be, for instance, an eighteen-year absence ended by chance and luck and the lepidopteristic intention to pin down the truth about Miss Crane, Miss Manners and young Kumar, and the events that seemed first to flutter and then to shatter Mayapore but actually seem to have left it untouched, massively in continuing brick-and-mortar possession of itself (if not of the landscape feebly invaded by its architectural, artisan formation). No, let it not be long, let it be short so that on renewed association the returning traveller will cry, possessively, even gratefully: Ah, India! Otherwise, after eighteen years and a too swift transition by Comet through the increasingly disturbing ambience of Beirut and Bahrein (the warmth correspondingly mounting, bringing the smell out like the warmth of a woman's skin releasing the hidden but astonishing formula of an unusual perfume) the nose – unused, but imagining itself prepared – will flex its nostrils against the grave revelation of the car or taxi drive from Bombay's Santa Cruz airport, along a road that leads through fields where the source of the wafting smell may be tracked to the squatting early-morning figures of male labourers casting their pellets upon the earth, there to lie, and harden, and encrust, and disintegrate, and lift in the currents of air into the generality of the prevailing winds.

Taking possession of the room to help, as Lady Chatterjee says, in the business of getting to know the surroundings that was Daphne's, left alone there, moving across the broad acres of uncarpeted floor, between the mosquito-net-shrouded bed and the door that leads into the private bathroom, one might – by attempting the journey from one island of Kashmir rug to another, not wetting one's feet in the striated sea of dark stained boards – play a variation of that old childhood game of not stepping on the cracks between paving stones and wonder if Daphne had time for similar absurdities. The bathroom is long and narrow. Green glazed tiles act on the walls from floor to shoulder height as shadowy mirrors of the room's contents and of its headless occupant. Perhaps Daphne, with her uncertain sight, was unaware of this and strode oblivious of truncated duplication by reflection from the door to the porcelain pedestal whose cistern, high up, is activated by one's pulling like a bell ringer on a long chain whose pot handgrip, moulded to the shape of the palm, emphasizes the luxuriousness of a comparatively rare machine. The porcelain tub is as big as an artificial lake, empty at this moment as if drained for an annual scraping. Its webbed claw feet are those of some dead, amphibious monster sentenced to support it like Atlas supporting the world. The immense brass taps suggest twin flows of piped-out water of ship's pump velocity, but only the cold tap works; the hot – when the stiff faucet is finally budged – produces a hollow rasping echo and a skitter of rust flakes. But the cold is warm enough. The bathroom is airless. There is no fan and only one window high up above the lavatory pedestal. At the opposite end of the bathroom – fifteen paces on bare feet across lukewarm mosaic that is slightly uneven and impresses the soles with the not unpleasant sensation of walking over the atrophied honeycomb of some long forgotten species of giant bee – there is an old-fashioned marble-topped washstand with an ormolu mirror on the wall above it, plain white china soap-dishes and a white jug on the slab; beneath the stand a slop-bowl with a lid and a wicker-bound handle. Here too is the towel-rack, a miniature gymnastic contraption of parallel mahogany bars and upright poles, hung with immense fluffy towels and huckabacks in a diminishing range of sizes, each embroidered in blue with the initials LC.

Returning to the other end, literally ascending the throne which is mounted on a broad dais anciently carpeted in the deep blue red of mouldy cherries, the splendour of the paper-holder fixes the attention. Here are lions, gilt-maned, gilt-faced, each holding in its gilt jaws an end of the bracket which supports the roll of buff, wood-chip austerity paper. The jaw of the nearer lion (and presumably that of its mate on the other side) adequately receives the ball of the little finger. Its head is as large as a clenched fist, so large that its cheek rests almost upon the cheek of its gilded counterpart. The effect is of two big cats grinning over the simple duty they have to hold, in readiness, something that is required for a cat-like but, because of the paper, ridiculous human function.

Lying in the bath, the eyes engage the single 75-watt bulb in a shade the shape of a pantomime Aladdin's hat, and attempt to see, above, the distant shadowy ceiling. A brass jug, dented from falls on to the mosaic floor, rests on the wooden rack that lies athwart the tub. The scoop. One remembers and, having soaped, stands and scoops and pours and scoops again and so, closing the eyes against the contrary evidence of the sex, attempts a re-enactment of Miss Manners refreshing herself after a hard day on the wards of the Mayapore hospital.

(To Lady Manners)   The MacGregor House,
                                              MacGregor Road,
                                                 Mayapore, I.
                                           26th February, 1942

Dear Auntie Ethel,

Please forgive me for not having written sooner. I hope you got Lili's telegram saying we'd arrived here safely. I'm sure you did. I can hardly believe it's a week since we said goodbye to you in Rawalpindi. It was sweet of you to let me come. The days have flown and looking back on them there scarcely seem to have been enough of them for us to have packed in everything we've done. I've just come back from my *second* day on the wards in the hospital which will show you no time has been wasted!

After Lahore the journey down was very interesting, much nicer than the one I did alone last year from Bombay to Pindi, which rather scared me because it was all so new and strange. I suppose I enjoyed this one because I've learned some of the ropes and anyway had Lili with me. She really *is* extraordinary, isn't she? Those awful English women in the carriage got out the next morning in Lahore. They were utterly beastly and never said a civil word to either of us. And those mounds of luggage they had that took up more than half the space! They hogged the little wc cubicle for over an hour after the train pulled out, and then sat up for ages drinking and smoking and talking as if neither of us was there while Lili and I were trying to get to sleep. (We had the upper and lower berth on one side of the carriage and they had the upper and lower on the other side.) I was so fagged I didn't wake up until the train had stopped at Lahore and there was all the fuss of them getting out. There was a chap to meet them, the husband of the one with her brains tied up in a scarf, I think. He came into the carriage at one point to look for something the one with the scarf was complaining had either been lost or *stolen*. They'd been out on the platform for some time while the coolies collected the luggage and he came in prepared to be rude. The poor chap looked awfully embarrassed when he saw *me*. They'd only complained to him about Lili, I expect. I was sitting up on the top bunk keeping an eye on *our* bags, with my hair all over the place. Lili had been up and dressed since five (so she told me afterwards) and was sitting there below me looking marvellous and cool as a cucumber, reading a book and pretending to be quite unaware of what was going on. Anyway he begged our pardon and thrashed about for a time, and the coolies thrashed about, searching under the seat and everywhere that didn't make it look too pointed that these women had suggested *we* might have pinched whatever it was one of them had lost. Then one of them called through the doorway, 'It's all right, Reggie, luckily it's been found.' I liked that 'luckily'! Reggie was as red as a beetroot by now and went out with his tail between his legs, and I think there was a row when he got back on the platform. The last thing we heard was the harpy saying very loudly, 'I don't care. The whole thing is a disgrace. I don't know what the country's coming to. After all first class *is* first class.' That word of Lili's is awfully apt, isn't it? Harpy.

It was marvellous from then on though. We had the whole compartment to ourselves and a lovely breakfast brought in. You know, until now I never did quite believe that story you told me about the time Sir Nello was turned out of a first-class compartment by a couple of box-wallah Englishmen. It seemed to me that if the railways allow an Indian to make a first-class booking then no one should be able to stop them using what they've paid for. I think if you hadn't been at Pindi station to see us off, though, there'd have been trouble with these two women about Lili and me actually getting in. Me only because I was with Lili. Was that why you got into the carriage first and condescended to them in that marvellous nineteenth-century way, before they had a chance of seeing her and realizing they were going to have to travel with an Indian woman?

When I remember how awful it is travelling at home in the blackout, with no heating in the trains, just a dim blue light, and the stations in darkness, people jam-packed in the corridors as well as in the compartments, but on the whole everyone helping everyone else and trying to be cheerful, I get really angry about the kind of thing that happens over here. Honestly, Auntie, a lot of the white people in India don't know they're born. Of course I never travelled first class at home, and there was sometimes bad feeling among the non-commissioned boys in the services when they were packed like sardines and the pinkest young subaltern fresh out of Octu travelled in comparative comfort, but that's service life. *This* is to do with civilians. Well, I mustn't go on about it.

It's much warmer here in Mayapore than Pindi. I only need a sheet at night and it won't be long before I have to have a fan going all the time. Lili's given me a marvellous room all to myself, and a super bathroom (although the seat's a bit wonky on the wc! and there's an inhibiting paper-holder guarded by lions). The MacGregor House is fascinating. I have to keep reminding myself that you never actually visited it because Uncle Henry had retired and left the province before Nello bought the place. But of course you remember Mayapore itself, although Lili says there have been lots of changes since then. The Technical College, for instance, the one Nello built and endowed and got his knighthood for, and the new buildings put up by the British–Indian Electrical. They're building an aerodrome out at Banyaganj which the English people say has ruined the duck-shooting! How Hitler would laugh! (There are some lakes out there which Lili says were a favourite European picnic spot.) A couple of evenings ago we went to dinner with the Deputy Commissioner and his wife, Robin and Constance White, who said they met you and Uncle Henry years ago, but didn't think you'd remember them because they were very junior. Mr White was under a Mr Cranston at the time, and they said you'd remember *him* all right if only because of the occasion when he was in camp, touring his district, and you and Uncle Henry, who were also touring, called in unexpectedly and found him bathing in a pool. Apparently you both stood on the bank talking for ages and he stood there doing his best to answer sensibly and be polite, standing very straight as if at attention, up to his waist in rather muddy water, and not daring to move because he had no bathing-drawers on. He thought afterwards that you and Uncle Henry *knew*, and were just keeping him in that awkward situation for the fun of it. I promised Mr White I'd mention this when I wrote to you, and ask if you really did know, because he's always wondered. It seems Mr Cranston never was certain. But it is one of the funny stories about the Governor and his Lady that went around for years and years – as you can judge, since it came up only the other night here in Mayapore, after all that time.

I liked Mr White, and his wife, although like all pukka mems *she* is a bit frightening at first. (I used to be frightened of *you*.) But they both seem to admire and respect Lili. It was a very private and friendly sort of party, with just two other men to balance Lili and myself at the table – Mr Macintosh the Civil Surgeon, who is a widower and another old friend of Lili's, and Judge Menen. He's married, but his wife is in the local nursing home at the moment. I liked the judge. He has a wonderful sense of humour, or so I realized later in the evening. At first I thought him a bit snooty and critical, and put it down to an inferiority complex about being the only male Indian present. He's much older than Mr White, but then of course it takes an Indian longer to rise to a position of authority, doesn't it? Anyway, after a bit I saw that he was pulling my leg in a way I'd have cottoned on to at once if he'd been English. It reminded me of when I first met Lili. Those dry amusing things she sometimes comes out with. If she were English, you'd laugh at once, but because she's not, then until you get to know her you think (as I used to think) What is she getting at? What's behind that remark? How am I supposed to reply or react without giving offence or appearing to have taken offence?

From what Lili tells me a lot of the English here are rather critical of the DC. They think of him as a man who does more than is absolutely necessary to show friendly to the Indians. They say he'll find himself taken advantage of, eventually. They talk about the 'good old days' of his predecessor, a Mr Stead, who kept 'a firm hand' and made it quite clear in the district 'who was boss'. This kind of attitude has been brought home to me in the two days I've worked at the hospital and I realize how lucky I've been so far, living with you, and not getting mixed up with average English people. Matron, a marvellous woman who's been out here for years and knows the score, said one particularly interesting thing when she interviewed me. The interview was fixed up by Lili through the Civil Surgeon who is medical overlord of everything that goes on in the district – but you know that! Matron said, 'You have three sponsors, Mr Macintosh, myself, and your own surname which is one people in this area remember as distinguished even if at the time there were a lot who disagreed with your uncle's progressive policies. If you're wise you'll trade on all three but avoid too obvious an association with the fourth.' Well, I knew what she meant by 'the fourth' and I must say I got my hackles up, and said, 'My *real* sponsor is Lady Chatterjee.' She said, 'I know. It's mainly why I'm taking you on. Even voluntary workers have to pass my personal test of worthiness. But this is a *British* general hospital, and I am its matron, and have long ago learned the lesson I had to learn if I were ever to do my job properly, and that lesson was to understand the necessity of excluding as extraneous any considerations other than those of the patients' well-being and the staff's efficiency' (she talks like that, rather officially, as if she has learned a speech). 'There's a lot' (she went on) 'that you may instinctively dislike about the atmosphere in which you'll be working. I don't ask you to learn to like it. I only ask, indeed demand, that your work won't be affected *by* the atmosphere.' 'Perhaps the atmosphere should be changed,' I said. At that moment, you know, I couldn't have cared less whether I was allowed to work at the hospital or not. After all, I wasn't going to be *paid*. She said, quick as a flash, 'I'm sure it should. I hope one day it will. If you'd prefer to delay working here until it does, and let someone else do the rewarding job of making sick people as comfortable as you can you only have to tell me. I shall quite understand. Although I'm sure that when you were driving an ambulance at home in the Blitz you never stopped to worry about what the wounded people you were taking to hospital felt about life or what their prejudices were. I imagine you were more concerned to try and stop them dying.' Well of course it was true, what she said. I stared at her through these awful glasses I have to wear if I'm to feel absolutely confident and I wished I was driving an ambulance still. I did get a kind of kick out of it, even if I was terrified a lot of the time. 1940. How long ago it seems! Only eighteen months, but an age and a world away, as they say. Here the war has only just begun – and sometimes I'm not sure a lot of people realize that it has. Back home it seemed in a curious way to be already over, or to be settled down to go on for centuries. In Mayapore I think more than ever of poor Daddy and poor David. The war that killed them has only just caught up with Mayapore. At times it's like waiting for them to be killed all over again, at other times like thinking of people who lived and died on another planet. I'm glad Mummy went before it all started. I can't, as most of the English here do, blame the Indians for resisting the idea of war, a war they have no proper say in. After all I've seen the real thing, in a minor civilian way, but most of the people who lay down the law here about beating the Jap and the Hun (those *awful* old-fashioned expressions that seem to give *them* heart but always depress *me*) haven't even heard a rifle fired in anger. British India is still living in the nineteenth century. To them Hitler is only a *joke*, because 'he was a house-painter and still looks like one even in uniform'. Three cheers for the Cavalry. Up the Navy! Sorry! I guess I've had one too many of Auntie Lili's gimlets. I've got to get the old glad rags on soon, because we're having a party to which no less a person than the District Superintendent of Police is coming. Lili says he's a bachelor. I hope a dedicated one! I can't bear the type of man who tries not to look as if he's noticed I'm not really attractive. Remember Mr Swinson?!! Auntie dear, I love you and think often of you and of us together in Pindi. I long really to be going up to Srinagar with you in May, but Auntie Lili seems deter-mined to keep me here, and of course I'm now committed to the hospital. And I am seeing more of India this way. There are a couple of other local voluntary bodies like me in the civilian wing, but the rulers of the roost are the official VADs and the QAs. You should see the airs some of the QAs give themselves. At home they'd simply be ordinary ward nurses, or staff nurses at most. Here they rank as sisters. Neither they nor the voluntary bods are supposed to do anything menial. That's all left to the poor little Anglo-Indian girls. Today, for the war effort, I rolled miles of bandages – I mean rolling bandages is *clean*. But I stood on my feet to do it, and they're killing me! Well, the boy has just come in to draw my bath. More presently. I'm loving it but finding it strange all over again, as I did when I came out last year. Mayapore is a bit off-putting in a way dear old Pindi isn't. Is it something to do with the fact that that part of the world is predominantly Muslim, and here it is Hindu? Please look after yourself and think often of your loving niece.

Daphne

The MacGregor House,
MacGregor Road,
Mayapore, I.
Friday, 17th July, 1942

Dear Auntie Ethel,

Many thanks for your letter and news of the goings on in Srinagar. Glad you got the photograph safely and in time for your birthday, but gladder still that you liked the dress length. The photograph seemed to me so awful that I had to send something else as well to make up for it, and then wondered choosing that colour whether I hadn't made everything worse! Not much clothes sense, I'm afraid, although I did feel that particular piece would suit you. Relieved you think so too! Hope old Hussein doesn't make a mess of it. Actually he's a better tailor than the man we have here. Lili and I had an iced cake in honour of your birthday, and a few people in to share it who stayed on afterwards for drinks (which I felt you would approve of!).

The rains have really set in now down here after a late start that set everyone in Mayapore hoarding foodstuffs in case of famine. I mean everyone in Mayapore who could afford it. Jack Poulson says it's the curse of India, the way the middle-class and well-to-do Indians swoop into the stores the moment a crisis even threatens. But that's apparently nothing to the corruption that goes on in higher circles where bulk foodstuffs are handled.

The grass at the front of the house is unbelievably green. I adore the rains. But how damp everything gets. The boy cleans *all* my shoes, every day, just to stop them from going mouldy.

I've bought myself a huge cape and a sort of sou'wester, not that I've had much need of either because I mostly get a lift to and from the hospital in Mr Merrick's car which he sends round with a police driver (a very militant Muslim who tells us all the Hindus have concealed weapons in their houses to chop off the heads of English and Mohammedans alike). If it's a petrol-less day (how we all complain about *that*) Mr Merrick sends his official truck, ostensibly on urgent duty (transferring prisoners from the jail to the courthouse). I find it a bit embarrassing and have told him several times that I can quite easily go on my bicycle on *any* day, or anyway get a tonga, but he insists that with all this Congress-inspired anti-British feeling boiling up again, and the MacGregor House being isolated on the outskirts of the cantonment, it's really his duty to see I don't come to any harm.

I like him better than I used to. I can't close my eyes to the fact that he's been kind and considerate. It's his manner that's against him (and something behind his manner, naturally). And of course a District Superintendent of Police *is* a bit off-putting. But now that I've got used to him – and got over something that I think I must tell you – I quite enjoy the times he takes me out. Except when he adopts an official tone, as on a night or so ago when he warned me against what he called my association with Mr Kumar, which he said had set people talking, not English people only but Indians as well. I'm afraid I laughed and thoughtlessly said, Oh stop acting like a policeman all the time. Which I realized at once was the last thing one ought ever to say to him because he takes his job very seriously and is proud of having got where he is and is determined to shine at the job and not to care who dislikes him for doing it properly.

I feel I must tell you, *but please keep it to yourself*, I've told nobody, not even Aunt Lili. About a month ago he invited me to his bungalow for dinner. He'd gone to a lot of trouble. It was the best English-style meal I've had in India (except that time when you had the Swinsons and they made such a fuss before-hand about hating Indian food). Another point in his favour from my point of view was that his houseboy is obviously devoted to him, and took pleasure in arranging everything properly for his sahib's candle-lit dinner for two. The excuse for the dinner, if there had to be an excuse, was for me to hear some of his records afterwards. You remember I told you at the time about the show put on by the military at the end of April, complete with band and parade? And about meeting Brigadier Reid who said he met us in Pindi? And how I went to the show with a couple of the girls from the hospital and on to the club afterwards with some young army officers? Ronald Merrick looked in at the club later that evening (he had had a lot to do, controlling the crowds, etc). Well we were all saying complimentary things about the music and the marching – it was rather striking – and I must have been more full of it than the others. Anyway Ronald turned to me and said, 'Oh, you like military bands? So do I.' Apparently he had piles of records. He said I must hear them some time.

So this was the occasion. I don't like them all that much! Not well enough to want to listen to records, so whenever he raised the subject afterwards I sort of put it off. Actually I'd almost forgotten about the records when he finally asked me to dinner. I said yes before I knew what I was doing, and when he said: 'Good, and afterwards you can hear some of those records I've been promising to play,' I thought Oh Lord! What have I let myself in for! In the event it wasn't too bad (the music I mean). We'd been around quite a bit together and there was tons to talk about. By now the music was just a part of a pleasant evening. I'd been to his bungalow before, but only with other people for a Sunday-morning beer party, but seeing it empty I realized how comfortable and pleasant it was. He doesn't smoke, or drink much, so I suppose his money goes further than that of men in similar positions who do. The bungalow is mainly PWD furnished, of course, but he has several rather glamorous things of his own. To begin with there was this super radiogram (on which he played a couple of Sousa marches). Then he had very nice tableware, and a marvellous Persian rug that he said he'd bought in an auction in Calcutta. His taste in pictures though was what really struck me. He's so very conventional in his behaviour you'd expect something nondescript on his walls. It's true there were pig-sticking and polo pictures in the dining-room and a David Wright cutie in his bedroom (he showed me round the whole bungalow but in such a sweet way that there wasn't anything awkward about the bedroom, as there might have been with another man) but in the living-room there was nothing on the walls except these two rather good reproductions of those Henry Moore drawings of people huddled in the underground during the Blitz, which I find difficult to look at, but do admire. He seemed touchingly pleased when I said, 'Oh, Henry Moore! What a surprising man you are!' One other thing that struck me – in the closet (the one used by guests just off the hall) he'd had the boy put out scented soap (Coty Chypre) and a little pink hand towel which was obviously brand new. I had the feeling it had been bought especially for the occasion. (The soap in his own bathroom was Lifebuoy, so don't jump to the wrong conclusion!)

There was another surprise too. After he'd played a couple of these Sousa marches he put on another record and said, 'I like this kind of thing, too,' and what do you think it was? The *Clair de Lune* movement from Debussy's *Suite Bergamasque*, played by Walter Gieseking. It was one of my brother David's favourites. When it began I thought: Whenever did I tell Ronald that David loved this? Then knew I never had. It was extraordinary. All that awful blaring (but sometimes stirring) Sousa and then this tender moonlit music that actually I could hardly bear to listen to, but loved all the same, although it seemed such an unusual thing for a policeman to like as well.

While it was playing the boy brought in the coffee – *Turkish*. There was a choice of brandy or liqueurs (curaçao or *crème de menthe*, very dull). All the bottles were unopened – fresh from the store, just for me. I expect if I ever dine there again the brandy will be at the same level we left it. While we were drinking it he asked me a lot of questions about my family, about how David was killed, and about daddy, and then about me, and what I thought about life and all that sort of thing, but in a chatty, sympathetic way that made me open up. (He must be a wizard at interrogation! That's not fair. But you know what I mean.) Gradually I realized he had begun to talk about himself. And I was thinking: People don't like you much, but you're fundamentally *kind* and that's why you and I have always got on surprisingly well. He said he came of 'a very ordinary family' and that although his father had done well enough, he was still only a grammar school boy and his grandparents had been 'pretty humble sort of people'. He had worked hard and done all right so far in the Indian Police which he thought of as an essential if

not especially attractive service, and his main regret was that
being in it he wasn't allowed to join up. His other regret was
that he'd never really had any 'youth' or met 'the right sort of
girl' for him. He was often 'pretty lonely'. He knew he hadn't
much to offer. He realized his background and mine were 'rather
different'. Our friendship meant a lot to him.

Then he dried up. I just didn't know what to say, because I
didn't know if I'd understood or misunderstood what he was
driving at. We sort of stared at each other for a while. Then he
said, 'I'm only asking whether after you've had time to think
about it you'd consider the possibility of becoming engaged
to me.'

Do you know, Auntie, that's the only proposal I've ever had?
I'm sure by the time you were my age you'd had dozens. Does
every girl find the first one oddly moving? I suppose it depends
on the man. But if he's, you know, all right, decent enough, you
can't not be touched, can you, whatever you *feel* about him as
a person? I don't think my feelings for Ronald Merrick could
ever be described as more than passingly affectionate. He's
fair-haired and youngish and has blue eyes and is really awfully
good-looking but there was and still is (perhaps more so than
ever) a distinct reservation (from my point of view) that must be
something to do with what I feel as the lack of *real* candour
between him and whoever he's dealing with. I never feel quite
natural when I'm with him, but can never be sure whether that
is my fault or his. But when he came out with this request (you
can hardly call it a proposal, can you?) I wanted very much to
have been able to make things *all right* for him and say 'Yes'. Do
men know how vulnerable they look when they slough off that
tough, not-caring skin they mostly seem to wear when there
are more than two people in a room? Far more vulnerable than
women, when *they* let their hair down.

What made it so extraordinary was that he never so much as
touched my hand. At the time, this *not* touching added to my
wish not to hurt him. Later, thinking about it, it added to the
sense I had of the coldness surrounding the occasion. We were
sitting at opposite ends of the sofa. Perhaps I ought to have
taken my specs out and put them on! Looking back on it I can't
really recall whether I felt that what had been said was a shock
or not. It seemed to be a shock, anyway a surprise, but in

retrospect the whole evening was *obviously* leading up to it, so I can't think why I should have been surprised, or even believe that I was. There must have been lots of things said before he came out with it that I inwardly took notice of. At some stage or other I decided that physically, in spite of his looks, he repelled me, but I think that came later, and was only momentary, when I'd established for both of us the fact that although I didn't want to hurt him I had never thought and never would think of him in the way he seemed to want me to. The feeling of faint repulsion probably came through because of the sense I had of relief, of having got out of a difficult situation and retreated *into myself* in a way that left no room for others whoever they might be. I was now more concerned about the possible effect of my 'refusal'. Honestly, I'm sure that all I said was 'Thank you, Ronald – but –' but that was enough. You know how people talk about faces 'closing up'? I think 'close-down' is nearer to it, because close up suggests a sort of *constriction*, a *change*, whereas what actually happens is that the face remains exactly the same but all the lights go out. Like a house where the people have gone away. If you knock at the door now there won't be any answer.

We had some more Sousa and presently he drove me home and we talked quite easily about nothing. When we got to the MacGregor House I asked him whether he'd like to come in for a nightcap. He said no, but escorted me up the steps to the verandah. When we shook hands he hung on to mine for a moment and said, 'Some ideas take some getting used to,' from which I gathered he hadn't yet given up, but it was a different man who said it. The District Superintendent of Police, the Ronald Merrick I don't care for. The same one who later – only a few days ago – annoyed me by warning me about my 'association with young Kumar'.

One of the servants was waiting on the verandah. I thanked Ronald for the evening, and then said goodnight to them both. I heard the car drive away and the servant beginning to lock up as I went upstairs. I knew Aunt Lili had planned an early night for once, so I didn't go to her room. The house was very quiet. It's the first time I've ever been conscious of the fact that it's supposed to be haunted. It didn't feel haunted in the eerie sense. Just big and empty and somehow desolate and occupied in the

wrong way. What am I trying to tell you? Not that I felt frightened. But that I suddenly wanted to be with *you*.

I never told you, but there was a time – my second month in
India last year – when if someone had offered me a passage home
I'd have accepted like a shot. Goodness knows I loved being
with you. But during that second month, perhaps not the whole
month but two or three weeks of it, I had what I can only
describe now as a permanent sinking heart. I hated everything,
hated it because I was afraid of it. It was all so alien. I could
hardly bear to leave the bungalow. I started to have awful dreams,
not *about* anything, just dreams of faces. They used to come up
out of nowhere, normal looking at first but then distorting and
exploding, leaving a blank space for others to come up and take
their place. They weren't the faces of people I knew. They were
people I invented in alarming detail – alarming because it didn't
seem possible to imagine faces so exactly. I suppose I was
obsessed by the idea of being surrounded by strangers and had
to have them even in my dreams. I never told you but I think
that day on the verandah with the durzi you guessed what I was
going through. I remember the way you looked at me when
I lost my temper and snatched away that blouse he was doing his
best to copy. You know, if I'd been living with the Swinsons
that would probably have been the point of no return for me.
I'd have been assimilated from then on into that inbred little
cultural circle of English women – men, too, but particularly
women – abroad in a colony.

I suppose it's only natural that wherever we go we should need
the presence of someone known and dependable and proven. If
there's no someone there has to be some*thing*. In Pindi during
those particular weeks I became ridiculously attached to my luggage, my clothes, as if they were the only things I could trust.
Even you, you see, seemed to have failed me. You knew everybody, everything, and I felt cut off from you because *I* didn't,
however much you took me out and about. And you took the
dirt and poverty and squalor in your stride, as if it didn't exist,
although I knew that's not what you actually felt about it. But
this is why I snatched the blouse from Hussein. I couldn't bear
to see him holding it up, examining it, *touching it with his black
fingers*. I *hated* myself for feeling that, but couldn't stop feeling
it, so I shouted at him. When I went to my room I sat down and

wanted to burst into tears and be rescued and taken home, home. I've never felt so badly the fact that I no longer have a home in England, with Mummy gone, and Daddy, and David.

Much the same thing happened to me the second week I was here at the MacGregor House, and my initial curiosity in my surroundings had been satisfied. But in Mayapore 'home' had become the bungalow in Pindi, and you. I hope none of this showed in my letters and worried you. I'm over it now. I love it all. But for a while I hated Mayapore. I asked myself what on earth had I done, coming to this awful place? I even suspected Aunt Lili of having me here only because I was English and it was a feather in her cap to have a white person staying in her house. (Isn't that disgraceful?) And I even thought back on that train journey and found myself less critical of those two beastly women. After all, I thought, how were they to have known that Lili wouldn't do something that *revolted* them? And in the hospital I realized how much easier it was to talk to another English woman, even if you disagreed with everything she said. People of the same nationality use a kind of shorthand in conversation, don't they? You spend less effort to express more, and you've got so used to the effortlessness that anything that needs effort is physically and mentally tiring, and you get short-tempered, and then tireder and more short-tempered from trying not to let the temper show.

I think this is why *I failed to keep my resolution never to go to the club. I made that resolution originally because it was impossible for Lili Chatterjee ever to go with me.* I have never liked the club, but it amuses me – it is so self-conscious about its exclusiveness and yet so vulgar. Someone is always drunk, the talk is mostly scurrilous, and yet its members somehow preserve, goodness knows how, an outward air of rectitude, almost as though there were inviolable *rules* for heartless gossip and insufferable behaviour. It was a week or two before I realized that because I lived at the MacGregor House most of the women I met at the club disliked me and a lot of the men were embarrassed by me. Not to have noticed the dislike straight away shows the extent of the relief I must have felt at first *simply to be there among my own kind.*

Mummy once said to me, 'You seem to like *everybody.* It's unnatural. It's also unfortunate. You're going to waste so much time before you've worked out who the people are *it's worth your*

while to know.' I used to think she meant worth while in the
ambitious sense. Now I wonder whether she meant worth my
while in the sense of the interests of *my* privacy and peace of
mind and sense of security. But either way she would be wrong,
wouldn't she? I'm sure this longing for security and peace is
wrong and that we should extend our patience time and time
again almost right up to its breaking point, put ourselves out on
a limb, dare other people to saw the limb off, whoever they are,
black or white.

But it isn't easy, is it? The night I came home from my evening
with Ronald Merrick I thought, as I was climbing the stairs, that
at the top I was in for something unpleasant and I wanted to
turn and run and get back to *him* of all people. I actually stood
still, half-way up, and looked down into the hall and there was
this servant, a boy called Raju, staring up at me. Oh heavens, he
was only making sure he didn't turn out the light before I got
up on to the landing, only doing his job, but I said to myself:
What are *you* staring at? I was in my long green dress, the one
you like that shows my awful shoulders. I felt – well, you know
what I felt. He was too far away for me to see his expression. He
was just a brown blob in white shirt and trousers, and then in
the place where his face was one of my imaginary faces came,
that of someone I'd never seen before. I called out, 'Goodnight,
Raju,' and heard him say, 'Goodnight, madam' (he's a South
Indian Christian so he says 'madam'), and then I continued up
the stairs and when I got on to the landing I think I expected
to see our resident ghost, Janet MacGregor. But there wasn't
anything. I've not seen her *yet*. I felt relieved, but also cheated.

One day I must tell you about Hari Kumar. So far in my
letters to you he's really just a name, isn't he? And I must tell
you about a curious woman called Sister Ludmila who wears
nun's clothing and collects dead bodies. I wish you were here so
that I could talk to you any old time. The gong's just gone for
dinner. It's raining frogs and the lizards are playing hide and seek
on the wall and making that peculiar chopping noise. Tonight
Lili and I are dining alone and afterwards I expect we'll play
mahjong. Tomorrow I hope to visit the local Hindu temple with
Mr Kumar.

Love, Daphne

*

I wish you could have been here in the rains (Lady Chatterjee says) and then you would have seen how Daphne loved it best. But I understand. You have to travel about and the wet season wouldn't have been the best time to do so. The garden is already beginning to look dry and tired and brown. I love every season, though. And I especially love it at night like this. I always sit on the front verandah because you don't get the smell of the river – which I never notice, but know that English guests do – and anyway you can see down the drive, which is nice, remembering the people who used to come up it, and anticipating those who might come up it now, and you can just make out the beds of canna lilies when we have the verandah light on like this. When there's a moon it's best with the light off, but when I give my party for you we'll have all the lights on, including those in the garden itself. I'd put them on for you now, for you to see the effect, but we're asked to conserve things as much as possible because of the war with China, and I suppose that includes conserving electricity.

Let me go on, then, about Miss Crane. She was an old school English liberal in the sense I grew to understand the term, someone who as likely as not had no gift for broad friendships. In Miss Crane's case I think it went further than this. I think she had no gift for friendship of any kind. She loved India and all Indians but no particular Indian. She hated British policies, and so she disliked all Britons unless they turned out to be adherents to the same rules she abided by. I suppose what I'm saying is that she made friendships in her head most of the time and seldom in her heart. To punish someone whose conduct didn't coincide with her preconceived notions of what he stood for she took his picture down. How ineffectual a gesture that was. But how revealing, how symptomatic of her weakness. As a gesture it lacked even the pathetic absurdity of turning the portrait of the black sheep of the family to the wall. At least in that gesture there was – and would be still if anyone ever did it nowadays – a flesh and blood anger, something positive. But she had courage. The Miss Cranes of the world often do, and I think at the end the reason for her madness was that she also had the courage to see the truth if not to live with it, see how all her good works and noble thoughts had been going on in a vacuum. I have a theory that she saw clearly but too late how she had never dirtied her hands, never got grubby for the sake of the cause she'd always believed she held dear, and that this explains why Mr Poulson found her like that, sitting in the rain by the roadside, holding the hand of that dead schoolteacher, Mr Chaudhuri.

Daphne, though, Daphne was different. Wouldn't you say? You've read those two letters now? Don't bother to make copies. Take them with you. Let me have them back one day when you've finished with them. I know them almost by heart. I only wish I'd known about them at the time. Yes, I wish it, but ask myself, Well how would it have helped if I had known, what could I have done if I'd seen them? She had to make her own marvellous mistakes. I say marvellous. *She* didn't ever shrink from getting grubby. She flung herself into everything with zest. The more afraid she was of something the more determined she was not to shrink from experiencing it. She had us all by the ears finally. We were all afraid for her, even *of* her, but more of what she seemed to have unlocked, like Pandora who bashed off to the attic and prised the lid of the box open.

Is this why I always sit here, on the front verandah? Those are the steps, you know. Well of course you do. You keep on looking at them, and looking down the drive, almost expecting to see someone who has run all the way in darkness from the Bibighar. On that night I was in the hall with Mr Merrick, just there by the entrance to the living-room. We couldn't see the steps from there. His car was parked away from the steps, in shadow. Afterwards, thinking about that, I wondered if he had left it so that it wasn't at once obvious to the outside world that he was here, actually at the MacGregor House when the whole of British Mayapore was seething with rumours about the riots in the sub-divisions, and rumours about Miss Crane who was already in hospital.

He said as soon as he came in, 'Are you all right, Lady Chatterjee?' which amused me really, because for the first time since we'd known each other he seemed to be treating me as one of you, as if I were Lady Green or Brown or Smith, living alone in a house only just on the fringe of safety. I gave him a drink, he said he hadn't much time, but drank it willingly enough, which I thought unusual, because he was an abstemious sort of man. I remember thinking: When you are worried, when you are concerned, when your face is alive, you're really quite good-looking. I said, 'I expect you've come to see Daphne, but she's at the club,' and he said, 'Yes, they said at the hospital she'd gone straight on to the club, but she isn't there.' 'Oh, isn't she?' I said, and I got worried too, but tried not to show it, so I said, 'But I'm sure she's all right.'

And then he asked outright, 'Is she with Hari Kumar?' I said, 'No, I don't think so.' I hadn't thought she was with Kumar. I'd even had the impression the association Mr Merrick warned her against had ended. I didn't know he'd warned her against it. I didn't know Mr Merrick had proposed to her. She'd kept all that from me. But she hadn't been able to keep from me the feelings she'd had for Kumar, nor the fact that she hadn't seen him for at least a week, in fact more like three weeks. So when Mr Merrick said, 'Is she with Kumar?' I replied, quite truthfully, 'No, I don't think so.' And then I wondered. But I said nothing. One did not voluntarily mention Kumar's name to Mr Merrick. He said, 'Well, at this time of night where can she be?' I said, 'Oh probably with friends,' and I went to the phone and rang several places where she might have been. It took ages. The telephone lines in Mayapore were blocked with official calls. Mr Merrick kept going to the verandah and coming back again each time I'd finished a call. 'She'll be in soon,' I said, 'come and have another drink,' and again, to my surprise, he said he would. He was in uniform still. He looked awfully tired.

'Is it serious?' I asked him. 'It seems to be,' he said, and then blurted out, 'What a damned mess,' and looked as if he was about to beg my pardon for swearing. 'Some of the people you know,' he said, 'are locked up.' I nodded. I knew which ones. I didn't want to talk about them. 'But here I am,' he said, 'having a drink with you. Do you mind?' I laughed and told him not a bit, unless when he'd finished his peg he was going to haul me off to jail in a black maria as a suspected secret revolutionary. He smiled but said nothing, and I thought: Oh, am I in for it? Then he came out with this special thing, 'I asked her to marry me. Did she tell you?' It was a shock. I told him, no, and realized for the first time how awfully dangerous the whole situation was. 'Is Miss Crane all right?' I asked. I didn't want to talk to him about Daphne, or Hari Kumar. Or about where they might be. Mr Merrick had always disliked young Kumar and I have to confess that my own feelings towards him were mixed. It always

seemed to me that he had too big a chip on his shoulder. And
he was in some trouble once. Mr Merrick had had him in for
questioning. At that time I didn't know the boy from Adam, but
a friend – Anna Klaus of the Purdah Hospital – once rang me
and said the police had arrested this boy for apparently no good
reason. So, well, you know me. I asked Judge Menen about it.
So far as I could see it all turned out to be a storm in a teacup
and he hadn't really been arrested at all but only taken in for
questioning. It turned out that my old friend Vassi knew him.
That's Mr Srinivasan, who still lives here, and whom you must
meet. Anyhow I asked young Kumar round one evening because
my curiosity had been aroused and that's how he came into my
life, or rather into Daphne's life. He was brought up in England.
His father had had tremendous plans for him, but the plans collapsed when the father died a bankrupt and poor Hari was sent
home here to Mayapore, only of course it wasn't home to him.
He was two years old when his father took him to England, and
eighteen when he came back. He spoke like an English boy.
Acted like one. Thought like one. They say that when he first
reached India he was spelling his name the way his father had
spelled it. Coomer. Harry Coomer. But probably his aunt
stopped that. She was the closest relative he had and I think in
her own rather orthodox Hindu way she was very good to him,
but that meant not disciplining him enough, letting him waste
his time which also meant letting him have time to brood about
his bad luck. It worried me a bit, the way Daphne seemed to
take to him, worried me because I couldn't be sure whether he
felt quite the same way about her. She knew I had these reservations. So did young Kumar. Perhaps I should have come right
out with it. But I didn't. And I think I must blame myself for
any note of furtiveness that crept into what Mr Merrick called
the association between Kumar and Daphne. And when Mr
Merrick was here that night and said that he had asked Daphne
to marry him and I realized how dangerous things could be,
I remembered that in the morning she had seemed especially
happy – not especially happy for the Daphne I knew, but especially happy for the Daphne who had been mooning about for
days and hardly going out anywhere except to the club and pretending in her typical way that nothing was wrong, and there
suddenly seemed to be no doubt at all that she *was* with Kumar,

that she had been happy because they'd agreed to meet again. No doubt in my mind, nor I think in Mr Merrick's. And believing I knew for sure that she was with Kumar I also believed I knew where and made the mistake of thinking that if *I* knew Mr Merrick might also guess, and go there and find them together, which I did not want. In fact it struck me that the less said the better, because the place where I guessed they were was also the place where Mr Merrick had first met young Kumar and taken him in for questioning, and so the whole situation had come full-circle and I felt that some kind of disaster was inevitable. So I made us both stop talking about Daphne and asked about poor old Miss Crane who had been taken to hospital. I said, 'Is she all right?' and he said yes, so far as he knew, and then looked at his watch and got up and asked if he might use the phone to talk to his headquarters. Before he got to it the phone rang. It was the Deputy Commissioner. Mr Merrick had told his people where he'd be. I remember Mr Merrick answering it and telling Robin White he'd personally checked all his patrols, that the town itself was quiet for the moment because nearly all the shops in the bazaar had closed and the people seemed to be staying indoors, almost as if there was an official curfew. Then he said, 'No, I'm here because Miss Manners is missing.' He made it sound as if I'd *reported* her missing, and it seemed to be such a ridiculous word to use, but at the same time true. He spoke a bit longer then handed the phone to me and said Robin would like a word with me and would I forgive him if he didn't wait but got off straight away. Robin said, 'Lili, what's this about Daphne?' I said I didn't really know, that I thought she had gone straight to the club from the hospital, but Mr Merrick said she wasn't there, so now I supposed I was worried too. I said, 'Are things bad, Robin?' and he said, 'Well, Lili, we don't know. Would you like to come and stay the night with us?' I laughed and asked, 'Why? Are people moving into the funk holes?'

There was a plan as you probably know to move English women and children into places like the club, Smith's hotel and the DC's bungalow if the threatened uprising really got going, and finally into the old barracks if things got as bad as in the Mutiny which some of the Jonahs said they would. Robin had had to work the plan out with Brigadier Reid, but this was the first time I'd ever heard him talk seriously about it. He said, 'No, not yet, but one or two of the women whose husbands are out of station have gone into the club.' 'Well,' I said, 'that's one place I can't go, isn't it, Robin?' He told me afterwards he hadn't quite known how to take that, he'd never heard me say anything bitter. But I didn't mean it to sound bitter. It just slipped out. It was just a case of my automatically stating my position. He said, 'Well, give me a ring, when Daphne gets back. Perhaps you'd ring in half an hour in any event?' I said I would. When I came away from the phone Mr Merrick's car was gone. It was nearly nine o'clock. Daphne had always rung if anything came up at the last moment that meant she couldn't get back at her usual time. I thought, well perhaps she's tried to ring, but simply hasn't been able to get through. But I didn't really believe it. I had only one clear picture in my mind and that was of Daphne and young Kumar, and of the place they used to call the Sanctuary. It was a place I had personally never been to, which was absurd of me. I had a horror of it, I suppose, in spite of what Anna Klaus used to say, and a horror of the woman who ran it, who called herself Sister Ludmila and collected people she found dying in the streets. Daphne was awfully impressed with Sister Ludmila. Anyway, I went round the back to see what the servants were up to, because I suddenly noticed none of them was about. They'd been very glum all day. There was no one in the kitchen, nobody attending to the dinner. I went to the kitchen door and shouted across the compound and after a bit Raju appeared. He said cook wasn't feeling well. I said, 'You mean he's drunk. Tell him dinner at nine-thirty or you'll all be looking for a job, including you. *Your* business is at the front of the house, Raju.'

I went back to the living-room and poured myself a peg, and then I heard Raju at the front. I thought: He's drunk too *and* incapable, the stupid boy's fallen flat on his face by the sound of it. So I went out to scold him. It wasn't Raju. I couldn't take it in at first. She was on her hands and knees. She'd fallen and hurt herself on the steps, but only fallen because she was already hurt and exhausted from running. She looked up and said, 'Oh, Auntie.' She was still in her khaki hospital uniform. It was torn and muddy and she had blood on her face. Even when she said, 'Oh, Auntie,' I couldn't take it in that it was Daphne.

*

The lights are on in the garden of the MacGregor House, in honour of the stranger. The shrubs, artificially illuminated by the manipulation of a battery of switches on the wall of the verandah, looking strikingly theatrical. There is no breeze but the stillness of the leaves and branches is unnatural. As well as these areas of radiance the switches have turned on great inky pools of darkness. Sometimes the men and women you talk to, moving from group to group on the lawn, present themselves in silhouette; although the turn of a head may reveal a glint in a liquidly transparent eye and the movement of an arm the skeletal structure of a hand holding a glass that contains light and liquid in equal measure. In the darkness too, strangely static and as strangely suddenly galvanized, are the fireflies of the ends of cigarettes.

The people in the garden are the inheritors. Somewhere farther away in time than in distance, the fire that consumed Edwina Crane spurts unnoticed, licks and catches hold. In this illuminated darkness one might notice this extra brilliance and hear, against the chat and buzz of casual night-party conversation, the ominous crackle of wood.

There was a shed in the compound behind Miss Crane's bungalow. In true English fashion she kept gardening instruments there. How typical of her to choose (on a windless day when the first post-monsoon heats had dried the wood out and prepared it for a creaking season of contraction and pre-cool-weather warmth) a site where a conflagration would not threaten the bungalow itself. She locked herself in and soaked the walls with paraffin and set them alight and died, one hopes, in the few seconds it took for the violently heated air to scorch the breath out of her lungs.

The story goes that for this act of becoming *suttee* (which Lady Chatterjee describes as *sannyasa* without the travelling) she dressed for the first time in her life in a white saree, the saree for her adopted country, the whiteness for widowhood and mourning. And there is a tale that Joseph, returning empty-handed from some wild-goose errand she had sent him on, fell on his knees in the compound and cried to the smouldering pyre, 'Oh, Madam, Madam,' just as, several weeks before, Miss Manners, falling on her knees, had looked up and said, 'Oh, Auntie.'

In such a fashion human beings call for explanations of the things that happen to them and in such a way scenes and characters are set for exploration, like toys set out by kneeling children intent on pursuing their grim but necessary games.

PART THREE

SISTER LUDMILA

HER ORIGINS were obscure. Some said she was related to the Romanovs; others that she had been a Hungarian peasant, a Russian spy, a German adventuress, a run-away French novice. But all this was conjecture. What was clear, at least to the Mayapore Europeans, was that saintly as she might now appear she had no business calling herself Sister. The Catholic and Protestant churches withheld their recognition, but accepted her existence because she had long ago won the battle of the Habit by declaring to the irate Roman priest who turned up to cast out this particular abomination that the clothes she wore were of her own design, that although a genuine religious had superior status and a larger stake in life eternal, she could not possibly have any exclusive claim to modesty or special vulnerability to heatstroke: hence the long light gown of thin grey cotton (unadorned either by cross or penitential cord, and tied at the waist by an ordinary leather belt obtainable in any bazaar) and the wide winged cap of white starched linen that sheltered her neck and shoulders from the sun and could be seen on the darkest night.

'But you call yourself Sister Ludmila,' the priest said.

'No. It is the Indians who call me that. If you object take your objections to them. There is anyway a saying, God is not mocked.'

In those days (in 1942), on every Wednesday morning, Sister Ludmila set out on foot from the cluster of old buildings where she fed the hungry, ministered to the sick, and cleansed and comforted those who for want of her nightly scavenging would have died in the street.

She carried a locked leather bag that was attached to her belt by a chain. Behind her walked a stalwart Indian youth armed with a stick. It was seldom the same boy for more than a month or two. Mr Govindas, the manager of the Mayapore branch of the Imperial Bank of India in the cantonment, which was the place she was bound for on these Wednesday outings, said to her once, 'Sister Ludmila, where does that boy come from?' 'From heaven, I suppose.' 'And the boy who accompanied you last month? From heaven also?' 'No,' Sister Ludmila said, 'he came from jail and has recently gone back in.' 'It is what I am warning you of,' Mr Govindas pointed out, 'the danger of trusting a boy simply because he looks strong enough to protect you.'

Sister Ludmila merely smiled and handed over her cheque made out to cash.

Week by week she came to Mr Govindas for two hundred rupees. The cheques were drawn upon the Imperial Bank of India in Bombay. The Imperial Bank has long since become the State Bank and Mr Govindas long since retired. His memory remains sharp, though. Since she never paid money in and was known by Mr Govindas to pay all her trade accounts by cheque as well, he could only assume that either her fortune was large or her account credited regularly from elsewhere. The long-standing instruction from the Bombay branch authorizing the cashing facilities at Mayapore described her as Mrs Ludmila Smith and the cheques were signed accordingly. By pumping a friend in Bombay, Mr Govindas eventually discovered that the money came from the treasury of a small princely state and might be reckoned as some sort of pension because Mrs Ludmila Smith's husband, said to be an engineer, had died while on the ruler's pay-roll. She took the two hundred rupees as follows: fifty rupees in notes of Rs. 5 denomination, one hundred rupees in notes of Rs. 1, and fifty rupees in small change. Mr Govindas estimated that most of the small change and a fair proportion of the one-rupee notes were distributed to the poor and that the rest went on wages for her assistants and casual purchases in the market. He knew that her meat, grain and vegetables were supplied on monthly account by local contractors, and that medicines were bought from Dr Gulab Singh Sahib's pharmacy at a trade discount of $12\frac{1}{2}$% plus 5% for monthly settlement. He knew that Sister Ludmila drank only one glass of orange juice a day and ate one meal of rice or pulses in the evening, with curds to follow, except on Fridays when she had a modest curry of vegetables and, on Christian festivals, fish. The rest of the food was consumed by her assistants and in meals for the hungry. He knew many such things about her. He sometimes thought that if he were to write down all the things he knew or heard about her he would fill up several pages of the bank's foolscap. But knowing all this he still believed that he knew nothing of importance. In this belief, in Mayapore, in 1942, Mr Govindas was not alone.

Her age, for instance. Well – how old was she? Under the nunnish pleats and folds and fly-away wings of starched linen her face described by some as inscrutable lived perpetually in an aseptic, reverent light. Her hands were those of a woman who had always directed the work of others. Time had barely touched them. A single ring, a gold band, adorned her wedding finger. Her throat was protected by a high-necked starched white linen bib that also covered her breast and shoulders. Her eyes were dark and deep set, and there was an impression of prominent cheekbones – proof perhaps of Magyar blood. Her voice, also dark and deep, matched the eyes. She spoke fluent but rather staccato English and a vile bazaar Hindi. Mr Govindas had heard English people say that her English accent was Germanic. It was also said that she possessed a French as well as a British passport. At a guess, it was assumed she was about fifty years old, give or take five years.

Having collected the two hundred rupees and deposited them in the leather bag that was chained to her waist, Sister Ludmila bade Mr Govindas good-day, thanked him for escorting her personally from his inner sanctum to the door, and set out on the journey home, attended by her young man of the moment who had spent the ten minutes or so that it took her to cash her cheque sitting on his hunkers in the street outside, gossiping with anyone who also happened to be waiting or idling his time away. Such talk as went on between the bodyguard and his chance companions was usually vulgar. The other men would want to know whether the crazy white woman had yet invited him to share her bed or when exactly it was that he planned to run off with the cash she hired him to protect. The ribaldry was good-natured, but behind it there might always have been detected a note of black uncertainty. To a man in health, her business seemed too closely connected with death for comfort.

From the Mayapore branch of the Imperial Bank which was situated in the arcaded Victoria road, the main shopping centre of the European cantonment, Sister Ludmila's journey back to

the sanctuary took her through the Eurasian quarter, past the
church of the mission, over the level crossing for which, like
Miss Crane – to whom she had nodded but never spoken – she
sometimes had to wait to be opened before she could continue
across the crowded Mandir Gate bridge. Once over the river,
outside the Tirupati temple, she paused and distributed money
to the beggars and to the leper who sat cross-legged, displaying
the pink patches of a diseased trunk and holding up lopped tree-
branch arms. On this side of the river the sun seemed to strike
more fiercely and indiscriminately as though the smells of
poverty and dirt would be wasted in shade. Colour was robbed
of the advantage of its singularity, its surprise. At ground level,
the spectrum contracted into ranges of exhausted greys and
yellows. Even the scarlet flower in a woman's braided hair, lacking its temperate complementary green, was scorched to an
insipid brown. Here, the white starched cap of Sister Ludmila
looked like some prehistoric bird miraculously risen, floating,
bobbing and bucking, visible from afar.

Beyond the temple the road forks into two narrower roads.
At the apex a holy tree shelters a shrine, ruminant cows, old
men, and women with their fingers held to their nostrils. At the
head of the road that forks to the right towards the jail the
Majestic Cinema announces an epic from the Ramayana (now,
as then). The left-hand fork is narrower, darker, and leads past
open-fronted shops to the Chillianwallah Bazaar. Down this
road Sister Ludmila, all that time ago, proceeded with the boy
behind her and a dozen children running by her side and to her
front, each hopeful of an anna. She walked upright, the locked
bag in her folded arms, and ignored the cries of the shopkeepers
inviting her to buy pān, cloth, soda-water, melons or jasmine. At
the end of the lane she turned left and entered the Chillianwallah
Bazaar through the open archway in the high concrete wall that
surrounds it.

In the middle of the walled area there are fish and meat mar-
kets – large open-sided godowns floored in concrete and roofed
with sloping sheets of corrugated iron supported by concrete
pillars. In the open, ranged along the enclosing walls, women
have set out their rainbow vegetables and spices on mats, and sit
among them holding their idle scales like so many huddled
figures of unblindfolded and so sharp-eyed mercantile justice.

From one of them Sister Ludmila bought green chillis and then marched on until she reached the exit on the other side of the walled square. Here, before passing through the exit, she turned aside and mounted a flight of rickety wooden steps to an open doorway on the upper floor of a building – a warehouse, obviously – whose side, at this point, forms part of the bazaar wall. Across the face of the building a sign in blue characters on a faded white background announces 'Romesh Chand Gupa Sen, Contractors'. Her bodyguard waited at the foot of the steps and smoked a bidi, squatting on his hunkers again, impatient of this unaccustomed interruption in the journey home. After ten minutes Sister Ludmila came out of the doorway and down the steps and led the way out of the bazaar, through another complex of lanes and alleys of old Muslim houses with shuttered windows above and closed doors at street level; until, abruptly, the houses gave way to open ground that was (still is) scattered with the huts and shacks of the untouchables. Beyond the huts there is a stagnant water-tank on whose farther bank are laid out to dry the long coloured sarees and murky rags belonging to the black-skinned, braceleted, bare-legged women who stand thigh-high in the water, washing themselves and their clothes. There are three trees but otherwise the land looks waste and desolate. Crows screech, flap and wheel aloft making for the river which is not visible from where Sister Ludmila walked, but can be smelt, and sensed – for behind a rise in the ground the land seems to fall away, then reappear more distantly. On the opposite bank are the godowns and installations belonging to the railway. The lane Sister Ludmila took lies roughly parallel to the winding course of the river and leads to a gateless opening in a broken-down wall that surrounds a compound. Within the compound there are three squat single-storey buildings, relics of the early nineteenth century, once derelict but patched up, distempered white, calm, silent, stark, functional, and accompanied (these days) by a fourth building of modern design. This was the Sanctuary, since re-named.

Sister Ludmila? Sister? (A pause.) I have forgotten. No, I remember. Put on the garments of modesty, He said. So I obeyed. The priest who came was very angry. I turned him away. When the priest had gone I asked God whether I had done wisely. Wisely and well, He said. And laughed. He likes a good joke. If God is never happy what chance of happiness is there for us? Such long dolorous faces that we pull. Never a smile when we say our prayers. How can one bear the thought of Eternity if in Heaven it is not permitted to laugh? Or come to that, permitted to weep? Is not our capacity to laugh and cry the measure of our humanity? No matter. It is not for this you have come. I have not thanked you. So I do so now. These days there are few visitors, and those that there are I cannot see. After they have gone He describes them to me. I'm sorry about your eyes, He said, but there's nothing I can do unless you want a miracle. No, I said, no miracle, thank You. I shall get used to it and I expect You will help me. Anyway, when you've lived a long time and can hardly hobble about on sticks but spend most of the day in bed your eyes aren't much use. It would need three miracles, one for the eyes, one for the legs and one to take twenty years off my age. Three miracles for one old woman! What a waste! Besides, I said, miracles are to convince the unconvinced. What do You take me for? An unbeliever?

It will be interesting, after you have gone, to find out who you are and what you look like. I mean from His point of view. It is almost a relief no longer to have sight of my own. I feel closer now to God. These days it is amusing to have the day described to me first by one of the helpers here and afterwards by Him. It is raining, they say; Sister, can you not hear the rain on the roof? Today has been hot and dry, He tells me after they have gone and I have said my prayers to summon Him. My prayers always bring Him. However busy He is, He finds time to drop by before I go to sleep. He talks mostly of the old times. Today in the heat and dryness you went to the bank, He says, surely you remember? Surely you remember your relief when Mr Govindas accepted your cheque and gave it to the clerk and the clerk came back with the two hundred rupees? And remember thanking Me? Thank God! you said in a voice only I could hear, the money has not been stopped; and remembered the old days in Europe and your mother saying, The money has been stopped, am I a woman to starve, am I not destined for splendour? I loved my mother. I thought her beautiful. When she was in luck she gave money to the Sisters. They are clothed like that, she said, in answer to my question, because those are the garments of modesty which God has bid them put on.

One day the Sisters passed by. Sister, my mother said to one of them, here is something for your box. But they continued. My mother called after them. She had recently had a special stroke of luck. I remember her telling me, This week I had a special stroke of luck. She bought gloves and good red meat. She would have given money to the Sisters, but they passed by. She cried out after them: Are we not all creatures of chance? Is one coin more tainted than another?

You understand...? Yes, you understand. This I am telling you about was in Brussels. I remember there was a fine apartment and then a poor one. We shall go back soon to St Petersburg, my mother used to say, but at other times she said we would go back to Berlin, and at others to Paris. Where then, I wondered, did we really live, where did we belong? There was about our lives a temporary feeling. Even a child of six could sense it. Since then I have always felt it. I am six years older than the century. It was 1900. I remember my mother saying, Today is the first day of the new century. It was an exciting moment. We had gloves and warm coats and stout shoes. The magic of Christmas was still in the streets. On everyone's face I could see a look of satisfaction at the thought of the new century beginning. My mother said: This will be our lucky year. Oh, the warmth of our gloved hands together! Our cosy reflection in the windows of the shops, my mother leaning down to whisper a promise or a fancy to me, her gloved finger on the pane, pointing out a box of crystallized fruits lying in a nest of lace-edged paper. A gentleman with a fur collar to his coat raised his hat to us. My mother bowed. We walked on through the crowded street. There was a park, and a frozen lake, and roast chestnuts sold at a stall. Perhaps that was another winter, another place. All the lovely things that happened to me as a child I seem to gather up and press together and remember as occurring on that first day of our lucky new century; our lucky new year after a warm, well-fed Christmas when a gentleman who smoked a cigar gave me a doll with flaxen hair and bright blue eyes. The things that happened that were not lovely I remember as happening on the day the Sisters refused to take my mother's charity. I was a bit older then, I think. Surely it was the time of the poor apartment?

With the money that the Sisters had refused my mother bought me barley sugar and sugared almonds. I watched her give the tainted coins to the shop assistant and take the bags in exchange. She held the bags for me in one of her gloved hands. I was afraid of the sweets because they were bought with money the Sisters had refused and this was the same as with money refused by God because I thought the Sisters were in direct communication with Him. Why are they dressed like that? That is the question I had asked. And my mother said they were dressed like that because God had bid them put on the garments of modesty. Whatever the Sisters did had the stamp of God's special authority on it. I did not fully know the meaning of tainted, but if the money given for the sweets was tainted then the sweets had become tainted and my mother's gloves had become tainted. The glove on my own hand held in hers would also be tainted, and the taintedness would seep through the soft leather into my palm. But the worst thing was the feeling that God did not want anything to do with us. The Sisters were His special instruments. He had used them to turn His back on us.

Ah, but then suddenly I saw the truth! How could I have been so blind? How angry He would be with them for refusing the money my mother had offered! I was not sure what modesty was, but if there had been a time when He had been forced to bid the Sisters wear its garments, had not this been a mark more of their punishment than their grace? Were they not also the garments of penance? What had they done to be made to wear those special clothes? What more dreadful clothes would He bid them put on now, as further punishment? They had refused money. The money was to help people God said should be helped, the poor, the hungry. And how poor, how hungry such people must be if they were poorer than us, and hungry all the time! And the Sisters, walking the streets in garments that betrayed some earlier shame, had condemned those poor to even greater poverty and sharper hunger. Would He now put some red ugly mark on their foreheads, so that the poor could get out of their way when they saw them coming? Or make them dress in the kind of clothes they'd not dare show themselves in for fear of being laughed at or having stones thrown at them? I clung to my mother's hand. I said, 'Mother, what will He do to them?' She stared at me, not understanding, so I repeated, 'What will

He do? What will God do to the Sisters this time?' She said nothing, but started walking again, holding my hand tightly. We went past a beggar woman. I hung back. We must give her some of the barley sugar, I said. My mother laughed. She gave me a coin instead. I put it in the old woman's dirty hand. She said God bless you. I was afraid, but we had good shoes and gloves and warm coats and God's blessing, and had made up to Him for what the Sisters had done wrong. The fire would be burning in the grate at home and there were the barley sugars and sugared almonds still to be eaten. I said to my mother, 'Is *this* our lucky year?' For the first time I felt that I knew what she meant by luck. It was a warmth in the heart. Without realizing it you found that you were smiling and could not remember what had made you smile. Often on my mother's lips I had seen this kind of smile.

The Sanctuary? Yes, it has changed. Now it is for orphan children. There is a new building and a governing body of charitable Indians. There are few who remember that old name, the Sanctuary. By God's grace I am permitted to stay, to live out my life in this room. Sometimes the children come to the window and stare through it, half-afraid of me, half-amused by the old woman they see here confined to her bed. I hear their whispers, and can picture the way their hands come up suddenly to cover their mouths to stifle a laugh. I hear when one of the helpers calls them, and then the scampering of their little bare feet and then farther away their shouts which tell me they have already forgotten the sight they have just found so enthralling, so funny. There is one of them, a little girl who brings me the sweet-sour-smelling marigolds whose stalks and leaves are slightly sticky to the touch. Her parents died of hunger in Tanpur. She does not remember them. I tell her stories from the Ramayana and from Hans Andersen and feel the way her eyes stay fixed and full of wonder, seeing beyond me into the world of legend and fantasy, the reality behind the illusion. What a blessing to the old is blindness. I thank God for it now. There was a time when I wept, for I have always loved to look upon the world, although I dried my eyes and would not bother Him with it, but smiled at Him and said Good Luck! when He came into the room to say He was sorry. Good luck, I said, the world You made is a wonderful place. What ever is Heaven like? Why, Sister Ludmila, He said, the same as here. He has got into the habit of calling me that for old time's sake and perhaps for His own. Am I forgiven? I asked. For what? He wanted to know. For calling myself Sister, for allowing them to call me Sister, for putting on the garments of modesty? What is this nonsense? He asked. Look, imagine that today is Wednesday. It has been hot and dry and Mr Govindas has honoured your cheque. Why should you think Mr Govindas would honour it and I refer it to drawer? He is, you know, a considerable Man of the world.

But you have not come to talk about this. Forgive me. Allow, though, a blind old woman an observation. Your voice is that of a man to whom the word Bibighar is not an end in itself or descriptive of a case that can be opened as at such and such an hour and closed on such and such a day. Permit me, too, a further observation? That given the material evidence there is also in you an understanding that a specific historical event has no definite beginning, no satisfactory end? It is as if time were telescoped? Is that the right word? As if time were telescoped and space dovetailed? As if Bibighar almost had not happened yet, and yet has happened, so that at once past, present and future are contained in your cupped palm. The route you came, the gateway you entered, the buildings you saw here in the Sanctuary – they are to me in spite of the new fourth building, the same route I took, the same buildings I returned to when I brought the limp body of young Mr Coomer back to the Sanctuary. Coomer. Harry Coomer. Sometimes it was spelled Kumar. And Harry was spelled Hari. He was a black-haired deep brown boy, a creature of the dark. Handsome. Such sinews. I saw him without his shirt, washing at the pump. The old pump. It is gone. Can you picture it where it was, under the foundations of the new building that I know from people's descriptions of it looks like a fantasy of Corbusier?

– but in the old days, before Corbusier, only the pump – and young Kumar washing there, the morning after we had found him lying as if dead in the waste ground near the river and carried him home on the stretcher. We always took the stretcher with us on those nightly missions. When we got him back Mr de Souza examined him. And laughed. 'This one is drunk, Sister,' he said. 'All the years I have worked for you I have said to myself: one night we shall lay upon the stretcher and carry home the useless carcase of a drunken man.' De Souza. He is a new name to you? He came from Goa. There was Portuguese blood in him somewhere, but a long way back. In Goa every other family is called de Souza. He was dark, darker by a shade or two than young Kumar. You prefer me to pronounce it Kumar. And why not? To hear him speak you might think him Coomer. But to see him, well, Coomer was impossible. And the name of course was rightly Kumar. He told me once that he had become invisible to white people. But I saw white women, how they watched him on the sly. He was handsome in the western way, in spite of his dark skin.

It was so with the policeman. The policeman saw him too. I always suspected the policeman. Blond, also good-looking, also he had sinews, his arms were red and covered with fine blond hairs, and his eyes were blue, the pale blue of a child's doll; he looked right but he did not smell right. To me, who had been about in the world, he smelt all wrong. 'And who is that?' he said. 'Also one of your helpers? The boy there? The boy washing at the pump?' This was the morning the policeman came to the Sanctuary; six months before the affair in the Bibighar. They were looking for a man they wanted. Do not ask me to remember who the man was or what he was supposed to have done. Published a seditious libel, incited workers to strike or riot, resisted arrest, escaped from confinement. I don't know. The British Raj could do anything. The province was back under the rule of the British Governor because the Congress ministry had resigned. The Viceroy had declared war. So the Congress said, No, we do not declare war, and had gone from the ministry. Anything that offended was an offence. A man could be imprisoned without trial. It was even punishable for shopkeepers to close their shops at an unappointed time. To hear of these things, to read of them, to consider them now, an element of disbelief enters. At the time this was not so. Never it is so.

And so there he was, Merrick, the policeman, with his hairy red arms and china blue eyes, watching young Kumar at the pump in the way later I saw Kumar watched on other occasions. I did not fully appreciate. Even if I had fully appreciated what could I have done? Foreseen? Intervened? So ordained things that the affair in the Bibighar six months later would not have occurred?

For me Bibighar began on the night we found young Kumar on the waste ground near the river, lying as if dead. Some distance off were the huts and hovels of the outcastes, but it was late and no lights were showing. It was by chance that we found him as we came back from the nightly scouring of the bazaar by way of the Tirupati temple and the river-bank, a journey that brought us by the other side of the tank where the untouchable women wash their clothes, as you will have seen on your way here. You can picture us as we always went, Mr de Souza in front with the torch, then myself and a boy behind with a folded stretcher over his shoulder and a stout stick in his free hand. Only once ever were we attacked, but they ran off when the boy threw the stick down and made for them, whirling the rolled stretcher over his head as if it weighed nothing. But that was a good boy. After a month the kind of boy I needed to take most of the weight of the stretcher would become bored, and when such a boy became bored his mind would usually turn to mischief. I never promised these boys more than four or five weeks' work. Towards the end of them I would begin to keep my eyes open for another lad wandering in the bazaar, sturdy and fresh from his village or some outlying district, a lad looking for work in a place where he believed fortunes were going for the asking. Sometimes such a boy would come to me, being told that there was easy money to be made with the mad white woman who prowled the streets at night looking for the dead and dying. Sometimes the previous boy would be jealous of the new boy and make up bad things about him, but usually the old one was glad enough to be off, with a bonus in his pocket and a chit addressed to whom it might concern extolling his honesty and willingness. Seeing the soldiers in the barracks some of the boys enlisted, others became officers' servants, one went to jail, and another to the provincial capital to become a police constable. The police were often at the Sanctuary. The boy who joined them had seen and admired the uniform and the air of authority. In the villages the police are local men. They do not have the same glamour for a boy as the police here in town. Some of these boys sent letters to tell me how they were getting on. Always I was touched by such letters because the boys were all illiterate and had paid good money to a scribe to send me a few lines. Only once did such a boy come back to the Sanctuary to beg.

We walked in darkness. 'Over there,' I called to Mr de Souza, 'flash your torch, there, in the ditch.' My eyes were sharper than anyone's in those days. I knew every inch of the way, where a hump should be, or a shadow, and where there should be neither. There are images that stay vividly in your mind, even after many years; images coupled with the feeling that at the same time came to you. Sometimes you can know that such an image has been selected to stay with you for ever out of the hundreds you every day encounter. Ah, you think, I shall remember this. But no. That is not quite correct. You do not think that. It is a sensation, not a thought, a sensation like a change in temperature for which there is no accounting and only some time afterwards, forgetting the sensation, do you think, I expect I shall always remember that. So it was, you see, that first night of young Kumar. In the light of the torch, his face; the two of us down in the ditch, kneeling. Above us, the stretcher boy with the rolled stretcher aslant his shoulder, a young giant, dark against the stars. I must have glanced up and asked him to get the stretcher ready. The smell of the river was very strong. On a still night, when the earth has cooled, the water continues warm and the smell near the banks is powerful. When there is a wind the smell reaches the Sanctuary. The river flows downstream from the temple past the place appointed for the outcastes. In entering the river for any reason at this point the outcastes will not pollute the water the caste Hindus bathe in, but this is to reckon without the pollution from other towns upstream of Mayapore. In the waste ground where we knelt, in the ditch, the smell of the river mixes with the smell of night-soil. At dawn, here, the untouchables empty their bowels. Without the blessing of God upon you it is a terrible place to be. Poor Kumar. Lying there. Such a place of human degradation. India is a place where men died, still die, in the open, for want of succour, for want of shelter, for want of respect for the dignity of death.

Who is it, Mr de Souza? I asked. It was the standard question. He knew many people. It was the first step in the drill of identification. Sometimes he knew. Sometimes I knew. Sometimes the stretcher-boy knew. For instance, a man known to be starving or dying of a disease, a man who would not go to hospital or come voluntarily to the Sanctuary, a man whose family were dead or lost or scattered, who had no hope of the world but only of a happier reincarnation or of an eternity of oblivion. But we usually knew where such men were to be found – such women too – and there would come the night when they could be lifted on to the stretcher, beyond protest, beyond defeat, and carried to the Sanctuary. For a fee the Brahmin priests would see to it that after they were dead they were suitably disposed of. The Hindus took their dead from us, the Mohammedans theirs, the State theirs. The State's dead were those we found dying, who were not identified. Such dead were taken to the morgue and if unclaimed after three days delivered to the students in the hospitals. Every morning at the Sanctuary there would be women whose husbands, sons, and sometimes I suppose lovers, had not come home the night before. And often, too, the police. But all this was none of my business. I left that side of things to Mr de Souza. My business was with the dying, not the dead. For the dead I could do nothing. For the dying, the little neither I nor the Sisters had been able to do for my mother: a clean bed, a hand to hold, a word through layers of unconsciousness to reach and warm the cold diminishing centre of the departing soul.

'Who is it?' I asked Mr de Souza. He was a man of heart and a man of talent, a lapsed Catholic, who took nothing from the Sanctuary except his bed and board and clothing. 'I don't know,' he said. He turned young Kumar over then, to see if there were wounds on his back. We had found him lying partly on his side, which is not usually the position of a drunken man. Someone, you see, had been ahead of us, and had been through the pockets, whoever it was from the huts who must have seen him staggering along the river-bank and had now returned home, possessing the wallet, turned out the lamps and feigned sleep. From the huts there was wakefulness, unnatural silence.

And we turned young Kumar back again, shining the torch on to his face again. And this is what I remember. This is the image. The face unchanged even after the body had been turned once, twice. The eyes shut, the black hair curling over the forehead which even in that state of his insensibility seemed to be furrowed by anger. Oh, such determination to reject! It was an expression you often saw on the faces of young Indians in those days. But in Kumar the expression had unusual strength. We got him on to the stretcher. I led the way back here to the Sanctuary. It was into this room where I lie and you sit that we brought

him. It used to be Mr de Souza's office. I had a room in the next
building where the clinic used to be, which is now the children's
sick bay. And here in this room Mr de Souza, bending over
young Kumar, suddenly laughed. 'This one is drunk, Sister!' he
said. 'It is what I have been waiting for all the time I have worked
for you. To find that only we have carried home the useless
carcase of a drunken man.'

'This one,' I said, 'is only a boy. To be so drunk he must also
be unhappy. Let him lie.'

And so he lay. Before I went to sleep I prayed for him. Each
night into sleep I took with me the memory of the face of one
of the rescued and it almost pleased me that for once it was the
face of a young man who was neither dying nor suffering from
injury. We went, you know, into places where the police did not
care to because they were afraid of being attacked, which is why
sometimes we brought home hurt and wounded. When we did
this we sent the police a message. Sometimes they came here on
their own initiative, as they did on the morning after we brought
young Kumar back. But never before had the District Superintendent come himself. If he had come the day before, the day
after, there might never have been Bibighar. You might then
have been able to say Bibighar to me now and I would have
nothing stronger than an impression of ruins and a garden. But
he came that day, Merrick, in short sleeves showing his red arms
and with a clarity in his blue eyes, a determination to miss nothing, a madness, an intention to find evidence. Ah, but of what?
'I want to see,' he said, 'the woman who calls herself Sister
Ludmila.'

And Mr de Souza replied, 'It is we who call her that.' Mr de
Souza was afraid of nobody. I was through there, in the little
room next door where now they hoard the clothing for the
children, the books and stationery, and games and rubber balls
and cricket bats, but where in those days we kept special medicines from Dr Gulab Singh Sahib's, under lock and key, and the
safe for the money I collected each week from the Mayapore
branch of the Imperial Bank, a safe for which Mr de Souza also
had a key. He slept here, where I am lying, with his desk there,
where you are sitting, and the table there by the window the
children stand at, under the light-bulb that at night no longer
glares at me. That was where we put the stretcher when we came

in. Sometimes we made more than one journey. He was standing there, Merrick, early on this Wednesday morning. I was opening the safe to get out the bag and the cheque book, and through the open doorway I heard him say this: 'I want to see the woman who calls herself Sister Ludmila.'

'It is we who call her that,' Mr de Souza said. 'Right now she is busy. Can I be of help?' And Merrick said, 'Who are *you*?' And de Souza smiled, I could hear the smile in his voice. 'I am nobody. Hardly worthy of your consideration.' In what they call a police transcript those words might look servile. To me they sounded defiant. So I came out and said, 'It is all right, Mr de Souza,' and saw Merrick there, carrying a little cane, dressed in shorts and a short-sleeved shirt, and a Sam Browne belt with a holster and a pistol in the holster, and his china blue eyes taking us all in. 'Mrs Ludmila Smith?' he said. I bowed. He said, 'My name is Merrick. I am the District Superintendent of Police.' Which already I knew, having seen him on horseback commanding the police who were controlling the crowds at the times of festivals, and driving in his truck over the Mandir Gate bridge. He had with him Rajendra Singh, the local subinspector who took bribes and stole watches from the men he arrested. Rajendra Singh had such a wrist-watch on. It was a finer watch than the one on Mr Merrick's wrist, but less serviceable perhaps. The Indians always had a tendency towards the tawdry, the English towards the apparently straightforward, the workable. But there was nothing straightforward about Mr Merrick. He worked the wrong way, like a watch that wound up backwards, so that at midday, for those who knew, he showed midnight. Perhaps no one could have cheated destiny by so arranging things that Kumar and Merrick never met. But I am sorry that it was here, although that was probably destined too, written on the walls when I first came here and saw the tumble-down buildings and recognized that they would serve my purpose.

'In what way can I assist you?' I asked him, and with a gesture I dismissed Mr de Souza, because I knew this would please Merrick. But also it confirmed that it was I who was in command. In my white cap, my garments of modesty. To match Merrick's uniform. One does not live in the world of affairs for nothing. One learns the rules, the unwritten laws, the little by-ways of the labyrinth of protocol. I offered Mr Merrick Mr de Souza's chair, but he preferred to remain standing. He said he wished to conduct a search. Again, with a gesture, I gave assent or at least indicated awareness that to resist such a thing was not worth the trouble, indeed that the search itself was the only troublesome thing, that it was he, Merrick, who was putting himself out, using up his time. I did not even ask him what or whom the search was for. There are so many things that one could say in such circumstances. With less experience of official interference I might have said all of them. And he was sharp. He looked at me and showed me with his eyes alone that he had instinctively divined the reasons for my unprotesting acquiescence. He guessed that I had nothing to hide that I knew of, but also guessed that I was a woman whose luck had often been better than her judgment but might not always be.

'Then where shall we begin?' he said. I told him wherever he wished. When we got outside I saw his truck at the gate of the compound and a constable posted there, and then, after he had been through the first two buildings and we were walking towards the third building, I remember the sight of young Kumar, without his shirt, bending his head under the pump. He straightened up. We were a hundred yards away from him. He looked round. And Merrick stood still. And gazed at him. 'And who is that?' he asked, 'also one of your helpers?' Over this distance he stared at Kumar. I called Mr de Souza who was following us. 'He spent the night with us,' I told Mr Merrick. 'Mr de Souza perhaps knows his name.' You understand, at this point I had not yet spoken to Kumar, but that morning had been told by de Souza only that the boy was all right but suffering from hangover and uncommunicative and not especially grateful for being brought to the Sanctuary, and had so far withheld his name. I thought that perhaps while Mr Merrick was conducting his search de Souza might have gone to the boy and said, Look, the police are here, who are you? and been told.

'Mr de Souza,' I said, 'the boy who spent the night with us —?' And de Souza said casually, 'As you see he is all right now and making ready to go.' 'I'm afraid no one can go until I say so,' Merrick said, not to me but to the sub-inspector, avoiding cleverly, you see, a direct engagement. 'Are we then all under arrest?' I asked, but laughed, and indicated that arrested or not

I wished to conduct him to the third building. He smiled and said that they were looking for someone, as no doubt I had guessed, and then walked on with me and Mr de Souza, leaving the sub-inspector behind. Some sign from Merrick had made the sub-inspector stay put, to keep an eye on Kumar. When we reached the third building Merrick stopped on the verandah steps and turned round. I did so too. The boy had resumed his washing under the pump. The sub-inspector stood where we had left him, his legs apart and hands behind his back. I looked at Merrick. He also was watching the boy. They formed a triangle, Merrick, Kumar, Rajendra Singh – each equidistant apart. There was this kind of pattern, this kind of dangerous geometrical arrangement of personalities. 'This building where we are now,' he said, but not looking at me, still looking at Kumar, 'is what is known as the death house?' I laughed. I said I believed that sometimes people who had never been to the Sanctuary called it that. 'Are there any dead this morning?' he asked. 'No, not this morning. Not for several days.' 'Homeless?' 'No, I do not house the homeless.' 'The hungry?' 'Those who are hungry know the days when there is rice. Today is not such a day.' 'The sick?' 'The clinic receives only in the evening. Only people who cannot afford to lose a morning or a day's work come to our clinic.' 'And your medical qualifications?' 'Mr de Souza is in charge of the clinic. He gave up paid work as a lay practitioner to work with me for nothing. The health authorities of the municipal board sometimes come to see us. They approve of what they find. As District Superintendent of Police you must know most of these things.' 'And the dying?' 'We have the voluntary services of Dr Krishnamurti, and also of Dr Anna Klaus of the Purdah Hospital. You can of course also inspect my title to the land and buildings.'

'It is a curious arrangement,' Mr Merrick said.

'It is a curious country.'

We went on into the third building. We had six beds in one room and four in another. In the year of the famine they were always occupied. Similarly in the year of the cholera. Now there was no widespread famine, no present outbreak of cholera. But scarcely a week went by that two or three of the beds were not in use. On this morning, however, they were all empty. The white sheets gleamed. He said nothing but seemed astonished.

Such cleanliness. Such comfort. What? For the dying? The starved unwashed dying? Such a waste! Go into the bazaar and look around and in a few hours you would find occupants for each of the beds – occupants who would benefit, get well. The world has a vested interest in those capable of being made well. At one moment he turned as if to say something, but thought better. The Sanctuary was outside his comprehension. He had not yet worked it out that in this so efficiently organized civilization there was only one service left that was open to me to give, the service that in a country like India there was no official time or energy left over for. The service that a woman such as myself could supply out of unwanted, unearned, undeserved rupees. For in this life, living, there is no dignity except perhaps in laughter. At least when the world has done its worst for a man, and a man his worst for the world, let him savour dignity then. Let him go out in cleanliness and such peace as cleanliness and comfort can give him. Which is little enough.

Perhaps in his bones, in his soul, Merrick was conscious of the meaning of the room he stood in, in his shorts and short-sleeved shirt and belt and holster. He looked at the polished floor and then with a sort of childish rudeness at my hands. Yes, they have always been soft and white. 'Who does the work?' he asked. 'Anyone,' I said, 'who needs to earn a few rupees.' Why should I do the work myself when I had unearned undeserved rupees that would help fill the cooking pot of one of the untouchable women you saw on your way here, washing in the stagnant tank? 'Where are these helpers today?' he said. I led him out into the compound behind the building where the helpers' quarters were. Perhaps there he saw it too, the distinction between the place of the living and the place of the dead: the smoky cook-house, the mud and thatch and the men and women who earned rupees and lived in what among the living passed as cleanliness but in comparison with the rooms for the dying was dirt. He made them come out of their quarters, and stand in the compound, and then entered those hovels, going alone and coming out empty-handed, having found no one in hiding.

He pointed at the people with his cane. 'These are your regular helpers?' he asked, and I told him that in the Sanctuary nobody was regular, that I hired and fired without compunction, wishing to spread whatever benefit it was in my power to give.

'Is Mr de Souza also irregular?' he asked. 'No,' I replied, 'because the Sanctuary is as much his as mine. He sees the point of it. These people are only interested in the rupees.'

'In life,' he said, 'rupees are a great consideration,' and continued to smile. But the smile of a man wearing a belt and holster is always a special smile. It was in the great war when I first noticed that an armed man smiles in a way that keeps you out of his thoughts. And this is how it was with Merrick. When he had satisfied himself that the death house had no secrets he said, 'Then there is just your night visitor,' and went back to the front verandah, to that dangerous geometrical situation, pausing at the head of the steps, glancing to where the sub-inspector still stood, and then at Kumar who was still standing by the pump, buttoning up his shirt. Smiling, Mr Merrick I mean, smiling and standing there. He said, 'Thank you, Sister Ludmila. I need take up no more of your time,' and saluted me by bringing the tip of his cane into touch with the peak of his cap, and ignored Mr de Souza who was waiting behind us, and walked down the steps. And when he began to walk the sub-inspector was also set in motion. And they converged, in this way, on young Kumar who also continued, standing, buttoning his shirt, doing up the cuffs. Waiting. Having seen, but making no attempt to avoid. Without moving I spoke quietly to Mr de Souza. 'Who is the boy?' 'His name is Coomer.' 'Coomer?' 'In fact, Kumar. A nephew by marriage, I believe, of Romesh Chand Gupta Sen.' 'Oh,' I said, and remembered having heard something. But where? When? 'Why Coomer?' I asked. 'Ah, why?' Mr de Souza said. 'It would be interesting, if not best, to go down.' So we went down, following a few yards behind Mr Merrick, so that we heard the first words, the first words in the affair that led to Bibighar. As we approached. Merrick. A clear voice. As if speaking to a servant. That tone. That language. The Englishman's Urdu. *Tumara nām kya hai?* What's your name? Using the familiar *tum* instead of the polite form. And Kumar. Looking surprised. Pretending a surprise not felt but giving himself up to its demands. Because it was a public place.

'What?' he said. And spoke for the first time in my hearing. *In perfect English. Better accented than Merrick's.* 'I'm afraid I don't speak Indian.' That face. Dark. And handsome. Even in the western way, handsome, far handsomer than Merrick. And then

Sub-Inspector Rajendra Singh began to shout in Hindi, telling him not to be insolent, that the Sahib asking him questions was the District Superintendent of Police and he had better jump to it and answer properly when spoken to. When he had finished Kumar looked back at Merrick and asked, 'Didn't this man understand? It's no use talking Indian at me.' 'Sister Ludmila,' Merrick said, but still staring at young Kumar, 'is there a room where we can question this man?' 'Question? Why question?' Kumar asked. 'Mr Kumar,' I said, 'these are the police. They are looking for someone. It is their duty to question anyone they find here for whom I cannot vouch. We brought you here last night because we found you lying in a ditch and thought you were ill or hurt, but you were only drunk. Now, what is so terrible in that? Except hangover.' I was trying to smooth over, you see, to make laughter or at least smiling of a different kind than Mr Merrick's. 'Come,' I said, 'come to the office,' and made to lead the way but already the Bibighar affair had gone too far. In those few seconds it had begun and could not be stopped because of what Mr Merrick was and what young Kumar was. Oh, if they had never met! If young Kumar had never been drunk, or been brought back; if there had never been that night-procession – the four of us, myself leading with the torch, Mr de Souza and the boy bearing the stretcher, and Kumar on it, but now recovered, standing there by the pump in the compound, facing Merrick.

'Is that your name: *Kumar*?' Merrick asked, and Kumar replied, 'No, but it will do.' And Merrick, smiling again, said, 'I see. And your address?'

And Kumar stared from Merrick to me, still pretending surprise, and said, 'What is all this? Can anyone just barge in, then?'

'Come,' I said. 'To the office. And don't be silly.'

'I think,' Mr Merrick said to me, 'we won't waste any more of your time. Thank you for your co-operation.' And signed to Rajendra Singh who stepped forward and made to take the boy by the arm but was brushed aside. Not with a violent motion, more with a shrug away to avoid distasteful contact. At this moment perhaps Merrick could have stopped it. But did not. Rajendra Singh was not a man to be shrugged off if Mr Merrick was there to back him up. And he was bigger than Kumar. He hit him across the cheek with the back of his hand. A soft, glancing

blow, done to insult as much as to sting. I was angry. I shouted,
'That will be enough of that.' It stopped them. It saved Kumar
from the fatal act of retaliation. I said, 'This is my property. In it
I will not tolerate such behaviour.' That sub-inspector – he was
a coward. Now he was afraid that he had gone too far. When he
struck Kumar he had also taken hold of his arm, but let it go.
'And you,' I said to Kumar, 'stop being silly. They are the police.
Answer their questions. If you have nothing to hide you have
nothing to fear. Come,' and again I made as if to lead them to
the office. But Merrick, no, he was not going to take the smooth
way out. He had already chosen the twisted, tragic way. He said,
'We seem to have got beyond the stage when a talk in your office
would have been a satisfactory preliminary. I am taking him into
custody.'

'On what charge?' Kumar said.

'On no charge. My truck's waiting. Now, collect your
baggage.'

'But I have a charge,' Kumar said.

'Then make it at the *kotwali*.'

'A charge of assault by this fellow with the beard.'

'Obstructing or resisting the police is also an offence,' Mr
Merrick said and turned to me. 'Sister Ludmila. Has this man
any possessions to be returned to him?' I looked at Kumar. His
hand went to his hip pocket. Only now had he thought to look
for his wallet. I said to him, 'We found nothing. We turn out
pockets, you understand, for the purpose of identification.'
Kumar stayed silent. Perhaps, I thought, he thinks it is we who
have robbed him. Not until his hand went like that to his hip
pocket was I certain that he had been robbed as he lay drunk the
night before, out there in the fields, near the river-bank. But in
any case a lesser man would have cried out, 'My wallet!' or 'It's
gone! My money! Everything!' drawing, attempting to draw a
red herring. Ah, a lesser man would have cried out like that, if
not to create a diversion, then in the little agony of sudden loss
that always, to an Indian, in those days anyway, looked like the
end of his constricted little world. And Kumar was an Indian.
But had not cried out. Instead, let his hand fall away, and said to
Merrick, 'No, I have nothing. Except one thing.'

'And that?' Merrick inquired, still smiling as if already
knowing.

'A statement. I come with you under protest.'

And all the time in those accents so much more English even than Merrick's. And in Merrick's book, this counted against him. For in Merrick's voice there was a different tone, a tone regulated by care and ambition rather than by upbringing. It was an enigma! Fascinating! Especially to me, a foreigner who had known an Englishman more of Merrick's type than Kumar's, and had heard this Englishman often rail against the sharp clipped-spoken accents of privilege and power. And here, in spite of the reversal implied by the colours of the skin, the old resentments were still at work, still further complicating the conflict. Kumar walked of his own accord towards the gateway and the waiting truck. But Merrick showed no sign of concern because he had the sub-inspector to trot after the prisoner. Another Indian. In this way mating black with black, and, again, touching his cap with the tip of his cane and thanking me for my services, keeping me talking, while I watched, at increasing distance, the affair between Kumar and the sub-inspector which was one of catching up, then push, and pull, and finally of what looked from where I stood like a violent meeting between Rajendra Singh, Kumar, a constable and the back of the truck with Kumar pushed, shoved, perhaps punched into the back of it, so that he fell inside rather than climbed. And the constable going in after him. And then the sub-inspector waiting, for Merrick. 'Why do you let them treat him like that?' I asked. I was not surprised. Only pained. For these were violent, difficult times. But Merrick had already turned and was on his way to the truck and pretended not to hear. When he reached the truck he talked to the sub-inspector and then the sub-inspector got into the back too. Well, so it went. Such things happened every day. And at this time, you understand, I had no way of telling what Kumar was suspected of, let alone of judging what he might have been guilty of. Only I had seen the darkness in him, and the darkness in the white man, in Merrick. Two such darknesses in opposition can create a blinding light. Against such a light ordinary mortals must hide their eyes.

It is good of you to come again so soon. Have you yet seen Bibighar? The ruins of the house, and the garden gone wild in the way most Indians like gardens to be? They tell me it has not

changed, that sometimes even now Indian families have picnics
there, and children play. The Europeans seldom went, except
to look and sneer and be reminded of that other Bibighar in
Cawnpore. And at night it was always deserted. People said it
was haunted and not a good place then, even for lovers. It was
built by a prince and destroyed by an Englishman. I'm sorry. You
are right to correct me. A Scotsman. Forgive me for momentarily
forgetting. Such nice distinctions.

Bibighar. It means the house of women. There he kept his
courtesans. The prince I mean. You have seen the Purdah Hospital here in the town, in the old black town as it used to be
called? Beyond Chillianwallah? Surrounded now by houses?
And changed. But it was a palace in the days when Mayapore
was the seat of a native ruler and the only foothold the English
had was one cut out by trade, need, avarice, a concern to open
the world God had given them, like an oyster suspected of a
pearl. Here all the pearls were black. Rare. Oh, infinitely desirable. But it must have taken courage as well as greed to harvest
them. Go into the old palace now, the Purdah Hospital, and look
at what remains of the old building, the narrow gallery of tiny
airless rooms, the kind of room these English merchants had to
enter to strike bargains, and there is an impression – from the
size of the rooms – of cruelty, of something pitiless. And it must
have been like this in the Bibighar. We cannot know for sure
because only the foundations are left and there never was an
artist's impression of the place as it was before the Scotsman
destroyed it. The Bibighar bridge was a later construction, and
so to visit his women the prince must have gone either by the
Mandir Gate bridge or by palanquin and boat, and so must his
father in order to visit the singer in the house that he also had
built on that side of the river, the house the Scotsman rebuilt
and renamed after himself. Indeed yes, the house where you are
staying. Before the Scotsman rebuilt and renamed it, was the
MacGregor House also a warren of tiny rooms and low, dark
galleries? Or was the singer given unaccustomed space, room for
her voice to spread, her soul to expand?

Go to the Purdah Hospital. Lady Chatterjee will take you.
Ask to go to the room at the top of the old tower. From there
you can see over the roofs of the black town across the river and
make out the roof of the MacGregor House. I wonder how often

the prince who loved the singer climbed the steps of the tower to look at it? And I wonder whether his son also climbed the tower to look across the river at the Bibighar? From the Bibighar also it must have been possible in those days to see the house of the singer. They are only one mile distant. Not far, but far enough for a girl running at night.

In those days, when Mayapore was a kingdom, on that side of the river there were no other buildings, and so those two houses were marks on the landscape, monuments to love, the love of the father for the singer and the love of the son for the courtesans, the son who despised his father for an attachment which, so the story goes, was never consummated. Day by day I think the son climbed the tower of the palace or to the highest room in the Bibighar to survey that other house, the singer's house, to glory in its decay, and said to himself, *Such is the fate of love never made manifest.* And night after night caroused in the Bibighar, his private brothel, aware of the ruin that grew stone by mouldering stone one mile distant. Now it is the Bibighar that is nothing and the singer's house that still stands, the one destroyed and the other rebuilt, in each case by this man, this MacGregor.

Let me explain something. In 1942, the year of Bibighar, I am in Mayapore more than seven years and knew little of Bibighar, little of MacGregor. This was the case with most people. Bibighar. MacGregor. These were just names to us. Take the road, we might say, over the Bibighar bridge, past the Bibighar gardens, and then turn into the MacGregor road and follow it along until you reach the MacGregor House which stands at the junction of MacGregor and Curzon roads, and Curzon road will lead you straight to the Victoria road and the cantonment bazaar.

This would have been the quickest way to the bank — it is only a short distance from here to the Bibighar bridge. But usually I went the other way, through the Chillianwallah Bazaar and past the Tirupati temple. The real life of Mayapore is on the Mandir Gate bridge side. I would go over the bridge and past the church of the mission and the girls' school, through the Eurasian quarter, Station road, Railway cuttings, Hastings avenue, and into Victoria road from that side.

But then, after that day in August 1942, the names Bibighar and MacGregor became special ones. They passed into our language with new meanings. What is this Bibighar? we asked. Who was MacGregor? we wanted to know. And then there seemed to be no scarcity of people able to tell us. Take Mac-Gregor. It was said of him that he feared God, favoured mosques and Muslims and was afraid of temples, and burnt the Bibighar because it was an abomination, burnt it and then knocked down what was left, leaving only the foundations, the gardens and the surrounding wall. It was also said that he did this following the poisoning of an Englishman at the prince's court, an event which was used as an excuse for the annexation of the state by the British government, the old East India Company. But Mac-Gregor did not burn the Bibighar so soon. The first record of MacGregor in Mayapore was in 1853, just four years before the Mutiny, but nearly thirty years after the annexation. In 1853 Mayapore was not the headquarters of the district. Mac-Gregor was not an official. He was a private merchant, of the kind who began to flourish after the old East India Company ceased to trade but continued to govern. He made his money out of spices, grain, cloth and bribes. His old factory and ware-house stood where the railway depot now stands and there is still a siding there that bears his name, the MacGregor siding. The railway did not come to Mayapore until ten years after he died, so obviously his influence was still felt, his memory fresh. You can picture his laden wagons setting off along the road that became the Grand Trunk road, and picture Mayapore at that time, before the railway. Still on that side of the river there were not many buildings, no barracks, no civil lines. There was, I think, a chapel where St Mary's is, and a Circuit house where the Court house stands. The District Officer lived in Dibrapur then. He would have stayed in the Circuit house when he came to Mayapore to hear petitions, settle cases, collect revenues. I wonder how many times he had to listen to subtle complaints which when he boiled them down he was able to see as com-plaints about MacGregor? I think of MacGregor as red-faced, his cheeks devasted by ruptured veins, virtual ruler of Mayapore, snapping his fingers at authority, terrorizing clerks, merchants, landowners, district officers and junior civilians alike; corrupt, violent – and yet in a few years lifting Mayapore out of the apathy it sank into after the annexation that should have transformed it from an old feudal backwater into a flourishing modern community, safe and happy under the rule of the Raj. I think he was the kind of man the merchants and landowners he dealt with would understand. It is said that he spoke the language of the greased palm, and this language is international. I think they would always know where they stood with MacGregor. But not with the austere, incorruptible, so perfect, so English District Officer.

You see how these facts about MacGregor do not fit the story that he burned the Bibighar because it was an abomination? But then this was the European version of the tale. Perhaps, also, it is the story he told his wife, whom he married and brought to Mayapore only after he had established his fortune and rebuilt the singer's house and called it by his own name. By that time he had already burned Bibighar, not, according to the Indian version, because it was an abomination in his eye and the eye of the Lord, an abomination even twenty or thirty years after its last occupation, but because he fell in love with an Indian girl and lost her to a boy whose skin was the same colour as her own. There are two versions of the Indian account of the burning of Bibighar. The first is that he discovered the girl and her lover met in the Bibighar, and that he then destroyed it in a fit of jealous rage. The second is that he told the girl she would have to leave the MacGregor House and live in the Bibighar. He took her there and showed her the repairs he had made to it and the furnishings and clothes he had bought for her comfort and enjoyment. When she asked him why she must leave the Mac-Gregor House he said: Because I am going to Calcutta to bring back an English wife. So that night she stole away with her true lover. When he found that she had gone he ordered the Bibighar to be burned to the ground, and then utterly obliterated.

And these stories ring truer, don't they? Truer than the tale that he burned Bibighar because it was an abomination. Poor MacGregor! I think of him only as a man of violent passions, and of emotions lacking any subtlety. If he had not burned the Bibighar like a child destroying a toy it had been told it mustn't play with, I wonder – would he have survived the Mutiny? The rebellious sepoys murdered their officers in Dibrapur and then roamed the countryside, eventually setting out for Mayapore with some idea of reaching Delhi, or of joining up with larger detachments of mutineers. It doesn't seem to be known where

MacGregor was killed, perhaps on the steps of his house or with the Muslim servant Akbar Hossain whose body was found at the gate. History was left the impression that nothing could have saved MacGregor because the sepoys knew he had burned the Bibighar and it was rumoured that his Indian mistress and her lover died in the fire. One wonders – did Janet know these tales? Was she happy with MacGregor or was her life in Mayapore a constant torment? Is it only for her dead child that her ghost comes looking? Or to warn people with white skins that the MacGregor House is not a good place for them to be?

It is curious. But there has always been this special connection between the house of the singer and the house of the courtesans. Between the MacGregor House and the Bibighar. It is as though across the mile that separates them there have flowed the dark currents of a human conflict, even after Bibighar was destroyed, a current whose direction might be traced by following the route taken by the girl running in darkness from one to the other. A current. The flow of an invisible river. No bridge was ever thrown across it and stood. You understand what I am telling you? That MacGregor and Bibighar are the place of the white and the place of the black? To get from one to the other you could not cross by a bridge but had to take your courage in your hands and enter the flood and let yourself be taken with it, lead where it may. This is a courage Miss Manners had.

I think at first she was not in love with Kumar. Physically attracted, yes, and that is always a powerful compulsion. But I saw other white women, the way they looked at him. Well, they found it easy enough to resist temptation because they saw him as if he stood on the wrong side of water in which even to dabble their fingers would have filled them with horror. Perhaps there were times when the girl felt the horror of it too, but resisted such a feeling because she knew it to be contradictory of what she first felt when she saw him. And then she rejected the notion of horror entirely, realizing that it was no good waiting for a bridge to be built, but a question of entering the flood, and meeting *there*, letting the current take them both. It is as if she said to herself: Well, life is not just a business of standing on dry land and occasionally getting your feet wet. It is merely an illusion that some of us stand on one bank and some on the opposite. So long as we stand like that we are not living at all, but dreaming. So jump, jump in, and let the shock wake us up. Even if we drown, at least for a moment or two before we die we shall be awake and alive.

She came several times to the Sanctuary. With him. With Kumar. She had said to him one day (at least I suppose she had said to him): Do you know anything about this woman, this woman who calls herself Sister Ludmila? Echoing something Mr Merrick had said to her. Or Lady Chatterjee. And young Kumar probably smiled and told her that he did; even that once I had found him and taken him for dead and carried him back drunk on a stretcher to the Sanctuary. Unless he kept that quiet. I think he did. But they came. And looked at everything. Walking hand in hand. Which had become natural for her but not I think for him. I mean he seemed to be aware of the effect such a gesture might have on those who observed it. But she seemed unaware. She came also several times by herself. She brought fruit and her willing hands. She had it in mind to help. Once she offered money. Her mother had died the year before the war and her father and brother had both been killed in it. She had a small inheritance, but all her aunt's money, Lady Manners's money, was to come to her when the old lady died. I said, No, I have no need of money, unless it is stopped. If it is ever stopped, I said, then I will ask you. She said, Then how else can I help? And I asked her why she wanted to. Surely, I said, there are countless other good causes you could support? I remember how she looked at me then. When she was alone with me she often wore spectacles. I do not think *he* ever saw her wearing them. Not wearing them for him was a vanity. She said, 'I have not been thinking in terms of good causes.' I acknowledged with a smile, but did not fully understand. Later I understood. I think, yes, later I understood. She did not divide conduct into parts. She was attempting always a wholeness. When there is wholeness there are no causes. Only there is living. The contribution of the whole of one's life, the whole of one's resources, to the world at large. This, like the courage to leap, is a wholeness I never had.

You know of course the image of the dancing Siva? He of the two legs and four arms, dancing, leaping within a circle of cosmic fire, with one foot raised and the other planted on the body of ignorance and evil to keep it in its place? You can see it there, behind you on my wall, carved in wood, my Siva dancing.

The dance of creation, preservation and destruction. A complete cycle. A wholeness. It is a difficult concept. One must respond to it in the heart, not the intellect. She also looked at my little wooden Siva. Peering at it. Putting on her glasses. She was a big girl. Taller than I. With that northern bigness of bone. I would not call her pretty. But there was grace in her. And joy. In spite of a certain clumsiness. She was prone to minor accidents. She smashed once a box containing bottles of medicine. On several occasions they met here. She and young Kumar. She came from her work at the hospital and while she waited helped with the evening clinic. Once he was late. We left the clinic and waited in my room until he came. I felt that he had intended not to come but changed his mind. So I left them together. And on that other evening, the night of Bibighar, he did not come at all. When it was dusk she went away alone. I saw her to the gate. She took the road to the Bibighar bridge, going on her bicycle. I begged her to be careful. The town was still quiet, but the surrounding countryside was not. It was the day, you remember, the day of the first outbreaks in Dibrapur and Tanpur. In the hospital that day she had seen the woman from the mission who had been found holding the hand of the dead man. She came direct from seeing her, from the hospital to the Sanctuary, to meet young Kumar surely. But he never came. We sat in my room and she told me about the woman from the mission who was ill with pneumonia because she had sat out like that, in the roadway, in the rain, holding the dead man's hand. Crane. Her name was Crane. Miss Crane. It was raining also while we sat and talked, waiting for Kumar who never arrived, but at sunset the rain stopped and the sun came out. I remember the light of it on Miss Manners's face. She looked very tired. As the light began to go she said she must be getting home. And went on her bicycle. By way of Bibighar. The same bicycle. I mean the same that was found in the ditch in the Chillianwallah Bagh near the house of Mrs Gupta Sen, where Hari Kumar lived. By Merrick. Found by Merrick. So it was said. But if Hari was one of the men who raped her why would he steal her bicycle and leave it like that, close to his home, as evidence?

And you see, when she left, wheeling her bicycle from the gate, turning to wave and then mounting and going into the twilight, I felt that she was going beyond my help, and remembered young

Kumar driven only a few months before in the back of Merrick's truck, going alone to a place where he also would be beyond reach of help. On that day when Merrick had driven away, taking young Kumar to be questioned, I said to Mr de Souza, Kumar? Kumar? The nephew of Romesh Chand Gupta Sen? This is what you think? And then went with him back to the office to finish the business Mr Merrick had interrupted me in, getting ready, it being a Wednesday, to go to the bank, saying a prayer to God that on my arrival Mr Govindas would not look embarrassed and take me on one side and say: 'Sister Ludmila, this week there is no money, we have heard from Bombay cancelling your facilities.'

But when I got to the bank, leaving the boy to wait outside, Mr Govindas came out of his inner room and smiled as usual and took me in, to sit and talk, while they cashed my cheque for two hundred rupees. 'Sister Ludmila,' he said, 'that boy outside. Where did he come from?' It was a joke between us. So I said, 'Why, from heaven I suppose.' 'And the previous boy? Also he came from heaven?' 'Well no,' I said, 'he came from jail and has recently gone back in.' 'It is what I am warning you against. Not to trust a boy simply because he looks strong enough to protect you.'

But of course I knew this. I knew that after a week or two such a boy would become bored and that when this happened his mind would turn to mischief. The boy on that particular day, already he was bored. When I got back outside with the two hundred rupees and the locked bag chained to my waist he was gossiping with people who had nothing better to do and was reluctant to leave them. But. He followed. He knew his duty. And so back we went, through the Eurasian quarter, past the church of the mission, and over the Mandir Gate bridge to the Tirupati temple. I have never been into the temple. The god of the temple is Lord Venkataswara who is a manifestation of Vishnu. And in the courtyard of the temple there is a shrine and an image of Vishnu asleep. It was of the image of the sleeping Vishnu that we talked, Miss Manners and I, that evening of Bibighar. Kumar had taken her there about two or three weeks before. Although he believed in nothing like that. But she wished to see the temple. His uncle had arranged it with the Brahmin priest. And so they had gone together and now she talked of it, to me who had never been. The rain stopped and the sun came out. It lighted her face, her tiredness, her own wish to sleep. I was able to visualize what she told me because of her tired face and because I had seen an image of the sleeping Vishnu in the temple at a place called Mahabalipuram, a temple by the sea, in the south, not far from Madras. Also there is in the south, you know, a very famous temple called Tirupati. High on a hill. The temple here in Mayapore takes its name from it. It is said that originally the people of Mayapore came from the south, that a Maharajah of Mayapore married a South Indian girl and built the temple to honour her and to honour the god she worshipped. Since then there has been so much assimilation it is impossible to divide and detect.

But in Mayapore there is the Tirupati temple. Mandir means temple. It is a word from the north. And so you have the meeting of south and north. The Tirupati temple, the Mandir Gate. In ancient days the town was walled. At night the gates were closed. The Mandir Gate then opened on the Mandir Gate steps. Coming from the north you would have had to cross the river by boat and climb the steps to the Mandir Gate. Later they built the Mandir Gate bridge. The steps remained but became simply the steps you see that lead up to the Tirupati temple. There were other gates to the south. There was never a Bibighar gate. The wall had gone, I think, before the Bibighar was built. The Bibighar bridge was built after MacGregor's day. What a mixture! MacGregor, Bibighar, Mandir and Tirupati.

Leaving the bank that day with the boy following, armed with his stick, I passed through the Eurasian quarters, and went past the church of the mission where the Eurasians worshipped. A little Church of England in miniature. And waited at the level crossing because it was closed to allow a train to pass. And eventually moved, going with the crowd over the Mandir Gate bridge, and paused on the other side, to distribute some money to the beggars and to the leper who always sat there, with his limbs cut back like those of a bush that had to be pruned in order to ensure the bloom. And then, taking the left fork from the holy tree, past the open shop-fronts, turning a deaf ear to the offers of pān, cloth, soda-water, melons and jasmine, and through by the open archway in the wall surrounding the Chilli-anwallah Bazaar, stopping to buy chillis which Mr de Souza had a liking for, and going then to the other side of the market square, past the loud meat and the stinking fish and the hunched figures of the market women with their scales lying idle like sleeping metal reptiles and up the stairway to the offices of Romesh Chand Gupta Sen, whose dead brother's widow, Mrs Gupta Sen, lived in one of those concrete houses built on the Chillianwallah reclamation, in the Chillianwallah Bagh.

'Arrested!' he said. The uncle-by-marriage. Romesh Chand. 'That boy,' he said, 'that boy will be the death of me. Who does he think he is? Why cannot he learn the ways of honour and obedience, the ways befitting a young Indian?' And called, ringing a little brass bell as though the office were a temple, so that I understood better young Kumar's disobedience, remembering from that morning the voice, the Englishness, and those northern sinews, that handsomeness. Do you understand? How it was alien, this background, this warren of little dirty rooms above the warehouses of the contractor? To him. Alien to him, to Kumar? Who spoke English with what you call a public school accent? Who had been taken to England by his father when he was too young to remember the place he was born in, and lived there, lived in England, until he was eighteen years old? But whose uncle back in India was a bania, sitting at a desk wearing the achkan, the high-necked coat, and with clerks under him, squatting in little partitioned cells, among grubby papers, one even holding paper money in his toes? For a time, after his father's death and his return to India, young Kumar was made to work there. But had rebelled and now did some work for the *Mayapore Gazette*. So much I gathered. I did not ask questions. Simply I went there to tell the uncle of Mr Merrick's action. So that steps could be taken. What steps I did not know. But he rang the little bell for his head clerk and sent him away with a chit, a note to a lawyer to come at once. There was no telephone in that place. One could tell that Romesh Chand was a man who did not believe in telephones, in the necessity for telephones, or in acting in any way that could be counted 'modern' or foreign. But who believed in his own power, his own importance. He asked how it was that his nephew came to be at the Sanctuary. I did not tell the whole truth. I said only that he had stayed the night there, that in the morning the police had come looking for a man they wanted and had taken Kumar away for questioning because he was the only stranger there. 'It is kind of you to take trouble to inform me,' he said. I said it was no trouble and came away. But all day I did not get young Kumar out of my mind. That afternoon I sent Mr de Souza into the bazaar to find out what he could and went myself to the Purdah Hospital to speak to Anna Klaus, the doctor from Berlin who came to India to escape from Hitler and who was my good friend. After she had heard my opinion of the kind of boy young Kumar was, she telephoned Lady Chatterjee who was on the hospital committee. And said after she had telephoned, 'Well, that is all I can do. Lady Chatterjee will speak to Judge Menen or the Deputy Commissioner. Perhaps. And your Mr Merrick will find himself asked questions. Which is all right as far as it goes. But it depends, doesn't it, depends on your young Mr Kumar, on what he has done? Or on what he is suspected of having done? If it is anything remotely subversive they can lock him up without a by-your-leave.' Which I knew. And came back here, and found Mr de Souza ahead of me. 'It is all right,' he said, 'the police only kept him a couple of hours. When the lawyer sent by Romesh Chand arrived at the police station they had already let him go.' I asked de Souza how he knew this. He said he had spoken to Romesh Chand's head clerk who was not supposed to have known what was going on but had found out by gossiping to the lawyer's clerk. So, Mr de Souza said, it is all right, and we can forget Mr Kumar. Yes, I said. It is all right. Dr Klaus, also she came that evening. And I told her. She said, 'Well, that's all right then. That's all over.' And again I said yes. But did not think so. When we went out that night with the stretcher I could not get it out of my mind that it was not all right and not all over. I asked myself, Did I then do wrong? To warn Romesh Chand? To get Dr Klaus to arrange it that important people would ask questions? Young Kumar was questioned and then allowed to go. And after he had gone his uncle's lawyer arrived. Merrick probably knew this but took no notice. An Indian lawyer was nothing. But later that day, when perhaps so far as Merrick was concerned the case of young Kumar had been settled and forgotten, he would have been rung by the Judge or Deputy Commissioner, or by someone ringing on the Deputy Commissioner's or the Judge's instructions and asked: Who is this boy Kumar you've got at one of the kotwalis for questioning? And

Merrick would have said, He's not there any longer, why do you ask? And whoever it was who was ringing would say, Well, that's probably a good thing. We have been asked what's happening. Your young suspect seems to have a lot of influential friends.

To be asked after by people in authority could undo all the good Kumar might have done for himself by answering questions properly once he got to the police station, would count against him in Merrick's book – in Merrick's books, where Kumar had already gone down as a boy who spoke better English than he, and would now go down as a boy who had friends who were able to speak to Judge Menen or the Deputy Commissioner, just as if he were a white boy, and not a black boy. And had stared arrogantly and said, Didn't this fellow understand it's no good talking Indian to me?

And later, yes, later, walked in public, here in the Sanctuary in view of anyone who cared to watch, hand in hand with the white girl, Miss Manners. And perhaps walked like that elsewhere, where Merrick would hear about it, or see it. I did not know until too late that Merrick also knew Miss Manners. All Europeans knew each other, but theirs, Merrick's and Miss Manners's, was a special way of knowing, it seemed. And that night of Bibighar I understood that it was this special way. Merrick came when it was dark. In his truck. Alone. He said, 'I believe you know a girl called Daphne Manners? I have just come from the MacGregor House. She isn't home yet. Have you seen her?' 'Yes,' I said. 'She was here. But left just before it got dark.' I did not think there was any personal interest in his inquiry. There was trouble in the district. And he was a policeman. I thought only of the girl. Of what could have happened to her. I assumed, you see, that Lady Chatterjee had rung the police because Miss Manners had not reached home.

He said, 'Why was she here?' I told him she sometimes came to help at the clinic. He seemed surprised and said, 'I didn't know that. I knew she came here once because she talked about it. How often does she come?' 'Very rarely,' I said. For suddenly I was cautious. And then he asked, did she come alone, had she been alone tonight, did I know where she had planned to go when she left at dusk? Yes, alone, I said, alone tonight, and home so far as I knew, back to the MacGregor House. By which route? 'Well, from here,' I said, 'it's quicker by the Bibighar. Didn't

you come that way from the MacGregor House?' It seemed that
he hadn't, that from the MacGregor House he had driven first
to the kotwali on the Mandir Gate bridge side, and then remembered she had once talked to him of a visit to the Sanctuary and
drove here from that direction. 'So you probably missed her,'
I said, and Merrick replied, 'But you say she left at dusk. I was
at the MacGregor House more than an hour after dusk and until
nearly nine o'clock and she hadn't got back.'

And then because I was worried for her and momentarily
forgot about Merrick and Kumar, I said what I had not intended
to say, said what could not help putting the name Kumar into
his mind. I said, 'Perhaps she called at Mrs Gupta Sen's.' Seeing
his face I wished that I had not said it. It was as if in mentioning
Mrs Gupta Sen I had actually pronounced the name Kumar. He
said, 'I see.' Behind his eyes there was a smile. And everything
fitted into place, fitted back into that dangerous geometrical
position I had had warning of, with Merrick and Kumar as two
points of a triangle, with the third point made this time not by
Rajendra Singh but by Miss Manners. I had that sensation which
sometimes comes to us all, of returning to a situation that had
already been resolved on some previous occasion, of being again
committed to a tragic course of action, having learned nothing
from the other time or those other times when Merrick and
I may have stood like this, here in this room where I am bed-
ridden and you ask your questions, with the name Kumar in our
minds and the name of a girl who was missing and who had to
be found. The revelation that Merrick was concerned as more
than a policeman and my own betrayal of the boy, of Kumar,
through talking of the house in Chillianwallah Bagh, talking of
Mrs Gupta Sen's – these were the springs that had to be touched
each time our lives completed one revolution and again reached
the point where Merrick and I stood in the room. And each
time the springs *were* touched, touched as surely as night follows
day, touched before they could be recognized for what they
were. I should have known that Merrick knew the girl. It was
stupid of me. It was the price I paid for devoting myself to the
interests of the dying instead of the living. I should not have
assumed that just because she was a friend of Hari Kumar she
could not also be a friend of Mr Merrick. If I had not been stupid
then we might have escaped from the cycle of inevitability and

Merrick would not have left, as he did, already convinced that Kumar alone could solve the mystery of the girl's disappearance.

But I had not known that Merrick knew the girl or that in his own curious way he was fond of her. But I guessed it then, after I had said, 'Perhaps she called in at Mrs Gupta Sen's,' and saw the excitement behind his otherwise blank but revealing china blue eyes. For he had long ago chosen Hari Kumar, chosen him as a victim, having stood and watched him washing at the pump, and afterwards taken him away for questioning, to observe more closely the darkness that attracted the darkness in himself. A different darkness, but still a darkness. On Kumar's part a darkness of the soul. On Merrick's a darkness of the mind and heart and flesh. And again, but in an unnatural context, the attraction of white to black, the attraction of an opposite, of someone this time who had perhaps never even leapt into the depths of his own private compulsion, let alone into those of life or of the world at large, but had stood high and dry on the sterile banks, thicketed around with his own secrecy and also with the prejudice he had learned because he was one of the white men in control of a black man's country.

Merrick had known for a long time about Miss Manners and Kumar. I realize that therefore Kumar was already in his mind as someone who might know where she was. But there is something that perhaps you do not know yet. Something I partly gathered when she came that night of Bibighar, the night when Kumar did not arrive, something I learned more fully of on a later occasion, when she came to say goodbye because she was going up north to stay with her aunt, Lady Manners, until it was all over. She was pregnant. She made no secret of it. For a time we spoke of ordinary unimportant things. I was greatly struck by her calmness. I remember thinking, It is the calmness of a beautiful woman. And yet she was not beautiful, as you know, as everyone you have spoken to will have told you, as you have seen for yourself from her photograph. At one point we both fell silent. It was not the silence of people who have run out of things to say. It was the silence of people who felt understanding and affection, who were only uncertain just how much at that moment the friendship should be presumed upon. It was I who made the decision. To speak of Kumar. I said, 'Do you know where he is?' meaning where he was imprisoned. I did not need actually to pronounce his name. She looked at me and the expression on her face told me two things, that she did not know but hoped, just for a second or two before the hope faded, that I did. She shook her head. She had asked. But nobody in authority would tell her. She had also called at the house in Chillianwallah Bagh, hoping that his aunt might know. But Mrs Gupta Sen would not so much as come out of her room to speak to her. More than this, I think, for the moment she had not dared to do in case she did him harm. He had been arrested, that night of Bibighar, with some other boys. Earlier that day, you remember, several people had been taken into custody for political reasons. It was said they had been put into closed railway carriages and taken away, no one knew where. It was also said that the arrests of five or six boys on the night of the Bibighar affair had caused the riots in the town. But the riots no doubt were already planned. Perhaps the riots were worse because of the rumours of the terrible things that were happening to the boys arrested after Bibighar. Or perhaps they seemed to be worse because among the English there was this belief that after Bibighar none of their women was safe. They said that it was because of Bibighar that the Deputy Commissioner was persuaded to see the situation as one that was out of hand and called in the military before it was actually necessary. Perhaps the truth of these things will never be known. Before Miss Manners came to say goodbye to me it had occurred to me that perhaps it weighed on her mind that unwittingly she had been at the very centre of all those troubles. But when she came she had this look of calmness, of concentration, the look, I think, of all women who for the first time are with child and find that the world around them has become relatively unimportant. I put my hand on hers and said, 'You *will* go through? Go through to the end?' She said, 'Why do you ask?' and smiled, so that I knew she would go through. I said, 'Have they tried to dissuade you?' She nodded. Yes, they had tried. She said, 'They make it sound awfully simple. Like a duty.'

But of course it was not simple at all. For them, perhaps, yes it would be simple. An obligation even. To get rid. To abort. To tear the disgusting embryo out of the womb and throw it to the pi-dogs. That's what I heard a woman say. A white woman. Is it true, she asked another – 'Is it true that that Manners girl is pregnant and has gone to Kashmir to *have* the baby?' They were in Gulab Singh's pharmacy buying cosmetics. Things were back to normal by then. And being told that it seemed to be true, she said, 'Well, what are we to make of that? That she *enjoyed* it?' Poor Miss Manners. How short a time it took for her to become 'that Manners girl'. Perhaps before Bibighar she had also sometimes been called this. But immediately after Bibighar her name was spoken by Europeans with the reverence they might have used to speak of saints and marytrs. But now. That Manners girl. And that ugly comment – 'Perhaps she enjoyed it.' And then the woman smiled and said in a loud voice, 'Personally, if it had happened to me, I would have had a public abortion outside their bloody temple and thrown the filthy muck to the pi-dogs. Or made them stuff it down their priests' throats.' And continued selecting powders and lotions for her white skin and succeeded, as that kind of woman always did, still does, in talking to the man who was serving her without once looking at him or letting her hands come within touching distance of his. One of the women, perhaps, that I had seen months before watching young Kumar when he accompanied me to the pharmacy, having met me on the way and stopped and talked for a while and offered to carry back to the Sanctuary the medicines I was going to buy, offered because that day I had no boy with me. Young Kumar and I had become friends. At least I felt that he was mine and I was his in spite of the fact that there was still an idea in his head that he had no friends at all. When he came out of the pharmacy he said, 'As you saw, I've become invisible to white people.' Perhaps he had not noticed the way the white women eyed him. Perhaps only he had noticed the way they pushed past him, or turned their backs, or called to the assistant he was already speaking to. He hated going into the cantonment shops for this reason. And yet I know for him there must have been a terrible longing to go into them, to become again part of them, because of their Englishness, because England was the only world he knew, and he hated the black town on this side of the river as much as any white man fresh out from England would hate it. Hated it more, because for him the black town was the place where he had to live, not the place he occasionally had to pass through with his handkerchief held to his nose on the way back across the bridge to the civil lines and the world of the club where white people gathered.

But Kumar is another story, isn't he? One that you must come to. I will tell you a name that might help you, that possibly no one heard of but myself, or has long ago forgotten. Colin. Colin Lindsey. Kumar told me about Colin when I saw him drunk on a second occasion. It was because of Colin Lindsey that he was drunk that first time, that night we found him and brought him back to the Sanctuary. In England Colin Lindsey was Hari Kumar's closest friend. They went to the same school. Colin tried to get his parents to look after Hari when Hari's father died and Hari was forced to come back to India. When he was not quite eighteen. With that Englishness. That English voice, that English manner, and English name, Harry Coomer. Speaking no Indian language. An Englishman with a black skin who in Mayapore became what he called invisible to white people.

But not invisible to the women in the pharmacy. Or to Miss Manners. Or to Merrick. And I was telling you something. About Merrick and what he already knew of the association between the girl and Kumar. I said to her, this day that she came to say goodbye, 'Miss Manners, I have a confession. It has been a lot on my conscience.' And told her how Merrick had come to the Sanctuary on the night of the Bibighar. How at this time I did not know that she and Merrick knew each other more than in the way one white person might know another on a civil and military station. But realized now that his interest was not only that of a policeman who had been told a white girl was missing. And then forgot, in my concern for what might have happened to her, that it was dangerous to mention the name Kumar to him, realized too late that it was especially dangerous to mention Kumar even obliquely in any connection with herself. And had said, 'Perhaps she called in at Mrs Gupta Sen's.'

'Why does it worry you,' she wanted to know, 'why is it on your conscience? I know Mr Merrick came here and that when he left he went to Hari's house.' I said: But later he went back. He left here and went to the house in Chillianwallah Bagh and asked for Hari and was told he was not at home. And then drove back to the MacGregor House. And found you had returned. In that state. And at once gathered patrols and surrounded the whole Bibighar area, and arrested the first five boys he found in that vicinity. *And went back to the house in Chillianwallah Bagh.* And went upstairs with constables and found Hari. With marks on his face, they say, bathing them, attempting to reduce evidence. And outside in the ditch, your bicycle.

Yes, she said. This is true. How did you know?

From Mr de Souza, I said. He has many friends and finds out a lot of things. Some are true, some are just rumours. This obviously is true. And it is on my conscience. That if I had not mentioned the house in Chillianwallah Bagh Mr Merrick would not have gone looking for Hari Kumar. Because *you* said nothing. We all of us know that you said nothing. That you said you did not see who it was who attacked you. We know that you have never implicated anyone. We know this from what Lady Chatterjee has said. I know it from Anna Klaus. We know that you even refused to attempt to identify the other boys who were arrested because you insisted you had never seen them properly in the dark. There is indeed one question in my mind. If Mr Merrick had not gone back to the Mac-Gregor House and found you, like that, would you have let it be known, at all, what had happened?

After a moment or two she said: 'Why should I keep it secret? A crime has been committed. There were five or six men. Four of them assaulted me. What are you trying to say to me? That you too think Hari was involved?'

No, I said. No, not that. Only I am trying to unburden. To ask you to help me to unburden. There is, you see, this other thing I remember. On that evening of Bibighar, when you came to the Sanctuary to wait for Kumar. While you waited you told me about the visit to the temple. As you talked I had an impression. An impression that you had not seen him since then. Had not seen him for two weeks or more. That on the day of the visit to the temple there had been some disagreement between you. A quarrel. That it disappointed but did not surprise you that by dusk he still had not come to the Sanctuary to meet you and you had to leave on your own. As you left, I had the idea that you would call at his house before going home. To see him. To put right between you whatever had gone wrong. Which was why when Merrick was questioning me I said that you might have gone to the house in Chillianwallah Bagh. And this made him think at once of Kumar, because he knew where Kumar lived. He would have remembered it clearly from the day he took him away to the police station for questioning. I was not able to put all this into words to myself at the time, at the time Merrick was standing here in this room on the night of Bibighar. But the words were there, waiting to come. And came later, when I heard that Kumar was among the boys arrested, Kumar among those who had been taken away, and then I remembered how Merrick's expression changed because I said that you might have gone to Mrs Gupta Sen's. And he looked round the room. As if he could tell that you and Kumar had been in the room on other occasions, had waited for each other here, that on this evening you had also been waiting for Kumar. As if at last he had discovered one of the places where you and Kumar met. I saw how important the discovery was to him, and that he was not just a policeman making inquiries about a missing girl. I had sensed this a moment or two before, when he seemed surprised to hear that you sometimes came to help at the clinic. It was the surprise of a man who felt he had a right to know all about your movements. Am I right?

Yes, she said. He seemed to think he had a right.

And he knew about you and Kumar?

Everybody on that side of the river knew, she said. Mr Merrick warned me against the association.

And after this warning, I said, perhaps it was that you and Kumar had the quarrel, when you visited the temple? And did not see each other again? So that Mr Merrick thought you had taken his warning to heart?

Yes, she said. I suppose that is the way it happened. The way it might have looked to him.

So then, you see, she could not unburden me. Of blame, of guilt, of treacherously saying to Merrick: Perhaps she has called in at Mrs Gupta Sen's? Of being instrumental in reviving in him the exciting suspicion that Miss Manners and young Kumar still met in secret, here in the Sanctuary. Of opening up for him a way of *punishing* Kumar whom he had already chosen, chosen as a victim. For Merrick was a man unable to love. Only he was able to punish. In my heart I feel this is true. It was Kumar whom Merrick wanted. Not Miss Manners. And it was probably her association with Kumar that first caused Merrick to look in her direction. This is the way I see it. And there is another thing I see.

This.

That young Kumar was in the Bibighar that night. Or on some other night. Because the child she bore was surely Kumar's child? Why else should she look, carrying it, like a woman in a state of grace? Why else should she refuse to get rid, refuse to abort, to throw the disgusting embryo to the mongrels? Why else? Unless having leapt she accepted the logic of her action, and all its consequences? Including the assault in darkness by a gang of ruffians. And believed that from such an assault she carried India in her belly? But would this fit the picture I had of her as she sat here, calm, concentrated, already nursing the child in her imagination, feeling that so long as she had the child she had not entirely lost her lover?

There was one question I longed to put to her. Partly I did not because I felt I knew the truth and partly I did not because I believed it was a question she would refuse to answer. For Kumar's sake. There are ways, aren't there, in which one person can enjoin another to her own silence? And she had surrounded herself, and Kumar's memory, with this kind of silence. They hated her for it. The Europeans. Just as they criticized that woman from the mission – Miss Crane – criticized her for being unable to describe the men who murdered the teacher. But in the case of Daphne Manners the situation was worse, because for a time, after the rape, she was for them an innocent white girl savaged and outraged by black barbarians and it was only gradually that they realized they were going to be denied public revenge. Because she would not identify either. Because at one point she was reported as saying that for all she knew they could have been British soldiers with their faces blacked like commandos. Because she asked if the boys arrested were all Hindus and on being told they were said that something must be wrong because at least one of the men who raped her was circumcised which meant he was probably a Muslim. She said she knew he was circumcised and would tell them why she knew if they really wanted her to. She said this in front of witnesses at the private hearing they held at the MacGregor House. The hearing was held because the whites were lusting for a trial. But what kind of trial could they have when it looked as if the victim herself would stand up in court and cast suspicion even on their own soldiers? And openly discuss such immodest details as a man's circumcision? So they got no trial. But what need did they have of a trial? The boys they arrested did not have to be found guilty of anything, but simply locked up and sent away, God knew where, with countless others. And with them, Kumar.

And then of course they turned on her. Oh, not publicly. Not to her face. Among each other. It would not have done for the Indians to know what they were thinking. But for the first time you would hear the English asking each other the questions Indians had been asking all the time. What was she doing at night in the Bibighar Gardens anyway? Obviously she had gone into the gardens voluntarily because nothing had ever been said about her being dragged off her bicycle as she rode past. And if she had been dragged off the bicycle wouldn't she have seen at least one of the boys who dragged her off? Wasn't there a street lamp on the roadside opposite the Bibighar? And wasn't there, not a hundred yards away, at the head of the Bibighar bridge, the level crossing and the hut where the gatekeeper lived with his family, all of whom are said to have sworn they had seen and heard nothing until Mr Merrick's patrols stormed in and lined them all up for questioning?

I will tell you the story that was finally told, that was finally accepted by all the gossips of British Mayapore as the unpalatable truth. You do not have to look far for its source of origin. No farther I think than to Mr Merrick. She had gone, they said, to Bibighar because Kumar had asked her to. Anyone could see the kind of boy Kumar was. The worst type of educated black. Vain, arrogant, puffed-up. Only by consorting with a white woman could his vanity be satisfied. And only a plain girl like Daphne Manners could ever have been inveigled into such an association. So confident did he become she would do anything he asked that he sometimes had the nerve to keep away from her for days, even weeks, at a time, the nerve to arrange a meeting and not turn up, to quarrel publicly with her, to humiliate her. And would then allow her the pleasure of being with him again for an hour or two. And all the time planning the biggest humiliation of all, which coincided, in all likelihood not by chance, with the time chosen by those Indians who thought to show the English who was master. For days before the planned uprising he kept away from her, working her to a fever pitch of desire for him, then sent her a message to meet him in the Bibighar. She flew to the rendezvous and found not only Kumar but a gang of toughs who then one by one systematically raped her. It was her shame and humiliation that made her keep silent. What English girl would want to admit the truth of a thing like that? But young Kumar was not as clever as he thought. That kind of so-called educated Indian never was. So arrogant and stupid had he become that he stole her bicycle and hadn't the common sense to leave it even a short distance from his own house. Perhaps he thought it didn't matter because by morning he expected the British would all be fighting for their lives. For one other thing was certain. A vain boy like that, for all his so-called English ways, was almost certainly playing a treacherous part in the uprising. Ah no, waste no pity on young Kumar. Whatever he got while in the hands of the police he deserved. And waste no pity on her either. She also got what she deserved.

This is what the English said. I spoke of it to Anna Klaus. Anna was fond of Miss Manners. It was Anna Klaus who treated her after the assault. I did not ask her the truth of the other rumour that went round. That Anna Klaus had told the Deputy Commissioner that in her opinion Miss Manners, before the assault, had not been *intacta*. For what could this prove either way about the affair of Bibighar? No doubt the Deputy Commissioner had his reasons for feeling he had to ask Dr Klaus the question. If he asked it. There was, you see, after everything was over, and the English had re-established their control, there was for a while, before other subjects of gossip took it out of their minds, a desire in Mayapore to destroy Miss Manners, her reputation and her memory.

And perhaps they would have succeeded. Except for this one fact. That Mayapore is an Indian town. And after a while when tempers had cooled and the English had forgotten the twenty-one-day wonder of the affair in the Bibighar, the Indians still remembered it. They did not understand it. Perhaps because of the punishments people said had been exacted they would have preferred to forget it too. But out of it, out of all its mysteries, to them there seemed to be at least one thing that emerged, perhaps not clearly, but insistently, like an ache in an old wound that had healed itself. That Daphne Manners had loved them. And had not betrayed them, even when it seemed that they had betrayed her. Few Indians doubted that she had indeed been raped by men of their own race. Only they did not believe that among the boys arrested there was even one of those responsible. And this, they felt, was a belief they held with her. A cross, if you like, that they shared with her. And so, after the event, honoured her for the things she was reported to have said which shocked them at the time as much as they shocked the English. And particularly they remembered how she had said: For all I know they could have been British soldiers with their faces blacked.

Well! What courage it took to say that! In those days! When the cantonment was full of white soldiers and the Japanese were hammering at the gates down there in Burma, and the British were prone to describe as treachery anything that could not be called patriotic. And you must remember that. That these were special days. That tempers were very short because consciences were shorn. What sort of white Imperial power was it that could be chased out of Malaya and up through Burma by an army of yellow men? It was a question the Indians asked openly. The British only asked it in the unaccustomed stillness of their own hearts. And prayed for time, stability and loyalty, which are not things usually to be reaped without first being sown.

Perhaps, though, your prayers were granted. Because you are a curious people. In the main very conscious, as you walk in the sun, of the length or shortness of the shadows that you cast.

PART FOUR

AN EVENING AT THE CLUB

THE MAYAPORE district of the province is still administered in five sub-divisions as it was in the days of the British. It covers an area of 2,346 square miles. In 1942 the population was one and a quarter million. It stands now, in 1964, at one and a half million, 160,000 of whom live in the town of Mayapore and some 20,000 in the suburb of Banyaganj where the airport is. From the airport there is a daily Viscount service to Calcutta and a twice-weekly Fokker Friendship service to Agra for the Delhi connection. The area in the vicinity of the airport has become the centre of a light industrial factory development. Between Banyaganj and Mayapore there are to be found the modern labour-saving, whitewashed, concrete homes of the new British colony, and then, closer to town still, the old British–Indian Electrical factory, newly extended but still controlled by British capital. From the British–Indian Electrical the traveller who knew Mayapore in the old days and came in by air would find himself on more familiar ground as he passed, in succession, the red-brick Mayapore Technical College which was founded and endowed by Sir Nello Chatterjee, and the cream-stucco Government Higher School. Just beyond the school the railway comes in on the left with the bend of the river and from here the road – the Grand Trunk road – leads directly into the old cantonment and civil lines.

Going from the cantonment bazaar which is still the fashionable shopping centre of Mayapore, along the Mahatma Gandhi road, once styled Victoria road, the traveller will pass the main police barracks on his left and then, on his right, the Court house and the adjacent cluster of buildings, well shaded by trees, that comprised, still comprise, the headquarters of the district administration. Close by, but only to be glimpsed through the gateway in a high stucco wall, similarly shaded, is the bungalow once known as the chummery where three or four of Mr

White's unmarried sub-divisional officers – usually Indians of the uncovenanted provincial civil service – used to live when not on tour in their own allotted areas of the district. Beyond the chummery, on both sides of the road, there are other bungalows whose style and look of spaciousness mark them also as relics of the British days, the biggest being that in which Mr Poulson, assistant commissioner and joint magistrate, lived with Mrs Poulson. Almost opposite the Poulsons' old place is the bungalow of the District Superintendent of Police. A quarter of a mile farther on, the Mahatma Gandhi road meets the south-eastern angle of the large square open space known as the *maidan*, whose velvety short-cropped grass is green during and after the rains but brown at this season. If you continue in a northerly direction, along Hospital road, you come eventually to the Mayapore General Hospital and the Greenlawns nursing home. If you turn left, that is to say west, and travel along Club road you arrive eventually at the Gymkhana. Both the club and hospital buildings can be seen distantly from the T-junction of the old Victoria, Hospital and Club roads. And it is along Club road, facing the *maidan*, that the bungalow of the Deputy Commissioner is still to be found, in walled, arboreal seclusion.

At half-past six in the evening the sun has set behind and starkly silhouetted the trees that shelter the club buildings on the western side of the *maidan*. The sky above the *maidan*, colourless during the day, as if the heat had burnt out its pigment, now undergoes a remarkable transformation. The blue is revealed at last but in tones already invaded by the yellowing refraction of the sun so that it is awash with an astonishing, luminous green that darkens to violet in the east where night has already fallen and reddens in the west where it is yet to come. There are some scattered trees on the edge of the *maidan*, the homes of the wheeling sore-throated crows which Lady Chatterjee says were once referred to by an American woman as 'those durn birds'. Certainly, in India, they are ubiquitous. Driving slowly down Club road with Lady Chatterjee, in a grey Ambassador that belongs to a lawyer called Srinivasan whom one has not met but is about to, one might indulge in the fancy of a projection from the provable now to the hallowed then, between which the one sure animated connection is provided by the crows, the familiar spirits of dead white sahibs and living black inheritors alike. At this hour the *maidan* is well populated by an Indian middle class that enjoys the comparative cool of the evening. There are even women and young girls. They stroll or squat and talk, and children play games. But the overall impression is of the whiteness of men's clothes and caps and of boys' shirts, a whiteness which, like the brown of the grass, has been touched by the evening light to a pink as subtle as that of that extraordinary bird, the flamingo. There is a hush, a sense emanating from those taking the air of their — well, yes, a sense of their what? Of their self-consciousness at having overstepped some ancient, invisible mark? Or is this a sense conveyed only to an Englishman, as a result of his residual awareness of a racial privilege now officially extinct, so that, borne clubwards at the invitation of a Brahmin lawyer, on a Saturday evening, driven by a Muslim chauffeur in the company of a Rajput lady, through the quickly fading light that holds lovely old Mayapore suspended between the day and the dark, bereft of responsibility and therefore of any sense of dignity other than that which he may be able to muster in himself, as himself, he may feel himself similarly suspended, caught up by his own people's history and the thrust of a current that simply would not wait for them wholly to comprehend its force, and he may then sentimentally recall, in passing, that the *maidan* was once sacrosanct to the Civil and Military, and respond, fleetingly, to the tug of a vague generalized regret that the *maidan* no longer looks as it did once, when at this time of day it was empty of all but a few late riders cantering homeward.

Not that the *maidan* did not find itself in those days — on certain occasions — even more densely populated than it is this evening. The British held their annual gymkhana here, and their Flower Show, and it was the scene of displays such as that put on by the military complete with band in aid of War Week, which Daphne Manners attended with other girls from the Mayapore General Hospital and several young officers from the military lines, which, like St Mary's Church, are to be seen on the far side of the *maidan*. The flower show is still held, Lady Chatterjee says; indeed until five years ago she exhibited in it herself; but the roses that used to be grown by English women who felt far from home and had infrequent hopes of European leave are no longer what they were and most of the space in the marquees is taken up with flowering shrubs and giant vegetables.

The gymkhana, too, is still an annual event because Mayapore is still a military station, one – that is to say – with a certain formal respect for tradition. Cricket week draws the biggest crowds, bigger even than in the old days, but then any event on the *maidan* now is bound to be more crowded, because although the British gymkhanas, flower shows and cricket weeks were also attended by Indians, that attendance was regulated by invitation or by the cost of the ticket, and the *maidan* was then enclosed by an outer picket of stakes and rope and an inner picket of poles and hessian (except in the case of the cricket when the hessian had to be dispensed with in the practical as well as aesthetic interests of the game) – pickets which effectively conveyed to the casual passer-by the fact that something private was going on. Nowadays there are no pickets other than those – as at the gymkhana, for instance – whose purpose is to separate the spectators from the participants, and there are influential Indians in Mayapore, the heirs to civic pride, who feel that it is a mistake to leave the *maidan* thus open to invasion by any Tom, Dick and Harry. Last year's gymkhana [Lady Chatterjee explains] was ruined by the people who wandered about on those parts of the *maidan* where the gymkhana was not being held but got mixed up with the people who had paid for seats and even invaded the refreshment tents in the belief that they were open to all. So great was the confusion that the club secretary, a Mr Mitra, offered to resign, but was dissuaded from such a drastic course of action when his committee voted by a narrow margin to reinstate the old system of double enclosure in future. As for the cricket, well, on two occasions in the past five years, the players walked off in protest at the rowdyism going on among the free-for-all spectators, and the last time this happened the spectators invaded the field in retaliation to protest against the players' high-handedness. There followed a pitched battle which the police had to break up with *lathi* charges just as they had in the days when the battle going on was of a more serious nature.

From problems such as these the British living in Mayapore today naturally remain aloof – so far as one can gather from Lady Chatterjee (who, when questioned on such delicate matters, has a habit of sitting still and upright, answering briefly and then changing the subject). It is rare (or so one deduces from her reluctance to swear that it is not) to see any member of the English colony at a public event on the *maidan*. They do not exhibit at the flower show. They do not compete at the gymkhana. They do not play cricket there. There would seem to be an unwritten law among them that the *maidan* is no longer any concern of theirs, no longer even to be spoken of except as a short cut to describing something mutually recognizable as alien. Indeed, you might ask one of them (for instance the English woman who sits with another in the lounge-bar of the Gymkhana club, turning over the pages of a none-too-recent issue of the *Sunday Times* Magazine – today's fashionable equivalent of *The Tatler* or *The Onlooker*) whether she went to the flower show last month and be met with a look of total incomprehension, have the question patted back like a grubby little ball that has lost its bounce, be asked, in return, as if one had spoken in a foreign language she has been trained in but shown and felt no special aptitude or liking for: 'Flower show?' and to explain, to say then, 'Why yes – the flower show on the *maidan*,' will call nothing forth other than an upward twitch of the eyebrows and a downward twitch of the mouth, which, after all, is voluble enough as an indication that one has suggested something ridiculous.

Apart from this Englishwoman and her companion there are several other English people in the lounge. But Lady Chatterjee is the only Indian and she has only sat where she is sitting (bringing her guest with her) because the first person met, as the club was entered and found not yet to house Mr Srinivasan, was an Englishman called Terry who had been playing tennis and greeted her gaily, with a reproach that she came to the club too seldom and must have a drink while she waited for her official host and so had led her and her house-guest to the table where the two English ladies already sat and then gone off to shower and change, leaving Lady Chatterjee wrapped in her saree, the stranger in his ignorance, and the table in awkward silence punctuated only by Lady Chatterjee's attempts at explanations to the guest of his surroundings and his attempts to engage Terry's waiting ladies in a small talk that grows large and pregnant with *lacunae*, for want of simple politeness.

A question arises in one's mind about the extent to which the club has changed since Daphne Manners's day. The servants still wear white turbans beribboned to match the wide sashes that nip in the waists of their knee-length white coats. White trousers flap baggily above their bare brown feet, and stir old memories of padding docile service. Perhaps in the decor of this particular lounge-bar, change of an ephemeral nature may be seen: the formica-topped counter instead of the old wood that needed polishing, glazed chintz curtains decorated with spiral abstractions instead of cabbage roses, and chairs whose severe Scandinavian welcome brings the old cushioned-wicker comfort gratefully back to the mind.

But it would be foolish to suppose that such contemporaneity is a manifestation of anything especially significant, or to jump to the conclusion that the obvious preference shown for this room by the handful of English members present proves, in itself, their subconscious determination to identify themselves only with what is progressive and therefore superior. This lounge-bar, giving on to a verandah from which the tennis can be watched, was always the favourite of the Mayapore ladies, and for the moment at any rate the only ladies in the club, apart from Lady Chatterjee, are English. If Indian ladies on the whole are still happier at home, who but they are to blame for the look the room has of being reserved for Europeans?

But then, why are there no Indian men in the room either? And why are some of the Englishmen not sitting with their own women in the lounge-bar but standing in the other room where drinks are served, talking to Indian men? And why do they manage to convey (even at a distance, in the glimpse you have of them between square pillars across the passage and through wide open doors to the old smoking-room) a sense of almost old-maidish decorum, of physical fastidiousness unnatural to men when in the company of their own sex? Why, whenever one of them breaks away, crosses the passage and enters the lounge-bar to rejoin his lady, is there presently a rather too noisy laugh from him and a shrug and secret little smile from her? Why does he now exude the aggressive, conscious masculinity that seemed to be held in abeyance in the smoking-room?

The arrival in the lounge-bar of a grey-haired, pale-brown man of some sixty-odd years puts only a temporary stop to such private speculations. Mr Srinivasan is of medium height, thin, punctilious in manner. His skin has a high polish. He is immaculately turned out. The light-weight suit, the collar and tie, point another interesting difference. The inheritors come properly dressed but the Englishmen expose thick bare necks and beefy arms. Mr Srinivasan makes a formal old-fashioned apology for being late, for having failed to arrive first and greet his guests. He also makes a joke (once current among the English) about Mayapore time which it seems is still generally reckoned to be half-an-hour in arrear of Indian Standard. One gets up to shake his hand, and meets the mild but penetrating gaze that reveals a readiness to withstand the subtlest insult that an experience-sharpened sensibility is capable of detecting. Lady Chatterjee who addresses him as Vassi, says, 'You know Terry Grigson's wife, of course?' and Srinivasan bows in the direction of the English woman who, still protectively immersed in the shallow enchantment of the *Sunday Times* Magazine achieves a token emergence by a slight lift of the head (which would be a look at Mr Srinivasan if the eyelids did not simultaneously lower) and by a movement of the lips (that might be 'Good evening' if they actually opened more than a gummy fraction). Her companion, also introduced, nods, and being younger and less inhibited perhaps by ancient distinctions looks as if she might be drawn into the general conversation, but Mrs Grigson, with a perfect sense of timing, turns the *Sunday Times* Magazine towards her and points out some extraordinary detail of Coventry Cathedral so that they are then both lost in the illustrated complexities of modern Anglo-Saxon art; and the uncharitable thought occurs that, for the English, art has anyway always had its timely, occupational value.

And it could occur to you, too, that Mr Srinivasan is not at ease in the lounge-bar, that if he had only managed to conduct his affairs in accordance with Indian Standard instead of Mayapore time he would have been waiting at the entrance when his second best car, the Ambassador, drove up and deposited its passengers, and would then have taken them into the old smoking-room, not had to leave them to the jovial Terry Grigson whose wife finds nothing to laugh about but with whom Mr Srinivasan and his guests are momentarily stuck, for politeness' sake, at least until Terry comes back from the showers and changing-room –

– as he does, beaming and raw-faced, in a creased bush shirt and floppy creased grey trousers, but not before Mr Srinivasan with a thin, almost tubercular finger, has summoned a bearer and asked everybody what they are drinking and sent the bearer off to collect it, having been answered even by Mrs Grigson, and by her companion who taking her cue from Mrs Grigson also said, 'Nothing for me, thank you.' Terry comes back between the sending away of the bearer with the curtailed order and his return with a tray of three lonely gins and tonics, by which time Terry has also been asked by Mr Srinivasan what he will drink, thanked him, and said, 'I'll go a beer.' When the gins and tonics arrive and Srinivasan says to the bearer, 'And a beer for Mr Grigson,' Mrs Grigson pushes her empty glass at Terry and says, 'Order me another of these, Terry, will you?' which he does, with a brief, almost private gesture at the bearer. The other woman, lacking Mrs Grigson's nerve for studied insult, would go drinkless did Terry not say, while Srinivasan talks to Lili Chatterjee, 'What about you, Betty?' which enables her to shrug, grimace, and say, 'Well, I suppose I might as well.' Since no money passes and no bills are yet presented for signing, one wonders who in fact will pay for them, but trusts – because Grigson looks almost self-consciously trustworthy – that he will see to it afterwards that Mr Srinivasan's bar account is not debited with a charge it seems his wife and her friend would rather die than have an Indian settle.

And now, perhaps abiding by yet another unwritten rule, perhaps having even received some secret, clan-gathering sign, a dumpy Englishwoman at an adjacent table leans across and asks Mrs Grigson a question which causes Mrs Grigson to incline her angular body by a degree or two and with this inclination fractionally shift the position of her chair, so that by a narrow but perceptible margin she succeeds in dissociating herself from those with whom she actually shares a table. It is difficult to hear what it is that so arouses her interest, because Lili Chatterjee, Mr Srinivasan and (to his lone, team-captain's credit) Mr Grigson are also talking with animation, and the stranger can only observe and make possibly erroneous deductions: possibly erroneous but not probably. There is nothing so inwardly clear as social rebuff – a rebuff which in this case is also directed at the stranger because he has arrived with one Indian as the guest of another.

And in the momentary hiatus of not knowing exactly what it

is that anyone is talking about, one may observe Terry Grigson's off-handsome face and see that old familiar expression of strain, of deep-seated reservation that qualifies the smile and points up the diplomatic purpose; a purpose which, given a bit more time, may not prevail against the persistence of his sulky segregationist wife. And this, perhaps, is a pity, considering all the chat that goes on at home about the importance of trade and exports and of making a good impression abroad.

'Well no,' Terry Grigson says, in answer to Mr Srinivasan's for-form's-sake inquiry whether he and his wife will join the trio of Srinivasan, Lili Chatterjee and her house-guest for dinner at the club, 'It's very kind of you, but we're going on to Roger's farewell and have to get back and change.'

The Roger referred to is, one gathers, the retiring managing director of British–Indian Electrical. Almost every month one more member of this transient European population ups stakes, retires, returns to England or moves on to another station. For each farewell, however, there is a housewarming, or a party to mark the occasion of a wife's arrival to join her husband in the place where for the next year or two he will earn his living. Whatever that living actually is – with the British–Indian Electrical, with one of the other industrial developments, or teaching something abstruse at the Mayapore Technical College, it will be earned by someone considered superiorly equipped to manage, guide, execute or instruct. He will be a member of that new race of Sahibs. He will be, in whatsoever field, an Expert.

'There is actually a most interesting but undoubtedly apocryphal story about the status of English experts in India nowadays,' Mr Srinivasan says in his rather high-pitched but melodious lawyer's voice when the party in the lounge-bar has been broken up by the quick-downing by Terry Grigson of his beer and by the ladies of their gin-fizzes, and their departure to change into clothes that will be more suitable for the purpose of bidding Roger God-speed. Upon that departure Mr Srinivasan has led Lady Chatterjee and the stranger across the lounge, through the pillared passage and the open doors into the comfortable old smoking-room that has club chairs, potted palms, fly-blown hunting prints and – in spite of the spicy curry-smells wafted in from the adjacent dining-room by the action of the

leisurely turning ceiling fans – an air somehow evocative of
warmed-up gravy and cold mutton. In here, only one Englishman now remains. He glances at Mr Srinivasan's party – but
retains the pale mask of his anonymity, a mask that he seems to
wear as a defence against the young, presumably inexpert Indians
who form the group of which he is the restrained, withheld,
interrogated, talked-at centre. It is because one asks Mr Srinivasan who this white man is, and because Mr Srinivasan says he
does not know but supposes he is a 'visiting expert' that the
interesting but perhaps apocryphal story is told.

'There was,' Mr Srinivasan says, 'this Englishman who was
due to go home. An ordinary tourist actually. He fell into conversation with a Hindu businessman who for months had been
trying to get a loan from Government in order to expand his
factory. A friend had told the businessman, "But it is impossible
for you to get a loan from Government because you are not
employing any English technical adviser." So the businessman
asked himself: "Where can I get such an adviser and how much
will it cost me seeing that he would expect two or three years'
guaranteed contract at minimum?" Then he met this English
tourist who had no rupees left. And the Hindu gentleman said,
"Sir, I think you are interested in earning rupees five thousand?"
The English tourist agreed straight away. "Then all you will do,
sir," the Hindu gentleman said, "is to postpone departure for
two weeks while I write to certain people in New Delhi." Then
he telegraphed Government saying, "What about loan? Here
already I am at the expense of employing technical expert from
England and there is no answer coming from you." To which at
once he received a telegraph reply to the effect that his factory
would be inspected by representatives of Government on such
and such a day. So he went back to the English tourist and gave
him five thousand rupees and said, "Please be at my factory on
Monday, are you by any chance knowing anything about radio
components?" To which the English tourist replied, "No,
unfortunately, only I am knowing about ancient monuments."
"No matter," the Hindu gentleman said, "on Monday whenever I jog your elbow simply be saying – 'This is how it is done
in Birmingham.'" So on Monday there was this most impressive
meeting in the executive suite of the factory between the Hindu
businessman who knew all about radio component manufacture,

the English tourist who knew nothing and the representatives of Government who also knew nothing. Before lunch they went round the premises and sometimes one of the officials of Government asked the Englishman, "What is happening here?" and the Hindu gentleman jogged the Englishman's elbow, and the Englishman who was a man of honour, a man to be depended upon to keep his word said, "This is how we do it in Birmingham." And after a convivial lunch the Government representatives flew back to Delhi and the English tourist booked his flight home first class by BOAC and within a week the Hindu businessman was in receipt of a substantial Government loan with a message of goodwill from Prime Minister Nehru himself.'

And one notes, marginally, that the new wave of satire has also broken on the Indian shore and sent minor flood-streams into the interior, as far as Mayapore.

Mr Srinivasan is the oldest man in the smoking-room.

'Yes, of course,' he says, speaking of the younger men – the Indians, 'they are all businessmen. No sensible young man in India today goes into civil administration or into politics. These fellows are all budding executives.'

Several of the budding executives wear bush shirts, but the shirts are beautifully laundered. Their watch-straps are of gold-plated expanding metal. One of them comes over and asks Lady Chatterjee how she is. He declines Srinivasan's invitation to have a drink and says he must be dashing off to keep a date. He is a bold, vigorous-looking boy. His name is Surendranath. When he has gone Mr Srinivasan says, 'There is a case in point. His father is old ICS on the judicial side. But young Surendranath is an electrical engineer, or rather a boy with a degree in electrical engineering who is working as personal assistant to the Indian assistant sales director of British–Indian Electrical. He took his degree in Calcutta and studied sales techniques in England, which is a reversal of the old order when the degree would have been taken in London and the sales technique either ignored or left to be picked up as one went blundering along from one shaky stage of prestige and influence to another. He is commercially astute and a very advanced young man in everything except his private life, that is to say his forthcoming marriage, which he has been quite happy to leave his parents to arrange, because he trusts to their judgment in such relatively minor matters.

'The thin, studious-looking boy is also a case in point. His name is Desai. His father was interned with me in 1942 because we were both leading members of the local Congress party sub-committee. His father told me last year when we chanced to meet in New Delhi that young Desai said to him once, "Just because you were in jail you think this entitles you to believe you know everything?" They were quarrelling about Mr Nehru whom this mild-looking young man had called a megalomaniac who had already outlived his usefulness by 1948 but gone on living disastrously in the past and dragging India back to conditions worse than in the days of the British because he knew nothing of world economic structure and pressures. My old friend Desai was secretary to the minister for education and social services in the provincial Congress Ministry that took office in 1937, and resigned in 1939. Before becoming secretary to the Minister he was in the uncovenanted provincial civil service and a lawyer like myself. But his son, this young man over there, is a potential expert on centrifugal pumps and says that people like us are to blame for India's industrial and agricultural backwardness because instead of learning everything we could about really important things we spent our time playing at politics with an imperial power any fool could have told us would beat us at that particular game with both hands tied. Such accusations are a salutary experience to old men like me who at the time thought they were doing rather well.

'Also you will have noticed, I think, that there are no old men in this room except for myself. Where are my old companions in political crime? Lili, please do not put on your inscrutable Rajput princess face. You know the answer. Dead, gone, retired, or hidden in our burrows grinding the mills of the administration exceeding slow but not always exceeding fine. You might find one or two of us at the other club. Didn't you know about the other club? Oh well, that is an interesting story. We sit with the lady whose husband was one of the founder members.'

'Nello put up money but rarely went,' Lady Chatterjee says.

'Also he chose the name, isn't it?'

Sometimes one could suspect Mr Srinivasan of deliberate self-parody.

Lady Chatterjee explains, 'They wanted to call it the MHC. All Nello did was get them to drop the H.'

'So MHC became MC, which stands simply for Mayapore Club. The H would have made it the Mayapore Hindu Club. No matter. An English wag anyway dubbed it the Indian Club which I believe is an instrument for body-building. Also it was known among Indian wits as the Mayapore Chatterjee Club, or MCC for short. But whatever you called it it was always the *wrong* club. Of course it was originally meant to be an English-type club for Indians who were clubbable, but it was not for nothing that the H for Hindu was suggested. It became a place where the word Hindu was actually more important than the word Club. And Hindu did not mean Congress. No, no. Please be aware of the distinction. In this case Hindu meant Hindu Mahasabha. Hindu nationalism. Hindu narrowness. It meant rich banias with little education, landowners who spoke worse English than the youngest English sub-divisional officer his eager but halting Hindi. It meant sitting without shoes and with your feet curled up on the chair, eating only horrible vegetarian dishes and drinking disgusting fruit juice. Mayapore, you understand, is not Bombay, and consequently the Mayapore club was not like the Willingdon club which was founded by your viceroy Lord Willingdon in a fit of rage because the Indian guests he invited – in ignorance – to a private banquet at the Royal Yacht Club were turned away from the doors in their Rolls-Royces before he cottoned on to what was happening. Ah well, perhaps dear old Nello imagined in Mayapore a little Willingdon? But what happened? One by one the type of Indian who would have loved the club because it was the nearest he was then able to get to enjoying the fruits of what he had been educated up by your people to see as just one but an important aspect of civilized life – one by one this type of Indian stopped going to the Mayapore and with each abstention the feet of the bania were more firmly established under the table – or rather, upon the seat of his chair –

'I think they are ready in the dining-room.'

'The point is, you see,' Mr Srinivasan says, having apologized for the absence of beef, the omnipresence of mutton, 'that these old men, my peers, my old companions in crime and adversity, those who aren't dead, those who are still living in Mayapore, now find themselves somehow less conspicuous at the Mayapore club than at the Gymkhana. Just look at the young faces that surround us. So many of these boys are telling us that we cannot expect to dine out for ever on stories of how we fought and got rid of the British, that some of us never dine out at all, except with each other, like old soldiers mulling over their long-ago battles. And when it comes to spending a few hours at a club, most of us – although not I – choose the company of men who rest on laurels of a different kind, men with whom it is easier to identify than it is with the members here because here everyone is go-ahead and critical of our past. I mean, for instance, that it is easier for us to identify with men like Mr Romesh Chand Gupta Sen, now a venerable gentleman of nearly eighty years and still going every morning to his office above his warehouse in the Chillianwallah Bazaar. To the chagrin of his sons and grandsons, I should add. And on one evening a week to the Mayapore club to discuss business prospects with men who were not interested in politics then, and now are interested neither in technical experts nor in theories of industrial expansion, but instead interested as they always were simply in making money and being good Hindus.'

There have been prawn cocktails. Now the curried mutton arrives. The chief steward comes to oversee its serving, but breaks off from this duty to walk over and greet a party of English, two of the men and two of the women who were in the lounge-bar. The steward indicates the table he has reserved for them, but they ignore him and select another more to their liking. Both the men are still wearing shorts. Their legs are bare to the ankles. The women have plump, mottled arms, and wear sleeveless cotton shifts. Without the knitted cardigans you feel they would put on at home of an evening over these summer dresses they have a peeled, boiled look. They are young. They sit together – opposite their husbands – an act of involuntary segregation that by now is probably becoming familiar to the Indians as they get used to a new race of sahibs and memsahibs from Stevenage and Luton but may still puzzle them when they recollect how critical the old-style British were of the Indian habit of keeping men and women so well separated that a mixed party was almost more than an English host and hostess could bear to contemplate.

The dining-room, like the smoking-room, has probably changed little since Daphne Manners's time. It is a square room, with a black and white tiled floor, and walls panelled in oak to shoulder height, and whitewashed above. Three square pillars, similarly panelled to the same height, support the ceiling at apparently random but presumably strategic points. There are something like a score of tables, some round, some rectangular, each with its white starched cloth, its electro-plated cutlery and condiment tray, its mitred napkins, its slim chromium flower vase holding a couple of asters, its glass jug filled with water and protected by a weighted muslin cover. There is a large Tudor-style fireplace whose black cavity is partly hidden by a framed tapestry screen. Above the fireplace there is a portrait of Mr Nehru looking serene in a perplexed sort of way. One can assume that when Daphne Manners dined here the frame contained a coloured likeness of George VI wearing a similar expression. Four fans are suspended from the ceiling on slender tubes that whip unsteadily with the movement of the turning blades. There are two arched exits, one leading into the smoking-room and the other into the main hall. There is also a third exit but that only leads into the kitchens. Against the wall, close to the kitchen exit, stands a monumental oak sideboard or dumb-waiter. On its top tier there are spare napkins, knives, forks and spoons, water-jugs, and on the lower tier, baskets of bread, bowls of fruit, bottles of sauce and spare cruets. Light is provided by stubby candle-style wall-brackets and a couple of wooden chandeliers with parchment shades, and during daytime by the windows that look on to the porticoed verandah at the front of the club, windows whose curtains are now pulled back and are open to let in the night air.

Well: it can be pictured all those years ago, especially on a Saturday evening, with a band thumping in the lounge-bar from which the old wicker tables and chairs have been cleared, and the dining-room rearranged to provide for a cold buffet supper. In the flagged yard at the back that fringes the tennis courts there are coloured lights slung in the trees, and couples used to sit out there to cool off between dances, waiting for the next foxtrot or quickstep. Some swam in the little floodlit pool that lies behind

the changing- and shower-rooms, the pool which, tonight, is in
darkness, in need of scraping (Mr Srinivasan says as he conducts
his guests on a tour of inspection after the ice-cream that
followed the curried mutton), and is seldom used because it is
open to all and neither race seems particularly to fancy the idea
of using it when it can't be guaranteed that the person last using
it was clean. There is a story that two or three years ago an
Englishman emptied all the chamber pots from the ablution
cubicles into it.

'But I was telling you earlier on,' Mr Srinivasan says, leading the
way back through the now deserted lounge-bar to the smoking-
room – which has filled up and even sports a few ladies in sarees
who are, one gathers, military wives – 'I was telling you about
the kind of man whom old fellows like myself who were reared
on briefs and files and nurtured on politics now find it easier to
fit in with than we find it here at the Gymkhana.'

Mr Srinivasan raises his finger and a bearer appears and takes
an order for coffee and brandy.

'And I mentioned Romesh Chand Gupta Sen,' he continues.
'He is a case in point. With Romesh Chand it has always been
a question of business first and politics last. Well, not even last.
Nowhere. He has made three fortunes, the first during the old
peace-time days, the second during the war and the third since
independence. None of his sons was allowed to continue education beyond Government Higher School. I asked him why this
was. He said, "To succeed in life it is necessary to read a little,
to write less, to be able to calculate a simple multiplication and
to develop a sharp eye for the main chance." He married a girl
who could not even write her name. She could not run a household either, but his mother trained her up to that, which is what
Hindu mothers are for. When his younger brother married a girl
called Shalini Kumar, Romesh prophesied no good coming of
the union, because she came of a family who allowed education
even if they did not wholly believe in it, and as a result Shalini's
brother went to live in England and Shalini herself could write
beautifully in English. She was widowed at an early age. You
may find this difficult to believe, but on her husband's death the
women of Romesh Chand's family did their best to persuade
her to defy the law and become *suttee*. Of course she refused.

What woman in her right mind wants to burn alive on her husband's funeral pyre? Also she refused to leave her dead husband's house in Chillianwallah Bagh. I tell you this because it is perhaps relevant to your interest?

'It was Romesh Chand who insisted that that Anglicized nephew of hers, Hari Kumar, should be brought back from England when her brother, Hari's father, died and left him homeless and penniless. Actually we suspected Hari's father of committing suicide when he realized he'd come to the end of a series of foolish speculations. Be that as it may, when Mrs Gupta Sen heard the news of her brother's death she went to Romesh and asked him for money that would enable Hari to stay in Berkshire to finish at his public school and go on to a university. This would be, what? 1938. She had almost no means of her own. She lived as a widow, alone in the house in Chillianwallah Bagh, mainly on her brother-in-law Romesh's charity. It was because she had always wanted a son, a child of her own, that she fell in with Romesh's counter-proposal that Hari should be brought home to live with her and learn how to be a good Hindu. To bring about this satisfactory state of affairs Romesh said he would even be willing to pay Hari's passage and increase Mrs Gupta Sen's monthly allowance. She had lived a long time alone, you know, seldom leaving the house. Almost she had become a good Hindu herself.

'She lived with great simplicity. Young Hari must have had a shock. From the outside the house in Chillianwallah Bagh looked modern. I suppose it still does. What I believe you used to call suntrap. All the houses on the Chillianwallah Bagh reclamation and development were put up in the late 'twenties. It was waste ground before then, and was called Chillianwallah Bagh because the land belonged to the estate of a Parsee called Chillianwallah. The Parsees have also always concentrated on business but they are much more westernized, hardly Indians at all. The land was bought from the Chillianwallah heirs by a syndicate of Mayapore businessmen headed by old Romesh Chand, who would never have lived in the sort of modern European-style house that was to be put up there, but saw nothing new-fangled in the anticipated profits. In fact it was to make sure of the amenities for development, such as lighting and water and drainage, and a Government grant-in-aid, that he saw to it his otherwise unsatisfactory younger brother – the one who married Shalini Kumar – got a seat on the Municipal Board. So, in time, up went these concrete suntrap-style monstrosities – suntrap only in the style because with so much sun about it's necessary to keep it out, not trap it, to have very small windows, you see, unless you have wide old-fashioned verandahs. And into one of them, into number twelve, Romesh's brother moved with his wife Shalini, the same house young Hari came to live in nearly ten years later and must have been shocked by, because inside they are dark and airless, with small rooms and steep stairs and no interior plan and Indian-style bathrooms. And in number twelve there was almost no furniture because although Mrs Gupta Sen's husband had bought a lot to go with the house, Romesh paid for it with a loan, and had since sold most of it to pay himself back. The house itself also belonged to him on mortgage. I know these things because I was what in England you would call the family lawyer.

'Yes, you are right. Lili bet me you'd cotton on. Indeed yes. It was I. I was the lawyer Romesh Chand sent for that morning Sister Ludmila went to his office and told him Hari Kumar had been taken away by the police. They thought he was arrested. This, of course, was about six months before my own arrest. It never bothered Romesh that I was politically committed. He understood the uses of politics in the same way that he understood the law of diminishing returns. After I had gone to the police station and found that Hari was already released I went back to my office, sent my clerk with a message to Romesh, and then went on to the house in Chillianwallah Bagh, to find out what it had all been about.

'Hari would not come down from his room to see me. But Mrs Gupta Sen and I were good friends. We always spoke in English. With Romesh I had to talk in Hindi. She said, "Tell Romesh everything was a mistake. There is nothing for him to go to botheration over." I asked her whether it was true, what the police had told me, that Hari had been drunk and taken by that mad woman to what she called her sanctuary. I had not known him ever to drink heavily. He was a great worry to his family but he had always seemed to be sober in his habits. She did not know whether he had been drunk. She said, "But I know that his life here, and therefore mine, is becoming unbearable."

'Young Hari Kumar, you know, was typical of the kind of boy Nello had in mind when he financed and founded the Mayapore club. But by Hari's time it was already choc-a-bloc with the banias looking like squatting Buddhas contemplating the mysteries of profit and loss. And of course there were no women. It wasn't intended to be a club for men only but that is what it had become and has remained. Which is one of the reasons why I am the exception to the rule, a staunch Gymkhana supporter! The lady over there is the wife of Colonel Varma. She is delightful. You must meet her. General and Mrs Mukerji aren't here tonight, but that is because no doubt they are invited to Roger's number one farewell. Next Saturday will be number two farewell and even I am invited to that.'

'So am I,' Lady Chatterjee says. 'I was supposed to go to number one with the other governors of the Technical Coll, but said I couldn't, so I'm at number two as well.'

'Then we will go together? Good. Meanwhile you, my dear fellow, have noticed, I expect, that all the English have now left the club?'

'To go to Roger's?'

'Oh, no. Of your fellow-countrymen who were here this evening only Mr and Mrs Grigson and the lady who was with Mrs Grigson will be at number one party. The Grigsons are senior. The other English you saw were junior. They will go to number two. Roger refers to them as foremen. In fact Roger has been known to call the Gymkhana the Foreman's Club. It was one of the gentlemen of the type Roger refers to as foremen who emptied the chamber pots into the swimming pool. After he had emptied them one of his friends had the idea of making a little Diwali, a parody of our festival of lights. So they got hold of some candles and stuck them into the pots and lighted them and set them afloat. A few of our Indian members who were present complained to the secretary, and one of our youngest and strongest members even complained directly to the gentlemen who were having such an enjoyable time at our expense. But they threatened to throw him into the pool, and used language that I cannot repeat. As an innocent bystander I found the whole situation most interesting. It was an example of the kind of club horseplay we had heard of at second or third hand and a person like myself couldn't help but remember student

rags from his college days. This particular demonstration was
hardly a student rag, however. Of course they were drunk, but
in vino veritas. They were acting without inhibition. Forgive me,
Lili, you find the subject disagreeable. Let us have Colonel
Varma and his wife to join us.'

The colonel is a tall wiry man and his wife a neat wiry woman
who seems to wear traditional Indian costume more for its theatrical effect than for comfort or from conviction. The tough little
shell of skin-thin masculinity that used to harden the outward
appearance of the British military wives also encloses Mrs
Varma. What terror she must strike in the tender heart of every
newly commissioned subaltern! Her wit is sharp, probably as
capable of wounding as her husband's ceremonial sword.
Tonight he is in mufti. They are going to the pictures, the ten
o'clock performance; the English pictures at the Eros, not the
Indian pictures at the Majestic. For a while the talk is of Paris,
because the film is about Paris – the film itself is said to be rotten
but the photography interesting – and then the Varmas say goodbye; Mr Srinivasan's party breaks up and Lili goes to powder
her nose.

'While we wait for Lili,' he says, 'let me show you something –' and leads the way into the black and white tiled hall
where between two mounted buffalo heads there is a closed
mahogany door with brass finger-plates and a brass knob. The
mounted heads and the door all bear inscriptions: the latter on
enamel and the former on ivory. The first buffalo was presented
by Major W. A. Tyrrell-Smith in 1915, and the second by Mr
Brian Lloyd in 1925. The enamel plate on the door bears the
single word: Secretary.

Mr Srinivasan knocks and getting no answer opens the door
and switches on the light and so reveals a small office with an
old roll-top desk and an air of desuetude. 'As the first Indian
secretary of the Gymkhana, from 1947 to 1950 actually, I have
a certain right of entry,' he says and goes to a bookcase in which
a few musty volumes mark the stages of the club's administrative
history. Among them are books bound like ledgers and blocked
on the spine in gilt with the words 'Members' Book', and in
black with the numerals denoting the years covered.

'You would be interested in this,' he says, and takes down the
book imprinted '1939–1945'.

The pages are feint-ruled horizontally in blue and vertically in red to provide columns for the date, the member's name and the name of his guest.

'If you look through the pages you will see the signatures of one or two Indian members. But they were of course all officers who held the King-Emperor's commission. By and large such gentlemen found it only comfortable to play tennis here and then go back to their quarters. The committee were in rather a quandary when King's commissioned Indian officers first began to turn up in Mayapore. It was always accepted that any officer on the station should automatically become a member. Indeed it was compulsory for him to pay his subscription whether he ever entered the place or not. And you could not keep him out if he was an Indian because that would have been to insult the King's uniform. There was talk in the 'thirties of founding another club and reserving the Gymkhana for senior officers, which would have made it unlikely that any Indian officer on station would have been eligible. But the money simply wasn't available. In any case the Indian officers more or less solved the problem themselves by limiting their visits to appearances on the tennis courts. One was never known to swim in the pool, seldom to enter the bar, never to dine. There were plenty of face-saving excuses that both sides could make. The Indian could pretend to be teetotal and to be reluctant to come to the club and not share fully in its real life. The English would accept this as a polite, really very gentlemanly way of not directly referring to the fact that his pay was lower than that of his white fellow-officer and that therefore he could not afford to stand what I believe is still called his whack. If he was married the situation was easier still. The English always assumed that Indian women found it distasteful to be publicly in mixed company and so there was a tacit understanding that a married Indian officer would appear even less frequently than his bachelor colleagues, because he preferred to stay in quarters with his wife.

'And really there was remarkably little bad feeling about all this kind of thing on either side. An Indian who sought and obtained a commission knew what problems he was likely to encounter. Usually it was enough for him to know that he couldn't actually be blackballed at the Gymkhana merely because he was Indian, and enough for the English members to know that he was unlikely to put in any prolonged or embarrassing appearance. And of course British commanding officers could always be relied upon to iron out any difficulties that arose in individual cases. It wasn't until the war began and the station began to fill up not only with a larger number of Indian King's commissioned officers but also with English officers holding emergency commissions that the committee actually had to meet and pass a *rule*. But then happily, you see, a realistic analysis of the situation provided its own solution. In the first place the influx of officers into the station obviously meant a severe strain on the club's facilities. In the second place the new officers were not only holders of temporary commissions but tended to be temporary in themselves, I mean liable to posting at almost any time. And of course among them there were likely to be men called up from all walks of civilian life, men of the type who, well, wouldn't be at home in the atmosphere of the club. And so for once the committee found themselves thinking of ways of keeping out some of their own countrymen as well as Indians. We, who were not eligible, watched all this from the sidelines with great interest. The rule the committee passed was a splendid English compromise. It was to the effect that for the duration of the war special arrangements would need to be made to extend club hospitality to as many officers on station as possible. To do this the compulsory subscription was waived in the case of all but regular officers and two new types of membership were introduced. Officers with temporary or emergency commissions could enjoy either what was called Special Membership, which involved paying the subscription and was meant of course to attract well-brought-up officers who could be assumed to know how to behave, or Privileged Temporary Membership which entitled the privileged temporary member to use the club's facilities on certain specific days of the week but which could be withdrawn without notice. Outwardly the no notice provision was meant to advertise the committee's thoughtful recognition of the temporary nature of war-time postings to the station. What it really meant was that an emergency officer who misbehaved once could be barred from entry thenceforth. The privileged temporary member had to pay his bills on the spot. He also had to pay a cover charge if he used the dining-room and what was called a Club Maintenance Subscription if he used the pool or the tennis courts. He was allowed to bring only one "approved" guest at any one time, for whom he paid an extra cover charge. Approved was officially held to mean approved by the committee but it also meant approved by the man's commanding officer who no doubt made it clear to these young innocents who were in uniform for a specific and limited purpose what kind of guest would be admitted. Officially it was said to be an insurance against a young man bringing the wrong sort of *woman*. Unofficially it meant bringing no Anglo-Indian or Indian woman, and no Anglo-Indian or Indian man unless that man was himself a King's commissioned officer. In any case, the expense of an evening at the club was usually reckoned to have been raised to the level that no war-time temporary officer would be able to afford more than once a month unless he was well-off. This was the period during which Smith's Hotel really flourished. So did the station restaurant, and of course the Mayapore Indian club enjoyed unaccustomed affluence. The Chinese restaurant in the cantonment bazaar made a fortune and you had to book a seat at the Eros Cinema two or three days in advance. As for the old Gymkhana club, well, it had its unhappy experiences, but by and large managed to maintain its air of all-white social superiority.

'The curious anomaly was, though, that even in those expansive days which the die-hards used to refer to as the thin end of the wedge, Indian officers of the civil service, even of the covenanted civil service, were not admitted as guests let alone as members. Which meant that the District and Sessions Judge, dear old Menen, such a distinguished fellow, couldn't enter, even if brought by the Deputy Commissioner. There was no written rule about it. It was simply an unwritten rule rigorously applied by the committee and if you take Menen as a leading example, never challenged by those who were excluded.

'Here in this book, though, you will see that as far back as May the twenty-second, 1939, the Deputy Commissioner, Mr Robin White, had the temerity to bring *to* and the luck to succeed in bringing *in* no less than three Indians who did not hold the King-Emperor's commission – the provincial Minister for Education and Social Services, the Minister's secretary – my old friend Desai – and myself. That is Mr White's own handwriting, of course. Perhaps you can judge character from handwriting? Well, but all this is a long story. We must leave it for tonight. Lili will be looking for us.'

Before the book is closed, though, a flick through the pages relating to 1942 reveals familiar names. The rule of the club has always been that a member signs his name on his first visit and then again on those occasions when he brings a guest. Brigadier Reid's almost illegible signature appears on a date in April; Robin White's on one or two occasions as host to men Mr Srinivasan identifies variously as members of the Secretariat, Revenue Settlement Officers, the Divisional Commissioner, and – once – the Governor and his lady. And there too on several occasions is a curiously rounded and childlike signature easily read as that of Mr Ronald Merrick, the District Superintendent of Police, and, in the same hand, the name of his guest, Miss Daphne Manners.

And on a date in February 1942 a Captain Colin Lindsey signed in, presumably on his first appearance as a temporary privileged member of the Gymkhana Club of Mayapore. Captain Lindsey's signature is steady and sober, unlike the signature that does not actually accompany it, but which one can see, by its side, in the imagination: the signature of his old friend Harry Coomer who round about this time was found drunk by Sister Ludmila in the waste ground where the city's untouchables lived in poverty and squalor.

At night the old cantonment area, the area north of the river, still conveys an idea of space that has only just begun to succumb to the invasion of brick and mortar, the civilizing theories of necessary but discreet colonial urbanization. From the now dark and deserted *maidan*, across which the uninterrupted currents of warm – even voluptuous – air build up an impetus that comes upon the cheek as a faintly perceptible breath of enervating rather than refreshing wind, there issues a darkness of the soul, a certain heaviness that enters the heart and brings to life a sadness such as might grow in, weigh down (year by year until the burden becomes at once intolerable and dear) the body of someone who has become accustomed to but has never quite accepted the purpose or conditions of his exile, and who sees, in the existence of this otherwise meaningless space so curiously and yet so poetically named *maidan*, the evidence of the care and thought of those who preceded him, of their concern for what they remembered as somehow typical of home; the silence and darkness that blessed an enduring acre of unenclosed common which, if nothing else, at least illustrated of its own accord the changing temper of the seasons. With here a house. And there a steeple. And everywhere the sky. Bland blue. Or on the march with armoured clouds. Or grey, to match the grey stone of a Norman church. Or dark: an upturned black steel receptacle for scattered magnetic sparks of light or, depending on the extro-verted or introverted mood, an amazing cyclorama lit only by the twinkling nocturnal points of a precise but incalculable geometry.

And there is, at night, a strengthening of that special smell: a dry, nostril-smarting mixture of dust from the ground and of smoke from dung-fires: a smell that takes some getting used to but which, given time, will become inseparably part of whatever notion the traveller, the exile, the old hand, may have of India as a land of primitive, perhaps even tragic beauty. It is a smell which seems to have no visible source. It is not only the smell of habitations. It is the smell, perhaps, of centuries of the land's experience of its people. It is to be smelt out there on the broad plains as well as here in the town. And because it is also the smell of the plains, to smell it – perhaps a degree or two stronger – as the car turns a corner and passes a roadside stall lighted by a naphtha lamp, only deepens the sense of pervasiveness, of ubiquity, of vastness, of immensity, of endless, endless acres of earth and stone lying beyond the area of the lamp's light.

This is the bigger car, the Studebaker. This is the long way home: northwards along the western boundary of the *maidan*, with the old Smith's Hotel on the left, built in the Swiss chalet style and dimly lit as befits an institution that has years behind it but isn't finished yet. This is Church road. It leads to St Mary's and to the military lines. It is the road that old Miss Crane cycled along, every Sunday, rain or shine, and it cannot have changed much, although the banyan trees that shade it during the day and clasp branches overhead to make a theatrically lit green tunnel at night, must have sunk a few more roots during the last twenty years. Church road is an extension of the Mandir Gate Bridge road and at this hour the car is slowed by the plodding pro-cessions of carts drawn by white humped oxen lumbering

homeward, back to the villages on the plains to the north of
Mayapore. The bells on their necks can be heard through the
open windows of the Studebaker – dulled by but insistent on
the hot wind created by mechanical movement. The carts return
empty of produce. The produce has been sold in the Chillianwallah bazaar. Now they are more lightly loaded with private
purchases and the farmers' children, most of whom lie huddled,
asleep, although a few sit upright staring with the fixity of
waking dreams into the headlights.

For a moment, as the Studebaker half-circles the roundabout
and takes the right-hand road along the northern edge of the
maidan, the spire of St Mary's may carry the stranger into a
waking dream of his own; so English it is. So perfect. It must,
surely, be very like the church in a district of the Punjab which
Miss Crane entered all those years ago, looking for an image of
herself that would not diminish her. The same grey stone. The
same safe comfortable look of housing the spirit of England's
personal protector. But few English now attend the services.
This has become the church of the Anglo-Indian community.
The minister is the Reverend A. M. Ghosh. Is there, perhaps, a
congregational joke about his holiness?

Close by St Mary's and its churchyard is the minister's house.
Like the church it is, tonight, in darkness. A few bungalows lie
back on the left, continuing the line of building from St Mary's
corner to the beginning of the military lines opposite the *maidan*.
From the air, by day, these are revealed as a geometrical complex
of roads and clusters of old and new buildings: the red, tree-
shaded Victorian barracks lying closest to the road the Studebaker travels on; the newer low concrete blocks farther back.
But from the road, at night, the impression is of space, infrequent
habitation marked by lonely points of light. It is not until farther
on that the large palladian-style mansion of the old artillery mess
comes into view, and the first jawans are seen: two soldiers on
guard duty at a white pole barrier that denies free entry by a left-
hand turn into the dark. The old artillery mess is now the area
headquarters. In 1942 it was the headquarters of the brigade
commanded by Brigadier Reid. Once past it, the sense of space
diminishes. Tree-backed stucco walls, and side-roads lit by infrequent street-lamps, mark the neat suburban area of the senior
officers' bungalows. And then, ahead, is the main block of the

ocean-liner-lit Mayapore General Hospital. The Studebaker turns right, into Hospital road, the road that runs along the eastern edge of the *maidan* and leads back to the T-junction of Hospital road, Club road and Mahatma Gandhi road – once Victoria road – the principal highway of the civil lines.

'Let us,' Mr Srinivasan says, 'extend the tour a little more. It is not very late,' and directs the driver to go on down past the chummery, the Court house, and the police barracks, into the cantonment bazaar and then to turn right again following the route that Sister Ludmila used to take, to and from the Imperial (now the State) Bank of India, through the narrower roads where the Eurasians lived in small bungalows backing on to the installations of the railway and out again, with a left turn, into the Mandir Gate Bridge road, past the main mission school and the church of the mission (both of which still flourish) to the level crossing where the car is halted to wait for the mail train that comes from the west and is due at any moment.

Beyond the level crossing lies the bridge and beyond the bridge the black town, still well-lit and lively. The steps leading up from the river to the Tirupati temple are floodlit by a neon standard. There are men walking up and down them, coming from, going into the temple precincts by the river gate. From here the river smell lying upon the warm air enters the open windows of the stationary car.

'They always close the level crossing gates,' Mr Srinivasan complains, 'at the precise moment the train is officially scheduled, even if they know jolly well it is half an hour late. Let me fill in the time by telling you the story of how Robin White took the Minister for Education and me and my old friend Desai to the club in May 1939.

'We were all at the DC's bungalow and at six in the evening after three hard hours of conference, Robbie said to us, "How about a drink at the club?" Naturally we thought he meant the Mayapore, but then he said, "The Gymkhana." We were astonished. The Minister begged to be excused. Perhaps he thought it was a joke. But Mr White would not hear of it. He said, "It is all arranged, the car is outside. Just come for an hour." So off we went. It was the first time I had entered, the first time any Indian civilian had entered. Also it was the last because Mr White was stopped by the committee from repeating his social indiscretion. But on the night when we arrived, you should have seen the porter's face when he opened the car door and saw us! Robbie said to the porter, "Hossain, tell the secretary I am here with the Minister for Education, and his party." It was quite a moment! We walked, Desai and I, slowly in the wake of Mr White and the Minister, slowly because Robbie was obviously giving the porter time to run in and find the secretary. On the verandah we all stopped and although it was nearly dark Robbie made great play of standing there and pointing out the amenities of the club's grounds, in fact he kept us there until he judged that the secretary had been found and warned. By now, you understand, it was clear to me that the visit had not been arranged at all, only considered as a possibility. The Deputy Commissioner had waited with typical British restraint to see what kind of a man the Minister for Education was before committing himself to the risky enterprise of taking him to the club. But it was all right. The Minister had turned out to be Wellington and Balliol, and to share with Mr Deputy Commissioner a love of Shakespeare, Mr Dryden and the novelist Henry James, as well as a concern for the Government Higher School and the schools run by the District Boards. Also they enjoyed a disagreement about Mr Rudyard Kipling whom Mr White thought poorly of but the Minister, anticipating Mr T. S. Eliot, thought well of. It is always necessary to have a mutual irritant, it's the best way of testing the toughness of individual fibre.

'And so the secretary came out. A man called Taylor, an ex-ranker of the Cavalry who had achieved gentleman's status by being commissioned Lieutenant Quartermaster and official club status because what he didn't know about organizing the annual gymkhana could have been written on the face of a threepenny bit. I saw him coming from his office into the hall. Robbie White had a great talent for seeing through the back of his head. He turned round and called out, "Oh, hello, Taylor, we have the honour of entertaining representatives of our provincial government. Allow me, Minister, to introduce you to our most important member, the Secretary, Lieutenant Taylor." Which left poor Taylor in an impossible position, because although he hated Indians he adored Deputy Commissioners and being thought important. Which Robbie knew. Robbie was a senior member of the committee but he had been clever enough to hold his fire for months, until the proper opportunity arose. I mean the opportunity to bring as guests men whom it was not socially inadmissible to describe as honourable. Even a provincial minister of state, after all, is a minister of state, and however much the run-of-the-mill English colonial might object to his colour, it couldn't be denied that the Minister had been appointed as the result of a democratic election, an election held with the full approval and authority of the King-Emperor's Governor-General. And all in accordance with the *official* English policy to promote their Indian Empire by easy stages to self-governing dominion status.

'All the same, Robbie White was sticking his neck out. A club was a club, a private institution no outsider could enter, even as a guest of the Deputy Commissioner unless a club official allowed it. Remember Lord Willingdon and the Royal Yacht Club fiasco in Bombay! But Robin knew his man. The secretary looked sick, but he was afraid to make a scene. He tried to lead us into the little ante-room along the corridor from here, but Robbie knew he had got us in now, so he stalked straight into the smoking-room and totally ignored the silence that fell like a stone.

'My dear fellow, shall I ever forget my embarrassment? The more acute, you know, because it was an embarrassment aggravated by a pride I cannot properly describe. There was I, a just-on-middle-aged man who had thought never to enter this sacred edifice. Do you know what struck me most about it? Its old-fashioned shabbiness. I can't think what I had expected. But it was a shock. Let me qualify that. By shock I mean the sort of shock you describe as one of recognition. I suppose that by keeping us out the English had led us too easily to imagine the club as a place where their worst side would be reflected in some awful insidious way. But the opposite was the case. And the opposite was what one recognized and what one saw at once one should have really expected. Perhaps you will understand this better if I describe Robin White to you as I remember him. He was quite a young man, still in his thirties, very tall, and with one of those narrow English faces which used to appal us when we saw them for the first time because they seemed to be incapable of expressing any emotion. And we wondered: Is it that this man is very clever and potentially well-disposed, or is it that he is a fool? If he is a fool is he a useful fool or a dangerous fool? How much does he know? What on earth is he thinking? When he smiles is he smiling at one of our jokes or at a joke of his own? Is it distaste for us that makes him put up his chilly little barrier, or is it shyness? Almost it was more comfortable to deal with the other type of English face, the extrovert face, even though we knew that the chances of it remaining open and friendly for more than six months were remote. At least in that sort of face there was no mystery to solve. The stages of its trans-formation were not only clear to see but also predictable. But with this narrow, introverted face, it took a long time to feel at ease. Often a man with a face like this would appear and dis-appear without our ever knowing the truth about him. Some-times we heard no more of him. At other times we heard he had succeeded to some important position, and then at least we realized that he had been no fool, although his subsequent repu-tation might also prove that he had been no friend either.

'For instance, with Stead, Robin White's predecessor, we all knew what we were up against. There were members of the local Congress sub-committee who preferred Stead's regime because Stead was almost a caricature of the traditional choleric Col-lector. We always said that he punished the district to avenge himself for what he considered unfair treatment by his own superiors in the service. If he had not been approaching retiring age in 1937 our first provincial minister for internal affairs would have tried to get him promoted to the relatively harmless posi-tion of Divisional Commissioner and pressed the claims of an Indian to succeed him. In which case we should not have had Robin White. We could have done worse, but not, I think, any better. This was my personal view. It was not shared by us all. Some of us, as I said, preferred Stead because he gave our com-mittee so many reasons to complain to Congress in Delhi where questions would be asked in the so-called central legislative assembly, and so many reasons for the District and Municipal Boards to complain to the provincial ministry. There were too many of us who preferred gnawing at the bone of short-term contention to pursuing a long-term policy that could lead from co-operation to autonomy.

'Stead, you know, was a Muslim lover, if lover is the right

word to describe a man who basically thought all Indians inferior. He made no secret of his preference, and this only added fuel to that ridiculous communal fire. Two of his subdivisional officers were Muslims. When the Congress Ministry came into power he transferred one of these Muslims from an outside area to Mayapore itself, which meant that this man was really acting as assistant commissioner and joint magistrate in the town. Unfortunately this Muslim Syed Ahmed was of the militant kind. All Muslim offenders either got off lightly in his court or were acquitted. Hindus were dealt with very severely. In retaliation the Hindu-dominated District Board decided that in the village schools all the Muslim children had to sing Congress songs and salute the Congress flag. Communal differences have always tended to snowball. There were riots in Tanpur, which was in the jurisdiction of the second of Stead's Muslim subdivisional officers, a man called Mohammed Khan. Our committee complained to the ministry that Mohammed Khan and Syed Ahmed were both inciting the Muslim community to create disorders. The ministries had no jurisdiction over the civil service but in certain circumstances pressure could be brought to bear, especially if you could make out a good case. Stead was eventually directed by the Divisional Commissioner to transfer Syed Ahmed to Tanpur. Mohammed Khan was posted to another district and Stead found himself with a young English assistant commissioner called Tupton, who was posted here from another district. It didn't make much difference because this fellow Tupton also thought Muslims manlier than Hindus, so Stead was laughing up his sleeve – until he was retired and we got Robin White. And it didn't take Robin long to cross swords with Tupton and arrange for him to be replaced by a man of his own choice, young John Poulson.

'In fact, I can tell you, it was the way he got rid of Tupton and brought in Poulson that first made us see that behind that not unfriendly but curiously expressionless face there was more than met the eye. To begin with, his getting rid of Tupton made it clear that there was an understanding of what constituted an unneccessary irritant. When it became clear also that he was not moving in a reverse direction, away from the Muslims towards the Hindus, but making a point of showing friendliness to both, we saw that he was strictly the fair-minded type. There was also

a statesmanlike air about him. He requested, in the most diplomatic terms, that the District and Municipal Boards should
reconsider the rule they had laid down about the compulsory
salutation of the Congress flag in the primary schools. I recall
the words in one part of his letter. "The Congress, I appreciate,
inspires the allegiance not only of a majority of Hindus but
of quite a large number of Muslims. I submit however that
although Congress is fundamentally an Indian national party and
that it is correct to lead Indian children towards a patriotic sense
of national duty by ritual observances, it is perhaps unwise to
leave an impression on their minds of the kind of exclusion the
Congress itself is rightly at pains to eradicate."

'Well, you see, he had us by the hip, or at least had by the hip
those of us who appreciated the subtlety of the English language.
As a member of the sub-committee – and he had had the foresight to send us a copy of his letter to the District and Municipal
Boards – as a member of the sub-committee who considered his
submission I argued for an hour over the significance of the
words "impression" and "exclusion".

'Perhaps to you Congress is synonymous with Hindu. To us
– originally – it was always the All-India Congress – founded,
incidentally, by an Englishman. But since there have always been
more Hindus than Muslims in India, it has also always gone
without saying that its membership is and was predominantly
Hindu. This did not in itself make it a party of Hindu policy.
Unfortunately, there is always an unmapped area of dangerous
fallibility between a policy and its pursuit. Do you not agree?
Well, surely as an Englishman, a member of a race that once
ruled us, you must agree? Was there not an unmapped area of
dangerous fallibility between your liberal Whitehall policies for
India and their pursuit here on the spot? What had Mr Stead to
do with official English policy without irrevocably violating it
by his personal passions and prejudices? Do you not agree that
the Mr Steads of your world kicked and swore against every
directive from Parliament and Whitehall that seemed to them to
be reprehensible? As reprehensible as it would be for the garrison
of a beleaguered fort to wave the white flag when plenty of
ammunition was still to hand? Did not such people always feel
themselves to be the quantity left out of the official equation,
the unofficial but very active repository of the old sterling

qualities they thought the politicians had lost sight of or never had? Don't you agree, my dear fellow, that those of your compatriots whom you have observed this evening, by and large, are still in the grip of some traumatic process that persuades them to ignore the directives of your government at home to export or die? Don't you think that we should get on better with the Russians and the Americans?

'Well, so it was, you understand, with members of the Congress. Perhaps even in a greater degree because the official Congress policy wavered between the extremes of that curious unworldly man and our sophisticated Kashmiri Pandit who realized always and perhaps still realizes that half a cake is better than no cake at all.

'So why should you expect the Congress to abide by rules no one else ever abided by? In countless places like Mayapore it became narrowly exclusive. In the same way that Stead became narrowly impenetrable, and your compatriots in the lounge-bar have become narrowly insular, needing the money they earn, the money we are quite prepared to pay them, but affecting to despise the people they earn it from.

'Forgive me. Lili is signalling me to shut up. But I am an old man. I am entitled, am I not, to say what I think? – and of course to stray from the point. I was telling of the Deputy Commissioner's letter and the perfect English flexibility of that sentence: "It is perhaps unwise to leave an impression on their minds of the kind of exclusion Congress itself is rightly at pains to eradicate."

'He was not only calling us to reaffirm the official party line which held Congress to be a body representative of all India, but pointing out very subtly what in our hearts we knew, that many of our local activities were contrary to the party line, if you judged the party line on its highest originating level, especially when those activities were directed at children. "It is perhaps unwise to leave an impression on their minds." This made us think of the kind of minds we left an impression on. The minds of children. Once we had to face the fact that we were acting as adults who knew the rough and tumble of everyday party politics, but acting in a world of children who didn't, also we had to face the fact that these children for a long time now had equated Congress with Hinduism and the singing of Congress songs and

the salutation of the Congress flag as an act of defiance not only
of the British Raj but of Muslim national aspirations. Because it
was we, their elders, who had simplified the issues in this convenient way.

'Unfortunately my arguments in favour of supporting the
Deputy Commissioner's submission, my arguments in favour
of dropping the morning ritual in our district schools, were
defeated by a five to two majority. And I was deputed, as a
disciplinary exercise, to draft the committee's reply to Mr White.
I remember only one sentence because the rest of my draft was
torn to shreds, and this sentence alone remained as mine. Let
me repeat it. It makes almost no sense out of context, but the
interesting thing is that the Deputy Commissioner recognized
its authorship. When he next met me he quoted it: "The salutation of the Indian National Congress flag should not be susceptible of any narrow, communal interpretation." He said: "I quite
agree, Mr Srinivasan. At least, on one point your committee
answered my letter." From that moment we were friends, which
is why when he heard that I was lunching with Mr Desai and the
Minister for Education he invited me to accompany them when
they went to his bungalow to discuss the extension of primary
education in his district. By then, as you probably realize, our
provincial ministries had got over their teething troubles. But of
course it was already 1939, although none of us could have
guessed on that evening he took us to the club that by the end
of the year the Ministry would have resigned over the ridiculous
point of order raised on the Viceroy's declaration of war on
Germany. Or guessed that we should then get thrown back
on to the old personal autocratic rule of British Governors
with a nominated council. That evening when we went to the
Gymkhana it seemed as if the whole world was opening up to us.

'But this is the point I am tortuously trying to make. It was
not until I came into the club with Desai and the Minister and
Mr White that I really understood what it was that men like
Robin White stood for, stood for against all narrow opposition.
I do not mean opposition in Whitehall. But opposition here.
On the spot. In Mayapore. I saw then how well he *fitted* the club.
How well the club fitted him. Like him, it had no expression
that you could easily analyse. It was shabby and comfortable. But
rather awe-inspiring – I suppose because the English as a ruling

class attached so much importance to it. And yet the majority of the people who were there – well, you felt that no matter how well they thought they were made for the club the club wasn't really made for them. In the club, in the smoking-room to be exact, for the first time I saw the face behind the face of Robin White. It seemed to go awfully well with the shabby leather chairs that looked forbidding but turned out to be amazingly comfortable to sit on. And Robin, you know, *looked* at the servants when he spoke to them. You could see him receiving a brief but clear impression of them as men. He did not feel superior to them, only more responsible for them. It was his sense of responsibility that enabled him to accept his privileged position with dignity. That is always the kind of attitude that makes for confidence. In one dazzling moment – forgive the dramatic adjective – in one dazzling moment I really felt I understood what it was the English always imagined lay but only rarely succeeded in showing *did* lie behind all the flummery of their power and influence. And that is why I have always loved the club since then –'

'Even now – ?'

'Oh well – I love it for what it was and even now it is really no different if you know what you are looking for. One always saw and sees through pretence. It is only that now that their responsibility has gone there is no longer any need for the average English person to pretend. And you have as well this very interesting situation in which emptying chamber pots into the pool can also be interpreted as a gesture of *your own* one-time under-privileged people against the kind of social forces that no longer work but used to keep them in their place. I mean, well, please forgive me, so many of your present-day experts are not what members of the club of twenty years ago would have called gentlemen, are they? They are what the English ladies of Mayapore would have called BOR types? British Other Rank? Well, you know, you send a chap like that to Mayapore today to teach us how to run one of those complicated bits of machinery and of course he is treated as a member of a superior race but I do not feel that he generally has much of a feeling of *responsibility* to teach, merely a need to earn a living in relatively pleasant surroundings and a feeling that what he finds so simple other people also should find simple, so that he is likely to become impatient. We cotton on very quickly to the superficial aspects of machinery, but not to its inner logic. This is what young men like Surendranath and Desai mean when they say we wasted time playing at politics. Anyway our shortcomings give the expert a feeling of considerable superiority and he also gets a bit of a kick, of which perhaps he is also slightly ashamed, to be automatically entitled to be a member of the Gymkhana. He laughs at what the Gymkhana used to represent – that old-fashioned upper-class English stuffiness and pretence – which is why I suppose he comes dressed in shorts and short-sleeved shirts and uses vulgar expressions. He knows almost nothing about British–Indian history, so writes off everything that seems to be connected with it as an example of old-type British snobbery. Which means also that in a way he writes us off too. And of course underneath all this there is this other thing, his natural distrust of us, his natural dislike of black people, the dislike he may think he hasn't got but soon finds he has when he's been out here a while, the distrust and dislike he shares with those old predecessors of his, but has the rude courage to express in physical action, like emptying chamber pots into the swimming pool. There is as well a more subtle complication. In his heart he also shares with that old ruling-class of English he affects to despise a desire to be looked up to abroad, and shares with them also the sense of deprivation because he has not been able to inherit the Empire he always saw as a purely ruling-class institution. If you said any of this to him openly he genuinely would not understand, and would deny what of it he did understand. But we understand it. To us it is very clear. But clearest of all now that there is no official policy of foreign government or mystique of foreign leadership that calls for pretence in public and private life, is the fact that behind all that pretence there was a fear and dislike between us that was rooted in the question of the colour of the skin. Even when we most loved, there was the fear, and when there was only the fear and no love there was the dislike. In this odd love-hate affair we always came off worst because you see – the world being what it was, what it is – we recognized and still recognize only too clearly that you were, that you are, far ahead of us in the practical uses of practical knowledge and we still equate fair skin with superior intelligence. Even equate it with beauty. The sun is too strong here. It darkens us and saps us. Paleness is synonymous with worldly success, because paleness is the mark of intellectual, not physical endeavour, and worldly success is seldom achieved with the muscles. Well – here already is the train.'

And presently, with a mechanical precision recognizable as one not wrought by local invention but by foreign instruction, the gates of the level crossing swing back and leave the road open to the bridge and the temple and the black town. The Studebaker (also a foreign importation, sold by its American owner for a handsome profit to a Brahmin friend of Mr Srinivasan's in Calcutta) glides forward and there below is the sweep of the river, glittering with the artificial jewels of the night's illumination. Obstructing the traffic that has been waiting to move in the opposite direction, from the black town to the civil lines (the old descriptive usages die hard), is another but shorter procession of carts drawn by white, humpbacked oxen. Their round eyes glint red in the headlights.

'Stop!' Mr Srinivasan cries suddenly. 'Would you like to see the temple? It is not too late? Oh no, come, Lili – let us show at least one thing tonight that is truly *Indian*,' and directs the Muslim driver to park wherever he can find a place.

At the bridgehead on the black-town side, with the Tirupati temple on the left, the road broadens into a square whose other end is marked by the holy tree and wayside shrine. On the right, almost opposite the temple, is the Majestic Cinema where the epic from the Ramayana is showing to packed houses. Beyond the square – it may be remembered – the road forks to the right in the direction of the jail and to the left to the Chillianwallah Bazaar. The square is lighted by a single standard close to the holy tree, but it is not dark because the shops are open-fronted and not yet shuttered, still open for custom, and lit by unshaded electric bulbs or glaring pressure lamps that hurt the eye to look at. Somewhere nearby – yes, from the coffee-house – there is the amplified sound of recorded music, a popular song of a celluloid civilization – a girl's voice, nasal, thin, accompanied by strings, brass and percussion. There are a cow or two, parked cycle-rickshaws, many people, and several beggar women who converge upon the Studebaker, carrying sleeping children aslant their bangled arms. Their eyes and the rings in their nostrils capture, lose, and recapture, shards of splintered light.

They reach the car and surround it, accompanying it, half-running, half-walking. When it stops their hands come through the open windows. It is necessary, in the end, for Mr Srinivasan to threaten them with the police. They retreat, but only far enough to allow the passengers to alight. The driver stays with the car and he is left in peace, but the party that now makes its way back towards the temple is followed by the most persistent of the women. Sometimes, making a way through the crowd, you think they have given up. A hand lightly touching your sleeve and then tugging it proves otherwise. To look straight into her eyes would be fatal. In India the head too often has to be turned away. 'You must not give them anything,' Mr Srinivasan says. An observer of the scene would notice that since leaving the car the beggar women have concentrated on the more vulnerable flank of the trio walking towards the temple: the white man. The observer would perhaps notice too that the woman who makes her dumb appeal through that gesture, that brief contact with the white man's sleeve, and who now keeps her voice down to a whisper and limits her vocabulary of begging to one urgently repeated word, 'Sahib, Sahib,' is the last to admit defeat, walking with the visitors almost to the entrance of the temple.

'I'm afraid,' Mr Srinivasan says, 'that you will have to take off your shoes. If you like you could keep your socks on.'

Socks? Ah, well, risk all!

The open gateway is fairly narrow, but it is deep because the gate is at the base of the tall stone tower that mounts in diminishing tiers of sculpted figures, the details of which cannot be seen at night. Inside the passage through the tower a temple servant squats by an oil-lamp, surrounded by chappals and shoes. With chalk he makes a mark on the soles and gives Mr Srinivasan a slip of paper. The stone floor of the passage is warm to the bare feet and rather gritty. The descent into the main courtyard of the temple is by a shallow flight of four steps. The feet come into contact with sand. There are people walking, people praying and people sitting on the ground who seem to be gossiping. The illumination is dim. In the centre of the courtyard is the square building of the inner sanctuary, with steps leading up, and carved pillars supporting an ornamental roof. Around the walls of the courtyard there are other sanctuaries. Some are in darkness; others are lit to show that the god or goddess is awake. The figures, often no bigger than dolls, are painted and garlanded. A bell is rung in the main sanctuary: by a devotee of Lord Venkataswara warning the god that he seeks admittance. Slowly the trio of visitors walks round the courtyard until the entrance into Lord Venkataswara's sanctuary is revealed. A man with a shaved head, bare chest, and the string of the sacred thread looped over his light brown shoulder stands near a pillar. He is one of the priests of the temple. The black-skinned, loin-clothed devotee stands at the open doors of the sanctuary in an attitude of prayer – both arms raised above his head, the palms together. The short length of rope attached to the tongue of the iron bell that is suspended from the roof still moves. It is possible to get only a glimpse of the inner sanctum: a gleam of gold, silver and ebony, in the heart of the stone. There is a bitter-sweet smell in the air. The sand beneath the feet varies from grit to velvet softness. Through the river entrance comes the smell of the water.

There are trees in the courtyard. In the day they afford some shade. Behind the main sanctuary is the sanctuary of the sleeping Vishnu. The stone of the sanctuary floor is rubbed black and shiny. Inside, in the dim light of the oil-lamps set in the walls the carved recumbent god sleeps through an eternity of what look like pleasant dreams. He is longer than a lying man would be. He is part of his own stone pallet, carved into it, out of it, inseparable from it. He is smooth and naked, with square shoulders and full lips that curve at the corners into a smile. The eyelids are shut but seem always to be on the point of fluttering voluptuously open. Once this imminent awakening has made its impression, the stiff limbs begin to suggest a hidden flexibility as though, at least, the god may be expected to ease the cramp of long sleep out of them. The delicately carved but powerful hand would then drop from the stone pillow and fall aslant the breast. And then perhaps the full lips would part and he would speak one word, speaking it softly, as in a dream, but revealing a secret that would enable whatever mortal man or woman happened to be there to learn the secret of power on earth and peace beyond it.

'I am sorry we cannot take you into the holy of holies,' Mr Srinivasan says, 'although I might swing it if I can convince the priest that you are a Buddhist. But perhaps some other time. Lili is looking tired.'

Not only tired but, oddly, out of place.

'These days,' Srinivasan explains, as shoes are found, socks retrieved from pockets and a coin given to the shoe-minder, 'the temples are all controlled by Government. In fact you could really say the priests have become civil servants. They are paid salaries, and collect fees according to official scales. It cuts down a lot on all that extortion that used to go on. This is one of the things we old congressmen insisted on ... that India should be a secular democratic state, not a priest-ridden autocracy.'

Before the car is reached, the same beggar-women encroach. Settled and safe in the Studebaker, Srinivasan says, 'Well, we are holy now, I suppose. It is in order to be charitable,' and throws some coins out of the window. The women scrabble for them in the dust, and the car, free of them, moves forward, taking the left fork from the square, where Sister Ludmila walked with her leather handbag chained to her waist. The lane is narrow, and harshly lit, and crowded. The bonnet of the Studebaker is like the prow of a boat, ploughing through a busy waterway. The chauffeur drives on the clutch and the horn. At the end of the lane, where it opens on to the walled square of the Chillian-wallah Bazaar market the town is suddenly dark and dead. The market is closed. The houses are shuttered. Only a few lights show. The headlamps create dense angular shadows. The smell off the river comes through the narrow openings between deserted buildings.

Turning a corner there is a glimpse of the old palace, the Purdah Hospital: a high wall, an iron gateway in it, foliage inside the grounds, a light showing behind the leaves. A dog with white and yellow markings crosses the road in front of the car. The sky ahead expands, displaying its stars in counter-attraction to the goods that were for sale in the shops. Somewhere, to the left, is the place once known as the Sanctuary and to the right the Chillianwallah Bagh reclamation.

'She died years ago, they say,' Mr Srinivasan explains, speaking of Mrs Gupta Sen who had been Shalini Kumar before her marriage. The car enters an area of well laid out but unmetalled badly lit roads, along which the suntrap houses of the rich merchants cluster in walled compounds, a few showing lights behind barred windows. Here there are the black, feathery silhouettes of coconut palms, leaning tall and drunken between the gaps in the houses. The car turns twice. But each road, each collection of dwellings, looks the same. Number twelve is an anonymous dark bulk. A grandson of Romesh Chand lives there for a few months in the year in the cold weather. The car, on Srinivasan's order, stops outside the iron, padlocked gate. There is nothing to feel except the night warmth and nothing to see except the shadows in the compound, and the culvert that leads from the road to the gate across the monsoon ditch in the bordering grass where the bicycle was found.

And young Kumar? Where is he now? Srinivasan shrugs. Dead perhaps. Upon Kumar's arrest after the rape in the Bibighar Romesh Chand disowned him. Perhaps, also, young Kumar disowned his family. Well, it is a vast country. Easy to get lost in. And again the sense of immensity (of weight and flatness, and absence of orientating features) blankets the mind with an idea of scope so limitless that it is deadening. Here, on the ground, nothing is likely, everything possible. Only from the air can one trace what looks like a pattern, a design, an abortive, human intention. The Studebaker noses forward, lost, at bay, but committed to automatic progression, out on to the Chillianwallah Bagh Extension road, which to the south leads to the now non-existent southern gate of the old walled town, and to the north of the Bibighar bridge.

The bridge has a low, stone parapet and is arched, as if perpetually tensed against the ache of rheumatism from having its supports so long in water. And so, down, to its northerly head, having led the traveller back across the invisible water (which in these less well-lit reaches does not glitter) to the second level crossing: having led across the eternal back to the transitory, from the waters that have their source in the snows of far-off mountain ranges to the parallel lines of steel that carry the trains eastward to the unimaginable coast.

And here is the hut of the level crossing keeper lit these days by a neon standard. The well-sprung car bounces luxuriously over the uneven surface of the wooden boards that have been set between the rails. It is not difficult to imagine the sensation of cycling over the crossing, with the light system showing green and, coming from the left, the smoky metallic railway smell that is the same anywhere in the world, and was certainly no different twenty-two years ago, so that it is possible to breathe in sharply and think: This is what she smelt as she cycled back from Sister Ludmila's Sanctuary.

But ahead, there is a change. The road is being re-surfaced. One remembers Lili Chatterjee having mentioned it. There are now warning lamps and mounds of chipped stone and x-shaped trestle ends that support long barricading poles: a familiar manifestation of public works in progress. The work in progress sends the car over to the right-hand side of the road, a few feet closer to the wall of the Bibighar Gardens.

An ordinary wall, such as you would find anywhere in India, a little higher than a man, stuccoed, greying, peeling. Old. With trees behind it screening an interior. As the car goes by nothing is said, but the silence is commentary enough.

Bibighar.

After a time even the most tragic name acquires a kind of beauty.

From here the car follows the route taken by the girl who ran in the darkness. Yes. This is what she must have felt: beyond the darkness of the buildings and the habitation, the space, the limitless territory. Through such ordinary ways, such unspectacular, unlit avenues. And all the time the curious smell – not of the railway now, but of the land – which perhaps she had learned to accept or not to notice, if not to love, to need.

PART FIVE

YOUNG KUMAR

WHEN HARI KUMAR's father died of an overdose of sleeping pills in Edinburgh and the lawyers told him that there wasn't even enough money to pay in full what was owed to Mr and Mrs Carter who ran the house in Berkshire he rang the Lindseys and asked them what they thought he should do. Although the lawyers insisted that he could put the notion right out of his head he had an old-fashioned idea that he was responsible for his father's debts, if in fact there were debts. The Lindseys found it as difficult to believe the lawyers' tale of bankruptcy as he did himself. They said he must come over to Didbury right away and stay with them. He was not to worry, because Mr Lindsey would see the lawyers and get proper sense out of them.

His father's death occurred in the middle of the Easter holidays of 1938, a few weeks before Hari's eighteenth birthday. The Lindseys were in Paris when it happened. If they had been at home Hari would probably have been with them and certainly have had their support at the funeral. He spent most of his vacations with the Lindseys. Their son Colin was his oldest friend. He had been with them up until the day before they were due to entrain for Paris. If his father had not written from Edinburgh and warned him that he was coming down to Sidcot and wanted to discuss plans for the future, he would have gone to Paris too, relying as usual on his father's agreement *in absentia*. Instead the letter had come and he had gone home and found his father not arrived and the housekeeper and her husband, Mr and Mrs Carter, in a disagreeable mood. He hadn't been expected and the Carters said they knew nothing of his father's plans to leave Edinburgh. He did not care very much for the Carters. In Sidcot the staff seldom stayed long. The Carters had been in residence for a couple of years, which was something of a record. He could not remember how many different house-keepers and handyman-gardeners his father had employed. In the old days, before he went to prep school and then on to

Chillingborough, there had been a succession of disagreeable
governesses and tutors as well as of domestic servants, some of
whom made it plain that they preferred to work for white
gentlemen. The house had never been to him what, since he
had got to know the Lindseys, he had learned to think of as a
home. He saw his father three or four times a year and seldom
for longer than a week at a time. He did not remember his
mother. He understood that she had died in India when he was
born. He did not remember India either.

The reason he found it difficult to believe what the lawyers
told him was that there had always seemed to be plenty of
money. When he was old enough to appreciate the difference
in degrees of affluence he realized that the house in Sidcot was
substantial, bigger and more expensively furnished than the
Lindseys'; and as well as the house in Sidcot there was a succession of flats in London which his father moved into and out
of, in accordance with some principle Hari did not understand
and took no interest in beyond what was necessary to record
accurately the change of address and telephone number, so that
his letters should not go astray and he could be sure of going to
the right place if his father rang the school and suggested lunch
in town on Hari's way home at the end of term. On such occasions he usually took Colin with him. And Colin once said,
looking round the sumptuous but unwelcoming flat, 'Your
father must be stinking rich.' And Hari shrugged and replied,
'I suppose he is.'

This was probably the moment when he began consciously
to be critical of his father who spoke English with that appalling
sing-song accent, spelled the family name Coomer, and told
people to call him David because Duleep was such a mouthful.
Duleep had chosen the name Hari for his only surviving child
and only son (the son for whom he had prayed and longed and
whose life had now been planned down to the last detail)
because Hari was so easily pronounced and was really only
distinguishable in the spelling from the diminutive of Saxon
Harold, who had been King of the English before the Normans
came.

The story is that Duleep Kumar, against the wishes and with
only the reluctant permission of his parents, went to England to

study for the law, just about the time that Miss Crane left the service of the Nesbitt-Smiths and entered the fuller service of the mission, about the time, too, that there died, in a penury as great if not as spectacular as Duleep's, the mother of a young girl who then entered an orphanage and in later years called herself Sister Ludmila.

The Kumars were landowners in a district of the United Provinces. They were rich by Indian standards and loyal to a foreign crown that seemed ready to respect the laws of property. There were many Kumars, but as a youth Duleep began to notice that no matter how much they were looked up to by people whose skin was the same colour as their own, the callowest white-skinned boy doing his first year in the covenanted civil service could snub them by keeping them waiting on the verandah of the sacred little bungalow from whose punkah-cooled rooms was wafted an air of effortless superiority. Power, Duleep felt, lay not in money but in this magical combination of knowledge, manner, and race. His father − one of those frequently kept waiting − disagreed. 'In the end,' he said, 'it is money that counts. What is a snub? What is an insult? Nothing. It costs nothing to give and nothing to receive. Hurt pride is quickly nursed back to health in the warmth of a well-lined pocket. That young man who keeps me waiting is a fool. He refuses gifts because he has been taught that any gift from an Indian is a bribe. At home he would not be so careful. But in forty years he will be poor, living on his pension in his own cold climate.'

'But in those forty years,' Duleep pointed out, 'he will have wielded power.'

'What is this power?' his father asked. 'He will have settled a few land disputes, seen to the maintenance of public works, extended a road, built a drain, collected revenues on behalf of Government, fined a few thousand men, whipped a score and sent a couple of hundred to jail. But you will be a comparatively rich man. Your power will be material, visible to your eyes when you look at the land you own. Your trouble will be a single one − the slight inconvenience of being kept waiting by one of this young man's successors who will also refuse gifts and in his turn wield what you call power and die rich in nothing except his colonial recollections.'

Duleep laughed. He laughed at his father's wry humour. But

mostly he laughed because he knew otherwise. When his father died the land so proudly possessed would be divided by his children, and later by his children's children, and then by his children's children's children, and in the end there would be nothing and the power would have dwindled away field by field, village by village. And a young man would still sit in the sacred bungalow, making himself ready to listen with an agreeable but non-committal expression to tales of distress and poverty and injustice; thinking all the time of his own career, planning to follow his predecessors one step at a time up the ladder to a desk in the Secretariat, or a seat on the Governor-General's Council, or to a place on the bench of the High Court of Justice.

Duleep Kumar was the youngest of a family of four boys and three girls. Perhaps a family of seven children was counted auspicious, for after his birth (in 1888) it seemed for several years that his parents were satisfied and intended no further addition. He was the baby, the last-born son. It could have been that his brothers and sisters grew up to be jealous of the attention and affection lavished on him. Certainly in later years, in the matter of his own son Hari's welfare, no interest was shown by and no help forthcoming from those of Duleep's elders who survived him. In the long run, things might have worked out better if there had been no surviving Kumar at all to take an interest; but there was Shalini, the little girl Duleep's mother bore when he was in his eleventh year. The evidence points to a special bond between the last-born son and the last-born daughter, one that in all likelihood originated in Duleep's sense of isolation from his older brothers and sisters, when the first flush of his parents' spoiling had worn thin, and caused him even at that early age to cast a critical eye upon the world around him and a restless one towards the world beyond. Of the four brothers only Duleep completed the course at the Government Higher School and went on to the Government College. His family thought that to study at the college was a waste of time, so they opposed the plan, but finally gave in. In later years he was fond of quoting figures from the provincial census taken round about this time, that showed a male population of twenty-four and a half million and a female population of twenty-three million. Of the males one and a half million were literate; of the females less than fifty-six thousand, a figure which did not include his three elder sisters. His father and brothers were literate in the vernacular, semi-literate in English. It was because as a youth Duleep had acquired a good knowledge of the language of the administrators that he began to accompany his father on visits to petition the sub-divisional officer, and had the first intimations of the secrets hidden behind the bland face of the white authority. There grew in him a triple determination – to break away from a landlocked family tradition, to become a man who instead of requesting favours, granted them, and to save Shalini from the ignorance and domestic tyranny not only his other sisters but his two elder brothers' wives seemed to accept uncomplainingly as all that women could hope for from the human experience. When Shalini was three years old he began to teach her her letters in Hindi. When she was five she could read in English.

Duleep was now sixteen years old. The Government College to which he had gained admittance was at the other end of the earth: a hundred miles away. His mother wept at his going. His brothers scoffed. His elder sisters and sisters-in-law looked at him as if he were setting out on some shameful errand. His father did not understand, but gave him his blessing the night before his departure and in the morning accompanied him to the railway station in a doolie drawn by bullocks.

And perhaps that is when what could be called the tragedy of Duleep Kumar began. He was a boy whose passion for achievement was always just that much greater than his ability to achieve. And it was a passion that had become used to the constant irritants of home. Far removed from there, in the company of boys of diverse backgrounds but similar ambitions, the original sense of frustration upon which these passions had thrived began to diminish. Here, everyone was in the same boat, but as the BA course progressed he became uncomfortably aware of the process that separated the quick-witted from the plodders. For the first time in his life he found himself having to admit that other boys, if not actually cleverer, could certainly be quicker. Analysing this he came readily to an explanation. The quick boys, surely, all came from progressive homes where English was spoken all the time. On the college teaching staff there was a preponderance of Englishmen. At the Government Higher School, most of the instruction, although in English, had been in the hands of Indians. He had always understood exactly what the Indian teachers were saying, and he had often felt that what they were saying he could have said better. But now he sat through lectures increasingly at a loss to follow not the words so much as the thinking behind the words. And he did not dare to ask questions. Nobody asked questions. They listened attentively. They filled exercise books with meticulous notes of what they thought had been said. To ask questions was to admit ignorance. In a competitive world like this such an admission would probably have been fatal.

He was, however, discovering a new irritant: the frustrations not of a hidebound orthodox Indian family, but of the English language itself. Listening to his fellow-students he was amazed that they seemed unable to comprehend the difference between the way they spoke and the way the Englishmen spoke. It was not only a question of pronunciation or idiom. He was too young to be able to formulate the problem. But he was aware of having come close to the heart of another important secret. To uncover it might lead to an understanding of what in the subdivisional officer looked like simple arrogance and in the English teachers intellectual contempt.

There came a time when he was able to say to his son Hari: 'It is not only that if *you* answer the phone a stranger on the other end would think he was speaking to an English boy of the upper classes. It is that you *are* that boy in your mind and behaviour. Conversely when I was your age, it was not only that I spoke English with an even stronger *babu* accent than I speak it now, but that everything I said, because everything I thought, was in conscious mimicry of the people who rule us. We did not necessarily admit this, but that is what was always in their minds when they listened to us. It amused them mostly. Sometimes it irritated them. It still does. Never they could listen to us and forget that we were a subject, inferior people. The more idiomatic we tried to be the more naïve our thinking seemed, because we were thinking in a foreign language that we had never properly considered in relation to our own. Hindi, you see, is spare and beautiful. In it we can think thoughts that have the merit of simplicity and truth. And between each other convey these thoughts in correspondingly spare, simple, truthful images. English is not spare. But it is beautiful. It cannot be called truthful because its subtleties are infinite. It is the language of a people who have probably earned their reputation for perfidy and hypocrisy because their language itself is so flexible, so often light-headed with statements which appear to mean one thing one year and quite a different thing the next. At least, this is so when it is written, and the English have usually confided their noblest aspirations and intentions to paper. Written, it looks like a way of gaining time and winning confidence. But when it is spoken, English is rarely beautiful. Like Hindi it is spare then, but crueller. We learned our English from books, and the English, knowing that books are one thing and life another, simply laughed at us. Still laugh at us. They laughed at me, you know, in that Indian college I went to before I came over here that first disastrous time to study law. At the college I learned the importance of obtaining a deep understanding of the language, a real familiarity with it, spoken and written. But of course I got it mostly all from books. A chapter of Macaulay was so much easier to understand, and certainly more exciting, than a sentence spoken by Mr Croft who taught us history. In the end I was even trying to speak Macaulayesque prose. Later I found out that any tortuous path to a simple hypothesis was known among the English staff as a Kumarism. And it was later still before I really understood that a Kumarism was not something admirable but something rather silly. But I think this notoriety helped me to scrape through. I was a long way down the list. But it was a triumph by my standards.'

And it was in the glow of this triumph that, aged nineteen, he returned home, not for the first time since going to the station in the doolie – naturally enough there had been the vacations – but for the first time as a young man of proven worth, and of ambitions that now pointed to the necessity of making the passage across the black water, to England, to sit for the examinations of the Indian Civil Service, which in those days was the only place where the examinations could be taken: a rule which effectively restricted the number of Indians able to compete.

He found his parents less jubilant over his academic success than they were concerned about his failure to fulfil a primary function: to be married, to increase, to ensure at least one son who could officiate eventually in his funeral rites and see him on the way, with honour, to another world.

The girl they had in mind, whose name was Kamala and

whose horoscope, according to the astrologers, was in an auspicious confluence with his own, was already fifteen; in fact, they said, nearly sixteen.

'Kamala!' he shouted. 'Who, what, is Kamala?' and would not even listen to the answer.

The Kumar home was a rambling rural agglomeration of low buildings built around a central courtyard, walled within a large compound, on the outskirts of the principal village within their holding, a distance of five miles from the town where the English sub-divisional officer had his headquarters. Five miles by buffalo cart to the nearest outpost of civilization, Duleep thought. Ah! What a prison! He played with Shalini and in intervals of playing retaught her the lessons he was pleased to find she had not forgotten in the three months that had gone since he last saw her. Between them now there was an adoration; she, in his eyes, such a sweet-tempered pretty and intelligent child, and he, in hers, a handsome, godlike but miraculously earthbound and playful brother whose wisdom knew no end, and kindness no inexplicable boundaries of sudden silence or bad temper; no temper anyway when they were together. But she heard his shouting at her brothers, quarrelling with her father. Once too, when he thought he was alone, she heard him weeping; and gathered flowers to charm away his unhappiness so that he should smile again, and tell her tales of Rama, the god-king.

In the end he decided to strike a bargain with his parents. He would agree in principle to the marriage with the girl Kamala. But there could be no question of actual marriage until he had completed his studies in England and sat for the examinations. He would submit only to a formal betrothal.

And how long, his father wanted to know, would he be away in England?

Two or three years, perhaps. His father shook his head. By then Kamala would be eighteen or nineteen and still living with her parents. Did Duleep want his wife to be a laughing-stock before ever she came to his bed? And had he thought of the cost of going to England to study? Where did he think so much money was coming from? Duleep was prepared for this objection. He would sign away to his elder brothers whatever proportion of his inheritance might be reckoned to equal the cost of his studies abroad.

'There are only so many maunds to a sack, and you cannot give up what has not yet come to you,' his father pointed out. 'Besides which your inheritance is what makes you an attractive proposition to your future parents-in-law.'

'My education, my career, mean nothing to them?' Duleep asked.

His father shook his head. 'What you call your career has not yet begun. Perhaps you have overlooked the advantage of the dowry your wife would bring to this household? With such advantage money might be found to send you to England. But you would have to marry first. You are nineteen already. And all your brothers were married before their nineteenth year. Your future wife will soon be sixteen. By that age all your elder sisters were already married. I have had to find three dowries already. I am not a man with a bottomless pocket. And in a few years there will be yet another dowry to find for Shalini.'

Family affairs were the one thing there was always time for. The negotiations with his father extended over many days. Towards the end of them Duleep went to him and said, 'Very well. I will marry Kamala. But then immediately I will go to England.'

For these interviews they met in the room his father had, these past few years, set aside for meditation – an act which might have warned them all of what was to come later. In this room there was no furniture. They sat on rush mats on the tiled floor. On the whitewashed walls there was no decoration other than a highly coloured lithograph of the God of Fortune, Ganesha, in a little rosewood frame, and, on the sill of the small unglazed barred window, a pewter jug that usually held a handful of marigolds or frangipani.

'I do not wish you,' his father said now, raising a new objection, 'to enter the administration. If you are not content to look after your property then I suggest that you become a lawyer. For this you can study, I believe, in Calcutta.'

'What have you got against the administration?' Duleep asked.

'It is the administration of a foreign government. I should feel shame for my son to serve it. Better he should oppose the administration in the courts to help his own people.'

'Shame?' Duleep said. 'But you do not feel shame to be kept waiting on the verandah of the little burra-sahib. You have said yourself: What is an insult? What is hurt pride?'

'I should feel shame,' old Kumar said, 'if the little burra-sahib were my own son.'

It was a subtle point. It took a day or two for Duleep to swallow it, to judge the actuality of his father's sudden antipathy towards the Raj which, if it was not sudden, had always been kept well concealed.

'All right,' Duleep told him a few days later. 'I have thought about it. I will become a lawyer. Perhaps a barrister. But for this I must study in England.'

'And first you will marry the girl Kamala?'

'Yes, Father. First I will marry Kamala.'

Of his close family only his mother and an aunt had seen Kamala Prasad, his future wife. To do so they had paid a visit to the Prasads' home. Pleased with what they saw and with what was known about her upbringing, they reported back to Duleep's father. Reassured by the astrologers and satisfied with the pro- posed dowry, all that remained from the Kumars' point of view – granted Duleep's obedient submission to their wishes – was to seal the arrangement with a formal betrothal and then to fix the date of the wedding.

Kamala Prasad lived some twenty miles away. For the betrothal ceremony only male Prasads made the journey to the Kumars' house: the prospective bride's father and uncles and two of her married brothers. They brought sweets and small gifts of money, but came in the main to satisfy themselves that the house Kamala would live in was up to the standard they had been led to expect. Duleep, who had watched his brothers perform the same duties, bowed to his future father-in-law and then knelt to touch his feet in a gesture of humility. The father-in-law marked Duleep's forehead with the tilak – the sign of auspiciousness. For a while the guests sat in formal conversation, took some refreshment and then went back to the station on the first stage of their journey home. The ceremony left little impression on him; it had seemed rather pointless, but for Shalini, with Duleep as the centre of attraction, it had been magical. 'On your wedding day, will you wear a sword and ride a horse, just like a king?' she asked.

'Well, I suppose so,' he said, and laughed, and privately thought: What a farce! His main interest lay in the arrangements he had begun to make with the advice and help of the principal of the Government College to go to England in September for the opening of what, fascinatingly, was called the Michaelmas term.

The betrothal ceremony took place in January, and then almost immediately there was difficulty over fixing the date of the wedding. The astrologers said that the ideal time fell in the second week of March. Kumar suggested the first week in September. The boat on which he had booked his passage through an agent in Bombay left in the second week. The astrologers shook their heads. If the wedding could not be managed in the second week of March it would need to be postponed until the fourth week of October.

'It is all nonsense,' Duleep insisted. 'All they mean is that by April the weather will be too hot and from June until October likely to be too wet.' He had no intention of spending nearly six months as a married man before setting out for England. In fact he had no intention of sleeping with a barely sixteen-year-old girl, however pretty, however nubile. He would go through the ceremony. He would even spend one night or two with her so that she would not be disgraced. But he would not make love to her. He would kiss her and be kind to her, and tell her that when he returned from England as a young man qualified in an honourable profession it would be time enough for her to take on the duties of a wife and the burdens of motherhood. He almost hoped that she would turn out to be unattractive.

Sometimes he woke in the middle of the night and thought that every step he had taken since leaving the college had been the wrong one. He had given up his plan to enter the administration. He had submitted to the demands of his parents to marry. He had undertaken to study for a profession his heart had not been set on. All he had succeeded in hanging on to was his determination to go to England. When he woke in the mornings the prospect of England was enough to enable him to enter the new day bright and cheerful, and he could not help responding to the warmth of parental approbation that had settled about him. He heard his father say once to an old friend, 'After his marriage, of course, Duleepji is to continue his studies in England,' as if that had been his father's wish, not his own, and he judged that paternal pride could grow like good seed in the most unlikely ground so long as that ground were first soaked with the sweat of filial duty. But, in the darkness of half-sleep and half-waking, he would search without success for a practical interpretation of that single, challenging word, England; for an interpretation that would ease him, bring comfort that extended beyond his general desire to his particular purpose. Power – in the sense he understood it – seemed to have been potentially lessened by his all too easy, equivocal agreement to enter the services of the law where power was interpreted, perhaps challenged, but never directly exercised. In myself, he thought, there is possibly a fatal flaw, the dark root of the plant of compromise that never bears any blossom that isn't rank-smelling; and turned over, to sleep again, his hand upon the firm breast of the submissive, loving girl who now always followed him into his dreams.

He had his way. The astrologers discovered an unexpected conjunction of fortunate stars. The marriage was arranged to take place in the first week of September. 'You see, Shalini,' he told his little sister, 'it was all nonsense, as I said,' but stopped himself from adding, 'Like the Kumars, the Prasads carry the burden of too many daughters and are only too anxious to have Kamala off their hands, even at the tail-end of the wet monsoon.' Looking at Shalini he found himself assessing the burden that she, in her ninth year, already represented in terms of the complicated sum of her necessary dowry and her parents' desire that she should be happy, and suitably matched, transferred to a household that would bring honour to them and good fortune to her, be given to a husband who would bless her with kindness and whom she would find it possible to feel affection for and be dutiful to, and so give satisfaction to him and to his family, and to herself and to hers.

'I hope,' he told himself, thinking of his own future wife, 'that I can find it in my heart not to hate her.'

The first list of guests on the groom's side which his father prepared ran to nearly three hundred names. After negotiations with the Prasad family the list was cut to just below two hundred. There would be twice that number on the bride's side. To the bride's family the cost would be crippling. In the middle of August the Prasads began to gather. The Kumars also gathered. They came from the Punjab, from Madras, from Bengal, from Lucknow and the home province, and from Bombay, from as far off as Rawalpindi. Duleep was the last of old Kumar's sons.

There would only be one other marriage in this particular generation: Shalini's. The house was full. The guest house that had been erected outside the compound for the weddings of Duleep's sisters was also full.

The journey to Delali was made early in the morning of the day of the wedding. Miraculously the rains had ended early, which was counted a good omen. In Kamala's home the first ceremonies had been going on for two days. Three coaches of the train to Delali were reserved for the groom's party. A delegation of Prasads was at Delali station to meet them. Duleep and his family were taken to the house of a brother of the bride's father. And there Duleep was dressed in the style of a warrior king, in tight white trousers, embroidered coat, sword, cloak and sequined turban upon which was placed a tinsel crown from which garlands of roses and jasmine hung, half shadowing his face, filling his nostrils with their sweet narcotic scent. As evening came he was led out to the caparisoned horse on which he mounted, with his best man, a young cousin, behind him in the saddle. The procession to the bride's house began at half-past six. It was accompanied by men with lanterns, drums, trumpets and fireworks. The evening was loud with the noise and explosion of their progression. It gave him a headache. The procession was followed by the people of Delali who wanted to see for themselves what kind of a husband old Prasad's youngest daughter had managed to get hold of. They shouted good-natured insults and Duleep's champions replied in kind.

Dismounting at the entrance to the bride's house, he was led through the compound to the married women's courtyard, sat down, and put through the first of his ordeals.

'So next week you are going to England,' one of the women said. 'Do you tire so quickly that you need to run away?'

'Oh no,' Duleep replied, entering into the spirit of the testing, 'but a young husband is wiser to accept the truth of the saying: Moderation in all things.'

'Perhaps the bride will have different ideas,' another woman said.

'The pot of honey,' Duleep said, 'tastes better after a long abstinence.'

'What if the honey should go sour?' an even bolder woman asked.

'To a faithful tooth even the sourest honey tastes sweet.'

The women laughed and hid their faces. Duleep was a man. The news was quickly carried to the bride who had sat for hours in her inner chamber, after her ritual purifying bathe, attended by the women whose job it was to clothe her in her red robes and heavy jewellery, put henna on her hands and feet and kohl on her eyes.

'As handsome as a prince,' they said, 'and bold with it. Ah, what eyes! But also gentle. Assuredly yes, you are fortunate. Such husbands do not grow on trees. He will be worth the waiting for, after the initial taste.'

The second ordeal was the ceremony itself which was due to begin at the auspicious hour of half an hour before midnight, in the main courtyard, and would go on for hours, in accordance with the Vedic rites. He sat next to his bride, facing the sacred fire on the other side of which the pandit sat. She was heavily veiled and kept her head bowed. Duleep dared not look at her. But he had the impression of her scent and smallness and temporary magnificence. The veil over her head was tied to the pommel of his sword which, in the olden days, he would have had to use to cut off the branch of a tree to show his vigour. Already they were united, indissolubly, throughout life and perhaps beyond it. And he had not yet seen her face. She had not yet looked at his. If she saw anything of him at all it could be no more than his gold, embroidered slippers and tight-trousered legs. Unless she had peeped. He did not think she had. The pandit was intoning mantras. Incense was thrown on the flames of the fire. Duleep and Kamala walked round the fire with Duleep leading, and then again, reversing the order, with Kamala ahead. She received rice into her cupped hands, and poured it into his, and he threw it into the flames. Together they walked the seven auspicious steps, and then the pandit recited their names and the names of their forbears, and Kamala was led away and he would not be close to her again until the night after the next when she would be led by his own mother into his room at home. But already it was morning. Tomorrow, then, Kamala would travel to Duleep's house, in clothes brought to her as gifts from the Kumars.

Duleep slept late, got up and broke his fast and inspected the dowry that was on show on trestle tables under awnings, in case a miserable, unexpected rain ruined the proceedings. There were clothes for himself and the bride, jewellery, small coffers of silver coins and one hundred rupee notes, family ceremonial costume, plate, household utensils, and, in a box, title deeds to land. He went to bed early, astonished by so much personal wealth, the cost to a girl's father of a husband for her, and in the morning was dressed again in his king's raiment, encumbered by his velvet sheathed sword and mounted on the caparisoned horse to lead the doolie procession to the railway station. The small figure of his still-veiled wife, dressed in scarlet, heavily jewelled, was supported by her father and mother out to the palanquin. He fancied that the moment before she entered she faltered and wept and was only persuaded to enter by some comforting, courage-giving words of her mother.

When the doolie curtains were closed the bearers took up the weight, and the women who followed the palanquin began to sing the song of the bride, the morning raga, the song of the young girl who leaves her childhood home for the home of her husband.

> *Dooliya la aō*
> *re morē babul ke kaharwa.*
> *Chali hoon sajan ba ke des.*

On the outskirts of their own village which they reached in procession from the railway station towards evening, they were met by what looked like the whole population. The married women approached the doolie (a doolie provided by the Kumars to replace the doolie left behind with the Prasads at Delali) opened the curtains and inspected the bride. From the way they looked at him afterwards he assumed that they had found no major fault. Of the family only Shalini had been left behind. She ran from the compound and clung to the bridle of his horse which, like the new doolie, had been waiting at the station.

'Duleep, Duleep,' she cried, 'oh, how beautiful you are. Why did you marry her? Why didn't you wait for me?' And walked proudly, possessively, leading the horse into the compound. But came later, long after she should have been in bed, to the room in which he prepared himself and said, 'I am sorry, Duleep.'

'Why sorry?' he asked, taking her on to his knee. She encircled her arms around his neck.

'Because,' she said, 'because I have seen her.'

'Then why should you be sorry?' he asked, his heart beating so loudly he could hardly bear the pain and uncertainty of it.

'Because she is like a princess,' Shalini told him. 'Did you fight for her? Did you slay evil spirits and rescue her? Did you, Duleepji? Did you? Did you?'

'I suppose I did,' he said, and kissed her, and sent her away, and then waited in the room into which Kamala would presently be led by his mother and given into his care.

The trouble was, he told Hari years later, that when he unveiled Kamala, and saw her, he fell in love with her. Perhaps this was true and accounted for the fact that his career in England reading for the law was a failure from the start. His final return, defeated, was hard to bear because no word of reproach was spoken by his father for the wasted years, the wasted money. Returning to India, he laboured under the weight of many burdens: the burden of knowing that his mind was incapable of adjusting itself to the pace set by better men, and the burden of knowing that time and again, in England, allowances had been made for him because he was an Indian who had travelled a long way, at considerable cost, and had so obviously set his heart on lifting himself by his boot-straps from the state of under-privilege into which he had been born. And then there was the burden of knowing that he could not blame his parents for the fact that in England he had often been cold, miserable and shy, and not infrequently dismayed by the dirt, squalor and poverty, the sight of barefoot children, ragged beggars, drunken women, and evidence of cruelty to animals and humans: sins which in India only Indians were supposed to be capable of committing or guilty of allowing. He could blame his parents for forcing him into a premature marriage that disrupted the involved pattern of his scholarly pretensions, but he could not blame them for this dismay, nor could he blame them for the constant proof he had that among the English, at home with them, he was a foreigner. He was invariably treated with kindness, even with respect, but always with reserve; the kind of reserve that went hand in hand with best – and therefore uneasy – behaviour. He found himself longing for the rough and tumble of life at home. To learn the secret of the Englishness of the English he realized that you had to grow up among them. For him, it was too late. But it was not too late for his son. He never anticipated successors in the plural. One son was enough. One son would succeed where he had failed, so long as he had advantages Duleep himself had never enjoyed.

The trouble was, Duleep thought, that India had made its mark on him and no subsequent experience would ever erase it. Beneath the thin layers of anglicization was a thickness of Indianness that the arranged marriage had only confirmed and strengthened. 'And for an *Indian* Indian,' he told Hari, 'there simply isn't any future in an *Anglo*-Indian world.' Of one thing Duleep was certain: the English, for all their protestations to the contrary, were going to hold on to their Empire well beyond his own lifetime and far into if not beyond Hari's as well. If he had a theory at all about the eventual departure of the English it was that they were waiting for Indian boys who would be as English, if not more English, than they were themselves, so that handing over the reins of power they would feel no wrench greater than a man might feel when giving into the care of an adopted son a business built up from nothing over a period of alternating fortune and disaster.

To Duleep, Indian independence was as simple as that, a question of evolution rather than of politics, of which he knew nothing. He believed in the intellectual superiority of the English. Manifestly it was not with physical strength that they ruled an empire. They ruled it because they were armed with weapons of civil intelligence that made the comparable Indian armoury look primitive by comparison. As witness to that was the example of the pale-skinned boy who sat on the verandah of the sub-divisional officer's bungalow. And no one had ever made *him* marry a sixteen-year-old girl. It did not matter to this boy, fundamentally, whether he went to the grave with male or female issue or without. He had never been distracted from his duty or ambition by the overwhelming physical sensation of finding, in front of him, a girl who had been thrust into the room by his own mother, a girl who when unveiled had filled him with the simple impulse to possess, to forget, to cast out the spirits of discipline and learning and celibacy, and enter, in full vigour, into the second stage of life which was attended by spirits of an altogether different nature.

'The fact that I fell in love with your mother,' he told Hari, 'proved one thing, which in itself proved many others. It proved my Indianness. It wasn't just a case of there being here opportunity for a young man to satisfy his sexuality in the terms you would understand it. What young man anyway could resist that excitement, of removing the veil and not being disappointed in what he saw, and of knowing that the girl who stood so meekly in front of him was his to do as he liked with? No, it wasn't as simple as that. At that moment, you see, I automatically entered the second stage of life according to the Hindu code. I became husband and householder. In my heart, then, my ambitions were all for my family, my as yet non-existent family of sons and daughters. Do you see that? Do you understand this strong psychological undertow? Oh, well, yes, naturally I would have pleasure, physical pleasure. But where else should this pleasure lead except to happiness and fulfilment for my own flesh and blood? Certainly it should not have been followed by another long period of celibacy, of learning and education. I was now, in an instant, already past that stage. In the Hindu code I was no longer a student but a man, with a man's responsibilities, a man's sources of delight, which are not the same as a boy's and not the same as a student's. And yet, in the eyes of the western world, which I took passage to, I was still a boy, still a student. In that old lower-middle-class English saying: I was living a lie. Isn't it?'

In such a way Duleep Kumar excused his failure, if failure it was in fact, but tortured himself with it because he was not reproached by his father or mother. Perhaps he was reproached by his wife, Kamala, who had also entered the second stage, having herself been entered, torn open, and then abandoned and left with recollections of her extraordinary and painful translation from child to woman, living at some seasons of the year with her own parents, at other seasons with Duleep's; and greeting him on his return with a humility that had gone a bit sour, so that Duleep felt it, and decided that if you looked at the situation squarely he had managed to get for himself the worst of both worlds. After all, he brought back no crock of gold, no princely raiment, no means to free her from the tyranny of a matriarchal household which his absence in England had probably given her expectations of. If she had no proper notion of the ambition that attended his departure she had, certainly, an understanding of the failure that attended his return.

'I went away,' Duleep said, 'a feared but adored Hindu husband. I returned as a half-man – unclean by traditional Hindu standards and custom because I had crossed the black water. But I had crossed it to no obvious advantage. To purify myself I was persuaded to consume the five products of the cow. Which includes the cow's dung and urine. Although not, of course, its flesh.'

In England he had never admitted to people that he was married. He was ashamed to. For a month or so he had anticipated and feared news of Kamala's pregnancy. His relief was relative to his disappointment. He could not have borne the distraction of knowing he was to be a father, but only with a sense of the reflection on his virility was he able to enjoy the freedom of finding he was not. He longed to receive letters, but their arrival filled him with frustration, even despair. His father wrote in Hindi, and addressed the envelopes in English in block capitals such as you would find figured by children in a kindergarten. Each letter was a sermon, a formal communication from father to son. The few letters he received from Kamala were as naïve as those of a child, the result of hours of labour and instruction. He knew that his own letters had to be read aloud to her. Only his letters to and from Shalini were pleasurable.

Restored to his wife, still unqualified even for the career he had not set his heart on, he set about the business of instructing her in lettering. She submitted ungraciously. She did not want to learn more than she already knew. She thought it a waste of time, an affront to her status as a married woman. Her sisters-in-law poked fun at her if they saw her with books. 'It is only because Shalini is cleverer than you that you act in this stupid way,' he said, when she pretended to have forgotten the lesson he had taught her the day before.

The old rambling house was a hive of inactivity. The women quarrelled among themselves. His mother's voice, raised above all in pitch and authority, brought only a brooding truce. His father spent hours alone in meditation. His brothers idled the days away, gambling and cock-fighting. For a time Duleep himself fell into a similar state of inertia. He need never lift a finger. He need do no work. He played with Shalini, now aged nearly twelve. We are waiting, he told himself, for our father to die. And then we shall have the pleasure of squabbling among ourselves over the inheritance. We shall squabble for three or four years and by then my brother's children will be old enough to marry and the money so carefully hoarded will begin to be squandered, land will be sold and divided and my prophecy will come true.

He had toyed with the idea of continuing his studies in India, and then with the notion that he could apply for a post in the uncovenanted provincial civil service. He had also thought to take his wife away and set up house on his own, but he did not want to leave Shalini behind. Her parents would not let her go to school. He tried to get hold of a teacher from the Zenana Mission, an organization that sent teachers into orthodox Indian homes to instruct the women privately, but the Mission lost interest when it was learned that only one young girl would attend the lessons. For a couple of years or more, he realized, Shalini's education would be his own responsibility. And by now Kamala was pregnant and he began to make plans for his son's future: a future which at times seemed very unlikely to take the shape he wanted it to. He could not imagine Kamala being persuaded to cross the black water. He could not imagine her living in England. In any case, he knew he would be ashamed of her. In England she would be a laughing-stock. Here it was he who was the laughing-stock. The problem looked insoluble. His son would grow up with precisely the same disadvantages he suffered from himself. He could have blamed himself for marrying such a girl. Or he could have blamed his parents for forcing him to marry her. He could have blamed India, and the Hindu tradition. It was easier to blame Kamala. Already she had become shrill and demanding. They quarrelled frequently. He was no longer in love with her. Occasionally he felt sorry for her.

Their first child, a daughter, survived two days. A year later, in 1914, in the first year of England's war with Germany, there was a second daughter; and she survived for a year. A third child, another daughter, was stillborn in 1916. Poor Kamala seemed to be incapable of bearing a healthy baby, let alone a son. Deprived in this way too, their quarrels became bitter. He discovered that she blamed him for her failure. To bear a strong son was her duty. She was determined to do it. 'But how can I do my duty alone?' she asked. 'It is *you*. All your years studying books have sapped your manhood.' Furious, he left the house, taking some money, intending never to return. He had a vague idea that he would join the army; but remembered Shalini and went home when the last of his money had been spent. He returned penniless and disgraced. In the month that he had been away Shalini had become betrothed to one Prakash Gupta Sen. The Gupta Sens were previously connected by marriage with the Lucknow branch of the Kumar family.

Shalini complained to him – not about her betrothal but about his absence during the ceremonial formalities. 'Why did you stay away, Duleepji?' she wanted to know. 'If you had been here you could have gone with my father and my brothers to Mayapore. And if you had gone you could have told me truly what kind of boy this Prakash is. *They* say he is intelligent and good-looking. Why cannot I know what *you* think? I could have believed you.'

'Is that all you can say? Is that all it means to you? What he looks like?'

But already she had become a woman.

'What else can it mean, Duleepji? Besides, I am fifteen. One cannot stay a child for ever.'

Shalini's marriage took place almost a year later – in 1917. Again the house was full. Duleep was astonished at the calm way she accepted the situation and even blossomed in the warmth of the formal flattery always accorded to a bride. When he saw young Prakash Gupta Sen he was horrified. Fat, vain, pompous, lecherous. In a few years this would be proved. Duleep avoided Shalini. 'My nerve has gone,' he told himself. 'Why don't I make a scene? Why do I let this terrible thing go forward?' And knew the answer. 'Because already I am defeated. The future holds nothing for me. I am only half anglicized. The stronger half is still Indian. It pleases me to think the future holds nothing for anyone else either.'

On the night of Shalini's wedding he slept with his wife again. She wept. They both wept. And exchanged undertakings that in future they would be kind, forgiving and understanding. On the morning of Shalini's ritual departure he watched from the gateway. She entered the palanquin without hesitation.

And Duleep saw one thing at last: that in helping her to open her mind and broaden her horizons he had taught her the lesson he himself had never learned: the value of moral as well as physical courage. He only saw her on two subsequent occasions: the first during the week she spent after her marriage in her parental home, with Prakash, and the second five years later when on the eve of his departure for England with his two-year-old son Hari, he visited her in Mayapore during the festival of *Rakhi-Bandan*, bringing her gifts of clothing and receiving from her a bracelet made of elephant hair: the festival during which brothers and sisters reaffirm the bond between them and exchange vows of duty and affection. By this time his wife Kamala had been dead for two years and poor Shalini was still childless. Her husband, Duleep knew, spent most of his time with prostitutes. He died some years later of a seizure in the house of his favourite.

'Imagine,' Shalini wrote to her brother at that time, 'Prakash's sisters actually suggested I should become suttee to honour such a man and acquire merit for myself!'

And Duleep replied from Sidcot, 'Leave Mayapore, and come to us in England.'

'No,' she wrote back. 'My duty – such as it is – is here. I feel, Duleepji, that we shall never see each other again. Don't you feel the same? We Indians are very fatalistic! Thank you for sending me books. They are my greatest pleasure. Also for the photograph of Hari. What a handsome boy he is! I think of him as my English nephew. Perhaps one day, if ever he comes to India, I shall meet him if he can bear to visit his old Indian aunt. Think of it – I shan't see thirty again! Duleepji – I am so pleased for you. In the picture of Hari I see again my kind brother on whose knee I used to sit. Well. Enough of this nonsense.'

These were all stories that Duleep eventually told to Hari. In turn, when Hari's father was dead, in the few weeks of English boyhood that were left to him, Hari told them to Colin Lindsey. He thought of them as stories which had no bearing on his own life – even then, with his passage to India booked, and paid for by the aunt with the peculiar name, Shalini.

There was one other story. This too he told Colin. It seemed incredible to both of them; not because they couldn't imagine it happening, but because neither of them could think of it as happening in Harry Coomer's family.

It went like this: that two weeks after Shalini's ritual return to her parents' home, and one week after her final departure to Mayapore with her husband, her father announced his intention to divest himself of all his worldly goods, to depart from his family and his responsibilities, and wander the countryside: become, eventually, *sannyasi.*

'I have done my duty,' he said. 'It is necessary to recognize that it is finished. It is necessary not to become a burden. Now my duty is to God.'

His family were shocked. Duleep pleaded with him but his resolve was unshaken. 'When are you leaving us, then?' Duleep asked.

'I shall go in six months' time. It will take until then to order my affairs. The inheritance will be divided equally among the four of you. The house will belong to your elder brother. Your mother must be allowed to live here for as long as she wishes, but your elder brother and his wife will become heads of the household. All will be done as it would be done if I were dead.'

Duleep shouted, 'You call this good? You call it holy? To leave our mother? To bury yourself alive in *nothing*? To beg your bread when you are rich enough to feed a hundred starving beggars?'

'Rich?' his father asked. 'What is rich? Today I have riches. With one stroke of a pen on a document I can rid myself of what you call my riches. But what stroke of a pen on what kind of document will ensure my release from the burden of another lifespan after this? Such a release can only be hoped for, only earned by renouncing all earthly bonds.'

Duleep said, 'Ah well, yes! How fine! In what way could you be ashamed now to find your son a little burra sahib? What difference could it make to you now, what I was or where I was? Is it for this that I gave in to you? Is it to see you shrug me off and walk away from me and my brothers and our mother that I obeyed you?'

'While there is duty there must be obedience. My duty to you is over. Your obedience to me is no longer necessary. You have different obligations now. And I have a duty of still another kind.'

'It is monstrous!' Duleep shouted. 'Monstrous and cruel and selfish! You have ruined my life. I have sacrificed myself for nothing.'

As he had found earlier, it was easier to blame anyone than to blame himself, but he regretted the attack. He suffered greatly at the recollection of it. He tried to speak about it to his mother, but these days she went about her daily tasks dumb and un-approachable. When the time drew near for his father to go he went to him and begged his forgiveness.

'You were always my favourite son,' old Kumar admitted. 'That was a sin, to feel more warmly towards one than to the others. Better you should have had no ambition. Better you should have been like your brothers. I could not help but exert authority more strongly over the only son who ever seemed ready to defy it. And I was ashamed of my preference. My exer-tion of authority perhaps went beyond the bounds of reason. A father does not ask his son to forgive him. It is only open to him to bless him and to commit to this son's care that good woman, your mother.'

'No,' Duleep said, weeping. 'That duty is not for me. That is for your eldest son. Don't burden me with that.'

'A burden will fall upon the heart most ready to accept it,' old Kumar said, and then knelt and touched his youngest son's feet, to humble himself.

Even in the business of becoming *sannyasi* old Kumar seemed determined upon the severest shock to his pride. He underwent no rituals. He did not put on the long gown. On the morning of his departure he appeared in the compound dressed only in a loin cloth, carrying a staff and a begging-bowl. Into the bowl his stony-faced wife placed a handful of rice. And then he walked through the gateway and into the road, away from the village.

For a while they followed him, some distance behind. He did not look back. When Duleep and his brothers gave up following him their mother continued. They watched but said nothing to each other, waiting for their mother who, after a while, sat down on the roadside and stayed there until Duleep joined her, urged her to her feet and supported her back to the house.

'You must not give in to sorrow,' she told him later, lying on her bed in a darkened room from which she had ordered the servants to remove every article of comfort and luxury. 'It is the will of God.'

Thereafter his mother lived the life of a widow. She gave her household keys into the care of her eldest daughter-in-law and moved into a room at the back of the house that overlooked the servants' quarters. She cooked her own food and ate it in solitude. She never left the compound. After a while her sons and daughters-in-law accepted the situation as inevitable. By such behaviour, they said, she was acquiring merit. They seemed content, then, to forget her. Alone, Duleep went every day to her room and sat with her for a while and watched while she spun khadi. To communicate at all he had to say things that needed no answer or ask simple questions which she could respond to with a nod or shake of the head.

In this way he brought her news: of the end of England's war with Germany, of business affairs he had begun to take an interest in, of his wife Kamala's latest pregnancy, of the birth of yet another stillborn child, a girl. Once he brought news, a rumour, that his father had been recognized but not spoken to by one of the Lucknow Kumars who had been travelling in Bihar and had seen him on the platform of a railway station with his begging-bowl. His mother did not even pause in her spinning. In 1919 he told her something of the troubles in the Punjab, but did not mention the massacre of unarmed Indian civilians by British-commanded Gurkha troops in Amritsar. In this same year he brought the news that Kamala was again with child, and in 1920, a few weeks after the festival of Holi, the news that he had a son. By now the old lady had taken to muttering while she spun. He could not be sure that she ever heard what he said. She did not look at him when he told her about Hari, nor two days later when he told her that Kamala was dead; that now he had a strong healthy son but no wife. She did not look at him either when he began to laugh. He laughed because he could not weep; for Kamala, or for his son, or his father or old mad mother. 'She made it, you see, Mother,' he shouted at her hysterically in English. 'She knew her duty all right. My God, yes! She knew her duty and did it in the end. It didn't matter that it cost her her life. We all know our duty, don't we? Just like I know mine. At last I've got a son and I have a duty to him, but I've also got you, and Father charged me with a duty to you as well.'

It was a duty that took another eighteen months to discharge. One morning he went to his mother's room and found the spinning-wheel abandoned and the old woman on her bed. When he spoke to her she opened her eyes and looked at him and said:

'Your father is dead, Duleepji.' Her voice was hoarse and cracked through long disuse. 'I saw it in a dream. Is the fire kindled yet?'

'The fire, Mother?'

'Yes, son. The fire must be kindled.'

She slept.

In the evening she woke and asked him again, 'Son, is the fire kindled?'

'They are making it ready.'

'Wake me when they have finished.'

She slept again, until morning, and then opened her eyes and asked him, 'Do the flames leap high, Duleepji?'

'Yes, Mother,' he said. 'The fire is kindling.'

'Then it is time,' she said. And smiled, and closed her eyes, and told him: 'I am not afraid,' and did not wake again.

It was in the October of 1921 that his mother died. A year later, when he had sold his property to his brothers and paid a visit to his sister Shalini, in Mayapore, he took his son to Bombay and there embarked for England. When he sailed he was comparatively well-off and during the course of the next sixteen years he managed from time to time to increase his capital and income with fortunate investments and lucky enterprises. Perhaps it was true that he had in him what he once referred to as a fatal flaw, although if there was a flaw like this it was not one that led to compromise, as he had thought. He had compromised, certainly, in his youth, but had stood by his duty in early manhood. The flaw was perhaps more likely to be found in the quality of his passion. There may have been impurities in it from the beginning, or the impurities may have entered with the frustrations that, in another man, could so easily have diluted the passion but in him roused and strengthened it to the point where the passion alone guided his thoughts and actions, and centred them all on Hari.

A stranger could look at the life, times and character of Duleep Kumar – or Coomer as he became – and see a man and a career and a background which in themselves, separately or in combination, made no sense. The only sense they made lay in Hari: Hari's health, Hari's happiness, Hari's prospects, power for Hari in a world where boys like Hari normally expected none; these were the notches on the rule Duleep used to measure his own success or failure: and these were what he looked for as the end results of any enterprise he embarked upon.

When Colin Lindsey's father kept his promise to see the lawyers, to try and make some sense out of the apparently absurd report that Duleep Kumar had died a bankrupt, the senior partner of that firm said to him:

'In his own country, Coomer would probably have made a fortune and kept it. He told me once that as a boy he'd only wanted to be a civil servant or a lawyer, and had never once thought of becoming a businessman. The curious thing is that he really had a flair for financial manipulation. I mean a flair in the European sense. It was the most English thing about him when you boiled it down. In his own country he might have knocked spots off the average businessman out there. He saw things in a broad light, not a narrow one. At least, I should say he always began every enterprise seeing it that way, but then narrowed it all down to a question of making money as fast as possible for that son of his so that he could become something he isn't. What a pity! In the last year or two when his affairs began to go down hill, I was always warning him, trying to head him off from foolish speculation. And I suppose this is where – well, blood, background, that sort of thing, finally begin to tell. He got frightened. In the end he went right off his head, to judge from the mess he's left behind. And of course couldn't face it. I don't think he committed suicide because he couldn't face the consequences but because he couldn't face what he knew those consequences would mean for that boy of his. Back home to India, in other words, with his tail between his legs. Coomer, you know, might have found himself in pretty serious trouble. I've said nothing to the son on that score. It's probably best that he shouldn't get to know. But there's one aspect of the business that the bank says looks like a clear case of forgery.'

Mr Lindsey was shocked.

The lawyer, seeing his expression, said, 'You can be thankful you haven't invested in any of Coomer's businesses.'

'I never had that sort of money,' Lindsey replied. 'And actually I scarcely knew him. We were sorry for the boy, that's all. As a matter of fact, it's a surprise to me to hear you say his father was so devoted to him. So far as we could see the opposite was true. I suppose we're a pretty soft-hearted family. My own son included. He asked Harry to spend a summer holiday with us some years ago when he found out that he was going to be on his own. It's been like that ever since.'

The lawyer said, 'But you see, Mr Lindsey, keeping himself out of Harry's light was Coomer's way of devoting himself to his son's best interests. I don't mean that he deliberately tried to give people the impression his son was neglected so that they'd invite him to their homes and he'd grow up knowing what English people were really like. He kept out of Harry's way because he knew that if Harry grew up as he wanted him to there'd come a time when Harry would be ashamed of him. For instance, there was the question of Coomer's accent. It seemed pretty good to me, but of course it *was* an Indian accent. He certainly didn't want Harry to learn anything from it. He didn't want Harry to learn anything from him at all. He told me so. He said he looked forward to the day when he'd see Harry didn't care much for his company. He didn't want the boy to be ashamed of him but too dutiful to show it. All he wanted for Harry was the best English education and background that money could buy.'

And not only money, Lindsey thought. The bitter seed had been sown. It was probably this as much as anything that finally dispelled whatever doubts he may have felt about the reasonableness of his rejection of his son Colin's impossible story-book proposal that Harry should come to live with them permanently if it could possibly be arranged – this – even more than the shock to his well-bred system of learning that young Coomer's father had put someone else's name to a document – this: that young Coomer's lonely situation had not been the result of neglect but of a deliberate policy that had a special and not particularly upright end in view – entrance into a society that stood beyond his father's natural reach to gain for him wholly on his own resources.

Now Lindsey remembered – or rather allowed to make the journey from the back of his mind to the front of it – the comments passed by friends whose judgments he trusted except when they clashed with his liberal beliefs (which were perched, somewhat shakily, on the sturdy shoulders of his natural clannish instincts). He could not actually recall the words of these comments, but he certainly recalled the ideas which lay behind them:

that in India, so long as you kept them occupied, the natives could be counted on very often to act in the common interest; that the real Indian, the man most to be trusted, was likely to be your servant, the man who earned the salt he ate under your roof, and next to him the simple peasant who hated the blood-suckers of his own race, cared nothing for politics, but cared instead, like a sensible fellow, about the weather, the state of the crops, and fair play; respected impartiality, and represented the majority of this simple nation that was otherwise being spoiled by too close a contact with the sophisticated ideas of modern western society. The last man you could trust, these people said (and damn it all, they knew, because they had been there or were related to people who had been there) was the westernized Indian, because he was not really an Indian at all. The only exceptions to this rule were to be found among the maharajahs, people like that, who had been born into the cosmopolitan ranks of those whose job was to exercise authority and were interested in preserving the old social *status quo.*

There had been a time when his son Colin had thought Harry's father was a maharajah, or rajah; or anyway, a rich land-owner of the kind who stood next to maharajahs in importance. Over the years the impression had gradually been adjusted (sometimes by these same friends who said that Hari's father was probably the son of a petty zamindar, whatever a zamindar was). But had the initial impression ever been adjusted to anything like the truth? Had the whole thing been a sham? Lindsey hated to think so. But thought so now, and returned home from his altruistic visit to the lawyers feeling that by and large he and his own son had been put upon, led by the nose into an un-savoury affair because they had been too willing to believe the best about people and discount the worst, ignored the warnings of those who had watched the Lindsey adoption of Harry Coomer with expressions sometimes too clearly indicative of their belief that no good could be expected to come of it.

At dinner that night, listening to his fair and good-looking son talking to black-haired, brown-faced Harry, he was surprised to find himself thinking: 'But how extraordinary! If you close your eyes and listen, you can't tell the difference. And they seem to talk on exactly the same wave-length as well.'

But his eyes were no longer to be closed. He took Harry on

one side and said to him, 'I'm sorry, old chap. There's nothing
I can do. The lawyers have convinced me of that.'

Harry nodded. He looked disappointed. But he said, 'Well,
thanks anyway. I mean for trying,' and smiled and then waited
as if for the arm Lindsey was normally in the habit of laying
fondly on the boy's shoulders.

Tonight Lindsey found himself unable to make that affectionate gesture.

His sharpest memories were of piles of leaves, wet and chill to
the touch, as if in early morning after a late October frost. To
Hari, England was sweet cold and crisp clean pungent scent; air
that moved, crowding hollows and sweeping hilltops; not stagnant, heavy, a conducting medium for stench. And England was
the park and pasture-land behind the house in Sidcot, the gables
of the house, the leaded diamond-pane windows, and the
benevolent wistaria.

Waking in the middle of the night on the narrow string-bed
in his room at Number 12 Chillianwallah Bagh he beat at the
mosquitoes, fisted his ears against the sawing of the frogs and the
chopping squawk of the lizards in heat on the walls and ceiling.
He entered the mornings from tossing dreams of home and
slipped at once into the waking nightmare, his repugnance for
everything the alien country offered: the screeching crows outside and the fat amber-coloured cockroaches that lumbered
heavy-backed but light-headed with waving feathery antennae
from the bedroom to an adjoining bathroom where there was
no bath – instead, a tap, a bucket, a copper scoop, a cemented
floor to stand on and a slimy runnel for taking the dirty water
out through a hole in the wall from which it fell and spattered
the caked mud of the compound; draining him layer by layer of
his Englishness, draining him too of his hope of discovering that
he had imagined everything from the day when the letter came
from his father asking him to meet him in Sidcot to talk about
the future. This future? There had never been such a meeting
so perhaps there wasn't this future. His father had never arrived,
never left Edinburgh, but died in his hotel bedroom.

Sometimes when a letter reached him from Colin Lindsey he
looked at the writing on the envelope as if to confirm to some
inner, more foolishly expectant and hopeful spirit than his own

that the letter was not one from his father telling him that everything was a mistake. He longed for letters from England, but when they arrived and he tore them open and read them through, first quickly and then a second time slowly, he found that the day had darkened in a way that set him brooding upon some act of violence that was motiveless; aimless, except to the extent that it was calculated to transport him miraculously back to his native air, his native heath, and people whose behaviour did not revolt him. In such moods he never replied to a letter. He waited until the acutest pain of receiving it was over, and, in a day or two, made a first attempt at an answer that would not expose him as a coward; for that would never do; it would be foreign to the scale of values he knew he must hang on to if he were to see the nightmare through to its unimaginable, unforeseeable, but presumably logical end.

In this way Colin Lindsey never had the opportunity of guessing the weight of the burden of exile his friend struggled under. In one letter, he wrote to Harry: 'I'm glad you seem to be settling down. I'm reading quite a lot about India to try and get a clearer picture of you in it. Sounds terrific. Wish I could come out. Have you stuck any good pig lately? If you do, don't leave the carcase in front of a mosque, or the devotees of the Prophet will have you by the knackers. Advice from an old hand! We drew the match with Wardens last Saturday. We miss that Coomer touch – those elegant sweeps to his noble leg and those slow snazzy off-breaks. Funny to think that your cricket will be starting just about the time the school here begins its football season. Not that I shall be seeing the football this year. Has it been decided yet what you are going to do? I'm definitely leaving at the end of this summer term. Dad says he'll stump up for a crammer if I want to matriculate (some hopes) but I've decided to accept my uncle's offer to go into the London office of that petroleum company he's something to do with.'

To this, after several days, Hari replied, 'The idea always was, you remember, that I'd swot for the ICS exams after leaving Chillingborough and sit for them in London, then come out here and learn the ropes. These days you can sit for the exams over here as well, but I don't think I'll be doing that. My aunt's old brother-in-law runs some kind of business in Mayapore and I gather the idea is that I should go into it. But first I'm supposed to learn the language. Although my uncle-in-law thinks my own language could be useful he says it's not much good to him if I can't understand a word of what 90% of the people I'd be dealing with were talking about. It's raining cats and dogs here these days. Sometimes it gives over and the sun comes out and the whole place steams. But the rain goes on, I'm told, until September, and then it begins to cool down, but only for a few weeks. It starts getting hot again pretty soon in the new year, and by April and May I gather you can't even sweat. I'm down with gippy-tum, and can only face eating fruit, although I wake up thinking of bacon and eggs. Please give my love to your mother and father, and remember me to Connolly and Jarvis, and of course to old Toad-in-the-hole.'

Sealing such a letter once he was tempted to tear it up and write another that would give Colin some idea of what it had meant to find himself living on the wrong side of the river in a town like Mayapore. Then he would have said: 'There is nothing that isn't ugly. Houses, town, river, landscape. All of them are reduced to sordid uniform squalor by the people who live in them. If there's an exception to this, you'd no doubt find it on the other side of the river, in what are called the civil lines. And perhaps you'd eventually get used to it, even enjoy it, because the civil lines are where *you*'d be; that would be *your* retreat. But I am here in the Chillianwallah Bagh. It's what they call modern. You're somebody by their standards if you live in one of these stifling concrete monstrosities. The whole place stinks of drains, though. In my room – if you can call it a room: with unglazed barred windows it looks more like a cell – there's a bed (a wooden frame with a string mesh), a chair, a table which Aunt Shalini has covered with a ghastly piece of purple cloth embroidered in silver thread, a wardrobe called an almirah with a door that doesn't work. My trunk and suitcases are mildewed. There's a fan in the middle of the ceiling. More often than not it stops working during the night and you wake up suffocating. My aunt and I live alone. We have four servants. They live in the compound at the back. They speak no English. When I'm in a room downstairs they watch me from doorways and through windows because I'm the nephew from "Bilaiti". My aunt, I suppose, is a good woman. She's not forty yet, but looks more than fifty. We don't understand each other. She tries to understand me harder than I can bother to try to understand her. But at least she is bearable. I detest the others. From their point of view I'm unclean. They want me to drink cow-piss to purify myself of the stain of living abroad, crossing the forbidden water. Purify! I have seen men and women defaecate in the open, in some wasteland near the river. At night the smell of the river comes into my bedroom. In my bathroom, in one corner, there is a hole in the floor and two sole-shaped ledges to put your feet on before you squat. There are always flies in the bathroom. And cockroaches. You get used to them, but only by debasing your own civilized instincts. At first they fill you with horror. Even terror. It is purgatory, at first, to empty the bowels.

'But the house is a haven of peace and cleanliness compared with what's outside and what goes on out there. We get our milk straight from a cow. Aunt Shalini boils it, thank God. The milkman comes in the morning and milks his cow outside the house, near a telegraph pole. To this pole he ties a dead, stuffed calf which the cow nuzzles. This keeps her in milk. The calf was starved to death because the cow's milk was taken by the milk-man to sell to good Hindus. Since I knew that, I take only lemon or lime in my tea when Aunt Shalini can get them from the bazaar. I've only been to the bazaar once. That was during the first week I was here, towards the end of May. The temperature was 110 degrees. I hadn't yet taken in what was happening to me. I went to the bazaar with Aunt Shalini because I wanted to be decent to her and she seemed keen for me to go. What was it? Some kind of nightmare? The leper, for instance, who hung about at the entrance to the bazaar and whom nobody seemed to take any special notice of. Was he real? Yes, he was real enough. What was left of his hand came close to my sleeve. Aunt Shalini put a coin into his bowl. She knows about lepers. They are part of her daily experience. And when she put the coin into his bowl I remembered that story my father told me, which I told you, and neither of us quite believed about the way my grand-father was said to have left his home and gone begging to acquire merit and become part of the Absolute. Well – did he end up as a leper too? Or did he just find himself communing with God?

'All those stories that my father told me; at the time they seemed to be simply stories. A bit romantic even. To get the full flavour of them you have to imagine them taking place here, or somewhere like it, somewhere even more primitive. I look at Aunt Shalini and try to see her as that young kid who was married off at all that cost to the fellow who died of syphilis or something. Died in a brothel, anyway. I wish Father hadn't told me about that. I find myself watching her at table, hoping she won't touch anything but the outer rim of the plate. Poor Aunt Shalini! She asks me questions about England, the kind of question you can't answer because at home it never gets asked.

'Home. It still slips out. But this is home, isn't it, Colin? I mean I shan't wake up tomorrow at Chillingborough or Sidcot, or in what we always called "my" room at Didbury? I shall wake up here, and the first thing I'll be conscious of will be the sound of the crows. I shall wake up at seven and the household will have been up and about for at least an hour. There'll be a smell from the compound of something being cooked in ghi. My stomach will turn over at the thought of breakfast. I'll hear the servants shouting at each other. In India everybody shouts. There'll be a pedlar or beggar at the gate out front. And he'll be shouting. Or there may be the man who screams. When I first heard him I thought he was a madman who'd got loose. But he is a madman who has never been locked up. His madness is thought of as a sign that God has personally noticed him. He is therefore holier than any of the so-called sane people. Perhaps underneath this idea that he's holy is the other idea that insane is the only sensible thing for an Indian to be, and what they all wish they were.

'The sun will probably be out in the morning. It hurts the eyes to look out of the window. There's no gradation of light. Just flat hard glare and sudden shadow as a cloud passes. Later it will rain. If the rain falls heavily enough you won't be able to hear the people shouting. But after a bit the sound of the rain sends you barmy too. Since coming here I've started smoking. The cigarettes are always damp though. About eleven o'clock an old man called Pandit Babu Sahib arrives, ostensibly to teach me Hindi. My aunt pays for the lessons. The pandit has a dirty turban and a grey beard. He smells of garlic. It sickens me to catch his breath. The lessons are a farce because he speaks no English I recognize. Sometimes he doesn't turn up at all, or turns up an hour late. They have no conception of time. To me they are still "they".

'You ask me what I'm going to do. I don't know. I'm at the mercy of my aunt's in-laws for the moment. There are some Kumars still in Lucknow, apparently, and a brother of Aunt Shalini's and his wife in the old Kumar house in the United Provinces. But they want nothing to do with me. Aunt Shalini wrote to them when she got the news of Father's death. They weren't interested. Father cut himself off from everyone but Aunt Shalini. He sold his land to his brothers before emigrating to England. This brother of his who's still alive is afraid – so Aunt Shalini thinks – that I plan to claim back part of the property. She suggests going to a lawyer to see if the original sale was in order. In this she's like every other Indian. If they can get involved in a long and crippling lawsuit they seem to be happy. But I want nothing to do with that sort of thing. So I'm dependent on her and her brother-in-law, Romesh Chand Gupta Sen, until I can earn a living. But what decent living can I earn without some kind of recognized qualification? Aunt Shalini would let me go to one of the Indian colleges, but it's not for her to say, because Romesh Chand controls the purse-strings. (After all, the Gupta Sens *own* her.) There's a Technical College here that was founded by a rich Indian called Chatterjee. Sometimes I think I might try and get in there and work for an engineering degree or diploma or whatever it is a place like that hands out.

'Do you know the worst thing? Well, not the worst, but the thing that makes me feel really up against it? Neither Aunt Shalini nor Romesh Chand, nor any of their friends and relatives, know any English people, at least not socially, or any who matter. Aunt Shalini doesn't know any because she doesn't have any social life. The others make it a point of principle not even to try to mix. This is a tight, closed, pseudo-orthodox Hindu society. I'm beginning to see just what it was that my father rebelled against. If they knew a few English I don't think it would be long before some kind of special interest was taken in my future. My five years at Chillingborough can't mean nothing, and there must be all kinds of scholarships and grants I could be put on to. But Aunt Shalini knows nothing about them, and seems afraid to raise the subject with anyone, and the Gupta Sens clearly don't want to know. Romesh Chand says I'll be useful to him in his business. I've seen his offices. I think I'd go mad if I had to work there. The main office is over a warehouse that overlooks the Chillianwallah Bazaar, and there's a sub-office at the railway sidings. He's a grain and fresh vegetable contractor to the military station on the other side of the river. He's also a grain dealer on his own account. And Aunt Shalini says he's got his fingers in a lot of other enterprises. He owns most of the Chillianwallah Bagh property. This is the India you won't read about in your pig-sticking books. This is the acquisitive middle-class merchant India of money under the floorboards, and wheat and rice hoarded up until there is a famine somewhere and you can off-load it at a handsome profit, even if most of it has gone bad. Then you sell it to the Government and bribe the government agent not to notice that it's full of weevils. Or you can sell it to the Government while it's still in good condition and there's no famine and the Government can let it go bad – unless of course it's stolen from their warehouses and bought up cheap and stored until a government official can be bribed to buy it all over again. Aunt Shalini tells me about such things. She is very naïve. She tells me things like this to make me laugh. She does not realize that she is talking about the people I'm supposed to feel kindred affection for, men like her husband, for instance, the late Prakash Gupta Sen. Somehow I must fight my way out of this impossible situation. But fight my way to where?'

Indeed, to where? It was not a question Colin could have helped him to answer because Hari never asked it of anyone but himself, and it was several months before he put it even to himself so directly, in such unequivocal terms. He had not asked himself the question before because he could not accept the situation as a real one. In that situation there was a powerful element of fantasy, sometimes laughable, mostly not; but a fantasy that was always inimical to the idea of a future stemming directly from it. In terms of a future, first the fantasy had to be destroyed. Something projected from the real world outside had to hit and shatter it. During this period he hung on to his Englishness as if it were some kind of protective armour, hung on to it with a passionate conviction the equal of that which his father had once had that to live in England was probably enough in itself to transform life. And because he now felt that his Englishness was the one and only precious gift his father had given him he liked to forget that he had once been critical of him and year by year more ashamed of him. He fell into the habit of saying to himself when-ever a new horror was revealed to him: 'This is what my father hated and drove himself mad trying to ensure I'd never be touched by.' Madness was the only way he could explain his father's 'suicide'. And he was old enough, too, to guess that loneliness had heightened the degree of insanity. If Duleep Kumar had not been lonely perhaps he might have found the courage to face up to the financial disaster which the lawyers had succeeded in convincing his son of but never in explaining to that son's satisfaction. In Mayapore, Hari saw that disaster as the work of the same malign spirit that now made his own life miserable.

Through most of his first experience of the rains he was chronically and depressingly off-colour. Whatever he ate turned his bowels to water. In such circumstances a human being goes short on courage. His indisposition and his distaste for what lay outside Number 12 Chillianwallah Bagh kept him confined to the house for days at a time. He slept through the humid after-noons as if drugged and grew to fear the moment when his Aunt Shalini would want his company, or suggest a walk because the rains had let up and the evening was what she called cool. They would go, then, towards the stinking river, along the Chillian-wallah Bagh Extension road to the Bibighar bridge, but turn back there as if what lay on the other side was prohibited, or, if not actually prohibited, undesirable. In all that time from May until the middle of September he did not cross over into the civil lines. At first he did not cross because there was no call to; but later he did not cross because the other side of the river became synonymous with freedom and the time did not strike him as ripe to test it. He did not want to tempt the malign spirit.

He crossed the river in the third week of September, in 1938, when the rains had gone and his illness was over and he could no longer find any excuse not to go through the motions of pleasing his uncle, Romesh Chand Gupta Sen; when, in fact, he had decided to please his uncle as much as was in his power, because he had talked to his uncle's lawyer, a man called Srinivasan, and now had hopes of persuading the uncle to send him to the Mayapore Technical College, or to the college in the provincial capital.

'I will become,' he told himself, 'exactly what my father

wanted me to become, and like this pay the malign spirit out. I'll become an Indian the English will welcome and recognize.'

His father's death had raised the question of moral indebtedness.

He went with some documents Romesh Chand told him were needed by a Mr Nair, the chief clerk at the warehouse near the railway sidings. He travelled by cycle-rickshaw. Few of the clothes he had brought from England were of any use to him. His aunt had helped to fit him out with shirts and trousers run up by the bazaar tailor. The trousers he wore today were white and wide-bottomed. With them he wore a white short-sleeved shirt, and carried a buff-coloured sola topee. Only his shoes were English; and those were hand-made and very expensive. One of Aunt Shalini's servants had polished them by now to a brilliance he himself had never achieved.

The traffic was held up on the Mandir Gate bridge. Immediately in front of the rickshaw, obstructing the view, was an open lorry loaded with sacks of grain. A sweating, half-naked coolie sat on top of the sacks smoking a bidi. Abreast of the rickshaw was another; behind, a bus. The rickshaw had come to a halt opposite the temple. There were beggars squatting in the roadway near the temple gate. He looked away in case he should recognize the leper. He heard the clanking of the train on the opposite bank but could not see it because of the lorry. Five minutes after he heard the train the traffic began to move. The bridge had a parapet of whitened stone. He had a brief impression of water and openness, and banks curving away in muddy inlets and promontories, and then the three wheels of the rickshaw were juddering over the wooden planks of the level crossing and he was translated into this other half of the world.

His disappointment was as keen as his anticipation had been. The road from the Mandir Gate bridge to the railway station was lined with buildings that reminded him of those on the Chillianwallah Bagh Extension road: but before the rickshaw boy took a turn to the right, ringing his bell and shouting a warning to an old man who was chasing a berserk water-buffalo, he saw a vista of trees and a hint, beyond the trees, of space and air. When the rickshaw boy drew up in the forecourt of the station goods-yard, which looked like all goods-yards, graceless and functional, he told him to wait. The boy seemed to object, but young Kumar could not understand what he said, and walked away without paying, the one sure way he knew of keeping him there. He entered the godown that bore across its front the sign *Romesh Chand Gupta Sen and Co., Contractors*. Inside there was the nutty fibrous smell of all such places. It was dark and comparatively cool. Labourers were carrying sacks of grain from a stack out into the sunlit siding on the other side of the warehouse and loading them into a goods wagon. The air was full of floating dust and chaff. Set into the wall closest to him was an open door and a bank of windows that overlooked the vast cavern of the godown. This was the office. It was lit by naked electric light-bulbs. He entered. The head clerk was not there. Two or three young men in dhotis and shirts of home-spun cotton sat at trestle tables writing in ledgers. They remained seated. In his uncle's office over the warehouse in the Chillian-wallah Bazaar the young clerks stood up whenever he went into their musty ill-lit rooms. That embarrassed him. All the same, suspecting that these clerks at the railway godown knew who he was, he could not help noticing the difference in their behaviour and momentarily feeling diminished by it. He asked where the chief clerk was. The man he spoke to replied fluently enough, answering English for English, but in a manner that was obviously intended to be offensive.

'Then I'll leave these papers with you,' Kumar said, and put them on the desk. The young man picked them up and threw them into a wire basket.

'They are marked urgent, by the way,' Kumar pointed out.

'Then why do you leave them with me? Why don't you take them with you and look for Mr Nair in the station master's office?'

'Because that's your job, not mine,' Kumar said, and turned as if to walk out.

'These documents are entrusted to you, not to me.'

They stared at each other.

Kumar said, 'If you're not competent to deal with them by all means let them lie in your little wire basket. I'm only a delivery boy.'

When he was at the door the other man called, 'I say, Coomer.'

He turned, annoyed to have it proved that the other man did know who he was.

'If your uncle wants to know whom you gave these papers to, tell him – Moti Lal.'

It was a name he expected to forget but in fact had cause to remember.

When he got outside the warehouse the rickshaw boy had turned nasty. He wanted to be paid off. Kumar climbed in and told him to go to the cantonment bazaar. He had worked out how to say it in Hindi. When the boy shook his head Kumar repeated the order but raised his voice. The boy took hold of the handlebars and wheeled the rickshaw around, ran with it for a few paces and jumped on to the saddle. Kumar had to shout at him again when he began to turn back along the way they had come. They had another argument. Kumar guessed the reason for the boy's objections. He did not want to take an Indian passenger so far. An Indian passenger seldom paid more than the minimum fare.

Eventually the boy submitted to his bad luck and turned towards the cantonment, and then Kumar found himself travelling along wide avenues of well-spaced bungalows. Here there was shade and a sense of mid-morning hush such as fell at home, between breakfast and lunch during the holidays at Didbury. The road was metalled but the pathways were kutcha. In the sudden quietness he could hear the rhythmic click of the pedals. He lit a cigarette because the odour of the leather cushions and the smell of the boy's stale sweat were now more noticeable.

The boy made a series of left- and right-hand turns and Kumar wondered whether he was being taken out of his way deliberately, but then – where the road they were now travelling on met another at a T-junction – he could see a section of arcaded shops, and one with a sign over it: Dr Gulab Singh Sahib (P) Ltd: Pharmacy. They had reached the Victoria road. He told the boy to turn left and indicated with a curt flick of the hand, whenever the boy looked over his shoulder to suggest that now was the time to stop, that the journey should continue. He wanted to see beyond the cantonment bazaar. He wanted to go as far as the place he knew was called the *maidan*.

There were English women in the arcades of the Victoria road. How pale they looked. Their cars were parked in the shade along one side of the bazaar. There was this shade to be had because at ten-thirty in the morning the sun was casting shadows. There were also horse tongas. The tonga-carts were painted in gay colours, and the horses' bridles were decorated with silver medallions and red and yellow plumes. Some of the English women were wearing slacks. Briefly he had an impression that these made them look ugly, but this was an impression that did not survive the warmth of the feeling he had that here at last he was again in the company of people he understood. He looked from one side of the road to the other: here was a shop called Darwaza Chand, Civil and Military Tailor; here the Imperial Bank of India; there the offices of the *Mayapore Gazette* which it interested him to see because Aunt Shalini had made a point of ordering the *Gazette* especially for him so that he could read the local news in English. The shops in the cantonment all advertised in the *Gazette*. The names were familiar to him. He wished that he had a lot of money so that he could tell the rickshaw boy to stop at the Imperial Bank, go in and cash a cheque, and then stroll across the road to Darwaza Chand and order some decent suits and shirts. He wished, as well, that he had the courage to go into the English Coffee House, drink a cup or two and smoke a cigarette and chat to the two pretty young white girls who were just now entering. And he would have liked to tap the rickshaw boy on his bony back, get out at the Mayapore Sports Emporium and test the weight and spring of the English willow cricket bats that were for sale there, at a price. The sight of the bats in the window made him long to open his shoulders and punish a loose ball. After he had selected a bat he would go across the road to the Yellow Dragon Chinese Restaurant and eat some decent food; and, in the evening, pay a visit to the Eros Cinema where at 7.30 and 10.30 that evening they were showing a film he had seen months ago with the Lindseys at the Carlton in the Haymarket. He would have liked the Lindseys to be here in Mayapore to see it with him again. Going past the cinema – a building with a white stuccoed façade and a steel mesh concertina gate closing the dark cavern of the open foyer, and set well back in a sanded forecourt – he felt the pain of his exile more sharply than ever.

He told the boy to go in the direction of the *maidan*. The cinema was the last building in the cantonment bazaar – or the first, depending which way you came. Beyond it there was a section of tree-shaded road with low walls on either side and, on the other side of the walls, the huts and godowns of the Public Works Department. The rickshaw boy got up some speed on this stretch, negotiated the crossroads formed by the Victoria and Grand Trunk roads and rode on past the Court house, the Police barracks, the District Headquarters, the chummery, the District Superintendent's bungalow and the bungalow which the Poulsons were to take over in 1939.

In this way Hari Kumar reached the *maidan*. He told the rickshaw boy to stop. The vast space was almost empty. There were two riders – white children mounted on ponies. Their syces ran behind. The crows were wheeling and croaking, but to Hari they no longer looked predatory. There was peace. And Hari thought: Yes, it is beautiful. In the distance, on the other side of the *maidan*, he could see the spire of St Mary's. He got down from the rickshaw and stood in the shade of the trees and watched and listened. Half-closing his eyes he could almost imagine himself on the common near Didbury. The rains had left their green mark on the turf, but he did not know this because he had never seen the *maidan* before; he had never seen it in May when the grass was burnt to ochre.

He wanted to mount and ride and feel the air moving against his face. Could one hire a pony from somewhere? He turned to the rickshaw boy. It was impossible to ask. He did not know the right words. Perhaps he did not need to know, or need to ask because he could guess the answer. The *maidan* was the preserve of the *sahiblog*. But he felt, all the same, that he would only have to speak to one of them to be recognized, to be admitted. He got back into the rickshaw and told the boy to go back to the cantonment bazaar. He would buy a few things at Dr Gulab Singh's pharmacy; some Odol toothpaste and some Pears' soap. Surreptitiously, he felt in his wallet. He had a five-rupee note and four one-rupee notes. About fifteen shillings. The rickshaw boy would ask for three but really be content with two.

On the return journey he became aware that there were very few cycle-rickshaws on the road. There were cars, cycles and horse-tongas. In the cycle-rickshaws the passengers were always Indians. In one rickshaw the passenger had his sandalled feet up on a wooden crate of live chickens. He felt the shame that rubbed off on to him because he travelled by rickshaw, so marking himself as out of his own black-town element because the cycle-rickshaws all came from the other side of the river.

When they reached Gulab Singh's he told the boy to stop, and got down, mounted the double kerb and entered the shadowy arcade. In Gulab Singh's window there were brand goods so familiar, so Anglo-Saxon, he felt like shouting for joy. Or in despair. He could not tell which. He entered. The shop was dark and cool, set out with long rectangular glass cases on table-legs, as in a museum. It smelt faintly of pepper and richly of unguents. At one end there was a counter. There were several English women walking round, each attended by an Indian assistant. There was a man as well, who looked a bit like Mr Lindsey. The Englishman's clothes showed his own up for what they were. *Babu* clothes. Bazaar stuff. The English were talking to each other. He could hear every word they said if he paid attention. The man who looked like Mr Lindsey was saying: 'Why hasn't it come? You said Tuesday and today is Tuesday. I might just as well have ordered it myself. Well, give me the other thing and send the rest up jolly sharp.'

Kumar stood at the counter and waited for the assistant to finish serving the Englishman. The Englishman glanced at him and then turned his attention back to what the assistant was doing: wrapping an unidentifiable cardboard carton.

'Right,' the Englishman said, taking the package. 'I'll expect the other things by six this evening.'

When the Englishman had gone Kumar said, 'Have you got some Pears' soap?'

The assistant, a man several years older than himself, waggled his head from side to side, and went away. Kumar could not be sure that he had understood. Another assistant came through the doorway marked *Dispensary*, but he was carrying a package which he took over to a woman who was studying the articles for sale in one of the glass cases. At the other side of the shop there was a photographic booth. Kumar waited. When he next saw his own assistant the man was opening another of the glass cases for a group of white women.

Kumar moved away from the unattended counter and took up a position from which he judged he would be able to catch the assistant's eye. He was right. He did. But the assistant's expression was that of someone who did not remember ever having been spoken to about Pears' soap. Kumar wished that the assistant's new customers had been men. He could have interrupted their conversation, then, without putting himself in the wrong. Instead, he found himself in the ignominious role of watcher on the sidelines, in a situation another man was taking advantage of: hiding, as Kumar put it to himself, behind the skirts of a group of women. He looked around and saw the man who had come from the dispensary going back there. He said to him, 'I asked someone if you had any Pears' soap.'

The man stopped: perhaps because Kumar's voice automatically arrested him with its sahib-inflections. Momentarily he seemed to be at a loss, assessing the evidence of his eyes and the evidence of his ears. 'Pears'?' he said at last. 'Oh yes, we have Pears'. Who is it for?'

It was a question Kumar had not expected, and one he did not immediately understand. But then did. Who did this fellow think he was? Some *babu* shopping for his master?

'Well, it's for me, naturally,' he said.

'One dozen or two dozen?'

Kumar's mouth was dry.

'One bar,' he said, trying to be dignified about it.

'We only sell it by the dozen,' the man explained, 'but you could get it in the bazaar, I expect,' and then added something in Hindi, which Kumar did not understand.

He said, 'I'm sorry. I don't speak Hindi. What are you trying to say?'

And was conscious, now, that because he was annoyed he had raised his voice, and other people in the shop were watching and listening. He caught the eye of one of the Englishwomen. Slowly she turned away with a smile he could only attach two words to: bitter, contemptuous.

'I was saying,' the man replied, 'that if you are only wanting one bar of Pears' soap you will find it cheaper in the Chillianwallah Bazaar because there they are taking no notice of regulated retail prices.'

'Thank you,' Kumar said, 'you have been most helpful,' and walked out.

*

The room in the Chillianwallah Bazaar office where Kumar worked was larger than the rest. He shared it with other English-speaking clerks. They were afraid of him because of his manner and his family connection with their employer. Proud of their own fluency in what passed among them for English – a language not generally in use at Romesh Chand's warehouse – they resented his intrusion but in a perverse way were flattered by the sense of further elevation his presence gave them. They were boys who, if they could help it, never spoke their mother tongue, and so looked down on the men in the small, airless partitioned cells, old clerks who conducted their business and correspondence in the vernacular. By arriving in their own midst Kumar had confirmed their superiority but threatened their security. In front of him they no longer dared to criticize Romesh Chand, or the head clerks, in case one of Kumar's jobs was to act as a family spy. And even when they felt reassured that it was not they could not help wondering which of them might lose his job to the Anglicized boy who knew nothing about the business but had the manner of a burra sahib. Their conduct towards him was a compound of suspicion, awe, envy and servility.

They sickened him. He thought them spineless, worse than a bunch of girls, giggling one day and sulking the next. He found it difficult to follow what they were saying. They ran all their words one into the other. They sang their sentences. Their pronunciation was peculiar. At first he tried to understand them, but then saw the danger of trying too hard. He wondered how long a man could work among them and not fall into the same habits of speech, not acquire the alien habits of thought that controlled the speech. At night, alone in his bedroom, he sometimes talked aloud to himself, trying to detect changes of tone, accent and resonance in order to correct them. To maintain the Englishness of his voice and habits became increasingly important to him. Even after the disastrous visit to Gulab Singh's pharmacy it remained important. He remembered what his father had said: 'If you answer the telephone people think it is an Englishman speaking.' There were no telephones at his uncle's office. There was no telephone at Number 12 Chillianwallah Bagh. Even if there had been telephones there would have been no Englishman to ring or to be rung by. But this absence of Englishness in his exterior public life he saw as a logical projection of the fantasy that informed his private inner one.

It was at this period, after the visit to the pharmacy, that the notion of having become invisible to white people first entered his head, although it took some time for the notion to be formulated quite in this way. When he had become used to crossing the river from the bazaar to the railway warehouse and used to the way English people seemed to look right through him if their eyes chanced to meet his own, the concept of invisibility fell readily enough into its place, but still more time was needed for that concept to produce its natural corollary in his mind: that his father had succeeded in making him nothing, nothing in the black town, nothing in the cantonment, nothing even in England because in England he was now no more than a memory, a familiar but possibly unreal signature at the end of meaningless letters to Colin Lindsey; meaningless because, as the months went by, the letters deviated further and further from the truth. The letters became, in fact, exercises by young Kumar to keep his Englishness in trim. He knew this. He knew his letters were unsatisfactory. He recognized the signs of growing-away that could be read in Colin's replies. But the association with Colin continued to be precious to him. Colin's signature at the bottom of a letter was the proof he needed that his English experience had not been imagined.

Where does one draw the line under the story of Hari Kumar, Harry Coomer: the story of him prior to Bibighar?

Sister Ludmila said that for her Bibighar began on the morning Merrick took Kumar away in his police truck; so at least Kumar has to be brought to that point, brought anyway to the moment when, in the dark, his body was turned over by Mr de Souza and his face lit by the torch. Such darkness, Sister Ludmila said; the kind of expression which was familiar to her on the faces of young Indians, but was, in Hari's case, especially significant.

And where does one go for the evidence of the story of Kumar prior to Bibighar? Well, there is the lawyer Srinivasan. There is Sister Ludmila. There is no longer Shalini Gupta Sen; no Gupta Sen who knows, or will admit to knowing. There are other witnesses: and, specifically, there is that certain signature in the

Members' Book of the Mayapore Gymkhana Club. There is also the signature of Harry Coomer in the Members' Book for 1939 of the Mayapore Indian Club. The Mayapore Chatterjee Club. The MCC. The other club. The wrong one. And this is to be found in a ledger somewhat similar to those used at the right club, under a date in May 1939, which oddly enough roughly coincides with the day the Deputy Commissioner challenged a tradition and made a forced entry at the Gymkhana.

'I put young Kumar up for the Indian Club' (Srinivasan said) 'because it was something I felt he needed. We only met a few times. I'm afraid he didn't like me. He distrusted me because I was his uncle Romesh's lawyer. Apart from that English manner of his which I found overbearing I quite liked him as a person, if not as a type. If we'd got on better, if he'd trusted me, perhaps I should have been able to do something for him, taken him to Lili Chatterjee's for instance and got him into a few mixed English and Indian parties. But by the time he got into what used to be called the MacGregor House set it was too late. He'd already got on the wrong side of the policeman, Merrick, and been taken in for questioning. The evening in 1939 I took him to the Indian Club wasn't a success. The banias were there, with their feet on the chairs. He hated it. I don't think he ever went again, and a few weeks later he left his uncle's office. He'd got wind of the marriage the Gupta Sens were thinking of arranging for him, and he'd given up hope of getting his uncle to agree to his going to the Technical College. I can tell you this, that if it hadn't been for his Aunt Shalini he'd have been in a bad way when he walked out of Romesh Chand's office. The old man was ready to wash his hands of him. I remember how she begged and pleaded with Romesh to continue the allowance he paid her. Well, he kept it going but cut it down. She pinched and scraped and went without things herself to give Hari something for his pocket; and of course she fed and housed and clothed him. I told her that as long as she did that she was stopping him from standing on his own feet. He was already nineteen. A man by our standards. But she wouldn't hear any criticism of him. And don't get the wrong impression. He didn't just sit back. I remember for instance that he applied for a job at the British–Indian Electrical. He had two or three interviews and for a time it looked as if he'd got in. Naturally they were interested. His English public school education didn't count for nothing. It didn't matter to them that he had no qualifications. They could have taught him what he needed to know, and trained him up on the administrative side. But he fell foul of one of the Englishmen there, so Shalini Gupta Sen told me. It wasn't difficult to guess why. In those days, you know, the commercial people were always looked down upon as the lowest form of Anglo-Indian life. Even schoolmasters ranked higher in the colonial social scale. The man Hari fell foul of probably spoke English with a Midlands accent, and resented the fact that an Indian spoke it like a managing director.

'After the British–Indian Electrical débâcle I tried to get Romesh to understand that the boy's talents were being wasted. But let me confess. It wasn't a problem I spent any sleepless nights over. You want me to be frank. And frankly I did not much care for the kind of Indian Duleep Kumar had turned his son into. Please remember that in those days I was only in my forties, also that my main interest was in politics. And I did not respond to Hari Kumar as a political animal. His father had taught him no doubt that Indian politics were all a nonsense, all window-dressing. Hari did not take them seriously. He had no real knowledge of them, no conception for instance of the step forward that provincial power had meant to the Congress. He scarcely realized that the province he lived in had once been ruled directly by a British Governor and a nominated council. He took democracy for granted. He had no experience of autocracy. Politically he was an innocent. Most Englishmen were. In those days I had no time for such people. Today, of course, I am a political innocent myself. It is the fate that awaits us all, all of us anyway who ever had strong views about political affairs when we were younger. Particularly it awaits those of us who paid for our views with imprisonment. Prison left its disagreeable mark. It made us attach too much importance to the things that led us to it.'

When Hari left his uncle's employment he also told Pandit Baba Sahib he no longer wanted Hindi lessons. He did this to save his aunt from spending money uselessly. He had picked up enough Hindi to give orders, picked up in fact what the average Englishman in India thought worth while bothering with. His series of interviews with the British–Indian Electrical Company took place in the early part of the rainy season of 1939. His rejection was a blow, even though he had expected it after his final interview. For the first time he wrote a letter to Colin that gave young Lindsey – or should have given him – a clearer idea of what Hari Kumar was up against.

'There was a strong likelihood of being sent back home to learn the technical ropes,' he told his friend in Didbury. 'First in Birmingham and then in the London office of the parent company. Things went swimmingly at the first interview with a pleasant chap called Knight who was at Wardens from 1925 to 1930. He played in the Chillingborough–Wardens match of 1929, when apparently they beat us by twenty-two runs. We didn't talk about the job at all, really, although it was Knight who mentioned London and Birmingham and got my hopes up. It sounded like the answer to a prayer, one that had been here on my doorstep all these months. I told him the whole thing, about father, etc. He seemed pretty sympathetic. The next interview was with the managing director, and that was stickier – probably because, as Knight had let slip, he was grammar-school with a university veneer. But even so, I still thought it was going well, even when he poured a bit of cold water on the idea of sending me home for training. He said there was a sort of understanding with the Technical College here to look primarily among their graduates for young Indians who had executive prospects, but that they were also working on a scheme with the college for extra-mural courses for their own "promising men", something to do with part-time training in the firm and part-time education at the college. If I got some kind of diploma from the college then it might be possible to send me home for more intensive instruction. He made rather heavy weather of my not having matriculated and said, "Of course, Coomer, at your age most young Indians have a BA or a BSc." I felt like saying, "Well, of a sort," but didn't, because I guessed anyway that he appreciated the difference between a BSc Mayapore and a man who'd been at Chillingborough on the classical side. Anyway, the second interview ended on an optimistic note. I saw Knight again for a few minutes afterwards and he said that in the month since he and I had had a chat he'd written to someone at the London office who'd been in touch with old Toad-in-the-hole, and that I'd been given a good reference.

'I had to wait another two weeks for interview number three which both Knight and the managing director had warned me about, but given me the impression was not much more than a formality, an interview with a fellow they called the Technical Training Manager, a fellow called Stubbs, who is best described as a loud-mouthed —. He began right away by shoving a little cylinder at me, across his enormous desk, and asking me to tell him what it was and what it was used for. When I said I didn't know but that it looked like a sort of valve he smirked and said, "Where are you from, laddie? Straight down from the tree?" Then he picked up a printed sheet and read out a list of questions. Long before he got to the end I said, "I've already told Mr Knight I know nothing about electricity." He took no notice. Probably I shouldn't have mentioned Mr Knight. He went on until he'd asked me the last question and I'd said, "I don't know," for the last time. Then he glared and said, "You some sort of comedian or something? Are you deliberately wasting my time?" I told him that was for him to decide. He leaned back in his swivel chair, and we stared at each other for what seemed ages. Then he said, "There's only you and me in this room, Coomer or whatever your name is. Let me tell you this. I don't like bolshie black laddies on my side of the business." I got up and walked out. Which is what he wanted me to do and what I couldn't avoid doing unless I wanted to crawl.

'So now you know what I am, Colin, a bolshie black laddie. (Remember that bastard Parrott, in our first year at Chillingborough?) I'm a bolshie black laddie because I know how to construe Tacitus but haven't any idea what that fellow Stubbs was talking about. And that wasn't the end of it. I had a letter from Knight about three days later asking me to go and see him. He told me that for the moment there weren't any vacancies. He was quite a different fellow. Puzzled and embarrassed, doing the right thing by an old Chillingburian, but underneath it all bloody unfriendly. Stubbs must have spun them all a yarn. And because Stubbs was a white man they felt they had to believe him. After all, for the job I was applying for, there were probably a score of BAs and BScs, failed or otherwise, who would be willing to jump when Stubbs said jump.

'The one thing that puzzled me was why it was Stubbs who was allowed to call the tune? Why him? Surely Knight knew what kind of a man he was? But he never so much as hinted he'd like to hear my side of what happened. He never referred to my interview with Stubbs at all. In fact when I came away I wondered why he'd bothered to call me in. He could have given me the brush-off by letter. Later I realized he probably wanted to have another look at me – sort of through Stubbs's eyes, bearing in mind whatever it was Stubbs had told them. And then I guessed that at this second interview with Knight I couldn't have made much of an impression, although it was hardly my fault because as soon as I sat down in front of him I could tell it was no go, and I was damned disappointed. Trying not to show it probably made me look as if I didn't care a damn. But I cared like hell, Colin. After a while the conversation just dried up because he had nothing more to tell me and I had nothing I could say except something like Please, sir, give me a chance. Perhaps he was waiting for me to say "sir". I don't think I ever said "sir" at the first interview, but if I didn't he hadn't noticed. But since he'd talked to Stubbs he was probably on the look-out for that sort of thing. Anyway, he suddenly stopped looking at me, so I got to my feet and said thank you. He said he'd keep a note about me in case something turned up, and stood up too, but stayed behind his desk, and didn't offer to shake hands. I think he had it in mind to give me some kind of tip about remembering that this wasn't Chillingborough and that I should start learning how to behave in front of white men. Anyway that was the feeling in the room. There was that desk between us. For me to be in his office at all had suddenly become a privilege. A privilege I ought to know how to respect. I don't remember coming away – only finding myself outside the main gate of the factory, and getting on my bike and riding back along the Grand Trunk road, over the Bibighar bridge, back to my side of the river.'

For a while after what Srinivasan called the British–Indian Electrical débâcle, Hari did nothing. He regretted writing that letter to Lindsey, regretted it more and more as week after week went by and he got no reply. Other things fell into place in his mind: Mr Lindsey's attitude to him towards the end of his last few weeks in England, which he had always attributed to the man's embarrassment at having been unable to do anything constructive for him financially; the experience on the boat, in which, once past Suez, the English people who had spoken to him freely enough from Southampton onwards began to congregate in exclusive little groups so that for the last few days of the voyage the only Englishmen he managed to talk to were those making the passage for the first time. He had shared a cabin with two other boys, Indian students returning home. He had not got on very well with them because he discovered that he had nothing in common with them. They asked his opinion on subjects he had never given a thought to. They were students of political economy and intended to become university teachers. He had thought them incredibly dull and rather old-maidish. It seemed that he shocked them by sleeping in the nude and dressing and undressing in the cabin instead of in the lavatory cubicle.

And so Hari came, one painful step at a time, to the realization that his father's plans for him had been based upon an illusion. In India an Indian and an Englishman could never meet on equal terms. It was not how a man thought, spoke and behaved that counted. Perhaps this had been true in England as well and the Lindseys had been exceptions to the general rule. He did not blame his father. His anger was directed against the English for fostering the illusion his father had laboured under. If he had felt more liking for his fellow-countrymen he might at this stage have sided with them, sought an occasion for paying the English out. But he did not care for any Indian he had met and what he knew or read of their methods of resisting English domination struck him as childish and inept. In any case *they* did not trust him. Neither, it seemed, did the English. He recognized that to the outside world he had become nothing. But he did not feel in himself that he was nothing. Even if he were quite alone in the world he could not be nothing. And he was not quite alone. There was still Colin, at home, and Aunt Shalini in Mayapore. The affection he had for her, grudging at first, when he first recognized it as affection, had become genuine enough. In her self-effacement he saw evidence of a concern for his welfare which was just as acute – perhaps more acute than Mrs Lindsey's which had been so effusively, openly and warmly expressed. He could not help knowing that in her odd, retiring way his Aunt Shalini was fond of him. The trouble was that her fondness could not reach him or encourage him outside the ingrown little world which was the only one she knew, one that stifled him and often horrified him. It was difficult for him to enter it even briefly to show her that he returned fondness for fondness. To enter it he had to protect himself from it by nursing his contempt and showing his dislike. He could not help it if often she believed the contempt and dislike were meant for her. When she gave him money he could not thank her properly. It was Gupta Sen money. Perhaps she understood his dislike of such money and the way his dislike grew in proportion to his increasing need; or perhaps he had hurt her by the curt words with which he acknowledged it. She took to putting the money in an envelope and leaving it on his bedroom table. It touched him that in writing his name on the envelope she always spelled it Harry.

It touched him too that she seemed to consider him as head of the household, head in the Hindu family sense because he was a man; potentially a breadwinner, husband and father; procreator. He could not imagine himself becoming a married man. Indian girls did not attract him. The English girls he saw in the cantonment seemed to move inside the folds of some invisible purdah that made their bodies look unreal, asexual. His lusts centred upon an anthropomorphous being whose sex was obvious from the formation of the thighs and swollen breasts but whose colour was ambivalent; dumb, sightless and unmoving beneath his own body which at night, under waking or sleeping stress, sometimes penetrated the emptiness and drained itself of the dead weight of its fierce but undirected impulse.

Four weeks after the final meeting with Knight, Hari applied for another job. He had spent the intervening time trying to work out the logic of a situation which he now accepted as real and not illusory. That precious gift from his father, his Englishness, was clearly, in many respects, a liability, but he still regarded it fundamentally as an asset. It was the only thing that gave him distinction. He was strong, healthy, and not bad-looking, but so were countless other young men. Where he scored over them was in his command of the English language. Logic pointed to a deliberate exploitation of this advantage. It occurred to him that he might well earn money by setting up as a private tutor and coaching boys who wanted to improve their speech; but such a life did not appeal to him. He doubted that it would be active enough or that he would have the patience it needed, let alone the skill. The other possibility, perhaps the only other one, was much more interesting.

Having read the *Mayapore Gazette* now for over a year he saw where his qualifications might gain him a natural foothold. Owned by an Indian, edited by an Indian, it was also obviously written and sub-edited by Indians. Its leaders and general articles were of a fairly high standard, but its reports of local events were often unintentionally funny. Hari imagined that the paper's reputed popularity among the Mayapore English was due to the fact that it gave them something to laugh at, as well as an opportunity to see their names in print on the social and sporting pages. For an Indian-owned newspaper it was shrewdly non-committal. It left political alignment to the local vernacular newspapers, of which there were several, and to an English-language paper called *The Mayapore Hindu*, which some of the official English read as a duty and others bought in order to compare its reports with the Calcutta *Statesman* and *The Times of India*, but which most of them ignored. It had been suppressed on more than one occasion.

Once Hari had decided to apply for a job with the *Mayapore Gazette* he spent several days copying out particularly bad examples of syntax and idiom from old issues, and then rewriting them. When he was satisfied that he could do the work he had in mind to persuade the editor to give him, he wrote and asked for an interview. He drafted the letter several times until he was satisfied that he had stripped it to its essentials. According to the headings at the top of the leader column on the middle page of the *Gazette* the editor's name was B. V. Laxminarayan. He told Mr Laxminarayan that he was looking for a job. He told him his age, and gave brief details of his education. He said that to save him the trouble of replying he would ring Mr Laxminarayan in two or three days to find out whether he could see him. He hesitated, but in the end decided, to add that Mr Knight of the British–Indian Electrical Company would probably be prepared to pass on the references that had been obtained from the head-master of Chillingborough. He signed the letter 'Hari Kumar' and marked the envelope 'Personal' to reduce the odds on its being opened and destroyed by some employee who was concerned for the safety of his own position. He had not worked in the office of his uncle for nothing. He doubted that Mr Laxminarayan would know Knight, or know him well enough to ring him, or – if he was wrong in either of these two suppositions – that Knight would have the nerve to tell an Indian any story other than that there had been several interviews but no vacancy. Also he relied on Knight's conception of what it was gentlemanly to say as one prospective employer to another about a young man who had played cricket against his old school.

Hari was right in the second of his suppositions. Laxminarayan knew Knight, but not well enough to ring him unless he wanted confirmation of a story about the British–Indian Electrical Company's activities. In any case he would not have rung him about Kumar's letter. Laxminarayan did not like Mr Knight, whom he described to himself as a two-faced professional charmer whose liberal inclinations had long ago been suffocated by his mortal fear of the social consequences of sticking his neck out. 'Knight,' he told Hari later, 'can now only be thought of as a pawn.' He had these harsh things to say about Knight in order not to have to think them about himself.

Laxminarayan was interested in the letter signed by Hari Kumar, but when he replied, 'By all means ring, although I have no immediate vacancy,' he had no intention of employing him. In fact he had been told by the absentee proprietor, Madhu Lal, who lived in Calcutta, to reduce the overheads and produce a more rational percentage of net profit to total investment. His own private view was that the *Gazette*'s circulation would be increased if the paper could be seen to commit itself to the cause of Indian nationalism. He knew that the *Gazette* was anathema to the members of the local Congress sub-committee, and that it was a bit of a joke to the English. He believed that he could sell it even more widely among the English if he could get up their blood pressure. The bulk of its present readership – self-consciously westernized Indians and snob English – would not be lost, because they were sheep by definition. But he reckoned that over a twelve-month period he could add five or ten thousand copies to the weekly circulation if Madhu Lal ever allowed him to make the paper a repository of informed and controversial local and national opinion – non-Hindu, non-Muslim, non-British, but Indian in the best sense.

Laxminarayan conscientiously believed in his paper. Believing in it was a way of continuing to believe in himself and frank criticism of its shortcomings was a more rewarding occupation than criticism of his own. He had found a way of substituting positive thought for negative action; which perhaps was just as well. He was too deeply committed to the compromise of early middle age to be able to rekindle – in a practical, sensible way – the rebellious spark of his youth. Certainly it was just as well from Hari's point of view. When Laxminarayan first met him it took no more than a few minutes of conversation for the smothered demon in the older man to kick out, to attempt – impotently – to take control of his judgment. The demon disliked Kumar: the manner, the voice, the way the fellow sat, with his head up, his legs crossed, one black hand resting on the other side of the desk – an embryo black sahib, talking with a sahib's assurance, the kind of assurance that conveyed itself as superiority subtly restrained in the interests of the immediate protocol. The demon only stopped kicking because Laxminarayan's internal flanks were inured to the pain of the demon's spurs and because he saw, in Kumar, a potential asset, an asset in terms of the type of periodical Mr Madhu Lal wanted the *Gazette* to be. And when Kumar handed him some papers, written proof of his talents as a sub-editor – paragraphs and columns that he recognized as extracts from old issues now transformed into the simple, clear, standard English that in times of stress even eluded the overworked editor, he knew that he would offer Kumar a job and probably get rid of one of the boys who worried him but for whom he cared most, one of the boys who had little talent but a lot of heart and would in all likelihood turn out eventually to be an embarrassment.

Laxminarayan. These days he lives in a bungalow that once belonged to a Eurasian family who left Mayapore in 1947 – a bungalow in the Curzon road. He is now an old man. He is writing a history of the origins of Indian nationalism that will probably never be finished, let alone published: his apologia for many years of personal compromise. He recognizes that the policy of Madhu Lal paid off because the *Mayapore Gazette* has enjoyed an uninterrupted existence. Left to him, to Laxminarayan, it might have been done to death in 1942, in which year *The Mayapore Hindu* was suppressed for the third or fourth time.

But he is amused, now, at the *Gazette*'s Hindu-National basis – its air of having always supported the causes it has become locally popular to promote. Its new owner is a Brahmin refugee from Pakistan. Its new editor is the owner's cousin. With regard to politics at the centre it gives most space to the speeches and activities of Mr Morarji Desai. It plans, next year, to publish itself in a simultaneous Hindi edition, as a first step towards dispensing entirely with English. This, more than anything, saddens Mr Laxminarayan who throughout his life has had what he calls a love-hate relationship with the English language. It is the language in which he learned to think his revolutionary thoughts, and the language which so readily lent itself to the business of making the cautious middle-way he took look and sound like common sense instead of like a case of cold feet.

'What am I now?' (he would ask you, if you went to see him at his home where he is surrounded by grandchildren whose high-pitched voices seem to come from every room and from the sunlit garden which – as the English would say – has been let go). 'Well, I will tell you. I am an old man who has lived through one of the greatest upheavals of modern history – the first, and I think the most passionate, of a whole series of upheavals, rebellions against the rule of the white man which have now become so commonplace they are almost boring. And I came through it without a scratch. A veritable Vicar of Bray, you understand. Retired now on pension. Honorary life member of the Mayapore Club where good Hindus forgather. Young journalists come to see me when they hear that I steered the *Gazette* through those stormy pre-independence waters and say, "Sir, please tell us what it was really like in the days of the British." Just like your own young people may occasionally say, What was it really like during Hitler and Mussolini? The old colonial British have become a myth, you see. Our young men meet the new Englishmen and say to themselves, "What was all the fuss about? These fellows don't look like monsters and they seem only to be interested in the things we are interested in. They are not interested in the past and neither are we except to the extent that we wonder what the fuss was about and aren't sure that our own government is doing any better, or even that it is a government that represents us. It seems more to be the government of an uneasy marriage between old orthodoxy and old revolutionaries, and such people have nothing to say to us that we want to hear."

'I gave Kumar a job and later got rid of a fellow called Vidya-sagar who was arrested in 1942 with several other members of the staff of *The Mayapore Hindu*, and was then put in prison. I was asked to take some steps in that disagreeable business young Kumar was involved in at the time of Bibighar. I'm afraid I refused. No one asked me to use my good offices in the cause of poor Vidyasagar who was given fifteen strokes for an infringement of prison regulations. Not that there was anything I could have done for either of them. But it stuck in my throat that when both of these boys were arrested, for different reasons, only Kumar had people to speak for him, people to ring me up and say, "Can't you get Hari out of jail? You were his employer. Can't you do something for him? Can't *you* prove he was nowhere in the vicinity of the Bibighar?" People like Lady Chatterjee. And that fellow Knight at the British–Indian Electrical whose conscience probably bothered him. Even the assistant commissioner, Mr Poulson, sent for me and asked me questions about what Hari Kumar's political affiliations really were. I said, "Mr Poulson, he is like myself. He has none. He is a lickspittle of the Raj." I was angry. I did not see why I should raise a finger to help him. If the British couldn't see for themselves that he was innocent, who was I to intervene? He was more British than they were.'

A week after Hari got his job on the *Mayapore Gazette* he received a letter from Colin Lindsey. It was dated towards the end of July 1939. Colin apologized for not having written for so long. 'A few months ago I joined the Territorial Army and your own last letter reached me in training camp,' he explained. 'We were pretty busy. If there's a war – and the odds are there will be – I shall put in for a commission; otherwise I get a kick out of just being an acting unpaid lance-corporal. (They made me up in camp, this summer.) I expect you'll be thinking of the army too, won't you, Harry? I mean if anything happens. I'm told the Indian army is quite an outfit, and no longer officered only by the British. Maybe we'll meet up in some dugout or other, like *Journey's End*! Sorry you had such an unpleasant experience at that factory or whatever it was. I can't understand why your aunt's in-laws wouldn't stump up to see you through the ICS. Dad tells me a friend of his says Indians can become

High Court Judges even, so the ICS seems to be the thing. That or the army. I recommend the latter. It's a great life. And honestly, Harry, you'd make a first-rate platoon commander – which is what I want to be if the war ever gets going. Then you could waggle a couple of fingers at that fellow Stubbs who was obviously other rank material only. Like me, at the moment! I've got a feeling that by the time you get this I shall be in France. Why the hell does it always have to be France? The feeling in my own unit is that the Jerrys ought to come straight over here. Then we could really show them a thing or two. Major Crowe, our CO, reckons that with all that guns–and–butter stuff the poor blighters are half-starved anyway and haven't got the strength to shoulder a rifle, let alone manhandle their artillery. Dear old Harry! Wish you were here. Then we could be in it together. For my money it's the only thing to be in, these days. The fond parents send their love.'

'One time he spoke to me of a letter from that boy Lindsey' (Sister Ludmila said). 'Why did he treat me as a mother-confessor? This I never earned. He spoke in that way he had, of believing in nothing, which was not natural to him, but was what he had acquired. "Sister," he said, "what would you have done if you had received a letter from an old friend that showed you suddenly you were speaking different languages?" I do not remember what I replied. Unless I said, "There is only God's language." Meaning, you understand, the truth – that this language matters and no other. He did not hold himself entirely free of blame for what happened because when he wrote he did not tell Lindsey what was in his heart. Perhaps he did not tell him because he could not. Did not tell him because he did not know himself.'

From the *Mayapore Gazette* Hari received sixty rupees a month, the equivalent of just over four pounds. He gave half to his Aunt Shalini because Uncle Romesh Chand reduced her allowance on the day Hari began work for Mr Laxminarayan. The sixty rupees were paid to Hari as a sub-editor. If Laxminarayan published any of Hari's original reports he was to pay him at the rate of one anna a line. For sixteen lines, then, Hari would earn a rupee.

All this he told Colin when he replied to young Lindsey's

letter. He was looking, perhaps, for a way of showing Lindsey that in Mayapore the threat of German ambitions seemed very far away, and Lindsey's curiously pre-1914 heroics strikingly out of tune with what Hari felt about his own immediate obligations and clearly recollected as the contempt for war which he and Colin had shared, or at least professed to share. Something had happened to Colin. It puzzled Hari to know what. There had been a time when they agreed that it might be necessary to pursue a line of conscientious objection to what they called compulsory physical violence in the interests of a nation's political and economic aims. Now, here was Colin talking nostalgically about *Journey's End*. Did the wearing of a uniform so corrupt a man? And what, anyway, in Colin's case had led him voluntarily to put one on? Colin had once said that patriotism, like religious fervour, was a perversion of the human instinct for survival. Chillingborough was a forcing house of administrators, not of soldiers. To an administrator a soldier represented the last-ditch defence of a policy: one to which, on the whole, it was shameful to retreat.

'I'm glad,' Hari wrote, 'that you're finding life in the TA not too wearing –'

That English subtlety! It struck him even as he wrote the words that they could be read either as manly understatement or bitchy criticism.

'– and I suppose if things come to a head India will be in the war too. Which will mean me.'

He sat and thought for a moment. He did not feel that it would mean him at all.

'It's difficult to apply a theory when faced with a situation that calls for some kind of positive reaction,' he continued. 'I suppose you've been faced with one in much the way that I have.'

He remembered the time when Mr Lindsey had described Adolf Hitler as a bloody housepainter, and later as a man who, 'anyway, got things done'. He also remembered that during Munich, which had coincided with his own act of appeasement of Uncle Romesh Chand, Colin had written him a letter which expressed relief that Mr Chamberlain's common sense had averted hostilities. To Hari in Mayapore, Munich had meant nothing. He judged retrospectively that to the Mayapore English, blanketed as they were in the colonial warmth of their racial indestructibility, it had meant nothing either. He did not doubt, though, that the tone of Colin's latest letter was an accurate reflection of a mood now shared by the English as a whole, at home and abroad. He tried to enter it himself, but could not. The inspiration for it was not to be found in the Chillianwallah Bagh, nor was it to be found in the cantonment, in the magistrates' courts, in the sessions and appeal court of the District Judge, or even on the *maidan*, places with which Hari had become increasingly familiar as a result of his job on the *Gazette*. It was not to be found in them because he entered such places as an Indian. He entered by permission, not by right. He did not care for what he saw. He did not care for what he felt – the envy of the English and their institutions that came to fill the vacuum left by the loss of his own English identity. He found it depressingly easy to imagine Colin in the place of the young Englishman who sat as a magistrate – not precisely with the power of life or death (because his judicial powers were restricted) – but with the power to send a man who was old enough to be his father to jail for a year; depressingly easy because in this young man Colin himself could be seen, if only symbolically, in an unpleasant light. On the other hand, he could not imagine himself presiding in the place of the Indian magistrate who appeared one day in the place of the Englishman, and conducted his court with no less acidity or assurance. For the first time Hari found himself asking: What is an Indian doing sitting there, fining that man, jailing this woman, sending this case up to the court of sessions? He felt an unexpected resistance to the idea of an Indian doing an Englishman's work. When he paused to consider this resistance he realized that he had responded as a member of a subject race. The thought alarmed him.

'Such a fuss,' he wrote to Colin two months later (when, far away in Europe, the war had already begun) about the resignation of those provincial ministries which had been dominated by the Congress. 'Of course you can see both points of view. The Viceroy had to declare war on India's behalf because he's the King-Emperor's representative, and the Germans now rank as the King's enemies. But since for some time now the British policy towards India has been to treat her as an embryo Dominion that only needs time to become self-governing, the

Viceroy might at least have gone through the motions of consulting Indian leaders. Some people say that under the 1935 Act
he was actually committed to consultation, but even if he wasn't
how much more effective it would have been if the declaration
could have been made with a simultaneous Indian statement of
intention to co-operate freely. And one can understand why
with all this talk going on about British War Aims the Indians
feel one of them should be independence for India immediately
the war is over. Failure to state that as a definite aim, with a
definite date, has led a lot of Indians to believe that independence should be insisted on *now*. They say that only a free country fights with a will. And they fear a repetition after the war of
all the prevarication that's been going on these last ten years or
more. But I think they're a lot to blame for the delay themselves.
The Congress says it represents all-India, but it doesn't. All this
disagreement among themselves about who represents what just
plays into the hands of the kind of English who don't want to
give India up – the kind of people my father always assumed
would get their way. On the whole I think he was probably right.
For instance, now that the Congress ministries have all resigned
most of the provinces are back under old-style rule of a Governor and a council, which seems to me the very sort of thing a
sensible party would have wanted to avoid because it puts them
back years politically. But then I have never been and probably
never will be able to make sense of Indian politics. As for the
effect of the war on the English here, so far as I can see there
hasn't been any. Frankly, it's something that seems to be taking
place in almost another world – if you can say that it's taking place
anywhere. To judge from the news nothing much is happening,
is it? The English here say that Hitler now realizes he's bitten off
more than he can chew and will end up by being a sensible chap
and coming to some arrangement with France and Britain. Some
Indians say that their own leaders, Nehru especially, have been
warning the West for years about the threat Hitler has always
represented.'

Apart from a short letter from Colin which was written over
the Christmas of 1939, a Christmas which Colin had spent at
home, after completing a course of training as an officer cadet,
Hari heard nothing for nearly a year. A note from Mr Lindsey
in the spring of 1940 informed him that Colin was 'somewhere

in France' and that Hari's last letter had been forwarded to him. He said that the best thing for Hari to do in future would be to write to Colin at Didbury so that the letters could be sent on to wherever he happened to be.

Hari could not help remembering the attitude Colin's father had taken in 1938, an attitude he had begun to see during the past two years as proof that the man had stopped trusting him. 'What will he do with my letters?' he asked himself. 'Read them? Censor them? Not forward them if I say anything he thinks might upset Colin, or if I say something he doesn't personally like?' The shadow of Mr Lindsey fell across the notepaper whenever he wrote. Here was a further disruption to the even flow of thoughts going out to his old friend. The belief that he and Colin were growing further and further apart as a result not only of circumstances but also of the intervention of the powerful force of the malign spirit that had driven his father to death and himself into exile, now took hold of him, but the letter he eventually received from Colin in the August of 1940 seemed to show that between them nothing had fundamentally changed. The structure of a friendship is seldom submitted to analysis until it comes under pressure; and when Hari attempted an analysis of his friendship with Colin he found it healthily straightforward. It was an attraction of like for like that had long ago outgrown whatever initial morbid or childish curiosity there had been in the colours of the skin and the magic of the genes. Colin's letter turned back the years. Here was the authentic voice of his friend Lindsey. Reading between the lines Hari understood that Colin had not had an easy passage. This pegged them level again. The letter gave him little general information. Young Lindsey had been at Dunkirk, and since then 'in hospital for a bit, not because I was badly hurt but because it took rather a long time to get the proper treatment and dressings, and things went bad on me, but are all right now'. The letter was written from home on a spell of leave between leaving hospital and returning to his unit.

'It was a bloody shambles if you ask me. It amuses me when I hear Dad say to people his son was at Dunkirk, as if that was something to be proud of. My lasting reaction is one of anger, but undirected anger because no one person or even group of persons could be held responsible more than any other person or any other group. I suppose it was our old friend Nemesis catching up with us at last. I lost one good friend. I went to see his sister the other day. Ridiculous how one gets involved in these trite melodramatic situations. We both hated it. When I got back from hospital Dad gave me a couple of letters from you that he'd saved up. We had a bit of a row about that. I was worried what you'd have been thinking, not getting any answers. At first he said he hadn't wanted to bother me, and that you'd understand anyway that I was otherwise engaged. Then he admitted he'd read them and thought them full of a lot of "hot-headed" political stuff. Hari, I only tell you this so that if you ever write letters to me care of home again you can bear in mind that they might be read. He's promised not to do that ever again, and sees that it was wrong, but he's got some funny notions in his head nowadays. I don't want to hurt the old boy but in lots of ways he seems like a stranger to me. And that's a cliché situation too, isn't it? So cliché that I almost distrust my reactions to it. But there are so many things he says and does that get on my nerves. He keeps a *Times* wall map, and sticks pins in it like a general. The pin that's stuck in Dunkirk has a little paper union jack on it. I have an idea it represents me. Write and tell me some sensible things.'

Sensible things? On the day Hari received this letter he had been in the District Court listening to the appeal against conviction of a man accused and found guilty in the magistrate's court at Tanpur of stealing another man's cow and selling it to a man who had given it away as part of his daughter's dowry. The accused man said that the cow had become his property because its owner refused to stop it wandering on to his land and it had fed constantly free of cost and consumed fodder in excess of its market value. The appeal was based on the grounds that the Tanpur magistrate had not admitted the evidence of two witnesses who would swear to the fact that the convicted man had given the original owner repeated warnings of his intention to sell. Judge Menen dismissed the appeal and Hari then left the court because the next and last case was an appeal against imprisonment under section 188 of the Indian Penal Code, and Hari's editor never published reports of such controversial matters.

'Sensible things?' Hari wrote back to Colin. 'I suppose that in wartime especially you can reckon it sensible if not actually fair to imprison a man for speaking his mind. But this is not a purely wartime measure. It is a long-standing one provided for in a section of the criminal procedure code. Section 144 enables the civil authority to decide for itself that such and such a man is a potential local threat to public peace, and thus to *order* him to stay quiet on pain of arrest and imprisonment. If he disobeys the order he gets prosecuted and punished under section 188. I believe he can appeal as far as the provincial High Court if he has a mind to. I was at the District and Sessions Court on the day your letter came. I left the court just before the Judge (an Indian) heard such an appeal, so I know nothing of the actual proceedings. But I saw the prisoner on my way out, waiting with two constables, and recognized him as a fellow called Moti Lal. He recognized me too and said, "Hello, Coomer," and was then hustled in through the door prisoners enter the court by. The last time I saw this man he was working as a clerk at my uncle's depot at the railway sidings. I made inquiries when I got back to the office. It seems my uncle sacked him a few months ago, ostensibly for inefficiency. But I guess from what my editor told me that the real reason was that my uncle heard from someone that Moti Lal was mixed up with what you could call the underground side of the Congress Party. I asked my uncle's lawyer, a Brahmin called Srinivasan, what Moti Lal had actually been arrested for. It seems he was always "inciting" workers and students to strike or to riot and had disobeyed an order prohibiting him from giving a speech at a meeting of senior students at the Technical College. He was also suspected of being the leader of a group of young men who were printing and distributing seditious literature, but no evidence was found. Anyway, he got six months. And his appeal was dismissed. An ex-colleague on the *Gazette* – a fellow called Vidyasagar who now works for a radical newspaper called *The Mayapore Hindu* told me about it when I met him in court yesterday.

'Vidyasagar is a pleasant chap whom I rather like but have a bad conscience about. The first few weeks I worked on the *Gazette* the editor sent me round with him practically everywhere, and then sacked him. Vidya took it well. He said he guessed what was in the editor's mind when he was detailed to show me the ropes. He said, "I don't hold it against you, Kumar, because you don't know anything." He chips me a bit whenever we happen to meet and says that given time I might learn to be a good Indian.

'But I'm not sure I know what a good Indian *is*. Is he the fellow who joins the army (because it is a family tradition to join the army), or the fellow who is rich enough and ambitious enough to contribute money to Government War Funds, or is he the rebellious fellow who gets arrested like Moti Lal? Or is the good Indian the Mahatma, whom everyone here calls Gandhiji, and who last month, after Hitler had shown Europe what his army was made of, praised the French for surrendering and wrote to the British cabinet asking them to adopt "a nobler and braver way of fighting", and let the Axis powers walk into Britain. The nobler and braver way means following his pre-scribed method of non-violent non-co-operation. That sounds like a "good Indian". But then there is Nehru, who obviously thinks this attitude is crazy. He seems to want to fight Hitler. He says England's difficulties aren't India's opportunity. But then he adds that India can't, because of that, be stopped from continuing her own struggle for freedom. Perhaps then, the good Indian is that ex-Congress fellow Subhas Chandra Bose who makes free-dom the first priority and is now in Berlin, toadying to Hitler, and broadcasting to us telling us to break our chains. Or is he Mr Jinnah who has at last simplified the communal problem by demanding a separate state for Muslims if the Hindu-dominated Congress succeeds in getting rid of the British? Or is he one of the Indian princes who has a treaty with the British Crown that respects his sovereign rights and who doesn't intend to lose them simply because a lot of radical Indian politicians obtain control of British India? This is actually a bigger problem than I ever guessed, because the princes rule almost one-third of the whole of India's territory. And then again, should we forget all these sophisticated aspects of the problem of who is or is not a good Indian and see him as the simple peasant who is only interested in ridding himself of the burden of the local money-lender and becoming entitled to the whole of whatever it is he grows? And where do the English stand in all this?

'The answer is that I don't really know because out here I don't rank as one. I never meet them, except superficially in my capacity as a member of the press at the kind of public social functions that would make *you* in beleaguered rationed England scream with rage or laughter. And then, if I speak to them, they stare at me in amazement because I talk like them. If one of them (one of the men – never one of the women) asks me how I learned to speak English so well, and I tell him, he looks astonished, almost hurt, as if I was pulling a fast one and expecting him to believe it.

'One of the things I gather they can't stand at the moment is the way the Americans (who aren't even in the war yet – if ever) are trying to butt in and force them to make concessions to the Indians whom of course the British look upon as their own private property. The British are cock-a-hoop that Churchill has taken over because he's the one Englishman who has always spoken out against any measure of liberal reform in the administration of the Indian Empire. His recent attempt following the defeat of the British Expeditionary Force in France to lull Indian ambitions with more vague promises of having a greater say in the running of their own country (which seems not to amount to much more than adding a few safe or acceptable Indians to the Viceroy's council) only makes the radical Indians laugh. They remember (so my editor tells me) all the promises that were made in the Great War – a war which Congress went all out to help to prosecute believing that the Crown was worth standing by because afterwards the Crown would reward them by recognizing their claims to a measure of self-government. These were promises that were never fulfilled. Instead even sterner measures were taken to put down agitation and the whole sorry business of Great War promises ended in 1919 with the spectacle of the massacre in the Jallianwallah Bagh at Amritsar, when that chap General Dyer fired on a crowd of unarmed civilians who had no way of escaping and died in hundreds. The appearance of Churchill as head of the British war cabinet (greeted by the English here with such joy) has depressed the Indians. I expect they are being emotional about it. I'd no idea Churchill's name stank to this extent. They call him the arch-imperialist. Curious how what seems right for England should be the very thing that seems wrong for the part of the Empire that Disraeli once called the brightest jewel in her crown. Liberal Indians, of course, say that Churchill has always been a realist – even an opportunist – and will be astute enough to change coat once again and make liberal concessions. As proof of this they point to the fact that members of the socialist opposition have been brought into the cabinet to give the British Government a look of national solidarity.

'But I wonder about the outcome. I think there's no doubt that in the last twenty years – whether intentionally or not – the English *have* succeeded in dividing and ruling, and the kind of conversation I hear at these social functions I attend – Guides recruitment, Jumble Sales, mixed cricket matches (usually rained off and ending with a bun-fight in a series of tents invisibly marked Europeans Only and Other Races) – makes me realize the extent to which the English now seem to depend upon the divisions in Indian political opinion perpetuating their own rule at least until after the war, if not for some time beyond it. They are saying openly that it is "no good leaving the bloody country because there's no Indian party representative enough to hand it over to". They prefer Muslims to Hindus (because of the closer affinity that exists between God and Allah than exists between God and the Brahma), are constitutionally predisposed to Indian princes, emotionally affected by the thought of untouchables, and mad keen about the peasants who look upon any Raj as God. What they dislike is a black reflection of their own white radicalism which centuries ago led to the Magna Carta. They hate to remember that within Europe they were ever in arms against the feudal *status quo*, because being in arms against it out here is so very much *bad form*. They look upon India as a place that they came to and took over when it was disorganized, and therefore think that they can't be blamed for the fact that it is disorganized now.

'But isn't two hundred years long enough to unify? They accept credit for all the improvements they've made. But can you claim credit for one without accepting blame for the other? Who, for instance, five years ago, had ever heard of the concept of Pakistan – the separate Muslim state? I can't believe that Pakistan will ever become a reality, but if it does it will be because the English prevaricated long enough to allow a favoured religious minority to seize a political opportunity.

'How this must puzzle you – that such an apparently domestic problem should take precedence in our minds over what has just happened in Europe. The English – since they are at war – call the recognition of that precedence sedition. The Americans look upon the resulting conflict as a storm in an English teacup which the English would be wise to pacify if they're to go on drinking tea at four o'clock every afternoon (which they only did after they opened up the East commercially). But of course the Americans see the closest threat to their security as coming from the Pacific side of their continent. Naturally they want a strong and unified India, so that if their potential enemies (the Japanese) ever get tough, those enemies will have to guard their back door as well as their front door.

'Working on this paper has forced me to look at the world and try and make sense out of it. But after I've looked at it I still ask myself where I stand in relation to it and that is what puzzles me to know. Can you understand that, Colin? At the moment there seems to be no one country that I owe an undivided duty to. Perhaps this is really the pattern of the future. I don't know whether that encourages me or alarms me. If there's no country, what else is left but the anthropological distinction of colour? That would be a terrible conflict because the scores that there are to settle at this level are desperate. I'm not sure, though, that the conflict isn't one that the human race deserves to undergo.'

So there were no 'sensible things' that Hari was able to tell Colin, but perhaps it was enough for each of them that over such a distance, of time as well as space, they still found it possible to make contact. There was a saying among young Indians that friendships made with white men seldom stood the strain of separation and never the acuter strain of reunion on the Indian's native soil.

'What would you do,' he asked Sister Ludmila, 'if you had a letter from an old friend that showed you were suddenly speaking different languages?' Perhaps it is odd that Kumar should have remembered this earlier *Journey's End* letter of Lindsey's, remembered it well enough to have it on his mind when he asked this question, as if the later one which Colin wrote after his baptism of fire asking him to tell him some sensible things was of less importance than the letter written in the nostalgic neo-patriotic mood Hari had been puzzled by. But then the unexpected side of a man's personality is more memorable than the proof he may appear to give from time to time that he is unchanged, unchangeable. The image of Lindsey as

someone who spoke a new language had made its mark on
Kumar, so that later he was able to say to Sister Ludmila:

'I should have challenged him then. I should have told him
what it had really been like for me in Mayapore. I should have
said, "We've both changed, perhaps we no longer have anything
in common. It's probably as ridiculous to believe that if I came
back to Didbury now we should be at ease with each other as
to believe that if you came out to Mayapore you would want
even to be *seen* associating with me." Yes, I should have said that.
I didn't say it because I didn't want to think it. We continued
to exchange letters whose sole purpose was to reassure ourselves
that there had been a time when we'd been immune to all pressures except those of innocence.

'When Colin came to India in 1941 and wrote to me from
Meerut, I felt a sort of wild exhilaration. But it only lasted a very
short while. I was resigned to what I knew must happen. If he
had come straight to Mayapore there might have been a chance
for us. But Meerut was a long way off. It seemed unlikely that
he would ever be posted to a station close enough to Mayapore
to make a meeting possible. And every week that went by could
only add to the width of the gulf he'd realize there was between
a man of his colour and a man of mine who had no official position, who was simply an Indian who worked for his living and
lived in a native town. He would feel it widen to the point where
he realized there was no bridging it at all, because the wish to
bridge it had also gone. I remembered my own revulsion, my
horror of the dirt and squalor and stink, and knew that Colin
would feel a similar revulsion. But in his case there would be
somewhere to escape to. There would be places to go and things
to do that would provide a refuge. He would learn to need the
refuge and then to accept it as one he had a duty to maintain, to
protect against attack, to see in the end as the real India – the
club, the mess, the bungalow, the English flowers in the garden,
the clean, uniformed servants, the facilities for recreation, priority of service in shops and post offices and banks, and trains, all
the things that stem from the need to protect your sanity and
end up bolstering your ego and feeding your prejudices.

'And then even if Colin had been strong-willed enough
to resist these physical and spiritual temptations and to come to
Mayapore to seek me out, where could we have met and talked

for longer than an hour or two? Since the war began the black town has been out of bounds even to officers unless they are on official duty of some kind. I could not go to the Gymkhana. And what would *he* have made of the other club when it's hateful even to me? If we had met at Smith's Hotel there could have been an embarrassing scene. The Anglo-Indian proprietor doesn't like it if undistinguished Indians turn up there. At the Chinese Restaurant officers are supposed to use only the upstairs dining-room, and no Indian is allowed above the ground floor unless he holds the King's commission. We could have gone to the pictures but he would have disliked sitting in the seats I would be allowed to sit in. There is the English Coffee House, but it is not called the English Coffee House for nothing. If he were stationed in Mayapore perhaps we could meet for an hour or two in his quarters. Or perhaps he could get permission to cross the bridge and visit me in the Chillianwallah Bagh. I considered all these possibilities because they had to be thought out. And of course I saw that the one constant factor was not so much the place of meeting but the determination to meet. And what friendship can survive in circumstances like that?

'From Meerut he moved to Ambala, and then to somewhere near Lahore. In his first letter he said that on the map Meerut didn't look too far away from Mayapore. In his second he said he wondered if he would ever be close enough to make a meeting possible. In his third he did not mention the possibility of a meeting at all. And then I guessed that it had happened, in just three months. He had seen what he would only be able to call *my* India. And had been horrified. Even afraid. How could he know that I had been also horrified, also afraid? How could he know that for three years I had hoped, longed to be rescued, and had confused the idea of rescue with the idea of my Englishness and with the idea of my friendship with an Englishman? How could he know any of this? In one respect I was more English than he. As an Englishman he could admit his horror if not his fear. As an Anglicized Indian, the last thing I ever dared to do in my letters to *him* was admit either, for fear of being labelled "hysterical". And so I saw the awful thing that had happened – that looking at what he would have to call *my* India, the suspicion that I had returned to my natural element had been confirmed.

'Well, I say I saw it, then; but did I? Didn't I still make excuses for Colin and excuses for myself? When there was no letter from Lahore, didn't I say, "It's all right, he's not a civilian who has nothing to do but wake up, eat, go to work and come back home to see what the postman has brought." And then when the war came close, when the Japanese bombed Pearl Harbor, invaded Siam and Malaya and Burma and even fluttered the English dovecots in Mayapore, didn't I say to myself, "Well, poor old Colin is in the thick of it again?" And even suffer pangs of conscience that I hadn't been man enough to stand by something that was sure at least, my English upbringing, and join the army, fight for the people I had once felt kinship to, even if out here they obviously didn't feel kin to me? And didn't I see what a damned useless mess I'd made of my life since 1938, sulking as badly as those poor clerks I despised, making no new friends, repaying Aunt Shalini's kindness and affection with nothing that she would understand as love or even thanks?

'And then I saw them. English soldiers in the cantonment, with that familiar regimental name on their shoulder tabs. In the January of 1942. Familiar from the letters from Colin, first from Meerut, and then Ambala, and then from near Lahore. Captain C. Lindsey, then the name and number of the unit, followed by the address, and ending with the words India Command.'

'It was,' Sister Ludmila said, 'the second occasion I saw him drunk that he talked so, about Colin. I told you there had been such an occasion. After he had been to the temple, with her, with the girl. This is when he told me these things. He had never told her. I said to her, that time she came to the Sanctuary to say goodbye, "Do you know of the man Lindsey?" and she thought for a while and then said, "No, tell me."

'But I said, "It's not important." It wasn't important by then. To you perhaps it is important. So long after. "I saw him," young Kumar told me, "or at least I thought I saw him, coming out of the Imperial Bank, getting into an army truck that had the same insignia on its tailboard that those British soldiers wore on their sleeves." But he was not sure. And even then made excuses for him. Already at this time, you see, with the war suddenly brought to our doorstep by the Japanese, India had changed. There was this air of military rush and secrecy – and on the day he thought he saw Colin he went home expecting a letter saying,

"Look, I'm stationed near Mayapore and sometimes come into the cantonment. Where can we meet?" But there was never such a letter. So as the days went by he thought, "No, the man I saw was not Colin. Colin could not come near Mayapore and send me no word at all. India could not have done that to him. Not that. How could India do that to anybody, let alone to Colin?"

'Can you imagine this? The feeling every day of Kumar's that if the post did not bring a letter then there would be a chance encounter somewhere in that area north of the river? Every day he cycled from the Chillianwallah Bagh to the office of the *Mayapore Gazette*, and on some days left the office and cycled to an event that he was required to report on. And this was another thing, another thing he told me. How even as a reporter he was invisible to white people. He would go to this event, that event. The gymkhana, the flower show, the Guides display, the Higher School Sports, the Technical College graduation, the Technical College cricket, the hospital fête. He knew nearly every important English civilian by sight and name and every distinguished Indian by sight and name, but they did not know him, for there was at these functions, you understand, what you call press officer or steward, and he, only, would be available to young Kumar, and sometimes not even him, because at an important function Mr Laxminarayan would also be in attendance. On this occasion, I mean the second occasion of his drunkenness he said, "– oh, there was a time when I thought I would make a name for myself. People would read the *Gazette* and say, What good English! How splendid! Who is this young Kumar? But they do not even know my name. At most I am 'the *Gazette* boy'. My name is never printed. No one really knows that I exist. I am a vaguely familiar face. But – I had it coming. He uses me. Laxminarayan. Sometimes he keeps me chained to the desk turning *babu* English into decent English. Sometimes he sends me out. But he keeps me as an anonymous cog in his anonymous machine. Once I heard an Englishman say to him, 'I say, Laxminarayan, what's happening to the *Gazette*? Apart from Topics by "Stroller" it isn't funny any more.' My editor only laughed. He did not explain why it isn't funny. He punishes me, you see, for Vidyasagar, for everything, for his own shortcomings."'

*

'It was at such a function,' Sister Ludmila said, 'that he saw this Lindsey for the second time. Saw and knew, beyond a doubt, standing not far away, close enough not to mistake the features, the expression, the mannerisms, the way of holding the body – whatever it was that had impressed itself indelibly on Kumar's mind as authentic Lindsey. What occasion? I forget. But remember it was February, the end of February. And that he mentioned the *maidan*. I have even still, this recollection, not my own but Kumar's. From Kumar I have inherited it. And feel almost as if I had been there. Am there. Towards evening. In Kumar's body. A dark face in the crowd. Has it been cricket? This I would not know. Cricket I do not understand. But I understand how towards evening on the *maidan* the races came uncertainly together in a brief intermingling pattern which from above, to God you understand, looked less informal than it looked from the ground because from above you would be able to see the white current and the dark current; as from a cliff, the sea, separating itself stream from stream and drift from drift, but amounting in God's Eyes to no more than total water.

'And he sees Lindsey. Ah well, as boys, what secrets of mind and body did they share? He told me of autumn in England. This too I see and feel. And am aware of young Kumar and young Lindsey as boys, running home across chill fields to come and toast their hands at a warm grate, just as I remember the blessing of gloves in a cold winter, and the way the breath could transform a window and fill the heart with a different kind of warmth. Ah, such safety. Such microcosmic power. To translate, to reduce, to cause to vanish with the breath alone the sugary fruits in their nest of lace-edged paper. To know that they are there, and yet not there. This is a magic of the soul. But it was a magic Kumar could not conjure, on the *maidan*, that hot evening, to make Lindsey disappear. Lindsey looked at him, and then away, without recognition, not under-standing that in those *babu* clothes, under the bazaar topee, there was one black face he ought to have seen as being different from the rest.'

I am invisible, Kumar said, not only to white people because they are white and I am black but invisible to my white friend because he can no longer distinguish me in a crowd. He thinks – yes, this is what Lindsey thinks: 'They all look alike.' He makes me disappear. I am nothing. It is not his fault. He is right. I am nothing, nothing, nothing. I am the son of my father whose own father left home with a begging-bowl in his hand and a cloth round his loins, having blessed his children and committed their mother to their care. For a while she followed him and then sat by the roadside and returned home to live out her days in her private fantasy.

So I go from the *maidan*, in my bazaar trousers, my bazaar shirt, my Anglo-Indian topee, knowing that I am unrecognizable because I am nothing and would not be welcome if I were recognized. And meet, also coming away, Vidyasagar. He also is nothing. I do not remember the rest. There was clarity up to a point. Drinking cheap liquor in an airless room in a house in a back street on our own side of the river. And Vidyasagar laughing and telling the others that soon I would become a good Indian because the liquor was bootleg and we drank it at Government's expense. The others were young men like Vidya, dressed as Vidya was dressed, in shirts and trousers, like mine. But I remember helping them to destroy my topee because it was the badge of all government toadies. I remember too that they kept refilling my glass. They wanted me to be drunk. Partly it was malice, partly fun. In that poky little room there was desperation as well as fervour.

Sister Ludmila said: 'He found out later that they took him back to the Chillianwallah Bagh, right to the gates of his house, so that he would not be robbed, or picked up by the police, and then left him, thinking he went inside, but he wandered out on to the road again, going back towards the river and into the waste ground. And must have stumbled and fallen down into the ditch and there become unconscious and had his wallet stolen by someone who had seen him and followed him.

" 'Who is it?" I asked Mr de Souza. "I don't know," he said, and turned him over to see if there were wounds on his back, and then turned him again, shining the torch on his face. And this is what I remember, of Bibighar beginning. The eyes shut, the black hair curling over the forehead. Ah! Such darkness! Such determination to reject.

'We got him on to the stretcher then, and carried him here to the Sanctuary. "This one is drunk, sister," Mr de Souza said. "We have carried home only a drunken man." "To be so drunk and so young," I said, "he must also be unhappy. Let him lie." And so he lay. And before I went to sleep I prayed for him.'

PART SIX

CIVIL AND MILITARY

I

Military

Edited extracts from the unpublished memoirs of Brigadier
A. V. Reid, DSO, MC: 'A Simple Life'.

LATE IN THE March of 1942 when we were still in Rawalpindi
and hard on the heels of the news that our only son Alan was
missing in Burma, I received orders to go to Mayapore and
assume command of the infantry brigade then still in process of
formation in that area. The news of this appointment was given
to me on the phone by General 'Tubby' Carter. I was to leave
at once and Tubby knew I should want a little time to break
the news to Meg who was still unfit and would be unable to
accompany me. I did not welcome the idea of leaving her on
her own at a moment when we were heavy of heart hoping for
further news of Alan and yet dreading what that news might be.
After talking to Tubby I went straight round to the nursing home
and told Meg of the task that had been entrusted to me.

She knew that in ordinary circumstances I would welcome
the opportunity of getting back to a real job of soldiering. It had
begun to look as if I would spend the rest of the war with my
feet under a desk, and with our son also in uniform I suppose
we had almost come to terms with this prospect and had
accepted the fact that age and experience must eventually make
way for youthful eagerness. But now, with Alan's fate uncertain,
it seemed as if some understanding deity had stepped in to redress
the balance and had called on me to play a part which – if the
news of Alan was the worst there could be when it came – would
at least give me the satisfaction of knowing I might strike an
active blow at the enemy in return.

Meg reacted to the news as she had always done at times of
crisis and difficulty – with no sign of any thought for herself.
Seeing how ill and pale she looked I wished that it had been in

my power to call Alan into the room, fit and well, his usual cheery self, and so bring the roses back to her cheeks. I am thankful that she was spared the news that he died working on the infamous Burma–Siam railway, news which for me darkened the days of our Victory, but I am grateful that she lived long enough to share with me the hope that was revived when we first heard that he was a prisoner-of-war and not dead, as we had feared. When I said goodbye to her on the eve of my departure for Mayapore there was also the burden of realizing that these were dark days for our country. There was a tough job ahead.

I arrived in Mayapore on April 3rd (1942) and immediately set about the first phase of my task, that of welding the (—th) Indian Infantry Brigade into a well-trained fighting machine which I could lead confidently into the field to play its part in a theatre of war where the Jap had temporarily proved himself master. The task was not going to be an easy one. The majority of the troops were green, and the surrounding countryside, suitable enough for run-of-the-mill training, very dissimilar from the ground we should eventually be required to contest.

I had been in Mayapore many years before. I remembered it as a delightful station with some lakes out at a place called Banyagani where there was excellent duck-shooting to be had. The old artillery mess was a fine example of 19th Century Anglo-Indian architecture, with a lovely view on to the *maidan*. It tended to get uncomfortably warm from March onwards but one could usually get away, down to Mussoorie or up to Darjeeling. It was not too far by train from Calcutta either, so one had plenty of opportunity to relax if one's duties allowed.

I did not have any illusions about relaxation now. Obviously there was a difference between a station as it once appeared to a young subaltern who had recently met the girl he was seriously thinking of asking to marry him, and the station, the same though it was, to which he returned nearly thirty years later as a senior officer at a moment when his country's fortunes were at a low ebb, and the country to which he had dedicated his life which represented the very cornerstone of the Empire had achieved considerable measures of self-government and stood virtually on the threshold of independence, an independence that had been postponed, for the moment, in the interests of the free world as a whole.

I went to Mayapore with every confidence in the troops, and with a fervent prayer that I should not personally be found wanting. I had been glad to hear from Tubby that there was a station commander on tap who would relieve the brigade staff of the general military administration of the district, and also to hear that the collector – called in this 'non-regulation' province a deputy commissioner – was a youngish fellow who was well thought of by Europeans and Indians alike. As senior military officer in the district, however, I knew I should be responsible in the last resort for the civil peace, and for the well-being of both soldiers and civilians, and the last thing I wanted was to become involved in the kind of situation that would distract me from my main job and give rise to the employment of troops on tasks that might have been avoided with a little forethought.

In view of the increasing unrest in India at this time, one of the first things I did after reaching Mayapore was to see the Deputy Commissioner, whose name was White, in order to listen to what he had to say about the state of his district and to tell him frankly that a lot of time and energy might be saved later if we agreed to show a firm hand at the first sign of trouble. I had already decided to bring the Brigade's British battalion – the (—th) Berkshires – into Mayapore and to move the 4/5 Pankot Rifles out of Mayapore, where I had found them, to the vicinity of Banyaganj where the Berkshires had been situated. My reasons were twofold. The British troops were newly out from home and I judged from my first inspection of them that they were far from happy in the rather primitive quarters which were all Banyaganj had to offer. There was an airfield in process of construction nearby (which I noted had denuded the lakes of duck), and scarcely a mile separated the far from salubrious coolie encampment from the battalion. More huts were being built but a lot of the men were under canvas and in April that was no joke. Conscious of the problem involved in appearing to make a distinction I nevertheless felt that Johnny Jawan would be less uncomfortable in Banyaganj than was Tommy Atkins. Also, in moving the Berkshires into the Mayapore barracks there was in my mind the belief that their presence in the cantonment might act as an extra deterrent to civil unrest, which at all costs I wished to avoid. I had, in any case, determined to use British soldiers in the first instance in the event of military aid being requested by the civil power.

In bringing the Berkshires into Mayapore I was also not unaware of the good effect this would have on our own people there – men and women doing difficult jobs at a time of special crisis. It was with this in mind too that I ordered an Army or War Week – complete with a military band – for the end of April, which was held on the *maidan* and was counted a great success. I feel that without immodesty (because the idea was mine but the fulfilment of it lies to the credit of those who organized or took part in it) I can claim that the excitement and 'lift' which the War Week gave to Mayapore distracted attention from the fact that the Cabinet Mission which Sir Winston – then Mr Churchill – had sent to Delhi to seek an end to the deadlock between the British Government and those Indian politicians who claimed to represent the Indian people and were demanding even further measures of self-government, had failed to come to any kind of reasonable understanding. This was the mission known as the Cripps Mission, after its leader, Sir Stafford Cripps, the socialist minister who eventually became Chancellor of the Exchequer when, after the war, our island race paid its peculiar tribute to the architect of our victory by ousting him from office. It was after the failure of the Cripps Mission in April 1942 that Mr Gandhi launched his famous Quit India campaign, which of course looked to us like an invitation to the Emperor of Japan to walk in and take over the reins of government!

Unfortunately I found White – the Deputy Commissioner – not wholly alive to the situation I believed might face us if Indian leaders were allowed to continue to speak out against the war effort and rouse the masses to adopt a policy of what Mr Gandhi called non-violent non-co-operation, a policy that could bring the country to a standstill. White seemed to be convinced that when the Indian National Congress talked about non-violent non-co-operation they really meant non-violent. He obviously had more faith than I in the ability of a demonstrating crowd to resist the hysteria that can turn it in a moment into a howling mob intent on taking revenge for some imaginary act of brutality perpetrated by the police or the military. He did not, in fact, appear to anticipate demonstrations of any magnitude, unless they were organized purely for the purpose of offering *satyagraha*, in defiance of the Defence of India Rules, so that the authorities would be bound to arrest the demonstrators and have their prisons filled to overflowing. My first meeting with White took place before Mr Gandhi had launched his Quit India campaign, but at a time when it was clear that the Cabinet Mission headed by Cripps was failing to reach agreement about the way in which Indian leaders could be identified more closely with the affairs of the nation. White still seemed to hope that at the last moment a working arrangement would be made. I had no such expectations. Right from the beginning of the war with Germany relations between ourselves and the Indians had steadily deteriorated. At the outset of that war Congress members of the central assembly had walked out to protest the sending abroad of Indian troops to the Middle East and Singapore and the Congress ministries in the provinces had resigned because the Viceroy had declared war without consulting them! Whatever our faults in the past, I as a simple soldier with only rudimentary political views could not help feeling that the sincere efforts we made in the years before the war to hand over more power to the Indians themselves had revealed nothing so clearly as the fact that they had not achieved the political maturity that would have made the task of granting them self-government easy. The act of 1935 which envisaged a federal government at the centre, representative of all walks of Indian life, and elected states governments in the provinces, seemed to a man like myself (who had everything to lose and nothing to gain by Indian independence) a statesman-like, indeed noble concept, one that Britain could have been proud of as a fitting end to a glorious chapter in her imperial history. Unfortunately it led only to a scramble for power and the central federal government scheme came to nothing. One could not help feeling that the heartrending cries for freedom sounded hollow in retrospect as one watched the scramble and listened to the squabbles that broke out between Hindus, Muslims, Sikhs, Princes and others. The Congress, for instance, openly admitted that they took provincial office in 1937 to prove that the federal scheme was unworkable at the centre and that they alone represented India. Unfortunately, this belief of theirs, that they were the democratic majority, seemed to be borne out on paper at least by their sweeping victory in the elections that were held prior to their taking provincial office. Be that as it may, one would have thought that two years of provincial power, with little or no interference from the Governors, who retained a watching brief on behalf of the central government and the Crown, would have moulded statesmen, but the resignations after the declaration of war – which left the Governors with no alternative but to assume personal control – struck most of my fellow-countrymen whose thoughts now lay principally with the safety of our homeland and the fight against tyranny, as proof that nothing had been learned at all of political responsibility, and that we could therefore no longer count on 'leading' Indians to take a broad view of the real things that were at stake in the free world.

I think it is true to say that we came to this realization with reluctance, and that it was a measure of our continuing hope for Indian freedom and of our readiness to extend our patience right up to its breaking point that even in our darkest hour – the defeat of our arms in South-East Asia – we opened the bowling once again on Mr Churchill's initiative and tried hard to find a way of giving the Indians a fair crack of the whip, which was more than Hitler would have done and more than we knew could be expected of the Jap. It was clear to us, however, that chaps like Gandhi had got on to our scent and were in full cry, heedless of the ravenous yellow pack that was on to *them*, indeed on to all of us. On April 6th a few bombs fell on Madras. Even that did not seem to bring the Indians to their senses, in fact they blamed us more than they blamed the enemy! Inspired by Mr Gandhi they had got hold of the idea that there was no quarrel between India and Japan and that if the British absconded the Japanese wouldn't attack her. A little later, it is true, Mr Gandhi very kindly suggested that the British army could stay in India and use it as a base from which to fight the Japanese, and that in ports like Bombay and Calcutta he could promise there wouldn't be any riots to disrupt the flow of arms and war material! – providing of course that we had otherwise left the country to be ruled by himself and his colleagues! What he thought the strategic difference was between ceasing to govern but continuing to use India as a base was not easy to tell if you looked at the situation from the point of view of the Japanese High Command! It was clear to most of us that at last his peculiar theories were being shown up for what they were: the impractical dreams of a man who believed that everyone was – or should be – as simple and innocent as himself. There were times, of course, when we found it difficult to put even this well-meaning construction on his speeches and writings.

When I looked out on to the *maidan* from the window of my room in the old artillery mess in Mayapore, or drove round the cantonment, I could not help but feel proud of the years of British rule. Even in these turbulent times the charm of the cantonment helped one to bear in mind the calm, wise and enduring things. One had only to cross the river into the native town to see that in our cantonments and civil lines we had set an example for others to follow and laid down a design for civilized life that the Indians would one day inherit. It seemed odd to think that in the battle that lay ahead to stop all this from falling into the hands of the Japanese the Indians were not on our side.

I remembered vividly the hours spent as a young man, exercising Rajah on the Mayapore *maidan*, and practising polo shots with Nigel Orme, who was ADC to General Grahame and won a posthumous VC at Passchendaele. Rajah, as readers may recall from an earlier chapter, was the first polo pony I owned, and Nigel Orme, although senior to me in rank and service, one of the best and truest friends I ever had. It looked to me as if fate had called me back to the place where I first got the 'feel' of India and first realized that whatever success or failure was in store for me in the profession I had chosen, there would always be a sense of oneness with the country and a feeling of identification with our aspirations for it. I remembered Meg as she had been in my thoughts then, all those years ago, so calm, so collected, kind and generous, ever ready with a smile – to me the most beautiful girl in the world. And I thought of our son, Alan, and of our daughter Caroline – safe now from Nazi or Japanese frightfulness, thank heaven, with her Aunt Cissie in Toronto. These three were truly my hostages to fortune and our fine boy seemed already to have been taken from us in part payment. More than anything else in the world I wished for victory to our arms, health and happiness for Meg, and to be reunited with her and darling Caroline and young Alan. I do not think that any of us older serving soldiers can be blamed if, at the time, we felt bitter that the country which had benefited in so many

ways from British rule appeared determined to hinder our efforts
to save it from invasion at a time when we could least spare the
strength. Pondering these matters on the level at which they
affected me personally I couldn't help wishing that I could be
left to concentrate on my main task and leave the politicians to
'muddle through' in their own mysterious ways. But I knew that
this could not be. The brigade was my responsibility, but so was
the safety of our women and children and the peace of the district as a whole. Those of us who were in contact with 'places
higher up' knew that it was thought we must be prepared to face
the gravest danger from within the camp as well as from outside
it; from the enemy in the tent as well as from the enemy at the
gate; and that it was not beyond the bounds of possibility that
the Congress planned the kind of open rebellion that could
snowball into a campaign of terror and bloodshed and civil war
such as we had not seen in India since the days of the Mutiny.
As events proved later our anxieties on this score were only too
well-founded. Before the summer was out the country was in
the grip of rebellion and in Mayapore the commotions got off
to the worst kind of start. It was in this pleasant old district that
two dastardly attacks on Englishwomen were made, within a few
hours of each other; the first upon an elderly mission teacher,
Miss Crane, and the second on a young woman, Daphne
Manners, who was criminally assaulted in a place called the
Bibighar Gardens.

Although on first acquaintance Mr Deputy Commissioner
White and I did not, as they say nowadays, hit it off, I came
presently to admire his tenacity. For me his physical courage was
never in doubt, and I judged, correctly as it turned out, that he
would never allow any personal reservations he might have
about official government policy to sway him in his dutiful
application of it in his own district. As a case in point, when
I asked him rather bluntly what he would do if he had orders to
arrest leaders of the local sub-committee of the Congress party
(I knew that District Officers had been warned to keep special
note of those of them whose prompt imprisonment might halt
the tide of rebellion), he replied, quite simply, 'Well, arrest them
of course,' but then added, 'even though I know that that is the
very worst thing we can do.'

I asked him why he felt this. He said, 'Because the kind of

men I would have to arrest are those who honestly believe in non-violence and have the power to move the crowd to self-sacrifice rather than to attack. Put such fellows in clink and you leave the crowd to a different kind of leader altogether.'

I could not agree, but recognized the sincerity of White's convictions. Of course to me, mass *satyagraha* was almost as harmful as open revolt. Naturally I asked him what he knew of or proposed to do about the kind of leader who might take the place of the Congressmen he had such faith in. He said, 'Oh well, that's like looking for needles in haystacks. A few are known. You can arrest those. But the others go free, and among them probably the most efficient because they've been efficient enough not to become known. You could spend your life working up a secret file and still miss the key chaps because Congress doesn't know them and you don't know them. They're nothing to do with Congress at all. They're young or middle-aged fellows with bees in their bonnets who think Congress the lickspittle of the Raj. Well, who has a life to spend detecting that kind of needle in this kind of haystack? Isn't it better to leave the fellows who have nothing to gain by violence free to control the crowd and direct it in true *satyagraha*?'

I told him that what he said probably made sense, so long as you could trust originally in the concept of non-violence, which I personally thought a lot of eye-wash. Pressed further, White admitted that he left what he called 'the needles in the haystack' to his District Superintendent of Police, a man called Merrick, whom I had met on a previous occasion and instinctively liked.

Although White's attitude left me in some uncertainty about the degree of determination to be expected from the civil power in the event of trouble in this district, I was confident that the police could be counted on to act swiftly and efficiently if need be.

White's thinking was wholly 'modern', typical of the new-style administration of the Thirties that had to take into account every half-baked notion that was relevant to the workable solution of a problem. The judge was an Indian called Menen, an old-school Indian I was glad to notice, but somewhat self-contained in true judicial style. Of the triumvirate only young Merrick, the District Superintendent of Police, seemed to me to have seized happily upon the greater freedom of action that

the war and the Congress provincial resignations had given to
district rule.

I had a special meeting with Merrick and told him that I relied
upon him to use his discretion, particularly in regard to what the
Deputy Commissioner had called 'the needles in the haystack'.
I put it to him bluntly that I had a brigade to command and train
for use against the enemy at the gate and not, if I could help it,
for use against the enemy in the camp. I told him I would
appreciate it if he stuck his neck out occasionally. I had not mistaken my man. He was young enough still to respond to simple
issues with the right mixture of probity and keenness. I could
not help but admire him, too, for his outspokenness. He was a
man who came from what he called 'a very ordinary middle-
class background'. The Indian Police had been the one job he
felt he could do. I knew what he meant, and liked him for his
total lack of pretence. Police duties are always disagreeable, but
they have to be carried out. Now that we were at war with the
Axis Powers he regretted the circumstances that had led him to
undertake service in a field that precluded him from wearing a
different uniform. He asked me, in fact, what chance there was
of strings being pulled to release him so that he could join up
'even as a private'. Thinking of Alan – whom physically he
somewhat resembled – I appreciated his patriotic scale of values,
but was unable to give him any hope of a transfer. In any case,
I realized that in the present situation he was more valuable to
his country as head of the local police than he would be as an
untrained junior officer, let alone as a private soldier. He promised to comply with my request to keep me informed, *sub rosa*,
of the temper of the district as he gauged it to be.

Having seen and talked to White and to Merrick I felt that
I had done as much as could be done for the moment to buy time
in which to concentrate on my job without too often casting a
glance in the direction of a local threat to our security. In any
case the arrival of my third battalion, the —th Ranpurs, gave
me plenty to do. Originally I had been promised a battalion of
Sikhs, but one from my old regiment was, needless to say, an
even greater boost to my morale! Bringing one company of the
Ranpurs into the Mayapore barracks (and so relieving the Berkshires of some of their station guard duties) I sent their remaining companies and the battalion headquarters into the area of

Marpuri, north-west of Mayapore, an area I had already selected as the best of two likely sites chosen by my brigade staff. Now that my command was complete I could really get down to work!

The Berkshires were settling down well. The move from Banya-ganj into the cantonment had certainly done the trick. The old barracks near the artillery mess were spacious and cool, and the men enjoyed the unaccustomed luxury of being able to avail themselves within reason of the ministrations of the native servants attached to the barracks, many of whom were the sons of men who had looked after an earlier generation of Tommies. They were now also closer on hand to the home entertainments so readily laid on by our ladies. It was, incidentally, many years since there had actually been a gunner regiment stationed in Mayapore, but the artillery mess had been famous in its day and naturally the name had stuck. In recent years Mayapore had been the home of an NCOs' school and the cool weather station of the Pankots. Since the war began it had turned itself virtually into a brigade staging point. Unfortunately, from the point of view of my brigade staff, the colonel-commandant of the NCOs' school who had also acted as station commander was on sick leave upon my arrival – a leave that turned out to be perma-nent because the school was transferred to the Punjab – so I inherited on paper at least the station commander's role. The Station Staff Officer (whom I managed to retain) had to do most of the work that would normally have rested on the station com-mander's shoulders, but he was an old ranker and a hard and dedicated worker.

I had elected to live in the artillery mess itself rather than move into the accommodation that was available to me, not only because my poor Meg was unable to join me and establish a household, which she had done so often before, in so many different parts of India, but because I felt I wanted to be on con-stant call and in a position to keep my staff on its toes. The rooms I occupied in the mess in the old guest suite which overlooked the *maidan*, were spacious but simple. There in the little sitting-room that I had turned into a private office, I could find a retreat from the press of routine to think out the best solutions to the many problems that confronted me. But it was in this room, towards the end of June, when the rains had just begun, that

Tubby Carter rang me with the news that Alan was reported a prisoner-of-war. Somehow one had always gone on hoping that he would reach India safely with one of the parties of our troops and civilians who had struggled back against great odds and in conditions of great privation to be restored to those who most sorely missed them. I asked Tubby if he would break the news to Meg. And here Tubby proved himself once again a good and true friend who, although my senior in rank, was always ready to use his seniority for the welfare of an old comrade-in-arms. He ordered me to Rawalpindi so that I could break the news to her myself. In less than thirty-two hours of Tubby's telephone call I was at Meg's bedside.

Neither Meg nor I had any illusions about what it meant to be a captive of the Japanese, but we found solace in the know-ledge that Alan was alive and – if we knew our son – probably kicking. Speaking of him to her, I felt the relief it was to do so knowing that at least it was in order to think of him in the present rather than the past tense. That evening Tubby came to the nurs-ing home with a bottle of champagne. In ordinary circumstances it might have seemed wrong to drink champagne at a time when our son was probably suffering hardship, but Tubby put things into perspective by raising his glass and inviting us to drink to Alan's safe return. I was proud of Meg when she raised her glass too and said simply, 'To Alan,' and smiled as if he were there in the room and the occasion of the toast a happy one. In the few long weeks that we had been separated she seemed to have gone down hill alarmingly. She had lost more weight and her eyes no longer sparkled. I realized suddenly that Tubby had not ordered me back to Rawalpindi only to break the news of Alan's capture to her but so that I could face up to the graver news that eventu-ally I would have to bear.

When we had said goodnight to Meg, Tubby took me in to Colonel 'Billy' Aitken's office and left me there. Billy said, 'I'm afraid there's no doubt. Meg's got cancer.' We had known Billy for years. In civilian life he could have risen to the top of his profession and become a rich man, but as he had so often said, he preferred to give his time to looking after those of his coun-trymen – and women – who lived ordinary lives doing often dull and unrewarding jobs abroad, than to prescribing sugar-pills for 'fashionable' but hysterical women in Harley Street. I asked him, 'How long?' For a moment we looked at each other. He guessed I would prefer to know the truth. He said, 'Perhaps six months. Perhaps three. Perhaps less. We shall operate, but the end will be the same.' He left me alone for a bit, for which I was grateful. I found it hard to believe that in just a few minutes I had to adjust myself to accept that darling Meg was to be taken from me by a fate even crueller than that which had taken Alan. Alan at least had had the satisfaction of getting in a blow or two. I think I realized as I sat there alone in Billy Aitken's office that I should never see Alan again either.

Billy and Tubby came back together and took me to Billy's quarters. Tubby asked me whether I wanted to relinquish my command and come back to 'Pindi. He hinted that there was a job going that was mine for the asking and would carry a major-general's hat. I asked him not to press me for an answer until I had had time to think it over. A room had been reserved for me at the club. They drove me back there and I made an effort to sleep so that I could wake up and make my decision in a clearer state of mind. In the morning I asked Billy the most important thing, which I had forgotten to ask the previous evening: whether Meg knew how ill she was. He said he had not told her but he was sure she was in no doubt. I said, 'Billy, *don't* tell her.' He knew then what my decision was, to go back to my brigade and to go back as soon as possible, so that neither Meg nor I would have to pretend for longer than we could manage. I knew this was my duty. I knew, too, that this was what Meg would want for us both. One cannot adopt a way of life without accepting every one of its responsibilities. It was hard to accept them at this moment, but I was sustained in the belief that Meg would understand and find strength herself in my decision. In spite of this, our parting was far from easy. I thought afterwards on the 'plane to Calcutta on which Tubby had wangled me a seat that it would have been easier if she had asked me not to go back to Mayapore. There seemed to be between us a terrible burden of things we had never said to each other. Before I left, Tubby assured me that he would send for me to be with Meg at the end, but this did not prove to be possible. I shall not write her name again. Goodbye dear Meg, cherished wife and mother of my children. God willing, we shall be reunited in a happier place.

*

I had laid it down that at the commencement of the wet monsoon our training should continue so far as possible without interruption. I had managed through constant pressure in the appropriate quarters to get the last company of the Pankots in Banyagani out of tents into huts before the rains began. The Ranpurs in Marpuri were less fortunate, but if they tended to be damp in one respect the same could not be said of their spirits!

In July our field training began to get under way and I was heartened by the keenness with which all ranks responded to the challenge of getting out on to the ground, even when the 'enemy' was only imaginary. My brigade major, young Ewart Mackay, proved worth his weight in gold. A regular, his enthusiasm was infectious. It spread throughout the Brigade Head-quarters staff. Cheerful, efficient and an all-round sportsman (he shone particularly at tennis) he was also a dedicated soldier and could be a stern disciplinarian. Later in the war he commanded with valour and distinction the 2nd Muzzafirabad Guides, his old regiment. His pretty wife, Christine (the elder daughter of General 'Sporran' Robertson) was with him at Mayapore and fulfilled the role of hostess with charm and grace. Christine and Ewart gave me 'open house' at the delightful bungalow they occupied in Fort Road, and it was Christine who organized the little dinner parties which, in other circumstances, would have been another and still dearer woman's task to arrange.

Heartened as I was on the two occasions in July when we took the brigade 'out' to test its mobility and degree of cohesion, I was still unable to lose sight of the role it played as a local force for order. In taking it out the fact was not lost on me that the resulting display of military strength (more impressive to those not in the know than to those who were!) could not but make an impression on the population who were being increasingly subjected to Congress anti-war propaganda. One of the most despicable aspects of that propaganda was the tale put about that in the retreat from Burma and Malaya the authorities had shown indifference to the welfare of Indian troops and the native popu-lation. To anyone such as myself who knew the affection the English officer felt for his sepoys and native NCOs, the imagi-nary picture painted by Congress of Indian soldiers left behind without leaders to be captured or killed, or of groups of

leaderless native troops and panicky villagers being pushed off
roads, railways and ferries to give priority to 'fleeing whites' was
laughable.

It was in the middle of July that my divisional (and area) commander told me that local civil authorities had received secret
orders from provincial governors to combat in every possible
way the poison of the insidious and lying propaganda of the
Indian National Congress. This was the occasion when I sought
yet a further discussion with the Deputy Commissioner.

From my point of view White was very much the unknown
quantity. I was confident in the police and sure of the loyalty of
our own Indian troops. Every man of the Berkshires had been
trained in the drill of duties in aid of the civil power, and at the
first sign of disturbances patrols and riot squads were ready to go
into action. Although these young English boys (many of them
civilians themselves little more than a year ago, and with only
a very sketchy idea of the problems of administering Imperial
possessions abroad) found the drill of 'duties in aid' rather
farcical, not to say puzzling when they recalled those of their
countrymen who had already laid down their lives to protect
India from both Nazi and Japanese tyranny, they very quickly
adjusted themselves to accepting the role they might have to
play as one more job to be done. When I gave this battalion of
'modern' young English lads an address on the subject of military
aid to the civil authorities I began by quoting those immortal
lines of the soldier's poet Rudyard Kipling:

> '– it's Tommy this, an' Tommy that, an'
> "Tommy, fall be'ind,"
> But it's "Please to walk in front, sir," when
> there's trouble in the wind –'

And I suppose a psychologist would say that I couldn't have
chosen a better way of putting the situation to them!

One could say that the basic thinking behind the military drill
for suppression of civil disturbance is as simple as this: that failing
the retreat of the crowd in the face of an armed might even
greater than that of the police, the life of one ringleader, for-
feited, equals the saving of many other lives. There have been
times in our history when this simple equation has not looked,

on the ground, as simple as it looks in the textbooks. I am thinking here, of course, of the *cause célèbre* of General Dyer in Amritsar in 1919, who found himself in a position not unlike that which I myself had to anticipate in 1942.

In 1919, as in 1942, the country was seething with unrest, and all the signs indicated open rebellion on a scale equal to that of the Mutiny in 1857. Ordered to Amritsar, Dyer came to a conclusion which the historians – fortified by the hindsight historians are fortunate enough to be able to bring to their aid – have described as fatal: the conclusion that in Amritsar there was to be found the very centre of an imminent armed revolt that could well lead to the destruction of our people and our property and the end of our Imperial rule. Learning that a crowd intended to forgather at a certain hour in a large but enclosed plot of ground called the Jallianwallah Bagh, Dyer prohibited the meeting by written and verbal proclamation in accordance with the rules laid down. This proclamation was defied and his warnings ignored. He took personal command of the troops he sent to disperse it. His on-the-spot orders to disperse also having been defied, he then ordered the troops to fire. The Jallianwallah Bagh, from a military point of view, was a death-trap, and many civilians died, including women and children.

Ever since the Dyer affair, which was seized upon by 'reformers' as a stick to beat us with, the army had naturally become supersensitive to the issues involved, and we were now in the unhappy position of finding ourselves in what practically amounted to a strait-jacket.

In the first place, unless the civil authority had collapsed or was otherwise non-operational – when it would be a question of proclaiming martial law – the military was powerless to intervene unless called upon, in writing, by the civil power, usually the senior civilian in the area. Such a request for aid was, in a sense, really only a call to stand by.

For example:

To: O. C. Troops

I have come to the conclusion that the Civil Authorities are unable to control the situation and that the assistance of the military has become necessary. I accordingly request such assistance.

Place:
Date: Time: Signature:
                                           Appointment.

Imagine now that having received such a request I had a platoon of infantry standing by. The civil authority might then ask me to give support at a point where trouble was imminent or had already broken out. Let us say, for instance (to choose one of the many incidents that occurred in Mayapore in August 1942) that a threatening crowd had gathered outside the main Hindu temple in the square upon which, having crossed the river by the main Mandir Gate bridge, there debouched the road that led from the civil lines.

The platoon of the Berkshires which had hastened by truck from District Headquarters, debussed some two hundred yards from the crowd who were crossing the bridge and hastily formed up on the road in a hollow square (there being shops and buildings on either side of the road whose roof tops or windows represented a threat to the flanks and the rear). In the centre of the hollow square thus formed by the sections of the platoon were to be found the following personnel:

> Platoon commander
> Representative of the Police
> Magistrate
> Bugler
> Bannermen
> Medical orderly
> Platoon Sergeant
> Signals orderly
> Diarist

The meaning of the word 'aid' comes into clearer perspective when you remember that apart from the platoon commander there was also a magistrate present. In the affair of the crowd crossing the Mandir Gate bridge the magistrate in question was a Mr Poulson, who was senior assistant to the Deputy Commissioner.

In the case we are considering, there were three distinct phases of operation. The first being what we might call the Testing phase, the second that of Decision and the third that of the Action which logically followed the decision.

Testing consisted first in the ordering by the platoon commander to the bugler to sound off, thus calling the attention of the crowd to the existence of a legally constituted force of opposition. The warning note having been given, the first of the bannermen raised the banner on which orders in English and the vernacular were inscribed. These were orders to disperse. Sometimes the raising of such a banner was enough to make a crowd obey. After the raising of the first banner a second note on the bugle was sounded and then, if the platoon commander considered that the situation warranted it, the second banner was raised. Upon this was inscribed again in English and the vernacular a clear warning that unless the crowd dispersed force would be resorted to. Since the crowd was usually making a pretty frightful din on its own account one could not rely on verbal warnings being heard: hence, the banners.

It was at the moment when the second banner giving warning of intention to fire was raised that both the platoon commander and the magistrate found themselves in the relative no-man's-land of having to make a decision which the text-books necessarily left to the man on the spot.

Fortunately, in the case of the first Mandir Gate bridge riot, the attending magistrate, Mr Poulson, did not hesitate to give the platoon commander the signed chit requesting him to open fire once it was seen that the crowd had no intention of falling back or dispersing. By the time all the necessary drill had been completed only a few yards separated the front of the mob from the forward file of riflemen, and brickbats were being thrown. From the town, on the other side of the river, a pall of smoke showed where an act of arson had already been perpetrated. (This was the kotwali, or police station, near the temple.) At the same time, unnoticed by the troops on the Mandir Gate Bridge road, a detachment from the crowd was making for the railway station along the tracks from the level crossing where the police had failed to hold them, and yet another platoon of the Berkshires was hastening to that area from District Headquarters to reinforce the police (commanded at that point by Mr Merrick, their District Superintendent).

Meanwhile, to return to our platoon on the Mandir Gate

Bridge road: as so often happened the mob had pushed old women to the front to inhibit the soldiers. It was the platoon commander's job to select as targets one or two of the men in the crowd, who, by their actions, he judged to be its leaders. There are occasions when only one of the soldiers, a man who has distinguished himself as a marksman, is issued with live ammunition, but the disturbances in Mayapore had gone far beyond the stage when such an insurance against a high casualty rate was considered wise. Nevertheless, in this present instance, the subaltern in charge now spoke individually to each man of the forward file, gave two of them specific targets and told the others to fire over the heads of the crowd when he gave his order to fire. It required considerable self-discipline and composure to go patiently through such motions while under attack, but badly bruised on the shoulder by a stone as he was the subaltern did so. He had to remember not to call any man by his name in case he was overheard by someone in the crowd which would lead to the man being identified! In the resulting volley both the marksmen found their targets and the crowd faltered, but only for as long as it took for new leaders to come forward and urge them in the Mahatma's current phrase 'to do or die'. This time the subaltern had no alternative but to order a second volley in which two civilians were killed and five wounded, including, as chance would have it, one woman. Seizing the initiative, the platoon commander ordered the detachment to advance and continue firing, but over the heads of the now retreating mob. The wounded woman was the first to be given attention by the medical orderly. The wound was found to be superficial because, no doubt, the soldier whose bullet had hit her had been sighting upon a man who had moved at the crucial moment.

Present at these proceedings there was one man, usually a member of the battalion or brigade intelligence section, whose duty was that of 'diarist'; that is to say, he was required to observe and make notes for later inclusion in the war diary of the unit or formation. This was a dispassionate factual report which did not take into account the thought processes leading to particular decisions which the subaltern's own report would do. The magistrate would also be required to submit a report on the incident to the civil authority. The representative from the police (an inspector or sub-inspector) would do likewise to his superior officer. In this way a number of reports on the same incident would be available if required by any court set up to investigate charges of brutality or excessive use of force. I must emphasize, however, that it was not always possible to fulfil, to the letter, all of the drill laid down for the employment of troops in these duties. As perhaps even the least imaginative of readers may judge, there could arise situations in which any one or even several of the 'required' personnel were not available, and only the need for instant action undeniably present!

In going into the above details I am conscious not only of digressing but of having moved my story, such as it is, forward to the point where the reader has found himself in the midst of action without knowing the stages that led to it. So I go back now to the day in July when I had a further meeting with Mr White, the Deputy Commissioner who, I knew, had recently received orders to combat the anti-war propaganda of the Indian National Congress, and whose attitude I felt it necessary to re-assess and, if necessary, confide to my divisional commander who, as area commander also, had virtually the entire province in his military jurisdiction.

I found White somewhat changed in regard to his appre-ciation of the situation. I personally had little doubt but that some kind of confrontation was inevitable, and was heartened to some extent to realize that the Deputy Commissioner also now seemed to believe that the situation had probably gone beyond the point where it could be retrieved. He was, however, still convinced that the 'disturbances', when they came, would be of a 'non-violent' nature, unless the leaders of the Congress were put away, in which case, he said, he felt unable to answer for the civil peace. I pounced on this and asked him point-blank, 'In the event of such arrests then, you would think it advisable to ask us to stand by?' He said at once that I had 'taken him up too literally'. He was in an uneasy frame of mind and I saw that there was no sense in pressing him, much as I should have liked to come away with a clear understanding. With regard to the Congress propaganda, he said he had talked to the editors of the various local newspapers and given warnings to those whose recent tendency had been to support the 'anti-war' line. This seemed to be satisfactory. I asked him to be good enough to bear

in mind as often as he could the situation from my point of view
– which was that of a man who was interested in the conditions
obtaining in Mayapore first of all as they did or did not affect
my training programme and then as they affected our people.

It was at this meeting that White said something that has
stayed in my mind ever since as an indication of the true sense
of vocation our finest colonial administrators have always felt.
'Brigadier,' he said, 'please bear one thing in mind yourself if my
attitude gives you any cause to feel dissatisfied. If your assistance
is asked for I know I can rely on it and upon its effectiveness. To
you, afterwards, it will have been an unpleasant task effectively
carried out and will therefore rank in your scale of values as one
of your successes. To me, in my scale, to have called you in at
all could never rank as anything but one of my *personal* failures.'
I protested that personal failure was putting rather too strong a
point on it but he smiled and shook his head. Most of the men
whom he had had to mark down for arrest if orders came from
government were his personal friends.

Then he said, 'But don't be alarmed, Brigadier. I am also a
realist. I use the word "failure" but I'm not a fellow to wallow
in it.'

With this I had to be content, and on the whole was, because
as I have said before I had come to respect White for the sense
of responsibility that after several meetings I could not help but
get an impression of from his very demeanour, which was
reserved, somewhat 'intellectual', but very down-to-earth and
practical in terms of action. White was fairly typical, I realize,
of the new race of District Officers who reached maturity just
at the moment when our Indian Empire was due to come of age
and receive 'the key of the door' from our government at home
– perhaps prematurely, but as a token of our patience and goodwill and historical undertakings.

After the failure of the Cripps Mission and the subsequent
opening of Mr Gandhi's Quit India campaign, I recollect that
the main question in the minds of most Englishmen was whether
or no Mr Gandhi would succeed in carrying the Indian National
Congress (certainly the strongest political force in India) to the
point where they would collectively identify themselves with
his curious doctrine and so give it the force and impetus of an
organized, nationwide movement. I have never been a close

follower of the ups and downs of politicians, but I was aware that Mr Gandhi had been 'in' and 'out' of Congress, sometimes pursuing a personal policy that the Congress endorsed and sometimes one that they did not. Mr Nehru, who was the actual leader of the Congress, had for some time been considered by us as a more sensible middle-of-the-way fellow who knew the international language of politicians and could possibly be counted on to see sense. A lot of his life recently had been spent in jail, but as I recollect it he had been freed in order to take part in the negotiations with the cabinet mission and was still at large and very much a force to be reckoned with. It was clear to us that he found Mr Gandhi an embarrassment and for a time our hopes rested upon his more practical and statesmanlike attitude winning the day.

Perhaps at this stage I should rehearse exactly what we knew was at stake and what we felt the opposition amounted to. In the first place we had our backs to the wall in the Far East and had not yet been able to regain the initiative and/or end the stalemate in Europe and North Africa. At any moment we expected the Jap to commence operations against the eastern bulwark of India. A Japanese victory in India would have been disastrous. Lose India and the British land contribution to what had become a global war would virtually be confined to the islands of our homeland itself, and to the action in North Africa, and the main weight of resistance to totalitarianism thrown on to the Americas. We regarded India as a place it would be mad-ness (as Mr Gandhi begged us) to make 'an orderly retreat from'! Apart from the strategic necessity of holding India there was of course also the question of her wealth and resources.

So much for what was at stake. As for the opposition, this amounted in the first instance to demands (inspired by Gandhi) that we leave India 'to God or to anarchy' or alternatively were challenged to hold it against a massive campaign of 'non-violent non-co-operation', which meant in effect that the native popu-lation would go on strike and in no way assist us to maintain the country as a going concern from which we could train, equip, supply and launch an army to chuck the Jap out of the Eastern archipelago!

Surely, we thought, men like Nehru would resist such a suicidal design?

At the beginning of August it looked like a foregone conclusion that Nehru had, as we say, sold the pass for reasons best
known to himself. He had not found in himself the political
strength to resist the Mahatma at this moment. Everything now
depended upon the vote of the All-India Congress Committee
on Mr Gandhi's Quit India resolution. This was made on August
the 8th. Historians since have attempted to prove that the passing
of the resolution was no more sinister than words on paper and
that Mr Gandhi hadn't even outlined in his own mind the precise
course that consolidated non-violent non-co-operation was to
take. My own belief was and remains that the non-violent non-
co-operation movement was planned down almost to fine detail
by underground members of the Congress acting on instructions
from those who wished to look publicly like that famous trio of
monkeys, 'hearing no evil, speaking no evil, seeing no evil'.

How else can I account for the violence in my own district
that erupted on the very day following the passing of the Quit
India resolution and the dawn arrests of members of the Congress party? A violence which immediately involved a European
woman, Miss Crane, the mission teacher, and on the same night
was directed at the defenceless person of a young English girl,
the niece of a man famous in the province some years before as
governor; a girl who was violently attacked and outraged by a
gang of hooligans in the area known as the Bibighar Gardens?
These two incidents were portents of the greatest danger to our
people, and coming hard on each other's heels as they did,
I could only come to one conclusion, that the safety of English
people, particularly of our women, was in grave peril.

As it so happened I was out at Marpuri with the Ranpurs when
I received a message early in the evening of August the 9th from
my staff captain to the effect that there had been civil commo-
tion in two outlying sub-divisions of the district, Dibrapur and
Tanpur, and that a detachment of police from Mayapore, accompanied by Mr Poulson, the assistant commissioner, had driven
out in that direction during the late afternoon and rescued a
police patrol and a group of telegraph linesmen from the police
post at a village called Candgarh where they had been imprisoned by rioters. Proceeding along the road towards Tanpur,
Mr Poulson had encountered first a burnt-out car and some

distance farther on the English mission teacher guarding the body of a dead Indian, one of her subordinates in the mission schools, who had been battered to death by, presumably, the same roaming mob. As Mr Poulson told me later, it was the sight of the mission teacher sitting on the roadside in the pouring rain that led him to believe that the troubles in Mayapore were to be of a greater degree than either he or Mr White had anticipated. I had spent the night at Marpuri with the Ranpurs, and did not know either of the Congress Vote or of the arrests of Congress leaders until my staff captain telephoned me about mid-morning on the 9th. He had had a signal from Division, and had also been informed by the Deputy Commissioner that a number of local congressmen in the district had now been detained as planned. During this first telephone call my staff captain told me everything was quiet and that the Deputy Commissioner had said there was no cause at present for alarm. I had therefore resolved to stay at Marpuri to watch the battalion exercise. But receiving the further communication from my staff captain about the incident near Tanpur, early in the evening, I resolved to return forthwith and ordered him to meet me at the Deputy Commissioner's bungalow.

I reached the Deputy Commissioner's bungalow in Mayapore at about nine o'clock. There was now further trouble in the offing. Mr White had recently had the news that this young English girl, Miss Manners, was 'missing'. Merrick, the head of the police, was out looking for her. White told me that following the rumours of violence out at Tanpur and the attack on the mission teacher several of the English women who lived in the civil lines had moved into the Gymkhana club – one of the sites previously selected as a collection point in the event of serious threat to lives and property. Taking White on one side I asked him whether he didn't think it wise for us to give a combined display of strength – joint patrols of police and military – either that night or first thing in the morning. He said he did not think so because the town itself was quiet. Most of the shops in the bazaar had shut down. This was against regulations but he felt it better to allow the population to remain indoors and not to provoke them. I questioned him about the mob violence in Dibrapur and Tanpur. He said he believed it was the result of a 'spontaneous reaction' to the news of the arrests, on the part of men who had the time and inclination to make a bit of trouble. Meanwhile communications with Tanpur and Dibrapur had been restored and the police there had reported that they were again in control of their sub-divisions. Several men had been arrested in Tanpur, among them, it was thought, one or two of those who had attacked the mission teacher and murdered her Indian companion. The teacher herself was in the Mayapore General Hospital suffering from shock and exposure.

Later, just as I was leaving, young Poulson came in. He had toured the cantonment as far as the Mandir Gate bridge, crossed the bridge and driven down Jail road to the prison to supervise the transfer of the jailed Congressmen to the railway station where he had seen them safely stowed away in a special carriage and sent off on the journey to a destination that was to be kept secret. I had a few words with Poulson who was obviously less sanguine than his chief about the immediate future. He was pretty concerned for his wife, because she was pregnant. They already had one little girl, and she was with them in Mayapore. The Whites' two children, twin boys, had gone back to school in England the year before the war began. One knew that Mrs White must feel the separation rather badly in the present circumstances, but she was a tireless and forthright woman – rather more commanding in 'presence' than her husband who was very much the 'thinker'. She never showed any sign of self-pity at the prospect of not seeing her sons again until the war was won, but I knew how much this must weigh on her mind.

I had hoped, as well, to see Merrick, but he was out searching for the missing girl – Miss Manners – who lived with a Lady Chatterjee, in one of the old houses near the Bibighar Gardens. Lady Chatterjee had been a friend of Sir Henry and Lady Manners when Sir Henry was Governor of the province. Sir Henry was dead, but I had known Lady Manners slightly in Rawalpindi and recollected that I had met the Manners girl on some occasion or other both in 'Pindi and in Mayapore. She had been in 'Pindi with her aunt and since coming to Mayapore to stay with Lady Chatterjee had been doing voluntary work at the Mayapore General Hospital. She had rather shocked the ladies of the cantonment by her attachment to a young Indian. I remembered Christine Mackay, the wife of my brigade major, saying something about it. On the whole, since coming to

Mayapore, I had been too occupied to pay much attention to cantonment gossip, but realizing who it was who was 'missing' I could not help feeling a serious premonition of trouble.

Asking White to keep me informed I then returned to my own quarters and put a call through to the Area Commander. I was heartened to hear from him that, as a whole, the province – indeed the country in general – seemed settled and quiet. The Congress committees had been banned by Government and many members of them detained under the Defence of India Rules as a precautionary measure. The General said he felt that the arrests had nipped the Congress revolt nicely in the bud and that we could now concentrate on our job of training and equipping our forces. I told him of the things that had occurred that day in my own sphere of command but he said they sounded to him like isolated incidents that had gone off at half-cock because the men who were supposed to have been behind them were now safely under lock and key. I went to bed in a relatively easy frame of mind and slept soundly, realizing how tired I was as a result of my twenty-four-hour visit to the Ranpurs.

My orderly woke me at seven, as I had instructed him, and told me that the District Superintendent of Police was waiting to see me. Guessing that something was up I gave orders for him to be brought to my room at once. Arriving a few minutes later he apologized for coming so early and for intruding on my privacy. Spick and span as he was I judged from his look of fatigue and strain that he had been up all night. I said, 'Well, Merrick, what's the grief this morning?'

He told me that the missing girl, Miss Manners, had been attacked in the Bibighar Gardens the previous night and raped by a gang of ruffians. Fortunately he had called at Lady Chatterjee's home for the second time that evening only a few minutes after the poor girl had herself returned after running all the way in a state of considerable distress through deserted, ill-lit roads. Merrick had at once driven to his headquarters and collected a squad and rushed to the Bibighar area. He had found five men, not far away, drinking home-distilled liquor in a hut on the other side of the Bibighar bridge. He at once arrested them (the distillation and drinking of such liquor was in any case illegal) and was then fortunate enough to find Miss Manners's bicycle, which had been stolen by one of the culprits, in a ditch outside a house

in the Chillianwallah Bagh. Entering the house he discovered
that there lived in it the Indian youth with whom Miss Manners
had been associated. This youth, whose name as I recollect it was
Kumar, had cuts and abrasions on his face. Merrick immediately
arrested him and then secured all six fellows in the cells at his
headquarters.

I congratulated him on his prompt action but asked him why
he had come personally to see me at this early hour. He said
there were several reasons. First, he wished to be sure that I had
the earliest possible notification of the 'incident' of which he
took the most serious view. Secondly, he wanted to know
whether he had my permission to transfer the detained men to
the guard room of the Berkshires if he judged that it would be
wise to move them to a place of greater security. Thirdly, he
wished to put it to me that in his opinion the Deputy Commissioner was seriously misjudging the gravity of the situation, a
situation which in a few hours had seen violent attacks on *two*
English women, and the murder of an Indian attached to a
Christian mission. He then reminded me that earlier in the
summer I had asked him to 'stick his neck out' if he thought it
necessary.

I could not help but ask him in what way he felt he was sticking it out now. He said he was convinced that the men he had
arrested last night were those who had assaulted Miss Manners
but that it might be difficult to prove. I said, 'Well, the poor girl
can probably identify them,' but he doubted it. He had asked if
she knew any of the men responsible but she said she didn't
because it had all been 'done in darkness' and she had not seen
them clearly enough to be able to identify them. Since one of
the fellows arrested was the man she had been associating with,
Merrick believed that for the moment at any rate she was not
telling the truth, but he hoped she would do so when she came
out of her shock and realized who her real friends were. Meanwhile he had the fellows under lock and key and had spent most
of the night interrogating them. They still protested their complete innocence in the matter, but he was convinced of their
guilt, particularly in the case of the man Kumar, who obviously
stole her bicycle and who was caught in the act of bathing his
face to reduce or remove the evidence of cuts and bruises
received when the girl fought back before being overpowered.

I asked Merrick if it was known how Miss Manners had come to be at the Bibighar. He said he was afraid it looked to him as if she had gone to meet Kumar there, an aspect of the case that he hoped could be glossed over for the girl's sake. He had met her himself on several occasions and counted himself as one of her friends, enough of a friend anyway to have warned her not long ago that her association with the Indian was one she would be well advised to end. But she seemed to be completely under Kumar's spell. Kumar, Merrick said, had once been taken in for questioning by the police when they were searching the town for a prisoner who had escaped from jail. During questioning it transpired that Kumar knew the escaped man, whose name was Moti Lal, but there was no evidence at that time that their acquaintance was more than superficial. Although 'westernized', Merrick considered Kumar to be a pretty unsavoury character, aware of his attraction for women and not above latching on to a white woman for the pleasure of humiliating her in subtle ways. He worked on a local newspaper, and gave no obvious trouble, but was known to have consorted with young men suspected of anarchistic or revolutionary activities – young men of the type of the other five arrested. Several of these men had been seen with Kumar on other occasions and they were all men on whose activities the police had been keeping an eye. Merrick's opinion was that Kumar and these five had plotted together to take advantage of Kumar's association with Miss Manners. Going to the Bibighar that night, expecting to find only Kumar, she found not only Kumar but five others – men who then set on her in the most cowardly and despicable way.

I was deeply shocked by this sorry tale and agreed with Merrick that the less said about her attachment to one of the suspected men the better, especially if things came to the head of a public trial. Meanwhile, I agreed, he seemed to have sufficient grounds to hold the men in custody on suspicion of this crime alone, which I thought was fortunate because once the story got round that an English girl had been outraged there wasn't a white man or woman in the country who wouldn't rejoice that the suspects were already apprehended. The effect on the Indian population of knowing that this kind of thing couldn't be got away with would also be exemplary.

Merrick said he was glad to feel that I approved of his actions.

He believed that the events of the previous day were simply a prelude to a violence which, if becoming no worse, would certainly become more widespread and would take all our combined efforts to resist. He had heard of my suggestion to White that both police and military patrols should be seen to be on the alert today and regretted that this proposal had been turned down.

I invited Merrick to have breakfast with me but he declined and said he must be getting back to work. Before he went I told him that if circumstances warranted it one or all of the six prisoners could be moved into the greater security of the Berkshires' guard room, providing that the police supplied their own guards and the Berkshires were absolved of direct responsibility for them. Merrick obviously feared an attack on his own jail by a 'do or die' crowd bent on releasing the men arrested for the rape. He had no doubt that by this morning the whole town knew of the incident. In India it was almost impossible to keep anything secret. Rumours began with the whispered gossip of native servants and spread quickly to the rest of the population. But a crowd attracted by the idea of rescuing their 'heroes' would have to show a lot of determination to try to penetrate the Berkshires' lines because this would mean a direct attack on a military installation – and on the whole this was something Indian mobs usually avoided. Much as I sometimes found it irksome not to take immediate control of this explosive situation – which an attack on the military would have entitled me to do without signed permission of the civil authority – the last thing I wanted was to become involved at this level, which is why I qualified my permission to move the prisoners into military lines with the phrase 'if circumstances warranted it'. But I certainly endorsed Merrick's opinion that the six prisoners must be held under maximum security. Their forcible release to go free and boast of their attack on an Englishwoman was at all costs to be avoided.

After breakfast I rang the Deputy Commissioner and told him that I had spoken to Merrick, and that Merrick had told me about the attack on Miss Manners. I again offered to co-operate with military patrols as a precautionary propaganda measure, but he said the district was quiet and that he was trying hard to maintain an atmosphere of normality. Most District Headquarters availed themselves of the services of what I suppose we must call spies or informers. White's informers reported to him that the population was more puzzled than angry, uncertain what their arrested Congress leaders really expected of them. To provoke them now was, he was sure, the very last thing a sensible man should do. Fortunately, for the present anyway, Muslim and Hindu communities were living together on terms of amity and although in a sense this could be counted a bad sign – since it suggested an alliance against the English – in another sense it was a good thing, because there was little or no danger of a communal situation developing that would snowball into something worse.

As usual, when I spoke to the Deputy Commissioner I was impressed by his calm and balanced thinking. I asked what he felt about the attack on Miss Manners and whether he didn't see it as a prelude to attacks on Europeans in general. He said it might well have been an isolated incident, such as that at Tanpur, the work of hooligans, men who had probably come in to Mayapore from one of the outlying villages expecting to find it in the grip of civil disturbance, only to be disappointed and therefore capable of taking it out on the first defenceless person they happened to see. I said the impression I got from Merrick was that the culprits were not villagers but young anarchists who lived in Mayapore. To this he did not immediately reply, so I asked him whether he thought the men arrested were not the real culprits. He said he had to keep an open mind on the subject and that a lot depended on the girl's own evidence once she was fit enough to give it. He thought Merrick might have made a mistake, but could not criticize him for his prompt action, at least not in the light of what Merrick himself had told him of the circumstances attending the arrests.

Having spoken to the Deputy Commissioner I then called my own staff together, told them of the situation as seen (a) by Merrick and (b) by Mr White, and finally (c) as seen by myself, that is to say one that was potentially grave but at present under the control of those whose duty it was to control it. In other words, for us, I said, it was 'business as usual', and I ordered my staff car for ten o'clock so that I could pay an unexpected visit to the Pankots out at Banyaganj. Taking me on one side when the others had gone, Ewart Mackay told me that he and his wife had already heard about the attack on Miss Manners and his wife's private view was that it was something the poor girl had been heading for, although naturally Christine and he were shocked and grieved. The point was, though, that Christine Mackay felt I should know that she did not see the attack on Miss Manners as evidence that European women generally were in danger. She had asked if the man Kumar had been involved and Ewart said she would be more than glad to hear that he had actually been arrested.

In other words, from this private source, I had confirmation of the reasonableness of young Merrick's personal suspicions but also of the Deputy Commissioner's broader impersonal attitude. I therefore set off for Banyaganj fairly confident that there was at least a breathing space for us to concentrate on more important things. In Banyaganj itself work was proceeding on the construction of the airfield. My heart went out to those poor and simple labourers, men and women, who needed every anna they could earn and did not lightly drop their tools and their baskets of stones at anyone's beck and call. I could not help thinking that if every one of the women working so hard in the heat and humidity of that August morning, with her ragged saree torn and mud-spattered, had taken the Mahatma at his word, and gone home to spin cotton she would have been hard put to it to feed her children – children for whose welfare, and hers, a committee of our own women had been set up and was actually represented that morning by young Mavis Poulson and the wife of the Station Staff Officer, who were doing their best to attend single-handed to the screaming wants of Hindu and Muslim babies of both sexes and to pregnant mothers who had collapsed under the weight of the baskets. Fortunately there were some stout-looking lads from the RAF in the vicinity so I felt that Mrs Poulson and Mrs Brown wouldn't come to much harm, and continued my journey to the headquarters of the Pankots. I spent a pleasant day there, watching their battle drill.

This was indeed the calm before the storm! I returned to Mayapore at about 5 p.m. and gave Mrs Poulson and Mrs Brown a lift, to save them the discomfort of the journey back to the cantonment in the RAF bus. Mrs Poulson also seemed to share Christine Mackay's view of the fate that had overtaken Miss Manners. Mrs Poulson said that the whole business must be extremely distasteful to Lady Chatterjee who probably felt a special degree of responsibility for what had happened, not only because Miss Manners was her house guest but because she herself was an Indian. I asked Mrs Poulson what she knew of the man Kumar and she said at once, hearing from me that he had been arrested, 'Well, you've got the right man. A trouble-maker if ever I saw one.' She thought that if poor Miss Manners had not been such an 'innocent' about India this distressing business would never have arisen, and she added how extraordinary and yet how logical it was that the two Europeans who had so far suffered injury in the present troubles were both women, and both women of radical, pro-Indian views. Mrs Brown, I noticed, was less positive on the subject, but I put this down to shyness. Her husband, as readers may remember, had risen from the ranks. I made a special point of trying to bring her into the conversation. I had a great respect for her husband's capabilities as Station Staff Officer. I am sure, however, that she felt much the same way as did Mrs Poulson, that is to say that they both thought the girl had been unwise but of course were dismayed by her fate and determined to stand by her. I was touched by this as yet further proof of our solidarity. Armed thus, one can face any crisis.

I dropped Mrs Brown in the cantonment bazaar where she had some shopping to do and took Mrs Poulson back to her bungalow. Declining her kind offer to come in and have a drink I left her to her task of supervising the putting to bed of her little daughter whose name, I think, was Anne, and ordered the driver to return to brigade headquarters. The rain had let up again and the late afternoon sun had come out. The *maidan* looked peaceful and I was reminded of those far-off days when I was a young man without a care in the world. That evening after dinner I wrote some personal letters and retired early to work on a field-training scheme that my staff had drafted for my consideration. Reading it through, and finding little to criticize, I felt a glow of confidence. If only the scheme had been more than a scheme! The Japanese would not have been resting so peacefully in their beds that night!

This was, however, to be the last comfortable night's sleep I was to enjoy myself for many days.

*

In the personal diary which I kept at this time the space allotted to the following day – August 11th – is blank, but there is a brief note on August 12th headed 2 a.m. which reads, 'A moment's respite after a day of widespread riots throughout the district. I received at 20.00 hours (Aug 11) a request for aid from the deputy commissioner. Cold comfort for our forces in Assam and Burma to know that those whose role is to supply and eventually reinforce them are being hindered in this way.'

Looking back to that day in August which marked the beginning of disturbances throughout most of the country, and remembering – as hour by hour reports of commotions, riots, arson and sabotage began to come in – the sense that grew of what we had feared and tried to stop finally facing us I cannot but be puzzled by the opinion still held in some quarters that the uprising was indeed a spontaneous expression of the country's anger at the imprisonment of their leaders. In my opinion, final proof to the contrary, if any is needed, lies in the words spoken by the Mahatma to his followers at the time of his arrest, 'Do or die.' Nothing, I feel, could be plainer than that. I did not hear of those words until the 11th, on which day the crowds that collected and attacked police stations, telegraph offices, and sabotaged stretches of railway line, were crying them as their motto.

Again the immediate seat of disturbances was in Tanpur and Dibrapur, and the police in those areas were sorely pressed. During the afternoon of the 11th the police in Mayapore, directed by mounted officers, were fully occupied in dispersing and redispersing the crowds that attempted to collect. Several constables were injured. A score of men were arrested and taken to jail. In a village just south of Mayapore an Indian sub-divisional officer of the uncovenanted civil service was attacked and held prisoner in the police post and was not rescued until the following day when our own patrols scoured the area. The Congress flag was run up in the village, and also over the court house in Dibrapur – a town that was cut off for several days. The post office in Dibrapur, which had been attacked on the 9th of August (the day of the attack on the mission school teacher) was this time destroyed by fire. Until our troops retrieved the situation on the 17th August Dibrapur – 70-odd miles away from Mayapore – was in the hands of the mob. In fact one of the mob's leaders declared himself Deputy Commissioner and district headquarters to have been transferred from Mayapore to Dibrapur! The sub-divisional officer who was legally and constitutionally in charge of that sub-division (again an Indian) was at first imprisoned but then released and installed in the court house as 'District and Sessions Judge'. He later claimed that he was forced to co-operate with the self-appointed Deputy Commissioner and that he had hidden most of the money from the local treasury to save it from falling into the rioters' hands. Restoration of the money and his previous good record probably saved him from paying the penalty of his apparent defection to the side of the rioters. There were, unfortunately, several cases spread throughout the country where magistrates and even senior Indian district officers complied with the orders of the mob leaders, and considerable sums of Government's money was stolen. In some areas the new self-appointed officials 'fined' townsmen and villagers and put the money into their own pockets along with revenues they had collected 'on behalf of free India'. There was not, I think, any instance of an English civil servant being coerced in this way, and there was, thank God, virtually no loss of European life. The one instance I remember was the murder of two Air Force officers (not in our own district) by a mob who – imagining them to be the pilots of an aircraft that had recently taken part in a punitive raid on a mutinous village nearby – immediately set on them in this foul way and tore them to pieces.

But to go back to the 11th, and to Mayapore itself: the District Superintendent of Police showed, throughout that day, considerable tactical ability. It was impossible for Merrick to have men everywhere they were needed, but there were three main danger areas – the area of the Chillianwallah Bagh Extension road which led from the south of the town directly to the Bibighar bridge, the 'square' opposite the Tirupati temple leading to the Mandir Gate bridge and the road leading west to the jail (the jail on the black town side of the river, not the cells at Police Headquarters in the civil lines where the six men suspected of the rape were being held). It was anticipated that there would be two main objectives of attack – the jail and the civil lines.

The day had begun normally enough until the police in the city reported that 'hartal' was being observed. At 8 a.m. however (an hour that more or less coincided with the renewed uprising in Dibrapur) a crowd was found to be collecting on the Chillian-wallah Bagh Extension road. This was dispersed by 9.30 a.m. but at once there was evidence that the dispersal had only led to the collection of another crowd in the vicinity of Jail road. Fortu-nately, Merrick had anticipated the moves that might be made in the event of any organized defiance of the agents of law and order and had already ordered his forces to deploy. There were several skirmishes. The post office on Jail road was threatened but secured. Meanwhile reports had begun to come in of 'iso-lated' acts of violence and sabotage in the district's outlying areas. At 1200 hours the sub-inspector of police in charge of the kotwali near the Tirupati temple received an 'ultimatum' to join the forces of 'free India' and co-operate in the 'release of the six martyrs of the Bibighar Gardens'. This ultimatum was delivered to him in the form of a printed pamphlet! The attempt to identify the rebellion in Mayapore with the Bibighar Gardens affair as though it were simply a crusade to release men whom the population thought wrongfully imprisoned was, I thought, not only a cunning move but proof of the existence of under-ground leaders of considerable intelligence. With this Merrick agreed. At first sight of the pamphlet he had at once raided the offices of an English-language newspaper called *The Mayapore Hindu* and found a press there that suggested that not only news-papers were printed on those premises but that they were also equipped to print in the vernacular. The type from which the pamphlet had been set up in English and Hindi had already been 'distributed' but Merrick felt justified in arresting every member of the staff actually on the premises and in destroying the press from which pamphlets of the kind distributed could have been run off.

This operation had been completed by 1300 hours, only 60 minutes after the delivery of the pamphlet to the kotwali in the temple square, which said a lot for Merrick's capacity for prompt action, as well as for his intelligence or 'spy' system. He told me that afternoon when I visited District Headquarters where the Deputy Commissioner and his staff were gathered in force, that one of the men on *The Mayapore Hindu* whom he had arrested was a close friend of the man Kumar, the principal suspect in the Manners case. He felt that it was very likely now that by interrogating this fellow (the note in my diary gives his name as Vidyasagar) Kumar's duplicity would be proved.

I confess that I felt sickened to realize the extent to which some of these so-called educated young Indians would go to defy and attack the people who had given them the opportunity to make something of themselves. I was also concerned about the capacity they had for violence in the sacred name of *satya-graha*. I said as much to Merrick who then reminded me that, in his job, he had to deal almost every day with fellows of this kind. If he sometimes 'bent the rules' and paid them back in their own coin, he believed that the end justified the means. He said he was almost 'off his head' at the thought that a decent girl like Daphne Manners, with every advantage civilized life had to offer, should have been taken in by a fellow like Kumar who had had the benefit of an English public school education. I was astonished to have this information about Kumar's background and felt that my own sense of values had been pretty well knocked for six.

Merrick described Gandhi on this occasion (when we drank a hasty cup of tea together) as a 'crazy old man' who had com- pletely lost touch with the people he thought he still led, and so was the dupe of his own 'dreams and crazy illusions', and had no idea how much he was laughed at by the kind of young men, he, Merrick, had to keep in order.

That afternoon at district headquarters I found the Deputy Commissioner calm and decisive in his reactions to the reports that were coming in. I told him that I was prepared to order the provost in charge of the military police to assist in the transfer of the six prisoners to the Berkshires' lines. This took White by surprise because apparently Merrick had not discussed such a possibility with him. He said he had no intention of aggravating racial feeling by placing six men suspected of raping an English woman under the noses of English soldiers. I grew rather heated at what I thought to be an unwarranted criticism of my men's capacity for self-restraint. He then assured me he had not meant any such thing, but simply that the job of guarding such prisoners could only be extremely distasteful and therefore bad for the morale of the Berkshires who, if called out in aid, would need to exercise a high degree of level temper and self-discipline. It was bad enough, he said, that the news of the attack on Miss

Manners had become current. He did not wish to have the Berkshires 'reminded hourly by the suspects' presence in their midst of an affair that can only excite strong basic emotions'.

On this subject we did not see eye to eye, and broke off conversation somewhat tartly. At eight o'clock that evening I received the expected request for aid, at once ordered what we had come to call the riot squad to report to district headquarters and the rest of the Berkshires to stand by, and drove to White's bungalow to which he had now returned and where I found him in conference with Judge Menen and members of his staff. Judge Menen looked as imperturbable as ever. I could not help wondering whether under that grave, judicial exterior lurked a heart that beat in unison with his countrymen's hopes for 'freedom'.

Since 4 p.m. it had apparently become clear to White that the available police were in insufficient strength to continue their task of discouraging the collection of crowds, particularly as a detachment of the city police had been sent to reinforce the police in Tanpur and attempt to re-establish contact with Dibrapur, thereby reducing their strength in Mayapore. Anticipating from the temper of the town's population that determined efforts might be made the following day to penetrate the civil lines, and getting some impression of the scale and nature of the revolt from his staff's collation of the day's reports from his own and other districts and provinces, the Deputy Commissioner decided, round about 7.30 p.m., to ask for military support. Reaching him at about 8.15 I was thanked for our prompt response. He said he still hoped that on the morrow it would not prove necessary to request the full weight of our strength. We agreed to keep the platoon of the Berkshires at District Headquarters on immediate call and to send some troops overnight to Dibrapur in the company of a magistrate and a police officer to see what was going on there and to try for pacification and reduction. Wishing to keep the Berkshires intact, I decided that the platoon going to Dibrapur should come from the Ranpurs at Marpuri. They were well placed to cross the river at a point some six miles west of Mayapore and to approach Dibrapur by a flank road from which they might catch the rebels in Dibrapur by surprise. I gave the orders at once by telephone to the duty officer at Marpuri.

I decided to be present myself at the rendezvous between the Ranpurs and the two representatives of the civil power and left with the latter in my staff car at 2200 hours. Making contact with the Ranpurs I then led the party to the bridge at a village called Tanipuram where we found the local police on their toes. The sub-inspector in charge reported that at dusk men had been seen approaching the bridge who had gone away at the sight of his men patrolling. The village had been quiet all day in spite of the rumours of Mayapore town being in a state of turmoil. Leaving the Ranpurs to proceed in the direction of Dibrapur I then drove back to the place of rendezvous – the railway halt that served the surrounding villages. I telephoned through to Mayapore and managed to get connected to District Head-quarters. I left a message that the Ranpurs were safely on their way, and then – feeling I had done as much as was possible that night – was driven home. By now we were in the early hours of the morning of the 12th and a steady rain was falling which I felt would do much to dampen the ardour of any potential night-raiders!

In the morning, after only three hours' or so sleep, my signals officer woke me with a message from the platoon of Ranpurs who had been on their way to Dibrapur that they had been held up on the road about ten miles from Dibrapur by a roadblock in the shape of a felled tree. No obstacle to the men, it was of course one to the transport. The tree had been removed with some difficulty because of the rain which was still falling and the slippery state of the road and kutcha edges. The subaltern in charge of the platoon, a young Indian, had proposed to send two sections ahead on foot to the next village one mile distant but the accompanying magistrate and the police officer had insisted on the party remaining intact while the obstruction was dealt with. If the subaltern had not been persuaded against his better judgment it is possible that the destruction of the bridge beyond the village – a bridge across a tributary of the main river flowing through Mayapore – might have been stopped. The bridge was blown some twenty minutes after they had begun work on clear-ing the roadblock. They heard the sound of the explosion. Reaching the village (which was deserted of all but a few old men and women) the subaltern had again got on to brigade signals and reported that the road to Dibrapur had now been rendered impassable for transport. He requested further orders.

This was the situation I was immediately faced with on the morning of the 12th. A glance at the map quickly confirmed that there was no alternative route to Dibrapur that did not involve a retracing of steps almost as far north as the bridge at Tanipuram, and the alternative route from there was little better than a good-weather track, from the point of view of mechanical transport. The bridge at Tanipuram only had to be blown now and I realized I had temporarily lost the use of two 3-ton lorries, a 15-cwt truck and valuable wireless equipment!

Fortunately my Brigade Intelligence Officer, a somewhat reserved but extremely able young man called Davidson, had already seen the danger and anticipated my orders for the police to be requested to make immediate contact with their post at the bridge at Tanipuram to check the situation there and give warning to be on the look-out for saboteurs. I rang the Deputy Commissioner and told him that I stood to lose valuable transport and equipment unless I had carte-blanche to secure the road. I told him why, and added that it seemed clear that the rebels in Dibrapur were led by pretty skilled men and that Dibrapur had obviously been chosen as the strong point for the rebellion in this district.

White gave the situation a moment or two's thought and then said that on the whole he agreed with me and gave me carte-blanche to command the road while the Ranpurs were 'withdrawn'. I told him that I had not necessarily been contemplating withdrawal, but instead the securing of the road during whatever period was required to re-bridge the river at the scene of demolition. We were sadly short of the necessary equipment, but even if it were several hours before the Ranpurs could proceed it was surely better late than never!

His answer amazed me. He said, 'No, I request withdrawal but agree to your commanding the road until your men are back this side of Tanipuram. I'll confirm that in writing at once.'

I asked him, 'And what if the bridge has gone at Tanipuram?'

He said, 'That will call for another appreciation, but speaking off the cuff it would look to me as if you had lost immediate use of three trucks and a wireless.' He then rang off. I dressed hurriedly and had breakfast, determined that if news came in that the bridge at Tanipuram had also gone I would order the Ranpurs to make their weight felt in that area, magistrate or no magistrate. But I was relieved, presently, to have a call from police headquarters to tell me that Tanipuram reported the bridge still standing and no sign of trouble.

I had decided not to withdraw the Ranpurs until the promised written request to that effect had come in from the Deputy Commissioner. I received this request by 0800 hours and at once told Ewart to order the transport and men to come back.

I then discussed the situation at Dibrapur with Davidson, my IO, who said he imagined that the view of the Deputy Commissioner was that if Dibrapur *were* the centre of the rebellion in the district, it could be left to stew in its own juice for a while, because the rebels had no 'troops' as such, and Mayapore was of greater importance. He thought that the Deputy Commissioner had decided that the pacification of his district should spread outwards from Mayapore.

Of all my staff, I suppose Davidson had achieved the greatest degree of frankness with me (except for Ewart who was by way of being a personal friend). When I first assumed command, the IO had been a young fellow called Lindsey, whom I took an immediate shine to. He had seen action in France with the ill-fated British Expeditionary Force. His association with the Berkshires dated back to his Territorial Army days before the war. He had come out to India with the new battalion as a company commander. On reaching India he had been sent for training in Intelligence duties, on completion of which, having expressed a wish to serve in a formation which included a unit of his old regiment, he was at once put in charge of our Brigade Intelligence Section. Early in April, a week after my arrival in Mayapore, he received posting orders to a G 3(I) appointment at Division. I made some fuss but Ewart persuaded me not to hinder the transfer. In his opinion, since coming to Mayapore, Lindsey had shown signs of restlessness and uncertainty and Ewart suspected that he had spoken to a friend on the divisional staff about getting a move. Lindsey's successor, Davidson, did not strike me as a particularly good substitute at first and we crossed swords on several occasions. Of Jewish origin, he had a layer of sensitivity that I did not at once comprehend.

After talking to Davidson, I decided to visit White. I drove first to his bungalow, and being told by Mrs White that he was touring the cantonment and the city, but expected to be back by ten o'clock, I decided to wait. I discussed the situation with her and found her own attitude shrewdly balanced between my own and her husband's. She said, 'Robin has always tried to see at least one year ahead. He knows that the people who oppose us now are the same we are going to have to live with and feel responsible for afterwards.' I said, 'Yes, providing the Japanese don't take over.' She said, 'I know. It's what I personally feel. But then I'm thinking of the twins and of never seeing them again. Robin thinks of that too, but knows that to think it isn't what he is paid for.'

I saw at once that between Mr and Mrs White there was the same fine sense of partnership which I had been blessed with in my own life.

When White returned, accompanied by young Jack Poulson, he at once apologized for any annoyance he might have given me earlier that morning about the Ranpurs and the bridge. I asked him whether I was right in thinking he had decided Dibrapur could be left to stew for a day or two in the hope that the successful reduction of unrest in Mayapore would leave it isolated and open to pacification. He seemed surprised, and thought for a moment, and then said, 'Yes, I suppose in military terms that is a way of putting it.'

I asked him what the civil terms were and he said at once, 'The saving of life and protection of property.' I asked him whether he therefore felt that the military were not to be trusted. He said, 'Your fellows are armed. My fellows have a few delaying weapons like explosives but otherwise their bare hands and their passions.'

I was surprised at his description of the rebels as 'his fellows', until I realized that just as I took my share of responsibility seriously so White took his, and I was aware of the curious enmity, as well as the amity, that could grow between two men of the same background, simply because the spheres of their responsibility differed. And yet, I thought, in the end, the result we both hoped for was the same.

The news that morning on the civil side was that the employees of the British–Indian Electrical Company were out on strike and that students of the Government Higher School and the Mayapore Technical College planned mass *satyagraha* that afternoon in a march across the Bibighar bridge and along the Grand Trunk road to the airfield at Banyaganj where work had also come to a stop following acts of intimidation against the men and women who had at first resisted the Congress call to cease work.

White intensely disliked action against students, whose volatile natures were unpredictable. They might be content to march in an orderly fashion and allow a number of their fellows to be arrested and then disperse, satisfied to have embarrassed the authorities and identified themselves with Congress ideals. But the slightest 'wind from another direction', as White put it, could lead them to throw themselves unarmed on the police or the military in a movement of mass hysteria that could only lead to a tragic loss of life. He asked, therefore, that his police be reinforced by troops and that the officer commanding them be asked to control the actions of the police as well as those of his own men. The police, White said, were inclined to be 'tough' with students. White then put it to me that the ease with which his informants had got hold of the details of these plans only led him to see the students' demonstration as a move to tempt our forces to concentrate mainly on the Bibighar bridge and the area of the colleges. He expected another attack, across the Mandir Gate bridge, by men and women of the ordinary population and one on the jail, and believed that these would coincide with the movement of the students.

I could not but admire his cool and, as I thought, sensible appraisal. I suggested that this morning might be a good time for a drumbeat proclamation by the civil and military authorities through the main areas of the city forbidding gatherings. He had considered this and now considered it again. Finally he said, 'No, it comes under my heading of provocation and reminds me too readily of the prelude to the massacre in Amritsar. It may also remind *them*. They don't need the proclamation because they know what is allowed and what isn't.'

I think that from this conversation – begun in an atmosphere of coolness almost amounting to distrust – I learned more about the workings of the civilian mind than I had ever done in a comparable time during my service in the country. I came away with a deep and abiding impression of the Deputy Commissioner's total involvement with the welfare of the people as a whole, irrespective of race or creed or colour. He must have had many doubts as to the various courses of action to be taken, but I think he had to solve them all with, in mind, what his wife had called the realization that these were the people we were going to have to live in peace with when the troubles were over. In the aftermath of the troubles in Mayapore I believe that he was criticized for having 'lost his head'. If this is true, I should like to put the record straight. White 'went it alone' for as long as he was able, and I, in the few days in which circumstances made his task almost impossible, tried to make the best of a bad job. I should also put on record my opinion that White would have 'worked himself into the ground' before admitting he was beaten if, on the evening of August 12th, he had not received direct orders from his Commissioner (who was situated two hundred miles away from him!) and who, in turn, acted on the instructions of the provincial governor, to employ 'to the utmost' the military forces available to him. I had a similar notification from my divisional and area commander. By the night of the 12th, the province, viewed as a whole, was certainly in a state of such violent unrest that without difficulty it could be called a state of rebellion – one which our immediate superiors could only view with the gravest doubts for the immediate future.

That meeting on the morning of the 12th was virtually the last between White and myself that has left any clear impression on my mind. I have already described on an earlier page – as an example of the drill of military aid to the civil power – the action that afternoon on the Mandir Gate Bridge road when, as White had anticipated, believing the authorities fully occupied in reducing the student demonstration, the mob attempted penetration of the civil lines from the temple square, set fire to the *kotwali* in the vicinity of the temple and deployed towards the railway station. Simultaneously to the action this side of the Mandir Gate bridge the police were desperately defending the jail. Two of them died and the mob in that quarter succeeded in breaking into the prison and releasing a number of prisoners before a force of the Berkshires, who were rushed to the spot, were able to regain the initiative.

As readers may recall from my earlier detailed description of the action on the Mandir Gate Bridge road, the troops 'in aid' followed up the advantage they had gained in breaking up the mob in confusion with their firing, by pressing forward. In this way, the main body of the retreating rioters was pushed back across the bridge, although small groups managed to escape along some of the side roads.

Halting on the civil lines side of the bridge, the platoon commander asked the magistrate, Mr Poulson, whether he should remain there or cross the bridge and enter the city to command the temple square where already he could see new 'leaders' exhorting the fleeing crowd to stand and form up again. Poulson, intent upon keeping the force of law and order intact according to the drill book, requested the Berkshire subaltern to remain at the bridgehead. Firing could now be heard from the direction of the railway station and Poulson assumed correctly that in crossing the bridge originally the crowd had split into two, with one body advancing along the Mandir Gate Bridge road and the other infiltrating along the tracks towards the railway station. He told the subaltern that if the troops crossed over into the square they might find themselves caught between the mob that was trying to re-form in the town and the mob retreating from the firing at the railway station. As it was, when men and women fleeing from the railway station came into view they found the Berkshires holding the bridge – their one line of retreat.

Unfortunately, in spite of Mr Poulson's prompt request and the subaltern's equally prompt response – to 'open a way' across the bridge for these unarmed fleeing civilians – the civilians panicked at the sight of the troops and misinterpreted as hostile the movements of the platoon, which were actually made to give them way. Those at the front of the crowd tried to fall back and were trampled underfoot. Many scrambled down the banks of the river and attempted to swim across, and I'm afraid a number of men and women were drowned. This incident was the cause of great misunderstanding. We were accused by the Indians, later, of deliberately setting a trap and of showing no mercy towards those who were caught in it. Attempts were made to bring evidence that the troops at the bridge had fired into the mob, thereby causing many of them to throw themselves into the river. So far as I could gather this 'evidence' rested entirely on the fact that several of those who were drowned were found to have bullet wounds when the bodies were recovered. These wounds can only have been incurred in the action at the railway station, when non-compliance with the orders to disperse, and attacks on the troops with stones and brickbats, had led to a volley from the troops. As I think I have mentioned, the police at the railway station were commanded by Merrick, the District Superintendent. He showed great energy and determination and recklessness for his own safety. Mounted, he continually pressed forward to scatter the crowd and stop it forming a united front. Only when he was forced to retreat did he give orders to his few armed police, and permission to the troops, to fire.

It was a bitter afternoon, the climax coming when news reached us at District Headquarters that the jail had been attacked and forced. By now a heavy rain was falling. Between five and six o'clock a storm raged overhead as if reflecting the one which raged on the ground. It was in these inclement conditions that yet another force of Berkshires (which I myself accompanied, along with the Deputy Commissioner) were rushed across the bridge in open transports, and closed in on the jail. The rain and the alarm spread by the news of the failure of the riots in the civil lines had reduced the size of the crowds on Jail road, and no doubt the spectacle of several lorry-loads of armed troops and the speed with which I had ordered them to proceed shook the determination of the men and women still in this area. Nevertheless the area in the immediate vicinity of the jail had to be cleared by debussing the troops and firing repeated volleys over the heads of the crowd. Once we were in control of the area of access to the jail itself, the picket-gate in the huge old wooden doors of the prison had to be forced with pickaxes. The insurgents had locked themselves in. They had also broken into the armoury, but fortunately their familiarity with such weapons as they found turned out to be practically nil, otherwise our men might have found themselves forcing an entrance under serious fire. Even as it was, one of our soldiers was wounded when, led by their platoon commander, the Berkshires entered the jail courtyard.

Their failure to hold the jail was the final blow to the rebels' hopes that day, and as was usually the case when reverses of this nature were suffered, anger turned inwards. On the night of the 12th/13th when it could not clearly be said who had the upper

hand in terms of civil control, factions of the mob took time off
from harrying us to settle old scores between each other. There
was looting and arson in the city, but it was directed this time
against native shops and houses, and even against persons. A dead
body found in the morning could so easily be claimed as that of
a 'martyr in the cause of freedom' who had been beaten to death
by the police or the military! There were also a few incidents in
the cantonment where small groups of men who had escaped
along side roads and found places of hiding, emerged after dark
and caused slight damage along the railway line. That night, too,
a fire broke out in one of the depots on the railway sidings.

By now, the Deputy Commissioner had received the instructions from his superiors to contest the rebellion in his district
with the full weight of the forces available to him, and I had
been informed of this development by my area commander. My
own 'private' instructions were that if in the next few hours
I deemed that the civil authority was no longer operational,
I had discretion to assume full command and declare martial law.
However, from what I had seen that afternoon, I believed that
between us White and I could restore order so long as we agreed
that the situation had deteriorated to below the point at which
either of us could be held responsible for a text-book reply to
every incident. I had told my area commander this, and added
that my greatest concern was with the situation in Dibrapur
which, after the day's experiences in Mayapore, I took an
increasingly serious view of.

I had a short meeting with White late that night. This was
one of the several meetings which I have no really detailed recollection of, because they were now all taking place hurriedly and
in an atmosphere of urgency, but I do recall his strained face and
his immediate question on seeing me, 'Well, you're taking over,
I suppose?' I said, 'Do you request that?' He shook his head, but
agreed to my sending, on the morrow, a force to Dibrapur by
the direct road south from Mayapore. But the area commander
phoned me again that night from his headquarters and asked
me to approach Dibrapur from the north-west on foot from the
demolished bridge which, meanwhile, was to be repaired as
quickly as possible by the engineers so that normal communications could be re-established along the road as soon as
Dibrapur was pacified.

The Ranpurs were held up constantly along that short ten-mile stretch of road beyond the bridge by roadblocks and home-made 'land-mines' from which they suffered several casualties. In this way, my belief that Dibrapur had been chosen as the stronghold of a planned uprising was upheld and it was not until the morning of the 17th that I was able to report to the Deputy Commissioner that the town was once again in the hands of legally constituted forces. To assist the Ranpurs I had to send a company of the Pankots along the direct route southwards through Tanpur, and by and large the operation assumed something of the nature of a full-dress military attack. I declared martial law in Dibrapur on the night of the 13th when the Ranpurs first entered the town. For three days they were engaged in restoring law and order. On the 17th an officer on the Deputy Commissioner's staff again took control on behalf of the civil authority, and those of our agents who had appeared to co-operate with the rebels (the Indian sub-divisional officer, a magistrate, and several constables) were brought back to Mayapore to be dealt with in the first instance by the Deputy Commissioner. This was the occasion when the sub-divisional officer, by restoring money he said he had hidden to stop it falling into the rebels' hand, was not proceeded against.

In the interim, throughout the district the rebellion had passed through increasingly violent stages of appearing virtually uncontrollable to a state when we could feel that the impetus that had set it in motion had been successfully counteracted. In any physical conflict the initial driving power needed to take active steps always seems to provide one with one's sharpest memories. Discipline and drill then take over and come into their own, proving their worth, but providing the individual with no especially memorable recollections. But I do recall that on the 14th of August, another serious attempt to penetrate the civil lines was made in the names of the 'Martyrs of the Bibighar and the Mandir Gate Bridge'.

One could not help but be moved on this occasion by the spectacle of crowds in which so many women, young and old, exposed themselves to the threat of wounds or even death. One detected in the attempts made on the 14th a closer adherence to the Mahatma's principles of non-violence. It was as if, over-night, these simple townspeople had become disenchanted with leaders who had encouraged them to grab any weapon ready to hand and to believe that the police and the soldiers could be overcome by such means. Now they came in a spirit of unarmed defiance, carrying banners which exhorted us to Quit India and deliver to them the 'innocent victims' of the Bibighar Gardens. The crowd that attempted to cross the Bibighar bridge was composed largely of women and children and so touching was the sight of them that our men were reluctant to fire, even although while the women were to the fore, the orders were to fire over their heads. I noticed a soldier of the Berkshires break ranks to comfort a little girl who was running up and down looking for her mother, one of the many women, no doubt, who had prostrated themselves on the road so that the soldiers would have to step over them when pressing forward to clear the bridge.

There is little doubt that the affair of the assault on Miss Manners in the Bibighar Gardens gave the population a 'popular' rallying cry, but I never took seriously the arguments which were put forward to prove that it was the action taken by the police to 'avenge' the rape that caused the riots in the town. The stories that the six arrested men had been brutally treated were, I am sure, quite without foundation, although once again I would add a reminder that the police, apart from the most senior officers, such as the District Superintendent, were themselves Indians, and there have been – it must be admitted – occasions in our history when white officials have been unfairly blamed for the actions of their native subordinates whom 'by the book' it was their responsibility to control. I doubt that even the Indians, however, took seriously the tale that was told about one or several of the arrested men (all Hindus) being 'forced to eat beef'. It is true that in the police you would find a fairly high proportion of Muslims, but if the populace had really thought the beef-feeding story was true, that would have given rise at once to a rumour that Muslim members of the police were responsible and hence to the kind of communal disturbance we were fortunate to be spared at this juncture. Such tales, in relation to the Bibighar affair, were no doubt the result of gossip after the event, when peace had been restored. Certainly no tales of this kind came to my notice at the time, and when they did there seemed to me to be no point in investigating them, which in any case it would not have been my job to do.

Unfortunately, as I think it to have been, the seriousness of the uprising in Mayapore which took all of us every ounce of our energy to combat, denied the authorities the proper chance to pursue and extend the evidence against the men who had been arrested for the rape, and the inability of the girl herself to offer evidence leading to identification left the case in a judicially unsatisfactory state. There was never cause to remove the suspects to the greater security of the Berkshires' lines, but, if they were truly guilty (and my mind remained open on that score) they must have counted themselves lucky to be disposed of in the way they were. The most that could be done, relying upon the evidence of their past activities and associations, was to deal with them under the Defence of India Rules and accordingly this was done. As for the attack upon the mission teacher and the murder of her Indian subordinate, here again a failure quickly to identify any of the men arrested that day in Tanpur as those responsible, led possibly to a corresponding failure of justice, although eventually one or two men suffered the supreme penalty.

According to official statements published later, the number of occasions throughout the country on which the police and/ or military had to fire upon the populace totalled over 500. Over 60,000 people were arrested, over 1,000 killed and over 3,000 severely injured. Indian authorities dispute these figures in regard to the numbers killed and put the figure even as high as 40,000! In the case of my own troops the figures were as follows: Number of incidents in which firing was resorted to: 23 (12 of these having been in Dibrapur). Number of people estimated as killed as the result of firing: 12. Number of people estimated as wounded as a result of firing: 53. I think these figures are proof of the restraint our men showed. I do not have figures relating to those arrested, because this was the task of the police. Nor do I have the figures of those in the district who were punished, for instance by whipping, a subject on which the Indians have always been tender-minded. The damage done in the towns and outlying areas of the district was severe and it was several weeks before order had been completely restored in the sense that a civil authority would minimally recognize as 'order' – that is to say, an uninterrupted system of communication, full and open access by road and rail from one point to the other, and local communities wholly in the control of the police and under the jurisdiction of legally appointed magistrates. As White said, it was, finally, the people themselves who suffered from the disruption to their normal peaceful way of life. It is said, for instance, that the Bengal famine of 1943 might have been averted or, if not averted, at least alleviated had the 'rebellion' never taken place. There were many cases of thoughtless destruction of shops and warehouses and food stores.

I am conscious that I have written perhaps over-lengthily of what in terms of my life as a whole was an affair neither of long duration nor of special significance from a military point of view. Perhaps the deep and lasting impression it has made on me can be related to the fact that it came at a time when I was facing the kind of personal loss it is still difficult to speak of. There were moments – as I went about these daily tasks – when I felt that my life, simple as it had been, had unkindly already distributed the whole of its rewards to me; and, seeing the strength and unity of the tide that seemed to be flowing against us, I could not help asking myself the questions: In what way are we at fault? In what way have I personally failed?

It was on the 18th of August, the day after I had been able to report to the Deputy Commissioner that Dibrapur was at last restored to his authority, and that my officers – by now scattered in many different areas of the district – believed that the worst of the insurrection was over – that a telegram reached me from Tubby Carter, ordering me to come at once to Rawalpindi. The telegram had been delayed because of the troubles, even although it originated in military channels. I knew, of course, that by 'ordering' me he was simply advising me of the necessity of returning. I spoke at once on the telephone to the area commander and he gave me leave to travel immediately by any means I was able. It was already evening. I left the brigade in the capable hands of young Ewart Mackay and the CO of the Pankots, and travelled all through the night to Calcutta in my staff car, not trusting to the railway, and, I admit, wearing a loaded pistol in my holster. I was accompanied by my batman as well as the driver. My batman was a Hindu, but the driver was a Muslim. I thought how salutary a lesson it was to those who talked so readily of 'differences' that in that car there could be found – travelling in perfect amity – a representative of each of the three main 'powers' in India – Hindu, Muslim and Christian. The journey itself, however, seemed endless. In the dark, with all these troubles freshly behind me I pondered the immensity, the strange compelling beauty of India.

Even now, that night remains in my mind as totally unreal. I did not reach Calcutta until well into the morning of the 19th, although the driver – sensing that something was personally wrong for me – drove recklessly. Armed too, I think he would have helped to sell our lives dearly had we been attacked. I went at once, on reaching Cal, to my old friend Wing Commander 'Pug' Jarvis, who had been warned by Tubby and had expected my arrival the previous morning. It was nearly midnight before the RAF plane he had got me on to took off from Dum Dum. Fortunately it was going direct to Chaklala, with only a short delay in Delhi. In the early morning of the 20th I was met by Tubby at Chaklala. He drove me direct to his bungalow and then to the resting place which she had come to just the day before, too soon for me to be present, which was an alleviation of my grief I had sorely hoped to be granted.

I returned to Mayapore in the second week of September, but about two weeks after my return I received orders to take command of a brigade which was already in the field, east of the Brahmaputra, preparing to face the real enemy. Of this brigade, and our preparations for action against the Japanese, I will write in another chapter. But in this welcome translation to a more immediately active role, I detected the understanding hand of my old friend in Rawalpindi, who knew that for me only one kind of duty was now possible

II

The Civil

An edited transcript of written and spoken comments by Robin White, CIE (Ex-ICS)

(1) I was interested in what you sent me of the late Brigadier Reid's unpublished memoirs describing his relationship with the civil authority in Mayapore in 1942. I didn't keep a diary, as Reid appears to have done, and it is a long time since I thought much about any of the events in question, but I am sure that

from a military point of view his account is a viable enough reconstruction of what happened. From the civil point of view there are of course some inaccuracies, or anyway gaps in the narrative or alternative interpretations, that would need attention if a more general and impersonal picture were required to emerge.

I doubt, however, that there is much I myself can contribute all this time after. I have not been in India since 1948 and have long since lost touch with both old friends and old memories. I can confirm that Ronald Merrick did indeed succeed in obtaining his release from the Indian Police, but I was not concerned in any way with this and knew of no official reason why the authorities should have agreed, in his case, to let him go. He was commissioned into an Indian regiment, I think, and was wounded in Burma in either 1944 or 1945. As I recollect it he was killed during the communal riots that attended partition in 1947.

I was interested to hear of your recent visit to Mayapore and glad to learn that Lili Chatterjee is still living in the MacGregor House, a name I had quite forgotten – although I remember the house itself. I am glad, too, to hear that Srinivasan is still alive and remembers our association. I never saw him again after the morning when I had to order him and other members of the local Congress party sub-committee to be taken in custody. I knew little of the 'Sanctuary' run by Sister Ludmila, which I'd also forgotten about, but I'm pleased to hear that now, as *The Manners Memorial Home for Indian Boys and Girls*, it perpetuates the name of a family which was once highly thought of in the province. You do not say in what way the Home was founded. Presumably on money left either by Miss Manners or her aunt, Lady Manners. Is it known, by the way, what happened to the child, if it survived?

I return Brigadier Reid's manuscript with many thanks. I was touched by several passages in it. Neither my wife nor I knew of the illness of Mrs Reid until we saw a notice of her death a few days after he was summoned back to Rawalpindi. We knew that his son was a prisoner-of-war, of course. It was something I bore constantly in mind in my dealings with him. I'm sorry to realize that the son also died. There were many occasions when Reid annoyed me (obviously he felt the same about me) and others when I respected him, but on the whole he was never quite my sort of person. We rather got the impression that his posting to the command of a brigade in the field was a move on the part of the military authorities to disembarrass Mayapore of a man whose reputation, after the troubles, was thought to have become locally over-controversial. I'm glad to feel that Reid was not given this impression himself. Since you did not send me the subsequent chapters of his book, I don't know what he had to say about his eventual return to a desk job. I believe he never did attain his objective of a 'confrontation with the true enemy'. For a time, naturally, I followed what I could of his fortunes with some interest. But, as I say, this is all a long time ago and my own career in India came to an end not many years after.

I am sorry that I cannot be more helpful.

(2) I have had a letter from Lili Chatterjee, and gather it is from you that she got my address. She tells me that at the end of your stay in Mayapore this year, she delivered into your hands, as well as two letters, a journal written by Miss Manners during the time she lived with her aunt in Kashmir, awaiting the birth of the child. Lili Chatterjee tells me that for some time she kept the existence of the journal secret from you, and that she would not have handed it over unless she had finally made up her mind that your interest in what you call the Bibighar Gardens affair was genuine. I gather that she received the journal from Lady Manners several years after the events it describes, and that Lady Manners, herself then approaching death, felt that of all the people in the world whom she knew Lili Chatterjee alone should take possession of it. Lili tells me that the journal makes it clear exactly what happened.

I gather that your concern with this affair arose from a reading of Brigadier Reid's unpublished book, which came into your hands as a result of your known interest in this period of British–Indian history. Lili tells me that you have been to some trouble to trace persons who would be in a position either to describe from personal experience, or to comment on, on the basis of informed personal opinion, the events of those years in Mayapore. I gather for instance that in an attempt to 'recon-struct' the story of Miss Crane, the Mission School superintend-ent, you visited, among other places, the headquarters of the

organization to which she had belonged, and browsed among
her unclaimed relics. I met Miss Crane once or twice, and my
wife knew her quite well in connection with local committee
work. I also met Miss Manners on a number of occasions, but
I'm afraid I knew almost nothing of the man Kumar. I met him
only casually, twice at most. Jack Poulson would have been able
to tell you more about him because after the arrests I gave Poulson the job of conducting the various inquiries. Unfortunately
I can't help you to trace Poulson. He emigrated to New Zealand,
I believe, and I have not heard of him for many years. However,
Lili tells me that you have traced and talked to a friend of Kumar's
in England, a man called Lindsey – the same Lindsey, perhaps,
who according to Reid's account applied for a transfer from the
Brigade Intelligence staff in Mayapore? My recollection is that
Kumar was originally sent to the jail in the provincial capital, but
if as you say his aunt left Mayapore years ago and not even his
old uncle or Srinivasan have heard of him since then, it looks as
though upon his release he began an entirely new life somewhere
in India or, perhaps, in Pakistan.

In view of what Lili Chatterjee has told me I am willing –
subject to a prior understanding that my memory cannot be
absolutely relied upon – to have a talk.

(3) Thank you for having given me the opportunity before we
meet to read a copy of the short extract from Daphne Manners's
journal in which she describes what actually happened in the
Bibighar, and the letter she wrote to her aunt about Merrick's
'proposal'. Thank you too for letting me see what you call the
deposition of the man Vidyasagar. I did not know this man at
all, and at this distance his name means nothing to me. I do
remember Laxminarayan and the newspaper. I was interested to
hear that Laxminarayan is still living in Mayapore, and I'm glad
he was able to put you in touch with Vidyasagar before you left
India. Miss Manners was obviously telling the truth (I mean,
writing the truth, in her journal) and if Vidyasagar's 'deposition'
is also true – and there seems small reason to doubt it since there
could hardly be much point in his lying at this stage – then I can
only express a deep sense of shock. One's own responsibility
isn't shrugged off lightly. I feel perhaps that I should balance
any adverse picture by explaining the ways in which I thought

Merrick a responsible and hard-working officer. However, I gather from what you say that on the basis of the various documents – Reid's memoirs, Miss Manners's journal and letters, and Sister Ludmila's recollections, not to mention Vidyasagar's deposition – you have pretty well made your mind up about the central characters in the affair and particularly about the kind of man Merrick was, and that my own contribution to your investigations should be confined to more general matters. A reading of these documents – which I now return – has certainly had much of the effect on me that you suggested it might. I find myself remembering things I have not thought of for years, and so perhaps, after all, I can be of some help.

(4) *Verbal Transcript*
Areas of dangerous fallibility between a policy and its pursuit? Yes, that sounds like Srinivasan. Is it this sort of dangerous area you want to try and map? Not only? I see. Very well, let's concentrate on the association between Reid and myself. But you'll have to ask the questions.

Well, I made one or two notes about inaccuracies in Reid's account, but what struck me finally was that quite apart from Reid's simple soldier attitude which antagonized me again just as much on paper as when we met face to face, he had somehow managed to make everything that happened look logical in his own terms, and I remembered more and more clearly the feeling I myself had in those days of not being able to rehearse the sequence of events that had led to a situation that seemed to be logical in itself but jolly well wasn't.

Every time Reid came into my office with that look on his face of being ready and eager to straighten us all out I felt like a man who had been playing a fish that might turn out to be either a minnow or a whale, and Reid's entrance, or even a telephone call from him, or from one of the officers on his staff, was just like someone suddenly tapping me on the elbow in midstream and telling me, quite inaccurately, what I was doing wrong. He had a genius for smothering any but your bluntest instincts, which is why I once lost my temper and told him rather rudely to leave me alone. He didn't bring that out in his book, but I'm not sure that this particular omission couldn't be traced to the fact that he had a hide like a rhinoceros and my show of temper had as much effect on him as the bite of a gnat. I know that his book gives an impression of a not insensitive man, but he was sensitive, broadly, only to major issues and *grand* emotions. In his daily contact with other human beings he did tend to bear pretty much the proportional weight of a sledgehammer to a pin.

When I first met Reid I saw him as a man it was going to take a lot of patience and energy to restrain. As so often happened when a man was taken from behind a desk, he had formed an opinion about what he was always calling his task or his role – as if it were pretty well cut and dried and took precedence over anyone else's, and I thought that having formed his opinion of his task he was also determined to carry it out *in toto*, however irrelevant some of its aspects turned out to be. I remember saying to my wife that if the Indians didn't start a rebellion Reid would be forced to invent one just so that by suppressing it he would feel he'd done his whole duty. She told me I'd better treat him gently because, as we all knew by then, his son was missing in Burma. I think I hoped as much as he did that the poor boy would turn up, and was even more concerned than he by the news that young Reid was a prisoner-of-war in the hands of the Japanese.

You could say that my association with Reid was fairly typical of the conflict between the civil and the military, so perhaps I was no less guilty of conforming to a generalized pattern of behaviour than he was.

No, you're quite right to correct me. I don't mean at all that the Civil were always progressive and the Military reactionary. I've fallen into my own trap, haven't I? Let me put it right. The drama Reid and I played out was that of the conflict between Englishmen who liked and admired Indians and believed them capable of self-government, and Englishmen who disliked or feared or despised them, or, just as bad, were indifferent to them as individuals, thought them extraneous to the business of living and working over there, except in their capacity as servants or soldiers or as dots on the landscape. On the whole civil officers were much better informed about Indian affairs than their opposite numbers in the military. In the later stages of our administration it would have been rare to find in the civil a man of Reid's political simplicity.

Put my finger on the main weakness of Reid's analysis of

the political situation in India from the beginning of the 'thirties – ? No, because analysis is the wrong word. He had an attitude, that was all. We all had an attitude but his struck me as pretty childish. It was emotional and non-analytical. But I was always taught that politics were people, and a lot of Englishmen thought as Reid thought and felt as he felt, which was why even when he was getting my goat most with his talk of Indians and Englishmen having to sink their differences in order to beat the Jap I recognized the *force* of his attitude. After all the Japanese were practically hammering at the door, and even though what Reid meant by Indians and English sinking differences was the Indians doing all the sinking, calling a halt to their political demands and the English maintaining the *status quo* and sinking nothing – one couldn't help admitting that the situation was very similar to the one a quarrelsome household would face if they looked out of the window and saw burglars trying to get in, or a gang of hooligans preparing to burn the house down. The head of the house would immediately feel obliged to take a lead and stand no nonsense from inside.

But straightforward as that situation might look – just a question of ceasing to squabble and presenting a united front to repel Japanese boarders – its straightforwardness depends on the nature of the squabbling in the house, doesn't it? On the whole I dislike analogies, but let's pursue this one a bit further. Let's imagine that the people in the house are a pretty mixed bunch, and that those who have the least say in how things are run are those the house belonged to originally. The present self-appointed owner has been saying for years that eventually, when he is satisfied that they've learned how to keep the roof repaired, the foundations secure and the whole in good order, he'll get out and give them the house back, because that is his job in life: to teach others how to make something of themselves and their property. He's been saying this long enough to believe it himself but ruling the household with a sufficiently confusing mixture of encouraging words and repressive measures to have created a feeling among his 'family' that by and large he's kidding, and that the only language he understands is the language *he* uses – a combination of physical and moral pressure. He's also said he'll leave – but stayed put – long enough to create factions below stairs among the people who hope to inherit or rather get the house back.

He hasn't necessarily intended to create these factions, but their existence does seem to suit his book. Deny people something they want, over a longish period, and they naturally start disagreeing about precisely what it is they *do* want. So he likes nothing better than to give private interviews to deputations from these separate factions and to use the arguments of minority factions as moral levers to weaken the demands put forward by the majority faction. He's got into the habit of locking up over-vociferous members of all factions in the basement and only letting them out when they go on hunger strike like Gandhi used to.

We were in India for what we could get out of it. No one any longer denies that, but I think there are two main aspects of the British–Indian affair which we prefer to forget or ignore. The first was that we were originally *able* to exploit India because the first confrontation – to use Reid's cant word – was that of an old, tired civilization that was running down under the Moghuls and a comparatively new energetic civilization that had been on the up-grade ever since the Tudors. English people tend to think of India as a Victorian acquisition, but it was originally really an Elizabethan one. And you only have to consider the difference between the Elizabethans and the Victorians to get an idea of the changes that took place in our attitude to our prize and therefore of the second aspect of the affair which we forget or ignore – the confusion surrounding the moral issue. The moral issue is bound to arise eventually and grow, and finally appear to take precedence in any long-standing connection between human beings, especially if their status is unequal. The *onus* of moral leadership falls naturally on the people who rank as superior, but just as a people over-endowed with power can explain that power away as God-given and start talking about morality and the special need to uplift the poor and ignorant – the people they have power *over* – so can a people who have had too long an experience of what today is called underprivilege pass the buck to *their* god. At almost precisely the same time that the English were developing their theories of the White Man's burden to help them bear the weight of its responsibility, the Hindus and the Muslims were taking a long hard look at *their* religions, not to explain their servitude but to help them to end it. A lot of nonsense has been talked, you know, about the communal problem in India as if we waited in vain throughout the centuries of our influence for the Hindus and Muslims to settle their differences, but the communal problem never really became a problem until Hindu and Muslim revivalists and reformers got to work in the nineteenth century, in much the same way our own did, to see what comfort and support and ways forward could be found in these old philosophies. I think the English, however unconsciously and unintentionally, created the division between Muslim India and Hindu India. More recently in Kenya we shrieked accusations of barbarism at the Kikuyu for their Mau Mau rebellion, but hit a man in the face long enough and he turns for help to his racial memory and tribal gods. The Hindus turned to theirs, the Muslims to theirs. It wasn't from *social* awareness that Gandhi identified himself with the outcastes of the Hindu religion. Untouchability was foreign to original Hinduism and in this attempted return by a subject people to the source of their religious inspiration it was bound to happen that untouchability should be chosen as the intended victim of a revival, and non-violence re-emerge as a main tenet of its revitalization. The Muslims' investigation of their religion was more dangerous, because Mohammed preached Holy War against the infidel. I think the English were perversely attracted to the idea of that danger. I always found it interesting that on the whole most English people were happier consorting with Muslims than with Hindus, but then fundamentally we've always been a bit embarrassed by the 'weakness' of Christianity. We saw the same weakness in Hinduism, but a sort of Eastern version of muscular Christianity in the religion of Allah.

In those days I was intensely *puzzled* by Gandhi. On the whole I distrust great men. I think one should. I certainly distrusted Gandhi – but not in the way Reid, for instance, distrusted him. I distrusted Gandhi because I couldn't see how a man who wielded such power and influence could remain uninhibited by it, and always make the right decisions for the right reasons. And yet I always felt his appeal to my conscience behind even my severest doubts about his intentions.

There's one story about Gandhi that I didn't know at the time, and it's particularly interested me since. Perhaps you know it too?

Yes. That's it. Do you think it relevant? It strikes me as fundamental to an understanding of the man. I mean to be declared
outcaste by his community merely because he expressed an
intention as a young man to go to England to study law! And
did you know this, that the leaders of his community declared
in advance that any fellow going to see him off or wishing him
good luck would be punished with a fine. Something like a
rupee each. And think how long he was abroad between first
departure and return. Nearly a quarter of a century altogether.
I wonder what he thought of India when he eventually got back
to it after all those years in England and all those years in South
Africa? Do you think his heart sank? Even though he returned
a hero because of what he had done for the Indians in South
Africa where he first initiated *satyagraha*. I mean India is far from
what Brigadier Reid called salubrious. Perhaps Gandhi took one
look at it and thought, Good God, is this what I've been longing
to return to? I mention this because presently we come to the
important question of *doubt* in public life.

I suppose it's also relevant that he returned to India just at the
time when friendly co-operation between the British and the
Indians was reaching the peak of its last notable phase, early in
the First World War. If I remember correctly he sailed from
South Africa to England in the summer of 1914 and got there
just about the time we declared war on Germany. He told Indian
students in London that England's predicament was not India's
opportunity – a healthy opinion which Nehru borrowed
twenty-five years later – and all through the Great War, in India,
he was in favour of the recruitment of young Indians to the
services. By and large India really went all out to help and not
hinder us in that war. There was a strong smell of freedom for
them in the air, and of self-government or measures of self-
government which they could earn by helping to fight Britain's
enemies, which they seemed happy to do anyway. It was in 1917,
wasn't it, that we actually declared specifically that the goal for
India was Dominion status? I think Gandhi got back to India
early in 1915, and rather crossed swords – as Reid would have
said – with people like Annie Besant. But even as early as this
he proved himself to be something of an enigma. In his first
public speech he said he was ashamed to have to speak in English
in order to be understood by a largely Indian audience. Most

Indian leaders prided themselves on their English. He criticized a prince who had just referred to India's poverty, and sarcastically pointed out the splendour of the surroundings – they were laying the foundation stone of a new University. Benares? Yes, the Hindu University in Benares. Then he said there was a lot of work to be done before India could think of self-government. That was one in the eye for the politically self-satisfied! At the same time he pointed at Government detectives in the crowd and asked why Indians were so distrusted. That was a snub to the Raj. He referred to the young Indian anarchists and said he was also an anarchist, but not one who believed in violence, although without violence he admitted the anarchists wouldn't have managed to get the decision to partition Bengal reversed. What a mixture of ideas this seemed to be! Mrs Besant tried to interrupt but the audience of students asked him to continue. The fellow in charge of the meeting told him to explain himself more clearly and he said what he wanted to do was to get rid of the awful suspicion that surrounded every move made in India. He wanted love and trust, and freedom to say what was in the heart without fear of the consequences. Most of the people on the platform left – I suppose they felt compromised or outraged or just publicly embarrassed – so he stopped speaking and afterwards the British stepped in. The police ordered him out of the city.

It must have been as it would be at a political meeting here, or in a television interview, if a well-known man actually got up or faced the camera and said exactly what was in his mind, without worrying how many times he seemed to contradict himself, and certainly without thinking of his own reputation, in a genuinely creative attempt to break through the sense of *pre-arranged* emotions and reactions that automatically accompanies any general gathering of people. In India that sense of pre-arrangement was always particularly strong because the Indians are normally the politest men and women in the world, which is probably why at a pinch they can be among the most hysterical and blood-thirsty. I suppose the widespread use of a foreign language has exaggerated their natural politeness. I've often wondered whether things wouldn't have gone infinitely better for us if all our civil servants had been compelled to acquire complete fluency both in Hindi and in the main language of their province and forced to conduct every phase of government in that language. Gandhi was right, of course, it was shameful that in talking to university students he had to speak a foreign language. The reason he had to speak it wasn't only because all the young men there had achieved their present status by learning and reading in English, but because it was probably the only language they *all* shared in common. We did nothing really to integrate communities, except by building railways between one and the other to carry their wealth more quickly into our own pockets.

Gandhi, you know, always struck me as the only man in public life anywhere in the world who had a highly developed instinct and capacity for thinking aloud – and this was an instinct and a capacity that seldom got smothered by other instincts. I'm sure it led eventually to the chap being completely misunderstood. People in public life are supposed to project what today we call an image, and ideally the image has to be constant. Gandhi's never was. The phases he went through just in the years 1939 to 1942 were inconstant enough for history to have labelled him as sufficiently politically confused to rank either as a band-wagoner or a half-baked pain in the neck. But I think what he was actually doing was trying to bring into the open the element of *doubt* about ideas and attitudes which we all undergo but prefer to keep quiet about.

And don't you think that can be partially traced back to the depression he must have felt way back in the nineteenth century at being able to leave his homeland only as an outcaste? Don't you think that the element of doubt entered very strongly at that moment as well as on his return? 'Am I doing the right thing?' he must have asked himself. After all he was only nineteen or so. To go to England and study for the law was something he could only do by being publicly rejected by his caste-community. Caste probably had a truly religious significance for him in those days. Going to England was significant only in terms of his worldly ambition. No man is without ambition, but perhaps few men have been forced to doubt the power for good that ambition represents as much as Gandhi was forced to do. I felt in the end that he was working out a personal salvation in public all the time. And of course the kind of doubt a man has of himself, of his actions, of his thinking, plays a prominent but invariably secret part in the actual events of the day.

It was right to bring it into the open for once. He was never afraid to say openly that he'd changed his mind or been wrong, or that he was thinking about a problem and would only express his views after he'd worked out some kind of solution.

What would have happened, I wonder, if I had publicly represented my doubts about the wisdom of imprisoning Congress leaders in August 1942? God knows. I can't have been the only district officer who felt that it was the last thing it was wise to do or the only one to write long confidential memoranda on the subject to his commissioner. But I didn't have the nerve to stand up in the open and rehearse in public the pros and cons of doing what I was instructed to do.

I sometimes wish that on August the 9th I'd gone to the temple square beyond the Mandir Gate bridge with a megaphone, called out to the people there and said, 'Look, Government tells me to imprison X Y and Z because the Indian National Congress has endorsed the Mahatma's resolution calling on us to Quit India and leave her to God, or to anarchy, in other words, so far as we are concerned, to the Japanese. But if I imprison these men, who will lead you? Will you be glad to be rid of them? Or will you feel lost? Congress talks about non-violent non-co-operation, but what does that mean? How won't you co-operate? How will you withhold co-operation without defending yourselves against us when we try to *force* you to co-operate? We'll try to force you because we believe we're fighting for our lives. When you defend yourselves how will you do so without violence? If I threw down this megaphone and struck one of your young men on the face, what would you do? What would he do? If he does nothing and I strike him again, what then? What if I then do it again and again, until his face is bloody? Until he is dead? Will you just stand by and watch? The Mahatma says so, it seems, but do *you* say so?'

But of course I never did go to the temple square with a megaphone. Doubts and all I locked up X Y and Z. And I think it was wrong. The men who ordered me to lock them up had probably had similar doubts before initiating the policy, but once it was laid on none of us was left with any official alternative but to carry it out.

I suppose true anarchy in public life is inaction arising out of the element of doubt as opposed to action following the element of decision. And of course between the doubt, the decision, the action and the consequences, I suppose you find what Srinivasan calls the areas of dangerous fallibility. Well, that's not a shattering discovery. We all know it. But Gandhi had the *courage* to operate openly on the ground of the dangerous areas, didn't he? Is that what you're getting at? Wise as we can be after the event, no one at the time pointed out that this was what he was doing: If he stepped too noticeably out of the acceptable line he was locked up, but released when it was thought his talents would be more valuable politically on a free rein.

What is clear to me beyond *any* doubt is that we turned him fundamentally into a power harmful to our policies when we resorted to the repressive measures of the Rowlatt Act, immediately after the Great War at a time when he and all Indians had every reason to expect a major advance towards self-government as a reward for co-operating so freely in the war with Germany. Were we mad? Or plain stupid? Or merely perfidious? Or terrified? Or just common-or-garden cocky after victory, thick-skinned and determined to give away nothing? What in hell was the good of declaring Dominion status as our aim for India in 1917 and not much more than a year later instituting trial without jury for political crimes and powers of detention at provincial level under the Defence of India Rules, ostensibly to deal with so-called anarchists but in practice to make any expression of free-will and free opinion technically punishable? What kind of a 'dominion' was that?

Well, you remember the result: riots, and then General Dyer at Amritsar and a return to distrust and fear and suspicion, and Gandhi emerging as the Mahatma, the one man who might provide an answer – but now it was going to be an Indian answer, not a British one. I'm sorry. I still get hot under the collar when I think about 1919. And I'm still deeply ashamed, after all these years.

No, I was too young at the time. I went out to India as a young civilian as we called ourselves in 1921. I had hardly a thought in my head. I'd done my swotting and passed the exams, and read all the the myth and legend. I wanted nothing better in those days than to get out into my first sub-division under the old pipul tree, puffing at a pipe and fancying myself no end as a promising administrator who would straighten out young and old and be remembered as White Sahib, become a legend myself and still be talked about fifty years after I'd gone as the fellow who brought peace and prosperity to the villages.

But of course I had to face reality at once. I simply wasn't cut out for paternalism. My superiors were the last of that breed. I disliked my first district officer. He probably didn't deserve it. But I hated India – the real India behind the pipe-puffing myth. I hated the loneliness, and the dirt, the smell, the conscious air of superiority that one couldn't get through the day without putting on like a sort of protective purdah. I hated Indians because they were the most immediately available target and couldn't hit back except in subtle ways that made me hate them even more.

And then one day, I remember it clearly, I was touring the district with the land settlement officer, going from village to village. On horseback, old style. I was fed to the teeth with village accountants who cringed and tahsildars who presumed and cringed all in the same breath, and I was critical of the settlement officer who obviously felt and acted like God going for a casual stroll, giving with the right hand and taking with the left. Then something went wrong with the camp *bandobast*. We were bogged down in some god-forsaken village and had to spend the night in a mud-hut. I was ready to cry from frustration and from my own sense of inadequacy. The settlement officer was drinking toddy with the village elders still playing at Christ and the Apostles, and I was alone in the hut. My bowels were in a terrible state and I couldn't face anything, let alone toddy. I was lying on a charpoy, without a mosquito net, and suddenly saw this middle-aged Indian woman standing in the doorway watching me. When our eyes met she made *namaste* and then disappeared for a moment, and came back with a bowl of curds and a spoon.

I was on my dignity at once, and waved her away, but she came to the bedside and spooned up a helping of the curds and held it out and made me eat, just as if I were her nephew or son and needed building up. She said nothing and I couldn't even look at her – only at her black hands and the white curds. Afterwards I fell asleep and when I woke up I felt better and wondered whether I hadn't dreamed it all, until I saw the bowl of un-finished curds covered with a cloth, on a brass tray by the bedside and a flower on the tray next to the bowl. It was morning then, and the settlement officer was snoring in the other bed. I felt that I had been given back my humanity, by a nondescript middle-aged Indian woman. I felt that the curds and the flowers were for affection, not tribute, affection big enough to include a dash of well-meant motherly criticism, the suggestion that my indisposition could be overcome easily enough once I'd learned I had no real enemies. I remember standing in the open doorway and breathing in deeply; and getting it: the scent behind the smell. They had brass pots of hot water ready for my bathe. Before the bathe I was sat down on an old wooden chair and shaved by the *nai*, the barber, without soap, just his fingers and warm water and a cut-throat. He scraped the razor all over my face and forehead, even over the eyelids. I held my breath, waiting for the cut that would blind me. But it was all gentle and efficient, a kind of early-morning *puja*, and afterwards my face felt newly made and I went to the bathing enclosure and scooped water out of the brass pots of hot water that stood waiting. Brooke had the right word for it. The benison of hot water. Later I looked among the women but couldn't tell which of them had come into the hut the night before and fed me as she would have fed her own son. There was another flower on the pommel of my saddle. It embarrassed me. But I loved it too. I looked at the settlement officer. He had no flower and hadn't noticed mine. As we rode away I looked back, and waved. The people made no move in reply, but I felt it coming from them – the good wish, the challenge to do well by them and by myself. I've never forgotten that. I expect that afterwards the bowl and spoon I'd eaten from had to be thrown away.

No. One did tend to spend the whole of one's career in the same province, but that village was not in the district where I eventually became Deputy Commissioner. Why? Did you think it lay close to Dibrapur?

(5) Thank you for sending me the edited transcript of the recording of our interview. I see you have ironed out a lot of the inconsistencies and repetitions but haven't been able to disguise the way that I kept leading away from the point. You were obviously right to end the interview when we got round finally to the business of Dibrapur, which probably needs more careful discussion than it would have got just then.

I don't know about Mary Tudor and Calais as you put it, but I certainly *remember* Dibrapur. There was terrible poverty there, the kind you would get in any region where an old source of wealth has retreated farther and farther. In the nineteenth century it was the headquarters of the district. I don't recall exactly when it was that they began to mine the coal, but gradually these particular veins were worked out and the adjoining district inherited the wealth and prosperity. Labour was still drawn from Dibrapur, but in decreasing quantities.

In any depressed area, anywhere in the world, you can assume that emotions and attitudes will be exaggerated. In one respect Reid was right and some kind of organized force *was* at work in Dibrapur, but how much was due to planning and how much to intelligent seizing of opportunity never was clear. Where he was wrong, I'm sure, was in attributing the force to an underground force of *Congress*, and I think Vidyasagar's deposition bears this out, and where I was right, I suspect, was in believing that *any* force of Indian national life could have been controlled by the Congress. The majority of Indians (excluding wild young men like Vidyasagar) have always respected authority – how else could we have ruled millions with a few thousand? Congress was the shadow authority. If we had not banned the Congress committees and imprisoned their leaders at the centre and in most of the provinces, I'm convinced that there would have been no rebellion of the kind that occurred. Gandhi, you know, didn't expect to be arrested this time. Politically, 'Quit India' was a sort of kite he flew. Morally, it was an appeal like a cry in the dark. But even if in places like Dibrapur there had been rebellion I am equally convinced that to contain it I would only have had to appeal to a man like Srinivasan for instance to go there and talk to the people and exhort them to non-violent non-co-operative methods. Strikes, hartal, that sort of thing. I honestly believe that the Indian is emotionally predisposed against violence. That would explain the hysteria that usually marks his surrender to it. He then goes beyond all ordinary bounds, like someone gone mad because he's destroying his own faith as well. We on the other hand are emotionally disposed *towards* violence, and have to work hard at keeping ourselves in order. Which is why at the beginning of our wars we've always experienced a feeling of relief and said things like, 'Now we know where we stand.' The other thing to remember about Indians, Hindus anyway, is that their religion teaches them that man, as man, is an illusion. I don't say that any more of them believe that than Christians believe Christ was the son of God or was talking practical sense when he said we should turn the other cheek. But just as the Christian ideal works on our Christian conscience while we're engaged in battering each other to death, or blowing each other up, so that we know that to do so is wrong, so I think when the Indians start battering each other they feel in the backs of their minds that the battering isn't quite real. I think this partly explains why unarmed mobs were always ready to face our troops and police. They themselves weren't real, the troops weren't real, the bullets were never fired and people didn't die except in a world that was an illusion itself. I agree that this doesn't explain why in such a non-existent world it was thought worth while opposing the troops in the first place.

But of course for me the people in the Dibrapur sub-division *were* real. They were bad farmers and poor shopkeepers. It wasn't their fault. The heyday of the coalmines was pre-Great War, but that heyday denuded part of the land permanently and led to unploughed fields, and the splitting up of families. There were several villages in that area where there were practically no young men. They'd all gone to the mining areas in the adjacent district. You know the sort of thing that happens as well as I do. We made special efforts there – I remember talking to Miss Crane about them once, because she had one of her schools near Dibrapur – but there was a lot of apathy as well as a lot of resentment. The young Indian I had out there in his own sub-divisional head-quarters was an extremely intelligent and capable man. It was the toughest sub-division in the district. He had a lot of problems but also a lot of *nous*. The fellow who appointed himself deputy commissioner was one of the local tahsildars who was also a local landowner. My own man had always had a lot of trouble with him. In his account Reid leaves a slight doubt in the reader's mind about the Indian sub-divisional officer's actual behaviour during the troubles. I know at the time people were going around saying that when it was all over the chap broke down in my office and spent hours crying and asking to be let off. No such thing. We talked the situation out quite unemotionally, and

I was satisfied that short of sacrificing his life – which I wouldn't have expected any sane man to do – the sub-divisional officer had made the best of a bad job, managed to restrain the self-appointed deputy commissioner quite a bit, in spite of the fact that as so-called Judge he was more or less kept prisoner. And he certainly saved a sizeable sum of money for the treasury. I expect the rumour about him crying arose from the fact that when we shook hands and parted there *were* tears in his eyes, and people probably noticed them as he left my bungalow. I hadn't been kind to him, just fair, I hope, but Indians have never been ashamed of responding to fairness in a way an Englishman would be ashamed to.

But that is jumping ahead. I know there was a failure in our intelligence system to pinpoint in advance the men who emerged as local leaders in Dibrapur and succeeded in cutting the town off for several days. I suppose I did use the expression 'needles in a haystack' when talking about such people to Reid, but I don't actually remember doing so. The police in the Dibrapur sub-division were – perhaps not unexpectedly in view of the toughness of their job – of a lower morale than elsewhere. Some ran away, and one or two constables took over and sided with the rebels. As you will have gathered, everything happened pretty quickly and our police – never numerous – were scattered very thinly in proportion to the area and the size of the population. I agreed to Reid sending troops on the night of the 11th in the hope that their prompt appearance at that particular moment would be as inhibiting as the appearance of troops usually was. Reid rather underplays the attempts made that day by the civil authority to get into Dibrapur with police and magistrates, and says nothing about the roadblocks on the *main* road. There were no blown bridges on the main road, but there was a series of felled trees that denied the road to the full use of transport, and the police found that the nearer they got to Dibrapur the less helpful the villagers were in helping them to clear the road. On the night in question the message I had had from Tanpur was to the effect that one truckload of police had 'disappeared'. It turned out later that they were locked up in the *kotwali* in one of the villages near Dibrapur. All the wires were down, of course, between Dibrapur and Tanpur.

The news of the blown bridge on Reid's flank road was

certainly a poser, but I couldn't help being rather amused because he had made the use of the flank road sound so professional and clever, and suddenly there he was in danger of losing two 3-ton lorries and a 15-cwt truck and his wireless. And he was mad as hell. I hope that my amusement didn't sway my decision. I requested the withdrawal of the troops on that road because I felt that if the rebels had the initiative and the means to blow a bridge (a fairly harmless occupation in itself, just a matter of destroying a ton or so of brick and mortar!) a meeting of the rebels and troops whose tempers had shortened might result in the very kind of bloody affair I wanted to avoid. I know that my decision is open to question, but I made it, and stand by it, and I think it was right. If there had not then been pressure from above to use troops to the full I should certainly have left Dibrapur to stew even longer than I did. That intelligence officer, Davidson, was right when he suggested to Reid that my idea was for pacification to spread outwards from Mayapore. But Reid was jumping on hot bricks. I don't offer this as an excuse, although perhaps I do offer it as a contributory factor to any decision of mine that I still have doubts about. When you have a man like Reid constantly at your elbow you do tend to lose your concentration. I think I would have withstood his nagging if the provincial civil authority hadn't begun to press too. It is difficult actually to recall the real sense of urgency that arose in a few hours when reports were coming in pointing to an uprising that was getting out of hand. Anyway there was the pressure from Reid, the pressure from provincial headquarters, and the pressure of my own doubts. So I let Reid have his way about Dibrapur. His little battle there was by no means uncontrolled. I have no complaints or accusations on that score. But I don't think it was accompanied by any *special* restraint, and I still believe, as I believed then, that the deaths of men, women and children in Dibrapur could have been avoided if the town had been allowed to 'stew' until the people themselves were of the temper (and it never took long for them to regain it) to make its *realignment* (and that is the proper word) just part of the day's routine.

Perhaps it was unfair that the action of his troops in Dibrapur (of which he does not give us the benefit of any detailed description in his book) should have been the main cause of the reputation Reid had afterwards for being over-controversial in the district 'during the current phase of pacification'. (The official jargon for 'let's all be friends again'.) My commissioner asked me to comment on Reid, confidentially. Complaints against any of us, civil or military, very quickly reached a high level as you know. I gave it as my opinion that Reid had at no time exceeded his duty and had been, throughout, a constant reassurance to me in the execution of my own. I added that, left to ourselves, and not ordered to make the fullest use of the means available, the force actually used might have been less and the result the same, or even better. I didn't see why Reid should carry the can back for people who had panicked at provincial headquarters. I don't think this comment of mine pleased anyone from the commissioner upwards. For a time I expected to be moved myself, but the luck or ill-luck of the game fixed on Reid – unless it were really true that his posting could be put down to the influence of friends of his who thought that following the death of his wife he would be happier if employed in a more active role. It is so easy – particularly when looking for a chosen scapegoat of an action you have taken part in – to hit upon a particular incident as proof that a scapegoat has been found when, in fact, the authorities have simply shrugged their shoulders, and a purely personal consideration has then stepped in and established the expected pattern of offence and punishment.

(6) Thank you for your reply to my written comments on the transcription of our interview. Yes, I do dislike the element of 'Yes, you did. No, I didn't' that all too readily rises to the surface. Reid had his attitudes and opinions and I had mine. One can't go on for ever justifying one's own and refuting someone else's with any kind of passion – but I'm sorry that the points I've been making notes of in the past few days in answer to specific statements in Reid's book don't come up now except extraneously. May I take one of them, though, and kill any idea Reid might have left that Menen, the District and Sessions Judge, was predisposed towards the rebels? Menen was predisposed towards nothing except the due process of the law which he had no special faith in, God knows, but certainly recognized his sworn duty to. I'm also slightly worried about any impression that could be left of my having either been in collusion with Merrick over – or turned a blind eye to – the

treatment of the Bibighar suspects. I feel I should be allowed to say something about this if you are going to publish Vidyasagar's deposition. Vidyasagar ranks as a self-confessed lawbreaker so that's neither here nor there.

In his deposition he is noticeably unforthcoming about the names of his associates. So to what extent we can rely on his statement that Hari Kumar was not one of his fellow-conspirators, neither of us can judge accurately. The picture we get from Miss Manners's journal (or rather from that short section of it which you have allowed me to see) is not in itself *evidence* of Kumar's non-complicity in the kind of activities Vidyasagar engaged in, and it's quite possible, reading the deposition, to imagine that Vidyasagar gave Merrick cause *genuinely* to disbelieve him during his interrogation. What worries me is that people should think I at any time, then or afterwards, knew about Merrick's treatment of the men suspected of the *rape*. He admitted to me that he had 'bent the rules' when dealing with the suspects – in order to frighten them and get them to tell the truth, for example threatened them with caning, and in one case had even had one boy 'prepared as if for punishment' – I think his expression was. He *volunteered* this information to me on the morning following the arrests, and when Menen approached me later and said rumours were going round that the boys had been whipped I was able to say how I thought such a rumour had arisen, and that I'd already warned Merrick to 'stop playing about'. More serious, in my opinion, was the second rumour, that they had been forced to eat beef. Merrick said he'd look into it, and he told me later that it was quite untrue, but might have been caused by a mistake made in the cells when one of the Muslim constables who was guarding them had his own meal sent in. Reid was quite right when he said that the job of suppressing the riots distracted our full attention from the boys suspected of rape and made it finally impossible to find any concrete evidence against them in connection with the assault. Menen did pursue the business of the rumours of caning and beef-eating. I gave him permission to have the boys themselves questioned on the matter. He told me that the lawyer whom he sent to talk to them reported that none of the boys, including Kumar, complained of having been either whipped or forced to eat beef. And none of them ever said anything about it to Jack Poulson, who had the job of examining them when we were preparing the political case against them. But all this time after I'm uncomfortably aware of having failed to investigate the rumours more fully. It seems pretty clear that they were ill-treated. However, I don't think that there was actually a miscarriage of justice. Merrick was obviously acting in the heat of the moment, believing them guilty of attacking a girl he was fond of. It didn't take long for us to realize that a charge of rape simply wouldn't stick, but the evidence available about their political activities was sufficient for us to feel justified in seeing whether they couldn't be dealt with under the Defence of India Rules. The case was referred to the Divisional Commissioner, and actually as high as the Governor. I've forgotten the details of the evidence, but it was pretty conclusive. So I still feel that the five boys first arrested were guilty of the kind of offences the rules were meant to cover. Only Kumar remains a conundrum to me. If he was treated as badly as Vidyasagar's 'informant' said, why didn't he speak out when Menen's lawyer talked to him? Why didn't he complain to Jack Poulson during the official examination? One can appreciate the silence of the other boys if what Vidyasagar says about police threats is true. But Kumar had already suffered – and presumably could prove it, and he was of a different calibre from the other boys surely? Perhaps the parts of Miss Manners's journal which you haven't shown me throw some light on this problem?

I suppose it is his silence on this subject that you have in mind when you say in your note to me that 'Kumar was a man who felt in the end he had lost everything, even his Englishness, and could then only meet every situation – even the most painful – in silence, in the hope that out of it he would dredge back up some self-respect'.

I quite see, from what you've told me about your 'reconstruction' of Hari Kumar's life, and from what I have read in Daphne Manners's journal, that Kumar might indeed have reacted in this way, but if Vidyasagar's informant was speaking the truth when he said that on the night of his arrest Kumar was caned on Merrick's instructions 'until he groaned' I should still have thought Kumar would have seized the opportunity to make charges when Menen's lawyer interviewed him and asked him point-blank whether it was true. To complain of having been unjustifiably and savagely beaten in the course of interrogation would not itself have been a betrayal of Miss Manners's request to Kumar to 'say nothing'. I mean, isn't there a limit to the stiffness of *any* upper lip?

But then I expect my objections to your conclusions are really based on my inner unwillingness to accept the unsupported evidence of Merrick's behaviour – or to admit my own failure to suspect it at the time. I have no comment to make on the figure you quote from 'official' sources that, excluding the United Provinces, there were 958 sentences of whipping after the insurrection, except to say that this was a legal punishment for people caught taking part in riots. If Kumar had been arrested during a riot he might well have been caned. I suppose what you are getting at is that this kind of punishment was 'in the air' and that Merrick seized an opportunity, bent the rules, and got away with it.

Having said all this I'll now confine myself, as you request, to the larger issue although before finally leaving behind the question of 'Yes, I did. No, you didn't', I would point out – perhaps unnecessarily – that one should not confuse the uncertainty that surrounds actions and events with the 'areas of dangerous fallibility' that lie *between* doubts, decisions and actions. Taking as an example the question of the forcible feeding – it either happened or did not happen. In attempting to map the 'dangerous area' we are not concerned with *facts* the truth of which, however unascertainable now, *was known to somebody at the time*?

I have thought hard about the true 'dangerous area' and must admit, somewhat reluctantly, that I can't grasp the issues firmly enough to come up with anything remotely resembling a premise from which you could work. I find myself too readily back-tracking into the old condition of statement and refutation and counter-statement. For instance, taking Reid's jejune account of the 1935 scheme for Federation – and his comment, 'It led only to a scramble for power', which leaves the unknowledgeable reader with the impression that we had made a handsome offer and then had to sit back and watch in dismay while the Indians proved themselves too immature either to understand the issues or to grasp their opportunity – all I can really turn my mind to are the alternative readings that show why, as *statesmen*, the Indians rejected Federation, and how the whole federal scheme and proposal could be seen in the light of our having offered the Indians a constitution that would only have prolonged, perhaps even perpetuated, our power and influence, if only as Imperial Arbitrators.

Similarly – again taking Reid's comments as a kind of basic 'norm' – one could write at length demolishing his casual inference that the Cripps Mission of 1942 failed because of Indian intransigence, or counter-state – equally casually and briefly and inaccurately – that this was a typical Churchillian move, made to dress the window and make friends and influence people abroad after the defeat in Asia, but which amounted in itself to no more than a grudging repetition of old promises and even older reservations.

And that's not what we're after, is it? Even though one is so tempted to cut away at the foundations of Brigadier Reid's apparently unshakeable foursquare little edifice of simple cause and simple effect in order to redress the balance and present the obverse, and just as inaccurate, picture of a tyrannical and imperialistic power grinding the faces of its coloured subjects in the dust.

In fact we are not at all after the blow-by-blow account of the politics that led to the action. Actually any one man would be incapable of giving such an account – if he confined himself to the blows. There were so many blows he would spend more than his lifetime recording them. To make the preparation of any account a reasonable task he would have to adopt an attitude towards the available material. The action of such an attitude is rather like that of a sieve. Only what is relevant to the attitude gets through. The rest gets thrown away. The real relevance and truth of what gets through the mesh then depends on the relevance and truth of the attitude, doesn't it? If one agrees with that one is at once back on the ground of personal preference – even prejudice – which may or may not have anything to do with 'truth', so-called.

Anyway, let me imagine (as you helpfully suggested in your note) that I am about to embark on a history of the British–Indian relationship. I would have to adopt an attitude to the mass of material confronting me. What would it be?

I think it would be as simple – childlike almost – as this: I would take as my premise that the Indians wanted to be free, and that we also wished this, but that they had wanted to be free for just that much longer than we had felt or agreed that they should be; that given this situation the conflict arose partly as a result of the lack of synchronization of the timing of the two wishes, but also because this, in time, developed into a lack of synchronization of the wishes themselves. Being human, the longer the Indians were denied freedom the more they wanted to be free on their own terms, and the more they wanted to be free on their own terms the more we – also being human – insisted that they must initially acquire freedom on ours. The longer this conflict continued, the more abstruse the terms of likely agreement became on either side. It was then a question of the greater morality outlasting and outweighing the lesser. Which was why, of course, in the end the Indians won.

Having put it in those simple words (and they form a mesh you could sift an enormous lot of detailed evidence through), I am reminded of what you said during our interview about 'the moral drift of history', and see how perhaps the impetus behind that drift stems in the main from our consciences, and that the dangerous area is the *natural* place for our consciences to work in, with or without us, usually without. The trouble is that the word dangerous always suggests something slightly sinister, as though there were an unbreakable connection at source between 'danger' and 'wrong'. 'Danger' does have this connotation, but I suppose it doesn't if we remember we only use the word to convey our fear of the personal consequences, the danger we'd be in ourselves if we followed our consciences all the time.

I remember that during our talk you referred to the 'beat' and the 'pause' and I think described these as the unrecorded moments of history. I wish I could relate this theory to a particular event in my life and see how I came out on the right side rather than the wrong, or that I could relate it to an event in Reid's. But even in attempting to relate it, I'm back again in the world of describable events. And when I attempt to relate the theory to all the events in the lives of all the people who were connected with the action – however directly or remotely – my mind simply won't take in the complex of emotions and ambitions and reactions that led, say, to any one of the single actions that was part of the general describable pattern. Perhaps though, the mind can respond to a sense of a cumulative, impersonal justice? The kind of justice whose importance lies not only in the course apparently and overwhelmingly taken, but in its exposure of the dangers that still lie ahead, threatening to divert the drift once more?

III

(Appendix to 'Civil and Military')

A Deposition by S. V. Vidyasagar

In my sixteenth year I was plucked in the matriculation and left the Mayapore Government Higher School with the reproaches of my parents and no prospects to a career. For nearly twelve months I was living a life of shame and wickedness, going with loose women and impairing my health. So bad did I become that my father turned me out of the house. My mother secretly gave me rupees one hundred which she had saved from the household expenses over many months. I regret that even this token of affection and motherly trust I squandered on drink and fornication. For many weeks I was at death's door in my squalid surroundings but upon recovery I was still only taking notice of girls and liquor. Many times I was praying for guidance and self-discipline, but only I had to see a pretty girl and at once I was following her and making immoral suggestions in front of everybody, so that my reputation was badly compromised and no decent person would come close to me, unless they were boys of my own kind whose parents were having nothing to do with them or not knowing that they were acting in this way until their neighbours or friends pointed it out.

In this manner I became seventeen and now, revolted by my way of life and resolving upon both moral and physical improvement, I went back to my father's house and begged forgiveness. My mother and sister wept at my return but my father was stern with me and called me to account for my past wickedness. I said that I could account for it only as a madness and that now I was trusting to recovery by God's grace and my own determination. Seeing me so sorrowful and humble of mien my father opened his arms to me once more. Beginning thus a new and upright life I took employment as a clerk with my father's assistance and recommendation and paid the whole of my monthly emolument to my mother, taking from her only a few annas for daily expenditure. At this time also I was bitterly regretting the irresponsibility and bad behaviour that had led me to well-deserved failure in the Higher School. At night I would read in my room burning the midnight oil until my mother begged me to be taking more care of my health and not running the risk of falling asleep in the office and losing my job.

So, determined not to be giving my parents any more trouble I drew up a chart which I pinned to the wall above my bed, allotting so much of my leisure hours to study, so much to sleep and so much to healthy exercise. On fine evenings I would stroll out to the Chillianwallah Bagh extension to look at the fine houses of our well-off neighbours and wander by the river-bank. There I saw and caught the eyes of many girls but always I drew back before the temptation to speak to them or follow them proved too much to be difficult. I avoided those parts of the town where I might fall in with my erstwhile companions, especially the street in which many prostitutes lived and whose glances from an upper room could be the ruination of any innocent and upright young man chancing to be in the vicinity.

I was now firmly set upon a course of life both bodily healthy and spiritually uplifting and even upon these walks I would take a book with me and sit down by the river-bank to study, casting but few looks at the black braids and silken sarees of the girls nearby. In this way, I happened to fall in with Mr Francis Narayan, who was teacher at the Christian mission school in Chillianwallah Bazaar and a well-known figure in Mayapore, always riding his bicycle to and fro and speaking at random. Falling into conversation with him I found myself telling him of my earlier bad life and reformed character and my hopes for the future. Learning that I was working as a humble clerk and sadly regretting my failure in the matriculation he said he would bear me in mind for any suitable post he heard about. But expecting nothing to come of this friendly meeting I continued to apply myself daily to my tasks and programme of self-improvement and further education. Now I began to feel somewhat of impatience and to cast covetous glances upon the books in the Mayapore Book Depot in the road near the Tirupati temple which I passed daily on my way home in the evenings. My father was head clerk to a contractor and the office in which I worked was belonging to a friend of my father's employer, a merchant with two marriageable daughters. One day I stopped as usual at the Mayapore Book Depot to browse among the many volumes. Under pretext merely of examining, I was reading chapter by chapter a book about 1917 Declaration of Self-Government. I had become interested in political affairs. Dearly I wished to possess this volume but its price was beyond my means although I knew that my mother would give me the requisite money were I but to ask her. As I stood that evening reading the next chapter, I saw that I was unwatched for the moment by the owner and his assistant and without conscious thought I went out with the book under my arm. Elated and yet afraid of being followed and apprehended as a common thief I wandered without due care and found myself in my old district. A voice called out to me and looking in that direction I saw one of my old friends, a young man senior to the rest of us who had talked and mixed with us but not accompanied us on our bouts of drinking and other bad things. His name was Moti Lal. Seeing the book under my arm he took hold of it and looked at the title and said, 'So you are becoming grown-up at last.' He invited me to have coffee in the shop where he had been sitting and I agreed. He asked me what I had been doing all these many months, so I told him. He also was a clerk, in the warehouse of Romesh Chand Gupta Sen. I asked him whether he had seen any of our other old friends but he said they had also become respectable like me.

On this occasion suddenly I was seeing that my old life was not so disreputable as my conscience was telling me. It was wicked no doubt to drink so much bad liquor and to go with immoral women without due discrimination, but now I saw that we had been doing such things because our energies were in need of special outlet. Fortified by this discovery I walked back to the Mayapore Book Depot, restored the stolen book to its rightful owner and said that I had taken it away in a fit of absent-mindedness. After this he allowed me to sit many hours in the back of the shop studying new volumes that had come in from Calcutta and Bombay.

I was in my eighteenth year when Mr Narayan, the mission teacher, called at my home and said that the editor of the *Mayapore Gazette* was looking for an energetic young man with good English who would act as office boy and apprentice journalist.

Mr Narayan confided in me that it was he who wrote the articles known as *Topics*, by 'Stroller', for the *Gazette*, which he did in order to augment his emoluments as a teacher. My father was against the idea that I should leave my present employment. He pointed out that in due course, so long as I attended carefully to my duties, I had prospects of becoming head clerk and even of marrying one of my employer's daughters if I showed application and diligence. In the past few months my father had become in very much poor health. Every day he would walk to his office, never even one minute late, but working frequently far beyond the appointed hour of closing and returning home to face my mother's complaints that his supper was spoiled. Since adopting a more manly attitude towards my own life I had learned respect for my father where before only there had been criticism. Also I was affectionate towards him because of his no doubt love for me. I did not want to displease him but also I wished to apply for the job Mr Narayan had already put in my way by speaking to the editor about me. Eventually my father gave his consent for me to apply to the *Gazette*. I feared greatly his death – which took place six months later – and I did not want to displease him in the twilight of his life or think of him leaving this world without a son to officiate at his funeral rites. Therefore I feared my own temper and resulting quarrel and being turned out again. But I thank God who moved him to give in to my wishes. In due course I became an employee of the *Mayapore Gazette*.

After my father's death I became 'head of the household' and had to arrange the marriage of my only surviving sister, who was then sixteen. These family obligations took up a great deal of my time in 1937/8. My mother and I were now living alone together. She was also always persuading me to become married. In those days I was somewhat innocent in these respects. I feared that my experiences with immoral women would make it dangerous for me to be a husband and father, even though I had not – by God's will – suffered any lasting disease. Also I was dedicating my life, after my father's death, to politics and to my work as a 'rising' journalist.

My duties now took me daily into the cantonment where the offices of the *Gazette* were situated and I was becoming familiar with the life on that side of the river. As a student also I had been going daily over the river to the Government Higher School but now as 'apprentice journalist' to Mr Laxminarayan I was learning things I was not bothering about or knowing before. For instance I became familiar with the administration of law and order, and of the social life of the English.

In this way as a young Indian of no consequence I suffered many social indignities and became bitter, remembering the care with which my father had needed to account for every penny and had feared to be absent from his profession even for one day. I became friendly with several young fellows of my age, and also again with Moti Lal, and we would talk far into the night about all this kind of thing often in my own home while my mother was sleeping. But it was not until Mr Laxminarayan employed in my stead Hari Kumar, the nephew of the rich merchant, Romesh Chand Gupta Sen in whose employment also was Moti Lal at one time, and I took up new employment with *Mayapore Hindu*, that I became involved with groups of young men who felt as I was feeling, leaderless in a world where their fathers were afraid to lose a day's work and even Indian politicians were living on a different plane from us. We decided to be on the alert to seize any opportunity that would bring the day of our liberation nearer.

By this time the English were at war with Germany and the Congress ministries had resigned and only we could imagine that once again our country would be forced to bear a disproportionate share of the cost of a war which was not of our seeking and from which we did not expect any reward but instead only promises coming to nothing. In those days we had to be careful to avoid arrest unless of course one of us decided to seek arrest deliberately by open infringement of regulations. Also we had to be careful when choosing our friends or casual acquaintances. Many innocent-seeming fellows were police spies and one or two of my friends were arrested as a result of information given to the authorities by people of that kind who were sometimes only interested in settling old scores and would make up tales to persuade the police to arrest one of us and put us out of harm's way. Moti Lal also was arrested, for defying order under section 144 prohibiting him from speaking at a meeting of students. He was sent to prison but succeeded in escaping.

When the Japanese invaded Burma and defeated the English

we felt that at last our freedom was in sight. Neither I nor my friends were afraid of Japanese. We knew that we would be able to make trouble for the Japanese also if they invaded India and treated us badly like the British. Many of our soldiers who were left behind by their British officers and captured in Burma and Malaya were given their freedom by the Japanese and formed 'Indian National Army' under Subhas Chandra Bose. If the Japanese had won the war our comrades in the Indian National Army would have been recognized everywhere as heroes, but instead many of them were severely punished by the British when the war was over and our 'national leaders' stood by and did nothing to save them.

In those days we were knowing that only young men who were ready to give life and take life could ever make India a 'great power'. We did not understand the ramblings and wanderings of our leaders. Unfortunately it was difficult for us to form anything but small groups. We told each other that if once the people rose against their oppressors we young men would be able to link up with each other and give an example of bravery and determination that would infect all.

This was the position at the time of the rebellion in 1942. With several other young men I had prepared myself for any kind of sacrifice. After my arrest I was interrogated for hours to give information about 'underground system', but if there was any such system I was not knowing of it, only I knew boys like myself who were ready to take the foremost place in facing the enemy. On the very day of my arrest, August 11, I and several fellows were planning to join and exhort the crowds who would be forming up later that day to march on the civil lines. News of such plans spread quickly from one end of town to the other. A crowd had tried to form up that morning on Chillianwallah Bagh Extension road but had been dispersed by the police who seemed to crop up everywhere at a moment's notice. I and my fellows were not among this crowd because at that hour we were engaged in printing pamphlets to distribute among the people exhorting them to help to release the boys unjustly accused of attacking an English woman. We delivered one such pamphlet to the police post near the Tirupati temple by wrapping it round a stone and throwing it through open window so that the one amongst us chosen for this dangerous task would have the chance of getting away without being seen. Having done this we then dispersed going each to our separate homes or places of employment. Only one hour later the District Superintendent of Police and many constables descended upon the offices of *Mayapore Hindu* where I was working. I and other staff-members present were immediately arrested because the police found an old hand-press in a back room that they said had been used for printing seditious literature.

This was not true and only I among those arrested was guilty of such an act to my knowledge, but I denied it. With those arrested was the editor, who told the police that I had been absent from work that morning and that his hand-press had been used only for innocent advertising purposes. I did not know about what the editor had said until later, because we were kept separately, but eventually I learned that they had all been released, although *Mayapore Hindu* was suppressed and the offices closed by order. Still I said nothing, because I hoped to keep secret the true whereabouts of the printing press and the names of my accomplices. I was removed from the kotwali to cells in police headquarters in the civil lines where the boys who had been arrested near the Bibighar two days before were being held, but I did not see any of them. I was kept in a cell secluded from others and then, after interrogation, taken to the prison in Jail road. I was in the Jail road prison when the people attacked it and overcame the guards and police at the gate and forced their way in. Several prisoners were released but unfortunately for me this act of liberation occurred in a different 'block' and soon afterwards the soldiers attacked the jail and our short-lived hopes of freedom were over. In this action many innocent people lost their lives which the authorities tried to disguise giving very low figures for killed and wounded.

I had been taken from the kotwali to the cells in the civil lines in the late afternoon of the 11th, and was interrogated there personally by the District Superintendent of Police. He was very clever with his questions but I had determined on complete silence. I knew that I would be locked up in any case, because I saw that he had a file about my suspected activities. He knew the names of many of my friends and even casual acquaintances and I wondered what spy had been in our midst. He kept asking me about Moti Lal. Also about Kumar and the other boys who had been arrested after the 'attack' on the English woman. It was no good denying that I knew Moti Lal and most of these boys because the Superintendent even had a note of dates and places where some of us had been seen together, or been known to have been together, beginning with a night in February when a few of us were drinking and Hari Kumar became too drunk so that we took him home only to hear later that he had wandered out again and been arrested and questioned. Two of the other boys arrested for the 'rape' were among those who were present on that occasion in February, and I could not help wondering whether after he was questioned Hari Kumar had agreed to spy on us and it was him we had to thank for our present predicament. Later I was ashamed to have had such thoughts, but I must be honest and mention that for a time I was suspicious.

None of the boys arrested for the 'rape' had been my accomplices in any of my own illegal activities, but the Superintendent also had 'on file' the names of three of the boys who were my accomplices and had been with me that morning at the secret press which we had taken over after Moti Lal's arrest. This press was in the house of one of the prostitutes. The police often visited this house themselves but were too alternatively engaged to notice anything of evidence that secret literature was also printed there.

When the Superintendent mentioned the names of some of the boys I had been with that morning I said (as it had been agreed between us if any of us were arrested) that we had not seen each other for two or three days. I admitted nothing to the Superintendent. I said that on that morning I had not felt well and so had gone to work late and in any case had been worried for my safety with all the troubles going on in the city.

After leaving the house where our secret printing press was, with the pamphlets which I had 'run off' and which my colleagues were now going to distribute, I had taken precaution of going to my home and telling my mother to say that I had been unwell and had not left home until now. My mother was very afraid, because this was proof that I was doing things against the authorities, but she said she would tell this story if she was asked. It was the first time I had kept away from my office duties to do this kind of work, which is why I took such a precaution. When the Superintendent asked me where I had been that morning

I knew that the editor or one of my fellow-staff members on *Mayapore Hindu* had mentioned my absence, but I told him about not having been well, and he looked annoyed and I could see that already he had had my mother questioned. I prayed that my real accomplices had all managed to tell satisfactory stories if they had been questioned also.

I was much afraid at this interrogation because of what we had heard about the horrible treatment of the boys arrested for the attack on the English woman. It was because of what we had heard that I and my accomplices hastened to print the pamphlet and distribute it during the day. The information about the dreadful behaviour of the police towards these boys came to us from someone who had spoken to one of the orderlies in the police headquarters who said that all the boys had been beaten senseless and then revived and forced to eat beef to be made to confess. But we believed they were not guilty and suspected that the story of the attack on the English woman was much exaggerated or even a fabrication because the boy 'Kumar' had been friendly with her and the English people therefore hated him. I knew nothing about Kumar's movements on the night in question but a friend of the other boys who were arrested said that except for Kumar they had merely been drinking home-distilled liquor in an old hut and knew nothing about the 'attack' until the police broke in and arrested them. This friend also had been drinking but came away a few moments before the arrests which he saw from a place of hiding. He thought that the level-crossing keeper at the Bibighar bridge had given them away because the keeper knew that they used the old hut to drink home-distilled liquor in and sometimes joined them and made them give him a drink to keep quiet about this illegal activity. I know that this is true about the hut and the drinking because I also sometimes went there. It was not the same place in which we drank on the night that Hari Kumar was with us and became intoxicated. To drink such stuff we had to find different locations to put the police off the scent. If we wanted a drink we could not afford proper liquor which is why we drank this bad stuff.

During my interrogation the Superintendent said, 'Isn't it true that you are a close friend of Kumar and that on the night of the 9th of August you and Kumar and your other friends were drinking in the hut near the Bibighar bridge and that then you left them because they were beginning to talk badly about going into the cantonment to find a woman?'

I saw that he was offering me a chance to ingratiate myself and bear false witness, and so much fearful as I was of being beaten, I said no it was not true, only it was true that I knew Hari Kumar and some of the boys he named, but on the night of the 9th August I was working late at offices of *Mayapore Hindu* 'subbing' the reports of outbreaks that had taken place during the day in Dibrapur and Tanpur, and that my editor would no doubt testify to this. I was speaking truth and the Superintendent was angry because he knew I was speaking it. He said, 'You'll regret your lying before I've done with you.' He then left me alone in the room. I looked round for ways of escape but there was not even a window through which I might attempt to regain my longed-for freedom. The room was lighted by one electric bulb. There was a table and a chair at which the policeman had been sitting and the stool on which I was sitting. In one corner there was an iron trestle.

When I realized that there was no escape I prayed for strength to endure my torture without giving away the names of my accomplices. I thought that in a moment they would come for me and that the Superintendent Sahib was even now ordering them to prepare things. But he came back alone and sat down at the desk again and started to ask all the same questions. I do not know how long all this went on. I was hungry and thirsty. After some time he left the room again without succeeding in hearing any different thing from me and two constables came in and took me into a truck and drove me to the jail in Jail road. On the way I hoped to be rescued by our people, but the truck drove very fast and there was no incident. I was in this jail for a week and was then taken to Court and charged with printing and publishing seditious literature. A police spy gave evidence of seeing me throw the pamphlet into the kotwali, which was not true, but I could not prove it. Also the illegal press had been found, no doubt also as result of spying, and all my accomplices apprehended. I was sentenced to two years' rigorous imprisonment. To serve my sentence I was sent to the jail near Dibrapur and locked at first into a filthy cell. I believed that the Superintendent in Mayapore had given orders for me to be especially harshly treated. At first I could not eat the disgusting food they gave me, hungry though I was. One day I quite lost my reason and threw the plate on the floor. The next day I was taken out of my cell and told that for infringing prison regulations I was to receive fifteen strokes of the cane. They took me at once into a small room and there I saw the same kind of iron trestle I had seen in the room where the Superintendent had questioned me. They showed me the cane they were going to use. It was about four feet long and half an inch thick. They stripped me of all my clothes, bent me over the trestle and tied my wrists and ankles and carried out 'the sentence'. Towards the end I could no longer support my suffering and fainted away.

I was sent later to another prison. I was allowed no communication with anyone, not even my family. They told me one day that my mother was dead. I wept and begged of God to be forgiven for the suffering I had caused her, in this freedom-work I had felt I had to do. I did not resent any of my punishment because I was guilty of all the 'crimes' I was punished for. I did not think of them as being crimes and therefore my punishment was not punishment but part of the sacrifice I was called upon to make.

It was towards the end of my imprisonment that one of the boys who had been accused of the attack on the English woman was brought also into this prison from another jail. These boys had all been kept in separate prisons because the authorities had wished to keep them apart no doubt so that two of them should not confirm the story of their unjust punishment to fellow-prisoners. When I saw this boy I cried out in amazement because I had thought they were all tried and condemned long ago. In prison I had heard once that they were hanged. But this boy told me there had never been any evidence against them. He thought it had been all a 'put-up job', and that there was probably no rape in the Bibighar at all. Finally the authorities had locked them all up as undesirables, all being known or suspected of indulging in subversive activities. We were not able to speak often to each other and he seemed too much afraid to talk about the rumours I had heard of torture and defilement.

When I was released from prison, my own home was no longer available. I had frequently to report to the police. My old employer Mr Laxminarayan found lodging for me and gave me some work so that I could keep body and soul together. I was in poor health and weighed only 97 pounds and was much troubled with coughing. In time I was able to regain some of my health and strength.

Of the boys arrested after the attack in the Bibighar only one of them I ever saw again who came back to live in Mayapore. This was the boy who came to the prison where I was. Hearing he was back in his home I visited him and asked him, 'Why were you afraid to speak much to me?' Even still he was reluctant to tell. He had suffered much and was afraid of the police who, he said, were always watching him. Still in those days the British were in power and had won the war and we wondered somewhat hopelessly about the future even though people kept saying that this time the British were really getting ready to quit.

This boy was speaking to me one evening in Mayapore, towards the end of 1946, and suddenly he said, 'I will tell you.' He spoke for a long time. He said that on the night of Bibighar when he and the other four who were still drinking in the hut were arrested they were taken at once to Police headquarters and locked in a cell. At this time only they knew that they had been caught drinking illegal liquor and were laughing and joking. Then they saw Hari Kumar brought in. His face was cut and bruised. They thought that this had been done by the police. One of them called out, 'Hello, Hari', but Kumar was not taking any notice. After that, except for my informant, none of the boys saw Kumar again. My informant was telling me all this in confidence, so I prefer to respect that and not divulge his name. These days all these things are forgotten and we are living different lives. Our young men today are not taking any interest in such matters. So I will call my friend 'Sharma' which is not his name nor the name of any of the other boys. Sharma was a fine, strong fellow, who like me had been 'a great one for the ladies' as a youth but had also somewhat reformed. He and his companions, other than Kumar, were locked in one cell, and taken out one by one. As one by one they went and did not come back, those remaining were no longer laughing and joking. They had also headache from too much drinking and were very much thirsty. Finally only Sharma was left. When his turn came he was taken downstairs by two constables and told to strip. When he was standing there naked one of the constables knocked at a door at the far end of the room and opened it and the District Superintendent came in. 'Sharma' was greatly humiliated to be forced to stand there so immodestly, especially in front of a white man. The constables now held Sharma's arms behind him and then the Superintendent – who carried a little stick – came over and held the stick out and lifted the exposed private parts and stared at them for some seconds. Sharma did not understand why this embarrassment should be done on him. He said, 'Why are you doing this, Superintendent Sahib?' The policeman said nothing. After inspecting the clothing which Sharma had been made to take off – also using the little stick to turn the clothing over and look at it – the policeman left the room. Later, of course, Sharma realized that the policeman was looking for evidence of rape practised upon a lady who had bled. When the Superintendent had gone the constables told Sharma to put on his underdrawers, but they did not give him back any of his other clothes. He was now taken out of the room by another door where he found his drinking companions in a cell, also wearing nothing but their underdrawers. Kumar was not with them. They tried to joke again, asking why the Sahib was so interested in certain parts of their bodies, but they were not feeling like laughing in this instance. Then one by one they were again taken away, and did not come back. When Sharma's turn came – and he was again the last – he was taken into the room where he had been stripped, and found the Superintendent sitting behind a desk. I think this was the same room in which Superintendent Sahib questioned me two evenings later. Sharma was not given a stool to sit on, however. He was made to stand in front of the desk. Then he was questioned. He did not understand the questions because he was thinking only of being charged with drinking home-distilled toddy. But suddenly the Superintendent said, 'How did you know she would be in the Bibighar Gardens?' and he began to see what might be behind all this rigmarole because of the word 'she' and the humiliation recently practised on him. But still he did not know what the policeman was trying to find out, until the policeman said, 'I'm inquiring into the attack and criminal assault on the English girl this evening, the girl who thought your friend Kumar was also a friend of hers.' Then there were many questions, such as,

'When did Kumar suggest all you fellows going together? Was she there when you arrived? How long did you wait for her? Who was the first man to assault her? You were led by Kumar, weren't you? If it hadn't been for Kumar you would never have thought of going to the Bibighar, would you? Were you just the fellow who was told to keep watch and never had the chance to enjoy her? Why should you suffer for the others if you just kept watch? How many times did you enjoy her, then? How many times did Kumar enjoy her? Why are you afraid? A fellow who has enjoyed drinking a lot of liquor starts thinking also about enjoying a woman, doesn't he? Why do you blame yourself for a perfectly natural thing? You shouldn't have drunk the liquor, but you did, and look what's happened. Why don't you be a man and admit that you drank too much and felt passionate? You're no weakling. You're a fine healthy fellow. Why be ashamed to admit your natural desires? If I drink too much liquor I also feel these things quite badly. There's no sign of blood on you or on your underclothes. She wasn't a virgin, was she? And you were the first fellow because you were the most passionate and couldn't wait. Isn't that it? Or perhaps you've been careful to wash? Or change your underclothes? Knowing what you have done was wrong? Knowing you would have to suffer if you were caught? Well, you are caught and have to suffer. Be a man and admit you deserve punishment. If you admit you deserve punishment you'll be let off lightly because I understand this kind of thing. And she wasn't a virgin, was she? She went with anyone who was able to satisfy her. And liked brown-skinned fellows. That's what young Hari Kumar told you, isn't it? Isn't it?'

This you see is what Sharma so much remembered. How the policeman finally kept saying, Isn't it? Isn't it? and banging his stick on the desk, because losing his temper at Sharma's all the time saying he knew nothing of what the Superintendent Sahib was talking about.

Then the policeman threw the stick on the desk and said, 'I see there's only one way to break *you*,' and he called out to the constables who took Sharma into the next room and through a door into another room. This room was even more dimly lit but he saw Kumar, naked, fastened over one of the iron trestles. In this position also I know it is difficult to breathe. Sharma said he did not know how long Kumar had been fastened in this way, but he said he could hear the sound of Kumar trying to breathe. He did not know at first that it was Kumar. Only he could see the blood on his buttocks. But then the policeman, the Superintendent, came in and said, 'Kumar, here's a friend of yours come to hear you confess. Just say "Yes, I was the man who organized the rape" and you'll be released from this contraption and won't be beaten any more.' Sharma said that Kumar only made 'a sort of sound' so the Superintendent Sahib gave an order and a constable came forward with a cane and gave Kumar several strokes. Sharma shouted out to Kumar that he knew nothing and had said nothing. He also shouted, 'Why are you treating this fellow so?' He said the constables then continued to beat Kumar until he groaned. Sharma could not look at this terrible punishment. After a while he was taken away and locked alone in a cell. Ten minutes or so later he was taken back into the room where Kumar had been. The trestle was now unoccupied. He was fastened to it after they had taken off his underdrawers. He said they then put what felt like a wet cloth on his buttocks and gave him nine strokes. He said the pain was so awful that he could not understand how Kumar had borne so much of it. They put the wet cloth over him so that his skin should not be cut and leave permanent marks. When they had finished he was taken back to the cell. Later he was put into another cell where his companions were. Kumar was not with them. He told them what had been done to him and to Kumar. The others had not been beaten but were afraid their turn was coming. The youngest of them began to weep. They did not at all understand what was happening. By now it was early morning. The Superintendent came down to the cell, with two constables. The constables were ordered to show the others what even nine strokes of the cane over a wet cloth could do to the buttocks. They held Sharma down and uncovered him. Then the Superintendent said that if any one of them so much as hinted at any time, to any person, during their 'forthcoming interrogation, trial and punishment' that any one of them had been 'hurt' or harshly treated, they would all suffer even more severely the punishment Sharma could describe to them both from personal experience and from having seen another man undergo it.

Half an hour later some food was brought in. They were

hungry and tired and frightened. They began to eat. After a few mouthfuls also they vomited. The 'mutton' in the curry was beef. The two Muslim jailors who were standing watching them laughed and told them that now they were outcastes and even God had turned his face from them.

PART SEVEN

THE BIBIGHAR GARDENS

Daphne Manners (Journal addressed to Lady Manners)
Kashmir, April 1943

I AM SORRY, Auntie, for all the trouble and embarrassment I've caused you. I began to apologize once before, when Aunt Lili brought me back to Rawalpindi, last October, but you wouldn't listen. So I apologize now, not for my behaviour but for the effect it's had on you who did nothing to deserve our exile. But I want to thank you, too, for your loving care of me, for voluntarily taking on the responsibility of looking after me, and for never once making me feel that this was a burden, although I know it must have been, and is as bad here where you see hardly anyone as it was in 'Pindi where so many of your old friends made themselves scarce. I sometimes try to put myself in your shoes and work out what it must be like to be the aunt of 'that Manners girl'. I know that's how people speak of me and think of me, and that it rubs off on to you. And all the marvellous things you and Uncle Henry did to make things seem right in India, for English people, are forgotten. This is really what I mean when I say I'm sorry. Sorry for giving people who criticized you and Uncle Henry the last word, for seeming to prove to them that everything you and he stood for was wrong.

The awful thing is that if you ever read this I shan't be here to smile and make the apology look human and immediate. If I get through to the other side of what I have to face we shall probably continue in the state we live in at the moment, of talking about as few subjects as possible that can remind either of us of the real reason why we are here. You won't in that case read this because I only write it as an insurance against permanent silence. I write it because I have premonitions of not getting through and I should hate to kick the bucket knowing I'd made no attempt to set the record straight and break the silence we both seem to have agreed is okay for the living, if not for the dead. Sorry about the morbid note! I don't feel morbid, just prepared. Perhaps I've felt like that all along, ever since the doctor in London told me to take it easy and stop driving ambulances in the black-out. Possibly the suspicion that I had to cram as much of my life as I could into as short a time as possible accounts for things I've done that people settled into the comfortable groove of three score and ten would reckon hasty and ill-advised.

If I'm right, and my premonitions aren't just morbid fancies, it would be odd, wouldn't it, how someone who looks so strong and healthy could be really just a mess of physiological sums added up wrong! After Mother died I used to be afraid of getting cancer. I've since been afraid of a tumour on the brain, to account for my poor sight and occasional headaches. All these sophisticated diseases also afflict Indian peasants but *they* are just statistics in the records of the birth and death rates and life expectancy charts. I often wish that I could feel and think myself equally anonymous, stricken (if I must be stricken) by God, and not by something the doctors know all about and can account and prepare you for.

But let me say this; medically I feel there is only one thing really 'wrong' with me, and that this may only be wrong for me because I'm not very efficiently put together. Like the doctor in 'Pindi, Dr Krishnamurti talks about a Caesarean. I've said that I don't want that. Maybe I'm just pigheaded, but you've no idea how important it is to me to try to do this thing properly. I don't want to be cut open, to have the child torn out like that. I want to bear it. I want to give it life, not have its life or my life or both our lives saved for us by clever doctors. I want to try my best to end with a good conscience what I began with one. I think Dr Krishnamurti almost understands this. He looks at me in such an odd way. And this is another thing I am so thankful to you for, that you've never even thought of distinguishing between an English and an Indian doctor, let alone resisted my consulting an Indian. Long ago (well, it seems long ago but can't have been much more than a year) I wrote to you from Mayapore saying how glad I was that I'd had the fortune to be with someone like you instead of like the Swinsons (whom I always remember as 'my first colonials'. And what a shock they were to me!) If I'd been their niece then even if they hadn't packed me off somewhere out of the way they'd never have allowed anyone but a white doctor to come near me. But perhaps if I'd been a niece of the Swinsons I'd have run a mile rather than see Dr Krishnamurti anyway. Or would never have got into what the Swinsons no doubt call 'this mess'.

Oddly enough there was a Dr Krishnamurti in Mayapore, a colleague of Dr Anna Klaus. I asked our Dr Krishnamurti whether he was any relation of the one in Mayapore and he said he expected so, if you traced the family far enough back. I told him that I was glad his name was Krishnamurti, because it was a link with Mayapore. He looked embarrassed and surprised. I'm not sure that he wasn't shocked, my saying that name, Mayapore, so casually. He's got over the embarrassment of having to touch me, but not the embarrassment of what it seems I represent to Indians as well as to British. This thing – whatever it is – that I represent has now passed from the purely notional to the acutely physical phase. In 'Pindi I saw how even the few people who came to see us – or rather came to see you in spite of me – couldn't keep their eyes off my waist-line. Now of course the distortion caused by the unknown child (unknown, unwanted, unloved it seems by anyone but me) is the most immediately obvious thing about me. If I went down into the bazaar, and didn't confine myself to the house and garden, I'd feel it necessary to go with a little bell, like a leper, so that people could go indoors and stay clear until I'd passed! If I'd been assaulted by men of my own race I would have been an object of pity. Religiously-minded people would probably have admired me as well for refusing to abort. But they weren't men of my own race. And so even the Indians in 'Pindi used to avert their eyes when I went into the canton-ment, as if they were afraid some awful punishment would pass from me to them.

Even you, Auntie, seem to keep your eyes level with mine these days.

Of course, I wasn't a virgin. Anna Klaus told me later that she had been asked and had given her answer. She wanted me to know that the question had come up and been dealt with. She didn't press me for any comment. I didn't make any. But I tell you, Auntie, to set the record straight. My first lover was a friend of my brother David. My second a man I met in London during the time I was driving the ambulances. Two lovers – but, you see, *not* lovers. We made love but weren't in love, although for a time I thought I was in love with the first man.

It is only Hari I have ever loved. Almost more than anything else in the world I long to talk about him to you, even if it were only to say, 'Oh yes, Hari said something like that,' or 'I saw that one time when I was with Hari.' Just to speak his name to another person, to bring him back into the ordinary world of my life. But I can't. I know that your face would go blank, and this is something I couldn't bear, to have him shut out like that, by you. He has been shut out enough. If I cry – and I sometimes do – it's because I know that I have shut him out as well. Is it true, I wonder, that you know where he is? I often think you know, that so many of the people I count as friends know, but won't tell me. I don't blame you, though. Your silence is for what you believe is my good, and mine has been for what I think is Hari's. God knows there have been affairs between people of Hari's colour and people of mine before, and even marriages, and children, and blessings as well as unhappiness. But this was one affair that somehow never stood a chance. I've given up hope of ever seeing him again.

This is why, especially, the child I bear is important to me. Even though I can't be positive it is his. But I think so, I believe so. If it isn't, it is still a child. Its skin may be as dark as Hari's or almost as pale as mine, or somewhere in between. But whatever colour – he, or she, is part of my flesh and blood; my own typically ham-fisted offering to the future!

A day or two since I wrote anything in this book. I write at night, mostly, huddled in your sheepskin, close to the dying log fire. It is a land of such marvellous contrasts. Tonight, in Maya-pore, the heat will be awful. One would sit under the fan, with all the windows open, but if I went to the little lattice window here and peeped through the cretonne curtains I would see the snow on the mountains. And yet in a few weeks the valley will be filled with people on leave. They will swim in the lakes and throng the river in their shikaras. Shall we move into Srinagar then, Auntie, and live on one of the houseboats and fill it with flowers and have our fortunes told?

*

Marigolds. How Bhalu hated it when I usurped his position and went gathering them early in the morning to put in a vase for Lili's breakfast tray! I was in Bhalu's bad books for trampling one of his flower beds and cutting marigolds the day Hari first came to the MacGregor House. Since I've never talked to you about Hari I don't know how much Auntie Lili told you. But soon after I went down to Mayapore with her she was asked by someone, Anna Klaus in fact, whether she knew a Mr Kumar, or Coomer as it was sometimes spelt, and if in any case she could ask Judge Menen what Mr Kumar had done to deserve being hustled away by the police, hit by a sub-inspector in the presence of witnesses and taken in 'for questioning'. Lili didn't tell me much about any of this but I gathered that she was taking some sort of interest in a young Indian who was in trouble simply for answering back, or something like that. Her not telling me much was all part of that attitude of hers we both know so well. Like at Lahore, on our way down to Mayapore, when she sat in our compartment cool as a cucumber pretending that nothing was going on while all the time those two Englishwomen were really accusing her of having pinched a piece of their beastly luggage. As you know, Auntie, it's difficult ever to get Lili to talk about the things Indians have to put up with, but that doesn't mean she doesn't feel badly about them, or that if she can help someone who's in trouble, as Hari was, she'll just sit back and do nothing.

In fact I never heard the full story of Hari's 'arrest' until Hari told me himself, long afterwards, one evening when we'd gone together to the Tirupati temple. *I didn't even know until then that the man who'd actually taken him in for questioning was Ronald Merrick.* I felt badly about that. I felt that everyone had deliberately kept it from me, Aunt Lili, Anna Klaus, Judge Menen, even Sister Ludmila – especially Sister Ludmila because it seemed it had all happened in the Sanctuary, in front of her. I felt badly because I had been out with Ronald as well as Hari, and it looked as if all the people I liked and trusted had simply sat back and watched and waited to see what might happen. Since then I've realized that it wasn't really like that. It was only like I think it always has been in India for people of either race who try to live together outside their own enclosed little circles. Inside those circles the gossip never stops and everybody knows

everybody else's business. But outside them it's as if the ground
is so uncertain that to stand on it is enough. Yesterday's mis-
understandings or injustices are best forgotten. You learn from
them but keep what has been learned to yourself, hoping others
have also learned. The important thing is to keep the ground
occupied, and once you start talking about anything except *today*
you're adding to the danger that's always there, of people turning
tail and scurrying back to the safe little place where they know
they can talk their heads off because in there they all have to
pretend to think alike.

But when I found out from Hari that it was Ronald Merrick
who had taken him into custody and questioned him, and had
stood by and watched a sub-inspector hit him, I felt I'd been
made a laughing-stock. I'd always assumed that Ronald was
much too high and mighty to have been involved personally
in such a local little matter as the arrest and questioning of a
'suspect'. I was angry with Ronald for warning me about my
association with Hari (as he had done only a few days before the
visit to the temple) without bothering to mention that he had
personally arrested and questioned him. I was angry with everyone, but most of all I suppose angry with myself. But what I said
to Hari that night made him think I was only angry with him,
and even accusing him of deceit, which is supposed to be a
typically Indian failing so far as the average stolid good old no-
nonsense Englishwoman is concerned. I suppose my reaction
struck Hari as typical too, typical of the roughshod-riding
English mem. After we parted I meant to have it out with Aunt
Lili when she got back, but she was late and I went to bed. I sat
up for ages, thinking of the times Ronald Merrick had been at
the MacGregor House, and the times Hari had been (but never
on the same occasion). I worked it out that the evening Ronald
came to dinner, after I'd come to stay with Lili (I remember
mentioning in my first letter to you from Mayapore that the
District Superintendent of Police was coming that evening and
that I had to change into my glad rags) must have been only a
day or two after Lili had been rung by Anna Klaus and asked to
speak to Judge Menen about 'Mr Kumar or Coomer', because
I know that happened in the first few days of my stay at the
MacGregor House. Perhaps if I'd been more settled I'd have
asked more questions about Hari, who he was, and what had

happened to him. But I didn't. On the night Lili had Ronald there to dinner, with several other guests, she must have known that *he* had been responsible for taking Hari into custody and probably knew he had stood by while Hari was struck by the sub-inspector. But she never said anything to him about it, either then or later, so far as I could tell. Neither did she say anything to Hari on the few later occasions he came to the house, at least not in front of me.

I wondered why. And why she had never told me the whole story. But wondering this I realized that no one who knew the story had ever said anything to me. I only knew that after Hari's first visit Lili had become reserved about him. I sensed her lack of real liking for him. And this had made me hesitant about telling her much about what Ronald came to call 'my association with Mr Kumar'. I saw the *extent* of the silence that had surrounded this association, and how I had automatically contributed to it. I'd also kept quiet – to everyone but you – about Ronald's 'proposal', and this was the same *kind* of silence.

This is when I knew that I really loved Hari, and wanted him near me all the time, and also when I began to be afraid for him. There seemed to have been a conspiracy among everyone I knew at all well to say nothing, but wait, almost as if holding their breath, perhaps wanting me to like Hari, for himself, simply as a man, but scared of the consequences and also of the other thing, that I was attracted to the idea of doing something unconventional for the hell of it, which of course would have hurt him more than me. But it was a conspiracy that seemed to be rooted in love as well as fear. I felt as if they saw my affair with Hari as the logical but terrifying end of the attempt they had all made to break out of their separate little groups and learn how to live together – terrifying because even they couldn't face with equanimity the breaking of the most fundamental law of all – that although a white man could make love to a black girl, the black man and white girl association was still taboo.

And then all my determination to have things out with Lili in the morning was undermined. Partly because there was nothing really to 'have out', partly because I was afraid. I couldn't see myself talking to Lili about any of this, because to talk would have been to introduce aspects of my 'association' *that had nothing to do with what I felt for Hari*. But thinking of what I felt for him, and looking in the mirror as I got ready for bed, I thought, Well – but does he love me? What *am* I? Just a big-boned girl with a white skin whose mother justifiably accused her of awkwardness, and whose father and brother were kind as the men of a family are always kind to a daughter or sister who is a good sport but not much else.

Sorry, Auntie. Not making a bid for *your* kindness. Just stating the truth, and explaining the awful doubts I had, the suspicion that perhaps what people said was true, that a coloured man who goes with a white girl only does so for special reasons.

When I first met him I thought him horribly prickly. He was supposed to come with his Aunt Shalini, but he came alone and was ill at ease. Later Aunt Lili said she wasn't surprised he'd come alone, because his Aunt Shalini was probably one of those embarrassingly shy little Indian women who either never went anywhere or cast a blight on any place they *did*. I'd virtually forgotten whatever Lili had told me about 'Mr Kumar'. It was some time in March and she'd decided to have a small cocktail party. When she made out her list she said, 'And we'll ask young Mr Kumar and see what he looks like.' I said, 'Which Mr Kumar?' and she said, 'Oh, you remember. The young man I was asked to speak to Judge Menen about because he got arrested by mistake.' Then she said, 'But don't for goodness' sake say anything to him about *that*.' Well, you know me! I've always tended to put my foot in it by coming out with things bald-faced. I used to be much worse, because I was so dreadfully shy and conscious of being clumsy, and the only thing I could think to do not to look awkward was to chat at people and say the first thing that came into my head, which more often than not turned out to be the wrong thing.

I've forgotten who most of the people were who came that time for cocktails. There was Dr Anna Klaus, I know, because that was the first time I'd met her, although I'd seen her talking to Dr Mayhew when she came to the Mayapore General for some consultation or other. And Matron was there. And Vassi (the lawyer, Mr Srinivasan, who was a friend of Lili's and also of Hari's aunt and 'uncle'). Hari's editor on the *Mayapore Gazette*, Mr Laxminarayan, was also supposed to be there but didn't turn up, probably because he found out Hari had been invited and he didn't feel the protocol would be right if he and a junior member of the staff were at the same function! At least that's what Hari said later. I know the Whites looked in for half an hour, and there were some teachers from the Higher School and the Technical College.

He was late turning up. He hadn't wanted to come, but had decided to face it. He was ashamed of his clothes. He didn't know any of us except Vassi and they didn't like each other much. When I say he didn't know any of us I'm wrong. He knew quite a lot of people by sight, because as a reporter on the *Gazette* it was his job to. He let slip to Aunt Lili that they had met before and that she had once answered a question he put to her when she won second prize for her roses at the flower show. I was standing next to her when he let on about that. He made it sound as if she ought to have remembered talking to him. She pretended to, but from the way she pretended I could tell that she disliked being *made* to pretend, which she only did because she thought he was hurt not to be recognized. And he saw through her pretence too. And at once became what I call prickly.

I put my foot in it too. When he spoke he sounded just like an Englishman. So I blurted out, 'Wherever did you learn to speak English as well as you do?' He just looked at me and said, 'England.' So of course I bashed on in a panic, expressing astonishment and interest, falling over myself to be friendly, but only succeeding in being inquisitive. Then Lili took me away and made me talk to some other people and the next time I saw him he was standing more or less alone, on the edge of a group of the teachers. So I went up to him and said, 'Let me show you the garden.' It was getting dusk and we were already *in* the garden, so it was a frightfully stupid thing to say. But it was this time of speaking to him that I really noticed how good-looking he was. And tall. So many of the Indian men I talked to I topped by an inch or two, which was something that usually added to my hysteria at a party where I was feeling shy and awkward.

But he let me show him the garden. Which is why I remember I'd been in trouble with Bhalu that morning. I showed him the flower bed I'd trampled on getting at the marigolds. I asked him whether he'd had a nice garden when he lived in England and he said he supposed it had been all right but that he'd never taken much notice of it. Then I said, 'Do you miss it all, though?' and he said at once, 'Not any more,' and sort of moved away and said it was time for him to go. So we walked back and re-joined the party which was breaking up. He said goodbye to Lili and thanked her rather brusquely and then just nodded goodbye to me. And I remember afterwards, when he'd gone, and one or two people stayed for dinner, all Indians, how forcibly it struck me that except for the colour of his skin he wasn't Indian at all – in the sense I understood it.

When everyone had gone and Lili and I were having a night-cap she said, 'Well, what were you able to make of young Mr Coomer?'

I said, 'I think he's a terribly sad man.' It was the first thing that came into my mind, and yet I didn't seem to have thought of it like that until then. And Lili said nothing except something like, 'Let's have the other half and then bash off to bed.'

I'm glad that I'm writing all this down, because even if you never read it it's helping me to understand things better. I think I've been blaming Lili for taking against Hari. No, let me be honest. I don't think I've been blaming her, I know I have. And I think I've been wrong. Reliving that first meeting with him I see how Lili, who was responsible for me to you, probably watched the way we left the party to inspect the garden, and didn't mis-interpret but responded to the little warning bell that she must have learned, during her life, never to ignore. Remembering all the wonderful things about Lili, I *must* be wrong to think that she could ever really have harboured resentment of Hari for the critical attitude he adopted towards her in those few insignificant moments when they first met at her party. And Lili, after all, is a woman too. She can't have been totally unmoved by Hari's physical presence. Nor unconcerned, when she saw us going off together (only for ten minutes!), about me, and how *I* might be moved by it.

I used to think the fact that she seemed to 'drop' him after that first well-meaning attempt to gather him into what was called the MacGregor House set was due to nothing more than her annoyance at his prickliness, or anyway to the stuffiness she can sometimes astonish you with if people don't behave in exactly the way she personally considers 'good form'. And knowing that she had put herself out to help him when he was

a total stranger to her I thought she was annoyed that he hadn't
shown the faintest sign of gratitude, and hadn't even said – as he
was so capable of saying because the language and the idiom and
the inflexions were natural to him – 'Thank you for the party,
and for everything', when he said goodbye.

Perhaps this apparent brashness contributed to her reservations about Hari, but I am sure, now, that if he and I had simply
smiled distantly at each other and passed each other by, the first
thing she would have said, when the party was over, would have
been something like, 'Poor Mr Kumar needs bringing out. We
need to knock that chip off his shoulder. After all, it's not really
his fault that it's there.' But she had seen that the chip on Hari's
shoulder was insignificant compared with the possible danger
that lay ahead for me, for him, if that clumsy but innocent walk
in the garden developed into the kind of familiarity which Lili,
as a woman of the world, saw at once as not unlikely.

Was it now that my dreams came back? Do you remember,
Auntie? Those dreams I wrote to you about once? The dreams
I had when I first came to India, and which I had again after I'd
left 'Pindi and gone to Mayapore? The dreams of faces, the *faces*
of strangers? Dreamed, imagined, constructed out of nothing,
but with an exactness that was frightening because they were so
real? The faces of strangers I had to take with me even into
dreams because I felt that I was surrounded by strangers when
I was awake?

The first two weeks or so in Mayapore, when everything was
new to me and I was getting to know my surroundings, I didn't
have those dreams. But as I told you in that letter, there was a
period when the newness had worn off, when I hated everything because I was afraid of it. I think the cocktail party marked
the beginning of this. I wanted to pack my bags and go back to
'Pindi – which interested me because when I was suffering this
kind of homesickness in 'Pindi I wanted to pack my bags and go
back to England. And just as I think you guessed something of
what I was going through, so I believe did Lili. But how much
of my restlessness – which I tried so hard to disguise – did she
put down to my thinking about Mr Kumar? How much, indeed,
was due to my thinking about him?

It was at this time that I broke my vow, never to go to the

club because Lili couldn't go with me. The girls I worked with at the Mayapore General were always on at me to go with them. And it was so easy to talk to them. I used to feel the relief of leaving the MacGregor House and cycling to the hospital and when I got there not caring what I said or how I said it, and being able to flop into a chair and complain about the heat – using all the little tricks of expression and gesture that you know will be understood, and which don't have to be thought about. The luxury, the ease, of being utterly natural. Giving back as good as you got if someone was edgy or bitchy. Being edgy and bitchy yourself. Letting it rip, like a safety valve.

So I started going with some of them to the club for a drink on my way home. They were usually picked up by young officers from the barracks, round about 5.30. There wasn't any serious attachment going. Just boys and girls getting together in their off-duty and maybe sleeping somewhere if it could be fixed. We used to drive to the club in tongas, or in army trucks if the boys could 'swing the transport' as they called it. Then we'd congregate in the lounge-bar or the smoking-room, or on the terrace. Or there was a games room, where they had a portable and a lot of old dance records, Victor Sylvester, Henry Hall, and some new ones, Dinah Shore, Vera Lynn, and the Ink Spots. Usually round about 6.30 I'd slip away and get a tonga home. I felt horribly guilty about going to the club because I'd told Lili I jolly well wouldn't. She'd always said, 'Don't be silly, of course you must go.' And I owned up at once, the moment I'd been, although on the way back that first time I was thinking up all kinds of excuses for being late. Once I'd owned up it made going again that much simpler, though. I felt less and less guilty and more and more at home in the club. Several times I stayed to dinner there, and only rang Aunt Lili at the last moment.

And then one day one of the boys who was a bit drunk and who'd insisted on coming with me to the phone said, 'She's not really your aunt, is she?' I said, 'No. Why?' And he said, 'Well, you don't look as if you've got a touch of the tar brush. I've had a bet on it.' And all kinds of little things fitted into place – oh, less in connection with what the boys and girls had said, but over the sort of things some of the civilian women had said, or rather *not* said. The way they'd looked when I said 'The MacGregor House' when they asked me where I was staying. The way some of the civilian men had chipped in and asked questions about you and Uncle Henry, as if (as I realized now) to test it out that I really was a niece of a one-time Governor and not some by-blow of Lili Chatterjee's family.

But there is this, too, Auntie – I think this kind of thing would have run off me like water off a duck's back if all the time, underneath the easy pleasure of being with the boys and girls, there hadn't been a sort of creeping boredom, like a paralysis. Basically I hated the way that after a few drinks everything people said was loaded with a kind of juvenile smutty innuendo. After a while I began to see that the ease of companionship wasn't really ease at all, because once you had got to know each other, and had then had to admit that none of you really had much in common except what circumstance had forced on you, the companionship seemed forced itself. We were all imprisoned in it, and probably all hated it, but daren't let go of it. I got so that I would just sit there listening to the things that were said, thinking, 'No, this is wrong. And I haven't got this time to waste. I haven't this time to spare.'

It was the evening I went to the club after the visit to the War Week Exhibition on the *maidan* that I first *admitted* this to myself. Was it just coincidence that I'd seen Hari again that afternoon, for the first time since the party? I suppose not. The two things were connected – the second meeting with Hari and my looking round the club and listening and saying to myself 'I haven't this time to waste'. And of course that other man was at the club too. Ronald Merrick I mean. Perhaps this wasn't coincidence either.

I went to the War Week Exhibition on the Saturday afternoon, at about four o'clock, with three or four girls from the hospital and two or three young subalterns from the Berkshires. We went to watch the parade and the military band which was the week's grand finale. There were the finals of the boxing, too, and the wrestling. The boxing was nearly all between English boys, but the wrestling was between Indians from one of the Indian regiments. One of the girls said, 'Oh no, I couldn't bear to watch *that*,' so we went to the boxing and watched these young soldiers dab at each other and make each other's noses bleed. Then we went into the tea-tent. The parade was scheduled for 5.30. I've never seen anything like that tea-tent. Flowers everywhere. Long trestle-tables covered with dazzling white cloths. Silver-plated urns. Iced cakes, cream cakes, jellies, trifles. One of the boys we were with whistled and said that 'some wog contractor was putting on a show and making a packet'. And of course this was probably true, and at once cancelled out the thought that only the English were having a beano, although it didn't cancel out the picture you had of people at home scuttling off to the shops with their dismal little ration books. And it didn't cancel out the thought of all the people who weren't allowed in the tent, not because they couldn't afford the price of the tea-ticket, but because this was the tent for 'Officers and Guests' only. There were a few Indian women there, the wives of Indian officers. But the mass of faces was white – except behind the tables where the servants were running up and down trying to serve everyone at once. And 'Officers' was really only a polite way of saying 'Europeans' because there were plenty of civilians and their wives there too, but only white civilians, like the Deputy Commissioner, and several men I recognized from Lili's parties as teachers or executives from the British–Indian Electrical.

The DC was standing talking to the Brigade Commander and as we passed them Mr White said, 'Hello, Miss Manners. You know Brigadier Reid, I think.' Why was I so pleased? Because at once the boys I was with sort of stood to attention and the girls looked as if butter wouldn't melt in their mouths. Apparently the Brigadier was previously stationed in 'Pindi and had met us once or twice at parties, but we only vaguely remembered one another. He asked after you and then the DC said, 'How's Lili?' and I said 'Fine' and felt that somehow I was vindicated and no longer ranked in our little group as the odd girl who lived with 'that Indian woman'. Because even if she was 'that Indian woman' the Deputy Commissioner called her Lili. And yet afterwards I was annoyed, too, because the DC hadn't said, 'Where's Lili?' He knew, without even having to think about it, that she was unlikely to be in the tent and therefore probably wouldn't be on the *maidan* at all because she wouldn't go to 'the other tent'.

Anyway, I introduced the boys and girls, which rather made their day, but also helped to make mine later, when we were on our way across the *maidan* to the parade and I saw Hari and went up to him and talked to him for about five minutes while the others waited where I'd left them, and were prepared to wait because they couldn't be sure who Hari might be if I was on chatting terms with the DC and the Brig. When I got back to them one of the subalterns said, 'Who was that?' so I just said, 'Oh, a boy who was at Chillingborough,' as if I had known him then and he had been a friend of my brother or some other male relation. Which shut them up, because none of them had been to anywhere as good. I was quite shameless. About being so snobbish, I mean. Because this was *their* weapon, not mine. I mean it was their weapon, then, in Mayapore, even if it wasn't at home. I enjoyed the brief sensation I had of turning their world momentarily upside down.

Hari was at the War Week Exhibition for the *Gazette*. I didn't recognize him at first – partly because I don't see people very well without my glasses, but mainly because he looked different. It took me several meetings before I realized that since the cock-tail party he'd spent money on new clothes – narrower, better fitting trousers (and not 'babu' white). In spite of his awkward-ness at that party, I think that after it he had expected more invitations, and spent money he couldn't afford so that he wouldn't feel so out of place. At one of our later meetings I said, 'But I'm sure you used to smoke. You had a cigarette at the party.' He admitted this but said he'd given it up. Even then I didn't immediately connect the new clothes and the money saved from giving up smoking, or see what these things meant in terms of the hopes Lili's invitation had raised for him.

He'd spent all his life in England, or anyway from the age of two when his father sold all his land in the UP and went to live there. His mother had died when he was born, and once they were in England his father cut himself off from everyone except this one sister, Hari's Aunt Shalini who had been married off at sixteen to a Gupta Sen, the brother of a rich Mayapore bania. In England Hari's father made a lot of money, but then lost it, and died and left Hari penniless and homeless. And so there he was, just in his last year at Chillingborough, quite alone. His Aunt Shalini borrowed money from her well-off brother-in-law to pay Hari's passage back to India. He worked for a time in the uncle's office in the bazaar, but eventually got this job on the newspaper, because of his knowledge of English. Aunt Lili told me a bit of this (she got it from Vassi) but for ages I assumed that because his aunt's brother-in-law was rich money was no problem to him, and I thought his working on a newspaper was from choice, not necessity. It took some time as well for me to understand that all the plans he and his father had had for him had come to nothing, because his 'Uncle' Romesh wouldn't spend a penny on further education, but set him to work, and his Aunt Shalini had virtually no money of her own. And then, of course, it took some time for the penny to drop that Hari's Englishness meant nothing in India, because he lived with his aunt in one of the houses in the Chillianwallah Bagh – which was on the wrong side of the river.

When I went up to him on the *maidan* that day I said, 'It's Mr Kumar, isn't it?' which the white people nearby obviously took note of. I misjudged the reason for his silence and the reluctant way he shook hands. I said, 'I'm Daphne Manners, we met at Lili Chatterjee's,' and he said, yes, he remembered, and asked how we both were. We chatted on like that for a while, with me doing most of the chatting and feeling more and more like the squire's daughter condescending to the son of one of her father's tenants, because that's how he seemed to *want* to make me feel. I wondered why. I broke off finally, saying, 'Come along any evening. It's open house,' for which he thanked me with that expression that meant he wouldn't dream of coming along unless specially asked and perhaps not even then because he took the invitation as a meaningless form of politeness.

So off I went and rejoined the gang and sat for an hour watching the parade and listening to the band. And in the club that evening I stayed on for dinner and we talked about the marching and the drill. All the boys were awfully proud of themselves because of the boxing and the regimental precision of the Berkshires. You could sense flags flying everywhere. When Ronald Merrick turned up he came straight over to me, which wasn't at all usual. Since the dinner party at Aunt Lili's, when we didn't particularly hit it off, we'd only exchanged a few words and had the odd drink or two for form's sake if we bumped into each other at the club. He always seemed busy and unrelaxed, and happiest in the smoking-room talking to other men and getting into arguments. He had a bit of a reputation for being on the quarrelsome side, and apart from a number of unmarried girls who chased him people didn't like him much. But this evening he came straight over to me and said, 'Did you enjoy the parade? I saw you on the *maidan*.' He sat and had drinks with us, and then came out with this semi-invitation to me to come along one evening and listen to his Sousa records, which the other girls chipped me about when he'd gone, coming out with that old joke about etchings, and never trusting a policeman. One of them said, 'Daphne's obviously got what it takes for Mr Merrick. I've been trying to land *that* fish for ages.' One of the boys made a joke about what she meant by 'takes', so the subject was back to normal. Being a Saturday there was a dance on too, and the usual horseplay at the swimming pool. And out on the terrace you didn't only *sense* the flags waving, you could see them. Scores of little flags strung among the fairy lights. There was an atmosphere of 'We'll show them'. The boy I was dancing with said that War Week had given the bloody Indians something to think about. Then he began to get amorous and I had to fight him off. I left him and went into the ladies and sat on the seat and listened to the scurrilous chat going on on the other side of the door and thought, No, it's wrong, wrong. And later, back in the lounge-bar, deafened by the thumping band, I thought, 'I haven't this time to waste. I haven't this time to spare.'

I felt as if the club were an ocean-going liner, like the *Titanic*, with all the lights blazing and the bands playing, heading into the dark, with no one on the bridge.

Auntie, promise me one thing, that if the child survives but you can't bear to have it near you, you'll try to see that the money I leave is used to give it some kind of decent start in life? I look around, trying to think where the child might go if it lives and I don't. I don't presume on your affection for me to extend to what is only half my flesh and blood, and half that of someone unknown to you – perhaps someone unknown to me, someone disreputable. I have got myself used to the idea that you won't want it under your roof, in fact, please don't worry on that score. It's inevitable that a child so badly *mis*conceived should suffer a bit for *my* faults. In any case, let's be frank, you probably won't live for as long as the child would need you to if he first came to a fully conscious, recollective existence while under your roof. I think of Lili. But wonder, too. Perhaps as the child grows, some likeness to Hari will become apparent. I so much hope so. Because that will be my vindication. I have nightmares of the child growing up to resemble no one, black-skinned, beyond redemption, a creature of the dark, a tiny living mirror of that awful night. And yet, even so, it will be a child. A god-given creature, if there is a god, and even if there isn't, deserving of that portion of our blessing we can spare.

I suppose the child – if I'm not here to nurture him – will have to go into a home. Couldn't it be as well my home in a way? There is that woman whom they call Sister Ludmila. I asked her once whether she needed money. She said not, but promised to tell me if she ever did. Perhaps as she gets older (and I don't know how old she is) she will spare a thought for the new-born as well as for the dying. It's a logical progression.

By 'decent start in life', I don't mean background or educa-tion, but much simpler things like warmth, comfort, enough to eat, and kindness and affection. Oh, all the things squandered on me.

If it is a boy, please name him Harry, or Hari if his skin is dark enough to *honour* that kind of spelling. If a girl – I don't know. I haven't made up my mind. I haven't thought of 'it' as a girl. But if she is please *don't* call her Daphne. That's the girl who ran from Apollo, and was changed into a laurel bush! With me it's been the other way round, hasn't it? Rooted clumsily in the earth, thinking I'm running free, chasing the sun-god. When I was in my teens Mother once said, 'Oh, for goodness' sake stop *galumphing!*' which puzzled and then hurt me because being tall I had an idea that I was a sort of graceful Diana type – long-legged and slender, taut as a bow, flitting through the forest! Poor Mother! She had a frightful talent for pouring cold water on people. It was David who taught me to see that she did this because she never knew from one minute to the next what it was she really wanted, so she felt that things were always going wrong around her, and had to hit out at the nearest likely culprit, usually Daddy, but often me. She adored David, though, which is probably why he saw through her more easily than Daddy and I did and was able to explain her to me. She never had her defences up for *him*. I suppose it was because even after years of living comfortably in England she still talked about India as if she had only just escaped from it a minute ago that I grew to feel sorry for it, and then to love it and want it for its own sake, as well as for Daddy's. When I was old enough to understand them he used to show me snaps and photographs and tell me what I thought were wonderful tales of the 'land where I was born', so that when I first came back out here I was always looking for the India I thought I knew because I had seen it in my imagination, like a kind of mirage, shimmering on the horizon, with hot, scented breezes blowing in from far-away hills . . .

It's funny how in spite of what you know about the rains before you come to India you think of it as endlessly dry and scorched, one vast Moghul desert, with walled, scattered towns where all the buildings are shaped like mosques, with arches of fretted stone. Occasionally from the window of a train – the one I went up to 'Pindi on when I first came out – there are glimpses of the country you've imagined. I'm glad I came before and not in the middle of the rains. It's best to undergo the exhaustion of that heat, the heat of April and May that brings out the scarlet flowers of the gol mohurs, the 'flames of the forest' (such a dead, dry, lifeless-looking tree before the blossoms burst) the better to know the joy of the wild storms and lashing rains of the first downpours that turn everything green. That is *my* India. The India of the rains.

There's another name besides Hari's that we never mention. Bibighar. So although you were in Mayapore once, and may have visited the gardens, I don't know whether you have a picture of them in your mind or not. There it is all greenness. Even in the hottest months, before the rains, there is a feeling of greenness, a bit faded and tired, but still green – wild and overgrown, a walled enclosure of trees and undergrowth, with pathways and sudden open spaces where a hundred years ago there were probably formal gardens and fountains. You can still see the foundations of the old house, the Bibighar itself. In one part of them there is a mosaic floor with steps up to it as if it was once the entrance. They've built pillars round the mosaic since and roofed it over, to make it into a sort of shelter or pavilion. Men from the Public Works come once or twice a year and cut back the shrubbery and creepers. At the back of the grounds the wall is crumbled and broken and gives on to waste ground. At the front of the garden there is an open archway on to the road but no gate. So the garden is never closed. But few people go in. Children think it is haunted. Brave boys and girls play there in the morning, and in the dry weather well-off Indians sometimes picnic. But mostly it's deserted. The house was built by a prince, so Lili told me, and destroyed by that man MacGregor, whose house is named after him, and whose wife Janet is supposed to haunt the verandah, nursing her dead baby. It was Lili who first took me into the Bibighar. Hari had heard something about it, but had never seen it, or realized that the long wall on the Bibighar Bridge road was the wall surrounding it, and had never been in it until I took him there one day. There were children playing the first time I visited it with Lili but they ran off when they saw us. I expect they thought we were daylight Bibighar ghosts. And afterwards I never saw anyone there at all.

Hari and I got into the habit of going to the Bibighar, and sitting there in the pavilion, because it was the one place in Mayapore where we could be together and be utterly natural with each other. And even then there was the feeling that we were having to hide ourselves away from the inquisitive, the amused, and the disapproving. Going in there, through the archway, or standing up and getting ready to go back into the cantonment – those were the moments when this feeling of being about to hide or about to come out of hiding to face things was strongest. And even while we were there, there was often a feeling of preparedness, in case someone came in and saw us together, even though we were doing nothing but sitting side by side on the edge of the mosaic 'platform' with our feet dangling, like two kids sitting on a wall. But at least we could be pretty sure no white man or woman would come into the gardens. They never did. The gardens always seemed to have a purely Indian connection, just as the *maidan* really had a purely English one.

Perhaps you say: But if you wanted to be with Hari, and he wanted to be with you, that was no crime, surely, and there were tons of places you could have gone and been happy together? Well, but where? The MacGregor House? His house in the Chillianwallah Bagh? Yes. But where else? Auntie, where else?

Where else that people wouldn't have stared and made us self-conscious, armed us in preparation to withstand an insult or a vulgar scene? The club was out. There was the other club, what they call the Indian Club, but Hari wouldn't take me there because there *I* would have been stared at by what he called the banias with their feet on the chairs. The English coffee shop was out. The Chinese Restaurant was out – after one visit when he was stopped from following me upstairs. I'd been there before with an English officer – and automatically, without thinking, began to go up. So we had to sit downstairs while I was subjected to the stage whisper comments of the people going to the room above, and the curious, uncomfortable stares of the British non-commissioned soldiers who shared the downstairs room with us. Even the poor little fleapit cinema in the cantonment was out because I wouldn't have had the nerve to try to take Hari into the sacrosanct little 'balcony' and he wouldn't have made me sit on a wooden form in the pit. Neither would he take me to the Indian cinema opposite the Tirupati temple, although I asked him to. He said, 'What, and sit through four hours of the *Ramayana*, holding our noses, getting fleas and sweating our guts out?'

Auntie, in Mayapore there wasn't anywhere we could be alone together in public that didn't involve some kind of special forethought or preparation. We spent a few evenings at the Mac-Gregor House while Auntie Lili was out playing bridge, and a couple of evenings with his sweet little Aunt Shalini, but a friendship between two human beings can't be limited in this way, can it? You can't not be affected by the fact that it's a friendship you're both having to work hard at.

And of course it was a friendship I began in a conscious frame of mind. Naturally, as I'd known he wouldn't, he never just dropped in to open house. I told Lili I'd met him on the *maidan* and invited him to come any time. In retrospect her reaction strikes me as that of someone who was subconsciously pleased, but afraid of the consequences for me, or, if not afraid, full of reservations. She told me more about him. Perhaps she was trying to warn me, but she only succeeded in adding fuel to my reforming zeal. She must have told me about his having been to Chillingborough before I met him on the *maidan*, because I'm sure he never mentioned Chillingborough at the party. But otherwise I've forgotten exactly how and when I fitted him together in my mind. All I know, what I admit to, is this – that I was conscious at the meeting on the *maidan* of doing a good deed. The thought revolts me now. I can't bear to remember that I ever condescended, even unintentionally, to the man I fell in love with.

When a couple of weeks had gone by and he still hadn't dropped in I wrote him a note. I got his address from Aunt Lili who had it in her book. As you know I've always been hopeless at bridge, and Lili was going round to the Whites to make up a four with Judge Menen whose wife was in the Greenlawns Nursing Home. Which left me alone on a Saturday evening. After the flag-wagging of War Week I didn't want to go to the club. I didn't know what I wanted to do. I thought of Hari. I'd been thinking of him a lot. It was Saturday morning. I wrote him a note and sent it by one of the servants to the Chillianwallah Bagh. The servant came back and said that Kumar Sahib hadn't been in but that he'd left the note. So I didn't know whether Hari would come that evening or not, which made Lili's silent criticism worse, and my determination to have everything ready stronger. I told cook to prepare dinner for two, chicken pulao, with piles and piles of saffron rice and onion pickles and mounds of lovely hot chappattis, and lots of iced beer, and what I called Mango-Melba to follow. I checked the cocktail cabinet and sent the boy to the liquor store for more Carew's gin. Then I went down to the cantonment myself, to the Sports Emporium, and bought a batch of records that had just come in, and a box of needles because Lili wasn't very good about changing them and used the same ones over and over and mixed the old ones with the new. We had a Decca portable she'd bought the last time she was in Cal. And when I got back I sent Bhalu crazy the way I bashed round the garden gathering armfuls of flowers! I felt a bit like Cho Cho San getting ready for Pinkerton! Lili went off to the Whites about six-thirty while I was still in the bath. She came into the bedroom and called out, 'Daphne, I'm bashing off now and will be back about midnight, I expect. Have a good time.' I cried out, 'Oh, I will. Give my love all round.' And then she said, 'I hope he has the good manners to turn up,' so I shouted back, 'Of course he will. He'd have sent a note by now if he hadn't been going to.' Poor Lili. She really thought he wasn't going to. So did I. I dressed in that awful electric blue dress that turns muddy green in the artificial light, but I felt I didn't care what I looked like. I knew I could never look anything but myself. And there was joy in not caring for once, but just being myself.

And he came, bang on the dot of 7.30, in a horse tonga. To get a horse tonga he must have gone to the station, because on the other side of the river you can usually only get cycle tongas. Or perhaps he had come from the cantonment bazaar, from Darwaza Chand's shop, and had waited there while they finished making the new shirt that made him smell of fresh, unlaundered cotton.

I'd cheated a bit in my note by not making it really clear I'd be alone. For all I knew he was the sort of Indian boy who'd think it wrong to dine alone with a woman, or if *he* didn't mind, that his aunt would refuse to let him come if she knew Lili was going to be out. I could see he was on tenterhooks at first, waiting for Lili to appear. We were on the verandah, and Raju was serving the drinks. It must have been on this occasion that he refused a cigarette and admitted he'd given it up. Not smoking made him more on tenterhooks, and suddenly I was on them too because I saw what a trap I'd laid for myself. He'd probably think Lili had gone out to avoid him because she disapproved of the idea of his coming to a meal, or, just as bad, that I'd asked him round secretly on a night she was going out because I knew she would disapprove. So before the situation got out of hand I told him the truth, that Saturday was one of Lili's bridge nights, and I hated bridge and had wanted a quiet dinner with someone I could talk to about home, but had cheated when writing my note in case he or his aunt thought it odd for a girl to invite a boy round on an evening when she was going to be by herself.

He seemed puzzled at first. It must have been about four years since an English person had spoken to him in the way that in England he'd have been used to and thought nothing of. I hated even being conscious of this fact, but I was, so there's no use in pretending otherwise.

Even on that first evening we were having to work at a basis for ordinary human exchange, although it was probably the only evening we met without feeling an immediate sense of pressure

and disapproval from outside. Within a minute or two of realizing Lili was out I could see him beginning to relax, beginning
to forget himself and start looking at and considering me. We
had about three gin fizzes and then went in and ate, sitting close
together at one end of the table. I'd worked it out before that
although it would have been nice for me if I could have just told
Raju to bring the food in and leave me to serve it, it would be
better for Hari's morale if we were *both* waited on hand and foot.
Raju of course tried to cut Hari down to size a bit by addressing
him in Hindi, but soon gave up when he realized Hari spoke it
really no better than I did! And I was glad to see how he also
relaxed at the table, once we'd made a joke about his inability
to speak the language, and tackled the grub! Like me. We both
waded in like a couple of kids. At Lili's parties I'd noticed how
the Indian men sort of held back, as if it was faintly indelicate
to eat hearty in mixed company. I kept sending Raju out to
bring more hot chappattis which Hari ended up by scoffing
without noticing how many he'd had. Later, when I had a similar
dinner at his Aunt Shalini's I realized that there was a difference
between our food and theirs, and understood better why Hari
ate as if he'd not had a square meal for weeks. I've never been
able to stand anything cooked in ghi, which affects my bile-duct
immediately and there was ghi in some of the dishes Mrs Gupta
Sen gave us.

But that is going on too far ahead. After we'd done right by
the grub, we sort of collapsed in the drawing-room and then
Raju brought in the brandy and coffee, and Hari did the honours
at the gramophone. All through dinner we'd talked and talked
about 'home'. We were almost exactly the same age, so remembered the same things in relation to the same phases of our lives,
I mean like seeing the *R101* blundering overhead. Aeroplanes
and Jim Mollison and Amy Johnson, Amelia Earhart lost in the
Timor Sea; films like *Rain* and *Mata Hari*. And things like cricket
and Jack Hobbs, Wimbledon and Bunny Austin and Betty
Nuttall, motor racing and Sir Malcolm Campbell, Arsenal and
Alec James, the proms at the poor old bombed Queen's Hall –
although Hari had never been there because he had no real taste
for music apart from jazz and swing.

When he first started putting the records on you could see
how much pleasure they gave him, but also how they suddenly

brought back his uncertainty. After he'd played two and put on a third, a Victor Sylvester, he got his courage up and said, 'I've almost forgotten how and was never much good anyway, but would you like to dance?' I said I was once described as an elephant with clogs on myself, but perhaps together we'd sort each other out, so we stood up and held hands and backs. At first he held me too far away for it to work properly, and we were both watching each other's feet all the time and apologizing and taking it awfully seriously, and when the record ended I think he expected me to sit down or suggest going on to the verandah, not only because it hadn't worked but because he thought I might have agreed to dance with him in order not to make it look too obvious that I felt it would be distasteful to be held by an Indian. But I asked him to find a particular record 'In the Mood', which, as you probably *don't* know, is quick and easy, an absolute natural, and waited for him, forced him to dance again, and this time we looked over each other's shoulders and not at our feet, and danced closer, and felt each other slipping into a sort of natural rhythm.

If you ever read this I shan't be around to feel diminished by your criticism. I can kid myself that I'm reliving it for no one except the one person who knows how far short of perfect re-enactment an account like this must fall. Perhaps as well as being an insurance against permanent silence it is a consolation prize to me, to give me a chance to have him with me again in a way that is more solid than unfettered recollection, but still insub-stantial. But second best is better than third — the third best of random thoughts un-pinned down. Oh, I could conjure him now, just with this scratchy old pen, in a form that might satisfy you better, but do more or less than justice to what he actually was. I could do this if I ignored the uncertainty I felt, the clumsi-ness we both shared; do it if I pretended that from the moment we held each other we felt the uncomplicated magic of straight-forward physical attraction. But it was never uncomplicated. Unless you could say that the opposing complications cancelled each other out — on his side the complication of realizing that the possession of a white girl could be a way of bolstering his ego, and on mine the complication of the curious almost titillating *fear* of his colour. How else account for the fact that in dancing the second time we stared (I think fixedly) over each other's shoulders, as if afraid to look directly into each other's eyes?

We didn't dance a third time, but in sitting out now there was no sense of physical rebuff as there would have been if I'd refused to dance at all or sat down after that first awkward impersonal shuffle. Our separation, our sitting, he in his chair and I in mine, was a mutual drawing-back from dangerous ground – a drawing-back from the danger to ourselves but also from the danger to the other, because neither of us could be certain that the other fully saw the danger or understood the part that might be played by the *attraction to danger* in what we felt for each other.

And that is how Lili found us when she got back, sitting companionably at the end of an evening we had both obviously enjoyed because we were still talking easily, with our tensions so well concealed we couldn't even be certain that it was tension the other one shared.

He stayed for no more than ten minutes after she got back; and yet during that time, while she talked to him, I could see his armour going back on layer by layer, and Lili change from faintly frosty to friendly back to frosty again – as if at one moment before he was fully re-armed she had seen the kind of vulnerable spot in him she was afraid of and so put up her own shutters, not to lock him out but to try – by putting them up – to lock me in, to keep us apart for everybody's sake.

One is not sensitive usually to the effect people have on one another unless one of them happens to be someone you love. In this case, I suppose, already I loved them both.

War Week was towards the end of April, so the evening Hari came to dinner at the MacGregor House must have been in the early part of May. One or two of the girls from the hospital went up that month to places like Darjeeling for a spot of leave. It was terribly hot in Mayapore. The moon was that curious lopsided shape which I think you told me is caused by dust particles in the atmosphere. There wasn't much leave going because of all the political crises that kept boiling up, simmering down and boiling up again. Matron said I could have a couple of weeks off and I think Lili would have liked to get away into the hills for a bit, but we were pretty short-staffed at the hospital and I didn't feel I was entitled to leave so soon after starting work. I suggested to Lili that she should go by herself and leave me to cope, but she wouldn't hear of it. So we sweated it out, as practically everybody else from the Deputy Commissioner downwards was doing. It became too hot, really, to have, parties – a few times out to dinner, and a few times having people in to dinner, that was about the sum total.

The day after Hari's visit he sent me a note, thanking me formally for the evening, and a few days later I got an invitation from Mrs Gupta Sen to have dinner at her house in the Chillianwallah Bagh the following Saturday. Lili had one too, but she said it was only for form's sake, and that anyway she was playing bridge again, so couldn't go. After I'd accepted I got another note, this time from Hari, saying that as the house was difficult to find (all the numbers were haywire and the Chillianwallah Bagh was really a system of roads, not just one road) he would call for me in a tonga at about 7.15, if that was all right. He said he hoped I wouldn't find the evening too dull, there was no gramophone or anything like that. I asked Lili if she thought this was a hint that he'd like it if I took ours along, with a few records, but she said that wouldn't do at all, you couldn't take a thing like a gramophone because not only might Mrs Gupta Sen think it wrong to have such a thing in the house (especially when the records were all European music, which probably hurt her ears) but she would more likely than not look upon it as an insult, a criticism of the kind of hospitality she had to offer. So I took Lili at her word, and I think she was right.

His Aunt Shalini was sweet, and spoke very good English. She said Hari's father taught her when she was a little girl and that she loved having Hari living with her because now she'd been able to pick it up again and improve her accent. She showed me some snaps of Hari taken in England, which her brother, Hari's father Duleep, had sent her from time to time. There were several taken in the garden, showing the house they lived in in Berkshire, which looked to me like a small mansion. Then there were later pictures of Hari, with some English friends, whose name was Lindsey.

I'd been pretty nervous, anticipating this visit to the Chillianwallah Bagh, and it didn't help when Hari was late picking me up and I was sitting alone on the verandah of the MacGregor waiting for him to arrive. Lili had already gone off to bridge.

She'd warned me to have at least a couple of drinks before Hari arrived in case Mrs Gupta Sen was teetotal, and I got a bit squiffy, drinking more than I needed because of the extra twenty minutes or so that I had to wait. He was awfully embarrassed about being late, which I think he thought I'd see as a typical Indian failing. He said he'd had difficulty getting a tonga because they had all seemed to be out ferrying people to the first house of the flicks. I was relieved when we got into the tonga and I saw the shapes of a wrapped bottle of gin and a bottle of lime or lemon in a little canvas bag on the seat. It was as good as dark by the time we got across the Bibighar bridge – actually it was as we went past the Bibighar wall that I asked Hari what he thought of the gardens. We had a bit of a laugh when it turned out he didn't even know properly what they were or that they were there. I said, 'I've only been in Mayapore a few months and you've been here for four years, and I know it better than you. But then that's like living in London and never going to the Tower.'

We turned off the Chillianwallah Bagh Extension road. The streets were badly lit and there was an awful smell from the river. I wondered what on earth I'd let myself in for, and I must confess my heart sank. It rose again a bit when I saw the type of house in the district we'd driven in to – cheek by jowl, but modern-looking and civilized, all squares and angles. I was amused the way Hari had to keep telling the driver things like 'Dahne ki taraf aur ek dam sidhe ki rasta' just like me, muddling through in pidgin Hindi. I chipped him about it and gradually he relaxed.

But then when we had stopped at his house he became un-relaxed again because one of the servants had closed the gate. He shouted out but no one came and the tonga-wallah didn't seem prepared to get out and open it himself. So Hari climbed down and opened it. It was only a few paces between the gate and the open area in front of the porch, which was lit by an unshaded electric light bulb, and we could have walked it, which might have been better because the tonga-wallah started making trouble about the tiny space he had to turn round in, which was something I had to leave Hari to deal with. Because his Hindi was as bad as mine I understood what was going on, and how he had to bribe the fellow to come back at 'gyarah baje' and refused to pay him meanwhile.

Suddenly I was fed up with the awful position Hari was being put in by a bloody-minded tonga-wallah, and was about to say 'Oh, tell the stupid man I'd rather walk home than put him to any bother,' but stopped myself in time, because that would have been taking charge and would have made matters worse, so instead when Hari had got his way and the man had reluctantly agreed to come back at eleven, I said, 'What a fuss they make,' as if I was personally used to it, which he probably knew I wasn't, and which made it look as if I was acting like a Mem, slumming. Sort of amused, at Hari's expense. Knowing what I'd done I wanted to get back into the tonga and go home, and have an enormous drink.

Instead we went indoors, encased in a sort of gloom, a sort of trembling expectancy of disaster, or if not disaster then awful boredom and discomfort, and unease. Thank heaven for Aunt Shalini, who came into the little hall like a miniature Rajput princess, beautifully and almost undetectably made-up, wearing a pale lilac saree, perfectly simple and plain, just cotton, but looking marvellous and cool. She shook hands, which made my feeble self-conscious efforts at *namaste* look silly. She said, 'Come in and have a drink,' and led us into the living-room, small but beautifully bare and uncluttered, with a rug or two, a divan and one tiny but very comfortable wicker chair which she made me sit in while, as she said, Hari 'did the honours' at the drinks table – a Benares brass tray on a carved ebony mother-of-pearl inlaid stand, on which there were exactly three glasses and the bottles Hari had taken out of the canvas bag as surreptitiously as he could. While she was talking to me I saw the physical likeness between herself and Hari, although of course she was tiny. In front of her I felt a bit of a gawk, big, clumsy, dressed unsuitably and showing far too much bare skin. Hari was wearing a grey cotton suit, but he had to take the jacket off presently because the fans were only working at half power.

When we'd had just one drink – and by this time I felt I really needed two – she said, 'Shall we go in?' and stood up and led the way next door to a small box-like dining-room. She called out to the boy to switch the fans on, and then we began to eat.

She'd taken so much trouble with the table, to make me feel at home. There was a bowl of water in the centre with frangipani blooms floating in it. And handwoven lace mats at the three places. She described every dish, but I've forgotten most of the names, and some of them I found difficult. When the main dish came on – Chicken tandoori – she said to Hari, 'Haven't we any iced beer?' and he got up and went away for a while and came back with the beer in bottles, followed by a servant with glasses and a tray. She said, 'Haven't we a jug, Hari?' So he sent the servant back for a jug, then went out himself again with the bottles. The boy brought the beer back decanted in a jug. The rest of the servants were watching from doorways and through the barred-window openings into the adjoining rooms. Aunt Shalini drank nothing, not even water, so Hari and I had the beer between us. My glass was an old tumbler with the Roman 'key' design, and his was smaller and thicker. He was conscious, overly-conscious, of the insignificant ways in which the table fell short of what he had once been used to and thought I would consider essential – but towards the end of the meal, when I had been watching him without realizing I did so, he caught my eye, and I think he saw then that whatever I noticed as 'faults' had only added to my feeling of being 'at home', and to my feeling for him and his aunt as people honouring me, expressing some kind of groping hope that one day our different *usages* would mean nothing, mean as little as they meant that evening to me.

After dinner was the time she showed me the snaps. I was longing for a cigarette but didn't dare open my bag. Suddenly she said, 'Hari, haven't we any Virginia cigarettes for Miss Manners?' How sensitive she was to every change of mood in her guests! How tolerant of any taste she personally found *dis-*tasteful – like the smoking and the drinking. And I think Hari was surprised too at the tremendous ability she had to entertain an English girl – her first English guest ever, so I discovered. What I admired Hari for was the way he didn't *press* things like drink and cigarettes, but left his aunt in control, in her own house, which an insensitive blustering boy intent on proving his Englishness probably wouldn't have done. The other nice thing he did was to have a cigarette too, so that I shouldn't feel I was the only messy person in the room, but I noticed how he just let it burn away without smoking it properly. He was afraid to get the taste for it again.

The only thing that went a bit wrong was over the business of going to the wc! When we got up from the dinner-table Hari made himself scarce for a while. I think he'd told Aunt Shalini to be sure to give me the opportunity to go, but that she didn't quite have the nerve to say anything to me when the time came. The next time I went to the house she had got over this embarrassment, but on this particular evening I think Hari's realization that I hadn't 'been' rather cast a blight on his evening. Round about 10.30 it began to cast a blight on mine too. I began to wonder whether they even *had* a wc of the kind they felt I could be invited to use. Actually it turned out that there was a downstairs as well as whatever there might have been upstairs. No seat, but she'd thoughtfully put a chamber pot on a little stool which I didn't dare use, and there was a bowl and a jug of water, on a table that looked as if it didn't always belong there, and some soap and towels and a hand mirror. I went in there after we heard the tonga-wallah come back and Hari went out to speak to him. I stood up and said, 'May I powder my nose?' So she took me into the passage near the kitchens and opened the door and switched on the light and said, 'Please, anytime you come, here it is.' There were a couple of cockroaches running up and down, but I didn't care. Lili shrieks blue murder if she so much as glimpses one, but although when I first got to India I was horrified to find them sharing places like bathrooms and wc's I no longer care.

When I said goodbye to Aunt Shalini I wanted to stoop down and kiss her, but didn't in case that offended her. Hari insisted on coming back in the tonga with me, but wouldn't come in for a nightcap. I think he was trying to avoid doing anything that would create an atmosphere of *Well, that's all over, now we can relax*. So after he'd driven off in the tonga I sat on the verandah and had a long cool drink of nimbo and waited for Lili to come home.

The next day I sent one of the boys round to Aunt Shalini's with an enormous bunch of flowers I'd raided the garden for, and a note of thanks. Bhalu was very cross with me, so I gave him ten chips and asked him not to complain to Madam and get me in trouble, which made him grin, the old rascal. After that he had me wound round his little finger. Perhaps he was wound round mine too, and we were partners in crime – crime because Lili paid all the servants extra when she had anyone staying in the

house and it was understood guests weren't to tip them. He
never complained again to Lili about my cutting flowers, but
round about the first of each month when he'd been paid his
wages he used to stand about saluting and grinning, until I gave
him a few chips. He bought a new pair of chappals with the first
lot of money I gave him, and looked very smart, but oddly more
tortoiselike than ever, with his khaki shorts and knobbly black
bare legs and these enormous army-style sandals, clopping about
on the gravel. You could tell he preferred bare feet, but the chappals represented status. He was once a gardener to a Colonel
James in Madras, and Colonel James's household has been
Bhalu's standard of pukka life ever since, even though I think he
knows the garden of the MacGregor House is far superior to any
other garden he's ever worked in, which may be why he has to
feel the whole of it belongs to him, and that he's tending it to the
honour and glory of James Sahib rather than of Lili.

I'm gossiping, aren't I, Auntie? Putting off the moment when
I have to write about the thing you really want to know. But
yet, not gossiping, because you can't isolate the good and happy
things from the bad and unhappy ones. And you see for me there
was a growing sense of joy, whatever there was for the people
who watched and waited.

It was now that Mayapore seemed to change for me. It was
no longer just the house, the road to the cantonment bazaar,
the road to the hospital, the hospital, the *maidan*, the club. It
extended to the other side of the river and, because of that, in
all directions, across that enormous flat plain that I used to stand
staring at from the balcony of my room, putting on my glasses
and taking them off, doing what Lili called my eye exercises.
I felt that Mayapore had got bigger, and so had made me smaller,
had sort of split my life into three parts. There was my life in the
hospital, which also included the club and the boys and girls and
all the good-time stuff that wasn't really good-time at all, just
the easiest, the least exacting, so long as you ignored the fact that
it was only the easiest for the least admirable part of your nature.
There was my life at the MacGregor House, where I lived with
Lili and mixed with Indians and English, the kind who made
an effort to work together. But this mixing was just as self-
conscious as the segregation. At the club you stood on *loud*,

committed ground. At the MacGregor House it was silent and determinedly neutral. With Hari I began to feel that here at last was ground wholly personal to me, where I might learn to talk in my own tone of voice. Perhaps this is why I felt Mayapore had got bigger but made me smaller, because my association with Hari – the one thing that was beginning to make me feel like a person again – was hedged about, restricted, pressed in on until only by making yourself tiny could you squeeze into it and stand, imprisoned but free, diminished by everything that loomed from outside, *but not diminished from the inside*; and that was the point, that's why I speak of joy.

Sometimes, knowing the effort it cost to squeeze into this restricted, dangerous little space, I was afraid, as I was that evening Ronald Merrick 'proposed' to me and brought me back to the MacGregor House, and I wanted to run back down the stairs and call out to Ronald, and was afraid of seeing the ghost of Janet MacGregor. This occasion, the occasion of his proposal after our dinner and my coming back to the MacGregor and being afraid, was in the middle of June. The rains were late. We were all exhausted, physically and mentally. That probably also accounts for my fear that night. That, and the feeling I had that Ronald represented something I didn't fully understand, but probably ought to trust. There's an awful weight still on my mind about Ronald. I feel that just as you and the others may know where Hari is, so there are things about Ronald that no one is prepared to discuss in front of me. I think about him a lot. He is like a dark shadow, just on the edge of my life.

Auntie, did he hurt Hari in some special horrible way? I think he did. But no one would say, at least would not say to me. And I didn't dare question anyone too closely. I was equally a party to the conspiracy to keep me a prisoner in the MacGregor House after that night in the Bibighar. I only left it twice, once to visit Aunt Shalini, who wouldn't see me, and then on the day before Lili took me up to 'Pindi and I went to the Sanctuary to say goodbye to Sister Ludmila. Ronald Merrick was on Sister Ludmila's conscience too. It seems she hadn't realized that he and I knew each other more than casually, hadn't realized that I might not know that it was Ronald who took Hari in for questioning that day he found him at the Sanctuary. But by then I was afraid to probe too deeply. I trusted no one. Only to my

silence. And to Hari's. But I remembered how after the Bibighar
on the one occasion we came briefly face to face Ronald would
not look at me straight, the time the Assistant Commissioner
came with Judge Menen and a young English sub-divisional
officer and held a sort of 'inquiry' at which Ronald gave evidence and I made everybody uneasy, perhaps angry, with my
answers to their questions.

Before I tell you what actually happened in the Bibighar,
I must say something about Ronald, and something about Sister
Ludmila. I think Ronald first took real notice of me that day on
the *maidan*, when I went to the War Week Exhibition; took
notice of me because he saw me go up to Hari and talk to him,
as a lot of English people did. If he already had his eye on Hari,
as some sort of potential subversive type (nothing could have
been farther from the truth, but Ronald had his job to do) he
probably looked at my going up to him like that, as a policeman
would, but also as an Englishman who didn't want an English
girl getting mixed up with the 'wrong' type of Indian. I mean
that would account for the fact that when he saw me in the
club that evening he came straight up to me and said, 'Did you
enjoy the parade? I saw you on the *maidan*,' when usually we
only nodded, or occasionally had a drink if circumstances made
it awkward for him not to offer me one.

He probably had an idea that it would be kind to head me
off, but also – because he was a policeman – wasn't above
looking at me as a possible source of information about Hari:
Do you remember my saying in a letter that with Ronald
I never felt there was any real candour between him and the
person he was dealing with? He took his job so seriously, and
I think he felt he had to prove his worth all the time, so that
nothing came naturally to him, nothing came spontaneously,
or easily or *happily*.

I wonder just *how* much, once he'd made the move of showing
friendly to me, wanting to head me off for my own good, he was
genuinely and quite unexpectedly attracted to me as a person?
Certainly from then on he began to pay attention. And although
I didn't appreciate it at the time I see now that he became my
new contact with the sort of world the club represented, the
flag-wagging little world – but through him it wore a subtler
mark – the Henry Moores, the Debussy. The one constant in

my life was Lili and the MacGregor House, the variants were
Hari on his side and Ronald on his. Those two seemed so far
apart I don't think I ever referred to one in front of the other.
But they weren't far apart at all. Which was why I was so angry,
felt such a fool, when I discovered the truth, that they'd been –
what? enemies – since that day in the Sanctuary, when Hari was
struck and dragged away, and Sister Ludmila had watched it all
happening.

She dressed like one of those sisters of mercy with huge white
flyaway linen caps. I'd seen her once or twice in the cantonment
bazaar, walking in front of a boy who was armed with a stick,
holding a leather bag that she kept chained to the belt round her
waist. I was with a girl from the hospital and I said, 'Whoever's
that?' She said, 'That's the mad Russian woman who collects
dead bodies and isn't a nun at all, but just dresses like one.' I was
only passingly interested, not only because India has its fair share
of eccentrics of both colours but also because it was during
that period of unhappiness, of dislike for everything around me.
A few weeks later I saw her again and mentioned her to Lili
who said, 'She doesn't do any harm, and Anna Klaus helps her
sometimes, and likes her, but she makes me shiver, bashing off
collecting people she finds dying.'

Aunt Lili hates anything grisly or sordid, doesn't she? She told
me that once as a young girl, the first time she went to Bombay
and saw the slums, she cried. I think well-off privileged Indians
like Lili have a sort of deep-rooted guilt that they bury under
layers of what looks like indifference, because there's so little
they can individually do to lessen the horror and the poverty.
They subscribe to charities and do voluntary work but must feel
it's like trying to dam up a river with a handful of twigs. And
with Lili I think there's also a horror of death. She told me about
going to the morgue in Paris with a medical student and how
afterwards she had nightmares of all the corpses rising up and
falling back and rising up again, which is why she hated Nello
to show off his cuckoo clocks in the museum room at the Mac-
Gregor House! The room where he put Uncle Henry's old briar
pipe in a glass case – the one Uncle Henry gave him to improve
his imitations.

I took Hari into the museum room once, round about the

beginning of the time when we knew that we both liked being together and so had to face the fact that there was almost no place we could be, except at his house or at Lili's. The Bibighar came a bit later. The time I took him in to the museum room we were joking about everything, but there was this sense already of cheating, of having to cheat and hide, buy time, buy privacy – paying for them with blows to our joint pride. I thought as I looked round the room, 'Well, Hari and I are exhibits too. We could stand here on a little plinth, with a card saying *Types of Opposites. Indo-British, circa 1942. Do not Touch.*' Then all the people who stared at us in the cantonment, but looked away directly we looked at them, could come and stare to their hearts' content. I think it was in Hari's mind too. We never went into the museum room again. I said, 'Come on, Hari – it's mouldy and dead,' and held my hand out without thinking, then realized that except for dancing, casual contact like getting in and out of a tonga, we had never touched each other, even as friends, let alone as man and woman. I nearly withdrew my hand, because the longer I held it out and he hesitated to take it, the more loaded with significance the gesture became. It hadn't been meant as significant – just natural, warm and companionable. He took it finally. And then I wanted him to kiss me. To kiss me would have been the only way of making the hand-holding right. Holding hands and not kissing seemed wrong because it was incomplete. It wouldn't have been incomplete if he'd taken my hand the moment I'd held it out. When we got out of the room he let go. I felt deserted, caught out, left alone to face something, like once at school when I admitted to some silly trivial thing several of us had done and found I was the only girl to own up, which made me look a fool, not a heroine. It was this sort of thing with Hari – these repeated experiences of finding myself emotionally out on a limb – that added up and made me feel sometimes – as I suppose I did climbing the staircase that night after Ronald Merrick's proposal – 'It's probably all wrong my association with Hari Kumar' – I mean made me feel it *before* Ronald put it into so many words. And added up in that other unfinished sum that posed the question, 'Well, what does he really feel for me? A big-boned white girl with not much to be said in her favour.'

*

And then there were the rains. They came fresh and clean, wild, indiscriminate. And changed the garden, Mayapore, the whole landscape. That awful foreboding colourlessness was washed out of the sky. I'd wake at night, shivering because the temperature had fallen, and listen to the lashing on the trees, the wonderful rumbling and banging of the thunder, and watch the way the whole room was lit as if from an explosion, with the furniture throwing sudden flamboyant shadows, black dancing shapes petrified in the middle of a complicated movement – a bit of secret night-time devilry that they returned to the moment the unexpected light went out, only to be caught and held still in it again a few moments later.

I was at the Chillianwallah Bagh on the last night of the dry. For two nights there had been sheet lightning and distant thunder. It was towards the end of June, about a week, perhaps less, after my dinner with Ronald Merrick when he had said, on the steps of the MacGregor House, 'Some ideas take some getting used to.' Sitting with Hari and Aunt Shalini this time I saw how unreal my life had become because there didn't seem to be any kind of future in front of me that I wanted and could have. *Why?* Holding one hand out, groping, and the other out backwards, linked to the security of what was known and expected. Straining like that. Pretending the ground between was occupied, when all the time it wasn't.

The tonga came at eleven and on the way home we suddenly saw her, lit by the sheet lightning – the wide white wings of the cap, a man ahead of her, and one behind carrying what looked like a pole, but was a rolled-up stretcher. I'd said – not wanting the evening to end – 'Let's drive back through the bazaar and past the temple,' and he'd agreed, and then I suffered pangs of conscience at the thought of the extra rupees the boy would want; because now I'd fitted Hari into place, and knew he hadn't any spare rupees to throw away. On the other hand I wouldn't have dared offer him even an anna. That time we went to the Chinese Restaurant I said quite without thinking, 'Let's go Dutch on a chop suey,' and his face closed down, the way Ronald Merrick's did when I rejected his proposal. The Chinese Restaurant was a far from happy experience, what with the insult it seemed I'd offered Hari suggesting Dutch and then the insult to us both when the proprietor stopped him from following me upstairs.

I said, 'That's the mad Russian woman who collects dead bodies, isn't it?' She was going away from us, turning up a side street. Hari said she wasn't mad and he didn't think she was Russian. He said, 'We call her Sister Ludmila.' He'd once written a piece for the *Gazette* about the Sanctuary, but his editor had refused to publish it because of the implication that the British were responsible for letting people die in the streets. So he'd altered the article, because that wasn't what he'd meant. He'd altered it to show that *nobody* cared, not even the people who were dying, nobody except Sister Ludmila. But the editor still wouldn't publish it. He said Sister Ludmila was a joke. I asked Hari if I could visit the Sanctuary. He said he'd take me there if I really wanted to see it, but that I mustn't be upset if she treated me like some kind of inquisitive snooper. She kept herself very much to herself and was only really interested in people who were dying and had no bed to die in, although she also ran an evening clinic that people could go to who couldn't afford to take time off from work to go to the day-time clinics, and she doled out free rice on certain days of the week, to children and mothers mostly. I asked him how he had got to know her and he simply said, 'By chance.'

She had an image of the Siva dancing in a circle of cosmic fire, carved in wood, and a framed biblical text: 'He that soweth little shall reap little, and he that soweth plenteously shall reap plenteously. Let every man do according as he is disposed in his heart, not grudging, or of necessity; for God loveth a cheerful giver.' There seemed to be a connection between the Christian text and the Hindu image, because *this* Siva was smiling. And the way the god's limbs are thrust out and jaunty-looking gives the image a feeling of happiness, doesn't it? The only immobile thing is the right foot (even the right leg is bent at the knee and springy-looking). The right foot is the one that presses down on the crouching figure of the little demon, which is why that foot has to be firm and unmoving. The left leg is kicking up, the first pair of arms are gesturing cautiously but invitingly, and the second pair are holding the circle of flame, holding it away but also keeping it burning. And of course the god is winged, which gives the whole image an airy flying feeling that makes you think you could leap into the dark with him and come to no harm.

These were the only bits of decoration in her whitewashed 'cell' – the Siva and the text. At our last meeting she gave the text to me, because she said she knew it by heart anyway. But I've always been too embarrassed to show it to you and I don't think I deserved to be given it anyway. It's in my big suitcase, the one with the straps round it.

What an extraordinary woman she was. When evening comes I think of her preparing to set out on that nightly expedition into the alleys and dark cul-de-sacs, and into the waste land between the temple and the Bibighar bridge. I got into the habit of going there about once a week straight from the hospital – to help with the evening clinic, not just because it was another place Hari and I could meet. I once asked her whether I could go with her at night on her missions. She laughed and said, 'No, that is only for people who have nothing else to offer.' I thought she meant I could offer money, but she said she had enough, more than enough, although promised that if ever she didn't and I still wanted to help I could.

We took to each other. Perhaps I liked her originally because she was fond of Hari and saw nothing wrong in our being there together. She used to let us sit in the office, or in her room. When it was dark he and I would cycle back to the MacGregor House, but he didn't often come in on those occasions. The days I knew I'd be going to the Sanctuary I went to the hospital on my bicycle and left early to avoid the car or van that Mr Merrick was always sending round for me. The same in the evenings, after work. I'd leave a message for the driver that I'd either gone or was working late. Sometimes, though, I'd let myself be driven back to the MacGregor, and then go on to the Sanctuary by cycle. I didn't want the hospital to know I helped at Sister Ludmila's clinic. It wasn't often that I did, but I guessed it was against the hospital rules or something. I saw Anna Klaus there one evening and said, 'Don't split on me!' She laughed and said people probably knew anyway because in a town like Mayapore it was almost impossible to keep anything a secret.

But not all the people who would have liked to know did. I mean people on our side of the river, people like Ronald Merrick. I kept it from Ronald because this was the part of my life I shared willingly with no one. Ronald was part of another life. Lili yet another. I didn't know I'd divided my life up into these watertight compartments, I mean I didn't consciously know. Subconsciously, yes, and I was aware of the subterfuge involved, but not aware of it in a way that ever allowed me in those days to use the word subterfuge – at least not until the evening when I went to the temple with Hari, and found out about Ronald's part in his arrest, and felt everyone had cheated, and then realized I'd been cheating just as badly myself, and became afraid, recognized that I'd really been afraid all along, afraid like everybody else of going out on a limb in case somebody sawed it off – which was ironic, wasn't it, because I used to kid myself that's what we all ought to do, kid myself it was what I was doing. But if I was out on a limb I had one arm securely round the tree-trunk.

I suppose I thought that everything I did was an adventure of some sort. An evening at the MacGregor House with Lili and a few 'mixed' friends, an evening at the club with Ronald or the girls and boys, an hour or two at Sister Ludmila's clinic, a walk with Hari on a Sunday morning to the Bibighar. Well, they were adventures, weren't they? because each of these things was done – unintentionally but for all practical purposes – in defiance of the others. I was breaking every rule there was. The funny thing is that people couldn't be absolutely certain which rule I was breaking in what way at what time because they were so hedged about with their own particular rule they could only follow me far enough to see that I'd broken it and gone away, and become temporarily invisible, so that when I came back, when I returned to their own fold they didn't know enough about what I'd been doing and where I'd been to make real charges against me, other than the general one of being – what? Unstable? Asking for trouble? Unaligned? Bad enough of course, but people do like to be able to define other people's instability and non-alignment, and if they can't their own fear of what you might come to represent forces them to make another bid for your allegiance.

To be rejected – which I suppose is one of the easiest ways of making your mark, you have to come *right out* with something they see as directly and forcefully opposed to what they think they believe in. To be accepted you have to be seen and heard to appear to stand for what they think they believe in. To be neither one thing nor the other is probably unforgivable.

But, Auntie, it was awfully difficult for me. I did genuinely *like* several of the girls and boys I mixed with at the club. I genuinely liked Ronald, when he was the closest he could ever get to being easy and natural with me. I even liked him when he was difficult and 'official' because I thought I knew why he acted like that. And I loved Lili, even at her most standoffish, when that old Rajput princess blood showed through and she sort of gathered up the hem of her cloak. Saree, I mean! I liked the *fun* of the English before it became self-conscious and vulgar and violent, and I liked the simple almost childish fun of the Indians, and their seriousness, before it became prissy and prickly and imitative of European sulks. With Hari I can't connect a word such as 'like', because my liking was hopelessly encumbered with the physical effect he had on me, which turned liking into love but didn't leave me insensitive to his pigheadedness and prickliness. All of which makes me sound on paper like a paragon of virtuous broad-mindedness, until you remember the horrible mess I made of everything.

I hate the impression we automatically get of things and places and people that make us say, for instance, 'This is Indian. This is British.' When I first saw the Bibighar I thought: How Indian! Not Indian as I'd have thought of a place as Indian before I came out, but Indian as it struck me then. But when you say something like that, in circumstances like that, I think you're responding to the attraction of a place which you see as alien on the surface but underneath as proof of something general and universal. I wish I could get hold of the right words to say just what I mean. The Taj Mahal is 'typically Indian', isn't it? Picture-book Moghul stuff. But what makes you give out to it emotionally is the feeling of a man's worship of his wife, which is neither Indian nor un-Indian, but a general human emotion, expressed in this case in an 'Indian' way. This is what I got from the Bibighar. It was a place in which you sensed something having gone badly wrong at one time that hadn't yet been put right but could be if only you knew how. That's the sort of thing you could imagine about any place, but imagining it there, feeling that it was still alive, I said, 'How Indian,' because it was the first place in Mayapore that hit me in this way, and the surprise of being hit made me think I'd come across something typical when all the time it was typical of no place, but only of human acts and desires that leave their mark in the most unexpected and sometimes chilling way.

Usually it was a Sunday-morning place, but one day Hari and I sheltered there from the rain, dashing in from the road in the late afternoon, on our bikes, and running up the steps that divided one level of old lawn from another, to the 'pavilion', the roofed-over mosaic. We stood under it and I had a cigarette. We'd been on our way to tea at Aunt Shalini's. It was a Saturday. I had a half-day off from the hospital and after lunch I'd cycled to the cantonment bazaar to see if those awful photographs I'd had taken for your birthday were ready at Gulab Singh's where that little man Subhas Chand had a booth. I saw Hari coming out of the *Gazette* offices and called out to him. I said, 'Come and help me choose my picture for Auntie Ethel, then if they're any good you can have one.' So we went to Subhas Chand and looked at the proofs. I said, 'Oh, Lord,' but Hari said they were all pretty good and helped me choose the one to make up cabinet size for you. Afterwards I made him come to Darwaza Chand's with me while I chose that dress length. There were hardly any people shopping at that time. Those who were stared at us in the usual unpleasant manner. When I looked at my watch and saw it was already four o'clock I invited him back to the MacGregor House for tea, but he said, 'No, come to see Aunt Shalini.' I'd not been to his house since the night before the rains set in. I told him I'd like to but I'd better change first. He said, 'Why? Unless you want to tell Lady Chatterjee where you're going.' But it was her purdah hospital committee afternoon, and there wasn't any need to tell Raju, so we set off. We went the Bibighar bridge side. He hated taking me over by the Mandir Gate bridge because that way we had to go through the bazaar. And that's how we were caught, cycling past the Bibighar. Down it came, as it does, and we dashed in there, expecting it to dry up in twenty minutes or so. But it went on and on, and blew up a storm.

I told him the sort of thing I felt about the Bibighar. It was odd, sitting there on the mosaic floor, having to shout to make ourselves heard, then relapsing into silence until the noise outside got less. I asked him to have his picture taken too, but he said he made a rotten photograph. I said, 'Don't be silly. What about those Aunt Shalini showed me?' He said he 'was younger then'! I asked him whether he still heard from those English friends of his, the Lindseys, but he shrugged the question away. He'd always been prickly about them when Aunt Shalini mentioned them. I thought they'd given up writing to him and he felt badly about it, but from something Sister Ludmila asked me the last time I saw her I got the feeling there was more to it than that, something to do with the boy, the Lindsey son, whom Aunt Shalini always described as Hari's greatest friend 'at home'.

Anyway, we were marooned there in the Bibighar and it began to get dark. We'd missed having tea, and I knew I had to be back by seven to change for dinner, because Aunt Lili was having Judge Menen and his wife in, to celebrate Mrs Menen coming out of hospital. I was shivering a bit, and I thought I'd caught a chill. I wanted him to warm me. An English boy would have snuggled up, I suppose, but there we were, with at least a foot or two between us. I got edgy. I wanted to take his hand and hold it to my face.

When we came away, that evening we sheltered from the rains, it felt just as if we had had a quarrel, a lovers' quarrel. But we weren't lovers and there'd been no quarrel. And again I thought: It's wrong, wrong because it doesn't *work*. He saw me home, and although the next day was Sunday neither of us mentioned any arrangement to meet. I was back at the MacGregor a few minutes before Aunt Lili and was soaking in a bath when I heard her calling to Raju on the landing. It was like hearing a homely sound after a long absence. I didn't see Hari again for over a week. I spent an evening or two at the club, once with Ronald and once with the boys and girls, and the rest of my evenings with Lili. But all the time I was thinking of Hari, wanting to see him but not doing anything about it. It was like sitting on a beach as a kid, watching the sea, wanting to go in but not having the courage. Yes – you promise yourself – when this cloud has gone by and the sun comes out then I'll go in. And the cloud goes by and the sun is warm and comforting, and the sea looks chilly.

I told myself the trouble was we'd run out of places to go where the risk of being stared at, the risk of creating a situation, could be minimized. In the club I was definitely getting the cold shoulder from the women. It was this thrashing about for ideas for new places that made me think of the Tirupati temple.

I asked Aunt Lili if English people were ever allowed in. She said she had no idea but imagined none had ever asked, because Mayapore wasn't a tourist town and the temple wasn't famous, but she'd have a word with one of the teachers at the Higher School or Technical College because if an Englishman had been in it would most likely have been a teacher or someone interested in art and culture. She wasn't sure about an English girl being allowed, though. I told her not to bother, because I would ask Hari. She said, 'Yes, you could do that I suppose,' and looked as if she was about to question the whole business of Hari, so I started talking about my day in the hospital to head her off. I wrote a note to Hari just saying, 'I'd love to see inside the Tirupati temple. Could we go together one day? Preferably at night because it always looks more exciting after dark.'

A day or two later he rang up from the *Gazette* office. They hadn't a telephone at Aunt Shalini's. He caught me a few moments before I was due to start out for the hospital and told me that if I really wanted to go he'd ask his uncle. His uncle was the kind of man who paid a lot of money to the priests in the hopes of buying the merit he didn't have time to acquire in any other way. At least that's how Hari put it. I said I really did want to go and that if he'd arrange it for the Saturday evening we could have a quiet dinner together at the MacGregor first, and then come back and play the gramophone. He sounded a bit cool. I had an idea I'd done the wrong thing asking him to take me to a *temple*. But we fixed it on a to-be-confirmed basis for the following Saturday when I knew Lili was playing bridge. Neither of us said anything about meeting meanwhile, although I thought he might turn up on the Tuesday evening at the Sanctuary. He didn't though, and I still hadn't heard from him by the Friday evening.

But I'd seen Ronald at the club, and stayed on to dinner with him. He drove me back to the MacGregor and on the way there he asked me to have dinner with him on the Saturday. I said I couldn't because I was hoping to visit the temple. When he stopped the car at the house there was no one on the porch, no sign of Raju, but he didn't get out to open the door for me. Instead he said, 'Who's taking you? Mr Kumar?' After I'd admitted it he was quiet for a bit, but then came out with what he said he'd been meaning to say for some time, that people were talking about my going out and about with an Indian, which was always tricky, but more tricky these days, especially when the man in question 'hadn't got a very good reputation' and 'tried to make capital out of the fact that he'd lived for a while in England', a fact which he seemed to think 'made him English'.

Then Ronald said, 'You know what I feel for you. It's because I feel it that I haven't said anything to you before. But it's my duty to warn you against this association with Mr Kumar.'

That's when I laughed and said, 'Oh, stop acting like a policeman.'

He said, 'Well, it's partly a police matter. He was under suspicion at one time, and still is, but of course you must know all about that.'

I told him I knew nothing about it at all, and wasn't interested because I'd met Hari at a party at the MacGregor and if Lili thought him the kind of man she could invite to her house that was good enough for me. I said I'd be grateful if people would stop telling me who could be my friends and who not, and that I personally didn't care *what* colour people were, and it was obviously only Hari's colour, the fact that he was an Indian, that got people's goat.

Ronald said, 'That's the oldest trick in the game, to say colour doesn't matter. It does matter. It's basic. It matters like hell.'

I started getting out of the car. He tried to stop me, and took my hand. He said, 'I've put it badly. But I can't help it. The whole idea revolts me.'

I don't know why I was sorry for him. Perhaps because of his honesty. It was like a child's. The kind of self-centred honesty a child shows. We call it innocence. But it is ignorance and cruelty as well. I said, 'It's all right, Ronald. I understand.'

He let go of me as if my arm had scalded him. I shut the door and said, 'Thanks for the meal and for bringing me home,' but it seemed to be the wrong thing to say. There simply wasn't a right thing to say. He drove off and I went into the house.

On Friday evening Hari sent round a chit saying that it was fixed for us to visit the temple the following evening, between 9.30 and 10.30, so I sent the boy back with an answer asking him to come to dinner at 7.30 for 8.

Came Saturday, he arrived promptly, as if to make up for past mistakes. He came in a cycle tonga, which explained the promptness but was probably also meant to point the difference between his life and mine. Somehow that difference became the theme of the evening. He was deliberately trying to put me off. I'm sure of that. For instance, he'd started smoking again, cheap Indian cigarettes – not bidis, but smelly and cumulatively unpleasant. I tried one but hated it, so we ended up smoking our own. He'd also brought a couple of records which he said were a present to me. I wanted to play them right away but he said, no, we'd wait until we got back from the temple, and looked at his watch. It was only 7.45 but he suggested that we ought to start eating. I said, 'Don't you want the other half?' He said he didn't but would wait while I did, which meant he didn't want to, so I told Raju to tell cook we'd eat right away, and we went into the dining-room. When we got in there he complained that the fans were going too fast. I told Raju to turn them to half speed. It got very hot. When the food came in he ignored the forks and began scoffing up mouthfuls with pieces of chappatti. I followed suit. He called out to Raju, 'Boy, bring water', and I began to giggle because it reminded me of the time you and I sat next to that rich Indian family in Delhi and how shocked I was at the apparently rude way the man talked to the waiter, 'Boy, bring this. Boy, bring that', but you pointed out that it was an exact English translation of the pukka sahib's 'Bearer, pani lao.' I thought Hari was having a game, taking off rich Indians of the English-speaking middle class, and wondered if he'd been drinking before he came. Our fingers and mouths were in a bit of a mess by the time we'd finished. Raju – who noticed what was happening even if he didn't understand it – brought in napkins and bowls of warm water, and we washed. I half expected Hari to belch and ask for a toothpick. In its way it was a perfect imitation. Normally he smiled at Raju but apart from his 'Boy, do so and so' he treated him as if he weren't in the room. And I began to wonder whether the Indians had got this habit from the English, or the English from the Indians, or whether the whole thing dated back to some time when servants were treated like dirt everywhere and the habit had only been kept up in the Empire by Sahibs and Memsahibs and modern Indians wanting to be smart.

The other thing Hari was doing, of course, was acting like an

Indian male of that kind, very polite on the surface but underneath selfish and aggressive, ordering the arrangements to his
own but not necessarily anyone else's liking – the curtailment
of the pre-dinner drinks, the early start on the meal – and now
the equally early start going to the temple which ended up by
being a late start because at the last moment he said perhaps we'd
better listen to the records he'd bought so that we could get into
the mood – a curious kind of hark-back to that dance record,
which made me suddenly wary, conscious that the mood Hari
was in was less comic than bitter.

And even over the playing of the gramophone he made us go
through a typical sort of modern Indian farce. Raju was told to
bring the gramophone out, but was shoved aside when it came
to winding the damn' thing up, and sent to look for the needles
which were in the compartment of the gramophone where they
were meant to be, all the time. Hari deliberately scratched the
first record by being clumsy with it and then pretended not to
notice the awful clack clack every time the needle jumped over
the dent in the groove. And he had chosen Indian music, something terribly difficult, an evening raga that went on and on.
What he didn't reckon with was the fact that I instinctively loved
it. When he saw that I did, he changed the record before it
was finished, and put on one that excited and moved me even
more. The odd thing was I could see it really made *him* savagely
irritated and seeing that, the idea that he had been having a joke
with me just wouldn't hold water any longer. I felt lost, because
I realized he had been trying in his own way to put me off, as
Ronald and everyone wanted, and that he was sufficiently fond
of me personally to believe that what he hated – the music, and
eating with your fingers – I would hate too. His discovery that
I didn't hate it, but loved it or didn't mind it, was another gulf
between us, one for which there was no accounting, because
I was white and he was black, and my liking for what he hated
or had never had the patience or inclination to learn to like, to
get back to, made even his blackness look spurious; like that of
someone made up to act a part.

He let the second record play to the end, and then *I* took
charge and said, 'We'd better go', and called out to Raju to bring
my scarf. I had an idea I'd need to cover my head to go into the
temple. Hari had brought an umbrella in case it rained while we

weren't under cover. On the way to the temple in the cycle tonga we said almost nothing. I'd not been in a cycle tonga before. To shift the weight of two people the poor boy had to stand out of the saddle and lean his whole strength on each pedal alternately. But I liked it better than the horse tongas, because we faced the way we were going. To travel in a horse tonga, facing backwards (which I suppose one does to avoid the smell if the horse breaks wind) always gives me a feeling of trying to hang back, of not wanting things to disappear. With the cycle tonga there was the opposite feeling, of facing the road ahead, of knowing it better and not being scared when you had to get out.

At the temple entrance there was a man waiting for us, a temple servant who spoke a bit of English. We took our shoes off in the archway of the main gate, and Hari paid some money over that his uncle had given him. I couldn't see how much it was but guessed from the attention we got that it was probably quite a lot, more than Hari had ever been given by his uncle before.

Well, you've been in temples. Isn't it odd how even with all that noise outside, to go in is like entering somewhere quite cut off – not a place of quiet – but cut off, reserved for a human activity that doesn't need *other* human activity to make it function itself. Churches are quiet in this way, but then they are usually quiet because they are empty. The temple wasn't quiet. It wasn't empty. But it was cut off. Once through the archway you walked into the *idea* of being alone. I was glad to have Hari with me, because my *skin* was afraid, although I wasn't afraid *inside* the skin. I was astonished by the sight of men and women just squatting around, under the trees in the courtyard, squatting in that wholly Indian peasant way, self-supported on the haunches, with arms stretched out and balanced on the bent knees, and the bottom not quite touching the earth. Gossiping. At first I was critical of this, until I remembered that the shrine in the centre of the courtyard was the real temple, and outside it was like the outside of a church where our Sunday-morning congregations gather and chat after the service.

Around the walls of the courtyard there were the shrines of various aspects of the Hindu gods. Some awake and lit, some asleep and dark. In those doll-like figures there's a look of what puritans call the tawdriness of Roman Catholicism, isn't there?

The dolls seemed to reflect that, but knowingly, as if pointing a moral – the absurdity of the need which the poor and ignorant have for images. Hari said, 'The guide wants to know if we'd like to make *puja* to the Lord Venkataswara.'

The holy of holies! I was excited. I hadn't expected to be allowed in there, and I was very conscious of the uniqueness of being allowed. Every so often one was startled by the ringing of a bell at the entrance to the central shrine. There were men and women waiting. Our guide forced his way through to take us in ahead of them. I hated that. He spoke to a priest who was standing watching us. Then he came and said something long and involved to Hari. I was surprised that Hari seemed to understand. When he replied to the man's question I realized Hari had learned more of the language than he was prepared to let on and only here, in the temple, couldn't keep up the pretence. He turned to me and said, 'I have to ring the bell to warn the god that we're here. When I've done so, look as if you're praying. Goodness knows what we're in for.'

I put my scarf on my head. The priest was watching us all the time. The bell was hung on a chain from the roof of the shrine at the head of the steps. I could see the inside now, a narrow passage leading to a brightly lit grotto, and the idol with a black face and gilt robes and silver ornaments. Hari reached up and pulled the rope that moved the tongue of the bell, then put his hands together. I followed suit and closed my eyes and waited until I heard him say, 'We go in now.'

He led the way. There were ordinary tubular steel bars in the passage, forming a barricade. We took up position round them with several other people – rather as at a communion rail, except that we stood and didn't kneel, and the bars formed a rectangle, with us on the outside and a space on the inside for the priest to come down from the little grotto. He was standing by the grotto while we were sorting ourselves out, and then came with a gilt cup. We held our hands out, as for the Host, and he poured what looked like water into them. He went to the Indians first, to make sure we'd know what to do. We raised the liquid to our lips. It was sweet-sour tasting, and stung a bit. Perhaps because our lips were dry. After we'd carried our hands to our lips we had to pass them over our heads, rather like making a sign of the cross. Then the priest came back with a golden cap – a sort of

basin, and held it over our heads, and intoned prayers for each
of us. He also had a gilt tray and when he'd finished with the
cap he put it back on the tray. Round the tray there were little
mounds of coloured powder and some petals. He stuck his finger
in the powder and marked our foreheads. The petals turned out
to be a small string of roses, and he gave them to me, putting
them round my neck. It seemed to be all over in a second or
two. On the way out Hari put some more money on a tray held
by another priest at the door.

I felt nothing while I was doing *puja*. But when I came out my
lips were still stinging and I could smell the sweet-sourness everywhere. I had a suspicion that we'd drunk cow urine. People were
staring at us. I felt protected from their hostility, if it was hostility
and not just curiosity, protected by the mark on my forehead
and the little string of red rose petals. I still have the petals, Auntie.
They are in a white paper bag, with Sister Ludmila's text, in the
suitcase. Dry and brown now. The faintest wind would blow
them into fragments.

There was one other thing to do, something to see, an image
of the sleeping Vishnu. Lord Venkataswara, the god of the
temple, is a manifestation of Vishnu, although the black, silver
and gold image looked to me far from that of a preserver. The
sleeping Vishnu had a grotto to himself, behind the main shrine.
The grotto was built into the outer wall. You had to go into it
and then turn a corner before you found the god asleep on his
stone bed. Only three or four people could get in at once. Inside
it was cool. The place was lit by oil lamps and the god was quite
a shock. One had expected something small, miniature, like the
rest: instead, this bigger than lifesize reclining figure that overpowered you with a sense of greater strength in sleep than in
wakefulness. And such good dreams he was dreaming! Dreams
that made him smile.

I could have stood and watched him for ages, but Hari nudged
me and whispered that there were other people waiting to come
in. We had to force our way through them, back into the courtyard. We went to the other gateway, the one that looked out on
to the steps leading down to the river. After *puja* one should
bathe, but there was only one man doing so at that moment. We
could just make him out, standing in the water up to his waist.
His head was shaved. Nearby there was a shed and platform

where the temple barbers worked, and where devotees gave their hair to the god.

Hari said, 'Shall we go and get our shoes?' He had had enough. Perhaps I had too, because I wasn't part of its outwardness at all. I felt like a trespasser. So we went back through the courtyard and collected our shoes. More money passed. I suppose it all goes into the pockets of the priests. At the gateway we were besieged by beggars. Our tonga boy was waiting for us and saw us before we saw him, and came pressing forward, ringing his bell and shouting, afraid that one of the other tonga boys would slip in and take us away. We were back in the din and the dirt. There was music from a coffee shop over the road. With my shoes back on, my feet felt gritty. Deliberately I'd not worn stockings.

When we got back to the MacGregor House we sat on the verandah. I asked Hari to send the tonga boy round to the back to get some food. He didn't look more than seventeen or so – a cheerful, pleasant boy who obviously felt that with this long evening hire his luck was in. Alone for a moment I went round the back and called Raju, and asked him to bring the boy to me. He appeared from nowhere, as if he'd been expecting me. I gave him ten chips. A fortune. But he deserved it. And it was part of my *puja*. I think Raju disapproved. Perhaps he extracted a percentage, or gave the boy short commons or no commons at all. In the end one can't bear it any more – the indifference of one Indian for another – and doesn't want to know what goes on.

It came on to rain, which drove us in from the verandah. Hari's earlier mood had gone. He looked exhausted, as if he had failed – not just at whatever he had set out to achieve that evening but at everything he'd set his heart on. I wanted to have it out with him, but it was difficult to know how to begin. And when we began it started off all wrong because I said, 'You've been trying to put me off, haven't you?'

He pretended not to understand and said, 'Put off? What do you mean, put off?' Which frustrated me so that I said, as if I were in a temper, 'Oh, put off, put me off, put me off *you*, like everybody else has tried.'

He asked who 'everybody else' was.

I said, 'Well, everybody. People like Mr Merrick for instance. He thinks you're a bad bet.'

Hari said, 'Well, he should know, I suppose.'

I told him that was a ridiculous thing to say because only he knew what kind of bet he was. He said, 'What's all this talk about anyway? What does it mean, bet? Good bet, bad bet? What am I supposed to be, a racehorse or something? Some kind of stock or share people keep an eye on to see if it's worth investing in?'

I'd not seen him angry before. He'd not seen me angry either. We lost our tempers, which is why I don't remember just what it was we said that led me to accuse him of criticizing a man he'd probably never met, and then to the realization that we'd been talking at cross purposes because no one had ever told me it was Ronald who took him into custody and stood by and watched him hit by one of his subordinates. I remember saying something like, 'You mean it was Ronald himself?' and I can still see the surprise on his face when the penny dropped at last and he knew I really hadn't known.

If only I'd contained my anger then. Well, I tried, because I wasn't angry with him but with Ronald, other people, myself as much as anybody. I said, 'Where did it happen, then?' and again he looked astonished. He said, 'Well, in the Sanctuary of course.' That was another blow. I asked him to tell me about it.

He'd been drunk. He wouldn't say why. He'd wandered out as drunk as a coot and collapsed in a ditch in that awful waste ground near the river and been picked up by Sister Ludmila and her helpers who thought he'd been attacked or was ill, or dying, until they got him back to the Sanctuary. He slept it off there, and in the morning Ronald came to the Sanctuary with some policemen, looking for a man who'd escaped from a jail, and was thought to have come back to Mayapore because that was where the escaped man used to live. He wasn't there, but Hari was. Well, you can imagine it, I expect, imagine how Hari would react to being browbeaten by a man like Ronald. The sub-inspector accompanying Ronald hit Hari in the face for not answering 'smartly', and in the end he was hustled away and punched and kicked when he got into the back of the truck.

One trouble was that he knew the man the police were look-ing for. This came out while Ronald questioned him in front of the sub-inspector at the kotwali. But he'd only known him as a clerk in his uncle's warehouse. Another trouble was that Hari deliberately made a point of confusing the police about his name. Coomer. Kumar. He said 'either would do'. Finally Ronald sent the sub-inspector out of the room and talked to Hari alone, or tried to talk to him, which was probably difficult because Hari had taken a dislike to him. I don't know why Hari got drunk. Perhaps from an accumulation of blows that had finally made him feel he cared for nothing and believed in nothing. He told me he was convinced he was going to be locked up anyway, so didn't watch his tongue. I think from the way he told me all this he was trying to help find excuses for Ronald that he couldn't find himself. Ronald asked him why he'd got drunk, and where. Hari wouldn't say where because he thought – and said – that where was none of Ronald's business – but gladly explained why. He explained it by saying he'd got drunk because he hated the whole damned stinking country, the people who lived in it and the people who ran it. He even said, 'And that goes for you too, Merrick.' He knew Merrick's name because he'd often been in the courts as a reporter. He said Merrick only smiled when he said 'and that goes for you too', and then told him he could go, and even apologized – sarcastically of course – for having 'inconvenienced him'. When he got back home he discovered Sister Ludmila had scared up some influential people to ask questions about his 'arrest' but this only amused him, if amused is the right word to use when he was really feeling bitter. He said it had amused him when eventually Lili invited him to a party, and also amused him to see Merrick watching the way I went up to him that day on the *maidan*. I didn't know Ronald had seen that, but it fitted in. Hari thought I had always known the whole story, and was only condescending to him when I broke away from the white officers and white nurses to throw a crumb of comfort to him.

I said, 'So it's amused you whenever we've been out together?'

He said, 'Yes, you could put it that way. If you want to. But you've been very kind, and I'm grateful.'

I said, 'I didn't mean anything as kindness,' and stood up. He stood up too. He would only have had to touch me, for the stupidity to have ended then, but he didn't. He was afraid to. He was too conscious of the weight that would have made touching a gesture of defiance of the rule Ronald had described a few evenings before as 'basic', and he didn't have that kind of courage, and so I was deprived of my own. The defiance had to come from him first, to make it human, to make it right.

I said, 'Goodnight, Hari.' Oh, even in that goodnight there was a way left open to him that 'goodbye' would have closed. But I mustn't blame him. He had good reasons to be afraid. I rehearsed them to myself upstairs in my room, sitting, waiting, determining to have things out with Lili. When I heard the cycle tonga go down the drive my determination began to go with it, and then I was worried, worried for him, because he was a man who would find it awfully difficult to hide, and I believed that was what he wanted to do. To hide. To disappear into a sea of brown faces.

That word Ronald Merrick used was the right one – association. Hari and I could be enemies, or strangers to each other, or lovers, but never friends because such a friendship was put to the test too often to survive. We were constantly having to ask the question, Is it worth it? Constantly having to examine our motives for wanting to be together. On my side the motive was physical attraction. I didn't have enough self-confidence to assure myself that Hari felt the same for me. But this didn't change what I felt. I was in love with him. I wanted him near me. I told myself I didn't care what people said. I didn't care what he'd done, or what people like Ronald Merrick thought he'd done or was capable of doing. I wanted to protect him from danger. If it helped him not to be seen with me any longer I was prepared to let him go, to let him hide. But because I was in love I kidded myself there was a time limit to 'any longer', a magic formula that took the sting out of the decision I made to let the next move come from him.

When Lili asked me next morning about the visit to the temple I chatted away as if nothing had happened. Several times I was on the point of saying, 'Did you know it was Ronald who arrested Hari?' But I didn't want to hear her say yes. I didn't want to pave the way to a discussion that might have forced Lili to confess for instance that she had since had doubts about Hari and regretted her haste in rushing to the defence of a man she didn't know but had since learned more of that made her feel Ronald had been right to suspect him and done nothing he need be ashamed of when he took Hari in for questioning.

I knew that Lili would be the first to realize something had happened between Hari and myself if the days went by without any word from him or meeting between us. I was aware of helping him by keeping quiet, aware of distracting attention from him, but not aware then of the truth of what I was actually doing – indulging my unfulfilled passion for him by weaving a protective web round him which even excluded me. I didn't feel that it excluded me. Later I did.

I went about my job, my ordinary life. No letter from him. To avoid having to answer Lili's questions, if she decided to ask them, I took to going almost every evening to the club. And people noticed it. I was glad they did. If I was at the club obviously I wasn't out with Hari. The first time I saw Ronald there he came up to me and said; 'Did you enjoy the temple?' I shrugged and said, 'Oh, it was all right. A bit of a racket, though. You can't say boo without it costing money.' He smiled. I couldn't tell whether he was pleased or puzzled. I wondered whether he saw through my casual pretence, but then decided that even if he saw through it he wouldn't see what lay behind it. I hated him that night. Hated him and smiled at him. Played the game. And again felt how easy it was, how simple. To act at conforming. Because all the time there was nothing to conform with, except an idea, a charade played round a phrase: white superiority.

And all the time wanting Hari. Seeing him in my imagination looking over the shoulder of every pink male face and seeing in every pink male face the strain of pretending that the world was this small. Hateful. Ingrown. About to explode like powder compressed ready for firing.

I thought that the whole bloody affair of *us* in India had reached flash point. It was bound to because it was based on a violation. Perhaps at one time there was a moral as well as a physical force at work. But the moral thing had gone sour. Has gone sour. Our faces reflect the sourness. The women look worse than the men because consciousness of physical superiority is unnatural to us. A white man in India can feel physically superior without unsexing himself. But what happens to a woman if she tells herself that ninety-nine per cent of the men she sees are not men at all, but creatures of an inferior species whose colour is their main distinguishing mark? What happens when you unsex a nation, treat it like a nation of eunuchs? Because that's what we've done, isn't it?

God knows what happens. What will happen. The whole thing seems to go from bad to worse, year after year. There's dishonesty on both sides because the moral issue has gone sour on them as well as on us. We're back to basics, the basic issue of who jumps and who says jump. Call it by any fancy name you like, even 'the greatest experiment of colonial government and civilizing influence since pre-Christian Rome', to quote our old friend Mr Swinson. It's become a vulgar scramble for power on their part and an equally vulgar smug hanging on on ours. And the greater their scramble the greater our smugness. You can't hide that any longer because the moral issue, if it ever really existed at all, is dead. It's our fault it's dead because it was our responsibility to widen it, but we narrowed it down and narrowed it down by never suiting actions to words. We never suited them because out here, where they *needed* to be suited and to be seen to be suited, that old primitive savage instinct to attack and destroy what we didn't understand because it looked different and was different always got the upper hand. And God knows how many centuries you have to go back to trace to its source their apparent fear of skins paler than their own. God help us if they ever lose that fear. Perhaps fear is the wrong word. In India anyway. It is such a primitive emotion and their civilization is so old. So perhaps I should say God help us if ever they substitute fear for tiredness. But tiredness is the wrong word too. Perhaps we haven't got a word for what they feel. Perhaps it's hidden in that stone carving of Vishnu sleeping, looking as if he might wake at any minute and take them to oblivion in a crack of happy thunder.

Was this the difference between my own emotions and Hari's? That he could wait and I couldn't? In the end I couldn't bear the silence, the inaction, the separation, the artificiality of my position. I wrote to him. I had no talent for self-denial. It's an Anglo-Saxon failing, I suppose. Constantly we want proof, here and now, proof of our existence, of the mark we've made, the sort of mark we can wear round our necks, to label us, to make sure we're never lost in that awful dark jungle of anonymity.

But in my impatience there was Anglo-Saxon planning, forethought, an acceptance that time went through certain fixed exercises that the clock and the calendar had been invented to define. The farther away from the equator you get the more sensitive you become to the rhythm of light and dark, the way it expands and contracts and organizes the seasons, so that time itself develops a specific characteristic that alerts you to its absurd but meticulous demands. If I'd been an Indian girl perhaps I'd have said in my note to Hari: Tonight, please. Instead I gave three or four days' notice. Three or four. I forget which, which shows how unimportant the actual number was, how unimportant as well the actual day suggested – although I remember that. As everybody probably does. August the ninth. In my note I said I was sorry for any misunderstanding, and that I wanted to talk to him. I said I'd go to the Sanctuary on that evening and hoped to meet him there.

I got no reply, but when the day came I felt happy, almost lightheaded. At breakfast time the telephone rang. I thought it was Hari and rushed to answer before Raju could get there. It wasn't Hari. It was little Mrs Srinivasan wanting to speak to Lili. I sent Raju up to Lili's bedroom to tell her to pick up the extension. When I went up to say goodbye to her Lili said, 'They've arrested Vassi.'

Well, you know all that side of things. We'd been prepared for it but it was a shock when it actually happened. When I got to the hospital the girls were acting as if they'd been personally responsible for saving the day by locking up the Mahatma and his colleagues and Congressmen all over the country. A year earlier most of them wouldn't even have known what Congress was. The atmosphere in the hospital that morning was like that in the club at the end of War Week. One of them said, 'Have you noticed the orderlies? They've got their tails between their legs all right.' Once this had been pointed out the girls seemed to go out of their way to find new methods of humiliating them. And there was a subtle change in their attitude to me, as if they were trying to make me feel that I'd been backing the wrong horse for months.

It wasn't until the afternoon that they began to get scared. First there was the rumour of rioting in the sub-divisions, then the confirmation that the assistant commissioner had gone out with police patrols to find out why contact couldn't be made with a place called Tanpur. It came on to rain. And about a quarter to five, when I was getting ready to go off duty, there was a flap because Mr Poulson had brought in the mission teacher, Miss Crane. At first we thought she'd been raped, but I got the true story from Mr Poulson. I saw him as I was going to Matron's office. Miss Crane had been attacked on her way home from Dibrapur, and had her car burnt out, and had seen one of her teachers – an Indian – murdered. She was suffering from shock and exposure. She'd sat on the roadside guarding the murdered man's body. As I'd met Miss Crane once at the Deputy Commissioner's bungalow I got permission from Matron to go in and see her. But she was already wandering and didn't recognize me. I thought she was for it. She kept saying, 'I'm sorry. Sorry it's too late,' mumbling about there having been too many chappattis for her to eat alone, and asking why I hadn't shared them, why had I gone hungry? I held her hand and tried to make contact with her but all she would do for a while was keep repeating, 'I'm sorry it's too late.' But suddenly she said, 'Mine's Edwina Crane and my mother's been dead for longer than I care to remember,' and then went off into a delirium about mending the roof and there being nothing she could do. 'Nothing,' she said, over and over. 'There's nothing I can do.'

It was raining when I left the hospital.* There was no sign of Ronald's driver or of the truck. He would have been busy that evening anyway. But I had my bicycle and my rain cape and sou'wester. I'd told Lili that I'd be calling in at the club and I'd also promised to see the girls there, but looking in on Miss Crane had made me late and so I cycled direct to the Sanctuary, down Hospital road, Victoria road, and over the river by way of the Bibighar bridge. Perhaps the rain as well as the rumours was keeping nearly everyone indoors, because I saw few people. I got to the Sanctuary at about 5.45. The rain was letting up a bit then.

I've never described the Sanctuary to you, have I? You turn off the Chillianwallah Bagh Extension road along a track that skirts the waste ground near the river where the poorest untouchables live in horrible squalid huts. Then you come to a walled compound in which there are three old buildings that date back to the early nineteenth century. One is the office, the other the clinic and Sister Ludmila's 'cell' and the third and largest the place

*Section of Journal shown to Robin White begins here.

where she tends the sick and dying. There must be nearly an acre of ground enclosed by those walls. The place looks derelict and you can smell the river most of the time. But inside the buildings everything is clean and neat, scrubbed and whitewashed.

She has one principal assistant, a middle-aged Goanese called de Souza, and several men and women whom she hires at random. I've always wondered where her money comes from.

Hari wasn't there. I went to the office first and saw Mr de Souza. He said Sister Ludmila was in her room, and that no one had turned up so far for the evening clinic, probably because of the rumours of trouble. I went across to the clinic and knocked at her door. I'd not seen her since the week of the visit to the temple. She knew Hari and I had been planning to go there. She asked me to come in and tell her about it.

The rain stopped and in about ten minutes or so the sun came out, as it often does, at the end of an afternoon's wet, but of course it was already setting. She said, 'Will Hari be coming?' I told her I wasn't sure. And then she asked me about the temple. She herself had never been inside it. I described our *puja* to the Lord Venkataswara and the image of the sleeping Vishnu. I wanted to ask her about the night she found Hari lying drunk in a ditch in the waste-land outside the Sanctuary, but didn't. As the minutes went by and he still did not come I thought, 'It's all going, going away before I've touched any of it or understood any of it.' I watched the wooden carving of the Dancing Siva. It seemed to move. There came a point when I couldn't watch it any longer because it was draining me of my own mobility. I felt I was becoming lost in it.

I turned to her. She always sat very upright, on a hard wooden chair, with her hands folded on her lap, showing her wedding ring. I never saw her without her cap so I don't know whether she'd shorn her hair. On other occasions when I'd been in her room its bareness and simplicity had always conveyed an idea to me of its safety, but this evening I thought, 'No, it's her safety, not the room's.' I felt this going away from me too. There was so much I wanted to know about her, but I'd only once asked her a personal question. She spoke English very well, but with a strong accent. I'd asked her where she'd learned it and she said, 'From my husband. His name was Smith.' One heard many different tales about her – for instance that she had run away from a convent as a young novice and wore the nunnish clothing in the hope of being forgiven. I don't think this was true. I think there was no tale about her that was true. Only her charity was true. For me it always outweighed my curiosity. When you spoke to her there wasn't any mystery. In herself she was all the explanation I felt she needed. And that is rare, isn't it? To be explained by yourself, by what you are and what you do, and not by what you've done, or were, or by what people think you might be or might become.

I stayed for an hour, until it was dusk. I told myself that Hari was probably working late, but I knew this didn't explain his silence. I wondered whether he had been arrested again but decided that was unlikely. The arrests that had been made were of prominent members of the local Congress, like Vasi. I thought of calling in at Aunt Shalini's but when I got out on the Chillianwallah Bagh Extension road I changed my mind and turned in the direction of the Bibighar bridge. It was almost dark. Thinking it might rain again I'd put my cape and sou'wester back on instead of strapping them to the carrier, and it was warm and clammy. I crossed the bridge and the level crossing. When I got to the street lamp opposite the Bibighar I stopped and took the cape off, and put it over the handlebars. It was stopping like this that made me wheel the bike across the road to look in through the gate of the Bibighar. When I stopped I'd had a strong impression of Hari in the Bibighar, sitting in the pavilion alone, not expecting me, but thinking of me, wondering whether I would turn up.

I went through the open gateway and along the path to the place where we always left our cycles – a place where we could lean them against the wall but keep an eye on them from the pavilion. When I got to this place there was no cycle. I looked across in the direction of the pavilion. At first there was nothing, but then I saw the glow of a cigarette being drawn on. I suppose the distance between the path by the wall and the pavilion is about a hundred yards. You can walk it straight by going up over what was once the lawn and the series of little steps. That's why we usually left our cycles against the wall, to save lugging them up the steps. The other way to the pavilion is by the path that skirts the grounds. I wasn't sure whether it was Hari in the pavilion and so I went up by the path.

When I got round to the side of the pavilion I could see the man standing on the mosaic platform. I said, 'Hari, is that you?' He said, 'Yes.' I turned the lamp off and left the cycle against a tree and then went up to the pavilion. When I got there I found I'd brought the cape with me.

I said, 'Didn't you get my note?' But it was a silly thing to ask. He didn't answer. I felt for a cigarette and realized I'd run out. I asked him for one of his. He gave it to me. It made me cough, so I threw it away. I sat down on the mosaic. The roof overhangs the edge and the mosaic is always dry. There was no need for the cape. I put it on the ground nearby. With so many trees around it sounds as if it's raining long after it has stopped. The water drips from the roof as well as from the leaves. Eventually he sat down too and lit another cigarette. I said, 'Let me try one of those again.' He opened the packet and held it out. I took a cigarette. Then I took hold of his hand, the one in which he held his own cigarette, and lit mine from his. I smoked without inhaling. After a while he said, 'What were you trying to prove? That you don't mind our touching?'

I said, 'I thought we'd got beyond that.'

'No,' he said, 'we can never get beyond it.'

I said, 'But we have. *I* have. It was never an obstacle anyway. At least not for me.'

He asked why I'd come to the Bibighar. I told him I'd waited for an hour at the Sanctuary, that I'd looked in on my way past because I thought he might be there.

After a while he said, 'You oughtn't to be out alone tonight. I'll see you home. Throw that disgusting thing away.'

He waited, then leaned towards me and held my wrist and took the cigarette and threw it into the garden. I couldn't bear it, having him so near, knowing I was about to lose him. That catching hold of my wrist was like the impatient gesture of a lover. For him it was like that too. I willed him not to let go. There was an instant when I was afraid, perhaps because he wanted me to be. But then we were kissing. His shirt had rucked up because he was wearing it loose over his waistband and my hand was touching his bare back, and then we were both lost. There was nothing gentle in the way he took me. I felt myself lifted on to the mosaic. He tore at my underclothes and pressed down on me with all his strength. But this was not me and Hari. Entering me he made me cry out. And then it was us.

*

They came when we lay half-asleep listening to the croaking of
the frogs, his hand covering one breast, my own in his black hair,
moving to trace the miracle of his black ear.

Five or six men. Suddenly. Climbing on to the platform. My
nightmare faces. But not faces. Black shapes in white cotton
clothing; stinking, ragged clothing. Converging on Hari, pulling
him away. And then darkness. And a familiar smell. But hot and
suffocating. Covering my head. As I began to struggle I could
think of nothing but the thing that covered my head. I knew it,
but did not know it because it was smothering me. And then
there was a moment – the moment, I suppose, when the man
holding me down and covering me with this suffocating but
familiar thing, lifted his weight away – a moment when I forgot
the covering and felt only my exposed nakedness. He must have
lifted his weight away when the others had finished dealing with
Hari and came to help. There was pressure on my knees and
ankles and then my wrists – a moment of terrible openness and
vulnerability and then the first experience of that awful animal
thrusting, the motion of love without one saving split-second of
affection.

I no longer dream of faces. In bad dreams now I'm usually blind.
This kind of dream begins with the image of Siva. I see him only
with my sense of recollection. Suddenly he leaves his circle of
cosmic fire and covers me, imprisons my arms and legs in darkness. Surreptitiously, I grow an extra arm to fight him or
embrace him, but he always has an arm to spare to pin me down,
a new lingam growing to replace the one that's spent. This dream
ends when I'm no longer blind and see the expression on his
face which is one of absolution and invitation. I wake then,
remembering how after they had gone I found myself holding
my rain cape, breathing, aware of the blessing of there being air
with which to fill my lungs, and thinking, 'It was mine, my own
cape that I use to keep the rain off, mine all the time, part of my
life.' I clung to the cape. I held it to my body, covering myself.
I thought I was alone. I had this idea that Hari had gone with
them because he had been one of them.

But then I saw him, the shape of him, lying as I was lying, on
the mosaic. They had bound his hands and mouth and ankles

with strips of cloth, torn for all I knew from their own clothing, and then placed him where he would have had to close his eyes if he didn't want to see what was happening.

I crawled like a kid across the mosaic and struggled with the knots, struggled because they were tight and difficult and because I was also trying to cover myself with the cape. I untied the gag round his mouth first, in case he was finding it difficult to breathe, and then the strips of rag round his ankles, and then the one round his wrists. And as I untied him he continued to lie as they had left him, so that presently I gathered him in my arms because I couldn't bear it. I couldn't bear the sound of him crying.

He cried for shame, I suppose, and for what had happened to me that he'd been powerless to stop. He said something that I was too dazed to catch but thinking back on it it always comes to me as an inarticulate begging for forgiveness.

I was suddenly very cold. He felt me shivering. Now *he* held *me*, and for a time we clung to each other like two children frightened of the dark. But I couldn't stop shivering. He moved the cape until it was round my shoulders and then covered me at the front. He got up and searched for things that belonged to me. I felt them in his hands and took them from him. He said, 'Put your arms round my neck.' I did so. He lifted me and carried me over to the steps and down them one at a time. I thought of all the steps between the pavilion and the gate, and then of the bicycle. I thought he was going to carry me across the garden, but he turned on to the path. When he went past the place where I'd left the bicycle I said, 'No, it's here some-where.' He didn't understand. I said, 'My bicycle.' He put me down but continued to hold me. He said he couldn't see it, that the men must have stolen it or hidden it. He said he'd come back in the morning to look for it. I asked him about his own bicycle. He'd left it in the bazaar to be repaired. He'd not had it all day. He picked me up again and carried me down the path. I felt myself becoming a dead weight in his arms. I asked him to put me down. He did so but then lifted me again. While we were in the garden I let him do this. If I'd asked him to carry me all the way to the MacGregor House I think he'd have man-aged it somehow. But when we got to the gateway and he put me down again – as if to catch his breath – the world outside the garden came back into focus. On the other side of the gate there was the beginning of what another white girl would have thought of as safety. It was safety of a kind for me too. But not for him. When he moved to pick me up again I pushed him away – as you'd push away a child who was reaching out to touch something that would burn it or scald it. Seeing the gateway I imagined him carrying me through it, into the light, into the cantonment.

I said, 'No. I've got to go home alone. We've not been together. I've not seen you.'

He tried to take hold of my arm. I moved away from him. I said, 'No. Let me go. You've not been near me. You don't know anything. You know nothing. Say nothing.' He wouldn't listen. He caught me, tried to hold me close, but I struggled. I was in a panic, thinking of what they'd do to him. No one would believe me. He said, 'I've got to be with you. I love you. Please let me be with you.'

If he hadn't said that perhaps I'd have given in. The thought that he was right and I was wrong and that the only way to have faced it was with the truth is one of the things I have to puzzle over now and carry with me – a burden as heavy if less obvious than the child. And you may wonder why when he said he loved me my determination to resist didn't come abruptly to an end. But love isn't like that, is it? It wasn't for me. It bewildered me. It sent me from panic to worse panic, because of what they might do to him if he said to *them*, 'I love her. We love each other.'

I beat at him, not to escape myself but to make *him* escape. I was trying to beat sense and reason and cunning into him. I kept saying, 'We've never seen each other. You've been at home. You say nothing. You know nothing. Promise me.'

I was free and began to run without waiting to hear him promise. At the gate he caught me and tried to hold me back. Again I asked him to let me go, *please* to let me go, to say nothing, to know nothing, *for my sake* if that was the only way he could say nothing and know nothing for his own. For an instant I held him close – it was the last time I touched him – and then I broke free again and was out of the gateway and running; running into and out of the light of the street lamp opposite, running into the dark and grateful for the dark, going without any understanding of direction. I stopped and leaned against a wall. I wanted to turn back. I wanted to admit that I couldn't face it alone. And I wanted him to know that I thought I'd done it all wrong. He wouldn't know what I felt, what I meant. I was in pain. I was exhausted. And frightened. Too frightened to turn back.

I said, 'There's nothing I can do, nothing, nothing,' and wondered where I'd heard those words before, and began to run again, through those awful ill-lit deserted roads that should have been leading me home but were leading me nowhere I recognized; into safety that wasn't safety because beyond it there were the plains and the openness that made it seem that if I ran long enough I would run clear off the rim of the world.*

It seemed so simple at the time to say, 'Hari wasn't there,' and to feel, just by saying it, that I put him out of harm's reach. It's all too easy now to think that his only real protection was the truth, however disagreeable it would have been for us to tell it, to have it told, however threatening and dangerous the truth would have been for him. Well, if he had been an Englishman – that young subaltern who began to paw me at the War Week dance, for instance – the truth would have worked and it would never have occurred to us to tell anything else, I suppose. When people realized what he and I had been doing in the Bibighar they would have stood by us while they tried to see justice done, and then when it had been done or when they'd pursued every possible line to an end short of justice because the men couldn't be caught turned round and made it clear that it was now our duty, mine in particular, to make ourselves scarce.

But it wasn't an Englishman. And of course there are people who would say that it would never have happened if it had been, and I expect they would be right because he and I would never have had to go to the Bibighar to be alone, we would never have been there after dark. He would have seduced me in the back of a truck in the car park of the Gymkhana club, or in the place behind the changing-rooms of the swimming-pool, or in a room in one of the chummeries, or even in my bedroom at the MacGregor on a night Lili was out playing bridge. And there are people who would say that even if this subaltern and I had made love in the pavilion in the Bibighar we would never have

*End of section of Journal shown to Robin White.

been attacked by a gang of Indian hooligans. Which is probably right too, although their reasons for saying so wouldn't be strictly correct. They'd invest the subaltern with some sort of superman quality that enabled him to make short work of a gang of bloody wogs, whereas, in fact, the gang of bloody wogs would have been made short work of by their own fear of white people. Miss Crane was hit a few times, but it was the Indian teacher with her who was murdered. They assaulted me because they had watched an Indian making love to me. The taboo was broken for them.

I think Hari understood this. I think this is what he saw and was ashamed of and asked to be forgiven for. All that I saw was the danger to him as a black man carrying me through a gateway that opened on to the world of white people.

I look for similes, for something that explains it more clearly, but find nothing, because there *is* nothing. It is itself; an Indian carrying an English girl he has made love to and been forced to watch being assaulted – carrying her back to where she would be safe. It is its own simile. It says all that needs to be said, doesn't it? If you extend it, if you think of him carrying me all the way to the MacGregor House, giving me into Aunt Lili's care, ringing for the doctor, ringing for the police, answering questions, and being treated as a man who'd rescued me, the absurdity, the implausibility become almost unbearable. Directly you get to the point where Hari, taken on one side by Ronald for instance, has to say, 'Yes, we were making love,' the nod of understanding that *must* come from Ronald *won't*, unless you blanch Hari's skin, blanch it until it looks not just like that of a white man but like that of a white man too shaken for another white man not to feel sorry for, however much he may reproach him.

And that is why I fought him, why I beat at him, why I said, 'We've not seen each other. You know nothing.'

So easy to say. 'I've not seen Hari. I've not seen Hari since we visited the temple.' That's what I told Lili when I was lying on the sofa in the living-room. She had understood at last what was wrong and had asked, 'Was it Hari?' And out it came, perhaps too glibly, but incontrovertible. 'No. No. I've not seen Hari. I've not seen him since we visited the temple.'

'Who was it, then?' she asked. I couldn't look at her. I said,

'I don't know. Five or six men. I didn't see. It was dark. They covered my head.'

Then if you didn't see them, how can you be sure one of them wasn't Hari Kumar? That was a question that had to be answered, wasn't it? She didn't ask it. Instead she said, 'Where?' and I said, 'The Bibighar,' and again there was a question. What was I doing in the Bibighar? It wasn't asked. Not then. Not by Lili. But the trap was beginning to close. It had been closing ever since I got back and stumbled and fell on the steps of the verandah.

I hurt my knee badly. I think I passed out for a few seconds. When I came to, and was trying to get up, Lili was there staring at me as if she didn't recognize me. I remember her saying the name Raju. I suppose she called him to help or he'd come out with her. The next thing I remember is being in the living-room and being given a glass of brandy. Raju and Bhalu must have carried me in. I remember Bhalu standing on the rug without his chappals. His bare feet. And Raju's bare feet. Black hands. And black faces. After I'd drunk the brandy Lili asked them to carry memsahib upstairs. When they came towards me I couldn't bear it and began to cry out and tell her to send them away. It was then that Lili knew what had happened. When I opened my eyes again she and I were alone and I was ashamed to look at her. She said then, 'Was it Hari?' and I gave her the answer I'd rehearsed.

And I'm still ashamed of the way I cried out when Bhalu and Raju came towards me. I cried out because they were black. I'm ashamed because this proved that in spite of loving Hari I'd not exorcized that stupid primitive fear. I'd made Hari an exception. I don't mean that I loved him in spite of his blackness. His blackness was inseparable from his physical attraction. I think I mean that in loving him and in being physically attracted to him I'd invested his blackness with a special significance or purpose, taken it out of its natural context instead of identifying myself with it *in* its context. There was an element here of self-satisfaction and special pleading and extra pride in love because of the personal and social barrier I thought my love had helped me to surmount. It had not surmounted it at all. No, that is not quite true. It had partly surmounted it. Enough for me to be ashamed then, as well as now, and to ask Lili to call Raju and

Bhalu back and help me upstairs. I thanked them and tried to
show them that I was sorry. In the morning, on my tray, there
were flowers from the garden, which Lili said Bhalu had cut
for me.

Before they helped me upstairs Raju had rung Dr Klaus. On
our way up to my room Lili said, 'Anna's coming. It's all right,
Daphne. Anna's coming.' Lili waited with me in my room. We
heard a car or truck drive up and Lili said, 'That will be her.' A
few moments later there was a knock on the bedroom door and
Lili called out, 'Come in, Anna.' I didn't want to see even Anna,
so I turned my head away when the door opened. I heard Lili
say, 'No, no, you mustn't come in.' She got up and went outside
and closed the door. When she came back she told me it was
Ronald, that he had been at the house before, looking for me.
I said, 'It's very kind of him, but I'm back now, so tell him it's
all right.' Lili said, 'But you see, my dear, it isn't, is it?' And then
she began to question me again, to get the answers to questions
Ronald had asked. In the Bibighar, but when? How many men?
What kind of men? Did I recognize any? Would I recognize any?
How did I get back?

She left me for a few minutes. I heard her talking to Ronald
in the passage. When she came back she said nothing but sat on
the bed and held my hand. Like that we heard Ronald drive
away. He was driving very fast. Without looking at her I said,
'You told him it wasn't Hari, didn't you?'

She said she had, so I knew Ronald had asked. The way they'd
both jumped to the conclusion that Hari was involved only
strengthened my resolve to lie my head off.

It was then just a matter of waiting for Anna. I was glad when
she got there, glad to be treated like a sort of specimen, clinically,
unemotionally. When she'd finished I asked her to tell Lili to
get one of the boys to run a bath. I had an idea that if only I could
lie in warm water for an hour I might begin to feel clean. She
pretended to agree, but she'd given me a strong sedative.
I remember the sound of running water, and passing into a half-
sleep, imagining that the running water was pouring rain. She
ran the water only to lull me. When I woke it was morning.
She was still at the bedside. I said, 'Have you been here all night?'
She hadn't of course, but had called in first thing. I always liked

Anna, but until that morning I'd also been a bit afraid of her, as one is of people whose experiences haven't been happy. One hesitates to question them. I never asked Anna about Germany. Now there was no need. We had found something in common. Which is why we were able to smile at each other, distantly, just for a moment or two, as if the connection between us was only just discernible.

I've told the truth, Auntie, as well as I know how. I'm sorry I wasn't able to tell it before. I hate lies. But I think I would tell them again. Nothing that happened after the Bibighar proves to me now that I was wrong to fight for Hari by denying I'd seen him. I know in my bones that he suffered. I know that he is being punished. But I mustn't believe that he is being punished more badly because of my lies than he would have been by the truth.

When I think of the contortions people went through in an attempt to prove I was lying and in an attempt to implicate him I tremble at the thought of what could have happened to him if just once, by a slip of the tongue, I'd admitted that we were in the Bibighar together.

But this doesn't help me to bear the knowledge that those other boys are unjustly punished. How can people be punished when they are innocent? I know that they went to prison in the end for reasons said to be unconnected with the assault. I hang on to that, in the hope that it is true. But if it hadn't been for the assault I think they'd be free today. They must have been the wrong men. I know I said I didn't see the men, and this was true. But I had an impression of them, of their clothes, their smell, a sense of them as men, not boys. They were hooligans from some village who had come into Mayapore for the hell of it. From what people said the boys who were arrested didn't sound like hooligans at all.

I didn't hear about the arrests until late the following day. Anna and Lili knew already. Ronald had come back the previous night and told them he'd got 'the men responsible under lock and key'. They said nothing to me at the time because I was asleep by then and nothing in the morning because one of the men was Hari. About half-past twelve Lili came in with Anna. She said, 'Jack Poulson has to talk to you, but he can talk in front of Anna.' I asked her to stay too, but she said it would be best for Anna and Jack to be alone with me. When Jack Poulson came in he looked like a Christian martyr who'd just refused to disown God for the last time. I was embarrassed by him and he was embarrassed by me. Anna stood by the open door on to the balcony and Jack stood close to her until I told him to sit down. He apologized for having to ask questions and explained that Mr White had given him the job of 'dealing with the evidence' since it was not merely a police matter but one that involved the station as a whole.

I had had time to think, time to worry about the questions Lili hadn't asked the previous night, but which I'd seen as ones that would have to be answered. What was I doing in the Bibighar? How did I know that Hari wasn't there if I didn't see the men who attacked me? I realized that the only way I could get through an interrogation without involving Hari was to relive the whole thing in my mind as it would have happened, as it would have had to be, if Hari hadn't been in the Bibighar with me.

My story was this: that after seeing Miss Crane I'd left the hospital and gone to the Sanctuary. I made a point of asking Jack Poulson not to say too much about the Sanctuary – if he could help it – because I went there to assist at the clinic and was sure this was a breach of hospital regulations even for a voluntary unpaid nursing officer. He smiled, as I'd intended he should. But then he stopped smiling and by his silence forced me to go on, unaided, to the difficult part of the story.

I left the Sanctuary about dusk. It had seemed clear that no one would come to the clinic because of the rumours of trouble. The whole town was unnaturally quiet. The people had imposed their own curfew. But far from frightening me it lulled me into a false sense of security. For once I felt I had Mayapore completely to myself. I cycled to the Chillianwallah Bagh Extension road and then over the Bibighar bridge and the level crossing.

At this point Jack Poulson said, 'Did you see anyone near the crossing?'

I thought about that. (I still hadn't been told about the arrests.) So far we were still dealing with fact, with truth, but I had to judge the extent to which I could allow myself to tell it. I saw nothing dangerous in the truth so far, so I tried to conjure an accurate picture of crossing the bridge and the railway lines. I said, 'No. There was no one about. The light showed green at the crossing – and I seem to remember lights and voices coming from the keeper's hut. When I say voices I mean a child crying. A feeling of some kind of domestic crisis that was taking up everyone's attention. Anyway, I cycled on. When I got to the street lamp opposite the Bibighar I stopped and got off.'

After waiting for a moment Jack said, 'Why?'

I said, 'I stopped originally to take off my cape. I'd put it on when I left Sister Ludmila's because I thought it was going to rain again, but it hadn't done, and you know what it's like wearing a rain cape for no reason.'

Jack nodded and then asked if I'd actually stopped *under* the street lamp. I thought: That means somebody saw me, either that or they're trying to establish that someone could have seen me. I wasn't bothered because I was still telling the truth. But I was wary, and I was glad that the half-lie I was about to tell was closer to the truth than the story I'd first thought of and rejected – that I stopped by the Bibighar to put my cape *on* because I thought it was going to rain, or because it had come on to rain and I'd decided to shelter for a while in the Bibighar. I rejected that story because it hadn't been about to rain, and didn't rain, and anyone could have proved that it didn't.

So I said, yes, I'd stopped under the street lamp and taken my cape off. And my rain-hat. I'd put my hat in the pocket of the cape and put the cape over the handlebars.

Mr Poulson said, 'What do you mean when you say *originally* you stopped to take off your cape?'

This was the first real danger point. Again I was glad I'd rejected the idea of a melodramatic attack by unknown assailants who overpowered me and dragged me into the Bibighar. I said, 'You'll think it awfully silly, or if not silly then foolish or careless.' Now that I was actually telling the lie I congratulated myself. In an odd way the lie was so much in character. Typical of that silly blundering *galumphing* girl Daphne Manners. I looked Jack Poulson straight in the eye and came out with it. 'The cantonment was so quiet and deserted I wondered whether I'd see the ghosts.'

'The ghosts?' he asked. He was trying to look official but only succeeded in looking as inquisitive as I was pretending to have been, the night before. I said, 'Yes, the ghosts of the Bibighar. I'd never been there in the dark' – that was dangerous, but it passed – 'and I remembered having heard that the place was supposed to be haunted. So I sort of said, Up the Army, Steady the Buffs, and crossed the road and went in. You can always get in because there's no gate. I thought it was a bit of a lark and that when I got back I'd be able to say to Lili, "Well, I've laid those Bibighar ghosts. Bring on Janet MacGregor." I wheeled my bike up the pathway to the pavilion, then parked it, turned the lamp off, and went up on to the mosaic platform.'

But Mr Poulson had never been in the Bibighar. He went later to inspect the scene, but for the moment I had to tell him what the mosaic platform was before he was in the picture. 'Anyway,' I said, 'I sat on the platform and had a cigarette' – (that slipped out and was also dangerous because if any cigarette ends had survived the night's rains they'd not be English ones) – 'and waited for the ghosts to show up. I was saying things to myself like, Come on, ghosts, let's be having you, and then began to think about Miss Crane, and wonder whether I hadn't been an awful fool. I suppose it *was* mad of me, sitting there, last night of all nights. But I didn't take what had happened in outlying parts of the district seriously, did you? I suppose they were watching me. I didn't hear anything – except the dripping and the croaking – I mean the dripping from the leaves and the roof and the croaking of the frogs. The men came rather suddenly. Almost from nowhere.'

Mr Poulson reassumed his Christian martyr face. He said, 'And you didn't see them?' Which was the other warning note. I said, 'Well, for an instant perhaps. But it was all so quick. I didn't have any warning. One moment I was alone and the next surrounded.'

Of course this was the part of the story Jack Poulson wanted to know about but found so acutely embarrassing he could hardly look at me while I told it. He kept glancing at Anna, for moral support, and at the time I wondered why she just stood there, obviously listening but staring at the garden, detaching herself from the interrogation, turning herself into an impersonal lump that would only spring into action and become Anna Klaus again if her patient's voice betrayed signs of distress.

Jack Poulson said, 'I'm sorry to have to press these questions.

But is there anything you remember about these men, or about any one of them, anything that will help you to identify them?'

I played for time. I said, 'I don't think so. I mean they all look alike, don't they? Especially in the dark,' and was conscious of having said something that could be thought indelicate, as well as out of character. He asked me how they were dressed. I had a pretty clear recollection of white cotton clothing – you know, dhotis and high-necked shirts, peasant dress, dirty and smelly. But the warning bells rang again. I saw *the danger to Hari if the men were ever caught.* I think that if I were taken to the Bibighar, at night, and confronted with those men, I would know them. You can recognize people again, even when you think there's been nothing to identify them by, even if there's been only a second or two to get an impression you can hardly believe is an impression, or at least not one worth describing or trying to describe. I was afraid of *being* confronted, afraid of finding myself having to say, 'Yes, these are the men,' because then they would plead provocation, they'd go on their knees and scream and beg for mercy and say that such a thing would never have occurred to them *if the white woman hadn't already been making love to an Indian.*

The trap was now fully sprung, Auntie, wasn't it? Once you've started lying there's no end to it. I'd lied myself into a position there was no escaping from except by way of the truth. I didn't dare tell the truth so the only thing I could do was to confuse and puzzle people and make them hate me – that, and stretch every nerve-end to keep Hari out of it by going on and on insisting that he was never there, making it so that they would never be able to accuse or bring to trial or punish the men who assaulted me because they knew that the principal witness would spike every gun they tried to bring into action.

But of course I was forgetting or anyway reckoning without the power they had to accuse and punish on suspicion alone. There was a moment when I nearly told the truth, because I saw the way things might go. I'm glad I didn't because then I think they would have proved somehow that Hari was technically guilty of rape, because he'd been there and made love to me and incited others to follow his example. At least my lying spared him being punished for rape. It also spared those innocent boys being punished for it too. I've never asked what the punishment for rape is. Hanging? Life imprisonment? People talked about swinging them on the end of a rope. Or firing them from the mouth of a cannon, which is what we did to mutineers in the nineteenth century.

So when Jack Poulson asked me how the men were dressed I said I wasn't sure, but then decided it was safer to tell the truth and say 'Like peasants' than to leave the impression of men dressed like Hari, in shirts and trousers.

Mr Poulson said, 'Are you sure?' which rather played into my hands because he said it as if my evidence was contradicting the story he'd been building up, or other people had built up for him, a picture with Hari at its centre. So I said, Yes, like peasants or labourers. And I added for good measure, 'They smelt like that, too.' Which was true. He said, 'Did any of them smell of drink?' I thought of the time Hari was found on the waste ground by Sister Ludmila. For the moment it looked safer to tell the truth again and say I didn't remember any special smell of drink.

Mr Poulson said, 'I'm sorry to have to subject you to this.' I told him it was all right, I knew it had to be done. For the first time in the interrogation we looked at each other for longer than a split second. He said, 'There's the important question of the bicycle. You say you left it on the path near the pavilion. Did you leave your cape on the handlebars?'

I couldn't immediately see the significance of this question. I assumed he knew that the cape had been used to cover my head because I'd told Lili and Anna. He'd got all this kind of detail from them. He never asked a single question about the assault itself. Poor fellow! I expect he'd rather have died than do so, magistrate though he was. But it was an English girl who'd been assaulted and his magisterial detachment just wouldn't hold out. I decided to tell the truth about the cape. I said, 'No, I'm pretty sure I took it with me on to the platform. In fact I did. I thought the mosaic might be damp, but it wasn't. So I didn't sit on the cape, I just kept it by me.'

He seemed to be satisfied with that, and later when the whole business of the bicycle and what had happened to it blew up in my face I realized what he'd been after. He was trying to estab- lish at what stage 'they'd' found the bicycle. If I'd left the cape on the handlebars that would mean they'd known the bicycle was there before they attacked me, because they'd used the cape. If I hadn't left it on the handlebars it could mean they didn't find the bicycle until they were making off along the path. And this would suggest that they had gone along the path and not out through the broken wall at the back of the garden. There couldn't have been any footprints though, because the paths were all gravel, and anyway with the rains and the police bashing about in the dark all that kind of evidence would lead nowhere. His next question was, 'You say you were suddenly surrounded. Do you mean they closed in on you from all sides of the platform?'

And again, the warning bell. If I said, Yes, from all sides, the next question wouldn't be a question at all, but a statement impossible to refute: 'So you never got an impression of the man or men who came at you from behind?'

I realized it was going to be difficult to kill completely the idea of there having been at least one man I never saw, especially if he was a man who kept out of sight in case I recognized him. Hari, for instance. The pavilion is open on all sides. I could only minimize the danger. I said, 'Well, no, not from all sides. Originally I was sitting on the edge of the platform, then I threw my cigarette away and turned round – as you would, to get to your feet. They were coming at me from behind. I don't know – perhaps I'd heard a sound that made me decide to get out of the place. It *was* pretty creepy. When I turned round there were these two just standing upright after climbing on to the platform and the other three or four vaulting on to it.'

Did I call out? No – I was too surprised to call out. Did any of them say anything? I think one of them giggled.

Mr Poulson questioned the margin of error there might be in my statement about 'the other three or four'. Was it three, or was it four? Was the total number of men five or six? I said I couldn't remember. All I remembered was the awful sensation of being attacked swiftly by as many men as there were, five or six. Men of that kind, labourers, hooligans, stinking to high heaven. I said it was like being thrown into one of those disgusting third-class compartments on an Indian train. And that I didn't want to talk about it any more.

Anna came to life then. She turned round and said, 'Yes, I think it is enough, Mr Poulson,' in that very forthright German voice of hers. He got up at once, glad enough to be out of it, if only for a while. Anna saw him to the door. She came back for a moment to make sure I was all right, then left me alone. Lili brought up some fruit and curds for my lunch and after that I dozed until late afternoon. I woke and found Lili in the room and Raju just leaving it. He'd brought up tea.

When I'd had a cup Lili said, 'I think Mr Poulson should have told you. Some boys were arrested last night. One of them was Hari.'

My bicycle had been found in the ditch outside Hari's house in the Chillianwallah Bagh. I didn't believe it. It was such a monstrous *fatal* intervention. I said, 'But he wasn't there! It wasn't Hari!' She wanted to believe me. I tried not to panic. If some men had been arrested I thought they must be the ones responsible and that they would already have talked about the Indian who'd been making love to me there. I was going to have to deny this, deny it and go on denying it, and hope that Hari would keep his promise to say nothing, to know nothing. I felt that he had *given* me that promise when he let me go. I asked Lili when he'd been arrested and why, and who by. When I took it in that he'd been in custody ever since the night before and that Ronald was responsible, that Ronald had found the bicycle outside Hari's house, I said, 'He's lying, isn't he? He found the bicycle in the Bibighar and took it to Hari's house and planted it in the ditch.'

Lili was shocked because she knew it *could* be true, but she refused to believe it. She couldn't accept that an English official would stoop to that. But there are only three possible explanations for the bicycle and only one is likely. I left the bicycle by the path against a tree. It was very dark on the path. You'd easily miss seeing the bicycle if you didn't know just where it was and if you had no lamp. I think when Hari carried me down the path we'd gone past the place before I said, 'It's here somewhere,' and he put me down. He wasn't interested in the bicycle. He was only concerned to carry me home. I suppose he had some dim idea that if the bicycle were there he could put me on it and wheel me home. But the bicycle was a bad joke, just at that moment, wasn't it? He hardly bothered to look. I think the bicycle was still where I'd left it, and that when Ronald rushed to the Bibighar with his police patrol they found it almost at once and Ronald put it into the back of a truck and drove to Hari's house and dumped it in the ditch. I think he was the sort of officer who let his men have a lot of elbow room and in return could get them to plant evidence like this for him and say nothing. Remember the incident of the sub-inspector hitting Hari and getting away with it? There was nothing to connect Hari with the assault in the Bibighar except his known association with me and Ronald's jealousy and suspicion and prejudice. What else made him go to Hari's house? And why when he got there did he spend time searching for the bicycle? If it was in a ditch outside it would have had to be *searched* for, wouldn't it?

If the bicycle *was* in the ditch before Ronald got there I suppose it's possible that one of his men found it during the course of whatever drill they go through when they go to a place to pick up a suspect. But the impression I got before the so-called inquiry was that according to Ronald they only went into the house because they found the bicycle outside it, and that it was only then that Ronald realized that the house was Hari's. If this was the impression he gave people at first he can't have been thinking very clearly because he wouldn't have to give English people any reason for going to Hari's house. Apparently he'd been there once that night already. He was probably not thinking clearly because Lili had repeated to him what I'd told her – that Hari wasn't with me, that Hari wasn't responsible. He wanted Hari to be responsible. I think he had to change the emphasis when it came to making a proper report, had to say that he'd gone to Hari's house and *then* found the bicycle, not the other way round.

I give Ronald this much benefit of the doubt, that after he left the MacGregor House, knowing what had happened to me, he went to his headquarters, collected a patrol, rushed to the Bibighar, found nothing, and then searched the area in the vicinity, arrested those boys who were drinking hooch in a hut on the other side of the river, and then headed straight for the house in the Chillianwallah Bagh, where he found Hari with cuts on his face and where his police found the bicycle. He went to the Chillianwallah Bagh because he thought I was lying, knew I was lying, and because the boys he arrested in the hut on the other side of the bridge were known to be acquaintances of Hari's. But he went mainly because he hated Hari. He wanted to prove

that Hari was guilty. And this leaves only the two other explanations for the bicycle. Either Hari went back for it after I'd left
him, found it, rode it home, then realized the danger and shoved
it into the ditch – which would mean he lost his head because
if he saw the danger he wouldn't leave the bicycle outside his
own house. Or one of the men who attacked me knew Hari,
knew where he lived, stole the bicycle and left it outside Hari's
house, guessing that the police would search near there – which
means that whoever it was who knew Hari also knew that Hari
and I were friends. And this leads, surely, to the proposition that
such a man anticipated that we'd be in the Bibighar that night.
But we didn't even anticipate that ourselves. The coincidence
of there being one man or several men in the Bibighar that night
who recognized Hari in the dark and thought fast enough to
steal the bicycle and leave it outside his house is too much to
swallow, isn't it? And who could such a man be? One of Lili's
servants? One of Mrs Gupta Sen's? One who might have been
able to read my note, in English, asking Hari to meet me on the
night of August the 9th, *in the Sanctuary*? No, it won't wash. It
won't even wash if you think – as I did for a while – of this
unknown but very clever or very lucky man or boy being one
of those stretcher-bearers Sister Ludmila used to hire, never for
more than a few weeks because after that they got bored and
'their thoughts turned to mischief'. On the day I went to say
goodbye to her I noticed that she had a new boy. She told me
about the boys who wrote to her after they'd left, and how only
one of them had ever come back to beg. And it did cross my
mind that perhaps the one who came back to beg was the one
who was with her and Mr de Souza the night they brought Hari
in to the Sanctuary. Such a boy might have taken an interest in
Hari, followed him around, got to know his movements, even
watched us on those occasions we went to the Bibighar. But
why? Such a boy, back in his village, might have talked about
the Indian and the white girl, and led a gang of fellow-hooligans
into Mayapore, attracted by rumours of trouble and the idea of
loot, and come to the Bibighar from the waste ground at the
back to shelter for the night, and seen Hari there, and me,
watched our love-making. The men who attacked us *had* been
watching. That is certain. But the coincidence is too much to
take. The men were hooligans. It was Ronald Merrick who

planted the bicycle. I know it. I don't think Hari had many friends, but I don't think he had any enemies either, except for Ronald – none, anyway, who would go to the lengths that were gone to to incriminate him.

If it wasn't Ronald, then it must have been Hari himself who took the bicycle, then panicked and left it outside his house. I don't think Hari panicked.

But I did. I told Lili to leave me alone. I wanted to think. It became quite clear. Ronald searched the Bibighar, found the bicycle, put it in the truck, then drove across the bridge, *towards Chillianwallah Bagh*, questioned the level-crossing keeper, found the boys who were 'friends' of Hari's, arrested them, drove on to Hari's house, planted the bike and then stormed into the house. And when Hari was arrested they probably searched his room. Had he destroyed my note asking him to meet me in the Sanctuary? The note was never mentioned so he must have done. This may have been the only thing he had time to do, if he hadn't thrown it away before. The photograph I gave him was mentioned. Ronald took it away, as 'evidence' – a copy of the same photograph that I sent you and which Hari helped me to choose from the proofs that day at Subhas Chand's. At the informal inquiry at the MacGregor House Mr Poulson said, 'Mr Kumar had your photograph in his bedroom. Was it one you gave him?' – you know – as if trying to establish that Hari was obsessed with me and had stolen the photograph to stare at at night, and as if giving me the opportunity to recant, to go on to their side, to get rid of my silly notions of loyalty and break down and admit that I'd been infatuated, that Hari had worked on my emotions in the most callous and calculating way, that it was a relief to tell the truth at last, that I had come to my senses and was no longer afraid of him, let alone infatuated, that he'd attacked and brutalized me and then submitted me to the base indignity of being raped by friends of his, and that then he'd tried to terrorize me with threats to my life if I gave him away, threats which he said would be all too easy to carry out because the British were about to be given the bum's rush. Oh, I know what was in their minds – perhaps against their personal judgment – but in their minds as the story they ought to believe because of what might be at stake. Of the trio who made up the board of private inquiry, or whatever it was officially called –

Mr Poulson, a startled and embarrassed young English sub-
divisional officer whose name I forget, and Judge Menen – only
Judge Menen, who presided, maintained an air of utter detachment. It was a detachment that struck me as that of fatigue,
fatigue amounting to hopelessness. But the fact that he was there
heartened me, not only because he was an Indian but because
I was sure he wouldn't have been there if there was any likelihood of the accused men coming in front of him in the District
Court. I suppose if the inquiry had led to what the board by
now had no hope of but the English community still wanted,
the case would have gone up for trial in the Provincial High
Court.

But I've gone a step too far ahead. I must go back for a
moment to the evening of the 10th – when I sent Lili out of the
room to give myself time to think because I was panicky about
what might have been found that could incriminate Hari, and
about who the other arrested men were, and what they might
have said. Then I was overwhelmed by the typically blunt
thoughtless English way I'd assumed everything would be all
right for Hari if *I* said he was innocent. I'd run away from Hari,
believing that just by putting distance between us I was helping
him. But I saw him now standing where I'd left him, at the gate
of the Bibighar. Auntie, what did he do? Go back to look for
the bicycle, and remove it, thinking he was helping *me*? Or begin
his journey home on foot? There was blood on my neck and
face when I got back – so Anna told me. It must have come from
Hari's face when we clung to each other. In the dark I didn't
see how badly or how little those men had hurt him. I never
asked. I never thought. He was bathing his face, apparently,
when Ronald burst into his room. Of course they tried to prove
he'd been hurt by me fighting back. But all I can think of now
is the callous way I left him, to face up to everything alone, to
say nothing, deny everything, because I'd told him to, but
having to say nothing and deny everything with those scratches
or abrasions on his face that he couldn't account for. When it
came out at the inquiry that his face was cut I said, 'Why ask me
about them? Ask Mr Kumar. I don't know. He wasn't there.'
Mr Poulson said, 'He *was* asked. He wouldn't say,' and then
changed the subject. Ronald was giving evidence at the time.
I stared at him, but he refused to look at me. I said, 'Perhaps he

had a scrap with the police. It wouldn't be the first time he was hit by a police officer.' It did no good. It was the wrong thing to say at that time in that place. It made them sympathize with Ronald rather than me. I didn't mind, though, because in any case I was beginning to hate myself. I hated myself because I realized Hari had taken me at my word and said nothing – quite literally nothing. Nothing. Nothing. Nothing. Said nothing in spite of evidence against him, which I hadn't reckoned with when I ran off and left him.

They hurt him, didn't they? Tortured him in some way? But he said nothing, nothing. When they arrested him he must have stood there – with the cuts on his face, my photograph in his room, my bicycle in the ditch outside, and said nothing. At one time during those days of question and answer Lili told me, 'He won't account for his movements. He denies having been in the Bibighar. He says he hasn't seen you since the night you both went to the temple. But he won't say where he was or what he was doing between leaving the office and getting home, some time after nine. He must have reached home about the time you did, Daphne.'

And of course these were the other things I hadn't reckoned with or known about: Ronald's first visit to the house in the Chillianwallah Bagh, his visit to the MacGregor House, his visit to the Sanctuary. When I left Hari at the Bibighar I suppose I assumed that all he had to do was to pretend to have been at home all evening, to persuade Aunt Shalini to swear he had been at home, if the question ever arose, or to make up another story, whatever he thought best, whatever he thought would work. But for Hari, no story worked. *I never gave him a chance to calm me down and say – as I would have let an Englishman say – 'Look, for Pete's sake, if I haven't been here in the Bibighar, where in hell have I been? How do I account for this swollen lip, or black eye, or scratched cheek,'* whatever it was.

I never gave him the chance because even in my panic there was this assumption of superiority, of privilege, of believing I knew what was best for both of us, because the colour of my skin automatically put me on the side of those who never told a lie. But we've got far beyond that stage of colonial simplicity. We've created a blundering judicial robot. We can't stop it working. It works for us even when we least want it to. We created it to prove how fair, how civilized we are. But it is a white robot and it can't distinguish between love and rape. It only understands physical connection and only understands it as a crime because it only exists to punish crime. It would have punished Hari for this, and if physical connection between the races is a crime he's been punished justly. One day someone may come along, cross a wire by mistake, or fix in a special circuit with the object of making it impartial and colour-blind, and then it will probably explode.

After Lili had told me about Hari's arrest and I'd thought for a bit I rang for Raju and told him I wanted Poulson Sahib sent for. I'd got over my panic. I was angry, even angry with Lili. I felt she'd let me down by allowing them to hold Hari in custody without doing a thing to stop it. She was very patient with me, but we were shut off from each other as we'd never been before. She said that if I really wanted to see Mr Poulson she'd ring him. I think she believed I was going to confess. She knew I'd been lying. But for her the truth would be as bad as the lies. She had brought Hari into the house, and he was an Indian. A fellow-countryman. For a day or two after the Bibighar, I felt like an interloper, one of her harpies who'd inexplicably become involved with the life of an Indian family, and had taken to sitting in her bedroom the better to keep what was left of her racial integrity intact.

Mr Poulson came after dinner. Lili brought him up. She asked whether I wanted her to stay. I said it might be better if Mr Poulson and I were alone. Directly she'd gone I said, 'Why didn't you tell me they arrested Hari Kumar last night?' Normally I liked him. Tonight I despised him, but then I was ready to despise everybody. He looked as if he wanted to fall through the floor. He said Hari had been arrested because the evidence seemed to add up that way, in spite of my 'belief' that he hadn't been involved. I said, 'What evidence? What evidence that can possibly contradict *my* evidence. You must all be mad if you think you can pin anything on Hari.'

He said that the evidence last night had pointed to Hari, and that it couldn't be ruled out that he was there, in spite of my belief that he wasn't.

I said it wasn't a question of belief. I asked him whether he really thought I wouldn't *know* if Hari had been among those who attacked me. That scared him. He was afraid of an intimate confession. When I realized this I thought I saw how to play the whole thing, play it by scaring them at the thought of what I might come out with, in court. I asked him about the other men. He pretended he didn't know anything about them. I smiled and said, 'I see Ronald is keeping it all very much to himself. But that's no wonder, is it? After all, it's pretty obvious he planted the bicycle.'

Lili had been shocked, but her shock was nothing to Jack Poulson's. He said, 'What on earth makes you say a thing like that?' I told him to ask Ronald. It seemed wiser to leave it at that, to leave Mr Poulson with something tricky to bite on. Before he went – and he went because 'in his view there was nothing it would be advantageous to pursue for the moment' – I said, 'Hari wasn't there. I doubt that any of the men you've arrested were there. It's the usual thing, isn't it? An English woman gets assaulted and at once everyone loses all sense of proportion. If Ronald or any of you think you're going to get away with punishing the first poor bloody Indians you've clapped hands on just to give the European community a field-day you've got another think coming. It'll never stand up in court because *I'll* stand up in court and say what I'm saying to you. Only I might be more explicit about a lot of things.'

He got up and mumbled something about being sorry and that everyone appreciated what a terrible time I'd had, that he was sure no one who was innocent could possibly be punished. I said, 'Then tell me this. Forget the *one* innocent man you've got locked up at the moment. Do the others fit my description of them at all?'

He said he didn't know. He hadn't seen them. But I wasn't letting him off so lightly. I was chancing my arm, but it seemed worth it. I said, 'Oh, come off it, Jack. You know all right. Even if you haven't seen them you must know who they are. Are they what I said? Smelly peasants? Dirty labourers? Or boys like Hari? The kind of boy Mr Merrick seems to have it in for?'

I'd hit the mark. But he still insisted he didn't know. He said he believed that one or two of them were known for or suspected of political activities of 'the anarchist type'. I pounced on that. I said, 'Oh, you mean educated boys? Not smelly peasants?'

He shook his head, not denying it but closing the way to further discussion.

Retrospectively, I'm sorry for the bad time I gave poor Jack Poulson. But it had to be done. I'm pretty sure he went away thinking, 'It won't stick. Not with those fellows Merrick's got locked up.' I don't know how much more he would say when he got back to the Deputy Commissioner's bungalow, which was almost certainly where he was headed. To Mr White probably all he needed to say was something like, 'Either she's lying, or Kumar is innocent, but if she's lying or continues to lie he ranks as innocent anyway because we'll never prove him guilty. The same goes for the others. Merrick's made a gaffe.'

Robin White detached himself from the affair, to the extent that he left Jack Poulson in charge of it up to the point where a final decision had to be made. If he'd been a man like his predecessor Mr Stead (whom men like Vassi loathed) God knows what would have happened. I suppose to Robin the assault on a silly English girl wasn't very important when he compared it with the other things he had to deal with. I don't know whether Mr Poulson ever said anything to Mr White about the bicycle and my accusation against Ronald. It wouldn't have been an easy thing for him to pass on. At the inquiry the bicycle was never mentioned, and the only time Hari was mentioned was when Ronald was giving evidence of arrest. He answered questions which Jack Poulson seemed to have worked out carefully in advance. In fact the evidence of the arrests struck me as ridiculous. Mr Poulson read out the names of the men arrested and simply asked Ronald where and at what time they'd been taken into custody, and what they had been doing. As I already knew from what Lili had told me, the other poor boys had been drinking hooch in a hut near the Bibighar bridge but at the inquiry the *unfairness* of it struck me all over again. According to Ronald, Hari was in his bedroom, 'washing his face on which there were cuts and abrasions'. I nearly interrupted and said, 'What about the bicycle?' but thought better of it. The bicycle not being mentioned was a good sign. I wondered if Jack Poulson had talked to Ronald in private and decided from the answers he got that he'd better keep the bicycle business quiet, not only for Ronald's sake, but for the sake of the Service, the flag and all that. But I did come out with the remark about the cuts on Hari's face when Jack Poulson asked me whether I recalled 'marking' any of the men who attacked me. I mean the remark about Hari probably having had a scrap with the police.

After the so-called evidence of arrests Ronald was dismissed and then they got down to the business of going over my statement again and asking questions, and I saw how the evidence of arrests was so thin that although it proved nothing it could also prove anything. Judge Menen had kept quiet – I mean he'd not asked me any questions so far, but towards the end he said, 'I must ask you why you refused the other day to attempt to identify the men held in custody,' which I had done, when the worst of the troubles in Mayapore were over and they wanted to push the case to a conclusion of some sort and get it over with. I said, 'I refused to attempt identification because they must be the wrong men. I shall say so in court, if necessary.'

Judge Menen said he understood why I should feel this in regard to 'the man Kumar' but the refusal to attempt identification of the other men might be interpreted as wilful obstruction by the principal witness and this might lead to the prosecution being able to prove its case in spite of that witness's evidence, because the wilful obstruction might be held as a sign of general unreliability.

I thought about this. Mr Poulson brightened up a bit. He didn't mind that Menen was an Indian and perhaps shouldn't speak to a white girl like that. It was the Law that spoke. He thought the clever old Judge had forced me into a corner by scaring me with a legal technicality, a reminder that even the principal witness couldn't obstruct the Crown in the pursuit of justice. But I thought I saw my way out. And I wasn't really convinced that Judge Menen was on particularly sure ground himself. I said, 'If my evidence is thought unreliable for that reason, does it become less unreliable if I go through the farce of looking at these men, with no intention whatsoever of saying I recognize them? You prefer me to go through that farce? You'd only have my word for it that I didn't recognize them. Simply looking at them isn't a test of reliability in itself, is it?'

Menen's poker face didn't alter. He said they would assume, continue to assume, that I was telling the truth, and reminded me that the whole inquiry was based on the assumption that I was telling the truth, that it was only the refusal to comply with the request to attempt identification which could raise the question of unreliability. He went on, 'In your statement you say you had a brief impression of the men who attacked you. You have described them as peasants or labourers. That being so, with such an impression in your mind, why do you refuse to co-operate in the important business of helping us, as best you can, to decide whether the men being held are held on sufficient grounds?'

Looking at him I thought: You know they're the wrong men too. You want me to go down to the jail and look at them and say, No, they aren't as I remember them at all. Either you want that, or you want me to make it *quite* plain, perhaps outrageously plain, that it's useless for anyone to expect to bring this case to court with these boys as defendants.

But I was still afraid of confronting them. I was sure they were the wrong boys, but I didn't know. I didn't want to face them. If they were the right boys there was a danger – only very slight, but still a danger – of their panicking at the sight of me and incriminating Hari. And if they were the right boys and I recognized them I didn't want to have to say, 'No, these aren't the men.' I wasn't sure I could trust myself to carry it off, even for Hari's sake. *I didn't want to tell that sort of lie.* There's a difference between trying to stop an injustice and obstructing justice.

I said, 'No, I won't co-operate. One of these men is innocent. If one innocent man is accused I'm not interested in the guilt or innocence of the others. I refuse absolutely to go anywhere near them. The men who raped me were peasants. The boys you've got locked up aren't, so they're almost certainly all innocent too. For one thing they're all Hindus, aren't they?'

Mr Poulson agreed that they were all Hindus.

I smiled. I'd prepared this one awfully well, I thought. I said, 'Then that's another thing. One of the men was a Muslim. He was circumcised. If you want to know how I know I'm quite prepared to tell you but otherwise prefer to leave it at that. One was a Muslim. They were all hooligans. Apart from that I can't tell you a thing. I can't tell you more than I have done. The impression I had of them was strong enough for me to know that I could say, "No, these aren't the men," but not strong enough for me to say, "Yes, these *are* the men." For all I knew they could have been British soldiers with their faces blacked. I don't imagine they were, but if by saying so I can convince you I know you've got at least one wrong man, well then I say so.'

Mr Poulson and the young man whose name I don't remember both looked profoundly shocked. Judge Menen stared at me and then said, 'Thank you, Miss Manners. We have no more questions. We are sorry to have had to subject you to this examination.'

He got to his feet and we all stood, just as if it was a courtroom and not the dining-room of the MacGregor House. But there the similarity ended. Instead of Judge Menen going out he stood still and made it clear that it was my privilege to leave first. When I got to the door Jack Poulson was ahead of me to open it. A purely automatic gesture, part of the Anglo-Indian machinery. But I could *smell* his shock. Bitter, as if he'd just eaten some aromatic quick-acting paralysing herb.

I went upstairs and poured myself a drink. I thought it was all over and that I'd won and Hari would be released in the next few hours, or the next day. I stood on the balcony as I'd done so often during the past two weeks. During the riots you could hear the shouting and the firing and the noise of trucks and lorries going from one part of the civil lines to the other. For a day or two there'd been policemen at the gate of the MacGregor House. They said the house might be attacked, but we'd been more worried about Anna Klaus than about ourselves. At one time she was practically a prisoner in the Purdah Hospital in the native town, and we didn't see her for a couple of days. Mrs White wanted Lili and me to move into the Deputy Commissioner's bungalow, but Lili wouldn't go. Neither would I. That's when the police guard appeared. The sight of the police guard made me feel like a prisoner too. Ronald never came near himself. He'd washed his hands of me. I felt that with a few exceptions the whole European community was ready to do that or had already done it. I didn't care. I got to the stage of believing that everything was coming to an end for us, I mean for white people. I didn't care about that either. One evening Lili told me the rioters had broken into the jail. I thought: That's how it will resolve itself. They'll free Hari. I didn't know he wasn't in that jail. But I thought: The Indians will take over. Perhaps they won't punish me. Perhaps Hari will come to the house. But I couldn't visualize it clearly enough. Nothing like that would happen. The soldiers were out and there was the sound of firing, and everything was only a question of time for *us*, hopeless for *them*. The robot was working.

But I was worried about Anna, and Sister Ludmila. They were the only white people I knew who lived or worked on that side of the river. Sister Ludmila told me later that she defied the curfew and went out every night with Mr de Souza and her stretcher bearer. There was plenty of work for them. The police turned them back once or twice but generally they managed to give them the slip. The 'death house', as people called it, was always occupied. And every morning the police went there, and the women whose husbands or sons hadn't come home.

I was worried for you, too, until Lili told me she'd got Robin White to send you a message through official channels that I was all right. They tried to keep my name out of reports that appeared in the national newspapers. Some hopes. Thank God we'd talked on the phone before my name was given away. Even so I was afraid you'd come down to Mayapore. I bless you for not doing, for understanding. If you'd come down I couldn't have borne it. I had to work it out alone. I bless Lili for understanding that too. At first I thought her detachment was due to disapproval, then that it was due to that curious Indian indifference to pain. But of course her 'indifference' was wholly 'European', wholly civilized, like yours, like my own. There are pains we feel, and pains we recognize in others, that are best left alone, not from callousness but from discretion. Anna's detachment was rather different. Hers also was European, but Jewish, self-protective as well as sensitive, as if she didn't want to be reminded of pain because to be reminded would transfer her sensitivity from my pain to what she remembered of her own. By keeping that amount of distance she was able to establish a friendship between us, trust, regard, the kind of regard that can spring up between strangers who sense each other's mettle. One shouldn't expect more. But affection comes from a different source, doesn't it? I'm thinking of the affection there is between you and me, which is not only an affection of the blood because there is the same kind of affection between myself and Lili. It's one that overcomes, that exists, but for which there isn't necessarily any accounting because trust doesn't enter into it at all, except to the extent that you trust because of the affection. You trust after you have learned to love.

I could never feel affectionate in that way towards Anna. Neither, I'm sure, could she towards me. But we were good and trusting, understanding friends. One develops an instinct for people. I wander on about this because when I stood on the balcony, drinking my well-deserved gin and lime-juice, I saw Ronald and Mr Poulson come out of the house and get into Ronald's truck. Judge Menen wasn't with them. He stayed behind to have a drink with Lili.

And I thought: How curious. Ronald and Jack Poulson are just *people* to me. I felt no real resentment, not even of Ronald, let alone of Jack who was obviously going off somewhere to chew the rag with Ronald. But I felt they were outside the circle of those people 'it was worth my while to know', as my mother put it once, probably meaning something else entirely. To me my own meaning was clear. I already *knew* them. They were predictable people, predictable because they worked for the robot. What the robot said they would also say, what the robot did they would do, and what the robot believed was what they believed because people like them had fed that belief into it. And they would always be right so long as the robot worked, because the robot was the standard of rightness.

There was no *originating passion* in them. Whatever they felt that was original would die the moment it came into conflict with what the robot was geared to feel. At the inquiry it needed Judge Menen to break through the robot's barrier – if break is the appropriate word to use to describe the actions of a man who made even getting out of a chair look like an exercise in studied and balanced movement. But he got through. At one moment he was sitting on *their* side, the robot side, and the next moment he was through. We were through together, he *brought* me through or joined me on the other side – whichever way you like to put it. So it seemed right, now, that he should have stayed behind to have a drink with Lili, and leave the robot boys to go off on their own and work out how to make it look as if the robot had brought the inquiry to some kind of a logical conclusion. They had to save the robot's face, as well as their own.

It was odd to find myself thinking this about Mr Poulson. Mr and Mrs White thought very highly of him. He was still pretty young, young enough to be cautious, which may sound silly, but isn't, because a young man has a living to earn, a family to support, a career to build. But it probably needs something like what came to be called the Bibighar Gardens affair to sort out the mechanical men from the men who are capable of throwing a spanner into the works. Which is another way of describing what I feel about Judge Menen. What is so interesting is that the spanner he threw into the works, the spanner that brought the inquiry to a stop was the right spanner. It must take years of experience and understanding to know which spanner to use, and the exact moment to use it. I think he knew so well, that in the end he handed the spanner to me just to give himself the additional satisfaction of letting me throw it in for him. He knew that the only way to bring the robot to a temporary halt was to go right to the heart of what had set it in motion – the little cog of judicial procedure which had been built into it in the fond hope that once it was engaged it would only stop when justice had been done. By going to the heart of the mechanism he exposed it for what it was and gave me the chance to bring it to a halt by imposing an impossible task on it – the task of *understanding* the justice of what it was doing, and of proving that its own justice was the equal or the superior of mine. But it was only a *temporary* halt.

Long before Judge Menen left I came in from the balcony and had my bath. I was finished and dressed for dinner before Lili came in and asked if I was all right, and if I would like to see Anna who had called on her way home from the Purdah Hospital. I said, 'Is Judge Menen still here?' She told me he'd gone about ten minutes ago. And had sent me his love. I'd never seen Lili *moved* before. I'd only seen her amused, or wry, or disapproving, or detached. I think it was Judge Menen who had moved her with whatever it was he said to her – or rather caused her to be moved directly she set eyes on me again after talking to him. I don't know what it was he had said. I never shall. That is typical of Lili. Typical of him too. And in a terribly English way Lili and I sort of got out of each other's light – put yards of space between us, but were together again.

I went down with her and greeted Anna. Lili asked her to stay to dinner. She said she would. For me it was like a sudden treat, a picnic plan confided to a child early on a golden summer morning. When Lili went out to tell Raju to tell cook it was dinner for three I gave Anna a freshener for her drink. She said, 'You look better. Please keep it up.'

And I said, 'I think I shall. I think we've won.' I said 'we' because Anna had stood by me all that time. I knew, before the inquiry, that she'd been asked that naked question: 'In your opinion was Miss Manners *intacta* before the assault?' And I knew what she had replied. When I said 'I think we've won', she raised her glass.

This was the last evening of happiness I had. After it I was optimistic but not happy. In the end even my optimism went. I needed Hari. I needed Lili too, and Anna, and you, but most of all I needed him. I'd built my own enclosed little circle, hadn't I? The one I'd feel safe in. A circle of safety in no-man's-land. Wherever we go, whatever we do, we seem to hedge ourselves about with this illusory protection. Hours went by. Days. More than a week. I never went out. When people came I escaped to my room. The MacGregor House was gradually filled again with vibrations whose source I had never pinned down before but now did and saw as inseparable from it: trust, compromise, something fundamentally exploratory and non-committal, as if the people in it were trying to *learn*, instead of teach – and so forgive rather than accuse. There is that old, disreputable saying, isn't there? 'When rape is inevitable, lie back and enjoy it.' *Well, there has been more than one rape.* I can't say, Auntie, that I lay back and enjoyed mine. But Lili was trying to lie back and enjoy what we've done to her country. I don't mean done in malice. Perhaps there was love. Oh, somewhere, in the past, and now, and in the future, love as there was between me and Hari. But the spoilers are always there, aren't they? The Swinsons. The bitches who travelled as far as Lahore. The Ronald Merricks. The silly little man who summed up his own silly little island-history when he whistled and said, 'some wog contractor is making a packet'.

Connie White came to see me one day. She brought Mavis Poulson with her. But she realized after ten minutes or so that she'd get nowhere because bringing edgy, virtuously pregnant Mavis had been a mistake. She sent her away. As the Deputy

Commissioner's wife she could do such a thing with no more than the personal courage it took to make Mavis dislike her for a day or two. When we were alone she said, 'My husband doesn't know I'm here. I shan't tell him I've been. And I oughtn't to interfere, I know. But they've sent Hari Kumar away. They've put him and the other boys in prison.'

It wasn't a shock. I was prepared for it. Days of silence from Lili had prepared me for it. I didn't understand it but that wasn't the same as not believing it could happen. I asked what they were putting him in prison for. She made a gesture that defined the futility of both the question and the answer. She said, 'All the papers went to the Commissioner, and it's out of our hands now. But I wanted to know if there's anything you can tell *me* that you wouldn't tell Jack or Robin, or Lili.'

I said, 'What sort of thing, for heaven's sake?'

Again she made that gesture, whose meaning we both knew. She said probably only I could tell her what sort of thing. I thought it was a trap. I smiled at her. She said, 'Well, you know what men are. They always tell themselves they can't afford the luxury of real curiosity. I mean curiosity about people. Oh, I know they solve all kinds of complex problems that prove we're made of water and gas or something, and that the universe is still exploding and travelling outwards at umpteen million light years a second which I suppose is fascinating, but of no practical use to *us* when it comes to trying to keep the servants happy and stopping them from making off just as effectively at a rate measurable in miles an hour.'

I laughed. It was so absurd. Small talk. Chat. Jolly jokes. Bless her. This was her armoury. The key – the chink in the armour – was that word 'curiosity'. I knew what I was supposed to say. 'What are you curious about?' I laughed again. I expect she thought I was bats. They say poor old Miss Crane went round the bend. Lili went to see her once while I was still at the Mac-Gregor. Perhaps twice. I don't remember. We didn't talk about it much. Miss Crane had taken all the pictures down from her walls or something, although she wasn't going anywhere. Later she committed suttee. You saw the report of it in *The Times of India*, I think. We both saw it. Neither of us mentioned it. Perhaps Lili wrote to you and told you more about it. Of course it's wrong to say 'committed' suttee. Suttee, or *sati* (is that the

right way to spell it?) is a sort of state of wifely grace, isn't it? So
you don't commit it. You enter into it. If you're a good Hindu
widow you *become* suttee. Should I become it, Auntie? Is Hari
dead? I suppose you could say we're hermits enough here to
rank as *sannyasis* anyway. But no. I've not done with the world
yet. I've still got at least one duty to perform.

And I knew I had a duty to perform for Connie White. After
I'd stopped laughing I said, 'Well then, what are you curious
about?'

You can't not pay for a joke. You've got to cough up the price
put on it.

She said, 'Well, it all seems to begin with a man called
Moti Lal.'

I'd never heard of Moti Lal, but it turned out he was the
man Ronald was looking for the first time he arrested Hari.
Moti Lal was once employed by Hari's uncle. He was always
haranguing groups of students and young men and labourers.
When he started trying to organize the staff at the place where
he worked old Romesh Chand sacked him. He also got served
with an order under section 144 of the Criminal Procedure
Code. I think Ronald instigated that. It's the one that calls on
you to abstain from an act likely to cause a disturbance in the
district, isn't it? Anyway, like so many other people were doing,
to keep the British embarrassed, he defied it, and was prosecuted
under section 188 of the Penal Code and sentenced to six
months. I remember all this jabberwocky because I latched on
to it while Connie talked about it, hoping it would explain what
could happen to Hari. It didn't, but I looked it up afterwards in
the law books in Lili's library.

Moti Lal was sent to the jail in Aligarh. He escaped. And
Ronald was looking for him when he called at the Sanctuary
on the morning Hari was there with a hangover. I asked Connie
what all this Moti Lal business had to do with an innocent man
being sent to prison for a crime he didn't commit. She said,
'But that's the point. Hari Kumar isn't being sent to prison
for the assault. He's being sent for political reasons. He knew
Moti Lal.'

Again I laughed. I said, 'Hari knew Moti Lal. I know Hari.
Why don't you send me to jail too? I suppose all those other
boys knew Moti Lal as well?'

She said she wasn't really concerned about the other boys. There were police files on all of them. They'd all been examined by Jack Poulson. Both Jack and her husband believed that they were the kind of boys who, if they hadn't been taken into custody on the night of the Bibighar, would have been arrested within forty-eight hours for rioting or sabotage. Whatever one felt about the justice or injustice of it, they were 'fair game' in present circumstances, and safer out of the way.

I said, 'Fair game is the right description. You could hardly release them now, could you? They were arrested for the worst crime of all, and everybody knows it. And the same goes for Hari, doesn't it? Only it's even trickier for him. Because everybody knows we used to go out together.'

She agreed that it was trickier for Hari, or rather had been trickier when it was still uncertain whether he'd taken part in the assault. But none of the boys was being charged with assault. That case was still open. The police were still working on it. But it looked unlikely that they'd ever catch the men who were responsible, unless the men began to boast – either back in their villages, or wherever they came from, or in the jails. You couldn't rule out the possibility that the men who'd assaulted me were among those arrested during the subsequent rioting. The police only hoped they weren't among those killed. Connie didn't think they would be because men of 'that kind' weren't likely to have risked their lives defying the military. If they'd been arrested they'd have been with the men who got caught looting. If they were still free they could, of course, be anywhere, and probably the only thing to hope for was an informer, someone with a grudge against them who heard them boasting. The trouble was that in India you could never rely on evidence when it was come by in this way.

I don't know what Connie was trying to do. Relieve me of the anxiety that Hari might still be punished for the assault; put me on my guard, because she guessed the truth and therefore also guessed that I didn't want the men caught in case they incriminated Hari; catch me *off* my guard, hoping for a careless word that would undo all the good I'd so far done. Perhaps she was trying to do none of these things. When you've lied your head off you suspect nearly everyone of cunning and evasion and deceit. I expect she was just curious, as she said, exercising her woman's right to satisfy her curiosity now that the men had made everything irrevocable.

She said Moti Lal had never been caught. He'd gone 'underground'. The boys who'd been drinking hooch when they were arrested all swore they'd not seen Moti Lal since he was sent to prison. Jack Poulson thought they were lying. The trouble was that Hari Kumar had 'gradually emerged' during all these investigations and interrogations as 'a young man of whom the gravest suspicions had to be entertained' (which also sounded to me like something Jack Poulson must have said). The police had kept a file on him for several months. He'd been had in for questioning at the time they were looking for Moti Lal. He'd 'made a mystery over his name', and had at first given the wrong one – which in itself was a punishable offence, although Ronald Merrick hadn't proceeded against him because the offence in Hari's case was only technical. But Hari had gone on record as saying, 'I hate the whole stinking country, the people who live in it and the people who rule it.' He'd worked in the same firm as Moti Lal. He was a one-time colleague of a young anarchist called Vidyasagar who'd been arrested for distributing seditious literature and delivering a pamphlet to the police calling on them to assist the people to 'liberate the martyrs of the Bibighar Gardens'. At the time of his arrest, after the assault on me, his room had been searched. The police thought it curious that there were no letters in his room; no letters, except one – a letter from someone in England who wasn't identified because he'd only signed his Christian name, but it was clear he was in the forces, and had been at Dunkirk. He described Dunkirk as a shambles. He asked Hari to bear in mind that letters might be opened. His father had opened some of them while this boy was in France and hadn't forwarded them because they were full of 'hot-headed political stuff'. Nobody could understand why Hari had kept just this one letter out of all the letters he must have had from time to time from different people. Of course they didn't intend to pursue the business of who this rather 'bolshie'-sounding English boy might be. It was enough that the letter more or less proved Hari was a bolshie himself. Without much difficulty a case had been made out to show that Hari Kumar – in spite of seeming to be such a quiet, uncommitted, well-educated young man – was a leading member of a group

of dangerous fellows whose early arrest alone had deprived
them of the opportunity to act openly against the war effort. The
papers relating to Kumar and the other boys had been sent to the
commissioner, and the commissioner had agreed with the decision Robin White had 'very reluctantly' come to: the decision
that these boys should be imprisoned under the Defence of
India Rules.

By the time Connie got to this point in her harangue I was
laughing in the way you do when the alternative is to cry. I knew
who the English boy must be. I said, 'But it's a farce! It's absurd!
Hari can prove it's a ridiculous *monstrous* farce!'

She said, 'But my dear, that's what puzzles *me*. The other
boys denied everything – everything except that they all know
each other, which they hardly *could* deny. They shouted and
wept and insisted that they were innocent of everything except
drinking hooch. And we knew they were lying. But Hari was
an altogether different matter. He was examined personally
by Jack Poulson. But to every question he said nothing. He
neither denied nor agreed. The only thing he ever said in his
own defence was "I wasn't at the Bibighar. I haven't seen Miss
Manners since the night we visited the temple." And of course
he only said that when they were accusing him of assault. To
all the other questions his only answer was, "I have nothing to
say." It's unnatural. I mean to me it's unnatural. The men simply
took his silence as a confession of guilt. I expect if I were a man
I'd have done the same. But I'm a woman, like you. I think of
Hari Kumar and listen to Jack talking to Mavis about him, and
to my husband talking to old Menen, and I think, "It's wrong.
A man doesn't say nothing, unless he's trying to put a noose
round his own neck. He fights for his life and his freedom. He
fights because he *is* a man."'

We were sitting on the verandah. Oh, everything was there –
the wicker chairs, the table with the tea tray on it, the scent of
the flowers, the scent of India, the air of certainty, of *perpetuity*;
but, as well, the odd sense of none of it happening at all because
it had begun wrong and continued wrong, and so was already
ended, and was wrong even in its ending, because its ending, for
me, was unreal and remote, and yet *total* in its envelopment, as
if it had already turned itself into a beginning. Such constant
hope we suffer from! I think the MacGregor House was built

on such foundations. The steps up to the verandah where I'd stumbled and fallen were only a few feet away. I had never seen Janet MacGregor's ghost, but I felt that she must have seen mine.

Connie said, 'I expect it's frightfully silly of me, but you know if Hari Kumar had been an Englishman I could have understood his silence better, although even then it would have had to be a silence imposed on him by a woman.'

I began to laugh again. I laughed because I saw that this time there really was nothing I could do – for Connie, for myself, or for Hari, for anyone. My legs – bare from the knee down – were an anachronism, an outrage. To play the scene with anything like *style* I needed a long dress of white muslin, and a little straw boater on my head. I needed to be conscious of the dignity of the occasion. I needed to be able to say, 'But Harry is an English-man,' and then to rise, put up my little parasol and detach myself from Constance White's company, so that she would *know* but say nothing because this was a world where men died in the open and women wept in private, and the Queen sat like a wise old lady on her throne and succeeded in that difficult feat of proving that there was a world where corruption also died for lack of stinking air.

Oh well, it was fine, wasn't it? Me sitting there in one chair and Connie White in another, showing acres of bare ill-looking flesh, sweating under the arms, and Hari sweating in a disgusting jailhouse, beyond the reach of either of us, wondering what he'd gained by acting like a white man should when a girl made him give a promise: a promise for his sake, yes, but for her own too. She wanted him. She wanted him to be around to make love to her again. It was marvellous. Marvellous because he was black. I wanted him and he was black so his blackness was part of what I wanted. Sitting there with Connie, laughing my head off, I hoped for one bitter, selfish moment that he suffered as much as I did, for putting his bloody acquired English pride above his compulsion to enter *me*. I wished him joy of his stupid sense of values. I thought: How typical! You tell an Indian to say nothing and he takes it literally.

Afterwards, of course, I knew he hadn't taken it literally. He'd interpreted it that way deliberately. To punish himself. To give him something new about himself that he could mock. When Connie had gone, no wit the wiser for her visit, but I suppose convinced I was unbalanced, Lili found me weeping in my room, because the comic mood had gone, the melodrama had exploded, not into tragedy but just into life and all the stupid cross-currents that tossed you indiscriminately from one thought to another but managed to keep you up. You can never drown. Never, never. Until you're dead. So why be so ridiculously afraid of the truth?

But with Lili sitting on my bed, wanting to comfort me but also wanting to chastize me for my absurdity, I was a child again. I wept and cried out, 'I want him, I want him. Bring him back to me, Auntie. Please help to bring him back.'

She said nothing. Like Hari. For them I suppose there *is* nothing to say. Nothing, that is, if they are intent on building instead of on destroying. Behind all the chatter and violence of India – what a deep, lingering silence. Siva dances in it. Vishnu sleeps in it. Even their music is silence. It's the only music I know that sounds conscious of *breaking* silence, of going back into it when it's finished, as if to prove that every man-made sound is an illusion.

What an odd concept of the world that is! We shall never understand it. They don't really understand it themselves, I suspect. Is it to try to understand it that Sister Ludmila wanders the streets collecting the bodies of the dead and the dying? Is it just a concept that could be traced to some long-forgotten overwhelming, primitive experience of pain and suffering? I ask because it struck me, a few weeks later, when I knew I was pregnant and I asked Lili to send for Anna Klaus, that Anna stood on the same edge of reality and illusion herself, because she'd been deprived and had suffered and continued to live. She's a great believer in anaesthetizing the patient, a great giver of sedatives. I remember how she stood in my bedroom frowning her little professional frown as she sorted things out in her black bag. Such a wealth of compromise there is in a doctor's bag! She seemed to be a long way away from me, and yet to be taking me with her – millions of miles away down long glazed white-tiled tunnels, subterranean passages of human degradation that were saved from filthiness because we northerners have learned how to make suffering aseptic and non-contagious. At first I had a silly idea she was preparing something for me to take to get rid of the child. I said, 'What's that, what's that?' She said, 'What a fuss! It is only to give you a quiet night. Expectant mothers must be contemplative. Like nuns.'

So I lay there, letting her get on with it. But suddenly I said, 'What am I to do, Anna? I can't live without him.'

She didn't look at me. She was measuring the potion. She spoke to the medicine, not to me. After all, this was the one thing she could really trust, really believe in, really love. She said, 'This you must learn to do. To live without.'

She handed me the glass, and stood by, until I'd drunk every drop.

Appendix to Part 7

Letters from Lady Manners to Lady Chatterjee

Srinagar, 31 May '43

My Dear Lili,

I hope you've forgiven me for not accepting your offer to come up last month, and for the silence since then that has been broken only by my two telegrams. When I wired you a week ago I promised I would write. If you would like to, do come next month. I shall be on the houseboat.

I'm afraid there are going to be endless legal complications. Poor Daphne died intestate, so I think the money becomes subject to the statutory trusts, on the child's behalf, unless the part of it which Daphne inherited from her mother is claimed by Mrs George's nephews and nieces. Mrs George Manners had a married sister, someone Daphne used to refer to as Auntie Kate, who was killed in a road accident. The husband married again, but there were two or three children from the first marriage – cousins of Daphne's with whom she remembered playing as a child. I expect if Daphne had died intestate but without issue the cousins would have had some sort of claim. I'm not sure what the situation is when the child in question is illegitimate. It will all have to be gone into and dealt with by the lawyers in London – which is where all the money is held anyway. Daphne was very careful with her small inheritance. She never touched the principal but drew on the income through the banks over here. Anyway, I have asked Mr Docherty in 'Pindi to do whatever has to be done to start sorting things out – but it will take ages before we know what properly belongs to the child and even longer before we know how use can be made of it over here.

Meanwhile the responsibility for her is mine. When you come up, Lili, perhaps you will be able to say whether you think the child is Hari Kumar's. I have a special reason for wanting to know. Not a reason connected with any legal claim or criminal charge. There is no question of attempting to establish paternity. Mr Kumar is beyond either our incriminations or our help, *and that is how I want it left*. But in giving shelter and affection to the child for Daphne's sake – and for its own – I should be happier knowing to what extent one might do so in the belief that its parentage wasn't surrounded by doubt as well as tragedy. I know I don't need to tell you that I want your *opinion*, not your reassurance, and that if you don't feel able to give one I shouldn't want you to pretend, simply to set my mind at rest.

She is a sweet and pretty child. Her skin is going to be pale, but not nearly pale enough for her to pass as white. I'm glad. As she grows older she won't be driven by the temptation to wear a false face. At least that is one thing she'll be spared – the misery and humiliation experienced by so many Eurasian girls. I intend to bring her up as an Indian, which is one of the reasons I have called her Parvati. The other reason is that I believe this is a name Daphne would like. Parvati Manners. Later she may decide to change that surname.

She was reluctant to come into the world but having done so seems equally determined not to let go of it. Dr Krishnamurti has found a wet-nurse, a pretty young Kashmiri girl who has lost her own first-born and lavishes affection on Parvati. She'd make a perfect ayah but says she won't leave Srinagar. She's the wife of one of the boys who paddles the shikaras during the season and I've promised him employment as soon as I move down on to the lake. Perhaps I can persuade them both to come to 'Pindi in September. He looks a frightful rogue but they're a handsome pair and she keeps him in order. It's touching to watch them playing with Parvati as if she were their own. While she feeds the baby he stays nearby, on guard. He's partly fascinated, partly embarrassed by the process, but intensely proud of his wife's talent, and I suppose of the part he played in filling her breasts with the milk now given to someone else's child. And I suppose they both see the money she earns as a compensation for their own loss; a gift from Allah.

It would please Daphne to watch them too. She only saw the child for a second or so. She was in labour for forty-eight hours. You and I have never had children so perhaps we can be classed as almost as ignorant of the process as men are – I mean anyway men who aren't doctors. Dr Knishnamurti was wonderful. Poor Daphne, to look at her you'd have thought her big and strong enough to have babies by the dozen, but the pelvis was wrong, and the baby was the wrong way round. He wanted her to go into hospital and have it turned, but she refused. So he did the whole thing here, bringing up a couple of nurses and an anaesthetist and loads of equipment. That was two or three weeks before she was due. He told me he'd turned the baby but that at the drop of a hat it could turn back again into a position that would lead to a breech delivery. He said he'd advised her to stand no nonsense and opt for a Caesarean so that directly it started the whole thing could just be got on with. But she refused. She had some idea that it was her duty to push the child out of her womb as nature intended. Krishnamurti and I have always been frank with one another. It's sad to think all this awful business was what was needed to make us friends. At the beginning I told him what your Doctor Klaus confided to you, that Daphne's heart was irregular. After examining her he told me it was nothing to worry about in itself, although he agreed that it was probably this irregularity that led to the doctors in London warning her off driving ambulances. It's odd that she never mentioned it. Well, no, not odd. Typical. She always pretended it was her eyesight that caused her to be what she once referred to as 'dismissed the service'. The point is, though, that the heart condition wasn't a complication in childbirth, only what Krishnamurti called 'a slight additional debit on the balance sheet'.

At one moment during that awful forty-eight hours I thought she wanted the child to die, or failing that to die herself. Since then I've changed my mind. She only wanted to 'do it right'. The child did turn again. I suppose because it couldn't get out. Krishnamurti had had the foresight to bring all the equipment back here. He turned the bedroom into an operating theatre. Poor Daphne wasn't compos mentis enough to know what was going on. It was I who gave permission for the Caesarean.

So I have that on my conscience. She should have been in hospital. Krishnamurti took every care. But she died of peritonitis.

For a couple of days afterwards I wouldn't even look at the child.
I'd seen it cut out. Krishnamurti let me watch. I was dressed up
like a nurse in theatre in a white gown, with a mask over my
mouth and nostrils. I needed to see this side of life. I'd never
have forgiven myself for being too faint-hearted to watch. When
it began I thought I'd never stand it. It seemed obscene, like
opening a can – which isn't obscene but is when the can is a
human abdomen. But then when the can was open and I saw
what they were lifting out I felt I was being born again myself. It
was a miracle and it made you realize that no miracle is beautiful
because it exists on a plane of experience where words like
beauty have no meaning whatsoever.

It also meant absolutely nothing to me that the curious
knotted little bundle of flesh that was lifted out of Daphne –
(perhaps prised is a better word because with their long rubber
gloves on they seemed to have to search for and encourage it to
emerge) – was obviously *not* the same skin colour as its mother.
The difference in colour was subtle, so subtle that were it not
for one particular recollection I'd now be persuaded that the fact
that the difference between them meant nothing was due to my
failing to notice one at the time. But I did notice it. The particular recollection I have is of thinking, Yes – I see – the father *was*
dark-skinned. But at the time this caused no emotional response.
I noted it and then forgot it. I only remembered it when Daphne
was dead and they tried to show me the child to take my mind
off things. But that wasn't the reason I rejected it. I rejected it
because in the state of mind I was in I blamed it for killing
Daphne. If anything its Indian-ness was what first made me feel
pity for it and start thinking of it as 'she'. I thought: Poor scrap
– there's not a thing she can look forward to.

I told you Daphne saw her for a second or two – between one
unconsciousness and another. The nurse held the child close to
her. She tried to touch it but didn't have the strength. But she
did smile. Which is why I really want you to see Parvati yourself
and judge if there is any resemblance at all to Hari Kumar. I'm
afraid I can't see Daphne in her – but perhaps you will. Relatives
are usually the last to see a family likeness.

Affectionately, Ethel

*

Rawalpindi, 5 Aug '47

My Dear Lili,

I have decided to leave 'Pindi. I refuse to live in a place whose people at the stroke of a pen will be turned into enemies of India – the country my husband tried to serve – and you can count on it that 'enemy' isn't overstating the case. The creation of Pakistan is our crowning failure. I can't bear it. They should never have got rid of Wavell. Our only justification for two hundred years of power was unification. But we've divided one composite nation into two and everyone at home goes round saying what a swell the new Viceroy is for getting it all sorted out so quickly. Which of course is right. But he's a twentieth-century swell – and India's still living in the nineteenth century – which is where we're leaving her. In Delhi they've all been blinded by him. I mean the Indians have. What they don't realize is that he was only intended to be the glamorous dressing in the shop window – a window we've been trying to get up attractively ever since the war ended. Behind the window the shop is as nineteenth-century as ever – albeit *radical* nineteenth-century. The slogan is still insular. India's independence at any cost, not for India's sake, but for our own.

I'm going down to the Residency in Gopalakand to stay with an old friend of Henry's, Sir Robert Conway, who is adviser to the Maharajah. The maharajahs are being sacrificed too – mostly their own fault, but the people who wield the knife are really the old Fabians and crusty Trade Unionists in London, *not* the Congress. Perhaps we can meet in Gopalakand? Little Parvati sends her love to Auntie Lili – and so do I.

Affectionately, Ethel

New Delhi, June 1948

My Dear Lili,

Can you possibly join me here? I'm at HH of Gopalakand's town palace, such as it is. I've been under the weather and there are a number of things I'd like to discuss. I also want to show you – and give you if you'll take them – certain items left by Daphne, writings of hers, etc., letters and a journal.

Under the terms of my new will I've made provision for Parvati and left money for the endowment of a children's home, thereby carrying out a wish expressed by Daphne. I've named you as one of the trustees and suggested that the home should be called The Manners Memorial Home for Indian Boys and Girls – which is a way of remembering my niece but avoiding the embarrassment that a name like The Daphne Manners Memorial Home might cause people who have long memories. I've suggested that the Home should be in Mayapore. One of the things we might discuss is the use of the site known as the Sanctuary. You told me last year that that woman's eyesight was failing. If it is possible and practicable to use the Sanctuary as a base for the home, one of the provisions of the endowment should be that Sister Ludmila is entitled to continue living there in grace and favour, as it were.

When you've read poor Daphne's journal – which I've kept to myself all these years, although I think you always suspected the existence of something of the sort – you'll understand better why my thoughts have run on these lines. The other thing we must discuss is Parvati's future. I don't want to sound morbid, but the time isn't far off when my death will leave her alone in the world. I am still of the opinion that nothing should be done to try and trace the man you and I are both certain is the father. Each time you see her you say she looks more like Hari than the time before. This is a comfort to me because I know you are telling the truth and not just reassuring me; but it doesn't persuade me that the poor boy should be tracked down and made to face evidence of his responsibility. I'm sure you agree. Without any difficulty I could have arranged for this to be done while he was in prison, and if he is still alive could still arrange it, I suppose, even though he must have been released two or three years ago. I think you are right to suspect that when his Aunt Shalini left Mayapore in 1944 she returned to her old home in the UP solely in order to set up some kind of household he'd have been able to return to when he came out – even if his sojourn there was not of long duration. Obviously someone knows the truth – probably that man Romesh Chand Gupta Sen. Your lawyer friend Srinivasan's assertion – when he came out of prison himself and asked after Mrs Gupta Sen – that Romesh Chand simply shrugged the question away and said she'd gone home to her village and that he'd broken off all connection with the Kumar family, probably amounts to no more than an attempt on the old man's part to disguise the fact that he knew what had happened but didn't care to say. My own belief is that when Hari was released he probably went to his Aunt Shalini's but then took himself off elsewhere, perhaps even changed his name. A boy imprisoned for the reasons he was ostensibly detained for would not lack friends in the new India. My guess is he wanted none of them. He might be dead – a chance victim of that awful savagery – that Hindu–Muslim blood-bath last year that marked the end of our unifying and civilizing years of power and influence.

No, my dear. Leave poor Hari Kumar to work out his own salvation, if he's still alive to work it out and if there's a salvation of any kind for a boy like him. He is the left-over, the loose-end of our reign, the kind of person we created – I suppose with the best intentions. But for all Nehru's current emergence as a potential moral force in world affairs, I see *nothing* in India that will withstand the pressure of the legacy of the division we English have allowed her to impose on herself, and are morally responsible for. In allowing it we created a precedent for partition just at the moment when the opposite was needed, allowed it – again with the best intentions – as a result of tiredness, and failing moral and physical pretensions that just wouldn't stand the strain of looking into the future to see what abdication on India's terms instead of ours was going to mean. Perhaps finally we had no terms of our own because we weren't clever enough to formulate them in twentieth-century dress, and so the world is going to divide itself into isolated little pockets of dogma and mutual resistance, and the promise that always seemed to lie behind even the worst aspects of our colonialism will just evaporate into history as imperial mystique, foolish glorification of a severely practical and greedy policy.

Do you remember dear Nello with Henry's pipe in his mouth, pacing up and down, copying Henry, saying, in Henry's voice, 'Policy? Policy? To hell with policy! What are you thinking and feeling, dear chap? That's the point! Don't let's waste bloody time on second-rate notions of what is *likely*. Let's consider the damned unlikely and see where we go from there.' How I laughed at the time. Remembering it now I don't laugh any more. Such a marvellous opportunity wasted. I mean for us, by us. Indians feel it too, don't they? I mean, in spite of the proud chests and all the excitement of sitting down as free men at their own desks to work out a constitution. Won't that constitution be a sort of love-letter to the English – the kind an abandoned lover writes when the affair has ended in what passes at the time as civilized and dignified mutual recognition of incompatibility? In a world grown suddenly dull because the beloved, thank God, has gone, offering his killing and unpredictable and selfish affections elsewhere, you attempt to recapture, don't you, the moments of significant pleasure – which may not have been mutual at all, but anyway existed. But this recapture is always impossible. You settle for the second-rate, you settle for the lesson you appear to have learned and forget the lesson you hoped to learn and might have learned, and so learn nothing at all, because the second-rate is the world's common factor, and any damn fool people can teach it, any damn fool people can inherit it.

What terrifies me is the thought that gradually, when the splendours of civilized divorce and protestations of continuing as good friends are worked out, the real animus will emerge, the one both our people just managed to keep in check when there was reason to suppose that it was wrong, because it could lead neither rulers nor ruled anywhere. I mean of course the dislike and fear that exists between black and white. And this is a fifth-rate passion, appropriate only to a nation of vulgar shopkeepers and a nation of fat-bellied banias. I remember that time dear Nello mimicked Henry, the look of awful shock on the face of one of Henry's aides (an awfully well-bred chap, whose grandfather made a fortune out of bottling sauce or something – not that this was against him, but he'd somehow never risen above it) and the way, while I was still laughing, this aide turned to me and seemed as if he were about to say, 'Good heavens, Lady Manners! Do you allow *that* in Sir Henry's own drawing-room?' And all he meant was that Nello was brown-skinned and poor Henry was white, although actually he was grey and yellow and ill, and on his way to the grave. I suppose everything gets stripped down to *that*, in the end, because that is the last division of all, isn't it? The colour of the skin, I mean; not dying.

Well, you and I have always tried to keep open house. *You* anyway, I suspect, will have to keep it open for a long time *yet*. What this letter is really all about, Lili, is this: When I'm gone, will you give Parvati a roof?

My love, Ethel

*

Imagine, then, a flat landscape, one that turns, upends, following in reverse the bends and twists of night flight 115, the Viscount service to Calcutta; a landscape that is dark but shows immediately below as a system of lights, clustering neatly round a central point with a few minor galaxies beyond its periphery – the flarepath of the airfield, the suburb of Banyagani, divorced from the parent body because the link with Mayapore, the Grand Trunk Road, is unlit except by the occasional night traffic (miniature headlamps moving at what looks even from this height like excessive speed) and a relatively small and isolated constellation about midway, where the new English colony live on hand for the Technical College, the factories, and the airfield which they use as casually as a bus terminal. Apart from the stranger there is one other Englishman on flight 115 – the same man who at the club that evening occasionally looked across at Srinivasan's private party; perhaps less from curiosity than from a desire to obtain momentary relief from the business of concentrating on questions being put to him by talkative young men like Surendranath and Desai who were trying to make up for the time they think their fathers lost.

Similarly surrounded as he has been in the airport lounge, this other Englishman now sits in the almost empty airliner several seats away from the stranger. The other passengers are Indian businessmen. They, too, sit separately from each other, on their way to deals in West Bengal. When the illuminated sign on the bulkhead goes out (*Fasten seat belts. No smoking*) portfolios will be opened and papers studied. The flight is of such short duration; the respite granted as precious to a man as the time he spends in more intimate surroundings reading the morning newspapers to find out what happened yesterday and judge how it might affect what could happen today. One of them – the man who sat in the airport lounge with his feet curled up on the interior-sprung chair – wears the dhoti. There is not room on the aircraft seat for him to continue in similar comfort, for which the stranger is grateful, because who knows where those feet have been in the past twenty-four hours?

The aircraft seems to be having difficulty attaining height. From the oval-shaped port the flarepath comes again into view, not much farther below than it was the last time of looking, and then the lights of Mayapore come back in focus, slightly blurred, which may be due to the condensation on the double glazing of the windows, but at least they conform to the pattern that is known and is now recognizable, because the watcher has had time to orientate himself.

One can even detect where the *maidan* lies: a dark space enclosed by evenly plotted points of illumination, Hospital road, Club road, Church road (a name unaltered in spite of Victoria having become Mahatma Gandhi), and Artillery road. The plane banks, nosing east, almost taking the course of the river that leads to Miss Crane's unimaginable coast. With this God's-eye view of the created world she never had to cope, which perhaps was a pity, because the topography she found so inhibiting from ground-level reveals itself from this height, and at this speed, as random and unplanned, with designs hacked into it by people who only worked things out as they went along.

The neon standard that lights the faithful from the Tirupati temple to the river and back again shows up relatively brightly, and plotting from this and the neon light above the keeper's hut at the level crossing at the northern head of the Bibighar bridge, the stranger (returning to Calcutta for a second inspection of mouldering missionary relics) is able to fix the approximate position of the Bibighar Gardens and the MacGregor House.

The Bibighar Gardens are dark (now, as then) – but from the MacGregor House there is the burst of light that Lili Chatterjee promised: all the lights turned on in the occupied rooms and all the floodlights in the garden; pale from here but suddenly unmistakable, so that foolishly one searches that distant area for signs of Lili herself, and imagines that she stands below the steps of the verandah with Parvati, staring up at the winking red, green and amber riding lights of the airborne commercial juggernaut.

This is the last image then – the MacGregor House – in which there are sounds of occupation other than those made by Lili and Parvati: of tinkling broken glass, of sensibly shod feet taking the rise from the black and white tiled hallway to the corridor above from which brass-knobbed mahogany doors lead into rooms that give their occupants the opportunity to view the reality for themselves and the dream for others, and to make up their own minds about the precise meaning of what lies beyond.

These sounds are ones that the casual visitor will today attribute to Parvati's presence, not to her mother's. But Parvati steps lightly and breaks nothing (except perhaps a young man's heart). She is another story, which is why her presence here is tentative, although this suits her, because of her shyness and the impression you get of her as a girl who has not yet met the world face to face, let alone subjected it to the force of her personality. To come upon her unexpectedly, to find her standing alone in a room of the MacGregor House or sitting in the shade in the garden counting the petals of a flower – to see her expression of intense but distant pleasure (distant because in spite of its intensity the source of it is obviously far away in some private world that trembles on the brink between her youthful illusions and her maturer judgment), to hear her early in the mornings and evenings practising her singing, to listen to the grave and studious application with which she attacks a difficult phrase, admits defeat with a low cry of exasperation, then re-attacks it, this is to leave the MacGregor House with an idea of Parvati as a girl admirably suited to her surroundings where there is always the promise of a story continuing instead of finishing, and of Lady Chatterjee as the repository of a tradition established for the sake of the future rather than of the past.

'Well, I don't know about that,' (Lady Chatterjee says, taking the stranger for one last look round the old place, accepting the support of his arm, shading her eyes from the late-afternoon sun with her free hand – and Shafi already waiting to take him in good time to the airport). 'I mean, a repository sounds like a place for storing furniture when you bash off to some other station. I suppose an Englishman could say that the whole of India is that sort of place. You all went, but left so much behind that you couldn't carry with you wherever you were going, and these days those of you who come back can more often than not hardly bother to think about it, let alone ask for the key to go in and root about among all the old dust sheets to see that everything worth while that you left is still there and isn't falling to pieces with dry rot.' She pauses and then asks, 'Has Parvati said goodbye to you properly?'

Yes, Parvati has said goodbye, and now runs down the steps

from the verandah (late, because she tends to work on Mayapore time instead of Indian Standard), making her way to her evening lesson with her *guru* who has sung in London, New York and Paris, and these days receives for instruction only the most promising pupils – girls who have both the talent and the stamina for a course of training that lasts eight years. One day, perhaps, Parvati will also sing in those western capitals, and then become a *guru* herself, instructing a new generation of girls in the formal complexities of the songs her English mother once described as the only music in the world she knew that sounded conscious of breaking silence and going back into it when it was finished. Before she goes out of sight – running in a pale pink saree – she pauses and waves, and the stranger waves back, wishing her well for the evening lesson. Twice a day she runs like this, and in the intervals locks herself up for hours of rigorous practice. Some- times a young man appears, bearing the twin drums, the *tablas*, to help her with the necessary percussion which otherwise she provides herself with sharp little flicks of her supple fingers on the onion–shaped tamboura. Her skin is the palest brown and in certain lights her long dark hair reveals a redness more familiar in the north.

Dooliya le aō re morē babul ke kaharwa.
Chali hoon sajan ba ke des. Sangaki sakha
saba bichchuda gayee hai apne ri apne ghar jaun.

Oh, my father's servants, bring my palanquin.
I am going to the land of my husband. All my
companions are scattered. They have gone to different homes.

(A morning raga)
Translation by Dipali Nag

THE DAY OF THE SCORPION

To Fern and John
with deep affection and regard

CONTENTS

PROLOGUE

THE WRITER encountered a Muslim woman once in a narrow street of a predominantly Hindu town, in the quarter inhabited by money-lenders. The feeling he had was that she was coming in search of a loan. She wore the *burkha*, that unhygienic head-to-toe covering that turns a woman into a walking symbol of inefficient civic refuse collection and leaves you without even an impression of her eyes behind the slits she watches the gay world through, tempted but not tempting; a garment in all probability inflaming to her passions but chilling to her expectations of having them satisfied. Pity her for the titillation she must suffer.

After she had passed there was a smell of Chanel No. 5, which suggested that she needed money because she liked expensive things. Perhaps she had a rebellious spirit, or laboured under a confusion of ideas and intentions. On the other hand she may merely have been submissive to her husband, drenching herself for his private delight with a scent she did not realize was also one of public invitation – and passed that day through the street of the money-lenders only because it was a short cut to the mosque. It was a Friday, and it is written in the Koran: 'Believers, when the call is made for prayer on Friday, hasten to the remembrance of Allah and leave off all business. That would be best for you, if you but knew it. Then, when the prayers are ended, disperse and go in quest of Allah's bounty.' Perhaps, when the service was over, it was her intention to return by the way she had come.

If she was going to divine service then she was bound for the Great Mosque, which lies in the heart of the city. Its minaret is not the only minaret in Ranpur, but it is the tallest and the only one from which the call to prayer is made nowadays; the other mosques of Ranpur are no longer in use as houses of worship. Some of them have decayed, others less ruinous are used as storerooms by the municipality. There are still Muslims in

Ranpur but the days are gone when the great festivals of the
îd al-fitr and the îd al-Adzha could fill the mosques with thousands of the faithful from the city and the surrounding villages
of the plain. The days are gone because thousands of the faithful
are gone. Some of those that remain still mourn friends and relatives who chose Islam but never reached that land of promise,
having died on the way, some of illness, many by violence.
Sometimes a train they travelled on would pass one coming out
of Islam, laden with passengers who had neither chosen Islam
nor been content to stay when they found themselves living
there, in the houses they were born in. These people mourned
too for what they had left behind and for friends and relatives
who started on the journey with them but did not live to finish
it. Some of the survivors settled in Ranpur which was, still is, a
sprawling city, seat of the provincial government. There are
temples and bathing places on the banks of the sacred river, with
steps and burning ghats. Bridges connect the north to the south
bank which is less densely populated than the north where lateral
and tangential industrial development has broken the landscape
with chimneys taller than any minaret. From the air this expansion outwards from the ancient nucleus falls into something like
a pattern. From the ground no pattern can be seen (except to
the east in the military precision with which the roads and
installations of the cantonment were built by a people who are
also gone) and the nucleus itself is a warren of narrow streets and
chowks in which one may too easily get lost and, being lost,
marvel that anyone could know of a short cut to the mosque or
to anywhere, let alone find it. Here, you might think no experience would be long enough to acquire such knowledge, in fact
that confusion seems to be almost deliberate, the result of recognition of a need to huddle together in order not to be destroyed
by a land that seems at best indifferent, at worst malignly
opposed, to human occupation.

To leave the narrow streets and crowded chowks behind and
enter the area once distinguished by the title Civil Lines, an area
of broad avenues and spacious bungalows in walled compounds
which culminates in the palladian grandeur of Government
House, the Secretariat and the Legislative Assembly; to continue, still in an easterly direction, past the *maidan*, the government college, the hospital and the film studios and enter the

cantonment, which someone once described as Aldershot with trees planted to provide shade instead of cut down to make room, is to pass from one period of history to another and to feel that the people from the small and distant island of Britain who built and settled here were attempting to express in the architectural terms that struck them as suitable their sense of freedom at having space around them at last, a land with length and breadth to it that promised ideal conditions for concrete and abstract proof of their extraordinary talent for running things and making them work. And yet here too there is an atmosphere of circumspection, of unexpected limits having been reached and recognized, and quietly, sensibly settled for. Too late to reduce the scale and crowd everything together, each road and building has an air of being turned inwards on itself to withstand a siege.

If you look in places like Ranpur for evidence of things these island people left behind which were of value, you might choose any one or several of the public works and installations as visible proof of them: the roads and railways and telegraph for a modern system of communication, the High Court for a sophisticated code of civil and criminal law, the college for education to uni- versity standard, the State Legislature for democratic govern- ment, the Secretariat for a civil service made in the complex image of that in Whitehall; the clubs for a pattern of urbane and civilized behaviour, the messes and barracks for an ideal of military service to the mother country. These were bequeathed, undoubtedly; these and the language and the humpy graves in the English cemetery of St Luke's in the oldest part of the cantonment, many of whose headstones record an early death, a cutting-off before the prime or in the prime, with all that this suggests in the way of unfinished business.

But it is not these things which most impress the stranger on his journey into the civil lines, into the old city itself (where he becomes lost and notes the passage of a woman dressed in the *burkha* in the street of the money-lenders) and then back past the secretariat, the Legislative Assembly and Government House, and on into the old cantonment in a search for points of present contact with the reality of twenty years ago, the repercussions, for example, of the affair in the Bibighar Gardens. What impresses him is something for which there is no memorial but which all these things collectively bear witness to: the fact that here in Ranpur, and in places like Ranpur, the British came to the end of themselves as they were.

More than two hundred miles south-west of Ranpur but still inside the boundary of the province of which Ranpur is the principal city lies the town of Premanagar, and – some five miles farther, marking the site of an earlier town of that name – the Premanagar Fort.

Premanagar is most easily prounounced Premman'ugger. Old-style British used to call it Pre*mah*'n'gh, strongly accenting the second syllable and all but swallowing the third and fourth, which gave the Fort status of the kind enjoyed by a tent when it is called a marquee. Originally built by the Rajputs, the Fort was partially destroyed and patched up by the Moghuls who held it against the Mahrattas but lost it to the British. In the mid-nineteenth century it was for a time the seat of an English free-booting gentleman of doubtful origin called Turner who raised a company of mercenaries which he styled Turner's Horse. His men terrorized the countryside and were said to be devoted to their leader. Apart from his Horse Turner had six wives, and a modest fortune which he lost gambling in Calcutta trying to buy a seventh. He died in a skirmish which most historians of the Mutiny of 1857 overlook, probably because so far as one can see nothing led up to it and it led nowhere itself. And old daguerreo-type reveals Turner as a man with side whiskers and fixed, pale-looking eyes that were probably blue. One suspects that he was murdered. His irregular cavalry either died with him or dis-appeared in search of further adventure, so no Turner's Horse lived on to perpetuate his memory. He was, it is said, a press-ganged sailor who deserted in Madras and sought his fortune up-country. But no matter. He is a body buried as it were in the foundations of that other ruined stronghold, the British Empire.

Real bodies were in fact buried in the foundations of the Pre-managar Fort. It was a fashion of the times, but the parents of young men (and sometimes the young men's wives) who were bricked up alive to give a fort an auspicious start in life were hand-somely rewarded. It is said, though, that the misfortunes of this particular fort were once traced to the fact that the treasurer at the court of the Rajput prince who built it – and bricked up a

promising young man and his child wife – pocketed the bereaved
family's pension for the five years it took the boy's father to
pluck up the courage to go over the treasurer's head and hint at
injustice. It is not known what then happened to the treasurer,
or the complainant. And anyway it is all conjecture. It has the
sound of a myth devised later to explain or anyway celebrate
misadventure. The British – as usual – had the best of it. They
inherited a partial ruin and preserved it with reverent determination as if awestruck at the thought of changing anything that
might then be turned to their disadvantage. Until 1939 the Fort
was a detention barracks, and a magnet for military schemes run
by grey colonels who had forgotten that as rosy subalterns they
had always found such exercises distracting to their sense of what
one was in the world to do.

After 1939, the Fort became a prison – a place of civil instead
of military detention. It comprised the foundations of the old
outer wall, a broken-down despoiled Hindu temple in what had
once been the precincts of the South Gate, a still stout inner wall,
a pretty mosque, two wells, a flagpole, and a walled courtyard of
red earth. Here, in the courtyard, between August 1942 and the
date of his release, the Fort's most distinguished prisoner created
a garden to pass the time. Traces of it still remain. Given better
luck than Turner his memory might have been perpetuated by
the habit, dear to Indians, of naming a place after its founder
or its most illustrious inhabitant. But it is not known now as
Kasim's Garden. Besides, it was only a patch.

Below the hill on which the redstone Fort rests in the massive
immobility of its functional decline are other ruins, the site of
excavations in 1926 by a team of Frenchmen whose leader
became *persona non grata* with the Deputy Commissioner and
the Provincial Governor when a complaint was lodged by an
English lady, a Miss Frayle, that Professor Lebrun had made
an improper suggestion to her while pointing out a recently un-
covered frieze of Hindu erotica. The expedition departed for
Pondicherry in amused, Gallic disgrace, collectively shrugging
its shoulders; and the inquisitive English who subsequently took
an archaeological interest in the diggings at Premanagar found
the erotica disappointingly mild, so mild in fact that Miss Frayle's
reputation suffered and she packed her bags and left for Persia.

Beyond the ruins is the plain, eroded by time, low rainfall, occasional floods and poor husbandry: a complex of old dry river-beds (nullahs) and scantily grassed hummocks over which herds of goats tinkled and still do, seeking the shade of infrequent trees and of bushes whose exhausted-looking leaves become yellowed by the dust blown up from the unmetalled strips on either side of the trunk road. This road stands out in the arid landscape, a hardened artery. The lifeblood of the country, traffic, flows along it thinly and irregularly. Even today you can stand on the roadside and hear nothing for an hour on end except some-times the goatbells and the wind in the telegraph wires. The wind is hot. At midday the Fort's outline is distorted by the shifting, shimmering air. At a suitable distance it takes on the look of a mirage and at certain times of the year, when climatic conditions are right, actually produces one – a replica of itself, hovering above ground, sometimes upside down. English people, observ-ing the apparition, used to find themselves thinking of Kipling or A. E. W. Mason, and looking forward to sundown, at which hour it was customary to refresh the body and relieve the spirit of the otherwise oppressive burdens of their duty.

Ranpur and the Fort at Premanagar are the first two images in the story to be told.

BOOK ONE

THE PRISONERS
IN THE FORT

PART ONE

AN ARREST, 1942

I

EX-CHIEF MINISTER Mohammed Ali Kasim was arrested at his home in Ranpur at 5 a.m. on August 9th 1942 by a senior English police officer who arrived in a car, with a motor-cycle escort, two armed guards and a warrant for his detention under the Defence of India Rules. The officer waited for ten minutes on the wrong side of the locked iron gates while the chaukidar went off to rouse one of the servants who in turn roused another who roused Mr Kasim. By the time the officer gained the entrance hall Mr Kasim was standing there in his pyjamas.

'Good morning,' the ex-Chief Minister said. 'I'm sorry they've dragged you out of bed. Is that for me?'

'I'm afraid it is,' the officer replied. Mr Kasim glanced briefly at the warrant, asked the Englishman to step inside and promised not to be long. Mrs Kasim came out and offered him an early-morning cup of tea which he felt he had to decline in the circumstances. She nodded, as if she quite understood, and then returned to help her husband get ready.

Ten minutes later Mr and Mrs Kasim came into the vestibule together.

'Where are you actually taking me?' Mr Kasim asked.

The officer hesitated. 'My orders are to drive to Government House. Beyond that I can't say.'

'Oh, well, that's just an initial formality. They'll hardly put me up there for the duration. I hope it's not going to be the Kandipat jail, though. It's so damp and depressing.' He turned to his wife, to embrace her, and the officer moved away and looked at one of the many portraits on the wall, a head and shoulders study of an elderly Indian wearing a number of rather splendid-looking decorations: the ex-Chief Minister's father, probably. He noted a likeness. The Kasims had always been rich and influential. The house was large and richly furnished, but had the spicy smell of Indian cooking and Indian perfumes which the Englishman always found disturbing, not quite civilized, or civilized in a way that suggested there was no distinction to be made between ancient and modern societies.

'I'm ready,' Mr Kasim said.

'Haven't you a bag?'

'Oh, that's here.' He pointed to a suitcase and a bedroll standing against the wall. 'I packed last night when I had news of the Congress Committee vote in Bombay. I thought it would save us time.'

The officer looked at the luggage and disguised his reaction – one of surprise and slight annoyance – by pursing his lips. Lists and arrangements for the detentions had been made secretly for some time, but the arrests, if they had to be made at all, were supposed to come as a surprise.

Saying nothing the officer stooped, picked up the suitcase and bedroll and carried them out to the waiting car where they were taken from him by one of the servants who had now all been alerted and stood around in the forecourt to see their master off to jail.

It was still dark. Mrs Kasim did not come out of the house. The Englishman waited until Mr Kasim was settled in the back seat of the car, gave a nod to the motor-cyclists and as they kicked their machines into life entered the car himself and closed the door. Now that the most embarrassing part of his job was done he would have liked a cigarette. He put his hand in his pocket. He would offer one to Mr Kasim to show him that he appreciated his co-operation. The last time he had arrested a member of Congress there had been a most objectionable scene: sarcasm, abuse and a lecture all the way to the jail about the iniquities of the *raj*. Mr Kasim was a model of restraint and good behaviour. But then he was a Muslim, and the Muslims were men of action, not words. You knew better where you stood with them and they knew when to bow with dignity to the inevitable. Remembering Mr Kasim was a Muslim, though, the officer realized he probably didn't smoke, and realizing that, he thought it would be better manners to deny himself as well.

'I'm sorry, Mr Kasim,' Sir George Malcolm said.

They were in the large lofty-ceilinged room where in 1937 Mr Kasim had presented himself to the preceding Governor and listened to formal and rather grudging words of invitation to form a ministry, and in the October of 1939 presented himself again to hand in his written resignation and the resignations of his colleagues. He had been in the room on many other occasions, but these were the two that came most significantly to mind.

'Please don't apologize,' he said. 'Are they arresting Gandhiji too?'

'Yes, so I understand.'

'And the Committee in Bombay?'

The Governor nodded, then said, 'Rather a broad sweep this time, as a matter of fact. Even chaps in your district sub-committees are going into the bag.'

Through one of the tall windows light was now showing. Kasim could just make out the distant bulk of the Secretariat. During his own ministry the lights had often burned there all night. A tale was told that on the occasion of his resignation the preceding Governor had waited until he was alone with his ADC and then said, 'Thank God, now for a bit of peace.' An English wit in the Secretariat had commented, 'Well, why not? The war is nearly two months old,' and like the rest reverted to the habit of leaving the office at 4 p.m. to get in a game of tennis and a drink at the club before going home to dress for dinner.

The Governor said, 'I gather you packed last night. Did your colleagues do the same, d'you think?'

'Perhaps. I don't know. Should they have?'

'Most of them.'

'Are they in the building?'

'No. They're elsewhere.'

'In Kandipat?'

The Governor did not answer. Kasim did not expect him to. In a case of mass arrests like this the British would be absurdly secretive about the places where leading Congressmen were to be kept under lock and key.

'If they are in Kandipat or elsewhere, why have I been brought here?'

The Governor took off his spectacles, dangled them, then placed them on the blotter. His desk was untidy. In his predecessor's day it had always been unpleasantly immaculate.

'I wanted to have a talk,' he said.

'Before sending me to Kandipat?'

'I think not Kandipat. Don't you agree?'

Kasim smiled. 'Do I have a choice, then?'

'Possibly.' The Governor leaned back in his chair and put one arm over it. With his other hand he played with the spectacles. 'What a damn' silly thing, isn't it? What did your people expect us to do? Sit back and let you bring the country to a standstill? Did anyone in his right mind really expect us to be blackmailed into granting independence just like that in the middle of a world war, with the Japanese preening themselves on the Chindwin?'

'Does anyone in his right mind think that arresting us all from Gandhi down will help?'

'If it stops you from inciting the factory workers to strike, the railways to stop, the ports to close, the soldiers to lay down their arms. That's what you voted for in Bombay yesterday.'

'I did not vote, Governor-ji.'

'No, you did not vote because you resigned from the Congress Committee last year. On the other hand you haven't resigned from the Congress Party. There have been rumours that you were considering it.'

'They are unfounded.'

'Are they? Are they, truly?'

Kasim folded his hands.

'They are mostly the result of one-time wishful thinking on the part – for instance – of Mr Jinnah.'

The Governor laughed. 'Yes, I heard about that. Is *that* true? That Jinnah promised you a portfolio in Bengal or Sind if you'd go over to the League?'

'Let us just say that his interest was aroused by my resignation from the All India Congress Committee. A certain gentleman was commissioned to ask what my further intentions might be. It is true that there were hints about a rosy ministerial future in one of the Muslim majority provinces, but nothing specific was promised.'

'And your reply?'

'Merely the truth. That I resigned from the committee in order to devote more time to my legal work and that in any case I was not an opportunist. Perhaps I should emphasize that I am not before we go further. You are thinking of offering me a loophole through which I could escape going to prison, I believe.'

'Not a loophole. But it would be an awful waste of your time and talent if you went to jail just when you were seriously considering resigning from Congress, wouldn't it?'

'I am not seriously considering it, Governor-ji. I am not considering it at all and have never considered it.'

'Will you consider it now?'

'Will you give me reasons why I should?'

The Governor sat forward, replaced his spectacles and picked up a pencil. 'Yes, Mr Kasim. I'll give you reasons, although as I see it they all point to one reason only – that you are no longer in sympathy with Congress policy. You haven't been in sympathy for a long time and grow intellectually and emotionally further and further away from Congress with every week that goes by. You were impatient with Congress when they won the provincial elections in 1937 but dithered about taking office. You were impatient with the face-saving formula which allowed them to pretend to take office just to show that the scheme for a federal central government wouldn't work. You were alarmed when you found yourself unable to form a provincial ministry which would have more accurately reflected the wishes of the electorate. The Congress majority in the province was slim enough to warrant a coalition. You wanted Nawaz Shah in your cabinet but none of your Congress colleagues would agree because he was a Muslim Leaguist. You were enough of a realist to bow to the inevitable, and a good enough party disciplinarian to make sure that on any major point of legislation in the Assembly your compromises were with the Muslim League and not the Hindu Mahasabah. You were criticized for that. People said scratch Kasim and you'll find one of Jinnah's men underneath. But you preferred to run the risk of that sort of criticism and to invite defeat in the Assembly than adjust your programme to ensure a comfortable majority of Congressites and Hindu right-wingers.' The Governor smiled. 'You see, I've done my homework. So let me continue. You knew what was going on in the districts, and knew that most of what the Muslims said was going on was gross exaggeration, but you recognized the dangers and were appalled at the evidence you had of what actual communal intimidation did exist. You saw that whatever the Congress professed to be, a national party, a secular party, a party dedicated to the ideal of independence and national unity, there were people in it who could never see it as anything but a Hindu-dominated organization whose real motive was power for the Hindus and who were coming into the open now that they'd got power. That alarmed you too. Every instance that came to your notice of a Muslim being discriminated against, of an injustice against a Muslim, of violence done to a Muslim, of Muslim children being forced to salute the Congress flag or sing a Congress hymn in school, you saw not only as reprehensible in itself, whatever the provocation might have been, but as another nail in the coffin, another wedge driven between the two major communities. And something else alarmed you, the realization that you were a man not with one master but two, the electorate to whom you were responsible, and the Congress High Command. It alarmed you because the High Command itself wasn't administratively committed. It wasn't answerable to an electorate, but it controlled and directed you who were. So when Britain declared war on Germany and the Viceroy declared war on Germany and the Congress High Command objected to having war declared over its head and called on all Congress ministries to resign, you resigned. You resigned at the dictate of a political organization that had no electoral responsibility to the country, except in the provinces through men like yourself. You saw the constitutional absurdity of this, but you handed your resignation in, handed it in here in this room to my predecessor, and he was a man who welcomed it because he was a man of the old school who thought India ungovernable except by decree, a man who'd sat back and laughed up his sleeve for two and a half years as he watched the farce of a ministry trying to serve both its electorate and its political bosses, and who sat back now, breathed a sigh of relief and assumed Governor's control which I've inherited. And it wasn't just the constitutional absurdity that struck you, it was the political folly of resigning, of having to resign. Without power, politics are so much hot air, and power is what your party got rid of. You knew what would happen and have seen it happen. How many seats in the Legislative Assembly reserved for Muslims were won in 1937 by non-League Muslims? A tidy few including your own. How many would be won now if we had an election tomorrow?

Any? Where would your slim Congress Party majority be with most of your non-aligned Muslims and even some of your Congress Muslims gone over to the League? Repeat that picture all over India and where is your party's proof of speaking for all India? Where is it, Mr Kasim? Where has it gone? You know the answer as well as I do. Up the spout. Down the creek. Sunk. Why? Because your party overlooked the fact that on the first assumption of political power the old battle was won and the new one begun. The old battle was for Indian independence and although you may not think so now, Indian independence became a foregone conclusion in 1937 when men like you became provincial ministers. Getting rid of us was still part of your programme but getting rid of us was no longer the battle. The real battle was to maintain and extend the area of your party's power. I've no patience with people, and they're chiefly my fellow-countrymen, who profess horror at what they call the sorry spectacle of the Indians squabbling among themselves because they're unable to agree about how the power they're going to inherit should be divided. Of course you must disagree. Of course you must squabble. It's a sign that you know you're no longer fighting for a principle because you know the principle has been conceded. You're fighting for political power over what has been conceded. It's logical. It's essential. It's an inescapable human condition. When you all resigned the power you'd got, in the belief that you were striking another blow for India's independence, you weren't striking a blow for that at all. You were striking a blow at your own existing and potential political power. You were narrowing the area you could hope to exercise it in. It isn't so much what you all did between 1937 and 1939 to make a lot of Muslims believe the League had been right and that a Congress-ruled India would mean a Hindu India that has made eventual partition of this country almost certainly inevitable, it's the fact that you relinquished power, and you relinquished it because you didn't understand the importance of keeping it. I say you, but I don't mean you, Mr Kasim. You well knew its importance and the folly of giving it up, just as you well know the latest folly your party has committed, the folly of not admitting the consequences of the first idiocy, of thinking you can put the clock back to 1939, ignore Jinnah and pretend the real quarrel is still with Britain and that the British are just playing that old game of dividing and ruling and hanging on like grim death. You well know that when Cripps came out in April your party had its last chance to retrieve its position. You well know that for the first time in all the long melancholy history of conferences, working parties and round table negotiations the Cripps Mission wasn't just *us* going through the old motions of palming you off with as little as possible. It was us again, but us under pressure from outside, from our allies, from America in particular, and I think you understood the peculiar advantages of negotiating with people under that sort of pressure. I think you understood too that the Cripps proposals were the best you are going to get while the war is on and that this was the last chance you had to contain Jinnah. But what happens? Your party shies like a frightened horse from the mere idea that any province or group of provinces should have the power to secede from a post-war Indian constitution and set up a constitution of its own. What does it mean, they ask? What but Pakistan? But who even a few years ago had ever heard of Pakistan let alone thought of it as practicable? Well, it's more than practicable now. It's damn' well certain. It needn't have been if you'd agreed to the Cripps proposals, come back into office, got on with the war and at the end of the war gone to a country you'd helped lead to victory and independence and trusted in the good sense of those people not to let their country be split down the middle. Instead of which you walk out on Cripps, spend the whole summer in cloud cuckoo land working up some absurd theory that if you make India untenable for the British they'll leave and the Japanese won't walk in. And while you're producing this ludicrous scheme you allow Jinnah to continue to extend the area of his power because in the Muslim majority provinces Jinnah's men have remained in office. And now comes the crowning folly, a resolution that's as good as a call to nation-wide insurrection. And you don't agree with that either, do you, Mr Kasim? You know the British simply aren't going to forgive all this Quit India nonsense going on while they're trying to concentrate on turning the tables on the Japanese, not – mark you – just to save themselves and their country but you and your country. You know all this, Mr Kasim, but you're still a pillar of the Congress Party, one of its most famous favoured Muslims, good propaganda and apparently living proof of the truth of their claim that they're an all-India party, the sort of man who's influential enough in this province for me not to think twice about locking you up as a potential inciter of riots and strikes, because your party, your party, Mr Kasim, yesterday committed high treason by conspiring to take steps calculated to aid and comfort the King-Emperor's enemies. And the one big question in my mind is why is it still your party, Mr Kasim? What official policy or policies has it adopted and pursued in the last three years that you have honestly felt to be either wise or expedient?'

'Perhaps none,' Kasim said.

'Exactly. And so, my dear Kasim, don't go into the wilderness with the rest of them this morning. However long it is, and my guess is it's for the duration, what a waste of your talent, what misplaced loyalty. Get out now. Write to Maulana Azad. Write this morning, write here and now. Send in your resignation. What more suitable moment? And the moment you write your resignation I tear up this stupid document authorizing your arrest. There's not a single act committed by you since you resigned office in 1939, not a speech, not a letter, not a pamphlet, not a thing said in public or overheard in private that warrants your being locked up. All that warrants it now is your continued allegiance to the Congress, your continued standing as a leading member of an organization we're outlawing.'

'I quite understand, Sir George.'

The Governor studied the expression on Kasim's face. Then he got up, walked to one of the long windows, looked out, and came back again, pacing slowly. Kasim waited, his hands still folded on his lap.

'I want you on my executive council,' the Governor said. 'If it were constitutionally possible for me to re-establish autonomy in this province I know whom I'd invite to head the administration. Short of that I want you *in*, I want to use your talents, Mr Kasim.'

'It is very kind of you, Sir George. I am immensely flattered.'

'But you refuse, don't you? You refuse to resign. You insist on going to jail. Forgive me, then. I hope you don't feel insulted. That wasn't my intention.'

Kasim made a gesture of dismissal. 'Please. I know this.'

The Governor sat down, took off his spectacles and played with them as before, but with both hands, leaning forward, with his elbows on the desk. 'Waste!' he exclaimed suddenly. 'Waste! Why, Mr Kasim? You agree with everything I've said, but you don't even ask for time to consider my suggestion. You reject it out of hand. Why?'

'Because you only offer me a job. I am looking for a country and I am not looking for it alone.'

'A country?'

'To disagree about the ways of looking for it is as natural as you say it is to squabble about how power will be divided when it is found. And as you say, I have disagreed many times about these ways, and people have many times expected me to resign and change my political allegiance. And if ways and means were all that mattered I expect Congress would have seen the back of me long ago. But these are not what matter, I believe. What matters is the idea to which the ways and means are directed. I have pursued this idea for a quarter of a century, and it is an idea which for all my party's faults I still find embodied in that party and only in that party, Governor-ji, nowhere else. Incidentally, I do not agree with you when you speak of Indian independence having become a foregone conclusion. Independence is not something you can divide into phases. It exists or does not exist. Certain steps might be taken to help bring it into existence, others can be taken that will hinder it doing so. But independence alone is not the idea I pursue, nor the idea which the party I belong to tries to pursue, no doubt making many errors and misjudgments in the process. The idea, you know, isn't simply to get rid of the British. It is to create a nation capable of getting rid of them and capable simultaneously of taking its place in the world as a nation, and we know that every internal division of our interests hinders the creation of such a nation. That is why we go on insisting that the Congress is an All India Congress. It is an All India Congress first, because you cannot detach from it the idea that it is right that it should be. Only second is it a political party, although one day that is what it must become. Meanwhile, Governor-ji, we try to do the job that your Government has always found it beneficial to leave undone, the job of unifying India, of making all Indians feel that they are, above all else, Indians. You think perhaps we do this to put up a strong front against the British. Partly only you would be right. Principally we do it for the sake of India when you are gone. And we are working mostly in the dark with only a small glimmer of light ahead, because we have never had that kind of India, we do not know what kind of India that will be. This is why I say we are looking for a country. I can look for it better in prison, I'm afraid, than from a seat on your Excellency's executive council.'

While Kasim was talking the Governor had searched for and found a folder from which he now took a paper. He handed it across the desk. Kasim unfolded his hands, took the paper, felt in his pocket for his spectacles.

'As you will see, Mr Kasim, that is a very short note which, if signed, will be your undertaking not to commit or cause to be committed any act whose effect is to disturb the peace or to hinder the defence of the realm. The undertaking would be valid for a period of six months from the date of signature. As you'll also see there's a rider to the effect that the signatory would, if called upon, use his best endeavours to inhibit the effects of any such acts committed within the province by others. You'll notice the paper says nothing about resigning from Congress. But sign the paper and I'll still tear this other paper up.'

'Yes, I see,' Mr Kasim said. He put the note back on the Governor's desk and replaced his spectacles in their case. 'You are expecting trouble, then. You have realized the disadvantages of having to lock us up to stop us rousing what you call the mob. But the mob perhaps rouses itself. And it is uncontrolled. It wants to know what you've done with us. All kinds of undesirable elements emerge. You want me therefore to become a sort of *ex-officio* peacemaker, armed with soothing words and no integrity. As you say, the paper says nothing about resigning from Congress, but it need not do so, of course. If I signed it I would be expelled. To sign it is tantamount to resignation. I could not sign it. You didn't expect me to, but I suppose you thought it was worth a try. I'm afraid you must cope with the mob without me.'

'Well we can do that and will.' For a while the Governor was silent, watching Kasim. Then he said, 'You are in a curious position.'

'I do not see it as curious.'

'I was thinking of your private position. Of your elder son, for instance, who holds the King-Emperor's commission. He fought in Malaya, and now he's a prisoner of war of the Japanese. It has always puzzled me why you allowed him to join the army.'

'Allow? He was under no obligation to seek my approval. It was his wish. India must have an army as well as a government. He became an officer. I became a minister.'

'And you both served under the crown. Quite. But you no longer do. He does. No doubt you have heard rumours of the pressures being put on Indian prisoners, officers and men, to secure their release from prison camp by joining units that will fight side by side with the Japanese. News of your imprisonment might well be used by the enemy to add to those pressures in your son's case. He was an excellent officer, I believe. He would be useful to them. His loyalty as an officer might be subjected to severe strain if he hears that we have put his father in jail. In his present circumstances he cannot simply resign his commission as you resigned your ministerial appointment. That is the difference, isn't it?'

'I think it is a difference he will appreciate. Just as he will appreciate that I cannot let personal considerations affect my political judgment.'

'Yes,' the Governor said, 'I expect it is,' and stood up in a way that conveyed to Kasim that the interview was at an end. He stood up too. In the pit of his stomach he felt the old familiar hollowness. He did not want to go to prison.

The Governor held out his hand. Kasim took it.

'I'm afraid that for the time being at any rate your whereabouts aren't to be made known, and this restriction must unfortunately apply in the case of your family. They will write to you care of Government House, and your own letters will automatically come here. I hope, Mr Kasim, that occasionally you will think of writing personally to me.'

'Thank you. Am I to be allowed newspapers?'

'I shall give the necessary instructions.'

'Then I'll say goodbye.'

'Goodbye, Mr Kasim.'

Kasim bowed his head, hesitated, and then walked towards the double doors behind which, he knew, the young police officer to whom the senior man had handed him over, and two British military policemen, would be waiting. But just before he reached the doors he heard the Governor call his name, and turned. The Governor was still standing behind the desk. He made a gesture with both hands, indicating the desk, the papers on it.

'May I send you away with an interesting thought that has suddenly struck me?'

'What is that, your Excellency?'

'That one day this desk will probably be yours.'

Kasim smiled, looked round the room. The thought, just at that moment, was almost sickening. He said, 'Yes. You are probably right,' and, still smiling, turned and took the last few paces to his more immediate prison.

At dusk Mr Kasim was taken from the upstairs room where he had been kept all day and driven to the sidings of the railway station at Ranpur cantonment. Here he was transferred to a carriage of the kind used to transport troops, most of whose windows had been blocked by steel shutters. The young officer in charge of him was joined by another. An armed sentry stood guard at the only door of the carriage that was still in use. When approaching the carriage Kasim saw that it was uncoupled. There were other soldiers and police in the vicinity. When he entered the carriage he expected to find other occupants, friends, ex-colleagues; but he was alone. The two young officers talked to each other in low voices and mostly in monosyllables. He made up his bed on one of the wooden benches. A tray was brought in with his dinner: soup, chicken and vegetables, and rice pudding with jam – obviously chosen from the European-style menu at the station restaurant. While he ate it one of the officers went for his own dinner. Half an hour later he returned and his companion went for his. Kasim's tray was taken by a British MP. Another armed sentry joined the first. At about nine o'clock the carriage was coupled to others, and the other officer returned from the restaurant. The two officers settled in the middle of the carriage leaving the guards at one end and Mr Kasim at the other. The train started. Kasim read. The officers continued to talk in low voices. They smoked cigarettes. Occasionally they shared a joke. A ten o'clock while the train was still moving slowly, uncertainly, picking its way across points and iron bridges, Mr Kasim gave the officers a start by rising suddenly and opening his suitcase. He sensed that they touched their holsters to make sure their revolvers were still there. From the suitcase he took out his prayer mat, then turned to them.

'I suppose neither of you can tell me which direction west is?'
He smiled, was rewarded with vague, uncomprehending but not
totally unfriendly negative replies, and then unrolled the mat on
the floor, stood for a moment and composed himself in order to
begin saying his Isha prayers in a peaceable frame of mind. He
then performed in full the four Rak'ahs prescribed.

During the night he woke several times. The officers and the
guards were taking it in turns to doze. He observed their faces:
slack, remote in the dim pools of light from the overhead bulbs
that had been left on. The light scarcely reached the end of the
carriage where he lay and once, because he had moved and
attracted the attention of the officer whose turn it was to keep
watch, he returned the man's incurious, dispassionate, half-
dreaming gaze for what seemed like an age before the man
suddenly realized that Kasim's eyes were also open and looked
away, stared down at his folded arms. When Kasim next awoke
this man was asleep, his companion sitting forward, elbows resting on his knees, contemplating his clasped hands in one of
which a cigarette was burning. Kasim raised his arm and looked
at the luminous dial of his wrist-watch. Nearly five o'clock. The
train was not moving but presumably wasn't at its destination.
Distantly, through the silence, he heard the cry of jackals. He
rose, aware of the sharp movement of the wakeful officer keeping a check on him. From his suitcase he took the waterproof
bag, leather case, soap-box, towel and shaving kit that he had
packed the night before last, and went into the cubicle. There
was no lock on the door. A single bulb illuminated dirty
green tiles and old, cracked porcelain. Iron bars were set in the
window. Behind them was a pane of frosted glass. He showered
and shaved, put back on the clothes he had travelled in. The
train had begun to move again. The motion set the door swinging open and shut. When he came out both officers were awake.
He nodded good-morning to them, returned his things to the
suitcase, got out his prayer mat and performed the two Rak'ahs
of the Fajr prayers. Making the last prostration he repeated to
himself a passage from the Koran. Oh God, glory be to You who
made Your servant go by night from the Sacred Mosque to the
farther Mosque. Praise be to Allah who has never begotten a
son, who has no partner in his Kingdom, who needs none to
defend him from humiliation.

Kneeling he rolled the mat up again, returned it to the case and snapped the locks shut. He made up his bedroll and secured the straps. Then he sat on the hard slatted bench. The officers went in turn to the cubicle at the other end of the carriage. The sentry who squatted at the door rose and woke the sleeping sentry, and then lowered the window and looked out. The train came to a halt. Rain was drumming on the roof. Kasim wondered whether his wife was yet awake. He thought of his married daughter in the Punjab, of his son Ahmed in Mirat, and of his elder son Sayed who was in God knew what hell-hole of a prison camp.

The train was, almost imperceptibly, once more in motion. Both officers had completed their ablutions. Now the sentries took it in turns to go into the farther cubicle. The officers mumbled at each other. One of them looked at his watch and stretched, went to the open window. The first light must be beginning to show, Kasim thought. The officer stayed at the window for some time. The overhead bulbs went out. The carriage was permeated with a grey mistiness that brought with it the notion of early-morning chill, and the faces of his guards were suddenly like those of strangers. The officer left the window and joined his companion. He must have made some sign. They began to adjust their belts. One reached for his cap. Kasim looked away, feeling the hollowness again. A few minutes later the train came to a halt. For a moment, because of the quietness, Kasim imagined they were held up by signals, but the silence was then broken by a voice speaking outside. Turning to look Kasim saw one of the officers at the window. He spoke to someone well below the level of the carriage. A moment later he opened the door and got down. His companion stayed in the carriage but stood at the open door. He lit a cigarette. One of the soldiers slung his rifle over his shoulder and studied the palm of his left hand as if he'd got a cut or a splinter. The carriage echoed metallically. It was being uncoupled. The rain had stopped falling. There was a whistle from up ahead. Kasim stood. The sentry stopped looking at his hand and the officer in the doorway glanced round, then back through the doorway again. He answered a voice from below and came away from the door. An officer with an armband round his sleeve hauled himself up into the carriage.

'Mr Mohammed Ali Kasim?' he inquired, as if making a formal identification.

'Yes.'

'This way, please.'

Kasim picked up his suitcase and bedroll. The others stood aside for him. At the doorway he looked down into the face of the officer whose eye he had held during the night. He said, 'I'd be grateful if you'd help me with my baggage.'

Standing below, near by, were two military policemen. The carriage was in a goods yard. A 15-cwt truck was parked at the shuttered entrance to a warehouse. Kasim smelt coal dust. The officer reached up and Kasim nudged the suitcase forward until he felt its weight taken. The bedroll followed. The officer set both down on the cinders. Kasim turned round to face inwards as he climbed down the narrow, perpendicular steps; then stood waiting. The officer with the armband came down. He indicated the luggage.

'This is all your luggage?'

'Yes.'

'Very well. My men will take you to the truck. Go with them, please.'

'May I be told where you are taking me?'

The officer with the armband hesitated.

'To the Fort,' he said abruptly.

'The Fort?'

Again the officer hesitated. Kasim thought he was surprised. 'You're in Premanagar,' he explained.

'Thank you. I didn't know.'

He glanced round. One railway siding looked like any other. He had not been in Premanagar since his tour of the province in 1938. He had never visited the Fort, but he had seen it from a distance. He had no clear visual recollection of it. Premanagar, he remembered, was not far from Mirat where his son Ahmed was. If they ever told his family where he was, and allowed him visitors, perhaps he would see Ahmed.

II

Major Tippit was a small man with very little hair. What was left of it was yellowy white. His face was lined and wrinkled. He

had a high complexion. 'I'm a historian really,' he explained.
'I retired from the army in 1938, but they dug me out. It was
decent of them to give me the Fort, wasn't it?'

Kasim agreed that it was.

'There's a lot of history in the Fort. I'm writing a monograph.
Perhaps you'd like to read some of it and give me an opinion,
one day when you have a moment.'

'I have a great number of moments.'

'I'm sorry I wasn't here when you arrived. Let us see, now,
how long has it been?'

Major Tippit glanced at the papers on his desk but did not
make any effort to find one in particular.

Kasim said, 'Nine days.'

'And you are comfortable?'

'I am comfortable.'

'Have you any complaints?'

'Several.'

'Oh yes. Lieutenant Moran Singh told me he'd made a note
of them. It's here somewhere I expect. I'll look into them.'

'Can't you look into them now?'

Major Tippit had very pale blue eyes. He gazed out of them
at Kasim as if he had reasons for not dealing with complaints but
couldn't remember what they were. He clasped his bony little
hands together on the desk – the kind of man, Kasim guessed,
who, lacking skill, energy or resolution, would make up for
them with a mindless, vegetable implacability. The unpleasant
young Sikh, nominally under Major Tippit's command, would
know exactly how far he could go, what would be allowed to
him by way of licence, and what disallowed.

'First of all,' Kasim said, 'is it really Government's intention
to keep me in solitary confinement? I understand the Fort has a
number of civil prisoners like myself. We are not criminals. We
shall probably be here for some time. The others seem to mix
quite freely. I can see them in the outer courtyard from the
window of my room. But since coming here I've been kept
isolated and have spoken to no one except my guards and Lieutenant Moran Singh. Is this state of affairs merely temporary or
is it to continue?'

'Yes, I see.'

Kasim waited.

'I am sorry you feel like that. The old zenana house is extremely interesting. I must come over one day and point out some of its more remarkable features.'

'Some of my fellow-prisoners would be interested in it too.'

'Oh, I don't think so. If I may make bold, they are not of similar intellectual calibre. The other prisoners here are very much from the rank and file of your movement.' A look of almost intense disappointment came on to Major Tippit's face, as if he had only just realized what they were talking about. 'We were told several weeks ago that we might have to provide accommodation for a VIP detenu. Of course we immediately thought of Mr Gandhi or Mr Nehru. At first I believed we had nothing suitable. Amazing how you can overlook something that's right under your nose. I had become so used to sitting here and looking through the window and seeing the zenana house, so used to going over there and using it for my own private purposes – I did a great deal of reading and writing and studying there – that I came to think of it really as an extension of my office. Then of course it struck me how eminently suitable it was. In the heart of the citadel, and if I may say so, constantly under my eye. One has that kind of obligation if one takes one's duties seriously. I made the necessary arrangements at once. It was the last thing I did before going on leave. One has to be prepared. I knew I would miss using the little house. I always found it so conducive to meditation. I confess I was a little sad when I returned last night and Lieutenant Moran Singh said that the zenana house was now occupied. However, I was most interested when he told me who you were. A member of the ancient house of Kasim. The Fort was once within the territory administered by the Kasim who was a viceroy of the great Moghul. But you know that? Your kinsman, the present Nawab of Mirat, is directly descended from him. I thought last night how interesting it was that a Kasim should have come back to stay in Premanagar. And frankly I was rather relieved that the occupant of the zenana house was of the Faith. Tell me, are you a Sunni or a Shiah Muslim?'

'Major Tippit, you have not answered my complaint. My impression is that the officers who conducted me from Ranpur brought a letter to you from Sir George Malcolm. Is there anything in that letter that suggested I should be kept isolated?'

'A letter?'

'I think the one near your left elbow. I recognize the heading.'

Tippit looked down, picked the letter up, glanced at it.

'Oh yes. Lieutenant Moran Singh mentioned a letter. I have not read it yet.'

'Would you do so now?'

Tippit looked down again, stared at the letter. His eyes showed no movement of reading. After a while he replaced the letter near his left elbow.

'Well?' Kasim asked. 'Is there anything that suggests or orders solitary confinement?'

'No.'

'Is there anything about newspapers?'

'You have permission to read newspapers.'

'Good. But I have not been given any. That is my other complaint.'

'I will speak to Lieutenant Moran Singh about it.'

'I've spoken to Lieutenant Moran Singh about it several times. I've given him a list of the newspapers I want. I've also written to my wife asking her to send newspapers. That letter and several other letters are still here. They are on your desk.'

'I'll read them as soon as possible. You understand that they must be read?'

'I understand nothing of the sort. They will be read in Ranpur, either in the censorship office at the Secretariat or by a member of the Governor's staff. Sometimes by both. I have not so far written personally to the Governor as he requested me, but I shall be doing so presently. I should like to be able to make some comments to him on whatever the current situation is.'

Major Tippit glanced up – not, it seemed, recognizing a threat. He said, 'Things have been very distressing, haven't they?'

'Major Tippit, how can I tell how things have been? I have no radio, no newspapers, my guards tell me nothing, Lieutenant Moran Singh tells me nothing and does not even post my letters. No letters have been given to me either. By now I should think there would be several.'

'Such senseless violence. It is difficult to know where to apportion blame. And that poor girl, that unfortunate woman. It has incensed people. Looting, rioting, burning. Yes, yes. One expects. Deplores but expects. But these other things ... I was delayed because the railways have been so uncertain. In Ranpur feeling is running high. In Mayapore the civil have handed over to the military. The whole country is seething. Will you have some tea?'

'No thank you.'

'It is ten o'clock. I always have tea at ten o'clock. A regular regime. While I'm away things get out of hand. It is five past ten.' He said this without looking at his watch. He made no effort to have tea brought in. Chapprassis were waiting on the bench outside, but he did not call one of them. He said, 'But they will be better now that I am back. Lieutenant Moran Singh has conducted everything with precision and now that I am back to say the word everything will fall into place. I'm afraid I cannot change the arrangements for your accommodation. Have you any other requests?'

'I should like further supplies of pen, paper and ink.'

'I will tell Lieutenant Moran Singh. He will arrange it with one of the clerks.'

'There are two habitable rooms in the zenana house, the one I have as a bedroom and the one I use as a study. I should like to share these rooms with one of your other prisoners.'

'Which one?'

'Any one. I don't know who you have got here.'

'As I said, rank and file. I cannot allow it. It is against my principles. I am surprised that you wish it. You are a man who has been in a position of authority. Well, well, that is a lonely business. I too am living alone in this fortress, Mr Kasim. I am glad you are here. We can talk together sometimes. I am interested in Islamic art and literature as well as in history. The early eighteenth-century Urdu poet, Gaffur, was also of your ancient family, so I understand. I have translated some of his verses into English. You might like to have a look at them.'

Kasim bowed his head.

'In one or two cases I believe I have managed to convey something of the splendour and simplicity of the original. You are well acquainted with the poems of Gaffur, Mr Kasim?'

'At one time, yes. As a boy. Since then other things have tended to occupy my mind. You said that the country is seething.'

'Looting. Arson. Sabotage. Policemen have been murdered.

Track has been torn up. Magistrates imprisoned in their own jails, Congress flags run up. Troops called out. Inevitable loss of life. Waste. Violence. Terrible violence. To no purpose. It's being stamped out. It's best forgotten. I should not talk about it.'

'You said something about a girl.'

'She was raped. Another woman was attacked. An elderly woman. The Indian who was driving her to safety was murdered.'

'Were they Europeans?'

'English. The woman was a mission school teacher. The girl who was raped was of good family. They have arrested the men.'

'Was this in Ranpur?'

'No. In Mayapore. The military have taken over. Your people have done terrible things. I do not understand you, Mr Kasim. Over this we are in opposite camps. We are enemies. But I am a humane man.' Major Tippit paused. 'I'm a historian, really. The present does not interest me. The future even less. Only through art and contemplation of the past can man live with man. I hope you will be content. Think upon the Fort as a refuge from life's turmoils and disappointments.'

Kasim waited, then when he saw that for the moment Tippit had no more to say, he rose, thanked his jailer for the interview and said, 'I have your permission to return to my quarters?'

He walked alone across the space that separated the Fort commander's office and the zenana house, under the eyes of the chapprassis and the armed sentries who patrolled the colonnaded verandah of the old barracks. In the centre of the courtyard a neem tree provided some shade. Puddles in the red earth reflected the blue of the sky. Puffs of cloud too light to cast shadows moved quickly, driven by the prevailing south-west wind. By midday it would probably rain.

The courtyard was enclosed to the east by the barracks, to the north, west and south by high crenellated red brick walls with bastions built into the angles. In the west and south wall there were gateways closed by studded wooden doors. Close to the southern wall was the square pavilion where Major Tippit lived. Abutting on to the northern wall was the old zenana house, a two-storey construction of stone and brick with fretted wooden arches shading the upper and lower verandahs. A wooden stairway gave access to the first floor. The rooms below were in use as storehouses. The dry smell of grain and sacking pervaded the place. Above, the verandah gave on to rooms all but two of which were ruinous. The farthest of these were boarded in. The two which were habitable were closest to the wooden staircase. Inside, they were lit by the open doors and by windows in the outer walls. These windows were blocked by fretted stone screens that gave the occupant views, through any one of their many apertures, of the outer courtyard and the inner and outer walls of the Fort. The courtyard where the zenana house stood had obviously been the women's. The barracks must have been servants' quarters. He could not see what lay behind the southern wall, other than the dome of the mosque, but from the outer windows of his rooms in the zenana he could see beyond the farther walls to the plain.

The walls of his two rooms were whitewashed. In one room there were a bed, a chair and a wardrobe; in the other a table, a chair and a calendar. The calendar was Kasim's own. He did not mark off the days. There seemed no point in doing so when the period of his imprisonment was not determined. 'I rise at six as usual, waking by habit,' he wrote now to his wife. 'They give me breakfast at eight. The two hours are spent bathing and dressing and reading. After breakfast I walk round the compound, unless it is raining, then write in my journal, and letters, until lunch. After lunch I doze for a while, then read until four, when they bring me some tea. After tea I walk again. After that I bathe. Then read. Then supper. Time of course hangs heavily. Today I expect letters at last. Please give my love to the children when you write to them. I am told there has been some unrest. I hope you are safe and unharmed by it. There must be a great deal for you to attend to. Do not write more often than you can well afford to. One thing I dislike is not being allowed to shave myself. They have taken my things away and send a barber every other day. Today is a bristly morning. I suppose they are afraid I might hurt myself with the razor. Even my little mirror is gone. I shall forget what I look like, no doubt. They have let me keep your and the children's photographs, because they are only covered with mica. I have the portraits on my desk. Pray remember every morning and night Ahmed Gaffur Ali Rashid. Our noble but eccentric ancestor! Looking at the photographs has reminded me of him.'

There was no such person as Ahmed Gaffur Ali Rashid. His wife would therefore see at once that this particular sentence contained the simple code message – an anagram – they had agreed upon to tell her where he was being held. He hoped the censors would not see it first. They would look for such codes in his first few letters to her. This was his fourth. He ran his hand over the stubble on his chin and then over his cheeks, wondering whether prison fare had made his face thinner.

So: Kasim's face. There was history in it; the history of Islam's holy wars and imperial expansions. He traced his genealogy back to a warrior-adventurer called Mir Ali who came from Turkey in the heyday of the Muslims' Indian empire just as years later young Britons came out in the heyday of their own. Mir Ali married a Hindu princess and they both adopted the new religion the great Moghul Akbar had devised in an attempt to establish a cornerstone on which to build the fabric of a dream, an India undivided by conflicting notions of God and the ways to worship God. Akbar wished his fellow-Muslims and the conquered Hindus to feel equal in one respect at least. But in the reign of Aurangzeb the Kasims re-embraced Islam. The empire was already running down but the Muslims still held the keys of the kingdom and under Aurangzeb the old proselytizing faith in Allah and his prophet was re-established as a buttress for the crumbling walls of state. A new wave of conversions, even among the proud Rajputs, showed that when belief is at odds with worldly ambition the former is the more likely to bow its head.

The reward for one of those Kasims who re-embraced Islam – the eldest grandson of Mir Ali – was the vice-regal appointment over a territory that stretched from Ranpur to Mirat. He was murdered by his son who had been one of his deputies. Internecine war, war against rebellious Hindu rulers and chieftains, war against the invaders from the west – the Mahrattas – marked the final years of the dying Moghul dynasty. The deputies of the great Moghul were carving out principalities and scrambling for power in the gathering darkness, unwittingly opening the gates that would let in the flood that was to swamp them: the flood of ubiquitous, restless foreign merchants whom they thought at first easy sources of income and personal riches,

French, British, Portuguese merchants who came to trade but stayed on to secure their trade by taking possession of the source of wealth, the very land itself. The merchants fought each other too, and there is no honour among thieves. A self-appointed prince, leaning on one of the foreigners to help him subjugate a neighbouring pocket-kingdom, too often found he was subjugated himself, imprisoned, then released by the forces of a different foreigner, set up as their puppet and in the end manipulated out of existence. By the beginning of the nineteenth century, of all those principalities that had been carved out of the territory administered by Mir Ali's eldest grandson, only one remained, and this was the tiny state of Mirat whose ruler, also a Kasim, had by wit and good fortune failed to arouse the acquisitive instincts of the British, had helped them at the right time rather than for the right reasons, secured his jagir and their recognition of his claim to be called Nawab. And since there was now no princely neighbour near enough for the British to look upon the Nawab of Mirat as a threat to their own peaceful mercantile and administrative pursuits he was allowed to continue, to blossom as it were like a small and insignificant rose in the desert of dead Moghul ambitions.

All this was in Kasim's face: a face of the kind that could be celebrated in profile on a coin – a forehead sloping to a balding crown, a fleshy but handsomely proportioned nose which stood on guard with an equally fleshy but handsome chin over a mouth whose lips were by no means thin, but were firm-set, determined, not unsensual. Full-face there was a broadness of cheek and jowl and neck, suggestive of a thyroid condition. The black hair that fringed his temples and the back of his head was flecked with grey. These, the thickness and the baldness, conveyed a different idea of Kasim; of a Kasim bearing the marks not of proconsular dignity and autocratic power but instead the marks of centuries of experience of duller but not unworthy occupations. This was a middle-class Kasim, a Kasim – as indeed Mohammed Ali was – of the branch that traced its connection to Mir Ali through the younger son of that Turkish warrior and his Hindu bride, and this was a branch that had rooted itself more modestly but more deeply in the adopted country. It boasted no viceroy, no Nawab, no captain of armies. It had prospered in other ways, in trade and in the professions. It might be called the Ranpur branch, and it had provided India with merchants, imams, scholars, lawyers, officials, philosophers, mathematicians, doctors, and a poet – Gaffur Mohammed whose verses Major Tippit admired. It had provided her more recently with a member of the provincial Governor's council, Mohammed Ali Kasim's father whose portrait an arresting officer took a moment off from duty to study, and with the first chief minister of the province, Mohammed Ali himself, a man in whom perhaps could be detected yet another inheritance, Akbar's old dream of a united sub-continent. For this he had come to prison. For this he had incurred the displeasure of Mr Jinnah whose name was also Mohammed Ali, who now had visions of a separate Muslim state but whose forbears were converts from Hinduism and had not come from Turkey.

One month after his incarceration in the Fort at Premanagar Mohammed Ali Kasim (known to the newspapers usually as M A K and to free and easy English as Mac) sought and obtained Major Tippit's permission to make a little garden in front of the zenana house. He also wrote his first letter to the Governor.

It took a little while (he wrote) for newspapers and letters to reach me, but presently I was inundated. Having caught up in quite a short while (since there was little else to occupy me) with the events (as reported) that followed the news of the nation-wide arrests, my immediate desire was to address you on the matter, because the newspapers invariably sought to establish that the rioting and disturbance only just now coming to an end were planned by Congress and indeed led by Congress in the shape of mysterious underground leaders people such as myself are thought to have chosen and briefed to carry out the job if we were arrested and couldn't carry it out ourselves. I recalled what I said during our interview about mobs that rouse themselves and, needing leaders, encourage the emergence of all kinds of undesirable elements. By and large I should say this is exactly what happened, although some of the incidents (in Dibrapur for example) show evidence of forethought. Those undesirable elements I mentioned do not of course come into existence overnight, but they are not underground elements of Congress. Neither can they be Communist-inspired, because the Indian Communists have become pro-war minded ever since Hitler invaded Russia, and would hardly do anything to disrupt the war effort against Fascism. They are inspired surely only by themselves, and are a danger to all of us.

There seems to be a general belief, however, that Congress had the wind taken out of its sails by the sudden arrest of so many of its leaders. The point is made that Mr Gandhi probably expected the Quit India resolution as it is now called to lead not to prison but to serious talks with the Viceroy. I am in agreement. (My own act of packing my bags directly I heard the resolution had been endorsed was the result of purely personal logic, and I confess I hoped it was an act I would look back on with that affectionate self-mockery we reserve for those of our fears which subsequent events show to have been groundless.) What I cannot see is how the two views can be reconciled. If the arrests came as a surprise (as I'm sure they did to most of us) surely the men who were arrested and surprised were not men who had planned for rebellion in their absence? Gandhi, you know, never said *how* the country was to be organized to withdraw from the war effort. As you know he has never been much of a chap for detail, and even those closest to him have often been puzzled to know exactly what it is he has in mind. People on your side who don't like him accuse him of deviousness and of course the general impression now is that his latest and most devious scheme has backfired. You yourself used the word blackmail, and the British in general have met the recent threats to their security in precisely the frame of mind of chosen victims of blackmail who refuse to be victimized. I hope that on reconsideration you will reject, if you haven't already done so, the blackmail theory. It's a theory that works two ways in any case. We could accuse the British of trying to blackmail us into putting everything into the war effort with false promises of independence when the war is won. You would answer that by saying they are not false, although you cannot prove that to us, and Churchill has made it clear that the rights and freedoms embodied in the Atlantic Charter do not apply to India so far as he is concerned. We, for our part, would answer your charge of blackmail by pointing out that the war is irrelevant to the situation because we are demanding nothing that we have not been demanding for years. The war perhaps has made us demand it with greater insistence and has strengthened your hand in not granting it yet, but it has not changed the nature of the demand, nor the nature of the resistance. It has merely added a different emotional factor and a new set of practical considerations; and on these our natures and our views widen our differences. What I hope you will be in agreement with me over is my belief that had we been allowed to continue at liberty the violent events of the past few weeks simply would not have occurred. You would have been faced with the far more onerous task of seeking a way round the deadlock created by a co-ordinated, peaceful, passive end to the co-operation of the Indian people in the war effort. This would have been the type of 'sabotage' Congress leaders, and Congress leaders only, could have directed. Perhaps it is Machiavellian of *me* to glimpse in Government's prompt arrests of leaders a Machiavellian intention: the intention of turning the onerous task into the simpler one of strong-arm tactics. It is easier to fire on rioters led by undesirable elements than to force resisting workers back into an arms factory, dockers back to the docks and engine-drivers back to the controls of their loco-motives. And Government must have realized that the people of India would be incensed by the wholesale arrests and imprison-ment of their leaders: incensed, at a loss, anxious to perform what their leaders wanted them to perform, but prey to anger, fear, and all the passions that lead to violence. I find it not at all difficult to accuse Government of deliberate provocation of the people of India: either that or of holding the insulting belief that the people of India are so spineless and apathetic that the disappearance from their midst of the men who have risen to positions of responsibility to them would at once leave them as malleable and directable as dull and unimportant clay.

That they are neither spineless nor apathetic has been proved all too well. I have read the accounts of the riots, burnings, loot-ings, acts of sabotage, acts of murder, the accounts of crowds of men, women and children attempting to oppose unarmed the will and strength of Government, and accounts of the firing upon these crowds by the police and the military, of deaths on both sides, of attempts to seize jails, derail trains, blow bridges, seize installations; accounts of what amounts to a full-scale but spontaneous insurrection – but with what a sad difference – for most of it has been conducted with the bare hands or with what the bare hands could pick up. There are Indians, I do not doubt, especially among those of us in prison (and our numbers have been considerably swelled since the morning of August 9th) who are proud of what the nation attempted. I cannot be one of them, for my chief reactions are anger and sorrow, and an emotion that I can't easily describe but which is probably due to a special sense of impotence, of powerlessness to do anything that will help to alter things in any way.

The reactions of sorrow and anger are by no means partisan. I feel them for and on behalf of people quite unknown to me, the young men for instance who are out here as soldiers, young Englishmen who as we all know have absolutely no idea about India except that it is a long way from home and full of strange, dark-skinned people. In many case soldiers like this have found themselves acting as you call it in aid of the civil power. Their principal feeling must have been one of bewilderment that changed swiftly to deep and burning resentment, because all they would understand was that the country they have come all this way to defend apparently didn't want them and was bent on getting rid of them. There was the terrible affair of the two Canadian Air Force officers who were literally torn to pieces by people from a village that had been bombed and who thought these men had flown the aeroplanes in question. Even if they were, the situation as I see and feel it is not changed. It is one that involves us all, as does the bombing, the entire scene and history of this lamentable business. In our own province I have been especially distressed by the two incidents involving English women, the attack on the Mission School Superintendent near Tanpur, and the rape of Miss Manners in the Bibighar Gardens in Mayapore. In this latter case I do indeed feel a personal involvement over and above any other. I knew, of course, Miss Manners's uncle, Sir Henry Manners, from the time in the early thirties when he governed the province and I sat by his invitation on several of the committees he set up in an attempt to break down some of the barriers between Government and people.

Manners was a Governor of great skill – tolerant, sympathetic, admirable in every way. His term of office in Government House was one of hope for us, a bright spot on a rather gloomy horizon. What enemies he made were reactionary English and extremist Indians. Perhaps without the opportunity he gave me, to make whatever mark I did make on those committees, my own party would not have given me the greater opportunity that led to office. You will understand then the weight of my personal distress at the news of the criminal assault on the niece of a man like that. It is an incident that seems all too understandably to have added fuel to the fires of violence in Mayapore, and perhaps in the rest of the province. The first reports I read, which did not disclose Miss Manners's name – referring to her merely as a young Englishwoman, victim of sexual assault by six Indian youths who had all been promptly arrested – struck me possibly as exaggerations because the reports were hysterical in pitch, and of course I hoped that they were not true. But it seems they were, at least in regard to the fact that the girl *was* attacked, and criminally used; and the eventual disclosure of her name and her connection with the late Sir Henry Manners came as a considerable personal shock.

I have since, however, become puzzled and vaguely disturbed by what I can gather of the consequences of this affair, and the piece in the *Statesman* yesterday, referring to the rape of Miss Manners (although mercifully omitting her name again – a first step towards some sort of privacy for the poor creature) does bear out my own feelings that some quite extraordinary veil has been drawn over the whole unfortunate business, but a veil that does not satisfy the lawyer in me. I had been reading the papers daily in expectation of further news about the six men who according to the early reports were arrested. Now, according to the *Statesman*, it seems that these six men were not charged with rape. The *Statesman* refers to a very brief paragraph in the *Mayapore Gazette* of one week ago which gave the names of two or three men recently imprisoned under the Defence of India rules, without trial of course. According to the *Statesman*, these men were among the six originally arrested as suspects in the rape. Again, according to the *Statesman*, which has been ferreting about, *all* six have been imprisoned under the rule. Quite justifiably, the *Statesman* asks whether the original reports that the suspected culprits have been arrested, thanks to the prompt action of the local police under their District Superintendent, were the result of wishful thinking or confusion on the part of the reporter, or whether subsequent investigation showed them to be innocent. If they were innocent, then as the *Statesman* again properly asks, is it not curious that six men suspected of rape should all turn out to be men whose political activities earned them imprisonment as detenus? Clearly now, there is unlikely to be any arrest or trial in connection with the rape itself and one must assume the real culprits have gone free. The question raised by the *Statesman* comes to this: Have six men been arrested for rape, found to be innocent either because they are or for lack of evidence that would hold up in a court of law, but have been put away under this convenient act because someone still believes them to be guilty, or is determined to punish them for some reason or other? I doubt that anyone will provide the answer the *Statesman* seeks and presently – although the affair itself will be a long time fading from memory – the legal aspects will quickly be forgotten; as will the curious side issues that stay in my own mind from my reading of the reports and collection of casual data: for instance the apparent fact that one of the arrested men, a man called Kumar, was a friend of Miss Manners; and the fact that Miss Manners (if the *Statesman* has interpreted correctly) declined, according to gossip, to give evidence because the men arrested were not the kind she remembered as the type who attacked her.

I imagine that the details of this distressing affair – which has exacerbated racial feeling throughout the country – have had something of your personal attention, more particularly in view of the victim's family connections in India. I presume she is the daughter of a brother of Henry Manners. One of the reports gave her address in Mayapore as the MacGregor House, which I remember as the home of Sir Nello and Lady Chatterjee who were friends of Sir Henry and Lady Manners. I take it Miss Manners was staying with Lady Chatterjee but that otherwise she normally lives with her aunt whom I knew fairly well and who, I believe, still lives in Rawalpindi. I have written a brief letter to Lady Manners, which I enclose. I should be most grateful if you would forward it. I have left it unsealed so that you can quickly assure yourself that I have written nothing to her apart from words of sympathy and regret for the terrible thing that happened to her niece. I cannot, I realize, expect any particular comment from you on the points I have raised in this letter. I offer them as someone whose enforced position as a mere spectator has in no way diminished his sense of involvement, curiosity, and concern with justice.

*

'His Excellency thanks you for your letter' (one of Sir George's secretaries wrote a month later), 'and wishes me also to convey to you Lady Manners's thanks for your personal message which his Excellency communicated to her.'

Kasim looked up; Lieutenant Moran Singh who had brought the letter over to the zenana house still stood in the doorway, smiling.

'Such influential people you are knowing,' Moran Singh said. 'Letters from Government House and such-like.' He turned and went out. Presently Kasim heard him shouting at one of the sentries. Moran Singh had relatives in Ranpur. He had offered to convey private messages to Mrs Kasim through those relatives, for a consideration. He took bribes, he sold Government stores. He had said to Kasim, 'Major Tippit is mad,' and had hinted that – again for a consideration – he could persuade Tippit to allow Kasim to be visited regularly by selected fellow-prisoners. Moran Singh represented everything in India that Kasim loathed. He had declined these offers.

Kasim wrote in his journal: 'A reply from Government House, which makes it clear that the Governor's request that I write to him occasionally wasn't really the friendly gesture I believed it to be. It is apparently to be a one-sided correspondence. He wanted me to commit my thoughts to paper but won't commit his own. He wants to keep track of me. I am a specimen under observation. They must be his orders that keep me isolated from other prisoners. He thinks isolation will give me time and opportunity to re-assess my position. Underneath that liberal man to man exterior is the indomitable public servant. Perhaps he is waiting for me to crack under the strain. I could be out of Premanagar by Christmas if I wrote to him and said I'd changed my mind and was willing to resign from Congress and accept nomination to his executive council. And God knows I might do useful work. But I must not be hard on him. They are only spiritual hardships I suffer here, and his policy in regard to me is dictated by good intentions and the determination to do everything he can to govern the province successfully and ease the condition of the people. The Governor buries himself neither in past nor future but in the present. It is an English trait. They will only see that there is no future for them in India when India

no longer fits into the picture they have of themselves and of
their current obligations. When that time comes they won't particularly care what happens to us. Sooner or later the Governor
will find that I don't fit in to whatever picture he has of the
current problems of this province. Perhaps I am already beginning to fade out of it. He would have written, I expect, if he
had seen an immediate way in which I could be useful to him.
One can't help admiring this barefaced attitude. We might learn
something from it. There is too much emotion in our own
public life. The English could never be accused of that. They
lock us up, release us and lock us up again according to what
suits them at the time, with a bland detachment that, fortunately
or unfortunately, is matched by an equally bland acceptance on
our part. They act collectively, and so can afford detachment.
We react individually, which weakens us. We haven't yet
acquired the collective instinct. The English send Kasim to
prison. But it is Kasim who goes to prison. The prisoner in the
zenana house is a man. But who is his jailer? The jailer is an idea.
But in the prisoner the idea is embodied in a man. From his
solitude the man reaches out to others. He writes to Sir George
Malcolm. He writes to old Lady Manners. But he cannot reach
them as people. They are protected from him by the collective
instinct of their race. A reply comes, but it is not from them. It
is from someone speaking for them. It has not been expedient
for either of them to write. I understand in both cases why this
should be. But to understand does not warm the heart.'

Several months later, the May of the following year, the prisoner
in the zenana house saw two notices in the same issue of the
Times of India. Under Births there was this entry: *Manners. On
May 7th, at Srinagar. To Daphne, a daughter, Parvati.* And under
Deaths, this: *Manners. On May 7th, at Srinagar; Daphne, daughter
of the late Mr & Mrs George Manners, beloved niece of Ethel and the
late Sir Henry Manners.*

There were times, Mr Kasim told himself, when he thought
he would never understand the English. What curious brand of
arrogance and insensitivity could lead an old lady to announce
to the world the birth of an obviously half-caste child to the
unmarried niece who, nine months before, had been raped by
Indians in the Bibighar Gardens? 'It is as if,' he wrote in his

journal, 'old Lady Manners were flinging an accusation into our faces, to make sure we know that this is an incident that cannot be forgotten and is one we have a continuing responsibility for. I do not remember her as the sort of woman who would make this kind of gesture; but of course the girl has died, presumably in childbirth. I suppose she is telling us that she will never forgive us for what a handful of our men did on that particular night. Or do these announcements mean that she has forgiven us now and taken the child, so tragically and violently conceived, to her heart, for India's sake? One cannot tell. The English have a saying, "He wears his heart on his sleeve," but this is something they never reveal except very occasionally to each other.'

PART TWO

A HISTORY

I

'SO IT WAS with Henry, and so now with poor Daphne,' Lady Manners murmured. And handed her niece's diary to Suleiman to lock up in the black tin box as he had locked up some of her husband's private papers, years before, with an air of reverence or anyway forbearance; but he took Daphne's book as if it were nothing special, put it in the box – whose lid was open – and stood, waiting, not catching her eye, still wearing the old astrakhan cap he had complained of months before in 'Pindi and had had money off her to renew.

Well, he is jealous, she thought, and still resents being sent for, travelling alone and uncomfortably on the bus all that way from 'Pindi to Srinagar, just to order the household for the journey back in the same direction, a beast-of-burden who has no burden worthy of the years, the centuries, the everlastingness of his service. He is an old man. His hair has gone grey, like mine. Why has he never grown a beard? If he grows a beard I must watch for signs of it and be prepared for the morning he will come to me and say, Memsahib, let me go, I am an old man. Before I die I must see Mecca, and having seen it dye my beard red, come back and live out my remaining years in peace and honourable retirement with the blessing of Allah the Merciful.

So, too, I would go, but not to Mecca. Where then? And how? I do not know how or where. Nor who has mercy to spare.

And she looked out of the window on to the placid waters of the lake, and heard the crying of the child. She made a gesture and said a word, both meaning the same thing. *Khatam*. Finished. Suleiman closed the lid of the box, turned the key and handed it to her. His old brown fingers were still supple from a lifetime of manipulative care of her property, and Henry's property, which were his gods, his ikons, but to care for Daphne's was nothing to him. It was all gone. But what? Well it has gone, she thought, whatever it was. And took the key from

him, and put it in her handbag, aware of the finality of the
gesture without understanding why she should think of it as
final. You were handsome once, she told Suleiman without
speaking. You had one wife we knew about and two concubines
you pretended were your wife's sisters. And were a rogue and a
rake, and had children, God knows how many, by whom, nor
where scattered. Now you are alone and I am alone, and we
cannot speak of it even yet as a man and a woman might speak
who share recollections. But if you were to die I should weep.
And if I were to die you would cover your head and speak to no
one for days. But here in the world where both of us live –
poised between entrance and exit, or exit and entrance – we will
maintain the relationship of mistress and servant, although we
have grown far beyond it and use it simply as a shorthand to get
through the day without trouble to one another.

Suleiman took hold of the box and carried it through into the
passage that ran along the side of the houseboat – the side adjacent to the bank of the island to which the boat was moored
– from her bedroom, with its single bed, past the empty guest
bedroom with its two beds, and into the dining-room, up the
two steps into the living-room beyond which was the verandah
with its view on to the water and the opposite bank where the
tongas waited, ready to transport the passengers from the shikaras
to the square where the buses and motor-cars halted.

In the water immediately below the verandah there was a
cluster of shikaras – one for the luggage, one for the passengers,
and upwards of half a dozen laden with Kashmiri art: woodwork,
shawls, carpets, flowers; and even a fortune teller – although it
was only 7.30 in the September morning, and the mist through
which a future might be seen to have substance had not yet
cleared. But in the last half-hour before a departure there was
always the possibility of a sale. From her room, Lady Manners
heard the cries of the vendors offering inducements, bribes,
to persuade Suleiman to go back in and bring her out to be
tempted.

And today, she thought, I am going to be tempted. And
followed Suleiman through to the verandah where he was standing, a thin, frail, stoop-shouldered man, in a moth-eaten fez and
floppy pyjamas, with Henry's old Harris tweed jacket hanging
on him to keep out the early-morning September chill, showing

his shirt-tail, blue against the baggy white trousers: and holding the box to his breast, like a reliquary, saying nothing, but watching the opposite shore, standing on guard over the piled luggage. Aware she had come, he spoke to the khansamar, ordered him to have the luggage stowed, and the khansamar beckoned to the man below who came scrambling. The vendors, seeing that departure was imminent, set up a new cry, making their appeal directly to her, holding up whatever it was they most wished her to be tempted by. She beckoned to the man who had sold her a shawl three years before, and had ever since been hopeful. She beckoned to him because of this, not because his shikara was closest (although it was, having been paddled into position early). He clambered, laden, across her own empty shikara and the luggage shikara, elbowing the men who were dealing with the luggage, reached the houseboat verandah and laid his bundle down, salaamed, untied the knot, opened and released a cascade of fine woven wool, with gold, silver and coloured embroidery. The khansamar had brought out a chair. She sat on it and watched the man – his skull-cap, and his touchingly dishonest eyes whenever he looked up to emphasize the truth of the lies he was telling her.

But Suleiman (she thought) stands detached from this foolery. Well, there was a time when he protected me from rogues, for he was our rogue, our beloved rogue, who never cheated us but knew rogues, being brought up with them; and their ways, being brought up in them; and saw lesser rogues off, and equal rogues, and bigger rogues. He taught me all I know about the ways of the bazaars and what he taught me is all that he knows too. He stands, holding the reliquary, and lets me get on with it as if I were a pupil old enough to know better, too old to be corrected. And does not look, but listens to the crying of the child.

And I choose this one, to warm my shoulders on a frosty night, for I am of an age that can grace a faint vulgarity, am I not? So much silver-thread, and too much scarlet silk. Shall I ever wear it? Perhaps that is doubtful. Or even this one? The green is a bit bilious, after such an early breakfast. Well, any of them? Am I too old, then, for this kind of gesture? For whose sake am I making it? My own? Henry's? Suleiman's? Daphne's? Or for Kashmir's because after all these years of arriving and departing

I feel it in my bones that I am going this time never to return? Or is it an insurance? To buy believing it the last, to ensure that it is not? Perhaps I buy for the child, for Parvati, whose crying Suleiman listens to and will not speak of. Has Suleiman yet looked at the child?

She chose a shawl that could have offended no one. But when she had paid for it and gone back inside after repeating the word and the gesture: Khatam: she regretted buying something that would give her neither pleasure nor pain, and wondered at the marvel of losing an opportunity to make a gesture others and she herself could have described later as out of character. In the end, she saw, habit became a vice, and good taste an end in itself: nothing could ever come of it.

Fifteen minutes later the khansamar knocked at the door of her room where she sat alone staring through the little window at the lake, her old-fashioned veiled topee already on her head, gloves on her hands, repeating to herself, with no outward sign that she was doing so, the little prayer she always offered up at the beginning of a journey. The khansamar told her that all was ready. She rose, thanked him for his service, and went out. She had distributed tips the night before. The staff of the houseboat, and of the house she had lived in from the November of 1942 all through the hard winter to June when she had come down to the lake, were gathered on the forward verandah and on the sunroof. Fifteen of them all told: twelve from the boat, and three from the house. She stood for a moment. They watched her in silence. Then she said, 'Thank you,' and allowed the khansamar to help her down the steps into the shikara which had an embroidered canopy and a spring mattress – the kind of shikara Henry once said made him feel when with her like Antony making himself at home with Cleopatra on her barge. At the foot of the mattress, the young ayah already sat, veiled for the journey from the valley she had never left before, nursing the child. When Lady Manners was settled Suleiman stepped aboard and sat in the narrow prow, still holding the reliquary. Behind her the three boatmen raised their pointed, elongated, heart-shaped paddles and began to negotiate a passage between the clustered boats of the vendors. She turned to wave, but the outline of the houseboat had become infuriatingly unclear. She realized, too, that she had forgotten to look at the flowers in the vase by her bedside, to make sure they were quite dead; and thinking of those flowers thought as well of Daphne's rhetorical question, written down while the snows still held, when the summer that had somehow never been was yet to come:

'Shall we go down to the lake, then, Aunty, and live in a houseboat and fill it with flowers, and have our fortunes told?'

I am leaving in two days' time (she had written to her old friend Lili Chatterjee in Mayapore), and so ends, as they say, a chapter – the burden of which you know and have lightened, not only by your too short visit this summer but by your wise counsel, and by the opinion you were able to express, after seeing the child. When I am re-established in 'Pindi, at Christmas-time for instance, perhaps you would come up and pay me a visit? I do not expect to be much invited out. My own race hardly knows any longer what to make of me and the existence of the child under my roof no doubt ranks as something of a scandal, such a lively, vocal repository for memories of events my countrymen are pretending it is best to forget – or if not best to forget at least wise to consider over and adequately dealt with. I don't make my appeal to you, or invitation, from any sense the last few months may have given me of isolation, but from that other more important sense of contact with a friend who speaks my language and with whom, over Christmas, I should so dearly love to exchange gifts of conversation, plans and recollections.

Today we are moving the houseboat down the lake from the isolated position you thought so pretty to its winter berth, to shorten the distance for the luggage shikaras the day after tomorrow. Since you were here I acquired neighbours. They are now gone back to Pankot where they are stationed. Their boat has been moved away and this last few days I have been alone again, which on the whole I prefer. These people who came and moored near by were punctilious about sending cards across when they arrived. I had Aziz return the compliment. Result: an almost tangible air of embarrassment and curiosity emanating from their boat; cautious nods if we happened to cross one another's bows when out in the shikaras. But no visit, except towards the end of their stay, and that by one of them alone, one of the two daughters, when the rest of them were out enjoying themselves one afternoon. She saw me reading on the sun-deck as she went past alone in their shikara, and waved, then had the boatmen come in close and asked whether she could come on board for a few moments. I couldn't very well refuse, although I thought it a bit offhand after the days that had gone by without a word exchanged. She came straight to the point and said it was embarrassment really that had kept them away, not knowing what on earth they'd be able to say to me that wouldn't make it obvious they were all avoiding any mention of poor Daphne ('the awful business of your niece' she called it). But they were going back to their station soon and she said she didn't like the idea of leaving without speaking to me. I thought it a rather thin excuse but not an uncourageous thing to do. She said she often heard the baby crying and would very much like to see her. So I took her down into the cabin where little Parvati has her cot. The girl – her name is Sarah Layton – looked at her for quite a long time without saying anything. Parvati was asleep and the ayah was adopting her possessive, on guard attitude, which probably added to the girl's uneasiness. I think she'd expected the baby to have the kind of pale skin that makes the mixture of blood difficult to detect unless you're looking for it. Eventually she said, 'She's so tiny,' as if she had never seen a four-month-old baby before, then thanked me for letting her see her. I invited her to stay and have some tea under the awning on the sun-deck. She only hesitated for a moment. On our way out she caught sight of the trunks with Daphne's name on them and hesitated again. She puzzled me. Nice young English girls in India don't usually give an impression of bothering their heads with anything much apart from the question of which men in the immediate vicinity are taking the most notice of them. Of course, they do go broody every now and again, but Miss Layton's broodiness struck me as odd and intricate, not at all the result of simple self-absorption.

The name Layton had vaguely rung my bell at the time of the exchange of visiting cards and directly she mentioned Ranpur and Pankot I remembered it as a name quite well known there but couldn't recall ever having met one of them. Henry and I were there for the five years of his appointment as Governor but one's social life was fairly crowded. Over tea she told me that she and her sister and mother were sharing the houseboat with an aunt and an uncle. Her father, Colonel Layton, is a prisoner of war in Germany. He commanded the 1st Pankot Rifles in North Africa. He was in prison camp in Italy for a time but as we've advanced from the south a lot of the prisoners have been moved back, so our recent successes there haven't brought Colonel Layton's release and return any nearer. The revelation that her father was a prisoner of war went some way to explain her sudden visit and attempt at apology. In her father's absence she was probably trying to do what was right and thought that coming to see me made up for the rudeness of the rest of the family. They may have believed that story themselves about not wanting to intrude on my privacy, but of course underneath this apparent delicacy of feeling is the deep disapproval I meet everywhere now and am used to. Perhaps dismay is more accurate a description, dismay that I should have stood by and let Daphne bear a child whose father might be any one of half a dozen ruffians, dismay that instead of bundling it off as unwanted to some orphanage when Daphne died bearing it, I take care of it, and have given it that name, Parvati Manners.

I asked Miss Layton whether she was enjoying her holiday. She said it was the first real one they'd had since the war began. Both girls have joined the WAC(I) and work in Area Headquarters at Pankot. They decided to come to Srinagar this year because the sister – the younger of the two – is to be married soon. I'd seen the usual crowd of young men visiting their houseboat so naturally I asked if the sister's fiancé was also in Srinagar. Apparently not. The engagement took place when he was stationed in Pankot, and originally the wedding was to have been there, towards Christmas of this year. But he was suddenly posted to Mirat and has written to say that the wedding must be brought forward and has to be in Mirat, the sooner the better, and the honeymoon can't be for longer than two or three days. Which means, of course, that he expects to be going back into the field (he was in one of the regiments whose remnants managed to get out of Burma in 1942). So the young bride will be a grass window almost directly she's married. This is why the Laytons have gone back to Pankot earlier than they planned. They'll be off to Mirat soon after they arrive and it seems they hope to stay in the palace guest house so the younger Layton girl is very excited. I told Sarah Layton she'd like Mirat, especially if they stayed there as guests of the Nawab, who entertained Henry and me when we were on tour in that area. Lending the guest house to service people who can't get accommodation in the cantonment is probably part of the Nawab's war effort. He must be getting on a bit, now, and so must his wazir, that extraordinary Russian émigré Count Bronowsky, or whatever his name was, whom the Nawab brought back from Monte Carlo in the twenties, at the time of the scandal over the Nawab's relationship with a European woman. I told Miss Layton to look out for Bronowsky, and how all the English used to hate him until they realized what a good influence he was on the Nawab. She asked whether I had any idea what they ought to take as a present, if the Nawab let them stay in the guest house. Apparently they've been arguing and discussing it for days. I told her the Nawab was distantly related to ex-chief minister M. A. Kasim, and that the famous classic Urdu poet Gaffur was an eighteenth-century connection of both; and suggested that the most flattering gift might be a specially bound copy of Gaffur's poems. She was very pleased by the suggestion and said she'd tell her mother and aunt and try to get hold of a copy. I told her she could buy one in Srinagar and might even get it bound here, in a few days. Alternatively that there used to be a shop in Ranpur, in the bazaar, which did excellent leatherwork and gold-leaf blocking.

After we'd finished talking about the book she looked at me with the most extraordinary expression of envy that I've ever seen in a girl so young. She said, 'What a lot you know.' I laughed and said it was one of the few advantages of old age, to be a repository of bits and pieces of casual information that sometimes come in useful. But she said she didn't really mean that, she meant know as distinct from remember. She couldn't properly explain it and got up and said she mustn't take up any more of my time. I told her to come again, and she said she would if there were an opportunity. I took it she meant there probably wouldn't be and as it turned out I never saw her again, except to wave to. I didn't see their departure but after they'd gone one of the boys who'd been on their cookboat brought round a little bunch of flowers with a card 'With best wishes and many thanks from Sarah Layton'.

I have been thinking over what she said about knowing as distinct from remembering. Perhaps all it amounts to is that as we talked and I trotted out these little bits of information I gave the impression, common in elderly people, not only of having a long full life behind me that I could dip into more or less at random for the benefit of a younger listener, but also of being undisturbed by any doubts about the meaning and value of that life and the opinions I'd formed while leading it; although that suggests knowingness, and when she said, 'What a lot you know' she made it sound like a state of grace, one that she envied me in the mistaken belief that I was in it, while she was not and didn't understand how, things being as she finds them, one ever achieved it. It would be interesting to meet the rest of the family, who from their general appearance and conduct I would describe as typically army if I hadn't learned that people are never typical. But what I mean is that one could probably plot a graph of typical experience, attitude, behaviour and expectations of an army family in India and find it a rough but not inaccurate guide to that girl's background and the surrounding circumstances of her daily life. I was touched by the flowers – and by the fact that they have not lasted and will be dead by the time I leave and go down to 'Pindi.

Picture her then, an old lady dressed in a fawn tweed jacket and skirt, a high collar to a cream silk blouse that is buttoned with mother-of-pearl. No longer agile she scarcely welcomes the luxury of the embroidered mattress in the shikara which she finds it difficult to get down to and stretch out on; difficult but not yet impossible for someone trained to the custom of not inviting sympathy, or causing amusement, with evidence of weakness or infirmity; so that now, reclining safely, propped against the back rest, her topee-covered head turned at an angle of dignified farewell, one hand raised and the other seeking and finding some kind of old woman's reassurance from the pleats and buttons just below her throat, there is an air about her of faded Edwardian elegance, Victorian even, for Victorian women were great travellers when they bothered to travel at all; and the early-morning mist swathed in the mountains and above the lake, the movement of the boat, the pointed paddles dipping and sweeping, the totem figure of Suleiman, the huddled permissive attitude of the Kashmiri girl nursing the child, all combine to make, as it were, a perpetual willow-pattern of the transient English experience of outlandish cultures.

II

If English people in India could be said to live in (in the sense of belonging to) any particular town, the Laytons lived in Ranpur and Pankot. Ranpur was the permament cool weather station of Colonel Layton's regiment, the 1st Pankot Rifles. Their hot weather station was in the hills of Pankot itself, a place to which the provincial government also moved during the summer. It was from the hills and valleys around Pankot that the regiment recruited its men: sturdy agriculturalists who had a martial tradition going back (it was said) to pre-Moghul times. Somewhere round about the sixteenth century the hill people turned their backs on the old hill gods, embraced Islam and intermarried with their country's Moghul conquerors. So far as the British were concerned they ranked as Muslims, although it might have been more accurate to describe them as polytheists. In the hill villages images of old local Hindu gods were still to be found. To these the women liked to make offerings – at sowing and harvest-times, when they were in love, when they were pregnant, after the birth of a son or the death of a husband. The men held aloof from such things, unless they were going a journey, when they made sure that a female relation left a bowl of curds and a chaplet of flowers at the local wayside shrine the day before.

The only mosque in the entire hill area was in Pankot itself. Many of the boys who made the trek from their village to Pankot to offer themselves as soldiers at the recruiting depot were unable to distinguish between the mosque, the Kali temple, and the Protestant and Catholic churches. They knew the names of Allah, and of their tribal gods, they accepted that Allah was all-knowing, all-seeing and all-merciful, more powerful than the gods of the hills; so powerful in fact that it was better not to involve him in everyday matters. When you died you would go to his abode. While you lived here on earth it was necessary to be honest, industrious and vigorous. If you lived a good life, did not drink or smoke, practised good husbandry, took wives, procreated, did not cheat or steal, kept your roof repaired, your family fed, then you would please Allah. To live such a life, how-ever, it was necessary to please authority as well – to pay your taxes, to offer gifts of money to minor officials and of loyalty to senior ones, to propitiate the gods of the hills who, being less powerful than Allah, had both the time and the inclination to make things difficult for mortal man by withholding rain, sending too much, making the earth sour, turning male children into female children in your wife's womb, poisoning your blood with sickness, filling the air with bad vapours. Since Allah was all-knowing obviously he understood this. To feed and flatter the hill gods was something you did to help in the business of making your life pleasant for Allah to look upon. All the same such things were best left to the women, because women did not really understand about Allah: they did not need to. For a man it was different; Allah was a man: the perfect husbandman, the supreme warrior. He blessed ears of corn and strengthened your sword-arm. To die in battle, fighting his enemies, was the one sure way of going to Heaven. There were people living on the plains below the hills, and even in Pankot, who did not understand about Allah either. Such ignorance meant that their men were not much better than women. The white man, however, understood about Allah. In Pankot there were white men's mosques. There was also Recruiting Officer Sahib's *Daftar*, where a boy could go to become a sipahi, a soldier. The white man's enemies were also Allah's enemies. The white man called Allah God-Father, but he was the same Allah. They called the prophet Jesuschrist, not Mohammed; but then did not the same sky cover the whole world? In Pankot did it not cover the mosque, the Hindi temple, the two churches, the Governor's summer residence, Flagstaff House and Recruiting Officer Sahib's *Daftar*? To the boys coming in from the Pankot hills these places were all seats of mystery and authority. And of them all Recruiting Officer *Daftar* was the one they recognized as the most important in practical as well as mystical terms.

Not one of them made the journey from his hill or his valley to Pankot who was not forewarned of and rehearsed in the incalculable mysteries of the *Daftar* by an older male relation. To make the journey to the *Daftar* was the first test of manhood. To be rejected was thought by some to be a shame a boy could never recover from. In Pankot bazaar there were men – it was said – who begged or starved because they had been rejected and were afraid to go home. To be accepted was imperative if – having chanced one's arm – one were ever again to look another man in the eye. And so they came, year after year, with stern faces (that in a moment could crack into a grin, because the Pankot people were of a happy disposition), blanket over shoulder, bare-foot, each – inevitably – wearing or bearing some token of an earlier family connection with the Pankot Rifles – a pair of carefully mended khaki shorts, a row of medals, a chit from an uncle who had risen to the rank of Havildar or Jemadar and who begged the favour of offering his nephew in the service of the King-Emperor (whom they confused, vaguely, with the great Moghul and Allah) and gave, as reference, the name of an Englishman who more likely than not turned out to be retired, or dead, although not forgotten. The *Daftar* had a long memory.

The main recruiting season extended from the beginning of April until the end of September and coincided with the civil and military retreat from the plains to the hills which – in the old days – brought to Pankot not only the Governor, his administrators, their clerks and their files from Ranpur but detachments of the Pankot Rifles and the Ranpur Regiment from Ranpur.

From April to September Pankot lived a full social life. One met the same people as in Ranpur but in different, more delightful surroundings. Receptions at the Governor's summer residence (built in the Swiss Gothic style, with a preponderance of wood, instead of as in Ranpur in stone and stucco in Anglo-Indian palladian with a preponderance of colonnaded verandah) were less magnificent but no less formal. The important clubs had Pankot duplicates (wood again, instead of stone) and there was the Pankot Club itself which subalterns and junior civilians preferred because there you met all the girls recently out from home who might turn out good for a lark.

Pankot was a place to let off steam in. It was thoroughly English. The air was crisp, the trees coniferous. India, real India, lay below. To the north – defining the meeting point of heaven and earth, distantly, was the impressive jagged line of the Himalaya (usually invisible behind cloud, but occasionally revealed, like the word of God). Summer in Pankot was hotter than summer in England, but the mornings and the nights were cool and the rains fell with nothing like the fury they fell with in the plains. Winter, during the hours between sun-up and sunset, was like an English spring.

As hill stations went Pankot ranked as one of the second class. It attracted almost no tourists and few leave-takers (who preferred Darjeeling, Naini Tal and Kashmir). There was a rail connection from Ranpur, narrow gauge and single track. The journey took eight hours up and six hours down. There was also a road which was used by the Indian bus and by the military who sent soldiers of the Pankot Rifles and the Ranpur Regiment up and down by lorry. In places road and rail converged, passed under or over one another or marched parallel. The ascent was slow. Embankments gave way to cuttings. Signs of habitation became fewer. The characters of villages changed. There were fewer water-buffalo, more white-humped cattle; many more goats. Rocky out-crops appeared; and then the road began to wind into the foothills, a dusty coil connecting the parched plain to the green-clad heights. Sound was muffled, amplified, thrown back – depending on the formation of hill-face, precipice, re-entry. There was a scent of timber.

Pankot was built upon three hills and their conjoint valley. The railway ended against a rocky face that the road found its way round, through a tunnel of trees, up, over the top and down into the enclosed vale – grassed acres scattered with hutments that bore the unmistakable signs of military occupation. Here, mists gathered in the evening and the early morning. Out of such mists, a mile ahead, emerged the Indo-Tyrolean architecture of the Pankot Bazaar – a V-shaped township of three-storey wooden buildings with fretted overhanging verandahs above open-fronted shops where they sold embroidered shawls, beaten silver, filigree wooden boxes inlaid with brass lotus designs. There were Indian coffee shops, fortune-tellers, the local branch of the Imperial Bank of India, a garage, a bicycle shop, the Hindu Hotel, the Muslim Hotel. At the tip of the V the buses halted. Here there were ponies and tongas for hire, even a taxi or two. This was the favourite place of pedlars and itinerant Holy men and small boys in rags and moth-eaten fur caps who competed with each other to shine the visitors' shoes. There was a smell of petrol, horse manure, cattle dung, incense and sandalwood, of spicy food being cooked in the open over charcoal fires. The shop signs were in English and in the vernacular in both the

Nagari and the Arabic scripts. Here, too, were the Kali temple and the mosque. In the centre of the square formed by the lower tip of the V, the temple and the mosque, stood a phallic stone monolith, erected in 1925, a memorial to the soldiers of the Pankot Rifles who had given their lives in the Great War. In November it received a wreath of poppies, offerings of ghi, buttermilk and flowers.

The arms of the V mounted quite steeply, reaching up into the hills behind the bazaar. The right-hand fork from War Memorial Square was the less steep, but it led finally to the majestic heights dominated by the Governor's summer residence. The left-hand fork led more abruptly to a lower area where rich Indians and minor princes owned chalet-style houses (a few of which had 'Mahal' in their names, to denote that they were palaces). This was an area the generality of the English had little knowledge of. To them Pankot was properly reached by taking the right-hand fork. Here were the clubs, the administrative quarters, the golf course, the bungalows and houses of seasonal occupation; most of them hidden by pines, marked by roadside posts at drive-entrances. And yet there was no feeling of enclosure. The road, at every turn, gave views. There were English people who said they were reminded of the Surrey hills near Caterham. Upon retirement from the civil or the military some of them came to Pankot – not to die (although they did – and were buried in the churchyard of St John's – C of E – or St Edward's – RC) but to enjoy their remaining years in a place that was peculiarly Indian but very much their own, and where servants were cheap, and English flowers could be grown (sometimes spectacularly) in the gardens, and life take on the serenity of fulfilment, of duty done without the depression of going home wondering what it had been done for.

It was in Pankot that Sarah Layton's childhood memories of India were chiefly centred. She and Susan were born there (in 1921 and 1922 respectively). Their christening was recorded in the parish register of St John's Church (Sarah in March, an Aries, and Susan in November, a Scorpio). The register also recorded the marriage in 1920 of their father John Frederick William Layton (Lieutenant, 1st Pankot Rifles, son of James William Layton, ICS) to their mother Mildred Rose Muir, daughter of Howard Campbell Muir – Lieut.-General (GS). Neither James

William Layton nor General Muir was laid to rest in the churchyard of St John, Pankot, but there were headstones there that
celebrated both names, those of General Muir's unmarried aunt
and James Layton's great-aunt – the former dead of fever, aged
nineteen, the latter in childbirth, aged twenty-three.

Sarah and Susan's father, John Layton, was in Pankot for the
second time in his life in 1913. He was then nineteen years
old, newly returned from Chillingborough and Sandhurst. His
choice of a military instead of a civil career was his own but
his choice of regiment had been dictated by a sense of family
connection. To begin with, Pankot had lain within his civilian
father's first district. Layton had no personal recollection of the
place. He had spent one summer there with his parents as a child
of three, when his father was working at the secretariat in
Ranpur and went up to Pankot with the provincial government
when it took its annual breather in the hills. Afterwards the
Laytons went down to Mayapore where Mr James Layton had
been appointed assistant commissioner and joint magistrate. A
later appointment still, as acting deputy commissioner, took the
Laytons down to Dibrapur and when that job was finished young
John Layton was eight and due to go home to England to school.
His parents, taking their long leave, accompanied him. During
school holidays he lived with his paternal grandfather in Surrey.
His parents returned to India. Shortly after their return Mr James
Layton was appointed Deputy Commissioner for the Pankot
District. During his tour of office there he made a name for
himself with the people of the hills. He had certain eccentricities
which endeared him to them. He used to escape from his office
and his staff and his wife and ride ten or twenty miles on his
pony between sun-up and sunset to talk to the villagers.

In India, as a child, young John Layton was inclined to be
sickly. He inherited his mother's constitution. Even in England
his health gave some cause for anxiety. There had been a plan,
indeed a promise, that in the long summer holiday of 1907 when
he was thirteen he would spend a month in Pankot with his
parents. His England-based grandfather advised against it and
suggested that instead his parents should take long leave and
come to England. Only Mrs Layton was able to make the
journey.

Sick before she set out (the ill-effects of life in places like

Mayapore and Dibrapur had become too deep-rooted for the healthier climate of Pankot to have made much difference) she was sick when she reached home. She was not the mother young Layton remembered. In later life he found it difficult to recall the conflicting emotions the sight of her actually aroused in him. As he said to his daughter Sarah (in a rare moment of confidence – rare but perhaps not unexpected because Sarah was her father's daughter while Susan was her mother's), 'I suppose I was disappointed. My mother looked old in the wrong sort of way. Well, I mean like someone on the stage made up for it. When she died it was like part of an act. I felt my real mother was still in Pankot, thousands of miles away, and this one was a feeble impostor – so when father married again and came back to England with his new wife Mabel in 1909 she was more real to me than my own mother had been. Why am I telling you this?'

Sarah's paternal grandmother, the first Mrs Layton, died in England of double pneumonia in 1907 after a bout of malarial fever six weeks after returning home to visit her son. Young Layton was then back at school, in his first term at Chillingborough. He went home to Surrey for the funeral and wrote a letter to his father in India saying he was sorry, and describing – with his grandfather's help – the headstone that was going to be erected on his mother's grave.

His father's second wife was the widow of a major of the 1st Pankot Rifles who had died heroically on the North-West Frontier. Young Layton met her in the summer of 1909 when his father brought her home on long leave. He liked her. In a curious way she reminded him of his real mother – the one he'd had a picture of. She treated him as if he were already a man, which in a way he was, being fifteen, a promising classical scholar, not bad-looking and growing out of childish debility. He was still thin, but he had bones, and his voice had broken. He was startled by his resemblance to his father, and flattered when his stepmother mentioned it. He had his father's eyes, she said. She was well-fleshed, heavier than he, but she often made him offer her his arm and when he did so she leant on it. She made him feel gallant. She asked him to call her by her first name, Mabel – a name he had not liked but liked now.

To his father's eventual question, 'Well, John, what do you

think of her?' he could only say in fullness of heart, 'Oh, she's topping,' and was amazed then when his father took his hand, as a woman might have done, and exerted a momentary pressure. They were lying on this occasion in his Surrey grandfather's orchard under an apple tree whose fruits were suspended in the branches – midway between their summer green sour and their rosy autumn ripe.

'What will it be, John,' his father asked presently, 'the administration or the army?'

'Oh, the army,' he said, thinking of his stepmother's first dead hero husband. 'The Pankot Rifles,' and then half sat up as if to apologize. His father lay back – eyes closed, smiling. 'I mean,' young Layton continued, 'if you agree, I'd like to, well, you know, not make capital out of your standing in the civil, but make a go of it on my own in something different. Do you mind?'

His father said, 'Not in the least,' then smiled more broadly and repeated: 'Not in the very least.'

When young Layton returned to India in 1913 his father was member for finance on the provincial governor's executive council. He and Mabel lived in a vast old bungalow in Ranpur. Layton stayed with them for a week and Mabel gave a dinner party for him at which he met the commanding officer of the 1st Pankot Rifles and the adjutant, and their wives. Before the guests arrived Mabel inspected him to make sure that the tailor in London had made his uniform correctly and that he was wearing it properly. It consisted of tight dark blue overalls that were strapped under the heels of wellington boots, a white shirt with a stiff narrow winged collar, a narrow black silk bow-tie, a black silk cummerbund, a waist-length jacket of dark green barathea frogged with black braid and clasped at the neck by a little silver chain. It was hot but not especially uncomfortable. He was proud to be wearing it and not put out when Mabel tapped his chest with her fan and said, 'Let it wear you, then you'll grow into it,' and kissed him and raised her arm in the way a woman did in those days to command the support of a man she approved of.

A week later he joined his regiment in Ranpur (the month was October) and a week after that went up to the Pankot Hills to the depot where he was initiated into the lore of recruitment, initial training, and transportation back to Ranpur of men returning from leave in their villages. In October and November boys still came down from the hills to Pankot to present themselves at the *Daftar*, often accompanied by an elder brother who had come up with his battalion in April from Ranpur and later gone on leave. The recruiting season was also the leave season. 2/Lieut. John Layton sometimes sat with the senior subaltern in the *Daftar*, learning the technique of selection and rejection. At others he watched the boys drilling under the depot Subahdar-major, or took command of the morning and evening parades. Apart from the subaltern appointed as Recruiting Officer Sahib there were two other British officers permanently at Pankot, the depot commander and his adjutant. Layton lived with the senior subaltern in a bungalow near the golf course. His military duties took up little time, but he had social duties. Social duties included calling (by leaving his card) on European officials and civilians (usually retired) and their wives, in order of seniority. Pankot was never empty but in the winter there was an air about the place of almost cosy relaxation. Wherever he went in Pankot he was known as James Layton's son and as Mabel's stepson. He did not mind having no special identity of his own. Life, in its fullest sense, was a question of service. He had an idea that his real mother, from ill-health rather than any other cause, had not fully understood this. In Pankot she also was remembered but as someone who hadn't been quite up to meeting the demands the country made on white people – certainly not up to meeting them in the way her successor, Mabel Layton, met them.

He was careful to take plenty of exercise. He rode and played tennis and at weekends went for long walks by himself; but solitariness, to Layton, was attractive only in prospect. He found the lonely hillpaths disturbing.

The house in which his father and Mabel lived during the summer was shut up. He looked forward to 1914 and hoped he would not have the bad luck to be left in Ranpur. He would have liked to spend at least one hot weather in Pankot while his father and Mabel were on station. By 1915 he would probably be on the North-West Frontier, because the 1st Pankots had not been there since 1907, the year Mabel's husband was killed and his own mother died in England. He also looked forward to the time – still further in the future because peace-time promotion was slow – when as senior subaltern he would live for a whole year in Pankot in charge of recruitment. Perhaps by then his father would have retired and come to live in Pankot permanently. Some people said that India was ruinous to familial devotion, because of the long periods when children were separated from their parents. Some people even tried the experiment of educating their children at special schools in India, but that didn't work very well. The children were marked, for life, as of the country. So far as young Layton was concerned, the years in England had only served to strengthen his devotion to his father, his stepmother, and the country they served.

In November he returned to Ranpur. He did not see Pankot again until the summer of 1919. In the hot weather of 1914 he was, as he had expected, left behind in Ranpur. By the time his parents came back from the hills war had been declared on Germany. In 1915 the 1st Pankots moved to Dehra Dun and then to Poona. There was some uncertainty about what role they were to play, and where, but eventually they were brigaded and sailed for Suez. They were in action in Mesopotamia. Subahdar Muzzafir Khan Bahadur was awarded a posthumous VC. The Colonel collected a DSO and two officers, one of them Layton, collected MCs. In 1918, somewhat depleted, they went to Palestine and in 1919 sailed back to India, where their return to Ranpur was temporarily held up because their arrival coincided with civil unrest in the Punjab, the consequence (according to the Indians) of the Rowlatt Acts which were intended to enable the Government of India (in spite of the 1917 declaration of Dominion status as its long-term political aim) to continue to exercise in peace-time certain war-time measures under the Defence of India Rules for the protection of the realm against subversion. These means included imprisonment of Indians without trial. According to the English the disturbances were simply a disagreeable sign of the times, proof that the war had ruined people's sense of values and let reds and radicals – white as well as black – get above themselves.

But the action of General Dyer in April in Amritsar in the Jallianwallah Bagh, where he personally led a detachment of Gurkhas who fired on an unarmed crowd of civilians who were defying his order not to hold a public meeting, killing several hundred and wounding upwards of a thousand, nipped the anticipated revolution nicely in the bud and in May the 1st Pankots left the staging camp where they had been halted and held in reserve, in case further troops were needed to act in aid of the civil power, and continued their journey home.

Pankot gave the regiment an official welcome – a full-dress military parade attended by the Governor and members of his council and by the General Officer commanding in Ranpur, Lieut.-General Muir. Subahdar Muzzafir Khan Bahadur's seven-year-old son and his widow (an unidentifiable figure dressed overall in a black *burkha* that made her look like an effigy) were presented to the Governor and the General (the widow through the medium of those officers' wives) and the son received his father's medal from the Governor. The officers who had been decorated stood on the saluting platform with the Governor and the General while the battalion marched past with fife and drum, followed by the 1st Ranpurs (second-in-command, Major A. V. Reid, DSO, MC) who had also seen service in the Middle East but had returned home sooner, and the scratch war-time Pankot battalions, soon to be disbanded. The rear was brought up, proudly, by the 4/5 Pankot Rifles who were destined to live on and go down to Mayapore and make it their permanent cool weather station.

Young Layton, as was his due, stood with the other decorated officers on the saluting platform.

'I remember thinking,' he told Sarah, 'that there was something wrong, something that meant all this pomp wasn't what we wanted, and that something irretrievable had been lost. Innocence I suppose. Perhaps I felt this only because father was dead, the war had been a mess and I'd done nothing to deserve my MC, or because Mabel was crying. Well, it was all splendid enough, I suppose.'

Layton's father had died unexpectedly in 1917 after a short illness caused by an abscess on the liver – the end result of a long-standing amoebic infection which had never been properly diagnosed or treated.

He died in the Minto Hospital in Ranpur and was buried in the churchyard of St Luke's. If he had lived another year, Mabel said, he would have got his KCIE. Since his death Mabel had altered, her stepson thought. There had always been a hard streak in her. Without it her gaiety would have seemed shallow. Now the gaiety had gone and the hard streak emerged when it was least expected: in private rather than in public. She cried at the ceremonial parade. But when she took her stepson to St Luke's to show him his father's grave her behaviour was off-hand. She seemed to have lost the knack, or the will, to make people feel at home in her company.

A year later, after her stepson's marriage to Mildred Muir and after there had been a committee of inquiry into the massacre in the Jallianwallah Bagh, a report by the Indian National Congress, a debate in the House of Commons on the findings of the Army Council, and General Dyer had been retired on half-pay (disgraced, whereas twelve months before he had been hailed as the saviour of India and was still thought of as such by all right-thinking people), Mabel Layton surprised everybody by refusing to identify herself with the ladies of Pankot and Ranpur who busied themselves collecting money for the General Dyer fund. These ladies had misinterpreted the tears at the ceremonial parade and the stony face over tea and coffee for patriotism of the most exemplary kind, and were shocked when by refusing either to contribute or help to collect money that would keep the wolf from the old General's door she appeared in an entirely different light: widow of a soldier who had died for the empire, widow – for a second time – of a civilian whose work for the empire had killed him, stepmother of a young officer who had fought for his country gallantly, step-mother-in-law of the second daughter of General Muir, but who was, it seemed, nevertheless insensible to the true nature of what the men in her life (including her father, who had been an admiral) had stood or still stood for.

When the total sum collected for General Dyer was heard to have reached the substantial fee of £26,000 the ladies of Pankot and Ranpur felt vindicated, justified. But Mabel Layton's comment was 'Twenty-six thousand? Well, now, how many unarmed Indians died in the Jallianwallah Bagh? Two hundred? Three hundred? There seems to be some uncertainty, but let's say two hundred and sixty. That's one hundred pounds apiece. So we know the current price for a dead brown,' and sent a cheque for £100 to the fund the Indians were raising for the families of Jallianwallah victims. But only young Layton and the Indian to whom she entrusted the money knew this.

'I'm keeping it dark for your sake,' Mabel told him, but with an edge in her voice that made it sound as if she felt he had personally driven her to secrecy. 'People would misunderstand. They usually do. You have a career to think of. You can't have a stepmother who seems to be going native, which is the last thing I'd do. I hate the damned country now anyway. It's taken two husbands from me. To me it's not a question of choosing between poor old Dyer and the bloody browns. The choice was made for me when we took the country over and got the idea we did so for its own sake instead of ours. Dyer can look after himself, but according to the rules the browns can't because looking after them is what we get paid for. And if it's *really* neces-sary every so often to shoot some of them down like ninepins for their own good the least we can do is admit it, just say Hard Luck to the chap who shoots too many, and see to it that the women and children who lost their menfolk, or the children who lost their parents don't starve. There were kids who got shot too, weren't there, at Amritsar? What do we owe them?'

She paid the £100 to one Sir Ahmed Akbar Ali Kasim, a wealthy Ranpur Muslim, one of her late husband's Indian colleagues on the provincial governor's executive council, whose son Mohammed Ali had already shown brilliance in his chosen profession, the law, and was inspired that year of the Jallianwallah Bagh massacre to join the Congress Party whose aim in that same year and for the same bloody reasons and under M. K. Gandhi's leadership was reversed from independence by peaceful co-operation to independence as soon as possible by non-co-operation.

'You are young,' Sir Ahmed Akbar told his son. 'Your heart is stronger than your head. When you are as old as I am you will not be so confused by these emotional issues. You think Jallian-wallah was a new experience? You are wrong. You think the Indian Congress can ensure that it will be the last episode of this kind? You will be wrong again. You think Jallianwallah proves that the British are lying, talking freedom but acting tyrannically and dealing destruction? Again you are wrong. Jallianwallah could never have happened if the British who talk freedom were not sincere. It happened because they are sincere. They have frightened their opponents with their sincerity. I do not mean us. We are not their opponents. Their opponents, the ones who matter but who will matter less and less, are also British. They are men like General Dyer. Why do you call that man a monster? He believed God had charged him with a duty to save the empire. He believed this sincerely, just as he believed sincerely that in Amritsar there was to be found an invidious threat to that empire. Why do you repeat parrot-fashion that the English are hypocrites? With this you can never charge them. You can only charge them with sincerity and of being divided among themselves about what it is right to be sincere about. It is only an insincere people that can be accused of hyprocrisy. Sometimes I think we are the hypocrites because we have lived too long as a subject people to remember what sincerity means, or to know from one day to the next what we believe in.

'Look' (the old man said, and showed Mohammed Ali a slip of paper), 'do you know what this is? It is a cheque for the rupee equivalent of one hundred pounds made out in my name by an Englishwoman. In exchange for it I am charged to send my own draft to the fund for the Jallianwallah widows and orphans, and not to reveal the name of the donor. Perhaps you think this smells a bit of hypocrisy. To me it smells only of sincerity. It is a straw in the wind which proves to me that for a long time I have been correct in my forecast of which way the wind would blow.

'You look at the English people you meet. Some of them you like. Some you hate. Many you are indifferent to. But even the ones you like do not matter. The ones who matter you will never see – they are tucked away in England – and they are indifferent to us as individuals. You think these officials over here rule us? These viceroys, these governors, these commissioners and commanders-in-chief and brigadier-generals? Then you are wrong. We are ruled by people who do not even know where Ranpur is. But now they know where Jallianwallah Bagh is and what it is, and many of them do not like what they know. Those of them who *do* like what they know are the ones you hear about and hear from. Like the General at Amritsar they are frightened people and frightened people shriek the loudest and fire at random.

'Ah, well, they were Indians who actually died at Amritsar,

but the Jallianwallah Bagh was also the scene of a suicide. There will be other such scenes. It takes a long time for a new nation to be born, and a long time for an old nation to die by its own hand. You will hasten nothing by failing to distinguish between the English who really rule us and the English who interpret and administer that rule. Haven't you yet understood that we are part and parcel of the Englishmen's own continual state of social and political evolvement and that to share the fruits we must share the labour and abide by the rules they abide by?'

'You mean,' Mohammed Ali said, 'submit to being shot down for protesting the freedom to speak our minds?'

'For this they have shot down their own people, and not so long ago. Out here we shall always be a step behind whatever progress the English make at home.'

Mohammed Ali smiled. 'No,' he said, 'we shall be several steps ahead.'

For a while the old man was silent, not because his son had stumped him. He was merely considering the violent landscape so casually mapped.

'Perhaps I am too old,' he said eventually. 'I can't see small print without my spectacles and even then I get a headache. I think the lady who donated this money also finds it difficult to read the small print. She is anyway only concerning herself with the capital letters of an ancient contract. In *your* contract is *everything* writ large, or is it that your eyesight is superhuman?'

John Layton was in his twenty-sixth year when he came back to India in 1919. In the last year of his service abroad he was acting adjutant of the battalion. On returning to Ranpur he relinquished the appointment to an officer of the 2nd Battalion who was senior to him. Temporarily he was without regimental employment. He was the natural choice for the role of Recruiting Officer Sahib. He went up to Pankot in May, with Mabel. They lived in the bungalow near the golf course that he had shared with the senior subaltern in the October and November of 1913.

Both Mabel and his father had talked of retiring to Pankot when the time came. They had had their eye on a place called Rose Cottage, inconveniently placed on the other side of the main hill dominated by the Governor's Summer Residence but to them the most attractive of the few privately owned houses and bungalows: attractive because of its garden, its views, and the fact that it was owned by an elderly widower who had been in tea in Assam and couldn't be expected to live much longer.

Layton's father had not been a rich man. What little he left Mabel inherited, but she had money of her own and money from her first husband who had died well-breeched in spite of having lived extravagantly. Since Mabel was childless he would eventually inherit everything. It would be useful. In peace-time an officer found it virtually impossible to live on his pay – he was not expected to – few attempted to however simple their tastes – he found it quite impossible to save. To serve the empire he needed money of his own. For the moment Layton had no worries on this score. Until his death his civilian father had paid sums of money into his account whenever he could afford them; and Layton suspected – surprised at the amount standing to his credit – that Mabel had contributed regular sums herself. Furthermore she declared her intention of handing over to him in full the principal she had inherited from his father, and the accumulated interest, directly he got married. Such funds together with what he had been able to save while on active service represented the kind of basic security without which a man of his kind would feel at a disadvantage when it came to thinking of the future in terms of fatherhood and of a proper education for his children.

When his Surrey grandfather died – and the old boy surely couldn't go on much longer – he imagined he would inherit the Surrey property into the bargain. His own children might spend part of their childhood there, with their mother (whoever she might be) or their grandmother Mabel, or some relation of their mother's. The long-term plan looked sound. In his twenty-sixth year he felt it was time to be thinking of marriage.

III

The GOC Ranpur, Lieut.-General Muir, had three daughters, Lydia, Mildred and Fenella. They were known as Lyddy, Millie and Fenny. 1919 was their first Indian season – the war had post-poned it. It was Mildred to whom Layton was most attracted. Fenny was boisterous and silly. Lydia had been engaged to a naval officer at home who was lost in the Atlantic. She bore her loss rather bitterly and Layton distrusted the element of sympathy that would initially enter any relationship a man could have with her. With Millie he felt at ease, even when they were alone and ran out of things to say to one another.

Mrs Muir was an expert chaperone. Opportunities to be alone with any one of her daughters were neither too few nor too many. It was said that she kept a list of eligible men and that a sign of being on it was the sudden myopia that afflicted that regal eye when you danced out of the ballroom on to the terrace of Flagstaff House and sat one of her daughters down in a place where the artificial light from the crystal chandeliers just failed to illumine the stone flags and the balustrade, but (ideally) lit her eyes and caught some of the facets of the jewellery she was wearing.

He decided after several such meetings that he was in love with Mildred Muir and – which was more important – that she was attracted to him. Eventually he declared his love, proposed to her and having got her acceptance asked the general for an interview, addressed himself to the older man with painstaking old-fashioned formality which (Mildred later told her daughter Sarah) swept the old boy off his feet.

The engagement was announced in September. The May of 1920 was chosen as the ideal time for the marriage. Layton would then have finished his twelve-month tour as Recruiting Officer, and he would be due for long leave. He and Mildred would honeymoon in Kashmir and then take a trip home to England to visit his grandfather in Surrey.

Of these plans his stepmother Mabel seemed to approve although he could not actually get her to talk for long about them. In November he took her back to Ranpur. On his return from the war he had found her living at Smith's Hotel and to this place she returned now, refusing an invitation from General and Mrs Muir to stay at Flagstaff House. After a weekend with the Muirs Layton went back to Pankot alone and this time found that solitude came easier to him. He rode and spent weekends walking in the hills. News of his progress on such occasions passed from village to village and wherever he went he found himself pressed to accept hospitality and knew that it would not do to refuse it. He was the only son of Layton Sahib and also the sahib who knew best how to tell the story of Subahdar Muzzafir Khan Bahadur's gallantry. Old and young men gathered round him in the evenings – and beyond the light cast by the flickering oil-lamps he was often aware of the veiled presence of listening women, and afterwards would sleep the sound sleep of satisfied appetite for food and drink and human correspondence that left in his mind an impression of the hill people's grave simplicity and cheerful dignity so that he thought 'Well, home is here,' and knew that for English people in India there was no home in the sense of brick and mortar, orchard and pasture, but that it was lodged mysteriously in the heart.

Late in the August of 1920, newly returned with his bride from England, he found Mabel still lodging at Smith's. They stayed with her there for a week before going on up to Pankot to join General and Mrs Muir and Fenny. Lydia had gone back to England with them after the Kashmir honeymoon and had stayed there, declaring that she would never go to India again. She never did. She took a job as secretary to a Bayswater physician, and later married him.

In October Mildred returned to the plains with her husband. Her first baby was due in the second half of March. By then it would be hot and she expressed a wish for the baby to be born in Pankot. There was a nursing home there, part of the hospital and convalescent home that was the Pankot extension of the general hospital in Ranpur. Still without regular regimental employment, Layton acted variously as his father-in-law's aide and as adjutant of the 1st Pankots, filling a leave vacancy. He sat on courts of inquiry and went on courses. In February 1921 he took Mildred up to Pankot. Mrs Muir accompanied them and so did Fenny. They stayed in the GOC's summer residence, a section of which was opened up for this unseasonable occupation. Five weeks later, on March 27th, Sarah was born.

Layton was only momentarily disappointed that his first child was a girl. She was a delicate rosy-cheeked image of Mildred and himself with none of that red ancient wrinkled look of the new-born baby. All that lacked to complete his happiness was a home of his own to bring her and her mother back to when they came out of the Pankot Nursing Home. They stayed throughout that summer in Flagstaff House. He wrote to Mabel asking her to

join them, but she seemed to have no liking for the hills now
and stayed in Ranpur. She did not see her stepson's first child
until late in the following October, when the Laytons went
down to Ranpur. They now had for the first time what could
pass as a permanent home – permanent in the transient, military
sense. The adjutant of the 1st Pankots had gone to the staff
college in Quetta and Layton succeeded to the appointment. He
moved his family into the bungalow that was to be their home
for the next few years, No. 3 Kabul road, Ranpur: a stuccoed
colonnaded structure, well shaded by trees in a large compound
with adequate stabling and servants' quarters, and a lawn where
Sarah and Susan (born in Pankot, in 1922) played – mainly under
the eye of Dost Mohammed the head *mali* who knew the ways
of snakes and scorpions so well that neither child ever saw a
live snake and only one living scorpion in the moment when,
encircled by a ring of fire created by Dost Mohammed, it arched
its tail over its body and (so he said) stung itself to death.

Sarah remembered the scorpion (she watched what Dost
Mohammed called its suicide with the detached curiosity of
a child) and the garden at No. 3 Kabul road – the shadowy
verandah, a dark retreat from the intensity of sunlight; the high-
ceilinged bedroom which she shared with Susan, twin child-
size beds under twin mosquito nets, and slatted doors which
Mumtez, their old ayah, closed at night and guarded, making
her bed up against them, sleeping across the threshold. Sarah
remembered being woken in the early mornings by the hoarse
screeching of the crows. She confused these memories of the old
bungalow in Ranpur with other more clearly sustained memories of Pankot; but neither Ranpur nor Pankot struck her when
she came back to them, a young woman, as having survived
the years of her growing up in England in the way she herself
survived them: to her eighteen-year-old eye, in the summer
of 1939, their reality was only a marginally accurate reflection of
the mind picture she had of them. There was too much space
between the particular places she remembered – places which
were strongholds of her childhood recollections – and the
strongholds themselves had a prosaicness of brick and mortar
that did not match the magical, misty but more vivid impression
they had left on her when young, so that returning to them,

Pankot and Ranpur – Ranpur particularly – seemed to have spread themselves too thin and yet too thick on the ground for comfort.

The sensation she had was one of insecurity which from day to day, and from moment to moment in any one day, could be cushioned by a notion of personal and family history. India to her was at once alien and familiar. The language came back slowly to her, in stops and starts. She was surprised by what she remembered of it, puzzled by what she seemed to have forgotten, but realized then that what she had ever learned of it was the shorthand of juvenile command and not the language of adult communication.

And yet (Sarah thought) over here in an odd and curious way we *are* children. I am aware, coming back, of entering a region of almost childish presumptions – as if everything we are surrounded by is the background for a game. But Susan and I are somehow left out of the game, as if even now we are not old enough to be depended upon to know the rules and act accordingly. Before we are allowed to play we have to know the rules. Without them the game can be seen to be a game, and if it's seen to be a game someone will come along and tell us to put our toys away. And this of course is what is going to happen. This is what I feel, coming back here. And directly it happens all the magic of the game will evaporate, the Fort will be seen to have been made of paper, the soldiers of lead and tin, and I of wax or china or pot. And Mumtez will not lie across the threshold, keeping our long night safe from ogres. Mumtez is gone long ago anyway. Where? Mother scarcely remembers her, which means perhaps that she was in our service for no longer than a year. She remembers Dost Mohammed but not the day of the scorpion. Instead she remembers the day of the snake who neither I nor Susan remember – I suppose because mother and Dost Mohammed between them kept the day of the snake well away from us.

But older children forget the toys that have been put up into the attic; only the younger ones remember and then they too in their turn forget and play games as if they were not games at all but part of life. But it is all a business of cobwebs and old chests and long days indoors that find us thrown back on our own frail resources, because we are afraid to go outside and wet our feet and catch a chill. Pankot is such a place. Pankot is a retreat. So is Ranpur. Not the real Pankot, not the real Ranpur, but *our* Ranpur and Pankot. We see them as different from what they really are which is why when we come back to them we are aware of the long distances that separate one place of vivid recollection from another. In Ranpur we become aware of the immensity of the surrounding plain and in Pankot of the very small impression we have made on hills which when we are away from them we think of as safe, enclosed and friendly but which are in reality unfriendly, vast and dangerous. That is our first shock when we return. It's not something we like to see or think about, so after a time we don't see it and don't think about it.

The house in Pankot and the bungalow in Ranpur which their parents were living in during the summer and winter respectively when Sarah and Susan returned to India in 1939 were not places either of the girls remembered. To begin with each was larger than its predecessor because Layton had now assumed command of the 1st Pankots after a fairly humdrum but not unsuccessful career, which during their daughters' absence at home had taken him (and his wife) from Ranpur to Lahore, and Delhi, Peshawar and Quetta, but since houses and bungalows were built very much to the same pattern neither girl was particularly aware of what made these homes different from those they lived in as children.

Sarah and Susan came back to India accompanied by their Aunt Fenny and Uncle Arthur – Major and Mrs Grace who had been taking home leave in 1939 – the year Susan finished with school, and Sarah, who had finished with school one term before, had come to the end of the short secretarial course she had insisted on taking, determined anyway to be prepared to be of some use to someone, somewhere.

Aunt Fenny, the youngest of the Muir girls, had married Arthur Grace in 1924. Her marriage coincided with her father's retirement. It had surprised people at the time that Fenny took so long to make up her mind between the several officers who from time to time laid siege to her affections. And her choice, coming when it did, in – as it were – the last year of her Indian opportunity (General and Mrs Muir having decided to retire to England) and lighting upon Arthur Grace, left an idea in people's

minds that she knew she had delayed too long. Arthur Grace
was possibly the least eligible of the subalterns who wooed her,
and the gossip was that at this last moment she panicked and said
yes to his proposal merely because he happened to make it on
a particular day, at a particular hour, when she was especially
concerned about her future.

His career had not been successful; they had not managed to
produce children, and Aunt Fenny had become year by year
more and more unrecognizable as the pretty but shallow girl
who had had a good time in Pankot in 1919 and 1920 – a bridesmaid who had caught her sister Mildred's bouquet when
Mildred and John Layton were married in the church of St John
in Pankot early one May morning, and who had been so solidly
surrounded by interested young escorts at Pankot station later
that day that she scarcely had time to wave her newly-married
sister off on her honeymoon.

Youngest daughter, bridesmaid, a godmother to Susan and
Sarah – these were the happy stages Fenny passed through before
joining the company of honourable matrons as the wife of
Arthur Grace. And then, in her turn, Sarah – being then but
three years old – acted as a bridesmaid to Aunt Fenny; although
of that she had really no recollection whatsoever beyond what
was evidenced by the family iconography, a photograph in Aunt
Lydia's house in London and the same photograph in her
mother's album in India.

It showed the Layton and the Muir families gathered together
in slightly self-conscious but handsome, well-dressed and orderly
array around a younger Aunt Fenny and a thinner Uncle Arthur
with Sarah standing there, a little to one side, in front of Aunt
Fenny, holding a nosegay whose scent she almost thought she
could reconjure (in isolation from the unrecollected event that
caused her to be holding it) and by her side the image of a five-
year-old boy in satin pageboy rig whom she could not reconjure
at all but whose name, apparently, was Giles, and who was the
son of her father's commanding officer.

Perhaps the group portrait was most notable for its inclusion of
Mabel Layton who stood next to her first husband's old comrade-
in-arms, by then the commanding officer of the 1st Pankots,
Giles's father, with on her other side an elderly Indian civilian
who was present at the wedding because of his connection with

the Governor who was also there with his wife shoulder to shoulder with General and Mrs Muir. The photograph was taken in the gardens of Flagstaff House at Pankot and in the background there could be seen the wooden balustrades and the kindly wistaria. Mabel Layton wore a wide-brimmed hat that all but hid her face, except for a mouth – held midway between repose and a smile.

As a child in India Sarah was afraid of Aunty Mabel (as she insisted on being called). This may have had something to do with the fact that Aunty Mabel was not really her grandmother, but her father's stepmother, and stepmothers were never nice people in story books. She liked Aunty Mabel in England better than she had in India, perhaps because she herself had grown up a bit. Mabel came to England with Major and Mrs Layton in the summer of 1933 when Sarah was turned twelve: the year great-grandfather Layton in Surrey was dying at last at the age of ninety-four.

Although in that long period of exile in England as schoolgirls, she and Susan lived in London with Aunt Lydia, they usually spent several weeks of the summer holidays with their great-grandfather. A casual observer might have thought that Susan was the old man's favourite child. It was Susan who sat on his knee to listen to his rather gruesome fairy-stories and his stories of their father's and grandfather's boyhoods in Surrey. Sarah did not mind this apparent favouritism. Between herself and her ancient relative there was a silent understanding that Susan needed looking after because she was the baby of the family. His stories either went over Susan's head or bored her, or frightened her. Towards the end of great-grandfather's life Susan decided that she was too old to sit on his knee although she enjoyed the preferential treatment his invitation – increasingly reluctantly accepted – always gave proof of.

Susan did not cry when great-grandfather Layton died; neither did Sarah but she felt they didn't cry for different reasons. He died towards the end of the summer of 1933, shortly before Sarah's and Susan's parents were due to go back to India with Aunty Mabel. Sarah believed Susan did not cry because Susan had never thought of her great-grandfather as a person, but as an old and rather smelly piece of furniture that had to be put up with in the summer and sometimes came to life in a way that was personally disagreeable to her but reassuring to her sense of self-importance and of everything in the house being at her disposal. In the summer of his death Susan had acquired other reassurances: her father's instead of her great-grandfather's knee, her mother's arms. It was the first reunion since the year of separation, 1930, when their mother, accompanied by Aunt Fenny, had brought the girls home to settle them at Aunt Lydia's and at school before rejoining their father in India; and Susan – in the few weeks before great-grandpa died – now tearfully seized the opportunity to tell her mother she hated everything in England. This puzzled Sarah. Sarah had stifled her own unhappiness in England because she didn't want it to rub off on to her sister who had seemed to take the uprooting and replanting (in what their parents always referred to as home – but which was as outlandish at first as Iceland would be to a Congo pigmy) as if nothing much had happened to her at all. The tears Susan now shed were counterfeit of those Sarah had kept in, and Sarah pondered the unfairness of it, the sudden inexplicable emergence of Susan as a little girl with a secretive side to her nature, who had not repaid Sarah for looking after her by trusting her enough to confide what was really going on in her mind but instead saved it all up to confide to her mother. From her state of puzzlement Sarah passed into one of distrust herself. Susan's outbust about the hatefulness of life in England, at Aunt Lydia's, at school, at great-grandpa's, was surely a pose, a bald-faced bid for the bulk of everyone's attention at a time when it should have been concentrated on great-grandpa who was dying, and it did not escape Sarah that she herself was being accused – although of what she wasn't quite sure. She felt out of things, cut off from her family by Susan's emotional claims on it and her implied criticism of the way she, Sarah, had tried in exile to represent it by looking after her sister as much like a grown-up person as she was capable of. And so when great-grandfather died, Sarah did not weep, because she felt – not necessarily understanding it – the final uselessness of giving way to an emotion: a life, well-spent, was over. It happened to everyone. It would happen to her mother and father, and to Aunty Mabel – to Aunty Mabel sooner than any of them, unless there were an accident or a war, or some special kind of Indian disaster such as cholera or unexpected illness. Susan, though, stayed dry-eyed – Sarah thought – because the death of anyone as old as great-grandpa was remote from her, relevant only to the extent it disrupted other people's concentration on matters she thought of as really important.

Susan did not want to go to the funeral. There was no difficulty about that. The difficulty that arose was over Sarah's resistance to the suggestion that she should not go either but stay behind and look after Susan.

'No, I want to go,' she told her mother – with whom, after the years of separation she had not yet established an easy relationship. 'Great-grandpa was very good to us. Mrs Bailey can look after Susan.' Mrs Bailey was the old housekeeper, who had been left three hundred pounds. 'In fact Susan can help her with the funeral meats.' Funeral meats was an expression Sarah had picked up in the last day or so from Mrs Bailey herself. She thought that as food it sounded unappetizing to eat and doleful to prepare and that it might do Susan good to be made to take a hand getting it ready. She hoped as well that the baking of funeral meats would get rid of the sweet odour in the house that reminded her of cut-flowers going bad in vases.

On the day of the funeral she shared a car to the parish church with Aunty Mabel and two of the elderly Layton relatives who had turned up earlier, had had to be met at the station and on the way to the church talked to Mabel about people Sarah did not know unless they were referred to as Mildred or John, which meant her parents. She did not cry at the service (no one did) nor later in the cemetery, standing by the amateur-looking grave that after a certain amount of necessary palaver received the coffin with great-grandpa in it; nor on the journey back. She cried later that night, in the dark, when Susan – who was not speaking to her – had gone to sleep. What made her cry was the thought that great-grandpa had put off dying until her father and mother and Aunty Mabel could get back home from India, but had not spun it out to put them in a position of having either to postpone their departure or leave England again still in a state of uncertainty. It seemed to be a thoughtful way of doing what the doctor had called 'going out'. No one's plans had been messed up. It struck her that he had deliberately stayed alive long enough to give them the satisfaction of believing they had made the last weeks of his life as jolly as they could be, confined to bed as he was, and then 'gone out' soon enough to give them time to do everything that had to be done, get over doing it, then pack their bags and catch the train and the boat their passages had been booked on months ago.

She cried at this evidence of consideration for others; and then at the thought that in some way she had failed Susan as an elder sister, because Susan obviously hadn't been as carefree as her behaviour had previously suggested, didn't feel enough consideration had been given to *her*. Sarah cried, too, because more than anything in the world at that moment she wanted to go back to India with her parents and Aunty Mabel and Susan. Without great-grandpa and the Surrey summer, England again looked to her like the alien land in which she and her sister had been sentenced to spend a number of years as part of the process of growing up. She felt grown-up enough now; quite ready, aged twelve, to tackle the business of helping her mother to look after father; quite ready to take Susan back, even alone, to the old bungalow in Ranpur where Mumtez guarded them against the dark and mysterious nights (for as such they now came at her). The knowledge that her parents no longer lived at No. 3 Kabul road, that Mumtez had long since gone, even been forgotten, that her mother and father were going back to a place called Lahore which was quite unknown to her, did not diminish the vividness of the picture she had of what a return to India would be like. She did not mind, either, that according to Aunt Lydia India was 'an unnatural place for a white woman'. In any case she did not believe it. Her mother was natural enough for anyone, and so was Aunty Mabel if you thought about it and didn't let it upset you when she averted her face when you went to kiss her (so that your lips merely brushed the soft part of her cheek near the earlobe). Aunty Mabel never let anyone get really close to her, but sometimes you found her looking at you, and felt the challenge of her interest in you; in what you were doing or thinking and in why you were doing and thinking it.

It was Mabel who told Sarah the truth about the scorpion; two days after great-grandfather's funeral (and Susan still not talking to her, so that she was alone in the orchard until Mabel, also walking alone, came upon her and said, 'Well, if you're doing nothing, take me for a walk').

They went through the orchard and through the gate in the

iron rail fence that enclosed it from the meadow. This meadow sloped down to a brook and a spinney. There was a path, worn by custom. The meadow was let to a man who kept cows there. Susan was afraid to walk down to the spinney unless the cows were all bunched together at the far end of the field, but Sarah liked cows. In India they were sacred. In England they weren't, but they were warm and sweet-smelling. She liked the way they tore at the tough grass with their thick curled tongues. She wondered how they avoided pulling it up by its roots and what they thought about when they looked up from their tearing and munching, flicking their ears and striking their flanks with their fly-whisk tails, and watched you watching them. Sometimes they took no notice of you at all, but cropped their way with ragged herd instinct from one part of the meadow to another without pausing to look up as you passed near by. At other times they all held their heads up or turned them to watch you pass behind their rumps. Now, as Sarah walked with Aunty Mabel towards the spinney they were pulling up grass on either side of the path. She could smell their breath and thought Aunty Mabel hesitated to pass through their midst. 'They're quite docile,' Sarah said, and took Aunty Mabel's hand, partly to reassure her and partly because just here the track was ridged and rather difficult for an elderly lady to negotiate. 'They're not great-grandpa's,' she said, forgetting for the moment that nothing was great-grandpa's any longer. 'They belong to Mr Birtwhistle. He lets us watch them being milked sometimes.'

'Do you enjoy that?'

Sarah thought. 'No. But I'm interested in it. I mean enjoy is how I'd describe liking something artificial like a book or a game. But milking is to do with actual life, isn't it, so I like it but I don't enjoy it. Does that make sense?'

'Of a kind.'

When they reached the brook Sarah showed Aunty Mabel the stepping-stones which gave access to the opposite bank and the woodland. 'It used to be our private wood,' she explained, meaning her own and Susan's, and private in the sense of pretend. 'There's a fence on the other side of the spinney. The land on the other side of that belongs to Mr Birtwhistle but it's all right to go in so long as you keep to the edges. I mean it's all right for me and Susan. Or has been. I suppose everything will undergo changes now. It's probably our last summer. Daddy's going to let the house and might even sell it.' She stopped, realizing that she was talking to Aunty Mabel as if she were a stranger instead of a member of the family who probably knew far more about her father's plans than she did herself. And she kept forgetting that Aunty Mabel had visited great-grandfather years ago, long before the 1914–18 war, with grandfather Layton, to meet her stepson, Sarah's father, and so must know the brook and the stepping-stones, the spinney, and the neighbour's land on the other side, and that this might be the last summer of all that any Layton would come here.

'Shall you miss it?' Aunty Mabel asked.

'I expect so, although we only ever come in July and August. I probably wouldn't mind not coming if I knew I could and had simply gone somewhere else for a change. It will be knowing I can't come that will make it seem sad, as if a phase of my life has ended for ever.'

They stood looking at the brook. Sarah didn't sit on the bank because Aunty Mabel was much too old for that sort of thing. Near the water the earth was always damp. It was a hot day, but shady here. Aunty Mabel had a coat on though. She was cold in England. Three years ago Sarah had felt the cold too but had got used to it. She had dreams sometimes, in colour, like a film, of herself in sunshine in Pankot. The brook babbling over the stones reminded her of Pankot in miniature. But then everything in England was on a miniature scale. She thought this had an effect on the people who lived there always. In comparison with her mother and Aunt Fenny and Aunty Mabel, for instance, Aunt Lydia – although taller than any of them – seemed to Sarah to lack a dimension that the others didn't lack. Lacking this dimension was what Sarah supposed came of living on a tiny island. She felt this, but also felt she hadn't yet developed the reasoning power to work it out in terms that would adequately convey what she felt to other people. So she kept quiet about it and was conscious of Aunty Mabel keeping quiet about something too, and noted this down mentally as one of the things she'd not noticed before that distinguished her Indian family from her English family – distinguished her father, mother, Aunt Fenny and Aunty Mabel from Aunt Lydia, Uncle Frank (Aunt Lydia's physician husband) and poor old great-grandpa.

Her English family kept quiet about nothing, but were always speaking their minds. Aunt Lydia sometimes presumed to speak other people's too. And all at once she saw the correspondence between (in particular) Aunty Mabel who never said very much at all and her sister, Susan, who said a lot, but hoarded important things up until someone came along (their parents for instance) whom she judged to be worth speaking her mind to.

Sarah did not understand this unexpected connection between her sister and Aunty Mabel but knew it was an Indian connection. The English who went to India were different from those who didn't. When they came back they felt like visitors. And the people they came back to felt that the connection between them had become too tenuous for comfort (tenuous was one of Sarah's favourite new words). There were areas of sensitivity neither side dared probe too deeply.

Sarah said, 'I think we'd better go back otherwise we'll be late for tea and make things difficult for Mrs Bailey.'

'If you think so,' Aunty Mabel said.

On their way to the house Sarah had what she secretly called one of her funny turns. All that happened in a funny turn (nobody ever noticed them because obviously there was nothing to see) was that everything went very far away, taking its sound with it. It was rather like looking through the wrong end of great-grandpa's field-glasses and at the same time getting the wireless tuned in badly. Sarah had decided that her funny turns were all to do with growing up. At any given moment (she imagined) her bones and flesh expanded a fraction beyond the capacity her blood had to pump itself into all the crevices it was supposed to get at, leaving her brain briefly deprived of nourishment and her eyes and ears in consequence fractionally just incapable of making an accurate recording of what was really going on. She had worked it out that there was no common factor to the turns. It wasn't a question of how cold or hot the weather was, or of how much or how little she had been exerting herself, or of how hungry or how overfull she was, or how she felt. She found the sensation very interesting, but if it happened while she was talking to somebody, she worried a bit about talking sensibly. When it happened now, as they went back into the orchard (Sarah taking care to shut the gate properly) she also worried about making sure that Aunty Mabel didn't fall on one

of the hummocks in the rough grass. She was never certain of
her own balance during a funny turn because balance depended
on getting your sense of perspective and distance right.

So she took her time closing the gate, hoping that in a few
seconds she would stop feeling like a giant in a tiny landscape,
that Aunty Mabel would come back into her proper proportions, bringing the orchard with her. She said (in a voice that
rang in her head but gave no impression of being loud enough
for Aunty Mabel to hear), 'I think there's a stone in my sandal.'
Sometimes it helped to bend down, because that sent the blood
into the head where it was needed. She bent down. A little to
one side of her feet there was a fallen apple. Her feet and the
apple were tiny, far away. One of the things about a funny turn
was that although you felt gigantic in relation to everything else
any part of yourself that you looked at was small and far away
too. When she had fumbled with her sandal she touched the
apple, fascinated by her distant hand; picked the apple up, and
was stung by the wasp that was searching its soft bruised
underside. The pain was sharp. Her brain recorded the message
accurately, but there was still a layer of insensitivity separating
her recognition of the pain and her realization that the pain was
happening to her. She heard herself cry out. She stood upright.

'What's wrong?' Aunty Mabel asked.

'I've been stung.'

She was all right then – the funny turn was finished. Her little
finger hurt. Aunty Mabel took the stung hand and looked at the
tiny red puncture – the originating centre of the swelling and
inflammation that was already beginning to show.

'A wasp or a bee?'

'Oh, a wasp. It was having a go at the apple.'

'Have you been stung by a wasp before?'

'Yes, twice.'

'That's all right, then. We'll get back and put something on it.'

'Mrs Bailey recommends lemon juice.'

'That will do.'

'Why is it all right that I've been stung before?'

'Because some people are allergic.'

'Does that mean they could die?'

'Yes. But it's very rare.'

'I thought only snake bites and scorpion stings were fatal.'

'No. And not always they.'

They walked side by side through the orchard towards the lawn and the house. On a day like this tea would normally have been in the garden in the shade of the cedar. Not having tea in the garden was one of the family's concessions to the formal discipline of mourning, or a sign anyway of their respect for the feelings of people like Mrs Bailey. Sarah was glad that none of her family seemed to believe in God. She didn't really believe in God herself. She didn't like religious people; rather she did not like them directly they stopped being ordinary and started to be religious. Truly religious people, like nuns and monks and saints were a different matter. She thought of them as truly religious because they gave up their lives to it, and giving up your life to it struck her as the only thing to do if you believed in it. If you didn't believe in it the most you could do was to be charitable and try not to be selfish.

She was worried because Susan had never been stung either by a wasp or a bee. Susan led a charmed life. Aunt Lydia said Susan would always fall on her feet. Sarah could not remember Susan hurting herself badly – not badly enough to leave a scar. Susan did not remember the day of the scorpion, although she had knelt by Sarah's side, watching Dost Mohammed build a fire round it.

'Is it true,' Sarah asked Aunty Mabel as they crossed the empty sun-struck lawn, 'that scorpions kill themselves if you build a ring of fire round them so that they know they can't get out?'

'No.'

Sarah was not surprised, in spite of having once seen what looked like proof that they did.

Aunty Mabel said: 'Their skins are very sensitive to heat, which is why they live under stones and in holes and only come out a lot during the wet. If you build a ring of fire round them they're killed by the heat. They look as if they sting themselves to death because of the way they arch their tails over their bodies. But it's only a reflex action. They're attacking the fire, and get scorched to death by it.'

After a few moments Sarah said, 'Yes, I see,' and was sorry it wasn't true that they committed suicide, even though for some time now she had ceased to believe old Dost Mohammed's story and in the practical experiment he conducted in support of it.

She admired intelligence and courage because she often felt herself to be lacking in both; and it had always seemed to her that the small black scorpion found in the servants' quarters at No. 3 Kabul road, Ranpur, had shown intelligence and courage of a high order; intelligence enough to know that it could never set about escaping without burning itself painfully to death, courage enough to make a voluntary end of it by inflicting on its own body the paralysing stab it knew would kill it. Sarah admired soldiers of ancient times who fell on their swords because they had lost a battle. She had a childhood nightmare of her father losing a battle one day and deciding to fall on his, or shoot himself, to avoid being captured.

Now that Aunty Mabel had confirmed what she already suspected about the death of the scorpion she was able to link one truth with the other: which was that the last thing she would want her father to do if he lost a battle was fall on his sword. It was an awfully impractical thing to do. And it would be impractical of the scorpion to kill itself. After all the fire might go out, or be doused by rain. It was more practical of the scorpion to attempt to survive by darting its venomous tail in the direction of what surrounded it and was rapidly killing it. Just as brave too. Perhaps braver. After all there was a saying: Never say die.

In the kitchen where Mrs Bailey was cutting cucumber sandwiches and watching the kettle Sarah had her hand seen to. After tea, which the family had in the drawing-room with all the windows open on to the flagged terrace that overlooked the garden, Susan sat in the window-seat reading one of her mother's magazines, and Sarah went upstairs to their bedroom. She sat in a window-seat too, which had a view across to Mr Birtwhistle's meadow. She had a pencil and an exercise book and drew a family tree, beginning with great-grandpa.

She had no idea why she drew the family tree but doing it made her feel better. It gave her a sense of belonging and of the extraordinary capacity families had for surviving and passing themselves on and handing things down. She extended the tree by mapping in what she described to herself as the Muir branch: giving her mother the two sisters Mrs Layton was entitled to (Aunt Fenny and Aunt Lydia, with their respective husbands, Uncle Arthur and Uncle Frank) and the parents they were entitled to, General and Mrs Muir. She and Susan were entitled to them too. They had Muir blood in their veins as well as Layton blood. At Christmas Aunt Lydia and Uncle Frank always took them up to Scotland where General and Mrs Muir lived in retirement. Sarah did not like Scotland. It was cold and craggy. Before her mother and father sailed back to India they were going up to Scotland too, but she and Susan weren't going with them. They were going back to Aunt Lydia's in Bayswater. Aunt Lydia and Uncle Frank had not come down for the funeral but had sent flowers. In her heart of hearts (as she put it to herself) she had never really taken to Aunt Lydia but had done her best not to show it because Susan didn't like Aunt Lydia much either and between them, Sarah felt, they could have made life miserable for themselves by exaggerating the things about Aunt Lydia they didn't like and were in mutual agreement about, and minimizing the things about her which they – Sarah anyway – did like.

When she analysed the pros and cons of Aunt Lydia she knew that it was Aunt Lydia's dislike of India that stood in the way of her feeling affection for her. She took a red and blue pencil and drew a red ring round her Indian relatives on the family tree and a blue ring round her English relatives. Great-grandpa had a blue ring and so did Uncle Frank and Aunt Lydia (although Aunt Lydia had spent eighteen months in India after the war). There was a warming preponderance of red crayon on the tree.

'That is my heritage,' Sarah said, then noticed that so far she had put no ring at all round Aunty Mabel. She put down the red pencil to pick up the blue and then paused.

'Why ever was I going to do that?' she asked herself. And retrieved the red pencil, ringed Aunty Mabel firmly with that fiery colour; the one denoting the Indian connection.

Six years later in the July of 1939 she came across the exercise book among other relics of her childhood that had been packed in a leather trunk and stored in Aunt Lydia's glory-hole. She sorted the trunk out now to make sure that nothing was worth saving from the bonfire – an incinerator, actually, at the far end of the untended weedy walled enclosure that Aunt Lydia called a garden – worth saving from the holocaust into which her English years were being thrown and causing her a degree of pain at separation she had not expected.

She sorted the contents of the trunk on a day when Aunt Lydia was out shopping with Susan and Aunt Fenny who was back again with Uncle Arthur from India. Susan was buying clothes for the tropics. Sarah thought that buying clothes for the tropics in Kensington was a waste of time. But Susan had set her heart on a topee with a veil swathed round its crown and hanging over the brim at the back to give extra shade to the neck; and on white shirts and jodhpurs to complete the outfit. Wearing these she would look like the heroine in The Garden of Allah. She also wanted some dresses in silk and georgette (which would be sweaty). And a shooting stick. And anything else that caught her eye and further excited the image she had of herself as a young girl – dressed and ready for a romantic encounter in an outpost of empire – whose father was a lieutenant-colonel, recently appointed to the command of the first battalion of his old regiment, the Pankot Rifles, and destined, no doubt, if there were a war – which seemed likely – to become a brigadier and then a major-general.

Possibly, she thought, the difference between herself and Susan was that Susan was capable of absorbing things into her system without really thinking whether they were acceptable to her or not; whereas she herself absorbed nothing without first subjecting it to scrutiny. Perhaps this was wrong. Perhaps she tried too hard to work things out. She didn't relax. She didn't have a talent for just enjoying herself, which was a pity because she must miss a lot that Susan never missed.

Finding nothing worth saving from the trunk she took the contents in several batches and several armfuls down the two flights of stairs and down the half-flight into the semi-basement and the kitchen whose door gave access to the garden.

There, on a warm July evening scented by warmed brick, bruised grass and the fumes of traffic in the park and on the Bayswater road, she set fire to the relics of a youth she did not understand but felt had given a certain set to her bones, a toughness to her skin, and caused her now (half-shielding her cheeks from the heat of the fire in the incinerator) to stand watching the conflagration as it were in her own right as a person who now inherited the conflicting attitudes of the Laytons and the Muirs, and of Aunty Mabel, and of great-grandpa who had 'gone out' on an August morning to the scent of cedars and stale flowers in vases, so that she had a vision of herself and her family as the thing she was burning, and of that thing, of that self, as an instrument of resistance and at the same time of acceptance. She could feel the heat on her bones, the heat on her skin. Within them remained the nub, the hard core of herself which the flames did not come near nor illuminate.

So I am really in darkness, she said, and this truly is the difference between myself and Susan who lives in a perpetual and recognizable light. The light that falls on Susan also falls on Aunt Fenny and Uncle Arthur. It falls, but in a way that makes different shadows, on Aunt Lydia and Uncle Frank. I do not know how it falls on Mother and Father – it is a long time since I have seen them – and I do not know who is in darkness except myself.

Two weeks later, accompanied by her sister Susan, her Aunt Fenny and her Uncle Arthur, Sarah Layton sailed back to India on the P & O.

PART THREE

A WEDDING, 1943

I

HAVING HANDED young Kasim a glass of the forbidden whisky Count Bronowsky said, 'So Mrs Layton drinks, you say. Do you mean in secret?'

Ahmed, taking the glass, held it well away from his nose. He disliked the smell of alcohol. In the palace there wasn't a drop to be had except what his servant or he himself managed to smuggle into his room there. He smuggled it on principle and had trained himself to drink a certain amount every day. It disappointed him that regular tippling hadn't yet given him a real taste for it let alone made him a slave of habit. A serious drinker, and finally an alcoholic, struck him sometimes as the only thing really open to him to become in his own right.

'I don't know about in secret,' he said. 'But she begins first, finishes last and has two drinks to anybody else's one. Also I've noticed that her behaviour is erratic.'

Bronowsky limped from the liquor trolley to the larger of the two cane armchairs that had been placed on the verandah, with a view on to the dark garden. He sat, settled his lame left leg on the foot-stool, raised his glass and looked at Ahmed with his right eye. The left leg and the blind left eye – covered by a black patch whose elastic, pitched at an angle, was countersunk by long use in a ring round his narrow head – were said to be the result of getting half blown-up in pre-revolutionary St Petersburg by an anarchist while driving along Nevsky Prospect to the Winter Palace.

'In what way erratic?'

Ahmed sat in the other chair and watched the Count select and light one of the gold-tipped cigarettes that came in rainbow colours from a shop in Bombay.

'She is irritable one moment, almost friendly at another. The almost friendliness occurs when she has a glass in her hand.'

'Her husband is a prisoner of war in Germany, you said?'

'Yes.'

'Is she still attractive would you say?'

'Her hair is not grey. She frequently powders her nose.'

'Ah – Her sister, this Mrs Grace, she is also erratic?'

'No. She is perfectly predictable. You can depend on her to be rude at any time. And she does not trouble to lower her voice.'

'Dear boy, what have you overheard her saying about you?'

Ahmed smiled. 'It seems I am quite efficient for an Indian.'

'But it was a compliment.'

'I would also make a good *maître d'hôtel* if I didn't stink so abominably of garlic.'

'I doubt Mrs Grace would know a good *maître* from a bad one. The English seldom do. But she meant well. And you *do*.'

'Garlic strengthens the constitution. My father used to carry an onion in his pocket to ward off colds. But that was mere superstition. Eating garlic is scientific. Also garlic is stronger on the breath than the smell of whisky. So you see it has its religious and social uses too.'

From a quarter mile or so away the drumming resumed. A Hindu wedding feast. Ahmed kept time on the arm of the chair with the fingers of his free hand. During Ramadan such a noisy manifestation of Hindu gaiety could cause communal trouble. He almost welcomed the prospect.

Bronowsky eased and re-settled the stiff lame leg. 'Tell me about the two Miss Laytons. Are they more to your taste? The one who is to be married – begin with her.'

'What an inquisitive man you are!' Ahmed thought. He was not inquisitive himself. To him people were remote, people and things and the ideas they seemed to find electrifying. But he quite enjoyed these regular sessions with Bronowsky, partly because the old wazir had taken him up as if he were someone worth giving time to, but mostly because Bronowsky's endless curiosity about other people helped him to form opinions about them himself, to consider them with greater objectivity and interest than he felt when actually dealing with them. The exercise, he found, enabled him to peel off a layer or two of his own incuriosity. True, when the sessions were over, he usually felt those layers thickening up again and was likely to tell himself that Bronowsky encouraged him to call and chatter mainly because he preferred (or was suspected of preferring) above all other the company of young men. Nevertheless each session left a residual grain of involvement.

'Oh, Miss Layton,' he said, and conjured a picture of Susan Layton holding a length of white material up under her chin and hectic-coloured cheeks. 'People do things for her. She must have trained them to think she can't do them for herself. Every time she lifts a finger to do something on her own she makes it look like an attempt at the impossible. People come running. It's not just the wedding, I think. She has probably always been the centre of attraction.'

'Is she fond of this Captain Bingham?'

Ahmed thought. How could he judge? He did not really know what fond was. His father was fond of his mother. His brother had been fond of the army. He himself was fond of chewing cloves of garlic. Bronowsky was fond of gossip. Fond seemed to be a combination of impulse, appetite and gratification. But even that didn't define it properly. He himself, for instance, had an impulse to make love to girls. He visited prostitutes. He had acquired a taste for sexual intercourse and had gratified it not infrequently. He was therefore, he supposed, fond of copulating as well as of eating garlic, but this was not what the world meant by fond or Count Bronowsky meant when he asked if the younger Miss Layton was fond of Captain Bingham. That kind of fond hinted at a capacity for denying yourself if self-denial was for the good of what you were fond of. He did not think Miss Layton had this capacity.

He said, 'No. I don't imagine she is really *fond* of Captain Bingham.'

'You mean it is merely a physical attraction?'

'On his part, yes. He is more attracted to her than she is to him.'

'How do you know?'

'I think, when he touches her, instead of being agitated she is irritated. Especially if she has her mind on the cut of a dress.'

'Embarrassment,' Bronowsky said. 'Obviously, what you saw was her reaction to a tender gesture made in front of others. The English are very shy of their sexuality. If you were a fly on the wall and saw Miss Layton and Captain Bingham together you might be surprised. Even shocked.'

Ahmed said nothing. He had been a fly on the wall; or rather

an unnoticed figure rounding a corner of the guest-house verandah where Miss Layton stood, holding up the length of white
material, reacting rather violently to Captain Bingham's two
waist-embracing arms and saying, 'Oh, Teddie, for God's sake.'
Which was interesting and quite contrary to Bronowsky's
supposition, because in public Miss Susan Layton submitted to
Captain Bingham's protective and possessive touch with equanimity, even with approval, in fact with an air of demanding it
quite frequently as if it were due to her at regular intervals. And
she was no less eager in such circumstances to give as well as
receive a caress. Only when they were alone, apparently, did the
exchange of caresses become distasteful. Fortunately for him he
had not been seen on the occasion of the breaking away from
Captain Bingham.

'What are you thinking?' Bronowsky asked.

Ahmed smiled, took another sip of the whisky, and said, 'Of
being a fly on the wall.'

'Does the idea appeal?'

'Flies on walls sometimes get swatted.'

'Every occupation has its hazards. Tell me about the younger
sister, the Miss Layton who isn't to be married.'

'But she isn't the younger.'

'Ah. That is always interesting. I imagine she isn't as pretty.
But perhaps more serious-minded?'

'She asks a lot of questions.'

'Questions about what?'

'The administration in Mirat. Native customs. Local history.'

'Is she so very plain then?'

'I find all white girls unattractive. They look only half-
finished. When they have fair hair they look even more
unnatural.'

'She is fair, then?'

'Yes. And to an Englishman probably as attractive as her sister.
And she is better-natured. Is that dangerous?'

'Why?'

'I understand it can be. This kind of English person invites
our confidence. They ask questions, at first of a general nature,
then of a more intimate kind. You think, well, he is interested,
she wishes to be friends. But it is a trap. One wrong move, one
hint of familiarity on your part, and snap. It shuts.'

'So says Professor Nair no doubt.'

'But don't you agree? I am asking you. I have no experience. It is what I've been told, not only by Professor Nair. Snap.'

'What are you really asking me? Whether you should be careful how you answer these fascinating intimate questions you anticipate Miss Layton asking you?'

'No. I am always careful. I was only asking your opinion of the belief generally held.'

'What belief?'

'That the friendly English are more dangerous than the rude ones.'

'Are you sure you mean English? Not white? Am I dangerous?'

'Oh, you are the most dangerous man in Mirat. Everybody says so. It goes without saying. One risks everything just talking to you. But then you are exceptional in every way, and I meant English, not white. If we had been subjugated by the Russians I would have said Russians. It isn't the whiteness that matters. It's the position of the English as rulers that makes their friendship dangerous. Dangerous on two counts. It weakens our resolve to defy them and it is against their own clan instincts. They are consciously or subconsciously aware of weakening their position by friendliness, so this friendliness always has to be on their own guarded terms. If we unwittingly think of it as mutual and go too far they are doubly incensed, first as individuals who feel they have been taken what they call advantage of, secondly as members of a class they fear they may have betrayed by their own thoughtless stupidity. Then, snap! They are indifferent to the effect of such a situation on us.'

'Is that what you believe?'

'It's what I am told. People are always warning us. It is well known. Fortunately, unlike my father I have never felt the urge to make friends with any Englishman, or Englishwoman. But it is interesting to observe them. It is interesting to come across one of the friendly ones, like the elder Miss Layton. It is like being a student of chemistry, knowing a formula, waiting to see it proved in a laboratory test.'

'Your glass is empty. Help yourself.'

Ahmed got up to do so. Bronowsky held his own glass out as Ahmed was passing him. Ahmed took it, but for a moment the older man retained his own hold on it.

'Have you kept your promise to me and written to your father?'

'No.'

'Why not?'

'The same reason as always. I begin writing and stop, there isn't anything to say, and even if there were every word would be read by someone else before the letter reached him. It is very off-putting. I write to my mother. She tells him what I am doing.'

'It isn't the same.'

Ahmed, in possession of Bronowsky's glass, went to the drinks trolley and poured generous measures of White Horse: two fingers for himself, three for Bronowsky. He filled both glasses almost to the brim with soda-water and came back to the chair where Bronowsky sat looking up with his good eye half shut as if measuring an effect. Ahmed offered him the replenished glass, but Bronowsky did not take it immediately.

'It isn't the same,' he repeated. 'Is it?'

'No, but he's used to the idea that I'm a disappointing sort of son.'

Bronowsky now grasped the base of the tumbler and when Ahmed felt it held securely he let go.

'You are more used to it than he is,' Bronowsky said. 'I think the idea that you're a disappointment to him has become your basic security. You'd feel lost without it. You know, dear boy, the most disturbing thing that happened to me when I was about your age was discovering that my father approved a particular step I proposed to take.'

'What step was that?'

'Marriage. The girl was my cousin, we weren't in love, but she would probably have made me a good wife and we always got on well enough together. I decided on marriage because I thought my father particularly disliked her. I anticipated the most vigorous opposition. Instead he embraced me. He almost wept. Really very alarming. I cooled off the idea at once. I felt some regret, of course. Perhaps I loved her after all. But I felt better directly I told him I'd changed my mind. He turned away without a word, but with his old comforting look of utter disdain. I felt secure again and never again felt insecure until he died. Then I had to earn his posthumous disapproval in a variety of ways, doing things I felt he would despise me for. Making liberal gestures rather popular at the time among intellectual landowners. Not gestures I had my heart in, but then you don't need your heart in good to do it. I did the right thing for the wrong reasons, which is what you are doing, efficiently carrying out the job you are paid for, even earning the approbation of the ungracious Mrs Grace. But you are carrying it out well because you think your father disapproved of your taking it and would be ashamed to know that a woman like Mrs Grace described you as a potentially first-rate hotel manager. You want him to be ashamed because his being ashamed of you is what you understand. You feel exactly the same about it as another boy might feel about his father being proud of him. Determined to keep it up. But the question you should ask yourself is whether he is ashamed. Has he ever been? Isn't it truer to say you grew up in a household where clear views were held on a number of questions that concern India, that you expected to inherit this clarity as you might inherit a share of the household goods and chattels and were startled to find you didn't. Startled is the wrong word. It was obviously a much slower process. But the upshot of it all was compensation for feelings of inadequacy, transference of your disappointment. You imagined the disappointment was your father's. But perhaps the truth was that he observed your struggles to take an interest with affection and compassion but didn't know how to help you. You didn't make things easier by withdrawing from him although what you were really doing was withdrawing from yourself. It's because you are fond of him that you don't write to him in prison.'

Ahmed smiled.

'You shouldn't be afraid of your emotions,' Bronowsky continued. 'In any case to be afraid of them is un-Indian. Now there's a danger for you if you like. You young men ought to watch out for it – losing your Indian-ness. It's a land of extremes, after all, it needs men with extremes of temperament. All this Western sophistication, plus the non-Western cult of non-violence, is utterly unnatural. One without the other might do but the combination of the two strikes me as disastrous. After all the sophistication of the West is only a veneer. Underneath it we are a violent people. But you Indians see no deeper than our surface. Add to that the non-violence cult and the result is emasculation.'

Ahmed grinned. Bronowsky said, 'Fornication can be a refuge as well as an entertainment. Your visits to the Chandi Chowk are no proof of your masculinity, dear boy.'

'Oh well, what am I to do? Raise an army to release the prisoners in the Fort at Premanagar?'

'You could do worse. In fact I can think of nothing more splendid. It interests me that it's the first thing that occurs to you. Such a passionate idea. How could the world fail to respond to it? It's what sons are for, to lead armies to deliver their fathers from fortresses. The British would lock you up for ever. They would laugh as well, of course, because projects obviously doomed to failure have their comical side, but they would laugh unmaliciously. They would respect you. On the other hand if you announced your intention to fast unto death if they didn't release your father they'd let you get on with it. They'd feed you forcibly. They'd be furious with you for attempting moral blackmail. I must say I'd sympathize with them. Non-violence is ridiculous. I'm not in favour of it. Can you stay to dinner?'

'No, I had a sudden invitation from Professor Nair.'

'What is he up to?'

'Nothing he tells me about.'

'Perhaps you don't listen hard enough. He's always up to something. Nawab Sahib expects to be kept informed. He will be back on Friday, incidentally.'

'Did you enjoy your visit to Gopalakand?'

'It was amusing. I left Nawab Sahib to enjoy himself a few days longer. He will be pleased with poems of Gaffur. Which of them thought of it?'

'I don't know.'

'Have they been into the palace?'

'I took them over the public rooms this morning. Will Nawab Sahib be going to the reception?'

'He will if I say so. I think I shall say so. What is arranged for tomorrow?'

'They are going shopping again. But in the morning before breakfast Miss Layton wants to ride.'

'Which Miss Layton?'

'The inquisitive one. Miss Sarah.'

'Alone?'

'I'm expected to ride with her I think.' Ahmed sipped his whisky. 'I shall keep a respectful few paces behind, naturally.'

'Do you think she has her mother's permission, or that of this Captain Bingham?'

'I didn't ask. I exist to carry out orders.'

'Don't be upset if you find you've got up early and had horses saddled for nothing. Her mother or Captain Bingham might veto her little jaunt if she's arranged it without mentioning it and they find out about it.'

'Oh, I shan't be upset.'

'Who else is there in the wedding party?'

'A Major Grace is arriving on Friday. He is the bride's uncle. Captain Bingham's friend sometimes visits – a Captain Merrick. He will be best man.'

'Merrick?'

'Yes. Do you know him?'

'I don't think so. Merrick. A vaguely familiar name. But in some other connection –? Well, you'd better be off if you're dining with Nair.'

Ahmed drained his glass and returned it to the trolley. 'Thanks for the drink,' he said, and stood for a moment looking down at Bronowsky, who never shook hands or exchanged formal greetings or farewells with people he looked upon as intimates. For a man of nearly seventy, Ahmed thought, he had worn very well. His face was unlined, his complexion pink. In the early years of his administration as chief minister in Mirat the anti-Bronowsky faction – said to have been headed by the late Begum – had nearly succeeded in poisoning him. His rows with the Nawab were almost legendary. They still occurred. But his influence over the Nawab was now thought to be complete.

Ahmed himself owed his position at the court to Bronowsky although it had taken some time for this to become clear to him. Originally he had thought it was the Nawab who had the notion of taking under his wing the unsatisfactory younger son of a distant but distinguished kinsman, a boy who had failed abysmally at college and showed no aptitude for any career of the kind open to a Kasim of the Ranpur branch: law, politics, the civil service. True, it was Bronowsky who had written the letters and even visited Ranpur but he appeared to do so in the capacity of agent, not principal, and gave no impression of himself caring one way or the other about the outcome of the Nawab's invitation. To Ahmed that invitation looked like one founded on charity rather than on interest and he believed it looked like that to his father, with whom discussion had been brief. His father was then still head of the provincial ministry, a busy man, and a worried man, almost entirely wrapped in the business of protesting the Viceroy's declaration of war on Germany without prior consultation with Indian leaders. By the time Ahmed reached Mirat his father, following Congress instructions, had resigned.

But, 'Well, *you* are safe,' the Nawab had said to Ahmed when they had news of M A K's arrest in 1942. 'You are under our protection. For this you must thank Count Bronowsky.' Why Bronowsky? Ahmed asked; and learned that it was the wazir's idea, not the Nawab's, that he should come to Mirat to learn something about the administration of a Native State. 'While you have been here,' the Nawab continued, 'you will have heard many adverse things about Bronowsky Sahib. It is not unknown for me to think and say adverse things about him myself. What you should know about him, however, is that his loyalty to the House of Kasim is without parallel even among Kasims, and that it is the future of the House he always thinks of.'

It was a loyalty Ahmed had not got the measure of, and he did not understand where he fitted in with whatever Bronowsky saw as the pattern of a scheme to promote the interests of Kasims. In the past year he had been aware of Bronowsky's appraisal; before that Bronowsky had scarcely taken any notice of him. His duties had been of an almost menial clerical kind, those of dogsbody to one official's secretary after another. The officials had grandiloquent titles. Ahmed had worked under the secretary to the Minister for Finance, under the secretary to the Minister for Education, under the secretary to the Minister for Public Works, under the secretary to the Minister for Health, under the chief clerk to the Attorney-General. Most of these ministers were related to the Nawab, two bore the name of Kasim. All were nominated by the Nawab and served as members of his Council of State.

The Council of State was Bronowsky's brain-child. In the twenty years of his administration he had transformed Mirat

from a feudal autocracy where Ruler met ruled only at periodical durbars into a miniature semi-democratic state where the
durbars still took place but where the machinery of government
was brought out of the dark recesses of rooms and passages in
the palace into, comparatively, the light of day.

He had separated the judiciary from the executive, reframed
the criminal and civil legal codes, created the position of Chief
Justice and during his chief minstership so far always succeeded
in appointing to it a man from outside Mirat whose impartiality
could be counted on – in one case an Englishman just retired
from the bench of a provincial High Court of British India.
Bronowsky had done all these things with a minimum of overt
opposition because it was to do them that the Nawab brought
him back from Monte Carlo in 1921. 'I must be a modern state,'
the Nawab was reported saying. 'Make me modern.' What
Bronowsky did by way of making the Nawab of Mirat modern
was also the means by which he gradually cut the ground from
under the feet of British officials of the Political Department
who objected to the appointment of a 'bloody *émigré* Russian'
as chief minister of a state with which, small as it was, they had
always had what they felt to be a special relationship. For all they
knew Bronowsky was a red, a spy, a man who would cause
trouble and feather his nest at the same time.

The Resident at Gopalakand who advised the Nawab of
Mirat as well as the Maharajah of Gopalakand had protested
the appointment of Bronowsky and the sacking of the Nawab's
brother to make room for him. Before the present Nawab
succeeded as Ruler the British had thought badly of him, had
favoured the brother who struck them as altogether more
amiable, a more malleable, more temperate man – not given as
the heir apparent was given to wild and extravagant behaviour
with money and women. The ruler in those days, the present
Nawab's father, was anxious for nothing so much as to live in
peace with the representatives of the paramount power. He
listened attentively to their stern warnings about his elder son's
sowing of wild oats, reacted as they intended he should react to
hints that if the boy didn't mend his ways he would never be
thought fit to rule Mirat – whereas the old Nawab's second son
was a model of a young prince. Such a model son, succeeding,
would certainly be confirmed by the King-Emperor's agents. In

his case there would be no danger of an interregnum, no danger of Mirat's affairs coming under the direct control of the political department. The old man began to manoeuvre for a position from which he could effectively disinherit his elder son in favour of the younger. The elder got wind of the plot, but it was luck that came to his rescue, luck in the shape of a proposal for marriage with the daughter of the ruler of a less ancient but far more powerful state with whom the British had an even closer relationship. The old Nawab was flattered. He attempted to arrange the alliance, but through the marriage of the girl to his younger son. The girl would have none of it. She had seen the man she wanted, through the zenana screen at a wedding celebration. The marriage took place as she wished. The old Nawab – and the British too – hoped that perhaps the marriage would see the end of the elder son's extravagances. It did not. He had only married the girl to secure his inheritance. The British, he knew, would never dare depose him now because to do so would outrage and insult the powerful father-in-law he had so fortunately acquired. When his father died he was confirmed in the succession. His Begum, headstrong as an unmarried girl became intolerable as his wife. He hated her. He hated the brother who had tried to steal his inheritance and who now, following the tradition, had become his chief minister – and a lickspittle of the British. The Nawab took mistresses, eventually a white woman. The scandal had begun. Out of the scandal Bronowsky emerged.

'Well, good night,' Ahmed said. Bronowsky said nothing, until Ahmed was at the bottom of the verandah steps, putting on his bicycle clips.

'Give my felicitations to Professor Nair,' he called. 'And be sure to mention the fact that you are going riding alone tomorrow with one of the Miss Laytons.'

'Why?'

'He will advise you more satisfactorily than I how to comport yourself, how to interpret accurately and safely her many little gestures and inflexions of voice which you might be in danger of misinterpreting. He will speak of such things as he speaks of all things – from the vast fund of his experience.'

Ahmed smiled, took his bicycle from the rack and prepared to mount.

'Oh and one other thing,' Bronowsky said, lowering his voice but enunciating carefully. 'Find out what you can about his visitor.'

'Has he got a visitor, then?'

'Yes. Two. A woman not identified and an elderly scholar by name of Pandit Baba Sahib. He comes from Mayapore. The question is, for what purpose?'

'Must there be a special one?'

'Professor Nair's visitors usually have a purpose, or if they don't have one when they arrive they have one when they go home.'

'Considering you only returned from Gopalakand today you're well informed.'

'I pay to be. And Pandit Baba is not unknown to us in Mirat. Have you had enough whisky to see you through an evening of fruit juice?'

'I think I shall manage.'

'Have a good time then, dear boy. And take care if you are tempted to come home by way of the Chandi Chowk.'

Ahmed waved, mounted and rode down the gravel drive of Bronowsky's bungalow to the gate which the watchman – already muffled in a shawl and armed with a stick – held open for him. Outside, he turned right, pedalled along the metalled road towards the city. To his left stretched the expanse of open ground which separated the city from the palace. Soft warm airs blew across it. The moon whose first appearance had ushered in the month of Ramadan was nearly full. It hung above the city, not giving much light, the shape and colour of an orange. It would wax and wane and become invisible. Its slender reappearance would announce the îd. During this month more than 1,300 years ago it was said that the Koran had been revealed by Allah to his Prophet. A good Muslim was supposed to fast from sunrise to sunset. Ahmed, remembering the whisky, stopped pedalling, stood astride and felt in his pocket for the clove of garlic. He popped it into his mouth and crunched, resumed his journey. The road was unlit, his cycle lamp out of order, but the night was luminous and he liked cycling in the dark. It could be a risky business and he preferred activities that had an element of danger in them, so long as the activities themselves were of a commonplace kind and only dangerous by virtue of some extraneous circumstance. Riding a bicycle in the dark or a horse over rough country were one thing, deliberately courting danger was another. To Ahmed, the kind of danger that added spice to a situation was danger that came suddenly and unexpectedly; only so could it retain what he thought of as essential to it: spontaneity, or mystery, or both. He had once suggested to Professor Nair that his attitude to danger could be summed up by describing it as one that distinguished between the danger to a man who joined a riot and the danger to a man who found himself involved in one in the course of moving peaceably between point a and point b. Ahmed had experienced both kinds of danger as a student. It was the unexpected riot he enjoyed. 'One did not feel,' he told Nair, 'that one had to take sides, one merely hit out in one's own defence, and there wasn't any moral problem to puzzle out either before or after. I was knocked off my bicycle by one faction and subjected to rescue by the other. I dished out bloody noses indiscriminately and felt fine, and nobody noticed or thought to wonder whose side I was on, so when I'd finished having my fun I just rode away and left them all to it.'

Closer in to the city the road became overhung on one side by the trees in the grounds of the Hindu Boys' College, an institution which like the Council of State owed its existence to Count Bronowsky. Numerically in a minority, a mere twenty per cent of the population, the Muslims of Mirat had maintained a firm grip on the administration since the days of the Moghuls. Until Bronowsky's day few Hindus had held any public post of any importance. There were more mosques than temples, not because the rich Hindus of Mirat were unready to build temples but because permission to build was more often refused than granted. The same restrictions had been placed on the building and endowment of schools for Hindu boys and girls, who were generally thought to be too clever by half. For the Muslim children an Academy of Higher Education had been established in the late nineteenth century, but its record was poor; there was a saying that a boy left there with no qualifications except for reciting passages from the Koran, but that this alone was enough to pass him into the service of an official – particularly of a tax-collector. Until the foundation of the Hindu Boys' College in 1924, non-Muslims whose parents wanted them educated above middle-school standards had to compete for places in colleges

outside Mirat, and having left Mirat the tendency was not to
return but to seek employment in the service of the Government
of India. Muslims, jealous guardians of their own entrenched
position in the administration of the State, saw no harm in this
draining of potential talent among the Hindus whose job, in
their opinion, was trading and money-lending. But Bronowsky
saw harm and persuaded the Nawab to see harm too, and to
allocate a modest annual sum from the State's revenue for a
college that would be open to the sons of rich or poor Hindus.
The rest of the money was provided by prominent Hindu
businessmen. The building that was erected reflected the combination of civic pride and sense of communal and personal
grandiosity with which the money was contributed: red brick
with white facings, Gothic windows and Gothic arches. Coconut palms were planted in the forecourt. From the beginning it
had been a success.

'Is that you, Ahmed?' Professor Nair called as Ahmed – having
passed the watchman at the gate of the college and walked his
bicycle off the drive that led to the main building and on to a
narrow path – came in sight of the Principal's bungalow. Nair
stood at the head of the steps, silhouetted by the light from the
open door. He was dressed in his white pyjamas.

'Yes, professor,' Ahmed called back. 'Am I late?'

'Oh no. At least only by a few minutes.'

'Count Sahib is back from Gopalakand. I had to call in. He
sent his regards by the way.'

Ahmed put his cycle in the rack, climbed the steps and let his
hands be taken in both of Nair's. The professor stood about a
foot shorter than Ahmed.

'I have an important visitor,' he whispered. 'Do you mind
taking off your shoes and socks? He's an awful stickler for ortho-
doxies. I'm afraid he won't eat with us.'

'Who is he?' Ahmed asked, bending to untie his shoe-laces.

'Pandit Baba Sahib of Mayapore. He is writing a commentary
on the Bhagavad Gita. I don't mean right now. I mean it is his
principal occupation. Please don't offer to shake hands, and
don't sit where your shadow will fall on him. It's all rather nerve-
racking. Frankly I came out to relax. I am longing for a cigarette
but daren't smoke one in case he smells it. At times like this one's

bad habits come home to roost. Had Count Sahib any interesting news?'

'None that he shared with me. May I keep my socks?'

'Oh by all means. The floors get so dirty. Come. Meet Panditji. Like me he is a great admirer of your father.'

The house smelt of incense, which was unusual. Pandit Baba Sahib had probably been in Mrs Nair's puja room. That was one of the rooms in Professor Nair's house that Ahmed had never entered. In fact he had only seen two rooms, the room where they sat and talked, which was entered from the right of the square hallway, and the room where they ate, which was entered from the left. An open door at the far end of the hall gave on to a courtyard, where Mrs Nair kept a tethered goat. Ahmed gathered that other rooms, such as the bedroom, bathroom and puja room were entered from this courtyard.

When he came into the living-room – Nair stepping aside and graciously waving him on – he saw that the chairs had been removed and cushions and rugs put down in their place. Pandit Baba Sahib was seated cross-legged on one cushion, resting his left elbow on a pile of three or four. He too was dressed in pyjamas. He had a grey beard and a grey turban. A pair of steel-rimmed spectacles with circular lenses were lodged half-way down his rather stubby nose.

'This is our young visitor,' Nair said. 'Son of our illustrious M A K. A young gentleman of many talents but currently Social Secretary to the Nawab Sahib.'

Panditji stared at Ahmed above the rims of his glasses. The whites of his eyes were yellow. He did not smile, he made no gesture of greeting. He simply stared. There was a certain kind of Hindu who inspired in Ahmed involuntary little twitches of distaste, the relics no doubt of the racial and religious animosity his own forbears had felt towards the forbears of men like Pandit Baba Sahib. It was no hardship to him to keep his distance or to stand where even his shadow could not reach the figure on the cushions who had made no attempt to acknowledge Nair's introduction and continued to stare up with an expression Ahmed would have thought genuinely disapproving had he not guessed it as probably an expression that Pandit Baba assumed automatically when meeting strangers, especially if the stranger was young. Ahmed gazed back, with Nair at his side still holding him by the elbow.

Presently Pandit Baba spoke. He had a high light voice. He spoke in Hindi.

'You do not look like your father.'

'Oh, you know him,' Ahmed said, but in English. 'Most people would agree with you. They say I take after my mother. Personally I never see any resemblance in myself to any member of my family.'

Pandit Baba frowned.

'Why do you answer me, and at such length, in a foreign language?'

'Because I speak Hindi rather badly.'

'You wish us to converse in Urdu?' Panditji asked, switching to it.

'I should prefer English, Pandit Sahib. It's the language we always speak at home. My mother is a Punjabi you see, and English was the only language she had in common with my father. Even in Urdu I express myself poorly.'

'Do you not feel shame to speak always in the language of a foreign power, the language of your father's jailers?' Pandit Baba asked – reverting to Hindi. At any moment Ahmed expected a bit of Bengali, a sentence or two in Tamil, perhaps a passage in Sanskrit. The Pandit was obviously proud of his facility. His refusal so far to speak in English did not mean he spoke it badly or was not proud of understanding and being able to speak it; but it was fashionable among Hindus of Baba's kind to decry it, to declare that once the British had been got rid of their language must go with them; although what would be put in its place it was difficult to tell. Even Pandit Baba Sahib would fare badly if he went out into some of the villages around Mirat and tried to understand what was said to him. He would need an interpreter, as most officials did. And the odds were the interpreter would interpret the local dialect in the language and idiom of the British.

'No,' Ahmed said. 'I'm not ashamed.'

'*Baitho*,' Professor Nair interrupted, and squatted on a cushion, motioning Ahmed to follow suit, which he did. His trousers made it an uncomfortable operation. Pandit Baba scrutinized him, this time through the lenses of his spectacles. The Pandit – Ahmed now saw – was sitting on a double thickness of cushions. His was a commanding position.

'I do not know your father in person, only I am admiring him from the distance,' he said suddenly, in English, 'and familiarizing myself to his photographs. It is a face after all much known in newspapers.'

Ahmed nodded. Pandit Baba, having spoken, subjected Ahmed to further scrutiny. It was extraordinary, Ahmed thought, how men distinguished in one field – and he assumed that Pandit Baba Sahib was distinguished – seemed to claim for themselves wisdom in all spheres of human activity; wisdom and the right to make pronouncements which they expected you to listen to and learn from. The most amusing thing was to see a group of distinguished men together, with no one but each other to make pronouncements to. They were as suspicious of each other, then, as children. He had seen such gatherings in his father's house while – outside the compound walls – crowds waited in patient homage, or simple curiosity, for a sight of these extraordinary, benign and powerful faces, and he had observed the change that came over those faces when they parted company with each other and went out to meet the crowds. He thought that if Pandit Baba smiled now he would look like them, as they came from the house to the verandah, their games, sulks, quarrels temporarily suspended, and their suspicions making way for the feelings of relief and pleasure at re-entering a familiar world whose plaudits reaffirmed the huge capacity they believed they had, individually and collectively, to solve its problems, its mysteries and its injustices. Perhaps (Ahmed thought, still meeting Pandit Baba's apparently unwinking gaze) it was his early experience of distinguished men that had led him to feel that there was distance between himself and other people and their ideas. Gandhi had once given him an orange, Pandit Nehru had patted his head, and Maulana Azad had taken him on to his knee; but oranges, head-pats and knee-rides – as he realized even at the time – were not the objects of those visitations, and the visitations themselves although promising excitement always left the excitement on the other side of the wall where the crowds waited. 'Why do they wait?' he had asked his elder brother Sayed. 'Because they know we are saving India,' came the steady reply. As a boy Sayed had been a bit of a bore. 'Saving India from what?' Ahmed said. 'Well, from the British of course.' But in the morning, as he went to school, he noticed that the British were still there and looking quite unperturbed. When he got to school he found there weren't to be any lessons because the teachers and the older boys were on strike to protest the arrest the previous night of people who had been carried away with enthusiasm at the sight of the Mahatma visiting Ahmed's father, and – after seeing the Mahatma off at the station – had got out of hand and thrown brickbats at the police who were jostling them, hitting them with lathis and treading them under horse-hoof. Two days later his father was arrested too – for making the speech the Mahatma had asked him to make – and was in prison – that time – for six months.

'Speak what is in your mind,' Pandit Baba commanded. What insolence, Ahmed thought. There are two categories of things in my mind, he should say, the stuff people like you have fed into it and my own reactions to that stuff. The result is cancella-tion, so I have nothing in my mind.

'I was thinking of my father in prison,' he said. After a moment or two the miracle happened. The Pandit's lips lifted at the corners. He was bestowing a smile of sympathy and of elderly approval of a young man's filial regard. Ahmed consid-ered its quality; it struck him as no less dishonest than the expres-sion of disapproval. How could Pandit Baba be moved to feel either approval or disapproval when the person who was the object of it was a complete stranger to him? Well, it is this that puts me off (Ahmed told himself), this ease with which people feel emotions, or pretend to feel them.

'I meant,' he continued, 'the first time, when I was quite young, a schoolboy still.'

The smile did not disappear. A man like Panditji could mes-merize you into submission, hypnotize you into regarding him as a source of spiritual comfort. It was undoubtedly his intention to try, and when you knew a man's intentions you were even more in danger of being subjected to them because to be aware of an intention somehow increased its force. I shall destroy you, one man might say to another; and at once he would have a confederate, the man himself. Ideas seemed to have a life, a power of their own. Men became slaves to them. To challenge an idea as an alternative to accepting it was to be no less a slave to it. Neither to accept nor challenge it was the most difficult thing of all; perhaps impossible. The idea of Pandit Baba as a personification of wisdom, a fount of knowledge and self-knowledge, which was presumably the idea the Pandit had of himself and worked hard at conveying, was not to be got rid of by privately or even publicly asserting that the man was probably a self-opinionated and pompous fool who relied on his venerable age and appearance to command what respect his behaviour and ideas in themselves could not.

'Do not think of it as prison,' Pandit Baba said, going back to Hindi. 'It is those who call themselves jailers who are in prison, and perhaps all of us who are outside the walls. For what is outside in one sense is inside in another. In time we must break the walls down. This duty to break them down is *our* sentence of imprisonment. To break them down will be to free ourselves *and* our jailers. And we cannot sit back and wait for the orders of release. We must write the orders ourselves.' In English he added, in case Ahmed had misunderstood, 'I speak metaphorically.'

Ahmed nodded. In India nearly everybody spoke metaphorically except the English who spoke bluntly and could make their most transparent lies look honest as a consequence; whereas any truth contained in these metaphorical rigmaroles was so deviously presented that it looked devious itself.

'You had a pleasant journey from Mayapore, Panditji?' he asked, to see how Pandit Baba would react to such a barefaced attempt to change the subject. The Pandit reacted, after a few seconds, with a vague gesture of the arm that rested on the cushions and then opened his mouth as if to continue his parable.

Ahmed said hastily, 'And is this your first visit to Mirat?'

Professor Nair answered for Panditji. 'Oh no, not his first visit. Panditji was at one time living in Mirat.'

Ahmed glanced at Nair and noticed the minuscule gems of sweat encrusted on his bald domed head. It was quite cool in the room. A table-fan, set on the floor in one corner, moved its round whirring wire cage from side to side like a spectator at a slow-motion tennis match – more interested, Ahmed felt, in the conversation than he was.

'But for the last few years,' Nair was saying, but looking all the time at Pandit Baba as if the Pandit had become a museum-piece suddenly and Nair his curator, 'he has been in Mayapore.'

'Yes, I see,' Ahmed said, looking again at the Pandit – and

the eyes, slightly enlarged by the spectacle lenses, that were still gazing at him. 'Then you were in Mayapore during the riots.'

'Which riots are you meaning?'

'The riots in August last year.'

Again Ahmed had to wait for a reply. Pandit Baba Sahib's sympathy had gone and his disapproval was undergoing a change. He now looked at Ahmed as if he felt he had been threatened with violence.

'You must be speaking of something that has escaped my notice,' he said at last. His heart had resumed the business of pumping cold blood. An old man like me, his expression now said, should not be put in danger of losing his temper. 'I am not remembering any riots in Mayapore in August last year.' He paused, continued. 'A riot – and since you are knowing English somewhat better than me, perhaps you will correct me or corroborate – a riot I believe according to English dictionary refers to the violent unlawful actions of unlawful assembly of people. In Mayapore and India in general only I remember spontaneous demonstrations of innocent and law-abiding people to protest against the unlawful imprisonment without trial of men such as your father, and in Mayapore, particularly, demonstrations against the unlawful arrest of innocent men accused of a crime none of them committed. If this is what you are mistakenly calling riots, then – yes – I was in Mayapore at this time, when many people suffered the consequence of resisting unlawful acts by those supposed to be in lawful authority.'

Ahmed inclined his head, a movement he had found useful in the last few years, a movement suggestive of submission without verbal acknowledgement of it. He had discovered that this combination often forced people to move from attack to defence. They felt compelled to justify the victory which had just been ambiguously conceded to them.

'It is necessary all the time to have the truth of things clearly in the mind, you see,' Pandit Baba said, 'and to speak of them in truthful terms. Loose speech leads to loose thinking. When you speak of riots you are speaking as the English speak. You must speak like an Indian, and think like an Indian.' The corners of his lips lifted again. 'I know it is not always easy. But to take only easy ways is often to end up with difficulties.'

Ahmed nodded and wondered what reason Nair had for

asking him at short notice on an evening when there was another guest, a guest Nair had failed to mention in the note of invitation sent round that morning but whose presence had not escaped the notice of Bronowsky, that was to say – of Bronowsky's spies. He wondered whether he would catch a glimpse of the woman Baba had brought with him, but doubted it. It was an all-male evening. He wouldn't even see Mrs Nair.

'Professor Nair tells me you are writing a commentary on the Bhagavad Gita. Does the work go well, Panditji?'

Again the gesture of the arm that rested on the cushion. Interpreting this, now, as a cue for Professor Nair to interrupt, Ahmed looked at their host. The sweat still shone on Nair's head. He still gazed at Pandit Baba. His smile had become fixed. He said nothing. He smiled, stared and perspired. Ahmed had the feeling that if Panditji got up and left the room it would take Nair several minutes to regain his normal composure – or lack of composure: he was a restless man, usually. Surely Panditji's presence in itself wasn't as nerve-racking as Nair's almost catatonic reaction to it seemed to suggest? Ahmed looked back at Panditji and found himself still under scrutiny.

'Your father, I believe, is in the Fort at Premanagar,' Pandit Baba said.

'So people say.'

'You have no comfirmation of this?'

'No.'

'You think he may be elsewhere?'

'Officially I have no information, Pandit Sahib. Unofficially it seems to be understood by people that he is, or was, in Premanagar.'

'But you are able to communicate. You write letters to him, and he writes back to you.'

'I usually communicate through my mother.'

'And the letters of course are directed through the prison authorities.'

'Of course.'

'And censored.'

'Naturally.'

'But occasionally you manage a more private kind of correspondence.'

For a while Ahmed did not answer. Eventually he said, 'I can't say whether my mother sometimes manages that. For myself the answer is no.'

'But before he went to jail, some kind of simple code was arranged, so that even a letter going through the authorities and the censor might contain some private or intimate information?'

Ahmed laughed, shook his head. Panditji raised his eyebrows.

'No such code was arranged?'

'No.'

'I am not an agent provocateur,' Panditji announced, and frowned. 'But let us talk of something else. Your father is in good health, I trust?'

'Yes, I believe so.'

'And your mother?'

'She is well, too.'

'Presumably she is not hopeful of being permitted to visit him.'

'No. She's resigned to everything. His being absent in prison is all a part of her experience of marriage.'

'You speak sadly or bitterly of that?'

Ahmed smiled. 'No. It is just the truth.'

Pandit Baba nodded. He said, 'It is perhaps more difficult for her – being of the Mohammedan faith – more difficult than for some other Congressmen's wives. Her family in the Punjab – they are perhaps more sympathetic to the policies of Mr Jinnah and the Muslim League than to those of the Congress?'

'That is correct,' Ahmed admitted.

'Since a long time, or since the political turncoating in the Punjab of Sir Sikander Hyat-Khan in 1937?'

'Perhaps, yes, since then.'

'This will no doubt be a sorrow to her, to have her husband imprisoned, to have no family member to turn to without feeling disloyal to that husband.'

'Actually I think my mother is angry sooner than sad.'

'What makes her angry?'

'Oh, quite a lot of things. For instance she loses her temper when she hears people describe father as a show-case Muslim.'

'Show-case? What is this? I have not heard this expression.'

'It means Muslims whom the Congress chose for positions of power in order to prove to everybody that they're not a Hindu-riddled organization.'

'Ah. Yes. I see. Show-case. And so Muslims who follow Mr Jinnah and his Muslim League say that Mohammed Ali Kasim, a Congress man, is a show-case Muslim?'

'They do I suppose, but members of Congress say it as well. Members who are jealous and think such Muslims have unfair advantages because of their propaganda value.' Ahmed hesitated. 'There is of course some truth in that.'

'Truth is not divisible, Mr Kasim. There cannot be such a thing as some truth. You are meaning to say that in some cases it is true that a Muslim had unfair advantages over a Hindu in the Congress because the high command chose him for his propaganda value first and his talents second. This may or may not be true. But it cannot be a matter in which there is *some* truth.'

Ahmed again inclined his head.

'You are staying in Mirat for a week or two, Panditji?'

Pandit Baba smiled, the smile of a man willing to be sidetracked because for him all paths led eventually in the direction he intended to go. 'It will not be so long. I shall return quite soon to Mayapore, I believe.'

'Only a short holiday, then.'

'I am not taking holiday.'

'There are texts in the college library that Panditji wants to have a look at,' Professor Nair explained. He was still smiling, but in the last few seconds had wiped the sweat off his head with a folded handkerchief, had come out of the catatonic trance. 'It is to inspect these texts Panditji is honouring us with a stay,' he added, quite unnecessarily; and then, more informatively, 'but before he leaves I hope to persuade him to address our students.'

Pandit Baba closed his eyes, inclined his head modestly to the right and then to the left.

Ahmed said, 'If you live in Mayapore, Panditji, perhaps you knew that English girl, Miss Manners? One gathers her circle of friends in Mayapore wasn't exclusively English.'

'No, I did not know her personally.'

'She's dead now. She had a child. There was a notice in the newspapers.'

'It did not escape our attention, Mr Kasim.' Pandit Baba paused. 'You have some personal interest in this matter?'

'No, but it was talked about a lot at the time, and when anyone mentions Mayapore these days you automatically think of Miss Manners – and the rape in the Bibighar Gardens.'

'It is not established that there was rape. Only that there were arrests, and imprisonment without trial of suspects, imprisonment not for rape but for so-called political activities.'

'So-called?'

'So-called. How can one say definitely when nothing is made public, when there is such a convenient regulation as Defence of India Rule?'

'Do you mean that the whole affair was invented, never took place at all?'

'I did not mean this. Simply I was speaking of evidence. Clearly it was thought that rape had occurred.'

'I expect the girl thought so herself,' Ahmed could not resist saying.

'I agree that it is not an experience the victim could be in doubt about.'

'You think that perhaps *she* made it up?'

'I do not think anything, Mr Kasim. Only I am saying that to speak of the rape of Miss Manners in the Bibighar Gardens is to speak of an affair as if it had happened when it is not legally established as having happened. If you say there was rape I would not agree or disagree. Also I would not agree or disagree if you said no, there was no rape, the girl was hallucinated or lying and making up stories for one reason or another. Only I can agree if you state simply that it was generally accepted through reports and rumour that there was rape, that certain men were arrested as suspects, that presently the British attempted to hush everything up, that no case was ever brought to court, that it was said the girl herself refused to identify those arrested, that in the end there was officially no rape and no punishment for rape.'

'Did you know any of the men who were arrested, Panditji?'

'Yes. I knew. They were boys of some education.'

'Did you know the one who was friendly with Miss Manners?'

After a moment Pandit Baba said, 'You are speaking of Hari Kumar.'

'I think that was his name. Did you know Kumar?'

Again a slight pause. 'Once when he first returned from England his aunt sought my assistance to teach him Hindi. Of all these boys I knew him best. He also could only speak properly English. He was not at all a good student. He had no wish to speak his native language. He employed himself on a local newspaper that was published in English. Always he was attempting to forget that he was an Indian, because he had lived in England since earliest childhood. His father took him there when he was two years old only. He went to English public school and had English friends. He did not understand why he could not have such friends here. His father died, you see, and he had no relative but his aunt in Mayapore. She paid for his passage and gave him a roof and was kind to him, being a widow with no children. But to him, she was a foreigner. All of us were foreigners to Hari Kumar. He knew only English people and English ways. Only he wanted these people and these ways. In Mayapore he could not have them. He was a most unfortunate young man. His case should be taken to heart.'

'But eventually he had one English friend, didn't he? I mean Miss Manners.'

'They were sometimes together. I do not know whether she was his friend.'

'People said they were friends and more.'

'I have no knowledge of this. I do not find it informative to take notice of idle gossip. They were sometimes together. This I can vouch for. People say she was unlike other English people. I do not know what they mean when they are saying that. English people are not mass-produced. They do not come off a factory line all looking, speaking, thinking, acting the same. Neither do we. But we are Indians and they are English. True intimacy is not possible. It is not even desirable. Only it is desirable that there should be peace between us, and this is not possible while the English retain possession of what belongs to us, because to get it back we must fight them. In fighting them we do not have to hate them. But also when we have got back from them what they have taken from us and are at peace with them this does not mean that we should love them. We can never be friends with the English, or they with us, but we need not be enemies. Men are not born equal, nor are they born brothers. The lion does not lie down with the tiger, or the crow nest with the swallow. The world is created in a diversity of phenomena and each phenomenon has its own diversity. Between mankind there may be common truth and justice and common wisdom to lead to amity. But between men there are divisions and love cannot be felt truly except by like and like. Between like and unlike there can only be tolerance, and absence of enmity – which is not at all the same thing as friendship. Perhaps the truth of this is most apparent to the Hindu who is born to understand and accept this concept of diversity.'

Ahmed waited a moment to make sure Pandit Baba had finished; then he said, 'A little while ago you said the people demonstrated against the arrest of Kumar and the others for a crime they hadn't committed, but how did they know they hadn't committed it?'

Pandit Baba smiled again.

'You are like your father in one way. You have perhaps some of his forensic skill. In a moment you plan to raise the question of riot again, you will say that it would be correct to describe the demonstrations as riots because the demonstrators had no means of knowing whether these boys were guilty or not at that time, and were only acting instinctively and therefore unlawfully, therefore riotously.'

'Isn't it a debatable point?'

'All points are debatable. But there are two things that must be taken into consideration. The first is that the demonstrations in Mayapore and the attacks on government installations were no different in main respect from similar demonstrations and attacks in other parts of the country, demonstrations against the arrest of Congress leaders – men such as your father. In Mayapore, however, there was additional weight and temper arising out of the arrests of these boys. But you see not out of the arrests as arrests but out of what quickly became known, that some of these boys were tortured and defiled by the police on the same night of their arrest in order to get them to confess. This knowledge came from the police headquarters itself, as did the knowledge that in spite of torture no confession was obtained. Some of these boys were whipped and they were forced to eat beef. They were Hindus, boys of some education. One was Kumar. We did not think it possible that such boys could set upon and rape an English girl. Also it was believed that all they had been doing was drinking illicit liquor in a hut on the other side of the river from the Bibighar Gardens. It was in

the hut that they were arrested. Kumar was not with them but
they were known to the police to be acquaintances of Kumar.
It was to find Kumar that the police went to the hut. The police
went to find Kumar because of his association with the girl who
was reported to have been raped. The head of the police in
Mayapore, the English District Superintendent, he also was
associated with the girl. It was the District Superintendent who
personally conducted the interrogations, who ordered the boys
to be beaten and forced to eat beef. All night he was there, in
the police headquarters, asking them questions. Meanwhile, if
there was rape, the real culprits, hooligans no doubt, made good
their escape. But District Superintendent was not interested in
them. Only he was interested in punishing these boys, especially
Kumar, because of Kumar's association with the white girl.
District Superintendent was an evil man, Mr Kasim. His cruelty
and perversions were known to his men and consequently to
some of us. It was one of his own Muslim constables who next
morning whispered the truth to people outside, because he was
ashamed of what had been done. He spoke too of a bicycle
which the police found in the Bibighar Gardens when they
searched there at night. It belonged to the girl. He said that
District Superintendent ordered the bicycle to be put in the
police truck. Later when they had arrested the boys in the hut
they drove to the house where Kumar was living. District Superintendent told them to take the bicycle out of the truck and
leave it in the ditch outside this house. Then they went into the
house and arrested Kumar, pretended to search the area and so
"found" the bicycle and said that Kumar had stolen it from the
white girl after raping her. Some of the police were thinking this
was a great joke. But the man who told of these things did not
think it was funny. Later, people were saying he became frightened and denied what he had secretly told. Perhaps if there had
been a trial for rape he would have been persuaded to tell the
truth of these things. But there was in any case no trial. District
Superintendent had been too clever. Even people like Judge
Menen and the Deputy Commissioner became suspicious that
the wrong boys had been arrested, and Judge Menen heard the
rumours of torture and defilement. He had the boys questioned
but they were too frightened to say anything, we understand.
Except Kumar who was not saying anything at all to anybody,

and did not even seem to want to save himself. But chiefly there was no trial because Miss Manners herself was saying the men arrested could not have had anything to do with it. So now District Superintendent produced evidence that all these boys were engaged in subversive activities and no doubt the English thought it was not possible to set them free in any event. So they were imprisoned without trial under Defence of India Rule, as your father and many others are imprisoned.'

'Surely it would be difficult to produce evidence of subversive activities, Panditji, unless it was actually there?'

'Not so difficult, Mr Kasim. But no doubt in all but one case these boys had done and said things that patriotic young Indians say and do, boys of some education, and of certain temperaments. The police had files on them as they had files on many such boys. In the other case, in Kumar's case, also they had a file because once he was taken into custody for refusing to answer questions and for making difficulties about giving his proper name. Unfortunately the police officer whose questions he refused to answer was this same Englishman, the District Superintendent. If Kumar had answered District Superintendent properly, if he had said "sir" and looked frightened and done some grovelling, District Superintendent would not have taken notice of him. But this was not Hari Kumar's way, who hated India, and wanted to be treated like an English boy, and spoke English and only English, and with what is called I understand Public School accent, and so was annoyed to be asked questions by District Superintendent who did not have such good education but expected to be treated all the time like a Sahib because of his white face. But to think of Hari Kumar engaged in subversive activities with other young Indians is to those of us who know him, Mr Kasim, only laughable. He did not like India. He did not like Indians. Only he liked England and his memories of being in England and having English friends. He was not a boy who would plot with other young Indians to get rid of the English.'

'Is he still in prison?'

'They are all still in prison, but I think not together. He is in the Kandipat jail in Ranpur, a long way from Mayapore. For many months his aunt did not know which prison they had sent him to. Now at last she is permitted to write and to send him some food and some books. He thanks her for them but she cannot be sure that he is allowed to eat the food or read the books. I know these things because I am in her confidence. Poor lady. Her sufferings are most sad to see. She was very fond of her English nephew as she called him.'

Suddenly Pandit Baba looked at Professor Nair.

'You say nothing, my friend.'

'Oh, but I am listening with a great deal of interest. I did not know you were so closely concerned with this very interesting case.'

'Yes,' Pandit Baba said. 'It is interesting. You find this also? It is the kind of case – by which I mean the case of the arrest and punishment of six boys – the kind of case our young friend's father here would have loved to take charge of in the days when he was so illustriously practising the law and defending countrymen of his who were wrongfully accused.' He looked again at Ahmed. 'Unfortunately it is a case that can never be subjected to the searching eyes of the law. But this does not mean it should be forgotten. And it is not only in the courts that justice is done. You look hungry, Mr Kasim. Let me not keep you and Professor Nair any longer from your supper. I shall have retired before you finish, for I have some work to do, so allow me to say good night.'

Nair rose, and Ahmed – somewhat stiffly – followed suit, bowed to Panditji and followed Professor Nair out of the room and across the hall and into the dining-room. A servant who had been squatting in the doorway that led out to the compound got up, went out and shouted orders to the cook. Nair set the fan going and they sat at opposite ends of the table which was dressed Western-style.

'Do you mind vegetarian?' Professor Nair whispered. 'It's the smell of cooking you see. One has to think of everything.'

II

The horses had been behaving badly. Sarah wondered whether young Mr Kasim had deliberately chosen them for their iron mouths and vicious natures or whether it had been a question of taking the best of a bad bunch from the palace stables. Her own mount, for instance, had shied twice at its early-morning

shadow, missed its footing on some shale and having reached the
promising openness of the comparatively flat turf in the middle
of the waste ground separating the palace from the city, resolutely come to a halt, stretched its neck and cropped grass. Mr
Kasim, who seemed to be having difficulty restraining his own
mount from surging forward in a gallop for the city gates, grew
nearly level but some feet away and held it there by what looked
like main force. She noted the ridged muscle on his bare forearms. The brim of his topee darkened his face and hid his
expression.

'Are you a Sunni or a Shiah, Mr Kasim?' Because of the distance between them she had raised her voice. She thought she
sounded like a games mistress.

'A Shiah,' Ahmed said, and wrenched his horse's head to the
left to stop it closing in on Sarah's.

'Is there a great deal of difference?'

'I beg your pardon?'

'Much difference?'

Pandering to his horse to make it feel it had got its way he led
it round in a tight circle and brought it to stand again in its
original position.

'Not really. The Shiahs dispute the rights of the three Khalifs
who succeeded Mohammed. You could say it's a political
division.'

'Who are the Shiahs for?'

'What?'

'Who do they say should have succeeded Mohammed?'

'Oh. A man called Ali. He was Mohammed's son-in-law. We
mourn his death at the beginning of Muharram. The Mohammedan new year. But then the Sunnis often join in the mourning too.'

'Is the Nawab a Shiah Muslim?'

'Yes.'

'Are there any Sunnis in Mirat?'

'Yes, a few.'

'I think if you rode on a bit this damned thing would stop
eating grass and at least pretend to do what I want it to.'

For answer Ahmed set his horse towards her and when he was
near enough reached over, took the reins from her and jerked.
The horse brought its head up.

'Keep him like that,' Ahmed suggested, holding the reins in short, so that the horse's neck looked painfully arched. She slid her left hand along the reins until her fist touched Ahmed's. She could smell the garlic on his breath. Perhaps he meant her to because he had heard what her Aunty Fenny said.

'Thanks.'

She set the horse at a walk. It jerked its head continually, trying to force her to lengthen the rein. Ahmed resumed his position, a few paces behind her on her left. Obviously he had no intention of making conversation; but was it shyness, dislike or indifference? At least, she felt, you could rely on him. He'd make no bones about disciplining the horse for her and, no longer dressed in a lounge suit but instead in short-sleeved shirt and jodhpurs, he looked like a man her future brother-in-law Teddie Bingham would describe as being 'useful in a scrap', than which for Teddie there was probably no higher praise of his own sex. Muslim men, after all, did have this quality. Sarah corrected herself: not Muslim men, but Indians who were descended like Mr Kasim from Middle Eastern stock: Arabs, Persians and Turks. They had retained the sturdiness of races whom extremes of heat and cold (she was thinking of deserts) had toughened.

England's climate had also toughened her people. Years ago Sarah had written an essay with the rather grandiloquent title: The Effect of Climate and Topography upon the Human Character. The idea, she remembered, had first come to her in the summer holiday of the year great-grandpa died and she had walked across Mr Birtwhistle's field encouraging Aunt Mabel not to be put off by the cows and then stood by the brook thinking how much like Pankot in miniature her surroundings were; the year when she was struck by the difference between her Indian family and her English family. 'England,' she had written when she was a couple of years older, 'although temperate climatically speaking, combines within a very limited geographical area a diversity of weather and natural features. Such conditions react upon the inhabitants to make them strong, active, energetic and self-sufficient. It is these qualities which they take abroad with them into their tropical and subtropical colonies, lands whose native populations are inclined because of things like heat and humidity to be less strong, less active, less energetic and more willing to be led, a fact which has enabled European races in general but the English in particular to gain and keep control of such territories. Upon the return of our colonial exiles to the land of their birth they are struck by the smallness of everything and by the fact that the self-sufficiency of their race, thus re-encountered, is really the result of the self-satisfaction of a people who have had comparatively little to contend with in the human struggle against nature.' She remembered the opening paragraph almost word for word and also remembered the red-pencil comment of the headmistress in the margin, 'An interesting essay and well developed so far as the question of climatic influences is concerned. I do not fully understand your reference to topography as an influence, however, and perhaps you fail to understand it yourself, as witness your failure to develop that aspect of your argument.'

'But I do understand it,' Sarah had assured herself, 'and it's all there, she just hasn't read it.' Reading it again, though, she thought that perhaps a bit of clarification would do no harm, then that it would be a definite improvement; finally that the headmistress was right and that clarification was essential, but in her mind first and only then on paper; and in her mind the clarification obstinately refused to come. She was stuck with that single recollection of a notion that had reached her out of the blue, that the place near the brook in the spinney beyond Mr Birtwhistle's fields was like Pankot in miniature and that this somehow explained why her Indian family were not like her English family.

Over to the right of the waste ground there were a few trees and a road and facing the road a substantial bungalow behind grey stucco walls. 'Who lives there?' she asked Ahmed, holding the reins tight in one hand and pointing.

'That's Count Bronowsky's house.'

'Is he really a count?'

'Yes, I think so.'

'Dare we gallop?'

'If you'd like to.'

'Where to? To the city gates?'

'There's a nullah. We'll have to bear left and join the city gate road.'

'I don't mind nullahs.'

'It's too wide to jump.'

'Come on then.'

She dug in her heels. A moment she loved: the slight hesitation, the gathering of propulsive forces in the animal she sat astride, the first leap forward that always seemed to her like a leap into a world of unexplored delight which she could only cut a narrow channel through and which she would reach the farther end of too soon but not without experiencing on the way something of the light and mysterious pleasure that existed for creatures who broke free of their environment. Ahead she made out the broken line of the nullah and as the horse did not at once respond to movement of wrist and pressure of heel had a second or two of fear that had itself broken free into a curious region of stillness and excitement; and then the horse began veering left; a quick glance over her shoulder showed her Ahmed. She felt an extraordinary, exhilarating sense of the perfection of their common endeavour. Together they galloped along the line of the nullah and charged through the gap where the nullah petered out a few yards from the road. From here she could see the city gate, isolated relic of the city wall, and how the road led to it and had come diagonally across the waste ground from the palace. They passed through splashes of shade from the trees that lined the road, drew level with and passed a line of lumbering carts drawn by humped white oxen, and then a file of women with baskets on their heads. The air was saturated by the pale smell of centuries of dung-fire smoke. The city was close. Why, it looms, Sarah thought, I don't want it: and exerted pressure with her right heel and right wrist to bring the horse round in a fine galloping sweep. She sensed the animal's bloody-minded resistance. It seemed as if it would neither turn nor slow, but would charge mindlessly on and dash itself and her to pieces on the city of Mirat. But then she felt the slight change of rhythm and the neat little spasm of adjustment to the centre of gravity, and Mirat began to swing towards her left shoulder. She exerted pressure to slow the horse to a canter, and then to a trot. At this end of the waste ground there was a group of three banyan trees, two of them with a fine display of rooted branches. She reined in beneath the youngest of the trees and looked round. Mr Kasim had reined in too, and waited exactly as before, a few paces behind her, to her left. Such precision! She smiled at him, pleased for both of them. The smile she got in return, though, was as distant as ever. Obviously he had not shared her pleasure; instead, probably, shared her moments of dismay, wondering what blame would be put on him if she fell and was injured. In his position Teddie would have felt obliged to say, Are you all right? or, You'd better go easy on that brute. And have got himself ready to complain to the head syce when they returned to the palace; all of which – Sarah realized – would spoil the morning for her by introducing the all-too-familiar note of criticism that day in day out acted in you and on you as part of a general awareness of being in charge, of having to be prepared to throw your weight about, so that really there was nothing you could enjoy for its own sake, nothing you could give yourself over to entirely.

She looked towards the town and said, 'It's funny, Mr Kasim, but I've not once heard the muezzin since I've been here, and yet there are all those minarets.'

'The wind's been in the wrong direction, I expect.'

'They do call then?'

'Oh yes. They call.'

'Five times a day?'

'Yes.'

'Will the îd al-fitr prayers be said in the mosques or out here?'

'Out here. Why?'

'I read somewhere that they're supposed to be held in the open air if possible.'

'You must have seen such meetings before, in open places?'

'No. I don't think so. I suppose because I've only been in places where they make them stay in the mosques in case of trouble. Or perhaps I've seen them but not known what was going on.'

'Last year the îd fell during the wet season. The prayers were indoors then.'

'Why is it preferred for them to be in the open?'

Mr Kasim paused, as if considering; but he might have been reluctant to answer so many questions about his religion. She, after all, was an infidel. When the answer came, though, it suggested mockery; mockery of her and of the beliefs of his own people.

'Because of the crowds, I expect. The idea is wholly practical.'

'You mean you have to cater for all the people who never go into a mosque normally?'

'Yes,' Ahmed said. And added, 'But I'm no kind of authority. The Imam at the Abu-Q'rim mosque would probably have a different explanation.'

'When exactly will the îd fall?'

'When the new moon is seen.'

'Supposing it's cloudy?'

'Then you calculate and usually make it thirty days instead of twenty-nine or thirty after the beginning of Ramadan, to be on the safe side. But it won't be cloudy this year and of course the calculation is already made. In fact the îd is due about a week after your sister's wedding.'

'Is it? But how nice. That means everybody will be happy.' She turned. It was uncomfortable having to sit askew in the saddle just to talk to him. She set the horse at a walk and then at a trot. Everybody will be happy. Everybody will be happy. Distantly she could see the roof of the palace. The sun was already hot and the short-lived freshness of early morning already staling. She noted the first phase of that curious phenomenon of the Indian plain, the gradual disappearance of the horizon, as if the land were expanding, stretching itself, destroying the illusion that the mind, hand and eye could stake a claim to any part that bore a real relation to the whole. It is always retreating, Sarah told herself, always making off, getting farther and farther away and leaving people and what people have built stranded. Behind her, she knew, Mr Kasim rode at a constant watchful distance, but as the land expanded it left them in relation to the horizon getting closer and closer together. She felt that a god looking down would observe this shortening of distance and wonder what it was about his lesser creations that made them huddle together when they might have emulated giants, become giant riders on giant horses. Why – Sarah cried to herself – that's how I used to feel! That's how I felt on the day of the wasp. And tried now to induce the feeling again, but failed. Well, I am full-grown, she thought, and those were growing pains. Full-grown. Full-grown. She persuaded the horse into a canter and thought of the men she might have married and the children she might have had since becoming full-grown, and wondered whether there was really such a thing as love and if there were what subtle influences it might have on the purely animal response, some men, but not Teddie, had wakened in her. She wondered if

Teddie had awakened Susan in that way, and Susan Teddie; and envied her not for being woken but for apparently being endowed with a nature that was ready to take all the rest on trust. My trouble is, she thought, I question everything, every assumption. I'm not content to let things be, to let things happen. If I don't change that I shall never be happy.

Again they moved left to avoid the nullah which on this side did not peter out but passed under the road, through a culvert. It was shallow, though, and the banks were easy. Sarah urged her horse down into it. The clay bottom was cracked, so quickly had the post-monsoon sun dried out whatever water settled here during the rains, but there was mud still in the shadow of the culvert. The ground bore the imprint of cattle, goat and horses' hooves.

'Do you come this way, Mr Kasim, I mean when you ride alone?' she called.

She did not hear his reply clearly. It might have been 'Some-times'. She took the rise back out of the nullah. They were now close to the house Mr Kasim said was Count Bronowsky's: new-ish-looking Anglo-Indian palladian, she noted; isolated in an extensive walled garden, probably built for him, by him. That sort of man knew how to feather his nest: a foreigner, a Euro-pean, in the service of a native prince, a throw-back to the days of the nabobs of the old trading companies – French, English and Portuguese. She did not think she would like old Count Bronowsky, although it was said he had done fine things. Fine things for himself too, she imagined, judging by the house. She could not imagine her father retiring to live in such a place, rather to a gabled villa in Purley, or a timbered cottage in Pankot if he chose to live the rest of his days in India. People like Teddie and Susan closed their eyes to the fact that her father's generation must be the last generation of English people who would have such a choice. War or no war, it was all coming to an end, and the end could not come neatly. There would be people who had to be victims of the fact that it could not. She herself was surely one of them, and perhaps Mr Kasim too.

Suddenly she wheeled the horse round in the same kind of tight circle Mr Kasim had described before they set off on their gallop. She caught him before he had time to hang back, and so confronted him in the act of reining in, but having done so she could not find an acceptable way of explaining her impulsive action, either to him or to herself. Curiously, though, in the moment before being embarrassed at finding herself at a loss, she thought that the world might be a more interesting and useful place to live in if there were more such empty gestures as the one she had apparently made. They were only empty in the sense that there was room in them for meaning to be poured. That kind of meaning wasn't found easily. It was better, then, to leave the gesture unaccompanied. To make words up just for the sake of saying something would be incongruous. So she closed her mouth and smiled, turned her horse's head and continued on at a walk, listening to the sound that never seemed to stop between sun-up and sundown, was taken for granted and seldom heard consciously at all: the sore-throated calling of the crows.

When they returned to the guest house she saw her future brother-in-law and his best man waiting on the terrace.

'Hello,' she called. 'What a nice surprise. Are you here for breakfast?'

The officer Susan Layton was to marry, Teddie Bingham, was the kind of man Mrs Layton would have preferred her husband to be on hand to approve of. She had complained to Sarah that it was bad enough having to write to Colonel Layton and tell him that his youngest daughter was getting married to a man he had never heard of, could not meet and might not like, without the additional worry of searching for the right sort of phrases to convey to him the idea that in his absence she had done every-thing necessary to be reassured about Captain Bingham's back-ground and found nothing amiss. She did not want to worry him. God knew he had worries of his own. Letters to a prisoner of war had to be cheerful and soothing.

'All you need tell him,' Sarah pointed out, 'is the name of Teddie's regiment and that Susan and he love each other. That's all he'll need to know. And that's all there is to tell. After all, nothing is amiss, is it?'

'There's the question of his parents. It's easier if a man has parents. All there seems to be is an uncle in Shropshire, a father in the Muzzafirabad Guides who broke his neck hunting and a mother who married again, had an unhappy time and died in Mandalay. Your Aunt Mabel says she knew some Muzzy Guides people but doesn't remember a Bingham, which is neither here nor there because she only remembers what she wants to. But it means all we've got to go on is Dick Rankin's word and Teddie himself.'

General Rankin was the Area Commander. Teddie had come to the Area Headquarters in Pankot from the staff college in Quetta. It was not a good posting for an officer who had commanded a company of the Muzzafirabad Guides in Burma, acted as second-in-command of the depleted battalion during the retreat. From Quetta he might have had a G2 appointment, or at least a posting to the staff of an active division. He admitted this himself. He hoped and believed the posting to Pankot was only temporary. The one good thing about it, he added, was that it had brought him and Susan together.

Before Susan it had brought him Sarah. She and Susan, both mustered into the Women's Auxiliary Corps, worked as clerks at Area Headquarters which had stationed itself permanently in Pankot for the duration to avoid the confusion and pressures of the yearly move from Ranpur to the hills and back again. Corporal Sarah Layton was the first of the two Layton girls he noticed, and for a time it seemed that he would prove to be the exception to the rule which, according to interested observers in Pankot, made it almost inevitable that any man first taking an interest in Sarah Layton would presently cool off her and start paying attention to Susan, who admittedly was prettier, livelier, always to be counted on to do what Pankot people described as making things go. The result was that one was never sure which group of men Susan would next be seen as the sparkling centre of, only certain that from time to time, in these groups, there would turn up a man who, briefly, had been conspicuous as a companion of her quieter, elder sister. Once he had succumbed to Susan's more obvious attractions he became one of a crowd; one ceased to notice him and, as a consequence, did not mark his disappearance. Susan, it was assumed, took none of her men seriously. They came, direct or via Sarah, danced attendance, and were replaced.

When Teddie Bingham showed signs of being Susan-proof it was to Sarah rather than to himself that he drew attention. The ladies of Pankot discussed this interesting situation over bridge, committee-teas, behind the counter of the canteen of the Regimental Institute for British soldiers of non-commissioned rank, and behind the scenes at rehearsals for their amateur theatricals. It was, they agreed, time that Sarah Layton settled down. She was all of twenty-two. She was very present-able, quite pretty, and well behaved. Her background was excel-lent, in fact impeccable within the context of Anglo-India in general and Pankot in particular. She was practically born in Flagstaff House (the senior ladies reminded those less well-endowed with detailed knowledge of Pankot history), her mother was a Muir, her maternal grandfather had been GOC Ranpur; her paternal grandfather had a distinguished career in the Civil, she was related by his second marriage to old Mabel Layton, and her father – now a prisoner in Germany – had commanded the 1st Pankot Rifles in North Africa.

And, in herself, Sarah Layton was upright, honest, and, one imagined, a tower of strength to her mother. Mrs Layton, it had to be admitted, had not borne up under the strain of separation from her husband with the ease and cheerfulness one had the right to expect of a senior military wife. One found her vagueness and general air of distraction difficult to deal with. It had become an aggravating duty, where once it had been a pleasure, to partner her at bridge, for instance. She was not always meticulous about paying her losses, either. Fortunately, a hint to Sarah Layton was known to be effective. It was rumoured that native shopkeepers like Mohammed Hossain the tailor, and Jalal-ud-din, the general merchant, had taken to referring overdue accounts to Sarah as an insurance against painful accu-mulation. Honorary secretaries of ladies' committees on which Mrs Layton sat had become used to mentioning the dates and times of meetings to Sarah, because this seemed to be the best way of reducing the odds against Mrs Layton turning up. On top of all this, there was – how should one put it? – a tendency in Colonel Layton's lady towards over-indulgence with the bottle.

Sarah Layton, it was obvious, was the temporary rock on which the Layton household had come to rest, and it seemed unfair that her mother should be demonstrably more alert to the existence of her younger daughter. One could not exactly describe Mrs Layton's attitude to Susan as fond – one gave her credit for retaining, in public, a proper manner of emotional detachment from the affairs of her children – but if one assumed

fondness behind the manner then Susan, clearly, was the favourite daughter – and seemed to know it. That she knew it was,
perhaps, the one major flaw in the bright little crystal. The
minor flaws – vanity and pertness – were probably marginal evidence of the existence of this major one. But one forgave her in
any case. She could not help it if people were attracted to her.
It would be unnatural of her to pretend this was not so and only
a girl with a remarkable capacity for self-effacement would not
take advantage of it.

All the same one was sorry for the comparatively – and it was
only comparatively – less attractive sister. One had never
doubted that eventually she would come across a man who, looking for more than a casual flirtation, would prefer the things she
had to offer. What made the association between Teddie Bingham and Sarah Layton so especially interesting to the ladies of
Pankot was the fact that Teddie, in their majority opinion, was
really rather good-looking; that is he was if sandy reddish hair
and pale eyelashes weren't on one's personal list of things in a
man one found disagreeable. The qualification was made and
accepted because one lady, a Mrs Fosdick, said she was allergic
to men with red hair and that she always counted pale eyelashes
a sign of weakness and untrustworthiness. Another lady, a Mrs
Paynton, said nonsense, pale eyelashes denoted an exceptionally
amorous nature, and if that is what Mrs Fosdick meant by weakness and untrustworthiness she was all for it. The ladies smiled.
Their interest in Teddie Bingham thus aroused in regard to a
specific point, they turned to a reconsideration of Sarah Layton
and agreed that in life it was the quiet and unassuming people
who in the end surprised one most. One had to remember, too,
that both the Layton girls had come back out with, as it were,
the dew of maidenhood still fresh on their young faces. Parents
in India, reunited with their daughters, were well aware of the
attendant dangers. On any station there were never enough
young girls to go round. Even the plainest poor creature might
expect attention from young men fired by climate and scarcity.
The girls were fired by the climate too, and the sensation of
power over herds of – as it were – panting young men could
easily go to their heads. The first year was the one to watch out
for. A girl needed her parents then. Wise parents stood by and
let a girl enjoy the illusion of having her head in the first six

months. One might expect anything up to six announcements that she had met the one man in the world for her. In the second six months one had to shorten the rein because this was the period when having found and discarded six Prince Charmings she could be expected to select as a seventh a man who had shown no interest in her at all, probably because he was already spoken for and had dropped out of the game of romantic musical chairs.

When the year was up and a girl had been through a complete cycle of seasons, it was time for her parents to take a hand. It was remarkable how docile the girls became, how easily they could now be led into the right sort of match. The second year was the year of engagements and marriages; the third year was devoted to maternity. With the first grandson or grand-daughter one could sit back with a sigh of relief that one's duty had been properly done.

The war had disrupted this ideal pattern. The Layton girls, for instance, were among the last girls to come out as members of what old Anglo-Indian wags used to call the fishing-fleet. These days one only got people like nurses. On the other hand the supply of men had become a torrent of all sorts where once it had been a steady dependable flow mostly of one sort only – the right. (Pankot, for instance, was full of the most extra-ordinary people.) One felt, as it were, besieged. Through the smoke and confusion one tried to maintain contact. One sought the reassurance that the old nucleus was still established at the centre. It was heartening to know that the elder Layton girl seemed to have chosen a man one could describe as pukka. He was a Muzzy Guide. His father had been a Muzzy Guide. If his association with Sarah Layton developed as one hoped, one could then say that Colonel Layton's departure from the bosom of his family long before the end of that first traditionally difficult year when a girl stood in need of the steadying hand of a father as well as of the guiding hand of a mother, had not had any real ill-effect. One might congratulate Sarah Layton on her own good sense.

In this way the ladies of Pankot, at bridge, at tea, behind the counter of the canteen of the Regimental Institute and in rehearsal breaks in their production of *The Housemaster*, discussed the various ramifications of Sarah's friendship with Teddie. They seemed to have set their hearts on an engagement. One could –

they said – always do with a really good wedding, and with a Layton girl involved one could expect a reception at Flagstaff House, perhaps count on the General to give the bride away. Life had become a shade drabber each successive year of the war. One was lucky if the Governor and his Lady spent more than May and June in the summer residence. Last year, 1942, when all that turmoil was going on down in the plain, there had hardly been even the shadow of a season. As for home comforts, those too were rapidly becoming a thing of the past. The influx of troops, the establishment of training camps, the departure of one's own menfolk, had driven one out of one's rightful bungalows to pig in at Smith's Hotel, the club annexe, or, if one was luckier than other grass widows, into (in Pankot idiom) grace and favour bungalows such as Mrs Layton and her daughters occupied in the vicinity of the old Pankot Rifles depot, although that meant one spent a fortune in tonga fares just to go to the club for morning coffee. By rights, the station felt, Mrs Layton and her daughters should have been living in Rose Cottage. As it was there was insufficient room there because old Mabel Layton, who had bought the cottage some time in the thirties, shared the place and expenses with Miss Batchelor, a retired missionary (and a born spinster if ever there was one) and both of them seemed destined to live for ever. On the whole, though, one envied the retired people who had their own places, although some of them had been reduced to taking in paying-guests, and as they died off the military requisitioned their bungalows for use as nurses' hostels and chummery messes.

Meanwhile, one coped and made what one could of any occasion that might briefly bring back memories of what life in India had been like before the war. In the heat generated by their expectations of the wedding, warmth was felt for the Laytons as a family and a symbol. One forgave Mrs Layton her vagueness, her forgetfulness, her understandable little indulgences. After all, she was still an attractive woman. Better a few too many chota pegs than the possible alternative.

The news that Teddie Bingham and Sarah Layton were no longer to be seen in each other's company came as a sad disappointment. Hopes that they had merely had a tiff and that a reconciliation would spur them on to a mutual declaration of affection were dashed when Teddie turned up at a club dance as a member of a trio of officers escorting Susan. It was calculated that he had more than his fair share of dances with her, including the last waltz. It was noticed that Sarah was not at the dance at all. Mrs Paynton reported an encounter with Sarah in Jalal-ud-din's shop the morning after and having received − in response to her friendly inquiry after Captain Bingham's health − an evasive reply that was barely polite. As Mrs Paynton said, Sarah Layton had always been punctilious in her observance of the rules laid down for the exchange of pleasantries − although (and perhaps the others would agree with her?) when one came to think of it she had never seemed entirely relaxed. In the present circumstances one had to make allowances. On the other hand perhaps one ought to consider more closely what it was about a girl who consistently lost men to her younger sister. Young men being what they were, nine times out of ten their desertion of Sarah in favour of Susan could be explained readily enough. But Teddie Bingham, surely, had been the one extra time, and ten out of ten suggested there was more to it than Susan's good looks and jolly temperament proving too strong as competition.

'If you ask me,' young Mrs Smalley said − and hesitated because she was never asked and had not been asked now. But she had searched for just such an occasion to make her mark with this group of her elders and betters. So, flushed but deter-mined, she contined − 'the trouble is she doesn't really take it seriously ...'

After an appreciable pause Mrs Paynton inquired, 'Take what seriously?'

'Any of it,' Mrs Smalley said. 'Us. India. What we're here for. I mean in spite of everything. In spite of her − well, what she was brought up to. I mean although men never talk about it they feel it, don't they? I mean in a more direct way than even we do. I think they're more sensitive than women are to, well, people − people like Sarah Layton. I believe that after a while they get a horrible feeling she's laughing at them. At all of us. Oh − I'm sorry. Perhaps I ought not to have said that ...'

There was silence. The ladies looked at one another. Poor Mrs Smalley wished the ground would open and swallow her. She − a Smalley (for what that was worth) had criticized a Layton, in public. And had talked about − *it*. One never talked about *it*. At least not in so direct a way.

Suddenly Mrs Paynton spoke. Mrs Smalley stared at her. She thought she might have misheard. But she had not.

'My dear,' Mrs Paynton had said. 'How extremely interesting.' Now she turned to the others. 'I'm not at all sure Lucy hasn't put her finger bang on the spot.'

Trembling, Lucy Smalley accepted a cigarette from Mrs Fosdick.

'It was last year I first felt it,' she said, having been persuaded to explain in greater detail what she meant when she said Sarah Layton didn't take 'any of it' seriously. 'I mean whenever we talked about all those dreadful things that were going on in places like Mayapore.' When she said 'we' she was speaking figuratively. She had rarely ventured a word herself. Because she had not, she had had more time to watch and listen. Whenever Sarah had been present with Mrs Layton, Mrs Smalley had taken special note of her because Sarah was the one woman in the group Mrs Smalley could treat as junior to herself. 'I thought perhaps she was a bit shy, so I always made a point of talking to her. It was never anything she said, but gradually I couldn't help feeling she was thinking a lot. I thought that sometimes she was bursting to come out with something, well, critical of us. Just as if she thought it was all our fault. And yet not, well, quite that. I mean I don't think she's a radical or anything. I think the best way I can describe it is to say that sometimes she looked at me as if I were, well, not a real person. I mean that's the reaction I had. She made me feel that everything we were saying was somehow a joke to her, the sort of joke she couldn't share.'

Again, the ladies exchanged glances. 'I think I know what you mean, Lucy,' Mrs Paynton said. 'And I think it's something like that, in the back of one's mind you know, that makes one feel even more strongly that it's time she settled down.'

The ladies agreed. Mrs Smalley was conscious that her moment of glory had passed its peak. The others, led by Mrs Paynton, now absorbed her suspicions of Sarah Layton, adapted them, and came to the conclusion that Miss Layton probably didn't mean to give people the impression of having unsound ideas and would be straightened out quickly enough if the right man came along. Perhaps Captain Bingham had been the wrong man. Things might be better for her when that little minx of a sister was married.

Three weeks later when Susan and Teddie took the station by surprise by announcing that they were to be married, Mrs Fosdick declared that a man who could woo one girl, switch his allegiance to her sister and end by marrying her was scarcely to be trusted to remain faithful for long, and that her opinion of the significance of pale eyelashes had therefore been vindicated. The other ladies said that Captain Bingham's choice, wavering though it might seem, was proof of there being something in the Layton girls that appealed to his deepest sensibility and that his final choice as between the two of them showed up even more clearly that the elder girl, although perhaps outwardly possessed of whatever it was that appealed in this way, was inwardly unsatisfactory in this other way that men sensed more quickly than women but which had at last been pinned down as unsoundness, if only of the incipient kind; and when it was noticed that Sarah Layton smiled at Teddie and Susan the idea the ladies might have had that she bore no grudge and took it all like a good soldier was edged out of their minds by this other idea – the faintly disagreeable one that she was smiling at them instead of with them.

All the same, they looked forward to the wedding. When Captain Bingham was posted quite suddenly as a G3 (Operations) to a new divisional headquarters stationed in Mirat, Mrs Fosdick said she wouldn't be in the least surprised if the whole thing now fell through and Susan, with so many other eligible men to choose from, decided she had made a mistake. The Laytons' departure for a late – last-fling-for-Susan – holiday in Srinagar strengthened her belief that Susan would soon find other fish to fry. The final surprise and disappointment came when the Laytons returned early from Kashmir and announced that the wedding, far from being either postponed or cancelled, had been hastened forward and would take place out of Pankot, in Mirat. One felt (the ladies said) that even taking into account the exigencies of war-time, and the fact that Captain Bingham was obviously soon returning to active service in the field, the Layton wedding had taken on a hole-in-the-corner air which it was somehow not easy to forgive.

'I'm not at all sure,' Mrs Paynton announced, 'that Mrs Layton should allow herself to be rushed like this. I get the impression she's really quite upset but is trying not to show it

for the girl's sake. Apparently Susan is coming back to Pankot
with them after the wedding because there'll only be a three-day
honeymoon and after that Captain Bingham is off. You don't
suppose...'

She did not say what was not supposed because she knew the
other ladies must have supposed it already, as she had done, and
rejected the supposition as too outlandish in relation to a Layton
to be considered seriously for a moment – unless, perhaps, the
Layton girl involved had happened to be Sarah. If Mrs Smalley
was right and had put her finger on what was wrong with Sarah
Layton, what was disturbing about her, then one could say that
nothing was beyond the bounds of possibility.

Teddie Bingham's posting to Mirat and his discovery soon after
arrival that if he wanted to get married his bride would have to
come to him, be content with a seventy-two-hour honeymoon
in the Nanoora Hills and prepared to kiss him goodbye as soon
as it was over, were not the only events that threatened to disrupt
the harmonious pattern of the wedding. Susan, somewhat to her
family's surprise, shrugged these disappointments away and said
that anyway being married in Mirat should be fun, especially if
– as was suggested – they stayed beforehand at the palace guest
house. They could go to Ranpur (she said), meet Aunt Fenny
and Uncle Arthur (who was to give her away), and travel to
Mirat as a party. So, provisionally, it was arranged, but soon after
the return from the Kashmir holiday Major Grace informed
them he could not get down to Mirat earlier than the Friday
before the wedding. He had to attend a series of conferences and
there was no getting out of this disagreeable duty. Mrs Layton
said she did not much care for the idea of travelling down and
staying for nearly a week in the guest house without a man to
look after them. Again Susan brushed the objection aside. The
guest house would be perfectly safe. According to Teddie the
Nawab of Mirat had handed it over to the station commander
for the duration, to provide extra accommodation for military
visitors (and their families) and although it wasn't in the cantonment it was in the grounds of the palace and was guarded. 'That
still leaves the train journey,' Mrs Layton pointed out. 'You're
forgetting Teddie's best man,' Susan reminded her. One of
Teddie's friends in Pankot was a man called Tony Bishop,

another old Muzzy Guide wounded in Burma and presently acting as ADC to General Rankin. Tony had already agreed to support him at the wedding. It would be the simplest thing in the world to get General Rankin to give him special leave so that he could go down to Mirat with them.

So Mrs Layton spoke to General Rankin and got his promise to allow Captain Bishop to escort them. But one week before the party was due to leave Tony Bishop went down with jaundice. Mrs Layton visited him in the military wing of the Pankot General Hospital.

'It's no good,' she said, 'he'll be there for three weeks, so now there's no best man. But it's a blow. Of all Teddie's friends Tony Bishop strikes me as the most sensible.'

'Best men are two a penny,' Susan retorted, and went up to Area Headquarters where she put a call through to Teddie at his divisional Headquarters and spoke to him personally. 'He'll get someone in Mirat, probably the man he shares quarters with,' she said when she came back. The remarkable thing, Sarah realized, was that for once Susan had done something herself instead of getting someone to do it for her. Her mother said no more about being unaccompanied on the train. It had never been a serious objection. There were bound to be plenty of officers on their way to Mirat and Susan would only have to stand a few moments on the platform with her mother, Aunt Fenny and Sarah, before a gaggle of subalterns approached them and inquired if any help was needed. Which was precisely what happened.

There were two Mirats: the Mirat of palaces, mosques, minarets, and crowded bazaars, and the Mirat of open spaces, barracks, trees, and geometrically laid out roads with names like Wellesley, Gunnery and Mess. The two Mirats were separated by an expanse of water, random in shape, along one side of which ran the railway and the road connecting them. The water and the gardens south of it were the Izzat Bagh, so-called because the first Nawab declared that Kasims would rule in Mirat until the lake dried up: a fairly safe bet because it had never done so in living memory. But it was a boast, and boasts were always considered dangerous. Providence ought not to be tempted. A man could lose face simply as a result of tempting it. The inhabitants of the city anticipated the worst. Instead, so it was said, for two successive years after the Nawab's announcement the wet monsoon was abnormally heavy and prolonged. When, in the second year, the lake flooded its banks and destroyed the huts of the fishermen, drowning several, people took it as a sign of celestial approval of the reign of the house of Kasim whose honour – or izzat – had been so dramatically upheld. The lake was adopted as a symbol of the Nawab's power, of his fertility, of an assured succession reaching into the far distant future. The mullahs declared the lake blessed by Allah, and the Hindus – eighty per cent of the population – were prohibited from using it even during the festival of Divali. A mosque was erected on the southern shore and a new palace was built with gardens going down to the water. The court poet – Gaffur Mohammed – celebrated the establishment of the new palace and its garden in this verse:

> So you must accept, Gaffur,
> That your words are no more than the petals of a rose.
> They must fade, lose scent, and fall into obscurity.
> Only for a while can they perfume the garden
> Of the object of your praise. O, would they could grow,
> Lord of the Lake, eternally.

It was in these gardens that a guest house in the European palladian style was built in the late nineteenth century, round about the time that a British military cantonment was established with the Nawab's approval in the area north of the lake.

There were two halts for Mirat: Mirat (City) and Mirat (Cantonment). The latter was the first arrived at if you travelled from Ranpur. The mail train was scheduled to reach Mirat (Cantonment) at 07.50 hours but was usually anything between half an hour and one hour later. Having deposited its passengers at Mirat (Cantonment) it took a half-hour rest and then chugged out, at a rate never exceeding 10 mph, negotiating points, junctions and level crossings until it reached the long isolated embankment that separated the lake from the waste land that had once – before the coming of the cantonment – been characteristic of the northern environs of the city. The train crawled along the bleak strip of ground that raised the railway to one level and the trunk road to another, slightly lower, with a kind of reluctance, as if the engine-driver expected subsidence or, anyway, signals showing green that would flash red at the last moment, scarcely leaving him time to apply his brakes. Between the presiding power and the old glory there was, as it were, a sense of impending disaster.

Although the Laytons and Mrs Grace were to stay at the palace guest house it was at Mirat (Cantonment) they alighted, on Teddie Bingham's instructions; 'Make sure,' he had written to Mrs Layton, 'you don't get carried on into the city. Of course I'll be there to meet you, and even if I'm unable to I'll get some-one to do so for me. But I thought it worth mentioning, just in case anything goes wrong, and remembering you're staying at the palace guest house you think you have to travel on into the city itself. No one ever does.'

'Things are looking up,' he said now above the din on the arrival platform. 'You're only twenty-five minutes behind schedule. I've got breakfast organized. I expect you're ready for it.' He pecked the cheek Mrs Layton offered, shook hands with Mrs Grace whom he had met only twice, held Sarah's hand for a prolonged few seconds as if the switch of his affections from her to her sister still needed some explanation, then turned and kissed and held on to pretty little Susan who had an air of being flushed and dishevelled in spite of the fact that not a hair was out of place and she had worked for half an hour on perfecting the pallor she had decided suited her as the wife-to-be of an officer who would soon be away to the war. It was on Teddie's cheeks a flush was actually visible, but he appeared brisk, fully in control of the problems posed by an arrival. The flush seemed to be one of pleasure combined with effort: the pleasure of see-ing his future wife again and the effort he would always put into doing even the most ordinary things right, more especially when there were members of the opposite sex depending upon him for their comfort and safety. He had an Indian NCO in attend-ance whose khaki drill shirt and knee-length shorts stood out from his limbs and body in stiff, starched, knife-edged perfec-tion. The man's pugree was an exotic affair of khaki cloth and diaphanous khaki muslin which gave his otherwise gravely held head a quirk of flirtatiousness and added a note of self-conscious gallantry to the way in which he stood by the open carriage and took charge of the mounds of luggage which the red-turbanned coolies were already fighting over.

'Don't worry about your things,' Teddie Bingham said. 'Noor Hussain's got the luggage *bando* taped,' and having thanked the officers in the adjacent compartment who had looked after Mrs Layton and her party on the journey from Ranpur and were now travelling on south, escorted the ladies through the crowd to the station restaurant, explaining that Noor Hussain would see the luggage safely stowed in a 15-cwt truck and taken to the guest house where they would find it waiting. For personal conveyance he had laid on a couple of taxis, and those too would be waiting directly breakfast was over.

Entering the restaurant behind her mother and Aunt Fenny, but ahead of Susan and Teddie who were obviously conscious of their duty as an engaged couple to stay close, Sarah concentrated on the smells coming from the kitchens. Whatever the day held in store breakfast was a meal she felt it was wise to give her undivided attention to. Once she was seated at the table, the orders given for cornflakes or porridge, egg and bacon, toast and marmalade, the first cup of tea or coffee drunk, and perhaps the first cigarette of the day lighted, she thought she would be able to view the sight of Susan and Teddie sitting together opposite her with more confidence in their future than she felt capable of drumming up at the moment.

There was (Sarah thought) something about Teddie Bingham that didn't wear well. He was not a man who grew on you. In this respect he was like the countless other young men to whom she had been mildly attracted and then lost interest in or lost to Susan with no hard feelings on either side. What was special about Teddie was the fact that Susan had agreed to marry him. Sarah could not understand why. She hoped, but did not believe, that they loved one another. She did not believe it because until they announced their engagement there seemed to have been nothing to distinguish him as a man apart, in the crowd of men round Susan.

'But then,' Sarah thought, 'we all have the same sort of history. Birth in India, of civil or military parents, school in England, holidays spent with aunts and uncles, then back to India.' It was a ritual. A dead hand lay on the whole enterprise. But still it continued: back and forth, the constant flow, girls like herself and Susan, and boys like Teddie Bingham: so many young white well-bred mares brought out to stud for the purpose of coupling with so many young white well-bred stallions, to ensure the inheritance and keep it pukka. At some date in the foreseeable future it would stop. At home you understood this, but something odd happened when you came back. You could not visualize it, then, ever stopping.

She looked across the table at Susan, at her mother, at Aunt Fenny, and remembered her Aunt Lydia saying that India was an unnatural place for a white woman. As a child she had not understood, but had understood since, and agreed with Aunt Lydia that it was. They did not transplant well. Temperate plants, in the hot-house they were brought on too quickly and faded fast, and the life they lived, when the heat had dried them out and left only the aggressive husk, was artificial. Among them, occasionally, you would find a freak in whom the sap still ran. She was thinking of her old Aunt Mabel in Pankot, and of the Manners girl's aunt in Srinagar who, in the midst of their conversation, had suddenly filled her with an alarming sense of her own inadequacy as a human being, so that on returning to her own houseboat she had sat in front of a mirror and stared at herself, wishing she were anything but what her outward appearance proved she was: an average girl whose ordinariness was like a sentence of life imprisonment.

'You are not going to tell us, I hope,' Aunt Fenny said to Teddie when she had taken her place, fussed about a stain on the tablecloth, studied the bill of fare, ordered porridge and poached eggs and returned her spectacles to their red leather pouch, 'that the wedding has to be even earlier, tomorrow for instance, because if so there'll be no one to give Susan away. Arthur simply can't get down until Friday.'

'No, don't worry, Mrs Grace, Saturday it is.'

'What about your best man, Teddie?' Mrs Layton asked.

'It's all fixed. I asked the chap I share quarters with if he'd stand in and he said he'd be glad to. Since then he's been bustling around making sure everything's all right at the guest house. He'll be along after breakfast to help us get sorted out. His name's Merrick. I hope you'll like him.'

'Merrick?' Aunt Fenny repeated. 'It doesn't ring a bell. What is he?'

'A gee-three-eye,' Teddie said, who took so many things literally.

Aunt Fenny turned to Mrs Layton. 'Millie, wasn't there a Merrick on General Rollings's staff in Lahore in thirty-one? It could be the same family.'

'Oh, I don't remember, Fenny. It's all so long ago.'

'Of course you remember. He married one of those awful Selby girls. No. I'm wrong...' Aunt Fenny paused. There was a family joke that Aunt Fenny kept the army List on her bedside table, and still referred to it whenever she gave a party and was in doubt about the seniority of one of her guests and consequently where to seat him and his wife. 'It wasn't Merrick. It was May-rick. I don't know a Merrick. Is he an emergency officer?'

'He got an immediate commission, I gather,' Teddie explained. 'He was in the Indian Police.'

'Isn't that unusual?' Aunt Fenny wanted to know. 'Young Mr Creighton pulled every string there is to get out of the civil and into the army for the duration, but they wouldn't let him go. He told me he'd only heard of one instance of it being allowed and I think that was a case of the poor young man in question absolutely pining away at the prospect of not being in on the shooting and becoming quite useless at his work. Perhaps it was Mr Merrick. What is his first name?'

'Ronald.'

'Ronald Merrick. What rank?'

Teddie looked faintly surprised. 'Captain.'

'My dear boy, I gathered that when you said he was a G3(I). I meant his rank in the police.'

'Oh, that. Superintendent or something, I think.'

'What district?'

'He did tell me. Now what was it? Is there a place called Sunder-something?'

'Sundernagar,' Aunt Fenny pronounced. 'A backward area. Relatively unimportant.' Captain Merrick thus disposed of she smiled blandly.

'Did you enjoy Kashmir?' Teddie asked.

'It was all right. The wrong end of the season and of course we had to cut it short.'

'I know. I'm sorry.'

'We had a vaguely unpleasant experience too. Millie wanted to move our boat up the lake to where she and John spent their honeymoon. There was only one other boat up there and it all seemed quite idyllic, if over-quiet and slightly inconvenient. Unfortunately our neighbour turned out to be someone on whom it was impossible to call. I'll give you three guesses.'

Teddie coloured up in anticipation of hearing something he'd rather not hear in front of Susan. Sarah glanced at her mother who was still reading the menu, apparently not listening. Only her mother knew about her visit to Lady Manners, and only for her mother's sake had Sarah said nothing to the others.

'I give up,' Teddie said.

'Old Lady Manners. And the child –'

'Oh, I see.' His blush deepened.

Mrs Layton put the menu down. 'What is the guest house like, Teddie?'

'I've only seen it from the outside, but the station commander says it's pretty comfortable. Ronald Merrick knows more about it than I do. He's been there a couple of times to check on the bando-bast. Incidentally, you'll have it all to yourselves. It's in the palace grounds and it's staffed by palace servants, but the Nawab's put it at the Station Commander's disposal for the duration, so it's really treated as cantonment territory and there's no need to stand on ceremony.'

'Shall we see the Nawab?' Susan asked.

Teddie assumed his playful expression. 'Why should you want to see the Nawab?'

'Because there was a scandal about him. He fell in love with a white woman and followed her all the way to the South of France.'

'Oh, did he? Who told you that?'

'I did, but I thought everybody knew,' Aunt Fenny said. 'The affair between between the Nawab of Mirat and Madame X or whatever they called her, was quite a *cause célèbre* in the early twenties. She was Russian or Polish and pretended to be of good family, but was probably a lady's maid. I don't know what originally brought her to India but she got her hooks into the Nawab, played him for what he was worth, cried off when he wanted her to marry him as his second wife and scooted back to Europe with the Nawab after her. They ended up somewhere like Nice or Monte Carlo. I remember there was a story about some jewellery which she claimed he'd given her – presumably for services rendered. He threatened legal action and they say this Count Bronowsky acted as go-between – so successfully that the Nawab brought him back and made him his prime minister.'

'Oh yes,' Teddie said. 'I've heard of Bronowsky. He's still around.'

'If he was really a Russian count I'll eat my hat but the Nawab's been under his thumb ever since and he's even dazzled the Political Department, according to Arthur. But then of course he had to, otherwise they'd have made the Nawab get rid of him years ago.'

'You haven't answered my question, Teddie,' Susan reminded him, 'but of course once Aunt Fenny starts it's difficult to get a word in edgeways.'

She smiled at Mrs Grace, but Sarah recognized the hectic little flush spreading over her powdered cheeks as a sign of the temper her sister seemed to find it hard to control whenever she felt even fleetingly neglected. Content, often, to sit and listen and think her thoughts, her most casual remarks or gestures demanded and usually received immediate responses, from women as well as men. Sarah sometimes marvelled at the way Susan could suddenly divert a conversation by throwing into it a comment or a question, and at the way she could then just as suddenly retire from it and leave people disorientated. It was as if she periodically and deliberately sought to test the strength of the impact of her personality.

'I asked,' Susan said, turning back to Teddie, 'whether we shall see the Nawab.'

'I don't know. He's away at the moment but may be back at the weekend. Colonel and Mrs Hobhouse – that's the Station Commander and his wife – say we ought to invite him to the reception, but that it's not certain whether he'll come.'

'Why? Because the reception is to be at the club?'

'No. He's allowed in as a guest, you know. Because of Ramadan. I mean he'll be fasting between sun-up and sundown.'

'I'd like to have a Nawab at my wedding,' Susan said, 'especially one who used to be wicked. Besides, if we make a bit of a fuss of him he'll have to send a wedding present and it might turn out to be a tray of super rubies or a fabulous emerald, or a few spare ropes of pearls.'

Teddie smiled, and glanced affectionately down at her left

hand, at the finger on which she wore his own modest cluster of engagement diamonds. She chose this moment to lean back in her chair, an indication that the others could again talk to each other.

Breakfast came to the table at last.

There were twelve tables in the station restaurant. Sarah counted them. Ten were occupied. The floor was patterned by black and white tiles. The ceiling was high; three four-bladed fans, suspended from it, revolved at half speed. The windows on the platform side were frosted to shut out the sight of trains, travellers and coolies. On one wall there was a portrait of the King-Emperor, George VI, and on another a pre-war poster of invitation to Agra to admire the stale image of the Taj Mahal. The bearers were dressed in white and had cummerbunds of green and black, white gloves and bare feet. At one table two Indian officers, Sikhs, sat together. A nursing officer of the QAIMNS was breakfasting with a captain of Ordnance, an Anglo-Indian girl with a subaltern of the Service Corps. The rest of the customers were British officers. Some had arrived on the 07.50. Others would be waiting for a departure.

And presumably (Sarah told herself) with the exception of the two Sikhs and the little Anglo-Indian girl, we all represent something. And looked at her own family, considering them for the moment as strangers to her, like the rest of the people eating English breakfasts in a flat and foreign landscape. There, she thought, watching Aunt Fenny, is a big-boned, well-fleshed woman. To look at her you'd say she has transplanted better than the thinner, sad-faced woman by her side, but her manner is a shade too self-assured, her voice a shade too loud, and when she stops speaking her mouth sets a shade too grimly, and the first impression that she has transplanted well is overridden by another, the impression that when she finds herself alone she will sit with a far-away look on her face, a look that would be gentle if it weren't for the mouth. However quietly or gently she moves or sits the mouth will stay fixed and grim so that all her thoughts and recollections will enter the room and surround her not with happiness but with regrets and accusations. Which means that even then you would not be able to feel sorry for her. The thinner, sad-faced woman is her sister. They have the same nose and a manner towards each other of intimacy that is neither casual nor closely affectionate and betrays a long but not necessarily deep experience of each other. Their real intimacy was over long ago. It ended with childhood, and was quite likely an intimacy only one of them felt, most likely the sad thin one who uses her hands with a curious vagueness, as if certain gestures which are habit are no longer appropriate because the person they were habitually made to, to express contentment, affection, to establish contact, to claim loyalty, to offer it, is no longer close to her.

Well, she was cheating, Sarah realized. No one looking at her mother could know that about her from her gestures. Would they know the other thing? Would they, by looking at her, be able to tell that the vagueness, the air of slight distraction, was proof – as Sarah knew it was – that Mrs Layton was already, at 8.30 in the morning, beginning to work out how long it would be before she could decently have a drink? You are still attractive, Sarah thought, and you are only forty-five. It is three years since you were with him. And India is full of men. So don't think I don't understand about the bottle in the wardrobe, the flask in your handbag.

She turned to Teddie and Susan. For her, the lightly but firmly sketched portrait of compatibility and pre-marital pleasure in each other's company which they presented in public, carried no conviction. In Teddie, Sarah was conscious of there seeming to be nothing behind his intentions – touchingly good on the surface – that gave them either depth or reality. In Susan she had become aware of a curious aptitude for deliberate performance. Susan was playing Susan and Sarah could no longer get near her. The distance between them had the feeling of permanence because the part of Susan called for a pretty, brown-haired, blue-eyed, flush-cheeked girl who entered, almost feverishly, into the fun and responsibilities of a life Sarah herself believed mirthless and irresponsible. It was mirthless because it was irresponsible, and irresponsible because its notion of responsibility was the notion of a vanished age. The trouble was, she thought, that in India, for them, there was no private life; not in the deepest sense; in spite of their attempts at one. There was only a public life. She looked again at the faces in the restaurant – ordinary private faces that seemed constantly to be aware of the need to express something remote, beyond their capacity to imagine – martyrdom in the cause of a power and a responsibility they had not sought individually but had collectively inherited, and the stiffness of a refusal to be intimidated; group expressions arising from group psychology. And yet they were the faces of people whose private consciousness of self was the principal source of their vitality.

Once out of our natural environment (she thought) something in us dies. What? Our belief in ourselves as people who each have something special to contribute? What we shall leave behind is what we have done as a group and not what we could have done as individuals which means that it will be second-rate.

She lit a cigarette and listened to Teddie and Aunt Fenny talking about Lord Wavell who was to be the new Viceroy and Lord Louis Mountbatten who was to be Supreme Commander of the new South-East Asia Command. Aunt Fenny was saying that it was a mistake to divest GHQ in India of its traditional military role. Teddie said Lord Wavell would make a good Viceroy because he was a soldier and people could trust him. New winds were blowing, but the dust they raised seemed to Sarah to be as stale as ever. Hot coffee was brought, the bearer sent with orders for morning papers: the *Times of India* for Mrs Layton, *The Civil and Military Gazette* for Aunt Fenny; nothing for Susan unless the new edition of *The Onlooker* was out; for Sarah the *Statesman* which Aunt Fenny disapproved of because although it was an English newspaper it was always criticizing Government or GHQ and was currently (she said) exaggerating the seriousness of the famine in Bengal, and blaming everybody for it except the Indian merchants who had hoarded tons of rice and were waiting for the market price to rise to an even more astronomic figure. 'Besides,' she said, 'the Bengalis won't eat anything but rice. There are tons of wheat going begging but they'd rather die than change their damned diet.'

Sarah tapped ash carefully into the glass ashtray and felt put off by the sight of the stub of her previous one, marked red by her lipstick, a sign of her personal private life, her none-too-hopeful message in a bottle cast back up by an indifferent tide on an island on which she sometimes felt herself the only one alive who still wanted to be rescued.

*

They were confronted by a forbidding openness, of water and unabsorbed light, a sort of milky translucence that deadened the nerves of the eyeballs and conveyed the impression that here one would live perpetually with a slight headache.

'There's the palace now,' Captain Merrick said. Sarah heard from her mother a low exclamation that could have been one of admiration or of disappointment. For the moment she herself was blinded by the vast area of sky and water.

'You're looking in the wrong direction, Miss Layton.' His voice was close. He was leaning forward. She had an impression that his fingers had touched her very lightly on the shoulder. The voice was resonant. There was something in its tone that acted as an irritant, although not an unpleasant one. 'I'm not looking in any direction,' she said. She raised her left hand to shade her eyes. 'There's so much glare.'

'I was afraid you'd find that, sitting up front. I'll tell the fellow to stop, then we can change places.'

Sarah shook her head. 'No. I can see the palace now –' Distantly, a dusty-rose-coloured structure with little towers, and a white-domed mosque with one slim minaret on the edge of the lake, reflected in the water – and – among the trees, at the end of the lakeside road they travelled on, a small palladian-style greystone mansion. The guest house.

The lake was on their left. Fishermen were casting nets from long low boats. The nets fell on the water, rippling its glassy surface as if sudden areas of chill were causing patches of gooseflesh.

Again the voice in her ear.

'You see where the reeds begin? That's the boundary of the fishing rights. They're not allowed to work closer to the palace. It's a traditional family occupation, the rights are handed down from father to son. They're quite a proud sect. Muslims, of course.'

Her mother spoke. When Captain Merrick replied his voice was no longer just behind her. He had sat back. But the voice was still resonant. It was a good voice, but not public school. Aunt Fenny had already commented on that fact, in the ladies' room at the station restaurant. 'Of course,' she said, 'you can get some peculiar people in the police. I don't suppose Captain Merrick's family would bear close inspection. But he's quite the little gentleman, isn't he, and terribly efficient over detail. That's a sign of a humble origin, too. Did you hear him tell Teddie the luggage has already arrived at the guest house? That means he called there to make sure, before coming to collect us. How shall we go? You, Susan and Teddie in one taxi, me, Sarah and Captain Merrick in the other?' But Mrs Layton said, 'No, I'll go with Sarah and Captain Merrick. Then I'll feel less like a mother-in-law.' She retired into a cubicle. Susan and Aunt Fenny went out. Sarah waited, gazing at her ordinary face in the mirror, combing her hair which was the same colour her mother's had been before it began to fade and she took to using bleach; a dark blonde, difficult to curl, badly in need of the permanent wave she would have to undergo before the wedding. She hated her hair. She hated her chin and cheekbones. They were too prominent. She repaired her make-up without interest. She envied Susan for having the kind of face that powder and lipstick could alter. Through these her own face always came back at her with a kind of dull incorruptibility, authentic bony Layton, quite unlike the rounder, more gently moulded Muir face. Well, she thought, it would wear better. There was a toughness in the Layton face that weathered storms. Her great-grandfather had had it, her father had had it, and now she had it.

Mrs Layton came out of the cubicle. She had her handbag with her. Through the mirror Sarah saw her mother glance at her, then look away. Without speaking she came across to one of the hand-basins, set her bag down, washed her hands, touched her hair and adjusted her hat. Silences between them were not unusual. They were strange silences which Sarah found difficult to break once they had set in. She sometimes thought of them as silences her mother used to establish between them a closeness that had never existed before and which she thought it too late to establish now except in this exchange of sentences unspoken and of gestures unoffered. There were occasions – and this was one of them – when Sarah felt a surge of almost hysterical – because pent-up – affection for this vague distracted woman who was her mother. The old forthright manner with its edge of sharpness that demanded respect, loyalty, more than it demanded love, was gone. It seemed now that nothing at all was being demanded and nothing given, except whatever casual things they were that were asked and given by habit – and these silences, which seemed to express a need that went much deeper than mere reliance on Sarah to forget she had not been loved as much as Susan and to give the kind of help Susan never could have given.

Following her mother and Aunt Fenny out of the restaurant – but this time in the wake and not the van of Susan and Teddie because Teddie's best-man-to-be had gravitated as if by a force of nature to the role of escorting her, seeing that doors were kept open for her to pass through, that any remark she made would get a suitable response, and of making light and suitable conversation himself should she seem to be in need of cheering up – Sarah remembered how within a few weeks of her arrival in Pankot in 1939 she had decided that India affected Englishmen in two ways: it made them thin and pale or beefy and red. Her father and – potentially – her new escort belonged to the former category, Uncle Arthur and (potentially) Teddie Bingham to the latter. The thin pale Englishmen were reserved and mostly polite to other people, including Indians even when they didn't like them; the red beefy ones acquired loud voices and were given to displays of bad temper in public. Between these two types of opposites there seemed to be no shades of colour or grades of behaviour worth noting. The young men fell potentially into one or the other of these categories directly they set foot in Bombay or went out to their first station. Their pinkness, you saw then, judging by its texture in each individual case, would fade or deepen; their flesh, depending upon built-in things like bone structure and muscle tone, would shrink or thicken; their good nature, according to the amount of self-control needed to sustain it, would become fixed and frozen, or would explode dramatically under the pressure of the climate and their growing inability – Uncle Arthur was a case in point – to take any real pleasure in the company kept.

But one thing was shared in common by these two broadly distinguishable types of men: their attitude to English women. After a time Sarah had been able to analyse it. They approached you first (she decided) as if you were a member of a species that had to be protected, although from what was not exactly clear if you ruled out extinction: it seemed to be enough that the idea of collective responsibility for you should be demonstrated, without regard to any actual or likely threat to your welfare. In circumstances where no threat seemed to exist the behaviour of the men aroused your suspicion that perhaps it did after all but in a way men alone had the talent for understanding; and so you became aware of the need to be grateful to them for the constant proof they offered of being ready to defend you, if only from yourself.

This collective public approach also affected their personal, private approaches. When young men talked to her, danced or played tennis with her, invited her to go riding, to watch them play men's games, to go with them to a show, became amorous or fumbled with her unromantically in the dark of a verandah or a motor-car, she had the impression that they did so in a representative frame of mind. 'Well here I am, white, male and pure-bred English, and here you are pure-bred English, white and female, we ought to be doing something about it.' The potential red beefy types were usually more enthusiastic for doing something about it than the potential thin pale types, but however hot or cold the degree of enthusiasm was Sarah could never feel it as an enthusiasm for her, but instead as an enthusiasm for an ideal she was supposed to share and which the young man in question apparently assumed was a ready-made link, a reliable primary connection between them that might or might not be more intimately strengthened according to taste. The ideal was difficult to define and Sarah had thought she ought to define it before deciding whether she should reject it or uphold it. She certainly had no intention of casually accepting it and becoming thoughtlessly implicated in it, which is what she believed Susan had done.

In the station concourse Sarah said to Captain Merrick, 'Mother would like you to come with us. Teddie can take Susan and Aunt Fenny,' and got her mother into the back of the first taxi. She saw Teddie approaching and wondered whether her mother's objections were not so much to being made to feel like a mother-in-law as to Teddie himself. She said, 'I want to ride in front, Captain Merrick. You go in with Mother.'

The driver was an Indian civilian. He would probably smell. Captain Merrick hesitated, but both doors were open and she got in. Teddie joined them. 'Are you all right?' he asked Mrs Layton. She said she was and told him to look after Susan. A few moments later they were settled and the taxi moved away, out of the shade. The heat coming from the engine and the hot air blowing through the open window combined with the glare and the baked musty stench of the taxi-driver to smother Sarah in that blanketing numbness which, in India, was a defence against the transformation of the illusion of exhaustion into its reality. She half-closed her eyes. They were going down a wide street of arcaded shops – the cantonment bazaar. The jingling harness of horse-drawn tongas, bicycle bells, the sudden blare of Indian music from a radio as they passed a coffee-house were sounds which this morning rubbed the edge of a nerve already raw from the irritation of feeling that everything was going inexorably forward and leaving her behind, that she could not catch up, could not cope. The taxi turned from the bazaar into a wide avenue. Ahead, the centrepiece of a roundabout, was the inevitable statue of the great white queen, Victoria, in profile to them on the line of their approach to it, the head slightly bowed under the weight of the dumpling crown and an unspecified sorrow.

The road was now shaded by trees, lined by the grey-white walls of compounds behind which gardens and old bungalows of military family occupation were occasionally revealed in glimpses of deep shadowy verandahs, patches of sun-struck lawns, beds of the ubiquitous crimson canna lilies. A scent of dew and strange blossom entered on the artificially created breeze and Sarah inclined her head, as if to a narcotic that might lift her spirits.

'We're coming to the church,' Captain Merrick said, and told the driver to slow down when they got to it so that the Mem-sahibs could see it better. His Urdu was fluent.

A greystone spire, Victorian Gothic; a churchyard, and lean-ing palm trees which always reminded Sarah of the India of old engravings. Behind their taxi the other taxi carrying Susan, Ted-die and Aunt Fenny, also slowed. Mrs Layton did not remark on the church. Presently they regained their former speed.

'The chaplain's name is Fox, by the way,' Captain Merrick said, and then began to rehearse the next few days' programme. A small party at the club tonight to introduce them to the General who would be out of station for the wedding itself, and to the Station Commander and his wife. Dinner at the Station

Commander's the following evening which the Chaplain would certainly attend. The G1 and his wife, the Station Commander and his wife, would have to be invited to the wedding. Teddie and Mrs Layton could work out between them who else among Teddie's fellow-officers and who else on the station should be invited. The club contractor was working on the basis of a small reception catering for between twenty and thirty people. Had Mrs Layton managed to get the cards printed in Ranpur? If not the printer Lal Chand who printed and published the *Mirat Courier* could produce them in twenty-four hours. The tailor Mrs Layton had mentioned in a letter to Teddie had been told to be at the guest house at midday to receive preliminary instructions. The steward in the guest house was under the control of the station staff officer, and would present the bill for meals and drinks at the end of their stay. Captain Merrick understood that these would be approximately at club prices. The rest of the guest house staff was supplied by the palace and there was no charge for accommodation, services or laundry other than personal laundry, all of which were to be accepted as part of the hospitality of the Nawab of Mirat to members of the services visiting the cantonment and unable to get accommodation in the club or the Swiss Hotel. The guest house was in the grounds of the palace, but there was a private way in and a separate compound. The private entrance, like the main entrance, was under armed guard, and there was a chaukidar. A palace motor-car would, Captain Merrick believed, be put at their disposal to help with things like shopping trips, and other motors from the palace garage would be lent for the wedding itself.

'I think that's about all, Mrs Layton, except that there's a young fellow who's distantly related to the Nawab and whose job it is to see that you have everything you need. He's an Indian, of course, a Muslim, and I think you'll like him. His name is Ahmed Kasim and he's a son of Mohammed Ali Kasim, the Chief Minister in the provincial government of 'thirty-seven to 'thirty-nine.'

'M A K? But isn't he locked up?' Mrs Layton asked.

'Exactly, that's the point. I mean it's something I think necessary to remember when dealing with young Kasim. He's an attractive young fellow, well-educated, speaks first-rate English, not in the least the usual surly type of Westernized Indian who thinks he's a cut above everybody – and believe me I've had some experience with that sort –'

Mrs Layton said, 'Yes, I'm sure you have. Teddie tells us you were in the police. My sister is dying to hear how you managed to get out of that uniform into this. She knows a young man in the Civil who's tried everything but still hasn't managed to swing it. Were you ever in Ranpur?'

'Yes, some years ago, in a very junior capacity.'

'And before your army commission?'

'I was DSP Sundernagar.'

'Ah yes. We lived there once. Rather a remote district. Was there much trouble there last year?'

'No, very little. Fortunately. It helped me persuade the powers that be that I could be more usefully employed.'

Presently Mrs Layton said, 'You were telling us about Mr Kasim's son.'

'Yes, I was.' A further hesitation. 'I don't quite know how to put this. In Ranpur he'd present no problem, but this is native sovereign territory and as a representative of the palace young Kasim is entitled to – well, certain consideration. One can't just treat him as a sort of errand-boy. The State's barely more than the size of a pocket-handkerchief but it's run on very democratic lines and has a tradition of loyalty to the crown. One of the Nawab's sons is an officer in the Indian airforce and of course the Nawab handed his private army over to GHQ on the first day of the war. It was mustered into the Indian Army as the Mirat Artillery, and got captured by the Japs in Malaya. In other words, officially the military in Mirat take an extremely good view of the Nawab.'

'And of all his entourage, including Mr Kasim. Oh, we promise to be well behaved.'

Presently Captain Merrick said, 'I beg your pardon, Mrs Layton. I've put everything very clumsily. The point I intended to make was that friendly and co-operative though Kasim is on the surface, it's as well to treat him cautiously as well as considerately because it would be unnatural if he didn't resent us a bit.'

'We probably shan't have time to let it worry us, Captain Merrick.'

'No.'

And then, suddenly, they had left the avenue of trees behind and were driving alongside the lake. Dazzled, Sarah heard his voice: 'There's the palace now,' her mother's low exclamation and then his voice again, close to her ear. 'You're looking in the wrong direction, Miss Layton.'

Beyond the reeds the lake curved away and the road became splashed again by shade from old banyan trees. A high brick wall, topped by jagged bits of broken glass, had come in from the left. The taxi was slowing. Ahead, a culvert marked the private entrance to the guest house. There was nothing to be seen of it, nothing to see at all apart from the long straight road which eventually led – Captain Merrick said – through the waste ground into the old city of Mirat. There were walls on both sides of the road now. They turned in through an open gateway. A grey-bearded sepoy with a red turban and red sash round the waist of his khaki jacket came to attention. The taxi continued along a gravel drive that was flanked on either side by bushes of bougainvillaea and curved towards the left. The bushes thinned, there were patches of grass, and through trees a glimpse of rose-coloured stone.

'Do you know,' Mrs Layton said, 'it reminds me of the drive up to grandfather's old place.'

'But that was all laurel and rhododendrons,' Sarah pointed out, remembering – none too clearly – her great-grandfather's house which she had last seen the year of his death, as a child of twelve.

'The effect is the same.'

Sarah did not agree but did not say so, content anyway that her mother had settled momentarily into the kind of nostalgic mood that suggested the actual arrival would go well, although later that night there might be a hint of tearfulness at lonely bed-going – a whiteness under the rouge unfashionably applied low instead of high on the cheeks, an inner disintegration betrayed by a marginal relaxation of the muscles of the jaw and neck that produced a soft little pad of tender ageing flesh under the courageous chin. Presently held high (as Sarah saw, looking over her shoulder) to receive a dab or two from the puff of a compact, there were, in its structure, the presentation to the world, signs of effort-in-achievement. Almost unconsciously bringing her hand up to stroke her own chin and neck in a gesture partly nervous and partly investigatory she marvelled at the havoc a few years would wreak on flesh so firm. There came a time when the face changed for ever, into its final mould. Hers had not done so, but her mother's had. Some faces then went all to bone, others went to slack, fallen, unoccupied folds and creases of skin. Her mother's would do that, and perhaps Susan's too, years hence. Her own would tauten. As an old woman she would probably have a disapproving but predatory look. Her mother would go on softening whereas she herself would harden exteriorly, become brittle interiorly. She would break into a thousand pieces, given the right blow. To kill her mother in old age would be a bloodier, more fleshy, less splintery affair. Her mother was protected already by incipient layers of blubber (like Aunt Fenny, but unlike Aunt Lydia). All the more credit to her therefore, Sarah thought, that she managed to convey a certain steeliness from within the softness.

Even at the most exasperating moments Sarah could feel, for her mother, a surge of love and deep affection that sprang goodness knew not from a long uninterrupted experience of her as a mother – the separation had been too long for that – but rather from a sensation of being able to treat her as if she were a human being towards whom she had a duty that was scarcely filial at all: almost as if she were a stranger of a kind suddenly encountered. She felt such a surge now, but as usual was unable to express it because her mother was not even looking at her, but putting the compact away. Well, so it goes, Sarah thought. And so it went: the taxi moving slowly through a tunnel of alternating bars of sunlight and strips of shadow and then coming out abruptly into the gravelled forecourt where the NCO with the diaphanous pugree stood by the side of the parked fifteen hundredweight that had brought their luggage. They drove in under a shadowy porticoed entrance and drew up at the bottom of a shallow flight of steps. At the head of the steps two men were waiting. As Captain Merrick spoke they were joined by a third.

'The chap in the scarlet turban is Abdur Rahman. He's head bearer and belongs to the Nawab. The little fellow holding his topee is the steward, his name's Abraham – an Indian Christian. He's the SSO's chap. And yes – there's Mr Kasim.'

Sarah, looking up, saw Ahmed emerge from the dark interior.

*

'Was it wise?' she heard her Aunt Fenny asking, and recognized her mother's first-drink-of-the-day voice: 'Was what wise?'

'Letting her go riding alone with Mr Kasim.'

'I didn't let her as you call it. I didn't know.'

'Didn't know? You mean she just sneaked off?'

'Oh, Fenny, what's wrong with you? My daughters don't sneak off. They go. They don't have to ask permission. They're of age. They do what they like. One gets married. The other goes riding. How am I supposed to stop them? Why should I try?'

'You're becoming impossible to talk to sensibly. You know perfectly well why it's unwise for Sarah to ride alone with an Indian of that kind.'

'What kind?'

'Any kind, but especially Mr Kasim's kind.'

Sarah said, 'What of Mr Kasim's kind, Aunt Fenny?' and shaded her eyes from the glare of the lake that at midday always seemed to penetrate the shade of the deep porticoed terrace on which her mother and aunt were sitting, on chairs set back close to one of the open french windows which gave access to the terrace from the darkened sitting-room, and through which she had now stepped. She could not see the expressions on her aunt's or mother's face, and did not join them. She stood near them, gazing at the lake, letting that milky translucence work its illusion of detaching her from her familiar mooring in a world of shadow and floating her off into a sea of dangerous white-hot substance that was neither air nor water.

'I'm sorry,' Aunt Fenny said. 'I didn't know you were listening. I was saying I thought it unwise for you to ride alone with Mr Kasim.'

From the midst of that buoyant, dazzling opacity she said, 'Yes, I agree — it was unwise.' When they returned the syce had been waiting. He followed them round to the gravel forecourt below the terrace on which she presently stood and held her horse's head while she dismounted. Mr Kasim dismounted too. 'Come in and have some breakfast,' she suggested. He thanked her and said, 'Some other time perhaps,' asked her if there was anything special that either she or her family wanted to do, to see, or to have him bring or make arrangements for. 'No, I don't think so,' she said, 'thank you for taking me riding.' She wondered whether for some reason or other they should shake hands. He remounted, touched his topee with the tip of his crop and brought the horse's head round — all, as it were, in the same capable movement. As she came on to the terrace she listened to the sound of the hooves on the gravel.

'We shan't go riding again,' she said and lowered her head, turned, looked at Aunt Fenny and found the older woman's face set in that extraordinary mould that was the answer to the need to express something beyond the private emotional capacity to understand.

Sometimes she hated Aunt Fenny, mostly she was irritated by her. For the moment she felt inexplicably close to her and to her mother who had her eyes closed, one hand at rest on the arm of the wicker chair, the other clasping a half-empty glass of gin and lemon, apparently waiting for the day to come into its familiar focus as one totally indistinguishable from any other.

Well, they are my family, Sarah told herself. I love them. They are part of my safety and I suppose I'm part of theirs.

'What happened?' Aunt Fenny asked. Her voice, normally rich and well-risen, sounded flat and dry.

'Nothing happened. I meant it was unwise because it made us both self-conscious. It never occurred to me that it might. It wasn't until we actually set out that I realized it was the first time I'd been alone with an Indian who wasn't a servant. And there seemed to be nothing to talk about. He only spoke when spoken to and kept almost exactly the same number of paces behind me from start to finish.'

The stiffness had left Aunt Fenny's face but this softening only emphasized the lines that years of stiffening had left permanently on her, the private marks of public disapproval.

And what I remembered on the way back (Sarah thought, half-considering this face that was Aunt Fenny's but also that of an English woman in India) was the luggage in the little cabin, with that girl's name on it. She was never real to me until I saw the luggage. She was a name in a newspaper, someone they talked about in Pankot. She began to be real when I saw the luggage in the houseboat in Srinagar. The child must belong to the Indian they said she was in love with, otherwise why should that old lady keep it? But it might have been any half-caste baby. The luggage was different. It was inert. It belonged only to her.

She was no longer alive to claim it, but this is what brought her to life for me. And this morning as I rode home, a few paces ahead of Mr Kasim, she was alive for me completely. She flared up out of my darkness as a white girl in love with an Indian. And then went out because – in that disguise – she is not part of what I comprehend.

'He is a perfectly pleasant young man,' Aunt Fenny said, 'and I understand his brother is an officer. But these days one simply can't tell what these young Indians are up to, let alone what they're thinking.'

'Perhaps they find the same difficulty in regard to us.'

'Yes, perhaps they do. But on the whole, my dear, we ought not to let that concern us. We have responsibilities that let us out of trying to see ourselves as they see us. In any case it would be a waste of time. To establish a relationship with Indians you can only afford to be yourself and let them like it or lump it.'

'Yes,' Sarah said. 'I suppose you're right. But out here are we ever really ourselves?'

III

There was, to begin with, the incident of the stone.

Apart from the black limousine travelling some seventy-five or hundred yards behind a wobbling bicycle ridden by an Indian carrying a raised umbrella as a protection against glare, there was no traffic on Gunnery Road; neither were there any visible pedestrians at the place where the incident occurred – the Victoria roundabout where a car coming down Gunnery Road and wishing to turn into Church Road had to slow down and describe a three-quarter circle round the monument. The driver of the limousine, an elderly man with a grey beard and wearing palace livery, having passed a file of peasant women with baskets on their heads going in the opposite direction, then began to concentrate on the cyclist and the possible obstacle he repre-sented. He began to decelerate. Gunnery Road and the three other roads meeting at the roundabout were well shaded by big-branched thick-boled trees. The wobbling cyclist turned left. The way now seemed clear for the driver of the limousine to negotiate the roundabout, but encroaching age and several minor accidents had made him cautious, distrustful of what an apparently empty street might suddenly conjure in the shape of fast-driven vehicles.

The sound, when it came, did not immediately register. He allowed the limousine to continue to glide towards a point on the roundabout where he would be able to see what threatened from the left and how clear it was to the right. When the sound did register he braked, stared at the bonnet and the windscreen, then twisted round to confront the pane of glass dividing him from his passengers and, finding it unblemished, only then looked through it.

The passengers, both British officers, were thrust back hard, each into his separate corner. Their arms were still held in half-defensive attitudes. They were looking from floor to window to floor and to the space between them on the seat: as one might look for some suspected poisonous presence – a snake for instance. The last thing the driver noticed was the shattered window on the nearside of the car – not the window in the door, which was lowered, but the fixed window that gave the passenger a clear view. It took the driver several seconds to realize that neither officer could have broken it, that something had been thrown. At this point both officers came to life, shouted something at him, each opened a door and jumped out. One word, one idea – half formed into the shape of an image actually seen – came into the driver's head. Bomb. He had heard of such things happening, but had no experience of them. He opened his own door, stumbled out and found himself climbing marble steps. He missed his footing, fell and lay motionless with his hands covering his head, waiting for the explosion.

After a while he sat up. Above him loomed the plinth on which the White Queen sat, hardened and sensitive, gazing up the length of Gunnery Road, which was still empty of traffic. The file of village women, now some four hundred yards away, continued their journey uninterruptedly. Turning he found both officers standing in the road a few feet from the car. They were looking towards and making gestures at the low grey stucco wall that marked the boundary of a compound. One of them had a handkerchief held to the left side of his face. They stopped looking at the wall and looked at him.

'Sahib,' he said to the one without the handkerchief, after he had picked himself up, walked down the steps and approached them, 'I thought you jumped out because a bomb had been thrown.'

The officer did not smile. He had blue eyes. The driver was always fascinated by Sahibs with blue eyes. The eyes of the other Sahib were not so blue, hardly blue at all, but he had very pale eyelashes. There was blood on the handkerchief.

He followed the Sahibs back to the car and watched while they looked at the shattered window and into the back. He went round to the offside door and helped them to look. He did not know what he was looking for. An object of some kind. He found the object wedged in a corner under one of the tip-up seats. He picked it up. A stone. He said, 'Sahib, this is it.' He handed it to the Sahib with the blue eyes. The Sahib took and showed it to the other Sahib.

Presently the unwounded Sahib looked across at him and said, 'Did you see who threw this?'

'I saw no one, Sahib. Only the women with the baskets but we had gone many yards past them before it was thrown. The person who threw it must have hidden behind that tree, Sahib. There may have been such a man. I do not know. My mind was not on this kind of matter. There was a man on a bicycle in front of the car. He was not making signals. My mind was on this man on the bicycle. He is gone. He went to the left. I did not see any other man. I am sorry, Sahib. It is not an auspicious beginning.'

'You're damned right it isn't,' Teddie Bingham said. 'For God's sake, Ronnie, is there any blood on my uniform?'

'It'll sponge out. Let me have a look at that cut.'

Teddie took the handkerchief from his cheek. Blood oozed out of a jagged cut below the cheekbone. Captain Merrick clapped the handkerchief back on.

'It may need a stitch and there may be glass in it.'

'But, Christ, there isn't time.'

'You can't get married bleeding like a stuck pig. Come on. Get back in and mind you don't sit on a splinter or you'll really be in trouble. When we get to the church I'll root out the chaplain and use his phone to get a doctor. There may be time to ring through and warn Susan and Major Grace. It'll mean putting the ceremony back a few minutes.'

Before sitting Merrick inspected his own and Teddie's side of

the seat for splinters, then told the driver to get on quickly to
the church.

'The bloody bastard,' Teddie said. 'Whoever it was. Bugger
him and bugger the Nawab. And bugger his bloody limousine.'

'Why?'

'Well, it's obvious, isn't it? A crest on the door as big as your
arse. A bloody open invitation for some bolshie Nawab-hating
blighter to heave a bloody great rock through the window.'

Merrick smiled; and was silent, contemplating the stone
which he held balanced on the palm of his right hand.

Nawab Sahib was having the frayed end of his coat sleeve
trimmed when Count Bronowsky told him there had been an
incident involving one of the motor-cars on loan to the wedding party. The car, a 1926 Daimler, once the property of the
late Begum, had been struck by a stone as it turned into Church
Road at the Victoria roundabout. A window had been shattered
and Captain Bingham cut on the cheek. The other occupant
of the car, a Captain Merrick, was unhurt. He had telephoned
the information through to Ahmed Kasim from the chaplain's
house where Captain Bingham was receiving attention from a
medical officer. The ceremony had been delayed for half an
hour and the reception at the Gymkhana Club would now
begin at 11.15 instead of at 10.45. There was therefore no need
to hurry.

Nawab Sahib, who was standing patiently in the middle of
the room – his left arm held out while his personal body-
servant snipped stray bits of thread from his cuff – glanced at
Bronowsky. The Count was dressed in a starched cream linen
suit, cream silk shirt and dove-grey silk tie. He had his best
ebony gold-topped cane to lean on. The Nawab then looked
at young Ahmed who wore a grey linen jacket and trousers,
noticeably less expensive but quite well cut and properly
pressed.

The silent inspection over, the Nawab returned his attention
to the make-and-mend operation on his own coat, and said,

'Has a substitute car been sent?'

'It was offered but declined. Captain Merrick insists the
damaged one is perfectly serviceable.'

'Has the chief of police been informed?'

'Ahmed has telephoned him, your Highness.'

'Will he think to make contact with the military police in the cantonment? Or will he rush about in the city arresting every likely culprit?'

The questions, recognized by the Count as rhetorical, were left unanswered. Ali Baksh, the chief of police in Mirat, was currently under the cloud of the Nawab's unpredictable but cautious displeasure. Another reason for Bronowsky saying nothing was his understanding that the Nawab's composure was deceptive and so best left untampered with. Bronowsky had trained the Nawab to think of himself as a man who had to deny himself the luxury of violent criticism, even of expressing an opinion about anything except strictly personal matters, and who had a duty to the one million people he ruled never to leap to a conclusion or take any unconsidered action. But Bronowsky knew that although the Nawab had so far made no comment on the incident of the car his sense of outrage had been disturbed and fired.

Bronowsky smiled. Within sight of the end of his own reign he allowed himself the full pleasure of self-congratulation. Nawab Sahib had been transformed, step by painful step, from a tin-pot autocratic native prince of extravagant tastes and emotions into the kind of ruler-statesman whose air of informed detachment and benign loftiness was capable of leaving even the wiliest mind guessing and the coldest heart warmed briefly by curiosity; and wily minds and cold hearts were the combination Bronowsky found most common in English administrators. Nawab Sahib was Bronowsky's one and only creation, his life-time's invention. He had fallen possessively in love with him and watched with compassion the struggle Nawab Sahib sometimes had to discipline himself to act and move – and think – in the ways Bronowsky had taught him.

Nawab Sahib removed his arm from the gentle support of the servant with the scissors and inspected the cuff. His private austerities were the last remarkable flowering of Bronowsky's design for a prince; remarkable because Bronowsky had not planned them. For Bronowsky, the austerities were to his design what the unexpected, seemingly inspired and unaccountable stroke of the brush could sometimes be to a painting, the stroke that seemed to have created the need for itself out of the combined resources of the canvas and the man who worked on it, and so was definitive of the process of creation itself and of the final element of mystery in any work of art.

The frayed cuff coats were not worn with the bombast of a rich miser, and it was difficult to say what emotion it was, precisely, that a man felt when he first noticed the spotless but threadbare cloth of the long-skirted high-necked coats, the clean but cheap and floppy trousers, the clean bare feet in old patched sandals or polished down-at-heel shoes; but Bronowsky believed that a major part of that response was made up of respectful wariness, much the same – possibly – as one's response would normally be to the sight of a gentleman down on his luck, but without the measure of pity and contempt such a condition evoked. The Nawab was rich enough for any but the most exaggerated taste. He was surrounded by proofs of his public comfort and of his private generosity. His austerities were reserved wholly for himself. They appeared at once as the badge of his right to lead a personal, private life and as evidence of how spare such a life had to be when so much of his interest and energy was expended for the benefit of the people it was his inherited duty to protect and privilege to rule. And it was this – the duality of meaning to be read into the Nawab's appearance – and the fact that the appearance was not deliberately assumed, that excited in Bronowsky the special tenderness of the artist for his creation. The austerities had been gradual, so that neither Nawab Sahib nor Bronowsky had ever commented on them. Equally gradual, Bronowsky supposed, had been the growth of dandyism in himself. It was as though the love that existed between him and the Nawab had exerted an influence to make them opposites, but what pleased him more was the realization that when they were together the comparative splendour of his own plumage looked like that of a slightly more common species. People, observing them, would be less inclined to believe what they heard – that Bronowsky was the power behind the throne. In Bronowsky, pride in what he had made was stronger than personal vanity. It was part of his pride that Nawab Sahib alone should be credited with the talents and capabilities Bronowsky had worked hard to train him to acquire and exercise.

He believed that Nawab Sahib was quite unconscious of there being any particular meaning to read into his habit of wearing old and inexpensive clothes. The Nawab had said once as they were preparing to go out on a public occasion for which Bronowsky had arrived dressed in his uniform of Honorary Colonel, Mirat Artillery (a uniform he had designed himself and which incorporated certain decorative flourishes reminiscent of the uniform of the old Imperial Guard to which Bronowsky had never belonged): 'Sit low in the carriage, Dmitri. Otherwise how will they tell that it is not you who is Nawab?'

'Should I sit higher than a man can sit, your Highness,' Bronowsky said, 'they would still know I was but Bronowsky. A wazir must dress to do honour to the State and the Nawab Sahib is the State. His raiment is Mirat.'

The Nawab smiled: the same slow, grave smile that had been one of the persuasions the Russian felt to follow the small, lost, dark-skinned man of passion, sorrows and absurdities to his curious little kingdom in an alien land. And since the occasion of this particular courtly exchange Bronowsky had noticed how whenever he entered a room where the Nawab stood the Nawab said nothing until he had taken in at one short or prolonged glance – depending on the amount there was to scrutinize – the details of his wazir's dress and accessories. The ritual had become one he felt the Nawab depended on for reassurance. For some time Bronowsky had encouraged Ahmed also to take an interest in his clothes (or, anyway, to submit to directions and suggestions because interest in anything seemed to be something Ahmed was incapable of taking, unless visits to the Chandi Chowk could be counted as an interest as distinct from a compulsion).

That Ahmed should find increasing favour in the eyes of the Nawab was a continuing concern of Bronowsky's present policy, one of whose objects was the marriage of Ahmed to the Nawab's only daughter, Shiraz, whom the late Begum had brought up, out of spite, in a rigidly traditional manner, with the result that Shiraz, after her mother's death, would not come out of the seclusion she had been taught to regard as obligatory for a woman. Her mother had died just before Shiraz reached the age of puberty, and so she had never gone officially into purdah. The Nawab, urged by Bronowsky, had withheld his permission for that step to be taken; but the girl was so timid her father did not have the heart to follow Bronowsky's advice further and insist on her adopting the modern ways of the palace. She was now sixteen, virtually untutored, and proved to be tongue-tied in the presence of strangers on the few occasions Bronowsky had succeeded in persuading the Nawab to command her out of her self-made zenana to pay her respects to visitors Bronowsky considered important. She had been taught by her mother to regard the wazir as an ogre, a man who had her father in thrall and whose private life was so wicked as to be unspeakable; and it was only with patience that he had gradually succeeded in removing from her mind the idea that simply to look him in the eye was tantamount to gazing at the Devil. Mostly, denied the privacy of the veil, she kept her eyes downcast and fled to the security of her rooms at the first hint that she had done her duty.

The sad thing, Bronowsky thought, was that she was ravishingly pretty. He assumed – because neither the Nawab nor either of his two sons was handsome – that this prettiness, like the perverted desire to hide it, was a legacy from her mother. Bronowsky had never been permitted to see the Begum. She submitted him to long and unkind interrogation from behind a purdah-screen which left him no notion of her except what could be gathered from strong whiffs of expensive imported perfumes, the glint of rich silks and brocades through the tiny carved apertures, and the harshness of a high-pitched voice in which passion, cruelty and bitchiness were in roughly equal proportions. From such one-sided interviews Bronowsky would retreat confirmed in his hatred of women, raging impotently against the enormity of their abuse of the moral weapons God had mistakenly given them as armour against the poor savage male and his ridiculous codes of honour. Sometimes, looking at Shiraz – a dark red blush under the pale brown skin of her cheeks, her eyes downcast, the fabric of her saree shimmering not from reflections but from the trembling underneath – Bronowsky wondered how much of her mother's temperament was concealed there and what it would take to release it and make some man's life – Ahmed's for instance – a misery. He comforted himself with the belief that the Begum, from all accounts, had always been a strong-willed woman and that what she had taught her daughter, once untaught, would release a temperament no more like the Begum's than the two sons' temperaments were like their father's.

Bronowsky thought little of either son. Both had eluded his

influence. Mohsin, the elder, the future Nawab, product of the English tutors and public-school-style college Bronowsky had agreed to early on as a sop to the Political Department, had acquired the pompousness of the English without the saving grace of their energy and without that curious tendency to iconoclasm which they called their sense of humour. He spent most of his time in Delhi, worthily and dully engaged in what he called his business interests, and as little as possible in Mirat, a place which his Westernized wife despised as socially backward. The younger, Abdur, similarly schooled, had acquired different English characteristics. He was a harmless young man who had graduated from an absorbing interest in cricket which he played badly to an equally absorbing interest in aeroplanes which he had not yet succeeded in learning to fly to the satisfaction of the Air Force.

Bronowsky admitted to himself that part of the reason for his letting the education and shaping of Mohsin and Abdur become the concern of others was to be found in the fact that neither of them had ever been well-favoured in appearance or manner. He thought, though, that it had been just as well. Their plainness and physical awkwardness had enabled him to concentrate the whole of his emotional impulse on the task of making a Nawab. A couple of handsome, active youths on hand could have caused his mind and will to wander in the bitter-sweet region mapped by his inclinations, explored by his imagination, but never – for many years – entered into. The discipline and self-denial involved in voluntary withdrawal from direct physical satisfaction of his needs had not been undergone only in order that he should never be guilty of corrupting another. He had come to recognize that the type of youth who attracted him was one whose attributes were wholly masculine and who therefore was attracted exclusively to women. The first sign that this was not necessarily so destroyed, for Bronowsky, the romantic fervour and loving admiration a young man could inspire in him, and left behind it only what he found grotesque. The man he could embrace was not the man for him. It had been as simple as that. The cessation of sexual activity had not been onerous. His affairs with men had been few: three in the twenty-one years between his nineteenth and fortieth birthdays. Physically there had been no women in his life.

Now, approaching seventy, he did not regret chances missed or opportunities wasted. He believed that if he had been born a woman he would have loved one man long, devotedly and faithfully. But having been born a man he did not now crave to have been blessed with normal appetites. He thought that anyway he had experienced to an extent few could claim the joy as well as the pain of loving unselfishly, from afar. He did not delude himself into supposing that his affection for Ahmed was the sentimental longing of an old bachelor for a son. He faced the truth. Ahmed was the latest manifestation of the unattainable, unattempted golden youth who came, sweetened the hour with his presence, and went unmolested into the arms of a deserving Diana, so that the whole world sang and the day was properly divided from the night. It amused him that this golden youth was brown, and touched him that in his old age the object of his undeclared and regulated passion should be someone his professional interest allowed a close connection with. It was as though the old Gods of the forest had rewarded him for his abstentions. He treated the reward with almost excessive care, conscious of the need to balance his emotional with his worldly judgment. Ahmed had become a feature of the policy he was formulating. It was a bonus that he filled so well Bronowsky's personal need: a bonus and a snare. It would never do to confuse the policy with the need or the need with the policy. And Bronowsky knew that if the interests of the need and the policy came into conflict for any reason, it was Ahmed who would be sacrificed because the policy, through all its shifts and changes to adapt to circumstances, was pre-determined by one thing that never altered: Bronowsky's devotion to his Prince.

'It is not auspicious,' the Nawab said. And sat down. 'A stone?'

'A stone, Sahib.'

'At one of the motor-cars?'

Bronowsky inclined his head. He motioned Ahmed to leave them. When Ahmed had gone the Nawab indicated a chair and said in the low voice Bronowsky automatically registered as a sign of special self-control, 'Please sit.' Bronowsky did so. He rested both hands on the gold knob of his cane. His white panama was on his lap. The Nawab sat with folded hands and crossed ankles, leaning his weight on his left elbow. The arms of the chair were carved with diminutive lion heads at the protruding tips. The room was dark from the closed shutters. A slanting column of sunlight, admitted by the gap between one set of shutters left partly open, fell just short of the Nawab's chair. The room was overfurnished. There was a preponderance of potted palms. Strangers coming to the palace were sometimes disturbed by a resemblance they could not quite give a name to. Only the elderly and well-travelled hit easily upon the explanation. The public rooms were furnished in the manner of a plush and gilt hotel of pre-Great War vintage on the Côte d'Azur. Only the dimensions of the rooms, the arched windows, the fretted stone screens, some of the mosaics and the formal courtyard around which the main part of the palace was built remained Moghul in spirit and appearance.

'I'm afraid I do not understand this incident of the stone, Dmitri.'

'No,' Bronowsky agreed. 'It is a puzzle.'

'It is ten years since a stone was thrown.'

Bronowsky nodded.

The Nawab looked towards the window.

'It was thrown at the Begum.'

Bronowsky nodded. He remembered the occasion well. It had enlivened his convalescence from a bout of gastroententis that laid him low for a week, an illness which his servants attributed to his having been given coffee and cakes during an interview in the Begum's apartment.

'From what young Kasim tells me,' the Count said, 'I believe it is one of the late Begum's motor-cars the stone was thrown at this morning.'

'Is that significant?'

'I should not think so – unless the culprit is a madman.'

'Do we understand correctly that he wasn't apprehended, and that there is no information about him at all?'

'That seems to be correct, Nawab Sahib.'

'Then it is unlikely that he will be caught.'

'Very unlikely.'

'One man alone is not usually responsible for such an incident. It is the kind of activity several people decide. Several decide. One acts. But this is relatively unimportant. What is important is to know why the stone was thrown.'

'May I suggest we put it another way, Sahib, and ask ourselves at whom, or even at what, the stone was thrown? If we can answer that the answer to the question why it was thrown probably follows.'

'Very well. At whom or at what was the stone thrown?'

'We know it was thrown at the car, but whether at the car or the occupants is the beginning of the puzzle. Let us assume it was thrown at the car. The car bears your Highness's crest. The symbolism would then be inescapable. Ergo – the stone was thrown at your Highness. The thrower may even have thought your Highness was riding in the car. But as you say, a stone has not been thrown for ten years and when it was thrown it was thrown at the Begum. Your Highness has never been subjected to any kind of personal or even symbolic attack. And it is Ramadan. A Muslim subject would not throw a stone during Ramadan. Your Highness's Hindu subjects are content. Those areas of the State of Mirat which suffered a poor crop are being assisted effectively by the Famine Relief Commission. Your Highness and I spent a week together in Gopalakand meeting the new Resident. I returned ahead, nothing untoward was reported to me when I returned. Your Highness was greeted on your own return last night at the station with the usual loyal address and popular demonstration. Ergo – let us assume from all this evidence that the stone was not thrown at the car but at the occupants.'

'Who are –?'

'Captain Bingham and Captain Merrick, both – so Ahmed tells me – staff officers in the divisional headquarters recently formed, temporarily stationed in Mirat, and due to leave in the middle of next week for special training prior to active duty in the field. In other words, officers without any military or administrative employment in the cantonment as such, detached from local affairs, virtually strangers to the population.'

'But British officers all the same, Count Sahib.'

'Quite so.'

'An anti-British demonstration –' The Nawab frowned. 'In which case, also an anti-palace demonstration. The wedding party are our guests.'

'We can't assume that the man who threw the stone at British officers riding in a limousine knew that they were on their way to a wedding, Sahib. Nor that the ladies in the wedding party have been staying at the guest house.'

'This nevertheless is the situation. The stone was thrown at our guests.'

'Beg pardon, Sahib. Captain Bingham is not a guest. He is the groom.'

'That is worse. It is a great mischief. They have given me a beautiful gift. We reply with a stone.'

'It happened in the cantonment, Sahib.'

'They are our guests wherever it happens. What am I to say to them when I meet them? That they have Mirat's hospitality but not Mirat's protection? I shall want a full report.'

'It will be as full as possible. Meanwhile your Highness can only express your regret. Your Highness might add that you are astonished and pained that such a thing should happen in Mirat, either in the cantonment or out of the cantonment.' Bronowsky paused. 'Even last August there were no anti-British demonstrations in Mirat. The prohibition of political demonstrations and meetings the previous July was extremely effective. Known agitators were made *persona non grata*. The police have been active in smelling out refugee-agitators from British India, and sending them back where they came from. The incident of the stone this morning is therefore a mystery.' Bronowsky glanced at his watch. 'If you are ready, Sahib, I think we should go. In the circumstances it would be a proper gesture to be at the reception early rather than late.'

A stone: such a little thing. But look at us – Sarah thought – it has transformed us. We have acquired dignity. At no other time do we move with such grace as we do now when we feel threatened by violence but untouched by its vulgarity. A stone thrown by an unknown Indian shatters the window of a car, a piece of flying glass cuts an Englishman on the cheek and at once we sense the sharing of a secret that sustains and extends us, and Teddie instead of looking slightly absurd getting married with lint and sticking plaster on his face looks pale and composed. The end of Teddie is not reached so easily after all. I was wrong when I thought he had nothing more to offer that he hadn't already given. He will always be ready to offer and willing to give himself in the cause of our solidarity.

And it was a special kind of solidarity, Sarah realized. It transcended mere clannishness because its whole was greater than all its parts together. It uplifted, it magnified. It added a rare gift to a life which sometimes seemed niggardly in its rewards, and left one inspired to attack the problems of that life with the grave simplicity proper to their fair and just solution. The hot-tempered words and extravagant actions that might have greeted the incident of the stone were sublimated in this surrender to collective moral force.

From her position behind Susan at the altar steps she observed the way Teddie stood, at attention, with a military rather than a religious deference to God. To her left, and a pace or two in front, stood Uncle Arthur who had just made the gesture of confirmation that it was he who gave Susan to Teddie. He was also at attention. He seemed to be staring up at the stained-glass window above the altar as if it might be through there that some light would fall to disperse the perpetual shadow of professional neglect it was understood by the family he suffered from and gamely plodded on in spite of. Glancing from Teddie to Uncle Arthur and back again Sarah thought: Why, what a curious thing a human being is; and was not surprised to hear Aunt Fenny sniff and to see that Susan was trembling as she put out her hand for Teddie to fit the ring on her finger. It is all over in such a short time, Sarah told herself, but in that short time everything about our lives changes for ever. We become something else, without necessarily having understood what we were before.

Teddie kissed his bride. Mercifully the cut had not been deep enough to need a stitch and the doctor had pronounced it free of splinters. Presumably it was not over-painful, but he cocked his head at an awkward angle, perhaps so as not to tickle Susan with any stray end of lint or sticking plaster. The kiss, Sarah noticed, was a firm one in spite of the angle at which contact was made. He did not wince; but breaking free smiled and touched the wound gingerly as if in a dumb show of apology for the inconvenience of it. It was the innocent gesture of a boy and the contrived one of a man with a sense of theatre who guessed that people were bound to wonder to what extent delayed shock or plain discomfort might impair the ardour of his performance, later, of private and more intimate duties.

Sarah stooped and gathered the folds of the bride's veil,

followed the family into the vestry. The organist was playing a tune she thought was probably 'Perfect Love'. 'Hello, Mrs Bingham,' she said, and kissed Susan on one flushed happy cheek. 'I wanted to say it first.'

'I couldn't stop shivering,' Susan said. 'Did it show? I felt everybody could see.' She kissed her mother, and Aunt Fenny, and Uncle Arthur. 'It sounds funny,' she said at one point. 'Susan Bingham.'

'Oh, you'll get used to it,' Teddie said. 'Anyway you'd better.'

They signed the register.

Within half an hour of the incident of the stone two NCOs of the British Military Police had arrived on duty outside the church. Mounted on motor-cycles they led the bride and groom from the ceremony to the reception at the Gymkhana Club where they were to remain until the time came for them to escort the bridal car to the station. Their instructions were to keep an eye open for any further attempted act or demonstration of an anti-British nature – for as such for the moment, it was thought, the incident of the stone had to be treated.

The roar of the motor-bikes and the stand-no-nonsense demeanour of the men astride them seemed to release in the people who had attended the ceremony and now watched the departure of Teddie and Susan and presently made their way to their own waiting cars and taxis (and in one case a military truck, logged out as on civil duties), an animus of a subtly different nature from the one which had made them feel calm, remote and dignified. It entered and stirred them like the divine breath of a God who had bent his brow to call forth sterner angels.

The affair of the stone, first reacted to with a sense of shock, then treated as lamentable, regrettable, a challenge of the kind to which the only answer was to rally round and make the young couple feel that after all their day had not been ruined, was now seen as contemptible; mean, despicable, cowardly. Typical.

The scene of the crime, the Victoria roundabout, significantly marked by the presence of a police truck and three armed MPs, caused among the occupants of the cars as they passed by it on their way to the club some speculation about the exact spot from which the stone had been thrown and the likely escape-route of the demonstrator. Neither young Bingham nor his best man had apparently seen a thing. They had been looking at the memorial or intent on what they were saying to one another. The shock of the stone coming through the window, the fact that young Bingham was hurt and that the car took some time to pull up – according to the best man who had to explain things to the guests as they arrived as well as get the doctor, ring the police, and warn the bride and her uncle to hang on at the guest house for an extra half-hour; all of which he had done with an admirably cool head – were contributing factors to the ruffian having got away unseen.

It was probably the work of some fellow with a grudge, someone who had been dismissed for stealing from his master as likely as not – and who had heard about the wedding from a friend still employed in the cantonment and had hung about hoping for a chance to get his own back, not caring who it was he actually threw a stone at. If the culprit wasn't a fellow of that sort he was some clerk or student whose head was crammed with a lot of hot air about the iniquities of the *raj*: the kind who needed a kick up the backside or shipping out to Tokyo as a present to Hirohito or Subhas Chandra Bose. If he was that kind of fellow he was probably a member of a group at work outside the cantonment, in Mirat City, where the cantonment police had no jurisdiction.

Some of the princely states were jam-packed with political agitators who fled from the British provinces at the time of the mass Congress arrests, over a year ago, and even a small place like Mirat was known to have had its share. There was probably still a nucleus that had escaped the Mirat city police net. In any case the city police were probably corrupt. The princes were loyal to the crown because the crown protected their rights and privileges. A prince's subjects were often only loyal to him because they were terrified of the consequences of not being. At heart a lot of them shared the same aspirations as the Indian nationalists of British India, or had been persuaded by propaganda to believe they did. Perhaps the incident of the stone was a warning shot, a sign that dear old Mirat was suddenly going to explode. On the whole that might not be a bad thing. The Nawab would come running to the cantonment authorities for help and that would give the police the opportunity to root out the hidden subversive elements.

The danger of such elements lay in the contact they might have with Indian troops. That had always been the nightmare. It was the finest army in the world. Subvert it and it could turn and destroy its creators like a man swatting flies. With the war the dangers of subversion had increased. The army's ranks had been swelled with recruits whose loyalty to the salt they ate could not be counted on as part of the martial tradition of tribe or caste. And yet its loyalty seemed as sure as ever, which seemed in turn to prove that pride of service could inspire men of any race and any colour, given the opportunity. Such thoughts, spoken or left unspoken, led to the third and final change of mood. This was a mood in which it was felt that the stone had not found its mark but had rebounded from its impact with the impenetrable and unbreakable defences that always surrounded any inviolable truth. The stone changed nothing. Someone ought to pay for it but in the meantime it had to be treated as a joke; a joke in bad taste, certainly, but what else could be expected?

The two MPs who had escorted the bridal car greeted the guests on their arrival in the forecourt of the old Gymkhana Club by stopping each car and indicating where it should be parked. The MPs were brisk, cheerful and efficient, and the guests accepted their polite but firm directives with the friendly nods of people who, used to giving orders, enjoyed obeying them in circumstances they knew called for attention to the small details of security and discipline. From their cars they entered the club by steps unfamiliarly but pleasantly got up in red carpet. They went in twos and threes into the dim fan-cooled entrance hall of busts, mounted trophies and padding barefoot servants; through the ante-room, a lounge, and out through one of the open french windows on the terrace with its view on to an emerald-green lawn where a sprinkler was still at work.

Just as Captain Merrick returned to Sarah with a replenished glass of fruit-cup, the club secretary pressed through the adjacent group of people and said, 'Excuse me, Miss Layton. Have you seen your mother and uncle?'

'Mother was here a few minutes ago. I don't know where Uncle Arthur has got to.'

'I think they'd better be found.' He showed Sarah a card

which she recognized as one of the wedding invitations. 'A servant just brought me this. One of the MPs sent it through. I'm afraid he's stopped the Nawab from coming in.'

'Stopped him? But why?'

'I suppose because he wasn't expecting an Indian to show up. I'll have to go out and start putting it right, but if your mother and uncle could be found and asked to come through I'd be grateful.'

'What's up?' a guest asked.

'The MPs have got the Nawab and his party stopped at the front door.'

'Good grief!' the guest said, laughed, and turned to pass the news on.

'I think I can probably find Major Grace,' Merrick said, ' – if you'd scout round for your mother.'

'I'll try and keep him happy in the ante-room,' the secretary called.

Sarah made her way through the guests to the far end of the terrace. She found her mother listening to Mrs Hobhouse.

'Mother, the Nawab's arrived,' she said, interrupting a flow of reminiscences about the 1935 earthquake in Quetta.

'Oh, my dear,' Mrs Hobhouse said. 'Down tools. Fly. We are honoured. He only got back from Gopalakand last night. I'd better come with you. He's an old dear, but terribly hard going. Thank God for the red carpet. He'll probably think it's for him.'

'I'm afraid he won't,' Sarah said – taking the glass her mother seemed not to know she had in her hand and putting it on a near-by table. 'He's been refused entry.'

'Refused entry?' Mrs Layton repeated. 'I don't understand.' Mrs Hobhouse grasped Sarah's elbow. 'My dear, whatever do you mean?'

'The MPs stopped him coming in. Captain Merrick's gone to find Uncle Arthur and the secretary wants us in the ante-room.'

She began to guide her mother back along the terrace. Mrs Hobhouse followed. 'But they can't have,' she said. 'I mean surely they were warned.' Suddenly she took Mrs Layton's other arm. 'Hold on. This is our job. Stay here with Sarah, and my husband and I will bring the old boy out. It's not right that either you or your brother-in-law should be placed in a position of

having to apologize. If it really has happened it's club business
or station business. Nothing to do with the wedding. Just stand
here close to the door. Or better still go down on the lawn.
I see Teddie and Susan are there. We'll bring the Nawab straight
through and down. He'll feel it's a more conspicuous place anyway, better than hobnobbing in this crush.'

'I think Mrs Hobhouse is right, Mother. Come on.'

She led her mother down the stone steps into the glare. It was
not unbearably hot. A light breeze had sprung up, was tangling
Susan's veil. She stood in the middle of a group of Teddie's fellow-officers, laughing. Sarah, catching sight of Captain Merrick
leading Uncle Arthur along the terrace, called out and beckoned
them down.

'I must say,' Uncle Arthur said when reaching them, 'this is
turning out to be the most jinx-ridden affair I've ever been
mixed up with, and that's saying something. Where's Fenny?'

'Shall I find her?' Captain Merrick asked.

'Well, that's easier said than done in this crush. I have a feeling
there are more people drinking our drink and getting up their
appetites for our food than were ever invited. Why couldn't they
have set up a marquee or something? Separate the sheep from
the goats. I'd swear half that gang on the terrace are just ordinary
members of the club muscling in on the festivities. I've been
having a word with the contractor's chap and warned him we're
not going to pay a penny over the quotation. He's making a
packet as it is. I say, cheer up, Mildred.'

'What?'

'You look half asleep.'

Mrs Layton stared at him, then said to Sarah, 'I'd better tell
Susan and Teddie what's happened.'

'Aren't we going to the ante-room?' Captain Merrick asked
Sarah, as her mother left her side and went over to the group of
men clustered round the bride.

'Mrs Hobhouse thought it better if we stayed here and she
and Colonel Hobhouse brought the Nawab down.'

'Good idea,' Major Grace said. 'Then we can pretend we
know nothing about this snarl-up or whatever it is. I say, is this
him now? Must be. How extraordinary. He looks like some
downtrodden munshi.'

The chattering and laughter on the terrace did not lessen, but

Sarah thought that abruptly it changed key. The Station Commander was walking slowly across the width of the terrace with a short little Indian, the top of whose truncated cone of a hat came level with Colonel Hobhouse's left epaulette – which in any case was lower than the right because the Colonel was bending slightly. The impression given by this sideways and downward inclination was one of deafness more than deference. Behind Colonel Hobhouse and the Nawab Mrs Hobhouse was similarly dwarfed by a tall thin man with an eye-patch.

'That must be Count Bronowsky,' Captain Merrick told Sarah, keeping his voice low. 'He's supposed to have been blown up by a bomb in St Petersburg but some unkind people say it's the result of peeping through keyholes. I'm told he's about seventy. He doesn't look it, does he?'

Behind Bronowsky and Mrs Hobhouse, the secretary walked with young Kasim.

At the head of the steps the Nawab paused, half turned with his left hand held in a gesture of command and invitation, and Ahmed detached himself from his position at the rear, came to the Nawab's side, made a firm elbow upon which the Nawab now placed his hand. Slowly they descended the steps. Sarah saw the thin face of the old man with the eye-patch twitch, as if something had both pleased and amused him.

When they reached lawn level the Nawab removed his hand and Ahmed stood back to enable Mrs Hobhouse and the Count to precede him.

'Mrs Layton,' Colonel Hobhouse said, 'his Highness, Nawab Sir Ahmed Ali Guffur Kasim Bahadur.'

Mrs Layton nodded her head and murmured, 'How do you do. I'm so glad you were able to come.'

The Nawab returned the nod and waited.

'Nawab Sahib,' Colonel Hobhouse said, 'Mrs Layton wishes me to say on her behalf and on behalf of her family how deeply she has appreciated your many kindnesses in regard to the arrangements at the guest house.'

'Indeed, yes,' Mrs Layton murmured again.

The Nawab raised one hand, palm outwards. The lids fell over his eyes. The head jerked fractionally to one side.

The Station Commander hesitated, as if he had not been fed with a line and felt he could not now say what he had rehearsed and make sense. Sarah guessed his predicament. He had expected the Nawab or himself to make some reference to the incident of the stone, to express regret or make light of it. But the stone and the insult just given at the door cancelled each other out. Thanks had been offered for hospitality, been autocratically dismissed as quite unnecessary and without the formal expression of regret and reassurance that might have followed in regard to the stone there had emerged a silence which although short-lived was profound. Sarah, narrowing her eyes against the sunlight, was moved to a special intensity of feeling for the texture of the clothes she wore. The breeze was pressing the ankle-length skirt of her bridesmaid's gown against her legs. She had a fleeting image of them all as dolls dressed and positioned for a play that moved mechanically but uncertainly again and again to a point of climax, but then shifted its ground, avoiding a direct confrontation. Each shift was marked by just such a pause and the wonder perhaps was that the play continued. But the wind blew, nudging her through the creamy thinness of peach-coloured slipper satin and she and they were reanimated, prodded into speech and new positions. The Count Bronowsky, Chief Minister in Mirat. My daughter, Sarah. My brother-in-law, Major Grace. Captain Merrick. And this is my younger daughter, Susan, now Mrs Bingham.

Almost imperceptibly they had moved closer to the group that had surrounded Susan and which had now opened out leaving her exposed, vulnerable, tiny and tender in the ethereal whiteness of stiffened, wafting net and white brocade, several paces away from the spot where the Nawab's slow progress had finally come to a halt. For an instant Sarah thought that her mother would allow the presentation to end there – as if her duty were to show the Nawab no more than an image of the bride, an effigy set up to demonstrate the meaning and purpose of an alien rite. Her mother made a gesture, vague, evasive, but it – or some instinct of Susan's own – prompted the bride into motion, the totally unexpected motion – charming, unprecedented – of a curtsy. She sank into the billowy whiteness, bringing the effigy to life, and causing a hush among the watchers on the terrace. An Englishwoman did not curtsy to an Indian prince. But the hush was only one of astonishment and disapproval for the time it took for the watchers to feel what those closer to her felt almost instantaneously: a little shock-wave of enchantment: and when the Nawab was seen to take a hesitant step forward and then a firm one, and offer his hand, keeping it there until, rising, she put her own into it, the prettiness of the picture she made was enhanced by recognition of the fact that her impulsive action – so delightfully performed – had achieved what words and formal gestures could not – the re-establishment without loss of face of the essential *status quo.*

'Thank you for coming to my wedding,' Susan said, and Sarah – losing the drift of the Nawab's response, his involved but courteous good wishes for the health and happiness of bride and groom – considering still what Susan had just said, sensing something odd about it, turned her head and let her gaze come to rest on Count Bronowsky. By his side Mrs Hobhouse stood, silently watching – with a contented smile – the exchange of pleasantries between the Nawab and Susan and Teddie who by now had also been introduced. Bronowsky had a panama hat in the hand unencumbered by the ebony, gold-topped cane. She imagined what he would look like with it on and wondered whether he had worn it in the motor-car. Perhaps, under the hat, the pale pink skin would look like that of a high-caste Hindu. If he wore a cap such as the Nawab had on he might look very like a wealthy Muslim from the north – so subtle sometimes was the distinction between that kind of Indian and thin gaunt Europeans who had lived for years out East. Additionally shaded by the brim of a hat, travelling in a car with two Indians, the MPs could have assumed there was no white man in the small party arriving and expecting admittance.

She tried to assess the degree of humiliation Bronowsky would be capable of feeling. If he was really a count, the white Russian *émigré* who had been found by the Nawab in Monte Carlo and made use of as a go-between in the affair the Nawab was having, or had had and was trying to continue, with a European woman, and considering the fact that he had served for twenty years in a position that must have been even more testing than that of a British political adviser to an Indian ruler, then he had probably acquired a degree of immunity from attacks on his prestige and self-esteem.

But then, Sarah reminded herself, it was impossible to assume anything when it came to such matters. And often it was the thoughtless action, the unintentional insult, the casual attack which, catching you off guard, hurt most. Remembering the twitch of amusement when the Nawab made his imperious but frail, attractive gesture of command to be helped down the steps, Sarah was struck by the idea that perhaps the crooked fleeting smile was one of amusement at the Nawab's expense, an involuntary sign of underlying resentment of the fact that he, Bronowsky, should be subjected to the same humiliation as the Nawab, his master, but be denied the opportunity to get his own back so swiftly. 'One never knows,' Mr Hobhouse had said recently, 'what to make of the Count, but of course it's probably important to remember he's a dispossessed Russian and that the Nawab is not, after all, a little Tsarevich saved from a cellar in Ekaterinberg.'

Sarah wished she had seen how he reacted to the sight of Susan curtsying to the man who was not a little Tsarevich, or could see his expression now, as he waited his turn to be introduced. He stood, slightly stooped, his head inclined to catch whatever Mrs Hobhouse next said to him, but looking away half right, so that Sarah saw only his eye-patch profile. Was a black patch, on its own, expressive? Sarah thought that it was. Seen by itself, thus, it looked like the round bulging eye of a nocturnal creature abroad in sunlight, staring myopically, alerted by some unexpected but familiar sound of which it awaited a repetition in order to be certain of the accuracy of its judgment of the source: and Sarah glancing in the direction indicated by the fixed intensity of the imaginarily luminous black patch, found that the source appeared to be Captain Merrick who, for the moment, stood alone, hands behind his back, unaware of the scrutiny he was under, taking a breather from the cumulatively exhausting duties of best man. Hatless, in full unflattering sunlight – the first time she was conscious of seeing Captain Merrick so – the years he could give Teddie showed. He was probably nearing thirty. In the company of Teddie and the young officers who surrounded Susan, he looked hardened, burnt by experiences distant from their own and placing him at distance now. He was not really Teddie's type. Chance alone – the sharing of quarters with Teddie and Captain Bishop's jaundice – had led to his presence at the wedding.

But the same could be said of all the other guests. And realizing that, Sarah understood what was odd about the thing Susan had said. The oddness was in that possessive phrase, 'my wedding'. She should have said 'our wedding' if the wedding had to be mentioned at all. She should not have said 'my wedding'. She should not have curtsied. She should not have been so composed, earlier, when she arrived promptly at the church at the postponed hour, and made no comment on the cause of the delay, walked slowly up the aisle on Uncle Arthur's arm and appeared not to see the damage to Teddie's cheek. Even in the vestry afterwards she had said nothing about the stone. She had said little about anything except to express concern that her shivering at the altar might have been too obvious and uncertainty about the suitability of the new name given her in exchange for the old one.

But she was guilty of all these acts and omissions, and 'my wedding' was – to Sarah – suddenly and touchingly significant, revealing as it did the extent to which Susan was conscious of the fact that no one else except Teddie seemed much concerned about it. Being married to Teddie was something she had set her heart on, presumably because in her mysterious self-sufficient way she was prepared to love him and be loved by him, but whatever the reason for the marriage the wedding was the one conclusive step she had to take to demonstrate in public the importance of what was happening to her. It was, on a much larger scale, like the gesture she made or sudden word she spoke which interrupted the flow of other people's thoughts and drew attention back to her existence. But the wedding, among strangers, in unfamiliar surroundings, already marred by the incident of the stone and the insult to the Nawab, was an affair that threatened to overwhelm her. She was fighting the threat with a single-minded determination, a tense, febrile assertion of her rights to her own illusion which Sarah, now that she understood, admired her for, loved her for, because she judged the amount of courage it took to close the eyes to the destructive counter-element of reality that entered any state of intended happiness.

She thought: That sort of courage is what distinguishes Susan from me, apart from her prettiness, and why men like Teddie have always finally preferred her company to mine. She creates an illusion of herself as the centre of a world without sadness and allows them entry. It is like when we are children. She is the little girl with the gift for making let's-pretend seem real; although when she was young it was the last talent I suspected in her. If she had it then she kept it secret, closely guarded. Now it has blossomed. One senses it in her as something tough and enduring but delicately poised, in constant need of fine adjustments so that it can contain or be contained, be shared, withheld, never diminished by exposure to ridicule.

The old protective instinct which she had thought atrophied by long disuse quickened and then lay still. All the outlets for it were overgrown and it understood it had woken to no purpose and must sleep again, become oblivious of its awakened hunger. Abruptly she moved away – taking the opportunity given by a general movement as the Count went forward to meet the bride and groom – and found herself facing Ahmed: a re-enactment in different dress and circumstances of the occasion on the waste ground when she rode at him, smiling and speechless, and he stared back, smiling less but just as silent: a meaningless situation then, equally meaningless now. They might have come from different planets. It was impossible to establish common ground; neither sense of duty nor personal compulsion would ever bridge the distance or shatter the glass from behind which they smiled and stared vacantly at one another like specimen products of alien cultures in display cabinets in a museum placed close together through an administrative oversight, or odd stroke of chance.

'He is very pleased with the book,' Ahmed announced suddenly.

'Oh yes. Gaffur. I'm glad.' She turned her head slightly, because of the garlic. It really was a revolting smell. The poems of Gaffur and the smell of garlic: a dark vision of an old lady under an awning on the sun-deck of a houseboat, and of trunks, musty, unclaimed, containing what was left of that girl passed over Sarah's consciousness of her presence on a sunlit scene – inconsequential but positive – like vapours casting actual shadows.

'It was a bit of luck,' she said. The old lady knew so much: more than facts – the shape and substance and significance of an accumulation of detail that so often, in the mind, passed by, as a procession of irrelevancies.

'What was a bit of luck?'

The voice was not Ahmed's but that of Captain Merrick who had arrived at her side.

'The poems of Gaffur,' she replied, glancing up at Merrick. 'Just something we brought for the Nawab. Someone we met in Kashmir told us that Gaffur was a Kasim too, so we had a copy bound up, we wouldn't have known otherwise.'

'I don't even know about Gaffur. Is he famous?'

'Oh, not is, was.' She turned to Ahmed again. 'I mean in the sense of "was, not is", because he's dead. But he's still famous as a classic isn't he?'

Ahmed put his head on one side, letting the eyes close. He rarely made a typical Indian gesture. He held and used himself with the stiff composure of an Englishman. She had absorbed that fact unconsciously, was only conscious of it now when he responded with the gesture of the head, like any other Indian deflecting a compliment to himself or his country from its target.

'But something tells me,' she went on, 'you don't go in much for poetry. What did Gaffur write about? Deserts and roses, and moonlit gardens? Jugs of wine?'

Merrick laughed. 'That's Omar Khayyam.'

'Oh, no, just Persian,' she said. 'I mean they all wrote like that surely, Persian poets, Urdu poets. Was Gaffur an exception?'

'No, I think he wasn't,' Ahmed said. 'Roses and deserts and moonlit gardens pretty well fill the bill from what I remember.'

'Did you have to learn him as a boy?'

'Read is a more accurate word.' Ahmed hesitated, then added, 'I never learned anything my teachers thought important. In the end they gave me up.'

'I know what you mean,' Sarah said. 'It's how I feel about me, more or less, except that I think I'd say I never saw the importance of what I was taught and always felt I wanted to be taught quite different things – the sort of things no one thought of teaching. I was the kind of child who automatically asked why when I was told the cat sat on the mat. My teachers said I ought to curb a tendency to squander curiosity on the self-evident.'

'Then from their point of view, you're in the right place, Miss Layton. In India nothing is self-evident.'

She looked at him, puzzled. Ask him a question and he would answer, usually with that brevity which made asking a further question a grindingly self-conscious business. She did not remember him making comments – of the kind that could remove verbal exchange from the level of an interrogation to that of a conversation – but in the last few moments he had made two, although the second had the familiar characteristic of those answers of his which seemed to kill a subject stone-dead, and left her suspended (she felt) like a vulture hovering over a carcass with no meat left on. She smiled, found herself tongue-tied, but hoped her silence would be interpreted as politeness and interest and would encourage him – if for once he was in the mood to talk – to continue. But it did not. He was not even looking at her now: instead at Captain Merrick, holding his head at an angle that disclosed an aggressive set of chin and jaw. He did not look angry but she wondered whether he was. He had been stopped at the door too, and had even less opportunity than Count Bronowsky to even up the score.

'Actually,' Captain Merrick said, 'that's something I feel bound to disagree with. I'd say things that are self-evident are common to all countries.' He was smiling and so now was Mr Kasim, but glancing from one to the other Sarah thought: No, you mustn't tangle with each other. She felt powerless to stop them. She saw Aunt Fenny hastening down the steps and moved to intercept her; but that was unnecessary. She was coming to them in any case.

'What's been going on?' she asked before she had quite reached them.

'Nothing's been going on, Aunt Fenny. The Nawab has arrived.'

'Well I know that. People up there are saying he had difficulty getting in.' She did not trouble to lower her voice. Aunt Fenny never did. She seemed not to have seen Mr Kasim standing almost next to her, but turned on him abruptly, thereby proving she had, and said, 'What a chapter of accidents!' and came back to Sarah, leaving her exclamation as it were – bouncing, to work its own way a position of rest. 'I've been putting out Susan's going away things. I can't find the hat-box.'

A room in the annexe had been set aside for the bride's use. Sarah and Aunt Fenny had brought Susan's luggage with them. 'It must still be in the car,' Sarah said. 'I'll go and see.'

'No, I'm sure Captain Merrick won't mind –'

Seeing he was wanted he came closer.

'A hat-box. We think it's still in the car. The one Sarah and I came in.'

'I know where it's parked. I'll check. What should I do with the box, bring it to you or take it to the annexe?'

'If you'd bring it to me? Well, whatever you think. So long as it's found. God knows what we'll do if it's not there or been stolen. There wasn't a servant in sight at the annexe just now. Anyone could have walked in. I've nabbed a spare body and made him stand guard on peril of his life.'

Captain Merrick nodded and went. 'Come,' Aunt Fenny said. 'I must meet the Nawab.'

As Sarah followed Mrs Grace she carried with her an impression of Ahmed alone, disengaged; standing restricted in the centre of a world she would never enter, did not know and could not miss. How lucky we are, she thought. How very, very lucky.

'Nobody told us you was expecting any Indian gentleman, sir,' the MP explained as he accompanied Captain Merrick to the place where the bridal cars were parked.

'I realize that. It was very remiss of us.'

'We didn't think you allowed Indian gentlemen into the club, so the corporal and me, sir, we thought those three gentlemen was havin' a lark. I mean anyone could've got hold of one of those cards, sir, and written a fancy name on it.'

'You did your duty as you saw it, Sergeant, no one is blaming you.'

'All the same we dropped a right clanger, didn't we, sir? Especially seeing one of 'em was a white gentleman after all and another was his nibs.' The sergeant grinned. 'Captain Bates'll have my guts for garters.'

'Is he your officer?'

'That's right, sir. But no sweat. We live and learn. And I'll know the nabob next time, won't I?'

They stopped at the line of limousines. One of the drivers left the circle of men squatting under one of the old trees shading the lawn, but the sergeant ignored him, opened the doors and presently found the box on the floor under one of the tip-up seats. 'Here you are, sir, one hat-box, brides for the use of.'

'Thank you, Sergeant. Are you staying with us or expecting a relief?'

'Orders are to wait and escort the cars to the station, sir.'

'In that case there'll be something for you and the corporal to toast the bride and groom in. I'll lay it on and send one of the stewards out to take you round and show you where. But you'd better go one at a time.'

'Thank you, sir. That'll be very much appreciated.'

'Well even a copper has to eat.'

The sergeant grinned again, came to attention and saluted. Merrick, encumbered by the hat-box, and capless, sketched the idea of a salute in reply and made back towards the club entrance. As he reached the steps he paused, looked at the hat-box, and then instead of entering continued along the front until he reached the corner of the building where a path led off through a shrubbery marked by a directional finger on which the word Annexe was painted black on white. He returned a few minutes later, without the box, and walked along the side of the club-house, between a flower-bed and the tennis courts where an old man in shirt and dhoti and a youth in a ragged pair of khaki shorts were restoring the lime-wash markings. Merrick stopped, reached into his pocket for his cigarette case, selected one, lit it and began leisurely to smoke and watch, as if concerned about the straightness of the lines that were reappearing, brightly, on their faded predecessors. The youth was doing all the work. It was not arduous but the sun was hot and the gleam on his shoulders showed that he was sweating. He became conscious of the spectator, made a mistake in the marking. The old man spoke to him sharply. Merrick did not move. He inhaled smoke slowly, deeply, continuing to watch until, growing tired of the scene, he threw the cigarette half-smoked into the flower-bed and continued along the path.

The lawn was now deserted. A single voice, a woman's raised in laughter, came from the almost equally deserted terrace. The wedding party had gone inside for the cold fork-lunch wedding breakfast and the ceremony of the cutting of the cake. Merrick looked at his watch. Ten minutes short of midday. He walked on the lawn, making for the steps, paused near them, stooped and picked up shreds of pink and white paper where someone had stood and brushed confetti from a dress or uniform.

Straightening, he saw himself watched by Count Bronowsky who had appeared at the head of the steps alone.

As Merrick joined him Bronowsky said: 'Ah, there you are, Captain Merrick. I suppose you have been undertaking yet another of the onerous duties of best man.'

'Just a small errand to recover a hat-box.'

'Well, you are a man for detail. I can see that. For instance, you share my compulsive instinct for tidiness. What was it, confetti?'

Merrick opened his hand.

'They say it's significant,' Bronowsky said, picking the scraps of paper from Merrick's palm and dropping them into the empty glass a guest had left on the balustrade. He picked the glass up too and placed it on a near-by table, for greater safety. While he did these things he continued to talk. 'I mean significant psycho-logically. Compulsively tidy people, one is told, are always wiping the slate clean, trying to give themselves what life denies all of us, a fresh start.' Having finished with the confetti and the glass he now looked at Merrick and, putting a hand on his shoulder, began to lead the way along the terrace towards the distant hum of conversation in the inner room where the bride and groom and guests had reassembled. 'You are married?' he asked casually.

'No –'

'Neither am I. Far better not. We'd drive our poor wives crazy, wouldn't we? Besides which, of course, there is this other thing about us – I mean about our tidiness. They say it's charac-teristic of someone who wishes to be the organizing centre of his own life and who has no gift for sharing.'

Bronowsky had stopped walking, but he retained his hold on Merrick's shoulder. The two men were of equal height.

'I am sorry,' Bronowsky went on. 'I am sorry about the inci-dent this morning. You were not hit yourself?' He removed his hand but stood his ground, keeping Merrick waiting.

'No, apart from Captain Bingham's scratch the only damage was to the car.'

The Chief Minister remained where he was and did not answer. Merrick also kept still. Presently he said, 'Is there some-thing you want, Count Bronowsky?'

'Yes. The answer to a question. But the question is imper-tinent. I hesitate, naturally –'

'Please don't.'

'Well. I have been wondering if you thought that perhaps the stone was thrown at you.'

'Oh? Why should you wonder that?'

'Mrs Grace tells me you were in the Indian Police.'

'That's quite true.' Merrick took out his cigarette case, opened and offered it to Bronowsky.

'No, thank you. I never smoke until evening.'

He watched while Merrick lit a cigarette then said, 'We shan't be missed for a bit, so let me tell you a little story. Years ago, when I was overhauling the administration in Mirat, I brought in a man who rather later in life than he felt he deserved had risen to be a judge of the High Court in Ranpur. I made him the State's Chief Justice, a grandiloquent title but with a salary to match. He retired in far greater comfort than would have been the case if he'd stayed in the ICS. He died peacefully in bed, but was once the victim of what the newspapers of my youth would have described as a murderous attack by a couple of ruffians who set on him in the dark as he walked from my house to his. I often warned him of the danger for a man in his position of walking alone, at night, in a usually deserted road. In fact for a time I made sure he was followed by a couple of my own stout lads. But he caught on to it and told me he would never visit me again if I treated him like that. So I withdrew the guards and then this thing happened. Two men whom he never got a proper look at jumped out at him. He was badly beaten.'

Merrick blew out smoke, and nodded his head.

'For a time,' Bronowsky continued, 'our police were completely at a loss because none of our known malcontents continued for long to be real suspects. The most likely ones had been arrested on suspicion of course, but protested their innocence vehemently – indeed with fortitude. In those days I had not yet succeeded in persuading the Mirat police to dispense with certain old-fashioned interrogatory methods. Anyway, for a time it looked as if the mystery of the attack on my highly prized Chief Justice would go unsolved, but then we had a stroke of luck. I was discussing the case with the poor fellow – who was still laid up and only just regaining his faculties – and he said, "You know, Bronowsky, I think I had a premonition about it." I asked him when and how. He thought for a bit and said he believed the premonition dated from a day about a week before the attack, when he was presiding over his court. It was a hot afternoon and the case before him was extremely complex. The people who had been admitted to the public seats were restless – fanning themselves with papers, whispering, that sort of thing, very distracting. He kept thinking, "In a minute I shall call them to order. In a minute I shall clear the court." But he somehow couldn't summon the necessary determination. He said, "I had an extraordinary sensation that something else" – and he didn't mean the case being heard – "– that something else had to be done first, done, or seen through, attended to. I felt I was being not watched exactly but waited for." After a while he stopped examining the faces of the pleaders and witnesses and the face of the accused and looked across at the public benches.'

Bronowsky had been holding his panama hat in the same hand that held the ebony cane. Now he took the hat in his free hand, hesitated, then gestured with hat and cane, raising his arms slightly as though conjuring an image of the courtroom and the judge's perplexity.

'Nothing extraordinary there, but after a while he noticed a young man who was not fanning himself, was not whispering to his neighbours, but leaning forward apparently absorbed. He found himself returning to meet this man's gaze many times. I asked him if the face of the young man had been familiar. Could it have been a man he had once sent to prison? He said no, not familiar, not exactly familiar. He never forgot a face, especially the face of a man he had sentenced. I asked him to think back carefully during the next day or two, particularly about the more sensational cases he had tried since coming to Mirat, because the young man might have been a relative of someone he had sentenced to hang or to prison for life. When I next saw him he said, "I've been thinking, as you told me, but not about sensational cases, nor about cases I've dealt with in Mirat. I've been considering the two cases I've never been able to shelve satisfactorily as over and done with because of the element of doubt. They were cases which *seemed* clear cut enough, but left me vaguely troubled. Both took place a long time ago, one when I was a District and Sessions judge and the other when I first became a judge of the High Court in Ranpur. In the Ranpur case I had to send a man to the gallows. The young man who watched me in court two weeks ago could easily have been his son. When you sentence a man to death you never forget the expression on his face while he listens to you. This was the same expression." I asked him to tell me the dead man's name, and suggested we got the co-operation of the police in Ranpur to find out whether the son or some other close relative had been in Mirat two weeks ago.'

Bronowsky stopped, again made the gesture of half-raising his arms.

Merrick said, 'And so you caught the chap.'

'Oh, no. The Chief Justice wouldn't hear of it. Because of the element of doubt that had stayed in his mind all those years. All the same I conducted private inquiries and established to my own satisfaction that the hanged man's son was in Mirat at the time of the attack. You see I was after the accomplice. The result of my inquiries in that direction pointed to the guilt of a young gentleman of Mirat of hitherto unblemished character, but on whom the police were now able to keep an eye. Their vigilance was rewarded later. You of course will understand the necessity of such precautions. Professional criminals and openly organized political agitators are one thing. One can always cope with them. It is these others – the dark young men of random destiny and private passions who present the greater difficulty. For instance, the stone this morning – ostensibly thrown at the Nawab Sahib's car. If it had happened in the city it could have sparked off a communal riot. The Muslims might have blamed the Hindus and set fire to a Hindu shop. The Hindus might then have retaliated by slaughtering a pig outside the Abu-Q'rim mosque. The police would then have had to break up the fracas with lathi charges and hooligan elements would then have attacked the police station. All this for a stone, thrown at you perhaps, by one of those young men because in the past you carried out some duty with a vigour he thought cruelly unjust.'

Merrick laughed. 'I'll shoulder the responsibility if that helps to explain the damage to the Nawab's car to everyone's satisfaction. When I was a police officer I had enough brickbats chucked at me during riots and demonstrations to learn you can't dodge them all.'

'My dear Captain Merrick. You totally misunderstand the reason for my waylaying you like this –'

'Yes, well, I realize it isn't a chance meeting.'

'Quite so. I came to look for you. But not to ask you to shoulder responsibility. To seek your help in placing it.'

'What does that mean?'

'It means that directly Mrs Grace told me you had been in the Indian Police a number of apparently unrelated things fell into a pattern for me and even pointed to a likely source of inquiry. My interest isn't in you or the stone or the damage to Nawab Sahib's car. My interest is in Mirat.'

Merrick shrugged slightly and smiled. 'Well, don't worry. If I was the target you can rest assured that by this time next week the target will be in quite a different place, a long way from here.'

'But can you say the same of the man or youth who threw the stone, or of the people who put him up to it, of the people he discussed it with, whose help he had in plotting the time and place and day? I hardly have to tell you that such an incident was almost certainly planned, and planned in concert.'

'Perhaps, but it seems a lot of trouble to go to, I mean just to get a crack at an unimportant, comparatively junior police officer who's no longer even in the force.'

Bronowsky said nothing for a while. He transferred the hat back to the hand that rested on the ebony stick, then looked up.

'But you are not unimportant. Surely you are the Merrick who was District Superintendent of Police in Mayapore last year, at the time of the August riots and of the rape of the English girl, Daphne Manners, in the Bibighar Gardens?'

Merrick, arrested in the act of carrying the cigarette to his lips, now completed the movement. He inhaled and expelled then held the cigarette in a position suggestive of stubbing. Bronowsky pushed forward the ashtray on the table they stood next to and waited while Merrick, accepting the cue, carefully extinguished the tip, tapping and then pressing, then letting go and rubbing thumb and finger-tips to clear them of clinging particles.

He said, 'How do you arrive at that conclusion?'

'I deduce it. My deduction is correct? You are that officer?'

'I've no reason to deny it.'

'Nor to advertise it? Mrs Grace says you were DSP in Sunder-nagar, which I take it is the district you were transferred to after the Mayapore affair, and which you mention when anyone asks where you were before getting your commission. I imagine you are ready to talk about Sundernagar and other places, but prefer for personal reasons to gloss over Mayapore. If so I'm afraid I inadvertently let the cat out of the bag. I was telling Mrs Grace how much we appreciated your thoughtful action in ringing through to Ahmed and she said you were an excellent man for detail, probably as a result of your experience as a police officer. Well directly she mentioned that, certain bells – which for reasons I'll explain were very ready to ring – rang loud and clear, and I'm afraid I said almost at once, Merrick? Police? Surely that's the fellow who was DSP in Mayapore at the time of the Bibighar Gardens affair? I was so positive that it took me aback when she looked surprised and said she only knew about a place called Sundernagar. I'm afraid I insisted I was right, and she was obviously so intrigued I thought it fair to try and have a word with you before you go in.'

'Well, it's a bit of a nuisance, but it can't be helped. You'd better tell me about the little bells.'

'To begin with there was just the name, Merrick. It was vaguely familiar when Mr Kasim first mentioned it to me on Wednesday evening. But a young army officer called Merrick meant nothing to me. In fact I doubt whether the same young officer described by Mrs Grace as late of the Indian Police a moment ago would have meant anything either but for two other things that I was thinking about on the way here, wondering whether there could possibly be a connection between them. The incident of the stone, and a report I had from Mr Kasim on Thursday morning. Tell me, Captain Merrick, does the name Pandit Baba mean anything to you?'

Merrick did not answer immediately, but his expression was that of a man sorting out a number of images conjured by the name rather than that of someone taking time to search the dim reaches of an uncertain memory.

'As a matter of fact, it does.'

'Please tell me what.'

'He's one of those so-called venerable Hindu scholars who manages never to get caught inciting his eager young disciples to commit acts of violence against the Muslims, against the British, against anything the Pandit currently disapproves of.'

'But he does incite them?'

'I'm sure of it. In Mayapore I could never lay a finger on him though. Anything he did in public, like making a speech to college students, was all sweet reason and high-mindedness. He was quite capable of criticizing the Congress Party, too. I think the line he took was that they were poisoning Hinduism with politics, but he shunned publicity and discouraged any attempt to turn him into a renowned local figure. He was the perfect dedicated scholar. As far as I was concerned he was too good to be true. I also think he was a snake. A lot of the educated young Indians who got into trouble in Mayapore were under his influence at one time or another. We once arrested a chap for handing out seditious leaflets among workers in the British–Indian Electric factory. He said his pamphlet only repeated things Pandit Baba had discussed with a group of young men about ten days before. I thought I'd got him at last. We picked up some of the other boys, and then hauled in Baba Sahib. Within ten minutes the Pandit had them all grovelling and weeping and begging his forgiveness for misinterpreting his teaching. The one we'd arrested actually said he deserved to go to prison for his stupidity and unworthiness and the Pandit made a great show of being willing to go to prison in his stead as a penance for being such a poor *guru* that his innocent words could lead boys into trouble. Of course he knew he was as safe as houses. All the same he was more cautious afterwards.'

'Good. Thank you, Captain Merrick. Then you'll be interested to know that Pandit Baba is in Mirat at the moment. Mr Kasim was asked to meet him the other evening, ostensibly to enable Pandit Baba to be introduced to a son of M. A. Kasim, whom he professed to admire, which I doubt. But according to Mr Kasim, the Pandit spent most of the time talking about the Bibighar Gardens affair, with particular reference to the activities of the District Superintendent of Police, whom he can't have named, otherwise Ahmed would have hit on the connection at once. No doubt the omission was intentional. He knew Ahmed had already met you. I find Ahmed a useful extra pair of eyes and ears because of his objectivity. He tells me what happens more or less exactly as it happens and I then consider the implications. In this case I wasn't very sure what the implications were. To involve Ahmed in something? To pump him about something? Something to do with Ahmed's father? Perhaps,

perhaps. But it made little sense. Neither did the stone-throwing. However, it all makes very good sense when the police officer whose reputation Pandit Baba was carefully tearing to shreds the other evening turns out to be one of the officers riding in the car that has a stone thrown at it. The venerable gentleman used to live in Mirat, incidentally. We felt very much the same about him as you did when you were in Mayapore. By we I mean the then chief of police and myself. He never actually became *persona non grata*, but things were going that way. I was glad when he made the decision for us, and went off to Mayapore.'

'And you believe he was behind the incident this morning.'

'Oh, I think so, don't you?'

Merrick turned, placed his hands on the balustrade and looked out across the dazzling garden. Bronowsky came to the balustrade as well but continued to support himself on the cane.

'Not that we should be able to prove it,' Bronowsky continued. 'I don't intend to try. The Pandit is playing a little game with me, I think. The opening move was his invitation to Ahmed. He knew every word would be reported back to me. He also knew that directly I realized he was back in Mirat I would set my spies on him. My spies tell me he didn't come to Mirat alone but with a woman, who keeps in seclusion in the private rooms of Mrs Nair, who is the wife of the principal of the Hindu College, in whose bungalow Pandit Baba is staying. My spies also tell me that this morning between nine-forty-five and ten-forty-five, Pandit Sahib was scheduled to speak to the students of the college on the subject of his new study of the Bhagavad Gita. No doubt he did so, in full view of several hundred youths, standing on a dais, splendidly detached from anything so violent and vulgar as stone-throwing. Where my spies have been less successful is in getting the names of any of the young men with whom he has had private conversations. Perhaps he has had none. Perhaps it was all done before he actually reached Mirat. He is almost certainly in touch with very many people, throughout India.'

'Aren't you exaggerating a bit?'

'Oh, am I? Was the stone this morning then the first evidence you've had that you've been carefully tracked since leaving Mayapore?'

Bronowsky waited. Presently, as if reluctantly, Merrick said, 'Go on.'

'There was an incident in Sundernagar, perhaps? An anonymous letter referring to the fate of what, if I remember correctly, were called the innocent victims of the Bibighar Gardens? And in your first military establishment – another letter, or something even more direct to suggest there was some well-wisher close at hand. For instance an inauspicious design drawn in chalk on the threshold of your quarters? Wherever you have been? Didn't it begin in Mayapore itself, and hasn't it continued, at intervals nicely calculated to make you believe that your last posting shook off whoever was intent on your discomfiture?'

Merrick allowed several seconds to elapse before replying.

'It's been much as you say. But it hasn't bothered me, and Mirat is their last opportunity. They can hardly go on persecuting me where I'm going unless some sepoy has been bribed to put a bullet through my head when nobody's looking.'

Bronowsky smiled. 'I don't think killing you is the idea, although I'm surprised they haven't thought of a more dramatic way of embarrassing you than throwing a stone. As you say, Mirat is their last opportunity for some time to come. The wedding would have been an excellent background for something colourful. I understand, incidentally, that you're not a close friend of the groom. Did it pass through your mind that taking part in the wedding might bring your persecutors out into the open?'

Merrick said, 'No, it was the other way round. I agreed to be best man and then realized I was probably the worst possible choice. But it was too late to withdraw and I wouldn't have known how. All that business is something I prefer to forget. I'm sorry you've identified me.'

'My dear fellow, why? All I can say is that if I've correctly judged Mrs Grace's reactions to my quite unintentional disclosure, you are now an object not only of interest but of admiring curiosity. They will remember how at the time the DSP Mayapore was singled out by the English press for praise and congratulation. One recalls it all well enough, the newspaper reports and the gossip here in the club, on this very terrace. Well you can imagine. An English girl criminally assaulted by Indians, not just any English girl – if there could possibly be such a thing in India

– but a connection of a one-time Governor in Ranpur who stayed at the palace in the thirties. Within – what was it, an hour or two – the police in Mayapore under their DSP had arrested the six culprits. Technically they were only suspects and not proven culprits but that hardly diminished the blaze of satisfaction at thoughts of revenge already afoot. It's all people talked about for days. Mirat has always had a floating population and we had people in from Mayapore who naturally enjoyed their reputations as experts on the rape and the riots, although these weren't really connected, were they? The rape was a local affair and the riots were on a national scale. Being a military and not a civil station, of course, the major focus of interest here was on that brigadier you had in Mayapore who took charge when the civil authorities decided they couldn't cope.'

'Brigadier Reid.'

'That's him. Reid. Most of the talk was of Reid but what it came down to in the majority view was that both the army and the police in Mayapore had acted with commendable vigour, whereas the civil had shilly-shallied. Well you know how people think these days – they say the civil has become so riddled with Indians that the old dependable type of English civilian has more or less died out and it's only the English army and police officer who can really handle an explosive situation. I remember a fellow sitting somewhere along there' – Bronowsky pointed to the far end of the terrace – 'one evening when I was having a drink with the Station Commander, not Hobhouse, his predecessor. There'd been a paragraph in the *Courier* about a farewell party in the Artillery Mess in Mayapore for Brigadier Reid, and, of course, the implication was that he'd got the sack. This fellow leaned across, pointed at the paragraph and said, "There you are. Reid saves the situation and then gets kicked out because he saved it his way, which probably means he killed twelve Indians where the Government thinks ten would have been enough. But the deputy commissioner who sat on his backside will probably get a plummy job in the Secretariat and a CIE."'

Merrick said, 'The Deputy Commissioner was a good enough man. And Reid didn't get the sack. He was given another brigade. It was a better job really. The brigade he had in Mayapore was only half-trained. The one he got was ready to go into the field. He's back at a desk now, though, so I've heard. Perhaps he didn't measure up. Perhaps he was a bit too old. His wife was dying when all that business was going on. We didn't know about that until afterwards.'

'Ah well, the truth is always one thing, but in a way it's the other thing, the gossip, that counts. It shows where people's hearts lie. Reid saving the situation and getting the sack is what they wanted to believe. Just as they wanted to believe that the fellow in charge of the police in Mayapore had arrested the right men in the Bibighar rape business. They blamed the civil for any excessive use of force the Brigadier was guilty of and they blamed the civil when it was gradually realized that the rape case was coming to nothing. Not even coming to court. They never thought of blaming the District Superintendent for arresting the wrong men because they were convinced they must have been the right men. And the people we got here from Mayapore during those few weeks following the rape took the line that it would have served the six suspects right if the rumours going round were true.'

'What rumours?'

'That the six boys were whipped and forced to eat beef to make them confess.'

'I see. That tale even reached Mirat, then?'

'Indeed it did.' Bronowsky paused. 'Was there any truth in it?'

'The beef business was a result of some minor confusion, I believe.'

'Confusion?'

'The jailers were Muslims and some food sent in for them was mistaken by an orderly for food sent in for the prisoners, who were all Hindus.'

'Ah, yes. A very reasonable explanation. And the whipping?'

'Judge Menen satisfied himself on that score by having the men examined.'

'Physically? Or merely by questioning?'

'I gathered questioning was all that was necessary. They all denied the rumour and swore they'd not been ill-treated.'

'You didn't examine them yourself?'

Merrick, who had answered most of Bronowsky's questions without facing him now did so. 'Why should I have? I'm the chap who was being accused of defiling and beating the prisoners.'

'Not actually accused, though? It was merely gossip, surely. Enough of it to cause the District Judge uneasiness?'

'Yes.'

'But not you?'

'No.'

'You ruled out the possibility of your subordinates having beaten the suspects?'

'I took personal charge of the interrogations. I knew everything that went on.'

'Except about the beef. You said there may have been confusion over the beef but you weren't present when the confusion arose?'

'I'm not in the witness-box.'

'Captain Merrick, I'm sorry. I don't mean to cross-examine you. But I have a natural curiosity. Would you satisfy it on one point? Were those men you arrested guilty of the rape?'

Merrick again looked across the balustrade, fixing his eyes, it seemed, on some intense but distant vision of incontrovertible truth.

'I think,' he said at last, 'that I shall believe they were until my dying day.'

After a while Bronowsky said, 'Our venerable pandit told Mr Kasim that he is acquainted with the aunt of one of your principal suspects, and was once engaged to try to teach him Hindi, the young man in question having lived most of his life in England.'

'Hari Kumar. That's quite correct. The aunt was a Mrs Gupta Sen.' He looked round at Bronowsky. 'Kumar wasn't just one of the principal suspects. He was *the* principal suspect. I believed then and believe now that he planned the whole thing. He'd been going out with Miss Manners for weeks, quite publicly. People were talking. In the end I warned her against that kind of association.'

'Oh, you knew her personally then?'

Merrick flushed. He took a fresh grip on the balustrade. 'Yes, I knew her very well.' He hesitated before continuing. 'Sometimes I blame myself for what happened to her because I think she partly took heed of my warning. She seemed to stop seeing him. She came more often to the club. She did voluntary work at the local hospital, and was living with an Indian woman. But that was all right, in its way. Lady Chatterjee was a very old friend of Miss Manners's aunt, Lady Manners. All the same, living with an Indian woman like that meant she came in contact with Indians socially. That was part of the trouble. But Kumar didn't run in those circles at all. He was nothing but a tin-pot reporter on the local gazette and gave himself airs because he'd been brought up expensively in England. I don't really know how she first met up with him, but I saw her go up to him once at one of those war week exhibitions that were all the rage last year, and it was obvious they already knew each other. I think he'd been once to the MacGregor House where she lived. But I knew him from the time I had to haul him in for questioning. We'd been making a search of a place called the Sanctuary where a mad old white woman used to take in the dying and starving. We were looking for a chap who'd escaped from prison, a fellow called Moti Lal who specialized in organizing subversive activities among well-educated youths. Needless to say he was an acquaintance of our venerable pandit. So was Kumar. Kumar was at the Sanctuary because that mad woman had found him drunk the night before. He needn't have been in any trouble the morning we found him but he chose to make a mystery out of his name. In England he'd been known as Harry Coomer. He thought he was too good to answer the questions of a mere district superintendent of police. I let him go because there was nothing to pin on him, but he went down on my list all right, and before long I'd connected him with most of our other suspected troublemakers, including of course our venerable pandit. I didn't like the idea of a girl of Miss Manners's kind – well, any kind of decent English girl I suppose – getting mixed up with Master Kumar. In the end I warned her. And although she said it was really none of my business who she chose to be friends with I think she realized she wasn't doing herself any good. And I think she tried to end the association. Kumar wasn't going to stand for that. And she must still have been infatuated. The way I see it is that he bided his time, then sent her a message begging her to meet him again at the place they apparently often met, the Bibighar, and waited for her there with those friends of his. She denied having gone there to meet Kumar and made up a cock and bull story about passing the gardens that night and being curious to see if there really were ghosts there, as the

Indians said. She and Kumar both swore they'd not seen each other for several weeks. She said she never saw the men who attacked her. Well, perhaps that was true. She said they came at her from behind, in the dark, and covered her head. Perhaps she simply wasn't prepared to believe Kumar could plan such a thing or be mixed up in it at all. In the end that infatuation of hers led to the whole damned thing going unpunished. When she found out we'd arrested Kumar she refused even to attempt to identify the other boys and started loading her evidence or threatening to load it, and if the thing had gone to trial she'd have turned it into a complete farce. I'd have been prepared to let her try but others weren't. She changed her story, only slightly, but just enough to turn the scales. She said she'd not seen the men because of the darkness and because they'd come upon her suddenly, but she had a clear impression of them as dirty, smelly hooligans of the kind who might have come in from one of the villages because of the news of the riots and disturbances that were just breaking out all over the province. She knew that the boys we had in custody were the last type you could describe as dirty and smelly. You can appreciate the visual impression there'd have been in court, with these six Indian youths in the dock in Western-style dress, most of them ex-students, and Miss Manners in the witness stand describing a gang of stinking whooping badmashes. She might have changed her tune if she'd seen them all as I did the night I arrested them. Five of them half pissed in a derelict hut where they'd gone to celebrate on home-made hooch, and Kumar back home, actually bathing his face to try and clean up the marks she made on it, hitting out at her first attacker.'

'How did Kumar explain the marks?'

'Explain? Oh, Master Kumar never explained anything. He was above explanations. His speciality was dumb insolence. He refused to explain the marks. He refused to answer any question until he was back at my headquarters and was told what he was being charged with. His answer to that was that he hadn't seen Miss Manners since a night two or three weeks before when he'd gone to a local temple with her. What struck me as extraordinary really was that she said exactly the same thing. They were both so specific about their last meeting having been the visit to the temple it was as if they'd rehearsed it, or rather as if he'd terrified her or hypnotized her somehow into using just those words: I've not seen Hari Kumar since the night we visited the temple: while he for his part said: I've not seen Miss Manners since the night we visited the temple. I thought it didn't ring true, but everyone else thought it would sound pretty conclusive in court. I always hoped we could get it into court because on oath and in those sort of surroundings the terror and shame I think she was suffering might have been lifted. I'm sure she was under a kind of spell. I'll never understand it. I can never get it out of my head either. The picture of her running home as she did, all alone along those badly lit streets. I expect you know she died nine months later, in child-birth?'

'Yes. As I recall it, her aunt inserted notices.'

'That was extraordinary too, wasn't it? Inserting notices. The death, yes. But the birth of an illegitimate half-caste kid whose father couldn't be identified?' Merrick raised his hands and let them fall again on to the balustrade.

'It shocks you?'

'Yes.' Merrick paused, as if considering the nature and depth of his reaction. 'It's like a direct challenge to everything sane and decent that we try to do out here.'

'It was a human life lost, and a human life beginning. Why not mark the occasion?'

'I'm sorry. I can't see it that way.'

'Most of your countrymen would agree with you,' Bronowsky said. 'I find it sad that in the end Miss Manners inspires more contempt than she does compassion, but I recognize that this is the way it has to be. You English all felt that she didn't want you, want any of you, and of course among exiles that is a serious breach of faith. It amounts to treachery, really. Poor lady. The Indians didn't want her either. There were those things that happened to Indian boys because of her. Happened or didn't happen. In any case they went to prison, and no one seriously believed their political affiliations or crimes or whatever it was that was used as an excuse to keep them under lock and key were of a kind to warrant detention. Even the English thought it a pretty transparent ruse to hold the suspects, a handy alternative to punishing the culprits. It was the kind of ruse that wouldn't have worked in more settled times. One forgets how highly charged the whole emotional and political atmosphere was.

There were English here who talked as if a new Mutiny had broken out. Later, I remember, some of your more liberal-minded people had prickings of conscience. There was an article in the *Statesman*. I expect you saw it. It interested me but I looked in vain for any further developments. I thought, well that police officer was sticking his neck out but no one is going to cut it off. He's weathered the storm. I'm sorry to realize you didn't. Sundernagar was something of a backwater, wasn't it? Tell me, if you'd had a chance to serve in the police force of an Indian state such as Mirat, would you have been interested? Or would the army have exerted a stronger fascination? I know how much many of you young Englishmen in the civil and the police dislike the general policy of treating these as reserved occupations.'

'Would *you* have given me such a chance?'

'I don't know. Perhaps not. But I've never been inhibited, by any reservations I might have about the consequences, in taking controversial action and making unpopular appointments, if that action or appointment attracts me strongly enough. My own appointment, after all, was monumentally controversial. Let me put it this way, rather. Were you not presently committed in quite a different direction, I should be interested to discuss such a possibility with you.'

'May I ask why?'

Bronowsky smiled. 'Because my instinct tells me you are something of an anachronism in this modern world of files, second-hand policies and disciplinary virtues. The Indian states are an anachronism too. The rubber-stamp administrator or executive is too advanced an animal for *us*, although ideally that is the likeness one looks for in the outward appearance. Detachment. Objectivity. Absolute incorruptibility – I don't mean in the venal sense of the word, or the word's opposite I suppose I should say. But a man can be – swerved – by his own passions, and to me incorruptibility always suggests a certain lack of concern. The concept of justice as a lady with a blindfold and a pair of scales someone else may lay a decisive finger on without her noticing has often struck me as questionable. It presupposes a readiness in those among whom she dispenses her gifts to keep their hands to themselves. You must agree that would be a perfect world and in such a world she would be a redundant

figure. But we are dealing in imperfection. Keep the figure by
all means, as a symbol of what might be achieved. Keep the
illusion of detachment. Cultivate its manner. But admit it cannot
be a controlling force without compromising itself. What is
detachment, if it's without the power to make itself felt? Ah,
that's the common factor – power! To exercise power in Mirat
you need eyes in the back of your head as well as an unblinkered
pair in front. And you need men around you who do not lack
concern, who have enough concern to be in danger of it getting
the better of them and leading them into error. God save us
anyway from a world where there's no room for passionate
mistakes.'

'You think I made one?'

'I think it's possible. For instance you haven't said what led
you to the hut where the boys were celebrating, or to Kumar's
house where you found him bathing his face. It strikes me as a
significant omission. It suggests that your only reason for visiting
Kumar so soon after you heard Miss Manners had been raped by
a gang of unknown Indians was that Kumar had been associated
with her in the past.'

'You think that reason insufficient?'

Bronowsky shook his head and looked down at his shoes,
considering. 'This hut,' he said, 'where the other boys were
found half-drunk. It was close to the Bibighar?'

'Just the other side of the river, in some waste ground.'

'And Kumar's house?'

'That was also on the other side of the river.'

'In roughly the same area as the hut?'

'No. But not far.'

'How soon after the rape, approximately, would you say you
found the boys in the hut?'

'At the time I estimated it at approximately three-quarters of
an hour.'

'Time enough for the five boys to get across the river to the
hut and open a bottle.'

'Of course.'

'And get half drunk.'

Merrick paused. 'I used the expression loosely.'

'All the same it was the impression you had. That they were
in liquor.'

'Yes.'

'And I suppose about ten minutes later you got to Kumar's house?'

'Yes.'

'So he had had at least three-quarters of an hour to get away from the Bibighar?'

'Yes.'

'And yet he was still bathing his face?'

'Yes.'

'Perhaps he hadn't gone straight home.'

'Perhaps.'

'He could have gone to the hut with the others and had a drink. Then one of them might have noticed the tell-tale marks in the light of whatever lamp they lit, and he thought it wiser to go home and clean up.'

'Very possibly.'

'There was a lamp?'

'Yes.'

'Did they say they'd seen Kumar that night?'

'They said they hadn't. Only two or three of them were friends of his so far as I knew. They insisted they'd spent the whole evening in the hut, alone.'

'Where might Kumar have gone if he hadn't gone straight home?'

'Anywhere. He might have waited in his own garden until he thought it safe to go in and upstairs.'

'Without being seen by his aunt, you mean?'

'His aunt, or a servant.'

'If he'd gone straight home how long would it have taken him?'

'About fifteen minutes. Twenty at most.'

'Walking?'

'Yes – walking.'

'Say ten or less if he'd had a bicycle?'

Again Merrick hesitated.

'Naturally.'

'I wonder about the business of bathing his face, you see. Working from the basis of the earliest moment he could have got home and into his room and started to clean himself up he would then have had a good half-hour before you arrived.'

'If he did go straight home then half an hour wasn't enough, was it? He was bathing his face. Do you really think I had insufficient reason for going to his home? The boys in the hut first, boys of Kumar's kind, two or three of them Kumar's friends, swilling hooch, laughing and joking. What more natural than that having started combing the area of the Bibighar and found them I should go straight to look for Kumar?'

'Well forgive me. That wasn't clear to me, the order and circumstances of arrest. All this is impertinent, I know, but perhaps not without interest to yourself, to talk about it again, with a stranger. And I am trying to get a picture. For instance, presumably you went immediately to the scene of the crime, the Bibighar, in case some of those fellows were still there and in any case to examine it. Now, if you stood in the Bibighar and said Yes, this is Kumar's work, would the route you then took to Kumar's house, presumably in a truck or jeep with some constables, would it have led you over the bridge and past the waste ground?'

'Yes.'

'So you saw the hut. I think earlier you used the word derelict. And perhaps we have established that there was a light showing *from* it?'

'Yes.'

'Well, is that the picture? That you saw the light, stopped the vehicle and rushed across the waste ground to the hut and found those boys?'

'Yes.'

'Well, wasn't there something strange about that? Didn't it strike you as odd? There you had a group of young men supposedly guilty of the most heinous crime of all, the rape of a white girl, getting on for perhaps an hour after they'd left her, but barely a few minutes away from the scene of the crime, in what sounds like a rather conspicuous place, a derelict hut in the middle of some waste ground, showing a light, laughing and joking and getting sozzled.'

'You find that inconsistent?'

'I do rather. It sounds to me more like the behaviour of boys who'd done what they insisted they'd done, and no more. Spent the whole evening in the hut, drinking illicit liquor, lighting a lamp when it got dark, just intoxicated enough to be careless about who saw it. The distillation and drinking of illegal hooch is not a very serious misdemeanour.'

Merrick smiled. 'You've drawn your picture out of context. You're forgetting what day it was and what had happened during the day. It was the ninth of August. On the eighth the Congress passed their Quit India resolution. On the morning of the ninth we arrested not only leading Congressmen but Congress members of sub-committees throughout India. Everything had come to the boil. In the afternoon in a place called Tanpur some police were abducted and an English mission teacher called Miss Crane was attacked by hoodlums. The fellow with her, an Indian, was murdered. We got Miss Crane back into the Mayapore hospital at above five o'clock. Nobody knew what would happen next. Shopkeepers put up their shutters and people stayed in their homes. I know the Congress has denied that there was any underground plan for rebellion. But I'd say later developments provided sufficient evidence of organized rebellion to make their denial look silly. Boys like the ones we arrested for the rape may not have been directly involved in that kind of organization, but that's what they wanted, that's what they had their hearts in, that's the kind of activity that appealed to them. They laugh at Gandhi, you know, all that crowd. All that passive resistance and non-violence nonsense is just a joke to them, just as it's a joke to the militant Hindu wing of the Congress and organizations like the Mahasabha and the RSSS. When you get down to the level of the educated fellow who thinks the world owes him a living in exchange for his matric or BA failed, the kind of chap who loathes the English who gave him the chance to rise above the gutters of the bazaar but is very happy to ape English manners and dress English style, then you're down at a level where nothing but anarchy reigns. When trouble comes decent people in the towns put up their shutters and close their doors. In the villages they harbour their cattle and guard their property and their lives. And out come the badmashes in the countryside, and the hooligans in the cities. But in the cities a lot of the hooligans can quote Shakespeare at you. When I went across the river that night I wasn't looking for people hiding in their homes, but footloose fellows like those in the hut. You see my interpretation of your picture of the fellows in the hut is quite different. What made them careless, showing a light, lounging around only a few minutes away from the Bibighar was an intoxication that only had a bit to do with the liquor. The rest was cockiness. They'd had a white woman. They thought the country was rising. Their day was dawning. They could see it quite clearly. The *raj* was on the run. The long knives were out. In a day or two the white man would be crawling, licking their shoes, and there'd be as many white women to rape or murder as they wanted.'

'And Kumar?'

'Kumar? Oh, Kumar! He was the worst of the lot. Have you heard of Chillingborough?'

'Chillingborough . . . yes. One of your big public schools at home?'

'Exactly. Well that's where Kumar was educated. To hear him speak, I mean if you looked away while he spoke, he sounded just like an English boy of that type. His mother died very early and his father took him to England when he was about two with the express intention of bringing him up not only to act and sound like the English, but to *be* English. The father was rich, but got involved in some sort of financial trouble, lost all his money and died leaving Kumar penniless. The aunt of his in Mayapore, a decent enough woman she was too, paid his passage back to India and tried to look after him. But nothing was good enough for him. He couldn't take what it involved, to be just another Westernized Indian boy in a place like Mayapore.'

'Poor Mr Kumar. It can't have been a happy experience.'

'Good Lord, you'd think a boy who'd had those advantages would have been man enough to face up to a set-back like that. I can't share your sympathy for him. But then I met him face to face. Kumar wasn't just a theory to me. I knew his type too well, and he was the type multiplied. To me it was quite clear what he was up to. He was out for revenge. Out to get his own back on us because in India he couldn't pretend to be English any longer. One of the executives in the British–Indian Electric factory told me he could have had a decent job there as sort of apprentice or trainee. But Mr Kumar refused to call the managing director sir, and was insolent to the man he'd have been working under. His aunt's brother-in-law was a merchant and contractor and for a time Kumar did some clerical work in the warehouse. That didn't suit him, but that's where he would have been first in contact with this chap I was telling you about who escaped from prison. Moti Lal. Moti Lal was a clerk in the same business.' Merrick suddenly slapped the balustrade. 'It's so damned obvious. Moti Lal. Pandit Baba. Going around with those boys who were drinking in the hut. Working as a journalist. And we found a letter in his room when we searched it. A letter from an English boy warning Kumar not to write bolshie things, because the boy's father had opened some of Kumar's letters and objected to his son getting such letters while he was still recovering from wounds got at Dunkirk. And he had a photograph in his room too. A photo of Miss Manners. Having a white woman running after him was the final perfect touch, from his point of view.'

Suddenly Merrick looked round at Bronowsky. He said, 'I didn't have to stand in the Bibighar and tell myself, yes, this is Kumar's work. I knew it was Kumar's work the moment I got to the MacGregor House and Lady Chatterjee told me Miss Manners had come back, in that state. I'd been at the house before. It wasn't the kind of night you allowed a white girl to be missing, and that's what it looked as if she was, missing. Sometimes I used to give her a lift home from the hospital. I was at the hospital that evening because of Miss Crane and when I left I looked for Miss Manners. They told me she'd gone to the club. Later I was at the club myself and inquired after her. I was told she'd not been in the club. I thought, so that's it, she's gone back to meeting Kumar. There was nothing I felt I could do about it, and with everything that was going on I had my hands full. But later I went round to the MacGregor House, which was a pretty isolated place. I thought I'd make sure they were all right. I found Lady Chatterjee alone, Miss Manners hadn't been back, and she was worried. At least, she was worried when I told her Miss Manners hadn't been at the club. I had to go back to my headquarters. It must have been getting on for nine o'clock. On my way back to headquarters I remembered Miss Manners sometimes went over the river to that place called the Sanctuary. She helped Sister Ludmila with the clinic. So I went to the Sanctuary and found she had been there, but had left before dusk. It's not far from the Sanctuary to the house Kumar lived in. I thought the situation was serious enough to go and see if she'd arrived at Kumar's. She hadn't.

And Kumar's aunt said Kumar wasn't at home either. Well that made it obvious to me. They were off somewhere together. I thought, well, God, she's welcome to him if that's what she wants, and drove back to the kotwali at the Mandir Gate. If I'd gone the other way, over the Bibighar bridge, I'd have come across her, running home along those dark streets. I'd probably have come across Kumar as well, and those others. But I went to the kotwali. It was chance that made me decide to detour to the MacGregor House when I finally set off back for my headquarters. I got there ten or fifteen minutes after she'd returned, exhausted, in that awful condition. Lady Chatterjee had sent for the doctor, but not the police because Miss Manners hadn't explained her condition. But Lady Chatterjee suspected and I made her go up and get confirmation. The message I got back wasn't clear, but it was enough. Attack, criminal assault, five or six men, in the Bibighar Gardens. I had to drive back to get a police patrol, and order a comb. A good thirty minutes or more must have passed between her leaving the Bibighar and my arriving there. We were probably ten minutes beating through the gardens, and another five at the level-crossing hut, interrogating the keeper and searching the area. And all the time I knew I was wasting time. I knew where I ought to be looking. When I finally set off for Kumar's house I very nearly ignored that hut, in spite of the light showing that someone was there. I think what made me stop was partly a sort of automatic professional response, a realization that nothing could be overlooked, and partly a twinge of conscience, a recognition of the unfairness of leaping to a conclusion. But the sight of those boys, the revelation of what they were, who they were – well I had them out of there and into a truck and on the way back to my headquarters before they knew what had hit them. And I went on in my own truck, with three or four constables, to get Kumar. The aunt tried to stop us going upstairs. She was scared stiff. I knew I was right, then.' Merrick laughed. 'And do you know what he said, when we went into his room? Well, there he was, stripped to the waist, bending over a bowl, holding a flannel to his face. He looked up and said – "Who gave you permission to burst into my room, Merrick?" '

Bronowsky laughed, and presently Merrick replied with a sour grin, looked at his watch and moved from the balustrade.

'I shall have to go in I'm afraid.'

'We both must,' Bronowsky said. 'I'm sorry to have kept you so long, but sorrier that all we had to discuss needed to be compressed into what amounts to no more than a brief encounter. Perhaps in the not wholly unforeseeable future we may have the opportunity to resume. Anyway, if you are ever in Mirat again, or disposed to contemplate coming back, I hope you will let me know.'

They began to walk down the terrace. The sound of talk and laughter from the inner room had become louder in the last ten minutes or so. 'You could do with a drink, I expect,' Merrick said, 'I know I could.'

'I could but I must not. You'll find Nawab Sahib holding a glass of orange or lemon for politeness's sake, so I follow suit to keep him company. He takes Ramadan very seriously and as a matter of fact I think he enjoys the discipline of holding a glass and not so much as moistening his lips. Tonight he begins a special period of fast and prayer and cuts his intake almost to nothing, even after sundown. The îd is in ten days' time. I'm sorry you won't be here for it and that the charming Layton ladies will be gone too. Nawab Sahib would have liked to have you as guests to a meal in the palace.'

'He's been more than generous as it is –'

They turned in at the french windows. Several guests stood in the room they entered, presumably having come in there to avoid the crush in the room beyond, through whose open door the wedding party could now be seen.

Bronowsky paused and made Merrick do so too by holding his arm in a way which a stranger, had he been watching, might have interpreted as proof of intimacy and of knowledge and interests shared.

'Tell me,' the count said in a low voice so that Merrick automatically bent his head closer. 'Who is the outstandingly handsome young officer with the dark hair, talking to the girl in blue?'

Merrick glanced quickly round the room.

Oh that, he seemed about to say, *that is –*

But as if suddenly unsure of something – the name of a man, the colour of a dress, his questioner's intention, he looked back at Bronowsky and for a moment the question itself seemed

to hang in the balance; and Bronowsky, observing the way
the colour came and went on the ex-District Superintendent's
cheeks, released his hold on his companion's arm and murmured:
   'Well, it doesn't matter. Come, let's go in,' and led the way.

'He was in love with her,' Aunt Fenny said, beginning the job of
unbuttoning Susan out of her wedding-gown while Mrs Layton
folded the veil and Sarah laid out the going-away clothes on the
bed in the little room in the annexe. 'A woman I met who'd
been in Mayapore told me. She said it was well known at the
time. The DSP definitely set his cap at Miss Manners, and everyone was surprised because they'd thought of him as a confirmed
bachelor and all the unmarried girls who'd been trying to hook
him wondered what he saw in her. I expect her background had
a bit to do with it, but when a man like that decides to take the
plunge he takes it terribly seriously. It must have been awful
for him when she became infatuated with one of those dreadful
Indian boys. I remember this woman saying he looked positively
ill after Miss Manners had been assaulted and they were trying
to make the charges stick. He must have been nearly out of
his mind at the thought of those men getting away with it. No
wonder he wangled his way out of the police and into the army
and never mentions anything about having been in Mayapore.
Count Bronowsky must have an extraordinary memory for
names. Captain Merrick was obviously upset having it all come
out like that. Did you see his face when he got back from fetching the hat-box?'
   'Stop it, Aunt Fenny!' Susan shouted. 'Stop it! I'm trying,
trying, *trying* to pretend that it's a nice day. I'm trying, *trying* to
remember that I'm being married to Teddie —' She jerked at the
dress — not yet completely unbuttoned down the back — and
pulled it away from her body, wrenched her arms out of the
sleeves and pushed the unwieldy billowing damask down over
her hips, breaking the thread of one of the buttons. Clothed now
in only her brassiere, pants and suspender belt, she twisted round
and kicked the discarded dress away from her feet. 'My dear
child,' Aunt Fenny began — but Susan, flushed of face and white
of body, snatched a sponge bag from the bed, said 'We've got
fifteen minutes, Mummy,' and grabbing the neat little pile of
fresh underclothes made for the bathroom.

'What have I done?' Aunt Fenny asked her sister.

'Nothing, Fenny. It's what you were saying, not what you were doing. The subject was hardly a suitable one in the circumstances, was it?'

'Oh dear. Yes, I do see. I am sorry. Poor pet. What are you looking for, Sarah?'

'One of the buttons came off.'

'I'll find it. Millie, you pack the dress away, and let Sarah get on with her own changing.' Fenny went down on her knees. 'I told him about our being moored close to Lady Manners's boat in Srinagar, but he never knew her. It was a bit of a relief because it slipped out, I mean about the houseboat business, and if he'd been a friend of old Lady M's it would have been rather embarrassing having to admit we'd not actually met her, he mightn't have understood how difficult it was for everybody. I was dying to hear something straight from the horse's mouth, but he was positively evasive when I suggested he come over to the guest house tomorrow or Monday and spend an evening with us. He said he might have to go to Calcutta. I mean go for good before Teddie and the rest of them leave next week. What a shame. He's been quite attentive to you, hasn't he, Sarah, pet?'

'Aunt Fenny, I just don't understand you.'

'Ah here it is. Millie, put it in your handbag for safety. Help me up, Sarah. What don't you understand?'

'You're still talking about that Manners business –'

'But Susan can't hear –'

'That's not what I mean. I mean you're quite prepared to gloat over the details, you're willing to sit Captain Merrick down, stick a glass in his hand and prise every last juicy bit of the story out of him, without any thought for his feelings at all. But when we had an opportunity to show friendly to the poor girl's aunt it was you who found the perfect excuse for keeping our distance. You said a visit would embarrass her.'

'Well, so it would,' Fenny said, turning to help Mrs Layton fold the dress into the suitcase. 'And if it hadn't embarrassed her it would certainly have embarrassed me. Everyone agrees that that woman's behaviour has been quite extraordinary.'

Sarah began to undress, contorting herself to get at the row of satin-covered buttons. She felt a tide of anger and frustration spread through her body.

'You could actually hear that revolting crying,' Fenny added. 'It was like being next door to some awful Indian slum. It made one feel quite sick, the thought of an English woman living in it.'

'I was in it too,' Sarah said, and as she did so seemed to discover, through her finger-tips, the secret of undoing the dress, and to touch, as well, the spring of some deeper secret that had to do with the unlocking of her own precious individuality. She let the slipper-satin gown fall to her feet where it lay like an unwanted skin. 'I spent a whole hour in the slum, talking to the extraordinary woman and looking at the revolting baby. Of course it wasn't a slum and the baby wasn't revolting. But I'd agree about Lady Manners. She wasn't ordinary.'

'You went to see her?'

'Yes.'

'What for?'

'To apologize for us. Perhaps the rest was just curiosity, like yours, Aunt Fenny.'

She picked up the sloughed dress. It was a garment she would never wear again. Suddenly, the waste no longer offended her; she was glad – glad Susan had insisted on peach slipper-satin, had resisted her own puritan preference for a material that, with adaptations, could have served secondary long-term purposes.

'Did you know about this, Milly?' Aunt Fenny asked.

'Yes, I knew.'

'And approved?'

'I find it difficult to approve or disapprove of what I don't understand. Let's just say I knew you and Arthur would understand it even less. I told her not to mention it. But it doesn't matter now. May we forget it, please? May we just concentrate on getting Susan safely to the train?'

'You're absolutely right. I don't understand. Apologized for *us*? My dear child, sometimes you worry me. You worry us all. You worry us very much.'

'Yes, I know,' Sarah said, packing the bridesmaid's dress and satin shoes into tissue. 'I worry me too. Shall I put Susan's veil in my case? There's more room.'

Automatically Aunt Fenny handed the folded veil and tissue over. Fragile, even insubstantial, its packed bulk yet called for two hands to support it. Carefully, Sarah placed it in the suitcase on top of the other things: the veil, the most important of all the trappings of Susan's determined illusion, now done with, put away. She remembered the day spent in Aunt Lydia's glory-hole, the armfuls of stuff taken down into the Bayswater garden and burnt in the incinerator from whose heat she had stood back, shielding her face with a grubby hand and thinking of the perpetual light that seemed to shine upon the members of her family.

Perhaps, she thought, I am no longer in darkness, perhaps there is light and I have entered it. But she did not know what light exactly, nor what entering it would already have laid on her by way of obligations. But if it was light she wanted to share it. She looked at Aunt Fenny and at her mother, snapped the locks of the case shut as if completing, with a happy flourish, some special conjuring trick.

'But don't let's worry just now,' she said. 'It's not only Susan's day, it's ours too.'

And to end it, adding a third link to the chain forged by the throwing of the stone and the barring of the club doors to the Nawab, there was the curious incident of the woman in the white saree who appeared from out of the crowd on the platform of the cantonment station where the train for Nanoora was drawn up, and who seemed intent on joining the group seeing Teddie and Susan off, although she stayed a few paces behind them.

At first only the officers on the fringe of the group noticed her, and they thought nothing of her presence. But now from farther down the platform a warning whistle blew and as Captain Merrick came down from the compartment, leaving Mrs Layton and Sarah and Major and Mrs Grace to make their private family farewells to the departing couple, the group moved to give him room, spreading out, leaving a clear space, so that Merrick, turning, found the woman a few feet away, and coming closer.

The saree was only of cotton, but being white, suggestive of widowhood and mourning, the cheapness of the material could not be counted a sign of poverty. The thought that she might be a beggar did not enter the heads of any of the officers near by. She was not very dark-skinned, and she looked clean, respectable. In fact the immediate impression everyone had, including Mrs Grace who now also left the compartment with her husband and

Sarah, was that an unpleasant scene was about to take place, with the Indian woman claiming a seat in the first class.

But she seemed to be a beggar after all. She had begun to speak, in Hindi, which the nearest of the officers got the drift of, and it was clear to others that Captain Merrick understood too because he answered her, also in Hindi. Help me, she had said, your Honour alone can help now. I beg you. Be merciful. To which Merrick replied: Please go away. There is nothing I can do for you.

She cried out, and fell to her knees – an alarming spectacle which, moving as it might have been on a stage to an audience already translated to a state of suspended disbelief, could only be a cause of embarrassment on a public platform. And the cry, the act of abasement, were not all. She pulled the saree from her head, revealing greying hair, reached out and grabbed poor Captain Merrick's feet and placed her forehead on the dirty ground, moaning and keening. It was impossible to touch her. One of the officers said, 'Jao! Jao!' and tried to help Merrick urge her away by pressing on her shoulder with his shin. She let go, but held her ground, scrabbled in the dirt and dust of the platform and symbolically smarmed her head with ash. She rocked and swayed, crying out the while inarticulately.

The extraordinary scene came to an abrupt end. An Indian railway official, the man who was checking reservations, emerged from a near-by compartment, saw what was happening and came at a run. He grabbed the woman roughly, pulled her to her feet, pushed her away, once, twice, as often as was necessary to press her back into the crowd of watching Indians, shouting angrily, threatening her with the police. Back among her own people she fell to her knees again, resumed her crying and gesturing, crazed by some grief that the bystanders could not understand or share, and which therefore seemed absurd to them. They watched her curiously, then parted as an elderly Indian with a grey beard and wearing steel-rimmed spectacles pushed his way through, approached her, spoke, raised her to her feet and led her away out of sight, down the platform.

'A madwoman,' the man in charge of reservations said. 'Please, no one is badly molested?'

That she was a madwoman seemed unquestionable, but to hear her so described by this particular man was like having official confirmation of the fact. It could be assumed that the woman was known: a poor, mad, harmless creature who pestered sahibs on railway platforms.

Teddie had his head thrust through an open window. A clean piece of sticking plaster adorned his cheek. 'What was all that?' he asked cheerfully. But he was not looking for an answer. There was another blast on the whistle. He turned back into the compartment.

'You'd better go, Mummy,' Susan said, and Mrs Layton broke away, pecked Teddie on the undamaged side of his face and allowed him to escort her to the doorway where Major Grace completed the task of handing her down. Teddie shut the door and Susan joined him at the open window.

'Somebody catch,' she shouted, and flung the tired little bouquet she had carried all morning into the air, but in Sarah's direction. She caught it and instinctively raised it to her nose to sniff the still sweet-smelling blooms. She looked up and found Susan watching her, waiting perhaps for some particular word or gesture but there was no word or gesture to find beyond a mouthing of the word 'Thanks'. All I can do as well, Sarah said silently, is wish you happiness.

And that seemed to be enough.

IV

Captain Merrick came to the guest house at the beginning of the short twilight. Sarah was alone on the terrace waiting, she explained, for the darkness to fall and the fireflies to come out. The rest of her family were still in their rooms.

'Haven't you slept this afternoon?' Merrick asked. She still wore the dress she'd changed into for the farewells at the station.

'Oh, I meant to rest but the place was too quiet. It's been such a hive of activity all week. So I wrote letters, well – one letter, to Father, about the wedding.' She looked at her watch. 'They'll be in Nanoora soon. Won't you ring for a drink?'

'If you'll have one too.'

'I may as well.'

Merrick went to the bell-push set in the wall near the french windows. He had changed out of best KD into a cotton bush shirt and slacks. After he'd rung he stood by the balustrade.

'The last place the light goes from is the lake,' Sarah said. 'But when it's really dark the lake's much darker than anything.'

'Water reflects the sky,' Merrick said, prosaically. He took out his cigarette case, came towards her. She shook her head.

'No, thanks. Not just now. But you do. It's part of the pleasure of this particular time of day. Smelling someone else's tobacco smoke.'

'You're very sensitive to atmosphere.'

'I suppose I am.' She thought for a moment. 'But not more than anyone else. Perhaps I think about it more.'

Abdur Rahman came out.

'What will you have, Ronald?' she asked, using his given name because for the first time it seemed natural to do so.

'Whisky if I may.'

'Whisky soda, Sahib *ke waste*, Abdur. *Burra peg hona chahie. Aur* Tom Collins *meri lie.*'

'Memsahib.'

When Abdur Rahman had gone Merrick said, 'You think I need a *burra peg* then?'

'I don't know about need. Deserve.'

'I used hardly to drink at all.'

He sat opposite her, lit his cigarette, then said, 'I'm off to Calcutta first thing in the morning, so I've really come to say goodbye to everybody.'

'Oh, I'm sorry.'

'The signal was in when we got back from the station. Three of us have to go, but it wasn't unexpected. The General warned us before he went himself. I think it means some change of location for the training and forming-up area. Perhaps things are on the move.'

Sarah said nothing for a while. The light, fading fast, perceptibly, had begun its tag-end of the day business of investing people you sat close to – Ronald Merrick in this case – with a curious extra density, a thickness and solidity that compensated for the darkening and fading of features, hands and clothes so that the person on whom darkness fell was not diminished but intensified. She thought of what he meant when he referred to things being on the move. Those things seemed to be so far away that they were almost unimaginable, and yet within a day or two he could be close to them and she could reach out and touch him now and he could carry the impression of her touch into areas of danger.

'Does it ever strike you,' she asked, 'how odd it is about war, I mean about the way it's concentrated in special places? And in between the places huge stretches of country, whole continents where life just goes on as usual?'

'Like here?'

She nodded. 'Like here.'

He said, after a while, 'I suppose the other curious thing is wanting to go to it. I needn't have.' He glanced at her. 'Will you write to me sometimes?'

She glanced back, ready to smile, taking it as a light-hearted, vaguely sentimental suggestion of the kind she could forgive him because he was, all said and done, a soldier; but she was aware, meeting his glance, of the request perhaps being as serious as it was unexpected.

'Yes, of course.'

'Thank you.'

He might have intended to add something but Abdur Rahman came out with the tray of drinks. Sarah took the cold glass, waiting until Merrick had said '*bus*' to the pouring soda water, then called 'Cheers'. The ice burned her lips, numbing them. This first moment of drinking chilled liquid always reminded her of the feeling in the lips as injections in the mouth wore off. She swallowed, closed her eyes and put her head back, making a faint exclamation of satisfaction she only partly felt.

Merrick said, 'I've enjoyed meeting you all, you know. It's been a long time since I was – with a family.' He sipped his whisky. 'I came to say goodbye but also with the hope of being able to apologize. I think I can to you. If you weren't alone I probably wouldn't think it opportune. It's not the sort of thing one can say to several people.'

Sarah had opened her eyes and turned her head, but he was looking doggedly in the direction of the lake.

'That stone someone chucked this morning was really thrown at me. I know it sounds childish and melodramatic but persecution of that kind has been going on ever since I left Mayapore. It's never bothered me but today all of you were involved. And that's what I want to apologize for, for two of the things that spoilt the day for Teddie and Susan, and all of you. The stone, and that unpleasant scene on the platform. I'm not sure I oughtn't to apologize for the insult to the Nawab too. I ought to have made sure those lads from the military police knew there were to be Indian guests. In any case they wouldn't have been on duty if the stone hadn't been thrown. I'm sorry. I was the worst best man Teddie could have chosen.'

'Oh, no! –'

'It's all to do with that Mayapore business.' He was looking at her now. 'You know about my connection with that?'

'Yes, I know.'

'I'm sorry – I mean for not saying who I really was and then being, well, faced with having to deny it and tell a lie or admit it and look as if I'd been telling one. It made me feel and look ridiculous, made it seem I'd something to hide or be ashamed of, but all I've wanted is to forget it, not have to answer questions about it in every new place I go to. I hope your mother in particular understands that. She's had me under her roof. I'm not unconscious of the obligation that has put me under.'

Sarah resumed her watch on the lake. She felt vaguely ill-at-ease, conscious of those things about Ronald Merrick that Aunt Fenny put down as signs of a humble origin. Phrases like 'under her roof' and 'not unconscious of the obligation' had a stilted, self-advertising ring that she didn't altogether care for. It alarmed her to realize that she could respond, as automatically as Aunt Fenny, to the subtler promptings of the class-instinct. Why should I question his sincerity? she asked herself; realizing that this was what she was doing.

'We all understood,' she told him. 'I'd say it was the natural thing to do.'

'Thank you.'

'But I don't really understand about the stone and the woman on the station. Was she the mother of one of the boys that got arrested?'

Merrick smiled, took another drink.

'Well, you do understand, you see. It's all quite simple once you know who I am. But she wasn't the mother of one of the boys, she was his aunt. Although pretty much like a mother to him. It wasn't pleasant seeing her like that this morning. I remember her as respectable and dignified.' He drank again. 'I shan't forget it in a hurry. But of course I'm not supposed to.

They want it to prey on my mind until I'm as convinced as they are that I made a terrible mistake, the kind of mistake I shan't be able to live with because it'll be impossible to correct it. But it's impossible now. They must know that. That poor woman was being used. She probably thought there's a chance I could work a miracle for her.'

Dim as the picture was Sarah comprehended vividly enough the essence of what it would convey if a whole light shone on it. She understood that he had carried a burden a long way, for a long time, had suddenly put it down and was intent on showing her – and himself – what it was before he shouldered it again and took it with him wherever he was going. Perhaps he hoped that showing it would lighten it, although – in the swiftly encroaching dark through which he was beginning to loom he looked capable of rejecting any claim that showing it might give a would-be sharer.

'Did you see that man who took her?' he asked. 'He's behind it. I heard he was in Mirat, and had a woman with him. He put her up to it, brought her all the way here from Mayapore, getting her hopes up that I could be moved by that kind of appeal, that I could do something. It's pretty cruel. He probably doesn't care a fig for her, or the boy, any of them. It's sheer pretence. The case is useful to him, that's all. It serves his purpose. But that's India for you. They're quite indifferent to one another's sufferings when it comes down to it, and we've become so lofty and detached, so starry-eyed about our own civilized values and about our own common-sense view prevailing that our policy has become one of indifference too. We don't rule this country any more. We preside over it, in accordance with a book of rules written by the people back home.'

'Yes,' Sarah said. 'Yes, I think that's true.'

Merrick drained his glass.

'When I was a youngster one of the first questions I asked the District Superintendent I worked my probationary period with was how much longer he thought we'd rule India. I was thinking of my future which was something I'd somehow never thought of as necessary when deciding to try for the Indian Police. But when I got out here it all seemed so unreal, like a play. I suddenly couldn't picture it as a thing I'd work at all my life. So I asked this extraordmary question, extraordinary I mean because it was absurd to be wondering about much more than learning the job I'd chosen and worked hard to get. He didn't think it extra-ordinary, though, and I've always remembered his reply. He said: "Don't bother your head about that, Merrick, because there's not a thing you can do. India will be ours until one day between questions and other business in the House of Commons the British people through their elected representatives will vote to get rid of it. The majority won't have the least idea what they're doing. Getting rid of India will be just one clause in a policy of reform dreamed up by intellectuals and implemented by the votes of mill-hands and post-office clerks, and if you think there's any connection between *their* India and the one you're going to help police you might as well go home now." '

He set his empty glass down.

'I've never accepted that,' he said. 'The fact, yes. But not the mentality that so often goes with it. Well, you know the sort of thing, I expect, although you don't really get it in the army because it's a tradition that you have your own self-contained community and a job to do that nobody outside thinks worth a button until the shooting begins. While there isn't any shooting you take it as all part of the game to be mucked about. You accept it philosophically. But in the civil and the police, in the business of daily administration of the country, there's the constant irritation of being strait-jacketed by policy from above. At the top the Government of India tries to fight the Secretary of State in Whitehall and at the bottom the district officer tries to fight the Government. But it's always a losing battle. You find yourself automatically implementing a policy you feel passion-ately is wrong and the only thing you can do short of resigning is detach yourself from the reality of the problem, from the human issues if you like. You become – a rubber stamp. That's the mentality I mean. It's something my first superintendent encouraged me to resist. Perhaps he was wrong. He was an officer of the old school. He'd seen what he called better times, times – he said – when you were master in your own bailiwick. I suppose I should have recognized that it was an older school, not mine, and that I live in a rubber-stamp age. And don't get the wrong impression, Miss Layton. I haven't been kicked out of the police. I applied for permission to transfer to the army at the beginning of the war. I pulled every string I knew, just like

Mrs Grace's friend. It needed the Mayapore business, needed me to become what's known as a locally controversial figure, to persuade them to release me for the duration, but I had to plead pretty hard even then. I sometimes think that if I'd done something terribly wrong the rubber stamp would have endorsed it. That's its danger. It's a controlling force without the ability to judge. Once you're part of the rubber-stamp process yourself you could almost get away with murder. And that's wrong. Must be. You ought to be answerable for your actions, but you ought to be able to act, you ought to be involved. As an individual. As a person. As a fallible human being.'

'There are times,' Sarah said, 'when I think I don't know what a human being is.' Times – she told herself – when I look up and see that heaven is empty and that this is an age when all of us share the knowledge that it is and that there has never been a god nor any man made in that image. It is an intensely bleak discovery because it calls our bluff on everything. 'But I know what you mean,' she continued. 'It's easier for men. Being involved. No. That's a facile remark. It's not easy for any of us.' She looked at him. 'What was *she* like? the girl. The girl in the Mayapore business.'

'Rather like you,' he said, without hesitation, as if he had expected the question and knew in advance what his reply would be. 'Not physically. Well, she was taller.' He fingered the empty glass, slithered it to and fro, a few inches, on the table. 'I suppose a bit clumsy. She knocked things over. She made a joke of it. But she was very sensitive. She said she'd been gawky as a child. She still felt like that. Unco-ordinated. But I only saw her as – peculiarly graceful. Grave. Slow. Beautiful almost, because of that. The kind of girl you could talk to. Really talk to. Or just sit with. Our tastes were – much the same. In music. Pictures. That sort of thing. Our backgrounds were quite different, because mine is very ordinary, but Daphne didn't give a damn who your parents were or what school you went to.'

Sarah felt compelled to say it.

'Were you in love with her?'

He played with the glass a few seconds longer, then gave it up, stubbed his cigarette, studied the hand that had moved the glass, holding it stiffly with the fingers splayed, rubbing the back and the palm with the thumb and finger of his other hand.

'I don't know. I thought I was for a while. But if I was it wasn't at first sight. I'd met her several times and not thought of her that way. In fact my first impression of her was a bit unfavourable. I thought, Here we are, another of those English girls who come out here with bees in their bonnets about the rotten way we treat Indians. Give her time to find they're taking advantage of her and she'll get over it, she'll go the other way, be worse than any of us. In a year she won't have a good word to say for them. She was living with an Indian woman. You had to take that into account. Lady Chatterjee was one of those Westernized aristo-cratic Rajputs, an old friend of Daphne's aunt, and Daphne had come down with her from 'Pindi to see what she called something of the real India. I can't say I cottoned much to Lili Chatterjee. She belonged to that top layer of Indian society that mixes with our own top layer, but that's not real intimacy. More like necessary mutual recognition of privilege and power. A banquet at Government House, a garden party at Viceregal Lodge. You'd find a lot of Lili Chatterjees there. You'd also find this particular one playing bridge in Mayapore with the Deputy Commissioner's wife. But not at the Mayapore club, not among ordinary English men and women when they were off duty. They pretend they don't care, the Lili Chatterjees I mean. Pretend they don't need to rub shoulders with the English middle class in their cosy middle-class clubs and homes. But they resent it. Daphne resented it too. She wasn't able to draw the distinction. She didn't see why a line had to be drawn – has to be drawn. But it's essential, isn't it? You have to draw a line. Well, it's arbitrary. Nine times out of ten perhaps you draw it in the wrong place. But you need it there, you need to be able to say: There's the line. This side of it is right. That side is wrong. Then you have your moral term of reference. Then you can act. You can feel committed. You can be involved. Your life takes on something like a shape. It has form. Purpose as well, maybe. You know who you are when you wake up in the morning. Well sometimes you can rub the line out and draw it in a different place, bring it closer or push it farther out. But you need it there. It's like a blind man with a white stick needing the edge of the pavement. Poor Daphne tried to do without all that. I attempted to stop her – well, crossing the road. She didn't seem to know she was crossing it. I suppose that's when I first really looked at her, first considered her. And found out she wasn't just another of those English girls with bees in their bonnets. She was *this* girl. And it wasn't a bee. I don't know what it was. It was quite beyond me. But whatever it was it destroyed her.'

He cocked his head, considering her.

'I'm sorry, I said she was rather like you, didn't I, but I've mostly been describing the things that made her different. I'm not sure I can put my finger on what it was about you that reminded me of her.'

'Does that mean I don't any longer?' Self-conscious under his scrutiny she defended herself from it with the thought that he was an appalling man whom she didn't trust. He had a lively intelligence, perhaps less lively than its activity within the confines of a narrow mind made it seem; but she did not have to pay for the pleasure, of listening to a man – an Englishman in India – talking seriously, by liking him. She was interested in finding out why she reminded him of Miss Manners, but did not care whether the reason was flattering or the opposite of that.

'What I'm going to say,' he said, 'may sound impertinent.'

'No – I'm sure it won't.'

'Well – that first morning. When I'd joined you all in the station restaurant and you sat in front of the taxi next to the driver. I felt from your manner you were making the same sort of judgments of us that she did. And I thought – please forgive me – here's another one who doesn't see why a line must be drawn. But it was none of my business. And I was wrong anyway.'

'Why do you say that?'

'Because I can see the line's been drawn for you. You accept it. Do you remember in the taxi how I made rather heavy weather of young Kasim's position, and your mother very understandably thought I was speaking out of turn?'

'Yes, I remember that.'

'Talking about Kasim. It was a sort of Pavlovian response on my part. I'd met him and I think subconsciously he'd impressed me as a man of Hari Kumar's type.'

'Who is Hari Kumar?'

'The chief suspect in the Bibighar Gardens case. The man she was friendly with.'

'Yes, I see.'

'And yet not Kumar's type. Physically, yes, but finally Kasim bears no more resemblance to Kumar than you do to Miss Manners. But in the taxi I think there was a sort of fantasy in my mind of Hari and Daphne being about to come together again. I'm sorry – it sounds awful, but there it was. You sat there in the front seat, shading your eyes – and that was like her. She had a way of standing, peering at things a long way off, with just that gesture. And at the end of the journey, the guest house, and Ahmed there, well – waiting. On the other side of the line.'

For an instant Sarah held in her mind's eye an exact image of Ahmed as she had first seen him at the entrance to the guest house, emerging from the dim interior, and of herself still dazzled by the lake whose glare had become trapped inside her head, making it ache; and then this vision dissolved into another, of herself and Ahmed riding across the waste ground with constant distance between them except at those two moments, Ahmed's seizing of the reins, herself wheeling round suddenly to face him.

'That morning you went riding with him,' Ronald Merrick was saying, 'and Teddie and I turned up unexpectedly for breakfast. When we saw you coming back I thought, Well, that's it, I was right, it's all happening again. But then when you both got off your horses I realized it wasn't happening at all. You were friendly enough, but the barriers were up. The way you stood I could see you weren't sure how to leave him, I could see it crossing your mind: What do I do now, how do I get rid of him politely? You invited him in to breakfast, didn't you? Now if it had been Kumar he'd have accepted. But Mr Kasim knows where the line has to be drawn too. It was a relief to you both when he got back on and rode off. Am I right?'

Sarah felt he was right for the wrong reasons. She did not answer him immediately. He aggravated a grinding impatience in her which she knew she must discipline.

'I can't speak for Mr Kasim,' she began.

'Then for yourself,' he urged. 'It was a relief.'

'I wasn't under pressure.'

'We're always under that. Resisting it or pretending it's not there only adds to it.'

'What are we talking about, Ronald?' – she used his name again deliberately, as a little punishment for calling her Miss

Layton after she had herself dispensed with that formality. 'The social pressure that keeps the ruled at arm's length from the rulers, or the biological pressure that makes a white girl think she mightn't like being touched by an Indian?'

Did he blush? She was not sure. The light was too far gone, absorbed, drained into the lake. He put up a hand and rubbed his forehead: a gentle action – a reflex, it seemed, of his mental registration of the need, now, to tread decisively but delicately on ground set with traps for the unwary.

'They are connected,' he said. 'If you visualize such a union, or if you consider its counterpart, the connection is quite clear. A white man, well, supposing I – or Teddie – I mean if one's tastes ran that way, to marry an Indian woman, or live with her. He would not be – what is the right word? Diminished? He wouldn't feel that. People would not really feel it of him, either. He has the dominant role, whatever the colour of his partner's skin. The Indians themselves have this prejudice about paleness. To them a fair skin denotes descent from the civilized Aryan invaders from the north, a black skin descent from the primitive aboriginals who were pushed into the jungles and hills, or fled south. There is this connotation paleness has of something more finely, more delicately adjusted. Well – superior. Capable of leading. Equipped mentally and physically to dominate. A dark-skinned man touching a white-skinned woman will always be conscious of the fact that he is – diminishing her. She would be conscious of it too.'

He relapsed into silence. Presently he said, 'I've said it all very badly. And I've broken one of the sacred rules, haven't I? One isn't supposed to talk about this kind of thing. One isn't supposed to talk about anything much.'

'I know,' she said. 'It's how we hide our prejudices and continue to live with them. Will you have the other half?'

'No, thank you. I ought to be going. I'm only half packed. Will you say goodbye and make my apologies to your family?'

Sarah glanced to her left. A light fell on the terrace from Aunt Fenny's and Uncle Arthur's room. A servant had wakened them. Her mother's room was dark.

'I expect Aunt Fenny will be out in a while.'

'I mustn't stay.'

He sat on for perhaps as long as half a minute, then rose.

'There's one,' he said. 'A firefly. The end of your vigil.'

But she did not see it. Standing, she thought of Teddie and Susan arrived already at the Nanoora Hills Hotel, observing the scene spread out below the balcony of their bridal room.

'The end of your vigil,' Merrick repeated, 'and the signal for me to depart.'

She smiled, went to the light-switch on the wall near the bell-push and flicked it on. Merrick, bathed in yellow light, lost that faded density. The sleeves of his bush shirt were still rolled up to the elbows. His arms were covered in fine blond hairs. Beneath the flesh on his cheeks the bone structure was emphasized by downward-pointing shadows. His eyes, his whole physical presence, struck her as those of a man chilled by an implacable desire to be approached, accepted. She felt reluctant to take the hand he slowly, consideringly held out as if uncertain that anyone would welcome contact.

'Well, goodbye,' she said, letting their hands meet. His felt warm and moist. The light had already attracted insects. They encircled the shade, distracting her. For politeness's sake she began to accompany him down the terrace but he said, 'No, please don't bother. Besides, you'll miss the next firefly.'

She watched him go – puzzled that by going he made her feel lonely. He did not look back. She returned her attention to the garden. After a while she heard the sound of the truck engine.

She paused in her walk below the terrace. The night air was India's only caress. She was among the fireflies now. One passed within a few feet, winking on and off. Since Ronald Merrick left she had bathed and changed, but still was the first out to begin the ritual of the evening at home – home being anywhere, any place there was – say – a verandah, a bit of a view and the padding slap of a barefoot servant answering a summons. Home, such as it was, was the passing of the hours themselves and only in sleep might one wander into the dangerous areas of one's exile (and perhaps, in one's thoughts, between one remark and another, one gesture and another). One carried the lares and penates, the family iconography, in one's head and in that sequestered region of the heart. Why we are like fireflies too, she told herself, travelling with our own built-in illumination; a myriad portable candles lighting windows against some lost wanderer's return.

She laughed, chasing one of the luminous pulsating bugs and then stopped, having remembered her father. 'I hope you are not lonely,' she said aloud. 'I hope you are well, I hope you are happy, I hope you will come back soon.' And turned back towards the terrace and was in time to see Aunt Fenny and Uncle Arthur come out and stand for a moment arrested by some unexpected thought, consideration, recollection. From this distance their exchange was all dumb show, and not much of it either. Two or more English together were very uninteresting to watch. Fenny left Uncle Arthur's side and went to her sister's room from which light showed behind the louvres of closed shutters. Fenny must have tapped. A vertical band of light appeared, widened, and Fenny went inside.

Alone, Uncle Arthur now sat in a wicker chair. Alone he relaxed. Alone he became almost communicative with himself. He shouted for the bearer, crossed his legs, jerked one rhythmically up and down, smoothed his balding head, scrubbed his moustache with the first joint of his left index finger, shifted his weight in the chair, drummed on the adjacent table with his right hand. Yawned. Eased his tie. Scratched his crotch. And hearing Abdur Rahman approach, stretched his neck back to speak to him. Perhaps he asked where she was because Abdur seemed to invite his glance to fall upon, to attempt to penetrate the darkness of the garden beyond the geometrical patterns of light falling upon gravel and grass.

Just then the vertical strip of light appeared again and widened and Aunt Fenny came out with Mrs Layton who brought her glass with her, and at once, so it seemed, a different pattern of the play was established and Uncle Arthur was on scene again, erect, sparing of movement. With the two women an element of grace entered. They sat, one on either side of Uncle Arthur who sank to his chair again, crossed his legs but kept the restless one still. Aunt Fenny was talking. The lone sound, the steady vibration of her voice reached Sarah, but not the words.

She began to walk towards them, conscious of coming at them from a great, a lonely distance away. She shivered a bit and the thought occurred that it was foolhardy to walk at night alone. She did not want to be alone. She remembered the sense she had had of being left behind when she saw that only one of the beds in her and Susan's room had been prepared for the night, mosquito net unrolled and draped, its counterpart left stiff and bunched above a smooth virgin counterpane.

'My family,' she told herself as she entered the geometrical pattern of light and the circle of safety. 'My family. My family. My family.'

BOOK TWO

ORDERS OF RELEASE

PART ONE

THE SITUATION

I

May 1944

THE CAR TOOK what she and her husband had called the House-hold Gate out of the grounds of Government House. Had it been called the Household Gate before her husband's term of office? She could not remember. She brought her hand up, seeking the reassurance of the pleated front of her blouse and the mother-of-pearl buttons.

The car was headed towards the city, but at the complex of roads that met at the Elphinstone Fountain the driver bore right, north, taking the road through the noisy, heavily trafficked commercial quarter. Behind the grandiose stone buildings of the offices and banks lay the labyrinth of the Koti Bazaar where she had shopped accompanied only by Suleiman, to the despair of Henry's *aides*. She glanced at the *aide* who accompanied her now and realized that she had already forgotten his name.

'You have a question, Lady Manners?'

How well trained he was. She nodded. 'I'm afraid I suddenly can't remember your name.'

'Rowan,' he said, without fuss.

'Rowan. It is a curious thing, memory. My husband had an astonishing one. Mine was only so-so. I used to try and bluff my way out of the awkward situations it seemed to lead me into, until I realized the situations weren't awkward at all, but the bluff was. The gate we left by, is it still called the Household Gate?'

'I've not heard it called that. H.E. calls it the side way. I think the official description is Curzon Gate because of the statue opposite.'

'But Government House was built before Curzon.'

'That's true. How about Little West?'

'It will do. But so will side way. The next Governor will call it something else. It's a way of making ourselves feel at home in an institution. Shall you return to active duty, Captain Rowan?'

Today he was wearing mufti but she recollected from their brief meeting the day before in the Governor's private office the ribbon of the Military Cross.

'No, I'm told not. But that's probably a good thing because I wasn't made in the mould of a good regimental officer.'

'Were you wounded?'

'Nothing so distinguished, I'm afraid. But I managed to contract a number of tropical things, one after the other.'

'What do you intend? A regular staff appointment?'

'No. I've applied to get back into the political department, which is what I always wanted. I was seconded before the war and served a probationary period, but then of course the army reclaimed me.'

'And you were in Burma?'

'Yes.'

They were through the commercial quarter, travelling along a tree-lined section of the Kandipat road with the railings of the Sir Ahmed Kasim Memorial Gardens on their right and on their left the houses of rich Indians, in spacious compounds. Most of the iron gates were padlocked, the occupants having retreated into the hills. An exception was number 8. She found herself uncertain which of the houses along this stretch of the Kandipat belonged to M A K. And another name was troubling her – the name of the girl with the look of envy who had sent a parting gift of flowers – a Pankot name.

She turned and said, 'Do you have the photograph, Captain Rowan?'

'H.E. gave me an envelope which he said you might ask for.'

'I'll have it now, if I may.'

He zipped open the leather document case on his knee, reached in and brought out a square buff envelope.

'Would you unseal it for me?'

She watched while he sought for an ungummed section of the flap. Having widened it he made a neat break with his finger. He handed the envelope to her. She had taken her reading-spectacles case from her handbag in readiness and now put the glasses on. From the envelope she withdrew a rectangular matt-surface print. There were two pictures on it, side by side; profile and full-face.

For a time she avoided the flat stare of the full-face, considered instead the side-view of it, the whorls of the neat, masculine ear, the black, apparently oily, neatly cut hair. In the processing the skin had retained the two-level density of a dark face under artificial lighting, the impression that negative and positive were aligned, one on top of the other. So that is what he looked like, she thought, and stared at the full-face, at the oddly expressionless eyes whose whites conveyed an idea that they might be bloodshot. She closed her own eyes to consider, uninfluenced, a different but familiar image and, having conjured it exactly, reopened her eyes and felt a stab of recognition which in the next moment she did not trust. She replaced the photograph in the envelope, took off her spectacles. They had entered a semi-rural area of hovels. There was a smell of human and animal excrement. A naked ash-smeared Sadhu leaned against a parapet and watched them go past, his arms folded, his head tilted. She saw his mouth open and his neck muscles swell, but could not distinguish his shout above the shouting of little boys who ran alongside the car calling for baksheesh; keeping up with it because it was slowed by a farmer's cart ahead and a string of cyclists coming in the opposite direction. The light was opaque: one particle of dust to one particle of air. The temperature was in the hundreds.

She returned her spectacles case to her handbag. The envelope was too big to go in too. She gave it back to Captain Rowan.

'I shan't want it again.'

Rowan put the envelope back into his briefcase. He looked at his wrist-watch and then at her. Their glances met. 'We have about ten minutes, Lady Manners. Would you like me to go through the arrangements so that you know what to expect?'

Again she sought the reassurance of the pleats and buttons. She looked through the double thickness of glass at the necks of the driver and his companion.

'I've no doubt H.E. has arranged everything as I would wish.'

'Not without a certain element of awkwardness being involved. Awkwardness for you.'

'I couldn't expect otherwise.'

'Before we reach the Kandipat I shall pull the blinds down over the windows. The man sitting next to the driver has all the necessary documents to pass us through the gates. The car will stop twice. When it stops the second time we shall be inside the prison. We should be immediately next to a doorway that leads into a corridor and eventually to the jail superintendent's private quarters. We shall go to the end of the corridor and into a room marked "O". I shall leave you alone in room "O". There are a few details about room "O" but I can explain those at the time. There is only the one door. The man sitting next to the driver will be on duty in the corridor.'

'And I shall be alone in the room – throughout?'

'Yes.'

'I understand. I shall see and hear but not be seen or heard?'

'Yes. Afterwards it will take me about five minutes to rejoin you.'

'And I should wait in the room until you come for me?'

'If you would, Lady Manners.'

'Shall I be required to meet anyone at all?'

'No one.'

'Thank you.'

'When we leave, the car will have been reversed in the court-yard and will be parked ready. We shall then drive straight out and back to Government House.'

Again Rowan checked his watch. He leaned far back in his seat, canting his head to get a glimpse of the area they were approaching. He said, 'I think perhaps we should lower the blinds now. We're coming into Kandipat.'

He reached forward, pulled down one of the tip-up seats and transferred himself to it, stretched across to the little roller-blinds on her side of the car. Gradually the back of the car was filled with sub-aqueous light. She lost the sensation of forward movement. When he had completed the operation he resumed his seat next to her, resettled the document case on his lap. She raised her hands, feeling for the veil, groped round its prickly edge until she felt the smooth round knob of the hatpin. She pulled the hatpin out, jabbed it gently into the buff cord uphol-stery and coaxed the veil out of its folds, until it hung loose, shading the whole of her face and neck. Retrieving the pin she replaced it in the back of her hat.

'In case I forget – afterwards – Captain Rowan, thank you for what you have done, are doing, and have undertaken to do. Can I rely utterly on your discretion?'

'Of course.'

'I understood from H.E. that he chose you for a reason that would become clear to me. If he meant your courtesy and efficiency it has already done so. But whatever the reason he had in mind, I'm grateful. Forgive me for raising the question of discretion.' She smiled, then wondered whether he would see that she did, through the veil, in the dim museum-like light. He was not smiling. But her compliments had not embarrassed him. Well, she thought, you are a man who knows his worth, accepts its obligations with interest and its rewards with dignity, and I particularly thank God for you today.

She thanked God too for Captain Rowan not talking, for not attempting to disrupt her contemplation of the mystery of the inhumanity of man towards man that a prison was the repository of and which was entered consciously even when the actual entry was made blindly, so: stop and pause, start and move and stop finally. At some point, when the back of the car was over-taken by a violently sudden darkness the line dividing contem-plation of the mystery from experience of it was crossed. A chill smell of masonry conjured the sensation of enclosure within walls sweating from a low but insistent fever – the fever of defeat and apprehension. The door on Captain Rowan's side of the car was opened. The cold damp smell of stone strengthened, came on a shaft of funnelled air with the implacable impact of an actual touching, so that Captain Rowan's hand, offering itself to hers, was a momentary shock, the flesh-touch of someone who had accompanied her into an area of distress. There were on either side of her glimmers of filtered light and, in front, steps and a narrow doorway that was open. She mounted the steps, grateful for his cupped hand at her elbow. The corridor was stone-flagged, stone-walled, lit by one naked bulb at its farther end where already she could make out the letter 'O' painted in white on a closed brown door. Reaching it she saw that the corridor turned at a right-angle towards flights of wooden stairs – up and down. After he had left her alone in Room O he would ascend or descend by one of those flights: descend, more likely.

He opened the door of Room O. A cold dry draught and a faint humming in the darkness, a subtle lethal scent as of chilled milk in frosted zinc containers – a scent that always caught her high up in the nostrils and made her conscious of the space between her eyes – distinguished the room at once as one whose atmosphere was regulated by an air conditioner. She thought: I shall catch a cold. Captain Rowan entered the room ahead of her and switched on the light – an act which registered in her mind as a consequence of particular rehearsal rather than of general familiarity.

The room was a square of bare whitewashed walls. It contained a table and a chair. On the table, which was covered by a piece of green baize, were a carafe of water with an inverted tumbler over its neck, an ashtray, a pad, two pencils, a table-lamp and a telephone. The chair had its back to the door. It stood close to and facing the farther wall. Into that part of the wall a grille was let in at eye-level for someone sitting in the chair. Above the grille was a smaller grille with a fine steel mesh. The table was set against the wall to the right of the chair.

Captain Rowan went to the table and switched on the lamp. It threw a small pool of light on to the white notepad.

'If you would sit, Lady Manners, I'll turn off the overhead light.'

She sat, lifted her veil. She could see nothing through the grille, but when the overhead light went off the grille was transformed into a faintly luminous rectangle. She felt Captain Rowan come close. He reached in front of her, manipulated a catch on the grille and opened it. Behind it was a pane of glass and behind the pane wide-spaced, downward-directed louvres of wood or metal. She found herself looking through the louvres into a room on a slightly lower level. There were a table, several chairs and a door in each of the three walls she could see. The table was covered in green baize. There were pads, pencils, two wafer carafes and – placed centrally – a telephone. Suspended above the table was a light. It was on and seemed to be powerful. There was no one in the room.

'Actually there's not much to explain,' Captain Rowan said. 'You can keep the table-lamp on without any light on this side of the window attracting attention from below. The light over the table down there is rather strong and the shade is adjusted so that the man sitting in the chair facing you tends to be a bit dazzled by it. I've tried it myself and I assure you that if you look up you simply can't see this grille let alone see anyone watching through it. But if the table-lamp here distracts you, just switch it off.'

'I think I should prefer it switched off.'

He pressed the button on the base of the lamp.

'Yes,' she said, 'now I feel less vulnerable.'

'Good. The microphone is in the telephone down there.' He switched the lamp on again. 'This is the speaker, above the grille. When I get down I shall ask whether you can hear. If you can, press the button that you'll find under the arm of the chair.'

She felt for it.

'Yes, I have it.'

'Would you press it now and watch the telephone downstairs?'

She did so. A green light on the instrument in the room on the other side of the grille came on in response to the pressure.

'That is also your line of communication. If the relay system breaks down all you need do is press the button. I will then pick up the telephone and say "Hello". Once the telephone is picked up there's a direct private connection between this room and that. All you need do is pick your own telephone up and tell me what's wrong. My reply may not seem relevant, naturally. But please don't hesitate to communicate if you think it necessary. The business can always be adjourned if you want to discuss any points with me.'

'Thank you, Captain Rowan.'

'Are you close enough to the grille?'

'Yes, and I shall put on my distance glasses.'

'Shall I turn the light off again?'

'If you would.'

Again the room darkened and the picture of the room below became brighter, clearer. She leaned forward.

'Then if everything is satisfactory, Lady Manners, I'll leave you.'

She nodded and said, 'Yes, please carry on with your own side of things.'

Presently she heard the door open. Light from the corridor came and went across the wall she faced. She fumbled for the clasp of her handbag, found it and opened a way for her hand into the familiar homely clutter. Without removing the case she opened it and took out her distance spectacles, put them on. Now she could appreciate the fuzzy quality of the baize, the contradictions of texture between the baize and the wood of the chair that would be the focus for her attention. There was a clock on the wall above the door behind the chair. It showed twenty minutes after ten.

Just before it showed twenty-five past the door below it opened and Captain Rowan entered. He put his briefcase on the table and sat in the chair the prisoner was to sit in and gazed at a point directly in front of him. His voice reached her rather metallically from the wall just above her head.

'The table is on a low dais and someone seated opposite sits slightly higher than the person in this chair. The head of the person in this chair is therefore raised a bit when he looks the other person in the eye. So.' Captain Rowan raised his head fractionally. 'You should now have a fuller face view. More chin and less forehead. If you have heard and understood please press the button twice.'

She did so. The green light on the telephone pulsed on and off, on and off.

'Good. Perhaps we should test the telephone connection.' He stood, leaned over and picked the receiver off the rest. She turned to her right, groped for her own instrument, found it, lifted the receiver and placed it against her ear. His voice was now in the instrument.

'Can you hear me?'

'Yes, thank you. It's working perfectly.'

'Shall we begin, then?'

'Please.'

'I'll wait until I hear you put your phone back.'

She replaced the receiver.

He looked up, narrowing his eyes against the bright light, put his own receiver down and said – his voice coming again through the speaker – 'I assure you no one can see the little window. I'm going outside for a moment. A clerk will come in. When I return I shall have an official from the Home and Law department of the Secretariat with me. The clerk and the official are both Indians. The clerk's duty is to make a shorthand transcript of the proceedings. The official from the Home and Law department is here because of the nature of the business which H.E. felt shouldn't be left entirely in the hands of someone on his private and personal staff.'

Rowan, while talking, had come round to the other side of the table and stood with his back to her. He took some papers from the briefcase. She saw him hesitate over the buff envelope which she had returned to his care.

He said, 'Although H.E. handed this envelope to me without explaining what was in it I gather it's a photograph of the man in question. I feel I ought to warn you that if so it was probably taken the year before last, sometime in August 1942. There are bound to be changes.' He put the envelope back in the briefcase. He looked round the table, then walked across to the door under the clock, opened it and went out.

She glanced at the clock. It showed about a quarter of a minute short of ten-thirty. The door on the left of the room opened. The clerk came in – a middle-aged Indian with a balding head and gold-rimmed spectacles. He wore a home-spun cotton shirt and dhoti. His feet, sockless, were tucked into black leather shoes. He came down to a chair placed several feet to the left-rear of the table almost out of her sight, and sat. The sounds he made were clearly relayed. She could just make out his crossed legs and the shorthand notebook which he held ready on his knee. He made a few marks on it with his fountain pen, testing the nib and the flow of ink. Satisfied, he put the cap back on the pen and began to adjust the folds of his dhoti. It seemed an act of vanity, like that of a woman wearing a long-skirted dress making sure it hung gracefully. She particularly noted the action. The clerk was unaware of the presence of an invisible audience. He coughed, cleared his throat, began to tap the pen on the notebook; puk, puk, puk. She found herself fighting a tickle in her own throat and then remembered that no one could hear her if she coughed to clear it. She did so. The tapping continued uninterrupted: puk, puk, puk, puk.

Abruptly the door under the clock opened again – the tapping stopped and the clerk stood – and Captain Rowan entered followed by the official from the Secretariat – a lean elderly Indian wearing a grey chalk stripe suit and a pink tie. He carried a black document case. He cast an upward glance in the direction of the grille, then came and sat with Captain Rowan. Their backs were towards her. They sat with plenty of space between them. Midway, on the other side of the table, the empty chair faced her directly and her view of it was not obscured. The crackling of the papers the two men were leafing through was now the only sound.

'Shall we begin?' Captain Rowan asked suddenly.

The lean Indian's voice was soft and low-pitched.

'Oh yes. I am quite ready if you are.'

'Tell them we are ready, Babuji.'

The clerk went to the door in the right-hand wall, opened it and spoke to someone in Hindi, then closed the door again and went back to his chair.

For an instant Lady Manners closed her eyes. When she opened them the room still contained only the three men. Her hand tugged at the pleats and mother-of-pearl buttons and then lay inert. She breathed in and out slowly in an attempt to slow her heart-beat. The door opened again. She could not see who opened it because it opened on a side that would hide whoever entered until he was inside the room out of range of the door's arc. For a moment or so the door remained as it was at an angle of ninety degrees to the wall and no one came from behind it.

When he did he came hesitantly – a dark-skinned man dressed in loose-fitting grey trousers and a loose-fitting collarless grey jacket buttoned down the front. He wore chappals without socks. Having emerged beyond the range of the door he stopped and glanced at the occupants of the table and then at a man who was holding him by the right arm – to guide or restrain, or both; it wasn't easy to tell. The other man was in uniform – khaki shirt and shorts. He wore a pugree and carried a short baton. The hand on the arm suggested authority but also aid or comfort such as might be given in an unfamiliar situation to a man who normally gave no trouble, whose mind and body were disciplined to routine and were slow to respond to unusual demands.

The hand was on the arm for no longer than a few seconds. The guard let go, came to attention and dismissed, closing the door behind him. The man in the floppy collarless jacket and trousers stood alone.

'Sit down, please,' Captain Rowan said. He indicated the chair.

It was the same profile as in the photograph: the same neat, masculine ear. But not the same. The face of the man in the photograph had been held erect, was well fleshed; a dark, handsome face with hair that curled – a bit unruly on the forehead. This man's hair looked as though it had been cropped some months ago and had not grown out in its former fashion. Under the brown pigment of the face there was a pallor. The cheek was hollow. The head looked heavy, as if long stretches of time had been spent by the man, seated, legs apart, hands clasped between them, eyes cast down, considering the floor, the configuration of the stone. He moved towards the table, stood by the chair, still in profile.

'Baitho,' the official from the Home and Law department repeated.

The man extended his right hand, clutched the back of the chair and then with an awkward movement twisted round and sat, holding the back until the weight and position of his body forced him to release it. He gazed down at the table. His shoulders were hunched. It looked as if he might have his hands between his knees.

'*Kya, ham Hindi yah Angrezi men bolna karenge?*' Captain Rowan asked.

Briefly she had an impression from the man's glance at Rowan of eyes startlingly alert, in sockets which compared to those she recalled from the photograph were large and deeply shadowed. The man looked down again.

He said, '*Angrezi.*' The voice was notably clear.

'Very well. In English, then.'

Rowan opened a file.

'Your name is Kumar, your given name – Hari.'

'*Han.*'

'Son of the late Duleep Kumar of Didbury in the county of Berkshire, England.'

'*Han.*'

'At the time of your detention you were living at number 12 Chillianwallah Bagh in Mayapore, a district of this province.'

'*Han.*'

'The occupier of the house in Chillianwallah Bagh being your aunt, Shalini Gupta Sen, *née* Kumar, widow of Prakash Gupta Sen.'

'*Han.*'

'You were taken into custody on August the ninth, nineteen forty-two by order of the District Superintendent of Police, in Mayapore, and detained for examination. On August the twenty-fourth as a result of that and subsequent examinations an order for your detention under Rule 26 of the Defence of India

Rules was made and you were thereupon transferred in custody to the Kandipat jail, Kandipat, Ranpur, where you have remained in accordance with the terms of the order.'

'*Han*.'

'I understood you elected to speak in English. So far you have answered in Hindi. Do you therefore wish to have these proceedings conducted in Hindi and not English?'

Again Kumar looked up from the table, but this time his glance was not brief and only now was she convinced that the man in the room was the man in the photograph and the conviction did not come from the speaking of his name or his acknowledgement of it but from the sudden resemblance to the photograph that had become superimposed on his prison face, the prison structure of bone. The resemblance, she thought, must lie in the expression. He gazed at Captain Rowan in the way that he had gazed to order into the lens of a camera – as into a precision instrument that could do no more than the job it was designed for and could not penetrate beyond whatever line it was he had drawn and chosen to make his stand behind, the demarcation line between the public acceptance of humiliation and the defence of whatever sense he had of a private dignity.

'I beg your pardon,' he said – and she shut her eyes, to listen only to the voice – 'it was a slip. I seldom have the opportunity of speaking English to anyone except myself.'

A pause.

'I understand,' another voice said above her head. She kept her eyes shut. The voices were those of two Englishmen talking. 'These proceedings,' the second of the two voices went on, 'are authorized by an order of the Governor in Council dated the fifteenth of May, nineteen hundred and forty-four and the purpose of the proceedings is to examine any facts relevant in your case to the detention order under the Defence of India Rule. You may if you wish decline to submit to the examination, in which case the proceedings will be terminated immediately. I am also instructed to advise you that the purpose of the proceedings is to examine and not to make a recommendation in regard to your detention. You should not assume that refusal or acceptance of the examination or the examination itself will have any bearing on the order for your detention or upon its eventual termination. On that understanding I now ask you whether you decline or submit to the examination.'

A pause.

'I submit to the examination on that undertaking.'

'Your submission is recorded. In the case of Kumar, Hari, son of the late Duleep Kumar, at present lodged in the Kandipat jail, Kandipat, Ranpur, under warrant dated August twenty-four, nineteen hundred and forty-two, Rule 26, Defence of India Rules, and in accordance with order dated fifteen May nineteen forty-four, of the Governor in Council, Government House, Ranpur, Captain Nigel Robert Alexander Rowan and Mr Vallabhai Ramaswamy Gopal examining. Examinee not under oath. Transcript of proceedings for submission on confidential file to His Excellency the Governor, copy on the confidential file to the Member for Home and Law, Executive Council.'

Again a pause. She opened her eyes. Kumar still sat with his shoulders hunched. He had returned to his contemplation of the table, as if in deference to a formal rigmarole that was no particular concern of his, but as the silence lengthened, was filled by nothing more enlivening to the ears than the sound of Captain Rowan adjusting and checking the papers in front of him, Kumar glanced up again to stare at his chief examiner and again she was struck by the alertness his eyes – and the clarity of his voice – were evidence of. She could not interpret it beyond that. Impossible to say whether he sensed danger or saw the examination as a source of hope. It could be either. It could be both. But whichever it was the alertness and the clarity betrayed the presence of the man inside the hunched submissive figure of the prisoner.

'Since a detention order under the Defence of India Rules is made without recourse to trial in the criminal courts,' Captain Rowan began, 'the documentary evidence in front of this examining board consists of summaries of evidence, statements and submissions by the civil authorities of the district in which you resided. In this instance, which involved five other men as well as yourself, the documents were submitted to the office of the Divisional Commissioner before the order for detention was made on you and these five other men. We are however only concerned with these documents as they relate to you. It is not within the terms of reference of this board to disclose the details of these documents to you, but it is upon them that we shall base our questions. I shall begin by reading to you a list of names. The question I ask in each case is – were you at the time of your detention personally acquainted with the man whose name I read out. I invite you to answer yes or no as the case may be, after each name. With the name I shall give a brief description – for example occupation – to reduce the risk of confusion. Is that understood?'

'Yes.'

'The first name is S. V. Vidyasagar, sub-editor employed on the *Mayapore Hindu*, originally employed as a reporter on the *Mayapore Gazette*. Were you acquainted with this man?'

'Yes.'

'Narayan Lal, employed as a clerk in the Mayapore Book Depot.'

'Yes.'

'Nirmal Bannerjee, unemployed, graduate in electrical engineering of the Mayapore Technical College, son of B. N. Bannerjee, a clerk in the offices of Dewas Chand Lal, Contractor.'

'Yes.'

'Bapu Ram, trainee at the British–Indian Electrical Company's factory, Mayapore.'

'Yes.'

'Moti Lal, last employed as a clerk at the warehouse of Romesh Chand Gupta Sen, contractor of Mayapore, sentenced to six months' imprisonment in 1941 under section 188 of the Penal Code. Escaped from custody during February 1942, and according to this document not apprehended at the date of the document's origin.'

'Yes.'

'Puranmal Mehta, stenographer employed in the office of the Imperial Bank of India, Mayapore.'

'Yes.'

'Gopi Lal, unemployed, son of one Shankar Lal described as a hotel-keeper.'

'Yes.'

'Pandit B. N. V. Baba, of B-1, Chillianwallah Bazaar road, Mayapore, described as a teacher.'

'Yes.'

'I shall now divide those names into two groups. In the first we have two names – S. V. Vidyasagar and Pandit Baba. The questions I shall ask relate to the kind of acquaintanceship you had with these men. In the case of Pandit Baba the records at my disposal, those on your case file, give me no idea why at the time of your arrest you were asked what you knew of him. Perhaps that would be clear after a study of the case files of the other men arrested at the same time as yourself, but those case files are not available to this examining board because they aren't pertinent to this examination. I would stress the latter point to you. This board examines you wholly on the basis of the file pertaining to your own arrest and subsequent detention. In other words, you are examined by a board unprejudiced by anything that is recorded in the cases of the other men arrested. My first question, with regard to Pandit Baba, is therefore this: Would you tell the board why – in your opinion – you were asked what your relationship with him was? I would remind you that your reply to this question as recorded in the file was to the effect that you had nothing to say. In fact ninety-nine per cent of your recorded replies to questions were to that same effect. I hope the same situation isn't going to arise this morning. Will you then answer the question? Why should you have been asked if you knew this Pandit Baba? Have you any idea?'

There was an appreciable pause but when Kumar spoke any initial hesitancy he might have felt to answer questions was quite absent from the tone of voice.

'I believe he was thought to have a lot of influence over young Indians of the educated class.'

'Who thought this?'

'The civil authorities in Mayapore.'

'Including the police?'

'Yes. The police once had him in for questioning because one of his disciples got into trouble.'

'Disciples?'

'Young men who gathered round him to listen to him talk.'

'What sort of trouble had this particular follower got into?'

'I believe he'd published or distributed a political pamphlet, or made a speech. I forget which.'

'Were you one of Pandit Baba's followers?'

'No.'

'Did you know the man who got into trouble?'

'No.'

'Then who told you about this affair?'

'I heard it as a matter of course. I was employed on the *Mayapore Gazette*. In a newspaper office you hear quite a lot that never becomes common knowledge.'

'What happened to the man who published this pamphlet or made this speech?'

'He was sent to prison.'

'What was his name?'

'I forget.'

'What happened to the Pandit?'

'Nothing.'

'How well did you know Pandit Baba?'

'I knew him as a man my aunt hired to try to teach me an Indian language.' A pause. 'He smelt strongly of garlic.' A pause. 'He was very unpunctual.' A pause. 'The lessons weren't a success.'

'When was this?'

'In 1938.'

'He tried to teach you Hindustani?'

'Yes.'

'Until then you knew no Indian language at all?'

'None.'

A rustle of paper. Then Gopal's voice: 'I have several points in regard to the detenu's early background and I should like to raise them at this juncture.'

Rowan nodded. Gopal addressed Kumar direct:

'Your father took you to England when you were aged two, according to this document. You were born in the United Provinces. Your father was a landowner there. Have you an inheritance in the United Provinces?'

'No. My father sold his interest to his brothers before leaving for England.'

'Your father never taught you your native tongue?'

A pause.

'He was at pains to try to teach me nothing.'

'Why?'

'He wanted me brought up in an entirely English environment so far as that was possible. I had a governess, then a tutor.

Then I went to a private school and on to Chillingborough. I didn't see much of him.'

'Why was he wanting this – did he tell you?'

'He wanted me to enter the Indian Civil Service, as an Indian, but with all the advantages of an Englishman.'

'What were those advantages, was he saying?'

'I think he thought of them as advantages of character, manner and attitude. And language.'

'Because he thought the English character, manner, attitude and language were superior to the Indian?'

'No. More viable in relation to the operation of the administration.'

'I am not fully understanding that reply.'

'It is an English administration, based on English ideas of government. He thought an Indian at a disadvantage unless he had been trained to identify himself completely with these ideas. He admired the administration as such. He thought it would be best continued by fully Anglicized Indians.'

'Did you share his ambition for you?'

'Yes.'

'Why?'

'I knew no other.'

'You wished to enter the Indian Civil Service and serve the administration?'

'Wish is the wrong word. It suggests the existence of an alternative choice and a preference for one of them. In my case I was never aware of an alternative.'

'From this document,' Gopal went on, 'I see that your mother died soon after you were born. Did the loss of your mother contribute to your father's decision to leave India and establish himself as a businessman in England?'

'It made it easier for him to put his plan into practice.'

'It was some two years after your mother's death that he took you to England. Presumably it took a little time for him to make the necessary arrangements?'

'He had to wait until his own mother died.'

'She was ill?'

'No. He had promised his father to look after her.'

'Your grandfather was dead?'

'He'd left home.' A pause. 'He renounced his worldly goods

and left home wearing a loin-cloth and carrying a begging bowl. He intended to become what is called *sannyasi.*' A pause. 'The family never saw him again, but my father kept his promise and stayed until his mother died.'

'I see. Had he always hoped to leave India and go to England?'

'If he had a son.'

'He had been in England before?'

'He studied law there before the First World War but failed the examinations. He had a business sense but no academic sense.'

'He was what we are calling Anglophile? He admired the English way of life?'

'He thought an intimate understanding of and a familiarity with it essential for anyone serving the administration.'

'What were his political views in regard to India?'

'We never discussed politics as such.'

'Was he in favour of constitutional development leading eventually to a form of independence or of more hasty means to that end?'

'The former I imagine. He said India would remain under British rule well beyond his lifetime and probably far into mine.'

'Would you then say that he was anxious that you should become the kind of Indian whom the British would be happy to see as one of their administrative successors?'

'Yes. In later years he talked much along those lines, whenever I saw him.'

'Was that also your ambition? To become that kind of Indian?'

'I had no recollection of India whatsoever. I didn't know what different kinds of Indian there might be. My upbringing was entirely English. There was probably little difference in my attitude to the prospect of coming to India when I was older and the attitude of the average English boy whose family intended he should have a career out here.'

'You had, then, no sense of coming home when eventually you came to India?'

'The sense I had was the exact opposite.'

'Were you perturbed by what you found?'

'Yes.'

'Perturbed by the condition of the people?'

'I was perturbed by my own condition.'

'You did not look around you and think – these are my people, this is my country, I must work to free them of the foreign yoke that weighs them down?'

'I wanted nothing more than to go home.'

'Home – to England?'

'Yes.'

'But later, perhaps, you were ashamed of this selfish attitude and began to listen to young men of your own age and kind, to be affected somewhat by their hot-headed but understandable talk and ambitions?'

'They might have been of my age. They weren't of my kind. I was a unique specimen.'

'Unique? Just because you had been brought up in England?'

'No. Because I came back to a family my father had cut himself off from – a middle-class, orthodox Hindu family.' A pause. 'My uncle-by-marriage tried to make me undergo a ritual purification to get rid of the stain of living abroad. The ritual included drinking cow-urine. It was a family that didn't believe in education, let alone Western-style education. Not a single member of the Kumar family or of the Gupta Sen family my aunt married into had ever entered the administration. They were middle-class Hindus of the merchant and petty landowning class. Against this background – yes, I was unique.'

Gopal said, 'Thank you, Mr Kumar. I have no further questions on this subject.'

Rowan nodded, glanced at his open file, then looked up at Kumar who slowly transferred his attention from Gopal. For a while the two men – whose voices sounded so alike – stared at each other.

'In England, you say, there was little difference between you and the average English boy who was being trained for a career out here. Why, then, were you so shocked by what you found? The average Englishman arriving in India isn't shocked at all. In fact, he's rather excited. How do you explain this difference?'

She saw Gopal look at Rowan, as if astounded that he should bother to ask such a question. She too wondered why he had. If Kumar's face had been capable of changing expression she imagined it would now reflect an astonishment the equal of Gopal's. Perhaps the time he took to reply reflected it. Eventually he said:

'The India I came to wasn't the one the Englishman comes to. Our paths began to diverge in the region of the Suez Canal. In the Red Sea my skin turned brown. In Bombay my white friends noticed it. In Mayapore I had no white friends because I had become invisible to them.'

'Invisible?'

'Invisible.'

Rowan looked down at his file.

'I see that your father died in Scotland early in 1938 and that you came out in May of that year and went to live with your father's sister, Mrs Shalini Gupta Sen, in Mayapore. Was she your only surviving relative?'

'She was the only relative my father kept in touch with.'

'Why?'

'He had personally supervised her education when she was a young girl. The Kumar women were all illiterate but he taught her to read and write English, and speak it. They remained very fond of each other. When she was about fifteen she was married to a man of more than thirty – Prakash Gupta Sen of Mayapore. He died before they had any children. She was always interested in her English nephew – which was the way she referred to me in letters to my father.'

'Your father's solicitors communicated with her and she agreed that you should live with her?'

'Yes. She borrowed the passage money from her brother-in-law.'

'The contractor, Romesh Chand Gupta Sen of Mayapore, whose office you worked in for a time?'

'For a time.'

'Was there no possible means of maintaining you in England to finish at your public school and then study for the ICS examinations as your father had wished?'

'The means perhaps, but they weren't offered. My father committed suicide. He'd had business failures. He tried to recoup but lost everything. That's why he killed himself. His English-style son existed only as long as the money lasted. He probably couldn't face telling me my English life had ended and my Indian life was beginning several years too soon.'

'Did you ever ask your relatives in Mayapore if they'd maintain you in England until you'd qualified?'

'The solicitor wrote to my Aunt Shalini, suggesting that.'

'I presume you had some friends in England whom you could have lived with?'

'It seemed like it – for a time.'

'The family of one of your friends at school perhaps?'

'Yes.'

Again the rustle of paper.

'In one of the reports on this file there's a reference to a letter which the police found in your room and took charge of. It was signed Colin and had a Berkshire address. Was Colin the boy whose family might have looked after you?'

'Yes.'

'But your aunt was unable to raise the money to keep you in England, until you'd qualified?'

'She had no money of her own. She was a childless widow whose husband died in debt to his brother. She depended on this brother of his for practically every penny.'

'We're speaking of Romesh Chand Gupta Sen, I take it?'

'Yes. He offered passage money, and offered her an allowance for taking me in. The solicitor said it was very generous. According to him I was probably only losing my last term at school. He said I could study for the ICS in India.'

'You still intended to enter the ICS then? You came out with that ambition unimpaired?'

'Yes.'

'You discussed it with your aunt, and her brother-in-law?'

'Yes. But it was made plain by Mr Gupta Sen that there was no money for any kind of further education. I was expected to start earning my living.'

'Which is when you started working in your uncle's warehouse?'

'Yes. In the office of his Chillianwallah Bazaar warehouse. I remember the leper.'

'The leper?'

'He stood at the gate of the bazaar.'

'Why do you remember this?'

'When I saw the leper I thought of my grandfather. I wondered whether he had become a leper too.'

'And it was during this period that you had Hindustani lessons from Pandit Baba?'

'Yes.'

'It must all have seemed very strange to you.'

'Very strange. Yes.'

'The next note on your file is that during the summer of 1939 you applied to be taken on as a trainee at the British–Indian Electrical factory. A trainee in what?'

'They had a scheme for training suitable young Indians for junior executive positions.'

'You failed to get taken on, I see. In fact the note says: "The applicant was turned down chiefly as a result of his sullen and unco-operative manner." Would that be a reasonable description of your attitude?'

'It would depend on who was describing it.'

'I infer from the note that the man who found you sullen and unco-operative was the manager in charge of technical training. An Englishman. What happened?'

'I'd already passed two interviews, with one of the directors and with the managing director. The interview with the technical training manager was supposed to be a formality but he insisted on asking me technical questions which I told him at the outset I wouldn't be able to answer. When he'd finished he insulted me.'

'How?'

'By suggesting that I was an ignorant savage.'

'Are those the words he used?'

'No. He said: Where are you from, laddie? Straight down off the tree?'

'What did you say to that?'

'Nothing.'

'And so the interview ended –'

'Not then. He said something else.'

'Well?'

'He said he didn't like bolshie black laddies on his side of the business.'

'How did you respond?'

'I got up and walked out.'

'Yes, I see.' Rowan turned a page of the file. 'The next note shows you as having taken employment as a sub-editor and reporter on an Indian-owned newspaper published locally in Mayapore in the English language. The *Mayapore Gazette*. I presume this went well because you were still employed there at the date of your arrest in 1942, some three years later. What led you to choose journalism as a profession?'

'I didn't think of it as journalism or of myself as a journalist. A few months living in Mayapore showed me I'd only one qualification to put to practical use. My native language. English. The *Gazette* was owned, edited and written entirely by Indians. The English it was printed in was often very funny. So far as I was concerned I worked on the *Gazette* as a corrector. I became an occasional reporter because I could earn four annas a line for anything I wrote which they published. In addition to my salary of sixty rupees a month.'

'Did your aunt and uncle-by-marriage approve of this job?'

'My aunt did. She used to buy the *Gazette* for me so that I could read about local affairs. She liked reading it too. She liked being able to talk English again. She was always very good to me. She did her best to make me comfortable and happy. It wasn't her fault that I was neither.'

'Your aunt approved but her brother-in-law didn't?'

'When I got the job at the *Gazette* he reduced my aunt's allowance.'

'Why?'

'He said I could contribute to my upkeep out of my salary. He gave me nothing when I worked in his office.'

'I now go back,' Rowan said, 'to the first group of names, which consists of two: Pandit Baba and S. V. Vidyasagar. It was in the *Mayapore Gazette* office that you met the second man, Vidyasagar?'

'Yes. It was Vidyasagar who showed me the ropes.'

'What kind of ropes?'

'Finding my way round the Civil lines. Where the District and Sessions court was, who the deputy commissioner was and where he lived. Which was police headquarters. Who to apply to for permission to attend and report on some social function on the *maidan*. Before I joined the *Gazette* there'd been no occasion for me to cross the river and enter the Civil lines and cantonment.'

'Your job on the *Gazette*, then, took you into what from your point of view were more pleasant surroundings, a happier environment altogether?'

'It was interesting to observe that environment.'

'You felt yourself no more than an observer?'

'I was no more than an observer. Perhaps I was even less than that. But it was interesting. Observing all the things English people did to prove to themselves they were still English. Interesting and instructive. It taught me to see the ridiculous side of my father's ambition. I realized he'd left an important factor out of his calculations about my future.'

'And what was that?'

'The fact that in India the English stop being unconsciously English and become consciously English. I had been unconsciously English too. But in India I could never become consciously English; only consciously Indian. Conscious of being something I'd no idea how to be.'

Again Rowan looked down and referred to his file.

'Vidyasagar is also described as a sub-editor on another Mayapore newspaper, the *Mayapore Hindu*. How long were you working together at the *Gazette*?'

'About three weeks.'

'Vidyasagar then left and joined the *Mayapore Hindu*?'

'He was sacked.'

'Do you know why?'

'When the editor of the *Gazette* took me on he did so with the intention of sacking Vidyasagar.'

'Did you know that?'

'No. But Vidyasagar did.'

Rowan hesitated. 'So there was cause there for some friction between you and Vidyasagar? Did he harbour any kind of grudge?'

'If he ever did he never showed it. When he was sacked he said he'd expected it and that it wasn't to worry me because he could easily get a job on the *Mayapore Hindu*. He always remained friendly.'

'Why did the editor of the *Mayapore Gazette* prefer you to Vidyasagar?'

'I wrote correct English. Vidyasagar had only been at the Government Higher School.'

'The editorial policy of the *Gazette* has always been pro-British, wouldn't you say? I mean in comparison with the *Mayapore Hindu* where Vidyasagar was subsequently employed. A note here mentions that the *Mayapore Hindu* had a history of closure by the civil authorities. In fact it was closed down for a time during the riots in August 1942. The *Mayapore Gazette* on the other hand has never been proscribed.'

'The *Gazette*'s policy was to print nothing that caused the authorities any misgivings. I don't know if that amounts to pro-Britishness.'

'I ask the question to find out if you think there'd be anything to be said for a view that as a young reporter and sub-editor your attitude to affairs in general was more in keeping with the paper's editorial policy than was the attitude of Vidyasagar, for example.'

'I had no comparable attitude. Vidyasagar was an ardent nationalist, like ninety-nine per cent of other young Indians of his age and class and education.'

'That's what I mean. The editor of the *Gazette* might have found such a young man an embarrassment. With you he felt on safer ground?'

'The editor never asked me if I had any political views or affiliations. He hired me because of my ability to transcribe copy into correct English.'

'Did you have any political views and affiliations when you joined the paper?'

'No.'

'I believe a great deal of the *Gazette* was taken up with reports of social and sporting functions organized by the English community in Mayapore.'

'Yes.'

'And you sometimes attended such functions in your capacity as a reporter?'

'In that capacity, yes.'

'You would be a more suitable representative of the *Gazette* at such a function than Vidyasagar −? I mean from the editor's point of view.'

'Perhaps.'

'And from the point of view of the people attending the function?'

'From their point of view I would be no different from Vidyasagar.'

'Why?'

'We both had black faces.'

A pause.

'But as time went by you were able better than Vidyasagar to break down this rather artificial barrier. You got to know a few English people.'

'I got to know one.'

'You're referring to Miss Manners?'

'Yes.'

'During your interrogation, whenever you were asked to describe the circumstances in which you became acquainted with Miss Manners you always replied: I have nothing to say. The question was simple enough, surely?'

'It was also unnecessary. The person asking it knew those circumstances as well as I did.'

'This board does not. So I ask the same question. What were the circumstances in which you got to know Miss Manners?'

'I was invited to the house where she was staying.'

'Can you remember the date?'

'Either the end of February or the beginning of March, nineteen-forty-two.'

'I see. Then that would have been soon after an occasion in February 1942 when you were taken to the police station at the Mandir Gate bridge and asked questions about your identity and occupation?'

'The invitation was a consequence of that.'

'You mean you were invited to the house where Miss Manners was staying because you'd been questioned by the police?'

'My being questioned by the police made certain people in Mayapore aware of my existence, yes.'

'Please elucidate.'

'I was arrested in a place called the Sanctuary –'

'Arrested?'

'I was dragged into a police truck, taken to the police station, held, questioned and then released. It seemed to me like being arrested.'

'Very well. Continue –'

'The Sanctuary was run as a private charity for the sick and dying by a woman known as Sister Ludmila. After I was arrested – taken away – she got word to Romesh Chand Gupta Sen. He sent for his lawyer, a man called Srinivasan. Srinivasan was a friend of Lady Chatterjee who lived in the MacGregor House.

Miss Manners was staying with her there. Sister Ludmila also mentioned my arrest to a German woman who was in charge of the Purdah Hospital. Doctor Klaus. Doctor Klaus was also a friend of Lady Chatterjee. By the time Mr Srinivasan got to the police station to ask why I had been taken there I'd been released. But Lady Chatterjee heard of the incident from Dr Klaus and asked Mr Srinivasan about me. So she became interested in my case.'

'Your case?'

'My personal history.'

'You mean she thought you sounded like a young man in need of some help?'

'I don't know. I assumed she was interested in what she was told about me by Srinivasan, otherwise she wouldn't have invited me to the MacGregor House to one of her mixed parties of British and Indian guests.'

'Lady Chatterjee has some influence in Mayapore?'

'She was the widow of the man who founded and endowed the Mayapore Technical College. That's what he was knighted for. She was a friend of Miss Manners's aunt, Lady Manners, the widow of an ex-Governor of this province. In Mayapore the British always accorded her respect.'

'To have her interested in you was an asset, would you say?'

'I imagine it could be.'

'When you accepted her invitation was it in your mind that Lady Chatterjee might help you?'

'I don't know.'

'It was an opportunity for you, surely, to meet influential Indians and English people socially?'

'It was an opportunity I was in two minds about grasping.'

'Why?'

'I'd been in Mayapore for nearly four years. It struck me as significant that it needed my arrest to open the door to that kind of opportunity.'

'Significant of what?'

'I wasn't sure. Perhaps it was to find the significance that I accepted and went along.'

'And did you find this significance?'

'Influential people are always anxious to exercise their influence. They enjoy helping lame dogs of the right kind. But they're also always very busy. Only lame dogs who have tripped up ever come much to their notice. By then, from the lame dog's point of view, it's usually too late. Lady Chatterjee was about three years too late. I'm not criticizing. It was simply so. Having me at the party wasn't a success.'

'Any particular reason?'

'Influential people like to be thanked. I didn't thank her. And it worried her when Miss Manners was so friendly to me.'

'There are two points there. What did you have to thank Lady Chatterjee for?'

'Nothing.'

'You mean nothing in your opinion. What in hers?'

'She asked Judge Menen to inquire why a fellow called Hari Kumar had been dragged into a police truck and carted off to answer stupid questions. I don't suppose it did me any good in Merrick's book.'

'District Superintendent Merrick of the Indian Police?'

'Yes. That Merrick.'

'And Miss Manners's friendliness towards you. You think it worried Lady Chatterjee. Why?'

'Miss Manners was in her care. She felt responsible for her to Lady Manners.'

'I quite understand that. I don't understand why Miss Manners's friendliness to you should worry her. Surely it was to make you feel that you had friends that she invited you to the party?'

'Miss Manners was a white girl. Her friendliness towards me was of a kind that embarrassed people to watch.'

Rowan hesitated. From her air-conditioned place of observation she thought she detected, in Rowan, a certain stiffening of the neck and shoulders. She felt it in her own.

'I'm not sure I understand,' he said. 'What are you suggesting?' He hesitated, then abruptly, coldly said, 'That Miss Manners threw herself at you?'

Kumar stared at Rowan. There was a muscular spasm low on one cheek.

'I'm suggesting that even someone like Lady Chatterjee was incapable of accepting immediately that a white girl could treat an Indian like a man. I found it difficult to accept it myself. For a time I thought she was making fun of me. She talked so readily.

Without any kind of artificiality – or so it seemed. Just as if we'd been back home. Lady Chatterjee very naturally treated me with caution after that.'

'Why "very naturally"?'

'She probably thought I might take advantage of Miss Manners. That's the popular assumption, isn't it? That an Indian will always take advantage of an English person who is friendly.'

'It may be an assumption generally held among certain types of English who come into contact with certain types of Indian. I can't think why Lady Chatterjee should think you'd take advantage of Miss Manners unless you gave her cause.'

Kumar seemed lost momentarily in thought. He said, 'I may have done for all I know. My behaviour at that time left a lot to be desired.'

'In what direction?'

'I'd forgotten how to act in that kind of company. Or if I'd not forgotten, trying to act as I remembered I should act seemed – artificial. I said very little. I was socially ill-at-ease. Miss Manners told me later that I stood and stared at her. I wanted to say things but the right words wouldn't come. I was a bit suspicious. I wasn't shy. Suspicious, and then astonished – to be treated as an equal by a white person. The comparison between this and what I'd just experienced was so extraordinary.'

For a while none of the three men at the table spoke. Gopal suddenly opened his file again and said, 'With regard to that recent experience I have a question –'

'Is it in regard to what he calls his arrest?' Rowan asked.

'Yes –'

'I should like to go back a bit further and come to that in its turn.'

'By all means.'

Gopal rested again.

'You mentioned the Sanctuary,' Rowan began. 'You called it a place run as a private charity for the sick and the dying. I have a record here of the occasion when you were asked to go with the police to the kotwali after you'd refused to answer questions put to you by police officers who visited the Sanctuary and found you there. The record has a note to the effect that according to the person in charge of the Sanctuary – here called Mrs Ludmila Smith, not Sister Ludmila – you had been found the night before by her stretcher party, lying unconscious in some waste ground near the river. Imagining that you were ill or hurt they took you back to the Sanctuary – as was their habit whenever they found someone ill, starving or dying in the street. It turned out, however, that you were merely dead drunk. Is that correct?'

'Yes.'

'It was your habit to drink excessively?'

'I had never been drunk before. I was never drunk again.'

'When you were questioned by the police at the kotwali you were not at all co-operative. But you admitted you'd been drunk and that your main drinking companion of the night before had been Vidyasagar, and that the names of the others were Narayan Lal, Nirmal Bannerjee, Bapu Ram. You were uncertain about Puranmal Mehta – but said there was a fifth man there who might have been called Puranmal Mehta. Therefore three if not four of the men you got drunk with on that night in February were among the five other men who were arrested under suspicion of being implicated in the criminal assault on Miss Manners. The question I must ask you is – for what purpose had you and these other men, including Vidyasagar, gathered together on the occasion you got drunk?'

'There was no purpose behind the gathering together.'

'It was simply your habit every so often to foregather with these men?'

'No. It was the first time – and the last.'

'But you said some while ago that you always remained friendly with Vidyasagar.'

'I said he remained friendly with me.'

'You met quite often.'

'Our occupation brought us into frequent contact.'

'You would meet – as reporters – at some function or, say, in the law courts. Then perhaps, when you'd done your jobs, you'd go off together – as acquaintances?'

'No. We would meet as reporters. Once or twice he invited me to have coffee. I always refused.'

'Why?'

'I didn't want to become involved.'

'Involved how? Politically?'

'Not politically. Socially.' A pause. 'In those days I was at pains

to preserve everything about me that was English.' A pause.
'I lived a ridiculous life, really. But I didn't see that. I thought
of their life as ridiculous.'

'Vidyasagar's and his friends'?'

'Yes.'

'You despised them? Because they hadn't had your
advantages?'

'No. I didn't despise them. But I thought them ludicrous,
through no fault of their own.'

Gopal interrupted. 'In what way, ludicrous?'

'They were always laughing at the English. They pretended
to hate them. But everything about their way of life was an
aping of the English manner. The way they dressed, the style
of slang, the things they'd learned.' A pause. ' "I say, Kumar old
man, let's dash in for a cup of coffee." Perhaps it was exaggerated for my benefit. I was a bit of a joke to them. But it seemed
ridiculous.'

'You say "they". You were – if only in a limited sense –
acquainted with these other men as well as Vidyasagar?'

'I came to Mayapore in 1938. I met Vidyasagar in 1939.
Obviously I saw something of them between then and August
1942. I knew them by sight, whether they were with Vidyasagar
or alone. After the night I got drunk I knew most of them by
name.'

'The night you got drunk was the beginning of a closer
relationship?'

'You don't get drunk with men without establishing something more intimate in the way of relationship. But it was still
distant. And shortly afterwards of course my life changed
completely.'

'How?'

'I became friends with Miss Manners.'

'What hasn't been dealt with yet is the reason for your sudden
switch in attitude to Vidyasagar and his friends. Until a night in
February 1942 you say you found them ridiculous – to the extent
that you would even refuse to have a cup of coffee with them if
one of them asked you when he met you in the street, or at
some official function. But that night you join Vidyasagar and
his friends not just for a cup of coffee but for a hard bout of
drinking – which ended so far as you were concerned in waste

ground near the river in a state of complete intoxication. What led to this sudden reversal of what we might call your policy in regard to men like Vidyasagar?'

'The realization that after all it was I who was ridiculous.'

'Please elucidate.'

'It is a private matter.'

'You could say that practically everything we are discussing is a private matter. I suggest that this is no more, no less private. If you find it difficult to talk about, to know where to begin for instance, suppose we begin by discussing the events of that night. How, for example, did you find yourself in the company of Vidyasagar?'

'We were both on the *maidan*.'

'As reporters?'

'Yes.'

'What was taking place on the *maidan*?'

'A cricket match.'

'Between which teams?'

'Teams from regiments stationed in the cantonment.'

'You were watching cricket with Vidyasagar?'

'No. We met as we were coming away.'

'He invited you to come and have a coffee?'

'He invited me to his home.'

'And you accepted?'

'Yes. I accepted.'

'Why?'

'There no longer seemed to be any point in refusing.'

Rowan said nothing for a while. 'Because your resistance was worn down at last or because something had happened to upset you?'

'I suppose it was a combination of the two.'

'Then what exactly was it that had happened to upset you?'

Kumar stared at the table.

'He was there.'

'Who was there?'

'Someone I used to know.'

'Someone you had known in England?'

Kumar nodded.

'Colin?'

Kumar nodded.

'Your old school friend? The boy whose parents might have given you a home after your father died?'

'Yes.'

'Why was this upsetting?'

No answer.

'You met and talked, and thought that he was less friendly than you remembered? Or did you only see him from a distance?'

'He was as close to me as I am to you.'

'Are you saying that he was close to you but didn't talk to you?'

'We neither of us spoke.'

'Are you sure it was this man, Colin?'

'Yes.'

'You knew he was in India?'

'He wrote to me when he first came out, in 1941. He wrote several times, from different places. He talked about coming to Mayapore. Later he talked about how unlikely it would be that he could travel so far. Later he didn't write at all.'

Gopal said, 'And what construction did you put on that?'

'I thought that he had gone on active service. I thought he was having a bad war. First Dunkirk, now perhaps the Middle East. But he came to Mayapore. I guessed he had come to Mayapore when I saw soldiers in the cantonment wearing the regimental flash.'

'The flash of the regiment you knew Colin was serving in?'

'Yes. When I started seeing the soldiers with the flashes I began to expect him any day. I mean expecting him to turn up at my house. Then I realized that probably wasn't possible, because my side of the river was out of bounds to soldiers stationed in the cantonment. So then I began expecting a letter asking where we could meet. There was never such a letter. So then I thought Colin hadn't come to Mayapore with his regiment.'

'Are you still sure that he did?'

'He was there, on the *maidan*, watching the cricket. I went up to him, to make sure. It was Colin. You don't forget the face of a man you grew up with.'

'Why didn't you speak to him?'

'He turned and looked at me.'

'Yes?'

'He didn't seem to recognize me. In India, you see, all Indians look alike to English people. It was the kindest construction I could put on it. Either that, or that he had been in India long enough now to understand that it would be hopeless for a British officer to have an Indian friend who lived on the wrong side of the river and had no official standing. But whichever it was the effect was the same. To Colin I was invisible.'

'I see. And that is why when you met Vidyasagar and he invited you home you accepted?'

'Yes. For all his faults – what I thought of as his faults – I realized he had a gift.'

'What sort of gift?'

'A gift for forgiveness.' Kumar looked up at Rowan. 'They still all laughed at my ridiculous English manner – at the absurd-ity of it in someone born an Indian, and still an Indian, incapable of being anything in India except an Indian – but their laughing at me was meant with kindness. That's why I got drunk. They used to get hold of home-made hooch. One of them sometimes distilled it himself. That's the sort of stuff we drank that night. They were used to it, but I wasn't. I don't remember much after they'd helped me burn my topee –'

'Burn your topee?'

'The topee was a joke to them too. They said only Anglo-Indians and Government toadies and old-fashioned sahibs wore topees. So we burned mine. Then I suppose I passed out. When I met Vidyasagar later he told me they'd taken me all the way home to my house in Chillianwallah Bagh, so that I wouldn't get picked up by the police. But after they'd left me in the com-pound I must have wandered out again, on to that waste ground where Sister Ludmila found me.'

Rowan nodded. He now turned to Gopal.

'You have a point or two about Kumar's questioning by the police after he was found at the Sanctuary.'

'I think perhaps it has been taken care of. I had intended to question the examinee about his apparent reluctance to answer questions when he was taken to the kotwali. The reason for that reluctance now seems quite clear. Please continue the examina-tion along whatever lines you decide.'

'Well, let's deal with that reluctance, nevertheless. When you were questioned at the kotwali you were not at all co-operative, according to the report on this file. You admitted that your main drinking companion of the night before had been Vidyasagar, though. Is that correct?'

'Admit is the wrong word. It suggests I'd felt I had something to hide and then changed my mind.'

'How would you describe your attitude to the police at the kotwali, then?'

'As that of someone responding quite naturally to a situation that involved him in unpleasantness without any explanation.'

'It was not clear to you why you were asked to accompany the police to the kotwali?'

'It wasn't clear to me why the District Superintendent had me forcibly taken from the Sanctuary, thrown into a truck, driven to the kotwali and then pushed into a room there.'

'Was he aware that force was used?'

'He watched it.'

'Isn't it true to say, though, that you brought it on yourself by being truculent when asked to identify yourself in the Sanctuary?'

'Perhaps. It wasn't easy that morning for me to identify myself.'

'What were you doing when first approached by the police officers who visited the Sanctuary?'

'Washing.'

'Where?'

'In the compound. Under a tap.'

'Getting rid of a thick head?'

'Yes.'

'Let me read from the report: "On being asked in Urdu what his name was Kumar affected not to understand any Indian language. Mrs Ludmila Smith then said – 'Mr Kumar, these are the police. They are looking for someone. It is their duty to question anyone they find here for whom I cannot personally vouch. I cannot personally vouch for you because all I know of you is that you were found by us last night unconscious from drink.' Kumar then made a gesture of defiance. The DSP addressed him directly as follows: 'Is that your name, then – Kumar?' To which Kumar replied, 'No, but it will do.' DSP then directed his sub-inspector to escort Kumar to the police truck. No evidence being found at the Sanctuary in regard to the escaped prisoner Moti Lal, DSP proceeded to the kotwali at the

Mandir Gate bridge and formally questioned the man Kumar."
Is that an accurate record of the events as you remember them?'

'Broadly. I don't remember a gesture of defiance unless I
shrugged. And the report omits to mention that the sub-
inspector raised his hand to hit me and would have done so if
Sister Ludmila hadn't objected in the strongest terms to any
violence being shown by anyone in her presence, on her private
property.'

'Why did you say "No, but it will do" when DSP asked if
your name was Kumar?'

'He pronounced it incorrectly. There was too much stress on
the last syllable. And I was still in the habit of thinking of myself
as Coomer, which is how we spelt the name at home. I mean,
how we spelt it in England.'

'Weren't you being unnecessarily obtuse?'

'Not unnecessarily. Merrick spoke to me as if I were a lump
of dirt. I wasn't in the mood for that. I had a hangover, to begin
with.'

'At the Sanctuary, then, you admit you weren't in the mood
– as you put it – to answer fairly and squarely questions put to
you by the police in the course of their duty?'

'The course of their duty didn't automatically give them
permission to treat me like a lump of dirt. In my view.'

'When you got to the kotwali, however, you became more
co-operative?'

'I answered questions as soon as Merrick explained why he'd
brought me in.'

'You mean the District Superintendent.'

'To me he was always Merrick. We came to have a special
personal association.'

'What do you mean?'

'It will become clear if you ask enough questions about my
various interrogations.'

'At the kotwali it was explained that the police were looking
for an escaped prisoner – one Moti Lal – who had lived in Mayapore and was thought possibly to have come back and gone into
hiding there. It so happened that although the DSP didn't know
when he took you in for questioning that you knew this man,
Moti Lal, you in fact did know him, and had to admit it when
questioned.'

'Again admit seems to me to be the wrong word. I'd met Moti Lal because he was once employed by Romesh Chand Gupta Sen in the office of the warehouse in the railway sidings. I also knew Moti Lal had been sacked. Romesh Chand disliked his employees being politically active. He thought all their energies should be devoted to their work. I knew that sometime after he was sacked Moti Lal was sent to prison for subversive activities. I was in the District and Sessions court when he was brought up for his appeal. I didn't know he had escaped. And I didn't know the man at all – apart from what I've just told you.'

'Didn't you know that Moti Lal had been a very popular figure among young men like Vidyasagar?'

'One couldn't help knowing. One knew of Moti Lal's popularity just as one knew of Pandit Baba's.'

'We now come to more detailed consideration of the names in group two. In group one there were Pandit Baba and Vidyasagar. In group two there are six names. The first is Moti Lal, who at the time of your arrest under suspicion of criminal assault was still apparently unapprehended as an escaped prisoner. The five other men are Narayan Lal, Nirmal Bannerjee, Bapu Ram, Puranmal Mehta and Gopi Lal. According to police records these men were all intimates of Vidyasagar's. And according to your testimony at least three of them were your drinking companions with Vidyasagar on the occasion in February after the cricket match on the *maidan*. You would in fact agree that you had some kind of relationship with all the men in the two groups – however passing a relationship you may judge it to have been?'

'Yes.'

'With the exception of Pandit Baba, these were all young men whom you would describe, more or less, as ardent nationalists who looked forward to an early end to a British-controlled administration?'

'They were all young men – Indians – therefore they would almost inevitably look forward to that.'

'After the night you drank with a certain number of them, would you say that you became more directly aware of their political desires and affiliations?'

'No.'

'Did you not in fact become privy to their political activities?'

'I never assumed that they ever did more than talk politics.'

'For what purpose then would you imagine they got together?'

'To drink bad liquor and exist for a while in a state of euphoria.'

'Are you aware that a couple of days after your arrest in August nineteen forty-two Vidyasagar was arrested in the act of distributing seditious pamphlets?'

'Yes. Merrick told me. He said Vidyasagar had confessed to acts of sedition and had implicated me as the leader of a plot to attack Miss Manners.'

'What was your reaction to that?'

'I didn't believe he had implicated me.'

'But you believed he had confessed to acts of sedition?'

'It didn't surprise me. The whole of Mayapore was by then engaged in such acts – or so one gathered.'

'You insist that neither before nor after the occasion when you drank home-made hooch with Vidyasagar and his friends were you involved in any way with their political activities.'

'Yes, I insist that.'

'But you saw quite a bit of them? I mean after the night you got drunk?'

'If anything I saw less.'

'How was that?'

'I've already said. I had become friendly with Miss Manners.'

'From a time towards the end of February or the beginning of March, until August, in nineteen forty-two, your social life became more or less exclusively involved with your friendship with Miss Manners.'

'It was the first time I'd had a social life. So it did not *become* exclusively involved with that.' A pause. 'And the date is wrong. It was from February or March until towards the end of July. At the time of my arrest on August 9th I had not seen Miss Manners since the night we went to the temple. About three weeks previously.'

'So you always insisted. But let us concentrate on these men, other than Moti Lal and Vidyasagar. And of course other than Pandit Baba. That leaves us with Narayan Lal, Nirmal Bannerjee, Bapu Ram, Puranmal Mehta and Gopi Lal. You say that you knew them as among Vidyasagar's friends but that if anything you saw less of them after the night you got drunk. I want you now to tell me about the last occasion you saw them. When was that?'

'I saw them last on the night of my arrest as a suspect in the criminal assault on Miss Manners.'

'In what circumstances?'

'They had also been arrested. I was taken through the room in which they were held.'

'Taken through a room at police headquarters?'

'Yes.'

'You were taken through the room as distinct from lodged in it?'

'I was in the room for about half a minute.'

'Did you speak to them?'

'No.'

'Did they speak to you?'

'One of them said, Hello, Hari.'

'You didn't reply?'

'No.'

'Why?'

'They were behind the bars of a cell in the room.'

'What was their demeanour?'

'They were laughing and joking.'

'And you were not?'

'No. I was not.'

'What happened then?'

'I was handed over by the two policemen who held me to two other policemen and taken to a room downstairs.'

'So you saw those five men in a cell on the night of August the ninth and recognized them all?'

'I recognized about three of them in the sense of being able to put a name to the face.'

'All the faces were familiar as men you knew but you didn't immediately recall all their names.'

'That is right.'

'You remembered all the names later?'

'No.'

'Please elucidate.'

'I was told the names.'

'By whom?'

'By District Superintendent Merrick.'

'Your memory is clear on that point, that District Superintendent Merrick told you the names of the men in the cell?'

'Yes.'

'He read out a list of names?'

'Yes.'

'And asked you whether you were acquainted with the men?'

'No.'

'No? What then?'

'He read out the list of names. Then he made a statement.'

'What was the statement?'

'He said: These men are all friends of yours and as you saw we have them under lock and key.'

'What did you say?'

'I said nothing.'

'Why?'

'It wasn't a question.'

'On reconsideration would you not agree with a statement to the effect that "when asked whether he knew the five other men in custody and with whom he had been confronted the prisoner refused to answer"?'

'No.'

'Would you not agree with the following statement? Upon being told dates and times and circumstances when he had been seen in the company of one or several of the other prisoners the prisoner Kumar refused any comment beyond the words: I have nothing to say.'

'Yes. I would agree with that.'

'Why did you have nothing to say?'

'I refused to comment on any statement because I didn't know what I was being charged with.'

'When did you ask what you were being charged with?'

'When I was taken into custody.'

'At number 12 Chillianwallah Bagh?'

'Yes.'

'Not at police headquarters?'

'I asked first in my room at 12 Chillianwallah Bagh. I asked again at police headquarters. I asked several times.'

'When were you first told?'

'After I'd been in custody for about an hour.'

Gopal suddenly interrupted. 'Please recollect carefully. Would it not be more accurate to say something to this effect': He glanced at his file and read out: 'At 22.45 hours the prisoner

Kumar, having continually refused to answer questions relating to his activities that evening asked for what reason he had been taken into custody. Upon being told it was believed he could help the police with inquiries they were making into the criminal assault on an Englishwoman in the Bibighar Gardens earlier that evening he said: I have not seen Miss Manners since the night we visited the temple. On being asked why he named Miss Manners he refused to answer and showed signs of distress.'

'No,' Kumar said, 'it would not be more accurate.'

'In what way is that statement inaccurate in your view?' Gopal asked.

'I may have asked at 22.45 hours why I was taken into custody but it wouldn't have been for the first time. I asked several times. It was probably at 22.45 hours when the District Superintendent finally told me. But it didn't happen in the way it's written down there. He said he was making inquiries about an Englishwoman who was missing. His words were: "An Englishwoman, you know which one." He then made an obscene remark.'

'Let us be quite clear,' Gopal continued. 'According to you the investigating officer did not say "We believe you can help us with inquiries we're making into the criminal assault on an Englishwoman in the Bibighar Gardens" – to which you replied "I haven't seen Miss Manners since the night we visited the temple".'

'No. It wasn't like that. He made the obscene remark and followed it with another.'

'Are you saying it was from these remarks that you gathered who the Englishwoman was and what had happened to her?'

'I'm not saying what I gathered, only what was said to me.'

'Are you saying that what was said to you accounted for what is described as your distress?'

'I don't know what he meant by distress.'

Gopal said: 'Then how would *you* describe your demeanour at this stage of your interview at police headquarters?'

Kumar looked down at the table. Presently he said, 'I was shivering. It would have been noticeable.'

'Shivering?'

'The interview was in a private room in the basement. It was air-conditioned.'

'This room is air-conditioned. You are not shivering now, are you?'

'No.'

'Why were you shivering on that occasion?'

'I had no clothes on. I had had no clothes on for nearly an hour.'

'No clothes?' Gopal asked. 'You were asked questions by a police officer in a state of undress?'

She was observing the hollow-cheeked face intently. A tremor passed over it. It might have been a smile.

'The police officer who asked the questions was fully dressed,' Kumar said. 'But I was naked.'

'That is what I said,' Gopal snapped. 'Why were you naked?'

'I had been stripped. My clothes were piled on the table.'

'I meant for what purpose were you stripped?'

'Originally for inspection I believe.'

'A physical examination?'

'Inspection would be more accurate. There was no doctor present.'

Gopal said, 'No doctor? Then who carried out the examination?'

'The District Superintendent.'

Gopal hesitated, then said, 'What kind of examination was it?'

'An inspection of my genitals. Doesn't it say so in the reports? He inspected my genitals for signs of blood.'

'Did he tell you that?'

'No. But it was obvious.'

'How?'

'When he'd finished he said: "So you've been intelligent enough to wash, we almost caught you at it, didn't we?" Later he said: "Well, she wasn't a virgin, was she, and you were the first to ram her?" So it was obvious the inquiry was about a woman who'd been assaulted.'

Captain Rowan interrupted: 'All this is, in a sense, irrelevant to the purpose of the inquiry. I should like to return to the main line of questioning,' but Gopal shook his head and said:

'All this is most important. It has a direct bearing on the detenu's statement that he was not immediately informed of the reason for being in custody and a direct bearing on the question of his distress as recorded. The impression I am getting here is that the physical examination and the references to other physical matters occurred before 22.45 hours. Hitherto the official suggestion has been that until then questions were asked in an ordinary line of interrogation and not answered and then at 22.45 hours the detenu was told the reason for the inquiries, appeared to incriminate himself by naming the woman and then showed signs of distress.'

'Perhaps,' Captain Rowan began, but she had pressed the button under the chair arm. The green light flicked on. Captain Rowan lifted his receiver as she lifted hers.

'Hello: Rowan here —'

'I have a question to ask — and something to say —'

'Oh, yes.'

'Does Mr Gopal know I'm listening? He glanced up at the grille when he came into the room.'

Rowan waited before replying, as if his caller had asked a longer question.

'The answer to that — the official answer — is no. But in that particular case I'm not sure. I'm in the middle of an examination. Is it urgent?'

'What I wanted to say is forget that I am here. You have your job to do. I don't want you to worry about trying to spare me from hearing unpleasant things.'

'Very well. I'll attend to it.'

'One other thing —'

'Yes?'

'Does Mr Kumar know that my niece is dead?'

'I'm not sure.'

'I should like to be sure.'

'Very well, and thank you. Goodbye.'

For a while after he put the telephone back on its rest no sound came through the speaker other than the slight rustle of paper. Then he spoke.

'Since we've had an interruption I think this is a suitable moment to break the examination off for five minutes.' He slapped the file shut. 'Babuji — tell the guard to hold the prisoner outside.'

The clerk got up and went to the door through which Kumar had entered, opened it and spoke to the guard. Kumar glanced

round. His movements suggested that he had not clearly understood what Rowan said.

'We shall call you back,' Rowan told him. Kumar stood up.
'In about five minutes we shall continue the examination.'

It was extraordinary, she thought. When he stood he gave the
appearance of a shambling man – one who might not be
expected to think clearly or speak precisely. He ducked his head,
then turned. The guard had appeared and now accompanied
him out. The clerk also went out – closing the door behind him,
leaving Rowan and Gopal alone.

Rowan said, 'Let's use these few minutes to consider really
what our terms of reference are. If I may say so these questions
about his interrogation by District Superintendent Merrick in
regard to the criminal assault tend to lead away from the main
point about his association with a group of fellows who were
clearly politically committed and politically involved –'

'I'm sorry to disagree with you, Captain Rowan. Perhaps
I have had less time than you to study the files of this curious case,
and it is most unusual for a detenu to be examined, in fact I
have never come across it before, neither has my superior.
I have assumed that since His Excellency personally ordered the
examination some serious doubt has arisen about the order for
detention. From my reading of the files – coupled with my recollections of the actual circumstances – I feel that the order rested
entirely on the original suspicion this young man was under in
regard to the criminal assault. For that reason I feel that the criminal assault aspect should now become the focus for our questions.
It would have been useful if you had agreed to a previous consultation, but my clerk told me you were unable to find the time.'

'Well let me put it to you that the man was never charged
with criminal assault although I agree the assault was the original
cause of his arrest. He seems on the other hand to have been
known to the police as a man to keep an eye on over anti-
government activities of a seditious nature –'

'– on the frailest evidence, in my opinion –'

'Well, that's really what we're out to examine. I think the
situation here is that at the *time* of his detention the circumstantial evidence of his implication in the assault was so strong
that neither the Deputy Commissioner nor the Commissioner
felt it reasonable to set him free –'

'– and used this ridiculous evidence of a connection with subversive elements as an excuse to imprison him without trial.'

'One has to consider the affair in the context of the time and circumstances. If the detention order was unjustly made we have the opportunity of seeing that now in clearer perspective. What we're not out to do is apportion blame among the several authorities who had the difficult job of investigating at the time. I am strongly against a line of questioning that can help the man to level accusations against particular officials. It will only confuse the issue from H.E.'s point of view. Kumar isn't under oath and the officials aren't here to answer. The man himself has never petitioned against the order and there's some cause to think he may have counted himself extremely lucky to get away with simple political detention.'

'Who has petitioned, then?'

'No one. No one can except the man in question.'

'Then why has H.E. suddenly ordered an examination?'

'I think chiefly as a result of private pleas – for instance by his relative – his aunt, Shalini Gupta Sen.'

'And perhaps by the late Miss Manners's aunt – Lady Manners? She, surely, must eventually have learned the truth?'

'That I wouldn't know,' Rowan said.

'I thought perhaps new evidence had come up and that the examination might be a preliminary to other proceedings.'

'Not to my knowledge.'

'Are the other five men to be examined?'

'I have no instructions. And their cases were different. They denied the criminal assault but never denied subversive political activity, even if they denied being engaged in such activities on the night in question which they said they'd spent drinking in a hut on some waste ground close to the Bibighar.'

'But Kumar did deny subversive activity –'

'According to the file his answer to every question was: "I have nothing to say".'

'It is somewhat different this morning, isn't it?'

'This morning he is not under suspicion of criminal assault. Which brings me back to the point. In my opinion the line of questioning should be confined as nearly as possible to facts bearing on the ostensible reasons for his *detention* – detention as distinct from arrest. The criminal assault is a dead file. The girl herself is dead. If she was intent on protecting him – for emotional reasons, as was thought at the time – we shall never know. A line of questioning that concentrates on facts relating to the assault and on the details of his arrest on suspicion of being guilty of rape can only be abortive, I believe.'

'I disagree. If there had been no rape he would never have been arrested. It is clear he was arrested only because he was known to consort with her. It has always been clear, Captain Rowan, if you will forgive my saying so, that Kumar was victimized by the British authorities in Mayapore for his association with a white girl. It is common knowledge.'

'Common knowledge isn't evidence. We must base our inquiries on the evidence in this file.'

'The evidence is worthless to a large extent, Captain Rowan. You have only to read it to see it is all too – what is the word you use?'

'Pat?'

'All too pat. Rigged. The girl knew what would happen. The record of her private examination before the District Judge and the Assistant Commissioner makes it perfectly clear that the case could never have come to trial with the six men who'd been arrested because one minute of her evidence in the witness-box would have killed the case for the prosecution stone dead. She remembered her attackers as men of the badmash-type – men who'd probably come in from the villages because of the rumours of riot and the prospect of loot.'

'Perhaps, but I think the prosecution might have built a lot on her *first* statement to the Assistant Commissioner, that it had been too dark to see who they were. It's clear to me that the case never came to trial for two reasons – firstly that the evidence against the arrested men was wholly circumstantial and secondly that the girl – presumably for emotional reasons – was obviously prepared – even to the extent of perjury – to explode the case in everyone's face if they attempted to bring it into court. As you will have read in the file, she even threatened to suggest her attackers could have been British soldiers with their faces blacked. It was never a serious suggestion but you can imagine what effect her making it, even as a joke, would have had on a jury. She could never have killed the case for the prosecution but with the chief witness working against the prosecution it's most unlikely that their case could have been proved.'

'And so the men would have gone free, Captain Rowan. The detention orders were made to ensure that never happened. The whole thing stank, Captain Rowan. You know it, I know it. H.E. knows it. That young man was as much a threat to the defence of India as I am. His only crime was to have been the friend of a white girl who got raped by a gang of hooligans or looters. What can we possibly turn up now that will shed any positive light at all on his political ideas and activities? The evidence on this file that attempts to point to political affiliations is laughable. I hardly see how one can even begin to frame viable questions from it. I will say frankly, Captain Rowan, that if we are to put this poor fellow through this examination we must give him every chance to tell us exactly what happened and not bother our heads about what it will look like on paper or what muck might be raked. I did not ask to be appointed one of his examiners, but since I am one I intend to examine and not be blinkered by any narrow interpretations of terms of reference that leave the record not worth the paper it's written on. Frankly I do not care anything about confusing H.E. with details about the assault. Once the examination is over we are both personally powerless to take any step or press for any step we think is justified. I shan't be surprised if the record simply goes on file and is conveniently forgotten and that poor fellow who may be having his hopes raised has them dashed again. But we are not powerless to pave the way for a justified step to be taken. Forgive me. I am perhaps overheated.'

As if by an association of ideas Gopal lifted the tumbler from one of the carafes and poured himself a glass of water. He sipped it delicately, then patted his lips with a folded handkerchief from his breast pocket.

'Very well, but if it's H.E.'s intention to review the detention order an examination that weighs heavily on the side of questions relating to the criminal assault may have a contrary effect. He may throw the record out as irrelevant. And of course you do realize that the examination might give grounds for renewed suspicion that the assault was an aspect of subversive activities plotted and executed by Kumar and others? You speak as if there was no evidence implicating Kumar in the rape. He was absent from home at the relevant time, never accounted for his movements and was bathing cuts and abrasions on his face when the police arrested him.'

'So the police record states. The first police report – the one signed by a sub-inspector – also mentioned that the girl's bicycle was found in the ditch outside Kumar's home. The second report, by the District Superintendent, dated one or two days later, states that this was an error and that the bicycle was found at the scene of the rape, in the Bibighar Gardens, and put in the back of the truck before the visit to Kumar's home. Which smells to me like an abortive attempt to plant evidence which the District Superintendent later realized wasn't going to wash. I personally have no faith whatsoever in the statements to the effect that Kumar was bathing his face when arrested. If Kumar's face was cut and bruised it was just as likely because the police hit him.'

'Then why didn't he say so? He was examined by the Assistant Commissioner, and by a magistrate appointed by Judge Menen, as well as by the District Superintendent.'

'Who would have believed him? He had listened to innumerable criminal cases in the courts as a reporter for the *Mayapore Gazette* and knew what he was up against. He is an intelligent man – a product of your own English public schools.'

'I know. I went to the same one.'

Gopal stared at Rowan – as if suddenly suspicious.

'Oh? Does he recognize you then?'

'No. I was in my last term when he was in his first. But I remember him. He was the first Indian Chillingborough ever took, a bit of a showpiece. A few years later I watched him play cricket for the school against the old boys. He was very popular. I have a vague recollection of his friend Colin, too.' Rowan poured a glass of water also. 'It's one of the reasons H.E. chose me to make the examination. Until the other day I'd no idea the chief suspect in the Bibighar case was the fellow I knew as Harry Coomer. I wish I'd known years ago what he was having to face. There must have been several old Chillingburians out here who'd have been willing to help him.'

After a while Mr Gopal said, 'Do you think so, Captain Rowan? Willing, perhaps. Able – no. He is an English boy with a dark brown skin. The combination is hopeless.'

'Yes,' Rowan said after a while. 'Perhaps it is.'

II

'The examinee's last statement, please.'

The clerk flicked back one page of his notebook.

' "So it was obvious the inquiry was about a woman who'd been assaulted." '

'No – the whole of it.'

The clerk cleared his throat and recited in a monotone, ' "When he'd finished he said – So you've been intelligent enough to wash, we almost caught you at it, didn't we? Later he said: Well, she wasn't a virgin, was she, and you were the first to ram her? So it was obvious the inquiry was about a woman who'd been assaulted." '

'Thank you. Mr Gopal – you were making a point.'

'Yes. It is really a question of the order and time at which the detenu alleges certain things were done and certain things said.' Gopal now spoke directly to Kumar. 'I should like to go back to the moment when the police came to your house and took you into custody. According to the police report this was at approximately 21.40 hours. Is that correct?'

'I expect so.'

'I see – also from the report – that some three-quarters of an hour earlier the DSP called at your home to see if Miss Manners happened to be there. He spoke to your aunt. She said she had not seen Miss Manners for several weeks. She said you had not yet returned from the newspaper office. Is that correct?'

'Yes.'

'Later when you came in she told you of DSP's visit and inquiry?'

'Yes.'

'At what time did you get home?'

'I didn't think to look.'

'Did your aunt not say something like, The DSP came here asking if Miss Manners was with us, because Lady Chatterjee has reported her missing?'

'She said the DSP had called wanting to speak to Miss Manners.'

'And you then asked how long ago?'

'Yes – I did. But she didn't reply.'

'Oh? Why was that?'

'Her attention was taken.'

'Taken by what?'

'She had noticed the state I was in.'

She sensed the little wave of Gopal's shock. Rowan's voice cut in, 'According to the police report that state was as follows: "An abrasion on his right cheek and a contusion on his left cheek, stains on shirt and trousers from contact with muddy ground or dirty floor." Is that an accurate report?'

'Yes.'

'Is it also correct,' Rowan continued, 'that when the police, led by District Superintendent Merrick, entered a room on the first floor of number 12 Chillianwallah Bagh, the shirt and trousers in which you'd come home were found discarded, that you were wearing a clean pair of trousers, no other garment, and were bathing your face in a bowl of water?'

'Yes.'

'After reaching home and speaking briefly to your aunt who told you DSP had called looking for Miss Manners you went upstairs, changed and began to wash.'

'Yes.'

'You were still washing when the police arrived, so you can't have been back home for longer than, say, ten minutes?'

'It would have been about that.'

'So if the police arrived at 21.40 you reached home about 21.30?'

'Yes.'

'According to the statement of Mr Laxminarayan, the editor of the *Mayapore Gazette*, you left the office of the *Gazette*, which was in the Victoria Road in the Civil lines, at approximately six-fifteen that evening.'

'Yes.'

'During interrogation, whenever you were asked to account for your movements between 6.15 and 9.40 p.m. your invariable reply was: "I have nothing to say." Do you have anything to say now?'

Kumar glanced down at the table. Gopal suddenly came to life. 'I have a point here,' he said. Rowan nodded. 'This contusion on the detenu's left cheek. There is a copy on this file of the medical report made out when the detenu was admitted to this prison. It was dated August 25th. It referred to traces of contusion still being visible on the face. Still visible, that is to say, after sixteen days. Unless further bruising was inflicted one might assume that the original blow or blows were therefore of considerable strength. Of course, it was never established what caused the contusion, but in the absence of any explanation by the detenu the impression the police reports seemed to leave was never counteracted. That impression was that the bruising was the result of blows by a woman defending herself from attack.' Gopal took out his handkerchief again, dabbed his lips. 'It is a point which a court of law might well have subjected to deeper consideration – the extent to which the contusion suffered could have been caused by a member of the female sex. I make the point in case it encourages the detenu to say what he was doing that led to his return home in the state described.'

'You have heard Mr Gopal's point. Are you prepared to comment on it?'

'I'm prepared to comment on it.'

Gopal nodded. 'Please do so.'

'It is a good point. I appreciate it being raised. I don't think it would have helped me in a court of law, if things had come to that.'

'Why?' Gopal wanted to know.

'Expert medical evidence would probably have held that a frightened woman can hit as hard as a man. But even if that had been expertly refuted the prosecution could have turned the point to my disadvantage.'

'How?'

'By suggesting that the men who assaulted Miss Manners fought among themselves.'

'Is that what happened?' Rowan asked casually.

Kumar stared at him. 'I have no idea.'

'Are you prepared to say where you were between 6.15 and 9.30 p.m. on the night in question?'

Kumar glanced at the table, then back at Rowan.

'No. I'm sorry. But I'm not.'

Rowan leaned back in his chair. Watching, she became aware – as though she sat at it herself – of the expanse of table-top that separated the interrogators from the interrogated. It was an area of suspicion that none of them apparently had the capacity to diminish – although Rowan was now attempting to do so.

'I find it difficult to understand,' he had begun. 'So far this morning you have been extremely co-operative. The impression you have made is of frankness and candour. Now suddenly you revert to that unhelpful attitude of "I have nothing to say" which nullified every attempt made at the time to allow you to state a case. I use the word unhelpful advisedly. It does not help us and it certainly doesn't help you. The purpose of this examination is to go over evidence which at the time seemed strong enough to warrant your detention. It may or may not be so that at the time other considerations – well let us call them suspicions – coloured the views of those whose responsibility it was, at a moment of acute crisis resulting from civil disorder, to weigh the evidence in regard to that detention. Such suspicions do not enter into what is being considered this morning. I hope that has become clear as the examination has gone forward. These suspicions do not enter into the question of what is being considered, but if the record suddenly disclosed a lack of candour that today might be called uncharacteristic you must see how that would allow room for suspicion once again to enter into the weighing of all the various considerations.'

'Yes,' Kumar said. 'I see that. But the suspicion is unavoidable. However hard you try to avoid questioning me about the criminal assault you'll find everything leads to it. And every time the question of the assault comes up the suspicion comes up too.'

'Well, need it? It's come up now, certainly. Perhaps it could be eradicated by your answering the question. I wonder if you realize how foolish your original refusal to answer was? I wonder if you realize how very close you were to being charged? Or if you realize the extent to which that charge – rather, I should say, the failure of the charge to be made – depended almost exclusively on Miss Manners's vigorous rebuttal of any suggestion that you were involved in any way whatever? lf she had shown the slightest uncertainty, if she had – however reluctantly – admitted that in all fairness she could not actually swear you weren't among those who attacked her, in the dark, suddenly, then you would have been charged and tried. I put it to you, if you had been charged and tried, in court, been put on oath, would you in those circumstances have refused to answer this question?'

'I should have refused.'

'In court that refusal could have been fatal.'

'I know.'

'Have you truly and deeply considered the reasonableness of this attitude?'

'I have truly and deeply considered the attitude. I have considered it daily, since the night of August the ninth, nineteen forty-two. For one year, nine months and twelve days.'

'And you still find it reasonable?'

'I have never said it was reasonable. It has never been a question of reason. It isn't now.'

'A question of loyalty, perhaps?'

'It's not a word I much care for.'

'Care for it or not, it gets us a bit further? Can we go a bit further still and establish to what or to whom you felt you were being loyal by maintaining what looked to everyone else like an unreasonable silence?'

'I'm afraid we can't go further. At least, not in the same direction.'

Rowan leaned forward again, and referred to his file. Eventually he spoke. 'Only two things of interest to the police seem to have been found in your room. A photograph of Miss Manners and the letter from Colin. The photograph was self-explanatory. She had given it to you. The letter from Colin is interesting though because – by your own evidence today – you had other letters from him. In fact I imagine that you heard quite often from him – at least until he came to India.'

'Yes.'

'I wondered why of all those letters you kept this particular one. It was an unfortunate choice because it was the one in which Colin told you two of your letters were opened by his father and not forwarded because his father thought them unsuitable reading for a young officer away on active service. The phrase "a lot of hot-headed political stuff" was the way he said his father described those letters. Why did you keep this particular letter from Colin?'

'It was the only one I ever had from him that really struck an authentic note. He went through various phases after he left school. But that one was from the man I remembered.'

'What sort of man was that?'

'The sort that found the liberal atmosphere of Chilling-borough the right kind of atmosphere.'

'You would call Chillingborough a liberal institution?'

'It wasn't a flag-wagging place. It turned out more administrators than it did soldiers.'

She smiled and wondered if Rowan smiled too to be reminded so unexpectedly of his own words – 'I wasn't cast in the mould of a good regimental officer.'

'But for a time after leaving school,' Rowan said, 'your friend Colin became what you call a flag-wagger?'

'He was infected by the atmosphere of 1939, I think. He joined the Territorial Army, and wrote of nothing else.'

'The letter which you kept was one he wrote after he'd been wounded at Dunkirk, I gather?'

'Yes.'

'His baptism of fire had an effect on him which you approved of?'

'The effect of making him sound like the friend I knew.'

'And what was the hot-headed political stuff his father objected to in your letters?'

'It must have been mainly what I wrote about the pros and cons of Congress's resistance to the declaration of war, and their resignations from the provincial ministries.'

'And what were your views on that?'

'I think it was to find out if I had any that I wrote to Colin about the pros and cons.'

'You would write that kind of thing to Colin. Would you discuss it with Vidyasagar?'

'No.'

'In spite of the distance between you, Colin remained your closest friend, your confidant?'

'In my mind he did.'

'It was a way of maintaining contact with – what shall we call it – your inner sense of being English?'

'Yes.'

Rowan sat for a while without speaking. Then abruptly he said: 'Have we been discussing in any way the question you said we couldn't explore further in the same direction?'

'We've been discussing it.'

'But not exploring it further?'

'But not exploring it.'

'So we are back to the moment when you were found by the police bathing your face?'

'Yes.'

'With this vital period between 6.15 and 9.30 p.m. un-accounted for?'

'Yes.'

'If you had been with Miss Manners that evening, where would you have been likely to meet?'

'The most likely place would have been the Sanctuary.'

'Why?'

'Apart from caring for the sick and dying, Sister Ludmila ran a free evening clinic. Miss Manners helped fairly regularly in the clinic in her spare time from the Mayapore General Hospital.'

'You both found the Sanctuary a suitable place to meet?'

'We were both interested in the work Sister Ludmila did.'

'Is that the frankest reply you can give me?'

'No. Let's say that the Sanctuary was one of the few places in the whole of Mayapore where we could meet and talk and not attract abusive attention.'

'Abusive attention?'

'The attention paid by Europeans to the sight of a white girl in an Indian's company.'

'Apart from these meetings at the Sanctuary you also visited one another's houses?'

'Occasionally.'

'Where else did you spend time together?'

A pause.

'Sometimes, on a Sunday for instance, we went to the Bibighar Gardens.'

'I gather from the descriptions in the file that these Gardens consist of a comparatively small, wild, overgrown area – the site of the old garden surrounding a building once known as the Bibighar – a building no longer in existence but where an open-sided pavilion or shelter has been erected on part of the old foundations.'

'Yes. It was a quiet and pleasant place to talk.'

'During the daytime –'

'During daylight.'

'You never went there together except in daylight?'

'Never.'

'Because of the old stories about it being haunted?'

'Because it was hardly a suitable place to go to at night.'

'How many people knew that you used to go to the Bibighar?'

'No one, so far as I know.'

'You were always alone there?'

'We once frightened some children playing there. Indian children.'

'How?'

'They thought we were ghosts I expect.'

'Daylight ghosts?'

'Yes.'

'It was usually quite deserted even in daylight?'

'It was the place only Indians went to – but it was on the Civil lines side of the river. I think Indians went there for picnics in the dry, cooler weather.'

'How many people other than Sister Ludmila and her staff knew you and Miss Manners used to meet at the Sanctuary?'

'Not many I think.'

'She mentioned the Sanctuary and her interest in it to District Superintendent Merrick, though?'

'She must have done.'

'Why must have done?'

'On the night she was missing he called there.'

'How do you know that?'

'He told me so himself – during my interrogation. He said he called at the Sanctuary because he remembered Miss Manners saying something about the place. I expect he made particular note of it because it was the same place he'd found me the previous February.'

'Did he tell you what he discovered when he called at the Sanctuary looking for Miss Manners?'

'He said Sister Ludmila admitted Miss Manners had been there but had left just as it got dark. So then he called at my house and spoke to my aunt.'

'Because Sister Ludmila told him that you and Miss Manners had often been at the Sanctuary together?'

'Perhaps. He would have called at my house anyway.'

'He was well acquainted with the fact that you and Miss Manners were friends?'

'Of course.'

'You have said that occasionally you visited Miss Manners at the MacGregor House. Did you ever meet Mr Merrick there?'

'No. She kept us well apart.'

'Kept you apart? Because of what had happened between you and Mr Merrick when he took you in for questioning that first time?'

'She didn't know until much later that Merrick had been personally involved in that. She kept us apart because she assumed in any case Mr Merrick wouldn't approve of our friendship.'

'I'm not sure why you use this expression – keeping apart.'

'He became a personal friend of Miss Manners too.'

'I see. You say became. You mean he became friendly with her after you and she had already established a friendly association.'

'Yes. He was on the *maidan* during the War Week Exhibition and saw her leave her English friends and come up and speak to me. Until then, so far as I know, he'd never taken any notice of her. After that he started inviting her out.'

'If his interview with you after your drinking bout left him under the strong impression that you were a man on whom the police should keep an eye – as seems to have been the case – it would follow, I think, that directly he saw you and Miss Manners were on friendly terms he would feel it his duty to try to protect her from what in his view was an undesirable association?'

'Yes, that could follow. It's a very reasonable explanation.'

'Did he in fact ever say anything to her about her association with you?'

'Yes.'

'She told you this?'

'Yes. It came up when I took her home after we'd visited the Tirupati temple.'

'She told you Mr Merrick disapproved of her going out with you?'

'She said Merrick's view was that I was a bad bet.'

'What was your reaction to that?'

'I said that Merrick should know if I was a bad bet or not.'

'Were you quarrelling?'

'Yes.'

'Why? Over something that happened at the temple?'

'Why do people who have grown fond of each other quarrel? I was in an over-sensitive mood. We both were. I realized what a ridiculous figure I made and what a lot of time she was wasting on me. She accused me of acting in a way calculated to put her off, which was true. That's when she told me Merrick said I was a bad bet. I told her he should know. I thought she always understood that Merrick was personally involved in that trouble I'd been in. It turned out she didn't. It made her feel she'd been made a fool of – unwittingly going out with Merrick as well as me. We parted on not very good terms.'

'But later you made it up?'

A pause.

'You're forgetting. We'd just come from the temple. I haven't seen Miss Manners since the night we visited the temple.'

'What night was that?'

'A Saturday. Three weeks before the night I was arrested under suspicion of assaulting her with five other men.'

Rowan leaned back again and turned to Gopal. 'I think we're now back to the question of the order and time at which he alleged certain things were done and certain things said. You were anxious to clarify that. Perhaps you would like to ask the questions.'

'Thank you.'

Gopal sipped water while reading a note on his file. Then he put the glass down, again dabbed his lips with the folded handkerchief. 'You were taken from 12 Chillianwallah Bagh at approximately 21.45, by truck to police headquarters in the Civil lines. You were held for perhaps a minute or less in a room where you saw five men whose faces you recognized even if you couldn't immediately recall all their names. You were then taken to a room downstairs. Up until this time, you allege, you were not told the reason for your removal from your home to police headquarters?'

'I wasn't told.'

'At 12 Chillianwallah Bagh the police entered the room and apprehended you without saying anything?'

'Things were said, but not about the reason for the arrest.'

'What sort of things were said? Can you recall, for instance, the police officer's first words to you?'

'He didn't speak for a while.'

'What then did he do?'

'He stood and smiled at me.'

'Smiled?'

'I also noticed a nervous tic develop on his right cheek.'

'A smile and a nervous tic.'

'Then he pointed at the clothes lying on the floor and asked me if I'd just taken them off. I told him I had. He told me to put them on again. I asked him why. He said – Because you're coming with me. We're going to have another of our chats.'

'Did you obey immediately?'

'Not immediately. I asked him what we were going to have a chat about. He said I would find out. Then he asked if I would dress myself or prefer to be dressed forcibly. There were several constables with him, so I changed back into the clothes I'd taken off. Then I went downstairs with two constables holding my wrists behind my back. My aunt was being held in the living-room. I could hear her calling out to me. I wasn't allowed to see or speak to her. I was put into the back of a truck and driven to police headquarters.'

'Where you saw the five other men who had been arrested, one of whom said, "Hello, Hari" – a greeting which you did not return because unlike these other five you were not feeling like laughing and joking. When you saw these men, saw them behind bars – what conclusion did you reach?'

'Conclusion?'

'You saw they had been arrested, as you had been. What did you think they'd been arrested for?'

'I assumed they'd been caught drinking their home-made liquor.'

'Their demeanour was commensurate with that of boys who had broken a minor law and were still under the influence of liquor?'

'Yes.'

'And what was going through your mind about the possible causes of your own arrest?'

'I felt it could only have something to do with Miss Manners.'

'Why?'

'Because Merrick had been at my house earlier asking for her. People were very edgy that night. A European woman had been attacked out in a place called Tanpur while trying to protect an Indian teacher from her mission. The man had been murdered and she had been knocked about. Some of the country police had been locked in their own stations by roving mobs. Telegraph wires were down and people were talking about a new Mutiny. As you know, there'd been a lot of arrests early that morning from Gandhi all down the line. For instance Mr Srinivasan had been arrested – as a leading member of the Local Congress Party sub-committee. I knew I couldn't be arrested for any political reason, but it seemed likely I'd be the first to get arrested if the police thought something had happened to Miss Manners.'

'So really your arrest was not such a puzzle to you, you are saying?'

'I'm merely telling you what was passing through my mind. I'm answering the question. I'm telling you that and stating again that I was in custody for a long time before the District Superintendent actually accused me of criminal assault. Once he'd done that I realized from other things he'd said and asked me that the five men upstairs were supposed to have been my accomplices in that assault.'

'Very well. Let us come to the moment when you were taken downstairs. What was the first thing that happened?'

'I was ordered to strip.'

'Who gave the order?'

'The District Superintendent.'

'In this room there were yourself, the District Superintendent and two constables?'

'At this stage, yes.'

'When you were stripped the DSP then inspected you as you have previously described?'

'When I was stripped the two constables held me with my arms behind my back, in front of Merrick's desk. Merrick sat on the desk and poured himself a glass of whisky. Then he just sat and smiled at me until he'd drunk it. He took about five minutes to drink it. After that he stood up, carried out the inspection and said, "So you've been clever enough to wash, we nearly caught you at it, didn't we?" I asked him why I'd been brought in. He said I'd find out. He said we had plenty of time. He told me to relax because we had a lot to talk about. He then ordered the constables to manacle my wrists behind me. When they'd done that he sent them out of the room.' Kumar paused. 'Then he began to talk to me.'

'You mean, to question you?'

'No. It was talking mostly. Every so often he put in a question.'

'What you describe as talking mostly' – Gopal said – 'what kind of talking?'

'He talked about the history of the British in India. And about his own history. About his ideas. About his views of India's future and England's future. And his future. And mine.'

Gopal appeared to be nonplussed. He hesitated before saying, 'Why should he talk about such things? You are remembering accurately? The impression one has been getting is that District Superintendent exerted himself a great deal first to find Miss Manners and then to bring her attackers to book. Now you are saying he sat and talked to you about such irrelevancies.'

'They weren't irrelevancies to him.'

'You are saying that to talk to you about the history of the British in India was just as important at that moment to District Superintendent as to question you about your movements that evening?'

'Neither talking nor questioning was of paramount importance to him.'

'Not of paramount importance? What are you suggesting was?'

'The situation.'

Gopal looked at Rowan and asked, 'What is he talking about? I don't understand him.'

Kumar answered before Rowan had a chance to speak.

'It was a question of extracting everything possible from the situation while it lasted.'

'The situation?'

'Yes.'

'But *what* situation?'

'The situation of our being face to face, with everything finally in his favour.'

'Finally? You are suggesting he anticipated this face-to-face situation?'

'Yes. That almost goes without saying.'

'Are you claiming – are you claiming that he was a rival for the friendly attention of Miss Manners and had therefore looked forward to a situation which would place you – at disadvantage? Is this what you allege? You claim that an aspect to be considered is that of jealousy?'

Kumar hesitated. 'That would be an over-simplification. And there'd then be the question, jealousy of what kind, and jealousy of whom?'

'I cannot follow these arguments. Let us leave the matter of what you allege he talked about and consider the questions you allege he occasionally put in. Perhaps those will be easier to understand. Can you remember any of those questions?'

'Broadly.'

'Then say what you remember broadly.'

'They were such questions as: Those fellows up there admire you a lot, don't they? They'd do anything you say. Who marked your face? Why didn't you go to the Sanctuary tonight? Who's Colin? She wasn't a virgin, was she, and you were the first to ram her, weren't you?'

'Did you reply to any of those questions?'

'I told him if he wanted answers he first had to tell me why I'd been brought in.'

'And these questions were interpolated, you are saying, into his talk on other matters?'

'Yes.'

'For instance he would be talking about the future of the British in India and would suddenly say, Who is Colin?'

'Yes.'

'And always you replied as you have described?'

'Not always. Some of the questions I treated as rhetorical.'

'But you said, more than once, that you would only answer questions if he told you why you were in custody?'

'Yes.'

'Gradually, however, you suggest, you got a clear impression that you and the others upstairs were suspected of criminal assault on a lady?'

'Yes.'

'And did you at the same time suspect that this lady was Miss Manners?'

'Yes.'

'Did you not ask?'

'No.'

'You were a close friend of Miss Manners. You knew the police had been looking for her, you knew of the troubles in the district, you guessed a woman had been assaulted and realized that this woman might be your friend Miss Manners, but you did not say, "Has something happened to Miss Manners?" '

'No.'

'Why?'

'I realized that's what he was waiting for me to do. I think it was a basic aspect of the situation.'

'Let us forget what you call the situation.'

'It's impossible for me to forget the situation. It had a very special intensity.'

Rowan spoke, taking advantage of Gopal's hesitation.

'I think we should do better to leave any inner significance the situation may have had for both DSP and the prisoner and concentrate on the form and order of the interrogation. If there was an inner significance it might even become clear to us what it was if we confine ourselves rigorously to the outer forms.'

'It is what I have been trying to do,' Gopal said. He rustled his papers; eventually spoke again to Kumar.

'There came a point when according to your previous testimony DSP said that he was making inquiries about an Englishwoman who was missing, and added "You know which one", and followed this with what you call an obscene remark. What was that remark?'

'I prefer not to say.'

'What did you understand from it?'

'That he was definitely referring to Miss Manners and to the fact that she'd been assaulted by more than one man, all Indians.'

'And it was at this point that you said you hadn't seen Miss Manners since the time you visited the temple?'

'Yes.'

'In that case I'm afraid I must press you to repeat the obscene remark. I must press you because without it your refutation of the official statement – that you yourself were the first to mention Miss Manners – is incomplete.'

'I'm sorry. I still prefer not to say.'

'Why?'

'It was slanderous as well as obscene.'

Rowan said, 'I think we needn't press this –'

'Oh, but I think we must,' Gopal said. 'I do not understand what detenu is getting at when he talks of a situation, but there is here a situation of which we are getting a picture and it is important that the picture should be as complete in every detail as possible. The situation I speak of is one in which the detenu, under suspicion of rape, is kept standing naked for a very long time by the senior police officer of the district, who sits on his desk drinking whisky and conducting an interrogation with, if detenu is to be believed, a total disregard for detenu's dignity as a human being, and asking questions in a manner calculated to insult, outrage, and to provoke to make comments which are then recorded as incriminating evidence of detenu's knowledge of events he could not have known about if he was innocent only. And the picture of this situation is not easy to believe. It is necessary that detenu should be examined closely on it because it arises only out of what he has been saying. He cannot suddenly stop saying because it suits him.'

Again she sought the reassurance of the pleats and buttons of her blouse. Gopal was making statements which on the record would convey an impression of doubting Kumar, of disbelieving that a police officer would act as Kumar had said. But Gopal did not want to doubt or disbelieve. Underneath that apolitical, civil service, collaborative exterior pumped the old anti-British fears, prejudices and superstitions. It came to her that Gopal disliked Kumar for the type of Indian Kumar was – which in every important way from Gopal's point of view was not an Indian way at all. It was not without pleasure that he assumed the hectoring tone, emerged suddenly, almost unexpectedly, as animated by a passion the record would show as one for a clinical sense of justice, the opposite of the real animus – a fastidious dislike of the white usurper on whose bandwagon he had a seat. Below her, yet another situation was in process. It fascinated, disturbed her, to have, suddenly, an insight into it. 'So I must press detenu,' Gopal was saying. It was the white man in Kumar he enjoyed attacking. But the objective was the revelation of the full outrage and unjust pressure Kumar the Indian had suffered.

'I am sorry,' Kumar said.

Gopal made an impatient gesture. How thin his fingers were, disapproving, permissive. They inspired her with dislike and pity: the twin responses to the odd combination of triumph and defeat the gesture implied.

Rowan took over.

'When – as you suggest – you understood from whatever it was you imply District Superintendent conveyed to you – that Miss Manners had been criminally assaulted and that you and the other men were under suspicion for that, you presumably made the statement as it appears in DSP's report. "I have not seen Miss Manners since the night we visited the temple." '

'Yes.'

'So the report is correct in that detail?'

'In that detail, yes.'

'And you are not inclined to dispute that this was at 22.45 hours?'

'No.'

'So a second detail of the report is correct.'

'Yes.'

'And you showed signs of distress, at this point, in that you were shivering, which makes the report accurate on three counts. I imagine, too, that you would not dispute the statement the report goes on to make that from that moment you reverted to the invariable reply to any question: "I have nothing to say." '

'I would not dispute that.'

'How long did your interrogation continue? How long were you in fact making this statement that you had nothing further to say?'

'I don't know.'

'Why not?'

'I lost track of things like time.'

'As long as an hour, two hours?'

'Perhaps.'

'Longer?'

'It could have been.'

'You were alone with the examining officer for two hours or more?'

'No. Other people came in after a bit.'

'The two constables?'

'Yes.'

'Anyone else?'

'One certainly. There may have been others.'

'Can't you remember?'

'I thought so. It seemed like it.'

'Are you saying you were confused? A bit giddy perhaps? And cold? Standing naked a long time in a cooled room?'

'I wasn't standing all the time.'

'You were allowed to sit?'

'No.'

Gopal re-entered the arena. 'I don't understand,' he said. 'You were not standing all the time but also you were not sitting. What were you doing? Lying down?'

'I was bent over a trestle.'

'Bent over a trestle?'

'Tied to it.' He hesitated, then added, 'For the persuasive phase of the interrogation.'

A pause.

Gopal said, 'Are you stating that you were physically ill-treated?'

'A cane was used.'

A rustle of paper. Captain Rowan's voice:

'Among the documents there is a copy of a report by a magistrate, Mr Iyenagar, who interviewed you at police headquarters on August 16th at the direction of the civil authorities. Do you recall that interview?'

'There were many interviews.'

'The one on August 16th was ordered by the civil authorities to inquire into rumours circulating in the bazaar of whipping and defilement of the prisoners held under suspicion of rape. Do you recall that now?'

'Yes, I recall it.'

'The report reads: *Iyenagar*: Have you any complaints to make about your treatment while in custody? *Kumar*: No. *Iyenagar*: If it were suggested that you had been subjected to physical violence of any kind, would there be any truth in that? *Kumar*: I have nothing to add to my first answer. *Iyenagar*: If it were suggested that you had been forced to eat any food which your religion made distasteful to you, would there be any truth in that suggestion? *Kumar*: I have no religious prejudices about food. *Iyenagar*: You understand that you have the opportunity here of making a complaint, if one is justified, which you need not fear making? *Kumar*: I have nothing more to say. *Iyenagar*: You have no complaint about your treatment from the moment of your arrest until now? *Kumar*: I have no complaint.'

Rowan looked up from his reading.

'Is that an accurate record of your interview with the magistrate?'

'Yes.'

'It is an accurate record, but you weren't telling the truth?'

'I was telling the truth.'

'You have just alleged that you were tied to a trestle and beaten with a cane.'

'Yes. I was.'

'Then why did you deny it when the magistrate asked you?'

'He asked if I had any complaint. I said I hadn't. I spoke the truth.'

'You had no complaint about being caned?'

'No.'

'Why?'

No answer.

Gopal said, 'Are you suggesting you were afraid of the consequences of complaining?'

'No.'

'What then?'

'It's difficult to explain now.'

'You did not complain, for reasons that now strike you as questionable?' Rowan asked.

'Not questionable.'

'What then?'

No answer.

'You are not on oath. The people you now complain about are not here to answer your accusations. Are you taking advantage of that?'

'No, and I am not complaining.'

Rowan's voice took on an edge. 'I see. You're merely stating facts. A bit late in the day, isn't it?'

'I don't know about late in the day —'

'Facts which you failed to state at the time for a reason you now find it difficult to give us.'

No answer.

'You say you were caned. How many times were you hit with this cane?'

'I don't know.'

'Six times? Twelve times?'

No answer.

'More than twelve times?'

'I didn't count.'

'On what part of the body were you hit?'

'On the usual place for someone bent over.'

'The buttocks.'

'Yes.'

A rustle of paper.

'On your arrival in Kandipat you underwent the routine physical check. The documents are here. The examining doctor found you physically A1. Judging by this document it seems no marks were found that would have pointed to your having received a number of strokes with a cane on your buttocks. There is a note about traces of bruising on your face. The examination was made sixteen days after your arrest and first interrogation. The caning perhaps was not so severe as to cut the skin? Sixteen days is not a long time. Wouldn't you say that if your skin had been cut the marks would still have been visible?'

'They were visible.'

'The doctor saw them?'

'I don't know.'

'You must answer more fully than that.'

'If he saw them he made no comment.'

'Nor any record. It is usual before the examination for a prisoner to be bathed. Were you so bathed?'

'Yes.'

'I understand such bathing is conducted under the eye of a prison officer. Was it so conducted?'

'Yes.'

'Did the prison officer comment on any marks there may have been on your buttocks?'

'No.'

'The marks were invisible to him too?'

'Indians of the lower class keep a pair of drawers on while bathing. I suppose it's because they're used to bathing in public. That's what happened when I was told to take a bath that day. I was told to keep my drawers on.'

Gopal said, 'It's a point I was about to make, Captain Rowan.

And in the case of the physical examination it is doubtful that the doctor – who I see from the medical report was an Indian – would have asked for the drawers to be removed for longer than was necessary to examine the pubic region. Was that the case, Kumar?'

'There was also an examination of the anal passage.'

A pause.

Rowan said, 'What you're suggesting then is that the doctor was either incompetent and failed to see what was under his nose, or saw the marks and ignored them in his report.'

'I'm not making a suggestion.'

'Are these marks you say you had still visible to any degree?'

'No.'

'You were not hit severely enough for the marks to be permanent.'

'I was hit severely.'

'To the point where blood was drawn?'

'I think it was when they started to draw blood that they covered me with a wet cloth. Then they carried on.'

A pause.

Gopal said, 'Who were "they"?'

'I couldn't see. It must have been the constables. They tied me to the trestle anyway. They started when Merrick gave the order and stopped when he said so. When they stopped Merrick talked to me. When he stopped talking he gave the order and they started again. It went on like that.'

Gopal said, 'Until you lost consciousness?'

'I didn't lose consciousness.'

Rowan said, 'But you have no idea how many times you were hit?'

'It's difficult to breathe in that position. It's all you think of in the end.'

Rowan continued: 'You allege that when the investigating officer told the constables to stop he talked to you. You mean he questioned you?'

'It was more like talking.'

'What was he talking about this time?' Gopal asked acidly. 'Not surely about the history of the British in India?'

'He was talking to encourage me.'

'Encourage you? To confess?'

'That was part of it. Perhaps not the most important.'

'But important enough for us to concentrate on,' Gopal said. 'What did he say to encourage a confession?'

'He said Miss Manners had named me as one of the men, that she said she'd been stopped by me outside the Bibighar and attacked while I held her in conversation, then that she'd been dragged into the gardens and raped, first by me and then by my friends. He said he didn't believe her. He suggested I should tell him the real truth. He told me he knew the truth but wanted to hear it from me first.' A pause. 'I'm sorry. I've got confused. He said that before he had me tied to the trestle. But after they tied me to the trestle he said it again, only this time he left out the bit about wanting to hear the truth from me. He said he'd tell me what he knew to be the truth and all I had to do to stop being beaten was confirm it.'

'And what do you allege he told you?'

'He said she'd obviously asked us to meet her, egged us on, that then we'd given her more than she'd quite bargained for, and that she was now trying to have us punished for something we'd only been technically guilty of.' A pause. 'He made it sound very plausible. He left me to think about it. He seemed to be away for quite a long time. When he came back he had one of the other men with him. He told me one of my friends had come down to hear me confess. I don't know which of the men it was. I heard this man trying to tell me he knew nothing and had said nothing. They started hitting me again.' A pause. 'After that I think Merrick sent everyone out. I think we were alone. He spoke and acted even more obscenely.'

Rowan said, 'The word obscene is open to different inter-pretations. Your allegation of obscenity – the second you have made – is against an officer of the Indian Police and is damaging to the reputation of that officer. You must give examples of obscenity so that anyone reading the record of this examination may form his own conclusion whether the word is justified in the context of the allegation.'

Kumar had slowly transferred his gaze from Gopal to Rowan. He said, 'He asked me if I was enjoying it.'

'Enjoying it?'

'He said, "Aren't you enjoying it? Surely a randy fellow like you can do better than this?"'

'Is that all?'

'He said, "Aren't you enjoying it? Surely a randy fellow like you can do better than this? Surely a healthy fellow like you doesn't exhaust himself just by having it once?" ' A pause. 'He had his hand between my legs at the time.'

Gopal seemed to recoil. Rowan spoke sharply to the clerk. 'Strike that from the record. Delete anything that followed the detenu's statement "I think we were alone". When you've done that leave your notebook on this desk and wait outside until I recall you.'

When the clerk had obeyed and closed the door behind him Gopal moved as if to protest, but Rowan said to Kumar:

'Why are you making allegations of this kind?'

'I'm answering your questions.'

'Are you? Or are you lying?'

'I'm not lying.'

'I put it to you that you are, that you are telling a pack of lies, very carefully rehearsed over the past year or so for just such an occasion as this, or to cause trouble on your release. If such outrageous things were done to you – really done to you – you would have said so when examined by the magistrate specially appointed to question you on just this kind of point. I put it to you that you did not say so because they had not happened. I put it to you that you are basing this story on tales and rumours you've heard since being imprisoned, rumours that were investigated at the time and totally unsubstantiated. I put it to you that you have made these things up in the belief that they may protect you from the danger you'd still be in if the charge of rape were made even at this late stage. I put it to you that your entire testimony this morning has been compounded of omission, exaggeration and downright falsehood and that your detention is no more than you richly deserve. You have now an opportunity to retract. I advise you to think most carefully whether you should or should not take that opportunity.'

'I've nothing I wish to retract. I'm sorry. I seem to have misunderstood.'

'What do you mean, misunderstood? Misunderstood the questions?'

'Not the questions. The reason for asking them.'

'The reason was made clear at the beginning.'

'No, the form the questions would take was made clear. The reason for asking them was left for me to guess at. I made the wrong guess. Something has happened to her, hasn't it?'

'Do you mean to Miss Manners?'

'Yes.'

'Why do you ask that?'

'Because the guess I made was that perhaps she'd finally managed to persuade someone I'd done nothing to deserve being kept locked up. But this examination increasingly smells of uneasy consciences. Something's happened to her and I'm the loose end someone thought it would be a relief to tie neatly off. I'm sorry. When we began you were so fair-minded it would have hurt if I'd still been capable of feeling hurt. And it would have been nice if I'd been able to answer your questions truthfully without it becoming clear that I can't be neatly tied off and that nobody's conscience can be soothed down. But I answer them truthfully, as truthfully as I can, and you begin to see that I'm the least important factor and that without intending to you're asking questions about what I call the situation. That's why you're annoyed and accuse me of lying, because the situation threatens to be more than any conscience can cope with. What's happened to her? Is she dead?' A pause. 'I've sometimes felt it but never let myself think it. If she is, you should have said so. You should have said –'

'We assumed that you knew. You're not cut off completely from the outside world. You exchange letters with your aunt. You have newspapers, surely? You talk to fellow-prisoners – new arrivals, for instance.'

'My aunt's letters are heavily censored. In any case she would never refer to Miss Manners. She's never forgiven her. I think she found it easier to blame Miss Manners than anything or anyone else for what happened to me. And I'm in the special security block here. We're allowed books, but not newspapers. Once a week they circulate a foolscap page of war news, full of victories and pious platitudes. How and when did she die?'

'She died of peritonitis. About a year ago.'

'A year ago? Peritonitis?' A pause. '– That's blood-poisoning, isn't it? Burst appendix, that sort of thing?'

'I gather the peritonitis was the result of a Caesarean operation undergone in far from ideal conditions.'

'A Caesarean? Yes. I see.' A pause. 'She married?'

'No. She didn't marry.'

'I see.'

'Do you still have nothing to retract?'

'Nothing.' A pause. 'Nothing.'

For a while after that he did not speak. He sat staring at Rowan. At first she did not detect it – there was no sound of it, no sign of it – except (and now she saw it) this curious un-emotional expulsion from the deep-set eyes of rivulets that coursed down his cheeks: opaque in the glaring light like phos-phorescent trails, a substance that released itself without disturb-ing the other mechanisms of his body. She shut her own eyes. She had had a sudden, astonishingly strong compulsion to touch him. No one had ever cried for Daphne, except herself; and this one person beside herself she could not reach. Between them there was a panel of thick glass and downwardly directed slats of wood or metal. The barrier that separated them was impenet-rable. It was as if Hari Kumar were buried alive in a grave she could see down into but could not reach into or even speak to, establish a connection with of any kind.

She opened her eyes again. The twin rivulets gleamed on his prison cheeks, and then the image became blurred and she felt a corresponding wetness on her own – tears for Daphne that were also tears for him; for lovers who could never be described as star-crossed because they had had no stars. For them heaven had drawn an implacable band of dark across its constellations and the dark was lit by nothing except the trust they had had in each other not to tell the truth because the truth had seemed too dangerous to tell.

In her mind was the image of Suleiman with the box held to his breast in the manner of someone holding a reliquary. The truth was in the reliquary and in the mind that held the image of Suleiman and in the mind of the man in the room behind the glass panel: the truth and memory of their having been in the Bibighar that night, as lovers, moving to the motion of the joy of union; and of the terror of their separation and of how, afterwards, she had crawled on hands and knees across the floor of the pavilion and untied the strips of cotton cloth the spoilers had torn from their own ragged clothing and bound him with. For a while they held each other like children afraid of the dark, and then he picked her up and began to carry her away from the pavilion.

I look for similes (she had written – secretly, in the last stages of her pregnancy, her insurance against permanent silence) for something that explains it more clearly, but find nothing, because there is nothing. It is itself; an Indian carrying an English girl he has made love to and been forced to watch being assaulted – carrying her back to where *she* would be safe. It is its own simile. It says all that needs to be said, doesn't it? If you extend it – if you think of him carrying me all the way to the MacGregor House, giving me into Aunt Lili's care, ringing for the doctor, ringing for the police, answering questions, and being treated as a man who'd rescued me, the absurdity, the implausibility became almost unbearable. Directly you get to the point where Hari, taken on one side by Ronald Merrick for instance, has to say, 'Yes, we were making love,' the nod of understanding that *must* come from Ronald *won't*, unless you blanch Hari's skin, blanch it until it looks not just like that of a white man but like that of a white man too shaken for another white man not to feel sorry for, however much he may reproach him.

The image sharpened. She understood it in an exact depth and dimension as if she were Daphne and the man sitting in the chair down there were actually standing, waiting to pick her up again after a brief rest. He tried to take hold of my arm. I moved away from him. I said, 'No. Let me go. You've not been near me. You don't know anything. You know nothing. Say nothing.' He wouldn't listen to me. He caught me, tried to hold me close, but I struggled. I was in a panic, thinking of what they'd do to him. No one would believe me. He said, 'I've got to be with you. I love you. Please let me be with you.' I beat at him, not to escape myself but to make *him* escape. I was trying to beat sense and reason and cunning into him. I kept saying, 'We've not seen each other. You've been at home. You say nothing. You know nothing. Promise me.' I was free and began to run without waiting to hear him promise. At the gate he caught me and tried to hold me back. Again I asked him to let me go, please to let me go, to say nothing, to know nothing for my sake if that was the only way he could say nothing and know nothing for his own. For an instant I held him close – it was the last time I touched him – and then I broke free again and was out of the gateway, and running; running into and out of the light of the street lamp opposite, running into the dark and grateful for the dark, going without any understanding of direction. I stopped and leaned against a wall. I wanted to turn back. I wanted to admit that I couldn't face it alone. And I wanted him to know that I thought I'd done it all wrong. He wouldn't know what I felt, what I meant. I was in pain. I was exhausted. And frightened. Too frightened to turn back. I said, 'There's nothing I can do, nothing, nothing,' and wondered where I'd heard those words before, and began to run again, through those awful ill-lit deserted roads that should have been leading me home but were leading me nowhere I recognized; into safety that wasn't safety because beyond it there were the plains and the openness that made it seem that if I ran long enough I would run clear off the rim of the world.

Well – she had gone. Yes, eventually, she had gone clear off the rim of the world – then or later; keeping faith with a promise that was as well an imprisonment. For him it would have been then that she had gone. He must have watched her, perhaps he followed, perhaps followed her nearly all the way to the house and then felt for himself something of the terror she had felt for him, so that he too ran home and in the privacy of his room began to bathe his face because it was cut and bruised by the men who had come at them out of the dark; the unknown watchers, the unknown spoilers, the men for whom a taboo had been broken by watching Hari love her. He had said nothing, explained nothing. 'Say nothing,' she had begged. He had kept faith with that. They had both kept faith. She wondered whether he would see her death as releasing him from a promise made and almost absurdly kept. The promise had betrayed and imprisoned them both. Considering this she felt soiled as from an invasion of territory she had no title to.

'Do you want a few moments to compose yourself?' Rowan asked.

'I am composed. But you should have told me. You should have made it clear.'

'Are you saying that if you'd known Miss Manners was no longer alive your answers to some of our questions might have been different?'

'I answered the questions because I thought the examination was the result of some effort of hers. I answered the questions because I thought she wanted you to ask them. If I'd known she had nothing to do with it, and that it was only a case of bad consciences I wouldn't have answered the questions at all.'

'There was one important question you didn't answer.'

'I shall never answer it.'

'Did it strike you at the time that your refusal to answer questions was unhelpful not only to you but to those five other men who were suspected?'

'Yes, I had to consider that. It was part of the situation.'

'Do you know what happened to them?'

'I was told they were sent to detention.'

'Did you think that justified?'

'No.'

'You believed them innocent of anything, except perhaps illicit distilling and drinking?'

'On that night I'm sure they were innocent of anything else. I don't know how or why they were arrested but I know none of us would have been arrested if it hadn't been for the assault. We were all punished for the assault, when it came to it. There was nothing I could do about that. Whether they deserved detention for political crimes, more or less than I do, I can't say. I wasn't able to let that enter into it.'

'Would it be in your power at all to remove the last shred of suspicion that they were implicated in the assault? It is accepted by this board that those suspicions were unavoidably part of the atmosphere in which your cases had to be examined when the question of detention under the Defence of India Rules came up. If you were being absolutely frank with us – for instance about your activities and movements on the night of the assault – would that frankness be helpful to those five men?'

'Are they still in prison?'

'Yes.'

'Are their cases also being reviewed?'

'That might depend a great deal on the result of the review of yours.'

'No,' Kumar said. 'You can't get rid of responsibility so easily. I think that is part of the situation too.'

The notion that Kumar could help five men who had never enjoyed Kumar's advantages seemed to interest Gopal.

'You are trying to cover everything with all this clever talk of a situation, but you are saying nothing about this situation. Time and again you leave an answer apparently complete but in fact it is only half-finished because of this so-called situation to which you relate it, and which you seem to want to mystify us with. What in fact was this situation?'

The rivulets were still visible. He did not seem to be aware of them and they now appeared to be motionless. She had an impression that they had ossified, that Rowan could have reached over and picked them away from Kumar's cheeks with his finger-nails, a piece at a time, and that each piece would fall with the light gyrating motion of something fragile, like an insect's wing.

'It was a situation of enactment.'

Gopal was impatient. 'Most situations are.'

'According to Merrick most situations are the consequence of one set of actions and the prelude to the next but negative in themselves.'

'These ideas of what you call the situation were DSP's not your own?'

'Yes. He wanted them to be clear to me. In fact from his point of view it was essential that they should be. Otherwise the enactment was incomplete.'

'And he made them clear?'

'Yes.'

'Perhaps,' Gopal suggested, 'you would be good enough to make them clear also to this board.'

'In a way that's impossible. The ideas, without the enactment, lose their significance. He said that if people would enact a situation they would understand its significance. He said history was a sum of situations whose significance was never seen until long afterwards because people had been afraid to act them out. They couldn't face up to their responsibility for them. They preferred to think of the situations they found themselves in as part of a general drift of events they had no control over, which meant that they never really understood those situations, and so in a curious way the situations did become part of a general drift of events. He didn't think he could go so far as to say you could change the course of events by acting out situations you found yourself in, but that at least you'd understand better what that situation was and take what steps you could to stop things drifting in the wrong direction, or an unreal direction.'

'An interesting theory,' Rowan said. 'But is it relevant to the events you've been alleging took place?'

'You ask the question the wrong way round. You should ask how relevant the events were to the theory. The theory was exemplified in the enactment of the situation. The rape, the interrogation about the rape, were side issues. The real issue was the relationship between us.'

'What exactly does that mean?' Rowan asked.

'He said that up until then our relationship had only been symbolic. It had to become real.'

'What in fact did he mean by symbolic?'

'It was how he described it. He said for the moment we were mere symbols. He said we'd never understand each other if we were going to be content with that. It wasn't enough to say he was English and I was Indian, that he was a ruler and I was one of the ruled. We had to find out what that meant. He said people talked of an ideal relationship between his kind and my kind. They called it comradeship. But they never said anything about the contempt on his side and the fear on mine that was basic, and came before any comradely feeling. He said we had to find out about that too, we had to enact the situation as it really was, and in a way that would mean neither of us ever forgetting it or being tempted to pretend it didn't exist, or was something else.' A pause. 'All this was part of what he talked about before he put me through what he called the second phase of my degradation. Before he had me strapped to the trestle. The first phase was being kept standing without any clothes on. The third phase was his offer of charity. He gave me water. He bathed the lacerations. I couldn't refuse the water. I was grateful to him when he gave me the water. I remember thinking what a relief it was, having him treat me kindly, how nice it would be if I could earn his approval. It would have been nice to confess. I nearly did, because the confession he wanted was a confession of my dependence on him, my inferiority to him. He said the true corruption of the English is their pretence that they have no contempt for us, and our real degradation is our pretence of equality. He said if we could understand the truth there might be a chance for us. There might be some sense then in talking about his kind's obligations to my kind. The last phase could show the possibilities. He said I could forget the girl. What had happened to her was unimportant. So long as I understood how responsible I was for it. "That's what you've got to admit," he kept saying, "your responsibility for that girl getting rammed. If you were a hundred miles away you'd still be responsible." What happened in the Bibighar Gardens he saw as symbolic too, symptomatic of what he called the liberal corruption of both his kind and my kind. He accepted a share of responsibility for what happened, even though there was no common ground between himself and the kind of Englishman really responsible. The kind really responsible was the one who sat at home and kidded himself there was such a thing as the brotherhood of man or came out here and went on pretending there was. The permutations of English corruption in India were endless – affection for servants, for peasants, for soldiers, pretence at understanding the Indian intellectual or at sympathizing with nationalist aspirations, but all this affection and understanding was a corruption of what he called the calm purity of their contempt. It was a striking phrase, wasn't it? He accepted a share of responsibility for the rape in the Bibighar because even the English people who admitted to themselves that they had this contempt pretended among themselves that they didn't. They would always find some little niche to fit themselves into to prove they were part of the great liberal Christian display, even if it was only by repeating *ad nauseam* to each other that there wasn't a better fellow in the world than the blue-eyed Pathan, or the Punjabi farmer, or the fellow who blacks your boots. He called the English admiration for the martial and faithful servant class a mixture of perverted sexuality and feudal arrogance. What they were stirred or flattered by was an idea, an idea of bravery or loyalty exercised on their behalf. The man exercising bravery and loyalty was an inferior being and even when you congratulated him you had contempt for him. And at the other end of the scale when you thought about the kind of Englishmen who pretended to admire Indian intellectuals, pretended to sympathize with their national aspirations, if you were honest you had to admit that all they were admiring or sympathizing with was the black reflection of their own white ideals. Underneath the admiration and sympathy there was the contempt a people feel for a people who have learned things from them. The liberal intellectual Englishman was just as contemptuous of

the Westernized educated Indian as the arrogant upper-class
reactionary Englishman was of the fellow who blacks his boots
and earns his praise.'

A pause.

'He said he was personally in a good position to see through
all this pretence because his origins were humble. If he hadn't
had brains he'd have ended up as a clerk in an office, working
from nine to six. But he had brains. He'd got on. In India he'd
got on far better than he could have done at home. In India he
automatically became a Sahib. He hobnobbed on equal terms
with people who would snub him at home and knew they would
snub him. When he considered all the things that made him one
of them in India – colonial solidarity, equality of position, the
wearing of a uniform, service to king and country – he knew
that these were fake. They didn't fool either him or the middle-
and upper-class people he hobnobbed with. What they had in
common was the contempt they all felt for the native race of the
country they ruled. He could be in a room with a senior English
official and a senior Indian official and he could catch the eye of
the English official who at home would never give him a second
thought, and between them there'd be a flash of compulsive
understanding that the Indian was inferior to both of them, as a
man. And then if the Indian left the room the understanding
would subtly change. He was then the inferior man. He said you
couldn't buck this issue, that relationships between people were
based on contempt, not love, and that contempt was the prime
human emotion because no human being was ever going to
believe all human beings were born equal. If there was an emotion almost as strong as contempt it was envy. He said a man's
personality existed at the point of equilibrium between the
degree of his envy and the degree of his contempt. What would
happen, he said, if he pretended that the situation was simply
that of a just English police officer investigating a crime that had
taken place and I pretended that I had no responsibility for it,
and that there was such a thing as pure justice that would see me
through, and if both of us recognized each other's claims to equal
rights as human beings? Nothing would happen. Neither of us
would learn a thing about our true selves. He said that the very
existence of laws proved the contempt people had for each
other.'

A pause.

'At one point he smeared his hand over my buttocks and showed me the blood on his palm. He said, "Look, it's the same colour as mine. Don't be fooled by that. People are. But prick an imbecile and he'll bleed crimson. So will a dog." Then he smeared his hand on my genitals. I was still on the trestle. After he'd had me taken from the trestle I was put in a small cell next door. It had a charpoy with a straw mattress. I heard them caning one of the others. Afterwards he came in alone with a bowl of water and a towel. My wrists and ankles were manacled to the legs of the charpoy. This was the third phase. I was still naked. He bathed the lacerations. Then he poured some water in a tin cup, pulled my head up by the hair and let the water come near my mouth.' A pause. 'I drank.' A pause. 'After I drank he told me I must say thank you, because he knew that if I were honest I'd admit I was grateful for the water. He said he knew it would be difficult to swallow my pride, but it had to be done. He would give me another drink of water. He would give it to me on the understanding that I was grateful for it, and would admit it. He pulled my head back again and put the cup close to my lips. Even while I was telling myself I'd never drink it and never say thank you I felt the water in my mouth. I heard myself swallow. He put the cup down and used both hands to turn my head to face him. He put his own head very close. We stared at each other.' A pause. 'After a bit I heard myself say it.'

A pause.

'That was one of the reasons why when they asked me if I had anything to complain about I said I hadn't. It was a way of making up to myself for thanking him for the water. After I'd said thank you he let go of my head. He smoothed my hair and patted my back. He said we both knew where things stood now. I could sleep now. There'd be no more questions for the present. I didn't have to confess tonight. The girl had incriminated me but it didn't matter. Tomorrow there would be questions. Tomorrow I could confess. When I woke up I'd be anxious to confess. My confession would show the girl up for a liar. I would be punished, but not for rape, because surely I could prove she'd agreed to the meeting, wanted the meeting? He would help me if I would confess to the truth. When I woke up I'd realize he was my one hope. I'd be grateful. I'd already thanked him for the water. That was enough for tonight. Now I could go to sleep. He rinsed the towel out and put it over my buttocks. Then he covered me with a blanket. I don't know how long I slept. I remember waking in the dark. My wrists and ankles felt as if they were still manacled to the charpoy. It was a shock to find they weren't. I had an impression of falling through space. I called out for help. The name I called was Merrick.'

A pause.

'Nobody answered. That gave me time to reason. The most humiliating discovery I made was that I'd believed what he said about Miss Manners incriminating me. I say had believed, but I was still believing it for minutes at a time, and then for another few minutes believing he was lying, then that he wasn't. Like that. Alternately. There can come a point, can't there, when the only attractive course of action for a man completely surrounded by others bent on his destruction is to help them destroy him, or do the job for them before they've quite mustered force for the final blow. It's attractive because it seems like the only way left to exercise his own free will. I made up my mind to confess to whatever he wanted. I thought, well anyway what's going to be destroyed? Nothing. An illusion of a human being, a ridiculous amalgam of my father's stupid ambition and my own equally stupid preferences and prejudices. A nonentity masquerading as a person of secret consequence, who thinks himself a bit too good for the world he's got to live in. He might as well be got rid of or, better still, get rid of himself, and who would feel there was any loss in that, except perhaps Aunt Shalini?'

A pause. She leaned back, closed her eyes, so that her understanding should come to her through only the unidentifying voice.

'But then, you see,' the voice said, 'the question arose – What did nonentity mean? And the answer was quite clear. It meant nothing because it was only a comparative – a way of comparing one person with another, and I wasn't to be compared, I was myself, and no one had any rights in regard to me. I was the only one with rights. I wasn't to be classified, compared, directed, dealt with. Nothing except people's laws had any claim on me and I hadn't broken any laws. If I had broken any it was the laws and not the people who operated them I had to answer to. There wasn't a single other person except myself I was answerable to for anything I did or said or thought. I wasn't to be categorized or defined by type, colour, race, capacity, intellect, condition, beliefs, instincts, manner or behaviour. Whatever kind of poor job I was in my own eyes I was Hari Kumar – and the situation about Hari Kumar was that there was no one anywhere exactly like him. So who had the right to destroy me? *Who had the right as well as the means?* The answer was nobody. I wasn't sure that they even had the means. I decided that Merrick had lied and that far from incriminating me she probably didn't even know yet I'd been arrested. That's the moment when I knew I was sick of lying passively there in the dark. I managed to crawl out of bed and grope round the wall until I found the light-switch. It was pitch black and it took me quite a long time just to stand upright. When I had the light on I noticed he'd left the tin mug near my bed. There was still some water in it. I put the towel round my middle and walked up and down so as not to stiffen up again. The water was warm, the room was probably stifling, there wasn't a window, only a ventilator high up, but I was shivering. Even after I'd drunk the water I went on walking up and down, holding the tin mug. What I was doing reminded me of something but for a while I couldn't think what. Then I got it. Like my grandfather, going off to acquire merit. The loin-cloth and the begging-bowl. It was funny. Aunt Shalini's in-laws were always on at me about becoming a good Indian. This wasn't what they meant but I thought, well, here I am, a good Indian at last. Up until then whenever I thought of that story my father told me about his father leaving home, shrugging off his responsibilities, it hadn't seemed possible that I was con-nected with a family where such a thing could happen. But walking up and down as I was, dressed in that towel, holding that cup, I understood the connection between his idea, and my idea that no one had any rights over me, that there wasn't anyone I was answerable to except myself. And I saw something else, something Merrick had overlooked. That the situation only existed on Merrick's terms if we both took part in it. The situa-tion would cease to exist if I detached myself from it. He could ask his questions but there was no power on earth that said I had to answer them. He could try and probably succeed in making me answer them by using force, but it would be my weakness and not his strength that made me speak. So I came to a decision

to go on saying nothing. I wouldn't answer his or anyone's questions except as it pleased me. I would never thank him again for
a cup of water. I'd rely on no one, no one, for help of any kind.
I don't know whether that made me a good Indian. But it
seemed like a way of proving the existence of Hari Kumar, and
standing by what he was.'

She opened her eyes and stared down into the room, was
struck again by that extraordinary incongruity: the hunched
submissiveness of the man's body, the alert and responsible
intelligence of the man himself.

'Walking up and down with the tin mug – that's how Merrick
found me when he came in. He looked as if he'd been home to
bathe and change but not to sleep. He was very pale. I thought
I saw the tic start up again on his cheek, but it was only for a
second or two. I asked him what the time was. His response was
automatic. He said it was six o'clock. Answering automatically
like that showed him that our relationship had changed. He
began to look puzzled. I walked up and down and every time
I turned to face him I saw this expression on his face, a sort of
dawning mystification, and I thought, my God, the risks he's
taken, he must have been very sure, he must have been absolutely convinced of my guilt. And he was still sure, still absolutely
convinced, but he guessed or knew it had all begun to go wrong,
and he couldn't work out why. I had a flash of admiration for
him. He was totally unconcerned about what I could say or do
that could get him into trouble. He said the constables would
bring me something to eat and some fresh clothes to put on that
had been collected from my home. They brought the food and
clothes. Then they took me to a new cell, the one that turned
out to be my home for a couple of weeks. I never saw anyone
all that time except the two constables and Merrick, unless I was
taken upstairs and examined by people like Iyenagar and the
Assistant Commissioner. When Merrick examined me it was
always in the room where the trestle was but there was never
any physical violence. He questioned me every day, sometimes
twice or three times, and I could tell that the conviction never
left him. I was guilty. The day he told me Vidyasagar had been
arrested he tried lying again, tried to make me believe Vidya had
incriminated me by accusing me of trying to get him to take
part in a plot to attack Miss Manners, but I had the impression

that making me confess didn't interest him any more. Our last full session was the day after I'd been examined by Iyenagar. Merrick said he understood what I was doing. He called it pretending nothing had happened, wasn't happening and wouldn't happen. He said I was wrong, it had happened, was still happening and would go on happening and that he had more contempt for me than ever before. It wouldn't have done me any good to complain to the lawyer, but it disappointed him I hadn't had the guts to accuse him when I had the opportunity. He wouldn't bother to question me again. He admitted he'd lied about Miss Manners accusing me. He said she'd told a cock and bull story about going into the Bibighar Gardens because as she strode past she had a sudden idea that she might see the Bibighar ghosts if she went in. So she'd gone and sat in the pavilion and then been attacked by five or six men she hadn't got a proper look at. Then he said, "But it's not true. You were together in the Bibighar. You rammed her. You know it, she knows it, I know it. She's lying and you're lying. She's lying because she's ashamed and you're lying because you're afraid. You're so scared you're trying to convince yourself the whole business is an illusion, like some naked Hindu fakir pretending the world doesn't exist. What price Chillingborough now?" Then he got up and stood very close to me and reminded me step by step of all the things he'd done to me. He invited me to hit him. I think he really wanted me to.'

Kumar slowly looked down, as if to indicate that he had finished. After a while Rowan said, 'I shall call the clerk back in. Do you wish to make a statement to this effect?'

He shook his head, then raised it. For the first time a smile was fully recognizable. 'I've said it all. The clerk wasn't here to record it. That's part of the situation too, isn't it?'

She felt the first wave – scarcely more than a milky ripple – of an extraordinary tranquillity the nature of which she had no energy to determine; instead only the temptation to surrender to as a runner tired of the race would give in to the temptation to fall out of it. It will end, she told herself, in total and unforgivable disaster; *that* is the situation. As she continued to look down upon the tableau of Rowan, Gopal and Kumar – and the clerk who now re-entered, presumably as a result of the ring of a bell that Rowan had pressed – she felt that she was being vouchsafed a vision of the future they were all headed for. At its heart was the rumbling sound of martial music. It was a vision because the likeness of it would happen. In her own time it would happen. She would live to see what she had been committed to enshrined in the glittering reality of an actual deed, and the deed itself would be a vindication of a sort. But it would never happen in her heart where it had been enshrined this many a year. The tranquillity she felt was the first tranquillity of death. For her the race had ended in the Kandipat in this room with its secret sordid view on to another. The reality of the actual deed would be a monument to all that had been thought for the best. 'But it isn't the best we should remember,' she said, and shocked herself by speaking aloud, and clutched the folds and mother-of-pearl buttons in that habitual gesture. We must remember the worst because the worst is the lives we lead, the best is only our history, and between our history and our lives there is this vast dark plain where the rapt and patient shepherds drive their invisible flocks in expectation of God's forgiveness.

The room was empty. Only the light remained, the dim light, and the glaring light that shone on the empty chair. Kumar had gone with the rest. A hand had touched her shoulder. Looking round she was aware of Captain Rowan and of his voice repeating a question, 'Are you all right, Lady Manners?'

'Yes,' she said, and let him help her out of the chair. Standing she put her handbag on the table, took off her distance spectacles and returned them to the case. She thought how odd such human preparations for departure were. In the passage the weight of unconditioned air threatened to extinguish her. Her legs were shaky from the long inactivity of sitting. They went by stages through degrees of cold and heat: from the cool room to the close, warm corridor, out into the oven-scorched air and the furnace of the waiting motor-car. She sat with her eyes closed, felt the subsidence of the cushion as he lowered himself into the seat's opposite corner. Then the movement: the villainous shadow of the prison gateway. No pause this time. Sun-fish swam across her lowered lids. She raised them and was blinded by a spike of light that pierced the blinds as the motor-car turned at an angle into the sunlight and smell of Kandipat.

'He told the truth,' she announced with a suddenness that caused him to glance at her sharply.

'I'm glad you felt that,' he said. 'Sitting so close to him it was painfully apparent to me that he did.'

'You never mentioned to him that you remembered him at Chillingborough.'

'It seemed unnecessary. It could have struck a false note, too.'

She stayed silent for a moment or two then said, 'I expect you've realized *why* H.E. asked you to look into the files.'

'I've imagined he did so because you asked him to.'

'Then you're probably wondering two things. You're wondering why I should ask him and why I should wait a year after my niece's death before asking him. Is it safe now?'

'Safe?'

'To have the blinds raised. I feel I'm driving to my grave.'

Why, and so you are, a voice told her. She recognized it from other occasions. Old people talked to themselves. From a certain age. No. Always. Throughout life. But in old age the voice took on a detached ironical tone. Passion had this determination to outlive its prison of flesh and brittle bone. As it made arrangements to survive it grew away, like a child from its favourite parent, impatient for the moment of total severance and the long dark voyage of intimate self-discovery. And so you are, her voice said. Driving to your grave. The parting of our ways. A release for both of us. One to oblivion, one to eternal life so unintelligible to either of us it ranks as oblivion too. And already our commitment to each other is worked out and nearly over. Momentum will carry you through what motions are left to you to show your grasp of situations and responsibilities.

'The child,' she said. 'But even now I can't be sure. Only surer. She was so sure. To look at her towards the end you'd think, how astonishing! That combination of ungainly ordinariness and state of grace. One has to make do with approximations. Lies and approximations. When we say he spoke the truth we mean this. Everything becomes distorted. When the child cries its needs are so simple. When he cried he scarcely seemed to know it. Who will read the record?'

'H.E.'

'And the Member for Home and Law?'

'He's an Englishman.'

'Why do you mention that?'

'Because it's pertinent. But Kumar will be released.'

'To what? In any case I don't want to know. I've had my amusement.'

'Amusement?'

'Isn't it all a charade? Over now. We go back into our corners and try to guess the word. Hari Kumar will have to guess it too. And Mr Merrick. Nothing can happen to Mr Merrick, can it? – everything in the file is the uncorroborated evidence of a prisoner. Nothing will touch him. That is part of the charade too.'

'It's safe now,' Rowan said. And began, one by one, to raise the blinds.

PART TWO

A CHRISTENING

I

March–June 1944

THE YEAR HAD begun quietly, but the death in captivity of Mrs Gandhi and her husband's own illness and release, ostensibly on compassionate grounds, marked a time which seemed, in retrospect, to be one of dreams and auguries.

Early in March, when he came in from a tour of his sub-division, young Morland, an officer on the staff of the Deputy Commissioner for the Pankot district, reported a curious tale that was being circulated in the hills; the rumour of the birth to a woman whose husband had abandoned her of a child with two heads. The mother had not survived an hour and the child – a boy – died before the sun set on the first and only day of its life. Morland, suspecting that the death of a child with any consider-able deformity might well have been assisted (although two heads had to be taken with a pinch of salt), had spent two weeks attempting to trace the rumour to its source, but had no luck. Everyone knew it had happened, but nobody was sure of the exact locality. Places were suggested, but going to them Morland was told: Not here, not here: and another village would be named, usually the one he had come from. The closer he tried to get to it the farther away the scene of the event became. But the effect on the people who discussed it with him was clear enough. Such things did not happen without a reason. It was a forewarning. But of what? Heads were shaken. Who could tell? On the journey home Morland noticed the constant freshness of the flowers placed on the little wayside shrines of the old tribal gods.

Having rid himself of the accumulated stains and strains of his tour, and taking his ease at the club, manipulating with excessive, youthful care that symbol of mature and contempla-tive manhood – a stubby briar – brick-red of face and bleached of head, Morland admitted he himself had come rather under the spell of the superstitious anxiety of the people of the hills and found his sleep disturbed by an odd sort of dream which, when he woke up, he never could remember anything of except that it seemed to have something to do with death by drowning. Morland always paused before he added, 'I don't know whether you know, but actually I swim like a fish.'

Within a week Morland was posted to the secretariat in Ranpur, his dream of death by drowning and the tale of the two-headed infant monster were all but forgotten, and Morland himself passed out of sight and mind (as he passes now into the limbo of only marginal images). But on March 18th, when the people of Pankot were startled by the news that the Japanese had crossed the Chindwin in force the day before, there were some who at once recollected the expectations of disaster Morland had brought with him from the remoter areas of the region. Five days later the Japanese crossed the frontier between Burma and Assam and stood on Indian soil, poised for the march on Delhi.

By the end of the month Imphal and Kohima and the whole of the British force in Manipur were isolated. Rumour ran that Imphal had fallen. In Delhi, the Member for Defence, Claude Auchinleck, assured the Assembly that it had not, that his information from the supreme commander, Mountbatten, was to the effect that it was still strongly held. In the Pankot club a wag said that Morland's tale of the monster with two heads was probably set going by natives who had heard about the separa-tion of GHQ, Delhi, from its old responsibilities in the field; that all this streamlining and modernization was a lot of poppy-cock; and that the Japs would never have invaded India if the army in India hadn't been put in the way of its right hand not knowing what its left hand was doing. The joke was ill-received, not because the joker was necessarily thought to be talking non-sense but because, pretty clearly, it was no time for laughter. At Area Headquarters a picture was emerging on the map in General Rankin's office of total encirclement of the forces in Assam, and of the movements of formations from other parts of the front and from training areas in India in reinforcement. Rankin was heard to say, 'Well, this is it.'

Morland's dream was not the only one Pankot heard of. In Rose Cottage for instance, Miss Batchelor, the retired mission-ary teacher who lived with old Mabel Layton, also dreamed; and, unlike Morland who had been reticent, told everyone who cared to listen all the details that she could remember. She dreamed she woke and found Pankot empty. She walked down the hill from Rose Cottage and saw not a soul until she got to the club where one solitary tonga waited. Between the shafts there was a lame horse. Well, not really a horse. The more you looked at it the more obvious became its resemblance to an ass, a creature such as Our Lord sat astride of for the entry into Jerusalem.

'You'd better jump in,' the tonga wallah said, 'they're coming and everyone's gone on ahead to catch the train.' She hesitated to accept the invitation because this particular tonga wallah was a stranger to her and she didn't trust him. 'What are you waiting for, Barbie?' he said, and she saw that it was really Mr Maybrick – the retired tea planter who played the organ in the protestant church – but with his face stained and wearing native costume. So she jumped in and made room for herself among the piles of organ music, and off they bowled at a smart and pretty pace down the hill, past the golf course, where there were people playing, carrying coloured umbrellas. 'Those are the fifth-columnists,' Mr Maybrick shouted at her. 'The golf course is the rendezvous.' It was known that the Japanese had stealthily surrounded Pankot during the night. 'We must take refuge, there's no time to catch the train,' she cried, trying to shout above the noise and rushing of air caused by the tonga's swift passage. Mr Maybrick was now driving four-in-hand. His whip whistled and cracked in the air above the wild-maned heads of a team of galloping black horses. 'To St John's! To St John's!' she shouted and was then at the reins herself and it was her own short-cropped grey hair that was wild and flying. 'Alleluia!' she called, 'Alleluia!' But the church had gone. 'You're just in time,' Mr Maybrick said – in his ordinary clothes now, but wearing a clerical collar. They were standing calmly, but sharing the knowledge that this was the eleventh hour. They were in the compound of a little mission school. 'It's really Muzzafirabad,' Miss Batchelor thought. Her old servant Francis was tolling the bell. They could see hordes of Japanese crossing the golf course, under cover of paper umbrellas. She turned to Mr Maybrick and said, 'We must save a last bullet each,' but when they looked back to the golf course the Japanese had gone and the children were coming to school, summoned by the bell. 'Come along,

children,' Barbie said, keeping her voice friendly but authorita-
tive. Francis said: 'The danger has not passed, memsahib.' But
she called to everyone, 'It's quite safe now.' They went into the
schoolroom, but it was a church again and Mr Maybrick was
playing the organ. She sat in an empty pew to give thanks for
their deliverance. 'And it was extraordinary,' she said, whenever
she told the dream, 'I've never felt so much at peace. I think it
was really a dream about poor Edwina Crane. I went to Muzzafirabad just after she'd left. That was a long time ago – 1914
actually. They were tremendously proud of her there. She really
did save the mission from rioters, she just stood in the doorway,
with all the children safe inside, and told them to go away and
not bother her. And they obeyed. The children used to show
me where she had stood, and I felt I'd never live up to *their*
special idea of a mission teacher. I think it was really a dream to
tell me that Edwina *is* at peace, in spite of that awful business of
her setting fire to herself, in 1942.'

And, presently, when Teddie was dead, a dream came to trouble
Sarah. In the dream they were saying goodbye to him and even
he knew that he would never come back. He had a look on his
face that expressed the most extraordinarily complete awareness
of the place he was going to. The look made him beautiful. They
were all stunned by it and by the knowledge that his presence
was some kind of trick, because he was already gone. 'Of course,
Sarah, it'll be up to you really,' he said, just before he left them.
They had to fight their way through a group of Teddie's friends
and avoid the figure of the prostrated woman in the white saree,
and after that Sarah was running alone through a deserted street.
When she got home her father was waiting. 'I suppose you did
your best,' he always seemed to say although his lips never actually moved. In this dream she was intermittently being made love
to by a man who never spoke to her. Who is that man? people
asked her – her mother or father, or someone who happened to
pass by. Oh, I don't know, she said. There was a superior kind
of mystery about the man.

The dream had begun a few days after they had the news that
Teddie was killed. The news was signalled from Comilla to
Calcutta and from Calcutta to Area Headquarters in Pankot
where it was intercepted by an alert signals corporal who knew

Corporal Layton, and liked her for not being standoffish with non-commissioned men, and thought it best to have a word with someone else before the message went by dispatch-rider to the Pankot Rifles lines where all the Laytons' mail was sent. And so at 10.45 on an April morning Sarah was told by General Rankin that there was some bad news he thought it best to tell her privately so that she and her mother could work out how best to break it to her sister. She remembered the time, 10.45, because when General Rankin sat down he no longer obstructed her view of the clock behind his desk. He had made her sit directly she came in and did not sit himself until he had told her about Teddie and reassured himself that she was going to take it with reasonable composure. To one side of the clock there was the map with tell-tale clusters of flags around Imphal and Kohima. She thought of Teddie as permanently pinned, part of the map.

'Is your mother at home or will she be out shopping?' the General asked.

'They're both at Rose Cottage. I think there's bridge.'

The romantic period of Susan's pregnancy had ended. She was showing. Before long, she said, she would be showing very badly. The grace and favour bungalow stood virtually unprotected from the military gaze in the lines of the Pankot Rifles. She had complained for several weeks that it was like living in a barracks. Now she felt she was showing too much to spend the day happily at the club and had acquired a liking for resting on the verandah at the back of Aunt Mabel's, knitting and crocheting and gazing across the flower-filled garden to the Pankot hills, while her mother played bridge inside with Miss Batchelor and whoever else could be persuaded to forsake the club and the well-stocked bar, and gusty invasions of male company.

Hearing that Susan and her mother were at Rose Cottage the General nodded. Mrs Rankin had played there on two occasions recently and it was scarcely a week since a hint had been dropped to Sarah that her mother's losses were unpaid up. In the midst of this new catastrophe the little debt remained as a source of vague irritation and restraint between the Laytons and the Rankins, not to be forgotten but temporarily overlooked.

'You'd better go up there and get your mother on her own if you can,' Rankin said. 'I'll tell the transport people to provide you with a car, and I'll have a word with your section commander.

Your mother may need you at home for a day or two I shouldn't wonder.' He paused. 'What a terrible, terrible thing.'

He went over to a cabinet, poured a small measure of brandy into a glass.

'Drink this. It's Hennessy three star, not country.'

She drank it down. She hated brandy. The smell reminded her of hospitals.

'Who looks after Susan?' Rankin asked, as if he too had been reminded. 'Beames or young Travers?'

'Dr Travers.'

'You may feel or your mother may feel he should be there when Susan is told. Meanwhile I'll ring my wife. We'll all do what we can.'

'Thank you,' she said and put the glass on his desk. 'I'd better go now.' She put the signal in her pocket. 'I think I ought to go by tonga. If I turn up in a car Susan may wonder and get alarmed before we're ready to say anything.'

'Would you like my wife to go with you? She'll be at the club. You could pick her up on your way.'

Ten rupees was what her mother owed. 'It's very kind of you,' she said, 'but it's not as if Mother and Susan are alone.'

'Wait a few minutes before you go. You've had a shock.'

'No, it's better like this. I mean better than just the telegram arriving.'

He saw her to the door. In the outer office the aide who had taken Captain Bishop's place opened the other door for her and accompanied her down the long arcaded verandah. He went with her all the way to the gravelled forecourt and out beyond the sentries who slapped the butts of their rifles. He hailed one of the tongas that stood lined up in the roadway. The sun was very hot, but the air was crisp; the famous Pankot air that always carried a promise of exhilaration and could be cold at night in winter so that fires were lit at four o'clock. Area Headquarters lay midway between the bazaar and the Governor's summer residence. Between these two were the golf course and the club. It was uphill, and the plumed horse took the slope at a nodding walk, jingling its bells and sometimes breaking wind. She remembered Barbie Batchelor's dream. She watched the road slipping by beneath her feet, her back to horse and driver and stable smell – a smell that was part of the smell of Pankot, the whole panorama of which was widening and deepening as the tonga gained height, disappearing as the road curved from the straight into the first of the bends on the hill on whose farther slope Rose Cottage lay with views to all the hills and valleys of the district her grandfather had ridden and her father had walked. Down on her left now was the golf course, come back into view, and, briefly visible, the bungalow where her father and Aunt Mabel lived after the First World War. More distantly she could see the familiar huts and old brick buildings of the Pankot Rifles depot, and the roof, among trees, of the grace and favour bungalow. Another bend in the road and the tonga, momentarily on the straight again, bowled past the flower-strewn embankment and then the open gateway of the club, giving a glimpse of white stucco columns and bright green lawns. Another turn and they were past the closed iron gates of the long driveway that corkscrewed up to the deserted summer residence. Climbing again now, slowly, past openings of private dwellings posted with familiar names: Millfoy, Rhoda, The Larches, Burleigh House, Sandy Lodge. At the top – Rose Cottage.

'Thairo,' she called, but the driver had already stopped. She got down, hidden from view by the high embankment. She wondered whether she should keep the tonga waiting, but decided not, gave him two rupees to save argument and turned into the steep little drive that was flanked by rockeries. Aunt Mabel was cutting roses, basket in arm, secateurs in hand, wearing old brogues, woollen stockings and a shapeless green tweed skirt. As a concession to the sun she had on a collarless sleeveless blouse, bright orange, that exposed her brown, old woman's mottled arms and neck. On her head there was a wide-brimmed pink cotton hat. These days you had to be careful not to come upon her too suddenly. The deafness that Sarah's mother thought of as assumed to match a mood had become more serious than that. But while Sarah was still several yards distant, her aunt turned. After a moment she put the secateurs in her basket and set it down on the grass, came to Sarah and took hold of her left arm, cocked her head to hear whatever it was Sarah had come at this unexpected time of day to say.

'Susan mustn't see me yet. Can you get Mother out here somehow?'

'What's wrong?'

'Teddie's been killed.'

Mabel's expression did not alter. After a moment she let go of Sarah's arm, then touched it again as a mark of reassurance, turned, picked up the basket and went inside. Sarah followed. The verandah at the front of Rose Cottage was narrow. It was cluttered with pots of flowering shrubs. The famous views were all at the back where the garden sloped to a wire fence, below which the land became precipitous. The cottage was one of the oldest in Pankot, built before the fashion came for building in a style more reminiscent of home. Stuccoed, whitewashed, with square columns on the verandahs and high-ceilinged rooms inside, it was a piece of old Anglo-India, a bungalow with a large square entrance hall. The hall was panelled. Upon the polished wood Mabel's brass and copper shone. The bowls of flowers gave off a deep and dusty scent, and Sarah, standing in the doorway, half-closed her eyes and imagined the drone of bees on a summer's day at home in England, which she had thought of as Pankot in miniature. But England was far away and Pankot was miniature itself. Rose Cottage was not big enough to contain Susan's loss and the gestures of sorrow that presently must be made. They would be offered and the whole of Susan's loss and other people's sorrow would balloon and Pankot would not be able to contain it. She could not hear any voices. She turned away from the hall and stood on the verandah, amazed at the bright colours of flowers in the sunlight and the antics of a pair of butterflies whom Teddie's death had not affected. She waited for her mother to come out. At this time of day she would be in her first drinks of the day state: languid but mettlesome, neither to be loved nor criticized, and requiring an explanation she would not ask for in so many words and which Sarah in this case could not give.

She heard her mother's footsteps.

Mrs Layton was frowning, puzzled by and impatient of an interruption. The frown meant that Aunt Mabel had not said why Sarah had come. That Mabel had said nothing was too char-acteristic to be called unfair. Quickly Sarah began to formulate words. There's awfully bad news, Mother. But that wouldn't do at all. Bad news could be about her father. Shot while trying to escape. Killed by a disease made worse by malnutrition; or dead of lost hope or broken heart.

She said, 'Teddie's been killed,' and reached in her pocket, gave the crumpled signal form to her mother who took it, read it, went inside and sat on a hard hall chair and read it again. Mabel came out of the living-room followed by Barbie Batchelor, Mrs Fosdick and Mrs Paynton. They gathered round Mrs Layton. Becoming aware of them, Mrs Layton looked up from the telegram and said, 'Teddie's been killed.'

Sarah went past them into the living-room. Cigarette smoke still hung in the area of the abandoned bridge-table. Here again there were bowls and vases of flowers and deep overstuffed chairs, and a sofa dressed in flowered cretonne. At the far end the french windows were open on to the verandah. She could see the upholstered cane lounging chair and Susan's bare feet crossed at the ankles in an attitude that suggested deep repose of all the body. Her sister's drowsiness and fleshy calm made the verandah momentarily unapproachable. But she had assured herself no movement inside the house had penetrated that quiet, upset that delicate contemplation of a world without trouble.

She went back into the hall. They were talking in low voices. Her mother still sat. She had the fingers of one hand pressed lightly against her forehead. Miss Batchelor was leaning over her, supporting her back with an arm, but the support was unnecessary. Her mother's back was stiff. She caught Sarah's eye. And Sarah knew. It was she, Sarah, who must find a way of breaking the news to Susan, and the way she found would probably be clumsy, in which case Susan might forgive her but never forget.

She said to Aunt Mabel, 'I'm going out to try and tell Susan now. I think someone should ring Dr Travers in case she takes it badly.'

To make Aunt Mabel hear she spoke clearly. The others turned. She had sounded hard but reliable. Such a combination was understood. If no member of the Layton family had been up to it one of them would have taken charge in just that way. Without waiting for Aunt Mabel's reply she went back into the living-room, edged past the chairs round the bridge-table and stepped out on to the paved verandah. Susan was asleep. A faint perspiration was visible on her upper lip. Her swollen belly tautened the cotton smock and the skirt of the smock was rucked up above her bare knees. The rest of her looked too fragile for the burden of disfiguration, but in her sleep she was smiling.

There was a faint upward lift to each corner of the moist closed lips.

Sarah could not wake her up and destroy such happiness. She sat on a near-by chair, watching her sister for the slightest sign that she was waking, and a ridiculous notion came to her that Susan should go on for ever dreaming and smiling and she go on sitting: in this silly uniform (she thought) with sleeves rolled up like a soldier's, but showing the white chevrons, and wearing sensible regulation shoes. One of her lisle stockings had a snag near the ankle. She wet a finger and applied it. It would do no good. It never did. The scent from the garden and from the ranges of hills where pine trees grew, oozing aromatic gums, came in waves with the faint breeze that here – even on the stillest day – could be felt on the cheek. Her father said that at eye level from the verandah of Rose Cottage the closest ground was five miles distant as the crow flew. He had worked it out with map and compass, sitting where she was sitting. That was the time he taught her to orientate a map with the lie of the land and take bearings to determine a six-point reference on the grid. He never taught Susan such things. But I am a grown woman, she told herself, not a leggy girl learning the tricks he would have taught the son he never had. In a letter at Christmas Colonel Layton said of Teddie, whose photograph they had sent, 'That son-in-law of mine looks all right. Not quite like seeing him in the flesh, but that will come, DV. Meanwhile I heartily approve and send my love to them both, and to you, Millie, and of course to Sarah.' Of course. Of course. She glanced back at Susan and saw under the book that lay open on the floor, pages down, a block of writing paper and the edge of an envelope that would contain the last letter Teddie wrote, the last she had received at least, to which she had not quite summoned the energy to reply, and so had put it by, to doze, and write later, beginning after lunch, and ending after tea, giving it then to Mabel's old servant Aziz to take down to the post.

She heard a faint sound and looked over her shoulder. Aunt Mabel was standing behind her, watching Susan too. She had never been able to tell what Aunt Mabel was thinking and now that true deafness was setting in even the old look of her sometimes watching you with inward curiosity about what you were thinking and why you were thinking it seldom appeared on the old but unwrinkled face. Her mother once said Mabel had no wrinkles because she cared for nothing and nobody, not even herself, and was never worried or concerned like an ordinary human being.

From the hall came the ring of the telephone. Mabel did not hear it. She moved to the balustrade and began to tend some of the flowers that were growing in pots and hanging baskets. Don't wake, Sarah told her sister. The telephone was promptly answered. She guessed the caller was Mrs Rankin. Mrs Rankin would be relieved that Mildred wasn't alone, but had Mrs Paynton and Mrs Fosdick to support her. In Mrs Rankin's book Mrs Paynton and Mrs Fosdick would count. And Sarah knew that she herself would count. While intending almost the opposite she was growing into a young pillar of the Anglo-Indian community. When they got back from the wedding she had been restless. It had been as if with Susan safely married her role of elder daughter had been taken from her. A married woman took precedence over a spinster. Sensing a release and a challenge she told herself: I must go to the war; and inquired about a transfer to the nursing services, which would take her as close to the war as a girl could get; closer than her clerking would ever take her. When she heard of it her mother made no comment; it was Mrs Rankin who took her aside and said, 'My dear, you mustn't think of it. It seems unfair because you're young, and want to do your bit, more than your bit if you can, but here's where it's going to be done. Have you thought of how much more your mother will need you if Susan has a baby?' And a week later Susan announced that this indeed was what she was going to do. Neither Sarah nor her mother ever said anything about the war Sarah could not go to, but between them now, in addition to the silences that hinted at need there were these new silences that were like a recollection of intended betrayal, silences of accusation, silences in which Sarah felt herself charged with having attempted to escape from her responsibilities, caring nothing for her mother, being jealous of her sister and forgetful of her father whose peace of mind depended on a certain picture of them holding a fort together. But these were charges she sometimes made against herself and needed no look in her mother's eye, no set of her mother's still lips, to remind her of.

She leaned back in the chair, turning her head to keep the silent watch: on Susan sleeping and smiling, and on Aunt Mabel taking dead heads off an azalea to give strength to buds not yet open. But that only worked with plants. The bud of Susan's belly wouldn't wax stronger with the cutting off of Teddie. Or would it? The image was grotesque but it had come and would not go away. It was merged with another, an image of a shapeless mindless hunger consuming Susan, consuming all of them, feeding on loss, on happiness and sorrow alike, rendering all human ambition exquisitely pointless because the hunger was enough itself.

Don't wake, she told Susan again, and closed her eyes to contribute to the persuasive arguments of the heat and scent and the siren whispers of the air. She opened them abruptly because Susan had stirred, shifted her legs and turned her head so that now she faced Sarah. After a while with eyes still closed she raised her right arm and made extra shade for her face with the crook of the elbow, then seemed to fall asleep again, but the weight of her own arm disturbed her, and her waking thoughts were more solemn than her sleeping ones. Unsmiling now she half lifted the lids of her eyes and observed Sarah through the fringes of her lashes and the shadow of her elbow. Sarah looked away. Presently she heard another movement – the sound perhaps of Susan lifting her arm to disperse the shadow, raising her head a bit to confirm the reality of Sarah's presence. A moment later Susan asked in a sleepy voice:

'Is it lunch-time already?'

Her eyes were shut again. She had moved her arm and made a pillow of both hands for her face.

'No. I've come back early.'

At the far end of the verandah Mabel stood watching, alerted by the movements Susan had made. She had kept an eye open. Sarah was grateful. In spite of the marked withdrawal from other people, when a real pinch came – Sarah had always thought so – Mabel could be relied on. She was a point of reference. You could not embrace her but you could lean against her and if you ever did so perhaps you would find that she was a shelter too, because she stood firm, and cast a shadow.

'Why have you come back early?' Susan asked, long after Sarah thought she'd dozed off again. And then, 'Anyway, what is the time?' Susan had stopped wearing her watch. She had read somewhere that mothers-to-be shouldn't allow themselves to be distracted by artificial divisions of time. Sarah looked at her own wrist. Was it only thirty-five minutes?

'Eleven-twenty.'

She glanced back at Susan and watched the eyes open yet again. They conveyed a slight annoyance.

'Have you come on badly, or something?'

Sarah shook her head. Since Susan had stopped coming on herself she either pretended not to know when Sarah had a period or spoke of it as if it threatened to disrupt her own routine. So Sarah thought. But perhaps she had become self-conscious and read into Susan's manner what she felt about them herself: that hers were the menstrual flows of a virgin, sour little seepages such as Barbie Batchelor had presumably sustained for a good thirty years of her unreproductive life.

She said, 'No,' and then, seeing an opportunity, added, 'It's not that.' She found herself studying the snag in her stocking again, and automatically wetted her finger, dabbed it, found inspiration from the firm contact. 'Let's help Aunt Mabel with the flowers.' She had an idea that Susan ought to be standing, that it would be bad for her to be told what she had to be told, lying as she was.

She stood up. Susan watched her and then looked round and noticed her aunt standing at the balustrade, attending to the flowers and yet not attending to them.

'Why should we do that?' she asked, but fully awake now, returning her right arm to its crooked position above her head, looking at Aunt Mabel who, Sarah saw, remained still, resisting any temptation to dissociate herself from the situation that was arising.

'Come on,' Sarah said, 'you'll get as big as a house if you lie around all day. You ought to take much more exercise.'

'I am as big as a house, and I've done my exercise.'

'Well, I'm going to push the back of your chair up anyway. You always lie out on it much too flat.' She went round behind and heaved the levered back higher.

'Oh, Sarah, no. What on earth are you doing?'

'Sitting you up.' She readjusted the holding rod. Her arms were trembling. She came round to the front of the chair. 'I'd

better lower the foot. Then you'll be almost respectable.' She
knelt, and did as she had warned. When she had finished she
continued kneeling. She said, 'Sorry. Have I made you awfully
uncomfortable?'

Her sister was leaning forward, her hands clasped to the chair
arms, her legs slightly apart with the smock ridden farther up
from her knees. She was not displeased by the attention but
puzzled by its suddenness and the absence of any immediately
clear reason for it. Now she leant back, but kept her grip on
the arms.

'What have they done, given you a day off?'

'Sort of.'

Susan waited.

'Well?'

Sarah reached for one of Susan's hands.

'Something's happened, which I have to tell you.'

The hand lay beneath hers, quite unresponsive.

'I don't know how to, but I've got to. I think I can only say
it straight. It's about Teddie.'

She paused, deliberately, to let it sink in. When she believed
that it had she went on:

'The signal came this morning and they stopped it being sent
over because they knew I was on duty. The signal says – it says
that Teddie's been killed. So that's what we have to start believing because there can't be any doubt. If there were any doubt it
wouldn't say that, but it does, and I'm sorry, sorry.'

Now she took both of Susan's hands. But they were pulled
away.

'No,' Susan said.

She stared down at Sarah.

'No.'

Mrs Fosdick came, and her mother, and Mrs Paynton, then
Miss Batchelor. 'No,' she said, rejecting them all, jerking herself
away from each touch of a hand on her arm or shoulder. 'No.
No. No.'

She kicked out with one foot, as if kicking Sarah away. Sarah
got up and the others closed in, filling the gap. They surrounded
her completely. 'No,' Sarah heard her say again; but her voice
was muffled now, as if she had covered her face.

Sarah went down the steps into the garden. At the end of the garden there was a place – a pergola dense with briar rose, and behind it a fir where there would be shade from the hot yellow light. As she went she heard a sound that made her stop: a drawn-out shriek, a desolate cry of anguish. When she reached the shade behind the pergola and under the fir she stood with her arms folded, and then sat and wondered whether Susan's cry had crossed the five measured miles to the other side of the valley, and wept – for what exactly she did not know – and it was over very quickly. She dried her eyes and did not want to be alone any longer. She got up, left the shade and reapproached the house with the sun heavy on her neck and heating her scalp. The situation was familiar. It had all happened before – people on a verandah and herself returning to join them. How many cycles had they lived through then, how many times had the news of Teddie's death been broken? How many times had Susan been taken indoors – almost dragged, stiffly resistant – in her mother's arms, while Mrs Fosdick and Mrs Paynton stood like silent supervisors of an ancient ritual concerning women's grief? Aunt Mabel had sat down, with the basket of dead heads on her lap.

'Are you all right, Aunty?' she asked, bending over her.

'Yes, thank you.'

'Can I get you anything?'

'No, thank you.'

'Let me take those.' She touched the handle of the basket but Aunt Mabel held on.

'Tell your mother she and Susan can have my room for the night if they would like that. I don't advise it, but Aziz can rig up extra beds and I can pig in with Barbie. You can have the little spare if they decide to stay.'

'Thanks, but I'll try and get them home.'

Mabel gazed up at her, then nodded. Sarah left her and joined Mrs Paynton and Mrs Fosdick who had gone into the sitting-room. There was no sound from anywhere in the house.

'They're in Barbie's room,' Mrs Paynton said, keeping her voice low. 'You mustn't be hurt, Sarah.'

'No,' said Mrs Fosdick. 'She didn't mean it, hitting out at you like that.'

'I wasn't hurt.'

A message had been left at Dr Travers's. Isobel Rankin had

phoned and offered to look after Susan and her mother at Flag-staff House. Everyone would do everything they could. It was difficult to tell how Susan was taking it. She hadn't cried yet. But there had been that sound. Sarah guessed that the sound had shaken them. It wasn't the kind of sound a Layton made. The servants had heard it. The sound was shocking, Sarah thought, to everyone but her. They would have preferred her sister to cry, quietly, in the privacy of her room. Well there, in her mother's arms, she could have wept to her heart's content and earned their eager sympathy. God knew they weren't hard women; but there was something intemperate, savage, about a grief that went unaccompanied by a decent flow of tears. They all three stood in the room that Barbie Batchelor had made cosy with chintz and cretonne. Miss Batchelor came back. Her tall thin body, iron-grey short-cropped hair and unhealthy yellow face – a network of lines and wrinkles – suddenly struck Sarah as ridiculous. Missionary India had dried her out. There was nothing left of Barbie Batchelor.

'She's just sitting there,' Miss Batchelor said. 'She won't answer us and she won't lie down on the bed. I feel that if only she would lie down it would be all right.' She hesitated. 'It's not like Susan. Not like Susan at all. Poor Mildred can't get through to her, and one feels so useless. One feels so useless.'

Surprisingly Miss Batchelor herself burst into tears, and sat heavily in one of the cretonne-covered chairs. No one in Pankot had ever seen Barbie Batchelor cry. She had come a few years ago, in retirement from the Missions and in answer to the adver-tisement old Mabel Layton put in the Ranpur papers for a single woman to share. Only once in her time in Pankot had she come into any sort of prominence, and that was at the time of the August riots down in the plains in 1942. She had cried: 'I know her!' when they read out the reports of the attack on the superin-tendent of the protestant mission schools in Mayapore, Edwina Crane, who, travelling from Dibrapur back to her headquarters, had seen her Indian companion murdered in front of her eyes and then been knocked senseless by the same mob and had her car burnt out; been found, later, holding the dead man's hand, sitting on the roadside in the pouring rain. 'I know her!' Miss Batchelor cried, and wrote, but had no reply, which was no surprise when eventually it was heard that Edwina Crane had gone very queer as the result of her terrible experience, and died by her own hand, setting fire to herself in a garden shed. 'Oh, poor Miss Crane,' Miss Batchelor was heard to say then. But she had not cried. 'I've always been useless, useless to everybody, how many of those little Indian children really loved God and came to Jesus?' Miss Batchelor said. They soothed her with murmurs of, 'Now don't be silly, how can you say that? There must be hundreds who are grateful to you.'

Sarah felt a suffocating claustrophobia, a tense need to destroy, and run, find air and light.

The claustrophobia was the beginning of the dream she was presently to have, where they were saying goodbye to Teddie, where she herself was running and being made love to by a man whose face she couldn't see and whom nobody seemed to know. He was there and then not there, then there again. He had a great, an insatiable, desire for her but it did not enslave her. He was a happy man and she was happy with him, not jealously possessive. He existed outside the area of claustrophobia, entered it and left it at random, without difficulty. He came to her because she could not go to him. A climax was never reached by either of them, but that did not spoil their pleasure. Disrupted as it was their loving had assurance. There was always the promise of a climax.

'She wants to go home,' young Travers said when he came out of Barbie Batchelor's room, where Susan was. He was not young, only younger than Beames, the civil surgeon to the station. 'And I think that's best, so I'll take her in the car with Mrs Layton.' She had refused a sedative. She had not lain down. She had hardly spoken. She did not speak in the car. When they reached home she went straight to her room. She lay on the bed then, while Sarah and her mother saw to the shutters and drew the curtains. She said, no, there was nothing she wanted, only for them to have their lunch and not bother with anything for her. She would be all right in a while.

The front compound of the grace and favour bungalow had a low wall and looked directly across the road to the back of the bleak Pankot Rifles mess, a rambling L-shaped structure, only partially concealed by trees. The Layton dining-room and master-bedroom had views on to this. At the back there were two other bedrooms and the sitting-room and these had kinder views on to an attempted garden – a square of lawn, a wall. Behind the wall were the servants' quarters. The bedrooms – Susan's and Sarah's – were small. They interconnected. They shared a bathroom that was reached from the back verandah. The black labrador, Panther, who had been a puppy when the girls came out in 1939, had mourned the absence of Colonel Layton, then attached himself to Susan, and these days marked the verandah outside her bedroom as his special territory. He whimpered at her door and Sarah told Mahmud to take him to the kitchen compound and try to keep him there. She told Mahmud what had happened. Mahmud was not one of Sarah's childhood memories but he had been in her father's service for many years, almost ten. When he went, pulling the protesting Panther, she knew that the circumstances of the family's mourning were complete. Sorrow would fill the house and compound with a kind of formality and even the dog would quieten. She went to look for her mother and found her wandering aimlessly in her bedroom with a glass in her hand which, with a wholly uncharacteristic gesture, she abruptly tried to hide, covering it with the palm of her other hand. The telephone rang in the hall. Sarah went to answer it.

Returning, she said, 'It was the padre's wife. She wanted to come round now, but I put her off until this evening.'

Her mother must have emptied the glass and put it away, out of sight. 'I never cared much for Teddie, you know,' she said suddenly. She was sitting erect, almost on the edge of the old PWD armchair, rubbing one bare elbow. 'So I can't pretend to be bowled over exactly. And I don't think Susan ever really loved him. She was very secretive about the honeymoon. At least she was with me. Did she say anything to you?'

'No.' This direct approach disturbed and embarrassed her.

'I shouldn't think Teddie was very – experienced. Not that that's terribly important. Although it is if there's a lack of consideration too. And that's how he struck me, as likely to be inexperienced and inconsiderate. I'd always hoped that Muzzy Guide friend of his, Tony Bishop, would cut him out. But he never even tried. I don't think he cared for Teddie much either or Teddie's attitudes. The one thing they had in common was a regiment.'

'We'd better eat,' Sarah said.

'There's some cold chicken and salad. Tell Mahmud to get up a tray for her. She can't not eat.'

But she did not eat. The telephone kept ringing through lunch, and afterwards the chits began to arrive. Mahmud was sent to Jalal-ud-din's to stock up on tick with country gin and bottles of lemon and lime, and cashew nuts, for the expected invasion of callers. They began to arrive from five onwards: Isobel Rankin, Maisie Trehearne, the wife of Colonel Trehearne who commanded the Pankot Rifles Depot, the Adjutant, old Captain Coley, whose wife had not survived the Quetta earthquake and who himself had not risen since because his ambition did not survive either; Lucy Smalley, Mrs Beames, Carol and Christine Beames who worked at Area Headquarters with Sarah; Dicky Beauvais, deputizing for the most recent batch of Susan's pre-showing grass-widow gallants, young officers who came ostensibly to claim the company of the unmarried sister but had tended to end up fetching things for Susan.

They came, spoke in low tones, and went one by one or two by two. The last to come were Dr Travers and the Reverend Arthur Peplow with his wife Clarissa to both of whom Dr Travers had given a lift; and only the doctor and the chaplain entered Susan's room, Travers first, and then Peplow, after Travers came out and pronounced her well enough and wanting to have a word with him.

'She has asked for a Memorial Service,' Peplow told them ten minutes later, accepting a gimlet, 'and I think that very suitable. I shall be very happy to arrange it.'

'Not happy, darling,' said Mrs Peplow, who was always correcting his way of putting things.

'Of course not. Happy to be of use; the circumstances are sad enough. I think on Saturday week, so that I can announce it next Sunday at matins and evensong. If you agree, Mrs Layton.'

'If it's what Susan wants.'

And Susan wanted it. She only referred to it once, the day after, when she asked her mother to send for the durzi and tell him to bring bolts of whatever he had in grey – silk and chiffon. 'It's for the service,' she said. 'I shan't wear black. And grey will always come in.' She drew the design herself, basing it on one of her smocks which the durzi had already made up. She chose a silk for the smock foundation, a chiffon for the outer drapes which she had the durzi cut to hang full and loose; and in it she hardly showed at all, but stood in the shade of the verandah – while the tailor knelt with pins in mouth and chalk in hand – a white-faced grey-clad little ghost. For her veil she made over a circlet of blue velvet and pale blue velvet flowers and hung it with soft grey net. A grey suede handbag, gloves and shoes, were the only other expense – and these would come in too.

And she made an impression, yes, an impression, walking unsupported by but next to her mother, up the aisle of the church in which she had been christened, with Sarah coming along behind, in uniform. The whole station was represented, the pews were packed. In the days preceding the memorial service Pankot had become conscious of a need and of an occasion coming that would satisfy it. At its centre, Susan, veiled, revealed what that need was, moved them to an intensity of determination to fulfil it; to reaffirm. They lifted their voices high to sing, Lord, While Afar Our Brothers Fight, Thy Church United Lifts Her Prayer; and lowered them to a grave and tender note of fervent understanding when they came to the third verse:

> For wives and mothers sore distress'd,
>   For all who wait in silent fear,
> For homes bereaved which gave their best,
>   For hearts now desolate and drear
> O God of Comfort, hear our cry,
> And in the darkest hour draw nigh.

But the last two lines were sung in mounting passion because the verse stirred them to a sense of what was owed to people like the Laytons. In India hadn't the Laytons always given of their best? In those two young girls, the one sad in grey, the other brave in khaki, there ran the blood of Muirs and Laytons and there were those two names on headstones in the churchyard, stones so old now that the names could only be read with difficulty. A time would come – the congregation felt it, as it were a wind driving them before it so that they had to cling hard not to be scattered – when all their names and history would pass into that same dark.

After the hymn Mr Peplow read the 23rd Psalm and as he finished General Rankin went to the lectern and read from

Corinthians: *Behold I show you a mystery, We shall not all sleep.* He read well until he reached the passage: O death where is thy sting? O grave where is thy Victory? when his voice became flat with self-consciousness. When he returned to his seat Mr Peplow said, very simply, 'Let us Pray.' They knelt and prayed for the deliverance from evil and the coming of the kingdom, for the whole state of Christ's church militant here on earth, for their sovereign George; and – after a pause – for the quiet repose of the soul of Edward Arthur David Bingham.

After the second lesson (*Man that is born of a woman hath but a short time to live*) which was read by Colonel Trehearne in his high, light, lilting voice, they rose to their feet again and sang 'Abide with Me', and it was remarked by those nearest to her that when they came to the opening lines of the last verse, *Hold Thou Thy Cross before my closing eyes; Shine through the gloom and point me to the skies,* Susan lowered her head and after the Amen sat down very quickly, with her head still bowed. She stayed like this throughout Mr Peplow's short address. He spoke of their sympathy for the young widow of a brave officer whom many of them had known, and remembered clearly for his cheerfulness, his kindly disposition. He had no doubt that Edward Bingham's was the kind of cheerfulness that adversity would not have diminished and it was this picture of him, young, smiling and in the prime of life that they must carry away with them. It would be a gallant soldier's best memorial.

He then spoke of the name Bingham, of the father who, like the son, had served in a famous regiment, and of the marriage only a short time ago of the younger Bingham into a family whose history of service to India went even further back. He did not need (he said) to speak at length about such things, for in this congregation the meaning of such service was fully understood and never had the meaning been clearer or the need to serve more pressing than now. This young officer had died, not in a foreign land, but on Indian soil, fighting off an enemy who had brought untold misery to the simple peoples of Burma and Malaya and would bring it to the Indians too if at what seemed like the eleventh hour we failed. But to fail, surely, was not possible, and already the tide was turning. Perhaps this time next year we should see the forces of evil and destruction swept into the sea, Burma regained, Malaya relieved, and India safe from threat, free to turn again to the ways of peace. The victory would not be without cost, but men such as he whom they had prayed this morning in remembrance of would, he hoped, not have died in vain. They were troubled times they had lived through, were living through, and yet had to face, and it was not only for victory to their arms they had to pray but for God to grant wisdom to those in whose hands chiefly lay the future happiness and progress of the great sub-continent, with all its complex problems and manifold differences of caste and creed and race. He asked them to join him presently in a minute of silent prayer, for the repose of the gallant dead, for the safety of the soldiers of India and Britain fighting – even as they sat there – shoulder to shoulder on the eastern frontier, for the peace and blessing of God upon the bereaved, and for wisdom in the councils of the world.

He left the pulpit and when he sank to his knees in front of the altar the congregation followed suit in their pews, prayed their prayers and thought their thoughts. It was said that on the eastern frontier the soldiers of India and Britain fighting shoulder to shoulder had found among their enemy Indian soldiers once captured by the Japanese but now fighting for them. The thought was bitter. Somewhere at the back of the church a coin, got ready for the collection, dropped on the tiled floor, but it marked the silence even more heavily and in itself conveyed an assurance of anxious, charitable intention. Rising once more Mr Peplow announced the last hymn, No. 437, 'For All the Saints, Who from their labours rest'. The collection was for the Red Cross. Four officers from area headquarters solemnly stalked the pews and were rewarded with the chink of coins and crackle of notes in the woven bags they offered on long wooden rods. As the congregation broke into the penultimate verse, 'But lo! there breaks a yet more glorious day', they delivered the collection to Mr Peplow, waited until he had raised it in humble offering and thanks, and then about-turned and regained their seats in time to join in:

From earth's wide bounds, from ocean's farthest coast,
Through gates of pearl streams in the countless host,
Singing to Father, Son and Holy Ghost.
            Alleluia.

Once more they knelt, for the blessing, and rose to restrained chords from the invisible organ, played by Mr Maybrick, the retired tea planter; and waited while, accompanied by Mr Peplow, the Laytons left. After a decent interval, they began to crowd the aisles, their faces stiff with dignity, automatically taking or giving precedence, so that the Rankins were the first to arrive in the porch where Mr Peplow stood holding one of Susan's hands in both of his. He let her go so that Isobel Rankin could embrace her, which she did, lightly, making a token kiss of the air near one veiled cheek and murmuring, 'It was a beautiful service, I hope you felt that.' Susan murmured in return and put out her hand to take the one offered by General Rankin to whom she said, in a low but firm voice:

'Thank you for reading the lesson so clearly, and for everything.'

The General nodded, touched – Sarah saw – that Susan should think of thanking him at all. Presently the Rankins went, with subdued farewells, and others took their place. Dicky Beauvais touched Sarah's shoulder and said, 'I'll ring you later. Where'll you be?' She told him they were going on to lunch at Rose Cottage and only had to wait for Barbie Batchelor so that they could all go up together in the car General Rankin had lent them for the occasion. He touched his cap and went. Sarah was away from the porch now and shielded her eyes from the sun, and then Miss Batchelor was upon her, grinning but blowing her nose. The others emerged from the porch. Mr Peplow accompanied them down the gravel path that led in a curve through the hummocky graveyard – downward, because the church stood, among pine trees and cypress, on an eminence.

At Rose Cottage Susan went with Barbie into Barbie's room to change into the flowered smock and sandals that had been brought up by Mahmud earlier in the day. Barbie came out and told them Susan had asked for lunch on a tray. She would eat it out on the verandah.

'It's been such a strain for her,' Barbie said. 'I don't think she feels up to talking. I'll tell Aziz and then I think the form is for us all to go in and eat.'

They did so. There were curried eggs and rice. Afterwards Mabel and Barbie went to their rooms and her mother to the spare, for the ritual of sleep. Sarah went out on to the verandah.

Susan had had her tray. She was resting on the same chair and in the same position Sarah had found her in ten days before. Sarah sat down, completing the pattern, presently turned her head and saw that Susan was watching her.

'What did Dicky Beauvais say?' she asked.

'Only that he'd ring.'

A pause.

'Is that what you're waiting for?'

Sarah looked away, towards the five-mile hill.

'No, Susan. I'm not waiting for anything.'

A pause.

'You're very lucky.'

'Why lucky?'

'Not to be waiting.' Susan's eyes were shut again. Gently, as if withdrawing into sleep, she turned her head into her folded hands.

At first Sarah did not notice the change in the rhythm of her sister's breathing; but then became conscious of it: conscious that the pauses between the rise and fall were unusually long, the rise and fall unnaturally abrupt. Sarah got up, went close, and understood what was happening. She reached out to touch Susan's head, but was afraid to. Close like this she could hear the suffocating attempts to deny the outlet for a pent-up misery. But what kind of misery? She could not tell. She thought: You have the courage of ten like me. And knelt, leaning on her hip, clasping one ankle, to wait and try to convey to Susan that she was there if wanted. And after a while, still making that sound as if she were suffocating, Susan took one hand away from her face, groped for contact and held on, moving her head from side to side behind the hand that covered it, as if she would wear it down to the skull and Sarah's shoulder to the bone, to relieve her agony.

'There's no one here,' Sarah murmured. 'Let it come out.'

'I can't,' Susan said. Her voice was almost unrecognizable, a hoarse moan below the breath, but emphatic in its conviction. 'I can't. I've got to hang on.'

Sarah bent her head until her cheek rested on the tense knuckles.

'Yes,' she said. 'Yes, if you want.'

'Then it may be all right. I thought the service would help it all come back. But it didn't. It didn't, and I don't know how to face it without. I don't know how to face it.'

She pulled her hand away and flung herself round so that she was on her back; and lay like that, with her eyes shut, turning her head from side to side, pressing down on her swollen belly with both hands.

'At the service I prayed for the baby to die. I want him to die because I don't know how to face it alone. How can I face it with Teddie never never coming back? I didn't want the baby, but it pleased him so, and he wrote and wrote about it, and I could face it like that. But I can't face it alone. I can't bear it alone.'

'You won't be alone, Su –'

'But I am. I am alone.'

Abruptly she sat up, doubled herself over her folded arms and began to move her body in a tight rocking motion. 'Just like I was before, just as I've always been, just as if I'd never tried. But I did. I did try. I did try.'

'What did you try –?'

'You wouldn't understand. How could you? You're not like me. Whatever you do and wherever you go you'll always be yourself. But what am I? What am I? Why – there's nothing to me at all. Nothing. Nothing at all.'

Sarah sat quite still, watching that rocking motion, held by it, and by the revelation, what seemed to be the revelation, of what had lain behind the game that seemed to have ended, the game of Susan playing Susan. Susan nothing? Susan alone? She pondered the meaning of: Whatever you do and wherever you go you'll always be yourself: and recognized their truth. She was herself because her sense of self, her consciousness of individuality was tenacious, grindingly resistant to temptations to surrender it in exchange for a share in that collective illusion of a world morally untroubled, convinced of its capacity to find just solutions for every problem that confronted it, a world where everything was accepted as finally defined, a world that thought it knew what human beings were.

But it did not know what Susan was. In grey and on her knees; yes, it knew that Susan; and it knew Susan in white with the wind catching her veil, or standing at a carriage window flushed and smiling and taking a last sniff at a bunch of flowers before throwing them in that bride's gesture which proved a readiness to share her luck and fortune. It did not know her in a coloured smock, rocking to and fro, and had no answer to her cry that she was nothing.

It did not know her and had no answer and Sarah did not know her either – not as Susan – but with something of a shock recognized in the girl crouched on the chair a sibling whose pretty face and winning ways had been, after all, perhaps, only a fearful armour against the terrors of the night, a shield that was not visible to her but deluded others into believing her protected. What else had they been deluded by? By everything, perhaps, but most of all by the signs and portents of self-absorption, that apparent trick and talent for creating a world around her of which she was the organizing determinedly happy centre. It had not been that at all. There had been no secret garden, but only Susan crying to be let in and building the likeness of it for herself because she believed the secret garden was the place they all inhabited, and she could not bear the thought that she alone walked in a limbo of strange and melancholy desires.

Shifting her weight Sarah reached and put her arms round her sister.

'You do amount to something, and you're really not alone,' she said, and Susan turned into the embrace, with the weird sound of someone inwardly recognizing and inarticulately acknowledging refuge.

II

Several images converge. That woman in the *burkha*, glimpsed in Ranpur, making her way to the mosque through the street of the money-lenders: one merely chanced upon her and noted the smell of Chanel No. 5; but – walking unhurriedly, in that enfolding garment – she defies her prosaic environment of time and place. She can be pictured years before, not in Ranpur but in Pankot, making her way along a section of the bazaar, like a ghost condemned to walk in a certain place, so many steps, presenting to the world a front, a proof of her existence, silently calling attention to herself; always appearing and disappearing in the same places, as though the route, as well as her presence, is significant.

There was such a woman in the dream Sarah had, but she was in widow's white, not purdah; and did not walk but remained prostrate. Yet, in the recurrence, in the uncertainty as to real intention, similarities existed. The whole of Sarah's dream was like the woman in the *burkha*. It came and went and stayed in her mind, so that sometimes, in daylight, awake, the visions of the dream would transpose themselves and she would find herself leaving Jalud-ud-din's and encountering, through the eyes of the woman who usually begged alms outside, this other woman, the one in white, lying in the dust, seeking for a mercy no one was capable of showing. For Sarah there came a time when the whole of that summer became inextricably entangled, as if, at this point, converging strands of circumstances met and intermingled but did not cohere; and woven into them were the patterns of her dream, and Barbie's dream, and the tale from the hills that had sent young Morland in his sleep to an unexpected death by drowning. She found it difficult later to remember things in the order they happened. There was a sense in which they became interchangeable.

For instance: did she fancy she saw Lady Manners in the bazaar before the old lady strangely announced her presence in Pankot (strangely because having announced it she remained resolutely in a purdah of her own)? Or had Lady Manners re-entered her sleeping and waking consciousness before she had made her presence known, so that the glimpse Sarah thought she had of her, leaving Jalal-ud-din's in the company of a distinguished-looking Indian woman, seemed like some special manifestation rather than a visual confirmation of a presence that was the subject of common gossip? And what came first? Lady Manners or the letter that revived the other image of the stone thrown into the car taking poor Teddie and his best man to the wedding? And when, why, was it first suggested that Susan was dangerously withdrawn and the tale was resurrected of Poppy Browning's daughter who, bearing her first child three months after being told her husband had died in the Quetta earthquake, promptly smothered it?

The most logical sequence would be one in which the letter reviving the image of the stone came first, because this might be seen as having had an effect on Susan that set people talking about Poppy Browning's daughter and the business of the

smothered child; and as having had the effect, as well, of reminding Pankot of the affair in the Bibighar Gardens in advance of
Lady Manners's arrival, so that the arrival had the special poign-
ancy Sarah seemed to remember as attaching to it.

There had been many letters: from all over India, from people
who had seen Teddie's death gazetted or the notice in the *Times
of India*. Most were addressed to Mrs Layton and she set about
answering them with an industriousness that Sarah fancied was
in part therapeutic, in part self-indulgent. All through the mornings, and on many an evening, Mrs Layton sat at the oak bureau
in the grace and favour living-room, writing, writing. Page after
page. There was apparently no end to the store of words, the
flood of words. And she became more directly communicative.
She discussed the letters with Sarah. She drank less.
    There were also letters to originate: to Aunt Lydia in Bays-
water, to Colonel Layton in Germany, to that uncle of Teddie's
in Shropshire whom the marriage had relegated from his old
status of next-of-kin and of whose nephew's death on active
service it had therefore become Susan's or Mrs Layton's duty
to inform him. The Shropshire uncle had promised a wedding
present after the war; it seemed doubtful now that Susan would
ever get it; he had not given an impression of a generous nature.
There were letters to send to Aunt Fenny too – now left Delhi
for Calcutta where Uncle Arthur had at last acquired a job
(a strange-sounding kind) that carried the pip and crown of a
Lieutenant-Colonelcy: the first to tell Fenny of Susan's loss and
the second to put her off coming up, as she offered.
    There were expected letters; one each for them from Tony
Bishop who, but for the jaundice, would have been Teddie's best
man, and who now worked in Bombay. There were unexpected
letters, a formal note of condolence from the Nawab of Mirat
to Susan and a less formal letter to Mrs Layton from Count
Bronowsky who said that the Nawab was deeply affected to hear
of the death in action of the husband of the charming girl to
whom and to whose family he had had the privilege and pleasure
of extending some small hospitality the previous year. He wanted
the Laytons to know that they were welcome at any time, now
or in the future, to stay as his guests again, at the palace, or in the
summer palace in Nanoora. 'How kind,' Mrs Layton murmured,

'but quite out of the question,' and wrote to thank the Nawab and his wazir, and explained that Susan was awaiting the birth of her baby.

Susan detached herself from the business of the letters. She asked her mother and Sarah to open them, answer for her, and keep by any of those they thought she might look at later. She specified only one exception to this rule. And this was the letter for which they waited. It came (Sarah thought later, unable quite to recall the order of things) in a batch of mail on the Sunday of the week following the Memorial Service. The flimsy envelope, addressed to Susan, was franked by a field post office, and attested for the censor by an officer whose rank alone was legible.

'I think this is it,' Mrs Layton said. She handed the envelope to Sarah who was helping with lists and priorities. Susan was at the back, playing with Panther, throwing a ball from the veran-dah and waiting at the balustrade while he went to retrieve it. They could hear the scuttering sound of the dog's pads and claws as it hurled itself down the steps and, after an interval, hurled itself back up them again to drop the ball with a *puck* at Susan's feet, panting from the exertion, and with the pleasure of having a mistress who again took notice of him.

Sarah handed the envelope back. 'It must be.' She looked round, alerted to a change in the rhythm of the game by the dog's anxious whimper. Susan was standing by the open window, watching them.

'It's come, hasn't it?' she asked.

Mrs Layton held the envelope out. 'We think so. Here you are, darling. You'll want to take it away.'

Susan came over, took the letter and went back to the veran-dah. They heard Panther growl and Susan say to him, 'Oh, all right, just once more.' She must have thrown the ball then. The dog scuttered away. Mrs Layton opened another letter. 'It's from Agnes Ritchie in Lahore,' she told Sarah. 'Put her on B list.'

Sarah entered Agnes Ritchie's name in the B column of her list and when her mother gave her the letter put it with others in the B folder. Susan must have thrown the ball into the bushes of bougainvillaea. It was some time before they heard the dog return. Ball in mouth, it came into the living-room, looked round and went out again. They heard then, faintly, from the far end of the verandah, the scraping of its claws on the closed door of Susan's room. In a while this sound of insistence died away. Sarah got up and went outside. The labrador raised its head and glanced at her. The ball was held securely between its extended paws.

'Come on, Panther,' she said, 'I'll throw your ball for you.'

But the dog rested its head again and waited.

Mrs Rankin rang and spoke to Mrs Layton about the Red Cross aid committee meeting, Mrs Trehearne sent a chit about the British Other Ranks Hospital Welfare and Troops Entertainments committee. Dicky Beauvais came round and asked Sarah for tennis at five with supper and pictures to follow. Mahmud complained that the dhobi had failed to turn up and asked permission to go into the lines and if necessary into the bazaar to find him. Distantly they heard the bells of St John's announcing matins, and closer, the strains of the regimental band of the Pankot Rifles at practice in the grounds of the officers' mess. The crows swooped and squawked. It was an ordinary Sunday morning. But an hour after she had taken the letter Susan was still in her bedroom, secluded with her evidence of war.

'I've done enough,' Mrs Layton said. 'I'm going to wash my hair.' She gave Sarah the pile of envelopes, the result of the morning's spate, and went into her room, calling for Minnie, Mahmud's widowed niece who helped him run things by taking care of the intimate details of a household of women. The call for Minnie roused the dog. It went padding past the window, making for the source of this evidence of renewed activity. Sarah finished stamping the envelopes, went into the entrance hall and left them on the brass tray where Mahmud would find them on his return from his quest for the lost dhobi. She went into her own room. Minnie had made the bed, tied the laundry into a sheet and pinned Sarah's list to it. The connecting door into Susan's room was closed and she could not hear her sister moving.

She tapped, then opened the door. Susan was sitting on the bed with an album on her knee which Sarah recognized as the one containing the wedding photographs and press cuttings. The letter was on the bedside-table, propped between the table-lamp and a framed picture of Teddie – Susan's favourite because it showed him looking serious, with the mere ghost of a smile.

'Mother's washing her hair and I thought I'd do mine,' Sarah explained. 'You don't want the bathroom for ten minutes, do you?'

Susan shook her head.

'Was it a letter about Teddie?'

'Yes.' She put the album down, picked up the letter and began to read it but seemed to give up half-way. She offered the sheet of buff army paper to Sarah.

'Dear Mrs Bingham, Since it was with me that your husband worked most closely it is, I think, my duty – a very sad one – to offer you on behalf of his divisional commander and fellow-officers, deep sympathy in the loss you have sustained by his death, of which you will by now have received official notification. He died as a result of wounds, having gone forward, under orders, with instructions to the commander of a subordinate formation then in contact with the enemy and under heavy pressure. With him at the time was Captain Merrick, whom you met in Mirat of course. Captain Merrick, although himself wounded – and at risk of his own life – rendered the utmost assistance to your husband, and stayed with him until the arrival of medical aid. Captain Merrick told the medical officer that your husband had not been conscious, and it may be some relief to you to know, therefore, that he did not suffer. Captain Merrick has now been evacuated to a base hospital and the Divisional Commander has been pleased to submit a report, in the form of a recommendation, in respect of Captain Merrick's action. Teddie – as most of us knew him here – ever cheerful and devoted to his task, is sadly missed by all of us. Those of us who met you, your mother and your sister, on the occasion of your wedding in Mirat, all send our special personal sympathies. Yours sincerely, Patrick Selby-Smith, Lt-Colonel.

Sarah returned the letter to its place by Teddie's portrait. Susan was going through the album again.

'I've never noticed it before,' she said, 'but there seems to be only one picture of him.'

'Of Colonel Selby-Smith?'

'No, of Captain Merrick. This is him, isn't it? It's really only half a face.'

Sarah sat on the bed next to her sister and studied the photograph. It was taken at the pillared entrance of the Mirat Gym-khana Club a moment or so before they left for the railway

station. It showed Teddie with his plastered cheek turned from
the camera and looking down at Susan who stood with her feet
neatly together, in a tailored linen suit, wearing a little pill-box
hat and holding the bouquet. Behind them on the steps, partly
shadowed, were Aunt Fenny and her mother, Uncle Arthur
and Colonel and Mrs Hobhouse. Behind these was the group
of largely anonymous officers of whom she only recognized
Ronald Merrick. Merrick was not looking into the camera but
down on to Uncle Arthur's neck. In that little crowd of grinning
young men he looked remote, humourless; but younger – she
thought – than she remembered him looking in full light, under
the sun. The camera and the shadows had smoothed out lines
and not recorded the weathered texture of the skin. As a youth,
at home, with his fair hair and blue eyes – she was sure they were
blue – he must have seemed to those near to him comely and
full of promise. 'She didn't care,' he had said, when talking that
evening about Miss Manners, 'what your parents were or what
sort of school you went to.' He must have been conscious of
them himself, though, and Sarah wondered about them, about
the ambition that had driven him and the capacity that had
enabled him to overcome what she supposed would count as
disadvantages if you compared them with the advantages of a
man like Teddie Bingham. She had never written to Captain
Merrick, but then he had never written to her. Once – or was it
twice? – he had sent his regards to them all through Teddie,
perhaps more often than Teddie remembered to say. She wondered how literally he had taken what she recalled now as a
promise to write sometimes. She had thought the request for
letters part of the attempt he seemed to make to convey to others
an idea that he was a man rather alone in the world, a man whose
background and experience set him somewhat apart but gave
him reserves of power to withstand what other men might feel
as solitariness. She remembered how they had sat on the terrace
the last time she saw him, waiting for the fireflies to come out,
and how as the light faded Captain Merrick's body had resisted
that diminishing effect, had intensified, thickened, impinged;
and how she felt that if she had reached out and touched him
then he could have carried the frail weight, the fleeting sensation,
of her fingers on his arm or hand or shoulder into those areas of
danger that co-existed with those of the impenetrable comfort

that surrounded her, protected her, and barred her exit. He had appalled her, she had not trusted him, although why that was so she did not know clearly. He had stood under the light that lit his face and his need, and his implacable desire to be approached; and offered his hand. He still impinged; what he had done or tried to do for Teddie, did not seem to alter – except in a curious way to emphasize – her picture of him as a man obsessed by self-awareness; but the request for letters might have been genuine.

'Yes, that's Ronald Merrick,' she said. 'Are you sure it's the only one?' She turned the pages of the album. It struck her as disturbingly significant of some kind of failing in all of them that he should have been missed out of the main wedding groups, that none of them had noticed his absence at the time, nor remarked it later when the proofs were chosen and the enlargements made. 'Yes, I remember,' she said, turning back to the one photograph in which he was represented. 'Aunt Fenny couldn't find your hat-box and he went to look for it and then immediately he'd gone there was the fuss about getting the pictures taken while the Nawab was still in the garden.'

'I didn't even know my hat-box was lost,' Susan said, 'but I suppose you'd call that typical.'

'Perhaps he didn't want his picture taken.'

'Oh, everyone likes their picture taken.'

'He may have thought of it being in *The Onlooker* and people recognizing him as the policeman in the Manners case.'

Susan considered this. She smoothed the photograph with one finger as if feeling for an invisible pattern she thought must be there, in the grain of the paper. She said, suddenly, 'Teddie was terribly upset. About that I mean. I don't think he ever forgave him. But I must, mustn't I? I mean I must write and thank him for trying to help Teddie. It's the right thing. Especially the right thing when he's not what Aunt Fenny calls one of us.' She smiled, as to herself, and continued smoothing the surface of the photograph. 'I think I envy him. Not being one of us. Because I don't know what we are, do you, Sarah?' She closed the album abruptly. 'The letter doesn't say which hospital or how badly wounded he is, but if it's a base hospital he must be pretty bad, mustn't he? If I enclose a letter for him when I write to Colonel Selby-Smith it would get sent back to wherever he is, wouldn't it?'

'Yes, that would be best.'

'I should write, shouldn't I?'

'It would be a kind thing to do.'

'Oh, not kind. I don't know kind. I don't know anything. I'm relying on you to say.' She was staring at the letter. 'I need help. I need help from someone like you, who knows.'

'Knows what?'

'What's right, and wrong.'

'Help with the letter?'

'Not just the letter. Everything.' She folded the letter and gave it to Sarah. 'Will you show it to Mother for me?'

'I will, but it would be nice if you showed it.'

'I know.' She was upright on the edge of the bed smoothing the counterpane now. 'But I'd rather not.'

'Why?'

'Mother didn't like Teddie. She didn't want me to marry him. She never said so, but it was obvious. She didn't really want me to marry anyone until Daddy comes back. She wants everything to be in abeyance, doesn't she? – because for her everything is. Everything – especially things about men and women. She didn't talk to me, you know.'

'Talk to you?'

'She made Aunt Fenny do it. Or anyway Aunt Fenny volunteered and Mother let her. I don't think that was right, do you?'

After a moment Sarah said, 'Was there anything you didn't know?'

'Oh, it isn't that. It was that Mother let Aunt Fenny. It made me feel she didn't care enough to make sure herself that I knew about the things I had to let Teddie do. She didn't want any of it to happen, so for her it wasn't happening. But at the time it just seemed to me to prove she didn't care, that nobody cared really.'

Sarah felt cold. Again she did not speak for a moment or two. Then she asked, 'Is that how you thought about it? That making love was just something you had to let Teddie do?'

Susan stopped the smoothing. 'I don't know. I didn't think about it much. All that was on the other side.'

'The other side? The other side of what?'

Sarah saw that her sister's cheeks had become flushed. She seemed, simultaneously, to become conscious of the warmth herself and brought her hands up and held them to her face. She no longer wore the engagement ring: only the plain gold band which had a thick old-fashioned look about it as if it might have been Teddie's mother's – the one relic of a life unhappily ended in Mandalay – although he had never said it was.

'I seem to have lost the knack,' Susan said.

'The knack of what?'

'Of hiding what I really feel. I'm out in the open. Like when you lift a stone and there's something underneath running in circles.'

'Oh, Susan.'

But she felt the truth, the pity of it, and was afraid. The wan hand of a casual premonition had stroked her neck.

Susan looked at her and, as if seeing the hand that Sarah only felt, at once covered her eyes and bowed her head. From under her palms her voice came muffled.

'I used to feel like a drawing that anyone who wanted to could come along and rub out.'

'That's nonsense.'

Susan uncovered her face and looked at Sarah, surveying – Sarah felt – her outline and density. She did not say: No one could ever rub you out. But such a judgment, held suddenly by Sarah of herself, briefly lit her sister's expression – calm, unenvious – without quietening the hectic flush that had reappeared after days of absence.

'No, it's not nonsense.' She looked down at her lap and her now folded hands. 'I felt it even when we were children in Ranpur and here, up in Pankot. I think it must have been something to do with the way Mummy and Daddy, everyone, were always talking about *home*, when we go home, when you go home. I knew "home" was where people lived and I had this idea that in spirit I must be already there and that this explained why in Ranpur and Pankot I was just a drawing people could rub out. But when we got home it wasn't any better. It was worse. I wasn't there either. I wanted to tell someone but there was only you I could talk to and when I looked at you I felt you'd never understand because you didn't look and never looked like someone people could rub out. Do you remember that awful summer? The summer they all came home and great-grandpa died? Well, I looked at them and felt no, they hadn't

come home, that they could be rubbed out too and that perhaps
I fitted in at last. So I longed to come out again, longed and
longed for it. When we did come out we weren't kids any more.
I wasn't frightened of India as I was as a kid. But everyone
seemed real again and I knew I still didn't fit in because there
wasn't anything to me, except my name and what I look like.
It's all I had, it's all I have, and it amounts to nothing. But
I knew I had to make do with it and I tried, I did try to make
it amount to something.'

'I never knew you were frightened.'

'Oh yes. I think I was very frightened. I don't know why
exactly. But I was always trying to get to the other side, the side
where you and everyone else were, and weren't frightened.
It was a sort of wall. Like the one there.' She nodded towards
the closed window where Panther had tried to get in and Sarah
glanced in that direction, saw that the wall she meant was the
one at the end of the patch of garden that hid the servants' quarters. 'Was there a wall like that in the garden at Kabul road?'

'Yes.'

'Dividing the servants from us?'

'Yes.'

'I know I was frightened of the servants. No one else seemed
to be. I suppose that was part of it. On the other side of the wall
it was very frightening but only frightening to me and I expect
I was ashamed and had this idea that if only I could get over I'd
be like everyone else.'

'Is that what you wanted? To be like everyone else?'

'Oh, I think so. We do as children. I think that's what I
wanted. Of course when we came out again I wasn't frightened
any more, I thought of it more as wanting to make a life for
myself that would add up just like everyone else's life seemed to
add up. I mean everyone seemed so sure, so awfully sure, and
I wasn't. I wasn't sure at all. I thought, if only I could make a
life for myself, a life like theirs, a life everyone would recognize
as a life, then no one could come along and rub me out, no one
would try. Marrying Teddie was part of it, the best part, even
though I didn't really love him.'

'I wondered,' Sarah said.

'Everybody wondered, didn't they? Well, that's the answer.
I didn't. I thought I was in love a score of times, but knew

I wasn't really, not inside where it's supposed to matter, and *that* frightened me too. It proved there wasn't anything inside, but I didn't want to go on being alone. I can remember it as clear as clear, the day I thought, why wait? Why wait for something that's never going to happen? I'm not equipped. Something's been left out. And I was always good at hiding what I felt, so I thought well, I'll get away with it and nobody will ever know. Whoever I marry will never know. And there was poor Teddie. He walked straight into it, didn't he? I married him because I quite liked him and I thought there probably wasn't much to him either. But I think there was. Yes, I think there was. He almost made me feel there might be something to me, in time. But he had a rotten honeymoon. Rotten.'

She turned, looked straight at Sarah and said:

'Not because I was scared or because he didn't *try* to make things different, but because I'd nothing to give him. That's why he was so pleased when I wrote and told him about the baby. He'd married a girl with nothing to her, but she'd given him something to make up for it. And having it to give him could have made *me* something, couldn't it? Who do I give the baby to now, Sarah? There isn't anybody. And I've nothing for it, except myself. And it's odd, awfully odd, but now when I think about what any of us could give it I can't see the answer.'

She hesitated, but held herself very still, and for a few seconds a half-formed picture came to trouble Sarah of Susan as a child holding herself like that, with the gritty surface of a faded red brick wall dark behind the halo of light on her hair; but the picture would not come more vividly or significantly to life and she could not say whether it was an Indian or an English memory.

'No,' Susan repeated. 'I try and try but I can't see the answer. I suppose the trouble is that people like us were finished years ago, and we know it, but pretend not to and go on as if we thought we still mattered.' Again she hesitated, then, looking full at Sarah again, asked, 'Why are we finished, Sarah? Why don't we matter?'

Because, Sarah thought, silently replying, we don't really believe in it any more. Not really believe. Not in the way I expect grandfather Layton believed – grandfather and those Muirs and Laytons at rest, at peace, fulfilled, sleeping under the hummocky graves, bone of India's bone; and our not believing seems like a betrayal of them, so we can't any longer look each other in the eye and feel good, feel that even the good things some of us might do have anything to them that will be worth remembering. So we hate each other, but daren't speak about it, and hate whatever lies nearest to hand, the country, the people in it, our own changing history that we are part of.

But she could not say this to Susan. Instead she asked, 'Why do you say *we*? *We* may be finished or not matter, or whatever it is. But you matter. I matter.' She wished she could believe it with the simple directness with which she said it. 'There's too much of it. Too much "we". Us. One of us. Oh I agree – one of us, I don't know what we are any longer, either. Stop thinking like that. You're a person, not a crowd.'

Again Susan studied her, calmly, but not – Sarah decided – unenviously, although the degree of heat generated by envy was slight, and said, 'How self-assured you are,' in a tone that reminded her – as a blow might remind – of that afternoon on the houseboat in Srinagar when she had looked at that old woman and heard herself say, 'What a lot you know.' What a lot you know. How self-assured you are. But I am not, not, not. Had *she* not been, that old fragile poised little lady, one of whose hands (she suddenly recalled) rested casually with faded Edwardian elegance on the little pearl buttons of a cream pleated blouse? Well, no, perhaps she had known nothing either, and been certain of nothing except that the years of belief were over and those of disbelief begun.

Sarah shook her head.

'I'm not self-assured at all. But I do know this – the baby matters too.' She meant, but did not say, that Susan had a duty to it. She did not want to use the word. There had been, still was, altogether too much talk of duty, almost none of love.

'Yes, I know,' Susan said. 'Everything must be done that can be. And there's something I've been meaning to ask you. Mother said that if you do it, Aunty Mabel will agree.'

'If I do what?'

'Ask her. About the christening clothes.'

'What do I have to ask about the christening clothes?'

'Whether she'll lend them.'

'What christening clothes are those?'

'Yours. Mine got lost or something. But she still has yours. Barbie told me. She saw them in one of Aunty Mabel's presses when Aziz was doing it out.'

'How did Barbie know they were mine?'

'She asked Aunty Mabel. And that's what Aunty Mabel said. And Mother told me she remembered Aunty Mabel was given your christening gown because it was made up mostly of lace that had belonged to Aunty Mabel's first husband's mother, and of course Aunty Mabel never had any children so the lace wasn't used and she wanted it to be used for you.' Susan paused. 'I thought perhaps you knew. Hasn't Aunty Mabel ever taken it out and shown you and said, "Look, this is what you were christened in?"'

'No, never.'

'I thought perhaps it might have been a secret you had with her.'

'I never knew Aunty Mabel and I had any secrets. Wasn't the gown used for you too?'

'No. I had something modern, so Mummy said. And it got lost, or didn't last. Not like the lace. I'd like it if the baby could wear the gown you were christened in.'

'I'll ask Aunty Mabel. But it might be old and a bit smelly.'

'No. Barbie said it was beautiful. And that Aunty Mabel must have taken special care of it. There's something else I have to ask. I mean about the christening. Will you be godmother? Mother says Aunt Fenny will expect to be asked, but I don't want that.'

'I shouldn't make a very good one.' Sarah hesitated. 'I don't believe in it.'

To say this she had averted her eyes and in her mind was an image of Aunty Mabel kneeling by a press (as she had never seen her kneel) and holding (as she had never seen her hold) the mysterious gown, inspecting it for signs of age and wear as though it were a relic the god in whom Sarah did not believe had charged her to preserve against the revival of an almost forgotten rite. And glancing back at Susan she thought she saw the convulsive flicker of an ancient terror on the plumped-out but still pretty face.

'I know. But if anything happened to me you'd look after the baby, wouldn't you?'

'Nothing's going to happen to you.'

'But if it *did*.'

'Well, there are plenty of good orphanages.'

'Oh, Sarah – not even as a joke.'

'Then don't ask silly questions. Of course the baby would be looked after.'

'That's not what I'm saying, not what I'm asking. Looked after, looked after. I'm asking if *you'd* look after it, not just to say it would be looked after.'

'Something might happen to me too.'

It was unkind, she thought, the effect that embarrassment had. Of course she would look after the baby.

Susan turned her head, seemed to stare at Teddie's picture. She said, 'Yes, something might happen to you. It will. You'll get married. You'd want your own children. Not mine and Teddie's.'

'You'll get married too.'

'Oh no. Not just to give the child a father. Not again, like that, without really loving. And how can I learn that?'

'You'll love the baby.'

'Shall I?' Susan faced her again.

'When you've got the baby it will be all right, and after a while someone like Dicky Beauvais will ask you to marry him.'

'Not someone like Dicky Beauvais.'

She made it sound as if one phase of her life had ended.

'No, all right. But someone.'

'I shouldn't want to be taken pity on and that's what it would be I expect. Poor Teddie Bingham's widow, a child herself really, how will she manage?' Again she glanced at her dead husband's portrait, searching perhaps for something in his hallowed face that showed not pity but compassion for those he had, without meaning to, left behind to manage as they might.

'I think,' she said, 'that after all it would be better if you wrote to Captain Merrick for me. You could thank him so much more kindly, make him understand how much the Laytons are *beholden* to him for what he tried to do for Teddie. Whatever it was. Whatever it was.' She frowned, getting it seemed no clearer picture from the picture of Teddie of the unwanted gift he had made her of his death; and Sarah – catching the frown, consider-ing the tone and rhythm of that repeated qualification, *whatever it was* – became aware of an element of doubt about the death that had entered for both of them.

'Well if you prefer it,' she said and then wondered: But what shall I say? and felt a little surge of resistance to the idea of saying anything, as though the act of writing would count as a surrender, proof that in the end he had succeeded in making her approach him – as herself, for herself, and as a Layton, for the Laytons.

'You could say I'm not fully recovered from the shock,' Susan went on, 'and tell him about the baby. Remind him, rather. He must have known about the baby. Teddie must have told them all about the baby. I expect they made one of those men's jokes about it. Ragged Teddie I mean, about him becoming a father. Perhaps he won't want reminding, but you'd better mention it, use it as one of the things that excuses me from writing to him myself. But I want him to know, I do want him to know that I am beholden.'

It was a word that apparently fascinated her. Spoken, it created, almost, a cloistered air of peace, of withdrawal from the fierce currents of an angry shock-infested world; it did not lay balm to the little wound of doubt, but the wound nagged less. Beholden, beholden. It was transcendental, selfless, forgiving.

'Who knows,' Susan asked, turning to Sarah with that kind of expression on her face, 'perhaps he's lying somewhere, feeling it, feeling it badly, that he was bad luck for Teddie. Last time it was only a stone, this time I suppose it was a shell or bullets, but they were together again. I want to find out. I think I want to know. I think I want to know because I owe it to Teddie to know what happened, otherwise it's just like someone going out alone. But Captain Merrick will know, then he can tell me. Then Teddie may know I know. Do you think –' but she broke off and had to be prompted.

'Do I think what?'

'Do you think it would be nice if we asked Captain Merrick to be godfather?'

'No, I don't.'

'Why not?'

'I don't know. I just don't think it would be.'

'You mean perhaps he doesn't believe in it either. But he did perform a Christian act, didn't he, and it's that that counts, not going to church and making a fuss. It says in the letter, rendered the utmost assistance in spite of being wounded, rendered the utmost assistance and stayed with Teddie until the arrival of medical aid. He was trying to save Teddie's life. Not just for Teddie's sake, but for the baby's probably, and mine too. So I think we ought to ask, and not care what people like Aunt Fenny would think.'

'What would people like Aunt Fenny think?'

'They might think he wasn't suitable, a suitable sort of person.'

'Because he isn't one of us?'

'Yes.'

But, Sarah thought, remembering the night of the fireflies, in a way he is, is, is one of us; the dark side, the arcane side. But at once recollected the question she had asked herself on that occasion: Why should I question his sincerity?

Her resistance ebbed and yet still, as she said, 'Well I shouldn't worry about what Aunt Fenny might say' – thereby implying her approval of the way being opened to god-relationship with him – she felt the backlash of that strange dismay which the thought, the remembered impact, and the new notion of him as the dark side of their history filled her with; and he became at once inseparable from the image of the woman in white, of someone – anyone – who found it necessary to plead with him for an alleviation of suffering of which – if only unintentionally – he had been the cause.

'It can be done by proxy, can't it?' Susan was saying. 'If he agrees. He can be godfather without actually being at the christening.'

'Yes, I think so.'

'And it might help him to get better, to know we wanted him for that. Teddie said he used to be sorry for Captain Merrick before all that bother he caused at the wedding. He never got any letters, or almost never. I think that's as much the reason Teddie asked him to be best man as the fact that they shared quarters. Teddie was very upset about the stone. But he had a tender heart.'

'Well, and so have you.'

'Oh, no.' She looked down at her hands. 'I have no heart at all.' Again she looked up. 'Will you do that for me, Sarah, then? Write for me and find out where he is?'

'Yes, I'll do that.'

But there was no need for that particular letter. The day following there was a note from Captain Merrick himself; a note to Sarah, which Sarah showed to Susan. And when Susan had read it she cried out because she was convinced from certain signs and portents in the note that Captain Merrick no longer had the use of eyes or limbs.

143 British Military Hospital
AFPO 12
17 May 1944

Dear Miss Layton,

By now I expect you will have been told that Teddie was killed, just three weeks ago, but in case there has been some error or delay I've thought it wiser to write to you and not to Susan. Perhaps I would have done so in any case. I'm not very good at expressing myself on paper and would find it difficult to write a letter to her. You will find the right words to convey my feelings to her, I am certain, feelings of sympathy and, I suppose, help-lessness in the face of what I know to her must be, for the moment, overwhelmingly sad circumstances. I am as you can see from the address and perhaps the handwriting which is that of one of the nursing sisters here, *hors de combat*, but my improve-ment is, I am told – and feel – steadily satisfactory. Perhaps some-one from the formation has already told Susan this, but in case not – I must tell you that I was with Teddie at the time. That of the two of us it should have been I who came out of it strikes me as supremely illogical – for there was Teddie with everything to live for, and I – comparatively – with something less than that. It should have been the other way round that it happened. Yes, indeed it should.

I am to undergo some more surgery, not here but in Calcutta, so they tell me, and after that can look forward to a period of convalescence and then some sick leave by which time it will have been settled about the future. I should be grateful, of course, to have news, some assurance about your sister's state of mind and health, if you could spare a moment to drop me a line (care of this place – it would be forwarded – I go within a day or two possibly). That business lies a bit heavily. All sorts of things go through my mind. I wish I could speak of them more directly to you. Meanwhile my kind regards to you both, and to your mother. I hope you have had recent good news of your father. Sincerely yours, (for) Ronald Merrick (S.P., QAIMNS).

'You could go and see him,' Susan said. 'You could stay with Aunt Fenny and go and see him when they take him to Calcutta.'

'Aunt Fenny could do that.'

'No, not Aunt Fenny. You. He didn't like Aunt Fenny. He didn't like me either. But he liked you. And it's you he's written to. He wants to talk to you.'

After this Susan relapsed into silence. She sat most of that day on the verandah, staring at the red brick wall, while Panther lay beside her, guarding her from those invisible demons which dumb animals perceive as ever-present in human sorrow and abstraction. And long before it began to be said in Pankot that Susan Layton had become dangerously withdrawn (so that among those who remembered, the name and history of Poppy Browning's daughter began to be spoken of) the servants who lived behind that wall observed this fact for themselves and recalled the fateful augury of the monstrous birth high up in the remote hills. In secret places about the bungalow garden they disposed offerings of milk to quench the thirst, and flowers to appease with sweet perfumes the uncertain temper, of both good and evil spirits.

At the entrance to Flagstaff House there was a narrow open-fronted wooden hut, almost the duplicate of the sentry box that stood inside the gateway, but sheltering a book, not a man. The book was chained to the shelf on which it rested. A pencil, also chained, lay in the groove formed in the middle by the open leaves. Every evening a servant came down the drive, unchained the book, took it back to the house and left it on a table in the entrance hall. In the morning the book was returned to the hut. As well as the book there was a small wooden box with a slot cut in its lid, wide enough to take a visiting card. The box, too, was taken every evening into the house and returned next day. The book and the box were the means by which a visitor to or some-one newly stationed in Pankot made an official call on the Area Commander. In the old days the call had been obligatory but nowadays a signature in the book or a card in the box was an

indication of the presence in (or departure from) Pankot of someone to whom the old forms were still important or who knew
them to be considered important to Flagstaff House and felt that
to displease its incumbents was not a dignified thing to do.

It was in the book that Lady Manners announced her presence, one day towards the end of May – Lady Manners, or her
ghost, or someone playing a joke, for no address was given
beyond the bleak indication of permanent residence, Rawalpindi; no one in Pankot had seen her or knew where she could
be staying, and the sentries who had been on duty between
9 a.m. and 5 p.m. could not recall, with the degree of certainty
Isobel Rankin hoped for when having them questioned by the
steward, anyone reaching the gate on foot, by car, by tonga who
had not entered but had gone to the book, signed and departed
and who answered a description suited to the name, the rank,
the whole condition which Mrs Rankin had in her mind as
definitive of that unhappy woman.

Well, the servants would know, anyone's servants would
know. But they did not, or pretended they did not, and so great
an incidence of pretence was unlikely enough to confirm their
denials. Where, then? Clearly not on the Pankot side of Pankot,
the side, the real side, reached by taking that right-hand fork
from the bazaar that led – gradually – to those majestic heights
on which stood the summer residence which Lady Manners had
once had the freedom of, all those years ago, longer than anyone
now on station including old Mabel Layton, who had not
bought Rose Cottage until a year in the thirties when the
Manners régime was over, could remember; and which now –
this season – once again stood empty. So, then, the other side,
where English people never went. Certainly, yes, that would be
like her, to come to Pankot and seclude herself among those
who belonged to the other side. In Pankot these days there were
several Indian officers, and some of them had wives (fragile, shy
creatures whom Isobel Rankin took pains with) and they might
know. But did not. It was a mystery. And why (if she were truly
there and it was no joke, no spirit-mark – that signature) had
she signed at all? And had she come alone, or with an entourage?
Where was the child? Was the signature a form of apology, a first
hesitant step back into the good opinion of her race? Or the
opposite of that?

And it was strange, Pankot thought, or if not strange certainly not uninteresting, that two of the marginal actors in the comedy or tragedy of the Bibighar Gardens affair (and it depended on what mood you were in, which label seemed the more apt) should impinge simultaneously on the consciousness of sensible people who thought it would have been nicer to forget that it had ever happened: Lady Manners who had stood by and let her niece give birth and then taken the revoltingly conceived child to her bosom, and Captain Merrick who was said to have done his duty and had no thanks and now lay wounded as a result of some attempt – the actual details were not clear – to help poor Susan Bingham's husband, the day he was killed in action.

That story of the stone, which Mrs Layton had brought back from Mirat (referring to it casually, as if a stone were thrown at every wedding); the odd little circumstance of Teddie Bingham's scratch best man turning out to be who he was; and the revelation that Merrick had been sent to a backwater after the failure of the police to establish guilt in the Manners case, and then been allowed to enter the army: these burgeoned under the warmth of approbation felt for a man who had stayed with a dying brother officer, until the stone itself became a symbol of martyrdom they all understood because they felt they shared it; and so, entering their consciousness, Merrick entered Pankot and was, for as long as interest in him lasted, part of the old hill station, at the still centre of its awareness of what was meant by the secret pass-phrase: one of us. One of us. And it did not matter that he was known, thought to be, not quite that by right. He had become it by example.

'Of course he was in love with her,' Barbie said – and it was through Barbie's more intimate knowledge and compulsive interpretation of things that were known casually to the Laytons that there filtered those elements of incidental intelligence which, even if their accuracy could not be proven, gave the facts the dark, ponderable glow of living issues. Yes, he had been in love with the Manners girl, but she had preferred that Indian, and she more than anyone else must have been to blame for the fact that he and his fellow-conspirators were never tried, never brought properly to book. She hadn't been able to stop them going to prison, but she had destroyed the case which had been built up so efficiently and swiftly by Mr Merrick. And obviously he had suffered for that, been made to pay for it, as men were made to pay. He had been sent to Sundernagar, just as though he was in disgrace. She had mined his career. Well, she was dead, and one must not speak ill of the dead, and perhaps before she died she had regretted her infatuation. 'And I do not,' Barbie said, 'well, as a Christian how could I, feel as strongly as some about the child. We are all God's children. But that child has not been brought to God.' Old missionary zeal shone on her ruined parchment face, and there was a picture to be had by anyone present when she spoke like this, of Barbie storming down the hill to seek old Lady Manners out and fill her with so much dread of the Lord that she would go penitent with the child in her arms to Mr Peplow; although what he would do if she did had to remain in the shadow of a half conjecture, the child having no known father, a heathen name, Parvati (which Barbie remembered because that was the name of Siva's consort), and being dark-skinned into the bargain (so it was said), in witness of the original sin of its conception.

'No, I wouldn't,' Sarah said, parrying by direct denial Barbie's question whether she would recognize Lady Manners if she saw her. She wondered if her mother had let something be known after all, about her impulsive action in Srinagar.

'But last year you were so close, your mother said.'

'A hundred yards.'

'You must have had a glimpse?'

'Yes, a glimpse.'

It was evening. They moved in the garden among Aunt Mabel's roses, waiting her return from one of the solitary walks she took, stoutly shod; a deaf old woman climbing steep hills, in silence.

Suddenly Barbie said, 'Who is Gillian Waller?'

'I don't know. Why?'

'I thought she might be a relation. Mabel mentions her.'

'Without saying who she is?'

'I mean in her sleep.' Barbie looked embarrassed. 'I go in you know. To make sure. She's become forgetful. Of the light. Her book. She falls asleep with her spectacles on. One is so afraid of danger. Breakage. A splinter in the eye. And on cold nights in winter of insufficient warmth, sitting up asleep not properly covered.'

'You tuck her up.'

'She doesn't know, but you see I owe her. I'm grateful. And I'm a light sleeper myself. The slightest sound wakes me. Of course in the old days in remote parts one felt vigilance laid on one almost by God as a duty and it's become a habit. I sleep best between two and four. I don't need much and I like to be sure. About *her*. I anticipated a *lonely* retirement, you know, most of us do, in the missions. Well, she knew that. She'd seen some of us, growing old and keeping cheerful and doing it on our own. So. Well, that's it. And recently she's become very restless. And then this talking. Well, muttering. Gillian Waller. As if whoever that is, is on her mind. I'm afraid to ask. I hate to seem to pry. She's such a self-contained person. When I first came to Rose Cottage she terrified me. I've always been a great talker. Talk, talk. God is listening, Mr Cleghorn used to say when I caught him out *not*. He was Muzzafirabad, head of the mission there when I took over from Edwina Crane and worried so because they adored her, and I was older than she. It made me talk the more. Talk, talk. It laps against her. I thought: she'll never stand it. And that made me talk harder. Waves and waves of my talking. Well, she's an edifice and I came to realize it didn't trouble her. She still likes to see me talk even if she can't catch all the words. Rock of ages. The sea pounds and pounds. There are people like that. She's one. Is Susan more cheerful?'

'Not cheerful, but holding on.'

'To what?' Barbie took Sarah's arm. 'To what?' And then, before Sarah could answer, asked, 'Who was Poppy Browning?'

'Poppy Browning? I don't know. Has Aunt Mabel talked about a Poppy Browning too?'

'No. It was gossip I overheard. Would you say that Susan is dangerously withdrawn?'

Sarah stopped, examined a red rose, bent her head to take its scent and again felt the touch of that casual premonition on the back of her neck, so that it seemed to her that she was arrested, suspended, between an uncertain future and a fading history that had something to do with bending her head like this to a bunch of sweet-smelling flowers: not those which Susan threw and she, Sarah, caught, but those there were evidence in an old photograph of her holding on the day of Aunt Fenny's wedding, while

Aunty Mabel, half-shadowed by a wide-brimmed hat, stood: an edifice, rock of ages.

'We endure,' she told Barbie. 'We're built for it. In a strange way we're built for it.' But was Susan? She faced Barbie. 'Is that what you overheard? People saying she's withdrawn?'

'Dangerously withdrawn. They stopped when they saw me. Mrs Fosdick, Mrs Paynton, Lucy Smalley. It was Lucy Smalley who was saying — "Yes, the last time I saw her I couldn't help but be reminded of Poppy Browning's daughter." Then they changed the subject.'

'Just talk then, Barbie, not serious concern. Otherwise they'd have roped you in. You're practically part of the family. You'd be the ideal person for someone really worried about Susan to have a word with.'

'Oh I wish,' Barbie said, holding Sarah's arm tight, then letting it go, abruptly, ' – but I can't. Go with you. My old head-quarters are in Calcutta, you know.'

Barbie's ministrations to Aunt Mabel were unobtrusive. She made herself scarce while Sarah followed Mabel along the rear verandah, holding the cradle-basket for the new crop of dead heads. The light had nearly gone. From inside Barbie touched the switch that turned on the globes on the verandah.

'When are you going then?' Mabel asked.

'Tomorrow.'

Mabel nodded, finished attending to the azalea. 'Where will you stay?'

'I rang Aunt Fenny. She'll put me up for a couple of nights.'

'I thought they lived in Delhi.'

'They moved to Calcutta in January.'

They went on to the next flower. Sarah said:

'I wanted to ask you something. Something special.' It was hard to speak up and still soften the blunt edges of a request. 'I wanted to ask you about an old christening gown.'

The capable old hands continued without pause, caressing, turning, searching, nipping; preserving the strength of the plant, coaxing it to vigour and ripe old age with the removal of those decayed relics of its former flowering. I am asking, Sarah thought, to take something like that from her, as well. And wondered if the same thought had occurred, shot home, a sharp wound swiftly healed by acceptance of its necessity – because without speaking Mabel suddenly turned and went inside, leaving Sarah alone there with the basket. There was silence inside the house but presently Barbie came to the french window and beckoned.

'She's in her room and wants you to go in.'

Sarah put the basket down by the chair that was Susan's favourite and followed Barbie through into the hall. The door of Mabel's room, which Sarah had seldom entered, stood open. She tapped, quite loudly. Mabel was on her knees by the open press at the foot of the bed, laying back folds of tissue paper – the same gestures, in exaggerated form, that she used to part foliage to expose the withered blooms on hidden stalks. She turned the last fold, wordlessly exposed the handiwork of a vanished generation. From a distance it was, as Sarah had predicted, yellowed, and perhaps close-to would be brittle-looking; but when she knelt and placed her hand between the lace and the fine lawn that lay beneath it the lace came alive against the pinkness of her skin.

'It's French,' Aunt Mabel said. 'If you like you can let Susan have it.'

'I didn't know about it,' Sarah replied. 'And it's for you to say.' She hesitated. 'It's exquisite.'

There were springs of lavender whose scent mixed with those of sandalwood. Around the hem of the lawn undergarment was a half-inch border of seed pearls. She marvelled at the industry gone into decoration that would not be noticed when the gown was worn. On that day, yes, that one day anyway, wearing this she had looked beautiful.

'My first husband's mother was French,' Mabel said. 'When we married he took me there, to see them. His mother's family. We sailed back to India from Marseilles. I never saw them again.'

'And they gave you the lace?'

'No, his mother gave me that in London. I never saw her again either. She was very handsome. He got his looks from her. And his courage. She was dying but we didn't know. She kept it from us. She saw he was happy.'

Sarah moved her hand under the lace. Astonishing. There was a motif of butterflies. They were alive, fluttering above her moving hand.

'It was an old château. Very old.'

'Where her family lived?'

'Yes. There was a tower.' A pause. 'She lived there. An old woman making lace. She was blind. She'd made lace all her life. I think she was a poor relation or an old retainer. I showed them this lace, this piece. His mother gave it to me – for a christening. And they said, It's Claudine's. Come and see her. Claudine made it, you can tell from the butterflies. So we climbed the tower and went into the room right at the top where she lived and worked. She ran her fingers over the lace, and put her hand under it like you're doing and said, "*Ah, oui, pauvre papillon. C'est un de mes prisonniers.*" And then something I didn't understand but which they told me meant her heart bled for the butterflies because they could never fly out of the prison of the lace and make love in the sunshine. She could feel the sunshine on her hands but her hands wove nothing but a prison for God's most delicate creatures.' A pause. 'I asked them to tell her that real butterflies might play in the sunshine but only lived for a day. It was rather silly and sentimental, but she smiled and nodded and took it as a compliment because she knew I was very young and didn't understand.'

Gently Sarah withdrew her hand. The butterflies were still. She thought of the christening to come and herself standing, perhaps by the side of Ronald Merrick, making vows in the name of a child swaddled in this lace, and knew that she did not want it used for such a purpose, for that occasion. She knew, but could not have explained.

'Please take it,' Mabel said. 'Anyway, I've meant that you should have it one day.'

Sarah began folding the tissue. She shook her head. 'I'm awfully grateful, but I think it should stay here.'

'No, take it,' Mabel repeated. She completed the folding of the gown into the tissue, lifted and held it so that, involuntarily, Sarah raised both hands to receive it. 'It's yours. It says so in my will. But take it now. I've no use for it. Things shouldn't be kept if they can't be put to use.' She got slowly but quite steadily to her feet, leaving Sarah kneeling, holding the bulked-up tissue. Their glances met, and held. Then, as she turned her head and began to move away, Mabel said:

'You are very young too, but I expect you understand better than I did at your age.'

*

The tonga was still waiting and the driver was lighting his lamps. She told him to drive down to the bazaar, to Jalal-ud-din's. As well as the christening gown Mabel had given her two hundred rupees to help, she said, with her fare and expenses. 'But they've wangled a travel warrant for me,' Sarah had protested, 'and even given me a movement order to make it look as if I'm on official business.' General Rankin, no less than other right-thinking people in Pankot, approved of Sarah Layton's mission. 'Well, it will help with bills,' Mabel had said, 'I expect your mother owes some.'

Between Rose Cottage and the club there was no other traffic. In early June, before the coming of the summer rain, even the Pankot air lost its bite. The heat of the day lingered on into the dark. She longed for rain. Susan's baby would be born in the early weeks of the rain. The mornings would be misty and on days when there was no rain the hills would be vivid green. She sat in the back of the slow-going tonga, holding the parcel, and fancied she could feel the slight pulsation, the flickering of tiny white wings. She became aware of the quietness of the road, its look of desertion, and remembered Barbie's dream of her gallant ride to St John's and her own dream that began with Teddie, who knew where he was going and struck them dumb because of that.

But at the club entrance there were other tongas and from there down the long stretch to the bazaar, with the golf course on her right, and on her left the bungalows that skirted the foot of Central Hill, dominated by the churches of St John's and St Edward's, they passed others, and a military truck, a taxi or two, and presently there were the lights that marked the beginning of the bazaar.

She got down at the tonga stand, told the driver to wait because she wanted him to take her on down to the Pankot Rifles lines. The shops were open, some of them brightly lit so that the few street lamps were paled to nothing. But it was not an hour for civil shopping. Groups of British soldiers eyed her but let her pass without comment, knowing she was not for them. The corporal's chevrons on her sleeves could never trick them into believing otherwise. A white girl was an officer's girl, and probably an officer's daughter. A chokra trotted by her side, offering his services as a little beast of burden. He waited outside

Gulab Singh Sahib's pharmacy while she went in and bought toothpaste and toothbrush to use in Calcutta and, as an after-thought, a bottle of toilet water to sweeten the journey. She paid what they owed and wondered where the line was drawn between necessity and luxury, the high cost of living and extra-vagance; and, outside, gave the three little parcels to the chokra but refused his offer to carry the parcel of tissue and lace.

'Jalal-ud-din's,' she told him and turned towards the store, walking down the arcaded frontage of Pankot's European-style shops; and saw her – the beggar woman who, for Sarah, had become interchangeable as a suppliant figure with the woman in the white saree. And afterwards, because she had concentrated on the figure of the beggar woman, recalled that embarrassing and distressing scene on Mirat station and Merrick's remote face, his muttered rejection of her plea in the same tongue the woman spoke in, she was unsure, as unsure as she was ashamed; unsure that the elderly white woman, half-hidden by a distinguished-looking middle-aged Indian woman, in the act of bending, climbing into a car through a door held open by an Indian driver, whose bulk almost immediately cut her off, was the woman from the houseboat; ashamed because the glimpse she had, the conviction that the woman was Lady Manners, caused her automatically to stop, half turn away, to avoid anything in the nature of a direct physical confrontation, as if – so – she might make up for an earlier impulsive action, eradicate it, rub it out, and identify herself with a collective conspiracy. She was ashamed to remember the way she stood, awkwardly poised, persuasively conveying in every exaggerated histrionic gesture and change of expression the portrait of a girl who feared she had left something behind at Gulab Singh Sahib's; so that the chokra, concerned, held up the three packages, inviting her to count. Then he pointed to the package she held herself, as though he thought some fit of absent-mindedness had caused her momentarily not to realize that she held it.

She smiled and nodded and faced towards Jalal-ud-din's again, the shame already warming her face; but there was no sign of the car. It had gone swiftly, silently, no doubt turning the corner of the inverted V to take the steep road into West Hill where people like the Laytons never went. She turned again, retraced her steps to the tonga stand and there gave the chokra his anna.

III

'Now tell me,' Aunt Fenny said, 'what have you really come for?'

The flat was air-conditioned. Perhaps that shadow of professional neglect which Uncle Arthur had always seemed to work under had not lifted; but at least he appeared to have reached the point of contact with the earth of its dark rainbow, and found a crock of fairy gold: the flat, its high view far above the roofs of old aristocratic houses, the like of which he had never secured for his and Aunt Fenny's personal use; and a war-time sinecure which, so far as Sarah could make out, involved him in giving lectures of a paramilitary nature to young officers, on the structure of Indian military and civilian administration. He was, she gathered, seconded to a branch of welfare and education which had its eye on the capacity some of these young Englishmen might show for identifying themselves with the problems of a country with which the war alone had brought them in contact. Behind the lectures was a blandishment: Stay on, stay on. 'We give them a picture you know,' Colonel Grace said, 'of what it's really like in peace-time, eradicate some of those impressions they have, that we're a load of blimps, sitting on our fannies under punkahs and shouting Koi Hai.' To counteract all that they gave them the stuff. The real stuff. Sarah nodded, and the young men – three of those in question – smiled easily. According to Aunt Fenny the flat was usually fuller even than Sarah had found it of Uncle Arthur's 'chaps'. He had conceived it part of the duties of the department he headed to bring the chaps home, or have them call, in groups, swapping the scratch amenities of the temporary mess out at the place where the courses were held, for the more considerable ones of a genuine Anglo-Indian *piedà-terre*, where they could imbibe, at breakfast, tiffin or dinner, those lessons that went deeper than any mere chat from a rostrum ever could. There had been no British intake into the ICS since the war began and the Indian army was dense with emergency officers of all kinds who had never thought of making a career of arms, least of all in India. Among them, surely, there were a few who would get the call, see the vision, understand the hard realities of imperial service and feel the urge to match themselves to them?

'They're mostly what Arthur calls in abeyance,' Fenny told Sarah as she showed her her room – a comfortable little white-walled box, as cold as a refrigerator, with the bulging grey Bengal monsoon sky – which Sarah had never seen in her life before – filling the hermetically sealed window. Overnight from Ranpur she had ridden into the June rain. It would not reach Pankot for a while yet. She felt, from this alone, that she had travelled into another world, so that it amazed her that it was ever possible to make the mistake of thinking of India as one country.

'What kind of abeyance?' (She was thinking of her mother.)

'Oh, you know, between postings, or getting better from jaundice, or just among the crowd that get stuck in depots and training establishments and apply for courses to stop themselves going barmy. We don't get many who are *born* slackers. At least Arthur doesn't bring them back here. Of course they're not usually quite our kind of people' – (Sarah nodded, again, gravely) – 'but then we're a bit of a dying species, aren't we, pet? And they're mostly nice cheerful chaps, and some of them are from good homes, and it's usually that kind who are seriously thinking of staying on after the war. Arthur's a great success with them – I think because he responds to them. He feels they genuinely want to know about India and what it's meant to the standard of life they enjoy back home and take so much for granted.'

'I expect you're a success with them too, Aunt Fenny.'

'Oh, I am! Do you know why? Because I'm happy. Isn't it gorgeous –?' She indicated not the room so much as the flat the room was a cold, rather remote, unlived-in part of. 'To be cool. Oh, to be cool.' There had been a time, surely, when Aunt Fenny had dismissed the more modern aspects of twentieth-century Anglo-Indian life as unwelcome signs of things going to the dogs. Sarah smiled. She herself preferred to be less cool, but it was nice to see Aunt Fenny enjoying something. This morning the lines of disapproval that fixed the mouth were like marks of an old illness, like smallpox, that had left no other trace. But it was at the moment Sarah was thinking this that Fenny stopped being happy about the flat and reverted to her older, probing, rather suspicious self.

'Now tell me, what have you really come for?'

Sarah told her. When she finished Aunt Fenny said, 'But, pet, couldn't I have done it for you and saved you all this trouble and expense?'

'They gave me a rail warrant.' She hesitated, observed Aunt Fenny's invisible hackles tremble with the effort she was making not to let them rise, and added, 'Susan has this idea he's lost a limb or his eyesight, and that if anyone goes to see him and then writes to her they might not tell her the truth, out of kindness.'

'But I could have seen him and then come up to Pankot.'

'That would have been expense and trouble for you and you could still have kept the facts from her out of kindness. I think she wanted it to be me because she believes she could see through it if I kept anything back.'

Aunt Fenny smiled, touched Sarah's arm.

'Do I detect six of one and half a dozen of another? I mean he took a bit of a shine to you in Mirat. Was it mutual?'

Sarah looked away, unable to take the opportunity to make Aunt Fenny feel less excluded from the question of Captain Merrick's bodily state of health. 'No, not at all. Anyway, I don't think he took a shine. I'm not really looking forward to it, but it seems to be important to Susan, and I'd like to get it over with as soon as possible. Do you think if I turned up this morning they'd let me see him?'

'You'll do no such thing. You'll tuck down here for the rest of the morning and catch up with some sleep. I'll ring the hospital and see what can be arranged for early evening or late afternoon, then you can have a relaxed day, see Mr Merrick at about five o'clock and come back here in time for drinks. Some of the boys are coming in for dinner. Do you really have to go back tomorrow?'

'Yes, I've booked my sleeper from Ranpur to Pankot for tomorrow night.'

'The old midnight special?'

'Yes.'

'So you'll have to be on the midday from Cal to get the connection? What about a reservation? It's not easy at such short notice.'

'Oh, I'll squeeze in. It's not difficult if you don't want a berth. Someone with a berth to Delhi will let me sit in. We get to Ranpur about nine in the evening, long before anyone wants to have their bed made up.'

'Yes, well, all the same I'll ask your uncle to pull some rank. He'll enjoy that. He's just like a boy about being able to say it's Colonel Grace speaking. But get your head down for now, pet. I can tell you didn't have a berth last night. Was it ghastly?'

'No, fun really. I sat up all night with some nurses who were on their way to Shillong.' And envied them, going to the war it seems I can never go to. We played cards and drank rather a lot of gin. And I listened while they discussed men in general and in particular the two officers who tried to get off with the two prettiest girls and had to be firmly ejected from the carriage when the train stopped at Benares. I fell asleep, near Dhanbad. The taste of the journey is still in my mouth.

She sat on the bed and at once knew how tired she was. Over-excited. Like a child. She was aware of Aunt Fenny stooping to unlace her shoes for her. She protested but it was done just the same. Weightless, her legs lifted easily on to the bed. Curtains were drawn. Comforted by all this evidence of family devotion and the softness of the pillow under her head, she fell asleep.

Before the taxi reached the Officers' wing of the military hospital the rain stopped. She arrived in bright sunshine and, mounting the steps to the pillared entrance, took off Aunt Fenny's heavy-duty macintosh. She had changed from uniform into mufti – a plain cotton dress whose lightness she was glad of in a humidity that was higher than she had ever experienced. After she had spoken to the English corporal at the desk and been asked to wait she sat and smoked, but the cigarette was damp. She dropped it, unfinished, into the sand-tray. The corporal answered the telephone, then spoke to a colleague whose uniform bore no chevrons. The private came across.

'Miss Layton for Captain Merrick?'

She nodded, followed him out of the reception hall into a corridor where there were lifts. The smell of ether-meth was settling on her stomach. She felt slightly faint. The private gave instructions to the Indian lift attendant then said to her, 'Sister Prior'll meet you at the top.' She thanked him, noticed – and was sorry for the embarrassment they must cause him – the septic spots on cheek and chin, vivid under the glare of the lift lights. He did not meet her glance. He smelt strongly of cheap hair oil. The attendant closed the mesh gates. Slowly they ascended. The letter from Ronald Merrick had been signed by a nurse in the QAIMNS. But she could not remember the initials. Had it been P for Prior? No. It might have been P, but not for Prior because the letter had come from Comilla. There had been no letter from Calcutta.

The lift stopped and the attendant opened the gates. She thanked him and stepped on to the landing. The smell was stronger than ever. A window gave a view of trees and light to a table with flowers on it and chairs for waiting. But she was the only visitor. There was no sign of Sister Prior; the corridors left and right of the waiting-room were empty. Had the lift man let her out on the wrong floor? Or the boy with the pimples mis-heard the corporal? She went to the window and stared at the trees and the view between them and the vast *maidan* beyond which was the low-lying clutter of the city. A door shut some-where along one of the corridors, and presently she heard the sound of a woman's footsteps. She turned, waited, and in a moment the woman entered the waiting-room area: a girl, rather, no older than herself, with dark hair rolled under a neat cap.

'Miss Layton? I'm Sister Prior.' She put out her hand, which Sarah took. The overall scrutiny she was under did not escape her. She wondered whether Sister Prior was the sort who would fall in love with a patient – in love with Merrick, for instance – and be jealously possessive of him. But she had scarcely had time.

'Am I upsetting regular visiting hours?' Sarah asked. Her hand had been let go of rather suddenly.

'That's all right. The message from your – uncle? Colonel –?'

'Colonel Grace.'

'Grace. Well, he said you'd come a long way.'

But Sister Prior made no move. They eyed each other levelly. The same height, Sarah thought, as well as the same age.

'I didn't quite get the relationship. You *are* a relative, aren't you?'

'No.'

'Well, I thought it was odd. I'd always understood he had none. I mean none at home let alone out here. But matron was under the impression from Colonel Grace there was a family connection.'

'I expect he mentioned my sister. Captain Merrick was best

man at her wedding.' She paused, intending not to explain further, but found herself doing so. 'I'm really here on her behalf. We had a letter from him when he was in Comilla.'

'Yes, I see. I haven't told him you're coming. I thought I wouldn't in case you didn't turn up and he was disappointed. But I'll go and tell him now. If I just say Miss Layton will that be enough?'

'Enough, but a bit of a surprise. I live in Pankot.'

'Where?'

'It's a hill station north of Ranpur.'

'Oh. Yes, you have come a long way, haven't you? Is your sister in Calcutta, too?'

'She couldn't travel.'

'Isn't she well?'

'She's having a baby. It's due in three weeks.'

'I see. I hope you don't mind my asking all these questions. Ronald is rather a special case with us. He's been wonderfully brave. But we think terribly lonely. Do you know anything about his family?'

'No, nothing.'

'His record shows his next-of-kin as a cousin of some sort. Both his parents died before the war. I think it was a late marriage. I mean they were quite old. And he has no brothers and sisters, and then of course he's never married himself. And until we heard from Colonel Grace today we were under the impression he had no close friends. I mean the only letters he gets are the official sort. And since he's been here he's never asked me to write a personal letter to anyone, so I've been wondering, I mean how you knew where he was.'

'He wrote us from Comilla and said he was being transferred to Calcutta. Someone on General Rankin's staff at Pankot checked for us and got the hospital in Comilla to send us a signal where we could contact him. My sister's concerned rather specially. Captain Merrick was wounded at the same time her husband was killed.'

'Oh, I'm sorry. About her husband.'

Sister Prior had not once let her glance fall away. Sarah felt her own fixed by it. 'I'm sure he'll be glad to see you, and I do appreciate your coming such a very long way, but I hope you won't find it necessary to ask him too many questions on your sister's behalf. We try not to let them dwell too much on what happened.'

'I haven't come to ask questions. I've come mainly to tell him how grateful my sister is for what he tried to do to help her husband, in spite of being wounded himself. We don't know exactly what it was he did do, and I'm sure he won't talk about it even if I ask, but it was something that led the divisional commander to send in a recommendation.'

'A recommendation?'

'Yes.'

'You mean for a decoration?'

'Yes.'

'Does he know that?'

'Probably not.'

'I hope you won't mention it.'

'I won't mention it.'

'I suppose decorations serve some sort of purpose. I never see what, myself. But then I've seen too much of what earning them involves. I always think a thumping great cheque would fill the bill better. What can you do with a medal except stick it on their chests and leave them to stick it in a drawer? I expect that shocks you. With an uncle who's a colonel.'

'My father's a colonel too.' About to add: And it doesn't shock me: she changed her mind and said instead, 'I'll wait here while you break the news to Captain Merrick that I've called to see him.'

Sister Prior nodded. A smile – of distant irony – momentarily broadened her pretty lips. Sarah turned, embattled behind the barriers of her class and traditions because the girl had challenged her to stand up for them. Hearing Sister Prior's retreating footsteps she realized the opportunity to prepare herself for whatever it was she had to face in Ronald Merrick's room had gone. Perhaps in any case it would have been deliberately withheld. The sight might be shocking, and it might please Sister Prior to watch how she took it. She lit another of the damp cigarettes, gathered her things together: Aunt Fenny's macintosh, the box of fruit, the carton of two hundred Three Castles cigarettes packed in four round tins of fifty each. She wished to be ready to go with Sister Prior directly she returned. But the minutes ticked by. It was nearly five o'clock. Occasionally there

were footsteps in the corridors, and the sound of doors opened
and closed. Voices, once. And the rising clank and whisper of
the lift. At five o'clock a dark-skinned Anglo-Indian nurse
appeared, coming from the direction Sister Prior had taken.

'Miss Layton? Captain Merrick will see you now.'

She followed the girl down the corridor. Reaching a door
numbered 27, which bore beneath a circular observation
window a card in a metal frame in which was written in black
ink, Captain R. Merrick, the girl tapped, opened and said, 'Miss
Layton to see you, Captain Merrick,' and stood aside. Entering,
Sarah halted abruptly, shocked to see him on his feet and coming towards her, aided by a stick, dragging the weight of one
plastered leg – until, coming to her senses, she saw the man was
not Merrick but a tall burly fellow who smiled and said, 'He's all
yours. Ignore me. I was just visiting.' Automatically she smiled in
return and looking beyond him saw Merrick in the bed by the
window – or anyway a figure lying there, propped by pillows.
A complex of bandage and gauze around the head, like a white
helmet, left only the features and a narrow area of the cheeks
exposed. The sheet that covered his body was laid over a semicircular frame. She could see nothing of him except the small
exposed area of the face and blue-pyjamaed chest and shoulders.
His arms were under the arch of the sheet. His head was inclined
a little to one side. He was looking at her. As she moved towards
him she heard the door shut.

She said, 'Hello, Ronald,' and was then at the bedside. The
down-draught from a fan whirling gently above held the sheet
pressed against the frame. She could see the pattern of the mesh.
She had an unpleasant idea that there was nothing beneath the
frame, that what she could see was somehow all that was left of
him, although she knew that was not possible. Embarrassed, she
switched her glance quickly back to his face, determined to hold
it there. He looked younger than she remembered, younger even
than in that one and only photograph, as if pain had smoothed
out his face and brought a glow of innocence to his complexion.
She could not see his chin, but the upper lip was shaved. She
wondered how he managed. And then remembered Sister Prior.

'I've brought some fruit and cigarettes. I hope that's all
right. I remembered you smoked.' She put the packages on the
bedside-table which was empty except for an invalid teapot from

which she imagined he was given water. She glanced at him again as she did so, and saw him swallow. Perhaps he had difficulty with his voice. His eyes were closed now, but as she moved round to sit on the chair at the other side of the bed he opened them and watched her. Yes, they were blue. Extraordinarily blue. He swallowed again.

'I'm sorry,' he said, 'I thought Sister Prior was playing some kind of practical joke, or that I was funny in the head because she's not really the joking kind. How is Susan?'

'She's fine. She sent her love. And Mother of course. And Aunt Fenny. She and Uncle Arthur are in Calcutta now. She'll come and see you in a day or two. She asked me to be sure to find out if there's anything you need.'

'That's very kind of her. And kind of you. Are you in Calcutta long?'

'No, I go back tomorrow.'

'To Pankot?'

She nodded.

He said, 'Do smoke. There are some in the drawer.'

'Can I light one for you?'

'I'm afraid it involves more than that. I can't hold anything yet.'

She lit a cigarette from her own case, then – overcoming the reluctance she felt to do so – a mixture of embarrassment and faint revulsion – she stood, leaned forward and held the cigarette near his lips. He moved his head to help her place the tip in his mouth.

'I'm afraid they're very damp.'

He released the cigarette, let his head back on to the pillow and blew out slowly, without inhaling. After a moment's hesitation she inhaled from the cigarette herself. The sharing of the cigarette was an unexpected intimacy. For a while they smoked alternately.

'Your hands,' he said, 'smell so much nicer than Sister Prior's. She's a bit of a dragon.'

'A very pretty dragon.'

'You think so?'

'Don't you?'

'A man in hospital's no judge. All the nurses look pretty, but it's their hands and throats and elbows that count in the end.

Sister Prior has very cold hands and red elbows. I'm not sure she hasn't got goitre too. The fact is she depresses me a bit. Sister Pawle in Comilla was much more like it. She's the one who wrote that letter for me. I was beginning to wonder whether it reached you. But this is miles better. Miles, miles better. And thanks for just turning up. You get used to taking the days as they come and it's better not to look forward to anything that isn't routine. But when you've gone I'll have something special to look back on, and count by, that I wasn't expecting.'

She held the cigarette for him but he shut his eyes briefly and thanked her, said he'd had enough. He couldn't actually stop smoking, but it did make him a bit dizzy. Sister Prior was slowly breaking him of the habit.

'What time do you go back tomorrow?' he asked.

'I ought to catch the midday train.'

'Then I shan't see you again.'

'I could come tomorrow morning. Would you like me to?'

His eyes were shut again.

'Oh, I should like it. But they wouldn't. They have other plans for me tomorrow. It's a good thing you turned up today.'

She waited for an explanation. When it seemed there wasn't to be one she asked him directly, 'Is it the surgery you mentioned in your letter?'

He nodded. He opened his eyes but didn't look at her. 'They were going to do it sooner. But I didn't travel as well as they expected. They made me feel like a bottle of wine when they said that. That I hadn't travelled well.'

'Did they fly you out?'

'Yes, it was fun. I've never flown in my life before, until all this. They flew me out of Imphal first, and then from Comilla. I've clocked up about three hours, I think. On my back though. It's an odd feeling flying on your back. You think of yourself as totally invulnerable. Well, you do taking off and in the air. Landing's a bit of a jolt. The chap who was in here when you arrived pranged on Dum-Dum a couple of weeks ago, coming in from Agartala. Extraordinary. The plane was a write-off, but he only bust a leg.'

She said after a while, 'Do you want to tell me about tomorrow, about what they're doing?'

He turned his head towards her, as if to study the depth of her interest.

'Oh, they'll poke about and come up with something and tell me afterwards. And don't be fooled. I look as weak as a kitten, I know, but I'm full of beans under this dopey exterior. Otherwise they wouldn't be doing it yet.'

'What time are they doing it?'

'Nine o'clock. Unless there's an emergency. I mean, not me. Someone else. I'm not a priority. Don't worry. I'm all right.'

'If I rang at about midday I expect they'd tell me how it went.'

'Yes, I'm sure they would.'

'Then I'll do that.'

'Thank you.' A pause. 'Teddie told me Susan was having a baby. He was very proud.'

'It's due next month. In about three weeks.'

He said, 'I expect she hopes it will be a boy.'

'I don't think she minds.'

Again he shut his eyes. 'What do you say?' he asked. 'She was such a happy girl. It's the happy people who are hardest hit when something like that happens. Teddie was a happy sort of man, too. They seemed made for each other. Well, I suppose that kind of happiness means there's a basic resilience, and that when she's got over the shock she'll come up smiling. Although –'

'Although what?'

'She struck me as happy in the way a little girl is. Perhaps that's a protection too. It interested me, the difference between you both.'

He brought the sentence to an abrupt end. She felt the full-stop. They had entered a zone of silence. For a moment she imagined he had fallen asleep, exhausted by the visit and unable to cope with the demands it made on him. Perhaps he was already under sedation, in preparation for whatever they were going to do to him in the morning. She felt a stirring of morbid curiosity, the beginning of a distasteful urge to draw the sheet away and observe the condition of his legs and abdomen, and arms from elbow downwards.

'I expect there are things you both want to know.'

She glanced up quickly.

'I hope my letter didn't worry you,' he added. 'Did you show it to Susan?'

'Yes, I did.' She hesitated. 'It did worry us a bit.'

'I'm sorry. Did anyone ever write to her from the division?'

'She had one the day before from Colonel Selby-Smith, so she knew you and Teddie had been together when it happened. He said you'd helped him. That's one of the reasons I'm here, to tell you how grateful she is. Well, all of us. And of course she's looking for reassurance, that you're all right, or going to be. The letter from Colonel Selby-Smith seemed to hint that what you tried to do to help Teddie made things worse for you. What worried us about your letter was that it had to be dictated.'

'Yes, I see.'

She waited, expecting an explanation, or a comment the re-assurance that she could take back to Susan. When it did not come it was, perversely, not concern for him – which might have filled her – but renewed reluctance to be drawn towards him which she felt; and this seemed to empty her. She thought, almost abruptly: He lacks a particular quality, the quality of candour; there is a point, an important point, at which it becomes difficult to deal with him. He isn't shut off. It isn't that. He's open, wide open, and he wants me to enter, to ask him about the legs I can't see, the forearms I can't see, the obscene mystery beneath the white helmet of bandages. But I won't. They, or their absence, their mystery – these I find appalling as well. It's unfair, perhaps inhuman of me. On the other hand, it can't be inhuman because I feel it, and I belong to the species, I'm a fully paid up member.

He had turned away, aware – possibly – that the purely phys-ical equation of their eyes, meeting, lacked a value. When he began speaking she wondered whether the way in was being widened; salted, like the way in to a dangerous, derelict mine. She found herself exerting pressure on the ground with the soles of her feet and on her chair with the small of her back.

'I thought it might be something else that worried you,' he said, 'that thing I said about the business lying heavily and want-ing to talk about it. Get it off my chest. As if I had some sort of confession to make.'

'Have you, Ronald?'

He turned again, stared at her. He smiled slightly.

'Well, we all have, I suppose. The fact is I feel responsible. Perhaps there's something about me that attracts disaster, not for

myself, but for others. Do you think that's possible? That someone can be bad luck?'

'Perhaps.'

'I was the worst best man Teddie could have chosen. Remember me saying that? That night I came to say goodbye and found
you watching fireflies?'

'Waiting for them. Yes, I do remember.'

'You denied I was the worst, but that didn't fool me. Teddie
wasn't fooled either. When I saw him again he'd cooled off.
I could see him putting distance between us. Oh, I'm sure there's
something in it. You find you have – a victim. You haven't
chosen him. But that's what he is. Afterwards he haunts you,
just as if he were on your conscience. The irony is that you don't
really have him there. You can question your conscience and
come out with a clean bill. But he sticks, just the same. Teddie
sticks. And that has a certain irony in it. I'm sorry. I'm making
it worse. I mean, giving you more cause to worry, not less.'

'It was Susan who worried. But just about you and how you
really are and how much of what is wrong is due to your staying
and looking after Teddie.'

'Staying?'

'She was told you stayed with him until the arrival of
medical aid.'

'I suppose that was one way of putting it, but there wasn't any
alternative. Well, make that clear to her. We were both up the
creek. The question is why? Whose creek?'

He closed his eyes again, and this time it occurred to her that
closing them was deliberate, part of a total effect he was seeking
to make. His voice was quite strong; it showed no real sign of
fatigue.

'You see, I ask myself, continually ask myself, whatever fault
it may have been of his, would it have happened if I hadn't been
with him? And the answer is no. It wouldn't. It was the stone
all over again. The stone that hit the car. Only this time it wasn't
a stone. And of course it wasn't thrown at me. Everything about
it was different, but the same. In effect.'

She said, 'You're imagining it. You ought to forget it and
concentrate on getting better.'

He lay for a while, not speaking, not looking.

'No,' he said suddenly, so that she was almost startled. 'One doesn't get better by not facing it. Besides, I was fond of him. I may have envied him too. You know how it is. He had all the attributes, didn't he? The game. Playing it. I mean really believing that it was. Astonishing, because it's not a game, is it? Unless you play it, then I suppose that's what it becomes. I keep on telling myself that it was playing the game that killed him, so that his death becomes a kind of joke. Only I can't see it. To me it was just a mess that he wouldn't have got into without me.'

He turned again and watched her.

'I'm telling you, not Susan. I couldn't tell Susan. For her I'd play the game myself. But with you it isn't necessary, is it?'

'No, it's not necessary.'

'Anyway, you'd see through it. I lack the attributes. You notice things like that, but I feel you don't mind, that it doesn't matter to you that I'm not — not like Teddie. It mattered to Teddie. It made him over-meticulous about the rules. He was trying to point the difference between us. He never quite forgave me for what happened at the wedding. He didn't say much, but he made me feel — intended to make me feel — that I'd done something not quite — pukka — getting involved in that sort of thing, accepting the intimacy he offered when he asked me to be best man but failing to tell him just who he was inviting intimacy with. It was the sort of situation you couldn't actually say was wrong. All you could say was it wouldn't have happened if, for instance, I'd been a Muzzy Guide — wouldn't have happened then because a fellow-officer in the true sense of the word wouldn't have any — what? Areas of professional secrecy? He wasn't blaming me. He saw how reasonable it was for me not to go round saying, Look, I'm the police officer in the Manners case, and I get threatening anonymous notes, and any day someone might chuck a stone at me and involve me and whoever I'm with in an embarrassing police scene. Yes, he saw that. All the same he resented *being* involved. He saw it as an unnecessary vulgarity, one that marked the difference between my world and his. He recognized that these two worlds had to meet, I mean in war-time, but that didn't mean he had to like it or encourage the intimacy to continue. We had one brief talk after he'd got back from Nanoora and joined the General and the advance party in the training area we went to, and of course he said all the right things, that I had absolutely nothing to apologize for or explain; but after that he never mentioned Mirat to me again. When I say he told me about Susan having a baby, that isn't strictly true. He told someone else, and it came up in mess – as a cause for general congratulation. Well, you know. One makes a sort of joke about it. It was quite a night. We were pushing the boat out because the orders had just come from Corps to move the division down into the field. They were all a bit high. Which is partly why Teddie let it out, that he was going to be a father. And that was the night I really knew that he did resent having got mixed up socially with a chap who wasn't a Muzzy Guide or its equivalent. He was laughing at the things the others said to him. But when I congratulated him and asked him to give you and Susan my kind regards he became frigidly polite.'

'You're exaggerating. Teddie wasn't like that.' But she guessed that Teddie had been. 'Anyway, he sent on your kind regards.'

'Oh, but he would. He said "Yes of course. I'll do that." And that was his *word*. The frigidness and politeness were due to him turning it over in his mind first, whether he should agree or say "No, I think not if you don't mind, Merrick".'

'You make him sound terribly old-fashioned.'

'He was.' A pause. 'He believed in the old-fashioned virtues. The junior officers in a war-time divisional HQ are a pretty hybrid bunch. They divide, you know, into the amateurs and the professionals. But there's a paradox, because the professionals are invariably the temporary chaps like me. The amateurs are the permanent men like Teddie, who see it as a game. But even among *them* Teddie stood out as an anachronism. He had old-fashioned convictions. So did a lot of them. But in Teddie you felt he had the courage that was supposed to go with them. And when I look at it squarely, it was having that kind of courage that killed him. But he died an amateur. He should have had a horse.'

'The Muzzy Guides used to.'

'I know.'

Again he closed his eyes.

She said, 'What do you mean, he died an amateur?'

'I'll tell you, but I don't want you to tell Susan.'

'I can't promise not to.'

He smiled, but kept his eyes shut.

She said, 'She may prefer to know he died that way.'

'Yes,' he said presently. 'In its way it had a certain gallantry.' He paused, opened his eyes, glanced at her. 'You know about the Jiffs?'

'Jiffs?'

'They're what we call Indian soldiers who were once prisoners of the Japanese in Burma and Malaya, chaps who turned coat and formed themselves into army formations to help the enemy. There were a lot of them in that attempt the Japanese made to invade India through Imphal.'

'Yes, I've heard of them. Were there really a lot?'

'I'm afraid so. And officers like Teddie took it to heart. They couldn't believe Indian soldiers who'd eaten the king's salt and been proud to serve in the army generation after generation could be suborned like that, buy their way out of prison camp by turning coat, come armed hand in hand with the Japs to fight their own countrymen, fight the very officers who had trained them, cared for them and earned their respect. Well, you know. The regimental mystique. It goes deep. Teddie was always afraid of finding there were old Muzzy Guides among them. And of course that's what he did find. If Teddie had been the crying kind, I think he'd have cried. That would have been better, if he'd accepted the fact, had a good cry, then shrugged his shoulders and said, Well, that's life, once they were good soldiers, now they're traitors, shoot the lot.' Merrick hesitated. 'A lot *were* being shot. Our own soldiers despised them. They were a pretty poor bunch, badly led, badly equipped. And I suppose underneath the feeling artificially inspired by their propaganda – that they were the real patriots, fighting for India's independence – they were, deep down, bent with shame. The Japanese despised them too. They seldom used them in a truly combatant role and left them in the lurch time after time. Anyway, that's the picture we were getting, and we were also getting a picture of our own troops, Indian and British, killing them off rather than taking prisoners. That wasn't what we wanted. The whole thing of the Jiffs became rather my special pigeon in divisional intelligence. And I was trying to get a different picture. I wanted prisoners. Prisoners who would talk, talk about the whole thing, recruitment back in Malaya and Burma, inducements, pressures, promises. Which Indian officers had gone for the thing and which had only been sheep. When it

came to the question of Indian King's commissioned officers
who had joined the Jiffs, Teddie preserved a sort of tight-lipped
silence. He made you feel an officer who turned traitor was
probably best dead anyway, unmentionable, quite unspeakable.
And perhaps not really a shock, because to him an educated
Indian meant a political Indian. But the sepoys, NCOs and
VCOs were a different matter. It's those he would have cried
for. All those chaps whose fathers served before them, and had
medals, and little chits from old commanding officers. Sometimes he said a lot of them probably joined so as to get back on
their own side, and that in any major confrontation the Jiffs
would come over and help kick the Japanese in the teeth. He
became obsessed with the whole question. He seldom talked of
anything else, to me anyway, because the Jiffs were my pigeon,
and in a subtle way he used the Jiffs, his views on them, and
mine, to point up the differences between us. Do you know
what distinguishes the amateur?'

Sarah shook her head.

'The affection he has for his task, its end, its means and everyone who's involved with him in it. Most professional soldiers
are amateurs. They love their men, their equipment, their regiments. In a special way they love their enemies too. It's common
to most walks of life, isn't it? To fall in love with the means as
well as the end of an occupation?'

'You think that's wrong?'

'Yes, I think it is. It's a confusion. It dilutes the purity of an
act. It blinds you to the truth of a situation. It hedges everything
about with a mystique. One should not be confused in this way.'

'Are you never confused, Ronald?'

'I am – frequently confused. But I do try to act unemotionally.
I do try for a certain professional detachment.'

'It's funny,' she said, 'I should have said you were actually
quite an emotional person. Underneath. And that it sometimes
runs you into trouble.'

He was watching her, but she detected nothing in his expression except – and this so suddenly that she felt she had observed
it the moment that it fell on him – a curious serenity. 'Well, of
course, you're right,' he said. 'I've certainly run into trouble in
my time. It's one thing to try to act unemotionally and quite
another thing to do so. No act is performed without a decision

being made to perform it. I suppose emotion goes into a decision, especially into a major decision. My decision to get out of the police and into the army was an emotional one, wasn't it? Just like the one I made as a boy, to try to get into the Indian Police. But I don't think I was ever an amateur, either as a copper or a soldier. I had no affection for the job, in either case. But I did the job. I tried not to be confused. That was the difference between Teddie and me – the *real* difference, not the one that had to do with the fact that Teddie was a Muzzy Guide and I was, well, what I am – a boy from an elementary school who won a scholarship to a better one and found it difficult later not to be a bit ashamed of his parents, and very much ashamed of his grandparents. But any difference that Teddie saw in our attitudes, he'd always put down to the fact that I wasn't the same class. You can't disguise it, can you? It comes out in subtle ways, even when you've learned the things to say and how to say them. It comes out in not knowing the places or the people your kind of people know, it comes out in the lack of points of common contact. People like me carry around with them the vacuum of their own anonymous history, and there comes a moment when a fellow like Teddie looks at us and honestly believes we lack a vital gift as well, some sort of sense of inborn decency that's not our fault but makes us not quite trustworthy. I'm sorry. I'm not speaking ill of him. That's what he thought. And that's why he was killed. I'm only trying to make it clear, make this background clear. He was killed trying to show me how a thing should be done, because he didn't trust me to do it right. Well, it was his own fault – but remove me from the situation and it wouldn't have happened.'

'What situation?'

He closed his eyes and turned his head away. 'What situation? It was a simpler one than – another I remember. It began with a fellow called Mohammed Baksh. A Jiff. He was captured by a patrol from one of the companies of the British battalion of the Brigade that was probing forward on our right flank. Overnight things had become terribly confused and by morning the British battalion had found itself out on a limb. The advance of the Indian battalion on their left had been held up and it looked as if the British battalion might get cut off or have its flank turned. They were astride a road in hill country and we hadn't got a clear picture of the enemy's strength, or of where the major enemy attack was likely to come from. And this particular Brigadier was suffering from a bout of jitters, he was jumpy about losing his British battalion and wanted to pull them back, but the General had other ideas, of pushing another battalion forward astride the road and deploying both battalions to encircle whatever enemy units there were in the immediate vicinity. But he didn't want to issue the order without personal contact with the Brigadier. He decided to visit the Brigade and get things moving from there, unless he judged the Brigadier's on-the-spot appreciation had something to be said for it, or he thought him incapable of pressing forward immediately with the right sort of enthusiasm. He took Teddie with him. And at the last moment he turned to me and told me to go with them to make sure the Brigade Intelligence Officer had a complete picture of what we knew, and to assess on the spot anything he might be able to add that would be new to us.' A pause. 'We went in two jeeps. There were three in the General's. The General, Teddie, and the Indian driver, two in mine, myself and my driver. Teddie drove the other jeep. He loved driving. A jeep particularly. And the driver liked sitting perched at the back, with a Sten gun. It was a lovely morning. Bright and crisp. During the day of course it got very hot. Have you ever been in Manipur?'

'No.'

'On the plain itself, around Imphal, it's like northern India up in the North-west Frontier, around Abbotabad; much the same view of hills and mountains. We were south of there, in the foothills. The road was pretty rough. Steep wooded banks one side, pretty long wooded drops the other – well, for much of its course. You flattened out every so often, when you went through a village. We reached the Brigade headquarters round about eight-thirty a.m. I wasn't in on the talk that went on between the Brigadier and General. I was with the Brigade Intelligence Officer and he'd just had the IO of the British battalion on the wireless, reporting that patrols had picked up this fellow Mohammed Baksh of the Jiffs. So far he hadn't given any information. They said he looked half-starved and had prob-ably deserted several days before. I wasn't so sure. The picture I had was that most of the Jiffs looked pretty exhausted. They didn't have the stamina of the Japanese. The whole force had crossed the Chindwin and come through hill jungle. The Japanese are old hands at that. Advance first and worry about your lines of communications and supplies afterwards. That's their technique. It worked in Burma and Malaya, but it didn't work this time because we were ready for it. That's why the General wanted to push the other battalion forward. He guessed the Indian battalion on the left of the British was misinterpreting the strength of the opposition they'd met in the night. I realized it was important to know more about this Jiff fellow. If all that stood in the way of the British battalion was a Jiff formation, then the General could perform his containing operation easily.'

'Didn't the British battalion know what was in front of them?'

'No, they'd reached their objective, and the only reason for the pause was their discovery that their left flank was unprotected, because the Indian battalion hadn't kept pace. The Indians were stuck about two miles back, apparently contained by a Japanese force of at least battalion strength. But the General thought that if the Indian battalion was pinned down by the Japanese, so were the Japanese by the Indians, a sort of tactical stalemate, and since the British battalion was astride the road the initiative was still very much with the Brigade. The British battalion had sent patrols forward, of course, but found nothing except this stray Jiff and their patrols reported no apparent threat to their flank or rear. Down there, you know, it isn't country you can stand and get a view of. You have to probe it more or less yard by yard. But they had found the Jiff, and I wondered whether the fact that he hadn't given any information was because he spoke no English and the IO of the British battalion spoke hardly any Urdu. I asked the Brigade IO what was happening about Baksh. He said he'd asked the battalion to send him back but the answer had been, Come and get him, we can't spare either the transport or the men just to look after a Jiff.'

He stopped, said, 'I'm sorry. Would you help me drink from that contraption on the table?'

She rose, went round by the bed for the teapot and held it for him.

'Thanks.'

'Would you like to share another cigarette?'

'No, but you have one. I enjoy the smell.'

As she lit one she remembered having said much the same thing to him, the night of the fireflies.

'Just then,' he went on, 'the General and the Brigadier came out from their conference. I could see there had been a flaming row. The Brig was about ten years the senior man and was all for caution because men's lives were at stake, the lives of men he loved. The General on the other hand was all for modern ideas of dash, surprise, throwing away the book, using your equipment to its optimum limit, loving the whole impersonal power-game of move and counter-move.' A pause. 'They were both amateurs because they were both hot-headed. They were trying to make a lyric out of a situation that was merely prosaic. It only seemed problematical because we lacked information. But because it seemed problematical all this free emotional rein was given to the business of its solution. Well, there you are. If there are things you don't know, you call the gap in your knowledge a mystery and fill it in with a wholly emotional answer. That morning it struck me as supremely silly because, do you know, there wasn't a single sound of warfare anywhere. It was quite still. Sylvan almost – with the sunlight coming through the trees. A phrase came into my mind. The sweet indifference of man's environment to his problems. Pathetic fallacy or no, I really felt it, an indifference to us that amounted to contempt. The Brig had installed himself in an old bungalow, probably a traveller's resthouse. There was a village near by but the people had fled. The Brigade transport was harboured in a kind of glade – command truck, signals truck. Well, you can probably picture it, just like a Brigade command post on a field exercise. I was never able to get the picture of an exercise out of my mind, even when stuff was flying. There's something fundamentally childish about the arrangements for armed conflict. And there they were, the General and the Brigadier, both red in the face, and Teddie looking pink and embarrassed. They went over to the command truck. The IO was still with me. I told him that if I could get the General's permission I'd go and collect that Jiff myself, and see what I could get out of him. The IO was all for it, glad not to be bothered with such a minor detail. I went to the command truck and saw that something had just happened to put the General back in a good temper. The CO of the Indian battalion had been on the radio. They now realized they'd got the Japanese into a pocket and had decided that the Japanese force wasn't much more than company strength. It meant the Indians could mop the Japs up, complete their advance and make contact with the British battalion. The General asked me if there was anything new on my side, so I told him about the Jiff and that I'd like to go up and try and get him to talk and in any case bring him back. He said, "Yes, you do that, and make sure they understand the operational picture." '

Again he closed his eyes, and said nothing for a while, as if conjuring the image of that morning. But she knew, instinctively, what was coming. Something Teddie had said that marked the beginning of the fatal occasion.

'Of course the operational picture was Teddie's side, not mine, but there was nothing about this picture that a G.3 I. couldn't tell the battalion commander just as clearly as a G.3 Ops could. But Teddie said, "I'll do that, sir, I'll go with him." And the General was in a good enough mood to agree. If he'd thought about it clearly he would have said no. It was absurd, two divisional staff officers going off to a forward battalion to collect one miserable prisoner and to confirm verbally operational information that the CO would get over the radio anyway. But there we were, doing just that, as a result of the General's euphoria following the solution to his problem, but chiefly because of Teddie's obsession, his belief that I was not the man to deal with an Indian soldier who had turned coat. I didn't understand, I didn't have the touch or the sense of the traditions that were involved. Teddie thought he did. The Jiff was the only reason Teddie volunteered to go.

'But before we set off something else happened that gave him a better reason. I suppose we were about five minutes, checking with the Brigade IO, making sure of the location and route. We were about to leave when we were called back. I thought the General had changed his mind, but it wasn't that. Division had been on. The whole operational picture had changed. The division had been drawn into what amounted in military terms to a blind alley. On the map it was advancing roughly south-west to oppose a threat from that quarter, but the major threat was now seen to be south to south-east. In less difficult country it would just have been a question of swinging round in the hope of cutting the advancing force in two, but it's difficult to swing across the grain of hills like that. The reserve Brigade was the only one of the three not faced with that problem. But I won't bore you with tactics. It's enough for you to know there was a bit of a flap, and that this trip of Teddie's and mine was suddenly much more important to both the General and the Brigadier. The Brigadier was already on the radio to the CO of the British battalion, telling him to send a company back to support the Indians who were going in to clear this pocket of Japanese, make sure they didn't break through on to the road, but he wanted definite information about the Jiffs. He wanted to make sure there were no Jiff units waiting their chance to come in and command the road when our own troops swung away from it. He told the CO I was coming along, that the two of us were coming, one to help sort out the Jiff situation and relieve them of the prisoner and the other to put them in the picture as the General now saw it.

'So off we went, in my jeep, the two of us and the driver. There were only three miles to go. That company of the British battalion must have moved. We met them debussing and scattering into the hill on our left. When we got to the battalion we found the headquarters bivouacked just beyond a village, commanding the junction of the road and a track that led off down into a valley on the right. The junction had been their objective the previous night. They had a company in the jungle between the road and the track and another company in the jungle on the left of the road. The whole thing was terribly brisk and businesslike, that is it was until you realized that there were probably no enemy ahead. The CO was one of those cheery types with a wide moustache and a scarf in his neck – navy blue with white polka dots. We found him sitting on a shooting stick, drinking coffee. He had two spare mugs ready and got his batman filling them when he saw us coming. The complete host. At pains to appear quite unflappable.

'I let Teddie talk first. When he'd finished the CO just nodded, made one or two marks on his map and said, "Well, I could have told them that. There's nothing down the road, except perhaps some stray Jiffs and if they're all like the one we've got they're no problem." He sent for the IO then and told him to take me to the mule-lines where they had the Jiff under guard. Teddie began to follow but the CO called him back. The

IO was a pleasant boy. He spoke French and German and had learned some Japanese, but he admitted his Urdu didn't extend much beyond what private soldiers who came out to India in the old days used to pick up in the barracks and bazaars. The only thing he'd got out of Mohammed Baksh was his name. He wasn't even sure whether Baksh had been an Indian prisoner of war or an Indian civilian in Malaya or Burma.

'But when I saw him I was pretty certain he'd been a soldier. He was squatting on his hunkers, under a tree, guarded by a young soldier on mule-lines picket, and directly he saw us coming he got to his feet and stood at attention, and stared straight ahead in that way old soldiers have, never quite meeting your eye unless you ask a personal question. He hadn't learned that as a civilian. He was a mess, though. Dirty, unshaven, under-nourished. His uniform had nearly had it. I started firing questions at him. Name, age, what village he was born in, what year he had joined, what regiment, whether he had any relatives serving in the army, whether his parents were alive, and what his father was. All very quickly, not waiting for the answers, but asking him nothing about the Jiffs or the Japanese or how he'd been captured. I wanted to start him thinking about his home. He'd probably not seen it for two or three years, and coming back to Indian soil could have made him pretty homesick. Then I started asking the questions again, but this time waited for answers. The family questions first, the name of his village, what his father did, was his father still alive? He said he didn't know about his father and I could see the question had got him. It was then that Teddie appeared and that was the signal for Baksh to shut up like a clam, just when I thought I'd begun to break him.

'I decided to leave the personal things aside for a bit and started asking questions about the past few days. Teddie's Urdu wasn't all that hot. He kept asking me what I'd said, and putting in questions of his own, if Baksh had been in the Indian Army, what regiment, who'd been his old commanding officer. The chap got very confused and nervous, looking at Teddie, but not quite at Teddie, at one part of Teddie. It took me a while to get it. That he couldn't keep his eyes off Teddie's regimental flash. And then I realized what was eating him and said, Baksh, you're an old solider of this officer's regiment, aren't you? He stared at me and then sort of collapsed. Teddie rounded on me, wanted to know what I'd said, so I told him. I said Baksh had once been a Muzzy Guide. He said I was making it up, he didn't believe it. No sepoy of the Muzzy Guides would ever turn coat, he'd rather die. He said there'd been one battalion in Burma and one in Malaya, that he knew every man in the Burma battalion, which had been his own, and all the officers of the one in Malaya. If Baksh was a Muzzy Guide he'd have been in the Malaya battalion. He told me to ask him the name of the Commanding Officer. Well I did so, and Baksh just shook his head and for a moment I thought perhaps Teddie was right, but I kept on asking him and in the end he said, "Hostein Sahib, Hostein Sahib." I thought well, that proved it, Teddie *was* right. The Muzzy Guides wouldn't have an Indian CO. But Teddie said, "Hostein Sahib was what they called Colonel Hastings", and stared at me as if we'd un-covered something terribly sinister, so sinister it was unbeliev-able. He asked Baksh what happened to Hostein Sahib. The answer was that none of them had seen either Hastings or any of the other officers since the night the battalion, or what was left of it, went into the bag, south of Kuala Lumpur. The Indian soldiers and their British officers had been separated by their Japanese captors. There was a rumour that Hostein Sahib had been shot, then another that he was in a camp up-country, on the Siam border. The Indian officer who came to talk to them later, in Singapore, said Hostein Sahib and the other officers had had plans to get away by themselves to Sumatra and leave the sepoys and NCOs behind, but being captured by the Japanese had stopped it. None of the sepoys believed this, and for weeks they'd refused to listen to men like the Indian officer who came and went in a Japanese staff car and was on friendly terms with the Japanese camp commander.

'What he was trying to do was get them to join the Indian National Army. Baksh said he was a Sikh called Ranjit Singh. He told them he'd been captured up in Ipoh, that the British officers in his regiment had all tried to save their own skins and left him commanding a rearguard action. He'd been a lieutenant. Now he was a major. He used to visit them two or three times a week and tell them about the free Indian Government that was being formed and which it was the duty of every patriotic Indian soldier to support by joining the new Indian Army that would march to Delhi and drive the British out. He said the Japanese were not India's enemy, only enemies of the British. Why pine away in the prison camps which British cowardice and inefficiency had driven brave men into? The British had always excused their imperialism by pointing out that their presence in India was a guarantee of freedom from invasion. But they hadn't kept the Japanese out of Burma and Malaya. The Japanese were freeing all Asia from the white man's yoke and self-respecting Indians couldn't just sit by and let another nation do their job for them.

'Baksh said that after several weeks other officers came, including a couple of Muslims who told them the whole of India was rising against the white imperialists and that men in the army back here were turning against their officers. I expect that would have been around August in 'forty-two. Some of Baksh's fellow-prisoners began to believe these tales and after a bit were taken out of camp and came back later in INA uniform, said how well they were treated and helped to recruit the rest. He said, "We were forced, Sahib – one man was tortured by an Indian officer because he refused to take the new oath. We didn't know what was true and what was not. We saw white sahibs working on the roads, like coolies. The world was turned upside down." '

Merrick paused.

'That was the kind of information I was after, I mean about the pressures and the officers responsible. There'll be a day of reckoning I suppose. God knows what will happen to all those chaps. The strength of the INA is three divisions. That's a lot of officers and a lot of men. A lot of sentences of death. Too many. It won't happen. I suppose we might hang Subhas Chandra Bose, who's at the head of the whole thing, but for the rest I expect it'll be a question of weeding out the hawks from the doves, tracking down those who've had their own men tortured. Baksh told me what they did to this chap who tried to stand out against them. It's too revolting to repeat.'

He closed his eyes, but when he continued his voice was still strong.

'I asked Baksh to describe what had led to his capture that morning and he told us that two days earlier the Japanese had ordered the officer commanding their unit to establish a listening post to keep watch on the track – the one that led down into the valley, and Baksh and two other men, both ex-Muzzafirabad

Guides like himself – had been chosen. Their unit was in a village about three miles south of the junction and the listening post was established in the jungle about a mile ahead of the village in a place where they could look down and get a good view of quite a long stretch of the track. Patrols were to visit the listening post every two hours, but if they saw anything going on one of the three men was to go back and report. Baksh said it was a stupid arrangement, the kind of thing they found themselves doing because the Japanese seldom gave them a proper job. Anyway they spent the whole day watching the track and reporting to the patrols. They thought they'd be ordered back when it got dark, but when the last patrol reached them the leader said he hadn't had any orders to leave the post unmanned. He'd see about it when he got back and in any case send up a hot meal. They'd been on iron rations all day, with only water to drink. But nothing happened. They didn't dare desert the post or even have one man go back and see what was up because their officer, Lieutenant Karim, was always on at them about obeying orders to the letter and showing themselves the equal of the Japanese in endurance and discipline. Karim had been a Jemadar in one of the Punjabi regiments. He'd adopted the Japanese method of slapping soldiers when he was angry.

'So there they were, according to Baksh, stuck all night on the hillside. When it got light they expected the patrol to turn up, but it never did. They had no food left and only very little water. They drew lots for which of them would go back when the sun had been up a couple of hours, and Baksh was the unlucky one. He expected Karim would beat him up.

'When he got back to the village he found it deserted. The unit had gone. It didn't surprise him because the Japanese were always ordering them to move at a moment's notice, usually in the middle of the night. He said it didn't even surprise him that Lieutenant Karim had packed and gone without thinking of the three men at the listening post, and that the patrol leader who'd promised to send a hot meal had forgotten all about them. He said, "In the jungle our doubts returned, each man was only thinking of himself. There was no good spirit in us." Well, it sounded plausible, and Teddie believed it. So did the young IO. I wasn't wholly convinced. I kept an open mind, whether he was telling the truth or trying to cover up the fact that he was a deserter or a spy. He said he scouted around, filled the water bottles from the stream they'd been using, and found some tins of food carelessly left behind, then went back to the post. When they'd eaten they decided to go back to the village thinking by now someone must have noticed their absence and they'd be sent for. In the village they tried to work out which direction the unit had gone. They were afraid of the Japanese appearing and treating them as deserters, or of some of the villagers returning and taking revenge on them for things the Japanese had done. I asked him then how large the unit was. He said it was about half company strength, and had been detached from an INA battalion for special duties, but he didn't know what the special duties were because apart from advancing up the road behind a company of Japanese they hadn't done anything. I wasn't so sure about that either, but I asked him to go on with his story. He said he and the two others had begun to quarrel. One man wanted to go back to the listening post, another wanted to stay hidden in the village and Baksh wanted to scout back along the road in the direction they'd come from a couple of nights before. So they drew lots again, and Baksh won. They tracked back for a couple of miles, keeping to the jungle along the side of the road, and found nothing. He said it was as if God had waved his hand and caused all the soldiers of their own and the Japanese armies to disappear. They went back to the village and on to the listening post. The two others suggested they should go down into the valley. They were sure their unit must have been sent in that direction. Why else should the track leading down to the valley have been kept a watch on? Baksh said there was no point in sending troops into the valley. There was nothing there except the surrounding hills. The road and the high ground on the other side of it were the only features of military value. They'd advanced along the road towards the village. In his opinion their troops had fanned out into the hills, not into the valley. He said they should cross the road and explore the hills, or stay where they were. In one case they'd at least be showing common sense and initiative, in the other obeying the last order received. If they went down into the valley they'd only be acting foolishly. They had a midday meal at the listening post and because they'd hardly slept at all the night before and were tired and hungry they decided to stay put and take it in turns, two men keeping watch and the other one sleeping. He said, "We had no strength left, Sahib, and no spirit. Through no fault of our own we had become deserters and were thinking and doing like that." It was agreed that at dusk they'd go back to the village. Baksh was the last to sleep. He said he woke when it was dark and found the others had gone. They had taken the rest of the food. He went to the village but knew they'd gone down into the valley and that they felt as he was feeling, that the end of the road had been reached and there was nothing for it now but capture by British or Indian troops. He slept in one of the deserted huts and woke during the night because of the sound of firing from the direction of the hill on the other side of the road. At least, he thought that was where it came from. It didn't sound close. When he woke again it was light. The firing had stopped but there were two British soldiers prodding him with their rifles. He was glad it was over. Now, he said, he would be shot, and knew he deserved death for being disloyal to the uniform of his father and fathers before him.' A pause. 'He broke down and wept and begged Teddie to shoot him then and there. That young IO was terribly embarrassed. Oddly enough Teddie wasn't. He held the man's shoulder and shook him a bit and said, "You're still a soldier. Act like one. You've done very wrong, but I am still your father and mother." The old formula. But Teddie meant it. He really meant it. In spite of what that man had done he felt it was his duty to do his best for him. And I suppose he felt compassion.'

'Did you?' Sarah asked. 'Did you feel that too, Ronald?'

'No. To me Baksh was merely a source of information. I had no feelings about the man himself. He'd made a choice. It hadn't worked out well. The law says he should be punished. Well, it happens all the time. You choose, you act, you pay or get paid. That's how I see it. Do you disapprove?'

'I can't, can I?' she said, then added, 'It's true after all. You pay or get paid. Although perhaps there are situations in which it's better for you to pay, more satisfying.' She thought: To the soul, whatever that is, more satisfying to the soul, if you know the choice was wrong. But what do I mean, *wrong*?

'Most people prefer to be paid. We're always looking for rewards. And Baksh got his. So did Teddie. It was a ridiculous scene in its way. It seemed to me to have nothing to do with the reality of what was actually happening. He knelt down and put his head on Teddie's boots, and that didn't embarrass Teddie either. I think it moved him. Very deeply. As if something he'd always believed in and put his trust in had been proved. He pulled Baksh to his feet, quite gently, and then they stared at each other. Measuring up. To each other, and to some standard of, well, what worked, what was possible about conduct. And Baksh gradually reassumed that old soldier look of not looking except into a middle-distance he wasn't even seeing. And Teddie nodded and said, "I remember Hostein Sahib, in Muzzafirabad. My name is Bingham, Bingham. Remember my name." It was a promise that didn't need explaining in so many words. They both understood that Teddie intended to do his best for him. The man felt he belonged again. You could see that. He might be court-martialled and shot, or imprisoned, but even in front of a firing-squad he would belong to the system that was executing him. I suppose it was months since he'd felt he belonged anywhere. It's extraordinary the lengths people will go to to convince themselves that they belong.'

He turned his head slightly and watched her, then said:

'Just then we heard firing on the hill. The Indians were going to clear that pocket of Japanese, with the company from the British battalion in support. The IO looked at his watch and asked me to question Baksh about the kind of arms this Jiff unit had and whether he thought it possible after all that they'd gone down into the valley and holed out there. The answer was that they had a mortar, a couple of machine guns. The rest carried rifles. They hadn't much spare ammunition. He looked back in the direction of the firing and then in the direction of the valley. I think we all got the same idea at once, that the Jiffs *had* gone into the valley and that they should have opposed the advance of the British battalion during the night or were supposed to harry the battalion once it was seen to have occupied the road junction. The firing on the hill might be their signal to attack. But a unit of only half-company strength was an absurdly small force. If Baksh hadn't lied about the strength, the Jiffs might have gone into the valley to join a Japanese force already holed out there. The IO said he'd better go and have a word with the old man, but before he'd gone more than a yard or so we heard the old man calling to him. I asked Baksh if he'd lied about the strength of the Jiff force. I suggested he'd lied from start to finish. He wouldn't answer me, but just looked dumbly at Teddie. Teddie said, "Leave the poor devil alone." But he asked a question himself. He asked the names of Baksh's two ex-Muzzy Guide companions from the listening post.' A pause. 'Aziz Khan and Fariqua Khan.' A pause. 'I expect I'll always remember them. The names. Not the men. We never saw the men.

'Presently I left Teddie to it and went to find the CO. There was the question of the valley, and who might be in it. If he intended to have a closer look I thought it worth staying for another half-hour. Not more. I'd done the job I came to do, so had Teddie. I knew we ought to be getting back to division and taking Baksh with us. I found the CO at the junction. Up along the road men were coming out of the jungle on either side. He told me he'd been ordered back about a mile and to leave a road block at the junction until the battalion from the reserve Brigade sent a company forward to man it. The little skirmish on the hill was nearly over and he was to move on through the hills, south-east. That was in line with the revised picture we'd had from division. I asked what he thought about the possibility of there being Jiffs or Japanese in the valley. He said the company manning the road block could deal with them, if there were any. Then he said I'd better get moving. He meant we were in the way. We were. Well, you can imagine, a battalion suddenly on the move. I went back to the mule-lines to get Teddie and Baksh. But they weren't there. The mules were being loaded and led out and I couldn't tell which of the men had been on guard, but the one I spoke to said the IO and the Jiff and the other staff officer had gone down by what he called the short cut. I went back to where we'd left the jeep. It wasn't there either. Neither was the driver. It took me a couple of minutes to find the IO. He seemed surprised to see me. He said he thought I'd gone with Captain Bingham and the Jiff-type to see if the other two Jiffs were anywhere around. When he saw I'd no idea what he was talking about he told me how when he went back to the mule-lines, by the short cut, he found Teddie alone with Baksh. Teddie told him Baksh thought the other two ex-Muzzy Guides were in the valley and would be looking for an opportunity to give themselves up, especially to a Muzzy Guide officer. The IO had said, Well, we're pulling out, take a look if you must, it's all yours. When he asked where I was Teddie said I'd gone down to the road and that he'd pick me up there. Perhaps he intended to. I don't know. At the time I could only think he'd gone off his head and I'm afraid I said as much to the IO. I'm sorry. I think it counted against Teddie afterwards. The IO asked me if I thought the Jiff was trying something on. I said I didn't know, but I wanted him back.

'Sometimes, you know, I lie here and realize I'd probably be all in one piece still if that young IO had been pigheaded or scared of his CO, if he'd said, "Well, it's your funeral," and gone about his own business. But he was the eager-beaver type. He took me to a jeep parked off the road and told me to jump in, he'd take me down the track. The jeep belonged to the CO but he wouldn't be needing it, not where the battalion was going. He meant for the march into the hills. What transport the battalion had apart from the mules would go back to the Brigade pool. He called out to a sergeant to tell the CO there might be something going on down in the valley and he was going to take a look and in any case check that the company in the woods between the road and the track were pulling out in good order. Then we set off and turned into the track. Men were coming out on to it from the jungle and marching up it in single file. When we got round the first bend we saw Teddie about half a mile ahead. He was in the driver's seat, going quite slowly, and Baksh was in the back with the driver beside him. You couldn't tell at that distance how alert the driver was, or if he had Baksh well covered with his Sten gun. There was a shallow ravine on our right, with a ridge beyond it, but Teddie was at a point where the ravine came to an end and there was a neck of flattish ground between the track and the ridge, most of it jungle, but making a fairly easy connection between the ridge and the track. Farther on the ground obviously fell away quite steeply into the valley. When we saw Teddie stop the IO said, "I think he's only taking a quick look-see. He won't find them there, we've patrolled all that." All the same Teddie stopped and a second or so later we heard him, quite clearly. Calling to them. Aziz Khan. Fariqua Khan. Aziz Khan, Fariqua Khan. It was as if Teddie himself gave the signal. There was a single rifle shot and not more than a second or two later an explosion in the woods on our left and then another one bang on the track

between us and Teddie's jeep, and then more or less continu-
ously, one after the other in the wood. The company that had
been located there and were still in there, moving out section
by section, were being mortared from the ridge over on the right
and there was more than one mortar, which meant Baksh had
lied or there were some Japanese there too.

'I hand it to the young IO. The temptation was to get out of
the jeep and dive for cover but he merely swore and started
swinging round. The track was narrow, it needed a three-point
turn. We were swung round with the wheels an inch or two
from the ravine before I realized he meant to drive back up the
hill. I remember shouting at him, "What are you doing? Didn't
you see?" I don't think he had seen. He shouted back for me to
hang on, but I jumped out and said I must get him. I don't think
he understood what I was on about. He realized later but at the
time he probably thought I didn't relish running the gauntlet
back up the track, and was going to ground in the wood, or
perhaps he wasn't thinking at all, just acting instinctively, getting
back himself as quick as he could to where he was supposed to
be and would be needed. The men who'd been marching up
the track had scattered. I saw a couple of them leaning against
the bank holding their faces. It was a sort of pandemonium.
I registered it, but not as someone who had to do anything about
it. I was thinking primarily of the other jeep and of what I'd
seen in the first few seconds, between the rifle shot, the first
mortar bomb explosion and the second one that fell slap on the
track. I saw three things. I saw Teddie duck, or appear to duck.
I saw the driver pitch over on top of him, as if he'd been hit.
And I saw Baksh staring at them, then jumping clear and running
on to that neck of flat ground. Then I couldn't see anything
because of the explosion on the track itself.

'And I don't remember anything awfully clearly between
jumping out of the IO's jeep and reaching Teddie's. I think
I ran down the track until I reached the mortar-bomb crater
and that the site of it acted as a warning signal. I must have
gone up into the wood then and run the rest of the way under
cover. I do seem to remember some difficult going, and falling,
picking myself up again. I know it was a sudden shock to find
the jeep was burning and that the driver was on the ground,
not slumped over Teddie any longer, and that Teddie wasn't

slumped forward but sideways. It wasn't at all how I'd last seen it. I realized another mortar bomb had fallen a few yards in front of the jeep and that the force of the explosion had hurled the driver off Teddie and also flung Teddie to one side. I don't know about the fire. I think the spare petrol cans had been hit and gone up. I don't really remember going up to the jeep, only being there, pulling Teddie out, trying to get a hold. I must have been hunched forward, protecting my face, reaching in and getting him by the waist or an arm. I don't remember being shot at, or know whether it was then, or when I got him out and dragged him into the wood, or when I had to go back and get the driver and drag him in too. I do remember there wasn't any sign of Baksh. They found him later. Dead of course. The other Jiffs must have shot him. They or the Japanese. It turned out there were Japanese as well.'

She thought: I don't know, I don't know, where that kind of courage comes from or why or what its purpose is, but I know it has a purpose. It's a kind of madness, a sublime insanity which even Ronald who's experienced it can't explain. He wanted to diminish Teddie for me but Teddie isn't diminished. He began to diminish himself, but now he isn't diminished either. For a moment they are both larger than life. Teddie calling stupidly for those men, and Ronald stupidly risking death to try and save him. And that's how I shall remember them. Without understanding why it makes them larger.

His eyes were shut again, had been for some moments, and that impediment in his throat was troubling him. He swallowed and said:

'I thought at first Teddie was dead too, but I'm afraid he wasn't, neither was the driver but the driver wasn't burnt. Teddie was.'

'But he was unconscious?'

'Not all the time.'

'Colonel Selby-Smith wrote that you said Teddie was unconscious and hadn't suffered.'

'Let Susan go on thinking that.' A pause. 'I got them both off the track and as far into the wood as I could manage. The driver's Sten gun was still in the jeep so I only had my revolver, and Teddie's of course, but I thought it was probably all up with the three of us anyway, either from another mortar bomb or from

the bunch of Jiffs I expected any moment to come down from
the ridge. I think it was becoming aware of that possibility that
made me notice my left arm was numb, but I couldn't see any
blood or any sign of having been hit. The arm and – other things
– made it difficult to do anything about the field-dressings and
I couldn't see where Teddie had been hit either. I had him on
his back and didn't want to turn him over. It's odd, about –
damage to people. I thought the driver was dying, that no one
could be such a mess and survive. I thought it would be Teddie
who might survive, although I hoped he wouldn't.' A pause.
'He would have been terribly disfigured.'

   She waited, then said:

   'You don't need to tell me anything you don't like talking
about, Ronald. I'd rather you didn't because I couldn't repeat it
to Susan, and if I know it she'll see I'm keeping something back.
And then she'll worry even more.' She hesitated. 'And you
haven't told me anything about you, about what's wrong or
what they've got to do to you.'

   'Oh, nothing wrong they can't put right. I was burnt a bit.
Shot up a bit. But in a few weeks I'll be back on my feet, which
I suppose is something.'

   She remembered the line from his letter: *There was Teddie with
everything to live for and I – comparatively – with something less than
that.* It no longer seemed like an affectation but a bare statement
of the truth. She would have liked to get him to explain but felt
the explanation was there, in front of her, and in her mind –
secreted in all the dark corners of her recollections of her brief
encounters with him, and with his reputation.

   She said, 'Was it a long time before you got any help?'

   'It seemed long. I think it was an hour. A bit more. But after a
while I felt quite safe because I realized the Jiffs wouldn't expose
themselves to our own direct fire by coming on to the track.
They might try to cross it, and of course they'd come on to it if
they thought they'd got the battalion pinned down, but somehow I assumed they'd do neither. It never struck me there might
be larger forces coming up from the valley. There weren't, but
I'm glad I didn't worry about it. I'm trying to make you see that
staying there with Teddie and the driver wasn't the death-and-
glory thing people might make out.' A pause. 'It was the snug-
gest place to be when you think of it. And there's this other

thing. If all this is a confession of some sort, that is what it's about, what I see about it now, I mean when lying thinking, going back, analysing it. I want you to know. So that you under-stand the difference, the difference between Teddie and me, and why I say he died an amateur. He went down there for the *regiment*. I told you there was a touch of old-fashioned gallantry in it. All that paternalist business really meant something to him. *Man-bap*. I am your father and your mother. It would have been great if he'd gone down there and called as he did and if they'd come out, hanging their heads, and surrendered to him, trusting in the code, the old code. That's what he wanted. I don't mean there was anything vain or self-seeking about it. He wasn't doing it for himself or for them. He did it for the regiment. He risked everything for it, his own life, the driver's life, Baksh's life, his job. So much. So much it's incalculable. Who knows, his going down there might have looked to that bunch of Jiffs and Japs, who'd been clever enough to get so near without being seen, like the beginning of an advance into the valley. It could have triggered the whole thing off. But in any case he was putting the regiment above his job. If it had come off he could have become one of those people a regiment remembers, celebrates, as part of their legend. Teddie Bingham? By jove, yes but that was before your time. There were these poor misguided fellows from a Muzzy Guides battalion that got cut to pieces in Malaya back in '41–'42 and had gone into the bag and been forced to join a bunch of renegades we called Jiffs. A lot of them came up with the Japs when they crossed into Indian territory early in '44. Our own chaps shot them out of hand if they had the chance, and there weren't many prisoners until this Muzzy Guide gave himself up, a chap called Mohammed Baksh. Young Bingham was a divisional staff officer at the time, but once a Muzzy always a Muzzy. He'd gone forward with a message from the General to the CO of a battalion that was in danger of being cut off and saw Baksh. Well, directly Baksh saw him the fellow went to pieces, and begged young Bingham to shoot him for his act of treachery, but young Bingham made him stand like a man and talked to him as if he were his own erring son, made him feel he still belonged. "Are there any others with you?" Bingham asked and Baksh said yes, two, both from his old battalion, starved, wretched, hiding out, too afraid to surrender. Well, there was stuff flying but young Bingham never hesitated. "Come on," he said, "show me where," and off they went right into the thick of it and when they got near the place where Baksh had left the other two Bingham said, "What are their names?" Aziz Khan and Fariqua Khan. Brothers I think they were. So what does young Bingham do? He stands up straight where everyone could see him and pick him off and calls out to them, ordering them to return to duty as soldiers of the Muzzy Guides. And, by jove, in a couple of minutes out they came and back he marched them. He didn't even take their rifles away.'

Presently Merrick said:

'But of course it didn't come off and nobody will ever tell the tale like that. And anyway that kind of tale has had its day. Is that why it didn't come off?'

'There's your tale,' Sarah said.

'Oh no, mine was a professional action.' He looked at her and again she thought she detected in his expression that curious serenity. 'It's only amateurs who create legends. There's nothing memorable about doing a job. I said mine was a professional act. I didn't go to save Teddie. I went to get Mohammed Baksh. I want you to accept that, and the fact that when it came to it I didn't have the courage to go looking for him. I pulled Teddie out because I was afraid of what people would say if I left him to fry.' A pause. 'I don't mean that all this went consciously through my mind, but in retrospect I see no other interpretation.' A pause. 'Do you?'

Do I? (she asked herself). Yes, I see a man who was in love with those legends, that way of life, all those things that from a distance seemed to distinguish people like us from people of his own kind, people he knew better. I see a man still in love with them but who has chosen to live outside in the cold because he couldn't get in to warm his hands at this hearth with its dying fire. And it is strange because I long to exchange the creeping cold for a chill reality but feel in my bones that my kind of cold would not be his kind, just as the warmth I knew as a child was different from the warmth he always imagined. I don't understand the distinction he makes between what he calls amateur and what he calls professional, but feel it's a distinction he's made to heal a wound. After all, there are only people, tasks, myths and truth. And truth is a fire few of us get scorched by. Perhaps it's an imaginary flame, and can't be made by rubbing two sticks together.

She said, 'Some people would have been more afraid of pulling Teddie out than of what people would say if he'd been left there. And I don't think you risked your life just to get Mohammed Baksh.'

'No?'

'You went down there without thinking why you went, Ronald. I mean when the shooting had started. You saw they were in trouble and needed help. What you call the game only looks like a game to people who aren't in the team. I'm sorry but even if it's only as twelfth man you're a member of the team after all, aren't you?'

He smiled, turned his head so that he need not look at her. He said, 'You are, when it comes to it, very much the Colonel's daughter, I'm afraid.'

'I was born that way.'

She waited. He did not respond. Again she felt the pressure of his willing her to enter and explore the mysterious areas of his obsession. To counteract it she considered other mysteries, or anyway questions that remained unanswered: The outcome of the battle, whether it had ever been proven that Baksh had lied, and why; what other prisoners were taken and, more grotesquely, the circumstances of his vigil, with Teddie burnt but not unconscious all the time, and himself in some unexplained condition of numbness which perhaps wore off before the time was up.

'Did the driver come through?' she asked. He nodded. 'And Teddie – was Teddie aware of what you'd done?'

'I don't know. I don't think so. If you could use a word like expression in a case like that I'd say his was one of blank amazement. He never made a sound. I'm not sure he could see me. But his eyes moved. At one time I thought he'd gone, but his heart was still beating. I'm sorry. I shouldn't tell you things like that. Burning's a terrible thing. I was glad when they told me he'd had a bullet lodged in his back. I suppose the fire had cauterized the wound. At the time I thought he was only dying from burns.' He looked round at her again. 'Sitting with him reminded me of the last thing I did as DSP Mayapore, just before I was – transferred to Sundernagar. There was an English mission

school superintendent living there who committed suicide.
Suttee, as a matter of fact.'

'Oh – do you mean Miss Crane?'

'You knew her?'

'No, but the woman my aunt lives with was in the missions.
She often talks about her. Edwina Crane.'

'That's her. Edwina Crane. A funny old bird. She'd been
around for years but no one knew her at all well except I suppose
the Indian children in the schools. If she had any friends they
were Indians and half-castes. So it was ironic, because she was
the first person from Mayapore to get hurt in the August riots.
She was on her way back from a place called Dibrapur with an
Indian teacher. A mob stopped them and murdered the teacher,
beat her up and burned her car out. We had her in hospital the
evening all that other business happened in the Bibighar. She'd
been found sitting on the roadside in the pouring rain holding
the dead Indian's hand. You couldn't get much out of her. She
was half-delirious when I saw her and couldn't remember anything. When she got better I think she was already off her head.
Melancholia. I heard she'd resigned from the mission and wasn't
seeing anybody. Then she did this dramatic thing, dressed herself
in Indian clothes, locked herself in a shed in her garden and
burnt herself to death. A symbolic act, I suppose. She must have
felt the India she knew had died, so like a good widow she made
a funeral pyre. I had to go along there, poke about among her
things, and question her old servant. There wasn't much to find,
she hadn't left a note. But in a chest I turned up an old picture
of Queen Victoria receiving tribute, a very stylized thing, with
the old lady sitting on a throne under clouds and angels, and
Indians of all kinds gathering round her like children. *Man-bap*.
I am your father and mother. And in another place I found the
little plate that had been taken off the frame. The picture must
have been a gift in recognition of some special service years
before. It went something like, To Edwina Crane, for her
courage. The mission was in Muzzafirabad. Oh and it dated back
years – I think before the First World War. But sitting there with
Teddie made it all seem to connect, I mean connect what she
had done all that time ago in Muzzafirabad and what he had just
done, or tried to do. And then there was the other similarity –
death by fire.'

He smiled at her. 'I think that made me feel – what you said. I mean for a moment there I was an amateur myself. I fell for it, really fell for it, the whole thing, the idea that there really was this possibility. Devotion. Sacrifice. Self-denial. A cause, an obligation. A code of conduct, a sort of final moral definition, I mean definition of us, what we're here for – people living among each other, in an environment some sort of God created. The whole impossible nonsensical dream.'

She waited. He had turned his head away again and when the silence continued unbroken the notion that he could have fallen asleep exhausted, nudged – but did not dislodge – the firmer belief she had that everything he said and did was rooted in acute awareness of himself as someone central to an occasion. And suddenly she had a vivid image of him on the platform of Mirat cantonment station, central to an earlier occasion that had been well marked by victims, although on that day, the day of the wedding, only the woman in the white saree had actually been present. But it was the significance of that lonely supplication that now struck her, for the first time, and re-created Bibighar in her mind as an occasion that continued, could not be ruled off as over, done with. Always, before, she had seen the white-clad figure as representative of an old misfortune that had left its mark; a sadness in a stranger's heart, an unknown and so unrecognizable grief; and it was only now, observing the faced-away figure of the man the woman had approached as if he were someone capable of granting an alleviation, that she understood the continuing nature of the misfortune, realized that the boy whom the woman pleaded for must, then at least, still have been paying a price, however far distant away in time had been the occasion of his fault, if there had ever been fault.

A new disturbing element of uncertainty stirred her. It caused her to press again with her feet on the floor and with the small of her back into the uncomfortable upright chair, so powerful was that sensation of not wishing to be drawn towards that central point of reference that was in Merrick, that *was* Merrick. She felt deprived of speech and then saw that this was a protection. Briefly she was adjured to silence by an exquisite tautening of nerves that promised, if only they could snap, to leave her vividly possessed by an absolute, an exemplary, understanding of what had been only partially revealed to her by that incident on the station.

But the moment passed. She was still possessed merely by unanswered questions. What was new and disturbing apart from her realization that the boy had still been paying for his fault, was the shadow of permanent misfortune she saw as fallen on him with the girl's death. Had the girl before, or her aunt since, attempted to reduce the price he paid, might still be paying? Or had a net enclosed him, so subtly, irrevocably, that nothing they could try to do would help? And was Merrick alone responsible for that? Was it these victims, not Teddie, who now lay like a weight on that conscience of his which he said he could examine but give a clean bill to? Perhaps that was the way in to him, to become his victim and then to haunt his conscience. But if so, it seemed to her that it was an approach without access at the end. There was, for some reason, no way into him at all, and all the people whom he chose as victims lay scattered on his threshold.

She thought: You are, yes, our dark side, the arcane side. You reveal something that is sad about us, as if out here we had built a mansion without doors and windows, with no way in and no way out. All India lies on our doorstep and cannot enter to warm us or be warmed. We live in holes and crevices of the crumbling stone, no longer sheltered by the carapace of our history which is leaving us behind. And one day we shall lie exposed, in our tender skins. You, as well as us.

It was extraordinary how like each other they were, and at the same time rigidly divided by an antagonism she believed was mutual. She could not bear the thought of this man clinging through a god-relationship to the family she loved, honoured, felt a strange irritated anguish for. He would, through that relationship, attach himself like lichen to a wall, the crumbling stone of the blind house that was doomed to become a ruin. At least, she cried to herself, let it be as noble a ruin as it can; and then laughed at her absurd pride, the fastidious distaste of this Colonel's daughter for a man she had decided, for no clear reason, she could not trust. And there was this problem too: that she had given her word to Susan that she would ask him.

She opened her mouth, but could not say it. She spoke the first words that came into her head.

'Did you ever know old Lady Manners, as well as her niece?'

And then remembered Aunt Fenny had already asked him that, the day of the wedding, and been told he didn't.

He turned his head towards her.

'No. Why?'

'I thought you might have. She's in Pankot.'

'Oh?' He waited. She did not explain. 'Is she well?'

'We don't know. None of us has actually seen her.' Did he look relieved? 'She signed the book at Flagstaff House.'

'Does she still have the child?'

'We don't know that either.'

'I see. Is Pankot such a large place, then?'

'She must be living on the west side. The Indian side. It's rather a mystery, why she signed the book.' She wondered what he would say if she told him now the story of what she had done in Srinagar. The white ward seemed full of shadows and echoes of departed voices. 'Incidentally,' she heard herself say, 'talking about children, before I go, I have a question from Susan,' and hesitated, struggling again with her reluctance and her sense of duty. 'She wonders whether you'd like to be one of the god-fathers.' She knew her voice was flattened by a cold formality. The same lack of enthusiasm must show in her face. Guilt pricked her. She might just as well have left the duty unperformed as perform it so badly.

'How very kind of her,' he said. He glanced away as if to turn the possibility over in his mind. She wondered if he felt the dead weight that had descended, the weight of the right-thing, like a stone pressing them down, sapping their strength. With one simple remark he threw the weight off. 'But in all the circum-stances it wouldn't be suitable, would it?' His glance returned, penetrating, implacable. She knew relief, felt only a small re-morse. She was at a loss to understand what it was about him that so appalled her.

'Are you to be godmother?'

She nodded.

He smiled faintly. She noted for the first time what it was that was so unusual about the blueness of his eyes. It was a blueness she realized she associated with the eyes of dolls: a demanding but unseeing blue, incapable either of acceptance or rejection. If the pillows were taken away, if he were lain flat, would they close and be incapable of opening until with inquisitive fingers you swung the delicately balanced lids up for a glimpse of those little mirrors with their grave but startling illusion of response?

'Well,' he said, 'you don't believe in it either, do you? But tell her – tell her I was touched and very grateful.'

'Is your not believing in it the only reason?'

She was denied an answer. The door swung open. 'I'm sorry, Miss Layton,' Sister Prior said, advancing towards the bed – trim, capable and asexually attractive – 'I'm told your uncle's come to fetch you. I'm afraid I wasn't able to let him up. Fact is I'm going to turn you out. How are we?'

'We are well,' Merrick said.

'Are you sure my uncle's here? It wasn't arranged.'

'Quite sure. Unless there are two Colonel Graces.'

'I think there's only one. I'll say goodbye, then, Ronald. I expect Aunt Fenny will be round in a day or two. Is there anything special you'd like her to bring you?'

'I don't think they're on the market.'

'What's that?'

'Nothing. Just my little joke. And thank you. Thank you for coming.'

'I'll ring tomorrow before I leave.'

'Well,' Sister Prior interrupted, 'tomorrow won't be at all a good day to ring us, will it, Captain Merrick?'

'No, Sister Prior. I suppose it won't.'

'The day after,' Sister Prior suggested.

'I shall be in Pankot the day after – I thought of ringing before I left.'

'Oh well, your uncle can keep in touch. I'm sorry to hustle you, but we have our little duties.'

Sarah laughed. Sister Prior in the ward, in front of her patient, was quite a different person from the one in the waiting-room. She did not like either, but preferred the bitterness to the professional coyness. She turned to Merrick.

'I'll write to you from Pankot.'

'Will you?'

The reply, meant – she believed – to shatter her, seemed to bounce off her. Never before had she been so conscious of the thickness of skin that was part of her inheritance. But consciousness of it at once began to thin it down. He had not meant, perhaps, to remind her of the earlier unkept promise, but had spoken involuntarily, out of genuine hope but lack of real expectation.

'Of course,' she said and then, determinedly, subtly stressing his Christian name because as yet he had not called her Sarah, she ended, 'Goodbye, Ronald.'

'Goodbye,' he said. For an instant there was a repetition of that difficulty with the throat. 'Goodbye,' he said again, and closed his eyes, as if he knew he had been played with long enough.

In the corridor Sister Prior said, 'He's marvellous, isn't he? You simply wouldn't know he's constantly in pain. He fights taking drugs. Is he a religious man?'

'Religious? No, I don't think so.'

'I ask because there are sects that think pain is something you have to bear. With Ronald we have to get up to all sorts of tricks. But the odd thing is him thinking he's not been drugged has the effect you'd expect if he actually wasn't.'

Sister Prior pressed the button to summon the lift. The Bengal sky beyond the window of the waiting-alcove was sodden with rain and cloud and evening. Below, waiting, was Uncle Arthur on whom fortune had smiled at last.

'Of course,' Sister Prior was saying – and this, surely, was a third persona? – the talkative, informed and uniformed bouncer? – 'it's all to the good that he's not over-dependent. He'll come through tomorrow that much better.'

The lift arrived. Sister Prior waited while the attendant clanged back the gates. Entering, Sarah placed her hand so that the gates should not be shut and the descent begin, and it all be over without having come to its logical end.

'I'm sorry,' she said, 'but we know nothing and he wouldn't say.'

'Oh, I realized that. And you ought to know, oughtn't you? The left arm.'

'The left arm?'

'They took the hand off in Comilla. Tomorrow we have to take off from just above the elbow. Third degree burns and a bullet in the upper arm and one in the forearm. The right arm's a mess too, but we can save that. His face will be scarred for life but his hair will grow again, of course. He might even look human without the bandages.'

As if stung Sarah removed her hand from the gates and Sister Prior took her opportunity and slammed them shut. The lift lurched and began to go down. You bitch, she shouted silently. You bloody, bloody bitch. And wondered, presently (as the lift arrived and she smiled automatically in reply to fat old Uncle Arthur's brick-red grin behind the mesh – strayed like a Cheshire cat into the infirm and unstable world of suffering), whether she meant herself or Sister Prior.

IV

'We've gone in,' Uncle Arthur had said. 'We landed in Normandy this morning and established a beachhead. Your mother will be bucked, won't she? I'd lay odds on your father being home by Christmas. We thought we'd have a special drink to that.'

In the vestibule, watched by the sergeant and the orderly with pimples, he introduced her to the officer he had brought with him – one of the men, she imagined, who was to enjoy or suffer dinner with the course leader and his wife and whose evening was probably further disorientated by being asked to help collect the niece who had visited a patient in the military hospital.

'This is Major Clark. For some reason that utterly escapes me I think he's sometimes known as Nobby. He was only a Captain a couple of months ago when he had to sit and suffer my interminable spouting. Decent of him to come back and visit us. My niece Sarah Layton. Be a good fellow and whistle the driver up.'

As Clark went out into the porticoed entrance she was aware of a broadness of back, a compactness of body, a physical wholeness. No burns, no bullets, no severance.

'How was young what's-his-name?'

'All right. Considering.'

'Good. Tell us all about it presently. I rang your aunt from the daftar. She said to see if I could pick you up. She's wondering if she should ring your mother.'

'Why should she do that?'

'To make sure she's heard.'

'Heard what?'

'The good news. But she's bound to have. I say, are you all right?'

'Yes, thank you.' She smiled. Her face felt made of elastic.

'It's these places. The smell gets on your tummy. Come on, the gharry's here.'

The gharry was Uncle Arthur's staff car. Clark saw them into the back and sat himself next to the driver. As they turned into the road the rain fell. Lightning scarred the horizon.

'When are you off then?' Uncle Arthur inquired, raising his voice to be heard above the sluicing rain and the long, trundling, skittle-ball rolls of converging thunder. But it was Clark he'd spoken to.

'First thing in the morning.'

Clark sat with one arm along the back of the seat, his back wedged in the corner of the seat and the door, so that he could talk and be talked to, see and be seen. Vaguely she registered the voice, the intonation, the air of ease, the appraisal she was under. She looked out of the window, scarcely listened to their conversation. They came out into Chowringhee, a place of lights and bicycles and trains. The window was misting up. The city lights hastened the approaching dark. With the edge of her palm she cleared a view for herself and felt like a child intent on observing, from a position of safety and comfort, an alien and dangerous magic.

'Well, what d'you think of the second city of the Empire?' Uncle Arthur asked. 'It's her first visit,' he explained, not waiting for an answer, something she usually thought of as a failing in other people but as a virtue in him. His lack of curiosity had always made him easy to get on with. It was, she supposed, a wholly avuncular virtue, common to that species. She thought that in its unpossessive uninvolved affection there might be felt something of the granite-rock of always available love. Should she weep – and for a few seconds, alarmingly, she felt like doing so – he would be desperately embarrassed but inarticulately sound, a speechless comfort. 'You should have been here a couple of months ago. Major Clark would have shown you the ins and outs. Wouldn't you?'

'Would I, sir?'

'Well, dammit, Clark, you had a reputation. I doubt he ever got to bed before dawn. But no one would have guessed. Always looked as fresh as a daisy.'

She glanced at Uncle Arthur, realized he had already had

a sundowner to celebrate that distant inaudible barrage of invasion, or had not quite recovered from a sumptuous lunch; and, catching Clark's eye, saw his judgment or knowledge corresponded with her own. There was, on his rather ugly face, an opacity, a semi-revelation of vanity and of amusement at someone else's expense which she did not understand and did not like. She thought of herself as pinned by its calculated directness. And looked back at the streaming window, burning with a ludicrous little sense of injustice that he should exist, unmarked, to pass silent comments on Uncle Arthur who seemed to find him engaging and anyway gave him lifts and invitations, good counsel and reports presumably; carried him into the circle of her safety that rested for the moment in the existence of Aunt Fenny in Calcutta; and there, in Pankot, dark, silent and undisturbed by rain or rumours of war and amputation – in Susan and her mother – and far, far away, beyond the streaming window, in the still centre of her father's patience and yearning for release and a quiet passage through the night.

She had not recognized the road. The driver's turn into the forecourt of the apartments was unexpected. She felt the curious flattening of inquiring spirit the traveller suffers from, knowing himself without occupation or investment in the fortunes of a strange city. Sandwiched between Uncle Arthur and Major Clark (who, she noted, smelt of some aromatic substance, an aggressive exudation of his naked body beneath the thin cellular cotton of his khaki bush-shirt) she thought of the lift as taking her from one level of non-experience to another. It came to her that like Ronald Merrick she did not travel well, and then that she was whole and, unlike Susan, unbeholden. I do not, she thought, no I do not, give a damn. The Furies were riding across an uninhabited sky, to their own and no one else's destruction. The real world was a tame, repetitious place: one part of it, when you really looked, was much like another, a chemical accident, a mine of raw material for the creation of random artefacts to house and warm or satisfy the need for sensual pleasure or creature comfort. The lift was one such. It jerked to a stop.

'No, a drink first and a bath second,' she told Aunt Fenny who was abroad in the flat in housecoat, slippers and tidy chiffon turban, midway in her preparations for the evening: a revelation to Major Clark of intimate domestic detail which Sarah put down as a further sign that Aunt Fenny had entered the new age, in which old Flagstaff House values were shrewdly to be readjusted as an insurance against the extinction of those who had held them. Gimlet and cigarette in hand and for a moment alone, Sarah was conscious of belonging to a class engaged in small, continual acts whose purpose was survival through partial sharing in an evolution which, of all the family, only Aunt Lydia back in Bayswater had anticipated and closely witnessed the process of. It was a survival of exiles. Their enemy was light, not dark, the light of their own kind, of their own people at home from whom they had been too long cut off so that, returning there briefly, a deep and holy silence wrapped them and caused them to observe what was real as miniature. In India they had been betrayed by an illusion of topographical vastness into sins of pride that were foreign to their insular, pygmy natures. From the high window of this concrete monstrosity you could see the tragedy and the comic grandeur of tin-pot roofs, disguised at street level by those neo-classical façades which perversely illustrated the vanished age of reason. What reason? My history (Sarah thought, drinking her sweet gimlet, then drawing on her bitter cigarette), my history, rendered down to a colonnaded front, an architectural perfection of form and balance in the set and size of a window, and to a smoky resentment in my blood, a foolish contrivance for happiness in my heart against the evidence that tells me I never have been happy and can't be while I live here. It's time we were gone. Gone. Every last wise, stupid, cruel, fond or foolish one of us.

She turned from contemplation of the rooftops, aroused by the sounds of more of Uncle Arthur's chaps arriving – among whom she sensed the presence of the next generation of her jailers. To avoid immediate confrontation she brushed past Major Clark who had been standing there as if about to speak and told Aunt Fenny – who was giving orders to the white-clad servant – that she'd finish her drink in the bath.

'I'll come in while you're dressing. I want to hear everything,' Fenny said. 'I've only got to slip into something and I'm ready. Have you anything pretty to wear? Iris Braithwaite from downstairs hopes to come, and perhaps Dora Pedley. They're always got up to kill. But the little party's for you, pet. Afterwards the boys will probably take you dancing or to the flicks, so do your

best –' this last in almost a whisper, on the threshold of Sarah's
room whose door she held open.

'Well I can't do more than my best, Aunt Fenny.'

'My dear, I'd forgotten. You look done up. Was it bad?'

'They're cutting off his arm.'

'Oh, no.'

The bath was already drawn. She rang the bell and, when he
answered, gave her glass to the bearer and told him to bring it
back refilled. She shivered in the bleak atmosphere of the air-
conditioned room, gratefully entered the steam and humidity of
the bathroom to undress in more familiar discomfort. Naked,
she put on her shabby bathrobe and felt caressed, but stubborn
in her refusal to succumb to a small passion for personal belong-
ings. For a minute or so, back in the ice-box of the bedroom,
she sat, smoked, combed out her hopeless hair and drank the
second gimlet, smoothed cleansing cream on to her incorruptible Layton face. So uncomely was it (in her eyes) that a wave of
pity for it released a succeeding wave of erotic desire to have it
loved, it and all her body – untouched beneath the robe Barbie
Batchelor had helped her choose the sensible material for. She
went and lay in the bath, the tumbler on its edge, within reach,
and wondered what else might be in reach.

No, I don't, she repeated, I don't give a damn. But knew she
did. Even for Aziz Khan and Fariqua Khan for whose names she
had already conjured faces, and – considering them now, their
staring eyes and speechless open mouths (as if aghast at the
injustice of no more than condign punishment) – she formulated
questions: *Why really did Teddie interfere? What made him so
anxious to be present when Ronald Merrick tried to get information out
of captured Indian soldiers? Had he witnessed an earlier interrogation?
Or was it merely, as Merrick seemed to suggest, because he had grown
not to trust him over anything?* When the water had cooled below
the point of comfort she got out, wrapped herself in one of Aunt
Fenny's new-age towels – which was as big as a tent, as soft as
down, fit only for a woman in love – and dried herself quickly
as if to avoid contamination; but remained swathed for a few
moments longer before substituting the shabby robe that had
strayed with her from shabby Pankot.

The air-conditioning enveloped her as she passed from bathroom to bedroom. She felt like a clinical specimen captured and

cosseted for some kind of experiment which Aunt Fenny, who knocked and entered, had already undergone and emerged from triumphantly, qualified to conduct on others.

'I've brought nothing long,' Sarah said. Fenny had on an emerald-green dinner gown.

'It doesn't matter. Mrs Braithwaite's just phoned to say Iris has gippy-tum and since they're over at the Pedleys it means Dora won't come either. So, pet, you'll be the only pebble on the beach. Now tell me about poor Mr Merrick.'

Sarah told her as much as it was necessary for her to know. When she had finished Fenny said, 'Why not stay a day or two longer? I mean if you could stand it. I'm sure it would cheer him up to see you again. He won't want to be bothered by me. Besides, I never know what to say to people in a bad way. I don't think I could. I've always been a terrible coward about illness. Arthur says that when he has only a cold even, I act as if I don't love him any more. I can't explain it but other people's physical troubles seem to strike me dumb. If you stay on a day or two and see him over the worst I promise I'll really put the red carpet out for him afterwards. I'm good at jollying people along.'

'Why?' Sarah exclaimed, pausing in the midst of applying foundation cream. 'Why should there be a red carpet? Why should we start getting involved at all?'

Aunt Fenny's face, reflected behind her own in the mirror, looked momentarily blank.

'Well, pet, you know the answer better than I do, I imagine. It's you who came all the way down here to see him.'

'For Susan.'

Fenny smiled. 'Only for Susan?'

'Yes.'

'Are you sure?'

'Yes, I'm sure. Why?'

'Well, he was awfully attentive in Mirat. I thought you might be a bit gone on him.'

'How could I be? He's not our class.'

The irony, she saw, was lost on Fenny.

'No. But he's made something of himself and that sort of thing doesn't matter like it used to, does it? I mean people say it's what a man does and is in himself that counts and I think that's true.'

'Am I really so unattractive, Aunty? A board-school boy with a brain and a gentlemanly veneer, and only one arm? Couldn't I do better than that?'

'Oh, Sarah.' Fenny flushed. 'Well, I was only thinking of you being happy. I thought you might be attracted to him and trying to hide your feelings because of what the rest of us might say. None of the things that are against him would matter to me if you did love him. I'd back you up, honestly, right to the hilt. So do you? Do you, pet?'

'As a matter of fact he appals me.' She finished her unreward-ing work with the cosmetic, stared at her own face and at the reflection of poor Aunt Fenny's which now seemed as bereft as her own. 'And it would be wrong to run away with the idea that he liked Teddie, by the way.'

After a bit Fenny said, 'I shan't ask you why you say that. I'll just accept it. But I will ask you this. I've wanted to for ages. Were you in love with Teddie? Did it hurt to lose him to Susan?'

'No. I wasn't in love with Teddie either.' She got up from the stool and went to the white-painted fitted wardrobe, took out the dress she had brought as best. Its absurd nice-young-girl look touched nerves that caused alternate chills of irritation and desolation. Removing the robe and standing for a few seconds in her underwear, acutely self-conscious under Fenny's appraisal of her figure, she put the dress on, hastily but reluctantly, like some kind of outgrown but necessary disguise that fooled nobody any longer. She recalled, from somewhere, but did not immediately connect it to the day of the wedding, taking a dress off and feeling she had entered an area of light. Dealing deftly with the simple buttons and the hook and eye of the kind she always chose – on the large side because she had no patience and seldom any help – she said, 'You see, Aunt Fenny, I don't know what it means when people use that word. But thanks for worry-ing about me. Just don't, that's all. I've met men I'm attracted to and some of them have been attracted back. That's simple enough. But this other thing, love, love, that's never happened. If it has I never knew it, so it must be over-rated. It must be a bit of a sell.'

'Well,' Fenny said, more brightly, 'that's all right then, isn't it? You've got it all to come. One thing's absolutely certain. You won't be in love and not know it.'

'Did you know it, Aunt Fenny? Did you?'

Fenny's smile contracted, but did not disappear.

'Several times I thought I did, once I knew.'

'You were lucky, then.'

'No, pet. Not lucky. It wasn't Arthur.'

'I'm sorry.'

'No you must never be sorry. No, never. Ninety-nine per cent of life is compromise. It's part of the contract. I've been perfectly happy. I won't say content. Contentment's a different thing. I think I've reached the stage where I could honestly say if I didn't still think of myself as a young woman, well, I *am*, that I've had a good life. Nothing marvellous has ever happened to me, but nothing bad either. I don't suppose I've done a great deal of good anywhere but I hope no one could say I've ever done any real harm. When I pop off there won't be a thing you could put your finger on to prove, you know, that I'd done more than earn my keep. It's not much, but even that takes a bit of doing, and it's about the most the majority of us can expect of ourselves.'

'I know.'

'Well, smile for me to show that you do.'

Sarah smiled.

'And if you come here I'll tell you my secret.' Sarah went. She sat on the bed and suffered the warm weight of Aunt Fenny's well-nourished hand on her own chill bony arm. 'It's not a secret to your mother. Has she never told you?' Sarah shook her head. 'I'm not surprised. Families are funny things. They have far more secrets from each other than you'd think likely, don't they? We know a lot about our friends, but not much about our kith and kin.' She paused, but she was still smiling. She said, 'The secret is that I adored your father.'

'My father?'

'But adored him. Not from afar, either, but he only had eyes for Millie. He thought me silly and empty-headed, a terrible little flirt and never took me the least bit seriously. He still doesn't. If I said to him now, John, do you know I loved you madly, he'd think it was a joke because he never noticed then and has never noticed since. In fact only Millie noticed and even she's forgotten just *what* she noticed. So have I, in a way, you know, in the way you do when it's all so long ago. But you see, pet, even now, I mean but even now, perhaps especially now, because it's ages since I've seen him, if he walked into this room my heart would take a funny little turn. Just for a second. Then, bump, back to reality because there never was and couldn't be anything between us. If there had been, if he'd felt the same, well even if we'd never married I'd never be able to say as I do that nothing marvellous has ever happened to me, but he didn't, so it wasn't marvellous. But it was this thing you say you don't know about, and it's not just physical attraction. And if it ever happens to you, you mark my words, you'll jolly well know.'

Sarah, who had stared for a while at her own clasped hands, glanced up. She found it difficult to take her aunt as seriously as she probably deserved. Like Sarah's mother and father, Fenny belonged to a generation of men and women – the last one there might ever be – who seemed to have been warmed in their formative years by the virtues of self-assurance and moral certainty; what, she supposed, she used to think of as a perpetual light, one that shone (thinking of Aunt Lydia) on their radical as well as conservative notions of what one was in the world to do. And weren't these things illusion of a kind? And this love, which Fenny said was not just physical attraction, an illusion too? Sex she understood, and even a grand passion because that, presumably, was a compound of physical desire, envy, jealousy and possessiveness. But love of the kind Fenny had described, the kind she herself and no doubt Susan had grown up to believe in as right and acceptable, now seemed to her like one more standard of human behaviour that needed that same climate of self-assurance and moral certainty in which to flourish; like all the other flowers of modest, quiet perfection which Susan had imagined grew on the other side of the wall, in the secret garden.

'Susan –' she began.

'What about Susan, pet?' Then, like Uncle Arthur, without waiting: 'I was thinking of Susan, too, of when we saw her and Teddie off at the station on their way to Nanoora.'

'Were you? Why, Auntie?'

'Because of a similar occasion, when we saw your father and mother off on *their* honeymoon. I coped with it awfully well. Later there was a family joke about it. They said I was so busy being the centre of attraction for all the young officers who came down to wave them off that I hardly had time to wave to them myself. In Mirat I watched you so closely, pet, because it brought it all back to me. I knew something had made you unhappy and I wondered if you were feeling the same about Susan whisking Teddie away as I felt about Millie whisking John. You looked so sad.'

'I wasn't sad.'

'Truly?'

'Truly.'

'Then everything's all right. Now.' A squeeze of the arm. 'Finish making yourself look pretty and come in as soon as you can. And do think over what I said. I mean about staying for a bit, just so that you can enjoy yourself, and meet a few new faces. I'm sure General Rankin will turn a blind eye to a few days' absence, and your mother can do without you very well. Just for once. Heaven knows when the baby comes you'll all be at sixes and sevens, so take advantage now, pet.' She hesitated. 'I know it's been difficult, for *many* reasons. In the old days coming out to India was a tremendous lark. All you've had is this dreary war and – what it's done to people.' People like my mother, you mean, Sarah thought. 'When your father gets home and realizes how much you've done to help your mother and Su, he'll be very proud of you, but awfully upset to know how little fun you've had.'

As if on cue the silence beyond the closed door was broken by a peal of men's laughter. Her aunt made a funny face. 'There you are,' she said. 'If you leave them too long they start telling each other horrid stories. Men simply aren't serious creatures at all, they make a joke of everything. I'd better go and keep them in order. What a shame Jimmy Clark's only here until tomorrow, he was one of Arthur's most promising chaps on the course and is such a nice man, but then he was at your father's old school. They're sending him down to do some special training in something rather hush-hush in Ceylon. He's only thirty but Arthur says he'll probably end up a lieutenant-colonel if the war goes on another year, which it probably won't. He got an emergency commission but we think he's the kind of man who may want to stay on in the army either here or at home. Incidentally, he's been asking all about you.'

Fenny rose, gave Sarah what was meant as a reassuring pat. Sarah smiled up at her, feeling it incumbent on her to remain where she was, like a tense little chrysalis from which – in the

ten or fifteen minutes of privacy that were left to her and
encouraged by homilies and the dutiful desire to shake off all
those dark and gloomy images of the world as a repository only
of occasions and conditions of despair – she would emerge as the
tough little butterfly of Aunt Fenny's affectionate imagination.

'No,' Aunt Fenny said, 'tonight the ladies will *not* withdraw. At
least not for more than a few minutes. There are only two of us
and frankly, Arthur, the walls in this flat are too thin for mutual
comfort.' The chaps, cheered by cocktails, an Anglo-Indian
curry, two bottles of South African hock and the expectation of
brandy or liqueurs, laughed dutifully. There were six of them,
including Jimmy Clark who sat on Sarah's right. On her left, at
the head of the table, was her Uncle Arthur, deep in but chin
above his cups. Opposite her, on Uncle Arthur's left, was a pale-
faced young officer with a lick of hair who had begun the
evening with what she had detected as intellectual reservations
but who was now, long before its ending, apparently entranced
and well on his way to what she knew men called being as pissed
as a newt. Why a newt? She had kept newts one summer at
Grandfather's, in a deep square blue Mackintosh's toffee tin and
all she could recall was that the water turned sallow and the
newts had died. Perhaps that was it. Sallowness, and death by
drowning, like Mr Morland in his dream.

   'We'll all withdraw and meet next door for coffee and what's-
it. Have you boys decided how you'll finish up this evening?
There's Ingrid Bergman and Gary Cooper at the New Empire.'

   'Send not,' the pale young officer intoned, 'to ask for whom
the bell tolls. It tolls for thee. I've seen it, it's rotten.'

   'And unless you've booked there isn't a chance,' another
man said.

   'Well, Arthur and I are going on to the Purvises,' Fenny
announced. 'We thought you young people might make up a
party of your own. I'm sorry Iris and Dora couldn't come because
then you might have preferred to stay here and dance to the
gramophone. There's plenty to drink and bits to eat if you get
peckish later, so do stay if you'd prefer to, or all go out somewhere.
You can talk it over with coffee. It'll be in in just a few minutes.'

   Catching Sarah's eye she nodded and rose. Noisily they
followed suit. Major Clark helped Sarah with her chair.

In the living-room Fenny said, 'The thing is, pet, just to fall in with what they decide and not express a preference. Men much prefer the helpless happy type. My bet is they'll plump for the Grand Hotel. It's an officers' hostel these days and they feel at home there. They might mix in with another party. Don't be too put out or standoffish if you find yourself in a gang that includes chichis. Boys like these from home think we treat girls like that awfully badly, and perhaps we do. They laugh at them too, but feel sorry for them, and can't bear it when English girls turn up their noses. But you're not like that, pet, are you? You'll have a lovely time. It's quite a thing for them to *have* an English girl, and they'll adore just being seen there turning up with you. And, pet, there's safety in numbers. Well, listen to me. Birds and bees. I shan't start worrying about you until long after midnight. Jimmy Clark will look after you. He'll know exactly why I put him next to you.'

'Who are the Purvises?'

'Oh just some rather dreary civil types Arthur has to keep in with. They're having a bridge party – Indians, not cards – and want to muster forces for after dinner when it gets tense and embarrassing because everybody's said everything twice.'

'I've never been to a bridge party.'

'Think yourself lucky. It's part of the price you pay when you get posted to a place like this. Let's powder our noses and get moving with the coffee. Some of them *need* it.' She hesitated, apparently struck by a conscientious thought. 'Oh dear. Ought I to let you? I *am* responsible for you to your mother, aren't I?'

'I've been out with tipsy boys before.'

'But it's different here. Calcutta's not Pankot and some of them are tipsy already. Well, one of them is.'

'I don't think we need worry about him.'

Fenny stared at her. A slight flush came and went. 'Don't we? Heavens.' She smiled. 'What can you know about such things? Well, anyway. Come on. Powder noses and into the breach.'

The Purvises' bridge party was an official affair so Aunt Fenny and Uncle Arthur used the staff car. They dropped Sarah and Major Clark at the entrance to the Grand Hotel. A following taxi brought the five others. Between the departure of car and arrival of taxi, Clark – shooing away small boys and bent beggars

– said, 'Be sure to tell me the moment you've had enough. It
can get pretty rackety in here. It may not be quite up your
street.'

'Oh, I don't know. Why not?'

'Well, I should say rather, it's not much up mine.'

'That didn't seem to be Uncle Arthur's impression earlier.'

'No.' She felt him glance down at her – not far down; he
wasn't tall. She caught sight of the taxi that was bringing the
others. 'It wouldn't be the first wrong one he's had. Let's go in.
It's a hell of a long walk. They'll soon catch up.'

The long walk was through a shopping arcade. At the end of
it was the reception hall. Near by a band thumped; a sound
Susan once described as only a degree or so less fascinating than
the sound of men *en masse*, waiting in the ante-room of a mess
for you to arrive on ladies' night. Bands attracted Sarah too,
but hearing this one prodded her alive to the fact that under a
wakeful surface, artificially stimulated by plenty to drink and
too much chatter, she was exhausted. Was it only yesterday at
this time that the train had left Ranpur? She smiled cheerfully
at the other five, as they came up, and went in the midst of
them through a lounge full of wicker chairs and tables, every
one occupied, predominantly by men in uniform, and out on
to a broad terrace where a band played to an almost empty
floor, under a temporary rainy-season roof. In the dry, presumably, you could dance under the stars. Bearers moved tables
together and arranged chairs. About to sit she felt herself held.

Clark said, 'I only dance where there's plenty of room and
other people can see, so now's your chance.' He took her on
to the floor. A quick-step. An over-familiar tune. Susan would
know its name. For the first few moments she felt a pleasure at
discovering he danced well and that she could follow. But after
one and a half circuits of the floor the old problem arose. She
had never been much good at talking and dancing together. The
two duties seemed incompatible. She tried to recall what questions she had asked him at dinner. Not many. Dinner had centred
mainly on conversation dominated by Uncle Arthur. She said
the first thing that came into her head.

'Aunt Fenny tells me you were at Chillingborough.'

He nodded. They were not dancing close, but the realization
that he never took his eyes off her was almost as inhibiting as

that over-close proximity men occasionally attempted and sometimes embarrassingly established.

'It's Daddy's old school,' she said.

'I know. I hope he survived the experience.'

'Yes, I think so.' She did not know what else to say.

'Good, I survived it too.'

A turn or so.

'Have you been in India long?'

'Six months.'

She wondered whether to him that was a short or long time. 'Aunt Fenny said you were in the desert.'

'Mostly a euphemism for Cairo. But yes, I was for a time in what's called the desert.' A pause. 'Shall I ask the questions now and give you a rest?' She glanced up. His smile was remote. His skin, close to, had a coarseness of texture which she felt she ought to dislike, but didn't. 'How was your boy-friend?'

'My boy-friend?'

'The chap you took goodies to.'

But just then the band stopped on an up-beat and a clash of cymbals.

He shepherded her to the table. A bearer was unloading glasses and bottles from a tray. Only three of the five other men were sitting there.

'Isn't it on the early side for dropping out?' Clark asked. The one with a blond moustache said, 'No one's dropped out.' The others agreed. She thought: They don't like Clark: and re-collected that he was a stranger to them. Perhaps they assumed from Clark's proprietary attitude that his earlier connection with Colonel and Mrs Grace was of a more intimate kind than their own and gave him rights in her which her aunt and uncle accorded formal recognition. It might not even be obvious to them that until today she and Clark had never met. She felt like saying something that would make the position clear, and was conscience-stricken by the fact that in spite of introduc-tions she was uncertain of their names. To the blond mous-tached one who asked her what she would drink (Freddie? She would have to listen more closely) she said, 'Do you get kicked out if you only want coffee?' He said something about letting them try and coffee it was but what about having something with it, for instance a sticky green? To please him she agreed before the penny dropped that he meant *crème de menthe*. The order was given, the music started up and Freddie (or was he Tony? Why were men so often called by their diminutives?) said 'May I?' and was on his feet as if he had recognized his possible sole opportunity. She responded automatically and was in his arms, waltzing, before she admitted to herself that dancing with the blond-moustached man was the last thing she had wanted to do. She had noticed the heavy perspiration while sitting at the table. Mercifully he kept his distance, but his hands were wet. Susan said heavy sweat was the sign of a beer drinker which was why British Other Ranks perspired worse than officers.

'Mrs Grace told me you've come miles to visit someone at the BMH.'

'Well, just from Pankot.'

'Where's that?'

She told him.

'I was there myself last month. The BMH I mean, not Pankot. Nothing romantic though. Appendix. These days they give you a spinal. Interesting looking up at the ceiling and sort of half feeling it all going on.'

'It must have been awful.'

'Oh, I don't know. Interesting. Looking up at the ceiling.'

She felt for him. Obviously he found dancing and talking incompatible too. She came out with it. 'I've met so many people tonight I've got the names mixed up.'

'Leonard.'

'Mine's Sarah.'

'I know. Just now I nearly made an awful bloomer. At home I've got a Labrador dog called Sarah. Well, I mean she's a she-dog. I nearly said, like you do when you're thinking of something to say, "I've got a dog named after you." I stopped myself in time but then my mind went blank.' Their ankles made fleeting contact. 'Sorry.'

She smiled. 'Where's home?'

'Shropshire. I'm a Shropshire lad. There are poems about it, but I've never read them.'

'What are you, a farmer?'

'How did you guess?'

An image of Mr Birtwhistle's fields and Mr Birtwhistle's

cows imposed itself behind Leonard's corn-stook hair and fiery, dripping face.

'I'm not really a farmer though. My father is.'

'It's a reserved occupation, isn't it?'

'Could be. But I'd only just gone in with him, and Dad's not so old. He's got Italian prisoners working for him. Says they're all right. I'm not missed. Well, not for that.'

'Will you go back to farming?'

'Expect so.' A pause. 'Your uncle makes India sound fascinating, though,' he added dutifully. They exchanged rather solemn glances. 'I suppose,' he said, 'you've lived here most of your life.'

'I went home to school. It works out about half and half.'

'Would you recommend it? Living in India?'

'Why, are you thinking about it?'

'Well, it sounds all right, responsible job, lots of servants. Your uncle says it will be years before the Indians can do without us entirely. Up in the Punjab I went round one of those experimental agricultural stations and I thought then there's a job I could do. A chap from England who knows a bit about farming looks at India generally and thinks he's back in the middle ages. I mean I don't know anything about politics or government or commerce, but I do know a bit about land. Some of the things you see make your hair stand on end. But then when I think of settling down here and getting married and having kids I don't think I'd like it much. I mean sending the kids back home wouldn't be my idea of having a family. Am I wrong?'

'I don't know.' She considered. 'I'd hate never to have been home. I'd feel I'd missed something important that I was entitled to, the thing that makes me English. You go back to claim an inheritance. Then if you have children of your own you send them back to claim theirs. It's part of the sacrifice parents have to make.'

'I couldn't make it. Even knowing that if I had a daughter, as well as a dog called Sarah, she might turn out like you if I did.'

She glanced up at him and felt his presence as a homely kindly man some girl other than herself would be fortunate to love and settle down with.

'But then,' he added, 'I don't think you're typical. Young memsahibs usually scare me to death.'

She laughed; but for the rest of the waltz they both seemed

to find it difficult again to think of anything to say. As he led her back to the table he said, 'Are you really going back tomorrow?'

'I should.'

'You mean there's a chance not? That film at the New Empire isn't rotten. I could sit through it again any day. But perhaps you've seen it too?'

'Oh, in Pankot we never get anything new.'

'May I ring you then, in the morning? You'll know by then, won't you, what you've decided?'

'Yes.'

'Then I'll ring you. At ten o'clock.' He delivered her up to Major Clark. On her section of the table there was coffee and brandy. 'I hope you don't mind,' Clark said. 'I changed the order because I didn't think you looked like a girl who drank sticky green.' The chairs had been moved, too. She and Clark were now subtly isolated from the others. There were still two absentees. They arrived as the band started up again – the pale officer who had been tipsy and now looked paler than ever and the dark-haired boy whom she was pretty sure was Tony. As they approached the table Clark whispered to her, 'Let's dance again. I'll tell you why presently.'

A foxtrot. She hated foxtrots. She longed just to sit and drink her coffee, but went back on the floor. Clark said, 'That man's been sick. They ought to send him home.'

'He was all right at dinner.'

'Not really. And the air's hit him. I've suggested to the others he ought not to stay.'

She looked in the direction of the table. The man in question was supporting his head in his hands. Two of the others were leaning towards him. The dark-haired boy had his hand on his back. It looked as if they were encouraging him to call it a day and leave while the going was good, before she and Clark returned to the table. Leonard sat watching with his arms on the table, dissociating himself from the argument. There were now more dancers, the floor was quite crowded. Her view was cut off. Clark said, 'When this dance is finished would you do something for me?'

'What?'

'Go to the powder-room. I'll show you where it is. I'll come back for you in about ten minutes. It shouldn't take longer.'

'I don't mind him being a bit high.'

He looked down at her.

'I mind. So would you if he stayed. So would he tomorrow. He's not just high. He's over the edge. He'll end up crying probably. Don't you think so? Don't you think he's the crying type?'

'I don't know.'

'Well I assure you he is.' A pause. 'I'd be grateful if you'd do as I suggest.' He smiled. This time there was no trace of remoteness. She felt exposed to a sudden, inexplicable but encouraging warmth. Leaving go as the music ended, guided back through the doors between terrace and lounge, she was conscious of his body and of her own under its control and protection. Her elbow was held. 'This way.'

'Ten minutes,' he said a few paces from a door. 'I'll be here. If I'm not, go back in and give me another five. Don't stand outside, unless you don't mind being pestered by strangers.'

She stayed in the powder-room for a quarter of an hour. Two Anglo-Indian girls came in. Her presence seemed to inhibit them. They talked in low voices but she caught the lilt which, if their skins were light enough, helped girls like these to pass themselves off as natives of Cardiff and Swansea. She wondered what she would find to say to them if they joined the party. She stayed at the mirror until they had gone and then, coming out, found him waiting.

She said, 'I thought I'd give it the five extra minutes.'

'I'm afraid even ten was too many, so there's a change of plan.' He took her arm and led her into the lounge with the wicker chairs and tables and noisy men, and through into the arcade towards the street.

'What's happened?'

'I'll explain in a minute.'

Again he shooed boys and beggars. A taxi door was held open by one of the hotel bearers. She entered, understanding that he had sent the man to make sure of one.

The man's 'Salaam, Sahib,' marked the passing of baksheesh. Clark spoke to the driver but she did not hear what he said. He might have given Aunt Fenny's address. He joined her. The taxi moved.

'What did you mean, ten was too many?'

'Just that. He wouldn't budge. And the others were no particular help. I'm sorry.' He offered her a cigarette. Automatically, although not wanting it, she took one. 'It's a dreary place anyway. But then it's all most of them have. I'll show you something better. Unless you want to go home. It's only ten-thirty, though.'

After he had lit her cigarette she gazed through the window at a dark sea, the *maidan* side of Chowringhee.

'See those lights way across?' he asked. 'That's where I first met you.'

'Oh.' She looked. 'You're not really telling me the truth, are you?'

'I think so. Yes. That's the BMH.'

'I mean about why we've left the others.'

'I promised your aunt I'd see you came to no harm, Miss Layton.'

After a while she said, 'My name's Sarah,' and turned to look at him in the odd, distorting lights that flickered in and out of the cab. She thought: It's about now he'll make a pass. But he didn't. He simply stared back at her. She said, 'Where are we going?'

'Across the so-called bridge.'

'What does that mean?'

'You'll see.'

What she saw was that in the politest possible way she had been abducted, that he had never had any intention of sharing her with the others, would have found a way of ditching them even if the pale officer had been sober. It would have taken a bit longer but the end would have been the same. She supposed she should feel flattered as well as annoyed. Perhaps that was what she felt, that or too tired to care much how she spent the rest of the evening.

As if he had followed her reasoning and wished to reassure her he said, 'I'll take you home if you'd prefer that,' but put his hand on hers in what she judged a pretence of consideration meant quite otherwise, meant in fact to have the effect it did, which was to leave her, when the touch was withdrawn, deprived of the source of a faint and therefore unsatisfactory physical response. 'The trouble is,' he said, 'if your aunt finds you there when she gets back she'll know the evening went wrong. That fellow doesn't deserve it but the less said about it all the better. Don't you agree? You and I are both leaving Cal tomorrow but they've got another week under your uncle's eye. I wouldn't want any of them to go back to their units with an adverse report, would you?'

'No.'

'I don't mean we should pretend the party never broke up or that you and I never went off somewhere else, but your aunt and uncle needn't be told why. If one of the others lets it out, that's their funeral. Now,' he ended, and touched her hand again, 'let's forget it and enjoy ourselves. This is the real Calcutta. I'm told this time last year these streets were littered with the corpses of people who came in to try and escape the famine. You have to hope the taxi doesn't conk out, they'd probably cut our throats and chuck us into the Hooghly.'

The taxi had increased speed. The road was ill-lit, a squalid urban area. Shrouded figures lay huddled under lean-to shelters and under arcades. Above, there were tenements. After a while the taxi took a road to the left, over a humped-back bridge. The darkness was now stabbed by the beams of the headlamps.

'All clear,' Clark said, 'we've passed the danger zone.'

The road became kuttcha. There were trees, then open spaces; clutches of houses came and went. 'All round here, in the old days, you'd find a lot of rich Indian merchants. But it's gone down. Don't let it depress you, though. We're not going slumming.'

They drove for another ten minutes, reached a crossroads marked by stalls and huts. Crossing another humped-back bridge the driver had to brake sharply to avoid a stray water-buffalo.

'That's India,' Clark commented. 'The internal combustion engine in confrontation with a creature evolved from the primeval slime.' Ahead there was a low stucco wall. They turned into it and through a gateway. She had an impression of a tall, rather narrow house, with many lighted windows. They drew up at an open doorway. When the engine died she heard the music of sitar, tablas and tamboura. He opened the door on his side, which was next the entrance, and helped her out.

'Walk right up and wait,' he said, 'I have to be persuasive.'

She climbed the few steps, smelling incense, but did not cross the threshold into the narrow hall in which she had a glimpse of curtained doorways guarded by a sleepy Buddha and agile Indian

Gods cast in bronze. She watched Clark bargaining with the driver, persuading him either to stay or return at a specified hour, and felt calm, which was odd, because standing made her realize that almost imperceptibly she was trembling, as if in the grip of a faint rigor. He came up the steps smiling vividly. 'Fixed,' he said, and harboured her in his right arm, leading her in. An Indian servant had come through one of the curtained doorways. Clark said, 'I've left a taxi-wallah out there, Billy. Try and see he doesn't get bored or go away, but don't give him anything stronger than beer.'

The man signified agreement. Clark led her through one set of curtains into a square room equipped like a bar. The music was coming from the room beyond.

'It's a free house,' he said, going behind a semicircular counter. 'So what'll you have, brandy? You never got to drink that other one, but this is better, Three Star. I'll make it long.' He popped a soda bottle, poured and came back out with two well-filled glasses. 'Cheers.' She answered by raising her glass. 'The house belongs to an Indian woman called Mira. While the music's on we just creep in and sit like mice.' Again he took her elbow, guided her through another curtained doorway into a room that surprised her by its length. Ceiling fans whirled sluggishly, wafting unfamiliar perfumes. A standard lamp at the far end illuminated a carpeted daïs on which the instrumentalists sat cross-legged. The rest of the room was unlit, but she clearly made out among the clutter of divans and couches men and women who sat with their faces towards the source of light. Clark took her on tiptoe to an unoccupied sofa against the wall just inside the doorway. A few feet in front of it a solitary Indian woman sat on cushions. She glanced round, seemed to smile, but returned her attention quickly to the music.

Sarah sat. Clark leant close to her and whispered, 'It's Pyari on the sitar.' She nodded, but only vaguely registered the name as one she might have heard mentioned as that of a famous man. She was never sure how much she liked Indian music or whether she agreed with the general opinion of the people she knew that it was a noise that showed more than anything else the hope-lessness of attempting to understand the people who made it. She had an instinctive feeling, though, that even if it was not really what she understood as music it was being performed with great virtuosity. The sitar looked more capable of playing Pyari than he, an ordinary human being with only so many fingers, of playing it. His struggles were immense but must be paying off, judging by the extraordinary ripples of sound. The tablas were smacked with matching agility by a round little man with a bald copper-coloured head. In the background a statuesque woman produced a resonant whining accompaniment on the upright tamboura.

Sarah sipped her brandy and soda. An evening of Indian culture was the last thing she had expected a man like Clark to offer her, but she was hopeful that, unresponsive to it as she was, the music would go on for some time because when it stopped she would find herself out of place, not knowing what to say to the woman who reclined so elegantly on cushions. She guessed that Indians like these laughed at English people like her. Again Clark leaned towards her and whispered, 'The woman on the couch down on the left in the spangled saree's a Maharanee, but she's suing for divorce. The elderly Englishman next to her had a distinguished career in the ICS. He's currently acting as her private legal adviser and escort while she's in Calcutta, but I don't imagine it goes further than that. That young white boy in mufti whose head he's fondling looks like an AB from a ship of His Majesty's Navy.'

Sarah glanced from the Maharanee to the man and stared, at first fascinated and then repelled by the hand that clutched, let go, and clutched again at the dark hair of a young man who sat at his feet uncomplaining. Clark whispered, 'It's one way for boys like that to see a few of the bright lights when they come ashore, and go back on board with a gold cigarette case like the officers have.'

The Maharanee turned, spoke to the retired civil servant, smiled and put her hand briefly on his free one, ignoring the boy and the older man's attentions to him. Sarah looked back at the musicians, and drank more brandy, felt hollow, embarrassed that in a roomful of Indians two Englishmen should so behave themselves. But the embarrassment was incoherent, less real than the curiosity which made not looking at them a conscious effort, a disciplinary exercise in tact that was also intended to display, for Clark's benefit, false proof of her inurement to all quirks of human taste and to evidence of their open satisfaction. She

thought Clark had her under scrutiny. She resisted the impulse
to find out, but a movement from him convinced her she had
been right and that he was deliberately putting her through a
test; but whether it was intended to confirm the presence of
a physical aptitude or the absence of a moral quality, she did
not know.

She decided to face it directly, and looked at him. He was, as
she expected, now watching the musicians. His right arm rested
on the back of the sofa. The hand – relaxed but too vigorously
formed to look limp – hung a few inches away from her shoulder. His face, in profile, just touched by light, as it might be far
back in the auditorium of a theatre with the play in progress,
reflected the same quality of assertiveness and self-possession.
She turned her head again, towards Pyari.

The music sounded as if it had reached a climax and would
end abruptly; which it did. The applause was remarkably loud
for such a thinly-scattered audience. She set her glass down and
joined in, for politeness. The musicians abandoned their instruments and made *namaste*. Light entered the room at several
points as servants rung curtains back and came in with trays.

The Indian woman on the cushions turned round.

'Jimmy, the movement control telephoned. The plane leaves
for Colombo half an hour earlier than they originally told you.'

'Thanks, Mira. By the way, I've brought someone along to
hear Pyari. Her name's Sarah.'

Sarah murmured hello. The Indian woman nodded, addressed
Clark again almost immediately.

'Pyari's in good form, isn't he? They've asked him at Government House. Did you hear?'

'No? Will he go?'

'What do you think? He said he might send one of his
third-year pupils because the people there wouldn't know the
difference. But none of his pupils wanted to go either, even as a
joke, unless he let them hide a bomb in the sitar. He said, "Why
should we ruin a good instrument?" So that was that.'

Clark laughed, ignoring the fact that the joke was partly on
Sarah. A bearer approached, offering pān. Sarah shook her head.

'You should,' he recommended, taking one and beginning to
chew. 'It cleanses the blood. Haven't you ever eaten pān?'

'I did as a child.'

'Have another drink instead then.'

She surrendered her glass. She had emptied it, nervously. The Indian woman got gracefully to her feet and went farther down the room to talk to a man and woman who sat with their arms round each other.

'Mira's a stunner, isn't she?' Clark said.

'Yes. Beautiful.'

'She keeps a husband in drink and pays all his gambling debts and hotel bills, and his mistress's clothes and jewellery accounts.'

'Does she? Why?'

'Why not? She's so rich she can't count it. Anyway, she likes his mistress. They used to be lovers themselves, but she's mad about the Maharanee now, and as that's quite mutual everything in the garden's lovely. You can always tell. When Mira's crossed she shuts herself up in her rooms for days on end. But one way and another this party's been going on since the day before yesterday. So I gather. I only got in this morning. She's probably paying Pyari a thousand chips for the music, so why should he perform at Government House for nothing? Not that he would anyway. He's very anti-government because they've never done anything to encourage the arts. Most of his students confuse art with politics, so he makes political gestures every so often as part of his duties as a good *guru*, but he couldn't care less about politics himself. In fact' – he looked round the room – 'no one here could. Politics are for the poor and the bourgeois middle class. Most of these people have fortunes stashed away in banks in Lisbon and Zürich. The existence of well-to-do little neutral countries is a pointer to what global war is really all about, or haven't you noticed?'

The bearer returned with drinks.

'I expect you wonder how I got to know this place,' Clark continued. 'Mira has friends in Cairo. They wrote her when they knew I was coming to India. So whenever I come in to Calcutta this is my unofficial address, which explains why your Uncle Arthur had that odd idea I was always out on the tiles. I expect somebody reported to him my bed was never slept in. I mean the one in the quaint monkish little quarters they gave me when I got myself sent on that course he runs. But as I was such a bright boy he obviously turned a blind eye.'

'Yes, I see.' She sipped the new, much stronger, brandy and

soda, looked at him and asked, 'Has Mira got friends in Ceylon too?'

'We both have.'

'Then you'll be nice and comfortable.'

'It's one of my aims in life. Isn't it one of yours?'

She stared at her glass and, after a moment's hesitation, allowed the absurd truth to enter like a chill draught through all the ill-fitting doors of her inherited prejudices and superstitions. 'I suppose I've never given it much thought.'

'I guessed you hadn't.' He hesitated. 'But you're refreshingly honest. I thought I wasn't mistaken. That honour-of-the-regiment exterior is paper-thin, isn't it?'

Yes, she thought, pitifully thin; but its thinness was less pitiful than the fact that it was there and could be seen and was the only exterior, the only skin she had. She felt her hand taken, and this time held on to.

'I wonder why?' he asked. 'Didn't the second injection take?'

'The second injection of what?'

'India and the honour-of-the-regiment. It's usually fatal, surely? I mean isn't the first one bad enough? Growing up with all the other po-faced kids in a sort of ghastly non-stop performance of Where the Rainbow Ends? Then having to trot back for a time to a little island that's gone down because it's become full of vulgar money-grubbers and people without standards and all sorts of jacks-in-office trying to paint out the pink parts of the map?'

She smiled, but said, 'I suppose that's how it looks. It's only half the truth.'

'What's the other half?'

She moved her hand from under his. She hated simplifications, especially those to which her own ideas of the complex nature of reality might be reduced. He did not reclaim contact.

'Extraordinary, isn't it,' he said, 'that the people in this country who feel most like foreigners to each other are English people who've just arrived and the ones who have been here for several years. Last Christmas, after I left here, I was up in 'Pindi staying with a friend of a friend back home who's been out here for about ten years. And there they were, the man, the wife, and two of the po-faced kids, and right from the beginning we felt towards each other like I suppose those people do who suffer from that odd racial prejudice thing, as if in spite of our being the *same* colour and class, one of us was black, me, and the others white, them. We were tremendously polite but simply had nothing to say to each other. I felt I'd met a family who'd been preserved by some sort of perpetual Edwardian sunlight that got trapped between the Indian Ocean and the Arabian Sea round about the turn of the century. Of course, having gone straight there from Mira's I was prepared to believe I'd struck something unusual. I hadn't, though, had I? It makes me want to say, Where have you all been? Come back. All is forgiven.'

She was still smiling. She said, 'Come back where? Forgiven by whom, and for what?'

But he was, after all, quite serious. 'I suppose one of the things you need to be forgiven for is deluding the Indians as well as yourselves into thinking that the values of 1911 are still current at home.'

'Why 1911?'

'Wasn't that the year of the Delhi Durbar? *Post*-Edwardian I grant you, but anything before 1900 would be a journalist's exaggeration and anything after 1914–18 quite irrelevant. And when I say deluding Indians I don't mean people of the kind you see in this room, I mean the kind who take you seriously, and that includes chaps like Gandhi and Nehru. Actually I hate the word Westernized, it's used so loosely. You could say Mira's Westernized, but she's modern West and that means a fair slice of modern East as well. Nehru and that lot, all the liberal-upper and bourgeois middle-class of India, they're one hundred per cent old-fashioned West. And it's all as dead as yesterday, isn't it? You ought to bury the body, or expose it to the vultures like the Parsees do. It didn't survive the Great War. It makes an awful smell. Of course there are still pockets of the stink at home, your kind of people go back to them and I was educated at one. Highly unsuccessfully. They went in a lot at Chillingborough for future colonial administrators, didn't they? They were even planning to have an Indian boy there – one who *wasn't* a Maharajah's son. He came round with his dad during my last term to have a look-see at one of the traditional founts of all liberal-imperial wisdom, and I thought, the poor little sod, he thinks this is where his future gets handed to him and unwrapped like a slab of chocolate. But he probably hadn't got a future.'

'Hadn't he?'

'As a tomb-attendant? I expect he's a sub-divisional officer now and wondering whether to stay in the executive or transfer to the judiciary. His deputy commissioner is more likely to be an Indian than an Englishman but the work he does and the attitudes that go with it will be the same as they were forty years ago when some pink-faced boy from Wiltshire sat under the same punkah and wrote many letters home to his mother.'

'What do you do for a living?'

'You mean in peace-time. The answer's the same in war or peace. I live.'

'On air?'

'No. I make money too.'

'At what?'

'At what? Do for a living? It's awfully unimportant, isn't it? Strip the guff from any job and what have you got? A way of making money. And please don't say, "Somebody has to run things." I know they do. Running things means making them pay. I run things to the extent I make things pay. To me a Viceroy is about as important or unimportant as a company secretary who drafts the annual report for the shareholders to tell them what the board's been up to. Your board's made a lousy job of running things out here. The place is a goldmine, but it's stiff with unemployed BAs and people who die in the streets of hunger. That's a legacy from all those blue-eyed Bible thumpers and noble neo-classicists who came out here because they couldn't stand the commercial pace back home. You had a per-fectly good thing going in that old merchant trading company who used to run things until the industrial revolution. What you wanted then was a bevy of steely-eyed brass founders and men of iron who'd have ground the faces of the Indian peasants in the dirt, sweated a few million to death and dragged India yelling into the nineteenth century. Instead of which you got the people who didn't like the smoke and the dark satanic mills because that sort of thing was vulgar, and after them you got the people who didn't like it because of the inhumanity that went with it. What you didn't get was the damned smoke. And that's the trouble. The Indian empire's been composed exclusively of English people who said No. Out here you've always had the negative side, the reactionaries and the counter-revolutionaries, but you've never had the bloody revolution. That's why an Indian urban dweller's life expectation is still thirty-five and why people die of starvation while the band plays at Government House, and Pyari plays the sitar at Mira's. Well, at home after the war we'll cut your empire adrift without the slightest compunction. It's a time-expired sore, a suppurating mess. From the point of view of people who really run things it's like a leg that you look at one morning and realize is too far gone in gangrene to be worth saving. Limping's better. It's going to be up to the Indians to grow a body from the limb. Of course most of them will make the mistake of thinking their independent body-politic is a whole, walking body. And at home we'll pretend we've fulfilled a moral obligation by giving it back to them. But that won't be the reason. We'll get rid of it because it doesn't pay and it's too late to make it pay. Give the war another year, the one in Europe anyway, and the one with Japan another year. Say summer 1946. You can expect a general election in England in the summer of 1946 at the latest, and the socialists will get in because the common soldier and the factory worker will put them in. Lopping off India is an article of faith with the socialists but when they see that keeping it doesn't pay they'll lop it double-quick. Who wants India's starving millions as one of what we'll all call our post-war problems?'

'Are you a socialist?'

'Good Lord, no. I'm what you'd call a low Tory, if you could call me anything at all.'

'Why are you so sure the socialists would win an election? Won't Mr Churchill's reputation count for anything?'

He laughed, and turned the question.

'Why do women always call him Mr Churchill? It makes him sound like a vicar who's been invited to judge the home-made calves-foot jelly. But the answer's yes, of course, his name *will* count. For everything patriotic, proud, victorious and time-expired. I don't suppose you've talked much to common British soldiers, have you? The fellows you refer to as BORs? You ought to. Ask them what they think of life out here, I mean the national service wallahs, not the regulars. Then you'll know. If there's one thing war shows the man in the street it's the difference between himself and the officer-caste. Back home it's obvious enough but on foreign service he feels it like a kick in the teeth.

I'll tell you what your BOR in Deolali or your cockney motor mechanic with the Desert Rats or your Brummagem door-to-door salesman with Wingate in Burma thinks. He thinks, "All right, mate. Have it cushy whenever you can and be a Boy Scout while the shit flies. Get on winning the war your lot started. I'll even give you a cheer at the end. And when you've got the whole stinking mess sorted out, be a good lad and bugger off, out of my sight, out of my government and out of my bloody life. But for ever." And what goes for the officer-caste goes for Churchill. Your poor blighter of a BOR thinks it's all real, you see. He hears the popping of corks in the officers' tents and goes back to his mug of tea or stale NAAFI beer with murder in his heart knowing everything would be all right if he could guzzle brandy, or if the Colonel had to choke on a mug of tea with bromide in it to stop him feeling randy. He thinks his own lot ought to run things because there are more of his lot drinking tea with bromide in it than there are what he calls la-di-dah poofs swigging brandy and getting hot for women they won't know how to poke.'

With an effort Sarah kept her eyes coolly on a level with his. She understood that the test and his use of gutter-slang, were part of a process of seduction. He would use different methods with different women. The words he chose for her and the whole gravamen of his argument were calculated to expose her as someone for whom, primarily, he felt contempt. He wanted her on her mettle. Or in embarrassed confusion. Or weak and defeated. She was not sure which.

'Go on,' she said.

He laughed, again reached for her hand and grasped it hard. 'You're quite a girl, Sarah Layton.'

'No,' she said, 'I'm not quite a girl. I'm this one,' and was aware of having jerked him into unexpected recognition of her as a person and not a type. She told this from his heavy hand which became, for a second or two, uncharacteristically inert.

'He's on the ball in one sense, your BOR,' Clark continued. 'The brandy's real enough and so's the tea and bromide. His mistake comes in thinking the difference between them has some kind of moral significance and proves his rights as a human being have been infringed. But what he calls his rights as a human being start where his honest sensations stop, don't they?

His honest sensations tell him to knock the Colonel down and pinch his brandy, but he's scared to do that and begins nursing a grievance and inventing a right, the right to a fair share. But when you cut out the moral claptrap your *fair* share of anything is what you're strong enough to grab. Or would you prefer the word earn? In practice it comes to the same thing. Your fair share is what you take. Don't you agree?'

Did she? She felt as if the effort she had put into facing up to him had reduced her power of concentration, that somehow she had missed some of the words and that her sudden inability to answer exposed for both of them the real reason why she sat there, unprotesting. With a gesture half-affectionate, half-mocking, he moved his hand and placed the knuckles behind her ear, ruffling her hair. Understanding that it would amuse him to see her shrink from such contact, she deliberately – but slowly – changed the angle of her head and body to force disengagement. The hand moved away, only to rest again on her bare neck.

'You're very tense,' he said. 'Did your visit to the hospital upset you?'

'I expect so.'

'Is he a bit of a mess, then, this fellow you went to see?'

'They're amputating his arm.'

'Oh. Yes, that *is* bad, isn't it? But it explains one thing that puzzled me. The fact that you appeared to take such an instant dislike to me. It means you must have noticed me and that the dislike was merely a transference of the physical revulsion you felt for the poor blighter they're going to cut up. It's quite common. Amputation *is* revolting, but a woman especially won't accept that it is until she sees someone she likes the look of, then she thinks, "You're disgustingly whole, why have you got two arms, blast you?" Or legs, or whatever it is the chap she used to like hasn't got any longer.'

'But I didn't like him.'

'No?' The hand on her neck moved an inch or so. 'You came an awfully long way to see him then, but I'll accept that and I don't think it makes any difference. The revulsion was there. You took it out on me. Shall I tell you something?'

'What?'

'You're not so tense now.'

It was true. Her body had become capable of controlled and fluid movement: a new feeling that added to her confidence and for which she felt indebted to him in a way she could not explain, except by acknowledging that it flowed from his hand. His eyes and line of cheek, lit obliquely, gave his face – now fully turned towards her – an irony which she thought she understood.

'You're still a virgin, of course, aren't you?'

The shocking directness of the statement caused her to jerk her glance away. She felt that he had hit her. Presently, she said, as clearly and levelly as she could, 'Yes, I'm still a virgin-of-course,' and by doing so arrested the retreat of warmth. But she could not bring herself to face him. For a while she was conscious of his continued observation and of the way her body was becoming increasingly dependent on the support of his hand for whatever air it had of self-possession. When he removed his hand and placed it momentarily on hers before removing it entirely, it seemed to her like a valedictory gesture, an acknowledgement of her as the person she had made him see behind the paper-thin exterior; the girl he had stalked, attacked, and tried to shock into a predictable herd-reaction. But when he took his hand away she felt he took that real self too and left her with nothing but her shell. She sat, coldly bereft, and then wondered if he had taken anything, had seen instead what she herself could not see, but began to have intimations of; that the shell was all there was because she had rejected all the things that had once filled it, and had not replaced them. One by one they had gone, the beliefs, affections and expectations of her childhood: but when? She stared across the room at the carpeted daïs where the unattended instruments lay and felt herself unattended too. Perhaps at her christening certain spectres had come like unbidden guests, spectres of that extinction-through-exile that awaited Muirs and Laytons and all their kind, and stolen away unseen, having cursed or blessed her with an awareness of their presence which would dog her footsteps and fill her mind, until, bit by bit, as she was bidden, she had cast out of herself all her inheritance and was left in possession – as it were of a relic – of a shell whose emptiness was the proof for future generations of where the fault had lain and why there could have been no other end, even for her. Perhaps especially not for her, because once – hunched on a window-seat – she had drawn her root and branch and ringed her Indian family proudly in red. Perhaps it had been a condition of the christening gift that what she discarded bit by bit should be discarded as proudly as it had once been put on, so that the possibility of looking for substitutes to ensure survival was excluded. If you went down you went down and the proudest way was not to go down fighting for eroded values but, simply, with them, however little you were responsible for them. Those values were your shell as well, what you were left with after you had rejected their substance. The shell was unalterable.

He said, 'I seem to have discovered the chink in your armour. But are you annoyed with me for asking, or because you have to admit you are? Or is it a bit of both? I can't believe it's that you're plain old-fashioned shocked or embarrassed. And you don't look like a girl who thinks a man should automatically assume the absence of a wedding ring on the hand of a well-brought-up young lady means she's saving it up for Mr Right. Or am I wrong?'

They were questions she could not answer except from a fund of outworn stock replies such as he would only receive with a gently derisive pretence of not having anticipated. The alternative was silence; which she chose.

'In any case,' he said, 'clearly I must apologize.'

The hand rested again on the back of her neck. The warmth flowed back in, revealing the one unchanging purpose to which she could be put, even as a shell. Her nipples hardened in simulation of giving suck, but she continued to stare at the daïs. There was sudden movement in the room. The man who played the tablas had come back in. A girl accompanied him.

'Mira *is* doing us proud,' he whispered, leaning close. 'It's Lakshmi Kripalani. She sings, in case you didn't know.'

She nodded, more in acknowledgement of his breath's faint palpations of her ear than of the words spoken. Mira was approaching. The Maharanee had also risen and was coming in her wake, but continued on towards the curtained doorway. Mira came to the sofa and leaned forward and spoke to her, excluding Clark.

'They'll be playing again soon. I'd better show you where you can freshen up.'

Clark removed his hand, relieved her of the unfinished glass of brandy.

'It's a good idea,' he said. 'They might go on for an hour. It depends on how inventive they're feeling. I'll keep this warm for you.'

Sarah got up with the half-formed intention of telling him that an hour was too long, that she should go home because they both had an early start to the day ahead; but she could not summon the determination. She followed Mira into the bar, through into the hall, then a passage, and up a staircase that turned twice. They came out on to a gallery whose barred windows were unshuttered and admitted the warm mulchy smell of the Bengal night. The gallery turned at right angles and continued along the length of the side of the house. Light came from naked bulbs fixed into sockets in the gallery roof. The Indians sometimes had a crude, uncluttered attitude towards electricity, Sarah thought. So often the bulb was accepted as a decoration in itself. Mira wore no chola under the dark saree. The elastic of a brassiere showed. At the end of the gallery she turned in at an open door. Sarah followed and paused – astonished at the room's opulence. A double bed, raised on a wide but shallow daïs and enclosed by a white mosquito net hung high and centrally so that the effect was of a regal canopy, was its main focus. The gossamer net shivered under the gentle changing pressures of air wafted by two revolving ceiling fans. The daïs was covered in white carpet and the bedcovers were of creamy white satin. The furniture was satin-walnut. Mira, still without speaking, had walked to a door, opened it and switched on a light.

'There's probably everything you want. If not, just ring and one of the girls will come.'

A fragrance, a chill; the bathroom was air-conditioned. It was larger than her bedroom at Pankot and marble-floored, with sheepskin rugs. Above the semi-sunken bath gilt faucets projected from marble green tiles. At one end of the bath pink frosted glass screened off the shower.

She looked at Mira, fearing her, chilled by her, but ready to praise what belonged to her. But Mira seemed quite indifferent and held the door open as if anxious to be gone. 'Thank you,' Sarah said, and went past her. The door was closed. The lavatory was in an adjoining cubicle. The cistern was the modern kind with a levered handle. It flushed quietly and immediately. In the pedestal wash-basin, piping hot water flowed. Back in the bathroom she sat on a luxurious stool with curved gilt claw legs and a padded green velvet seat. The legs of the marble-topped table matched the legs of the stool. She studied herself in an immense mirror, a flattering one. Glancing at the array of bottles and sprays and jars she opened her handbag with misgivings about the quality of its contents but determined to use nothing that didn't belong to her, and then was held by a delayed reaction. Her eye had caught objects that struck her as incongruous. Among the scents, lotions and other items in a toilet battery of wholly feminine connection were two wood-backed bristle hair-brushes and a leather case. The zip was half undone. She reached out, zipped further, then completely, and lifted the cover, stared at the contents – four gold-plated containers and a matching safety razor.

She turned round, considered the bathroom, searching it for other clues to masculine occupation without much idea of what to look for, and noticed in one corner a bin with a padded seat that obviously lifted. She turned back to the mirror and went to work with powder from her compact, occasionally glancing at the bin's reflection. A dab of lipstick completed her repair operations. She shut her handbag. The click echoed. She sat for a while and felt in need of some show of kindness, such as Aunt Fenny had made, taking her shoes off, making her rest, and again remembered that she had not slept properly for two days; three, if she counted the night she last slept in Pankot, disturbed by a gift of lace, a meeting avoided, and expectation of new ground and a long journey. She looked at her watch. Eleven-thirty. Less than six hours since she had said Goodbye, Ronald, and got in return a goodbye that was not coupled with the blessing and absolution of her name.

Her name – she got up from the stool – her formidable, bony, yearning name – and walked to and opened the bin; stared down at the soiled expensive briefs, those meshes of mysterious and complex cellular imprisonment. She closed the lid, knowing that both bath and bedroom were tainted by his casual presence and the ludicrous talent he had for casual contemptuous excitation.

I am sensible now – she decided – after Pyari has played I shall go home, alone if necessary. She reached for door-handle and light-switch, intending to flick the one after opening the other, but when she opened the door a whole field of darkness faced her. She stood arrested by it and by the notion that darkness always contained dangers and presences.

Instinctively, but without conviction, she blamed Mira, who had apparently not even left the door open between bedroom and gallery. There would have been light enough then. Momentarily she was without a sense of direction. She felt along one wall, searching for another switch. Her elongated shadow probed the slant of bathroom light across the floor and up a blank wall. There was no switch. But she had her bearings. The five-mile hill, the five-mile door. Over there, she told herself; and was rewarded then by the suddenly visible pale strip of light making the boundary of bedroom and gallery. She walked towards it, and stopped.

'You're going the wrong way,' he said. 'I'm over here.'

His voice came from behind, from some intensely organized, centralized point of reference. Turning towards it she was dazzled by the light from the decoy bathroom. The bed was darkly shadowed by one of the bathroom walls, which jutted into the room.

'You seem startled. Weren't you expecting me?'

'No.'

She turned and walked towards the slit of light, anticipated the driven-home look and the absent key. She jerked the handle. The absurdity of the handle's obedient but unfunctional mobility nullified her attempt to convey composure. Nothing looked sillier than trying to open a door the person watching you knew you knew was locked. She turned back, facing that equally absurd dark central point of reference.

'That's a pity,' he said. 'I thought you understood we had an appointment. Mira did, so you mustn't worry about our absence causing comment. Is it the dark that puts you off? I thought you'd prefer it. At first, anyway.'

'We have no appointment. Please turn the lights on and open the door.'

As she spoke she realized that her eyes had become more used to the dark areas beyond the shaft of light coming from the bathroom. There was a slow rhythmic movement and in the second before the restored bedside lamp reversed the negative image into a positive one she detected the stretched arm, sensed the manipulative action of his hand on the switch, and understood from the spare density of his form that he was naked.

He was seated on the edge of the bed, staring back at her across a still extended arm, caught and held in the ageless classic pose of a figure from some Renaissance ceiling. The shock he gave her was that of astonishment that in the flesh a man could look as he had been depicted for centuries in stone and paint. Lowering the arm he exposed a sculptured chest.

'Are you sure you want the door opened?'

'Yes.'

'The key's here on the table. I've also been thoughtful enough to bring our glasses. Have I miscalculated? I don't often, but it wouldn't be the first time. It's an occupational hazard of the male. You get a few more slaps in the face than you deserve, but you also get your screws, so you can't complain. Are you quite sure you don't want to lose that cherry?'

'Quite sure. I'll give you a minute to unlock the door.'

She moved, making for the bathroom. Casually, he got up and was there before her. She stood still. Naked, the earlier and only slight advantage he had in height was further diminished. In her high heels she eyed him almost levelly, but her manifest disadvantage in strength and weight was pressed home on her as if by an actual pressure of his limbs. She turned, sat on a padded satin-covered chair. Doing so disclosed to her the shameful fact that she was trembling. She faced him again, deliberately. She observed him dispassionately, from head to foot. Having quartered him she looked again to her front and said, 'I've seen you now, so may I go?'

'That wasn't the object of undressing. I turned the light off, remember? The only reason I'm like this is that making a pass at a girl and getting her hot and then introducing the devastatingly practical note of pausing to take your clothes off always strikes me as highly comic. When a man wants a screw he ought not to beat about the bush. It's different for girls because their clothes can come off so gracefully. Have I really wasted my time?'

'Yes.'

'Well, that's an occupational hazard too.'

There was a pause. Presently he crossed her line of vision. When he reached the bed he felt under the mosquito net and drew something out. Blue material. His pyjama trousers. He put them on. The bunched tops of the trousers thickened his waist slightly. He lit a cigarette, then brought their glasses of brandy over. He put them on the floor, went back to the table for an ashtray, returned and sat on the floor himself, and gazed up at her.

'You're not really plain, are you? In fact you're quite pretty. And you've got thin shoulders. In the buff I expect your breasts look much more prominent.' He put his head on one side, considering her. 'But your hips are a shade too narrow. I bet you've got a hard little bottom. What I like best about you though is you never say anything too obvious. I know the dialogue that can go with this particular situation by heart and it gets pretty boring. So that's what I like best. Your not saying anything obvious and your Colonel's daughter's guts. It makes an unusual combination.' He drank, indicated her own glass. 'Drink up. It'll do you good. I never screw them when they're pissed so you're quite safe. I mean don't *not* drink because you think I'd take advantage if you had too much. But I don't suppose you ever have too much, do you? That's another point in your favour. Your aunt told me you have a thin time at home because your mother drinks. It's embarrassing, isn't it? My father drank a lot. He used to cry too. Does your mother cry? What she ought to do is give up drinking and find some young officer who'll screw her whenever she wants and bow out without making a fuss when the Colonel comes home. After all, that would be better for the Colonel, wouldn't it? To come home to a placid, loving woman, instead of a neurotic alcoholic who gets her screws out of bottles.'

'Like your father?'

'Yes, like him.'

'And what did *your* mother do for screws?'

'Oh, Mother was never hard up. She went in for handsome chauffeurs. When I was eighteen I put my foot down, though, and insisted that even if the chauffeurs went to bed with her they still had to call me either Master James, or Sir.'

'And did they?'

'Yes, but I expect it cost her an extra small fortune at the men's shops in Bond Street.' He smiled. 'Go on. You're doing very well. For one awful moment I thought you were going to say something like "Kindly leave my mother and father out of this." I hope you're not too cross with Aunt Fenny, by the way. She was only trying to paint a little picture of you that would bring out my protective instincts. She said more than she intended, but that was my fault.'

'I realized that.'

'Do all your family view you with the same mixture of alarm and affection as she does?'

'Probably.'

'Why are you shivering?'

'Because I find it difficult to control myself.'

'And you feel you must? What do you find difficult to control? Your temper?'

'Yes.'

For the first time since coming to sit on the floor he freed her from her self-imposed obligation not to let her glance waver. He looked down at his glass and for a moment she escaped into the safe oblivion of private darkness. When she opened her eyes again he was watching her. She said, 'I'd be glad if you'd open the door now. If the taxi's still waiting I can go home without putting you to any trouble. If it's not I'm afraid you'll have to organize one. I don't know where we are.'

'Don't worry about the taxi. You're forgetting I promised Aunt Fenny you'd come to no harm.'

'She's my Aunt Fenny, not yours.'

The comfortable angle of his head and trunk, the casual, easy, disposition of his limbs created confusing images in her mind of strength and languor and confident patience. They were confusing because she herself felt she had come to the end of a tether.

He took his hand from his glass, stubbed his cigarette and rose. She anticipated a physical attack on her, but he did not make it. Instead he went back to the bedside table, picked up the key and returned. He resumed his former position on the floor, tossed the key two or three times like a coin, then placed it on the floor between them.

'*My* key for *your* Aunt Fenny,' he said. 'I pay the forfeit and keep Aunt Fenny. There's not much going on in her, but what goes on is tough as old boots. I like that. If she were five years

younger and I were five years older we'd screw. She knows it.
In that cosy closed-in little corner of her bird-brain mind where
the real Aunt Fenny lives she knows it, just as she knows in the
same cosy little corner that asking me to look after you was the
most risky thing she could do if you wanted to hang on to that
cherry of yours. Obviously what she really thinks is that you
ought to get rid of it. Which means she thinks the same as I do,
only with her the thought's subconscious. I'll tell you another
thing. You're tougher than she is. Far tougher than you probably
realize. With you the toughness goes an awfully long way in
because you haven't got a bird-brain. It thinks. Potentially
you're worth twenty Aunt Fennys. But the thinking and the
toughness aren't worth a bag of peanuts if you lack joy. And
that's what Aunt Fenny has that you haven't. Joy. Not much.
She's too shallow to have much of anything, but I bet you she
was a scorcher as a girl. I bet she went for joy first and let the
thinking and toughness come later, and that means that in her
late middle-age she still remembers how to get a kick out of life.
It doesn't really matter which way round you do it, if you do it
both ways. But why not do it both ways from the start? Isn't that
sensible? Isn't the place already overcrowded with people who
have thought for so long they've forgotten how to be happy, or
with people who've spent so long trying to be happy they
haven't had time to think, so end up not knowing what happiness is? For pete's sake, Sarah Layton, you don't know anything
about joy at all, do you?'

'No,' she said. 'No, I don't,' and reached for the key and then,
stupidly, lost sight of it because her eyes had responded – as if of
their own accord – to a humiliation, an unidentifiable yearning,
and a dim recollection of an empty gesture that had something to
do with wrenching the reins of a horse and wheeling to confront
imaginable but infinitely remote possibilities of profound contentment. She felt the metal of the key under her fingers and the
flesh-shock of his hand on her knuckles.

'You're crying,' he said. 'Why? Because you really want me
to make love to you? I couldn't promise that. Not love. You
couldn't either, could you? Not with me. If you liked we could
pretend that it was love but it wouldn't be honest and your
honesty is part of what attracts me. You don't belong, do you?
And the trouble is you know it, but I suppose while your

father's away you feel you have to pretend you do belong, for his sake.'

'No,' she said. 'I do belong. That's what I know. That's the trouble. Please take your hand away.'

He did so. She grasped the key. It weighed nothing. What it would open was a prison of a kind.

'Wait,' he said. He got up, went to the far side of the bed. Through the net she saw blurred pictures of a stranger dressing. There was a superior kind of mystery about him. In her dream there had been no problems, no threat of violence. She had surrendered to him casually. The absence of a climax struck the one familiar note; that and an awareness of her father's unspeaking presence, his silent criticism of her failure to hold back for him the tide of changing circumstances, her failure to hold in trust days he had lost which belonged to him; days that must, to him, be an incalculably dear proportion of those few left in which the once perpetual-seeming light would shine on undisturbed by the brighter, honest, light whose heat would burn the old one to a shadow.

The stranger came from behind the net and stood for a moment watching her. Who is that man? people asked her in the dream. And her reply had always been, Oh, I don't know. She had never been convinced that she spoke the truth, but in any case now knew the answer. Who is that man? Why, one of us, one of the people we really are.

'Well,' he said, 'shall we go, Sarah Layton?' He came closer. 'If so you ought to bathe your eyes. My Aunt Fenny would think the worst had happened if she saw you now.'

She was holding the key in one hand and her handbag in the other. The blurred opaque image of his face cleared. Presently he bent forward, grasped the exposed end of the key and carefully took it from her. He held out his other hand and, when she did not move, reached further and touched the strap of the handbag, then grasped it. Her own grip loosened. She felt the smooth strip of leather slide from her fingers and watched him stand back, holding the two things she had surrendered and which he now seemed to be showing her, waiting for some kind of confirmation that she understood he had them. He transferred the key to the hand with which he held the handbag then stooped and picked up the ashtray and, with his free hand, their glasses, holding them from the insides, rim to rim, between thumb and fingers. He went to the bedside-table, placed the glasses and the ashtray by the lamp and, after a moment's hesitation, placed the handbag there as well. Still holding the key he went over to the door and inserted it in the lock but did not turn it. He came back and stood in front of her in further brief consideration and then went over to the bedside-table again and switched the lamp off so that the room was as it had been at the beginning of their encounter. The shaft of light from the bathroom stretched across the floor, separating them until he emerged from the shadow on the other side of it and crossed over on to her side, and squatted. He touched her right ankle, gently lifted and eased the shoe from her foot and then the shoe from the other foot, and placed the shoes neatly together on one side of the chair. The hand in which she had held the key was cupped and taken, and then the other, and both carried and held to his face, so that it seemed she had reached out and put her hands on his cheeks with a gesture of adoration. She closed her eyes, exploring the illusion of possession which such an adoration might create between two people and was then aware that her hands were no longer held except by the desire to explore. Her own head was taken. For a while they stayed so, enacting the tenderness of silent lovers, and then slowly bending her head she allowed him to deal with the old maid's hook and eye.

V

His hand was on her arm gentling her from sleep and in the second or two before she woke she knew the sweet relief of this evidence that she had only dreamt the scene in which Aunt Fenny told her Susan was in premature labour brought on by shock; and that the reality was this warm quiescence with which her body came back to life and consciousness, flesh to flesh with the body of the man who had penetrated it, liberated it, and was waking it again from profound rest so that it might enclose and be enclosed and go again, rapt, to the edge of feeling.

'I'm sorry,' the voice said. 'But we're nearly there.' A strange, unbelievable, soundless splintering; an extraordinary convolution of time and space. Her eyes opened and she saw the woman whose name was Mrs Roper. 'We're coming into Ranpur, Miss Layton. I'm sorry to disturb you.'

She pulled herself upright, understanding completely where she was and yet not understanding it at all, but she knew she was indebted to Mrs Roper and to Mrs Roper's friend, Mrs Perryman, and that this was because they had let her share the coupé and had even had the top bunk lowered so that she could rest properly. She knew from the lights in the ceiling, close to her head, that it was night, whereas it had been day when the bunk was lowered. Her uniform was crumpled.

'Can you manage, my dear?'

Mrs Roper's head scarcely came to the level of the bunk. The fans whisked the stray ends of her grey hair which was set in a way that suggested Mrs Roper remembered she was pretty as a girl. Mrs Roper's husband had been a Forestry Officer in Burma. He sent her back to India in 1941 and as she hadn't heard a word since the Japanese invasion she believed he was hiding out with one of the hill-tribes who had been their friends. Mrs Perryman's hair was brassy-blonde. Her husband had been in the medical service and died of cholera in 1939. She took in paying-guests, one of whom was Mrs Roper. They had been staying with Mrs Roper's brother's family on leave at Ootaca-mund and were on their way back to Simla, having returned by way of Calcutta to visit a friend of Mrs Perryman's whose husband was in jute. It was their first holiday since the beginning of the war, and they had saved for it, presumably. But they had not mentioned money.

Sarah knew all these things about them because they had talked incessantly from midday when the train left Howrah station until an hour after lunch. They had talked for kindly reasons because Uncle Arthur had taken them on one side to thank them for letting her share the coupé and to ask them to look after her because her great-aunt, of whom she had been very fond, had died suddenly in Pankot and the shock had sent her sister into premature labour. She swung round on the bunk and was held by a reaction in her bloodstream, unexpected but familiar. Sound and sight became miniature, far away. From behind brass screens she heard Mrs Roper say, 'Now don't rush. I just thought you'd want plenty of time because we only stay in Ranpur ten minutes.'

With her foot she felt for the top of the nest of steps, far down in the distorted well of the coupé, and finding them, made the descent.

'You've had a nice long sleep. We nodded off too. Now don't bother about us. Is there anything we can do?'

'No thank you, Mrs Roper. I'm fine.'

'Leave the bunk. Directly we've had dinner Mrs Perryman and I are going to tuck down.'

In the cubicle she bathed her face in slow-running tepid water. There were specks of soot. The train was going over points, intersection after intersection. She steadied herself on the handgrip and confronted her mirror image. Did it show? Could anyone tell? That she had entered, like other women? Yes; to her it showed; vividly; more vividly than her anxiety for Susan, more strongly than the grief cushioned by disbelief that she felt for Aunty Mabel who walked in and out of her mind, condemned by a memory to go on performing the task to which so many hours of her last days had been stubbornly devoted; more strongly than the concern for her mother who had been alone to cope and for her father for whom Aunty Mabel was now an irretrievable part of a time she had been unable to hold back for him. She did not know why she should have wanted to hold it back. She did not even know she had tried to until she saw that it had gone. She had failed but she had entered. She had entered her body's grace.

Mrs Roper personally selected the coolie to carry Sarah's single suitcase. Thirty years of experience had given her an eye, she said; an eye for the kind of coolie an unaccompanied white girl could rely on not to intimidate her into paying him more than he deserved, and to make sure, in such a case as this, that the transfer from one train to another was smoothly accomplished.

'Shouldn't we find an escort for you?' Mrs Perryman asked. 'There must be at least one young officer on the platform we could whistle up.'

But Sarah was already at the open door of the carriage and there were nearly two hours to go before the train for Pankot left Ranpur. 'I'll go to the restaurant and then to the waiting-room if necessary. I'll be perfectly all right. Thank you for all your kindness.' She shook hands with them and stepped down. The platform was crowded. She saw bearers threading their way through with loaded trays, and called up to Mrs Roper that their meals were coming. Then she waved and followed the elderly coolie who had her suitcase on his head. Her childhood delight in travelling at night was still a potent force. She had always loved the noise, the risk, of railway stations. The journey to Calcutta was the first she had ever made alone. The case, hovering at eye level – and as bodies interposed themselves between her and its bearer looking as if it moved of its own accord without support – was a symbol of childhood's end. It struck her how curious an object a suitcase was. To it you consigned those few essential portable things that bore the invisible marks of your private possession of them; but the case itself was destined to live most of its useful life under the public gaze and in the hands of strangers.

At the door of the station restaurant the coolie halted. The turbanned head, which earned him an anna for all that it could carry at any one time, was set in a rigid thrust-up position that gave his eyes, under wrinkled, hooded lids, a preoccupied, anxious look. She changed her mind about going to the restaurant first. The Pankot train would be waiting at its special platform. She could look for her reservation and, if she were lucky, get the compartment opened and have a tray sent in. She gave the coolie instructions and once more followed him, to the end of the main platform, to the point where two subsidiary tracks came in to a bay, to sets of buffers, with a platform separating them. On one track there were three lit coaches, one of them painted blue and white, colours she had never seen before, and on the other the Pankot train, which she recognized because of the coaches: old-fashioned, squarer-cut, and with decorative flourishes in the woodwork. There were a few people on the platform, among them two Indian police, and a station official with a white topee. The Pankot train was in darkness. Some way along the platform under a lamp, a group of private soldiers were playing cards. Men off leave or on posting; perhaps both kinds. Tomorrow night they would be playing cards or writing home at the regimental institute and perhaps Mrs Fosdick or Mrs Paynton would be among the women who manned the tea-urns. She felt the first lick of a wave of nostalgia for the Pankot hills, but fought it down because upon its ripples grief could ride in. She spoke to the Indian in the white topee. No, the train was not ready yet. No, he did not have the key to unlock the compartments. But he went with her, looking with a torch for that strange advertisement of her name, noted and written on a piece of card by someone she would never see and placed in its metal bracket on the side of the carriage by someone she might see but never know.

Closer to the group of card-players this other card was found. A coupé. The discovery gave her childish pleasure, as did the fact that there was no name on the card but her own. Miss Layton. She would sleep undisturbed. She turned to the patient coolie and used the old old words of command. *Idhar thairo. Idhar thairo.* Stay here. Stay here. Dutifully he lowered the case and then squatted beside it as though it were a child he had carried far, out of some ancient servitude which he himself still had the habit of but hoped not to entrust with the other burden of the genes; and would not, for the genes of the case were hers, not his.

'What's the blue and white carriage?' she asked the man in the white topee.

'Oh, that is private. It belongs to a maharajah.'

'Which maharajah?'

'I do not know. There are so many.'

She thanked him for finding her compartment and walked back towards the restaurant, anticipating light and noise. This platform was sour and gloomy. Clark's words came back to her. 'A tomb-attendant?' Ahead of her a man was getting out of the blue and white carriage, a man in a white suit and panama hat. He had a stick and took the descent carefully. She noticed him because he might be the maharajah but quickly realized he could not be. The lamp on the platform revealed the fact that he was a European. He took out a cigarette case. He had got out of the carriage to smoke. Perhaps the maharajah was inside and did not like him smoking. He glanced at her, but concerned himself again with his cigarette, as if quite uninterested in her presence. He was oblivious of the fact that she had entered. Had entered. To him, perhaps, all women were assumed to have entered. Into their bodies' grace.

But beyond him she hesitated and turned. Her action caused him to look in her direction, with his one available eye. The other was the blind buffed eye of a nocturnal animal. She retraced her steps.

'Count Bronowsky?'

Already he had lifted his hat, but it was clear to her he did not recognize her, and for a moment she was afraid she had spoken to a man who looked like Bronowsky but was not. He said, 'Yes, I am Count Bronowsky.'

'I'm Sarah Layton. We stayed at the guest house last October when my sister was married.'

'Miss Layton? Well, forgive me. Why didn't I recognize you? But I know. It's the uniform. I see indeed it is you.' He held out his hand and, when she gave him hers, carried it with an old man's courtesy to his lips and held on to it. His accent, which she did not remember having remarked in Mirat, struck her as comic, exaggerated. She had a sense of charade which probably emanated from him because she had had it on the morning of the wedding when he joined the group on the lawn of the Mirat Gymkhana club; a sense of charade, of puppet-show; of dolls manipulated to a point just short of climax.

'Nawab Sahib and I were so very distressed to hear of Captain Bingham's death,' he said. How clever still to remember Teddie's name; but then the old wazir could count a memory for names among his many – obviously many – talents. He had remembered Merrick's too.

'It was kind of you to write. Have you been staying in Ranpur?' She assumed that like herself he was on the point of departure.

'No, not staying.' He let her hand go. 'Have you?'

'I'm only changing trains. I've just got in from Calcutta.'

'That train is going to Pankot?'

'It is at midnight. I came along to make sure my booking was fixed. Now I'm going to have some supper.'

'In the restaurant?'

'Yes. It's still open.'

'And are you alone?' She nodded. 'My dear Miss Layton, I cannot allow it. We can do better for you than that. In the restaurant you will wait for twenty minutes for something badly cooked, I'm quite sure of it. And then you will not sleep a wink, and what dire consequences might ensue from entering such a place unaccompanied I do not know.' He took her arm, holding hat and stick and unlit cigarette in his other hand, and began to guide her to the steps of the Nawab's coach.

'But –'

'But I am inviting you. On behalf of Nawab Sahib, who is not here by the way. I invite you into more compatible sur-roundings. Besides, apart from my own pleasure there is that of a handsome young Englishman who is already bored by my company but too well bred to show it. Only his sense of duty persuades him to sit and listen to me as if every word I speak is of importance to him. And Ahmed will be here presently. You remember Ahmed? You rode horses together. Do you like champagne? Of course you like champagne. With perhaps some caviar. And some cold game pie. Or smoked ham with melon. When Nawib Sahib is not in the coach it is possible for me to indulge a taste for smoked ham. The champagne is from my personal pre-war stock. I have been eking it out this past year but the Allied invasion of France encourages me to hope for fresh consignments before too long. You know the story of the true princess?'

'The one who needed twelve mattresses?'

'That is she. But even through twelve mattresses she felt the discomfort of one little pea from the pod. How can I let you suffer the discomfort of entering a public restaurant?'

'Well, I'm used to it. But thank you.'

The way in was like the entrance to a Pullman coach, but a thickness of carpet at once pointed a private superiority. The door that led into the main interior was closed and she waited until Bronowsky had negotiated the steps and joined her. His lameness, like his accent, was new to her. Perhaps it was only noticeable when he had something more agile to perform than walking. He opened the door on to a saloon of red and gold – a travelling throne-room such as she imagined the last Tsar Nicholas would have felt at home in. There were tables lit by crimson-shaded lamps, gilt chairs with crimson backs and seats, footstools, and salon sofas. At the far end an open doorway, hung with looped velvet curtains, gave a view of a dining-table set with a snowy white cloth and decked for a buffet.

As they went in the man Count Bronowsky had forewarned her of looked up from the document he was reading. Her arrival obviously surprised him and to get up he had first to secure the document to the briefcase on which he had been resting it, and uncross his legs. An army officer, he was wearing best KD.

'Allow me to introduce Captain Rowan,' Bronowsky said. 'This is Miss Layton whom I have just rescued from going alone to the restaurant. Nawab Sahib and I had the pleasure of her company at the Palace guest house last year on the occasion of her sister's marriage.'

Rowan nodded. Sarah thought she would not describe him as handsome. Her main impression of him was of a man, perhaps a little younger than Clark, who would be extremely difficult to get to know. There was something in the careful way in which he had overcome his surprise, temporarily withdrawn his interest from the document, and risen, still in possession of it and of the briefcase, that suggested a controlled expenditure of energy, a distrust of any kind of instant reaction, a firm belief in the importance of keeping reserves of whatever particular capacities he had. She judged that probably they were considerable.

A steward appeared in the doorway of the dining saloon. 'First,' Bronowsky said, 'champagne. We were going to wait for Ahmed, but only as a puritanical exercise in self-discipline. With champagne there should always be a sense of occasion, which you have kindly supplied. Come, sit. Do you smoke?' He offered her a silver box of pink cigarettes with gold tips. When they were settled he went on: 'I myself smoke only in the evenings, and then I'm afraid I smoke too many, but these are mild. My introduction to smoking was of a most unusual nature in that I was chastised by my father not *for* smoking but for showing an aversion for tobacco which he thought unmanly. All through one summer, when we were in the country, and I but sixteen, I was made to sit opposite him in his study at ten o'clock each morning and smoke a cigar under threat of a beating from my English tutor should I but turn a paler shade of pale. The fact that my tutor would not have hurt a fly and that I knew the threat no more than a threat, mere bombast, on the part of a man for whose moral cowardice I had the greatest contempt, did not diminish my valiant struggles to disguise my nausea. It became, you understand, a point of honour to smoke the disgusting thing to the bitter end and retire – apparently in good order. But my repugnance for cigar-tobacco has never left me. That winter, in St Petersburg, I took a perverse fancy for the gold-tipped cigarettes smoked by the lady who frequently visited us. I should perhaps explain that my mother died when

I was ten. I would steal one of these cigarettes from this lady's handbag whenever I had the opportunity. She kept them in a tortoiseshell case. I remember the case quite clearly, the smooth feel of it in my fingers. And having stolen one I would smoke it after I had gone to bed delighting in the fact that I had stolen it from her and that, unwomanly as smoking was considered at that time, these particular cigarettes looked revoltingly effeminate. Hence my life-long habit – gold-tipped cigarettes, preferably pink, and after sunset. In such small ways we preserve the memories of our youth and remain to that extent forever young. What memories, Miss Layton – or I should say, what habits that will become memories do you think you will still celebrate when you are my age?'

'I don't know, but I'm sure there are some.'

'With girls perhaps it is different. They grow up and marry and have children of their own and everything from their own childhood is put by. Perhaps this is sad because much later what was put by as done with and forgotten may come back to plague them with an intense nostalgia. Their children grow up and go away and all the years a woman devotes to them are as if they have never been. Women are more courageous than men though. Perhaps they accept that their life's work, I mean in the biological sense, is very quickly over. But a man and his career, that is different. His career is the whole of his life. He can afford to introduce notes of absurdity. Perhaps he needs to. His body undergoes no biological change, his life is not divided in that way, nothing physically dramatic happens to him. He never carries his own creature inside him, the poor man has to make do with the one he was born as. Perhaps this explains why he cherishes the memory of its different stages of growth and hangs on to them, in the hope of seeing something whole.'

The champagne cork popped. They were all three silent witnesses of the ritual of pouring. The steward wore white gloves. He handed the glasses on a silver tray. Bronowsky said, 'Captain Rowan, I had not intended tonight to introduce a personal note, but there was a private reason for the champagne and Miss Layton's gift of her company prompts me to share my secret with you both. Today is my seventieth birthday, and I have a toast.' He grinned. 'As an Englishman you will probably appreciate it more than Nawab Sahib would – who touchingly remembered the day and sent me a telegram this morning from Nanoora.' He raised his glass. ' "It is little I repair to the matches of the Southron folk, Though my own red roses there may blow; It is little I repair to the matches of the Southron folk, Though the red roses crest the caps, I know. For the field is full of shades as I near the shadowy coast, And a ghostly batsman plays to the bowling of a ghost, And I look through my tears on a soundless clapping host, As the run-stealers flicker to and fro, To and fro; O my Hornby and my Barlow long ago!" '

He raised his glass still higher, then lowered it and drank; and, when they followed suit (both – Sarah thought – rather put off their strokes by the unexpectedness of the occasion and the obscure, indeed incongruous, connection between the words and the man who spoke them) Bronowsky went on: 'The poem was explained to me by the charming boy from whom I learnt it in 1919, but I fear my own private interpretation is the one that remains with me. He was just eighteen and his parents had sent him from England to stay with a French family who were holidaying on the Italian Riviera. He learned, or was supposed to learn, French conversation from them. I, a poor Russian *émigré*, was hired to teach him the language's grammar and syntactical complexities, not I fear successfully because he fell madly in love with the Spanish maid of a neighbouring family. His other interest, his only other interest, was cricket. He came to me one day and said, Monsieur Bronowsky, please teach me a French poem. Well, I knew why. I had seen them together, holding hands and staring into each other's eyes, quite dumb, because the girl really only spoke her own language and what little French they might have exchanged quite deserted him the moment he was in her adorable presence. "But if she speaks only Spanish," I said to him, "what purpose will a French poem serve? Why not recite to her in English?" He said he'd thought of that but he only knew one poem, which happened not to be suitable. I begged him to let me be the judge of that and made him recite it. I was extraordinarily moved and told him to repeat it to her in just the same manner, but perhaps a little slower and with slightly more expression. I also got him to write it down for me.'

'And was it successful?' Sarah asked. 'I mean with the Spanish maid?'

'Alas. He found her that same afternoon holding hands with a fisher-lad. He told me of this disaster when he came for his evening lesson. He was stunned, well, you could see it, but also well controlled, in the way of the English. He went home very soon after that in order, so he said, to get in some more cricket before the summer ended. You could tell he was quite finished with women. At least for a week or so.'

'What a sad story,' Sarah said.

'Isn't it? I'm delighted you see that it is sad as well as comic. And I've always thought how much that flirtatious young lady's memories were impoverished by the chance she missed to have her hand held and her ears simultaneously enchanted by a poem she would not have understood a word of but could hardly have failed to know was spoken from the heart. You see he felt quite romantic about cricket, and so long as she didn't know what the poem was about, it was the perfect vehicle for him to express one passion through the medium of another. She would have heard the rhymes, and the slow alliterative and repetitive cadences which seem to be holding on to memories to stop them slipping too soon away. She would have heard the strange hard burr of a northern language, softly spoken, and so different from the loudly spoken languages of the south, which the sun seems to have melted so that they flow ever quickly onwards, with hardly a pause, like time itself. Above all, how could she not have detected the note of pride ringing through the lamentation! Oh, if I had been she, no doubt I would have positively swooned away.'

'Anyway,' Rowan said, 'congratulations. Your own journey south has been capped by conspicuous successes.'

'Ah,' Bronowsky exclaimed. 'I have understanding companions. Thank you. Steward. More champagne. Miss Layton, what news of your father?'

'We haven't heard for some time, but we believe he's well.'

'And he'll be home soon, surely? And your mother and sister? Particularly your sister?'

'Yes, they're both well.' She would not intrude her anxiety. Or her grief.

'And what took you to Calcutta, alone?'

'My aunt lives there now.'

'Ah yes, I recall. Mrs Grace? And your uncle who gave your

sister away? They are both in Calcutta?' She nodded. 'And the officer who was best man, Captain Merrick, have you had news of him?'

She hesitated, again reluctant to introduce a sombre subject on the old man's birthday. In any case he was probably only being polite.

'He interested me considerably,' Bronowsky went on, as if prompting her. 'I thought him an unusual man.'

'Actually it was to visit him in the hospital that I went to Calcutta.'

'Really? What is wrong with him?'

'He was rather badly wounded at the same time Captain Bingham was killed. My sister was anxious to find out if there was anything we could do because she was told he'd tried to help Teddie. There's been a recommendation. I mean for a decoration.'

'Yes,' Bronowsky said after a moment's thought. 'Courage. He had physical courage. You could see that. I'm distressed to hear he was wounded. How badly?'

'He's lost an arm. He pulled Teddie out of a blazing truck while they were under fire.'

'Ah.' A pause. 'Yes. Which arm?'

'The left.'

A pause. 'Then that is something. I observed him picking up bits of confetti, also stubbing a cigarette. He was right-handed.' He turned to Rowan. 'You may remember the man we're speaking of. Merrick?'

'No. I don't think so.'

'I don't mean you would remember him personally. He went into the army from the Indian Police. He figured rather prominently in that case involving an English girl, in Mayapore in 1942. The Bibighar.'

Rowan was drawing on his cigarette. He nodded. 'Oh yes. That case.'

'He was District Superintendent. In Mirat I had a long and interesting talk to him and found him still utterly convinced that the men he arrested were truly guilty. I myself and I suppose most people since have come to the conclusion they couldn't have been. It would have been understandable if Merrick had begun to waver in his opinion – unless you accept that he left the police temporarily under a cloud and he harboured a grudge. But he had tried for years to get into the army. He was a very ordinary man on the surface but underneath, I suspect, a man of unusual talents. Are those boys still in prison?'

'Which boys are those?'

'The ones arrested, not tried, but detained, as politicals.'

'I'm afraid I don't know, Count.'

'I hope they are not forgotten and just being left to rot. The provincial authorities have an obligation in this matter, surely.'

'I'm sure they are not just forgotten.'

'The Indians remember. Unfortunately not only Indians of the right sort. There is a venerable gentleman of Mayapore who last year visited Mirat and engaged in some tortuous processes of intimidation. The stone – Miss Layton, you recall the stone – was almost certainly thrown at the instigation of this slippery customer. He is one of those on whom we keep a watchful eye. I am told he has recently left Mayapore, but I am not told where he has gone, or why. Forgive me, it is an uncheerful subject, and Miss Layton must eat. We shan't wait for Ahmed. In any case he's probably only going to be interested in the champagne.'

Rowan looked at his watch and Bronowsky, who was rising, touched his arm. 'We shall be able to leave on the scheduled time. Ahmed will see to it. Come.' He led them to the dining saloon. Two stewards removed covers from the waiting dishes.

'I must go, I'm afraid,' Sarah said, putting down her coffee cup. Her watch showed twenty minutes to midnight and for some time now she had been nervously aware of mounting activity on the platform. Once she had parted the crimson velvet curtains that covered the window she sat near and had seen more soldiers, and officers directing them; Indian families with mounds of roped luggage, some of the women in purdah. The lights were on in the Pankot train but the view was too oblique for her to make out her patient coolie, who would still be waiting.

'Another five minutes,' Bronowsky pleaded. He had regaled them with more champagne and talk of pre-1914 Russia and post-1918 Europe, but for the last ten minutes she had been too conscious of the narrowing gap between the minute and hour hands of her wrist-watch to take in much of what he said. She believed that Captain Rowan was similarly preoccupied, but disguising it better. Occasionally he glanced at her as if to say: I know how you feel, but don't worry.

'If I stay another five minutes I shall never want to go, and I've got my compartment to get unlocked.'

Bronowsky put down his glass. 'Then I mustn't be selfish. But Ahmed will be disappointed. He often talks about you.' They all three stood. He took her hand and kissed it. 'Thank you for my birthday present. You will return to Mirat? One day, very soon?'

'Yes. I should like to,' she said, and realized quite suddenly that she meant it, and knowing how unlikely it was that she would ever go again, felt a wrench at parting that was out of all proportion to the real loss or lack of expectation. She turned to Rowan.

'Goodbye, Captain Rowan.'

He took her hand, but not in farewell. 'I'll see you to your compartment,' he said, but Bronowsky intervened, insisted that this was a privilege he claimed for himself. She thought Rowan's face betrayed a momentary blankness, as if the refusal by Bronowsky of his offer to accompany her had made it necessary for him to dismiss from his mind some line of thought or plan of action he had wished to pursue; but since they had only just met and were unlikely ever to meet again, she knew she must be mistaken. But the impression remained, after they had said goodbye and while Bronowsky was handing her down on to the platform. Once down it vanished to the back of her mind, driven there by surprise.

'Why, they've cordoned us off,' she said.

'It saves us from being boarded and from constant explanations that we are not a public conveyance,' he said, and guided her inside the cordon of ropes that held the crowds away from the three coaches, to a point where a policeman was on duty. Originally there had been only two policemen. There were four or five now. The policeman let them through. She felt she would have understood the cordoning off and the presence of police if the Nawab had been travelling. But he was in Nanoora. She had assumed from some of the things said by Bronowsky and Rowan in the past hour and a half that Bronowsky was going to Nanoora too.

She glanced up the platform. They were level now with the

front of the first of the three coaches which a locomotive was slowly approaching.

'There is our engine,' the Count said, pointing with his stick. He walked on her left, holding her left elbow. 'We are due to leave at half past midnight, so we must hope Ahmed isn't much longer delayed. If we fail to leave at twelve-thirty the railway people can't fit us in to their schedule again until two a.m. That is your coolie attracting our attention. Now, where is an inspector to unlock your compartment? The fellow over there in the white topee?' Bronowsky waved his stick. The coolie humped the suitcase and stood with that same upward-strained rigidity of neck and head.

It was the same kind of topee but a different man under it, and he had the key. He unlocked, entered and switched on lights and fans, and the coolie climbed up and deposited the bag, returned, touching his turban. She had two rupees ready but Bronowsky restrained her and gave the old man a folded note, which looked like five and must have been because after he salaamed he did not go away but waited near by as if accepting an obligation to see that the train carried her safely out of his hands and into those of God.

In the compartment adjacent to hers three young subalterns who looked like new postings from an OTS eyed her curiously, no doubt assuming that the elderly man with the eye-patch and ebony cane was her father, a sahib of the old school. No, she wanted to say to them, it's not as you think you see it. What you see is a trick, everything here is a trick. She turned to Bronowsky, feeling for questions.

'Have you a blanket and things like that?' he asked before she could speak.

'Yes, they're in my case.'

'And you haven't left the key of the case behind in Calcutta?'

She laughed, looked in her handbag and reassured him. The question eluded her. 'Please don't stay, Count Bronowsky,' she said, and held her hand out. 'Thank you for a marvellous supper and for rescuing me from the restaurant. And – Happy Birthday.'

He took her hand, but was silent for a while, looking down at her through his one eye.

'How self-contained you are! I don't remember that when

you were in Mirat. But of course we did not exchange many words and you were somewhat overshadowed by the occasion. A bride is always the centre of attraction. But Ahmed noticed you. He affects not to be susceptible to the charms of white ladies. But after you had gone I observed how on many mornings he rode across the waste-ground opposite my house and retraced exactly the course you had taken together, stopping under the same trees, cantering along the same stretch.' He smiled. 'I am confessing, aren't I? That I watched you from the window of my bedroom. I did, but not intentionally. I caught sight of you by chance, but was held by the spectacle. I was amused to see he was doing as he had warned, the night before, when he told me he was to take you riding. He said: Oh! I shall keep my distance, I shall keep my place. It was a joke, of course. Not a bitter one. He has great objectivity, perhaps too much. He is somewhat like an actor who knows every line in a play and plays his part to perfection but cannot light the character up from inside, so with him it is always a part. Well here is Ahmed Kasim, he says, committed to go riding with this English girl. What is expected, what does the world say? Yes, of course. Five paces behind. How amusing! Only he is perhaps less amused than he would have us think. You understand?'

'I understand, yes.'

'You understand what I am saying, but not why I am saying it. To tell you the truth I am not sure. It's probably the champagne. On the other hand, unlike the majority of people I am the opposite of tongue-tied by railway stations and scenes of departure. It must be due to a fear implanted in my mind years ago that even the simplest goodbye may turn out to be for ever and leave you with a feeling of remorse for big and little things you left unsaid. Not that you should ever say everything. Perhaps I am talking to stop you asking those questions you want to ask which I can't answer. I must beg forgiveness. I am only adding to the mystery. But mysteries are no bad thing, especially for the young. They warm the powers of perception and in themselves can be quite beautiful.'

A warning whistle blew. Bronowsky gripped her hand more firmly, reassuring her there was still time – far more for her than for him. 'But don't misinterpret. That picture you have in your mind now, of Ahmed retracing the course you took across the waste-ground. I did not intend a romantic allusion. I said he had great objectivity. He is a spectator, an observer, and when the need arises he can take a part, but not with his heart in it because he doesn't know what part he wants to play or, if he has an inkling, he doesn't see where it fits in. He's indifferent to all the passions that most arouse people in this country. I suppose with a family like his that's lived, breathed and thought nothing but politics it's not unnatural. But in India it's rare. And because it's rare he thinks of it as a disease peculiar to him. He said to me once: "My mother tells me to think hard about something my father once wrote to her – We are looking for a country. But when I think about it I can only make the comment that the country's here, and so am I, and shouldn't we stop squabbling over it and start living in it? What does it really matter who runs it, or who believes in Allah, or Christ, or the avatars of Hindu mythology, or who has a dark face and who has a light?" '

'Yes,' Sarah said, 'what does it matter?'

Bronowsky considered her, and for the first time she noticed how concentrated, how single-minded, a one-eyed man had to be, how deprived he was of the tragi-comic human right to laugh on one side of his face and cry on the other, like the king in the fairy tale. She felt pierced, as if by a singularity of purpose and intent. But that was a mystery too. Perhaps it was beautiful. She did not know. In a few minutes the chance to know would have gone, would have joined the sad jumble of all the other limited chances which (panic-stricken by the thought that the train would suddenly be gone without her), she felt everyone was given.

'He told me about his father's letter and his reactions to it some time *after* you rode together, after you had left Mirat.'

The whistle blew again.

'And you see, he had never spoken to me so frankly before. And I remembered those solitary rides he took, which I did – I must confess – see at first in a superficially romantic light. But now when I look at that picture of him over and over re-enacting that morning ride, I seem to see him trying to recapture something. Some moment he missed, or did not seize, and only understood later was significant.'

'Yes,' she said, 'there was a moment.'

'Tell me.'

'I can't. It wasn't clear. It was to do with the way he kept behind.'

'Something you said?'

'No. Didn't you see?'

'Beyond the mullah, when you galloped, you were outside my range. Two blurred specks. But coming back I thought you once had difficulty with your horse.'

'Not difficulty. I tricked him. I closed the gap. Just for a moment.'

'And then?'

'That was all. He waited for me to ride on.'

The third whistle. 'Thank you, Miss Layton,' he said. 'Now – you had better take your seat, but don't close the door. My steward has some extra luggage for you.' Looking behind she found the steward waiting with a small hamper held to his chest. 'Come.' He handed her up. She stood back and let the steward come in and place the hamper on the floor. When he left the compartment Bronowsky closed the door. She stood at the lowered window. 'There is some champagne,' he said, raising his voice, 'for a christening, which if my arithmetic is correct will take place in the quite near future. But there are also a few things for you to nibble if you get hungry. Shut the windows tight, lock the door and lower the blinds. And if you are in trouble knock loudly on the wall between you and the young officers next door who have been watching with very understandable interest. When next you write to Captain Merrick please remember me to him and tell him I recall our conversation. He will know what I mean.'

'Yes, I will. And thank you again.'

'Now. Please pander to an old man and an old Russian superstition. The circumstances are wrong but the gesture may overcome them. Just sit quietly for a moment, as one always should before setting out on a journey.'

She sat and exchanged smiles with him through the window. Presently the whistle sounded again – a sustained and urgent note. She got up. When she reached the window of the door the train was moving. Bronowsky stayed motionless – his panama hat held to his breast – but gliding away from her, becoming partially obscured by groups of people who slid past as if the platform were being pulled backwards by some strange law of lateral gravity. As the view of the station expanded she saw distantly the three coaches of the Nawab's private train, marooned under dwindling points of illumination. She thought, but could not be sure, that two figures were passing through the cordon, a man and a woman in purdah; but the glimpse was scarcely a glimpse; perhaps a brief hallucinatory image switched by her eye from one part of the platform to another.

When she had closed windows and meshes and lowered blinds, secured locks, it was twenty-four hours since she had entered her body's grace. She made up her bed with sheet and blanket, blew up her air pillow, but then sat, tracing the red and green tartan pattern of the pillow's cover with her right forefinger. Why red and green? Why tartan? She held the pillow to her, then lay down, letting it cushion her head.

Are you happy? he asked. I'm content. Then we're friends? Not friends. Enemies? No, not enemies – strangers still. Shall we make love again? She turned her head into the pillow, wanting him because she knew no other man. The pain of wanting was exquisite. She opened her mouth to receive an image of his but found only the warm flesh of her own hand that was not cunning or quick enough to hold back days or rescue a single firefly from all those that rode the night emitting signals of distress; the signal lights of souls gathering like migrant birds for a long journey because the home they knew had become inhospitable.

She dozed, woke, covered herself with the blanket as an insurance against the chill that would accompany their entry into the hills, but could not summon the resolution to turn off lights and fans. She dozed again, but sleep was held back by an instinct to keep watch on the night's dissembling progress. Ten minutes short of half past two. Going with him now, back into the danger zone. Are you sad? he asked. Just silent. Content and silent, he said, it's a good basis to build on, you will have a good life. And already up there in the hills (these hills) Aunty Mabel had gone, and been quickly buried, as was customary. And who knew whether hers had been a good life? I waited up, Aunt Fenny said, I waited up, pet, your mother rang. It was twenty-four minutes to three. At five it would be thirty-six hours since she had stood waiting for Sister Prior, and since Susan – lying on the verandah of Rose Cottage – had watched Aunty Mabel suddenly put down her basket on the rail between two of the azaleas, and sit, and die, as quietly as she had lived.

VI

At four Ahmed was woken by one of the stewards; and at half
past, wearing a new dark grey tropical suit made up by Bronowsky's tailor, he went along the corridor and tapped at the door
of his mother's compartment. She was lying fully dressed on her
bunk. On the opposite bunk her maid snored with her back
turned to the single light that lit his mother's head.

'Is it time?' Mrs Kasim asked, keeping her voice low.

'Yes, Mother. Don't get up.'

'Have you slept at all?'

'Yes. Is there anything I can get you?'

'No, Ahmed, nothing.'

'You shouldn't have stayed awake.'

She held on to his hand. 'It wasn't difficult. Stay with me until
the train stops. But don't let's talk. Poor Farina's exhausted.' He
sat on the edge of the bunk. His mother nodded, closed her eyes.
'You look very smart,' she murmured, and gripped his hand
more tightly, as if to thank him for taking trouble. Her hair was
greyer than it had been even six months ago. He didn't know –
had never known – what she really thought. She had always
seemed content to echo his father's words. What have you got
out of it, he wanted to ask, out of all this struggle and dedication
and sacrifice? What have your compensations been? Are they so
small that you notice a suit and get comfort from having me sit
and say nothing?

After a while it began to worry him that perhaps the train was
behind schedule, that he was committed to stay for a long time,
uncomfortably perched; but there was now a change in the
rhythm of the rapidly moving coach. His mother noticed it too.
Deep – too deep – lines of concentration appeared on her forehead. Speed was being lost. Presently they had slowed to that
tentative pace which always made Ahmed feel that a train had
transformed itself from a mindless piece of careering machinery
into a sentient intelligent creature, probing forward through a
maze of obstacles.

His mother opened her eyes and leant up on one elbow. 'You
had better go.'

He bent for her kiss.

'You've got the letter safely?'

'Yes, Mother, I've got it safely.' He patted his breast pocket.

She watched him until he pulled the door to between them. In the corridor he lit a cigarette. The dining-saloon still savoured of old festivity, too recent to have gone stale; but it seemed to belong to another time. A nodding steward jerked awake as Ahmed passed him. He found Bronowsky awake in the saloon, reading a small leather-bound book, smoking one of his pink cigarettes.

'I have been indulging several of my most private vices,' the Count said, 'wakefulness while the world dreams, the poetry of Pushkin and an unfinished bottle. There is still a glass left. Or would you prefer something stronger? Yes. Steward. Bring Kasim Sahib a large scotch and soda. Or no soda? No soda.'

'Is Captain Rowan up?'

'I hope so. He was woken at four-fifteen. I have kept watch as well. But that's a virtue. Has your mother slept?'

'No. She promises to.'

The scotch was brought. Ahmed took a generous gulp.

'Here,' Bronowsky said, reaching into his pocket. 'I have a present for you.' He offered a clove of garlic. 'Chew it before you reach the Circuit House.'

'Thanks.'

'Take care not to get close to Captain Rowan, though. He would be too polite to turn his head. He's expecting an appointment in the Political Department, he tells me. We talked for a while after you went to bed. I expect Sir George Malcolm has entrusted him with this present business mainly to help him get his hand in. He should do well. He has a talent for finding out what he wants to know without appearing to encourage conversation to rise above the level of casual chat, and for feigning indifference to the information when he gets it.'

'What did he want to know tonight?'

'He was fascinated by Merrick and the stone and Pandit Baba Sahib. His dismissal of Merrick's name as one that meant nothing to him was disingenuous. I'm too old a hand not to react when feigned indifference is set off by an aura of alertness. I sensed it when Miss Layton and I were talking and sensed it again when I told you in front of him about Merrick's loss of an arm. When we were alone he worked skilfully back to the subject. He began by asking me how and where I lost the sight of an eye. But of course I helped him. We are both professionals.'

'Are you warning me not to speak too freely to him? You know I never do that.' Ahmed smiled, and took another mouthful of the whisky. Had he really got a taste for it yet? He wasn't sure.

'I am giving you, possibly, an example of the discreet way in which the English set to work to re-establish a principle of justice, for their own peace of mind, while attempting to preserve the *status quo* resulting from the breaking of the principle. If Rowan knew of Merrick, which I firmly believe, his pretence otherwise suggests that the files on the six unfortunate detenus in the Manners case have quite recently been on His Excellency's desk. Which means that the detention orders are being reviewed, and possibly that poor Mr Merrick's reputation has suffered a set-back far more serious than the one that saw him packed off to a backwater by a department anxious to keep its mistakes from reaching the ears of more powerful departments which need to ensure that the principles of impartial justice are *seen* to be held sacrosanct. Assuming my interpretation is correct, do you understand Captain Rowan's interest in the recent history of the ex-District Superintendent in Mayapore?'

'No. It's too early in the morning, Count Sahib. And he'll be here in a minute.' The train was still at a crawl, single-mindedly solving the Chinese puzzle of steel links that unfairly confronted it.

'Sometimes, Ahmed, you are so deliberately obtuse that I could send you to bed for a week on bread and water.' The Count paused. 'The reason is – and you would do well to remember it – that Captain Rowan has recognized with the sure instinct of his race, that Mr Merrick's recent history is the key to the preservation of the *status quo*. It has probably already been decided that the six boys are unjustly detained and must be released. That is the principle of justice re-established. But how preserve the *status quo* when clearly a mistake was made by Merrick and compounded by superior authority? On paper your prime scapegoat is Merrick. But how unpleasant to have a scapegoat at all. Imagine the relief with which Captain Rowan will go back to Ranpur and initiate discreet inquiries – with the Governor's approval – into the truth of what he has heard tonight. A citation for bravery in the field and an amputated arm. What luck! It wipes the blot from the escutcheon and solves the problem of Mr Merrick's future civil or military employment. The boys go free, the files are closed, and all is – as they say – as it was before. The one thing the English fear is scandal, I mean private scandal. If Mr Merrick had ever been asked to account for his actions the outside world would never have heard of it.'

'You think he had actions to account for?'

'Undoubtedly.'

The train jerked to a halt. From somewhere beneath and a few feet behind, something clanked. Ahmed went to the window, parted the curtains and saw pools of diffused light on cinders, and under one of the standards that shed the light a limousine from the palace and an army truck. He pulled the curtain to, drained his glass and looked at Bronowsky.

'*Courage, mon ami,*' Bronowsky said, '*le diable est mort.*' Ahmed repeated the words to himself, to translate them. He smiled. 'Is he?' he asked.

They waited for Rowan.

Eventually they were beyond the town. The windows of the limousine were lowered half-way. Sheet lightning spasmodically lit the night sky and the barren landscape.

'It's very close,' Rowan said. 'With any luck it'll be raining tomorrow.'

Ahmed agreed that with any luck it would, and mentally put up his guard. But where could a civilized exchange about the weather lead except to a mutual recognition that they had nothing to say that would destroy their all too ready-made images of each other? Rowan – the archetypal Englishman, unemphatic in speech and gesture but warmed inside no doubt by the belief that what he did would have its modest place in the margins of history; and himself, younger son of a veteran Congress Muslim, the son who failed and got packed off to kick his heels in one of the old princely states where he could embarrass no one; known to drink and to womanize, to be indifferent to politics, a potential wastrel and living proof of the continuing validity of the classic formula of misfortune that could afflict respected parents.

'Is there any point you think we ought to discuss before we arrive?' Rowan asked.

'No, everything is clear.' Clearer to him, he thought, than perhaps Rowan realized; although it would be wrong to make too firm an assumption on that score. He felt in his pocket for the clove of garlic and self-consciously carried it to his mouth. Rowan gave him a quick glance, as a guard would who had to bring a prisoner to a place of interrogation and keep alert for attempts at suicide. The car rode the unrepaired tarmac more evenly than the truck ahead in whose canvas-roofed interior two British military policemen sat stoic under the hypnosis of the twin sources of pursuing light.

Abruptly the gap between truck and limousine shortened.

'We're there, I think,' Rowan said. The truck turned across a culvert that separated the road from the eroded landscape. The limousine followed. They were in a compound that had no walls. There were lights on in the Circuit House. Figures moved on the verandah. There were two other vehicles parked. Getting out of the limousine Ahmed surveyed the land beyond the compound, but the night was black and there was no view of the fort. He followed Rowan to the verandah. Rowan shook hands with an Englishman in civilian clothes and with one in the uniform of the civil police, but when he turned, wishing to make introductions, Ahmed said, 'I'll wait down there, if you don't mind,' and walked to a place where a chair and a table were set, and took up his position.

Presently Rowan joined him. 'Don't you wish to meet the Divisional Commissioner?'

'Not just now, unless it's essential.'

'Very well,' Rowan said, and left him.

Very well. It was one of the English phrases Ahmed had never understood. Rowan and the others would probably intepret his withdrawal and isolation as a sulky attempt to show them that after all he had a patriotic nature. They could not know that he isolated himself to preserve for as long as possible his sense of detachment from the issues of a situation not of his own devising.

And after a while there was a light, far off; gone as soon as seen; but his muscles had tensed, as though to force his body to leap up and stretch an arm to glean the light before it was extinguished. But he continued to sit still and it was a long time before the light reappeared, moving and unmistakable, a mile down the road and coming at speed.

He got up and stood by the verandah rail, then went to the head of the steps, ignoring Rowan whose shadow fell aslant the floor from the open doorway. He heard Rowan go back in and say something to the others. The approaching car slowed, turned in across the culvert. He was dazzled by the abrupt glare of the headlights and the lingering penumbra as they were doused. An officer got out of the front passenger seat and opened the near door at the back. Ahmed felt his way down the steps.

An old man emerged, grasped the young officer's arm and slowly straightened. Light from the verandah revealed sunken eyes wide open with the shock of transition to a strange environment. With his free hand the old man shaded them.

'Ahmed? Ahmed? Is that you?' The voice did not belong to the old man. It was his father's voice. The officer stood away and Ahmed felt his left arm taken in both the old man's hands.

'Ahmed?'

'Yes, Father.'

'Your mother, Ahmed. Your mother. What news of your mother?'

'She's well, you'll see her very soon.'

'They let the Mahatma out. Poor Kasturba was dead.'

'I know. But there's nothing like that.'

'Then God is good to me.' He clung to him. Ahmed felt him trembling. The officer turned his back.

'Come and sit,' Ahmed said.

Presently the old man released him and stood back, looking suspiciously towards the house. 'Who is there?'

'An officer on the Governor's staff and two others I don't know.'

'So many people? But there is a room where I can be alone?'

'We can talk on the verandah.'

'No. Please ask for a room. I must be alone for a few minutes, then we must talk. After that I will see them. Not before. Ask this officer to go and tell them.'

'I'll go myself. Wait here.'

The room he entered was barely furnished. Rowan and the others were standing round a deal table. He spoke to Rowan, ignoring the Commissioner and the policeman.

'My father asks for a room where he can be alone for a while.'

Rowan turned to the Commissioner. 'Is there another room, sir?'

'There's one at the end, where Mr Kasim was sitting. It's not locked.'

'Is it for devotional use?' Rowan asked, looking in Ahmed's direction.

'Apparently no one at the Fort bothered to reassure him my mother was neither ill nor dying. He's been expecting to hear the worst. So he's not yet ready to talk to anyone.'

'The Fort commander would have had the minimum instructions necessary, but I regret any worry he's been caused.' Again he spoke to the Commissioner. 'I think it would be better if we made this room available to Mr Kasim and wait in the other one ourselves. Is there a way to it other than along the verandah?'

The Commissioner mumbled and led them out through a back door. Ahmed waited until the sounds they made were no longer audible, then went back to his father. He found him sitting in the car. He helped him out and up the steps. Inside the room, in the glare of the light, the physical toll exacted by nearly two years in prison was fully revealed. The long-skirted high-necked coat that had once shown up a comfortable thickness of body, hung loosely. The flesh of the thickened jowls was fallen, the fringe of hair was wholly grey. The white cap of Congress seemed too big. The hawk-like nose had a hungry questing look.

'I'll leave this with you, Father.' He gave him the envelope which contained his mother's letter. 'It's from Mother. She wrote it a few hours ago.'

'Is she near by?'

'Not far. Let me know when you want me.'

For the first time since entering the room his father looked at him.

'No, I am all right. Stay here. We must talk. You are taller. And broader. How long has it been?'

'Nearly three years.'

'You have your full growth. You quite dwarf me. Quite dwarf me.'

The moment was over then. In the few seconds sitting in the car his father had recovered and put back up the barriers.

'They told me nothing until five o'clock yesterday, and then only to pack my things and get a few hours' sleep. Am I free, or on my way to another jail?'

'You are free,' Ahmed said; but he had hesitated.

'On what conditions? Is there an amnesty? No – don't answer. Let me read your mother's letter. Sit down.' His father sat at the table. Ahmed chose a seat near the door, which was still open. The room was very warm. The fan was not working. Unhurriedly his father brought out his spectacle case and put the spectacles on. A slight tremor of the hands was the only sign that his composure was incomplete. The letter was very short but he lingered over it with the concentration Ahmed remembered as characteristic. Briefs, minutes, resolutions, correspondence: they had all been subjected to this slow searching analysis. Why does he take so long? Ahmed had once asked. His mother replied: He reads between the lines.

Kasim folded the letter and put it back in the envelope. He took his spectacles off, returned them to the case and the case to his pocket.

'Your mother says she hopes I will agree but that I'm not to be swayed by emotional or private considerations. You had better tell me what I'm being asked to agree to. All I gather otherwise is that she is on her way to Nanoora to stay with my kinsman, the Nawab, and that this could be the scene of our immediate reunion. I too am invited to Mirat?'

'Yes.'

'As a guest of the Nawab?'

'Yes. They call it – under his protection.'

'I see.' Kasim sat back. 'While in the sovereign state of Mirat I would be free to enjoy my rights as a private citizen, providing I did nothing to embarrass my host, which means nothing that incurs the displeasure of the Indian Government. Should I set foot outside the State on the other hand, and go back to Ranpur, then I should probably be arrested.'

'They haven't said so, Father.'

'They?'

'The Governor in Ranpur.'

'You've seen the Governor?'

'Not personally. Neither has Mother. But he sent representatives. One of them is here tonight.'

'On whose instigation did he send representatives? On the

Viceroy's? From newspapers and letters received I gather Wavell is anxious to break the political deadlock of the past two years. Who else is being released into this kind of protection? Nehru?'

'The Viceroy knows, but the initiative's been with Malcolm. It's not a general arrangement.'

'I am the only Congressman of any importance being paroled?'

'Yes, Father. So far as I know, you're the only one.'

'Why?'

The question was snapped. In the past such a tone and such a whiplash of a word had entangled perjured witnesses and intimidated honest ones. There was no way round the truth.

'Because of my brother.'

A pause.

'There is news of Sayed, then?' Kasim asked calmly.

'Yes.'

'Of his death? He has died in prison camp?'

'No, Father. He's been captured.'

'I know he was captured. He was captured by the Japanese in Kuala Lumpur in 1942. It is a long time since we had any word.'

But the old man seemed suddenly older. 'We've had word now,' Ahmed said. His father might never forgive him for saying what he had to say. Sayed had always been the favourite son, the one in whom hope had been placed, whose life had not been a source of disappointment. It should have been Sayed who sat here. The old man would then not have looked so old. 'Sayed was captured a month ago in Manipur,' he went on. 'We don't know where he is except in a prison camp in India with some of the others. Directly the army knew who he was they told the civil authorities in Calcutta and those authorities told the authorities in Ranpur. Malcolm invited Mother to Government House, but didn't say why. She refused to go so he sent someone to the house. Then she wrote to me in Mirat. She said she'd suspected for some time that Sayed had joined the INA. About six months ago she had an anonymous letter delivered by hand, telling her Sayed sent his love and would see her soon. I think I know who might have sent it, but that doesn't matter. And previously one of Mother's friends told her they thought they'd recognized Sayed's voice on the Japanese radio.'

'The INA —?'

'The Indian National Army.'

'I know what the initials stand for. I was about to say – the INA? Sayed?' The old man smiled. 'Captured in Manipur? Yes. Perhaps a man with this name, Lieutenant Sayed Kasim.'

'He was Major Kasim.'

'There you are then. Prisoners of war don't get promoted.'

'Major is his rank in the INA.'

'Rank? His *rank* in the INA? Is there such a thing? No. Sayed is not a major in the INA. He is Lieutenant Kasim and his regiment is the Ranpur Rifles. Why have you believed this ridiculous story? Someone has made a mistake, a ridiculous mistake, as a result of all this feeble propaganda which the British have rightly tried to scotch. Now they are believing it themselves, it seems. The Indian National Army? What can that be? A handful of madmen led by that other madman, Subhas Chandra Bose, who was never any good to Congress. He always had delusions of grandeur. First he escapes from India, then turns up in Berlin and then in Tokyo. He sets up an absurd paper government-in-exile and perhaps a few Indians living in Malaya put on a uniform and help him kowtow to the Japanese, fooling themselves that if the Japanese ever defeat India they will allow Subhas to set up his paper government in Delhi. But it is all wishful thinking and propaganda, there is no Indian National Army deserving of the name. If a Major Kasim was captured in Manipur he would be some unlucky fellow who foolishly accompanied the Japanese as an observer for Bose. He would not be Sayed. And Sayed would not be fighting and killing Indians. He would not be helping the Japanese to invade his own country.'

'There were thousands of Indians taken prisoner in Burma and Malaya. A lot of them felt they'd been deserted by their British officers. There were tales of a white road out and a black road out.'

'You are speaking up for them? You think your brother is one of them? You are calling your brother a traitor?' Kasim got up, Ahmed felt it obligatory to rise too. But they came no closer to one another. 'You forget that Sayed is an Indian officer. He holds, unless he is dead, the King-Emperor's commission. It was his choice. He was a good officer, the first Indian officer in his chosen regiment. It concerned me that he should choose to take a commission, but then I am a politician. He wished to be a soldier. I said to him once, Do you regret it? He only laughed. In the mess he said they were all equal, that there was only one standard and if you measured up to it you were accepted. To me it all seemed simple and naïve, but Sayed *was* naïve. He was naïve, he could never have made a success of politics, but he did not have it in him to be a traitor. In 1939 he said to me, "You are a minister of state, I am an officer in the Indian army. We are both necessary people." He had no complaints, he encountered no difficulties. It was I who encountered difficulties because a son of mine had taken the King's commission. But I did not see them as difficulties. The world is full of fools who don't see an inch in front of their noses. What kind of independence will it be when we get it if we can't defend it? And how shall we be able to defend it if there aren't boys like Sayed willing to train and discipline themselves faithfully and steadfastly to inherit that side of our national responsibility? What are we living in, a jungle? When the British invited Indians to take the King's commission they were proving what my father called their sincerity. You do not hand your armed forces over to the command of men who will turn it against you. What kind of an army will it be if its officers think of their commissions as meaningless bits of paper? It is a contract, a contract. All of Muslim law is based on the sanctity of contract, of one man's word to another. You must be prepared to suffer and die for it. It is written. It is revealed. It is in our hearts. What are you telling me? That it is not in Sayed's? That he is not a man to keep his contract? That he is an opportunist? A cowardly scoundrel? Without a thought for his own honour or for mine, or his mother's, or for yours? Are you telling me this is the kind of India I have gone to prison for? If you are, you had better leave me here. I do not know that kind of India. I do not know that kind of man. He is not Sayed. He is not my son.'

'We've had a letter, Father. He's written to Mother.'

'A forgery.'

'He says you will help him.'

'Does he?'

'Eventually there'll be court-martials.'

'Will there?'

'In his letter he says he refused to join until they told him you'd been arrested.'

'Well?'

'He asked us to give you his love. He's sorry he failed.'

'Failed?'

'Failed to complete the march on Delhi.'

His father's mouth was working. 'The march on Delhi? What is that? Some city on the moon? Or do you march nowadays on your own capital? He thinks perhaps the Moghul empire still exists and has been ravaged by barbarians? And that I languish in some medieval dungeon, clanking my chains, crying out to my son to muster an army and ride to my rescue? God save me from such a deliverance. I would fear for my life. Such a son would strike me down. He would drag me from prison and have me trampled to death. I don't accept his love. I don't listen to his apology.'

The old man's voice had strengthened and risen to the pitch that had swayed juries, brought order to a noisy Legislative Assembly and sent ministers scuttling at midnight through the corridors of the Secretariat. Ahmed closed the door. The action calmed him and hardened his resolution. He could not escape involvement. He had to speak out.

'I've closed the door because it would be better if they don't hear. There *is* an Indian National Army and it isn't just a few madmen. It would suit the British very well if every Congressman said what you've just said. But do you think they will? A dozen Indian officers helping the Japanese would have no political significance. The British could shoot them for treachery and no one would need to raise a finger in protest. But hundreds of officers and thousands of men do have political significance. Whatever the members of your party feel individually, collectively you're going to have to stand by them, because the ordinary Indian won't see any difference between men like these who grabbed rifles and marched up through Burma with the Japanese and men who said the Indians had no quarrel with the Japanese and called on the whole country to sabotage the British war effort. Except that the young men who grabbed rifles and marched will look more heroic than the old men who went to jail and suffered nothing but personal inconvenience.'

'Then I had better go back and continue in that relatively comfortable state of personal inconvenience.'

'You can't go back, Father. They won't let you. I know Mother talks about hoping you'll agree, but she's got into the

habit of thinking you have a choice, and knows you'd choose
what you see as the honourable way. But the plain fact is they're
chucking you out of the Fort. They pretend it's a compassionate
release and men like the Governor may actually feel sorry for
you. He obviously knew you well enough to guess you'd feel
disgraced, and not proud, about Sayed. But if he knows you as
well as that, the kindest thing would have been to keep you in
prison, because being in prison is your one current public badge
of honour, isn't it?'

'You have never thought so!' the old man cried. 'You have
always been ashamed. Why? Do you think I have not been
ashamed too? You think it is a matter of pride to look out of a
window and know that this is as much as you will be allowed to
see of the world? No! It is not a badge of honour, it is one of
humiliation. But there are circumstances in which you weigh
one humiliation against another, and choose. I have chosen
many times before and I can choose again.'

Kasim sat. He took the white cap off and placed it on the table.

'No, Father. You can't choose. At least I don't think so.'

'You don't think so. We'll see. Let them take me forcibly to
Mirat. But then let them stop me returning to Ranpur.'

'To do what? Something that will force them to arrest you
again? What sort of thing will that be? They only arrested
you last time because of your loyalty to the Congress. Wouldn't
most of your time be spent persuading your friends and the wives
of your colleagues who are still in prison that your release isn't
a reward for making a deal with the Governor, or with Jinnah?
When a man comes out of political detention and there's no
amnesty to explain it his friends want to know why.'

'There is always the truth.'

'About Sayed? What will you do? Talk to your Congress
friends as you've talked to me? Call Sayed a traitor? You might
just as well write your letter of resignation now, and apply to
Jinnah for membership of the League. Not that Jinnah would
touch you with a barge-pole if you took that line with him.
He'll have to call Sayed a patriot too, if he values his career as a
future minister.'

Kasim looked up from contemplation of the cap. The sunken
eyes glittered. 'To whom have you been talking? Obviously not
your mother. To these representatives of Government? To

my feeble-minded kinsman, the Nawab? To that European paederast, that *émigré* Wazir?'

'I've talked to all of them, but not about this.'

'No?'

Kasim looked again at the cap. 'Then I must apologize for having underestimated you. I had assumed your dissociation from the kind of affairs that have been the central concern of my life was a mask for your failure to understand them. But your assessment of my present position is shrewd, and I am indebted to you for bothering to open my eyes to it. Since one of my sons turns out to be a deserter and a traitor, it is some compensation to realize that the other one is not stupid, as I thought.'

Ahmed glanced down at the floor. He supposed he had invited it. It was only fair that his father should hurt him too. But when he looked up again he found his father's eyes closed and head bent forward. For a long time neither of them spoke. It was his father who broke the silence.

'I am sorry. You did not deserve that. Forgive me. And you have come all this way to meet me. In prison you forget that time doesn't stand still, that circumstances change and that without your knowing it you yourself are carried forward with them. It is a shock to come out and discover it. It is difficult to adjust. I must thank you for perhaps having saved me from too hastily making impractical or anachronistic gestures.'

He put his hands on the table, folded, attempting an illusion of unimpaired competence and capacity. But Ahmed guessed that the hands clasped one another to disguise evidence of a sudden and frightening lack of confidence.

'Presently,' the ex-chief minister said, 'you must call in these patient English officials, but there are a few points I wish to be clear on first. Was it the Governor or the Nawab who suggested I should be released from the Fort and sent to Mirat?'

'The Governor, through his representative. Mother asked me to find out if the Nawab would agree.'

'Then we need not concern ourselves with the Nawab's or his Wazir's motives, but only bear in mind what future political advantage they may see accruing from their generosity. Secondly. What reasons did the Governor give for making the suggestion?'

'None. At least, not in so many words, but the connection

was clear enough, I suppose. The representative told Mother the
news about Sayed and then said that the Governor had taken
advice –'

'Advice?'

'The inference was that there had been a discussion with the
Viceroy. The Governor said he'd be prepared to release you into
the protection of anyone acceptable to both sides, and suggested
the Nawab. He promised Mother that if she got the Nawab's
approval the release would be arranged immediately.'

'But –?'

'There weren't any buts. Except for the condition of secrecy
until the release had taken place. The Government will then
report it as due to a concern for your health.'

'*My* health?'

'From their point of view it must be more acceptable that way
round. I imagine they don't want an epidemic of Congress wives
with fatal illnesses certified as authentic by Congress-minded
doctors.'

'You miss the point that the Governor imagines it is also more
acceptable from my point of view. He offers me an alibi that
might stand me in good stead later on when my less fortunate
colleagues are released.'

'No, Father. I hadn't missed that point.' He hesitated. 'There's
one other thing, the Governor said that arrangements could be
made for you to talk to Sayed.'

They stared at one another.

'And this is all?' Kasim asked suddenly, ignoring Ahmed's
last remark. 'Nothing is said about the expected duration of my
illness, nor about the conditions in which I am to live?'

'You'll have a private suite of rooms in the summer palace in
Nanoora. We'll drive first to Mirat. The Nawab's private train
will be waiting there for us. Mother is on it. So is Bronowsky.
The Nawab's at the summer palace.'

'Which of course is heavily guarded.'

'Not heavily.'

'But where nevertheless I shall be incommunicado. I hope
Bronowsky understands that Nanoora will suffer from a slight
increase in the population in the form of inquisitive news-
papermen anxious for every scrap of information they can pick
up or invent about my state of health and mind?'

'He's going to issue bulletins. You won't be pestered.'

'You mean I shan't be allowed to be pestered. Well – my kins-man the Nawab of Mirat will be a more considerate jailer than Government, and in this matter you are right, I have no choice. But I am still their prisoner and this time your mother joins me. It is a sacrifice she will willingly make, but it is one I would have spared her. Do you understand that, Ahmed?'

'Yes, I think so.' He waited, but his father seemed to have no more to say. He was staring at the white cap again. 'Shall I go and tell them you're ready?' The old man nodded, but when Ahmed was about to open the door he was stopped by the sound of the voice continuing.

'What have you been trying to tell me?'

Ahmed turned round.

'That I should bow to the inevitable as I bow to this new humiliation? That I should prepare myself to play along with the crowd and so ensure my political future? Or that I should acknowledge defeat and retire from politics and grow onions to ward off the chills of old age? Have you ever tasted onions that flourish in the dry weather on mugs of shaving water begged from the prison barber on every second day? It is an interesting flavour. Perhaps it is only in the imagination that one tastes soap. But then the imagination of an ageing man is severely limited and prey to all kinds of quaint illusions and expectations.'

Kasim looked up. 'Unfortunately,' the old man said, 'we have only one life to live and we are granted only one notion of what makes it worth living. It isn't easy to write that notion off as mistaken or the life we live in pursuit of it as wasted.'

'I know.'

'Do you? You will. But not yet. You're young and your life is all before you.'

Yes, but what kind of life? Ahmed wondered. The life he lived now wasn't his own because he lived it in the dense shadows of his father's life and of the lives of men like him. He longed to grope his way out and cast a shadow of his own. The longing was so intense that his blood stirred. It was as if a voice inside him cried out: Rebel! Rebel!

But Rebel against what? In India only one kind of rebellion was possible, and that kind had become an old man's game. They had played it a long time and it wasn't over yet. The game and the men had grown old together and India had grown old with them.

'Well?' Kasim asked. 'What are you waiting for? Go and fetch them, or are you going to explain what you've been trying to tell me? Which of the two alternatives you think I should choose?'

Ahmed hesitated. The game had gone wrong but his father had always played it honourably. No doubt he would do so to the end. What was sad was the fact that his father was not looking for a country for himself but for his sons, and they could never inhabit it because a country was a state of mind and a man could properly exist only in his own. In his father's India, the India his father *was*, Ahmed felt himself an exile; but an exile from where he didn't know. His mind was not clear enough to penetrate the shadows of other men's beliefs which lay across it; and before these beliefs – so sure and positive, so vigorously upheld by words of challenge and acts of sacrifice – he felt stupidly unformed and incoherent. Perhaps it was a beginning of coherence for him to have understood the nature of his father's problem, and to have spoken out. But farther than that he could not go. Could not? Should not, rather. The problem was his father's, not his; and the hands the problem was in were safe enough. The old man would never compromise. Neither would he give up the fight. The sight of him sitting there, waiting to confront three men he thought of as his country's oppressors, moved Ahmed to despair and melancholy pride. The bizarre notion struck him that if only there were a mirror in the room he would take it down from the wall and put it on the table and say: 'There's the India you're eating out your heart looking for.' In the shape of his father's prison-diminished body, he felt for such an India an undemanding, a boundless love, and for an instant in his own heart and bones he understood his father's youthful longing and commitment and how it had never truly been fulfilled, and had never been corrupted, so that even in an old man's body it shone like something new and untried and full of promise.

But there was something missing; and knowing what it was and how he could cover up his silence and indecision and at the same time convey to his father something of what he felt he went to the table, picked up the white Congress cap and offered it.

'You've forgotten this,' he said. 'They pretend to laugh at it, but of course they're afraid of it really. If they see it on the table they might come to the wrong conclusion.'

His father stared at the cap, then bent his head. Ahmed put the cap on for him, gave it a jaunty tilt. His father's hands touched his, seeking to impose an adjustment. 'No, straight,' he said. 'And firm,' and muttered something which Ahmed only partly caught.

But outside, on the verandah, he caught the whole of it. The sky was lighter and the Fort stood immense and dark and implacable; mercilessly near. 'Straight and firm,' his father had said – 'like a crown of thorns.'

EPILOGUE

AND AFTER ALL it seemed that Susan had held somewhere in the back of her mind a memory of the day she once told Sarah she had forgotten: the day Dost Mohammed made a little circle of kerosene-soaked cotton-waste, set light to it and then opened a circular tin, shook it, and dropped the small black scorpion into the centre of the ring of fire. Poised, belligerent, the armoured insect moved stiffly, quickly – stabbing its arched tail, once, twice, three times. Sarah felt the heat on her face and drew back. When the flames died down the scorpion was still. Dost Mohammed touched it gingerly with a twig and then, getting no response, scooped the body into the tin.

'Is it whole?' Susan asked. For a while she had this strange idea that it couldn't be because it had been born nearly a month too soon. She received the child in her arms reluctantly, fearing that even at this stage one of them might destroy the other; or, failing this, that she would find some vestigial trace or growth which a few more weeks' gestation would have taken care of. What will you call him? people asked. 'I don't know,' she said. 'A name is so important. How can I choose an important thing like that entirely on my own?'

Susan had had a bad time. 'But,' Mrs Layton said, 'she was a brick.' And so it was generally agreed. A brick. Like her mother. Among those who knew the Laytons only one person withheld praise of the way in which Mildred Layton had coped in Sarah's absence and this was Barbie who maintained a tight-lipped, red-eyed silence, and made preparations for departure from a place of refuge that had not proved permanent. Perhaps it was to Mr Maybrick that she spoke confidentially and through Mr Maybrick that a story gained subterranean currency that Mildred Layton had ridden roughshod over her suggestion that Mabel had wanted to be buried in St Luke's cemetery in Ranpur, next to her second husband, and not in the cemetery of St John's. Had Mabel ever expressed such a preference? Perhaps she had, but only to Barbie, and there was nothing in the will to confirm it. Even if there had been, who could blame Mildred for the hasty arrangements made to inter her stepmother-in-law's body in Pankot within twenty-four hours of the old woman's sudden death? What else could she have done, with Susan in labour brought on by the shock of witnessing that death, alone, on the verandah of Rose Cottage? The expense, the inconvenience (the sheer horror, if you liked) of packing the old woman with ice and transporting her to Ranpur would have been intolerable, and it was more important to help a new life into the world than to be certain that the remains of a spent one were buried in a place one had only an old maid's word had been the place desired by the departed.

And so Mabel Layton had gone to her last resting place in the late afternoon of the day following her death. There were mounds of flowers on the grave to make up for the thin scattering of people who managed to get away for the service. Mrs Layton's flurried presence was noted and respected. She would have been forgiven for not attending because Susan still lay in a room of the Pankot nursing home, as yet undelivered. Her mother had spent the night there and would return directly the funeral was over to spend another night, if need be. Was it, people wondered, a false alarm? It would be quite understandable, if so. It was a terrible thing for a young girl so far advanced in pregnancy to find herself sitting on a verandah with a dead woman. It would have been better if there had been some warning, if old Mabel had cried out or fallen or at least shown signs of being unwell; instead of which she had simply stopped tending the plants on the balustrade and sat down in a chair close to the one Susan was lying on, and given up the ghost. Well, she was an old woman and it was a good way to go; but not good for Susan who had only gradually become puzzled and then alarmed by the angle of the old woman's head. 'Are you awake, Aunty Mabel?' she asked, raising her voice because of the deafness. And, three hours later, when Rose Cottage was almost empty again of all the people Susan had sensibly and courageously helped to summon, her mother found her in the little spare, with her hands pressed to her abdomen and her eyes wide with terror and incomprehension.

'It can't have,' she said, when Dr Travers told her twenty

minutes later that her labour seemed to have begun. 'It can't be. It isn't time. The baby isn't finished.' For thirty-three hours she lay in a room of the nursing home which Isobel Rankin had seen was made available – a lovely room, marked down on the official lists as exclusive to the wives of officers of senior field rank. And at five o'clock in the morning – as Sarah slept fitfully on the train from Ranpur, keeping watch on the night's progress (and Ahmed Kasim sat on the verandah of the Circuit House near Premanagar, keeping a different kind of watch) – Susan was delivered of a boy who looked absurdly, touchingly, like Teddie.

'It doesn't matter,' Susan said when Sarah told her Mr Merrick was grateful but felt he couldn't accept. 'I'm going to ask General Rankin, but there have to be two godfathers for a boy so you'd better ask Dicky. At least he's got two arms.' It was the only thing she ever said that showed how little or much she had taken in of Sarah's story about Teddie's death and Merrick's action and misfortune; but thereafter she began to show a tender devotion to the child which Dr Travers said was a sign of her having come through, of her confounding those Jeremiahs who once talked about her as being dangerously withdrawn like the daughter of a woman called Poppy Browning. Who said that? Mrs Layton demanded, not having heard the rumour but remembering Poppy Browning well enough from the old days in Lahore. Miss Batchelor had mentioned it, Dr Travers thought. 'That woman!' Mrs Layton cried; and another nail was driven into Barbie's coffin.

On the day before Barbie quit Rose Cottage for temporary sanctuary with the Peplows, Sarah found her wandering in the garden with Mabel's cradle-basket and Mabel's secateurs. 'I should have kept my mouth shut,' she said, 'I mean about St Luke's in Ranpur. But she *did* wish it. She *told* me. Quite clearly. Last year. I suggested we should go down to Ranpur to do some Christmas shopping but she said, Oh I shall never go back to Ranpur, at least not until I'm buried. I thought your mother knew all about it but was forgetting it in all the rush and confusion. But there you are. I've opened my mouth once too often. Rose Cottage is yours now, and it's not as if I expected to stay on or have longer than a week or two to make other arrangements if Mabel died before I did. What hurts is being misunderstood and leaving a place I've been happy in, under a cloud. I know it was

unfair to you, my being here. If I hadn't been, there'd just have
been room for you and Susan and your mother. I said so to
Mabel. More than once. Oughtn't I to go, Mabel? I said. After
all I'm not family, and they're not comfortable down there in
the grace and favour. But she wouldn't hear of it. I don't know
why. She lived a life of her own, didn't she? I never knew what
she was thinking. It sometimes seemed to me she'd *found* herself,
I mean her true self, and just wanted to be alone but have someone who would talk to her. Heaven knows I did that. Well, it's
all over now. I've written to the Mission. I thought I might do
some voluntary work. There are people starving and dying,
aren't there? There must be something I can do, even if it's only
laying out bodies. I shouldn't want paying. I've got my pension
and the little annuity she'd left me. Not that I'm happy about
that. Nor is your mother, I shouldn't wonder.'

'You mustn't think that, Barbie. You made Aunt Mabel's last
years very pleasant. It's the only way she could repay you. And
we've still got plenty. We're well off now.'

Barbie looked round the garden. Mabel's presence was like a
scent. 'Shall you be happy here, all of you?'

'I don't know. I don't know at all, Barbie.'

'Will she marry Captain Beauvais?'

'Susan?'

'People think so. They say the child should have a father: I'd
encourage it if I were you. If she doesn't marry again you'll never
get away.' Suddenly Barbie flushed and grasped Sarah's arm.
'That's what you want, isn't it? To get away. But some people
are made to live and others are made to help them. If you stay
you'll end up like that, like me. Worse probably because all
this' – she released Sarah's arm and made a broad gesture at the
garden and the hills – 'it's coming to an end somehow, isn't it?
Very soon.'

Abruptly Barbie left her and Sarah did not see her again until
the morning of the christening when she sat alone in a pew near
the altar while Sarah and Dicky, General and Mrs Rankin, and
Sarah's mother, stood at the font and Mr Peplow received the
new Edward Arthur David Bingham as a lively member of Holy
Church. The baptism was hurried, almost furtive; and when it
was over the Rankins went their way and the Laytons went
theirs. There was no party but Dicky went back with Sarah and

her mother to the grace and favour bungalow where the business of packing private possessions into crates for the move to Rose Cottage had been interrupted the day before. The child was placed in the care of Minnie who had been promoted to the position of ayah and had already notably proved her worth; but it was Sarah who dealt with the milk and the bottle and the rubber teat while Minnie watched, anxious to learn but so far unsuccessful in persuading the child to accept this substitute for his mother's breast.

In the afternoon Dicky drove Sarah to the nursing home – a week to the day and almost to the hour that he had driven Susan home from there with the child in her arms. He did not go in and Sarah told him she would get a tonga home. 'Shall I come and see you tonight?' he asked. She did not want him but thought it might be better, if only for her mother's sake, to have someone in the house to whom both of them could talk. 'Yes,' she said, 'come in time for drinks.'

'I do hope you find her better,' he said. 'Oh, I do hope so.' He turned away and Sarah went in. Twenty minutes later, escorted, she entered the room where Susan was, which was not a pretty room at all. There were bars at the window. Susan sat on an upright chair, hands folded on her lap, watching the gently falling rain and smiling. Another chair was placed near by and on this Sarah took up her position and waited until Susan slowly turned her head and looked at her.

'Hello, Su. I've come to see if there's anything you want.'

How pretty you look, Sarah thought. Pretty and happy. No, more than happy, profoundly content, totally withdrawn. You've found your way in. Why should that cause us pain and sorrow? Why should it hurt to think that you don't recognize me? Or only recognize me as someone belonging to a world that's become unreal to you and isn't to be compared with the one you've always imagined and imagine now, and smile at because you feel its protection all round you like a warmth?

Now you look back at the window, through the bars which you don't see. The little flush on your cheeks which used to look hectic no longer does so; it's a flush of pleasure and the smile is a smile of happiness, almost of beatitude. Why do we call it sickness? And pray for you to come back to us? When you come back you may remember what you did or tried to do, and why.

And we are selfish enough to want you to remember and tell us because we're not people who will accept mysteries if we think there are explanations to be had.

But you scare us. We sense from the darkness in you the darkness in ourselves, a darkness and a death wish. Neither is admissible. We chase that illusion of perpetual light. But there's no such thing. What light there is, when it comes, comes harshly and unexpectedly and in it we look extraordinarily ugly and incapable.

She glanced round and spoke in a whisper to the young psychiatrist who stood waiting with Dr Travers. 'May I touch her?' The man nodded. Sarah had no faith in him; not because he was young – that was a good thing – but because his work was exclusively with men. She leaned forward.

'Susan? It's me – Sarah.'

But Susan did not look at her again and Sarah shrank from touching her. She did not want to intrude or disrupt the pattern of her sister's absorption. After a while she said, 'Goodbye, Susan. I'll see you again tomorrow,' but the words went unheeded or unheard and she rose and went with the doctors to the door. 'Can you keep her here?' she asked. Travers said they hoped so. The alternative – as Mrs Layton so much feared – was a place in Ranpur. But the patient was very quiet. It was probably only a passing phase. Travers said he could have sworn that a week ago her attitude to the child was normal; maternally loving and possessive.

It wasn't normal, Sarah wanted to say, but none of them had seen it; except Mahmoud's widowed niece, Minnie; and it had not been her place to say but only to watch and learn and be on her guard, and make offerings to the old tribal gods of the hills, which it seemed she and the other servants had got into a habit of doing, secretly, to ward off a rumoured evil of monstrous birth, and which she now continued to do because as far as Minnie was concerned the affliction which she had detected in the young memsahib's devotion to the child was of divine origin, as all madness was, a sign of God's special concern and interest.

Sarah waited until the rain stopped, then left the nursing home and took the first tonga in the line. 'To St John's,' she told the tonga-wallah. She did not want to be alone with her mother.

When they reached the church she asked the man to wait and went into the churchyard, past the hummocky graves – old lichen-eaten crosses aslant in long wet grass. She took the path round the south side of the church, to the newer part of the cemetery and stood at Aunt Mabel's grave with its mounds of withered wreaths. Her own little posy, gathered from the garden of Rose Cottage after the funeral, was withered too. The ink had run on the cards, leaving ghostly traces of anonymous remembrances. *Ah, oui. Elle est une de mes prisonnières.* That too had been a nail in poor Barbie's coffin because she had told Susan about the butterflies in the lace. Had she been listening or had Mabel repeated the story to her after Sarah had gone? No matter. 'Little prisoner, little prisoner. Shall I free you? Shall I free you?' Susan had said, touching the baby's cheek with her finger. But even that had passed them by as no more than a tender admonition.

Sarah left the graveside and on impulse went into the church through the south door which Mr Peplow always left open during the hours of daylight. She sat in a front pew and after a while had the curious feeling that she was not alone. Little prisoner, little prisoner, shall I free you? Is that what she had meant to do? And was it only yesterday that, finding herself alone with the servants in the grace and favour bungalow while Sarah was at the office and her mother at Rose Cottage measuring curtains, Susan had sent Mahmoud to the bazaar for blue ribbons and then sent Minnie after him to tell him white, not blue?

Uneasy, Sarah looked behind her but saw no one and turned back to her contemplation of the image of her sister's madness; but in the stillness she heard from outside the church the squeaking sound of a motor-car or taxi coming to a halt and then, after a second or two, the short note of summons on its horn; and presently, much closer, the unmistakable sound of footsteps on tiles, within the body of the church. She turned again. A woman in an old-fashioned veiled topee was coming down the aisle towards the altar, making for the south door; a woman who must have been there all the time on the darker side of the nave, and whom Sarah recognized. At the end of the aisle the woman genuflected, supporting herself with one hand on the end of the pew.

Why, what a lot you know, Sarah told her silently, what a lot, what a terrible, terrible lot. But now I know some of it too, and know that this kind of knowing isn't knowing but bowing my head, as you are bowing yours, under the weight of it.

The woman came towards her, one hand held to her breast clutching a cross that wasn't there except in the form of pleats and buttons. Level with her the woman hesitated. Sarah could make out little of the face through the veil, but smiled because she felt beholden, as Susan would have said. The woman said nothing but half raised a hand in a gesture that stopped short both of greeting and farewell, and then went out through the south door to the waiting transport. And when she had gone Sarah moved, stumbling over the hassocks, wanting to ask, to ask; but just what she didn't know. She hesitated too, and was lost. Outside, rounding the buttressed corner of the church she saw the old woman opening the lych-gate, began to run, and stopped. The rain was falling again; gentle rain. All the hills of Pankot were green and soft. She ran down the gravel pathway, past the graves of Muirs and Laytons, understanding that this was part of her dream, the running and the absence of an end to the journey. When she got to the road the car was gone.

Little prisoner, shall I free you? Divine intervention! Well, Minnie had understood and not gone beyond the gate in Mahmoud's wake, to change an order for blue ribbons, but crept cautiously back to the end of the verandah where she had been sorting bundles of laundry for the dhobi, and where Susan Mem was dressing the baby in the lace he was to wear on the morrow, talking to him in her strange guttural tongue.

Divine intervention; odd, alien custom. Which? How could Minnie know? All she could do was watch and wait. After a while the dressing was over. The mother hugged the child to her and then walked out into the bright sunshine of the rain-free afternoon, across the patch of grass towards the wall that hid the servants' quarters. There, for many days, Mahmoud had lit bonfires to destroy the accumulation of unwanted years. And there Susan placed the child on the grass, took the ready-to-hand tin of kerosene and sprinkled a wide circle around it. For a time Minnie stared, fascinated, believing herself a hidden witness of a secret initiation. But when Susan Mem set fire to the kerosene and the flames leapt, arcing their way round in a geometrical perfection, Minnie snatched a sheet from the dhobi's bundle and ran, threw the sheet on to the flames, entered the circle and picked the child up and carried it to safety.

She stood some way off. Susan Mem had not moved. She knelt and watched the flames dying and did not appear to notice the trampled sheet or the fact that the child was no longer there. The grass was too wet for the flames to catch hold. Only the spirit burned, and left a scorched smouldering ring.

'Pankot Rifles Depot *ki taraf jao,*' Sarah told the tonga-wallah who snapped his whip and clicked his tongue. They bowled down the lane from St John's, from the eminence towards the valley. As they went past the nursing home which was set far back from the road in wooded grounds Sarah leant her head against the canopy and imagined herself Susan, leaning her head against the bars that separated her from the window pane. She closed her eyes as perhaps Susan was doing, even now, and after a while felt the quietness of her own happiness and grace welling up inside her; and smiled, ignoring the rain that seemed to be falling on her face.